ROWENA CORY DANIELLS

The FALL of FAIR ISLE

BROKEN VOWS // DARK DREAMS // DESPERATE ALLIANCES

This edition published 2015 by Solaris
an imprint of Rebellion Publishing Ltd,
Riverside House, Osney Mead,
Oxford, OX2 0ES, UK

www.solarisbooks.com

Broken Vows first published 1999 as *The Last T'En*
by Bantam Australia.
Dark Dreams first published 2001 by Bantam.
Desperate Alliances first published 2002 by Bantam.

US ISBN 978 1 78108 303 1
UK ISBN 978 1 78108 302 4

Cover by Clint Langley

10 9 8 7 6 5 4 3 2 1

A CIP catalogue record for this book is available from the
British Library.

Designed & typeset by Rebellion Publishing

Printed in the US

BOOK ONE
BROKEN VOWS

To D, who always believed in me.

Chapter One

GENERAL TULKHAN STRODE the halls of the stronghold, triumphant. But even though the last of the T'En royal family had surrendered, he experienced no thrill of victory. His father, the Ghebite King, was dead.

Shattering glass broke his concentration. Heart pounding, he spun around. Nothing.

According to the terms of surrender, he had promised there would be no wanton destruction. Senses strained, he made out the muffled sounds of jeering male voices a little way down the passage. Scuffling noises were followed swiftly by a man's frustrated yelp of pain.

Tulkhan cursed in three languages. He had forbidden his soldiers the rights of conquest. There was to be no looting, no women. It was hard on the men who had followed him so faithfully. They expected – no, they deserved – the rewards of victory, but Tulkhan had granted terms and, besides, he wanted to study the renowned T'En culture, and that meant preserving it wherever possible.

Suppressing his annoyance, he strode toward an ornate set of double doors. He heard one of his men shout a warning, followed swiftly by a dull thud and more curses.

Throwing the doors open, he took in the carnage – smashed pots, exposed scrolls and the overwhelming stench of preserving fluid. Two of his men stood with their backs to him, restraining a tall woman. Three of his elite guard circled the captive, nursing various injuries.

Tulkhan immediately dismissed the possibility that the haggard old man in the corner, who was watching all of this with bright eyes, could be the cause of this mayhem. It had to be the female his men were attempting to subdue. He cursed silently. It wasn't like his elite guard to disobey an order.

'Halt! What is this?'

An ominous silence descended on the room. His men looked almost sheepish. For an instant, amusement pierced Tulkhan's irritation.

'A veritable wildcat, General,' one man ventured.

With a flick of his wrist Tulkhan signalled the Ghebite guard to turn the captive toward him and prepared to be lenient. He could afford to be magnanimous, his army was victorious.

But this was no ordinary captive. His guards restrained one of the legendary T'En. Jolted, Tulkhan swallowed. His instinctive revulsion warred with his innate curiosity.

The female was a pure T'En – in his own language, an accursed Dhamfeer – a dangerous alien creature with mysterious powers.

Dishevelled but defiant, she glared at him, her torn bodice revealing small, firm breasts that rose and fell with each short breath. But it was her unnatural gaze which captivated him. The old superstitions were true. The eyes of a pure Dhamfeer were dark as red wine, red as the blood which ran in a rivulet from her swollen lips down her long neck and over her high breasts. He should have been repelled, for she was the antithesis of a Ghebite woman.

Instead of a rich coppery sheen, her flesh was as white as milk. A fine tracery of blue veins ran underneath the skin's surface like marble. Absently, he wondered if her skin was as flawless to stroke as that silky stone. His fingers tingled in anticipation of an exploratory touch.

Riveted by the sight of the Dhamfeer's milky flesh, streaked red by her own blood, Tulkhan felt his body respond. A rush of lust which was equal parts fascination and fear gripped him. Shocked, he licked dry lips. Never had he known such an immediate reaction.

By all that was holy, he should be repelled. She was not even a True-woman. According to the Ghebite priests, women possessed weak, inferior souls. Tulkhan smiled grimly. He was sure the priests would declare this female Dhamfeer possessed *no* soul. After all, she was little more than a beast.

If so, why did he read intelligence in her strange eyes?

Taking a deep breath, he put theological questions aside and considered the situation. He had personally viewed the remains of several half-blood Dhamfeer during this campaign, but never come face to face with a live specimen. To see one who was not only very much alive, but so obviously pure Dhamfeer, reminded him that this was a foreign land, recently ruled by the legendary T'En.

He shuddered, and became aware of a strange scent that made his heart race. It was not the taint of fear – having been soldiering since he was seventeen, he knew that intimately. This scent was rich and slightly musky. And he felt an overwhelming urge to lose himself in its source.

With a start he realised it was coming from the Dhamfeer. Why didn't she fear for her life? Why did she respond to threat with this heady, sensual scent?

He recalled the survival ploy of a little marsupial, a native of his homeland. When threatened by its natural predator, the creature gave off a scent which mimicked the mating scent of a predator. In the resulting confusion the marsupial had a chance to escape. Instinctively he sensed that the Dhamfeer was trying to protect herself by seducing him.

'Stop that!'

She blinked, confused. 'Stop what?'

Tulkhan cursed under his breath, unable to explain. How could he prove his suspicion? Who would believe him, since it meant that the Dhamfeer could control her scent?

Just what *could* the Dhamfeer do?

Superstition held that one of her race could possess a True-man such as himself with the sheer power of their will. The hardened soldier in Tulkhan shrugged this aside – a great deal of nonsense was said about this almost mythical island. They'd said it was impregnable, and he had proved them wrong.

Command meant never revealing weakness, and years of experience came to the fore. Stifling his disquiet, the General turned on his men. 'So it takes five of you to subdue a mere female?'

They wilted under the attack, resentfully eyeing the ground.

The Dhamfeer smiled and he caught a glimpse of her sharp white teeth. She was enjoying the guards' discomfiture, the vixen. He itched to wipe that sly smile from her face, to subdue those defiant eyes and see that proud chin fall.

Superstition also said that the eyes of the Dhamfeer could ensorcell you. Tulkhan held her wine-dark gaze, meeting those feral eyes with a challenge of his own.

Nothing. He experienced no tingling apprehension of ensorcellment. Even better – for an instant he thought he read a flicker of fear, quickly cloaked.

Having proven folklore wrong, Tulkhan assessed his captive. This Dhamfeer was very young. Her own people must have considered her too young to fight, or she would have died at their side on the battlefield.

He grimaced – how barbaric of these people to train women for their regular army, and condone their slaughter on the battlefield.

The elite guard waited with bated breath as the conquering Ghebite General confronted the last of the royal line.

Imoshen met General Tulkhan's eyes, desperate not to reveal how he unnerved her. She'd heard he was a freakish giant, far bigger than a normal Ghebite warrior, but seeing him in the flesh was startling. His massive dark form dominated the room. She had to look up to meet his eyes, and this annoyed Imoshen. Being pure T'En, only the tallest of True-men could look her in the eye, and she hadn't realised till now how much she enjoyed looking down on people.

But it was more than that. This Ghebite General appeared utterly alien in his flamboyant war finery. He'd removed his crested helmet to reveal dark, sweat-dampened hair, which clung in fine tendrils to his broad cheekbones. With his strange, coppery skin and obsidian black eyes, he was the antithesis of her own kind – extrinsic, unknown and unknowable.

But what unnerved her most was the sharp intelligence she perceived in his calculating dark eyes; the cynical twist to his mouth. Here was a man who believed in nothing, who would stop at nothing.

As she held his gaze, she realised he was studying her, assessing her. A prickle of fear moved over her skin. This Ghebite was too clever for her liking. She feared perceptive intelligence in an invader more than brutality.

Worse. She was his captive. Her heart sank, but she would not reveal her weakness to him. She raged at the ignominy of her position – to confront her captor like this, restrained and half-naked.

She would not grovel.

If only she had heeded the Aayel's advice. Not so long ago, she had been unwilling to face the reality of their defeat. If only she could go back and retrace the impetuous steps that had led her to this.

IMOSHEN'S SIX-FINGERED HANDS closed in fists of rage. 'I hate him! I –'

'Imoshen!'

With a guilty start she turned to face the Aayel. Her great aunt had received the title on her hundredth birthday. As the Aayel, she was a living repository of their society's shared history. It was an honour for her family. A minor branch of the royal line, they were second cousins to the Empress.

Where were her kin now, murdered on the battlefield by that man? White hot rage ignited Imoshen. Her gaze flew to the plains beyond the stronghold's walls. She raised the farseer and peered through it.

There he was, the Ghebite General, resplendent in his barbarian battledress. A defiant red crest topped his helmet, rippling in the breeze. Linked plates of armour emphasised his broad shoulders. Long tendrils of his dark hair had come loose from his braid. They lifted in the breeze, twining around the strong column of his throat.

Even from this distance, the farseer enabled Imoshen to make out the severe planes of his arrogant face, burnt to a coppery sheen by the blazing sun of his northern homeland, Gheeaba. It was a word to strike fear in the hearts of peaceful people everywhere.

The General sat astride a magnificent black destrier, a massive creature trained to trample the enemy beneath its hooves, ready to die for its master. Imoshen grimaced. She had heard his men were happy to die for him too, such was the devotion he inspired.

'Barbarians,' Imoshen hissed.

'Come here, Shenna.' The voice was soft. But Imoshen knew even though the Aayel used her pet name, it was a command.

Slapping the farseer closed she slipped off the window seat and padded cat-light across the bare boards. The Aayel despised the trappings of luxury. According to her they were a symbol of weakness, a sign of how the royal line had succumbed to indolence and in-fighting, making it ripe for invasion by the northern barbarians.

'The Ghebite General stands on the field with his army and demands we open our stronghold gates.' Imoshen's throat was tight with emotion. Logic told her that for the General to have come this far, her family must be dead. Even the Emperor and Empress, who had led separate armies in a pincer attack, a last-ditch attempt to crush the invaders, must have failed.

All lost.

Other than the Aayel, every relative she had lay dead, fallen between Umasreach Stronghold and the coast.

A vision of a bloodied battlefield swam before her mind's eye. Sickened, she saw the carrion birds pecking at the flesh of the dead, heard the screams of the horses dying and the moans of the wounded.

Was it a true Seeing or all her too-vivid imagination? Imoshen did not know. The Aayel was the one who had the gift for scrying. Imoshen's gift was the more mundane but useful ability to hasten healing.

'If only our mainland allies hadn't deserted us.' Imoshen's hands closed in fists of frustration. 'I don't understand. The Empress sent for their aid in plenty of time. Why didn't they come to our aid?'

'The *why* does not matter.'

'It matters to me!'

The Aayel sighed. 'I am old and cynical, Shenna. I have seen too much. True, the southern kingdoms have not honoured the treaty of alliance, but it is not surprising. Fair Isle is small, and richer than they. Gheeaba stretches across the north of the mainland like a great canker, growing more powerful with every country it absorbs.

'Meanwhile the southern kingdoms withhold their support. They watch and wait to see if Fair Isle will fall. Whatever happens, they cannot lose. If we stand against the Ghebites, it halts their southern march and leaves us weakened, eager to accept our allies' help on any terms before the Ghebites renew their attack in the spring. Think of your lessons.'

'How can you talk of history when the General stands at our gates, demanding our surrender?'

The Aayel smiled. 'One day this will be history. But listen.' She caught Imoshen's hand in her own six-fingered hand and held her gaze with time-worn, mulberry eyes.

Below them in the courtyard Imoshen could hear the fearful moans of the people who had fled before the invaders, retreating within the fortress's walls, believing themselves safe in Umasreach Stronghold.

'Imoshen, heed me. To have come this far the General must have conquered all resistance. We can expect no aid. We must surrender the stronghold.'

'There are still the southern nobles.'

'A handful of stubborn men and women. They are no use to us here, today. We must surrender.'

'The church? Surely they will –'

'Protect us?'

Imoshen tried to interpret her great aunt's expression and failed.

'If the Ghebite General knocked on the door of the basilica itself, do you think the Beatific would pause to consider for more than a heartbeat before turning us over?' the old woman asked.

'But the Beatific is head of the T'En church, which reveres our gifts. We are the last of the pure T'En, sacred vessels of –'

'Pretty words, Imoshen. But think. The Beatific is a True-woman, not a throwback like you and I, not even a half-blood. If the church lived up to its vows I would be the Beatific, not her. No, the church is for True-people, while we are nothing but inconvenient reminders of an earlier time.' The

Aayel hurried on before Imoshen could draw breath to argue. 'We are on our own. We must surrender our stronghold.'

'No!' Imoshen gasped. Her head spun as her perception of the world tilted from its axis. 'Umasreach has never fallen. What right has the Ghebite General to march his armies across our lands and take by force what is ours?'

'The same right T'Imoshen the First had six hundred years ago, when she marched across these fertile lands and defeated the simple farm folk to lay claim to Fair Isle – the right of might.'

Imoshen's skin went cold with the logic of it. She had never thought of her namesake's acquisition of this island as anything other than a glorious victory. That it had been an invasion, which stripped True-people of their ancestral homes and rights, was an unwelcome revelation.

The Aayel nodded wisely, her pale face like parchment. Imoshen felt those old, thin claws tighten on her hands.

'It is hard to be marked as different, I know. You could be the child I was never allowed to have.' Fondly, she stroked Imoshen's long hair. 'The blood of the first T'Imoshen runs as strong in you as it does in me. Mark the signs – the silver hair, the six fingers, the garnet eyes. But over six hundred years our people have interbred with the locals, our language and culture have interwoven with theirs and we have lost our fierce will. We have grown content, ripe for plunder. This Ghebite General is only doing what the first T'Imoshen did, bringing fresh blood to a fertile island.'

Imoshen shook her head, blinking back tears of fury. She could not see it that way. This was her home, her people, and she would die for them.

'Better to live and protect them,' the Aayel insisted, skimming her thoughts. She glanced to the door as the sound of booted feet marching on stone and the jingle of metal heralded the arrival of the stronghold guard.

'Will you do a scrying to see if Umasreach can stand against him?' Imoshen pleaded.

The Aayel waved her words aside impatiently. 'It is never so precise. Besides, I need no gifts to see what logic tells me will happen.' She fixed Imoshen with her sharp eyes. 'The General will offer us terms. We would be wise to accept. At least we will have something to bargain with. If we force him to lay siege to our stronghold and take it by force he will punish our defiance by systematically killing all who opposed him.'

Imoshen bowed her head in acknowledgment, but resentment burned in her as her great aunt signalled that she would meet with the defenders to hear the Ghebite's terms.

Retreating to the window embrasure, Imoshen picked up the farseer again. A compulsion which was equal parts fascination and revulsion drove her to study the True-man who had destroyed her world and stolen her future.

General Tulkhan was the first son of the Ghebite King's second wife. Imoshen sniffed disdainfully. *Wife!* That word smacked of slavery. What could you expect of a culture where men had more than one bond-partner and called them *wives* not equals?

These barbarians had complicated family lines. Being the first son of the second wife, the General had not inherited the kingship when the old King died during the spring campaign. Instead, the first son of the first wife, Tulkhan's younger half-brother, had assumed the title.

Young King Gharavan followed the main army at a more sedate pace with his own contingent of men, consolidating the General's rapid victories. This much Imoshen had heard. Rumour ran wild concerning the Ghebite General, his cunning and his prowess in battle.

But she could not discount any of it, for General Tulkhan was here at the gates of her family's stronghold. He had defeated stronghold after stronghold. Often with a lesser army, he had met and surrounded opposing forces in the fields and vanquished them. If half of what she'd heard was true, Imoshen had to conclude that he was a brilliant tactician.

It was said that the men who served under the General adored him, that he had led a charmed life, working his way up through the ranks on ability. Loyal to the old King, he had subjugated nations, collected bounty and annexed countries, all in his father's name.

Creeping south-east across the mainland like a plague year by year, the Ghebites under the young General's leadership had advanced steadily, devouring all resistance in their path.

Through brilliant strategy and, Imoshen suspected, tactical errors on the part of her complacent blood-relatives, in one short season General Tulkhan had defeated the T'En. He was on the brink of ultimate victory. Fair Isle, the centre of T'En culture and learning, was within his grasp.

Once he had captured Umasreach he would ride into the capital, and the citizens, with nothing more than their city patrol to protect them, would lay down their weapons and the jewel in the crown would be his to lay at the feet of his half-brother, King Gharavan.

From this fertile, strategic island General Tulkhan could command the trade routes of the world, just as Imoshen's people had done for six centuries.

Studying the rows of men standing at attention in orderly ranks, she had to admit that despite their constant battles and enforced marches they looked fresh, and their pride was obvious.

Closing the farseer, Imoshen swallowed uneasily. She did not relish her position. It would have been better to die on the battlefield than live a captive.

She bitterly resented her parents' decision not to allow her to fight alongside them. Though she had been trained in the martial arts, they had considered her too young to ride to war with them.

She had offered to travel behind the army to serve as a healer, but her elder brother and sister had objected. Imoshen had not been surprised. She knew them well enough to understand that though they loved her with one breath, they resented her with the next. This war was their chance to win honour and recognition on the battlefield, to outshine her.

They had not found it easy to watch her outgrow them in size and ability. And when her T'En healing gift surfaced during puberty, they had withdrawn even further, excluding her from their social life with cruel taunts and whispered jibes.

Imoshen knew she had been more of a burden than a blessing to her family – the throwback daughter who was forbidden to take a bond-partner, who could not hope to advance the family by bonding to form a powerful alliance.

Even now, her face grew hot as she remembered the last time she had spoken with her family. She had turned on her siblings in a rage, accusing them of not caring about the men and women who served them. If they did, they would take her along, for the lives she could save and the suffering she could ease. But no, all they cared about was their own advancement.

After that outburst her parents had banished her from the strategy meetings. Their parting had been strained with resentment on both sides, and now they were all dead. She could never take back those words, or make amends.

Imoshen didn't know how she felt. So much had happened since spring. This war had come upon Fair Isle like a storm at sea, sweeping all before it. It was four hundred years since the T'En had led an army into battle, and that had been to quell local resistance to T'En rule. Since then her people had relied on threat and coercion, otherwise known as diplomacy. The Aayel was right – her people had grown complacent.

But not Reothe. Her betrothed had sailed far and wide, discovering new trading routes, returning with knowledge and riches.

A cold hand closed around Imoshen's heart. She fought a wave of nausea as the realisation struck her – Reothe must be dead.

Impossible. He was so alive, so intense. Her heart raced with the memory of him.

Her family had been honoured when Reothe chose to ally his line with theirs. But when he made it plain he wanted Imoshen and not her elder sister, her parents had baulked; for Reothe was a throwback like herself, exhibiting all the T'En traits, and pure T'En women did not bond. The church expected them to be celibate in honour of the first Imoshen's celibacy.

T'Imoshen the First had decreed that the T'En males, both full-bloods and half-bloods, and all half-blood T'En females, were to take bond-partners outside their own people. The policy had been designed to assimilate the settlers with the native population of Fair Isle. It was an old law which had been followed without question, until the T'En race was spread far and wide but was diluted to a point where it was almost negligible.

T'En throwbacks from half-blood unions were so rare everyone had thought the Aayel was going to be the last pure relic of their race. That was until Reothe's parents announced his birth but, unlike Imoshen's arrival, his hadn't been so unexpected.

His eccentric, first-cousin parents were a tolerated oddity. Their fascination with everything T'En was considered in bad taste.

After years of infertility the birth of a pure throwback son was seen as retribution. When they retired from court life to live quietly on their estates and raise the child, their extended family had been relieved.

All this she had overheard. As a child, Imoshen had missed few of the nuances of adult conversation. And what she had failed to understand had been thoroughly explained by her sister, who never passed up an opportunity to make sure Imoshen understood her place.

She'd always felt her parents could not understand why they had been blessed, or cursed, with a throwback. All her life she had been an object of fascination, distrust and derision.

She had never expected to take a bond-partner.

But Reothe had anticipated everyone's objections. He had brought with him a document of dispensation signed by the Emperor and Empress, witnessed by the Beatific. Relieved, her parents had given their consent for Reothe to approach Imoshen.

Assuring Imoshen it was a good alliance, they had pointed out that she and Reothe were second cousins, both related to the royal family. And, with two voyages mapping new trade routes to his credit, Reothe already had a reputation for brilliance and daring. He would go far.

She had not been so sure. Something about Reothe made her senses quicken with a presentiment of danger. It had all happened while the Aayel was away at Landsend Abbey serving the church in her official capacity. With no one to consult, Imoshen had been forced to make a decision.

She recalled how she had last seen Reothe, striding toward her, his fine silver hair lifting in the breeze, his piercing wine-dark eyes fixed on her. It was an eerie sensation, seeing a male mirror of herself. Had he experienced the duality of their people? He must know what it was like to be both loved and feared.

Imoshen had longed to let her guard down. All her life she had been a barely tolerated outcast in her own family. Even the Aayel had kept her at a distance. In Reothe she hoped to find a kindred spirit. If so, why didn't she trust him?

Was she unnerved by his Otherness? How absurd, when she was as pure T'En as he.

But he was different, and it made her wonder if the people she lived with found her as unnerving as she found him.

A shift had occurred over the six hundred years since the first T'Imoshen and her explorers set foot on Fair Isle. Where once the vanquished people were the underclass, recognised by their language, their religion, their slight frames and golden skin, through interbreeding and the interweaving of everyday life the T'En had grown to be one with the locals, just as the original inhabitants had assumed a fierce loyalty to their once-invaders.

It was odd, Imoshen thought. She had never regarded her people as invaders, but honesty forced her to admit the truth.

The Ghebites' primitive chanting carried on the wind. The men were singing a deep, repetitive passage which stirred her blood despite herself.

Yes, she could sense their virility and passion. No wonder they drove the complacent and over-fed Fair Isle army before them. Sated with life's pleasures, her people had been no match for the primal hunger of the battle-hardened Ghebites.

In other circumstances, she might have admired the vitality of these barbarians. Imoshen had studied the tactics of mainland invasions. Unlike many of her peers, she had learnt the ancient T'En art of armed and unarmed combat, as well as diplomacy of state.

Her brother and sister had teased her, contemptuous of her old-fashioned dedication to knowledge for its own sake. But Imoshen felt more at home immersed in the ancient manuscripts, communing with long-dead people, than dealing with the sly smiles and whispers of her peers. While her brother looked for recognition with his poetry and her sister prepared herself for the acid frivolity of court life, Imoshen retreated to the library and read of old battles.

Having heard the many tales of the Ghebite General's tactical brilliance, she was curious to get a closer look at the man who had subdued the warring northern kingdoms, allied Gheeaba to the Low-lands and then in one summer campaign conquered Fair Isle, once thought impregnable.

Raising the farseer, she located General Tulkhan again, the Ghebite standard billowing behind him. His commanders gathered around him; gloating over the stronghold's surrender, no doubt. Imoshen's lips curled with contempt, for she did not see one woman in the ranks. So it was true. The Ghebite males shut their woman away from life.

Instead the warriors bonded to each other – the Ghebites believed it made for a fiercer fighting unit. Ghebite women were either wife-slaves or a harmless diversion for their males.

She had heard they kept their wives and daughters in seclusion to produce sons or to marry off to further family alliances. Ghebite women were merely instruments of birth. The males ran their barbaric society, and look where it had led them: on a pointless path of destruction, acquisition of territory for its own sake.

Imoshen's stomach churned as anger threatened to consume her. It was a sad day for the her people, reduced to Ghebite rule. She was no man's slave. The Ghebites were fools if they underestimated the women of Fair Isle.

Wincing, she felt heat flood her cheeks as she heard the Aayel accept the terms of surrender. Against her will, Imoshen's gaze was drawn to the tableau. Having delivered the General's message, their own stronghold guard stood with despair written clear in their faces. The men and women she had trained beside now faced defeat with her.

'...and in return for a bloodless victory,' the Aayel was saying, 'General Tulkhan must appoint someone to meet with me and discuss the welfare of our people. There will be no looting, no wanton killing, or we will defend this stronghold to our last breath.'

The old woman's dark eyes flashed fiercely and hope surged in Imoshen. Defeat was ignoble, but if they could rescue some honour from this surrender...

When the defenders had gone, the Aayel beckoned and Imoshen came forward, head held high, rebellion in her breast.

'You are the last pure T'En. I am old, but you hold the seeds of the future. If you die, our line perishes. Now is not the time for heroics, Shenna. Keep quiet, attract no attention.'

Imoshen would have spoken, but her great aunt silenced her. 'I will negotiate an honourable surrender. The fields are ripe with crops which must be harvested, or the winter snows will find us all starving. Already from here to the northwest coast the land lies black and ruined. Unless we move now, famine will stalk us this winter. Go, and heed my warning. I rely on your good sense.'

Her great aunt's aged hand trembled as she lifted it in the T'En sign of blessing, causing Imoshen a stab of guilt. The light touch of the Aayel's sixth finger, the one closest to her heart, brushed Imoshen's forehead.

Impulsively she caught that hand between hers. 'I will heed your words, but –'

'I know it is hard, Shenna. You are my sister's grandchild, yet you are more mine than anyone's. I thought I had years to watch over you, but now... There is much I wanted to tell you, only your parents would not have it. They wanted to ignore the pure T'En in you –'

They were interrupted by anxious stronghold servants. The Aayel dismissed her and Imoshen was left to wander, angry and heartsore. It was bitter to have confirmed what she had always suspected. Her family had tried to deny what she was.

Throughout Umasreach the inhabitants went about their tasks in trepidation, unsure whether the General would honour the terms of surrender. They came to Imoshen – some merely touched her hair or her sixth finger in passing, others asked for verbal reassurance.

The irony of it made her smile. In good times they had barely tolerated her, but when they felt threatened they turned to her.

She had to cloak her own fear and mistrust to bolster the courage of her people, but she was practised at this. All summer, as word had come of defeat after defeat, she had lived a lie of reassurance while she watched her world crumble. Since spring her life had changed direction irrevocably.

She should have been taking her formal vows with Reothe in the coming spring, creating history as the first pure T'En female to take a bond-partner, a pure T'En male. Imoshen shivered.

Banishing her betrothed's intense wine-dark eyes from her memory, she stood at the window of her tower room to watch a different, unwelcome history unfold. The stronghold's inner gates opened and the General entered astride his black warhorse, flanked by his commanders.

The people watched sullenly as their barbarian conquerors filed into the courtyard, without a drop of blood being shed.

General Tulkhan was followed by his elite guard, who oversaw the laying down of arms and the formal surrender.

Impotent rage seared Imoshen as she stood at her tower window. The autumn sun sank, cloaking her in its red glow, staining her with the unshed blood of their ignoble surrender. And she hated General Tulkhan with all her heart.

Shut away from everyone, she brooded, feeding the fires of her anger until shrill cries of excitement told her the General was making his way to the formal chamber to meet the Aayel.

Imoshen knew she was supposed to remain out of sight, but she wanted to hear the terms and judge the man for herself. So she slipped a cloak over her shoulders and joined the scurrying workers in the stairs and corridors of the conquered stronghold.

Truly, she meant to follow the Aayel's advice and hold her tongue but, as she entered the passage leading to the great library, she heard a terrible commotion.

Impulsively, Imoshen tiptoed quickly down the passage and slipped into the library. All the knowledge of Umasreach was stored in there, along with treasures, treatises on herbal cures, plays and profound philosophies, held in trust by the Keeper of Knowledge and the invaders were destroying it.

Before she could take in the chaos around her, the old scholar threw his frail body between the barbarians and his charges. Already the Ghebites had broken open several earthen jars and tipped the oil on the stones to expose the ancient scrolls to the air. When they broke the seal of the next jar the Keeper screeched in dismay. The Ghebites laughed raucously.

A flash of fury ignited Imoshen. These men were animals!

One Ghebite lifted a glass jar of preserved organs and smashed it on the floor. The pungent aroma of its preserving fluid filled the air. Where it met the oil a slow fusion occurred, hissing and fizzing menacingly – two vastly different substances in contact with one another, destroying each other. Was it an omen foretelling the fate of her race, the T'En and the Ghebites?

The largest male snatched up another precious canister and prepared to break the seal.

'Cease!' At Imoshen's command he stopped. The men looked over at her, startled. 'You must stop the wanton destruction immediately. The knowledge in this room has been collected over –'

They recovered and laughed. Imoshen strode toward the soldier who held the old man, and cuffed him across the head as she would an errant stable boy. Though she was only seventeen, she looked down on the man. 'This is an outrage. Release the Keeper of Knowledge. Have you no respect?'

The Ghebite and his partner released the old man. Leering, they turned on Imoshen, who instantly realised her mistake as both men were armed. But they ignored their weapons, seeking instead to grab her.

She ducked under the guard of the first and swung her foot at his knees, sending him to the floor. The second caught her arm, but instead of pulling away she went with his strength, darting inside his guard, to elbow him in the ribs. She jerked her head back into his face. His nose broke with a satisfying crunch.

These were both simple manoeuvres, learnt in early childhood by those who revered the old ways. A female might not have the muscle of a male but she had speed and could use their own strength against them.

The Keeper of Knowledge gave a shrill laugh which spurred the other three on to attack Imoshen. She knew the odds were against her. The floor was littered with broken pots and glass, and covered by a thin film of oil. She had little opportunity to manoeuvre.

Experience told her the only way to fight superior odds was to place them so that they impeded each other and were reduced to attacking her one at a time.

With this in mind she stepped back toward the shelves and kicked the closest man in the knee. He went down cursing.

Her aim was to disable. It felt good to take action after her enforced idleness since spring.

One of the men yelled something and the other two tried to encircle her. She saw their intention and charged the man who blocked her path to the door, but her foot slipped on the oil slick floor and he caught her. She'd only just broken away from him when two more were upon her.

Furious, she twisted and writhed in their grasp – all silent rage. Twice she drew blood with her sharp teeth. One man cursed and a fist caught her in the mouth. She tasted her own sweet, salty blood.

Two of them succeeded in pinioning her arms and the others, all nursing various injuries, surrounded her, keeping beyond range of her kicks. Their expressions told her they were intent on exacting revenge. Imoshen knew her situation was desperate.

One tore the neckline of her gown, baring her breasts. She felt her nipples tighten on contact with the cold air and heated looks.

They uttered eager, throaty laughs. Outrage roiled in her belly and with it came cold dismay. Their laughter made her skin crawl. So it was true, these Ghebites raped captive females. Such an act was an abomination to her people.

'Barbarians!' she hissed.

The nearest balled his fist.

That was when the General himself had arrived. She writhed under his calculating gaze, caught at a disadvantage. She wanted to rage defiantly at him, but already her impetuous actions had cost her her dignity. Imoshen knew she must not anger this barbarian. If he chose, he could order everyone in Umasreach Stronghold put to the sword, and nothing and no one could stop him.

Channelling her fear, she tried to think clearly. She could not afford to allow her anger to take over. This was war – she had to use every weapon she had. The Aayel claimed everyone had a weakness. She had to find the General's weakness.

Meeting his eyes, Imoshen made her stand. 'According to the terms of surrender...' She swallowed. How it galled her to use that word. 'There was to be no wanton destruction. I found these fools smashing the pots which preserve our most ancient parchments. I call on you to honour the terms and preserve this knowledge. Our people have a saying, *Knowledge knows no loyalty. It is the tool of the wise.*'

She let the words flow, but her mind was concentrating on what lay behind his penetrating gaze. Focusing on the man, she tried to read any nuance in his expression, any unguarded thought that might reveal his weakness.

It was rumoured that sometimes in moments of great stress, the pure T'En could call on their gifts to see into another's heart, but she could discern nothing from this Ghebite. His face was guarded, like his too-black eyes which hid his thoughts from her. He was physically different from any of the men she had known, but something in her recognised his type. He was a soldier, a man of action used to command, physically and mentally disciplined.

The elite guard waited to hear their General's response.

Tulkhan shifted, irritation eating at him. He didn't need this girl-woman to lecture him on the terms of surrender. What rankled most was the knowledge that she was right. His men had been in the wrong. He would have to discipline them.

Already he had confronted an aged crone, who seemed to think she would be representing her people to negotiate terms. Once he would have laughed outright, but many years in foreign countries taught him to hold his tongue and watch.

His own men had snickered, for in Gheeaba an old woman past childbearing age was good for nothing but minding the babes or feeding the dogs.

Tulkhan experienced a painful flash, a memory of his old mother hobbling around the royal courtyards, dodging blows. How proud she had been of him. Yet he had never acknowledged her, even when he had felt her glowing eyes on him. And she, in turn, had not expected so much as a kind word from him in passing. Then, during one of his numerous summer campaigns, she had died, unmourned, buried in a communal grave for the fever victims.

After all this time he thought he'd forgotten, yet the sight of proud old Aayel had reminded him of his mother. Though he did not know why, when his mother's demeanour had been that of a servile dog waiting to be kicked, as was appropriate for an old woman who had no value to society.

Yet when Aayel spoke, these odd people had blanched and watched with fear in their eyes as though she might strike him down with her withered arm. Did they know something he didn't? A quiver of disquiet moved through him. The old woman was throwback too, pure Dhamfeer.

Now he faced another of these Dhamfeer women, one who had taken on five of his elite guard in defence of an old bag of bones and a library of knowledge.

It amused him, though he was not about to show it. 'Who are you to lecture your captor?'

'Release me.'

He stiffened, irritated by her demand. To give ground was to show weakness, but his men had been in the wrong, and now was the moment for compromise. He nodded to his men. 'Release the Dhamfeer and no more destruction –'

'They can help the Keeper of Knowledge restore the manuscripts,' his captive interrupted, in the tone of one used to giving orders.

He knew she had to be one of the royal line, yet he'd been eliminating them as he did battle, first the Emperor and his wife, then their heirs. Who was this Dhamfeer? Even the Emperor and his kin had looked more like True-people than she did.

The guard stepped away from her. She tossed her head and shrugged her shoulders as if to rid herself of the imprint of their hands, but she made no move to cover her breasts, making him wonder if what they said was true – Dhamfeer women did not know modesty because they considered themselves above True-men, allowing none to sully their perfect, pale flesh.

Heat suffused him. It was also said if the Dhamfeer chose to take a lover they were insatiable, that a True-man could die trying to satisfy one. Again his soldier training surfaced. Superstition and nonsense. He wanted answers.

'Very well,' he said. 'Who are you?'

A prickle of excitement moved over his skin as he noted fury flame in her wine-dark eyes.

'I am T'Imoshen,' she said, using the T'En prefix, which translated roughly as *princess* in his own language.

Lifting her chin, she held his eyes defiantly. A well-bred woman of his race would have looked down out of deference, especially an unmarried female.

Tulkhan stiffened. The 'T' she had claimed was a sign of the royal house, which meant this vixen was directly related to the Emperor – by rights, he should have her killed.

A member of the royal household would foster insurgence, and provide a figurehead for the rabble to congregate around in the event of rebellion, even a female.

'Imoshen,' he acknowledged, intentionally ignoring her title. She was too sure of herself, he needed her more malleable. If he was to use her, he had to frighten her. Deliberately rude, he nodded to the man at her side. 'Lock her in with the old crone, the one they call Aayel.'

He caught a flicker of triumph in her carefully schooled features. Was she pleased because he had ordered her locked away with the old woman, or was she pretending? He didn't know. He didn't understand these people, least of all a Dhamfeer throwback.

Tulkhan felt his mouth tighten in a grim line of annoyance. Privately he might find her unsettling, but he must not show a moment's indecision before her, or his men. To maintain command, he must always appear to be in command.

He would have to decide what to do with her. Killing a female did not bother him. He had seen what these females were trained to do in battle and he would order her execution without compunction.

But after nearly eleven years with the army, he was beginning to feel that he had seen too many deaths. He was sick of the stench of destruction. More importantly, he could make use of this Dhamfeer. She was his direct source for the cultural treasure of this island. But to be of use to him, she had to fear him. He wanted to see fear crawl across her features, he needed to see it. With a flick he indicated her cloak on the floor. 'Cover yourself, woman.'

She bent down and lifted the cape, a little smile playing around her swollen lips. As though it made no difference to her, she swung the cloak over her shoulders and pulled it closed. Then, before his men expected it, she stepped forward so that her face was near his, her eyes level with his mouth.

She was much bigger than a woman of his race, tall even for a man.

Her six-fingered hand closed on his bare forearm. He had a flash of cool white fingers pressed around his coppery skin.

Her wine-dark eyes fixed his, searching intimately, and he felt... naked.

Again, he caught that foreign scent on her skin, not unpleasant but carnal. It sliced through his civilised exterior, through his educated mind to the primal male in him, eliciting an urgent response from his body, a response so immediate it unnerved him.

His physical vulnerability was a revelation and he hated it. Tulkhan had not been unnerved since his first campaign. Irritation flashed through him so that he had trouble distinguishing her words.

'I see an old woman.' She grimaced as if in pain and Tulkhan went cold to the core. 'The fever troubles her –'

Before she could finish, the soldiers jerked her away from him, cursing her and apologising profusely to him.

'Fools! If she'd wanted to kill me I'd be dead by now!' Her other hand had been only a finger's breadth from his ceremonial knife.

Her comments had to be a trick, a lucky guess. Yet honesty forced Tulkhan to admit she had dipped into his mind and plucked an image of his mother – not as he had ever seen her, since he had been leading the army in another country when she died, but as he imagined the old woman had lain, alone, unloved, dying, with no one to mourn her passing.

Guilt surged through him. He hated the Dhamfeer woman for stealing the image from his mind and using it to pierce his defences. All his life he had prided himself on his control, even in the heat of battle he assessed the odds, the enemy's capabilities and his own men. Next to the King, his word was absolute.

Now, looking into her pale face, he faltered, but he could not afford to reveal his trepidation. She must never know he feared her, and his men must never suspect this chink in his armour.

The Dhamfeer frowned, her eyes widened and she asked as if genuinely confused, 'Why did they refuse the old woman medicine to ease her passing?'

General Tulkhan's mouth went dry – this was his private torment. If he had been there, if he had shown one shred of feeling, he would have insisted they treat his mother, but it was the custom not to physic the old women. Only a girl or a woman of child bearing age would be treated. The old females must live or die depending on their strength.

'Take her away,' he snarled.

The Dhamfeer stepped back, surprised by his tone. Even his men flinched. Furious, he gestured. '*Out!*'

Head held high, she walked past him as though the men who stood to each side of her were there to serve her, not to imprison her.

Defiant Dhamfeer.

Tulkhan fought an urge to grab her slender throat and crush her. He longed to see her at his feet pleading, as he had crushed the defending armies. He had dealt with kings and noble men. He had seen honourable defeat and cowardly defeat, but he had never feared his captive before, and he felt a loathing that went bone deep.

She defied him on every level, made him doubt his very image of himself. Only once before had he been forced to question his place in the world. When his half-brother was born and his position as the King's heir was supplanted, General Tulkhan had seen his erstwhile mentors withdraw their support. Human nature was fickle, he discovered. As the son of the King's second-wife, any chance of inheritance had died with the birth of his half-brother. He had no rights, only those which he took and held.

Swallowing this bitter knowledge, he had chosen to walk alone and make his own future.

As a matter of political necessity, he gave lip service to the Ghebite religion. He had sworn fealty to his father, the King, and striven to prove himself. Every time he returned triumphant to present his father with the news of another victory, he had looked for one particular expression in the old man's eyes. But the King had died without acknowledging him as anything more than the son of his concubine.

After this campaign was over he would swear an oath of fealty to his half-brother, King Gharavan, but inwardly he raged against a system that acknowledged a man's birth and not his worth.

In his heart Tulkhan called no man master.

In the deepest recess of his being he recognised that same defiant quality in the Dhamfeer woman and he had to admit a certain reluctant admiration.

It could not be easy to find oneself a captive, confronted by the victor.

The Dhamfeer were an ancient race. They had come out of the rising sun six centuries ago and taken this land of the True-people by force. They'd made use of written language and created art and music when his ancestors were still eating their enemies' hearts to acquire their courage.

Much was whispered of Dhamfeer powers, their ability to read minds and to see the future. How much of it was true, Tulkhan did not know. A good tactician did not reveal the extent of his power, and he had assumed it was all bluff, until now. After all, their armies had not outwitted him on the field of battle.

Yet this young woman had plucked a long-buried image from his mind.

'Give the Keeper of Knowledge the aid he needs,' the General ordered as though he wasn't dizzy with the implications of what he'd just learnt.

He stepped into the passage and went to a narrow window. He could not deny the evidence – his skin crawled with the knowledge. She had touched him and, with that contact, delved into his thoughts. He felt violated, more frightened than the first time he had faced death on the battlefield, because his mind was private, his only sanctuary.

His tutors had filled him with the lore of his homeland and the strategies of great battles. In the years he had travelled with the army, he had kept an open mind, learnt all he could about his enemies. Knowledge knew no allegiance, knowledge was power.

Curse her, she was right.

His Dhamfeer captive had invaded his mind and laid open his vulnerable self – he should kill her.

A shudder passed over his body at the thought. In his mind's eye he saw his old mother lying on the mat, suffering in silence.

The image came more clearly to him than ever before. He tried to bury it as he had done repeatedly in the last few years, but the Dhamfeer had exposed it and, in doing so, she had laid open his hidden grief.

Tulkhan gripped the window frame till his shoulders ached with tension. Moisture gathered in his eyes. Eyes that had witnessed countless deaths on the battlefield burned with unshed tears for a mother he had loved but had never acknowledged.

In Gheeaba, a man had no time for tears – they were a female weakness. The Dhamfeer had defied him. She had emasculated him.

He had to kill her.

THE AAYEL'S SURPRISINGLY strong hands closed on Imoshen's arm, stopping her when she would have risen to leave with the other women.

They had the use of a wing of chambers, but effectively they were prisoners in their own stronghold. The other women retreated to dress for the evening meal. The Aayel had said they were to be very formal and carry on as if they were not living on a knife's edge.

As the connecting door closed on the last woman, Imoshen prepared for the worst. She felt her cheeks grow hot. Had the Aayel heard about her meeting with the Ghebite General? She had no excuse. Her impulsiveness had led her into trouble, again. Imoshen opened her mouth to apologise but the Aayel spoke first.

'We haven't much time.' Her voice rustled like dry leaves on paving stones. 'We need to find this General Tulkhan's Key.'

Imoshen felt a rush of excitement. The Aayel was talking about using her gift. And it wasn't a simple scrying, either. Right now they needed all the help they could get. Despite the terms, they faced possible execution. It would only take a small shift in some factor, perhaps something they could not predict, for the General to justify their deaths. 'What will you do? Can I help?'

The Aayel's garnet eyes fixed on Imoshen's face. 'No, better not. I want you out of the way. If I'm worried about you, it will break my concentration. Contrary to what is rumoured, the T'En gifts aren't very powerful. You can heal a little and I can scry imperfectly.

'If I maintain body contact and concentrate very hard I can sift a True-person's mind to find their deepest fear or secret wish – the key to controlling them. It is not easy, and the General might resist. He strikes me as a man who is used to keeping to himself. He is no fool, Imoshen.'

'I know that.' She eyed the Aayel resentfully.

The old woman squeezed her arm. 'Go, get dressed. I want you looking very regal tonight. We are the last of the T'En and must look the part. Appearance is everything to the susceptible.'

Imoshen nodded and touched her lips briefly to the old woman's forehead. But in her heart she raged against the unfairness of it. She wanted to be there to see how the Aayel used her T'En powers.

Resentment burned in her. Her parents had forbidden the Aayel teach her about her T'En heritage, condemning her to suffer all the subtle slights and indignities of her accidental birth and none of the advantages.

Imoshen had to know how the gifts worked. She wanted it so badly she could taste it. Well, her parents were dead, so their strictures no longer counted. In the changed future she would have to rely on herself and whatever skills she had, which meant she had to learn all she could about her T'En gifts.

Grimly determined, Imoshen chose to disobey her great aunt.

Rather than waiting for the maid to return from fussing over the other women, Imoshen dressed quickly. Choosing a fine skull cap, made of wired metal and inlaid with pearls, she brushed her long hair and set the circlet in place so that the large pearl drop hung, centred on her forehead. It was the sort of headdress she would normally have worn on a special occasion. The Aayel was right, it did help give her confidence.

Then she slipped her feet into the soft-soled boots and scurried back to the connecting door, making no sound on the polished floor.

A screen of scented wood blocked her line of sight, but it offered the perfect cover to prevent the room's inhabitants from seeing her open the door a crack. The General was already there, speaking with the Aayel. Imoshen caught her breath.

His low voice, with its faint Ghebite accent, rumbled to a stop as the Aayel interrupted.

'...be best if you interfered as little as possible with the running of the stronghold.'

He muttered something short and sharp. 'My men have been campaigning since spring. They expect their rights of plunder. You are in no position to lay down –'

The Aayel gave a cry. Heart thudding with concern, Imoshen pushed the door open and stepped forward to peer over the screen. She was in time to see her great aunt gasp and clutch the wall for support, but her fingers slipped. The Aayel fell headlong into the General's arms.

Tulkhan cursed as he caught the old woman. She was so light, nothing but a bag of bones. What should he do with her?

'Barbarian! What have you done to her?'

He whirled around to see the Dhamfeer girl running across the room toward him. She was no longer the untidy feral wench who had confronted him in the library, but a graceful princess dressed in rich brocade and pearls. Yet she was no less dangerous, he reminded himself.

'I did nothing. She collapsed –'

'Browbeating her, no doubt,' the Dhamfeer snapped, placing a hand gently on the old woman's forehead. She gave a soft grimace as if stung and pulled back, rubbing her hand thoughtfully. 'Bring her through here.' Gesturing imperiously, she led the way through a door to what he surmised was her own bed chamber. 'Sit here, before the fire. No. Don't put her down, you must hold her upright.'

He resented her tone. 'Why?'

'I am the healer. Do you want her life on your conscience?'

Tulkhan sank onto the seat before the empty fireplace. The old hag was held in high esteem by the people of Umasreach Stronghold. He didn't want the old woman dying in his arms. Even if he had done nothing to cause her death, rumour would have him blamed for it, making his task more difficult. The least he could do was cooperate with the Dhamfeer healer, but he would not let his guard down.

Imoshen was only a female, and a mere girl, not yet married. Girl or woman? By Ghebite standards she could not be given the title of woman until she was of marriageable age.

Surely she was more than fifteen summers?

Then why wasn't she married like a Ghebite girl? Of course, she was pure Dhamfeer – untouchable. Perversely, he felt a surge of defiant lust for what he knew he could not have.

He put the thought aside and concentrated on the situation. Foreign customs never ceased to amaze him. The men of Fair Isle treated their women with a strange mixture of licence and contempt. Revering them one instant, then sacrificing them in battle the next.

If the Dhamfeer had been a Ghebite girl, he would have considered her harmless, but he had learnt not to make snap judgments. His every instinct warned him to be on guard against the heathen healer.

He studied Imoshen's concerned face as she examined the old woman. Strange, the Dhamfeer were not beautiful by Ghebite standards. Their faces were too narrow, their cheekbones too high and features too pointy. Yet there was something about the girl's face that fascinated him. Was it the contrast of her pale skin and wine-dark eyes?

Abruptly she glanced up, meeting his gaze.

He swallowed, his heart thudding uneasily. Tulkhan saw the knowledge in Imoshen's eyes. She had felt it too. It was hard to define the sensation – a metallic taste on his tongue, a tingling which made his skin crawl, his teeth ache and his temples throb.

A seed of panic stirred in his belly. 'What's happening?'

Imoshen licked her lips. 'It is the T'En gift you feel. I... I am seeking the source of my great aunt's weakness.'

He nodded, gritting his teeth. The sensation was unpleasant. It felt like a ruffling of his senses, much the way a cat might feel if someone rubbed its fur against the grain. He swallowed, forcing his tense throat muscles to work.

Imoshen poured water into a bowl, sprinkled herbs on the surface and dampened a cloth, using it to sponge the old woman's temples and wrists.

It didn't appear to do much good, but the sensation of discomfort persisted; Tulkhan thought she must be working on two levels.

'What is wrong with Aayel, girl?'

'Not Aayel, *the* Aayel. It is a title, not a name,' Imoshen corrected. 'And I have a name. You know it. I give you leave to use it. As for what ails the Aayel, it is old age. She had her hundredth birthday the year before I was born.'

It was on Tulkhan's lips to deny this, but the simple way the Dhamfeer girl spoke told him she believed it. In Gheeaba, fifty was considered old.

He concentrated on the healer, Imoshen. She gave him *leave* to use her name. How condescending of her. In any case, he did not trust her. Who knew what trick she might try? She seemed focused on the Aayel.

Tulkhan shifted to ease the muscles of his shoulders.

Interesting, if they weren't stoned to death by their own people, the Dhamfeer could live for a century. His father had been considered an old man when he had died at fifty-three. He left behind him only two sons, but his seven daughters by his first wife and two concubines had married well, extending the royal family's network of support throughout the Ghebite aristocracy.

Tulkhan grimaced. For there too, he had failed to win his father's approval. He had not been able to cement the alliance of his only arranged marriage. It had been annulled by custom, three years from the date it began, when his wife produced no children. He had refused another marriage, fearing...

The old woman stiffened in his arms. Immediately the unpleasant pressure behind his eyes eased.

'She recovers?'

Imoshen nodded, letting the cloth fall into the bowl.

Gently, Tulkhan eased the old woman off his lap. Propping her against the back of the deep chair, he crouched at her side to observe her. The Aayel was awake and aware, even if she seemed a little bewildered.

'How did I get in here?' she demanded feebly.

He patted her thin shoulder. 'You passed out, old one. I carried you in.'

The Dhamfeer healer came to her feet. 'You may leave now. Whatever you were discussing can be put off until tomorrow. I will escort the Aayel down to the great hall. It will ease the fears of the stronghold if you join us at the table and break bread with us.'

Tulkhan also rose. He was growing used to the way this Dhamfeer girl simply assumed command, but it still annoyed him.

'I will be back to escort you both down to the great hall.'

She inclined her head, as though this wasn't important. He left having had the last word, but it didn't give him any satisfaction.

Imoshen walked the General to the door then shut it after him. She turned back to her great aunt, hardly able to contain her excitement.

'I thought he would never leave. What did you learn?'

The Aayel smiled, her eyes as bright as a bird's.

'Well?' Imoshen prompted.

The Aayel frowned at her with mock severity. 'You deliberately disobeyed me, Shenna.'

'Yes. And just as well I did. He felt it when you used your gift. I had to pretend it was me seeking to heal you.'

The Aayel waved this aside and rose, but she wavered for a moment. Instinctively, Imoshen offered to support her.

'What is it, grandmother?' she asked.

The Aayel laughed. 'Foolish child. I am old. I overextended myself. But you were right, you did distract him for me. He was so busy watching you, making sure you weren't playing some trick on him, that he wasn't worried about a frail old crone.'

Imoshen had to smile.

The Aayel patted her arm. 'He is a clever man, but he is trapped by his own culture. He is hardly able to believe you are a threat to him. And since I am not only female but old as well, he disregards me altogether.'

'Foolish man,' Imoshen purred, delighted with her great aunt. 'So, what did you learn?'

The Aayel straightened, stepping away from her. 'I must dress for dinner.'

'Why won't you tell me?' Imoshen called to her retreating back.

'You will know soon enough.'

'When will you teach me how to do that trick?'

The Aayel spun around to face her, dark eyes snapping fire. 'It is not a trick. The gifts are never to be taken lightly. I have seen what can happen when a pure T'En oversteps the mark. I was twelve the last time one of us was stoned. And the Beatific of that time ordered that I witness it. I shall never forget.

'The rogue T'En male stood in the courtyard and held my eyes, held me captive. I had no defence from him. He sifted my mind freely, seeking something. I... I never understood what he wanted, but I felt every stone that hit him. I felt his agony, his fury and despair.

'I died with him that morning, stoned to death, and I have never trusted a male T'En since. I –'

'Is that why you refused to meet with Reothe?'

The Aayel looked away. 'I can tell you now that he is dead. T'Reothe was dangerous. Your betrothal to him was a mistake.'

'If you believed this, why didn't you tell my parents? Why didn't you warn me? Why didn't you teach me the ways of the T'En, even if my parents had forbade it?'

The Aayel took several paces forward, her dark eyes flooded with anger and grief. Her fierce expression silenced Imoshen.

'I can see it in you, all restless fire. You wonder why I never rebelled? Why I followed the edicts of the church?' She gestured sharply. 'How can you stand there and judge me? You cannot know what I have witnessed. I grew up living in fear for my life. Nothing, not royal birth, not even the Empress's favour, could have saved me from the power of the church, had the Beatific declared me rogue!'

Imoshen bit her lip. 'I am sorry. But that was over a hundred years ago. It is not like that anymore. Besides, everything has changed now. The church is as much a victim of the Ghebites as we are.'

The Aayel nodded slowly. 'True, the rules have changed so we must make our own.' She paused to study Imoshen critically. 'Try not to look too Other. The General finds your differences disturbing.'

Imoshen snorted but nodded.

After her great aunt left to dress, she used the bowl of useless, sweet-smelling herbs to bathe her flushed face and neck. For some reason the Ghebite General made her feel gauche. When confronted by his calculating gaze, her instinct was to attack, and she could tell he didn't like it.

So he found her unnerving? Good.

If the truth be told she found the General equally unnerving. Considering that he held Umasreach and all of Fair Isle in the palm of his hand, the less she irritated him the better.

Imoshen vowed to be on her best behaviour – her life depended on it. But the thought of pandering to the whims of a barbarian Ghebite filled her with rebellion.

Chapter Two

IMOSHEN WAS INTRIGUED. Why had the Aayel woken her so stealthily? The night candles had been doused long ago and she had fallen asleep after enduring a painfully tense meal at the General's table.

The household servants who waited on the Aayel and herself were asleep in the antechamber. Imoshen's great aunt drew her aside to the window seat where they sat in a patch of moonlight.

The Aayel's voice was low, intense. 'He believes he must have you killed.'

'You did a scrying without me?'

'No –'

'You read it, when he helped you? I saw how you pretended to stumble when you rose from the table. What secrets did you discover when you touched him?' Imoshen gave a disgruntled sigh. 'I took his arm when he escorted us down to the great hall with the intention of trying to skim his mind, but I felt nothing.'

The Aayel patted her shoulder. 'It is not easy to read a person. Don't be discouraged. I've had years to hone my skill. I did get an insight into the Ghebite General when I touched him, but no, I did not read him.

'This time I used logic, Shenna. I am old and in his eyes useless. You are young and even though *only* a female,' her voice grew rich with laughter, 'you could be used to unite those loyal to the Old Empire.'

'But I –'

The old hand clasped hers, willing her to silence.

Heart hammering with the injustice of it, Imoshen held her tongue.

'Don't despair, there is hope. He came to see me again after you retired tonight. He came on an excuse, but he was looking for you. He's drawn to you.'

'I despise him!' Imoshen leapt to her feet and prowled the length of the room. What could she do? She felt trapped. She could feel the Aayel watching her thoughtfully. It irritated her.

'A strong emotion moves you,' her great aunt acknowledged. 'But listen, time is short. If we are to survive, you must think with a clear head and make difficult decisions which will require great fortitude to fulfil.'

'I will do whatever I must.' Imoshen strode back to the window eagerly. Her hands clenched and unclenched. How she wanted to take action. 'Show me the way and I will follow it without fail.'

'No matter how hard it may be?'

She grasped the old woman's hands. 'I will not fail you. I will not fail the T'En blood that runs strong in me.'

The old woman nodded then walked stiffly to the recessed cabinet and used her personal key to unlock it. Imoshen felt a stirring of hope as she watched the Aayel remove different medicinals.

Her great aunt knew them by touch and by smell, and did not need to light a lamp. Imoshen had learnt her herbal-lore from the Aayel who, though she did not have the gift to hasten healing, had a lifetime of practical knowledge.

Imoshen darted eagerly across the room to join her great aunt. Already she felt optimistic. 'A slow, debilitating poison? I will find a way to slip it to him.'

'No.'

'Much better.' Imoshen nodded. 'A quick-acting poison which mimics a natural illness.'

'No.'

'Then what?'

'Hush and listen. You know your medicinals. What's this?'

Imoshen sniffed and concentrated. She wanted to please the Aayel to show that she had learnt her lessons well. 'A woman's herb, it has something to do with the bleeding cycle. It's not for inhibiting fertility.'

'No. It brings on fertility.'

Imoshen's lips formed a question but she held it back, fearing the answer.

As if her silence was expected, the old woman continued speaking in a voice that was no louder than the rustle of leaves on an autumn breeze. 'This must be taken each night for fourteen days to bring the body into cycle. Remember this whatever happens –'

'What do you mean?' Imoshen's skin went cold, her voice rose.

'Hush. The General leads through the loyalty of his men. He must show himself to be all-powerful and without doubt, but he is a True-man with all the human frailty that a man possesses. He must cloak his weakness, just as you must hide your thoughts when you have to take a path you may despise to achieve your ends.'

'I don't understand you.' Agitated, Imoshen turned and walked to the window. 'I wish the General had never come to invade Fair Isle! Oh, why did our armies fail? We had the numbers, we had –'

'We had grown arrogant in our complacency. Hubris is fatal. Humility is a painful lesson.'

'Hubris, humility – what have these to do with it all?' Imoshen muttered, resentfully. Was the Aayel mocking her?

'If you live long enough, you will understand.'

Imoshen grimaced. That was a cheerful thought.

She sank onto the padded window seat with a sigh. Her fingers clasped the casements as she turned to look up to the twin moons.

The smaller represented woman; the larger, man.

They performed a dance around each other, sometimes one was in ascendant, sometimes the other. Then, four times a year on the cusp of the seasons, both moons would fill the sky with a blaze of light so bright that night was almost as clear as day, bathed in silver.

Soon it would be that time, the time of the Harvest Feast, of ancient rites the people still performed after six hundred years of foreign lords, a time when the T'En performed ancient ceremonies dating back to the customs of their homeland.

Imoshen flinched, recalling her history lessons.

The first T'Imoshen had ordered their ship burned to the water line so that none could desert her and flee back to their distant homeland. That took courage. It was a hard decision which had forced them to succeed or die trying.

Pride surged through her. She could be as unflinching as her namesake if need be.

'Here it is.' The Aayel recalled Imoshen's attention and offered her a small stoppered decanter and a vial. 'Pour out this much each night and drink it when you retire.'

'What would you have me do, Aayel?' Imoshen's hands closed in fists on her knees. She made no move to take the small measuring vial. The dark liquid glistened. Its pungent smell stung her nostrils, making her stomach churn.

The old woman looked through the window.

'Double full moon, a propitious time. You are blessed. You must convince the General to send his men out into the fields to assist the farmers to harvest the crops. Our people have made great sacrifices for us. On the farms there are few able-bodied people, mainly the very old and the very young.

'The food must be harvested and stored in our central granaries, from whence you will dole it out. Hundreds, even thousands, will come down from the north, pitiful and starving. There may not be enough to feed everyone, but you must share it fairly, between our own refugees and the barbarians as well as the locals.'

'What are you talking about?'

'Survival. Drink this.'

'No.'

A silence grew between them. Imoshen could hear her own pulse rushing in her head. She felt sick at heart. 'Isn't there another way?'

The old woman's voice was implacable. 'You have no choice. You must ensure your survival. Tulkhan means to kill you. He must, or you will become a figurehead for rebellion. To save your life you must lie with him and conceive a child, a son. You know the way to ensure the child is a boy.'

'Lie with the barbarian?' Imoshen swallowed hard. Must she compromise her principles to live?

Would General Tulkhan even want her? She shuddered, recalling how he had stared at her with cold, calculating eyes. He was not a foolish youth driven by the first flush of lust.

'Even if I did somehow trick him into planting his seed, why would that stop him from killing me?'

'Listen. I question and I learn, you must do the same. Knowledge is power. General Tulkhan has no son. The Ghebites place great significance on having a male heir. If Tulkhan is to hold this land, he must take it into his heart, into his bed, to become one with it. You represent the land, you are the last of the T'En. If you and he are joined, you will be the mother to the future heir.'

'But from what I've heard, the King is young. He will have heirs of his own.'

'The King has dominion from here across the mainland to the north as far as Gheeaba. He must maintain control over all of this and ensure his conquered lands remain loyal. What has been won by might can only be held through forethought. Remember your lessons.'

'Yes. But the General despises me!' It was a cry from the heart. 'I see it in his eyes.'

The Aayel closed Imoshen's cold, reluctant fingers around the glass vial and raised it toward her lips. 'Drink. Fourteen nights in a row you must take this and, on the last, trick him into his planting his seed.'

Imoshen's blood rushed in her head. She felt herself go hot and cold as she considered the steps she would have to take. She had never lain with a male. For most of her life it had been taken for granted that she would never do so.

She had never told of her secret shame, how Reothe had come to her before their formal betrothal and suggested they go riding. How innocently, because she had never known anything but circumspect treatment from the males of the stronghold, she had gone with him.

The memory of it still made her cheeks burn, for she, who previously spurned all males, had been captivated by Reothe.

He had challenged her to a race across the plains, then along the forest paths. She'd let her horse have its head and matched him, leap for leap. She never could resist a challenge. When they had dismounted, panting with excitement, the blood was singing in her body.

He'd challenged her to perform the formal defence-offence manoeuvres with him, but it had been a ploy. He'd abandoned the standard responses and tricked her, blocked strikes. When she realised he was playing with her, she grew angry. He'd proved that though she knew her moves she could not defeat him physically.

Finally, he'd laughed at her outraged expression. She'd struck him while he was off-guard, knocking him to the ground. When he looked up, his expression told her she would pay for it.

She'd turned and run, almost mounting her horse before he pulled her from it. He'd tripped her and pushed her to the mossy ground. She'd fought him fiercely. But she hadn't intended to hurt him so she hadn't used the blows to his eyes or throat which might have freed her. Still, she had made it clear with the force of her resistance that she was not giving in.

At last, panting with exertion, she ceased to struggle and looked up at him. Despite her intention not to cause him harm, she saw that his lip was bleeding and she experienced a ridiculous pang of guilt. But it was the intensity of his expression which unnerved her. She had never seen naked desire written clearly on a man's features before.

When his lips claimed hers she remained still, unsure. She tasted his blood on her tongue, experiencing the velvet softness of his lips for the first time. It felt strange.

He explored her mouth with tantalising little touches that left her wanting more. His breath, his scent and his essence enveloped her, imprinting him on her. A sweet languor stole surreptitiously through her limbs.

Curious, she had returned his touch, surprised by a savage surge of desire which claimed her. Suddenly lost, she had forgotten herself in his embrace, forgotten all caution. Seared by a passion she did not know existed, she gave herself up to sensation.

When their lips parted she had moaned in protest.

He could have taken her then, but he hadn't. He had laughed, a wild, passionate laugh which both frightened and fascinated her. And though she could tell it cost him, he had held back.

It seemed he was pleased with her response to him.

It was then he revealed that he'd always intended to make her his. A formal request to bond with her fell falteringly from his lips and she'd agreed without prevarication, surprising herself by the surge of heat which flashed through her body. His eyes had widened, as if he sensed her response, and he had smiled.

At that moment she realised Reothe did not intend a cool, political bonding but a bonding of the blood, of the soul.

Looking back, Imoshen decided he must have sensed a sensual liability in her. Maybe it called to him and he had recognised it for what it was – a wild, wanton streak. He had deliberately passed over her elder sister, who by rights should have been bonded before her. He had come to Umasreach prepared with the dispensation which allowed him to break six hundred years of custom and take her for his bond-partner.

During their formal betrothal ceremony, Reothe had touched her and she him, they had shared their scents and mingled their blood symbolically, for the approval of the witnesses.

This was the sum total of her experience with men.

Because she had been born a throwback, destined to live a celibate life like the Aayel, no man had shown an interest in her. The idea of dying chaste had not bothered her. She could not understand the way her sister and friends eyed the young men of their acquaintance. Her own reaction to Reothe's touch was a shock. He appeared to have awakened something in her.

Imoshen licked her lips. Before the betrothal she had not received the same formal training as her sister.

Once she was betrothed, she began new instruction. Other young people of a comparative age and social level had started lessons years earlier to prepare them for the pleasures of bonding. She'd had to make up those lessons to train her in the arts of lovemaking. These sessions did not hint at the depth of sensation she felt in Reothe's embrace, and they had certainly not prepared her to undertake the seduction of a Ghebite barbarian who despised her.

Imoshen shuddered.

'Drink,' the Aayel ordered. 'You have it within your power to supplant the barbarian's victory with a victory of your own, to blend our blood with his, to rule through him and his son.'

The glass vial felt cold against Imoshen's lips. It smelled strongly of herbs she'd never had reason to use. What choice did she have? It was not her way to accept her fate calmly, bowing to the inevitable. She would fight it every inch of the way. Even if it meant this.

She held her breath and drained the vial in one gulp. It burned all the way down, finally spreading to an intense ball of heat in her belly.

Imoshen closed her eyes. She'd made her decision. It was begun. She would turn surrender into victory.

Fire surged through her veins, a passionate conviction. She felt an awareness of her body, a tension which coiled within her. Was it a presentiment of what she intended for the General?

THE NEXT MORNING Imoshen sought him out. Somehow she had to ensure her survival for another thirteen days and during that last night she must seduce General Tulkhan. The knowledge weighed heavily on her.

In the cold light of day she did not feel so confident.

Pausing in the courtyard entrance, she watched him talking to his commanders. She studied the way they interacted. They were all seasoned veterans, some younger, most older than he.

It was obvious from the timbre of their voices and the way they stood that they deferred to him, not just because of rank or his freakish size but out of respect. In their eyes he had proved himself. She would do well to remember that.

Whatever she might think of him and his coarse barbarian ways, he had proved himself to his peers.

She would not approach him until the men parted, for to accept the advice of a female would demean him in the eyes of his men. Imoshen felt a little smile tug at her lips. Already she was learning to think like a Ghebite. As the Aayel said, to know your enemy is to know how to manipulate him.

She did not want to weaken the General's position. It would force him to make a show of strength, perhaps force him to sacrifice her to shore up his hold on the men.

General Tulkhan threw back his head and laughed. Imoshen shivered. The Ghebites echoed his deep-throated laughter.

For an instant she experienced an unfamiliar pang – they shared a camaraderie. On the battlefield they were equals. Yet when the General looked at her she read his reaction despite his guarded expression. He despised her.

Resentment burned in her breast and all her good intentions were forgotten as she stepped into the morning sunshine.

The men parted and the General spun on his heel, his cloak billowing. She noted how his sharp eyes scanned the courtyard. Imoshen knew instinctively that he missed nothing.

A shiver of awareness crept up her spine. He was a dangerous animal and she had to seduce him, trick him into spilling his seed in her. In that moment she became aware of her body in a way she had never been before.

The bustling courtyard surged around the General. His soldiers were victorious, but forbidden their rightful plunder. Consequently, they laughed too loudly, swaggered too much and looked threateningly on the frightened people who had sought shelter within Umasreach. The stronghold soldiers stood by unarmed and resentful, bristling at each unspoken threat. Amid all this ran geese, ducks, dogs and small children. The place was packed with humanity, brimming with tension.

Tulkhan inhaled the rich autumn air, savouring the scent of wood-smoke. This fertile southern island was so different from his homeland, where it would not grow cold for another small moon. Already he could feel a chill on the air, and it quickened his senses with a strange anticipation.

He stiffened as the Dhamfeer stepped from the shadows. Her silver hair held an unearthly radiance in the pale, early morning sunshine. When she lifted her chin and met his eyes he felt his body tense in response. His heart rate lifted a notch as if anticipating battle.

There was no mistaking it, she meant him to see her. She was approaching him here, where any of his men might see. Had she no shame, no fear?

She gave none of the signals of deference a Ghebite women would have given when approaching a high-ranking male. Her rudeness was sure to irritate his men on his behalf. Tulkhan understood she did not know his country's customs and so did not know any better. Obviously, she considered herself the equal of any man. She would never have grown so bold in Gheeaba. Any sign of independence would have been beaten out of her. Strangely enough, that thought caused him a moment's disquiet.

As she strode toward him, he could not help but admire the very boldness that set his teeth on edge. Yet, for her own protection, he should lead her away, find a private place his men could not observe her lack of respect.

Again he felt an inexplicable surge of desire. Obviously he had been without a woman too long, to respond this way to a female, especially a Dhamfeer, a creature learned men regarded as less than human.

Less than human she might be, but the intelligence which gleamed in her feral red eyes was unmistakable and dangerous. His mouth went dry as he sensed her anger, held in tight control.

When she stepped within what was considered polite speaking distance, he caught a faint hint of her scent.

There was no doubt about it. He would have to find one of the stronghold women and bed her tonight – anything to rid himself of this unnatural longing for the Dhamfeer woman.

Inclining her head in a gesture which was the nearest she had come to deference so far, the Dhamfeer met his eyes, yet another unintended insult. 'I would speak with you, General.'

Tulkhan stiffened. She accorded him his title, but her face revealed no deference and her body shouted a challenge to his. What trickery did she plan?

'Speak.'

She glanced about, wishing perhaps to go somewhere private. Perversely, he decided to confront her here in the midst of the bustling courtyard. Let her show him what she made of it.

'In thirteen days it will be Harvest Moon –'

'The conjunction of the moons.'

'Yes. It takes time to harvest the grains. Normally by now we would be mid-way through it, preparing for our Harvest Feast. I don't know what it is like in your homeland, but here winter can come on rapidly. Soon the snow will lie thick on the ground and the days will grow short. If we do not fill the store rooms with grain, my people, your people – everyone will starve before the thaw. The fields between here and the northwest coast lie ruined and the farm animals slaughtered.'

He tensed. 'A travelling army must eat.'

'And empty fields mean little resistance from hungry people. I know.' She eyed him narrowly.

A frisson of danger danced across his skin as he sensed her animosity. She did not defer to him. She met his eyes, met his challenge. Her mind was as sharp as his and he resented having to acknowledge it.

'You think like a man.' It annoyed him.

Her eyes widened, then narrowed. 'And you think like a Ghebite.'

What did she mean by that? Why did she invest it with such mockery? He had the uncomfortable feeling that he had not bested her in that exchange and he resented it. 'Make your point, Dhamfeer.'

She flinched. Good. He had meant the name to be an insult. He wanted to unnerve her.

But she continued in a measured tone. 'Even your elite guard must eat, and the lands from here south to the coast are the only untouched fields where the grain hangs heavy, spoiling to be harvested. We can't afford to lose this harvest, but the farmers are reduced to the very young and the old. They cannot bring the crops in.

'You must order your army out into the fields to help harvest the grain, thresh and winnow it. The harvest must be brought in here to be stored, for in no time survivors from the north will come here pleading for food. We must be able to feed our own people, your army and the refugees.'

'We?' He bristled. She stood there, telling him what to do without deference to her position as the representative of a conquered people. But as much as he resented her tone, he knew that she was right. He did not know the climate of this southern island and, during his long campaigns, he had learnt the folly of not listening to those who knew the land.

'Your men grow restless. Only this morning I had to stop one of them from raping a kitchen maid.'

'It is the custom for the conqueror to take the women. It is their right of conquest.'

'It is uncivilised. By the terms of our agreement –'

'Your surrender, you mean!'

Her wine-dark eyes flashed with rage and colour stained her pale cheeks. He could see her chest rising and falling under her thin garment, visibly reminding him of her high, milky white breasts. He felt his body react instinctively and scorned his physical response.

Why, she was hardly a real woman by Ghebite standards, tall and scrawny instead of small and rounded. What was wrong with him?

The silence stretched between them and the clamour of the crowded courtyard seemed to fade as the moment hung in the balance.

Imoshen had seen the blaze of desire in his eyes, followed by the contempt he felt for her. The desire boded well for her plans, if only she could but get past his disdain. With an effort of will, she dropped her voice and continued, projecting a calm she did not feel. 'By the terms of our surrender your men are to respect our property and our people. Your men have been well disciplined for the most part, but they grow restless.'

'This is a poor excuse for a victory, no victory feast, no rights of conquest –'

'Debauchery.'

'Rights of conquest.'

'I won't argue!'

Tulkhan smiled. 'What do you call this?'

She flashed him a look. She knew what he was doing. 'I am here only on behalf of my people and yours. Your men need activity, we all need the grain. Occupy them with a task, have them bring in the harvest. With your army on the move it could be done in half the usual time. By custom we would hold our Harvest Feast on the night of conjunction, let this be your victory feast. Thus they will have their victory celebrations without engendering ill feelings –'

A girl screamed as she ran into the courtyard, her long golden-brown hair matted with blood from a cut to her forehead, her budding breasts bared.

Blind fear filled her face. She took in the crowded Ghebites, and fled in terror as several soldiers lurched after her. In no hurry to catch her, they were enjoying the chase.

With a moan of despair, she staggered toward the General and Imoshen, falling at Imoshen's feet. 'Lady T'En, save me. I am bound until the Harvest Feast.'

She gasped as Imoshen impatiently pulled her to her feet.

'Don't plead! Stand tall. You will be safe with me.' Curbing her anger,

Imoshen pressed her fingers over the girl's wound to stem the blood. Her eyes sought the General's, offering an unspoken challenge. 'According to the people's religious beliefs, they must abstain from pleasures of the flesh while they are harvesting the grain to appease the gods.' She did not add that this abstinence culminated in the Harvest Feast, where the peasants indulged in ritual intercourse as a way of giving thanks and ensuring the fertility of the fields the following spring. Theirs was an old religion, tied to the earth.

Instead, she held his eyes and nodded toward his men who had come to a sheepish, resentful halt. She was sure he could read her unspoken words, *so this was what his elite guard had been reduced to?*

'Explain,' he snapped at the men, and they blinked, swaying slightly.

It was obvious they'd been drinking. They were nothing but Ghebite barbarians. Rage flowed like fire through Imoshen's veins.

Let them argue their way out of this one, Imoshen thought with relish. If the General was an honourable man, as he professed to be, he had to chastise his men. Yet, she realised he might hesitate to do so in front of her, for his men would resent her witnessing their dressing down. She should leave.

As though the outcome of the interchange did not concern her, Imoshen led the girl away to treat her wound.

After she entered the darkness of the doorway, she heard the General bellow, using the soldier's coarse cant. A smile escaped her. They were rough men and they understood rough treatment. It was only as she escorted the girl back to her chamber that Imoshen realised the General spoke her tongue. That meant he was fluent in least two languages – he was not an uneducated man. Had he deliberately learned their language before attempting the invasion? If her guess was right, it suggested a cold, calculating mind, and a determination to succeed which made her shudder.

How was she to seduce this strange man?

Pushing her own troubles to one side, she took the reluctant girl to her chamber to treat her.

After summoning a servant to bring fresh water, she turned to the girl. 'What are you called?'

'Kalleen, but please don't.'

Imoshen hesitated. The girl was typical of her people, small with warm golden skin and eyes the same shade of light hazel. At this moment she appeared intensely embarrassed, because one of the royal family was caring for her.

'Nonsense,' Imoshen said. 'You are in need. It is my place to serve the needs of the people.' When her servant returned with a bowl of water Imoshen sprinkled purifying herbs in it and rinsed Kalleen's cut.

As she worked, it occurred to her that she had been learning the healing arts at the Aayel's side since she was a child, yet she had only brushed the surface of the old woman's knowledge. She was lucky her T'En talent was for healing. It was so practical.

'If I'd had a knife I'd have gutted them, one by one,' the girl muttered.

Imoshen snorted. 'If you'd had a knife you'd have been dead. The General's men are battle-hardened veterans, not farm boys out for fun.'

The girl sniffed as though unconvinced.

Imoshen smiled. She supposed Kalleen was her own age or a trifle younger. She could sympathise with her.

Rising, Imoshen went to the camphorwood box and removed the hidden panel. Selecting a small, well-balanced knife, she returned and offered it to the girl.

Kalleen swallowed eagerly and rose, her deft brown fingers closing around the handle.

Imoshen gripped Kalleen's narrow wrist and tilted her hand so that the blade angled up. She positioned it just below her own ribs.

'There, like that. Strike for the heart,' Imoshen advised. 'You will only have one chance, make it count.'

The girl's eyes widened but she nodded.

'And wear it like this for quick access.' Imoshen shifted the brocade panel of her tabard to reveal her own knife, strapped to the front of her thigh. The central seam of her loose pants was open, allowing her easy access to the weapon. 'Speed may mean the difference between life and death.'

Kalleen's golden eyes shimmered with understanding.

Imoshen let the panel drop and turned to clear away her healing possets. She felt the girl observe her and looked up.

Kalleen slipped the knife inside her sleeve for safekeeping then caught Imoshen's free hand in hers.

'Lady T'En, you give me back my pride.' And she kissed Imoshen's sixth finger.

A LITTLE LATER Imoshen heard the General's voice in the courtyard below, ordering his men to prepare to move out. So he had taken her advice to heart.

The Aayel sent Imoshen a speaking glance.

She felt dizzy with relief. Their gamble had paid off. She had distracted him from ordering her execution and relieved the tension in the overcrowded stronghold by finding a fruitful task to occupy the invaders.

With his army out in the fields harvesting the crops and delivering the grains to Umasreach, their winter food source was secure.

It was a small victory, but Imoshen was determined it would be the first of many. All she had to do now was remain in the background and avoid the General for the next thirteen days.

Unfortunately, that was not to be.

IMOSHEN PACED THE store rooms overseeing the cleaning and preparation for the influx of grain. When she heard the approach of booted feet on the stone floor a shiver of fear overtook her.

The Ghebites rounded the corner and stopped. She knew they were Tulkhan's elite guard because they wore his personal insignia.

Her own stronghold guard and servants straightened. Again she felt that undeniable tension. Her people had surrendered, but they had not accepted their defeat. The ignominy of it seethed beneath the surface, needing only a spark to bring it to flame and open rebellion.

The General must be aware of it too.

'Lady T'En. General Tulkhan requests an audience.' The young soldier who spoke obviously found it hard to be civil. He would not meet her eyes and though it was phrased as a request, Imoshen knew it was an order.

She wiped her hands on the smock she wore over her gown and undid the ties, placing the pinafore to one side.

'See to the other storerooms and stop all rat holes. I shall expect it done on my return.' The order was unnecessary as her people knew their job, but she must appear in control, just as the General must maintain that aura of command. She turned to the soldiers. 'Where is the General?'

'With the one called Aayel.'

'*The* Aayel. It is a title, not a name,' she corrected instinctively. 'It translates as Wise One. You may escort me.'

Thus she strode before them, aware that she had outmanoeuvred them. What was meant to be the escort of a prisoner had become an escort of another kind.

What did Tulkhan want? Imoshen refused to let fear undermine her composure. She would take her cue from the Aayel.

When she arrived General Tulkhan was standing before the fire, hands clasped behind his back. The Aayel, as befitted her great age, was seated stiffly in her hard-backed chair. Imoshen had noticed that in the presence of the Ghebites, her great aunt continued to affect a physical weakness which was misleading. This amused her, but she hid her smile.

At the sound of her approach, the General turned. 'Pack your travelling kit. I'm taking you with me.'

'But my place is here, looking after my people –'

'Exactly. If my men ride up to these farmers, very likely they will run into the woods and hide. I need their co-operation, so I'm taking you with me as ambassador. You know the farmers' dialect, they'll trust you.'

Imoshen's eyes flew to the Aayel who gave an almost imperceptible nod of encouragement.

She drew breath. It was unexpected, but he was right. 'In that case, we will visit the nearest village and speak to the Elders there. They can send runners to the outlying farms.'

The General nodded and it was agreed. A shiver of anticipation moved over Imoshen's skin. She had meant to keep away from him for the next thirteen days, but now she would be in his company, forced to socialise with him, bedding down in his camp each night. She would have to tread very carefully. But maybe she could turn this to her advantage.

*   *   *

THE REST OF the afternoon was spent packing and preparing their escort. That night Imoshen took her draught as the Aayel watched.

Wincing at the taste, she sealed the decanter. It was their first chance to speak freely.

Imoshen wiped her mouth with the back of her hand. 'You put the idea in his head?'

'No, he came to me. He is no fool. I merely suggested one of us would make a good ambassador. He chose you because I am so frail.'

Imoshen chuckled, then sobered as the old woman clasped her hand.

'You will be with him day and night, Imoshen. It is a chance to observe him. He's proud and he does not like to rely on others, but he is also a practical soldier. Learn, ingratiate yourself with him. Hush. I'm not finished. Go as far as Landsend. From there the abbey can send out messengers, who will be trusted. The southern highlands raise little grain. We cannot rely on them for food.

'Once that is done, you must return here in time for the Harvest Feast.'

Imoshen nodded. She saw the logic of it, but she still felt sick at heart. Would the simple folk view her as a traitor, aiding the invader?

There was an almost imperceptible noise from behind the hangings. Both the Aayel and Imoshen stiffened. With a deft flick, Imoshen slipped her hand under the panel of her tabard and retrieved her dagger. Padding softly across the stone floor of the chamber, she positioned herself in front of the tapestry.

The Aayel nodded. Imoshen tugged the hanging from the wall, dragging their eavesdropper forward by one arm. With the ease borne of years of practice, she twisted the spy's arm behind her back and held the dagger to her captive's throat.

'A traitor?' Imoshen hissed.

The Aayel stepped forward to view the eavesdropper. A strange expression flitted across her face. 'I don't think so.'

'Never, my lady,' Kalleen whispered fiercely. 'I am yours. Let me serve you. I want to go with you. I know the farmers, they're my people.'

The Aayel nodded and Imoshen released her. The girl fell to the floor and kissed the brocade hem of Imoshen's tabard.

'Oh, get up!' Imoshen pulled her to her feet.

Kalleen tilted her head in surprise.

Imoshen felt a reluctant smile tug at her lips. 'My mother despaired of ever teaching me court protocol,' she confessed.

Kalleen laughed. 'Protocol could not make the goose boy a prince.'

Imoshen did not know what to say. The household servants knew their place, unlike this impudent girl from the fields.

'How true,' the Aayel observed dryly. Imoshen met the old woman's eyes above the girl's head. The Aayel approved of Kalleen. 'Go and get some sleep. You leave at dawn.'

*   *   *

THEY SET OFF riding into the rising sun. The smoke fires of the morning meal hung on the still, cool air. General Tulkhan felt the chill as he signalled to his men on the stronghold ramparts then urged his horse to one side and let the main body of his army file away into the morning mists.

The Dhamfeer sat astride her horse, riding loosely in the saddle accompanied by the serving girl whose forehead was already healing. He had placed the last member of the royal family under an escort of his elite guard in case an attempt was made to free her. There were still rebel bands wandering the plains, remnants of the once mighty T'En army who refused to accept the surrender.

The Aayel had explained to him the reason for people's abstinence at this time and he had told his men to restrain themselves until the feast where, according to custom, they would be able to indulge themselves freely. It amused him to think that Imoshen had chosen not to tell him the form the celebration took.

But this religious forbearance meant he'd had no chance to take his release with a willing woman and he shifted in the saddle, only too aware of the tension in his body. His gaze went to the Dhamfeer. At his signal the elite guard parted, allowing him to weave his way to her side.

Apart from his uneasiness with everything T'En, all was going well. Tulkhan expected any day now to greet a messenger who bore the news that the capital had fallen to his half-brother. T'Diemn lay two days' journey on the River Diemn, which provided a safe berth to ocean-going vessels of the mainland, just as Landsend provided safe harbour for those from the eastern archipelago.

Imoshen looked up, her face bathed in pure, early morning light, and he was taken aback. She was so young and, at that instant, so transparent. She glowed like a child with a treat.

The air echoed with the rhythmic jingle of the horses' saddles and bits, the soft mutter of the men and the early morning cries of the birds. It was utterly peaceful, giving a lie to the tension which brooded beneath the surface.

Imoshen wondered why the General had fallen in beside her. He gave an odd reluctant grin and she smiled. She felt a reluctant surge of excitement. She knew her position was perilous, but she couldn't cower forever, and she couldn't contain her exuberance for life.

Soon she would see the ocean again and visit the villages on the road to the abbey. Joy filled her at the thought of once again seeing the beautiful port of Landsend. She tried to feel resentment, told herself it was a shame she was forced to do this as the ambassador of the invader, in reality a prisoner whose cooperation was 'requested,' but her naturally buoyant spirits wouldn't allow her to feel downcast.

The elite guard fell a little behind them, only Kalleen remained stubbornly at Imoshen's side. They rode in silence, amid the sense of excitement which came with an army on the move.

'I wish to learn the farmers' speech. From what I've overheard it has much in common with your tongue,' General Tulkhan announced. 'You will teach me.'

Imoshen felt a flash of annoyance, but even his high-handedness could not deflate her good spirits this morning. She chose to be amused.

'Our tongue is a hybrid of the two, not the original High T'En we first spoke. It evolved to facilitate commerce between the T'En and the locals,' Imoshen said. She had always enjoyed tales of the past. 'You speak our tongue very well, General. I gather you learned it from our trading partners on the mainland to the west? Surely you don't make it a habit to learn the language of every nation you conquer?'

He cast her a swift glance and she gave him a bland smile, determined he should know she might be his captive, but she would not be his slave.

The General laughed.

Tulkhan's reaction was so unexpected Imoshen stared at him. Heat flooded her body, colouring her cheeks.

'It's no hardship,' the General told her. 'I have a gift for languages. When I take a country I stay long enough to establish a regional governor, build garrisons and ensure the smooth running of the colony. Gheeaba supplies the administrators, which leaves me free to take the time to learn the customs of their culture.'

'What of your own home, Gheeaba? Don't you miss it?'

He was silent for a moment and she thought he wouldn't answer.

'There is nothing for me there.'

'But the old woman who died?' She could have bitten her tongue.

He frowned and shifted in the saddle. His eyes met hers fleetingly, unwillingly. Imoshen realised she'd found the chink in his armour and she knew instinctively that he didn't like revealing his weakness. It was lucky she had attempted to read him or she would never have discovered his hidden guilt.

Without a word, he kicked his mount's flanks and rode forward at an angle. The troops parted for him so that in a few moments he was out of the column and galloping toward the outlying scouts.

Imoshen ground her teeth, annoyed with the General for being so proud and with herself for not minding her tongue.

All day, Imoshen watched General Tulkhan surreptitiously. She had time to observe the easy way he rode and how he used the strength of his powerful thighs to guide his black destrier with barely perceptible signals. As he rode, he held his head so proudly, his long dark hair streaming behind him. He was a magnificent male, she couldn't deny that.

But he was also a warmongering, Ghebite barbarian who held her life in the palm of his hand. Worse still, she'd alienated him, for he did not come near her again.

When she caught his dark gaze as he galloped past to speak to those bringing up the rear with the supply wagons, she felt a shiver of anticipation, but he made no move to acknowledge her.

In the late afternoon they entered the first village.

The inhabitants had come out of hiding to meet the invaders, silently watching the procession advance on the village square with a mixture of apprehension and curiosity.

News of the General's arrival had preceded them. An army this large could hardly travel without being noted. There were few able-bodied women who weren't laden down with babes. Mothers stood with their little ones at their sides and the old men and women watched from seamed faces. There were no young men.

The Ghebites remained mounted, filing out to each side of the small village square. Their horses shifted restlessly, sensing water and feed nearby.

When they reached the square, the elite guard moved apart, clearing a path for the General and Imoshen.

As she rode up, considering how she should handle this moment, Imoshen sensed that the villagers were wary but reassured by her arrival.

General Tulkhan met her eyes. Before he could tell her what to do, she urged her mount forward. Careful not to appear threatening, she swung lightly from the saddle. Out of courtesy to the farmers she chose to approach them on foot, so that they did not have to crane their heads up to look at her.

Her confident stride gave no sign of her thudding heart or the sickly fear in her belly – fear that they would spit on her for siding with the invaders, for betraying her people, for surrendering when Umasreach could have held out for days, maybe even into the winter. She made the sign of deference used when approaching those of great age and greeted the Elders of the village, an ancient bonded couple.

She could tell the villagers were pleased to see their Elders treated with respect. Then Imoshen began her explanation, slipping quite naturally into the patois of the people. She found its sweet lilting sound soothing; it reminded her of her childhood nurse.

The old man and woman exchanged glances. Smiles of relief lightened their faces as the purpose of the visit became clear. Imoshen realised her fear of rejection was unfounded. These people were realists. They needed the grain harvested, so they would accept help.

Did they really care who ruled, so long as the rulers were just? Imoshen wondered. It was a sobering thought.

Acting as interpreter for the General, she learned the number of men the village and surrounding farms would require to bring the grain in and prepare it in time for the Harvest Feast. Several pigs had been slaughtered in their honour, and it would have been discourteous to leave. The villagers wanted to entertain them.

Tulkhan felt impatient with the delay, but understood the political necessity of accepting the villagers' hospitality. He ordered his men to pitch the tent for Imoshen. He would bed down in the open with his men as he always did. It was a necessary part of his command strategy to forge and strengthen the bonds of brotherhood.

As soon as Imoshen's tent was erected, he observed a queue of villagers and many others he suspected had been hiding out in the woods or come in from nearby farms, making their way to her tent. Some entered obviously ill and left carrying little bags of herbs. At one point he saw Imoshen's maidservant open the tent flap to throw out a bowl of bloodied water.

So the Dhamfeer was carrying out her heathenish healings. No word had been sent out. It appeared to be a custom, almost a service the villagers expected of her.

He sent for a man he trusted, Wharrd, a commander who was renowned for his ability to set bones and sew flesh on the battlefield. Together they approached the tent. The people watched them warily, but held their ground. Small children clung to their mothers' legs, and there was even a boy with a puppy.

Tulkhan's skin prickled unpleasantly as he touched the tent flap. He tasted a metallic tang on his tongue.

It reminded him of the time Imoshen had healed the Aayel. He knew enough of unseen powers from his travels to realise that something more than simple healing was going on here.

Without waiting for a welcome he tossed the flap open and strode in to find Imoshen kneeling beside an old woman. They were both peering into a dull mirrored surface which held a thin film of water – scrying. The maidservant moved forward to prevent him interrupting, but Tulkhan signalled her that he was no threat and she stepped back.

Silence stretched within the tent. Only the murmur of voices outside, the distant shouts of his men as they relaxed around their camp and the sounds of animals as they settled for the night filled the air.

A great sadness filled Imoshen as the vision faded. She lifted her eyes from the water's surface. Even with her poor skills, she knew it was hopeless. It had been the same as her own vision when she had searched for her family. The pain cut just as deeply. This sort of task required an effort of will and openness which left her no protection from the emotions of those she served. The old woman looked at her hopefully.

She was aware of the General and another person watching, but ignored them. Taking the old woman's hand she spoke gently. 'I am sorry, grandmother. The one you seek will not be returning.'

The old woman's shoulders sagged, then she straightened. She nodded once and rose stiffly, pressing a bag of dried herbs into Imoshen's hands. It was not the custom to pay for the T'En's services, but a gift would be welcomed.

The old woman shuffled out and Imoshen rose to her feet, feeling dizzy. 'Yes?'

Since puberty she had assisted the Aayel at the season cusp festivals, but she had never had to bear the burden of the healings alone. Her gift was small and her skill with it raw. The effort drained her. If only the Aayel were here now. She needed her great aunt's keen insight and the wisdom gathered from over a century of life.

As Imoshen fought the ache in her chest, her throat closed painfully and tears stung her eyes. When she tried to pour a drink of honeyed wine, her fingers shook so badly, Kalleen came to her side protectively. The young woman took the jug from Imoshen's hands and poured it. Imoshen nodded her thanks, glad her back was to the General so he could not see her weakness.

Greedily she gulped the sweet liquid.

'My man Wharrd is a bone-setter,' Tulkhan announced without preamble. 'He will assist you.'

It was not a request, it was an order. Imoshen turned, her face flushed with anger. She met Tulkhan's eyes and saw that he knew she didn't want help. She looked her unwelcome assistant up and down. He was a grizzled campaigner, a capable man who at the moment appeared very uncomfortable. Her contrary nature made her feel a flash of understanding.

She put her wine aside. 'I need no assistant, only the privacy of –'

'You are wearing yourself out. We must travel tomorrow. Wharrd will help you.'

'Very well.' Imoshen could see the General was determined to outmanoeuvre her. For now she would tolerate his spy at her side. She straightened and gestured to the flap. 'You may leave and send in the next one.'

She knew the General hated it when she told him what to do, but since he had achieved his goal of foisting an unwanted observer on her, he carried out her order good-naturedly, which succeeded in annoying her further.

She eyed the Ghebite called Wharrd. Despite her resentment of him, she must make the most of it, must somehow turn this to her advantage. General Tulkhan would learn not to cross her.

A woman entered with a small girl who held her arm at an odd angle. At a glance Imoshen knew the shoulder had been dislocated and had not been put back properly. She flinched, imagining the pain the child had already endured. Then she smiled grimly. This was a chance for Tulkhan's spy to earn his keep. Using her voice to soothe the woman and child, she directed the mother to sit down with the child on her lap and gently removed the little smock to reveal the child's deformed shoulder joint.

As she talked, Imoshen crushed and burned a pungent herb. Inhaling the herb would help them to relax. She knelt to wave the smoke towards the mother and child with a small fan, speaking all the while, weaving a spell of enchantment with her words. The Aayel had told her it did not matter what you said, only that you built up a feeling of trust with the one you sought to help.

When this was done Imoshen put the bowl of cinders aside and took the child's hand, holding her gaze. Calling on her gift, she impressed her will on the child, eventually inducing a state of waking sleep. Over and over she repeated that the child would feel no pain. The mind was a powerful thing. She had seen people undergo excruciating procedures and not feel the pain, as long as they believed they wouldn't.

Rising swiftly, Imoshen placed a hand on the mother's shoulder and nodded to Wharrd. 'This is where your superior strength is useful.'

He nodded grimly.

Doubtless he had sawn off wounded soldiers' legs as they screamed in agony. He was a hardened veteran, but he seemed reluctant to touch the trusting child. The little girl stared drowsily at him, her wispy golden head tucked into her mother's chest as Imoshen's soothing chant continued to weave its spell. Imoshen understood his reluctance, but it had to be done.

He wiped his palms and grasped the child's arm and pulled it out sharply. There was an audible click as the joint landed back in place but no scream from the child, only a look of mild surprise.

The mother gave a soft gasp.

Imoshen waved Tulkhan's spy aside and knelt to strap the little arm against the child's torso. She gave the mother some advice, sending her away with herbs which would help the child sleep that night.

It pleased her to know the little girl would now live a normal, useful life. This was the joy of her gift. Imoshen closed tired eyes, thinking how lucky she was. She could hear Kalleen thanking the woman for some eggs and escorting her out.

Weariness overcame her, bringing with it a faint nausea. She knew she was taking on too much with these healings, but the people expected it of her and she could not let them down, not when they had been let down so badly by the Emperor and Empress.

Imoshen felt a tentative touch on her upper arm. Startled, she opened her eyes to see Wharrd, his eyes wide with awe.

'The child didn't scream. She didn't even wake,' he whispered.

'No.'

He went pale. 'Sorcery?'

'No.' Imoshen shook her head. 'It is a skill I was taught. With the herbs to aid concentration, I coax the patient into a sleep-like state. While they are suggestible they can be told they won't feel pain, or even that they will not lose too much blood. It saves much suffering.'

His eyes widened and he licked his lips eagerly. 'What must I give you to teach me?'

'Nothing,' Imoshen answered, then smiled at his surprise. His urgency did not stem from greed. Instinct told her it came from his nature. This man was a true healer, serving his general as best he could.

She repressed a shudder.

How could a healer choose soldiering as his vocation? How could he inflict pain and kill when in his soul he wanted to ease suffering? She touched his hand, feeling the conflict in him. With joy she realised she could ease it. 'Simply watch and learn.'

He dipped his grizzled head to kiss her hand. A rush of embarrassment flooded Imoshen. She didn't want to become involved with this Ghebite warrior, yet already she could feel a bond forming. Her fingers brushed his grey hair.

'Please don't. There must be things you can teach me.' With a tug she urged him to straighten and held his eyes. 'I am only the Aayel's student in herb lore. I am sure we can learn from each other.'

THERE WAS NO chance for Tulkhan to speak with the Dhamfeer. He had wanted to discuss their plans and begin his language lessons, but she was occupied until the food was prepared, then courtesy meant he had to join her at the long plank tables set up in the square to partake of the feast.

His supply wagon had provided part of the food, but his men mingled freely with the villagers. He only hoped as the music and dancing began that his men remembered his rule and did not force the women. Diplomacy was not a foot-soldier's strong point.

Some of his men would be billeted in the village, others would go out to the farms on the morrow. Many had been travelling since their early teens, fighting on behalf of their homeland, so this would be a change. How would they react to simple farm life?

All around him the villagers celebrated and so far his men had not offended anyone. He began to relax.

This was not his home, but strangely enough Tulkhan felt a tug of recognition. Though the music was unfamiliar the feeling around the fires was oddly seductive. It spoke of a day's honest hard work and the reward of home and hearth. It was so long since he had been back to his homeland it took him a few moments to pinpoint the sensation. Then he acknowledged what he felt was a rush of homecoming.

What surprised him was Wharrd's reaction to the heathen healer. He had expected scepticism, at the very least resistance, but the Dhamfeer seemed to have won over one of his most trusted men in a single afternoon. Tulkhan encouraged his sense of irritation to fester. He did not want to feel at home here. This was not Gheeaba. It was a deceptively peaceful island which would turn on him the moment he faltered. He could not afford to reveal weakness.

Music warmed the chilly night air and flickering firelight lit the people's happy faces. The same firelight danced over Imoshen's narrow features, warming her pale skin, making her wine-dark eyes pools of mystery. He caught her watching him several times and each time he felt a sense of unease, as if he was being weighed up.

Once she raised her farmhouse cup to him in silent salute, and sipped as though she drank from fine crystal. He returned the salute, amused and intrigued. Was she acknowledging the success of their plan, or mocking him because she had won over his bone-setter?

He did not know what to think. Her mystery both annoyed and fascinated him.

The farmers called forth their storyteller, who regaled them with a long and involved tale, which Imoshen translated for Tulkhan, who translated for his men. Even so, he had time to study the people. They wore their best clothes. No rags here, but ornately embroidered vests and bodices. He saw fine examples of carved wood and pottery so elegantly turned and painted it could have graced a Ghebite lord's table.

This was a prosperous island where even the simple farmers enjoyed good food and wine, and took the time to create things of beauty. There was much he could learn from this culture.

Long before the festivities showed signs of dying down Tulkhan noted that Imoshen made her excuses and slipped away. She seemed tired, paler than usual. Tulkhan observed the way the people touched her shyly, stroking her sixth finger for luck.

What must it be like to live in a land where legends walked amongst men? Tulkhan shuddered. The mainland stories of Dhamfeer powers varied from place to place, but some of the rumours had to be based on truth. He had already experienced Imoshen's insidious mind touch. Logic told him he should keep well away from her.

But after Imoshen was gone, he felt restless. The scene seemed less intense and much less interesting once she was no longer there to explain a song or translate a question.

Tulkhan rose and stretched. With no real destination in mind he left the tables and found himself wandering away from the noise into the darkness and towards the welcome glow of the tent, illuminated against the trees by the light of a single candle.

He paused. Through the thin walls of the canvas tent he heard Imoshen singing softly. She was alone, her maidservant had joined in the fun.

He watched the Dhamfeer's silhouette on the tent's wall as she stripped, unaware of the effect she was having. Her hair fell like a curtain, obscuring the line of her pert little breasts and the curve of her hips and buttocks.

True, she was tall and scrawny for a woman, but somehow it didn't matter. He liked the length of her legs, her slender waist. It made it more tantalising to know that her perfect pale flesh was considered sacred, too precious to be desecrated by the sweaty touch of a lustful male.

Tulkhan shifted, aware of a growing tension in his body.

Innocent of any guile, Imoshen turned with natural grace to pour a drink and drained it before dousing the single candle.

Tulkhan stood in the quiet of the night as the sound of music drifted to him, laced with shouts and laughter.

He ached to go to her. Imoshen was his by right of capture. Yet he knew she had never surrendered, and would never surrender in the true sense of the word.

Every conversation she'd ever had with him reinforced her resistance. It was a tangible wall between them. The hard-headed realist in Tulkhan sneered at his traitorous body's demands. Did the Dhamfeer tempt him because she was unattainable?

According to the Ghebite priests, he should not feel this physical pull. Yet, it made his mouth go dry and his body burn. The practical soldier in him said she was all woman, whatever her race and her body called to his.

Tulkhan ground his teeth. He despised himself for his weakness. He would not let his flesh rule his mind. Frustration boiled in him. He despised her for bringing him to this.

In desperation, he turned and stalked off, determined to burn off his desire, only to find himself back at her tent a short while later. Equal parts rage and fear filled him. Had the Dhamfeer bewitched him? Was his soul no longer his own?

Chapter Three

WITH AN EFFORT of will, Tulkhan held firm. One small, sane part of him did not believe Imoshen, who after all was only a female and a mere girl at that, had cast a spell on him. This tug was simply too physical.

It disturbed him to find the demands of his flesh threatening to outweigh his rational mind. All his adult life he had prided himself on his control. He had simply gone too long without a woman. It was affecting his judgment.

Eventually he won a hollow victory.

The hard ground was cold comfort especially near dawn when a chill mist stole over the land. Perversely, Tulkhan rejoiced in the discomfort. He had to purge his body of its unruly desires.

At the first hint of dawn he stripped and bathed in the village pond, much to the amazement of the few villagers out doing their early chores.

There was a frost on the ground and the water was bitterly cold, forcibly reminding Tulkhan that this was not his northern homeland. For a moment he felt nostalgic, recalling the thick walled houses and a sun so bright, that the light hurt your eyes.

The cold might have put out the fire in his body, but it did not cool his temper. His men felt the sharp edge of his tongue that morning as he rounded up those who'd slept overlong after their night of drinking and dancing.

It annoyed him to find Imoshen already mounted and waiting, her breath misting in the fresh dawn air.

'Lady T'En,' Tulkhan acknowledged as he approached her, manoeuvring his mount to her side. He saw her eyes narrow warily. He never addressed her by her royal title. 'It is obvious you haven't made a practice of camping.'

'No, when we travelled my family and I stayed in lesser noble houses,' she replied cautiously. 'Why, what have I omitted to do?'

'Nothing, if it was your intention to display yourself to my men last night,' Tulkhan said, savouring her shocked expression. 'The next time you disrobe, put out your candle first, then you will not to cast your shadow on the tent wall for all to see. Unless it was your intent to entice my men.'

Imoshen's eyes flashed red as she flushed to the roots of her pale hair. 'You know very well it was not!'

He shrugged, even though his accusation was unjust and he was secretly pleased that he had been the only man to witness her innocent display.

'It won't happen again, I can assure you.'

She went to urge her horse past him, but he caught the bridle and pulled it closer so that their thighs were pressed together. She glared at him, her lips white with fury.

'It had better not happen again, because my men are due their rights of conquest. I've told them to wait until Harvest Feast, but with you flaunting your body before them I cannot answer for their deeds. They might forget you're a precious Dhamfeer, sworn to celibacy, and recall only that you are a woman!'

For an instant he caught a flicker of fear in her eyes, quickly cloaked, and regretted baiting her.

Then she lifted her proud chin and fixed those exotic eyes on him. 'The females of Fair Isle aren't compliant Ghebite women fit only for breeding sons. I'm more woman than any of your barbarians could handle!' With a flick of her reins she freed the mare's head and forged past him. Tulkhan watched Imoshen's stiff straight back, his heart pounding with the intensity of their exchange. She was magnificent. She hadn't backed down. Instead she'd met him with a challenge of her own and he did not doubt her boast for a moment.

Irritated by the turn of his thoughts, he cursed and pressed his knees to his horse's flanks. His men were in formation, waiting. He stood in the stirrups and bellowed the signal to move out. As he watched the column file from the clearing of the village, he found he had to consciously relax his grip on the reins.

There she went, infuriating Dhamfeer.

Honesty made him admit no one but he had seen her disrobe so enticingly. No one but he had ached for her, torn between duty and desire.

What was wrong with him? Never in all his years campaigning had he let his emotions rule his head when dealing with the enemy. And Imoshen was definitely the enemy. He only had to look at her to see her differences. She was one of the *feared and revered Dhamfeer,* as the children's rhyme went.

But she was no nursemaid's invention to scare naughty children. This Dhamfeer was all too real. He shuddered, recalling how she had plucked a thought from his mind.

Tulkhan compressed his lips in annoyance and vowed not to let the Dhamfeer pierce his guard again. He would be polite but distant. The gods knew he had enough responsibilities to occupy him without complicating things by acting on his base physical desires.

Imoshen seethed as she rode away from the General without so much as a backward glance. Her shoulders ached with tension and she could still feel his eyes on her, but she refused to acknowledge him.

She was furious with herself. What had possessed her? The General must think her a wanton creature, boasting like that. She, who had never lain with a man, who had only theoretical knowledge of the procedure, claiming to be more woman than any man could handle. Her cheeks flooded with heat as she recalled her ridiculous challenge.

In fact, she hadn't even been particularly good at her studies. It had all seemed a little bizarre to her when she had looked at the illustrated texts.

She pressed the back of her hand to her mouth, appalled at the implications of her boast. Why, she had all but challenged him to bed her!

Was she any better than the Ghebite women she had so cruelly mocked? She planned to trap the General, bait him with her body and steal his seed. The conception of a child should be a joyous event, shared by bond-partners. Shame flooded Imoshen, for she planned to conceive General Tulkhan's son and use him as a tool to save her own life.

Just then Tulkhan galloped past her, rounding up the last of the men as the column moved out. She felt her gaze drawn to him, despite herself.

What if the Aayel was wrong?

What if he thought nothing of his own flesh and blood? Would he order her execution, knowing she carried his unborn child? Could he be so inhuman? She didn't know.

The Aayel's gift was scrying, interpreting what she saw and reading people. Imoshen could only trust the old woman's advice and hope. She vowed to keep a rein on her tongue when next Tulkhan spoke to her.

But when Tulkhan did join her it was only for his language lesson, and he was scrupulously polite. Imoshen found it easy to instruct him. He was a fast learner, quick to pick up the nuances of the language. She would do well to remember that.

THE SHORT DAYS passed uneventfully for Tulkhan, and each village they entered wanted to entertain them. Minor noble families vied to outdo their neighbours in providing hospitality. They shed more and more men as they progressed, leaving groups behind to bring in the crops. Everywhere they went the locals consulted Imoshen, with Wharrd at her side. The man even slept on the ground at the entrance to her tent, much to Tulkhan's irritation.

His plan had backfired. Instead of inserting a spy he had provided the Dhamfeer with a willing servant and lost one of his most trusted men.

They were only a few hours' ride from Landsend when Tulkhan called for a pause to take lunch. They were skirting an expanse of high country covered with virgin wood, which, according to Imoshen, took days to traverse if you were lucky enough to reach the other side. The men eyed the encroaching forest warily.

Like the wooded ranges of the southern highlands this forest was ancient and for the most part untouched. It was said ancient spirits roamed the thickly clustered trees, unfriendly spirits which took a human toll from those who passed through their domain.

More superstition, Tulkhan cursed impatiently, as he signalled his troops to stop. He knew the value of presentation. He ordered his men to clean their weapons and deck themselves out in full regalia, so that when they marched into Landsend that afternoon they would be an impressive sight.

They had stopped in a pleasant glade. Great shafts of autumn sunlight fell through the canopy, illuminating the silver trunks of the trees that ringed the clearing. As the men ate, the camp grew quiet and the vast silence of the deep, virgin forest seemed to absorb every man-made sound.

Imoshen didn't feel hungry. She felt restless and strangely uneasy. She looked around the clearing. The midday sun was brilliant but gave little warmth.

Kalleen was teasing Wharrd, and as usual he was trying to outdo her. Imoshen listened absently as they compared the kinds of food their countries considered delicacies.

The girl snorted as he described how a mainland beast with a single horn would be killed solely so its horn could be crushed into a powder believed to help men maintain their sexual potency.

If he thought to embarrass the farm girl, he failed, for she winked at Imoshen and asked innocently, 'Of course a man like you would never have need of that horn's medicine, now would you?'

For once Wharrd had no reply and Kalleen preened, having won the encounter.

Imoshen found it confusing. The Ghebite men were quick enough to talk of their prowess with women, but confronted by a woman who would talk of such things, they became offended. It was not like the court of the Old Empire, where the Empress and her friends had recommended each other's lovers.

Not that she had belonged to that circle. Her family had preferred the quiet of their country estates and held old-fashioned values such as fidelity between bond-partners. She hated to think what they would say about her plan to seduce the General and steal his son.

Imoshen stood, arching her back, and decided to stretch her legs. She wasn't planning to wander too far away, but then she caught the scent of a familiar herb and on impulse followed her nose, intending to pick some leaves to supplement her supplies. Next she noticed the heart-shaped leaf of a plant renowned for treating conditions of the heart, and another which was ideal for bringing down fevers and protecting against the poisons which could take root in a wound.

As she picked the leaves, she hummed the little songs the Aayel had taught her to use when selecting herbs. She twisted the leaves neatly upon themselves and tucked them inside her jerkin to keep her hands free.

Pleased with her find, Imoshen didn't pause to wonder why the locals hadn't come by to collect herbs so near the main path to Landsend. She supposed the plants had survived this late in the season because this was a northern slope and caught the sun for most of the day.

Around her the insects hummed, filling the air with their busy song. She came to the top of a small rise and carefully picked her way down the slope, through waist-high ferns surrounding the massive trunks of trees, which rose above her like the columns of a great building. She could no longer hear the occasional comment from the Ghebites or the snicker of their horses.

The ground sloped and, in between the cleft of the two great rocks, a bracken-cloaked spring seeped from the ground, pooling in small rock ponds as it made its way down hill.

Pleased, Imoshen picked up her pace. This was excellent, just the place she needed to find the moss which aided the healing process. She got down on her hands and knees to crawl amid the bracken, turning over the smooth river stones, searching out the best specimens. She was careful to leave some moss so that it could regrow.

Imoshen followed the little stream downhill between the rocks. Despite the shafts of autumn sunlight the cold was intense near the water's edge. The brook grew wider, spreading into a pool bordered by large rocks.

It was so good to escape the Ghebite General's presence. For days she had been on her best behaviour.

The villagers and minor nobles expected her to be the T'En, a healer who could advise them, while the General treated her with aloof indifference. But his gaze, when he thought she wasn't looking, devoured her. She had been controlled and circumspect, never acting without thinking of the consequences.

It wasn't natural for her. Here, she could let her guard down and delight in simply being herself.

Unbraiding her hair, she massaged her scalp, feeling the faint warmth of the sun seep into her skin. The cool water tempted her, but she wasn't foolish enough to strip off. The cold would be intense, and besides, the General might send one of his men to bring her back.

Imoshen sighed. The Aayel would be pleased with her, she was behaving with great maturity. Still, it couldn't hurt to paddle her feet. Slipping off her boots, she dipped her toes in the pool. The cold was fearful. It was also invigorating so she splashed some on her face and drank from her cupped hand.

Feeling observed, Imoshen looked up.

A presentiment of danger made her mouth go dry. She had the distinct feeling that someone or something was watching her, yet she was alone. Instinctively, she froze and strained to hear.

Her heart thudded in her chest. A prickle of fear lifted the hairs on the back of her neck. It was not the immediate, natural response to danger she'd felt when she first confronted the General. This was an eerie, preternatural sensation.

Listening intently, she could not discern the faintest sound from the men in the glade. Even the knowledge that if she were to scream they would hear and come crashing through the undergrowth brought her no comfort. Instinct told her that steel and sinew could not protect her from what threatened here.

She had teased the General with old tales about special places where ancient spirits dwelled, spirits which predated even the locals. Her old nurse, long dead now, had told tales of a dawn people who predated the golden-skinned locals and worshipped a race of Ancients.

Fleetingly, Imoshen wondered if it was an eternal cycle. Fair Isle was taken by force and settled, then the invaders were absorbed by the island, so that they in turn were subjugated by new invaders. The thought made her head spin, but she had no time for such questions.

Something was threatening her here and now.

She had heard rumour of places the locals avoided in the deep woods, places of power – evil, greedy power – but she had dismissed these stories as superstition. They were traditionally associated with the hot springs where steam seeped from the cracks in the stone.

Slowly Imoshen rose to her feet. There was definitely something here, and her T'En senses told her that this something was not friendly. She wished it were a product of her imagination.

Tightening the laces on her jerkin to keep her herbs safe, Imoshen bent and hastily re-tied the straps of her boots. As yet there was no evidence to back up her terrible sense of foreboding. Finally, she straightened and shaded her eyes against the sparkle of the autumn sun on the pool's surface.

Her every instinct screamed, *leave.*

She backed away from the pool but the feeling did not ease, instead the space between her shoulder blades ached. Slowly, she turned to face the unseen threat.

Her eyes widened as she took in a patch of bare earth where nothing grew. It was surrounded by tall slender-trunked trees, which towered over her. The trees and bracken grew right up to the bare circle, but from that point nothing flourished, not even a weed. Instinctively she knew it was a sacred, accursed place where innocent blood had been shed. No seed could take root on such soil.

Bordering the empty patch was a circle of low, worn stones. Her heart lurched as her theoretical knowledge confirmed what her senses had known all along. This was not a natural phenomenon – it was an ancient site where the dawn people had worshipped.

Imoshen focused, trying to pierce the veil of time. This was not her skill, the Aayel would have been better at it. She frowned in concentration, her heart thudding erratically. At first there was nothing but the writhing squiggles in her mind's eye, then a brooding darkness gathered. Distant voices grew closer, chanting, bringing with them the unmistakable scent of fresh blood.

A hand closed on her shoulder. Imoshen gasped, reacting instinctively. Clenching her fist, she brought her arm up and swung the point of her elbow back to catch her attacker in the midriff. Even as she darted forward she heard a grunt of surprised pain. There was only one way to run, across the clearing, so she did.

A man cursed.

Through the thin soles of her boots, she felt the impact of her running feet on the bare earth. She caught the scent of her attacker. It was familiar but the need to escape dominated all thought.

The impact of a heavy body knocked her off her feet. Flying forward, she flung her hands out to take the force of her fall. Even as she hit, she attempted to writhe out of his grasp, but he had her upper thighs wrapped in his arms. His heavy chest pressed on her buttocks.

The chanting grew stronger as the darkness closed on her. The smell of blood was nauseous, overpowering.

They had her!

'Imoshen, it's me.'

She twisted, desperate. A flurry of images filled her mind – blood, death, a great power grown old and vindictive.

Because she was pinned she couldn't reach the knife strapped to her thigh. Arching up, she tried to bring the back of her skull into contact with his face, to smash his nose.

'Imoshen, it's Tulkhan. Stop!'

The General?

Panting, she froze. The confusion faded from her mind. She'd panicked, the Ghebite meant no harm. Or did he?

'General?'

Her voice hung on the air as she lifted her upper body and twisted beneath him. Grudgingly, he released her, letting her slide from under his weight. She was aware of the hard planes of his belly and thighs.

Relieved to escape him, she came to her knees to catch her breath. He remained crouched before her, watching her thoughtfully. She could still feel the imprint of his body on hers and it filled her with a strange languorous longing.

Blood on the stones. Passion in the voices.

A surge of excitement flashed through her. Imoshen gasped and licked her lips. She saw a flicker of awareness in his coal-black eyes. He felt it too, for all that he was a True-man.

For an instant the victor and vanquished faced each other in the centre of an older, greater power, grown malevolent with the passage of time.

Tulkhan had felt the ridge of a hidden knife on Imoshen's thigh as she slid from underneath him. He knew if she could have retrieved the weapon his life would have been forfeit. The Dhamfeer had been a heartbeat away from slitting his throat.

Until now he hadn't known she carried a knife. He should punish her for concealing a weapon. His heart raced at the thought of taking her in his arms and exacting payment for all the tortured nights he had lain awake tormented by his need for her.

Her eyes widened, and she went to spring to her feet.

But before she could, he tackled her, driving her backwards onto the leaf litter.

She grunted, the air knocked from her lungs.

With her body pinned beneath his, he felt the hard ridge of her knife. She sucked in a painful breath and writhed furiously, trying to slide from beneath him, forcibly reminding him of her feminine curves and the weapon.

He must not let her get to it. Fury darkened her T'En eyes to a mulberry black.

She wore the blade strapped to the front of her left thigh. How did she get through her clothing to it? It would be useless unless she could reach it quickly in an emergency.

Slowly, his hand travelled beneath her tabard. The panel of brocade material offered no barrier. His mouth went dry with longing. He felt the soft material of her leggings. Then he found the cunningly hidden slit in the fabric. Beneath him her body quivered with tension. He felt the silky smoothness of her skin. With a flick he released the catch and pulled the knife from its sheath, bringing it out into the light between them. It felt hot in his hand, hot from her body.

She struggled convulsively, but he tightened his hold, pinning her to the ground. He thought he caught her faint womanly scent on the knife.

'Was this for me?' His voice sounded strange.

'This is a very bad place,' she whispered.

He hesitated. What was she talking about? Her eyes were wide with fear and he could smell it on her skin. Why?

His body tensed against the unseen threat. Was he reacting to her fear, or to an outside source?

Tulkhan didn't know. He only knew that despite the heat of the knife which burned into his hand like a brand and against all his better instincts, he ached to bury himself in her.

Her wine-dark eyes searched the clearing and she flinched at what she saw, but when he looked around there was nothing, just emptiness and few old stones.

'We must leave here, General.'

Her voice came to him from a great distance, ordering him about yet again. He had an overwhelming urge to take the knife's sharp point and part the strings of her jerkin, slice through the fine material of her shirt. He wanted to see the pale rise of her breasts. Since that first time he'd seen her, held captive by his men, bloodied but not bowed, he had wanted her.

If he were to lower his head, he could bury his face in her soft feminine curves, inhale her unique scent. A savage surge of desire gripped him. He had the knife, the superior strength and she was his by right of conquest.

Her lips drew back from her teeth and her eyes narrowed as if she knew what he was thinking. Instinct told him she would fight with the last breath in her body. Tulkhan knew then that he would have to kill her before he could subdue her.

His free hand sought her breast beneath the material and encountered something else. A puff of heady herbs engulfed them both. Inhaling the sharp pungent scent, he winced. It stung his nostrils, clearing his head.

What was he thinking?

He had never forced himself on a woman. They were always willing, only too willing, for all the good it did him.

Shocked by the path his thoughts had taken, he sat up slowly to crouch on his heels. It cost him dearly to pull away from her. He felt as if an invisible cord joined their bodies, reeling him ever tighter to her. So fierce a pull must be sorcery.

She also came to her knees, drawing closer to him. Her hands closed over the knife he held. Deftly and without apology, she pressed her fingers into his thumb, breaking his hold. He didn't resist as she slid the knife from his hand and calmly replaced it in its sheath. He caught a flash of white thigh before the tabard fell back into place. He fought a convulsive urge to lick that flesh.

'It's the rocks.' Her voice was a warm breath caressing his skin.

Rocks? He could only make sense of her words through a supreme effort of will. His whole being was focused on the raging need in him – a need so violent it had nothing to do with casual dalliance. What possessed him? He had to break free of this compulsion.

'Rocks?' He forced himself to follow the arc of her arm as she gestured and finally noticed the worn stones in a circle around them.

'Blood on the rocks,' she whispered.

Why was there a tremor in her voice? Tulkhan watched uneasily as she dipped inside her jerkin to pull out a handful of leaves, crushing them between her fingers. Again the spicy, sharp scent flooded his senses and his thoughts focused.

Her troubled eyes held his, willing him to listen. 'It is older than the locals, ancient and hungry for our bonding, our blood –'

'Imoshen!' She had never seemed more Dhamfeer to Tulkhan than at this moment, yet he still desired her. What had almost happened here was wrong. It went against all his natural instincts. Shuddering violently, he fought for control. The force of his need frightened him. Was his raging desire fed by an outside source? The idea was unnerving and repellent. He hated to think his actions had been dictated by an unseen presence. Shocked, he forced himself to concentrate on what she was saying.

Her fingers bit into the tense, corded muscles of his forearms. He could see Imoshen was terrified. A surge of protectiveness banished the urge for primal violence.

'We have to get out of here. Come, General.'

'There...' His voice was a croak. He had to swallow before he could continue. 'There's something here?'

'It lured me to the stone circle.' Intense dark eyes held him. 'It nearly invaded you, but you resisted it. I think the moment has passed.' In a lithe, circling movement she came to her feet, eyes searching the clearing. The length of her thick hair fanned out as she moved.

She extended her hand in a friendly, boyish gesture which seemed odd to him considering his behaviour had been less than brotherly. But he rose, brushing the dirt from his knees and thighs.

'So we're safe?' He was irritated with her, with himself, and he didn't know why.

She was right, there had been some force acting through him. No matter how much he might desire her, he would never have contemplated forcing himself on her.

'I'm not like that,' he said.

She cast him a swift calculating glance and once again he was aware of her intelligence and what remained unsaid between them.

'Let's go, while we can.'

He laughed but the sound was hollow on the still air.

Imoshen strode across the barren ground and he fell in behind her. When she came to the stones, she made several signs on the air and whispered something under her breath, then crushed more of the leaves on the ground.

Tulkhan watched all this with a certain scepticism.

But when they stepped between the worn stones he realised with a jolt that the soft sounds of the deep woods hadn't pierced that fell circle, for now those sounds rushed in on him.

He stiffened, recognising the scent of an animal – a rank, fetid scent. A predator was close, very close. There was no breeze, so the beast could not disguise its presence by approaching downwind.

They had escaped one threat to face another, but at least this one could be defeated with a man-made blade.

Imoshen froze as her heart hammered. She knew that scent – a wildcat on the prowl.

'What is it?' Tulkhan's voice was a whisper.

'A hunter. It won't attack while there are two of us, unless it's desperate. But it is very close and it is watching us.'

She was glad of the General's presence. Imoshen didn't question why she knew she could trust him to protect her back, she simply accepted it. Once again she drew her knife. 'Watch behind, I'll watch ahead.'

They walked uphill, striking away from the brook toward the rise beyond which they knew the others waited. The beast kept pace with them, only falling back as they entered the clearing where the horses shifted uneasily, showing the whites of their eyes. Several of the handlers whispered soothingly to calm them.

The return of General Tulkhan and his captive was greeted with relief and some ribaldry. Their extended absence had been marked. The men were amused, tolerant. Imoshen's hair was hanging loose, filled with bracken, her clothes dusty and dishevelled. Tulkhan was also dirt-stained.

The General escorted her to her horse, ignoring the jibes. The men were ready to move out. As one of the foot soldiers passed Imoshen the reins she saw a knowing smirk in his eyes. Her hands tightened convulsively, but she restrained herself because she noticed the man's expression when he met the General's eyes.

With a jolt she understood the Ghebites' amusement and it gave her an unwelcome insight into their world. They thought their General had been bedding her, too eager to restrain himself. Imoshen's cheeks stung with heat.

Didn't they know pure T'En women were sacred? She would never consider bedding a man for idle enjoyment.

She had thought the Ghebites despise her kind. Yet the men were not offended. It appeared that despite her Otherness, she was female enough for them to tolerate the idea of their General lying with her.

Tulkhan held her gaze, his dark eyes sparkling with amusement.

She gritted her teeth and swung into the saddle. Tulkhan gave her a rueful grin and she realised he was not only aware of her chagrin but he was enjoying it. With all her being she wanted to wipe that arrogant masculine gleam from his eyes. Instead she lifted her chin and held her head high, daring anyone to comment.

The General might be grinning now, but she knew better. He had almost raped her at the insistence of an ancient force. She was lucky those herbs had been tucked into her jerkin. Their pungent scent had helped clear his head and she'd been able to use the moment to distract him.

But honesty forced her to admit it had been the General's willpower which had conquered the unseen force and freed him. As much as she wanted to, she had not been able to help him. Frustration filled her. Unlike the Aayel, who could scry the future and read people, Imoshen's T'En powers were weak. Only once had she sifted a conscious mind and that was when she was first confronted by the General.

Then she had been in a heightened state of awareness, fearful for her life. It had been an unconscious act of self-preservation. If only she had more control over her T'En gifts.

Tilting her head forward, she caught her hair and began to braid it.

'No.' Tulkhan grabbed her elbow. 'Leave it loose.'

He raised his hand and drew his fingers through the first part of the braid, separating the strands. Her scalp tingled with the slight tug. His hand travelled the length of her hair and came free with a small piece of brown bracken. Laughter lit his eyes as he held it up for her to see, then tossed it aside.

'Your people expect you to look like the T'En princess you are,' he told her.

She opened her mouth to argue, but it was true. He moved away, satisfied that she would obey him.

Kalleen's saucy eyes met Imoshen's and the serving girl curled her top lip, silently giving her opinion of men, the General in particular. Imoshen had to smile.

She stole a glance in his direction, watching as a soldier helped Tulkhan into his battle regalia. She should despise the Ghebite General, but she had to admit he had all the makings of a leader. For one, he looked so fine in full battle dress. She had to admire his easy stride, the grace of his body as he swung onto the back of the black war horse.

The column moved out and it was a relief when they finally left the forest. Soon they were riding into a cool breeze, sharp with the salty tang of the sea.

Tulkhan felt the chill in his hands as he held the reins. His men had never travelled this far south before and the autumn chill promised a cold winter.

'So...' he shifted in the saddle. 'If the farm folk see the twin moons as a mother and child, what do the T'En see them as?'

He knew the answer but he wanted to hear the Dhamfeer's explanation. She never missed a chance to lecture him on the superiority of her culture, and he never missed a chance to confound her with his knowledge of other cultures.

'As a man and woman,' she replied, plucking a long strand of silver-blonde hair from her lips and tossing her head. Obviously, she enjoyed the bracing sea breeze. 'Like man and woman, the moons vie for supremacy, first one is in the ascendancy, then the other. Their relationship is strongest and thus at its most powerful when both shine freely, so it is with a man and woman.

'While there are things one does better than the other, they are strongest when they can stand side by side, equal in each other's eyes.' Her fierce wine-dark eyes met his and held. 'I will call no man my master.'

A shiver moved over his skin. He found a laugh. 'Neither will I!'

She laughed, then eyed him narrowly. 'I've heard your people see the moons as two half-brothers, who battle constantly for supremacy.'

'Yes.' He shifted in the saddle. 'One is the son of the first wife, the other the son of the second. Both want the father's love, so they try to outshine each other.'

'Are they not equal?'

He grimaced. He was the King's eldest son, but his mother had been the second wife, not the first taken to consolidate political power. So his younger half-brother, Gharavan, was now the ruler. But he had known this would happen ever since the boy was born. He had seen the marked difference in his treatment once the King's first wife produced a male heir. He had known then who his true friends were, and since that day he had learnt enough of human nature to be grateful for that early lesson, cruel though it had been.

As concubine-son Tulkhan had no birthright. His general's rank and the respect of his men had been earned and he was proud of this. 'The first son of the first wife inherits the father's property, while the second gets nothing.'

'What if the first born was a daughter?'

He snorted. 'Females don't inherit.'

'Why not?'

He shrugged casually to irritate her. 'They just don't. They don't own property, they don't sit on council...'

Imoshen laughed, startling him. 'Then Gheeaba is the poorer for that policy, because you lose the skills of half your people!'

She urged her horse forward and galloped a little ahead. He stared at her shoulders, admiring the way she rode. Curse her, she'd done it again. Honesty forced him to admit she was probably right. If he felt disinherited, how did his elder half-sisters feel? He hardly knew them. They'd been married to consolidate his family's position during the long years he had spent on the campaigns.

Imoshen urged her mount forward, delighted to have gotten the better of

Tulkhan. He was looking far too fine and pleased with himself in his battle regalia. She understood why he had ordered his men to dress for their arrival at Landsend. His army made an impressive spectacle, none more so than the General himself. But she was on edge after what had happened and she didn't want to ride too near him.

She thought she recognised a rocky outcropping and urged her horse toward it. The elite guard parted for her, used to her conversations with their general, her coming and going freely. Several had consulted her on the matter of old wounds that hadn't healed.

Imoshen leapt from her mount, tied the reins to a low bush and ran to the top of the outcropping. The view was just as she remembered it. From where she stood the ground fell away, a chequerboard of rolling grain fields and winding lanes which led to the port of Landsend. In the distance she could see the magnificent abbey that dominated the bluff and overlooked the large bay. The horizon was an endless blue. Somewhere beyond that ocean and to the north lay the original home of the T'En.

She was looking at history. Landsend, where her namesake, T'Imoshen the First, had made landfall.

Inhaling deeply, she rejoiced. The scent of the sea made her heart race. The stiff breeze pressed her clothes to her body and filled her chest.

She sensed the General at her side and pointed.

'There it is!' She had to raise her voice to be heard over the sea breeze. 'This is where the first T'Imoshen ordered her ship burnt to the water line. She had a much smaller army than yours, made up of the old and the children. They were explorers, looking for wealth and knowledge.

'Within a generation, the T'En had captured the whole island. Sporadic uprisings occurred for around two hundred years, but we brought culture, music, art, written language, medicine and science to this land.'

She turned to him, pride blazing in her eyes. A smile of triumph curved her lips.

Tulkhan knew then that Imoshen would never yield to him. Beauty lay spread out below them, but he did not see it. He stiffened, stung by the implications of her comment – she considered him a barbarian.

'What have your people done since then?' he demanded. 'Grown lazy and self-indulgent?'

'While the T'En ruled, no one, not even a landless drifter, lived in fear of starvation. If anyone, male or female, was wronged, they could bring their grievance before the church to be heard. There was justice for all.'

Tulkhan tensed as she caught his hands in hers, fixing her glittering eyes on him.

'I admit that you've bested our army, General, but don't throw out what is good. Keep the best, build on it. Be a leader with vision!'

He searched her eyes, startled by her vehemence. True, in the rare idle moments during his many years of campaigning, he had compared the way different kingdoms drafted and enforced their laws. The weak gave their loyalty to the strong for protection, and in doing so gave up their freedom.

But Imoshen was talking about justice for all regardless of gender or social status, an individual's right. Tulkhan's head reeled at the concept.

'Fair Isle is renowned for its culture, the music, the arts –'

'The decadence!' Tulkhan would not let her compare their homelands and call him a barbarian by default.

Imoshen's hands tightened on his. 'Discard the bad, build on the good. Gather the greatest minds in Fair Isle...'

'I have met great thinkers on the mainland, too. Men who were working on ways to heal, men who turned their farseers to the night sky or who designed machines to do the work of ordinary men.'

'Then invite them to Fair Isle. Knowledge knows no master, knowledge is power!'

As Tulkhan stared into her upturned face, a vision of Fair Isle's future swamped him. Was it possible to eliminate disease, free the worker from endless toil, and create an island where the weak did not fear the strong?

She lifted their clasped hands, squeezing them in her excitement. 'You *do* see it!'

He flinched.

The Dhamfeer had done it again. She'd reached into his mind and invaded his thoughts. He felt defiled.

Revulsion flooded him. He flung her hands away. Fury goaded him to inflict the same measure of pain on her. Catching her by the upper arms, he shook her, pressing his fingers savagely into her flesh.

'Don't ever do that again.' Even as he spoke, he registered the confusion in her face. She didn't understand his anger. A sheen of unshed tears glistened in her eyes and he realised he'd hurt her.

She'd offered him a vision of the future and he'd thrown it aside. Curse her!

Curse her beautiful, trembling mouth.

He had to kiss her. It made no sense. One kiss would never be enough. Instead of heeding common sense he let the need which had been steadily building within his body guide his actions.

He caught her to him, capturing her lips with his.

She tasted so good. Her skin was soft, her mouth hot. The curves of her slender body pressed against his. He felt her quicken under his touch and recognised her raw and uninhibited reaction. Her ragged breath fanned his face, her hands caught his neck as she strained against him. She was an innocent wanton. The thought inflamed him.

Drunk on sensation, he felt like laughing till he heard a silken whisper in his mind. Tulkhan registered her unspoken plea for more. He froze. She'd done it again – she'd invaded his mind.

He broke the contact abruptly, thrusting her aside. As he pulled back, he noted her flushed face, her lips swollen by his kisses.

'Get on your horse, Dhamfeer.' But his hands held her close, pressed to his body, thigh to thigh.

She blinked.

He realised that she didn't understand his abrupt change. Was it possible that she didn't even know she was doing it? Were her abilities intuitive, rather than controlled? The analytical part of Tulkhan's mind put this thought aside for future consideration.

A ragged cheer broke from the elite guard. It surprised Tulkhan. Their embrace must have appeared spontaneous and passionate to his men, who were too far away to have caught the undertones.

He met Imoshen's eyes, saw her flush.

Sliding his arm around her shoulder Tulkhan turned her to face the men, who cheered again. He felt the first stirring of resistance and when Imoshen would have shrugged free of him, he tightened his grip.

Still grinning, he told her, 'Never disappoint your people, Imoshen. Didn't they teach you anything?'

She turned into his embrace and caught his face in her hands. 'More than you think, General.'

This time when she kissed him the unexpectedness of it ignited his passion, bypassing all logic. His body was ready for hers.

Then snap, her teeth closed painfully on his bottom lip before she pulled back, Dhamfeer eyes alight.

Stunned, he released her.

Laughing, she jumped lightly to the ground and freed her mount's reins.

Tulkhan tasted blood on his tongue. The pain was nothing, but the challenge consumed him. Curse her vow of celibacy. He would have her, and she would beg him for more.

THEY RODE INTO Landsend as the sun set. Tulkhan had timed it perfectly; the sun gilded their polished armour and weapons. A curious populace escorted them up the winding rise to Landsend Abbey, cheering. It appeared the purpose of their visit was already known. Good news travelled fast.

Though the Dhamfeer was his captive, she was greeted with honour, almost reverence, by the abbey scholars, reminding Tulkhan forcibly that Imoshen was the last of the T'En race.

The abbey leader, the Seculate, was a woman who wielded the power of her office with quiet authority. Again, he was reminded of Fair Isle's differences. In Gheeaba a woman would never have commanded a man, yet here the male priests not only listened attentively to the Seculate's every word but they scurried to do her bidding.

The troops were housed in the township itself, only the elite guard were quartered within the abbey. Tulkhan remained outwardly impassive, but he was on edge. If she planned treachery, the Seculate could have them all murdered in their sleep and leave his men leaderless.

Yet the more he saw of these people the more he was impressed by their culture, their architecture and by their reverence for knowledge. Their meal was simple but delicious, and they were entertained in the courtyard by music and obscure plays which he found hard to follow. He would have much preferred to follow Imoshen when she withdrew with her maidservant.

The sounds of revelry drifted up the stairwell as Imoshen and Kalleen made their way to their chamber.

Imoshen noticed how Kalleen tilted her head to catch the noises from the courtyard. She realised the poor girl would rather be out there, joining in the fun, than helping prepare a bath, so she dismissed her. Kalleen didn't need to be told twice.

In the bath chamber Imoshen stripped.

Ha, she thought, *let Tulkhan pretend to be unimpressed by hot running water!*

Even she was impressed. Her family's stronghold did not indulge in luxuries. For the first time she wondered why the church, devoted to serving the T'En, should allow its members this kind of luxury. A niggling worm of disquiet troubled her and the Aayel's talk of the Beatific returned to her.

But the Beatific was far away in T'Diemn, and she was here in Landsend.

Imoshen sank into the water, revelling in its heat. She washed her hair with scented soap. It was a luxury to be clean. After delaying as long as she could, she climbed out and dried herself.

Taking her time, she inspected her bruises caused by the fall when Tulkhan tackled her. Her heart still thudded when she recalled how her life had hung in the balance.

Yet, for a moment, when they looked out over Landsend, she'd felt he shared her vision. She'd seen the leap of understanding in his eyes. Then he had thrust her aside. Just when she thought there was something more to him, he had proved her wrong.

As for that kiss...

Her lips tingled and her body thrummed with the memory. She had to admit he had moved her, but the man was such an odd mixture of scholar and barbarian. He could learn a country's language before invading it, then have to cloak his surprise when he saw the abbey's leader was a woman.

Imoshen frowned. What must he think of *her*?

She stalked from the mosaic tiled bathing room into her chamber. Tightening the drawstring of her night gown under her breasts, she knelt in front of the fire, enjoying its warmth. Methodically, she spread her hair over her fingers to dry.

She would not think about him.

Yet, the General had withstood the effects of that ancient evil. He'd pretended scorn after their encounter but she sensed he'd been unnerved, even a little frightened by what he'd experienced. She had been truly afraid he would attack her, that she would have to fight for her life and it wouldn't have been him she was fighting. Imoshen tried not to dwell on her strange reluctance to hurt him.

Somehow Tulkhan had found the strength of will to throw off the ancient power's domination. Her hands slowed as she finger-combed her hair. She could tell he disliked being out of control. He was truly a man of rational thought, a man ahead of his time, ahead of his own people.

Not that he wasn't a barbarian, she amended, then grinned, aware of her twisted logic.

The Aayel had said he was a man trapped by his own culture. The General could barely believe her great aunt was a threat to him. From what she had overheard, Imoshen knew the Ghebite religion regarded the 'Dhamfeer' as less than human. Though Tulkhan was a contradiction, a soldier who strove to learn, he was still a product of his upbringing. The Ghebite priests would have taught him to despise the T'En and their innate powers, that must be why he feared her. Imoshen frowned.

She was still his captive, for all that the Seculate had presented her with this room and had asked her to perform the ceremony over the meal tonight.

Yet Tulkhan feared her?

She shook her head wearily. Too much had happened.

The fire was warm and she spread her hair to dry, running her fingers through its thick waves, which hung past her waist. She wouldn't think about him again.

Perversely, her mind presented her with a picture of General Tulkhan watching her during the meal tonight. Twice she had caught him staring, his gaze calculating, weighing. She knew he didn't trust her, she was too well liked by the people. Her life hung by a thread. Imoshen shivered, despite the fire. Yet the desire in Tulkhan's eyes had been real enough tonight and there had been no mistaking his intention when he kissed her.

A soft click made Imoshen turn. Her heart thudded as she scanned the room. A panel beside the fireplace slowly slid to one side.

Light-footed, she darted over to the travelling bag and drew out her knife as the panel opened. A figure stood in the darkness of the secret passage.

Imoshen raised the knife, prepared to use it. Should she throw and risk missing a fatal blow or wait until she could aim for the attacker's heart?

A soft chuckle made her skin prickle.

Reothe stepped into the dim glow of the firelight. He was dressed in battle gear but had discarded his armour, leaving only leggings and chest leather. His slender, sinewy arms were bare and his narrow intelligent face watched her closely. The fine silver tendrils of his hair glistened in the firelight as he moved towards her, one side of his mouth lifted in a mocking smile.

'If you mean to use that knife, throw it now, because I'll disarm you if you let me get within arm's length,' he warned.

'This knife isn't for you.' She found his assurance annoying, but her body reacted to him as it had done once before. What was it about him that made her heart race and her head swim?

She let the knife point drop with an odd reluctance and he smiled, his eyes brilliant pools in his pale face.

'You don't seem surprised to see me? Did you guess I'd survived?'

'Hardly. General Tulkhan –'

'Tulkhan? That northern usurper?' His harsh tone made her wince. He stepped nearer, still not touching her, but close enough for his breath to stir the fine hairs on her forehead. 'I've been thinking of you. Imagining you. We would have been bonded this spring if the Ghebites hadn't invaded. Now I'm a renegade, my estates forfeited, and you're a captive. But I've come for you.'

Imoshen swallowed, trying to concentrate. His scent was achingly familiar, reminding her of the day they took the oath of betrothal – how his eyes had consumed her, how he had promised to bond to her and no other.

Reothe represented her people, her loyalty was to him and her family, her land. Wasn't it?

He lifted one long hand and pulled undone the drawstring at her throat so that the neck of her gown loosened and slid over her shoulders to fall below her breasts where the second drawstring held it in place. She heard his sharp intake of breath and felt her skin tighten. Her nipples hardened under his gaze. A wanton heat suffused her, confused her.

When he spoke, his voice was deeper, thicker. 'I've lain awake in the fields, hidden in caves, and imagined you like this, imagined claiming you. You gave your word and I gave mine. I've come for you.'

'What, now?'

'Now! You must come away with me. I'll take you south. I have followers who are loyal, contacts in the southern mainland kingdoms who will help me raise an army as well as friends on the islands of the archipelago. Come spring, we can return to retake our island. We'll drive these Ghebite barbarians out!'

Imoshen's head swam. She hadn't considered raising an army of mercenaries. Was it possible to retake their land, to fight at Reothe's side?

He snatched her hand and took the knife. Lifting its sharp blade to his lips he kissed it.

Imoshen swallowed. No, he couldn't mean to make a formal bond here and now.

'With my blood,' he whispered and slit his left wrist, the one nearest his heart. 'I vow to bond only unto you, Imoshen of the T'En.'

She stared dumbfounded as the blood oozed from the cut, gathering momentum. He lifted her left hand.

And she knew she didn't want this. 'No.'

'Yes.' He was implacable. 'I made a promise to your family, to you.'

She gasped as the blade cut through the flesh of her left wrist and he pressed the two wounds together.

'By the joining of our blood, by the breath in my body. I cleave to you.' His fierce eyes held hers. He gave their bonded wrists a little shake. 'Say it. Say the vow. I have a boat waiting in a hidden cove below. We can escape through the passage to the sea –'

'I can't do it.' The words were torn from her.

'Why not?'

'I can't leave them now.' Imoshen felt a rush of heat take her as she thought not of the people who trusted her, but of General Tulkhan as he listened so intently to her language lessons. 'If I go now, the people will think me false. They will revolt, and the Ghebites will turn on them. The harvest will fail, blood will stain the fields and starvation will stalk the snows. Better I stay and be the General's prisoner, a guarantee of their behaviour, then leave them to their fate.'

'Farmers?' he repeated incredulously. 'I'm offering you a chance to retake our lands, to drive the Ghebite General and his army out.'

'More fighting, more bloodshed; and what will the people eat? Will you war till not a house stands, till weeds cover the fields because no one is left to plough them? No!' She wrenched her wrist away and grasped it to stop the flow of blood. She needed to bind it and take something against the poisons getting into her blood.

'We made a vow.'

'In another world, when my family still lived and –'

He grabbed her around the waist, lifting her off her feet, so that she felt his hard thighs against hers and how much he wanted her.

'I made a vow,' he ground out. 'I don't go back on my word, Imoshen.'

'I can't do it. I pledged my word to the General, the people trust me. They depend on me.'

'Your word to General Tulkhan?' He gave an odd, strangled laugh. 'What is the word of a captive? What choice did you have? You aren't bound by it. Our vow stands true, being of an older making.'

She watched the blood from her wrist trickle down across the muscle of his shoulder so that it appeared he was bleeding. He was probably staining her gown. Her breasts pressed against the leather of his jerkin and she could smell his unique male scent. Her head spun with an intoxicating passion. What was it about Reothe that called to her? Was it because he was one of her own kind?

His voice changed, softened. 'You want me, don't deny it. Come away with me now.'

Before she knew he meant to, he lowered his head and inhaled her scent, a ragged groan escaped him. His involuntary moan made her body shudder, then his lips were on hers and it was like the other time in the woods, only this time she was as good as naked, with nothing but a thin gown fixed under her breasts, and he did not restrain himself, he devoured her.

Did he hope the force of his passion would convince her, obliterate all but his will?

His passion frightened her, even as it ignited her. His scent was so familiar, all the things she had learnt about him before returned as if some deep inner truth were being confirmed.

'Imoshen,' he breathed her name, his lips on hers. 'You can't stay here.'

'I can't leave my people.' This time it was a plea for understanding. 'They need me.'

He uttered a groan and let her weight slide down his body till her toes touched the ground, then he released her and stepped back. She could see what it cost him to maintain his control. Right at this moment her body raged against her mind.

'You have a hard head, Imoshen.'

'I must –'

'What about your heart? The honour of your family?'

'I...' She swallowed. 'Practicality guides me. Honour is useless if you're dead, and... and I have no heart.'

He nearly laughed. 'A lie. Very well. I will come again.'

'No. They'll catch you and kill you.'

This time he did laugh. 'I'm going now, but I'll be back and next time I'll claim you and take you with me.'

He caught her wrist and pressed it against his, reaffirming the bond. His eyes held hers.

Imoshen felt her body yearn for him, but she refused to succumb to the power of his will. 'I haven't taken the vow.'

'I have. I knew you were meant for me when I saw you in the palace. When I came to Umasreach last autumn, I felt it in my body, and you did too.'

'No, no I –'

'Don't bother to deny it.' He lifted her wrist to his mouth and she thought he was going to kiss her wound, but he closed his eyes. 'Seal flesh.'

Then ran his tongue across the torn flesh.

A flash of heat stung her and she snatched her hand from his. There was a new pale pink scar on the fine white skin of her inner wrist where the wound had been.

She gasped. 'How did you do that?'

His wine-dark eyes which were so like hers, held her. 'There's much I could teach you. We're the last of our kind, we can't let our line die out, we can't let the knowledge and the gifts die with us.'

He lifted his own wrist and held it to her face. 'Heal me.'

'I can't –'

'Nonsense. You can do it. Heal me.'

Tentatively she caught his hand, feeling the bones, the strength in him. She turned his wrist to her mouth and touched the tip of her tongue to his wound, tasting his blood as she drew along the torn skin. In her mind's eye she saw the skin closing and sealing. When she looked again, a fine pale scar was all that remained of his bonding-wound.

'It's healed!'

'It will never heal until you lie with me and complete the vows. I still bleed, but you can't see it, Imoshen.'

This time when he lifted her face she knew he was going to kiss her and she found a strange reluctance gripped her. His mouth was firm, his tongue tasted of blood, and she knew he must be able to taste his blood on her tongue. She felt a surge of fear. He was a feral creature, implacable and alien.

She was afraid of him. What else could he do? Did he know what his body did to hers? Obviously he had recognised it long before she did. She didn't like being at a disadvantage. It was frightening not knowing the extent of another's ability, not knowing if they were manipulating you.

No wonder Tulkhan feared her.

Reothe pulled away from her. His eyes narrowed and she knew he had sensed her thoughts.

She opened her mouth but hesitated as his lips set in a hard line.

'What game are you playing, Imoshen?'

'I... nothing.' She felt at a loss, a child caught in an adult's game. 'I seek only the best for my people.'

Noises in the hall alerted them. There was so much left unsaid. The door creaked on its hinges.

Reothe gave her an intense look, which promised this was unfinished. Then he darted through the narrow gap, ducking his head to pass into the passage. The wooden panel slid shut.

Imoshen pulled up her gown and kept her back to the fire to hide the blood stains from Reothe's bonding wound. She could still smell his scent on the air, on her skin, but her maidservant wasn't so sensitive. Imoshen could tell Kalleen was weary as she gave her pithy opinion of the abbey and of Wharrd.

She offered her services to Imoshen, who refused, saying she wanted to sit up a little longer. Kalleen curled up on the low bed at the foot of Imoshen's bed. Soon she was fast asleep.

Thoughtfully, Imoshen dropped her gown to the floor and studied the blood stains on the small of her back where Reothe had held her. She lifted the material to her face and inhaled his scent.

He was her other self. Her loyalty should be to him and to her family, to regaining the kingdom, yet she could not abandon the people of Fair Isle. She was torn. She'd given her word to General Tulkhan.

Her word? She had also given Reothe her word and all but made the vow of bonding. What was wrong with her? Opposing loyalties clawed at her. She felt as if she would tear in two. What could she do? She tossed the gown into the fire and watched it burn, the flames casting shadows across her naked, pearly white flesh.

It seemed symbolic – the burning of her innocence. She knew whatever path she took one of the two men would grow to hate her, and one of them would die.

Chapter Four

IMOSHEN LIFTED HER hand and looked at the wound on her wrist. Reothe had been right. She had healed him after he had done the same for her. She would not have thought it possible. Perhaps that type of healing would not work on True-men and women, perhaps it was only effective because of her racial affinity with Reothe?

Frustration gripped Imoshen. Her parents had kept her birthright from her, forbidding the Aayel to instruct her in T'En ways, and there was so much she did not know. And Reothe did. He'd had longer to hone his natural skills, but healing had always been her gift. His skill surprised her.

Was he more gifted than she? The Aayel's fearful voice returned to Imoshen as she described how she had witnessed the stoning of the last rogue male T'En. He had captured the Aayel, invaded her mind and forced her to experience his pain. His death had nearly been hers. How cruel. Imoshen felt anger on behalf of the twelve-year-old child her great aunt had been. She might sneer at the Ghebites, but she must not forget it wasn't so long ago that her own people had practised barbarism

Her great aunt had had good cause to fear that rogue T'En male. Now Imoshen understood why the Aayel had chosen to absent herself during Reothe's visit.

Did the Aayel have a good reason to fear Reothe? Surely not?

Imoshen shivered. She would not rest until she knew the extent of Reothe's gifts and how to defend herself from him. He had all but read her mind. She hated knowing her thoughts were open to him.

Was that how the General felt?

Her hair was almost dry. Feeling strangely distant, she separated the long strands and began to plait them together. As she did, a flicker of firelight reflected on the knife blade, attracting her eye.

Imoshen flushed.

Reothe had challenged her to use it, knowing she wouldn't. He had risked his life to come back for her. She owed him something. Yet his intensity frightened her. When he held her, she couldn't think clearly.

Was he trying to force his will on hers by subtle use of his powers? Her skin went cold at the thought.

Had her confusion been due to the strength of his gifts and not her natural response to him? Had he chosen her from the first because she was susceptible?

Back home at the stronghold, she had searched the library for works which predated the first T'Imoshen's invasion of Fair Isle. But there was very little information on the T'En. What she did find was too obscure to be useful.

It appeared that there had been great workers of the T'En gifts in their ancient homeland, but the histories were strangely silent on exactly what these gifts were.

Yet the Aayel had said the T'En gifts were poor, unreliable things, that those who used them unwisely faced the wrath of the church – *their* church – which was supposed to revere the T'En.

Imoshen shuddered, recalling the Aayel's eyes as she spoke of the stoning. The horror of that event had stayed with her for over a century, colouring her actions for the rest of her life.

Anger flashed through Imoshen and she directed it towards the long dead Beatific who had ordered the Aayel to witness the stoning. Imoshen understood that it had been a precautionary measure, to ensure the young Aayel's cooperation, but the consequences were far more damaging to a young child. If its purpose was to ensure that the T'En would remain repressed, then it had succeeded.

Was the church protecting the people of Fair Isle from the T'En? Imoshen shivered. Suddenly she felt very alone.

All her life she had been an object of curiosity. The people were both fearful and fascinated by her. It had been a burden she'd borne with growing resentment. But perhaps the True-men and women had good reason to fear the T'En? She did not know. So few throwbacks had been born, only two in the last one hundred years...

No, it was all a fabrication of her over-tired mind. She was no monster and neither was Reothe. They might have small useful gifts, but these benefited True-man and T'En alike. Her priority was to ensure her own survival under a barbarian invader.

Imoshen kept her own counsel while at Landsend Abbey. She performed her duties, but remained aloof from Tulkhan and the abbey seniors because for Reothe to have access to the abbey's secret passages, someone had sided with her betrothed.

Did they consider her a traitor?

Was she?

THE RETURN JOURNEY was made swiftly. Already, loaded wagons of grain were wending their way to Umasreach Stronghold, where their loads would be stored and catalogued. Imoshen knew there was work ahead of her.

The easy companionship which had developed on their ride out was gone. Tulkhan's elite guard watched her closely. Had they heard a rumour of Reothe's visit? Was she condemned without trial? Imoshen didn't know what to think.

Should she have run away with Reothe when she had the chance to save her own life, even though it meant deserting the people who trusted her? Again, Imoshen had no answer.

They entered the stronghold late one afternoon on a cool, autumn day that held a foretaste of the winter to come. When the Aayel came out to greet her, Imoshen tried to mask her disquiet, but her great aunt sensed it. General Tulkhan did not exchange one word with her as he rode off to the stables with his men.

'You're chilled to the bone. Come inside, Shenna.' The Aayel led Imoshen to her chambers, where the servants waited.

It was all so normal, so soothing – an illusion. But Imoshen let them fuss over her, glad to relinquish all responsibility this once.

The Aayel dismissed the women, then sprinkled healing herbs in the hot water. While Imoshen bathed, she sat and watched.

'It did not go well?'

'It did at first. I learnt a great deal. He is not a stupid man.'

The Aayel gave a snort. 'So, you discovered that!'

'He's stubborn and he hates... no, fears me.'

'So he should. You could be the death of him and the downfall of his hold on Fair Isle.'

Imoshen gnawed her bottom lip. Should she tell the Aayel about Reothe and the dual tug of the familiar against the unknown? She desperately wanted the Aayel to confirm that she had made the right decision. Imoshen stole a look at the wizened old woman. Would she look like that in a hundred years from now?

She almost laughed – she would be lucky to live that long.

The Aayel watched her, silent, appraising but uncritical. It was reassuring.

'I've been taking the potion,' Imoshen said.

'I know. I can see it in you. You're blooming with health and fertility. Perhaps that is why the General is distancing himself from you. He fights his instincts.'

Imoshen grimaced. She was not so hopeful. Her instincts were totally confused. Duty and the General, or duty and Reothe?

As she stood and took the drying cloth from her great aunt, the old woman's hands brushed hers.

'What has Reothe to do with this?' the Aayel demanded.

Imoshen opened her mouth to lie but she couldn't.

Instead, she lowered her voice. 'Reothe entered the abbey. I believe he has a supporter or two there. He came to my room. He...' She felt vulnerable, because she did not understand. Why was she drawn to him? To hide her confusion, she dried herself vigorously. 'He wanted to bond with me. He tried to perform the ceremony, but I wouldn't give him my vow and refused to flee with him.

'I told him I had to stay for the people. He said I was betraying them by not leaving with him to help raise an army to retake Fair Isle. But I had to refuse. It tore me in two!' She tossed the cloth aside, lifting her hands to the Aayel in supplication. 'I've been going over and over it. One moment I think

I have failed the memory of my family, yet I feel I cannot fail the people. Please, tell me, did I do right to refuse him?'

The Aayel ran her paper-dry fingers down Imoshen's cheek. 'He is very gifted, that Reothe.' Her sharp eyes held Imoshen's. 'What do you feel?'

'I don't know...' She turned and walked away from the Aayel towards to the fire. The warmth attracted her, but she also used the movement to cloak her intimate feelings. She hardly dared admit to herself this secret yearning for Reothe. It seemed a weakness, because it made her vulnerable to him and she could not afford to let anything but cool rational thought guide her decisions, not if she was to survive this crucial time. 'He calls to something in me, but he frightens me.'

'Your instincts are good. I knew his parents, their parents and their parents. There is bad blood in his family, a brilliance, but also an unsteadiness. It sometimes surfaces in the pure T'En. His mother and father were first cousins. They were scholars of history. I know despite the concerns of their family they bonded to keep the blood pure. They risked social stigma to bring Reothe into the world. I suspect that is why he wants you, you're so obviously of the old race.'

Was it true? Was that the only reason Reothe wanted her? Would his body call to hers with such ferocity of purpose if it was only a logical choice? Instinct told Imoshen his need for her went deeper than logic.

She dropped her nightgown over her head and pulled the drawstrings. 'You didn't answer me. Who should have my loyalty, my betrothed who wants to rekindle a war, or the people who only want to live out their lives free from war? And what of General Tulkhan? He is the invader, yet I have given him my word. Reothe said a vow given under duress is no vow at all, and that my betrothal promise to him is of an older making. I want to do the right thing but... Tell me, what should I do?'

Imoshen turned hopefully to the Aayel. Surely her great aunt would vindicate the decisions she had made?

'There are no easy answers, child.' The old women poured the potion. 'You must survive, concentrate on that. You are blooming. Drink.'

Imoshen downed the medicine. Was there a visible difference in her? Her breasts had grown more sensitive. She felt impatient with those around her and she had caught herself watching General Tulkhan when he rode through the ranks, when he prowled around the fire circle. She liked the way his body moved and she couldn't help recalling how he had pinned her to the ground, his arms around her thighs, his weight on her.

An impatient exhalation escaped Imoshen.

She had one desperate gamble, one throw of the dice in another three days. Maybe her heightened sensitivity, the slight change in her scent, the ache in her core were all her imagination, and the potion wouldn't work. Then what would she do?

Imoshen returned the empty vial to the Aayel. 'I want you to try a scrying. I must know if I am doing the right thing.'

The old woman sighed. 'It doesn't work like that. It's never that simple –'

'I must know. This is tearing me apart.'

The Aayel signalled her to lower her voice. The old woman sighed. 'Very well. Bring me my scrying platter.'

She hurried to obey.

When Imoshen returned, she knelt at the old woman's knee, her heart pounding. What would she learn? Would she see herself with Tulkhan or with Reothe? Should she lead her country into war, or keep the peace with the invader at a price almost too steep to bear?

The Aayel scooped up a handful of the scented bath water.

'Bath water?' Imoshen wrinkled her nose.

'It's your future,' her great aunt muttered dryly.

Imoshen lifted the knife she had selected for this purpose and pricked her finger, adding two drops of her own blood. She had noticed any working of the gifts was stronger if blood was spilt, and the more you gave of yourself the more you got back in return.

The Aayel stiffened.

'I have to know,' she insisted. 'I don't care what the price is.'

'Don't be too quick to make that claim, Shenna,' the Aayel muttered, swirling the water around on the plate to mix the blood. 'You don't know the price the gifts may demand.'

Imoshen tensed. Did she read some hidden knowledge there? Was the Aayel hinting that the gifts had more potential than she had previously claimed? An unwelcome thought came to Imoshen. Had the Aayel deliberately kept a deeper, more potent form of knowledge from her in an attempt to control her?

'Take it,' the Aayel urged.

Automatically, Imoshen accepted the scrying plate. 'Me?'

'It's your future. Take responsibility for it.'

Stung by the implied criticism, Imoshen concentrated as she tilted the scrying platter this way and that, observing the thin film of water which covered its surface.

Nothing. She was useless.

No. She had to know. Gritting her teeth, Imoshen peered through the film to the platter's reflective surface, searching for a form, a hint. Still nothing.

'What do you see?' she asked the Aayel in desperation.

'What do *you* see?'

'Me? I am no good at scrying.'

'And never will be, if that's the attitude you take!'

Goaded by her great aunt's tone, Imoshen focused. At first she only saw the glint of candle flames distorted by the thin film of water in the shining metal of the platter.

'Bring to mind what concerns you. Guide it,' the Aayel whispered.

Imoshen nodded. She had to know if her decision was the right one.

Her heart lurched as the General's broad features appeared. His coppery skin darkened, flushing with anger and exertion. He grimaced and dodged as someone struck at him. More and more figures attacked.

'They'll kill him!'

'What do you see?' the Aayel pressed.

'The General. He's being attacked in a narrow hall. They look like our people.' Imoshen gasped as one of the assassins leapt forward shouting a name. 'Reothe!'

'Is Reothe there?'

'No, they attack in his name.'

'Assassins?'

Imoshen shuddered, water spilling onto her nightgown.

The Aayel took the platter and tipped the remaining water into the tub. She used her apron to dry the surface. 'So.'

Imoshen felt cheated. 'But I don't know any more than I did before.'

Her great aunt shrugged. 'Now do you believe me? Scrying is not an exact science. Concentrate on what you do know. The General desires you.'

Imoshen made a noise in her throat. 'He hates me –'

'He wants you. I can see it in him. True?'

She nodded reluctantly. 'But he also hates and fears me.'

''Twould be worse if he were indifferent.' The old woman seemed pleased. 'You must seduce him three days from now when we host the Harvest Feast. You know what the people will want that evening, a formal consummation.'

'No!' Imoshen was shocked.

The Aayel shrugged philosophically. 'It is an old custom and most cultures have something like it to ensure the fertility of their fields the following spring.'

'But we've never taken part in that side of the festivities. We left it to the people to choose the male and female to consecrate the –'

'So?'

Imoshen folded her arms. 'I won't do it. I... I've never even lain with a man.' She flushed. 'I wouldn't know what to do.'

Birdlike, her great aunt tilted her head. 'You've had the lessons.'

Imoshen snorted helplessly.

The old woman gripped her arm, eyes intense. 'Don't live a life bounded by fear like I did. Seize the moment.'

Imoshen licked her lips reluctantly. 'Tell me how to go about it.'

The old woman gave a hoot of laughter. 'You ask me? By law I had to remain celibate or risk death.'

'Didn't you... I mean, weren't you tempted? Did you never love someone enough to –'

'Risk death for the love of a man?' the old woman mocked.

Imoshen watched her great aunt and wondered what memories caused the bitterness in her voice.

'Maybe I was too comfortable, too timid to risk everything for love. But you... you have nothing to lose and everything to gain.' The Aayel took

Imoshen's hand. 'This is your great gamble and you will only get one throw of the dice. If the General suspects you are manipulating him, he will be furious.'

Imoshen shuddered. She did not need her great aunt to spell out what she meant. 'Very well. But all I have is theoretical knowledge. I am not very experienced. Should I lie with –'

'No!'

'It was only a thought.' Imoshen felt her face grow hot. 'I will never succeed in seducing him. He despises me.'

'He burns for you.'

'He has a strange way of showing it.' She felt cornered. Resentment seared her. She wasn't ready for this. Life had been simple before General Tulkhan and is Ghebite army invaded.

'What if he rejects me?' Imoshen whispered.

The Aayel said nothing.

Imoshen felt her body flood with heat. General Tulkhan maintained a wall of indifference between them, yet she would be lying if she did not admit to sensing his attraction to her. As much as she hated to admit it, she burned with the same reluctant desire for him.

'Listen not to what he tells you, but what his body says,' the old woman advised and would say nothing more.

EVERYONE HAD HELPED to bring in the grain before the snows came. The harvesting was nearly over. The weather watchers forecast an early, bitter winter and already there were frosts in the hollows of a morning.

With most of the army out in the fields, those who remained behind in Umasreach Stronghold were busy cleaning out the grain stores and making the usual winter preparations.

Ten times a day the stronghold servants came to General Tulkhan asking directions. His own men waited to be told their tasks. Trained from childhood in the arts of war, he faced the task of ordering the lives of a thousand people, administering to the needs of a small civilian army.

He found himself constantly referring to the Aayel and to Imoshen, who had been raised for this responsibility. Indeed, the Dhamfeer seemed able to keep a dozen strands of thought in her head, to know instinctively which tasks needed priority, much as he would have done on the battlefield. He saw her as a general in times of peace. Before he knew it, she was his right hand, running the stronghold and half his elite guard.

Tulkhan watched with a growing sense of satisfaction as the wagons rolled in, heavily laden with grain. In the courtyard, his men were working side by side with the people and the stronghold guard.

He was surprised by the pleasure this simple yet vital task provided him. In the past he had left the day-to-day tasks to underlings. He'd moved on once a nation had been conquered and his curiosity about their culture had been satisfied. His administrative involvement had gone only as far as selecting places for forts and garrisoning them. Intent on taking the next country, he'd been happy to leave the holding of the conquered lands to the administrators appointed by his father.

Now he realised to conquer was one thing, to hold was another.

He turned towards the stairs. When Umasreach was built six hundred years ago, access to these storerooms, which were designed to double as prisons, had been through a hole in the ceiling and a ladder. But over time the inhabitants of the stronghold had sacrificed defensibility for practicality. He had seen evidence of similar compromises over and over during his inspection of Umasreach.

The walls of the original circular keep were three times as thick as man was tall, with no windows or doors on the ground floor. It had been designed primarily to repel attack, with only the third and fourth floors set aside for living quarters. But as the stronghold grew, the tower's role became less vital and it was reduced to one of many. Once the T'En hold on Fair Isle was more secure, the defenders had enlarged Umasreach, joining outer walls with battlement walks to the keep, and reducing its defensibility. But all these battlements between the towers could still be isolated by dropping the collapsible walks which circled the towers, so that if one section of the stronghold's walls were breached, the area could be cut off and the threat from attackers minimised.

Tulkhan had made a point of studying the defences of every country he travelled through, and Umasreach impressed him. Running water piped up from an underground reservoir was supplied to every floor of the new section. The reservoir was filled by a stream which had been diverted around four hundred years ago when the new section was built.

Before this, their water had come from a well, which stretched down below ground level to a depth of four stories, all dressed with stone, with foot and hand holds to the water level. Tulkhan knew because he had climbed down there.

He had also instructed Imoshen to show him the main gate defences. Access holes had been provided above the outer gates so that the stronghold defenders could pour water on them if potential invaders tried to set fire to the wooden frames. Reinforced with iron bands, the outer gates opened into a long passage to the inner gates. The portcullis at each end could be dropped to trap invaders in the passage and the holes in the ceiling opened so that the stronghold guard could pour scalding water or boiling oil, or shoot arrows into their attackers. If the invaders made it into the courtyard, the passage turned sharply so that they were forced to present their unshielded right sides to attack.

Even when the new section of the stronghold had been built all access to the buildings had been on the second floor, with stairs so steep attackers could easily be sent crashing to the cobbled courtyards below.

He had seen the more recent additions, the broadened steps with stone balustrades. He had seen where lower floors had been opened for ease of access. Tulkhan had personally walked every passage of Umasreach, the old, the new and the additions to the new.

It was the same story all over Fair Isle – towns had outgrown their fortified walls and the inhabitants had not bothered to build new ones or maintain the old. This was what four hundred years of peace did to a people. It made them soft.

Tulkhan's old tutor had spoken the truth when he said that all things being equal, it was not the strength of the defences but the strength of the defenders' hearts which decided a castle's fate. If all of Fair Isle had shared Imoshen's passion for freedom, his task would have been nearly impossible.

Where was she now? Ordering his elite guard about, no doubt.

He cursed softly. Over the past few days he had experienced a strange restlessness. Even now, something that was more than hunger gnawed at him. He felt irritable and tired because he couldn't sleep at night. With both moons nearly full it was almost as bright as day, but this had never bothered him in the past.

Despite his best efforts, he could not avoid Imoshen as she worked beside her people in the granaries, taking stock of what had come in, offering receipts to the farms, organising places for the constant stream of refugees from the north. As his men returned from the harvest and the new arrivals flooded in, the plains below the stronghold became dotted with makeshift houses. Smoke from their fires filled the sky day and night. Umasreach had become the centre of a town which rivalled the island's capital, T'Diemn.

With a sixth sense acquired through years of living with death, Tulkhan froze. He had entered a stone passage which led from the courtyard to the granaries. In the distance he could hear the people working, their voices raised in an ancient chant.

The hairs on the back of his neck lifted. There it was – a furtive step. Assassins?

Before he could back up, they were upon him. Two men, one woman. From their garb, he guessed they were escaped soldiers of the Emperor's army. The nearest lunged, his dirk passing harmlessly through the thick wadding of the General's jerkin.

Tulkhan cursed himself for a fool. He was unarmed.

Twisting the man's hand he kneed him in the face, tearing the knife from his fingers. The woman lunged for him with a knife, screaming a name. Her suicidal leap would have had him, but at the last instant he managed to twist from under her and felt her land heavily on the dirk. It was torn from his fingers, now slick with blood, as the third uninjured attacker leapt in with a short, pointed weapon which Tulkhan knew by custom carried poison. One scratch and he would die a lingering death.

There was no time for nicety. Grunting with the effort, he thrust the woman's body between them and saw her jolt as she took the spike in her back.

Clenching his fist, he thumped the man in the side of the head even as the first one leapt on his back. He heard the thunder of feet on the passage as his own guard arrived. They hauled the man off his back and slit his throat in an excess of zeal before Tulkhan could question him.

The last attacker turned to flee, but a dagger thrown by one of his guards caught him between the shoulder blades.

Panting with the exertion, Tulkhan looked at the bodies.

It was as he feared. The name on the woman's lips as she leapt, intent on his death at the cost of her own life, was *T'Reothe*, rumoured to be the leader of the rebels.

Silencing the angry comments of his elite guard, Tulkhan indicated the bodies. 'Bring them into the courtyard. Send for the Aayel and Imoshen.'

IMOSHEN KNEW BY the smack of metal and the sharp thump of boots that this was no ordinary summoning. Kalleen ran into the room gasping something about an assassination attempt on General Tulkhan.

'What?' Imoshen's first thought was to consult the Aayel, but fear closed her throat so that she could not speak. She crossed the room and knelt beside her great aunt's chair, silently seeking reassurance. The Aayel would know what to do.

The old woman clutched her hand. 'Time has run out, Shenna. I thought we had longer. There is so much I did not tell you. I'd meant to –'

Imoshen's heart sank as the elite guard marched through the open doors. Without deference, they ordered Imoshen and the Aayel out.

Their leader would not meet her eyes. *He knows*, she thought. *The General means to have us killed.*

But she came to her feet with outward dignity, while inside she raged at the unfairness of it. Another two days and she could have spun her web.

Imoshen helped the Aayel to stand. She realised her great aunt was playing for time. The old woman walked slowly as if weighed down by her great age.

Imoshen's mind whirled with images, half-formed plans. Should she have warned General Tulkhan about the scrying? It had been on the tip of her tongue so many times, but she knew how he held such things in contempt. He might even have assumed she knew something of the plot, or worse still, was the instigator. In the end she had kept her own counsel.

She took a deep breath and stiffened her back. Come what may, she would not beg.

Kalleen would have accompanied them, but the elite guard pushed her aside.

They were led downstairs. Imoshen imagined the great hall where the General would have them summarily executed. Now she would never have her chance to seduce him and save her people from servitude. She should have run away with Reothe when she had the opportunity!

What? And left the Aayel to die alone?

As if sensing Imoshen's thoughts, the Aayel squeezed her hand.

To Imoshen's surprise, they were led out into the courtyard, where a sea of faces turned to them, refugees from the north, loyal locals returned with their harvest, the household servants and stronghold guard, and the Ghebites.

General Tulkhan did not meet her eyes as he leapt onto an empty dray and signalled for quiet. He indicated the parapets where, much to her horror, she saw three round objects, heads.

'Rebels!' he roared, and there was a hushed intake of breath from the crowd.

Imoshen's thoughts spun. No traitors' heads had been spiked there for hundreds of years. Nausea swept her. These Ghebites were barbarians. Truly, she and the Aayel were about to die.

A buzzing filled her head as the General shouted something about treachery and death to all those who opposed him. He paced on the dray's boards, all eyes drawn to him.

With bravado he told how, unarmed, he had fought off three armed attackers. She realised it would become part of the mythology which surrounded him. Even the locals and her household guard were in awe of him.

Suddenly he turned to the captives and beckoned. The men who surrounded Imoshen pushed her forward. They would have lifted her bodily onto the dray, but she thrust their hands aside and leapt lightly up, her heart hammering.

With great deliberation she turned and helped the Aayel, steadying her as the men thrust her up. There was a concerted hush, an inarticulate moan from those loyal to the Old Empire.

Imoshen looked out over the sea of faces. Sections of the crowd were shifting uneasily. The camaraderie of the harvest was forgotten.

So she was to die here, slaughtered like a pig by a butcher in the courtyard of her family's stronghold. She never imagined herself dying except with a weapon in her hand. She cursed. If the truth be told she'd never imagined herself dying.

The General was speaking, and she tried to concentrate.

'...some amongst you who would cling to the old rulers, who do not accept my right of conquest.' General Tulkhan raised one hand. 'The old ways are dead. Know this.'

He drew his ceremonial dagger. Someone shrieked.

The crowd surged forward. Instinct told Imoshen they were on the verge of revolt. Tulkhan must have sensed it too, because for an instant his eyes met hers in silent understanding.

Whereas this morning the locals and stronghold guard had worked beside the elite guard laughing, singing as the food was stored, now the people stood circling the dray, their work tools raised as weapons.

If the General put Imoshen and the Aayel to the sword, not only their blood would stain the courtyard stones.

Tulkhan tensed as he realised how tenuous his hold on Umasreach had become. Here, in the packed courtyard, hand-to-hand combat would be butchery. The resentment that seethed just beneath the surface would erupt into outright rebellion. It was conceivable that he could be brought down and killed in the struggle. He could lose the jewel in the crown, Fair Isle, and his very life.

Yet all his experience told him the last of the royal house must die. He turned to the two women, one on the verge of life, the other older than he believed possible.

Imoshen's face was blanched white, her lips compressed. As the stronghold guard surged forward, the General caught a flicker of anticipation and realised she did not intend to let him kill her without a fight. She meant to precipitate a rebellion, and she would take him down with her. He acknowledged this with a flash of admiration.

There it was – he had to kill them both, yet the minute he raised the knife he was a dead man. The crowd would riot, the stones would run with blood. He saw no way out of this dilemma.

A withered hand pushed Imoshen aside and the Aayel met his eyes. She stepped forward, her hand extended.

Tulkhan looked from her hand to her shrewd, implacable face.

'Your code demands a death to assuage the dishonour of this attack,' the Aayel stated simply.

'Yes.'

'No!' Horror closed Imoshen's throat as she realised what the Aayel intended. 'I won't let you –'

Those old eyes turned to her. 'You have no control over my actions. This is the only path and my chance to die with honour.'

Imoshen watched her great aunt extend her hand for the knife. The General gave it to her.

The Aayel lifted the ceremonial dagger high, her thin voice carrying in the sudden hush. 'I release you from all guilt and take on the guilt of those who attacked the General.'

Imoshen wanted to protest against the injustice of it. It was only with a supreme effort of will that she remained outwardly impassive. Inside she was reeling, though her feet remained rooted to the spot. Her heart thundered in her ears.

In a movement too swift to stop, the Aayel plunged the knife up under her own ribs.

A terrible cry, an outpouring of raw and angry pain, rose from the crowd. The Aayel had seen the oldest of them born, she had seen their parents born and buried. She was a living historical link to their communal past.

And now she was gone.

Tulkhan stepped forward but Imoshen thrust him aside, catching the frail old body in her arms. She sensed the life leave the old woman on a whisper of a breath.

How could this be? How could someone so intense and knowledgeable pass from this world to the next with so little sign?

'She died well,' Tulkhan said softly.

Imoshen glared at him. 'She saved your skin, barbarian.'

She saw him flinch but did not care. He went to take the Aayel from her.

'No. This has to be done properly to honour the dead.' Amazingly, she was dry-eyed, though inside she wept. Raising her voice, Imoshen shouted over the rising babble of the crowd. 'The Aayel must not be touched by any but one of the blood. We must honour her passing with the proper ceremony.'

Burdened with the frail husk, Imoshen knelt on the dray. 'Take us out onto the plain.'

The General himself took the reins, urging the workhorses forward. The elite guard fell back and the people parted as the dray's wheels thudded over the cobbles. As they passed through the inner gates into the passage, they were plunged into darkness. Imoshen blinked, momentarily blinded. She could see Tulkhan's silhouette dark against the light of the plain beyond the outer gates. It seemed fitting that he should honour the Aayel's sacrifice by taking the reins of the dray.

Golden afternoon light enveloped Imoshen as the wagon rolled out onto the well-worn road to the plain. When they were well clear of the township, she ordered a halt and firewood brought to build a funeral pyre around the dray.

As servants from the stronghold unhitched the horses and dragged wood from nearby shacks to make the pyre, Imoshen remained seated, her arms protectively around her great aunt's body. She dispatched a message to Kalleen to bring the Aayel's ceremonial robe and the sacred oils needed to perform the death rites.

Imoshen wrapped the frail old body in the robe then placed the Aayel on her funeral pyre. She would let no one else touch her kin. Awkward and stiff with grief, she climbed down.

The chill of winter came through the thin soles of her indoor shoes, sending a creeping cold through her bones. Imoshen stepped back and turned to the west to see the sun setting beyond the hills. It seemed fitting that the last Aayel should die as the sun set and the winter closed in on the end of the reign of the T'En.

In Imoshen's family, the Aayel had held the reins of religious power; hers was the voice which had called down a blessing. Other families not blessed with a throwback had the services of members of the T'En church. The Aayel had never trusted the church. She would have preferred Imoshen to say the words.

Tears stung her eyes, but she blinked them away. She did not have time for grief now. This had to be done properly.

All around her they waited, the stronghold servants and guards, the refugees, the locals and the Ghebites. They waited for her signal.

Imoshen shuddered. She was without guidance now, in a world where all the rules had changed and death stalked her.

With an effort, she recalled the blessing and spoke the words. From a great distance she heard her voice carry on the still evening. Then she stepped aside and retreated to stand on the rise and watch the sun.

Around her the people sang their ancient songs, songs which were old when her namesake invaded their land and placed them under her yoke of servitude. Was it human nature to take and take?

As the sun sank in a blaze of autumn glory, Imoshen sprinkled oils from the Aayel's private cabinet, then raised her hand. On her signal a servant of the royal household ignited the Aayel's funeral pyre.

As the greedy flames laid claim to the pyre, Imoshen retreated, her cheeks scorched. She fingered the cupboard key in her hand. The Aayel's private medicinals were hers now. She could mix a potion to kill General Tulkhan as easily as she could mix a healing posset.

She need not continue tonight and tomorrow night to take the herb of fertility.

Cold crept up through her bones. She felt chilled to her very heart, despite the heat of the pyre. What did it matter if the elite guard turned on her and killed her, so long as she took General Tulkhan with her?

All around her the refugees, the harmless, blameless people of Fair Isle, raised their voices in an ancient song of lament as glowing cinders spiralled upwards from the leaping flames.

Soon the skies would grow leaden with snow and these same refugees of the war would freeze in their makeshift homes on the plain. Imoshen flinched. There would not be enough wood to keep them warm. It was a terrible thing to see the old, the very young and the injured suffer, and they all relied on her.

She glanced around her at the scene, and noted that the General and his men kept their distance, perhaps sensing that they'd had a lucky escape, saved from rebellion by the Aayel's actions.

All about her, as the plain grew dark, faces were turned to the funeral pyre, its pungent smoke floating on the still autumn air as the sky faded to a pearly opalescence.

Finally all that remained of the funeral pyre was its glowing embers. The twin moons, male and female, met in union to flood the plain with silver light, cloaking its squalor and its desperate inhabitants.

Trembling with the effort of will, Imoshen signalled it was over. Later the royal household servants would gather the ashes and sprinkle them on the stronghold's sacred garden.

IMOSHEN RETREATED TO her rooms where she ordered hot water and placed oils in the bath. She took no food and no drink other than the drug the Aayel had entrusted her to take. And she didn't know why she took that.

After dismissing Kalleen, Imoshen sank into the hot water and stared into the flames of the open fireplace. She was numb. Without the wise counsel of the Aayel she was truly alone, and it frightened her more than she wanted to admit.

On the parapets were three round objects – the heads of those who would have killed the General in Reothe's name, in her name. She shuddered. The grisly trophies mocked General Tulkhan's claim to culture. Truly, he was a barbarian. He'd been ready to kill her.

Imoshen pressed cold fingers to her burning eyes. A soul-deep ache settled in her core. Her great aunt was gone. How could she go on without the Aayel's advice?

But the old woman's choice of death made her smile with grim pride. She could only admire the Aayel and hope if she ever had to face the same choice, her decision would be as honourable.

Imoshen sighed. In a way, death was simple. It was living that was hard. With her death, the Aayel had succeeded in buying them time, but the risk was still present.

Noises came from the hall outside. Imoshen heard Kalleen's voice raised in angry denial. Heart pounding, she twisted around in the bath, looking for her robe. Before she could find it, the door to her chamber was thrown open and General Tulkhan marched in. Bounding around him like a small, ineffectual puppy, Kalleen made a valiant effort to stop him.

The General was alone, which relieved Imoshen of her immediate fear. If he meant to execute her, she sensed he would send his elite guards for her.

The immediate danger past, she felt a burst of anger. What was he doing here? Was it not enough that the Aayel should die by her own hands? Did the man have no consideration?

When Kalleen tried to block his view the General brushed the girl aside.

'You may leave, Kalleen,' Imoshen said, coolly.

As her serving maid backed out bristling, Imoshen decided how to handle this encounter. Rather than rise and attempt to cover herself, she remained in the tub. 'Whatever you may do in Gheeaba, here we do not invade a person's bedchamber –'

'Who is T'Reothe?'

Despite the warm water, Imoshen's skin went cold but she remained outwardly impassive. Only she could feel the pounding of her heart. 'Why do –'

'Answer me.' The General's voice was a whip crack.

Imoshen took a slow deep breath to steady herself. 'He was one of the Royal House, reared by the Emperor and Empress, a second cousin of mine. You must have met and defeated him in one of your battles during this campaign. As far as I know, he lies unburied on a bloodied field somewhere.'

'Then why did the assassin scream his name as she tried to gut me?'

So her scrying had been accurate? Reothe had sent the assassins. Didn't he realise he'd put her life at risk? Would Reothe discard her so easily? She doubted it. Maybe the assassins were zealots who had acted independently of him, but in his name.

Imoshen did not know what to think. She looked down, only to find her shoulders grasped ruthlessly by General Tulkhan as he hauled her to her feet. Bath water cascaded out of the tub onto the floor, hissing where droplets hit the embers of the fire.

Tulkhan was furious. He had seen the flicker of knowledge as Imoshen lowered her eyes. The Dhamfeer was hiding something.

He'd hauled her to her feet and out of the tub before he knew he meant to do it.

Now he shook her. 'Look at me!'

For an instant he stared into her startled face. Her eyes were luminous dark pools, like red wine held to the candle flame. His large hands gripped her white shoulders, his fingers dark against her skin. He could feel her fine bones.

Her hands hung at her side. She was too proud to cover herself. Her damp hair clung to her body in long tendrils. Dark nipples peeped from the tenuous covering but his gaze returned to her mouth.

She dragged in a ragged breath, parting red lips to reveal those sharp little teeth, and he was forcibly reminded yet again that she wasn't one of his race, that she was T'En, from the mythical land beyond the rising sun.

Irritation gripped Tulkhan. He could feel the heat exuding from her body. That carnal scent he'd come to associate with her made his nostrils dilate. It called up a primal response in him. It was a response that went beyond rational thought, and one that had to be crushed.

He shook her once again. 'Who is T'Reothe? Has he been in contact with you?'

She gave a wild laugh, unshed tears glittering in her eyes.

'T'Reothe was my betrothed!' Her eyes narrowed, tears spilling unheeded down her cheeks. 'He's probably dead like everyone else I ever loved, killed by you and your king.' With a practised flick she bought her arms up inside his guard and used his own strength against him to break his grip on her shoulders.

Her six-fingered hands curled into fists and she struck him fiercely, repeatedly on the chest, weeping freely. 'They're all dead. My mother, father, brother, sister, and now the Aayel!'

The blows were not meant to hurt, but to express her frustration and anger. As they thudded into him, his heart lurched, each strike slipping further past his guard so that he felt her despair.

He caught her elbows and pulled her forward, pinning her to his chest. Her hands were caught between her breasts, her fists closed. She gasped, lifting a shocked face to him, the tears glistening on her cheeks like crystals.

As he looked into her eyes, he felt a terrible yearning. He wanted her. How he wanted her, this Dhamfeer woman. Who would have thought he would find her Otherness alluring, intoxicating even? Yet here he was, ready to take her, to throw aside all sense and caution. Wasn't she his by right of capture?

The fire crackled on the hearth. The scented oils of the bath hung on the steamy air.

Pinned to Tulkhan's chest, Imoshen was transfixed by the twin flames of desire in his eyes. He smiled down at her in anticipation.

No.

She was not a victim, certainly not *his* victim!

Her heart pounded and fury heated her blood, singing in her veins. She sucked in a breath then pulled back sharply, transferring her weight, but he anticipated in time to twist his hips so that her raised knee skidded past his broad muscled thigh, allowing that hard male thigh to press intimately between her naked legs.

Imoshen froze.

The sudden pressure triggered a wave of unexpected heat. She gasped and saw his eyes widen as he registered her response.

He was going to rape her, here in her own bedchamber.

'That's right,' she hissed, rage making her voice tight. 'Take me by force, just like you took my lands by force. You haven't the wit to be anything other than a brutal plunderer.'

His great arms tightened so that she gritted her teeth as the air was forced from her lungs. Star points of light danced across her vision.

He held her so close she felt his voice rumble in his chest when he spoke. 'You surrendered.'

'Only to save my people.' A roaring filled her ears. Each short breath was hard won. 'I will never surrender to you. You can never subdue me. Not by brutality, not by forcing yourself upon me, not –'

Her mouth was covered by his and she knew a moment's despair. She was too close to wrestle, arms pinned against his chest. She had no leverage when her toes barely touched the ground.

His presence overwhelmed her senses. She registered his distinctive male scent, the heat of his body, the abrasive material of his jerkin against her breasts.

His hard thigh pressed between her legs lifted her ever higher. A strange and unfamiliar sensation swamped all conscious thought. His demanding mouth overwhelmed hers, its hot velvety depths so alien, so unknown.

She was drowning in him, barely able to think.

His ragged breath filled her mouth as he groaned.

The utter abandonment of the sound tugged at something deep inside her, robbing her limbs of their strength. She heard an answering moan, and realised that it was her own.

How could she feel any desire for this man when only a few nights ago she had been stirred by her betrothed? What kind of woman was she?

Tulkhan lifted his head and his eyes blazed with triumph. His expression pierced her delirium.

No. She would not be his conquest!

She sucked in a breath and bared her teeth, lunging for his throat. He barely had time to bring his hand up to protect himself before her teeth found his flesh. With delight she felt the small bones of his hand crack and tasted his blood.

Suddenly she was released. Her feet hit the ground, but she would not relinquish her hold. She clung to him, her hands twined through his clothes, her teeth embedded in his flesh.

With a snap Imoshen registered a direct blow to her forehead. Stunned, she staggered back, colliding with a low seat.

Even as she fell, her head was clearing and she recoiled, springing catlike to her feet. She didn't know this wild creature she had become.

Delight flared through her as she saw his eyes widen in alarm. He stood there breathing as raggedly as she, his injured hand clasped protectively to his chest. Blood seeped from between his fingers.

Fear and disgust travelled across his face.

His eyes narrowed and she knew he meant to kill her.

For the second time that day Imoshen faced death.

General Tulkhan slowly drew his ceremonial dagger as he wondered what had possessed him.

A heady intoxicating desire still rode his body, but before him he saw a feral, alien being. Even now she called to him to give up all rational thought, abandon himself in her flesh, drown in her exotic scent.

Naked and defiant, the Dhamfeer stood before him, poised for attack, her long silver hair hanging in twirling tendrils. Her intelligent, calculating eyes flashed feral red. Her lips and breasts were stained with his blood, confirming that she was no more than a beast, with merely the outward trappings of a True-woman.

Tulkhan tried to flex his injured hand. He grimaced as pain lanced through it. He'd sustained enough injuries to know there were broken bones.

For an instant he debated calling his men to hold her, but it would demean him to reveal that she had injured him. He should be able to better a mere woman, a naked, unarmed female at that, even if she was a Dhamfeer.

He licked his lips. Unbidden, his mind presented him with the image of her writhing beneath him, not in agony but in abandonment.

Without warning she straightened and the animal in her retreated to be cloaked by the regal woman. 'My people venerate the old. We appreciate their wisdom, we treasure them. We would not deny our old ones medicinal herbs.' Her voice vibrated with contempt and she stepped forward. 'You were saved a mutiny this afternoon when the Aayel took her own life. Our people would have risen up and the stones would have run with blood.'

He swallowed as he watched her approach with disbelief, making no attempt to cover herself.

The dagger stayed poised between them as he hugged his throbbing hand to his chest. Even now he could smell her distinctive scent.

She was breathing as rapidly as he, her pale shoulders lifting and falling, her lips parted. 'You must kill me to be sure of your command.'

He didn't deny it.

She continued. 'Just now, you would have taken me by force.'

'It is my right.'

'Rights that make a person less than human?'

'Dhamfeer!' He made the word an insult.

Her eyes narrowed. 'Barbarian!'

He gulped as she flicked her long hair back over her shoulders to reveal her pale, strong body. She stepped closer until the tip of the dagger pressed into her bare breast.

His eyes were fixed on the delicate mound which rose and fell with each quick breath. The sharp blade of the dagger dug into her flesh, not cutting it as yet.

There was nothing but the sound of her rapid breathing and the pounding of his own heart as he raised his eyes to her face. Those intense, wine-dark eyes were fixed on him. Her skin was so unnaturally pale and her lips were stained by his blood.

Something stirred within him, acknowledging the power she had over him.

Tulkhan flinched. This was his chance; one determined thrust between the ribs and he would be rid of this infuriating female, this source of rebellion – yet he couldn't move.

He could see the pulse fluttering in her throat.

She was taking a terrible gamble. Reluctant admiration stirred in him.

He didn't want to kill her, he wanted to *claim* her.

Time stood still as their fates hung in the balance.

Imoshen couldn't hear for the blood rushing in her ears. Every sense was strained, focusing on him, watching, evaluating. She could hardly breathe. Then she saw it, the slightest waver of determination.

A ragged gasp escaped her. She almost fainted with relief.

The General uttered a heartfelt groan and covered his face with his forearm in despair. He could not bring himself to kill her, and she realised that by his standards she had shamed him.

With a cold shudder she understood she was just as much at risk this instant as a moment before. To cover his shame he might turn on her. He might call his men in to kill her.

She cleared her throat. 'A great leader must know when to show mercy.'

He glared at her. 'A leader must know when to be ruthless.'

'And when to bind her people to her with acts of kindness.' She felt light-headed. 'Your teacher must have studied the same manuscripts as mine.'

He gave a grimace that might have been a smile. 'Only my master was not speaking of a female leader.'

'Man comes from woman. She makes up half the world. Would you deny half of yourself?'

He shrugged this aside and she knew the moment of knife-edged danger had passed.

She dared to take his crushed hand in hers. At first he stiffened then he let her examine it. 'You will need treatment.'

'My –'

'I have the unguents here in my chamber. Your people need not know.' Imoshen led him by his ruined hand across to the window seat. She had succeeded in facing him down, now she had to win his trust.

She shivered. It had been close. If she hadn't fought him, he would have raped her there and then. Imoshen knew instinctively tonight would have been wrong. The Aayel had been specific. She must seduce him tomorrow night, after she had taken the last of the brew.

With simple unhurried movements, Imoshen lifted a plain night gown over her shoulders and knotted it under her breasts. Gathering her hair, she combed it with her fingers and tilted her head to watch him. Good, the spark was still there. She could see the desire in the tight planes of his face.

Let it simmer. Tonight was not the night.

Taking her private key, she unlocked the medicine cabinet and made her selection of herbs, powders and fluids.

'How could this Reothe be your betrothed? Aren't the females of your kind sworn to celibacy?'

It was a fair question.

'Normally, yes. But Reothe was granted special dispensation by the Emperor and Empress. The Beatific witnessed the –'

'Did you love him?'

Startled, Imoshen's gaze met his. Did she love Reothe? She burned at his touch, but perhaps it was her body's sensual frailty and not some deeper, pure emotion?

'I... I don't know. It was so long ago. For all I know he is dead.'

'So you'll forget your betrothed as easily as that?' he demanded.

She grimaced, annoyed with him. According to the General she could do no right. 'I have enough to worry about with a stronghold full of hot-headed Ghebites, without borrowing trouble.'

Placing the medicinals on a low table before him, she explained what they were for as she worked. 'This one will bring down swelling. It is used on the skin. This one aids the knitting of flesh and bones. You drink it. This one sprinkled on the flesh stops the ill-humours that cause the flesh to poison.' Seeing how his hand pained him, she called on her gift to hasten the healing, then bound the wound with great care before strapping his hand gently to his chest in a sling. Finally she presented him with the liquid.

'Drink this.'

'You could be poisoning me.'

She felt a reluctant smile tug at her lips. 'I had considered it.'

'And decided against it? Why?'

Imoshen licked her lips, unable to come to terms with her conflicting emotions. Yet the words flowed from her. 'I know you. If I kill you it will not change matters. Your elite guard will turn on the castle and kill as many of us as it takes to put down the rebellion and there will still be the King to reckon with.'

'Honest, at least.' A wry humour lit his face, eliciting a smile from her.

Still he hesitated to drink. The General held the small cup in his hand, his dark eyes on her. Finally she took the cup from him, lifted it to her lips and sipped half of it, wrinkling her nose at the taste.

He accepted it from her then, turning it so that his lips touched where hers had been. Deliberately he met her eyes as he drained it.

A strange sense of fear and anticipation rushed through her, settling low in her belly, an insistent reminder of her secret plan.

The General could not know he had unwittingly shared with her one of the bonding ceremony symbols. If it was an omen, it was a good one.

LATER, AS IMOSHEN lay in her bed, she recalled that moment and many other things about the evening. Her body sang with an unexpected energy and her breasts ached. Her nipples felt tender, irritated by the light garment.

Was this all part of the brew's effects?

Tomorrow night she must seduce the General. She would use the mental tricks her instructor had taught her to ensure she conceived a male child.

Imoshen buried her face in the cool material of her bedding.

Her life hung by a thread. She could only hope the Aayel had read General Tulkhan correctly. For the T'En, life was sacred, but she seriously doubted the Ghebites held life in such high esteem. Why would the General value the life of an unborn child?

She mustn't doubt herself or the Aayel's plan. Doubt was deadly.

Tomorrow night was her one and only chance. If he rejected her, she was lost.

Chapter Five

THE DAY OF the Harvest Feast dawned bright and cold. Tulkhan's elite guard complained of the chill, which made Imoshen smile; this was mild compared to full winter.

She dressed with care, aware that tonight she would seduce the General, take his seed and begin a boy child who, according to the Aayel, would ensure her survival by binding Tulkhan to her.

Imoshen felt fragile and alone. She missed her great aunt, this cold morning on the cusp of the seasons.

Her breasts were tender and her head felt thick and muzzy, probably from lack of sleep, for she seemed to have spent most of last night tossing and turning, waking from fevered dreams, recalling her close escape. Just the thought of how he had forced his hard muscled thigh between hers made her heart race.

Hearing the General's voice in the courtyard, she ran to the window to observe her prey, taking in the way he strode through the throng, the way the others stepped back from him. He spoke to his elite guard, then broke off and turned to look up at her window. She remained motionless, hidden in shadow. She saw his dark brows crease, almost as if he could sense her plotting to ensnare him.

When the General turned his back on her to consult with his guards, she felt an irrational annoyance. This was not like her. It must be the Aayel's potion that made her restless and her thoughts like quicksilver. She wanted to run down into the courtyard to taunt him and elicit an angry response from him. She wouldn't be ignored, wanted him to admit his attraction to her and to take her in his arms like he had last night.

She knew the General was not impervious to her. As much as he seemed repelled by her, he was also fascinated. Last night he had desired her, but instinct told her she had done the right thing in fighting him off. Not only was it wrong to let him take her before the appointed time, but if he had done it in that manner the basis of their battle would have changed. And she would have lost the initiative.

She might have surrendered Umasreach Stronghold to the Ghebite General, but theirs was a personal battle which was still being fought.

General Tulkhan gestured in answer to one of his men and Imoshen stepped back from the window, released from her own spell. She called Kalleen and hurriedly finished dressing.

The day was a frenzy of activity for her. As head of the stronghold, she had to vet all plans for the Festival of Harvest Moons, then personally oversee the decorations and aspects of the food preparation, because they were part of the time-honoured religious rites of this ancient festival.

Massive bonfires were being built on the plain. Normally the people would have thronged to their local villages, but because so many refugees had clustered around the stronghold it had become a township, almost rivalling the T'En capital in population, if not in size.

Homeless, hungry and fearful for their future, the people were more eager than ever to celebrate the Festival of Harvest Moons. Imoshen understood their need. The familiar feast offered reassurance. If the festival went well tonight they could expect a good crop next year. Food and shelter, that was what these people cared about, not the identity of their rulers. And who could blame them?

As was the custom, she fasted all day. By rights her great aunt would have conducted the ceremony, but her people had made it clear they expected her to do it, even though she was not recognised by the T'En church.

One of her first and most important responsibilities was to oversee the construction of the harvest bower. It was essentially a primitive hut, decorated with fresh hay and the last ripe fruits and flowers of the season. Here the participants would consummate the union of the double moon. Usually the elders of the village chose a young man and young woman. They were singled out because they best represented the future of the village – young, healthy, ripe. After much feting they would be escorted to the bower to consummate their brief but vital bonding. Their joining in the field both ensured fertility the following spring and thanked the powers for the recent harvest.

While she dealt with practical matters, on a deeper level Imoshen fought to come to terms with what she must do this evening. If Tulkhan guessed for an instant that she was manipulating him into her arms, he would resist, and she couldn't afford to miss this opportunity.

She studied the small, low-roofed hut, inhaling the scent of the fresh hay. Her cheeks flooded with heat as she imagined what would take place here tonight. Her body craved a mating and that disturbed her. She didn't like to think her actions were dictated by her body. It must be the Aayel's potion that was making her feel this way.

With a word of congratulations to the eager refugees who had constructed the bower, she stepped out into the chill of late afternoon and took a deep breath to steady her thudding heart.

There he was, striding toward her. Did his step falter slightly as he caught sight of her? She hoped so. The General gestured to the man at his side, indicating the fire pits.

Food for the crowd was being prepared in great fire pits. The night before the heated stones and coals had been raked over the meat and vegetables. Feeding the masses was a nightmare of logistics, but the Harvest Feast had to be done properly.

As she watched Tulkhan pace the plain, giving orders, Imoshen realised he was not wearing the sling she'd fashioned for him. He wore dark leather gloves and he was careful about how he used his injured hand. She understood immediately why he was disguising the injury. To explain how it had happened would diminish him in the eyes of his men and undermine his power. And, above all, he had to maintain control.

She had to admire his tactics and the force of his personality. No other leader, not even the Empress herself, had impressed Imoshen with their ability to inspire respect and loyalty the way General Tulkhan did.

Mentally she amended that. Reothe had impressed her with his courage and daring. Among all their kin, only he had gone voyaging to open new trade routes, seeking adventure.

T'Reothe, last T'En Prince.

Had she made the right choice?

A little shiver passed over her skin. Only time would tell.

It was growing dark. Imoshen left the fields and walked towards Umasreach. A different flag flew over the battlements, but the sounds and scents were familiar enough. If she ignored the occasional Ghebite accent she could close her eyes and pretend it was last autumn and her family were inside, preparing for the ceremony.

A twist of pain curled inside her, intimate and intense. She hadn't had a chance to mourn their loss and she was unlikely to have the opportunity now.

In the great hall a central dais had been erected to sacrifice a pig or lamb. Rumour had it that long ago the sacrifice had been more than this.

Many ancient customs and rituals had been absorbed by her people. After the initial invasion, the original inhabitants had continued practising their ancient ways, but over time their earth-close secrets had intertwined with the more formal customs of the T'En so that it was difficult to know where one left off and the other began.

Looking back over six hundred years, Imoshen wondered if the original inhabitants of Fair Isle had not vanquished the T'En in the end, through sheer force of numbers. Through interbreeding, the pure T'En had all but disappeared. The language, customs and values of the golden-skinned locals had gradually permeated even to the highest levels of society, so that now a throwback like herself was an outsider amongst her own people.

Would this happen to the Ghebite barbarians?

She smiled at the irony of it. Six hundred years from now who would care whether Imoshen, last T'En Princess, cemented her future by seducing General Tulkhan?

'My lady?' Kalleen appeared at her side. 'They told me to tell you that the room is ready for purification.'

Imoshen felt a grin tug at her lips. The girl's tone told her Kalleen's ongoing battle with the long-established servants of the stronghold had flared up again. They resented a farm girl being raised above one of their own to the position of Imoshen's private servant.

'Then we mustn't disappoint them.' Imoshen smiled.

She followed the young woman, mentally preparing herself for the task ahead. Whatever her personal opinion of the T'En church, the people of the stronghold expected her to follow tradition. She could not dishonour them.

Imoshen stripped and entered the little wood-lined room. Herbs had been sprinkled over the stones so that when water was poured on them a heady, humid scent engulfed her.

She had fasted since the death of the Aayel, preparing her body for the purification ceremony. Her hair hung in heavy damp ropes over her bare shoulders and down her back. She cleared her mind and sought to recall each step of the ceremony, praying that she wouldn't forget a line or gesture.

In the past, her parents had shared the ceremonial roles with the Aayel right up until the final stage of the ceremony, when the Harvest Feast platter carrying the ritual corn sheaf and bull's horn were presented to her father and mother, who passed it to the Aayel to ceremoniously bless the items before returning the platter to the village elders. The elders then presented these items to the chosen male and female. The young man received the bull's horn. It was a symbol of potent masculinity, associated with the beasts of the fields.

Imoshen's stomach growled with hunger, but the only thing she planned to swallow was the last portion of the potion the Aayel had prepared for her, and later the sacramental wine, which she had to bless during the ceremony.

To her surprise the enforced idleness and privacy did bring her a measure of inner peace, and after the prescribed time she left the heated room feeling calm and restored. Kalleen escorted her to the sacred garden to fulfil the last step of the purification ceremony.

'THERE SHE IS,' Wharrd whispered.

Tulkhan's heart lurched. He was not spying, he told himself. He had asked for an explanation of the ceremony tonight, and Wharrd had learnt the details from Imoshen's maid so he could instruct his master.

That was how they came to be in the secluded balcony of the private courtyard that housed the stronghold's sacred garden. Even through his boots he could feel the chill of the stones. The sun's setting rays no longer reached the walled garden and Tulkhan shivered in sympathy as Imoshen dropped her cloak to stand naked by the pool.

Her pale skin glowed eerily in the twilit courtyard. Kalleen took the cloak and retreated to the entrance, leaving her mistress alone. Imoshen raised her arms and her small breasts lifted, the darker tips peeping through her long silver hair.

The General felt his body stir in response. He wanted her even more after last night. His injured hand throbbed as if to mock him. What would have happened if her teeth had closed around his throat? She would have crushed it, killing him; possibly at the expense of her own life, but he doubted she would count the cost too great.

He wished Wharrd gone, he wished Imoshen's T'En religious rites were his to witness alone. He didn't want anyone else seeing her strong, perfect body. How could he have thought her too tall and scrawny? True, she was long-limbed and more slender than the women of his race but the more he saw her the more her form pleased him. It became the standard by which he judged all else.

'Leave me.' He found it hard to speak and was grateful when he sensed Wharrd moving off through the connecting doors to the inner chambers.

Alone, General Tulkhan, leader of the invading forces, watched the last of the T'En with an intensity which ate at him. His heartbeat hastened until it was a heavy, solid drum which reverberated through his body. He was enthralled, unwilling for the moment to end.

Why was she standing there? She held something in her hands, crushed it, then sprinkled what looked like petals on the surface of the dark, stone-edged pool.

Then she surprised him by stepping off the edge down a number of shallow steps into the icy pool. Pausing to take a breath, she sank below the waters until only the swirl of her long hair remained on the surface. Then even that grew heavy with moisture and sank.

There was no sign of her presence other than the gently moving petals on the dark surface. Alarmed, his hands tightened on the stone-work.

He was about to leap over the balustrade and drop the body length to the soft garden bed below when Imoshen rose from the depths. She glided up to the rim like an albino seal he had seen while making the crossing to Fair Isle.

As Imoshen surged up the steps he could hear her fey laughter. It made his skin prickle with fear and excitement. She called out to Kalleen, who ran forward with the cloak. Tulkhan could see Imoshen was shaking with cold as the little serving maid enfolded her mistress in the cloak.

'I'm glad that part's over!' Imoshen's voice carried, echoing off the stone walls of the courtyard. They hurried from the courtyard.

Ritual purification. The phrase returned to him. According to Wharrd, as the last of the T'En, Imoshen would lead the ceremony tonight right up until she was presented with the symbols of fertility for plant and beast, the corn sheaf and bull's horn.

Tulkhan shifted, staring down into the empty courtyard. He was as tense and apprehensive as a bridegroom. Her continued presence and the unspoken challenge in her eyes only made it worse. He was as bad as any of his foot soldiers. They were excited, edgy. Rumours of the excesses condoned on the night of the Harvest Feast abounded. There had been much boasting in the ranks. Tulkhan suspected even his men might be astonished at the behaviour of these Fair Isle farmers.

Not much longer, he told himself, not bothering to specify what he meant.

※   ※   ※

IMOSHEN CLASPED THE simple white robe around her shoulders and tied the plaited belt around her waist. She wore her hair loose. It had been brushed until it had a life of its own, lifting and clinging to objects.

She went barefoot because she was supposed to feel the earth beneath her feet. Her first task was in the fields with the refugees, where the stones had been raked back from the fire pits. There she blessed the feast as the Aayel would have done, barefoot, bare-headed, at one with the primitive people who surged around her, muttering eagerly. Their earthy excitement was strangely contagious. It made her stomach flutter with expectation.

Then she accompanied her own people into the stronghold and a more complex ceremony borrowed from the ancient T'En culture followed. Blood was spilt to ensure new life. She tried to focus all her attention on the tasks at hand, to channel her meagre gifts, but all the while she was aware of General Tulkhan watching her.

When she lifted her arms to signal for silence, she felt her nipples press against the material and flushed, knowing that he must have seen her traitorous body's involuntary signals. Deep inside her, a slow burn threatened to consume her.

The bitter after-taste of the last portion of the Aayel's potion still lingered on her tongue. In a daze of heat from the open fireplace and the expectant press of the hushed crowd, she repeated the words her mother would have said and slit the pig's throat as her father would have done. A little of the blood was mixed with red wine and presented to her in the ceremonial chalice.

When she sipped it, the tangy fluid went straight to her empty stomach, triggering a soporific feeling which spread through her limbs. The chalice felt heavy, significant in her hands. It made her think of the way the General had taken the drink from her and turned it so that his lips touched where hers had. The memory warmed her. Before she meant to, her eyes sought his face and she read the same need there.

His gaze burned with unspoken promise, threatening to banish all else from her mind. For a moment she faltered with the chant, then recalled it and went on.

The initial ceremony over and the food blessed, the revellers moved to the tables. Great platters of food were bought out, voices rose, wine flowed freely. Soon the long tables were groaning with food. A heady rush of music and excitement filled the large chamber.

Imoshen knew she could eat now, but she felt so tense she couldn't swallow a morsel. Instead, she looked around, marvelling at the strange assortment of people gathered in the great hall tonight. Minor nobles who had fled the invading forces with their entourages were scattered around the hall, vastly outnumbered by the stronghold guard and Ghebite soldiers. There was much laughter and crude comments from the elite guard.

To a casual observer, the inhabitants of the stronghold might be mistaken for convivial company as the food was shared around, and toasts drunk.

Imoshen watched, feeling strangely detached. Who would have thought that only yesterday the Aayel had averted mass slaughter by ritual suicide? Violence seethed below the surface, valid anxieties warred with petty rivalries.

Imoshen's fingers tightened on her crystal goblet. In her heightened state of awareness, she felt the raging emotions and sensed how this apparently peaceful scene could change in a heartbeat to one of bloodshed. The Aayel had averted one crisis, but there would be others. She needed a bargaining tool to hold over the General.

She should make her move.

Imoshen winced. Now that the time had come, she felt gauche, unsure of herself. To delay the moment, she lifted her wine goblet and sipped, silently vowing that she would not fail the Aayel, would not fail herself. The warmed wine slipped down her tight throat and into her belly, adding fire to the furnace below. She eyed General Tulkhan's profile. Somehow she would seduce him.

After all, he was only a man.

But now that the moment was upon her she didn't know what to do. Soon the village Elders would come forward to present her with the symbols of fertility. Already she could see the old couple waiting in the shadows. Once this part of the ceremony was over, the refugees would retreat to the fields to mimic the rituals of the bower.

As for the stronghold inhabitants, they would conduct a slightly more circumspect celebration of their own. Anything was condoned on the night of the harvest moons – it was a night for madness. She had always been sent to her room at this time. The untouched, untouchable T'En.

Imoshen's heart lurched as she saw the old man and woman approach. The corn sheaf and the bull's horn lay proudly displayed on the platter.

She started to rise. Her head spun. Had she drunk too much on an empty stomach, one goblet of warmed wine?

A hush fell over the hall. All eyes were on the Elders. It was clear to Imoshen that even the Ghebite barbarians understood the significance of the platter.

After licking her strangely numb lips, she said the blessing over the symbols. As the Elders waited patiently for her next move, Imoshen felt the weight of their expectation. She must not falter. Resolve strengthened her and she silently vowed she would not fail her people.

Tulkhan watched Imoshen, tension crawling through his body. She looked ethereal standing there in the simple white shift, her hair a glowing nimbus over her shoulders. She also looked slightly unfocused, as if she was having trouble concentrating. If he hadn't known better he would have said she was tipsy. The thought made him smile to himself. The Dhamfeer was young and inexperienced, despite what she might think.

He'd been watching her all day and knew she had been on her feet since dawn. It had been a day full of responsibilities for the last T'En. He also knew she'd taken no food since the Aayel died by her own hand the afternoon before. Imoshen must be close to collapse. An oddly protective urge surprised Tulkhan.

As he watched her intone an arcane T'En chant over the two objects, a premonition gripped him. Anticipation made his heart race.

When Imoshen presented the Elders with the platter the old man turned and lifted the bull's horn.

Tulkhan sensed more than heard a whisper pass through the ranks of his men. It was his own name. Then it grew to a deep repetitive chant. The chant captured his drumming heart's beat, urging it on.

This wasn't how the ceremony went. According to Wharrd, the Elder was supposed to present the horn to the most virile young man of the village, some fellow out there in the makeshift town was probably waiting right now, hard and ready.

The Elder's dark eyes, set deep in his seamed face, fixed on the General. Tulkhan's mind cleared of every extraneous thought, and he understood the forces at play with utter clarity. It came to him much like a decision made in the heat of battle. He could seize the prize if he seized the moment. He was on his feet before he knew it.

The chanting fell away. The silence stretched, broken only by the scuff of his leather boots on the stone as he strode through the gap in the long table and out into the centre of the hall. He looked down into the Elder's wise old face. Behind the man, his woman made a slight movement which drew Tulkhan's gaze to her face. Devilment twinkled in the depths of her hazel eyes. They knew what they were about, this old pair. They were playing politics for the sake of their people.

Instinctively, Tulkhan dropped to one knee. There was a hushed murmur of approval. The Elder held the horn out to Tulkhan. His hands closed possessively around the cool grainy surface. It was his, and for tonight he was their symbol.

The old man placed the leather thong over Tulkhan's neck. The horn rested on his jerkin, heavy with significance.

He came to his feet and caught the old woman's eye. With an almost imperceptible flicker of his eyes he indicated Imoshen. The old woman nodded and walked across the stones. A buzz of excitement rose from the tables.

Imoshen was still standing. Two bright spots of colour flamed in her cheeks, but she didn't look down. Instead her eyes flew to meet his, glittering with something Tulkhan couldn't read. They held a knowing intelligence that both frightened and excited him.

A smile almost touched her lips. If he didn't know better he would have sworn her expression held triumph, then the old woman's silver head came between them, blocking his vision.

He saw the old woman's shoulders move as she lifted the corn sheaf. The excited whispers dropped away. The moment stretched. For a heartbeat it seemed the Dhamfeer would refuse to accept the symbol.

Whatever she might feel, Tulkhan knew Imoshen had to accept. His men would take it as a personal insult if she refused him. The fragile illusion of peace would be shattered.

Then the hall's inhabitants let out a collective sigh of relief. Their sibilant whispers grew progressively louder as the old woman stepped back and bowed before rejoining her mate. Tulkhan was left alone in the centre of the hall, his heart beating wildly in his chest.

He could not take his eyes from Imoshen.

She held the corn sheaf stiffly in both hands. He knew she was pinned, helpless as a butterfly, trapped by events beyond her control and the expectations of those present. But he wanted her. He'd wanted her since the first moment he saw her bloodied and defiant, restrained by his men.

Only last night she had refused him at risk to her own life. Now she must accept him, or destroy the brittle peace. Already she had given much for her people's safety. Would she give herself?

Did he want her on those terms? He almost laughed. Knowing Imoshen as he did, there were no other terms, and he vowed to have her any way he could.

Tulkhan beckoned Wharrd and quietly ordered his horse brought forth, bridled but unsaddled. He knew the next step – they would be escorted to the bower. To the people their joining was a symbol, a sign to the gods to ensure a good crop come spring. This Harvest Moons, the joining would be more than symbolic. It held significance for the whole island, the joining of the conquered with the conqueror.

Intent on claiming his prize before she could escape him, Tulkhan stepped forward and extended his hand to Imoshen across the feast table. He could see the racing of the pulse in her throat, and for an instant he thought he caught a glint of fear in her eyes.

If she had been a Ghebite woman of comparable social position, she would have been a shy virgin, terrified by the events forced on her. A pang of pity prompted him to turn his hand over in a gesture of entreaty. His action caused a flicker of uncertainty in her eyes.

A buzz of speculation spread through the hall.

He watched Imoshen lift her chin. Her nostrils flared as she took a deep breath. Her free hand rose to settle in his palm. The physical contact triggered a tug of recognition deep inside him. His fingers closed possessively over hers.

Her flesh was so pale against his coppery, scarred skin he felt as if he were holding a rare prize just within his grasp, one wrong move and he might crush her. Yet he knew her air of vulnerability was deceptive. Imoshen had an innate, immutable strength. He'd clashed with her and experienced the force of her will on more than one occasion.

But at this moment she felt fragile to him. He had won this round and, perversely, he wanted to make her path easier. Tulkhan gestured to the left, intending to escort her the length of the table and around into the open centre of the hall.

A half smile flitted across Imoshen's face. Before he could guess what she was thinking, she stepped lithely onto her chair and up onto the table. Stunned, he stared down at her slender foot and narrow ankle. Her bare toes looked incongruous, nestled amid the platters of food. As she stepped forward her white gown parted to reveal the long, shapely length of her pale thigh.

His mouth went dry. He looked up into her face and saw her smile. It was a hungry, feral smile. Imperiously, she dropped his fingers and placed both her hands on his shoulders. Instinctively his arms rose, his hands encompassing her slender waist. He felt the flare of her hips, the tight muscles of her abdomen as he took her weight, bringing her forward to him.

He held her there, her hips pressed to his chest, her feet far from the ground. Then, very slowly and with great deliberation, he lowered her, letting her slide down the length of his body. He cursed the thick jerkin which prevented him from feeling her soft curves against his flesh.

When her toes touched the ground she smiled a small satisfied smile and lifted her arm regally. He offered his and she laid her forearm along his arm, her fingers over his hand. As her eyes met his, he realised that never for a moment did she acknowledge him as her conqueror. She considered herself his equal.

A surge of raw desire clawed at him.

His head rang with his men's ragged cheers. He knew they had been laying bets on how long before he claimed her for his bedmate.

He had neither admitted nor denied seducing her that day in the forest. In that instant Tulkhan recalled the odd sense of menace which had pervaded the clearing and Imoshen's terror. She had seen more than he, things a True-man could not see. She was Dhamfeer, privy to arcane gifts.

What was he thinking? He could not deny what he had experienced. More than once, he had felt her words inside his head. When it had happened, he had hated her intrusion, because she had breached his defences. His mind was the private bastion of his thoughts. Insidious fear curled through him.

Tulkhan hesitated. If he were to lie with Imoshen, would it give her even greater power over him? Would the joining of their bodies allow her access to his inner thoughts?

He searched her face for duplicity, but saw only the flush of desire mingled with embarrassment in her cheeks and the uncertainty in her eyes. She was wanton one moment, pure innocence the next, and he wanted her.

Tulkhan banished his misgivings – Imoshen was all woman, and his by right. He had waited long enough.

Wordlessly he indicated that they should leave and she nodded. They stepped forward in unison, escorted by an enthusiastic rabble of elite guard and minor aristocracy into the courtyard where Tulkhan's magnificent black destrier waited, shifting nervously.

He caught the bridle firmly in his hand and leapt across the beast's back. It took a moment for him to regain control as the horse sidled away and the crowd scurried back, then he extended his hand to Imoshen.

Tulkhan flexed his booted foot. She used it like a stirrup, stepping up and taking his extended hand. With a graceful leap she sprang up onto the horse and settled into place before him.

The scent of her freshly washed hair rose around him, its silver tendrils tickling his nose. She swayed with the movement of the horse, rubbing against him, tantalising him with her nearness, with the knowledge of what was to come.

They were through the passage and outer gates, down onto the plain before he knew it. Torch lights danced on the still air, the refugees cheered and sang as they formed a living sea around them. A primal, almost wordless chant rose from the masses, as if from one great communal throat. The air was rich with the scent of roasted meat.

The bower was nothing more than a primitive hut, fashioned from thatched straw, yet it looked like a haven to him. The black horse stopped before it and Tulkhan tossed the reins to Wharrd. Swinging his weight over his mount's back, he leapt to the ground and lifted his arms to Imoshen. An inner urgency seemed to animate her. The dancing torch lights reflected in her dark eyes, filling them with restless points of fire.

She swung her leg across the horse's back. When she slid forward into his arms her dress rode up so that he caught a flash of her firm white thighs. Then she was in his embrace, real flesh and blood.

This time he pressed her hips to his chest and buried his face between her breasts, eager to inhale her distinctive feminine scent. He felt her fingers lace through his hair, pressing him to her breast in an oddly protective, intimate gesture. When was the last time a woman had held him with such gentleness?

Tulkhan raised his face and looked up into hers. Wisps of her hair floated on the air as if alive, her eyes glittered and her lips parted in a gasp. Imoshen looked into his eyes, her soul naked. He felt a tug of recognition as if he had always known her and suddenly he understood she was as vital to him as the very breath he drew, or could be, if he let down his guard.

Stunned by this revelation, he let her weight slide down against his body, bringing her face closer to his. Cupping his face in her hands, she traced his eyebrows with the soft pads of her thumbs, pressing gently on his closed eyelids. Momentarily blinded, all his senses focused on touch, smell and sound, he felt her lean forward and her lips brush his closed lids, first one, then the other, in a benediction of tender desire.

Again, he was disturbed by the intimacy of her touch. He had meant to claim her body, not to lay his soul bare to her.

When he opened his eyes to look into her face she seemed to glow with an inner radiance. He wondered if, when she touched her lips to his closed eyes, she had laid some sort of magical charm on him in order to make herself appear even more beautiful than nature had made her.

He was mad to want her, mad to lay himself open to her tricks. Yet he had no choice. He was mad for her. He *had* to have her.

A rush of desire blazed through his body, obliterating all thought. Caution played no part in what he felt. The primitive chant drummed on the air, seeming to vibrate on his flesh, making it throb in time to the sound. Suddenly impatient, he released her waist to take her by the hand. Without preamble he strode towards the bower's open flap, urgency driving his steps.

At the entrance Imoshen planted her feet and caught his arm, indicating he should wait. She hung her corn sheaf on a hook above the opening and looked at him expectantly. He had no idea what she wanted.

Her gaze fell from his eyes to the bull's horn which hung around his neck and he realised he was supposed to remove it, to place it with her corn sheaf.

At her signal he inclined his head and she lifted the leather thong from around his neck, hanging the masculine symbol next to the feminine.

'They burn the bower afterwards, along with the symbols.' Her voice was raw, bereft of all pretence.

Afterwards.

The significance of the word hung in the charged air.

Imoshen wouldn't meet his eyes and he wondered if she was suddenly shy. But she took a quick breath and stepped into the bower without any urging from him. He followed her, letting the flap fall so that they were alone in the half dark.

Tulkhan marvelled. It was so strange to find himself here in a dirt floored primitive hut, alone with the deposed princess of the mythical T'En. He had only to lay a hand on her to claim her as his prize. She had been untouchable, unattainable. But for tonight she was his. Surely the fates were playing with him, promising him heaven only to dash his hopes.

Her pale hair and white gown glowed as his eyes adjusted to the dark. He smelt fresh herbs, dried flowers.

Imoshen stepped forward into the centre of the hut, under the smoke hole. The twin moons' brilliant light fell on her, bathing her in its silver glow. She lifted her hand, beckoning him. To him she was an ethereal glowing object, enticingly Other.

Tulkhan tensed. This was Imoshen, a girl not yet a woman. Why was she was so matter of fact? Did she know no shame? A woman of his own people would have wept, begged him not to dishonour her. A woman of his own kind would not have accepted the corn sheaf.

Anger sparked in him. He could smell her distinctive scent, so familiar yet so unlike Ghebite women. There was no point fighting it. He had to admit her differences aroused him. But he also desired her simply because she was who she was. He had never met anyone like Imoshen of the T'En.

Tulkhan hesitated, strangely reticent now that they were alone.

She touched the shoulder clasps on her gown and the material fell to her feet in a pool of pale luminescence.

He heard his own sharp intake of breath. His body carried him forward two steps, so that he joined her in the circle of radiance. Her pale hands lifted to his chest as if to help him disrobe, but he caught her hands in his.

'I don't understand. You held me off at knife-point last night.' He gestured to the bower around them, the furs on the floor. 'Why does this make me acceptable?'

Silently, she placed her cheek on the back of his hand. He felt dampness, tears on his skin. Something twisted inside him and he despised himself. Was she weeping because she hated him, because he had given her no choice?

What did he want from her? Forgiveness? An invitation?

A surge of desire seized him and he had to admit it. He wanted her to want him, to welcome him into her arms and into her body.

She kissed his knuckles. He felt her warm breath caress his flesh. Her tongue rasped across his skin and a ragged groan escaped him. He pulled her to him, feeling the warm curves of her body wrapped in the silken cloak of her hair.

Outside he could hear the dull roar of the people's chanting. The knowledge that they were waiting for him to lie with her before continuing their ceremony irritated him. He knew he could not take Imoshen against her will as part of a ritual, yet he could no more stop breathing than call a halt to what was about to happen.

He could not fail now.

When his hands tugged at the laces of his jerkin he found his fingers strangely numb. Her deft hands undid the ties and slid the material over his shoulders. His shirt followed.

He held his breath as her flesh pressed against his bare chest. He could feel the tips of her breasts on his skin.

Silently, she stepped back, pressing the fingers of one hand to her chest as if she was short of breath. He could see her eyes glittering strangely. She stood just out of reach.

Heart pounding, he drew off his boots, unlaced his breeches and freed himself. Naked at last, he stood before her. The little bower was full of heated air and the heady scent of arousal. Impatience seized him.

He caught her hand and pulled her close against his hard body. She shuddered on contact, malleable but not taking the initiative. It was as if she wanted him to claim her, as if she was holding back.

He wanted her to touch him, to want him. He willed her to seduce him so that he could despise her. But she remained passive, his captive, betrayed into this. He guided her hand to cup his shaft, closed her fingers around his length, felt the outrush of her hot breath on his throat. Even so her hand remained still, encased in his.

He recalled the strangely gentle touch of her lips on his closed lids. Had it only been an illusion? Why wouldn't she touch him like that now? He craved her willing touch.

The pallet of furs was at his feet. He sank slowly to his knees, inhaling her scent as he went. Her breasts brushed his face. His lips traced a path across the silken flesh of her abdomen. His tongue dipped into the indentation of her belly button and he felt her tremble.

Lower still he sank. The soft curls of her mound tickled his face. He wanted to taste her, but was afraid to invade her so intimately. He knew instinctively that to take would negate the prize and he desperately wanted the gift of her willing touch.

Sinking back onto the furs he pulled her with him, bringing her body over his, her face to his throat. Her hair spilled across his chest, a silvery blanket.

'Touch me.' Naked desperation laced his voice. She slid away from his body to lie beside him, her weight supported on one elbow. One of her thighs lay over his. He could feel the heat of her on his flesh.

He had revealed himself with that plea and he felt utterly vulnerable, afraid she would mock his need.

Cupping her cheek in her hand, she peered down into his face. Her features were bathed in the up-glow of the moons' twin light. Her eyes, usually so dark, were pools of silver radiance. He saw the flash of her teeth as she licked her lips. If only she would touch him.

As if curious, her warm, dry fingers caressed his face, traced the line of his eyebrows, defined the curve of his lips. Her touch was balm to him. It held a degree of intimacy, yet was almost asexual in its tenderness.

'Why do you hesitate?' she asked softly. 'You chose me. For this one night I am yours.'

It was enough. Desire flared into action. He felt the fragile bones of her shoulders as he caught her to him, claimed her lips. Even as he kissed her, he seemed to hear her laughter in his head. Then he couldn't think for the urgency in his body.

Somehow she was under him, slender and soft, yet surprisingly strong. And this time she was not fighting him. She met his need with a need of her own which made him strive to conquer her. As their bodies joined he felt her resistance but instead of tensing, she welcomed him.

When he buried himself deep in her it was enough, for a heartbeat. Then the urgency took him again.

Their limbs entwined, their breath mingled, their bodies strained against each other. Before he even realised the moment was upon him he was swept over the edge into a cascade of ecstasy so intense that when he regained control of his body, he was surprised to find her beneath him, the world unchanged. He knew a moment's savage triumph. She might be T'En and sacrosanct, supposedly too pure to tolerate a man's touch, but she was still a woman.

Her body had welcomed him despite the pain he caused her.

'You were untouched.'

She closed her eyes in silent agreement. When she did not open them, he watched her face. She seemed to be concentrating. The air inside the bower shimmered around them. Tulkhan's heart skipped a beat.

He knew that sensation all too well. The Dhamfeer was calling on her gifts, and he didn't want to be a part of it. But when he tried to withdraw and roll to his feet her thighs locked around his hips, trapping him.

Startled, he looked into her now open eyes only to find they glowed with an inner radiance. The sight both fascinated and repelled him. There was a strange taste on his tongue and his head ached as if a thunderstorm were about to break.

Suddenly she gasped and tensed beneath him. He felt her inner muscles convulse around him. A groan escaped him. He could feel the tension solidify within him once more. He wanted her again.

This time he needed to affirm she was his.

Tulkhan tried to speak but she embraced him, drawing his face to meet hers. Her lips sought his, eagerly, hungrily. The strange metallic taste was strong on her tongue.

Was this the taste of T'En magic?

He couldn't think. She was in his mouth, in his head. Her scent was in his nostrils, her heat enveloped him. Her laughter rubbed across the back of his skull like velvet. Every instinct screamed *Beware* but he couldn't escape her, couldn't escape her triumph.

'I felt the flare of your son's life force!'

Her words were sensation, nonsensical slivers which barely registered in his fevered mind. His body urged him to claim her once more, yet his head warned him to stop while he still could.

He had tasted her and he was drunk to have her again. Why was she so triumphant? What had she said?

'What?' His words were slurred.

Little ripples ran through her body and her inner muscles tugged on him so that even though he made the effort to still his urges, she drew him deeper into her.

He couldn't afford to drop his guard. A short bitter laugh escaped him. Was it already too late?

'What did you say?' He tried again, his voice harsh.

Moonlight brimmed in her eyes, illuminating her face. She answered him, so sweetly serious. 'I have your son. I felt his life begin just as I was taught I would –'

'Impossible!' The exclamation was out before he could stop it.

She tilted her head curiously. 'No, I would have said inevitable, considering.'

Stunned, he pulled away from her and this time she released him, observing him curiously.

Rolling out of the circle of moonlight, he crouched defensively in the shadows, watching her.

She sat up, negligently naked, her hair draped over her body like a gossamer shawl. At that moment she was totally Other, alien and implacable, yet... her luminous form still called to him. His traitorous body urged him to rejoin her and bathe in the radiance of the twin moons' glow.

Mouth dry and heart pounding, he clenched his fists, determined not to fall under her spell again. This was a trick.

He knew she must be able to smell the fear on his skin and hated himself for the weakness. Tulkhan sensed that if he went to her now he would belong to her, body and soul.

'What is it?' In one fluid movement she came to her knees, flicking her long hair over her shoulder. 'Why do you fear me?'

He could not answer. Had she plucked from his mind his impossible dream, buried deep behind walls of bitter denial? His shame revealed, did she now seek to manipulate him?

She tilted her face to the opalescent glow, held out her hands and bathed in the silver light. A soft laugh escaped her as she played with the moonlight.

'I can feel their power. I've never felt like this before. I have been half asleep all my life.'

In her voice Tulkhan heard innocent wonder, and the Imoshen he had come to know returned. He lunged forward and caught her, pulling her into his arms, out of the moons' direct light as if they were the enemy. When he touched her he knew she was only flesh and blood, distractingly beautiful flesh and blood, but real, capable of fear and pain like himself.

'What do you mean, you have my son?'

The moonlight still seemed to live in her eyes and their luminous quality captured him as she looked at him almost pityingly.

'Every act has its consequence, General. You came to me willingly, you gave him to me.'

'Impossible.'

'How can you say that? You chose me for this bonding.'

Tulkhan shook her, feeling the tensile strength of her body. She did not have the brute strength he had, but there was a tenacity to her flesh, as if her fierce will imbued her body with an added power.

T'En power?

'How can you know when a life starts?' he demanded.

She tilted her head studying him. 'Don't your women know when they are with child? This is my fertile night. I felt the new life flare within me, just as I was taught –'

'You planned this, but you can't trick me!' He thrust her aside so violently that she fell back into the patch of moonlight. He sprang to his feet, rigid with fury but still unable to ignore her beauty as she crouched there in the circle of silver moonlight. He paced back and forth across the dirt floor.

Imoshen watched the Ghebite General, unable to understand his reaction. He was deeply disturbed. Prowling back and forth, he spun to face her, chest heaving. She could see a glowing form reflected in his dark eyes like the twin moons and realised it was herself.

Why did he deny she carried his child?

He swore softly and appeared to come to a decision. Imoshen watched as he fumbled in his haste to pull on his breeches and boots. She could have sworn he was shaking with anger. Or was it fear?

Had the Aayel miscalculated when she Read General Tulkhan? Apprehension settled in Imoshen's core, drowning the last warm flare of the new life she had felt quicken. Had she been mistaken? Was it simply hope she'd felt? No. That flare of new life was too intense to be misunderstood.

Why then was the General denying her?

He scooped up his jerkin and thrust his arms in, not bothering to lace it before he turned to look down at her. 'Well, get up. We have to walk out there together or this thing won't have served its objective.'

Imoshen flinched, but rose to her feet. He had purposefully and cruelly distanced himself from her. As she pulled her shift over her head and tugged her hair free, letting it drop down her back, she sensed him watching her. He was devouring her with his eyes. His gaze caused a physical sensation on her flesh. She was glad the moons' silver radiance did not reveal her flaming cheeks, her tear-laced eyes. For all the world she would not admit he had hurt her.

His desire for her was like a heady drug. She could feel her body responding to his unspoken need. He wanted her, but it was her own response which surprised Imoshen. She had naively thought once the moment of conception was passed, she would be free of this distracting desire for him. But it was not to be.

'Come.'

The Ghebite General stood by the door flap of the bower, a dark brooding presence. Try as she might, she could not begin to understand him. She wanted to refuse, to make a stand, but it would negate what she had achieved so far. The fragile peace must be kept and her hold on the General must be tightened.

So she stepped into the shadows by the bower entrance to join him, mentally preparing herself for what was to come.

The General caught her hand and pulled her close to him. She'd thought he meant to march straight out, but his hands encircled her waist, then slid down to cup her buttocks.

She felt him swell, pressed into the soft flesh of her belly. His need for her was like a fever, contagious, consuming him and her, consuming all rational thought.

He cursed and plunged through the flap. There was a ragged shout, which turned into a cheer, and by the time they had climbed astride his war horse, the bower was aflame.

Amid a sea of celebration, Imoshen watched the bower burn, isolated, alone. Somehow it seemed fitting to her that her son should be conceived on the field like this, caught betwixt the invader and the conquered, under the twin harvest moons.

A flush of fierce determination inflamed her. In that moment Imoshen understood what she had begun. A helpless new life depended utterly on her. She knew she would do everything in her power to see that her child lived to claim his place. It amazed her to discover that without a qualm of conscience she could contemplate lying, even murder, to protect her flesh and blood.

Was this why the Aayel wanted her to fall pregnant, because it would focus her will? Imoshen did not know. But she felt terribly vulnerable. How was she to save her unborn child when her own life hung by a thread?

Flames leapt high into the night sky, sparks spiralled upwards.

Tulkhan felt Imoshen stiffen in his arms. She turned to him. The leaping patterns of the fires illuminated her pale skin, creating shadows that haunted her features.

A shudder ran through her body and she surprised him by pressing her face into his chest. Her arms slid around his body. Wordlessly, she clung to him and he was surprised by a strong protective urge.

Around them the gathered refugees mingled with his own Ghebite soldiers. They watched the bower burn in almost total silence. When the roof and walls collapsed and sparks flew upwards into the still air, a sibilant sigh of satisfaction travelled through the masses.

Someone struck up a tune and the dancing began.

Tulkhan knew the night would get wilder and wilder, even by Ghebite standards. He turned his beast toward the Umasreach Stronghold. Imoshen rode across his thighs, her face buried in his chest. He guided the horse with his knees, holding her in one arm.

No one paid them any attention as they entered the stable courtyard. The servants had done their duty and been dismissed, and now the night was turned over to revelry. Already he heard raucous laughter and shrieks from the stables.

The anger which had driven him to distance himself from Imoshen had dissolved, departing with the sparks of their bower on the still night air. The Dhamfeer had tried to trick him, but he would not be taken in. He would not allow himself to hope for the impossible.

The twin moons' light fell so strongly in the courtyard before the stables that Tulkhan cast a shadow as he swung his weight off the horse's back. Imoshen slipped down before he could help her and ran inside. Strange, he had expected another confrontation. It was out of character for her to avoid him.

He had to admit he wanted another confrontation, another reason to rail at her, to take her in his arms and... his face grew hot at the thought. He must have been a fool if he thought one bedding would get her out of his blood.

Impatience raged in his body, but he forced himself to tend to his horse, to leave it safely stabled and rubbed down. Before he could make his way through the great hall, he was hailed by several of the elite guard who wanted to drink his health. Much ribald comment was directed to him concerning the Dhamfeer. They wanted to know if she was as wild as rumour had it.

Strangely, Tulkhan couldn't join in the jest. He felt as if he was watching everything happen to someone else, as if there was something he should be doing elsewhere.

He knew what it was. His blood was boiling for her. Perversely, he made himself stay in the great hall and jest with his men. He knew the value of bonding. He might be the son of the King's second wife, but he was a soldier first and they respected him for that.

Slightly drunk, though not near enough considering the ale he'd consumed, he climbed the stairs to his bedchamber. Wharrd was sleeping in the outer room, his limbs entangled with those of Imoshen's small serving maid. Tulkhan stared morosely at them.

He could remember when his life was that simple, when he thought success of the field of battle would win him his father's love and acknowledgement. Impatient with himself, he forged ahead, but in his slightly hazy state he stubbed his toe on the door jamb. His curses woke Kalleen, who fled.

Wharrd sat up, his protest dying on his lips when he met the General's eye.

'Bedding the enemy, now?' Tulkhan asked. It was meant to be a jest, but he saw the man flinch.

Wharrd opened his mouth, then clearly thought better of making the obvious reply. Tulkhan gave a rueful smile, acknowledging Wharrd's unspoken comment.

'I should cut out my tongue,' Tulkhan muttered and tried to make amends. 'Wine?' He'd had more than enough, but it didn't ease the continuous ache which thrummed through his body. It seemed no amount of wine could dull that need.

The bone-setter nodded and accepted a mug. Tulkhan stirred up the fire and built it higher. He wouldn't sleep tonight. To lie alone, without her in his arms, would be agony. He could still smell her on his skin, feel her flesh on his fingers. The silken caress of her hair haunted him.

He clenched his fist and stared into the flames, resting his forearm on the mantelpiece. He'd forgotten the older man.

'I've seen you grow from a boy to a man. I've served you all these years, but now I want to step aside. This is how I see it,' Wharrd said without preamble. 'I've followed the army for nearly thirty years. I was but a lad when I first saw men die. I've sewed men up, sawn off their arms and legs, watched them die in agony. I'm tired of it. I want a quiet little cottage somewhere, a wife who'll warm my bed and my heart, who'll give me strong, healthy children. And I pray to the gods they will never have to live through what I've seen.' He met Tulkhan's eyes, his face an odd mixture of defiance and apology. 'I'm tired of fighting. I want peace.'

Tulkhan said nothing. The events of the night were pressing in on him. His most trusted friend was stepping down. His father was dead, his younger half-brother had become King. He had conquered every country from the north to Fair Isle. What was left for him?

Should he return to the mainland and lead the army into the southern kingdoms? What purpose would it serve? His father was dead. Even after all he'd achieved in his father's name, he had not won the old King's love. Why should he lead an army to conquer land for his half-brother?

What then?

Should he build some ships and sail off to the archipelago in search of wealth? The idea did not cause his blood to ignite with passion. Personal fortune had never meant much to him.

For the first time in his life he felt lost, without purpose. An emptiness and a sense of dislocation filled him.

Yet, echoing through the stronghold, he could hear shouts of revelry, laughter and music. The only thing worse than a rowdy drunk was a morose drunk, and Tulkhan did not like his own company.

IMOSHEN PROWLED THE moonlit room, cat-light on her bare feet. Kalleen huddled before the empty fireplace, watching her. The rest of the stronghold had cast care aside to indulge in the revelry.

'Something is wrong, I can feel it.' Imoshen spun around, her hands opening and closing in futile fists. She strode to the window, but the sight of the twin moons offered her no comfort. 'If only the Aayel were here. She could tell me what I feel.'

The little serving maid said nothing.

'Of course!' Imoshen spun to face her. 'Bring me the scrying platter.'

While the girl hastened to obey, Imoshen took her knife and pricked her finger, squeezing several drops of dark blood to the surface. 'Here, Kalleen.'

She knew she was worrying her maid and one part of her regretted this, but she had to do something. Her T'En senses screamed a warning.

The blood fell on the silver platter. Imoshen added a little water, watching the two liquids mingle. She walked to the moonlit window seat and leant there in the embrasure, swirling the water lightly over the plate's surface.

Scrying rarely worked for her. Tonight she couldn't focus her thoughts. Dread of what she might learn and impatience with her lack of skill warred within her. She felt as if there was something important she was missing, something she should sense.

Kalleen hovered just out of reach, breaking Imoshen's concentration. It was pointless. Dispirited, she stopped pushing for a vision and let her thoughts drift.

Too late now to flee with Reothe, she had made a commitment to save herself and her son as well as the people of Fair Isle.

Imoshen was about to throw the water out the window in disgust when something appeared in the plate. Bodies writhed, people fled in terror, women, children, horses screamed. Their stomach-churning cries filled her head. Acrid smoke from the burning buildings stung her throat.

Panic seized her.

They were being hunted through the streets. There was nowhere to run. Metal clattered on stone. Imoshen screamed. She fled with her people, her heart pounding.

One of the invaders grabbed her gown, tearing it. He trapped her arms. She writhed in his vicious embrace, a parody of love. She struggled in silence, full of desperate fury. Somehow, she must escape, but his grip was unbreakable.

Weeping. Someone was pleading, calling her name. Another voice, this time masculine, pierced the screams of those around her.

'Imoshen!' The familiar deep voice was filled with concern.

She recognised the scent and realised it was the General who held her. With that knowledge, the terrifying vision faded.

'Put out the fire!' he bellowed.

What fire? Imoshen strove to see through the grey mist that enveloped her. The General was holding her against his body, her back pressed to his chest. She twisted in his arms and caught sight of Kalleen. The small, nimble figure darted forward, slapping the flaming bed curtains with a blanket.

Imoshen blinked, the last wreaths of grey mist fading as her sight returned. Her bedchamber was alight?

'What happened?' Imoshen tried to sidle out of Tulkhan's grasp.

'You tell me.' He swung her around to face him. 'Kalleen screamed for help. We found your chamber like this!'

Imoshen thrust his hands aside and turned to survey the damage. It looked worse than it was. Wharrd and Kalleen almost had the fire out. Who would set fire to her bedchamber?

She had no idea.

Impatient with the blank in her memory, Imoshen paced across the room. Her bare toe caught the serving plate. It went skittering across the stone like a live thing flashing silver, clattering sharply. The sound scraped on her raw nerves.

Imoshen gasped. Her heart jumped, then began to pound rapidly. Kalleen yelped with fright. Wharrd cursed.

Imoshen shuddered as echoes of the slaughtered innocents' screams filled her head.

What had she seen, or more worryingly done?

She turned to Kalleen, grabbing the girl's wrist. 'Tell me what happened?'

The little maid's mouth twisted with reluctance. She fixed her golden-hazel eyes on Imoshen's face, then glanced sharply towards the men, and Imoshen instantly regretted her demand. The Ghebites were still their enemy. Kalleen's instincts were correct, she did not want to reveal any weakness before them.

Wharrd pulled down the last of the bed curtains and rolled them up, still smouldering.

Forcing herself to behave calmly, Imoshen let Kalleen's wrist go and stepped away, turning to the men. 'Thank you for coming in, General, but everything is under control now. You may leave.'

He gave a short impatient laugh. 'You haven't answered my question.' Abruptly he turned on Kalleen. 'What happened, girl?'

She jumped with fright and looked to Imoshen, who saw that the girl would lie for her.

Why? Why should she inspire such loyalty?

Imoshen put this thought aside and rubbed her temples trying to think. The General would not be put off. He had come to her aid, saved her from something. What? She frowned. Perhaps he deserved an explanation.

'There are a dozen jumbled images in my mind. I remember standing by the window under the light of the twin moons and searching the scrying plate, but I saw nothing...' Even as she said this, the memory returned, cleaving her tongue to the roof of her mouth, closing her throat with fear.

'You began to scry,' Kalleen said softly. 'Suddenly you dropped the plate and screamed.'

'I saw women, children being hunted down through the narrow streets and slaughtered. There was nowhere to run. Then I was running with them.

'One of the invaders lunged for me. His hand raked my shoulder. I tried to run between the blazing buildings toward the square. But it was a trap.' Imoshen bit her lip, aware that the General was watching her closely. It would not do to reveal the extent or, in this case, her inability to harness her gift. He already feared her T'En powers. What would he do if he thought she was unable to control it?

'You ran about the room, as if trying to escape someone,' Kalleen whispered.

'And then?' General Tulkhan prompted the little maid, who looked to Imoshen for the signal to proceed.

Imoshen nodded. A cold certainty settled in her chest. She was sure the bed curtains had not been set alight by natural means.

'Then?' Kalleen echoed, her eyes widening with terror as she remembered. 'My lady did not know me. She screamed and the bed curtains burst into flames. I went for help.'

Several slightly drunk, but reasonably alert soldiers charged into the room half-dressed. One was naked except for his sword.

Tulkhan swore under his breath. He swung his cloak from his own shoulders, to clasp it around Imoshen's. Before she could speak, he was marching toward the men.

'What drunken revelry is this?' he demanded.

'We heard a scream. We thought it was another assassination attempt!'

'Nothing like that.' Tulkhan laughed, his voice rich on the charged air. 'The Princess had a nightmare. She cried out in her sleep –'

'I smell burning.' One man eyed Imoshen suspiciously.

'I knocked over my candle. I'm sorry.' It galled her to let them believe she was frightened by her own dreams, but Tulkhan was containing the disturbance and she had to do her part.

He ushered the men out, shut the door, then turned to meet her eyes across the chamber. Imoshen realised the General had given her the Ghebite equivalent of her title. Did that mean he was acknowledging her as his equal? Did he even realise he had done it?

'Explain,' he growled.

'Explain what? I had a bad feeling. I did a scrying. I must have knocked over my candle.'

Kalleen went to speak, but reconsidered. Aware of what the girl might have revealed, Imoshen was grateful.

Tulkhan strode toward Imoshen, his long dark hair streaming behind him. Her heart leapt to her throat. She felt an instinctive fear, mingled with admiration. Even now she wanted him.

His hands sprang to her neck. She flinched but held her ground as he tore the cloak off her shoulders. 'Explain this!'

He spun her around to stand before the polished metal mirror. By the candlelight she could see nail marks on her bare shoulder. The material of her simple shift had been torn, rent as if someone had attempted to grab her and she'd only just eluded them.

Chapter Six

FEAR MADE IMOSHEN'S skin go cold. Had the vision felt so real because it *was* real? But how?

She did not know. Truly, her life had been in danger. Here was the evidence. Yet... it had only been a scrying. Nothing like this had ever happened when the Aayel did her scryings. What had she done wrong? Why had the bed curtains burst into flames?

Confusion overcame her, shredding her confidence. Her heart sank. She was a danger to herself and those around her. What was happening to her?

'Who attacked you?' Tulkhan demanded, his voice vibrating with repressed emotion.

Imoshen realised the General was holding himself on a very tight rein. It was clear he thought someone, perhaps one of his own men, had attempted to rape her. It was a logical assumption. Unless she wanted him punishing his men unfairly, causing further resentment, she would have to tell him the truth, and that meant admitting her own lack of control over her gifts.

Imoshen hated to admit her weakness, but there was nothing for it. She must face the consequences of her actions with dignity.

'Kalleen, take Wharrd out and offer him some wine. I'm sure he could do with refreshment,' Imoshen ordered and walked to the empty fireplace. It was cold and dark, the wood laid ready to strike the tinder. She missed the fire's welcoming warmth. When had they lit the candles? Last she recalled the room was bathed in moonlight.

As she turned to confront the General she saw a moment of silent communication pass between him and the bone-setter. Yes, she must remember that as kind as Wharrd was, he was still Tulkhan's man sent to spy on her. *Not that he needed to do much spying,* Imoshen thought grimly, *when she set her own bedchamber alight.*

On his General's signal, Wharrd left with her maidservant. Imoshen swallowed. Where to begin?

She didn't want to meet Tulkhan's eyes. Surely he would despise her for her weakness? She was torn. She only had to look at him to recall his arms around her. Her body thrilled at the memory, and ached for his touch. She frowned – at this moment the last thing she needed was this physical distraction. It made her feel awkward and vulnerable, because he had known her body and now he would know her weakness.

To hide her discomfort she resorted to social etiquette. 'Wine?'

He waved a hand as if the answer didn't matter, then strode to the fireplace. Imoshen crossed to the low table and poured two goblets. Turning to offer him one, she saw him building up the flame. When had he had time to strike the tinder?

Tulkhan came to his feet. 'I want an explanation now.'

He made Imoshen feel small and she wasn't. She resented that. She enjoyed looking down on men.

Licking her dry lips, she began. 'The Aayel could have explained it. She knew so much more than I. Maybe it is normal. But it never happened before. My scrying has been erratic. Healing was always my gift.'

'You're saying this wasn't done by one of my men?' Tulkhan asked, clearly trying to contain his exasperation.

Imoshen touched his arm. She told herself it was to ask his forbearance, but the moment she felt the hard muscle under the fine material, she knew she'd touched him because she had to. The warmth of his skin went through her fingertips, travelled up her arm and settled in her core. She felt a tingle of excitement move over her body. The intensity of her physical reaction startled her.

Her eyes flew to his and she knew he felt it too. The General stepped away to pick up his wine. But she sensed it was an excuse to escape her.

'What happened tonight?' he asked. 'Were you in danger –'

'Yes. Something went wrong.' Imoshen flushed. She had to tell him. He deserved the truth. 'You asked if it was one of your men who attacked me. It wasn't. But I think he was a Ghebite. He nearly caught me.

'I was in a narrow street. All about me the buildings were ablaze. The choking smoke... I couldn't breathe. It was so very real. I don't know how...' She heard her voice rise and bit her lip, taking a deep breath to regain control.

Someone hammered on the door. Imoshen gasped and stepped closer, clutching the General's arm. Tulkhan's hand closed over hers. She snatched it away, already regretting her weakness.

With exaggerated patience General Tulkhan put his wine aside and cursed in three languages, making Imoshen smile. The hammering came again.

Their eyes met and something passed between them – a rueful acknowledgement of their situation. Whatever they might feel personally, their positions meant they were always on duty, at the beck and call of their people.

Imoshen raised her voice. 'Come in.'

The door swung open and half a dozen of Tulkhan's elite guard staggered in with a bloodied individual between them. She felt the General stiffen. Another assassination attempt?

'My Lady T'En?' The man writhed in his captors' grasp, twisting to pin his one good eye on her.

As Imoshen stepped forward, all the unease she had been feeling settled into one lump of leaden fear in her belly.

'Put him down. Step back!' Fear and fury made her voice ring like steel.

The elite guard obeyed instinctively. Imoshen simply accepted their obedience, her mind on their captive. The man was bleeding freely but he was not badly hurt. She took her own goblet and sank to her knees, offering it to him. With a jolt she realised he was only a youth, not yet out of his teens.

'Lady T'En?' His fingers closed on her wrist as his eyes searched her face. 'You must save T'Diemn. The Ghebites surrounded it. Our mayor parleyed for terms. We laid down our arms and opened the city gates. They marched into our streets, into the palace.

'Then they beheaded the mayor. They called for all the heads of the guilds, bade them come to the square with their families. First they killed the leaders of the guilds, then –'

'Then they slaughtered the women and children,' Imoshen muttered, understanding her vision.

'No.' He frowned at her.

Imoshen shook her head. It would have taken him at least a day to reach the stronghold. Instinctively, she knew slaughter of the innocents was happening right now. And she was helpless to prevent it.

'When I left, they were calling for the first-born son of every family. My mother wouldn't let me go. They'd already killed my father, the silversmith guildmaster. She told me to slip away to the docks, and swim down river to escape.'

Imoshen sprang to her feet. The goblet fell to the stone floor, rattling in a half circle. It was all horribly clear at last. 'They're killing women and children, hunting them through the streets –'

'Who?' The General caught her arm, swung her around to face him.

'Your half-brother and his army. It's a massacre. If you want the rest of the country to turn against you, go join the King and murder the townspeople of T'Diemn!'

She saw the General blanch. He did not question her claim.

'We ride at dawn,' he bellowed. 'I want every man of my elite guard ready to move out. I'll select a core guard to hold the stronghold. Move!'

As his men headed for the door, the General strode past her to follow them and she caught his arm. 'What are you going to do?'

His dark eyes met hers. 'Save the city. If I don't make a move I'll lose the kingdom.'

She nodded. 'You may have already lost the kingdom. When word of this gets out, the people of the south will fight to the death rather than be slaughtered after surrender.'

'I keep my word,' General Tulkhan ground out. 'Hasn't the stronghold met with a fair treatment?'

Rage flared through Imoshen. She wanted to deny him his answer, but honesty forbade it.

'You have been fair.' The words left a bitter taste in her mouth.

A muscle jumped in his cheek. His obsidian eyes blazed and she realised his honour was at stake. At that moment she had an insight into the General's warrior code. It was so alien to hers in some ways, and yet so similar in others.

'What will you do? You are not King and people are dying.'

'What can I do? I am only a True-man, without T'En gifts. Let me go!' His voice was harsh.

She realised she had been holding his arm, though he could have easily thrust her aside. Fury burned in his dark eyes. Was he angry with her because of her ability to scry, or with his half-brother for risking what he had fought so hard to gain? Imoshen could not tell.

Now was not the time for a battle of wills. For once they were both on the same side. She wanted General Tulkhan to save the townspeople of T'Diemn. She released his arm and stepped back. He swung away from her, striding from the room.

Imoshen's bedchamber was suddenly empty except for the wearied, bloodied youth, who had knelt there at their feet watching all this. She offered him her hand. 'Come to the fire.'

'My lady.' He clasped her hand and bought it to his lips, raising a weary face to hers. 'My mother is a half-blood. She said the Aayel would know what to do. But they tell me the old one is dead. Do you trust this Ghebite General? How can you? When –'

'Nothing is that simple.' She stared down at his bruised face, exasperated. 'We can trust General Tulkhan to take steps to hold this island. And that does not include murdering the townspeople after they've surrendered. It goes against the principles of warcraft and statecraft.' She tightened her grasp on him. 'Now let me clean you up.'

He staggered a little as he came to his feet. His eyes were level with hers. 'No. It would not be right for the last of the T'En to tend me.'

Imoshen almost laughed. She pushed him toward the fireside. 'Sit down.' Then she turned to get her medicinals. He reminded her of her brother, an odd mixture of earnest and cocksure. That thought made the laughter die on her lips. Her brother was dead. Every member of her family lost to her. She was the last T'En, struggling to survive.

Even if she was able to forge an understanding with the General, he was not the King. Tulkhan's younger half-brother Gharavan held the power and he was sacking T'Diemn.

Imoshen felt she understood the General on one level at least. He was an honourable man by his own standards and a statesman. But what if this King Gharavan ordered Tulkhan to raze Umasreach Stronghold, execute her and her supporters? Her skin went cold. What would he do? Would he commit treason and betray his half-brother for her, a mere Dhamfeer?

It was a while since she had seen the contempt in his eyes, but he had a lifetime of prejudice to overcome and she was not one of his people. He owed her no allegiance. He owed her nothing. He did not even believe she carried his son.

So much for the Aayel's plans!

She shivered as she poured a few herbs into the bowl and dipped the cloth to cleanse the lad's face.

'It isn't right,' he said.

'What isn't right?' She concentrated on the wound above his right eye, which had swollen shut. The gash in his forehead was bleeding freely still. Scalp wounds were notorious for bleeding.

'It isn't right that you should serve me.'

Imoshen met his good eye then, surprised to see it was the golden-brown of a True-man's, even though his skin was pale like her own. He was the result of six hundred years of interbreeding.

'You have a name?' she asked.

'Drakin – uh, Drake.'

She smiled. His mother would have called him Drakin, little Drake. She wrung out the cloth and pressed the wound's edges together. Instinctively, she used her gift to urge the flesh to knit and felt the warmth flow through her fingers into his skin. He didn't flinch, seemed unaware of it.

Why did the healing come so easily to her? Imoshen didn't have time to wonder.

'It is as it should be, Drake. I am one of the last T'En. I live to serve the people. You are one of my people. Yes?' She smiled when she saw his bemused expression. He nodded briefly. 'Then let me serve you.'

She took the cloth away, pleased to see the wound had stopped bleeding. Applying crushed leaves to prevent it festering, she wrapped clean cloth around his head and saw to the lesser cuts on his lip. All the while she felt his eyes on her.

'Yes?' she asked at last.

'You are very like him. You could be his sister.'

Even before she spoke, she knew who Drake was referring to, but she pretended not to understand. 'My brother is dead.'

'No. T'Reothe. He came to my parents to have his silver valued when he returned from his first voyage. I was only a lad then, but I was allowed to stay. He spoke kindly to me, told me tales of things he had seen while my father weighed the silver.'

'Really?' Imoshen knew so little about the man she had been betrothed to. So Reothe had been kind to a boy who could do him no favours. The thought hurt her and she realised she would rather not know Reothe's good qualities.

'My mother has your eyes. She told me tales of T'Imoshen the First. In T'Reothe I saw them come to life and now again in you,' Drake whispered shyly. He touched her sixth finger and his gaze lifted to her hair. 'I heard he was betrothed to you and I wondered. Now I see. You were meant for him, to bring back the great –'

'Hush.' She pressed her fingers to his lips, distressed by what she knew he would say. If she wanted Drake and other young men like him to live, she must lie. Those lies sprang easily to her lips. 'That was another lifetime. Reothe is dead. I have made my peace with the General.'

'Murderer. His king called the guildmasters to the square. He had them beheaded before their families. My mother...' He moaned, unable to go on.

Imoshen felt his terrible pain as if it was her own.

When healing she had to open herself to the injured person's feelings. It left her vulnerable. But to dwell on it would only bring more suffering and anger. 'You did the right thing in coming here. How did you manage it so quickly?'

He gave a rueful grin. 'I stole a soldier's horse, rode it then walked it and rode it again. I tried to sneak into the stronghold but the General's men caught me. They beat me.'

'I see... Kalleen?' Imoshen came to her feet. She'd sensed the farm girl's curious presence for some time now. Her maidservant stepped forward. 'This young man has done us a great service. Find him a room, someone to see to his needs.'

He protested faintly, his cheeks burning with embarrassment, but Imoshen ignored him. With some final instructions to Kalleen about preparing a healing broth, she left him by the fire with a blanket around him.

RESTLESSNESS PLAGUED IMOSHEN. She had followed the Aayel's plan to success only to have her peace of mind destroyed by a petty Ghebite king.

She dragged a full-length white fur cloak which had been her mother's around her shoulders and made her way to the stairs. She needed to escape the confines of the stronghold.

It was nearly dawn and the festivities of the Harvest Feast were over. In the courtyard by the stables the elite guard were already stirring. Imoshen could hear their excited voices, the champ of horses and the jingle of harness.

Driven by something she did not understand she made her way up to the battlements and paced their length. She could feel the sting of the cold predawn air on her cheeks and bare feet, but her body was warm within the cloak.

Hundreds of fires still dotted the fields below her stronghold. Her heart sank with the enormity of it all. Thousands of people sought shelter down there, expecting safety on her doorstep. And she had no magical path to safety, not even for herself. Covering her face with her hands, she withdrew into the stone crevice between the battlements, tears stinging her eyes.

Her ancestors had planned well, creating little stone nooks behind the battlements so that defenders could hold off their attackers protected on their unshielded sides. But they had not anticipated a time when Umasreach would surrender without a fight. Shame and frustration gnawed at her. While she stood here the people of T'Diemn suffered at the hands of King Gharavan.

If only the Aayel lived. She could have asked her great aunt's advice.

A shudder shook Imoshen. She dared not attempt another scrying. Now that she was facing her darkest fears she had to admit it – the thing had gotten beyond her control. She had run with the woman who fled her captor.

Unleashed by her terror, a fire had sprung up spontaneously and engulfed the bed curtains. And what of that poor woman?

She was probably dead now. Imoshen had not saved her, could not even save herself. Scalding hot tears slid unheeded down her cheeks, as she sank to sit with her back to the stone.

Lack of sleep made her weary, lack of food made her light-headed. When she pulled the cloak tighter about her, she caught a faint scent of her mother. She closed her eyes, seeking comfort.

But the dead offered no comfort.

Only Reothe still lived. He had known his gifts longer than her. He was familiar in a haunting way, a mirror to herself. If only she could ask his advice.

She felt sleep creep up on her, making a mockery of her racing thoughts.

As she drifted, the sounds from the courtyard below interwove with her dream, so that she thought she was lying in a cold hollow in the woods, hearing the enemy pass by. There was no fire to warm her or her companions, for they couldn't risk one. They were rebels.

Then she recognised the identity of the person who lay beside her in the hollow, felt his warmth down her length.

'Reothe?'

His eyes gleamed in the dark woods.

'Imoshen?'

It was so real, but sometimes dreams were like that.

She needed to unburden herself. 'The General goes to stop his half-brother, the King, from slaughtering the townsfolk of T'Diemn. I fear for my life, for his.'

'And for mine?'

Imoshen opened her mouth to speak, then it occurred to her that she had already named him a dead man tonight.

Reothe clutched her shoulders, pulling her close to him. At his touch, she realised she was naked. She felt his hard thigh between her legs. His face, coarse with its unshaven growth, scraped her cheek. His mouth was hard on hers. Yet it moved her to feel him like this, needful and urgent. She let herself go, savouring the fire of his touch, the fire created by his body's need for her. His mouth claimed hers.

He pulled back sharply, inhaling.

'What have you done this night?' His breath fanned her face. 'I can taste him on your mouth, smell him on your skin. How could you give yourself to him? You were mine. Promised to me!'

His rage both frightened and aroused her. She wanted to laugh.

'Such arrogance...' Only in her dream would she dare to speak like this to him. 'The world has changed. I am a caged captive, awaiting my death sentence. You are a woodland mouse fleeing before the raptor.'

'How could you do this?' he whispered, running his hands down her body. She felt the hard length of him against her, the possessiveness in his body, and understood that he wanted her. 'How is it that I can I touch you?'

She lay there, watching his face by the twin moonlight filtering through the trees. There were other shadowy forms in the hollow with them. She could smell their unwashed bodies. The cold was seeping into her bones.

And Imoshen knew this was no dream.

She went to move, but he restrained her.

Reothe lifted on one elbow, his other arm stretched possessively across her. She heard him send the others to scout the party they were tracking. They scurried away through the woods, leaving her alone with Reothe.

She shrugged out of his grasp, pulling herself up to hug her knees. He sat watching her. His pale face and hair glowed in the twin moonlight. It was a bad night for hunting, too much visibility.

She shivered.

He took his cloak from his shoulders and draped it around her. As he pulled back, he was smiling. 'If you have given yourself to him, why did you come to me?'

She opened her mouth to speak, but did not want to admit her fear.

He crouched before her in the deep debris of the forest. She could smell the dying leaves, taste the tang of winter on the air. But overlaying all that was his scent and his hunger for her.

'You came to me because you are bound to me. We are the last of our kind. Your body calls to mine. I felt it the first time I saw you, saw it waken in you that time in the woods when you quickened at my touch. You came to me because I call to you –'

'No.' She tried to think through the rush of desire which warmed her body. Once again she did not know if what she felt was her own natural reaction to him, or some trick he used to seduce her.

Imoshen hated her uncertainty, hated feeling out of control. Confused, she rolled to her feet and stepped around him, pacing across the clearing in the dappled light of the twin moons. It was as if a thin band joined them – the further she moved from him, the more painful the sensation was.

She spun to face him. 'What are you doing, Reothe?'

He came to his feet, a pale silver figure. He exuded a menace she hadn't recognised before. Still she stood her ground as he walked slowly, almost silently, through the leaf litter toward her.

'You gave him that which should have been mine.' Reothe voice was low, a corrosive caress. 'I want you. Come to me now. Join with me. We will be so much more paired than apart.'

She felt the strength of the bond which joined them, felt it tighten, drawing him to her, preparing her for him. In a flash Imoshen understood what he wanted.

Fear gripped her. Even though she had never lain with Reothe, he had this ability to cloud her mind and arouse her body. How much more power would he have over her if she were to take him willing into her arms, into her body and into her mind?

More importantly, if he had her at his side the people would see them as a viable alternative to the Ghebite invaders. All her plans would go astray. General Tulkhan would...

Reothe cursed. He sprang forward to cover the distance between them.

She knew if he laid a hand on her she would not be able to resist his strange allure. Everything slowed. Like some feral being from a nightmare, he covered the distance between them. She saw him passing through the patches of moonlight alternately illuminated and dark, his face twisted in a grimace of determination.

The realisation hit her – she could not stand against him.

'No!' The cry was torn from her.

Imoshen turned and tried to run.

Thud. Her head struck the stone of the battlements. Tears of pain stung her eyes. Heart still raging in her chest, she staggered to her feet, trying to take stock of her surroundings. She was alone, on the ramparts of her family's stronghold.

Anxiously she searched the long walk, but it was empty. Reothe was not here, could not follow. Realisation hit her. If he had been able to move as she had, he would not have had to use the secret passage in the abbey. No wonder he wanted her to join forces with him. Yet, she had no idea how she had travelled to him. Had she really been present in the glade? Everything had seemed so real.

One thing was clear, Reothe considered their vow still stood. He wanted her. More than that, he needed her to regain Fair Isle. Had she made the right choice?

Feeling the dawn breeze lift her long hair, Imoshen pulled the cloak more tightly about her. Grimly, she turned to go inside. A dark figure strode towards her. Her heart lurched. For a moment she thought it was Reothe come for her. Then she recognised the set of General Tulkhan's broad shoulders, his outline unfamiliar in full battle regalia.

'T'Imoshen,' he said, using her full royal title. He performed something she assumed was a formal gesture of greeting in his own land.

She felt utterly vulnerable, frightened by what she had learnt, afraid of being left alone for fear Reothe would find a way into the stronghold. She was afraid for the General, because he went to meet King Gharavan and possibly oppose him, and last of all she feared for her own future and that of the child she had begun this night.

If General Tulkhan was not strong enough to stand against his half-brother and win him over, her position was untenable.

'I have come to ask something of you,' the General said and she could tell he did not like to ask. 'I must take most of my men to confront my half-brother. A small force will remain here –'

'You have my word we will not rise against you.' Imoshen cut him short. She stepped forward, covering the distance between them. She wanted to feel his hands on her, feel his reality once more before she was left to deal with her fears alone. 'You will not be fighting a war on two fronts.'

She heard his ragged intake of breath, felt his rough soldier's hands on her flesh as she drew them inside her cloak. The simple shift she wore parted for him. His breath caught in his throat as she placed his palms on her flesh.

She strained against him.

'Take care when you move against your king,' she whispered, her lips moving on his skin where his jaw met the tendon of his throat.

His unshaven chin scraped her face as their lips met and his words came in a puff of breath over her face. 'I don't fear him. He's poorly advised. Gharavan will listen to me. I taught him to ride and to fight.'

His calloused palm brushed her taut breast. A moan escaped her. The material of her shift tore. It was a shocking sound, punctuated by their ragged breathing, his guttural groan.

He shuddered as she boldly cupped his arousal through the material of his breeches. Wrapped in their twin cloaks, the trapped air between them grew hot. She felt the hard stone at her back as he pinned her there.

She wanted him now, as much of him as she could have. It did not matter if this was illogical. She didn't want him to leave, to face danger alone as she would be doing. Her unspoken desperation seemed to call to something in him.

He shuddered as he stepped away from her. She followed, pressing her face into his neck. Her tongue touched his throat where she felt the tight cords of his neck, the pounding of his pulse.

She wound her fingers through his cloak. He stepped back again, though she could feel how much it cost him.

Why was he rejecting her?

He was about to ride out. Imoshen flushed. Was she so desperate for him that she would join with him here on the battlements?

The answer was simple. Yes.

Shame heated her cheeks. What had possessed her? She must not lose sight of her real purpose here. 'The rebels will look for any sign of Ghebite dissension –'

'Don't you think I know that?' He grimaced. 'Where do you stand on this, Imoshen?'

She sucked in her breath. Where did she stand? Not with Reothe, not with futile fighting and more bloodshed. But did she truly stand with the Ghebites?

Could she lie? No.

'I stand for the people of Fair Isle, for their right to live without fear and oppression.'

He nodded once as if this was no more or less than he expected. 'And you will back me so long as I follow that course?'

This time she could answer without hesitation. 'Yes.'

There were cries of greeting from the courtyard below, the sound of men gathering. General Tulkhan strode to the stone work and waved down to the men. They responded with the Ghebite battle cry.

'Come to my side, Imoshen.'

It was a show for his men, for those of her personal stronghold guard who would remain here and might be tempted to take a stand. Imoshen hesitated, understanding the significance of her public support of the Ghebite General, but she joined him. Whatever her personal feelings, they must present a united front.

The General's men fell silent at the sight of her at his side, but those of her retinue, the servants who had prepared the food for the journey and the stable hands who had saddled the horses, gave a ragged cheer.

'Kiss me,' Tulkhan whispered. 'Pull me into your arms and kiss me.'

She was shocked by the naked hunger in his voice and by the unspoken message he wanted to impart to those below.

'Do it.' He turned to her.

Imoshen faltered. To lie with him at the Festival of the Harvest Moons when she had been chosen was one thing, but to accept him like this before their people was another thing entirely. Would her own people despise her for taking the invader willingly into her bed?

'I must have your support if I'm to stop the bloodshed,' he whispered.

The General was right. She stepped forward, her eyes fixed on his grim mouth. She felt the breadth of his chest on her hands as she reached for him, felt the longing of her body to cleave to his. When his mouth sought hers she was ready to open for him. His broad hands found the small of her back, pulling her into him, pressing her body intimately against his.

Dimly, she heard the cheering from below, but there was a great rushing in her ears. She felt both frightened and exhilarated. There was nothing half-hearted about his response. His hunger for her had never been in doubt. It was a physical reaction which, if her own body was anything to go by, he had little control over. But whatever the reason for his need, he was certainly not above using their attraction for political gain.

Even knowing this, she longed for him as their lips parted.

General Tulkhan waved to the men gathered below and shouted: 'Time to ride.'

They cheered.

'Ride safely, ride swiftly,' she gave him the formal reply.

He strode off, cloak lifting. Imoshen remained where she was to see him off.

She was still standing on the battlements when the sun rose and the tail end of the Ghebite General's men entered the distant thick woods.

Her gaze travelled the fields, taking in the campfires and makeshift dwellings. The land below the stronghold walls teamed with refugees, desperate people who had come to her for safety.

A new phase in her life had begun. Whether she had intended it or not, she had made a commitment to General Tulkhan and she had to see it through.

Just as she had done whatever was necessary to ensure her personal survival, she would do whatever was needed to ensure the survival of her dream. The people of Fair Isle had no one else to care for their future.

As far as she knew, T'Reothe, General Tulkhan and King Gharavan were following their own plans for their own ends. True, she wanted to survive, but she wanted more.

Fair Isle and its people were hers to protect.

GENERAL TULKHAN'S TROOPS were used to moving quickly and they made good time despite a chilling downpour the following day.

The scouts spotted the desperate townsfolk on the great eastern road out of T'Diemn. Those who were able to run fled from the Ghebite scouts, but several, mainly the old and injured, were captured and delivered to Tulkhan. He knew the value of information and ordered the columns to stop while he questioned them.

He had a hard time convincing the poor wretches he was not going to summarily execute them. They spoke of cruelty, of mass murder. Rumour had it every inhabitant of T'Diemn was dead.

Tulkhan's army marched on, leaving the people he'd questioned by the side of the road. They watched him and his men with dull eyes, seething with the hatred born of powerless desperation.

He'd spoken to them personally, struggling with the local patois, but many of them spoke the more common language of trade. Tulkhan told them to go home, to tell the people who had fled their farms to return to their homes and villages, that there would be no more killing.

They did not seem convinced.

It was late afternoon when Tulkhan saw the fabled T'Diemn for the first time. The setting sun painted the domes and spires, cloaking the destruction caused by the invaders with a deceptive golden haze. Some of that haze had to be smoke hanging heavy on the still air.

The city had sprawled beyond its original fortified walls. From the rise where his party stood, Tulkhan could see that the more recent outer buildings of T'Diemn still smouldered in places.

As they rode down the paved road he recognised the signs of a prosperous city. Beside the road stood little shrines made of dressed stone and they were clearly well cared for. But as he came closer to the outlying buildings he could see the devastation.

In the steadily growing twilight the stench of smoke hung on the air, rich with the stink of death. No children ran in the burnt out streets, no chickens or pigs. What buildings remained were boarded up and shuttered. The General sensed hostility and fear, as if the city were drawing its collective breath to face another onslaught.

A deep and pervading anger settled in Tulkhan's core. He knew from experience that sometimes a show of force was necessary, but he abhorred senseless cruelty and destruction. Behind him his men were silent; the only sounds were the chink of their weapons and the creak of their horses' gear, punctuated by the steady thud of the horses' hooves.

When he crossed the bridge and approached the great gates which pierced the wall of the inner city Tulkhan saw the heads on the pikes and his fury rose a notch. Making an example of three assassins who had attempted to take his life was one thing, killing townsfolk who had laid down their weapons after surrendering was unacceptable.

Tulkhan tried to imagine his charming young half-brother giving the order and could not. Gharavan was not vindictive. When Tulkhan had last seen the youth he would have sworn he did not have the ruthless nature required for this.

No one opposed them as General Tulkhan and his men entered the oldest part of the city and made their way up through the winding streets to the tall spires of the royal palace.

The nearer they came to the city centre, the less destruction Tulkhan saw. He noted his brother's men lying drunk in the streets. His own men rode by without answering their bawdy cries.

Here, not every place was boarded shut and the taverns were open, doing a roaring trade. No doubt the women of the street were busy as well. But the respectable townsfolk made their opinion clear by their absence.

Tulkhan entered the main square where the rain had washed most of the blood from the stones. He paused to study the royal palace. Which building was it? A great multi-domed structure stood on the west side of the square, facing a large, many-towered building on the east. Smaller but equally spectacular buildings faced the square on the north and south sides.

He had read of the wonders of Fair Isle. Its wealth and culture was legendary on the mainland. This was why he had diverted. After the Low-lands negotiated a surrender without resistance, the southern kingdoms had expected him to continue south on the mainland to consolidate his hold but Tulkhan had other plans. He wanted Fair Isle. He believed that if Fair Isle fell, it would demoralise the southern kingdoms. Strike swiftly, strike unexpectedly, that was his credo, and look where it had led him – to the very palace of the T'En.

Triumph and contempt made him smile, for these legendary rulers of Fair Isle had not felt the need to build their palace as a defensible last stand. In their arrogance they had created a palace of fragile glass and delicate stone towers.

At that moment the clouds parted and the setting sun bathed the white stone of the building crimson. The palace blazed with a welcome glow of light against the blue-black clouds of the retreating storm.

But Tulkhan did not mistake this for an omen. He knew the real storm lay inside. Dismounting, he ordered his commanders to have the men camp in the square. They could have taken shelter in the palace or claimed any building they took a liking to, but Tulkhan wanted his men isolated from the rot he had found in his half-brother's army. Leaving the commanders to make camp with their usual efficiency, Tulkhan entered the palace by one of the largest entrances.

A young, slightly drunk Ghebite soldier straightened at his approach.

Recognising Tulkhan, he blinked and tried to draw his weapon in formal salute. The General brushed past him wordlessly, too angry to speak.

He followed the bawdy music, laughter and feminine squeals down a series of long formal galleries. Hundreds of candles were already alight, filling the air with their scented wax.

His boots crunched on the smashed glass and crockery, which littered the brilliant floor mosaics. Wall hangings so rich the colours glowed, hung lopsided from their frames. The destruction reminded him of animals invading a home, smashing, eating and fornicating at will, unable to appreciate the beauty of their surroundings.

How Imoshen would mock him if she could see this.

Imoshen... he felt a yearning deep within him, and was glad she was not there to witness this destruction.

Shame filled him, quickly replaced by anger.

Tulkhan thrust open double doors to see half a dozen Ghebite soldiers drinking and gambling. He took in their state of undress and inebriation. Amongst them he recognised a number of the small-boned, golden-skinned males and females of Fair Isle decked out in borrowed finery. Their overbright, frightened eyes watched him carefully.

Tulkhan marched straight across to a young Ghebite noble and pulled him upright by his fancy vest. 'Where is Gharavan?'

The young noble gasped and tried to focus his wine dulled wits. 'General Tulkhan?'

'Where is my brother?'

Startled, the youth plucked ineffectually at Tulkhan's hands, but his voice held a note of reprimand when he replied. 'The King is in the far chamber, entertaining.'

Tulkhan tossed the youth back onto the ornate couch with the others. Before this campaign the young men who had associated with his halfbrother had respected him. To them he was the triumphant General Tulkhan, almost a legendary figure.

In those days the young nobles as yet unblooded by war had been eager to hear stories of his battles. Tulkhan cursed softly. Now his half-brother ruled and he was expected to show respect to these puppies!

'Take me to him,' Tulkhan ground out, hardly able to contain his fury.

The youth stood and straightened his clothes.

'This way, *General.*' He made the title an insult.

As Tulkhan entered the throne room of the T'En Emperor he was only dimly aware of the white walls inlaid with pale golden designs. His gaze was drawn through the tall multi-paned windows to the leaping flames of a huge bonfire in the courtyard beyond. The hungry blaze cast bizarre moving patterns over the room's inhabitants. Leering, leaping shadows danced along the walls. Tulkhan felt as if he had entered a waking nightmare.

This room was even more crowded than the outer chamber. Hundreds of scented candles hung from ornate candelabras or littered the tables. They were crusted heavily with several days' wax and some were dying in their own wax puddles. The room's inhabitants consisted of his half-brother and his advisors. Some were old, wily men Tulkhan recognised as advisors to his father, others were ambitious and brash, barely out of their teens like his half-brother. They were dressed in what he assumed was the latest fashion of the Ghebite court.

Food was piled high on several low tables. Fair Isle musicians played unfamiliar instruments. Pretty young locals, both men and women, were scattered amongst the Ghebites, who ceased their revelry when they caught sight of Tulkhan.

The silence spread. It was not a welcoming silence.

Sprawled on a luxurious day-bed surrounded by sycophants, Gharavan's face settled into petulant lines. Tulkhan's heart sank.

News of his father's death had come to Tulkhan on the battlefield. He had sent his sworn fealty to his half-brother and continued the campaign. Now that Gharavan was no longer the boy-heir, Tulkhan was ready to accord him the respect due to the ruler of the Ghebites. He strode forward purposefully, his boots striking the tiles loudly in the hushed silence. He felt the eyes of the assembled elite of King Gharavan's travelling court on him. Some were amused and curious, but others were openly contemptuous.

Tulkhan tensed. He had never been a courtier, content to play lap dog at his father's side. There was no warmth in his half-brother's eyes, only wary resentment.

Where was the happy-go-lucky boy he remembered?

Tulkhan dropped to one knee. King or not, he really wanted to haul this weak youth outside and douse his head under a water pump before knocking some sense into him.

Instead, General Tulkhan placed his hand over his chest and bowed his head. 'The last royal stronghold is taken, the people from this town to Landsend swear allegiance to you, my king. As do I, your half-brother, General of the Ghebite army.'

The relief in the room was palpable.

His half-brother swung his feet to the floor and sat up on the day, pushing a partially clad girl away.

'Tulkhan!' His eyes blazed with drunken fondness and a certain sly satisfaction. 'So you've finally torn yourself away from your campaigning to come and swear fealty.'

Tulkhan rose and glared down at his half-brother, seeing the old familiar pettiness, the inclination to self-indulgence, written in his features. These were things he had always regarded as youthful excesses. What might have been charming and forgiven in a young boy were dangerous weaknesses in a king. But Tulkhan knew this was not the time to berate his half-brother.

'You will wish to hear how the campaign went,' he announced. 'Where will we go?'

Clearly Gharavan had no such wish but he came to his feet, overcome as always by Tulkhan's stronger will.

'The antechamber at the far end would be suitable, my king,' a Vaygharian of about Tulkhan's age advised. 'I will have food and wine sent through to you.'

King Gharavan hesitated, then seemed to decide to make the best of it. Swinging his arm through Tulkhan's, he ambled toward the far door, waving to the musicians. 'Continue.'

As Tulkhan drew nearer he could read fear in their faces. Though the Fair Isle musicians smiled and inclined their heads in obedience to the invading King, their hearts were closed. They hated him. His half-brother had done irreparable damage to the peace. It was one thing to capture a land, quite another to hold it.

When they entered the antechamber, a servant was hurriedly scurrying out after lighting a sconce of scented candles. The far door had barely closed when Tulkhan rounded on his half-brother.

'What were you thinking, to murder your subjects like this?'

'I had to teach them respect. These townsfolk were over-proud. True, they surrendered, but they smirked behind my back and called me a barbarian!'

'So you proved them right?' Rage flooded Tulkhan. 'What possessed you?'

'I had to break them, to show them I had ultimate power. Only fear would bring them to their knees –'

'With hate in their hearts and a knife at the ready behind their backs!' Tulkhan paced to the tall windows and looked into the courtyard, where embers from the fire blew on the breeze. What was Gharavan burning? A charred manuscript lay in the cinders. Tulkhan ground his teeth, knowing the evidence would only confirm Imoshen's opinion of the Ghebites.

'Now they jump to do my bidding,' Gharavan insisted, surly and defensive.

'Only because they fear you.'

The young King laughed, an odd high sound almost unsteady. 'And don't they fear you, Tulkhan the Ghebite General?'

Tulkhan turned and caught his half-brother by his rich brocade vest. He smelled wine on Gharavan's breath. It disgusted him.

'They respect me. I keep my word.' He watched as his half-brother blinked uneasily. 'I can't believe you gave this order. Who advised you on this mad venture? Didn't you realise you were fostering insurgence?'

'Insurgence?' a voice repeated.

Tulkhan spun to see the dark-haired Vaygharian who had suggested they use this room. He had always distrusted the Vayghars. In his father's youth, the Vayghar nation had chosen to form an alliance with Gheeaba rather than do battle. Since then they had grown rich feasting on the wealth of Ghebite conquests, and their merchant-aristocracy had infiltrated the upper echelons of Gheeaba.

Tulkhan turned to his half-brother, who made the introduction.

'My advisor, Kinraid of the Vayghar.'

Kinraid inclined his head, offering the merest civility of greeting. Tulkhan felt an instinctive dislike.

'You spoke of insurgence?' Kinraid smiled. In Gheeaba it was said a Vaygharian could smile while he traded you out of your home and wives. 'You, who harbour Imoshen, last T'En Princess? Even now rebels gather in the forested highlands to the south, plotting to steal back Fair Isle. The Princess will be their rallying point, a throwback, a Dhamfeer bitch. Was bedding her worth the risk?'

Anger blazed through Tulkhan's veins. He wanted to cross that space between them, take the Vaygharian by the throat and throttle the life from him. He'd already taken two steps when he collected himself.

The Vayghar smiled.

The man was no fool – Tulkhan could read malevolent intelligence in Kinraid's gaze. With a start he realised this Vayghar was his real enemy. This was the man who had been whispering poison in his half-brother's ear.

Tulkhan felt them both watching him, waiting for his reaction. If he were to answer the provocation now, his half-brother would be justified in calling the guards. Gharavan could have him executed in self-defence and his own men would be helpless to come to his aid. They would be fed a pack of lies they wouldn't believe, but their allegiance was to the throne and if their General was dead, what was the point of opposing their king?

All this flashed through Tulkhan's mind in less than a heartbeat. He must tread warily.

'T'Imoshen has given me her word.' He used her title. 'She will not urge the thousands of peasants who have fled to Umasreach Stronghold to rise against us.'

'And why should we believe this Dhamfeer bitch?' his half-brother asked, belligerence lighting his dark eyes.

Tulkhan met Gharavan's gaze and knew at that moment he trusted Imoshen, the Dhamfeer woman, more than his own flesh and blood.

He had made this boy his first wooden practice sword and taught him to fight. He had picked him up when he fell off his horse, dusted him off, soothed his hurts and loved him like a father. Their own father had been too obsessed with ruling his growing lands to take the time to father his sons.

Tulkhan lifted a hand and saw his half-brother flinch, but he laid it gently on Gharavan's shoulder. 'Unless you want the whole country rising against you, you must stop this vindictive slaughter. Offer them an honourable peace. There is much we can learn from these people. Theirs is an ancient culture.'

Gharavan searched his face and for a moment Tulkhan was reminded of a younger, charming youth who had listened breathlessly to tales of his campaigns.

'It is much easier to rule by love than fear. Fear must be enforced, love is given.' They were old lessons, learnt at the knee of his tutor who had stood in for his absent parent. Gharavan nodded and Tulkhan forged on, hope rising in his chest. 'We must win back their trust and respect. Make reparation to the families of the guildmasters, call on the leaders of the city to help govern T'Diemn. They know the needs of the city and its people –'

'And all of this will stop the rebels?' Kinraid asked.

Tulkhan turned to him. 'No, but it is better to fight on one front than two. We need to secure the townspeople's loyalty.'

'And what of your loyalty?' The Vaygharian strode toward them, placing a protective hand on the young King's shoulder. 'I did not see you swearing fealty when Gharavan was crowned. You walk in here, criticise his judgment and order him about. Who is the King here?'

A spasm of anger gripped Tulkhan. He could already see the doubts taking root in his half-brother's febrile mind. 'My loyalty is not at doubt. I serve the King. I have secured Fair Isle for his glory –'

'Secured it?' Kinraid sneered. 'Not when the rebels congregate in the southern highlands and prepare to make forays against us.'

'True.' Gharavan was ready to find fault with Tulkhan. 'What of this T'Reothe? I hear he's the last Dhamfeer Prince, betrothed to the bitch you are so hot for.'

Tulkhan winced. The Vaygharian's eyes gleamed with satisfaction.

They could not know whether he had bedded Imoshen or not. It was simply speculation, but it revealed the way their minds worked. They were united against him and unwilling to listen to reason.

Tulkhan could see the Vaygharian's manoeuvrings as clearly as if they were laid out on a chart before him, but could think of no way to avoid the coming confrontation.

'If you were truly loyal to King Gharavan,' Kinraid announced, 'you would take your men and lead them in the service of your king. Clear out the rebel camps.'

'Yes. Wipe them out like the vermin they are.' Gharavan's face glowed at the thought.

Tulkhan could not afford to hesitate, it would only confirm his disloyalty. Yet... 'The highlands are inhospitable. In places, a whole army could disappear and not find its way out. The rebels have chosen well.'

'You refuse my order?' his half-brother demanded.

'No.' Tulkhan tried not to let reluctance show in his voice. 'I serve my king, and my advice is not tainted by personal gain. Remember that, Vanny.' He deliberately his brother's childhood nickname. The Vaygharian might be a clever, cunning man, but he did not have their shared history. 'I will stay a few days and help to restore order and placate the townspeople. Then I will take my forces south to seek the rebels.'

It took four days to calm the people of T'Diemn. Tulkhan lost count of the number of times he needed Imoshen's sage advice. He did not know these people, their customs or their beliefs.

Acting under vague orders from his half-brother, he saw to it that fires were extinguished, food distributed and the damaged homes were rebuilt by the King's own soldiers.

He met with the various leaders of the city, from the civil administrators and guildmasters to the head of the T'En church. The Beatific was a woman, which once again reminded him of the differences in their cultures. In T'En society there were many women in positions of authority. They were mature women, who by Ghebite standards would have been considered non-persons. But they spoke with the weight of experience and he could not fault their advice.

He saw to it that businesses and produce markets reopened and normal services were resumed.

Tulkhan offered his personal apology to those who had lost loved ones, and through it all he focused on the outcome. If he did not win over the people of T'Diemn and the rebels roused the countryside against him, the townspeople would welcome them into the capital at the first opportunity.

He could not afford to lose the support of the people of T'Diemn.

If there was an overwhelming swing against the Ghebites, he was doubtful of Imoshen's loyalty. She was a pragmatist, and he had to admit that if he were in her position, he would side with the winning army whether it was invader or rebel. Imoshen wanted peace for her people, not years of protracted warfare.

On the evening of the fourth day, Tulkhan strode into the private entertainment wing of the royal palace, looking for his half-brother. He wanted to return to the stronghold to be certain of Imoshen's loyalty, but he told himself this was unnecessary. Unless other factors changed, Imoshen would keep her word.

It had been a harrowing six days since he'd ridden out of Umasreach Stronghold, six days apart from Imoshen when he had been living day and night with her. He could have used her reassuring presence and her diplomatic skills on many occasions. While dealing with the townspeople, he had even considered sending for her.

But the knowledge that he had sworn to enter the southern highlands to hunt the rebels stopped him. Much as he needed her, he could not bring Imoshen to the palace and leave her at the mercy of his half-brother and that treacherous Vaygharian.

Tulkhan grimaced as he heard the usual sounds of revelry. The room was full of young Ghebite nobles for whom the campaign had been one good billet after another, one party after another while the foot soldiers moved on ahead and cleaned up resistance. Sprinkled amidst them were the fawning advisors who curried favour with King Gharavan, offering him the words he most wanted to hear and nothing else. Tulkhan was surprised by a surge of hatred for them all.

Those nearest the entrance looked over at him. No one offered a friendly greeting.

He had noticed a definite change in these young men. Where once the youths had hung on his every word, now a subtle rot had set in. They cast him sly, mocking looks, and there were barely whispered jokes about the man who lay with the Dhamfeer. His part in the Harvest Feast was common knowledge, not that he regretted it.

Despite this, Tulkhan remained hopeful. On the few occasions he had been alone with his half-brother he had managed to talk some sense and plan for the future of Fair Isle. Now he hoped for one last talk before he left. He had to impress his loyalty on the youth.

The smaller antechamber where he and Gharavan had had their first private meeting seemed a sensible place to look for his half-brother. Someone tittered as he strode toward the door. Tulkhan ignored them. There wasn't a man amongst them he would choose to have at his back in a fight.

He thrust the door open and stepped inside, expecting to catch his brother with one of the wenches. Instead he found Gharavan and the Vaygharian naked on the fur before the fire.

Gharavan lifted his head, visibly annoyed at the interruption. Tulkhan cursed. This was worse than he expected. It was common for young Ghebite men to take male lovers. It was encouraged in the ranks, because it cemented the bonds and made a stronger fighting force. But now Tulkhan understood the hold the Vaygharian had over his half-brother. No wonder he would not listen. As long as Kinraid was Gharavan's lover, the youthful King would always give more weight to his words.

The Vaygharian raised himself on one elbow and studied Tulkhan calmly, making no attempt to cover his nakedness.

'What do you want?' Gharavan snapped.

'I ride at dawn,' Tulkhan's voice revealed nothing of his feelings. 'The townspeople are resigned. They will bring their disputes to your tribunal for satisfaction. It is your chance to prove just.' His brother waved this aside, irritating Tulkhan. He wanted to say more, but with the Vaygharian's insolent eyes on him he knew it was pointless. 'I will go to my bunk. Good night.'

'So early? Why don't you take one those willing girls or boys?' Gharavan's smile was vicious and vindictive. 'Ah, but I forgot, your tastes do not run that way. I'm afraid we haven't any Dhamfeer to indulge you. In my court we draw the line at bestiality!'

The insult was delivered with more venom than Tulkhan had expected of his half-brother and he knew from the satisfied smirk on Kinraid's face that something similar must have passed his lips recently.

Seething with anger, Tulkhan turned and left them, marching through the cluster of men and women. They watched him, amused by his disgrace. It struck him with a savage sorrow that he was watching the decline of his father's power. The old master who taught him tactics was right – a monarchy is only as strong as its king.

IMOSHEN FINISHED BRAIDING her hair and tossed the heavy plait over her shoulder. So far so good. Nothing had arisen that she could not deal with. As leader of Tulkhan's elite guard, Wharrd reported to her. The Ghebites had responded to her orders promptly, without a grumble. They were vastly outnumbered by her own stronghold guard and the refugees, and very aware of it.

To keep everyone occupied and because it served a useful purpose, she had set the able-bodied adults to building a new town on the plain below Umasreach. Sturdy wooden houses were springing up, with broad paths between them. If the refugees were to survive the bitter winter as well as the threat of disease through overcrowding, simple sanitation had to be observed, fresh water supplied and waste disposed of.

Already people were setting up shops to supply their trades. She'd spotted the signs for seamstresses, carpenters, bakers and cobblers. From the battlements yester-eve she had marvelled to see a town emerging, one that would rival T'Diemn in size and population, if not in cultural accomplishments.

'My Lady T'En,' Kalleen gasped as she ran into the room. 'I would have been here to do your hair, but you did not ring.'

'I could not sleep.' Imoshen rose and stepped closer to her maid. She could smell lovemaking on Kalleen's body and recognised the scent of the youth, Drake. 'Should I look to find a place for Drake in the stronghold? Since old man Larkin died and his apprentice went off to war and got himself killed, we've been without a silversmith.'

Kalleen shrugged, her cheeks very pink. 'It's early days yet.'

Imoshen laughed and swung her cloak around her shoulders. Even inside the stronghold it had grown colder. The sooner they finished the shelters the better for those on the plane.

She was climbing the stairs after taking inventory of the food stores when Drake stepped from the shadows. His intense gaze held hers, their faces level. Something was amiss. His over-bright eyes worried her.

Imoshen touched his forehead, checking for fever. 'What is it, Drake, are you unwell?'

He caught her hand, his trembled with energy.

She assumed he had come to speak of Kalleen and nervousness held his tongue. 'Tell me what you wish.'

'Lady T'En.' He fell to his knees, bringing her hand to his lips. 'I am here to serve you. I know how General Tulkhan has forced you to serve him. But he is gone and I'm well enough now. I have two horses saddled. You can escape, to the forests, to the rebels. I hear T'Reothe himself leads them –'

'Hush!' Imoshen stiffened. For the moment the elite guard were obeying her, but she knew their ultimate loyalty was to Tulkhan. If they knew Reothe was nearby... 'You mustn't speak his name here. The stronghold and all who live here are sworn to General Tulkhan's service. Besides...'

She hesitated, looking into his earnest face. The bruising over his eye had faded to a greenish yellow now. He was so young, so sincere and so eager to die for a cause.

Even though they were about the same age, she felt immeasurably older than him. With a tug she urged him to rise. 'Who knows if Reothe lives? They say he leads the rebels, but it could be some imposter using his name. Winter will be upon us soon and the rebels will have to suffer through it in the deep woods, without shelter or safety from pursuit.'

Drake did not look convinced.

'The stronghold needs you.' She tried again. 'We have no silversmith.'

Servants came up the stairs eager to consult Imoshen about household arrangements. The youth uttered an impatient exclamation. She smiled and squeezed his hand, then turned to deal with the servants. When she had finished he was gone.

Imoshen sighed. Instinct told her Drake had not been persuaded.

That evening, as she sat before the fire calculating how to bring water from the underground caverns into the new town, Kalleen came to prepare her for bed. The young girl's hair was untidy, her face truculent and her eyes red-rimmed. Intent on her work, Imoshen didn't notice the signs at first.

'I need an engineer like the one who...' she ran down as she looked up. 'Why, what is wrong, Kalleen?'

The girl brushed her cheek impatiently. 'He's gone.'

'Drake?' Imoshen's heart sank. She did not have to be told where he had gone – in search of Reothe, glory and death. 'I offered him a place here.'

'I know.' A bitter sob escaped Kalleen. 'It was not enough. *I* was not enough for him.'

Imoshen came to her feet, hugging the girl. There was nothing she could say.

FAR TO THE south in the treacherous highlands, Tulkhan led his mount up the steep incline. Behind him his men were scattered over the slope. The noise of their passage was enough to wake the dead. Spread out as they were, they offered a prime target for ambush.

He felt the sweat of fear drying on his skin. Here on the northern slope of the hillside he was shielded from the cold wind and the sun was a welcome change from the chill that crept up through a man's boots into his bones, stealing his very passion for life.

The same chill had seen dozens of his men come down with a bone-shaking fever. He'd had to leave them in the small villages that dotted the southern highlands and trust they would not be murdered in their sick beds.

He reached the crest and looked out to the south over the densely wooded ridges that stretched like frozen green waves, rolling all the way to the distant southern ocean. It was impossible to march an army through land like this. The rebel leader would find it ideal for ambush.

Tulkhan was only too aware of their vulnerability. If he'd been Reothe, instead of the pursuer on this fool's errand hunting shadows, he would have harried his pursuer till not a man stood.

Only two nights ago he and his men had accepted the hospitality of one of the T'En southern nobles. It did not take Tulkhan long to recognise the signs. The man and his family were giving lip service to the Ghebites, but their true loyalty lay with the rebels.

When the nobleman claimed he knew nothing of the rebels' whereabouts, Tulkhan could have threatened to execute him. This might have loosened the tongues of his three daughters, but it would have made them hate him and strengthened their resolve to stay loyal to the old regime.

The eldest girl reminded him of Imoshen even though she was only part Dhamfeer. He caught himself wishing Imoshen were with him, riding at his side. The local villagers would have answered her questions and she would have known if they were lying.

Mist clung in the hollows between the ridges. There were no visible signs of the rebels' passage, nothing to tell the General he wasn't wandering pointlessly through these accursed blue hills.

Only the fact that seven nights ago one of his advance parties had been massacred to a man told him he was on their trail. After that he'd sent two commanders out with a number of his men on alternative routes, in the hope of flushing the rebels out.

But his men had not returned. They had local guides who knew the paths and the caves, much good it did them.

His local guide was proving annoyingly obtuse. Not that the man actually lied to him, as far as Tulkhan could tell, but getting information from him was like extracting teeth.

Tulkhan cursed softly. 'What is that slim column of smoke?'

A finger of smoke hung on the still air in one of the deep ravines. When it reached the turbulent upper air it vanished.

The guide shaded his eyes and gave a non-committal shrug. 'Could be bush fire. Lots of fires this time of year.'

'Could it be the rebel camp?' Tulkhan persisted.

The guide turned burnished gold eyes on him. The man was a True-man like Tulkhan, but of a baser race, one of the very old stock who had settled Fair Isle so long ago they had grown apart from their mainland cousins. His colouring, his accent all marked him. In his own way he was as alien to the Ghebites as Imoshen.

'If you were leading the rebels would you leave a smoking cooking fire to mark your camp?' the guide asked.

Tulkhan cursed. 'Then it's a small crop holder?'

'Could be.' His guide shrugged.

'We'll go there.'

The guide shifted and Tulkhan thought he sensed reluctance. Was the man hiding something?

'How long will it take us to get there?' Tulkhan asked. It seemed only a short way, but he had learnt that distances were deceptive, particularly in these dense highlands. There were two ridges between them and the deep ravine. With no paths, the ravines could prove impassable. The army could lose a whole day in backtracking.

The guide shaded his eyes and studied the terrain. 'Go that way. All day.'

Tulkhan frowned. The rebels would be long gone if it was their camp, but at least he would be able to tell if he was on their trail.

He signalled to the men to move out. Stoically, they responded.

He should have left the horses quartered on the planes. But who was to say they would be there when he returned? He hadn't known that the southern highlands would be so impassable.

They travelled for the most of the day. As far as Tulkhan could tell, the guide might have purposefully chosen the roughest, most uncomfortable path for him and his men. But he could see no easier route, so he held his peace.

The cold was seeping up through the ground and the sun no longer reached the ravine's deep valley floor when they neared their destination. It was time to find a place to camp. Every night he tried to select a spot they could defend if attacked. It was rarely ideal.

As they advanced in the steadily growing twilight, Tulkhan felt on edge. He paused and sniffed. There was a strange tang on the air and he could have sworn the valley floor was not as cold as it had been before.

He turned to the guide, only to see him making a sign across his chest and eyes.

'What's this?'

'Holy place.' The guide would not meet his eyes. 'Not a good place to go.'

Tulkhan wondered if the guide was trying to divert him. 'Move on.'

He forged ahead, rounding a bend in the ravine floor to find a relatively open space where the new scent was even stronger.

A low mist clung to the stones and spindly trees, making it impossible to see more than a few feet ahead of them.

But there was a stream and it would provide a relatively safe place to camp for the night. Tulkhan strode over to the brook and dipped his hand in. His cold fingers registered the warmth of the water. It was almost hot enough to bathe in. His eyes narrowed. This wasn't mist. The place was shrouded in steam which rose from vents in the rocks.

'What manner of place is this?'

But the guide had moved ahead, leaping from smooth river stone to stone, over the stream. Tulkhan followed, growing uneasy as the mist thickened and visibility dropped.

He found the guide crouched before a flat-topped stone, blackened by fire.

The guide made a complicated sign and left some of his hard cakes on the stone. 'For the Guardian. We go now.'

'Wait. What is this place?'

'Old. Older than the T'En, older even than my people. Not a good place to stay.'

Tulkhan was inclined to agree, but it was almost dark and they couldn't risk stumbling about in the ravines. He'd already lost men and horses due to falls.

'We camp here for the night.'

The guide stifled an involuntary exclamation.

Tulkhan's eyes narrowed. 'I'll have one of my men leave an offering on the stone for the Guardian. Satisfied?'

The guide said nothing.

Retracing his steps across the stream, Tulkhan went to check on his men. They filled the ravine floor. With practised ease they were selecting places to make campfires, places to bed down and spots for lookouts.

Tulkhan beckoned the soldier who handled the cooking. He chose a fine pullet hen, 'donated' from the nobleman's kitchen.

'Will this do?' Tulkhan asked the guide.

The man glanced to the bird, then away. He gave a shrug.

Exasperation made Tulkhan impatient. He was trying to meet these people half way.

He had always made it his policy to pay lip service to the religion of conquered countries. Men who had lost everything would risk everything. Men who had scraps feared losing even those. Give the masses food and religion and it would keep them quiet, if not content. 'Come.'

The guide followed silently, almost reluctantly.

Grabbing the chicken by its legs, the General stalked off with it squawking indignantly. He felt ridiculous, hungry and tired as he crossed the stream and returned to the sacrificial stone. He wished he had never come to the southern highlands to hunt rebels. But he was determined.

Tulkhan laid the bird on the stone and took out his ceremonial dagger. 'Is there any formal observances I should make?'

'A little of your own blood should mix with the sacrifice's.'

Tulkhan grimaced. It was like other religious procedures he had witnessed. Every country thought their religion superior.

He snorted. By the gods, he had grown cynical. Pricking the ball of his thumb, he squeezed out a drop or two onto the stone. 'Like so?'

But when he looked up the guide had backed away.

The man made the sign over his eyes and again over his chest. Tulkhan shrugged. Whatever he might think of their religion, the guide at least believed in its power.

Tulkhan's stomach rumbled. He wanted to get this over and done with and have his dinner.

With one slash, he sliced off the chicken's head, letting its blood flow over the stone. The blood poured hot on the stone, so hot it bubbled. Hissing steam rose, obscuring everything, even the guide who stood only a body-length from him.

The hairs on the back of Tulkhan's neck rose in protest. His heart hammered as he recognised a creeping sensation. He could feel a tingling on his tongue, that familiar metallic taste he associated with a gathering of power.

'What's happening?' Tulkhan hated the note of panic in his voice.

The guide's answer came from a great distance. He was no longer subservient, but insolent and pleased. 'You have fed the Ancients. Now they will feed on you. Feel the Guardian's power!'

The steam almost blanketed out all noise, but Tulkhan could hear the guide scrambling for his life. He dropped the body of the chicken and turned. But a wave of dizziness swamped him.

He could not tell which way the camp lay, no sound came through the mist. An ominous sense of expectancy hung on the air. Tulkhan cursed himself for a fool.

He drew his sword, vowing to sell his life dearly, but in his heart of hearts he suspected the Guardian could not be hurt by cold steel.

Blood pounded through his head, drumming in his ears. Was it really his own blood, or the sound of a drum beat and the chanting of voices? Red leaping shadows filled the mists.

His mouth went dry with fear.

Incongruously he saw the mists before him part to reveal a sexless, naked child of eight or nine. This apparition raised ageless, ancient eyes to study Tulkhan.

A great oppression settled on him.

He wanted to drop to his knees and beg the child's forgiveness.

Abruptly the drum beats faded and the steam swirled behind the child, who turned as someone or something approached. Glowing opalescence travelled through the mist in expanding waves.

Then, as if the mist were a living thing, it exhaled, revealing a tall, slender T'En male who stepped from its embrace. Tulkhan blinked, shielding his eyes. The man seemed to carry his own inner illumination.

Squinting into the glare, Tulkhan gasped. He was looking at a male version of Imoshen. The man was pure T'En. He had the same narrow nose, high cheekbones and wine-dark eyes, and he was clad for war.

The warrior frowned at him. 'What mischief have you been working, Ghebite? Don't you know the Ancients are greedy once awakened?'

Tulkhan glanced around, but the child was gone. Had that sexless creature been one of the Ancients? Was this man the Guardian? Was he some past T'En warrior bound by a curse to patrol this place?

'Well?' the intruder demanded.

'I sought only to honour the local's beliefs.' Tulkhan was surprised to hear the firm tone of his voice. Who would guess his heart was hammering? 'Who are you, the Guardian?'

'Guardian?' The feral red eyes gleamed and Tulkhan could have sworn the T'En was laughing silently at him. 'In a way. Who are you?'

'General Tulkhan, half-brother to King Gharavan.'

This time the T'En warrior did laugh, a bitter rueful laugh. 'I should have let them devour your soul, General.'

Tulkhan's hand tightened on the sword. 'Who are you?'

'I am your death. You do not know it, but you are a dead man who walks and talks.' He executed a mocking bow. 'I am T'Reothe of the T'En.'

Tulkhan leapt forward, sword slashing to take the warrior in the gut. The blade travelled through Reothe's insubstantial body. The T'En's laughter poured over Tulkhan, scraping along his raw nerve ends as the momentum of his lunge met nothing and he staggered forward into the swirling mists. His boot skidded on the wet stone and he went down on one knee.

Even as he fell, he turned and lifted the sword point between them. But T'Reothe was gone.

Shouts. He heard his men calling his name. They charged through the mist, swords drawn, carrying burning brands.

Rising stiffly, Tulkhan favoured his injured knee and tried to calm his men. They had heard him give his battle cry and come to his aid.

By the time he had settled the camp and arranged the watches, Tulkhan was not surprised to learn their guide had disappeared. He would have liked to move camp but it was after dark and he had to satisfy himself with posting extra watches.

He shuddered, knowing that mere metal would be poor defence against an attack led by this T'Reothe.

As the men settled down for the night, Tulkhan paced the length of their scattered camp along the ravine floor. Huge fern trees rose above his head, dripping moisture from the heated misty air. His men were forced to spread out because the ravine was so narrow. They were vulnerable to ambush.

He hated this southern highland. He should never have come here. Driven by impatience, he kept patrolling, pausing to exchange a word here and there with the sentries. The spirits of his men always improved when they saw him.

But Tulkhan had no such faith in himself. He had seen his enemy in the flesh, or at least the insubstantial flesh. T'Reothe of the T'En was pure Dhamfeer. His skin crawled at the memory.

Tulkhan had experienced Imoshen's tricks first-hand. What more could this Reothe achieve? Even the ancient one had fled at the T'En warrior's approach. When Reothe had called him a dead man who walked and talked, somewhere deep inside Tulkhan felt as if a light had gone out.

He had looked into himself and discovered he was hollow, and he hated it. He had never felt inadequate before. How could he, a True-man, compete with the T'En warrior when cold steel could not wound insubstantial flesh?

But there was nothing insubstantial about Reothe's existence.

What if Imoshen discovered her betrothed was more than a rumour? If she knew Reothe lived, would she feel bound to honour her earlier vows? Would she see her male counterpart as the likely victor and change allegiance?

TWO DAYS LATER, Tulkhan spotted smoke and led his men to a ravine floor where they found the remains of one of his other contingents. More than forty men lay dead. The lone survivor was their commander, who had been tied to a stake unharmed.

When he saw them approach, his eyes rolled in terror, and he wept and laughed.

Tulkhan stepped forward as his men cut the survivor down and helped him massage sensation into his limbs.

'Leave me!' he shrieked, almost falling when they released him. The man stared at Tulkhan with a mixture of horror and relief. 'He said you would come. He said I would not have to wait long –'

'Who?' Tulkhan asked, although he suspected he knew the answer.

'T'Reothe. Two nights ago he led his people into our camp just before dawn. He left me with a message for you.'

The commander clamped his lips shut and his body shuddered.

'What message?' Tulkhan grimaced.

The man shook his head. 'The moment I tell you I will die.'

'Nonsense!' Tulkhan felt the men around him stir uneasily as a terrible sense of foreboding gripped him. He had to know the message. 'There is not a mark on you. No festering wound, nothing. You are untouched and healthy. Take heart. Give me the message.'

Tears slipped from the man's eyes, falling unheeded. He pulled his jerkin open to reveal his chest, marred only by a small burn. 'The T'En Prince touched the skin above my heart with the sixth finger of his left hand. He looked into my eyes and he said the moment I tell you his message my life will flee my body.' He dropped to his knees. 'Please don't make me tell you.'

Tulkhan hesitated. He could not afford to show weakness, yet the man's fear was very real. It made his own skin crawl with dread. 'Is it an important message?'

The commander nodded once. He took a deep breath, came to his feet and looked Tulkhan in the eye, giving the Ghebite salute. 'T'Reothe is going north to claim his betrothed, the Princess Imoshen.'

The words left his mouth in a great rush. He gasped, pressed his hands to his chest and stood absolutely still.

Tulkhan stared, unable to look away, unable to offer aid. Surely this Reothe could not kill by mere suggestion.

Tulkhan placed his arm on the man's shoulder in a gesture of solidarity. Silently the commander shook his head, clasped his own hand over his General's then frowned.

His body jerked once.

The breath left him in a long sigh. He swayed. Tulkhan cursed. His men swore by their many gods as their fellow soldier fell to his knees and pitched forward into the dirt, dead. Not one man tried to break his fall.

Even as Tulkhan knelt down to feel for the man's heartbeat, he knew what he would find. He had seen death too many times to be mistaken.

Fearful whispers told him Reothe's little ploy had done its damage.

'Get moving!' he bellowed. 'I want a funeral pyre for the fallen and the words said over them.'

He watched as his men worked efficiently, gathering dead wood to burn the bodies. Was Reothe headed north to Umasreach to claim Imoshen, or was he simply diverting Tulkhan?

The General had no way of knowing. How did you defeat someone who could move in mists and kill with a touch?

Despair gripped Tulkhan but he clamped down on it, knowing this was what Reothe wanted.

When the men lit the funeral pyre, he rose to his feet, his decision made. He would find the rest of his men before Reothe slaughtered them too. Then he would return to T'Diemn and report to his half-brother before going to Umasreach Stronghold.

He needed to warn Imoshen and, more than this, he needed her to tell him what manner of man he was fighting. Did Reothe have a weakness? Of course he did. If anyone knew T'Reothe's weak points it would be Imoshen.

Tulkhan tensed. What was he thinking? How could he confront Imoshen with the news her betrothed still lived and in the next breath demand she tell him, the Ghebite invader, how to defeat her T'En kin? How could he ask her to betray Reothe?

Did she love her betrothed? Did love enter into the proceedings of a T'En marriage of alliance? In Gheeaba a man looked for compliance and good family connections in his wife. Family loyalty...

Who would Imoshen choose to support, her once betrothed and near kin, or himself, the invader who had taken her stronghold by force?

Did he really want to know?

IMOSHEN AND HER mount made the crest with energy to spare. It was good to escape the confines of Umasreach along with the constraints of her position. She turned her horse to face the distant settlement. From here she could see the great walls and towers of the stronghold and the new town which sprawled at its feet.

Because the town had been designed, not grown, there was a broad avenue leading directly to the outer gates of the stronghold and wide streets which fanned out to ring the outer walls. Smoke rose from the many chimney tops. The familiar reassuring smell of baking and humanity carried on the afternoon breeze to her.

The sky held a heaviness which promised cold, perhaps even snow, tonight. She shivered. Soon winter would grip the kingdom. She shuddered to think how many people they would have lost without the efforts of the last large moon cycle. There was still work to be done. She had been busy settling disputes, while greater and lesser guilds had been formed and guildmasters elected to deal with their internal problems.

She sighed. There was still no word from General Tulkhan. But she had heard how he had calmed the townspeople of T'Diemn, and knew that despite the rumour that it was the King who had ordered these changes, she recognised Tulkhan's hand in them. She also knew that he was in the southern highlands, hunting the rebels, and she was troubled.

On a purely practical level, if Tulkhan should die, her position would be precarious. She would have to deal with young King Gharavan who, from what she had heard, would not be easy to reason with.

With the passing of the large moon cycle she knew the Aayel had been right. She had conceived. If Tulkhan died while she carried his son where did that leave her and the child? Her hands tightened on the reins as frustration filled her. She was still a piece in a larger game with no security.

Imoshen's horse shied and snickered. She stood up in the stirrups, twisting in the saddle to survey the woods behind her. The refugees' voracious need for timber for fuel and building materials meant the undergrowth had been cleared and suitable trees taken. Consequently the woods had retreated farther from the stronghold. She had travelled quite a distance to reach this knoll.

Come spring she hoped to see tilled fields below the knoll, stretching from here to the outskirts of town. They'd be needed to supply food for the new township. With a shudder she realised her world was changing. Her home would never again be as it was during her childhood.

Truly, she felt as if the person who had watched General Tulkhan's army march across the rolling grass was someone else. She had seen so much since then and so many others depended on her now.

It was a relief to get away from the constant demands of the stronghold, to be truly alone, her own person. Imoshen wondered if she would ever be as free as the child-woman who had unwittingly ridden into the woods with Reothe.

Knowing a little more now, she wondered if her parents had realised who he really was. They couldn't have known the extent of his abilities, else they wouldn't have let her ride off with him. She flushed and bit her lip.

He could have had her there on the grass and she would have welcomed him. The knowledge stung her pride, stained her cheeks. But even now the memory stirred her body and she could feel the tug of like to like.

Out here, away from the mundane demands of her position, she could face her fears. Was it true? Did she crave Reothe because only in his arms could she know her true mate, one whose abilities meshed with her own?

Something stirred and flickered to life in the back of her mind. She swallowed, noting a strange taste in her mouth, the way her heart pounded in her chest. Sounds and colours seemed unnaturally clear and bright. Scents became stronger.

Fear curled through her body, intimate as a lover, insistent as pain. No. She would not call on the T'En gift which lay dormant in her. She dreaded releasing what she did not understand and could not control. Worse, every time she flexed her powers it appeared to make her more vulnerable to Reothe. For an instant she seemed to hear his mocking laugh echo on the cry of a bird. She shuddered and banished him from her thoughts.

Since the night of the harvest moons nothing strange had happened. She had studiously avoided any use of her ability. She hadn't even tried to use her gift for healing. It was fear which held her back, fear of the unknown. If only the Aayel still lived!

With a sigh, Imoshen urged the horse off the crest and down into the woods behind. The path she had forged led back around the base of the knoll and down onto the plane.

So preoccupied was she that she had no presentiment of danger. When the body darted from the undergrowth and grabbed the horse's bridle there was nothing she could do. Before she could aim a kick at his head, another body tumbled from a low branch onto the horse, pulling her to the ground.

She fell with his weight atop her, knocking the wind from her chest. Stars spun in front of her eyes. Desperately, she fought to drag in a breath.

Someone pulled her upright into a sitting position and she blinked, trying to focus on the face.

'My lady?'

She knew that voice. 'D... Drake?'

He grinned, well pleased with himself. He looked leaner and scruffier. He was dressed in a farmer's practical winter furs, as were his two companions. They also smiled, pleased with themselves and with her.

Imoshen had a sinking suspicion. 'I'm glad you are safe, Drake. You know you and your friends can claim sanctuary in Umasreach any time –'

'No. You don't understand.' He gripped her arm, pulling her to her feet with the strength of a fanatic. 'Reothe sent me to bring you. We ride now.'

Chapter Seven

HER FIRST IMPULSE was to refuse him, emphatically. She had already refused Reothe once when he had come to her, and a second time when she had unwittingly gone to him.

But now it appeared her once-betrothed had tired of waiting. Imoshen knew a moment's panic.

She did not want to spend the winter hidden away in the deep woods, snowed-in with Reothe for company. It would give him the chance to work on her, claim her physically and then try to lay claim to her will and her gifts. What kind of abilities would they have if they were bonded? Was that why Reothe had been so eager to become betrothed?

For an instant, she had a vision of Reothe and herself – beautiful, terrible dictators ordering the lives of the inhabitants of Fair Isle. She shivered. No, she could not spend the winter in his camp, in his arms. Who knew what would be left of her *self* come spring?

But she could not begin explain this to Drake. She must play for time.

'You found him?' She searched the young man's face for any sign of doubt. Her hands went instinctively to his hand, to feel his bare flesh. But all she received in response was a flash of overwhelming certainty.

'I found him and others. More join us every day. The whole island would rise if it was known the last of the T'En rode together,' he assured her.

'And what would happen if I left Umasreach after giving my word? Think, Drake. Don't you care about the fate of our people there? Thousands rely on me. General Tulkhan would be justified in making an example of them. Would you have me abandon my people?'

She glanced swiftly to the other two, recognising their origins. Farmers were practical people, unlike Drake, who had known the comfort of town living. It was easy to be idealistic when you had enough to eat.

Drake looked stunned.

Imoshen pressed home her advantage. 'I can't abandon my people.'

'Your people?' his voice rose. 'You abandoned them to these Ghebite barbarians. Your betrothed, the last of the T'En, waits for you, T'Imoshen. The people would rise behind the true rulers. Now is the time to think on a grander scale. What is the fate of one stronghold when the whole Island is at stake?'

Imoshen's heart sank. The other two nodded, convinced by Drake's rhetoric. She looked down. Now was not the time to resist – she was outnumbered three to one.

'Come, the others are waiting.' Drake caught her arm. 'I promised Reothe I would not fail him.'

One of the men led her horse. Drake held her arm in what was meant to be a courteous grasp, but in effect he restrained her.

As they stumbled down the slope into the deeper woods, Imoshen's mind spun with ideas. She had to get away before they joined their larger party.

Her horse whinnied and another answered from behind the thicket. Four mounts as scruffy and ill-fed as their riders waited patiently with a fourth man holding the reins. His eyes widened when he saw her and he made the deep obeisance.

'Truly,' he whispered. 'She has the same look as our leader.'

Drake laughed. 'Why do you think he chose her?'

'We were betrothed,' Imoshen corrected.

Without warning, Drake spun her around, pulling her arms behind her back.

'Reothe warned me that the Ghebite General has influenced your mind, my lady. Forgive me.' He signalled the men. 'Bind her.'

One of them moved behind her and she felt him tie her hands with a leather strip. Imoshen resisted the urge to struggle, and instead managed a shaky laugh. 'Is this how you deliver Reothe his bride, bound?'

'Only a precaution, Lady T'En,' Drake said.

He helped her climb onto her horse and took the reins. She could have struggled, but that would have reduced them to rolling in the damp leaf litter in an ungainly heap and served no purpose. No, when she made her bid to escape she would make sure it was successful. Anger flashed through her, sharpening her senses, making her aware of that strange taste on her tongue and the tingling in her body as her gift gathered.

Drake mounted his own horse and pulled on the reins of her mount. One of the rebels rode before them and another two behind as Drake led her through the woods.

Imoshen's innate sense of direction told her they were heading away from the stronghold. Dusk closed in early as the temperature dropped, promising snow.

Imoshen shivered. She was not dressed for this. Soon her own people would wonder where she was. Would the stronghold guard turn on Tulkhan's elite guard? Would Wharrd assume she had betrayed them? It would be his duty to report her defection to the General.

What would Tulkhan think? Would he believe she had betrayed him? Her heart sank. How could he think otherwise? He wouldn't know she had been abducted.

Imoshen ducked her head as they wove under the branches of winter bare trees. It was growing darker by the moment and colder, yet they pushed on. Their destination must be nearby.

Her skin prickled with fear. She didn't want to face Reothe, didn't feel she had the resolve to resist the force of his will. She had to make a move soon.

'I'm cold,' Imoshen complained. 'Here I am, without even my winter cloak. I'll be wanting a word with Reothe when I see him. How much further till we reach him?'

'Not far, my lady,' Drake answered automatically. 'I'm sorry, I have no cloak to loan you.'

It was as she'd suspected. Imoshen leant low on the horse, feeling the warmth of its body. Fleetingly, she wished she was as unimportant as this horse.

A rush of alien images flooded her mind. Scent. Man smell. Cold, mingled with eager images of food and a warm stall, and underneath that, a dislike of the woods, a fear of predators.

When she lifted her head, her mind had cleared and she knew what to do. It was quite simple, really. They were deep in the woods now, with poor visibility. A light snow fell, coating everything with its soft white powder. Would it interfere with the scent? She wasn't sure. She made herself recall the rank smell of the predator which had stalked her and General Tulkhan that day near Landsend, how it had made her feel, the sheer terror she had fought to control. She recalled retreating up the slope with Tulkhan at her back, her knife at the ready. Then she projected that memory.

She couldn't have said how she did it, only that by reliving it, her body reacted as if she were experiencing it again and her horse reacted to the change in her body's scent. Her mount's fear communicated itself to the other horses and to the men with them. They drew closer.

'Strike fire!' Drake ordered, climbing off his mount. No one asked why.

Imoshen couldn't let them regain the security the naked flame offered. If only the snow would break a brittle branch...

Something snapped nearby, triggering a rush of raw energy.

From the dark undergrowth there came a muffled crack and the rapid pad of a heavy carnivore charging. Imoshen's heart leapt in her breast. 'It comes!'

Her mount reared, reacting to her terror. She clamped her knees, leant forward, and managed to keep her seat. The other horses snorted, pivoting as their riders fought to maintain control.

'Hurry with the torches!' Drake cried.

It wasn't enough. Panic flared in Imoshen. She needed a real attack, a leaping, snarling shadow which...

Even as she thought it, a white snow leopard broke from the trees, all grace and ferocity.

Horses and men screamed.

The last she saw was the cat leaping for the throat of the nearest horse. Then her mount bolted through the tree trunks and it was all she could do to huddle low in the saddle and hug the horse's heaving sides with her knees.

Behind her she heard the terrible screams of a dying horse and the knowledge that she had called forth the beast frightened her as much as the knowledge that it was real. Once again her gifts had outreached her ability to control them.

In the mad rush she did not know which way they were going. Snow fell in a thick curtain. It was so dark the tree trunks were only darker shadows in a dark grey world.

She glimpsed tightly packed trees with no possible gap between them. Blinded by fear, her mount charged straight ahead. She tried to plunge into its mind as she had unwittingly done before, but a solid wall of terror held her out. Or was it her own terror? Too late, the wall of trees were upon them.

She could only hunch down and hope.

The impact stunned her.

Her side ached, and she heard something thunder away.

Imoshen lifted her head to see the hooves of her mount disappearing into the deep shadows. She was lying on her side in the snow with no memory of how she got there. She must have lost consciousness briefly. Something blocked her vision in one eye and she blinked it away, then looked down to see dark droplets staining the snow. Blood.

She was bound, wounded, lost in the woods without a cloak in the first snows of winter. But at least she was free.

Fuelled by determination, she rolled to her knees, amazed to find nothing was broken. True, she staggered as she came to her feet and there seemed to be a lot of blood, but she could still move.

Blood would attract predators.

Exhaustion threatened to overcome her, but she drove herself to follow the retreating hoof beats.

Somewhere nearby, Drake and the men would be regrouping.

Imoshen looked up, trying to catch a glimpse of the stars, but they were obscured by the clouds and her head was spinning so she couldn't sense which way to go to reach the stronghold.

Her mount would know. She followed the churned snow, hardly able to distinguish anything in the grey-black world. Again she tried to call the horse, concentrating on its scent, its sense of self, which she had experienced so briefly.

There, a flicker a recognition illuminated her mind.

The horse had slowed to a steady walk not far away and was thinking, if it could be calling thinking, of food and its stall. Relieved, Imoshen broke into a run. Her mount was like a bright beacon in a world of silver shadows. She was so relieved to have discovered the horse nearby, tears stung her eyes.

A whinny greeted her, then it changed to a snort of fear. Icy fingers of dread travelled up Imoshen's spine.

Something was hunting her, just as she had hunted the horse. She could feel it now, probing the preternatural night. She stopped and spun around, searching the woods.

Odd, the night was not inky black as it should have been. She could make out the fall of the land, the trunks of the trees, everything had a silverish-green cast.

What was after her?

Without knowing she intended to do it, her mind sent out a questing probe, following the sense of pursuit to its source.

Flare!

She met the mind which sought hers and recognised its pure essence, free of the trappings of a mortal body.

'Reothe...' Her knees crumbled. Terror robbed her of coherent thought.

His thoughts sliced like a blade through her identity, shutting down all rational thought. Communication went beyond words. She recognised his anger and his determination. He would not relinquish her, not while he still lived.

While he held her thus she could not even lift her head, let alone flee and, now that he had located her, he was coming to claim her. She sensed his triumph.

Despair flooded Imoshen. Fool! By using her powers, she had unwittingly drawn him to her.

Something soft and moist touched her cheek. Horsey breath engulfed her face, making her choke. And just like that, she was free, blinded by the night but alone with her horse, kneeling in the steadily building snow.

The horse was a dark bulk. Its soft nostrils nuzzled her face. She didn't need to probe its mind to know it wanted food and thought she would provide it. Tears of relief stung her eyes as she staggered to her feet. She had to get away, and to do that she had to be invisible to Reothe's questing talent.

She was just another grey patch, as grey as the snow which fell in the inky blackness, just another piece of the night. She pressed her face into the horse's flank, savouring its warmth, for she had grown deathly cold while Reothe held her in thrall.

Then frustration seized her as she realised that without her hands she could not climb into the saddle. Still, it was reassuring not to be alone and maybe, just maybe, she could use her mount to deflect Reothe.

Her horse shied, its animal intelligence recognising the T'En power Reothe was wielding to search for her. She could feel it too. It made her teeth ache and triggered that strange taste on her tongue again. She almost wanted to answer it, to feel that flare of mental recognition. Until that moment she had never known how completely alone she was.

The temptation to touch minds was insidious, startling her with its intensity. She thrust the thought aside, clamping down on it. Placing her face in the hollow of the horse's neck, she inhaled its earthy scent.

She would hide her presence by assuming the horse's identity. She was anxious for warmth, for her stall and food. The beast began to move and she moved with it, her booted feet already numb with cold. But the thought of what lay ahead of her drove her on, while the thought of what lay behind drove her to push herself when cold and weariness threatened to overwhelm her.

Time passed. The ground passed beneath her boots. Walking became automatic.

Thought was a luxury she did without. The night stretched out before her.

When she raised her eyes and saw the huddled outline of the houses below the stronghold, the smoke lifting from their chimney tops and their lights almost hidden behind the shuttered windows, she was too weary to feel joy, only relief.

Her horse hastened and she kept pace with it, stumbling forward on numb legs.

The snow-mantled streets of the new town were empty, the houses tightly shuttered. The wide avenue that led up to the outer gates of the stronghold stretched before her, one last obstacle. The heavy gates were open and at the far end of the passage dark the courtyard glowed.

Strange. Why weren't they searching for her? Why weren't they alarmed? Where were her stronghold guard and General Tulkhan's elite guard?

She stumbled down the passage, thinking it was not that long since Tulkhan had entered these gates at the head of his army to lay claim to Umasreach, yet it felt like a lifetime ago to her.

No one challenged her, which was odd.

The horse threaded its way through the courtyards towards the stable, where the soft glow of lamplight told her someone was waiting. She watched the horse go, deeply grateful for its unwitting protection.

Imoshen could hear the sounds of revelry in the great hall, but everything sounded wrong to her ears. Why were they celebrating? Why weren't they searching for her? She felt an odd sense of dislocation, as if this wasn't her stronghold at all. Had the use of her T'En gifts distorted her perceptions so that she would never feel normal again?

She shuddered with more than cold.

Would every use of her gifts cause her to drift a little further from True-people until she lived, isolated, in a trap of her own making?

She was shivering uncontrollably now, partly with delayed reaction to her ordeal.

The great hall held a crowd of brightly costumed people. Music played, but it was not her native music. It had the vivid intensity of the Ghebites. So unexpected was the scene that greeted her, Imoshen wondered if she had unwittingly transported herself to another time. She did not know these brightly garbed young men. They were Ghebites, that much was certain, but wearing those outlandish clothes? Then amidst the newcomers she was relieved to recognise her own stronghold servants scurrying about to serve the newcomers.

Strange. Her people looked right through her.

A Vaygharian came to his feet and shouted for silence. The general din died away. He lifted a goblet in salute to his companion, another man, a young man who reminded her vaguely of Tulkhan. 'To King Gharavan and to the jewel in his crown, Fair Isle!'

There was a shout as the others drained their drinks and called for more.

The young King rose, good-naturedly accepting their shouted comments. 'To my half-brother, may he find the rebels and kill every last one!'

They roared.

'And to my loyal courtiers. I lay claim to Umasreach Stronghold and declare the Princess Imoshen a traitor, to be hunted down and executed without trial.'

The breath left Imoshen's body in an exclamation of amazement. She felt the constriction of the dried blood on her face as she frowned.

The Ghebites roared, while Imoshen noted her own servants kept their eyes downcast.

This had gone far enough.

Rigid with anger, she strode forward into the centre of the hall. This time her people noticed her.

'My lady,' a lad cried, dropping his jug. It smashed on the stone floor, shockingly loud.

An old woman would have come to her, but Imoshen shook her head, her eyes fixed on the young King's face. She watched his features go slack with surprise, then harden with a mixture of fear and hatred.

'Welcome to Umasreach, King Gharavan,' she greeted him formally. 'On behalf of General Tulkhan, with whom we made our terms of surrender, I bid you and your people welcome. And if someone will cut my bonds and bring me some warm food, I'll tell you how I was abducted and how I escaped.'

She noticed the young King cast a swift glance to the man who had first spoken and recognised him as the power behind the throne.

'Abducted you say, yet you are here?' The Vaygharian's insinuation was clear.

She felt someone slit the bounds which held her arms from wrist to elbow and bought her arms forward. Her shoulders ached fiercely. Lifting her hands she stared at them. They were blue, the fingers curled like the furled petals of a flower. She couldn't feel a thing. It was as if they belonged to someone else.

She tried to rub them together but though she was able to move her arms and her wrists met, her hands remained useless. Would she get frostbite? Lose her fingers?

Imoshen did not know, but she understood she could not afford to show a moment's weakness here.

'I was abducted.' She stepped closer to the table and held her hands out toward the King and his confidant. 'Or do you think I would strap my hands behind my back and stagger through the deep woods in the snow till my feet and hands went numb for the joy of it?'

'Who tried to abduct you?' the King asked. There was no more talk of doubting her word.

Imoshen went to speak, but even now she could not bring herself to turn Reothe over to these self-serving barbarians. 'Rebels. My horse bolted. I was knocked from the saddle. My head...' She tried to feel the extent of her head wound, but her hand wouldn't open and she only succeeded in starting the bleeding again.

Warmth seeped into her, melting the ice on her clothes. Little droplets landed on the stones at her numb feet, which were beginning to burn as circulation returned. She was so hungry she could feel her body trembling at the sight and scent of food, but she couldn't use her hands to feed herself and she would not bury her face in the nearest platter of food like an animal.

Imoshen lifted her gaze from the meat on the table, aware that the gathered Ghebites were staring at her in horrified fascination. If she didn't get help soon, she would fall at their feet, and she couldn't afford to do that. Unlike Tulkhan, these men had no compassion. They saw weakness as an opportunity to be exploited.

'Forgive me greeting you like this. I will go to my chambers and clean up.' She stepped back and made formal obeisance then turned and walked from the great hall.

As she stepped through a doorway, her knees buckled, and she sagged against the wall in the shadows, listening to the din of voices raised in exclamation.

The woman who ran the kitchen was there to meet her, as well as the housekeeper who oversaw the bedchambers and galleries.

The cook clutched her arm. 'They arrived at dusk, my lady. Just marched in and took over.'

The second massaged Imoshen's free hand. 'They ordered us about and you could not be found. We had no idea you'd been...'

Imoshen lifted her hand for silence. 'Treat them as honoured guests, of course.'

'My lady!' Kalleen ran down the steps to join them. 'I thought they'd taken you.'

Was Kalleen in league with the rebels? Imoshen frowned. Had the girl betrayed herself to the other women? But no, they were still chattering on, excusing themselves for serving King Gharavan. A laugh escaped Imoshen. She bit it back when she heard the odd lilt to her voice. In another breath, she would be crying.

Kalleen hugged her, then studied her face. 'I heard you'd been abducted by rebels and escaped. How –'

'I need a warm bath and food, and then I will tell you.'

On the stairs her legs gave way and several of the servants who had followed her ran forward. Kalleen pushed them aside, offering her slender shoulder.

Imoshen accepted her help, amused by the way the girl took charge.

Up in her room, Imoshen waited while the hot water was carried in and poured into her bathtub. She had to clench her teeth to stop from crying out as Kalleen massaged sensation back into her hands and feet.

'We did not know what had become of you. Last anyone saw of you, you were down in the town speaking with the blacksmith,' Kalleen said reproachfully. 'Then, when the King rode in, you couldn't be found. Wharrd was worried but he would not admit it. There has been no word from General Tulkhan and now King Gharavan is here. What does it mean?'

Imoshen did not know, but her instincts told her it was not good.

Once the tub was full she sprinkled soothing herbs on the warm waters. 'Send the servants away, Kalleen.'

When the girl returned, Imoshen lowered herself into the tub. She winced as she attempted to bathe the blood from her hair, studying her progress in the polished metal mirror which Kalleen held. In the royal palace they had real glass mirrors and hot running water, but her family had not believed in such things.

'I saw Drake today,' Imoshen said, watching the girl's face closely.

Kalleen leaned closer. 'Was he well? Does he regret leaving?'

'He abducted me.'

'No!'

'Yes. He's with the rebels.' She caught Kalleen's hand as the girl put the mirror aside to rinse Imoshen's hair. 'I need to know where your loyalty lies. Do you stand with me or against me?'

Kalleen golden eyes widened with hurt, her body stiffened. 'How can you ask!'

Imoshen flushed. 'I'm sorry, Kalleen, forgive me. All about me I see enemies. That young fool the King for one, but even more so his companion. Then...' She bit her lip. She feared Reothe more now than before. 'Where is the General?'

'Hunting rebels in the southern highlands,' Kalleen answered automatically.

Fear for General Tulkhan assailed Imoshen and her heart sank. Did he still live? They'd had no word from him.

Her once betrothed was T'En and his men were fanatics. While Tulkhan was a canny leader of True-men whose soldiers loved and respected him, he did not have T'En gifts. How could the General hope to stand against Reothe?

In a flash it came to Imoshen.

If she stood at Tulkhan's side, she could help him defeat the rebel leader. Was this what Reothe feared?

No wonder her betrothed would not take no for an answer. She could not be neutral. She had to take sides, had to choose which man would live or die.

Imoshen groaned.

'Are you hurt, my lady?' Kalleen whispered. 'I will call Wharrd.'

Imoshen laughed. 'My hurts can't be healed by a bone-setter.' Morosely she watched as Kalleen laid out her night garment and warmed the bed with a pan of hot coals. Such luxury. She was sure Reothe did not have his bed warmed, if he slept in a bed at all.

But she did not want to think of him. Thinking of him called to mind the memory of his essence when their minds touched. Imoshen shuddered. What would she give to know such a bonding? What would it be like to share a mind-touch that was bathed in love instead of fear and dominance?

Imoshen now believed that if she and Reothe were to bond, they would be able to defeat the invaders, and she suspected Reothe had known this all along. But at what cost to the people, and where would it end? Would Reothe be content with Fair Isle?

Her head hurt and her limbs trembled. 'I'm hungry, Kalleen. Find me something to eat.'

'Now?'

'Yes, now!' Imoshen winced. 'I'm sorry.'

'You seemed... strange,' Kalleen confessed. 'For a moment I did not recognise you. It must be the bruising.'

But when the girl left and Imoshen looked in the reflective metal, she knew it wasn't that. Something inside her had changed. She had lost her innocence tonight. She was no longer so naive and trusting.

Tonight she had used her T'En skills to lure a predator to kill True-men. She had faced Reothe with her naked mind and run from the pain of his knife-sharp gifts.

If she had to choose sides, and it appeared she did, then let Tulkhan be her general. Strangely enough, she did not fear him. But they were all threats – the King, his Vaygharian advisor, Reothe and the General. She would use whatever tools came to hand to ensure her survival.

It shocked Imoshen to realise she was planning to use people just like Reothe did, and she shivered.

Thoughtfully, she stood before the fire to rub her body dry. Apart from a few bruises and the gash in her hairline, she had survived the ordeal physically, but her inner certainty was gone.

She knew buried T'En power lay deep inside her and that it could surface in times of stress, and if it did, Reothe would know, because the same ability lay in him.

And he was hungry for her.

TULKHAN SAT TALL in the saddle despite his weariness. His men slumped, wrapped in their inadequate northern winter cloaks. The snow still fell and the outriders he'd posted on their flanks were lost in the whiteness. They were probably so weary they didn't have the energy to keep watch.

Was it less than two small moons ago that he'd left his half-brother in T'Diemn and entered the southern highlands to hunt rebels with three companies of men behind him?

He had led pitifully few of those men back to the capital. Ever since they'd seen one of their own commanders drop dead two days after T'Reothe's touch, the men had whispered of black sorcery.

They spoke of haunted dreams.

Meanwhile Tulkhan dare not reveal his secret fears. Reothe had said he was the man destined to kill the General. He seemed so sure... Tulkhan told himself it was only bluff. But his sword had passed through the Dhamfeer, while that unnatural being's laughter mocked him.

The rebel army had proved as insubstantial and impossible to catch as its leader. Even knowing that Reothe's warning about Imoshen might be a trick, Tulkhan had chosen to believe him and had returned to T'Diemn with the pitiful remains of his three companies, only to find his half-brother had left for Umasreach Stronghold.

Why did that worry him?

Surely he could trust Gharavan?

He feared for Imoshen. Was Reothe the real threat or was it the lies of Kinraid, the Vaygharian? It would not take much skill to weave a story to convince his lackwit half-brother that Imoshen was a liability.

Tulkhan grimaced. He'd nearly had her killed himself. Yet now he was driving his weary men in a forced march to reach the stronghold in an attempt to avert that very thing.

Imoshen was a focal point. The fate of Fair Isle lay in her lap and his fate was entwined with her choices.

Tulkhan didn't like feeling helpless. He was used to taking the initiative, rather than reacting to the challenges of others. Urging his horse on, he breathed a sigh of relief when he saw the tower of the original keep rising above the naked branches of the trees. The stronghold was still distant, but they would be there before sunset.

His men and their horses seemed to sense their journey would soon be over and their pace increased. When they broke from the trees and rode down into the basin of the plain, he marvelled at the changes. A real town had sprung up. The steep pitched roofs were coated with snow. The same white snow hid the newness, and the bare earth he guessed he would find in the streets instead of paving.

People saw him approach with his men and though he did not expect cheers or happy greetings, he was surprised to see the doors and windows being shuttered.

His own men muttered uneasily. Tulkhan was grateful he'd left the wounded and sick behind, taking only those well enough to travel. It had been a difficult balance to strike. If he approached his half-brother with the better part of his army at his back, the young King might take alarm. Now was not the time for a show of strength. Tulkhan knew the loyalty of the army lay with him. He smiled grimly. At least he believed it did.

So he rode through the streets of the new town with a mere sixty men, all of whom had seen service in the woods fighting rebels. There were practicalities involved in his decision to bring such a small force. When he reached Umasreach he would have to house and feed the men he brought with him. He knew the stronghold's resources were overstretched.

The lookouts on the battlements watched their approach stonily. Tulkhan knew news of their arrival would have been reported long ago. It galled him to think he was walking into the stronghold which he thought of as his own, more his own than any other keep he had taken, to report failure to his half-brother who was only looking for a reason to find fault with him.

A deep sorrow gripped him as he passed through the claustrophobic passage to the courtyard beyond.

When had it changed? Once Gharavan had looked up to him and loved him.

Tulkhan swung down from the saddle weary and stiff, but he couldn't show it. Wharrd and the members of his elite guard who had been left to maintain the stronghold had contrived to be present in the stables on his arrival.

Amid the jostling of horses and stable lads, Wharrd made his report. The grizzled bone-setter's careful choice of words told Tulkhan that Wharrd believed the King was a threat.

But he didn't know the boy like Tulkhan did.

In the time it took to unsaddle his horse, the General learnt the number and nature of the men his half-brother had brought with him.

As usual Gharavan had surrounded himself with a court of young unseasoned nobles, but he had also brought a company of men who had served under Tulkhan on other campaigns. They were seasoned fighters, loyal to Gheeaba.

If it came to trouble, would they stay loyal to Tulkhan?

The General was still considering the ramifications when Wharrd lowered his voice and told him the rebels had attempted to abduct Imoshen only yesterday.

It rocked him to learn Reothe's men had nearly succeeded. So the T'En warrior's challenge hadn't been a bluff. Apparently only Imoshen's determination to elude her captors had foiled the rebel leader's plans. That she had rejected her betrothed and returned to the stronghold gave Tulkhan a fierce surge of satisfaction.

But he forced himself to look at Imoshen's actions rationally.

She had given him her word that she would not lead an uprising of stronghold guards against him while he was calming T'Diemn, but at Reothe's side she might have been at the forefront of a rebel army determined enough to retake Fair Isle, aided by their accursed Dhamfeer gifts. Why hadn't she joined her betrothed?

Was it loyalty to Tulkhan, or was it simply that she had weighed the odds and thought the Ghebite was more likely to be the victor?

He felt a cynical smile tug at his lips. At least Umasreach Stronghold was still under his control. If it had fallen and Imoshen had turned against him, the King would have had good reason to doubt his general's judgment.

Whatever Imoshen's true reason for not joining the rebels, Tulkhan could now face his half-brother secure in the knowledge that Umasreach was behind him.

He hesitated, confronted with the enormity of it. He'd been preparing to challenge his king's authority. No, impossible. His half-brother would never turn against him. It must not come to that.

He was a warrior, trained to think in terms of battle tactics. His mind had been automatically weighing factors – nothing more. It was an almost instinctive response arising from years of campaigning.

As Tulkhan strode through the stronghold halls, rounding the now familiar corners, he found himself thinking of Imoshen when he should have been preparing for his interview with the King. The escort led him upstairs to the great library where he had first met Imoshen.

A vivid memory returned, a flash of her beautiful white breasts stained with dark red blood returned to him. It made his body race in anticipation. He ached to claim her. Time and distance had not dulled his craving for her.

Even as he made his obeisance to the King, his gaze slid past Gharavan's, searching for Imoshen's familiar, tall form. For a brief moment she held his eyes, her wine-dark gaze urgent and compelling. The intimacy of it made his heart leap. Then she looked away, her expression carefully neutral.

He was very aware of her standing behind the Ghebite conquerors. On a purely physical level the sight of her jolted him. An almost painful longing to touch her swept over him.

Tulkhan came to his feet. He had been weary beyond belief but now his body answered his commands without complaint and his mind felt startlingly clear.

'My king,' he acknowledged his half-brother.

Abruptly he registered what he had seen and again his gaze was drawn back to Imoshen's face. A great purple bruise marred her forehead. The thought of anyone hurting her was abhorrent to him and his hands flexed as outrage flooded him.

Imoshen's eyes narrowed. She tilted her head ever so slightly toward the King in what Tulkhan interpreted as a warning. His heart pounded. Imoshen was warning him against his half-brother?

She was an enemy who had vowed never to surrender to him. If he believed Imoshen only dealt with him because it suited her purposes, why should he heed her warning against his own flesh and blood? Perhaps it suited her to divide them. Yet, Wharrd...

'Well, General?' Gharavan prodded. 'What have you to report?

'When you stop lusting after the Dhamfeer bitch!' the Vaygharian muttered.

The General stiffened as Gharavan gave a snort of laughter.

The casual insult had been directed at Imoshen as well as himself. Tulkhan swallowed his instinctive reaction. Had his preoccupation been so obvious? Offence was always the best defence.

He focused on his half-brother. 'I looked for you in T'Diemn –'

'Well I am here, as you can see.' The youth indicated the ancient manuscript which lay open on the table. 'You advised me to study this island and its inhabitants.'

Was Gharavan saying, *I am king, not you? I have this island, this stronghold and this woman you want. It is all mine to do with as I will.* Or was his younger half-brother following his advice?

Perhaps he was seeing threat where a young man stood, merely flexing his new-found power?

Tulkhan felt the sands shifting beneath his feet.

He knew his arrival at Umasreach had been noted when he entered the valley. His half-brother had had time to set up this meeting in the chamber of knowledge and chose the participants. Was Gharavan planning on using Imoshen against him?

And as for the Vaygharian, Tulkhan wished him elsewhere. How was he to reason with Gharavan, when the Vaygharian stood there undermining Tulkhan at every turn?

'As you see, the Princess has been translating the history of Fair Isle for me,' Gharavan remarked, indicating the illuminated vellum. He flicked a page of the heavy tome with an idle finger. 'But the first chapter of a new and glorious book will have to be written in our tongue, not some long-dead script.'

Another insult, or youthful bravado?

'The island has seen many invaders. They came to conquer but stayed to become one with the land,' Imoshen remarked. 'Only Fair Isle endures.'

Tulkhan saw his brother flinch.

Why was Imoshen drawing his brother's anger? The young King slammed the book shut and slid it across the polished wood to the Keeper of Knowledge, who shuffled off with it, stroking the tome as it to reassure himself it was unharmed.

The Vaygharian's hand rested lightly on Gharavan's shoulder. The youth drew a slow breath, then turned glittering dark eyes to Tulkhan, who read impatience, anger and an underlying fear in his half-brother's face. 'Well, General? Have you brought me the rebel Reothe's head, or at least news of his death?'

Tulkhan stiffened. He hated reporting failure, but it was best to be frank. Besides, Imoshen knew the man she had been betrothed to still lived and, despite that, she was here facing Gharavan with him and not in the woods with Reothe and his rebels.

'Reothe escaped. The southern highlands are a death trap and the rebels know them intimately. They ambushed my men, then disappeared without a trace. We weren't properly provisioned to camp out in the depths of winter. The cold was so intense our water-skins froze.' While he spoke he felt Imoshen's eyes on him. He wanted to look at her, but he disciplined himself to make his report. 'If the rebels didn't kill us, cold and fever would have. I decided to call the hunt off until spring.'

King Gharavan came to his feet slowly. '*You* called off the hunt?'

Tulkhan was weary of games. Why should he explain himself to an untried youth and a conniving merchant?

'A good tactician knows when to retreat,' Imoshen said softly but forcefully.

Tulkhan noted that his half-brother and the Vaygharian both ignored her. Was it because she was female and Dhamfeer? Or was it because her comment, though true, was not what they wanted to hear?

'I won't risk my men uselessly,' Tulkhan stated. 'Besides, our latest information places Reothe far from the forests where we were hunting. He's come north, this way, if my informant could be believed.'

Tulkhan repressed a shudder, recalling the way the breath had left his commander's body, taking his life with it. One touch from the T'En warrior and a man was dead.

The Vaygharian's eyes narrowed. A flash of something passed swiftly across his face and Tulkhan wondered what it meant. But his head buzzed with conflicting thoughts.

He realised his half-brother was speaking.

'...take fresh men into the southern highlands –'

'No. I won't risk any more men until the thaw. The rebels will go to ground through winter. We'd never find them.' With a start Tulkhan realised he had interrupted and contradicted his king, spoken to him as if he was still the boy he had once been.

Gharavan rose, anger suffusing his face.

Tulkhan considered apologising, but he knew warcraft. He was right to refuse to obey a foolhardy order.

Imoshen moved around the table, filling the ominous silence. 'I will have food prepared and see that the General's men are quartered.' She stepped between the two brothers. 'King Gharavan, you do not know this land. Your Ghebite soldiers do battle with more than the cold or the rebels or the predators in the highlands. There are ancient powers in the deep woods, dating from a time before the dawn people came here. And the Ancients do not like to have their peace disturbed.'

A flicker of something akin to fear travelled across the young King's features, even the Vaygharian's knuckles whitened on the table top. Tulkhan recalled the stone circle he and Imoshen had stumbled into on their way to Landsend and his more recent encounter with the Ancients' powers when he had unwitting tripped the guide's trap. He shuddered.

He had thought the strange, sexless child had fled from Reothe, but could Reothe be in league with the Ancients?

Was Imoshen guessing? Or was she using basic statesmanship and bluffing to distract the attacker?

Since when had his half-brother become his enemy? If he could only get the lad alone and talk some sense to him. Tulkhan fumed.

'Dhamfeer bitch!' Gharavan sneered. 'Do you think to frighten me with nursery tales? Ancient evils!'

Tulkhan saw Imoshen's shoulders stiffen. She did not flinch when his half-brother strode around the table to glare at her, his face only a hand's breadth from hers.

'Milk-faced whore,' he snarled. 'Don't try to play your Dhamfeer tricks on me. If your people had such great powers, why didn't they use them to stop my general and his army? No. They died like the dogs they are on the battlefield, bathed in their own blood. Kneel!'

When Imoshen remained frozen, Gharavan lifted his hand to strike her.

Even as she went to block the blow, Tulkhan moved. His knee struck the back of her knee so that she fell to the floor at his half-brother's feet.

A gasp of surprised pain escaped her. Tulkhan winced. She would hate him, but it couldn't be helped. His half-brother was just looking for an excuse to execute her.

'Bow, woman,' Tulkhan commanded. His fingers bit into her shoulder, holding her down. He could feel her fine bones grinding. He knew he must be hurting her.

Slowly, Imoshen's head of intricately knotted silver plaits, dipped before his half-brother.

King Gharavan's dark eyes gleamed with satisfaction. His gaze went to Tulkhan, demanding an unspoken response. The General sank stiffly to the floor to kneel at Imoshen's side.

'I swear, the rebel Reothe will be captured and executed in your name, King Gharavan,' he ground out.

Tulkhan was aware of Imoshen at his side. His hand still rested on her shoulder, though not gripping as cruelly as it had before. Her profile was a perfect mask, hiding her fury.

'Very good,' Gharavan purred.

When Tulkhan heard the satisfaction in his half-brother's voice, the crazy pounding of his heart began to ease. How had it come to this?

He must get his brother away from the Vaygharian. Given the chance, Tulkhan was sure he could make Gharavan see reason.

'You may go.' The young King gestured dismissively.

Tulkhan came to his feet, his fingers linked around Imoshen's arm, so that he drew her upright with him. He expected to see hatred in her eyes as they both bowed and turned to leave, but instead her expression was carefully guarded. Two spots of colour burnt high on her cheeks. Her eyes glittered and her mouth was a tense line.

When they stepped out into the hall, Tulkhan was aware of his half-brother's courtiers gathered in clusters. Their conversations died and the hangers-on turned, watching and weighing, awaiting the return of their king. How was he going to get Imoshen past them before her temper erupted?

'General Tulkhan?' Imoshen's voice was an imitation of itself, but only he knew that. She offered him her arm. 'Allow me to show you to your chambers. A bath has been drawn for you.'

He took her arm. Avid, unfriendly eyes watched them. He searched his mind for a neutral topic. 'The number of buildings outside the stronghold surprised me. There will be a thriving town in no time.'

As they walked the length of the gallery, maintaining their innocuous conversation, Tulkhan sensed their every word was being memorised, every gesture observed and catalogued. He hated it.

Now that the threat had passed, his heartbeat returned to normal and weariness fogged his brain. They turned the corner to enter the wing where he had slept last time. Several stronghold servants scurried past with empty buckets.

Imoshen opened the door to his chamber, inspected it and dismissed the rest of the servants. Tulkhan watched her, waiting for the outburst, willing it to come. He found the tension unbearable.

There was a bath already drawn before the fire. She stepped toward it, her back to him. 'Strip. You smell of horse sweat and death. And your brother hates you.'

He lifted his hands. 'I had to do it. He was only looking for an excuse to have you executed.'

She spun to face him, eyes blazing, chest heaving. 'Do you want me to thank you for saving my life? Very well. I thank you.' She shuddered. 'My knees will be bruised for a week. I should have knelt faster but my stupid pride wouldn't let me. There, are you satisfied?'

He could see a sheen of unshed tears shimmering in her eyes and he longed to take her in his arms, but he suspected that if he took one step closer she'd pull her knife on him.

She drew a deep ragged breath and blinked fiercely. 'How does it feel to kneel to a brother who hates you?'

'*Half*-brother,' he corrected. 'And he doesn't hate me; at least, he didn't. He's been led astray, badly advised by that Vaygharian –'

'Is that what you call it?' She laughed bitterly, then seemed to hear the hysterical edge to her voice and clamped her mouth shut.

There was a charged silence in the large chamber.

Imoshen shivered, then moved closer to the fire. Tulkhan watched her. True, she was one of the Dhamfeer, but he could not regard her as less than a True-woman. She was a challenging mix of vulnerable and fragile, yet she exuded an inner strength, which he could not ignore.

Today she was ornately dressed in an elaborate embroidered gown which was laced under her breasts and fell in heavy brocade folds to her knees over a fine under dress of soft white material. Strands of her pale hair were plaited and threaded with small, semi-precious stones into a crown. She looked every inch the T'En Princess, regal and somehow older than he remembered her.

Imoshen had changed since they were last together. Was this the girl-woman who had clung to him on the battlements?

'Why are you looking at me like that?' she asked.

So many things threatened them both, so many things stood between them, at that moment he wished he was simply a soldier and she a camp follower who had come to bathe him.

'I don't trust that smile,' she whispered, an answering smile lifting her lips.

By the gods, he wanted her. 'Why are you here?'

She indicated the bath. 'Strip. The bath is going cold. I'm here to speak without being spied on.'

'You're going to watch while I bathe?'

'Does it bother you?'

'No.' He gestured to the corridor, his tiredness suddenly gone. 'But what will they think?'

'Since they already think that I warm your bed, what does it matter?'

Her reply held an odd tinge of defiance and despair.

Tulkhan could not understand why this troubled her.

From what he had seen, the women of Fair Isle took lovers without impunity. Their men didn't mind and, since the Ghebites despised all women, what did it matter if they thought Imoshen was his bed-mate? They might even despise her less. But he wisely chose to keep this observation to himself.

He had yet to find his way with this new Imoshen. He had been finding his way since the first time he confronted her. The memory of that meeting made his body quicken.

'If you're staying, you might as well help me undress.' He waited, watching for her reaction. He wanted her to touch him, wanted to feel her hands on his skin. Any excuse would do. 'You've dismissed my servants.'

She laughed, then stepped forward. 'What barefaced brass. I suppose you are waited on hand and foot while on campaign, a hot bath drawn every night and food served on golden plates?'

He laughed. It felt good to laugh.

As she spoke, her hands moved deftly across his chest, unlacing his vest. She tossed it aside and turned back to him.

He sat and lifted one booted foot imperiously. Her reaction was just what he'd hoped. Amusement and fury mingled in her face as she stepped astride his leg to work his boot off.

It slid over his foot and she dropped it, turning as he lifted the other leg.

She snorted. 'I hope you're enjoying this –'

'Immensely!'

A flash of fire lit her eyes, igniting a surge of dangerous desire in him.

Wordlessly, she stepped astride his other leg and worked his boot off. It fell with a thud.

He rose, standing in nothing but his breeches and undershirt.

She stepped back.

If he hadn't known better he would have said she was suddenly shy with him. A silence hung between them, heavy with unspoken questions.

'You should know,' she told him. 'Yester-eve, when I could not be found, without sending out a party to see if I had been thrown from my horse or lost my way, your half-brother had all but declared me a rebel and authorised my execution. I was abducted.' Her fingers indicated the bruise on her forehead. 'I was lucky to escape.'

Tulkhan peeled off his undershirt, aware how the material stuck to his grimy skin, and tossed the garment aside. Her gaze flew to his breeches and colour suffused her pale cheeks. At that moment, she seemed very young and uncertain.

It amused him, but the amusement vanished when he noticed that the flesh around the wound on her forehead was already turning green, as though the bruising had happened days ago. She must have been treating herself. A prickle of wariness travelled across his skin. He must not forget she was Dhamfeer, and all that this implied. The hastened healing was all the evidence he needed.

But instead of sensible wariness, he felt a deep anger. It annoyed him to think anyone had a raised a hand to Imoshen.

Her eyes widened as he stepped closer and lifted his hand to touch her bruised face. 'What did they do to you, Imoshen?'

'My horse bolted and ran into a tree. That was how I escaped the rebels.' Her off-hand comment was at odds with the tension in her body.

He wanted to break through her defences. Some devil prompted him to take her hands in his, guiding them to the laces at his belly. 'The bath is going cold. Undress me.'

Startled, her lashes lowered as she glanced down to his breeches and the arousal they could not hide.

Her face was a comic mixture of reluctance and curiosity.

He nodded, unable to speak, his heart hammering. This battle of wills was more testing than any encounter on the battlefield.

'Very well,' she whispered.

He let her hands drop.

She reached for the knife she wore strapped to her upper thigh. Her hand emerged from the slit in her under gown, armed with the naked blade.

His heart missed a beat as the knife's wicked edge moved close to his loins. He swallowed. She caught the waist of his breeches in one hand and pried the knife blade under the lacing. With a snap, snap, snap the laces gave, falling aside.

'There.' She stepped back, her voice unsteady.

He took a deep breath as if relearning how to breathe, and dropped the breeches, stepping out of them. Her eyes widened and he realised that she had not seen him this way before, had probably never seen an aroused male.

He untied the leather thong which held his hair and stepped forward. Before he could reach for her, she darted around the far side of the bath and he had to smile.

When he'd lain awake shivering in the snow, waiting for the rebels to spring from their hideout and slaughter them all, he'd thought of Imoshen, imagining her in his arms, pliant and willing. But when had she ever been like that? She was a firebrand, deadly one minute, sweetly unsure the next, and he wanted her desperately. But for now he was willing to enjoy the chase.

At fifteen he'd wooed and tamed one of the wild ponies of his homeland. He knew when to feign disinterest. So he sank into the tub and reached for the soaping sand. It was scented with sandalwood and something else he didn't recognise.

'Did you mean what you said about Reothe and the powers of the deep woods, or was it just a ploy to divert my half-brother?' he asked.

She didn't answer, but he sensed her coming closer and hid a smile when she knelt behind him. Lifting the ladle, she poured warm water over his neck and shoulders.

He could see the fingers of her other hand. The knuckles whitened as she gripped the rim of the bath. 'You risked death in the woods.'

He laughed softly. 'I've risked death every day since I was seventeen –'

'Don't you know what Reothe is?'

Startled by her intensity, Tulkhan twisted to study Imoshen's face. 'He's Dhamfeer, like you.'

She rolled her eyes. 'You don't know what that means. Neither did I until...' Seeming to recollect herself, she didn't finish what she'd been about to say but lifted her hand to indicate he should pass the bath scrub.

He gave it to her, watching as she rolled up her sleeves, then worked up a lather. His skin tingled in anticipation. 'Explain what you mean about Reothe.'

On her knees she moved around the side of the tub next to him. 'You can't defeat him in the woods. And you can't trust your half-brother at your back.'

He gave a grunt of amusement. 'And I can trust you?'

'Yes.'

'Why should I believe that? You surrendered the stronghold, but you've made it clear you never surrendered to me.' He waited. What did he want from her, some admission of commitment? Ridiculous, she wasn't even one of the True-people. Yet...

'I want to survive,' she said with simple sincerity. 'I don't want to see Fair Isle reduced to years of civil war. You can trust me because I'd rather deal with you than your half-brother and that Vaygharian. At least you listen to reason and see beyond your own immediate goals.'

'What of Reothe?' He had to know. Her reasoning was logical, exactly the path he would have taken in her position. Sometimes an enemy you could trust was better than a friend who might betray you. But where did that leave the man she'd been betrothed to?

She looked down.

'He was your betrothed, the last T'En Prince,' Tulkhan pressed. 'And now that you know he still lives...'

She sighed and he thought she was going to lie to him. Instead, she stroked the lather along his shoulders. Her fingers massaged his tense shoulders, manipulating the slabs of muscle, working wonders. She moved behind him to run her fingers up the nape of his neck, and he did not object. No one had ever pampered him like this.

He felt the knots of tension and tiredness seep from his weary body. When her fingers worked through his scalp, lathering his long hair, every sensation was somehow intensified. Her fingers were magic, he could lose himself in her caress.

'You are a wonderful witch,' he whispered, his voice hoarse.

'If I am a witch, then Reothe is a warlock.'

There was a tremor in her voice. It chilled him despite the warm bath water. He tried to twist his head so he could see her face, but she wound her fingers through his wet soapy hair so tightly it was almost painful.

'Listen, General!' Her breath tickled his ear, making the little hairs on the back of his neck rise. He sensed her whispered words were torn from her at great personal cost. 'Reothe has powerful T'En gifts, things I am only just discovering. He... he nearly trapped me out in the woods, and if he had I would not have been able to fight him.'

Reothe had come here in person and she was afraid of him? 'I don't –'

Abruptly, she tipped a ladle of water over his head, indicating the conversation was over. Warm water cascaded around his shoulders.

So Reothe was a sore point with her. Biding his time, Tulkhan let Imoshen rinse out the soap. When she'd finished, he rubbed the water from his face and caught his long hair to wring the excess from it.

He looked across the bath to where she now knelt opposite, watching him warily. Imoshen was not telling him everything. He knew he should pursue it, yet he was so weary he found it hard to concentrate. The only thing he could think of was how beautiful she looked despite the bruise over her troubled eyes.

He indicated the puckered skin along her hairline. 'You'll have a scar.'

'I'd rather be interesting than pretty.'

He laughed. 'You are nothing like the women of my homeland.'

She looked at him as if she didn't know how to take this. The damp heat of the bath made the short elf locks around her face tighten into ringlets. Even her eyes looked bruised. Fear gave them a shimmering quality. He wanted to erase that fear, to know that she trusted him for himself, not because she had no choice.

The thought of someone striking her face so hard that it split the skin and drew blood was physically distressing to him. Was this wound the reason she feared the male Dhamfeer? 'Did Reothe hit you?'

She made an impatient gesture. 'I told you. I was trying to ride a bolting horse with my hands tied behind my back. No, if only it were that simple. Since...'

Colour stained her face and she looked down to lather her hands once again. Shifting to the side of the tub beside the fire, she prepared to soap his chest. He sensed she wanted to speak but couldn't.

Tentatively, he touched her arm. 'If we are to be allies, you must trust me.'

Her eyes met his. Then her pale hands began to work their magic again, slowly circling the skin across the broad planes of his chest, working deeper and deeper. The sensation was so intense he had trouble concentrating on what she was saying.

'You call me Dhamfeer, we call ourselves the T'En,' she said softly. 'Six hundred years ago there were several hundred of us. We were blown off course far across an ocean thought to be too broad to traverse, so my namesake claimed this island for the T'En. She took it by force, but in the end the island has taken us.

'Reothe and I are the last of our kind, throwbacks born because of in-breeding in the royal line. There is no one to teach me how to use the gifts the T'En knew. And since the night I lay with you, something has wakened in me. It stirred to life, quickened by our joining.'

The glance she cast him was swift and unsure. It stirred something deep and primal within him. He caught her hands before they moved lower on their self-appointed task. Her touch was too intoxicating. He wanted a clear head.

'Is that... normal?'

She shrugged. 'The Aayel is dead. I don't know. I know only that certain things happened the night of our joining which frightened me –'

'The scrying, the bedding bursting into flames?'

She ducked her head and nodded as though ashamed to admit a weakness, which he supposed it was, from her point of view.

'I don't know how to control what has woken, so I've chosen not to use it, even when I felt it stir like a restless beast in the dark caverns of my mind. But yester-eve when they captured me I was frightened. They said Reothe was nearby. I knew once he had me in his power...' She looked up to Tulkhan. 'I don't know how it is with your people. But Reothe and I were betrothed. There was a bond formed that day. And he uses it to draw me to him.'

'I don't understand.' Tulkhan was afraid he did, and he didn't like it one bit.

She rinsed the lather from her hands and straightened. 'Hold out your hand and close your eyes.'

It was a strange request, yet Tulkhan complied without question. He realised it was a measure of how far he had come since taking Umasreach Stronghold. He felt her fingers lace through his. Her hands were soft, still damp from the bath water. He wondered what it would be like to taste her skin, to run his tongue up between her breasts, inhale her subtle feminine perfume. He wanted to see her eyes darken with desire and hear her gasp of appreciation.

'Well?'

'Well, what?' he asked, hoarsely.

'What were you thinking of?'

This time he felt his face grow hot. 'Nothing. Why, what was I supposed to think of?'

She looked closely at him. Her fingers went to the laces which held her over-dress tightly cinched beneath her breasts. With deft fingers she undid the lacing, letting the stiff material drop away to the floor.

His breath seemed to falter in his throat. Next her fingers tugged on the string which held the neck gathering of her under-dress. His blood drummed in his ears as she loosened the material, letting it fall from her shoulders to reveal her perfect small breasts. The nipples peaked.

Unable to look away, he watched her fingers circle those tight nipples. 'This is what you were thinking.'

His mouth went dry with fear, not desire.

'How?' One word escaped him.

'Good. I haven't tried that before.'

'Curse you...' He sprang to his feet, dragging her upright.

Bath water slopped over the rim onto the floor. On contact with his damp skin the material of her under-dress clung to her body. Her bare breasts brushed the dark matted hair of his chest. He could feel her warm flesh, as good as naked next to his.

Anger and desire warred within him. 'Keep out of my head!'

'How do you think I feel?' She jerked as if to escape him, but he wouldn't release her, not while there was still breath in his body.

Pain travelled across her face, shadowing her eyes.

'I hated it when Reothe invaded my mind. At least I admitted it to you. He played with me, manipulating my senses without thought for my feelings. How do you think I feel, knowing he can do that?'

'Reothe manipulates you?'

She nodded, and stepped back as he released her. Tulkhan hated to acknowledge the terrible feeling of foreboding stealing over him. The rebel leader had laughed as Tulkhan's sword sliced through insubstantial mist. Reothe vowed he would be the Ghebite General's death, had even called him a dead man who walked and talked.

Somehow the Dhamfeer rebel leader had evaded Tulkhan's army in the highlands, yet killed or wounded half his men. And then there was the inexplicable death of the commander.

Reothe had arranged for Imoshen to be plucked from the land around her stronghold in broad daylight and nearly succeeded in abducting her.

What manner of man was T'Reothe?

Dhamfeer. Other and dangerous.

If so, then so was Imoshen. The knowledge that she had invaded his mind still rankled Tulkhan.

He caught her shoulders, drawing her near to search her face.

'You were betrothed to him, destined to be his bed-mate.' The thought of another man planting images of seduction in Imoshen's mind incensed Tulkhan. He wanted to strike out.

But Imoshen had freely given her vow to Reothe, while Tulkhan had to admit he had laid claim to her body through trickery. He had no real claim on her. His throat closed with bitterness, choking his voice. 'What does it matter if he seduces you with mind tricks, surely it is his right as your betrothed?'

He watched her eyes widen, knew he'd hurt her and cursed himself, because he didn't want to cause her pain.

'You don't understand.' She pulled away from him as if she'd been stung.

If he hadn't been standing in the bath, Tulkhan suspected she would have kicked him.

'I'm afraid he'll seduce my mind. If joining with you that once gives me this much access to your thoughts, can you imagine what joining with Reothe would do? He wants to use me to regain Fair Isle!'

'And I want to use you to hold Fair Isle,' Tulkhan ground out. 'What is the difference?'

She stiffened, her face beautiful and mask-like in its stillness. She was shocked beyond pain.

He had pushed her till she reacted, but it was a hollow victory.

'Choice!' The word fell from her lips, startling him with its force. 'I choose to ally myself with you.'

'But you were betrothed to him, promised –'

'In another time, before the Old Empire fell!' Her voice was low and intense. 'You must understand, for all our sakes. Reothe tried to use the betrothal as a lever on me and I refused him. Now he has tried force. If he gets me in his power I will have no defences against him. I don't know how to use the T'En gifts and he does.' The confession was torn from her. 'How do you think I feel, knowing he can manipulate my mind?'

'How do you think I feel knowing you can do the same to me?' Tulkhan demanded raggedly.

She blinked, and he could have sworn she was surprised.

'But I'm not going to hurt you.' Her sincerity was obvious.

He almost laughed. 'As long as I'm useful to you, as long as there are other threats like my half-brother and his lover, or Reothe.'

Tulkhan could hear the mockery in his own voice. He didn't want to stand here arguing with her. Suddenly nothing mattered but his desire for her, his need.

He had missed her presence while in T'Diemn, missed her advice while in the southern highlands dealing with sly locals. More than that, he had yearned to feel her warm, compliant body next to his at night, to sleep with her in his arms. He blinked. Where had these thoughts come from?

Furious, he turned on her. 'Curse you, Dhamfeer. Are you playing with my mind now, planting suggestions?'

Imoshen was surprised by the General's sudden savagery. His face conveyed such anguish that she longed to convince him his thoughts were his own.

'Of course not!' she said. But why should he believe her? 'It wouldn't be right.'

'You deny tampering with my thoughts before?'

'No. But that was done to prove a point. To tamper with your thoughts to change your mind wouldn't be right.' She drew herself up, not deigning to cover her breasts. The damp under-gown clung to her thighs and abdomen. 'If you were having lustful thoughts, they were your own –'

'Ha!' He stabbed an accusatory finger at her. 'How did you know they were lustful thoughts?'

She bit her bottom lip to hide the smile which threatened to undo her. Now was not the time to mock him. Wordlessly she pointed.

Hastily, he covered himself with the drying cloth.

He stepped from the bath, the cloth held securely in place. She couldn't help but admire his long flanks and the curve of his taut buttocks as he turned his back, pointedly ignoring her.

His coppery, battle-scarred hands rubbed the cloth firmly across his shoulders. She wanted to feel those hands rub as firmly across her flesh, wanted to feel him clasp her with a passion that would ignite them both, and banish all fear and doubt.

'You are angry with me.'

The firelight danced on his tall frame, illuminating the many small scars where old wounds had healed. She hated every one of those scars, because they were evidence of his life before she knew him.

He wanted her; that was plain enough. What did she have to do?

Imoshen licked her lips. When she spoke her voice was almost hoarse. 'I would not mock you.'

He gave a single grunt. It conveyed a world of meaning.

'General Tulkhan?' She breathed his name, her heart hammering with tension as she released the material of her under-dress. It fell at her feet.

Mortally afraid he might reject her, she closed her eyes, unable to meet his. Naked physically and emotionally, she held her breath until she heard his ragged gasp then she braved his gaze.

The planes of his face were taut with need, his eyes twin fires of dark desire. Yet he stood there, rigid with contained urgency.

Did he want her to beg? Unable to speak, she took a step and put her hand tentatively on his chest. She felt the fevered hammering of his heart beneath her palm. With her other hand she caught his wrist and lifted his hand to press his palm over her own raging heart.

'Please.' The word was a whisper. It hung on the super-charged air between them.

'Why?' Desire and despair warred in his voice. 'So you can control me as Reothe seeks to control you.'

Imoshen shook her head. 'I wouldn't... couldn't do that.'

'You expect me to believe you?'

She could only nod.

With a groan he caught her to him.

Chapter Eight

IMOSHEN'S HEART SANG. She felt lightheaded with relief. A delicious anticipation tingled through her limbs. The length of Tulkhan's hard thighs pressed on her legs, the heat of his arousal melded into her belly. His hands circled the small of her waist, lifting her to him.

Tears stung her eyes.

Blindly she searched for his lips, felt the graze of his unshaven beard on her cheek, then the heat of his mouth on hers. There was nothing tentative about his kiss. It was possessive, demanding. She revelled in the knowledge that he wanted her despite his better judgment, because it was the same with her.

What did the rational mind have to do with this? It went beyond thought to a primal source deep within. Her fingers wound through the damp silk of his long, dark hair.

His mouth parted from hers. When he spoke his lips grazed hers, his breath caressing her skin. 'Is it true?'

What was he talking about? She shook her head, blindly seeking his lips only to have him clasp her face between his hands.

His fierce obsidian eyes searched her features, as if to probe her soul. 'Is it true?'

'Is what true?' She could hardly think.

'Are you with child?'

She blinked, surprised by the question. 'Of course. I told you so.'

A flash of something that might have been anger travelled across his face, then he bent to kiss her and she was lost in sensation. This time his passion was bruising, but she met it with the white hot fury of her own.

When he raised his head, she twisted out of his arms and stepped backwards, wordlessly beckoning him toward the bed. But he stood unmoving, watching her as she slipped under the down-filled covers. Hugging the cool material to her chest, she looked at him expectantly, her body alive with anticipation.

Silent, unable to speak, she waited for him to come to her.

He prowled across the room, lean and dark, urgent. 'Have you no shame? You were untouched when I took your maidenhead.'

A shiver ran through her body. She didn't understand his anger.

A nervous laugh escaped her. 'I want you. Why should I deny it?'

'Why indeed?' He gave a strange laugh and stepped toward her.

Relieved, she held the covers back to welcome him, drawing him down to her. The long length of his body met hers. Their legs entwined. Impatience gripped her. Feverishly, she guided him into her.

There was a flash of pain but she ground her teeth rather than admit it.

'I hurt you?' He seemed startled.

'No. Not much. Don't pull away.'

He lay still in her, supporting his weight on his elbows. She wriggled under him, experimenting with the extent of her discomfort.

It was nothing compared to the thrill of having him like this.

But when she reached for his face and her lips met his, his manner had changed again. This time he was tender and she revelled in it, relaxing so that the pain of accepting him faded until it was swamped by the ever-increasing excitement of her impending release.

This time he lingered with her, bringing her slowly to her peak. She forgot everything in the moment of their joining, forgot herself in him. The power of their meeting left her breathless and dizzy. It was frightening to be so vulnerable to someone she didn't really understand or know, someone who only recently was her enemy.

She watched as he slid from her embrace and knelt above her, inspecting the bedding. She sat up, not surprised to see that she'd bled again.

'It didn't hurt as much as the first time.' She tried to reassure him.

He seemed stunned. 'It's true, then. If you carry a child, it's mine.'

She looked at him curiously. 'Of course it is.'

'How can this be?' His eyes searched her face.

She almost laughed. 'A child is usually the consequence of what we did, unless the woman uses –'

He caught her shoulders. 'You don't understand. I've never fathered a child. I thought I couldn't!'

Imoshen felt her skin go cold. So this was what the Aayel had seen – his secret shame, his one weak point. How cunning of her great aunt not to tell her, for she might have doubted her ability to conceive.

Now the babe was a foregone conclusion.

He placed a tentative hand on her belly. 'You are sure?'

She covered his hand with hers, touched by the wonder in his voice. She had meant to steal this child as a bargaining tool, but now she understood it was much more than that. It was the greatest gift she could give him.

He seemed so hopeful, but the healer in her had to temporise. 'You will see your son born, unless I miscarry.'

THE FIRE HAD fallen down to ashes. Imoshen lay nestled in the curve of the General's body, listening to the soft rise and fall of his breathing. At that moment she felt tender toward him, but more than a little indignant. He had suspected her of trying to pass off another man's child as his own!

Now she understood his private bitterness.

Stretching against him she felt him harden and nudge the crease of her buttocks. He uttered an appreciative noise in his throat and she smiled. She was sure if she were to...

A ragged shout made her heart falter. The sound came from the corridor, followed by the repetitive thud of booted feet. A woman shrieked.

Imoshen sat bolt upright.

The General lifted his head, his dark eyes startled, hair wild over his shoulders. 'What is it?'

'I don't know.' She licked dry lips. 'Soldiers in the hall outside –'

The door to the chamber flew open, crashing against the stone wall. Armed men poured into the room.

Tulkhan rolled out of the bed, running naked for his sword. Imoshen knew her dagger lay discarded by the cold bath. There was no time to reach it and they were outnumbered. Violence would not free them from these Ghebites. None of them were Tulkhan's men.

Several of the guards drew their weapons, preventing the General from reaching his. He cast a quick glance to her. Their position was hopeless and they both knew it.

Tulkhan straightened. 'This is my private chamber. Explain the intrusion.'

The Vaygharian stepped forward, his eyes alive with malicious triumph. 'Arrest these two by order of the King. They were plotting treason.'

'No!' General Tulkhan roared. But whether it was to deny the accusation or the knowledge that his half-brother had ordered their arrest, Imoshen did not know.

'On what evidence?' she asked. Pulling a soft blanket from the bedding, she wrapped it around her. Fear pounded through her veins, but she refused to show weakness as she stepped from the bed to confront her accusers. 'There can be no evidence, because the accusations are untrue.'

'You were convicted by your own words, both of you.'

The Vaygharian was enjoying himself. She could sense it oozing from him. He strode toward Imoshen but not near enough for her to jump him, or within Tulkhan's reach.

'The Dhamfeer withheld information. Her former lover, Reothe the rebel leader, was in the woods. Had she told us, we could have sent men out to capture him and his followers. His head would have been sitting on a pike on the battlements even now.'

Imoshen went cold with fear. Yes, she had withheld information which Tulkhan had unwittingly revealed, implicating her.

'I knew only that rebels had captured me, not how near their leader was,' she lied. 'And you're lucky you didn't venture into the woods after Reothe, because if you had, not one of you would be here to tell of it.'

The men stirred uneasily. Her conviction carried weight.

'So it is a groundless charge.' Tulkhan stepped forward. Though he was naked, the mantle of leadership was still visible in the set of his shoulders. Imoshen admired his assurance. The General was used to giving commands. Men were used to obeying him. Perhaps there was hope.

'Step away from the Princess. She is innocent of treason.' Tulkhan was firm but not strident. 'As am I.'

'You deny you refused a direct command of your king?' the Vaygharian cut in swiftly stilling the voice of reason. 'He ordered you into the highlands to hunt rebels.'

'And I refused,' Tulkhan agreed. 'To go would have been to murder my troops. I gave a commitment to hunt the rebels in the spring.'

'Convicted by his own words. Arrest him!'

The shouts of Gharavan's men drowned Tulkhan's voice. They surged forward, secure in the knowledge that they outnumbered the unarmed, naked man.

Imoshen stiffened. She refused to fight them, but this didn't stop them pawing her body on the pretext of subduing her. The blanket was torn from her so that she was clad in nothing but her long, pale hair. She refused to cower or plead as they pulled her towards the Vaygharian.

The General received worse treatment. Though he did not resist, their sheer numbers bore him down, arms were raised and the flat of their swords struck him repeatedly. She wanted to cry out, but she held her tongue and ground her teeth.

It was just as well. She found the Vaygharian's eyes on her, enjoying her anguish, feeding on her distress.

'Enough,' he said finally. The men drew back, hauling Tulkhan to his feet.

The General was bleeding freely and barely able to stand. Even so, he straightened with painful dignity. 'I demand to speak with my brother –'

'The King does not wish to be disturbed.' Kinraid cut him short. 'Take them below and secure them.'

Someone shoved Imoshen between the shoulder blades so hard that she staggered forward, falling to her knees at the Vaygharian's feet. The pain in her already bruised knees was sharp and immediate.

'You see,' he purred. 'It grows easier to kneel before your masters.'

Hatred surged through her. What she would give to hold a knife in her hands right now. He would be dead before his next breath. But then so would she, and where would that leave the General?

Imoshen's mouth went dry. What was she thinking?

It startled her to realise she had put Tulkhan before her people. They were her priority. She had to survive for the sake of Fair Isle and the child she carried, though in truth the babe seemed unreal to her at this moment.

The Vaygharian seized her arm, hauling her to her feet. His fingers caught in her long hair, pulling it so that tears of pain stung her eyes. She blinked them away, determined not to let him see even the slightest weakness.

He released her arms. With his black gloved hand, he tilted her face to study her features. His eyes were level with hers and, as she watched, she saw his gaze darken with desire. Instinctively, she knew this was a man who liked to inflict pain. It aroused him.

'Is it true what they say about the *pure* Dhamfeer women?' he purred.

'Well, General? Is this celibate bitch as hot to bed as rumour has it? No snivelling pleas, no martyred silences, just hot thighs and eager lips.'

She would have pulled back, but the men behind her pinned her arms.

Smiling slightly, the Vaygharian lifted his free hand and caught the tip of each finger-glove in his teeth, tugging on the leather till the glove slipped off his hand.

Imoshen stiffened as his warm, dry fingers brushed her breast, delicately tracing her nipple. To her shame her body responded and his smile broadened.

She hated him with every fibre of her being. Rage flooded her, blotting her vision. She wished him dead.

Sparks flashed before her eyes as if she were about to faint, but instead she realised they were the sparks of a raging fire. She saw the Vaygharian spin to face her, the flames at his back. He could not escape. Panic flashed across his face, sheer terror. Then his features hardened. He turned and with a shout of despair leapt into the roaring fire.

A cry of horror escaped her and she stiffened, panting.

Her vision cleared to see the Vaygharian's pleased face. Imoshen realised that he thought she was afraid of him, and she smiled with the foreknowledge of her vision.

'Why do you smile?' he snarled.

'You will die by your own hand, in flames of agony,' she told him.

It was very satisfying to see fear tighten the planes of his face. His hand swung in an arc, which she tried to dodge, but her captors restrained her. His balled fist caught her in the side of the head.

Dimly she heard Tulkhan roar as everything faded.

COLD CLAWED ITS way into her bones. Imoshen shivered and fought the need to wake. Her head hurt. Fear slept like an unwelcome twin in the back of her mind. To return to consciousness would mean a return to the real world of pain and... treachery.

It came back to her in a rush. The King, Tulkhan's own flesh and blood, had betrayed him.

She lifted her head and winced. Mercifully it was dark, but terribly cold. Shivers wracked her body. Nausea roiled in her stomach. Fighting the waves of pain, she tried to focus on a dim grey shape in the darkness and felt around her.

Her fingers encountered cold stone. She was lying on a floor lightly sprinkled with stale straw. Something scurried away and she knew she'd had company.

A soft laugh escaped her – how ironic. She was a prisoner in her own dungeon. She must remember to have the place cleaned, the rat-dogs released and fresh straw sprinkled. It was even more ridiculous when she did not know if she would escape this trap.

'Imoshen?' the General hissed.

She stiffened. A wave of longing enveloped her. She wanted him to hold her, to tell her everything would be all right, even though she knew it wouldn't.

'Imoshen, are you all right?'

She snorted.

When he spoke, she heard the answering smile in his voice. 'Come closer.'

She crawled toward the sound of his voice, but her fingers met cold, old wood. Dragging herself upright she found metal bars and saw a dim shape beyond.

They were separated by a passageway. So she would not have the luxury of warming herself in the General's embrace.

'What time is it?' she asked, when she could trust her voice not to betray her.

'Near dawn.'

Something in his tone warned her. 'What are their plans? A trial first, then execution, or simply execution?'

She heard him chuckle softly.

'Imoshen?' Dimly, she made out his outline, pressed against the bars opposite her, and saw his hand waver in the space between them.

By thrusting her arm through the bars of her own prison, she could just touch his fingers. Her shoulder ached abominably. Then she remembered how he had forced her to kneel to his petty king. Even that had not saved them.

His fingers were cold but gripped hers firmly.

'They will hold a trial. I am the King's half-brother. He couldn't have me executed without the formality of a trial.'

'And me?'

He hesitated.

'I see.' Her throat was tight with anger. 'When will they come for me?'

'Dawn.'

'So little time?' Her heart faltered.

She had dodged death many times in these last few moons, how ironic to die at the hands of a petty king and his vindictive lover.

Would her people revolt? What would General Tulkhan's elite guard do? Would they remain loyal to their rightful king, or to the man they had served so faithfully?

She'd been right. Gharavan was not to be trusted.

Rage warmed her. Would she have the chance to take that spiteful tyrant with her? If she did, she would only have the one opportunity.

Imoshen considered her options. Hopefully they wouldn't bind her. Seeing how contemptuous they were of a mere female, they probably would leave her arms free. Then if they let her get near enough to King Gharavan, she would go for his throat. A killing blow would crush his wind pipe and he'd suffocate even as his men gutted her.

She smiled, that was a pleasant thought.

'Imoshen?' General Tulkhan interrupted her. 'I... I should have heeded you when you warned me not to trust him.'

She knew it was true. What did he want from her, absolution? Strangely enough, she felt compelled to give it. 'You loved him.'

'Yes.' The word was torn from him. 'Even though he was my half-brother and destined to inherit what I could not earn.'

Her arm ached, but she didn't want to release the General's hand. That contact was her one point of humanity. Without him she was nothing but a weapon primed to kill. She was glad he would not see her die. Once she had killed Gharavan, there would be confusion. Tulkhan's elite guard would surely revolt. The General was next in line for the kingship. If the elite guard turned on the King's Vaygharian adviser... Was that the meaning of the foretelling she'd seen?

Imoshen's heart raced in anticipation. She would like to have a hand in his death. Of course, it meant her own and that of the child she carried. A cold chill ran through her body. Did she have the right to decide the fate of her unborn child? A black laugh rose inside her. What was she thinking? She was as good as dead anyway.

If only she had let Drake take her to Reothe, but what then? She would be her betrothed's captive as surely as she was King Gharavan's. What did it matter if the cage was stone or silk? It was still a cage.

Imoshen sighed, the Aayel had been right. There were no simple answers.

The General squeezed her fingers. 'The first time I saw you, your breasts so pale, your eyes so fierce... I wanted you.'

Imoshen swallowed. 'I hated you.'

'I know.'

She could tell he was smiling. 'But you proved an honourable enemy and' – her voice grew thick – 'a true friend.'

She wanted to tell him that he had become so much more to her, but the words stuck in her throat. She did not want to weep before him. She had to remain strong, to focus her will on killing Gharavan.

There were muffled footsteps and voices, the glow of an approaching torch.

'So soon?' Imoshen whispered, flinching as Tulkhan's fingers tightened their grip on hers.

'Imoshen?'

She could see the outline of his bruised face, his mouth and throat stained with dry blood. She knew she must look as battered.

A group of the King's men strode into the narrow corridor. Their two torches blinded Imoshen and their cruel laughter seared her.

Through a blur she saw one of them dart forward, weapon drawn ready to slash her extended arm. Though stiff and sore, she pulled back, aware how easily her arm could be broken even with the flat of the sword. She needed the use of her limbs if she was to carry out her plan.

Several cloaked figures blocked her view through the door's grate, but she could hear them shouting insults at General Tulkhan.

'Lady T'En?' a soft voice whispered.

Imoshen looked to see Kalleen restrained between them and her heart sank. What were these barbarians planning? The girl was innocent.

One of them moved forward to unlock Imoshen's prison door. Stiffly she stepped back.

On seeing her, Kalleen gave a soft cry of distress. 'What have they done to you, my lady?'

Imoshen tensed at her tone. The Kalleen she knew was not so weepy. Had they been brutal with her?

The youth who had opened the door was barely seventeen, richly dressed, out to conquer the world on a great adventure at the King's side. Imoshen saw it all in his face, and knew instinctively that he had never shed blood in anger or fear.

He flinched when Kalleen turned on him.

'How could you mistreat my lady so? She is the last of T'En, a princess in her own right. Get out while I help her dress!'

Shuffling, his face hot, he backed out.

Imoshen caught a glimpse of the others pressed against the far prison door, taunting General Tulkhan, then her door swung shut.

'My lady,' Kalleen whispered and Imoshen found the girl pulling her into the shadows.

'I'm all right.'

The girl hugged her fiercely.

Once released, Imoshen indicated the basket. 'So I am to die dressed, they allow me that much dignity.'

Kalleen stepped back and tugged at her cloak, dropping it to the stones.

'What are you doing?' Imoshen asked uneasily.

'I'm here to take your place.'

'No. I won't do it –'

'My lady,' Kalleen said sternly, her voice a fevered whisper. 'They will behead you at dawn. If you leave now, you can slip away from the stronghold, run into the forest and contact the rebels.'

Even as she spoke she was pulling on Imoshen's rich fur coat. Urgently, the young woman dragged the poorer cloak over Imoshen's shoulders.

'They will kill you,' Imoshen croaked.

Kalleen blinked, her face barely visible in the spears of light which came through the grate. 'They will be angry and probably beat me. It does not matter.'

Imoshen's heart twisted within her. They both knew Kalleen was lying.

'I am taller than you, fairer –'

'Pull the cloak up, hunch down.' Kalleen gave a start as the door shook on its hinges. 'They come.'

There was no time for more. It was a trick they were sure to expect. Yet hope fluttered in Imoshen's breast. If she managed to escape, she could turn on the King, rouse the stronghold guard. She had to succeed.

Her captors must believe she was the serving maid. They must perceive Kalleen as the captive Imoshen.

The girl proudly turned away from the door, acting her role. Someone tugged on the back of Imoshen's cloak. Her heart pounded with urgency.

What should she do? She'd never tried to befuddle the minds of men before. Her great aunt had said some True-men were more susceptible to the gifts than others, but that was all she knew.

If only the Aayel had lived long enough to help her to understand and harness her T'En power. Panic threatened to steal her wits then, like a fog lifting, her mind cleared and only ice-cold determination filled her.

She would be Kalleen, the faithful servant distraught because her mistress was to die. A thousand stinging ants picked their way over her skin.

The youth dragged her away from the proud, fur-cloaked figure.

'My lady!' Imoshen wept and thumped the youth. He caught her hands and looked down into her face. It seemed she was smaller than she had been. Fear flickered in the back of her mind, but she was Kalleen and words leapt to her tongue. 'Ghebite barbarian!'

He laughed and pushed her through the open door. 'Get out, or you can stay and keep your mistress company with the headman's axe.'

Imoshen dared not glance in Tulkhan's direction and risk breaking her concentration. She was Kalleen the former farm girl, an unimportant creature in the scheme of things.

With every step she took out of those dank, oppressive chambers, terror warred with elation. The guards jostled her in their eagerness to escape the dungeon. Any moment now she was sure they would look into her face and see through the illusion.

At the entrance to the kitchen wing they marched off, talking amongst themselves. Imoshen sniffed and scurried away into the warren of storerooms and then past the great kitchen itself, where the woman who ruled this domain was already up, preparing fresh bread and warm broth for their first meal of the day.

Imoshen paused to catch her breath. How long did she have? Dawn could not be far away.

Running lightly through the empty corridors, she headed for the wing she had put aside to house the elite guard. Wharrd was pacing the floor, arguing with several of the men when she entered.

A man grabbed her as she ran into the room, lifting her off her feet.

'Kalleen, what are you doing here?' Wharrd rounded on her. 'Have you a message from Tulkhan?'

As she slid from the man's grip Imoshen remembered Kalleen and Wharrd had had a falling out over Drake and, as far as she knew, they had not made up their difference. But she was no longer Kalleen. She must resume her own identity now.

At this thought her skin crawled with a thousand pinpricks of pain.

She must take control of the stronghold defenders, trap Gharavan's men and convince the elite guard to...

Wharrd swore softly, then made the sign to ward off evil. Several men turned their faces away, others went for their weapons.

By their reaction Imoshen knew the change must have taken effect, she felt like herself again. The cloak did not brush the ground as she drew it tightly about her.

'Princess,' Wharrd made a soldier's attempt at a bow.

Dhamfeer, someone hissed behind her.

She ignored him. 'I need clothes, breeches, boots and a jerkin. Kalleen has taken my place. I won't let her die in my stead. And I won't let them make a mockery of the General's devotion to his king. Tulkhan is innocent of treason.'

'I know,' the grizzled campaigner muttered. 'We all know that.'

Imoshen moved towards the bone-setter. He flinched as she approached, though he tried to hide it. She didn't have time to reassure him. 'The Vaygharian poisons Gharavan's mind with lies. The King is weak, not half the man General Tulkhan is. Where does your loyalty lie?'

Wharrd did not hesitate. 'With Tulkhan.'

'Aye, the General.'

'General Tulkhan!'

Their voices joined the bone-setter's, gaining conviction.

Imoshen's hand closed on Wharrd's arm. 'Will you fight beside my people?'

'What would you have us do?'

She smiled. 'First find me some clothes.'

TULKHAN SHIVERED. HE had called to Imoshen repeatedly, but she would not answer. She was going to die at dawn and the knowledge was bitter. He would also face the headman's axe once they were through with the mockery of his trial. And he had only himself to blame. He had thought he could reason with his half-brother, wean him from the Vaygharian, but he'd overestimated his influence with Gharavan.

On the battlefield you could not afford to underestimate the enemy. But this was not the battlefield, and backroom politics was not his style.

He had thrown away Imoshen's life and his own, as well as Fair Isle, which should have been his. He had won it while his half-brother and his army had ridden on his coat tails, mopping up survivors, swaggering through crushed villages.

He had misjudged his man and must face the consequences.

Shivers wracked his body. He despised himself. But it was the empty cold ache within that troubled him most. They would lead her away, proudly defiant to the last, and he would never see her again.

Tulkhan did not believe in an afterlife. He had seen too many religions in too many kingdoms to hold onto the faith of his Ghebite homeland. But just this once he wished he was a believer, that there was some way he could ensure they would be reborn and meet again in another life.

Contempt seared him. It was this kind of woolly thinking which had led him astray. He should have assessed his half-brother's character flaws and recognised his weakness for what it was. A stronger mind could lead Gharavan to great things, but it could also lead him to evil.

Booted feet struck the stones.

'Imoshen, answer me. They come!'

But she stubbornly refused. Was she frightened? Tulkhan longed to offer comfort. Yet he dared not. She probably despised him for leading them into this. Self-disgust seared him. What right had he to offer her anything?

Knowing they would taunt him, he moved back from the grille, but not too far. He wanted to catch sight of her face this one last time.

'Let's see this Dhamfeer Princess,' one of them growled.

'See her die like any other woman. Where is your Dhamfeer magic now, Princess?'

They flung the door open.

Tulkhan could see nothing but their backs. The after image of flickering torchlight danced on his night-blinded eyes.

Why the silence? He had expected cruel mockery. The King's men staggered back. One of them cursed. Between their shoulders Tulkhan saw Kalleen's truculent, frightened face as she walked determinedly out of the cell.

The men broke into a gabble of accusations and counter-accusations. They swore the switch was impossible.

One of them grabbed Kalleen and shook her. 'She's real.'

'The last one was real too, remember I looked into her face,' the youth cried. 'Dhamfeer magic!'

They cursed and called on their gods to protect them. Typically, their greatest fear was who would tell their king.

Tulkhan rejoiced. Imoshen was free. But he dared not draw attention to himself. The men were angry and frightened. They would turn on anyone.

One of them grabbed Kalleen, twisting her arm so that she cried out. They dragged the girl away and Tulkhan knew there would be no mercy for her. Gharavan would be enraged.

In the same breath, fierce joy coursed through him. Imoshen was free.

What would she do?

What could she do, an outlaw in her own stronghold? The servants would be on her side, unless his half-brother had them all cowered by brutal threats. No, he doubted if they would betray her.

What was he thinking? He had seen the King's men lead Kalleen away twice and he had not known one of them was Imoshen. He'd had no idea she could cast illusions. She constantly surprised him. He shivered as he remembered how she had described the Vaygharian's death.

Was she using foreknowledge? She had said it with the same certainty that Reothe had spoken of his own death.

Tulkhan repressed a shudder.

What was the extent of Imoshen's Dhamfeer heritage? Could she retake Umasreach on her own and leave him to rot down here?

Self-loathing filled Tulkhan.

She didn't need him. She had said herself she'd only taken him as an ally for practical purposes.

Why had she taken him to her bed, then? He flinched. Was that quicksilver passion of hers an incandescent coal, ready to leap into flame for any man who knew how to ignite it?

Imoshen had admitted Reothe moved her.

Even now she was probably far from the stronghold. Why shouldn't she flee into the woods and take Reothe's side? If this was but a glimpse of her T'En gifts, how much more powerful would the two Dhamfeer be when joined?

No wonder she had abandoned him. He had proved himself incompetent, so she had cast him aside.

Despair cut through Tulkhan. He was a fool.

Love for his half-brother had undone him. Love had clouded his vision. That would never happen again, he vowed. He only wished he might live long enough to see his half-brother brought low by Imoshen's hand. A grim smile tugged at his lips.

King Gharavan had made a bad enemy in the Dhamfeer woman. Tulkhan knew as surely as the Vaygharian's days were numbered, that Gharavan would meet death before his time.

Marching feet sounded on the stones again and he tensed. Surely it was not time? They couldn't have summarily executed the little maid already.

Three different King's men approached his cell. Tulkhan wondered grimly what had happened to the others. The men flung the door open and hauled Tulkhan out. He tried not to flinch, but the torchlight hurt his eyes. Chilled to the marrow by the cold, he tried to walk with dignity down the length of the dungeon chambers.

He expected them to be rough with him, but they were circumspect. Still, a pair of breeches wouldn't have gone astray. If he was to meet death he'd have preferred to do it clothed.

He was sure the oversight was deliberate. But if they thought to cower him they would discover they were wrong.

The upper floors of Umasreach were abuzz with activity and suppressed excitement. Servants scurried about, but he could not see his own men or the stronghold guard. He understood why when the men marched him into the great hall.

His own man, Wharrd, stood behind the King's chair, flanked by the elite guard who it appeared had sworn allegiance to Gharavan. Tulkhan's gut twisted at the thought. He had believed his men, especially the elite guard, were bound to him through years of service, years when he had sweated in the sun, shivered in the cold, slept on rocks and faced death at their sides.

Did it count for nothing? Fury made him stand taller. He would not flinch before his half-brother. He would meet his end with dignity.

He met Gharavan's eyes and something travelled between them, some acknowledgment of his humanity. Was there a chance he could reason with the youth?

Then he noted the arrogance in the Vaygharian's stance and saw the way the man's hand rested on Gharavan's shoulder. The hopelessness of his situation threatened to overwhelm Tulkhan. His brother had sold his soul to a soulless man who wanted only power.

Tulkhan surveyed the hall. The King's men were gathered around in clusters, some still buckling on their weapons, adjusting their cloaks. He was right – he had been called prematurely.

Little Kalleen was a miserable creature. Unbound, she knelt at Gharavan's feet. Where was Imoshen now? Half-way across the woods, running to Reothe, no doubt.

He felt anger on Kalleen's behalf. She had been willing to give her life for her mistress, only to be abandoned.

'The Dhamfeer has escaped, thus confirming her guilt. What say you, General?' Gharavan asked.

Tulkhan wondered why his half-brother felt it necessary to prolong this mock trial. 'I knew nothing of it. I ask one thing only. Spare the maidservant.'

His half-brother stiffened and glanced down at Kalleen, who ducked her head as if expecting a blow.

'If she is so eager to take her mistress's place, she can die in her place.'

'No!' It was out before Tulkhan could stop himself.

'No?' Gharavan stiffened in the seat.

Tulkhan ground his teeth. His own life was forfeit, but he might yet save the girl. 'I taught you to ride. I made your first wooden practice sword. If you have any memory of the love we once shared, grant me this one request. Release the girl.'

'What of yourself?' Gharavan asked. 'What do you ask for yourself?'

Tulkhan ignored the glittering eyes of the Vaygharian, who was relishing every moment of this.

'Nothing?' pursued his half-brother. 'Do you deny you refused to obey my command?'

Stung, Tulkhan glanced to the men who had served under him. He knew he must look a pitiful sight in their eyes, naked, almost blue with cold, bruised and bloodied. They had followed him because they respected him. It irked him to lose their respect.

'Well?' Gharavan prodded.

'I would not lead my men to certain death in the southern highlands in the depths of winter. I've given a sworn undertaking to hunt Reothe and his accursed rebels come the thaw. But why continue this? We all know it is a mockery. You...' Anger threatened to choke his voice. 'You had my father's love. You were his chosen heir, yet you fear me. Why? I've served our father loyally. I rose to that position through skill, not favour. Never once have I done other than serve in his name. I would have honoured you with the same service –'

'Say you,' hissed the Vaygharian. 'But what of the Dhamfeer Princess? You took her to your bed. The country is behind her. You could have taken Fair Isle for your own. Admit that this is what the pair of you planned!'

Tulkhan was stunned. What the Vaygharian said was true, he could have used Imoshen to unite the people. But it was never his intention to take Fair Isle for himself. 'You twist my words –'

'Enough!' The Vaygharian strode forward. 'This man calls me a liar because he lies. He plots to further his own ambition.'

Rage gripped Tulkhan, ridding him of the last shreds of despair. To be unjustly accused of the very crimes the Vaygharian was committing was the ultimate irony. Giving the formal signs, he challenged the Vaygharian. 'I call you liar, you are dishonoured.'

Kinraid laughed. 'I won't accept a challenge from a condemned prisoner. There is no honour in that.'

He was loudly seconded by the King's men, making Tulkhan wonder how many of them owed their position to the Vaygharian.

Gharavan came to his feet. 'Who says General Tulkhan can't challenge Kinraid, the Vaygharian?'

It was a strange question, one that surprised Tulkhan and made the King's men hesitate. They looked to each other.

'Who says he is a dog without honour and should be beheaded?' roared the Vaygharian.

His shout was taken up by the King's men, who followed his lead eagerly. Tulkhan noted the silence from his elite guard, the silence from the rest of the stronghold servants and guard scattered through the great hall. They were unwilling witnesses to his trial and execution.

Quickly he scanned the room, once again on familiar territory. This was a battle with the odds against him, but one which he recognised and understood. Now, he knew who was loyal and who would stab him in the back given a chance.

Gharavan's expression caught his attention. Odd, it was almost sympathetic.

The young King stepped forward, pulling Kalleen to her feet. 'Go home to your people.'

She stared at him, her mouth open with disbelief.

Kinraid started and strode toward Gharavan, obviously about to disagree with the King's order. Tulkhan heard a shout from the back of the hall.

His half-brother gave Wharrd a signal. 'Arrest the Vaygharian.'

'No!' Kinraid spun. 'What manner of –'

'Imposter!' A scream echoed to the vaulted roof as someone charged through the throng by the kitchen door.

Tulkhan stared. It was his half-brother, dishevelled, frantic to reach them.

The Vaygharian spun to face King Gharavan. 'Then who? You!'

He drew his sword and lunged toward the false Gharavan, who thrust Kalleen aside and drew his own sword.

Even as Tulkhan watched, his half-brother's face wavered and slipped to reveal Imoshen in breeches and jerkin, her hair tightly bound at the nape of her neck. She parried Kinraid's wild thrust.

The hall reacted to the sight with gasps and curses.

Wharrd darted forward with a bundle for Tulkhan. He found clothes and a sword thrust into his hands even as the great hall erupted. Men screamed, servants ran or turned on their oppressors.

It was the stronghold guard and his own elite guard against the king's men. The outcome was inevitable. But Gharavan's men were well armed and desperate. They rallied around their king.

Tulkhan discarded everything but the breeches. He dragged them on and laced them in moments, then leapt forward to engage the Vaygharian.

Before Tulkhan could reach him, one of the King's men staggered into him. The man went down to his knees, dragging Tulkhan with him. Imoshen brought the hilt of her sword down onto the man's head and offered Tulkhan her arm. A wild, fey smile split her face. Her wine-dark eyes were alight with battle fever and he shivered, recognising it for what it was. Once he had wielded a sword in an ecstasy of killing. When had he lost that thrill? Now he hated bloodshed, hated death.

Wordlessly, he took her arm and pulled himself up. Where was the Vaygharian? Bodies obscured his vision, threatened to overwhelm them both. Men were dying all around them.

Turning, he plunged into the fray with one aim in mind.

His half-brother fought desperately with his back to the wall and his men going down around him. Tulkhan swept through, hitting with the flat of his sword, kicking men aside as they went down.

At last he faced his half-brother who stood, chest heaving, blinking with shock. Gharavan wore nothing but a night shirt. Tulkhan could only suppose Imoshen must have surprised him in bed, subdued him then made the switch.

The King dragged in a ragged breath and lifted his sword point in the defence position as Tulkhan had taught him.

Years of training on the battlefield guided the General's sword. The blow sent the young King's weapon flying from his numbed fingers. Then Tulkhan's sword tip pressed at his half-brother's throat.

'Tell them to put down their arms,' Tulkhan said.

'Surrender!' His half-brother swallowed, his Adam's apple bobbing close to the sword point. 'Lay down your arms!'

The terror in Gharavan's voice communicated itself to those around him and the swordplay ceased. There were repeated clangs of metal on stone as the King's men were disarmed or voluntarily downed their weapons.

Tulkhan stepped back. 'This way.'

'What will you do?' Gharavan whispered.

Tulkhan had no idea.

He didn't want to kill his half-brother. Yet his instinct and all his experience told him letting Gharavan live could be a fatal error. The youth's death was needed to consolidate his position.

When had it come to this?

Tulkhan turned his back on his half-brother and walked away. Would Gharavan attack him from behind? Was he hoping Gharavan would? Then he could strike the lad down in self-defence and remain guiltless of his half-brother's murder. Tulkhan did not want to carry that burden.

Imoshen strode toward him, her face feral with the heat of battle. 'Kill him!'

Tulkhan touched her cheek sadly and searched her eyes, looking for something, though he could not have said what it was.

'If I took life as easily as that, you would be dead,' he told her softly.

She blanched, recoiling as if he'd slapped her.

'Tulkhan?' Gharavan pushed through his kneeling, wounded men. 'Tulkhan, blood-kin –'

'Don't tempt me, Gharavan,' Tulkhan warned.

'He would have killed you,' Imoshen's eyes were dark pools of anger. Tulkhan knew he had hurt her, and after she had saved him.

The enormity of what the Dhamfeer had done hit him. How she must be laughing at him. She had held them all in the palm of her hand during that masquerade. He shuddered at the thought. How could he trust Imoshen when he would never know what she was capable of?

'Tulkhan?' Gharavan seized his arm. 'It was Kinraid's idea, he –'

'Where is the Vaygharian?' Tulkhan yelled and thrust his half-brother aside. But though everyone looked for him, Kinraid had escaped the great hall.

Gharavan did not seem surprised.

'Wharrd?' Tulkhan turned to his elite guard, grateful to know that they had been loyal all along. 'Send men out to the stables. Find the Vaygharian. Kill him if he resists, but I fear he has already escaped.' He turned to his half-brother. 'As for you. I renounce all kinship with you. To me you are as one dead. You may take that which you can carry on your back, a horse and your wounded. Make haste to Northpoint.' He named the port where he knew his half-brother's ships had made landfall. 'Never set foot on this island again. If you do, your life is forfeit.'

He knew Imoshen would object. His half-brother was about to speak, but Tulkhan overrode them both. 'Go now. My elite guard will escort you. Stay clear of the capital, T'Diemn.'

The King's men were eager enough to flee, knowing they would escape with their lives. They hurried out of the great hall, escorted by the elite guard.

At last Tulkhan turned to Imoshen, visibly seething at his side.

'He would have killed you!' she repeated.

'He's still my half-brother –'

'You're sending him back to rule an empire seven times the size of this island, seven times as wealthy. Do you call that punishment?'

The Dhamfeer stood there questioning his judgment as if she was his equal, as if it was her right. A strange double vision overcame Tulkhan. He saw Imoshen as a Ghebite male would view her. Once he would have thought her an ignorant female who had no right to question his authority. Now he knew not only was she trained in matters of state and battle tactics, but her T'En gifts gave her the ability to manipulate True-people.

Fear of her Dhamfeer powers rippled through him. Why did she even bother to argue? How long before Imoshen stopped arguing and simply wrenched control from him? A bitter smile made him grimace.

But he answered her question. 'Gharavan is going back to an empire made up of conquered nations. My father held it together by the sheer force of his personality. It will take only one uprising for the whole house of cards to come crashing down. If I am lucky, Gharavan will spend the rest of his life losing the countries I annexed since I became general of my father's army.'

He watched her face, saw her assess his words and nod slowly. 'Very well.'

So she was convinced, for now.

He was banishing one weak enemy, but he still faced internal threats, Reothe and his rebels and... he watched Imoshen as she absently cleaned her blade and re-sheathed it.

Dare he trust her?

After this night he dare not turn his back on her.

It galled him to see how, unlike him, his own people turned to her. Even his wounded men limped or were carried to the Dhamfeer for treatment. She simply accepted this as her duty, sending Kalleen for her medicinals.

Brooding, Tulkhan watched Imoshen go about her self-appointed task as healer. She was as much a threat to him as Reothe. Other, unknowable, she could befuddle his mind, plant thoughts in his head, even confuse a hall full of people with her illusions.

She was a dangerous enemy but a good ally. It was wiser to keep her close, to observe her.

He realised with a jolt that Gharavan had been right. While Imoshen stood at his side, the island would remain behind him.

Wharrd returned to report no sign of the Vaygharian. Tulkhan shrugged his shoulders, easing his bruised body, and tried to concentrate. There was so much to do. Events had forced him to lay claim to Fair Isle for himself.

Grim determination seized him. All his life he had served his father as the first son of his second wife. He had taken pride in his skills as a general. He had sought to win his father's respect by his service and what had it led to? This debacle.

From now on, he would serve no one. He was his own man. His hands tightened on his sword hilt. This island was his, and what he took, he held.

IMOSHEN TENDED THE wounded until she was so weary she could hardly think. Each time she closed a wound, she exerted a little push to help the skin knit, adding a little warming glow that would close off the bleeding and fight infection. It was instinctive, something she had done in the past with an effort. One part of her mind marvelled at the growth in her gift, or at least in her ability to control it.

But she was also physically exhausted after lying awake all night, shivering with cold and dread. The mental effort to maintain the deception in Gharavan's form had taken every fibre of her being. Numbly, she regretted the lost opportunity. She might have won them over, fooled the King's men and had the Vaygharian executed, all without bloodshed, if Gharavan hadn't escaped.

She should have had him killed. The fact that he was General Tulkhan's half-brother had stayed her hand. The General's loyalty was sadly misplaced, but it sprang from his true heart and she'd had to respect that.

Her hands trembled as she straightened and sensed Tulkhan's piercing eyes on her. He looked distant, brooding. Suspicious even?

The thought was unwelcome. Why should he be suspicious of her? Hadn't she stood by him? Hadn't she proved more trustworthy than his own flesh and blood? Why then, was he standing there in the shadows tight-lipped, the planes of his face taut with tension?

She tried to put herself in his place, not literally since she knew he didn't like her invading his mind, but figuratively.

In one night General Tulkhan had lost his half-brother and his place in the world. But he had laid claim to Fair Isle. That gave him a purpose, yet the freshly taken island was seething with rebellion. His hold was a fragile thing. Was he capable of holding Fair Isle?

For one terrible moment, Imoshen wondered if she had made the right choice. After all, Reothe was one of her own kind. True, his T'En gifts were greater than hers and she feared his single-minded determination. But he had never threatened her personally. Back before this invasion, he had been kind to her when she was nothing but a gauche child-woman out of her depth in the Royal Palace.

Reothe had even risked his life to rescue her from the Ghebite army at Landsend Abbey. He was not to know she did not want to be rescued. Her choice to stay at Tulkhan's side for the sake of her people still seemed the right decision. But was it?

It was the old dilemma. If only the Aayel were here to advise her.

'That's the last of them, my lady,' Kalleen said, her voice breaking with weariness.

Imoshen felt guilty. She took the girl's small golden-skinned hand in her own. 'You saved my life this night, and I won't forget it. Is there anything I can do for you or your family?'

Imoshen winced as Kalleen stiffened, offended. 'I did not do it for gain, Lady T'En!'

'I know.' Imoshen squeezed her hand. 'But we can't eat principles. Give it some thought. You're tired, so am I.' Tired beyond thought. 'We'll rest now.'

'No.' Tulkhan stepped forward. 'Send warm water to your mistress's room, Kalleen. See that she is dressed as befits her station.'

Imoshen was made aware of her Ghebite male attire, and the grime and blood on her hands and clothes. She stiffened. If Tulkhan didn't approve of her, that was his problem. But what was he planning? 'Why can't I rest?'

'I must ride to the capital. The army awaits, and if I don't lay claim to it, my half-brother or that Vaygharian may well stir up trouble.'

'Kinraid is probably riding the fastest horse he could steal to the coast,' she countered. But Tulkhan was right. The army was leaderless and probably rife with rumour. Now was the moment for him to take command. 'Very well. You go to the capital and secure the army.'

She felt him study her face and wondered what he was looking for.

'You're coming with me,' he said.

'But there is work for me here. The township is still being built. As the winter tightens its grip, more people flock here every day looking for food and shelter. I cannot leave my people when they need me.' Imoshen saw his closed expression. 'You must go to T'Diemn and assume command of the army, see to it that they are settled in for the winter, that there is enough food for everyone and the soldiers are occupied so they don't cause trouble for the townsfolk during the idleness of deep winter. But you don't need me to –'

'I do.'

Imoshen laughed. 'What for?'

Wharrd returned to tell his General that the King and his men were about to leave.

Tulkhan nodded. His hand slipped around Imoshen's upper arm. 'Kalleen, go fetch your lady's white fur cloak. And I'll need my cloak, too. Wharrd, have our horses saddled –'

'What are you doing? We can't leave yet.' Imoshen planted her feet and twisted to free her arm

'Hold still.' The General stepped behind her. She could feel him undoing the leather thong which held her hair. The skin on the back of her neck prickled as his fingers brushed her flesh. She ached for his touch, and hated herself for the weakness.

Turning a little to face him, she could see the bruises on his chest overlaying the old scars. Was he badly hurt by the beating?

His distinctive male scent came to her. It was intoxicating. Like strong wine it went straight to her head, clouding rational thought. Her body urged her to take that one step which would bring her into contact with him. She wanted to feel him down the length of her, to tuck her face into the crook of his neck and taste the salty tang on his skin. A shudder of longing ran through her.

Surely he could sense her reaction to him? Yet he remained unmoved. Shame stung her.

It startled Imoshen to admit that her body's needs could almost override her good sense. She knew the General had withdrawn from her, though she didn't know why. Tulkhan should have been grateful for her help, but instead he was grim, his dark eyes impassive as he unbound her long hair. He lifted the tangled tresses to run his fingers through the knots, freeing them.

If she were to lean back she could press her shoulders to his chest, feel his arms around her. Instead she felt the insistent little tugs on her scalp as he unravelled her hair.

Kalleen returned, breathless, with their cloaks. Imoshen didn't know how long they had been standing there. For her, time had stopped as she battled against the force of her body's need. It was an unwelcome complication when she had to have her wits about her.

She should have felt relief, now that King Gharavan had been dispatched and banished to his own lands, but instead she found General Tulkhan had once again become her enemy.

Weariness and something else made her breath catch in her throat. She was so tired, physically and mentally. Would she ever know a safe harbour where she could let her guard down, where she could be accepted for herself?

Tears flooded her eyes. She blinked them away fiercely, despising her weakness.

Calling on her reserves of strength, Imoshen lifted her chin and stood tall while Kalleen adjusted her cloak, spreading the mantle of her hair across her shoulders.

She watched Tulkhan swing his deep red cloak around him. The Ghebite cloak was not warm enough for this southern winter. His hair hung in long matted strands down his shoulder, dried with caked blood in places.

Irrationally, she longed to tend him as she had done last night. The words sprang to her lips, but she contained them. She wanted to order a hot bath prepared so she could sponge the dried blood from his hair, see to his wounds. She ached to do it. Instinct told her the General needed a tender touch, but his manner was so forbidding she knew it was impossible. She was not welcome and the knowledge hurt.

Wharrd handed Tulkhan his helmet.

She watched as the General wound his hair into a knot and pulled the helmet over his head, wincing.

He was once again the distant barbarian invader, his eyes hooded beneath the helmet's ridge, his height increased by the crest that arched across the top.

He offered her his arm and she took it as understanding came to her.

He had banished his half-brother the King and laid claim to Fair Isle in reality, but not yet officially. This was a show of strength. He had to look the part and she was playing her role at his side.

He needed her to bolster his position. Not by so much as a glimmer did he reveal anything as they walked from the great hall. The corded muscles of his forearm were like bands of steel under her fingers.

Before she knew she meant to do it, Imoshen used the physical contact to probe. She had to know why he deliberately distanced himself from her. But she met a wall of iron will that held her probing gift at bay.

Startled, she looked at him and saw only the grim line of his jaw, the chiselled tip of his nose and broad angle of his cheekbone. The General had not consciously resisted her, yet he had excluded her from his mind.

This was interesting, and daunting. It meant she could not gauge his mood and motivations. Not that she would have done it, she amended hastily. But honesty forced her to admit the temptation would always be there.

Uncertainty had prompted her to try dipping into his thoughts just then and how soon would she have slipped into the habit of monitoring his mind?

This frightened Imoshen. She did not want to become so removed from Tulkhan and those around her that she thought nothing of stealing into their thoughts to gain a lever over them.

It was just as well Tulkhan did not sense her subtle probe. Or had he? Was that why he stepped back from her so stiffly now? But no, he offered her his hand. She swung into the saddle of her horse, then watched him mount. Only she saw his slight grimace of pain, and her heart contracted.

He was such a magnificent creature. Only she knew how bruised and sore he was as he sat astride the black destrier. Under that red cloak his chest was naked and he was clad in nothing but breeches and boots.

If he was in pain or cold, he would not reveal it.

At General Tulkhan's signal the party moved out. Gharavan and his men wore cloaks, and their horses were heavily laden with clothes and stores. They were escorted by a select number of the elite guard. Tulkhan urged his mount forward, signalling Imoshen was to ride beside him.

It was a crisp early morning. They moved down the slope away from the stronghold at a slow walk, and the inhabitants of the township lined the broad street's edge, staring and silent. Rumour would have kept them informed of what had passed. King Gharavan had invaded Umasreach Stronghold and tried to execute the General and the last T'En Princess. In less than a day he had been vanquished and was being banished from their island.

Imoshen could sense the relief of the crowd and their animosity toward Gharavan. With a start she realised that if she and Tulkhan had not been there to add dignity to the escort, the townspeople might have picked up clods of snow or refuse and thrown it at the deposed King and his men.

She had to admit Tulkhan was wise, far wiser than any other Ghebite.

They left behind the last of the rude shelters hastily built by the recent arrivals, and came to a halt on the empty snow of the white plain. A finger of winter sunlight found its way through the sullen low clouds, illuminating them with its cold brilliance. A thousand diamonds of light sparkled on the cold snow. Their breath hung in clouds on the still air. Their horses snorted and shifted, bodies steaming in the cold.

Tulkhan nudged his mount forward. At his signal, Imoshen followed. Light reflected off the snow and off her white cloak so that it felt as if she was bathed in a cold silver brilliance. The moment had a timeless quality that seemed to stretch forever. The significance of the night's events struck Imoshen, stealing her breath for a moment.

They were living history.

On this bitterly cold winter's morning General Tulkhan had faced death, routed his half-brother and laid claim to Fair Isle, all with her help.

What would Reothe say if he knew how instrumental she had been in the night's events?

Imoshen squinted and scanned the line of the woods. Like benevolent giants the massive evergreens rose above the bare deciduous trees. Scattered through the forest they stood head and shoulders above the bare black branches, defiantly green still. In deep winter they would be cloaked in a protective layer of snow which insulated their foliage from the cold.

A horse snorted and her mount shifted uneasily.

Was Reothe himself watching this tableau from the safety of the woods? Would Gharavan ever reach the northwestern port and his ships?

The words exchanged between General Tulkhan and his half-brother washed over her. She heard only their tone, resentful on Gharavan's part, cold and uncompromising on Tulkhan's. Then the General raised his hand and Wharrd gave the cry to move off.

Tulkhan's horse shied and would have joined the others, but he held it back, wheeling the beast around to rejoin her. Side by side they sat their mounts, he in his barbarian battle finery, resplendent in red and black, she in white-tipped fur and silver hair.

What was General Tulkhan thinking? Imoshen wondered. Was he mourning his dead father, his half-brother and his Ghebite homeland lost to him forever now? Or was he thinking of warmth, food and rest, like she was?

When they could no longer see the banished men and their escort, when the outcasts had become one with the dark trunks of the woods, the General turned his horse and she followed suit. She was cold under her cloak and she knew he must be colder still. But they rode solemnly into the township, down the main street. People had drifted out to watch the King leave and now followed them back through town in a mass.

The place seemed pristinely beautiful coated in snow, glistening in the pale sunlight. You couldn't see how hastily it had been cobbled together. Snow coated the scarred earth which had recently been rolling grasslands.

Everything was so beautiful Imoshen's eyes stung with unshed tears. Perhaps it was her. She hadn't expected to see this day dawn and, now that she did, she found life very precious.

They had almost mounted the rise to the stronghold when someone gave a ragged cheer. As if this was a signal, the townspeople took up the cry. It was a mixed babble – some called on General Tulkhan, others called on the language of Fair Isle, but the meaning was clear.

Not only had the General and Imoshen delivered themselves from death this last night, but they had delivered the people from persecution.

At the outer gate, General Tulkhan slowed and turned his mount to face the populace. Imoshen again followed his cue. Her heart swelled with an emotion she didn't try to name, and the tears she had been holding back flowed freely down her cheeks, scaldingly hot on her cold skin.

She told herself the people were weary of war, that they wanted peace and prosperity, not oppression. She and the General had shown that they could maintain peace and deal fairly. Was it more than self-interest which prompted this show of loyalty from her people? Imoshen did not know. Her head might hold doubts but her heart could not help responding, soaring with their cheers. She felt a rush of comradeship for her people who had suffered under the Ghebite invasion. Lifting her hand in salute, she smiled through her tears.

At last Tulkhan turned his horse and they entered the passage, passing through the inner gates to the courtyard where the servants, remaining elite guard and stronghold guard greeted them enthusiastically. It warmed Imoshen because she knew these people personally. Fresh tears made her vision swim.

She was so tired. She wanted nothing more than a warm bath and food, then to crawl into bed.

The General swung from his saddle and turned to her, holding out his arms.

She wanted to feel his hands on her waist, to feel the length of his strong body as he lowered her to ground. She wanted to lay her head on his chest and know that she had nothing to fear, but she couldn't afford to lower her guard.

Disdaining his help, she swung her leg over the saddle and leaped to the ground.

Tulkhan caught her arm, his fingers biting sharply into her flesh. He raised their joined arms to acknowledge the greetings of the stronghold. She knew he was annoyed with her show of independence. They had to present a united front. Their every move was being assessed, watched by servants, petty nobles and members of the stronghold and elite guards.

When the cheer died down General Tulkhan raised his voice. 'I thank you for standing true. I will not forget this night, or your loyalty.'

Again they cheered and Imoshen grimaced to herself. Other than the elite guard, the stronghold's loyalty had been to her and Tulkhan had benefited from it. By relieving them of Gharavan, the General had become a hero. And what of her?

As they moved toward the steps to the great hall, the people surged forward, jostling to get near her. They stroked her hair and touched her sixth finger.

'T'En,' they whispered reverently, proudly. 'Lady T'En.'

But they wouldn't meet her eyes.

Then Imoshen understood. She had become their talisman – a creature to be revered and feared, the T'En of nursery rhyme.

It stung her to the quick, but it also amused her, because she was the same person today she had been yesterday. Only their perception of her had changed. A rueful smile tugged at her lips. She glanced at General Tulkhan, expecting him to be amused as she was, but instead she read suspicion in his obsidian eyes, quickly masked.

Imoshen couldn't fathom his reaction. Her head spun with weariness. Rest... that was what she needed. Later, when she could think clearly, she would deal with General Tulkhan and his suspicions.

He took her arm. 'Prepare yourself. We ride for the capital before the next bell.'

Imoshen's heart sank.

Chapter Nine

BUT IT TOOK longer than that to prepare to ride out. Imoshen had to speak to the stronghold staff and the guildmasters of the new township. A representative had to be elected from the townsfolk to make requests on behalf of their people.

Several officers of the stronghold guard loyal to Imoshen volunteered to accompany them to T'Diemn, along with a large force of Tulkhan's elite guard. A small contingent of Ghebite soldiers remained at the stronghold to serve as Tulkhan's eyes and ears. The good behaviour of the stronghold inhabitants was ensured by Imoshen's presence at the General's side.

Imoshen did not want to leave her home. All her instincts were against this hurried departure, and the weather suited her mood. The sun had given up its unequal struggle with the advancing mist and the sky hung heavy with snow-laden clouds. The air was still and charged with foreboding.

Once the immediate threat to her life had passed, Imoshen felt exhausted. A strange lassitude enveloped her, making concentration almost impossible. Voices echoed in her head and everything seemed to be happening at a great distance. Dimly, she realised she had overextended herself by casting the illusion of the young King's form.

But the events of the last few days were too fresh to think on. She felt only a mild irony. She had never expected to make her way to the capital at the side of a Ghebite conqueror.

This was very different from her first visit to T'Diemn and the Royal Palace. Riding into T'Diemn two summers ago for her first midsummer festival, she had been so eager. She could remember her excitement, her anticipation of the delights offered by the sophisticated town. At barely sixteen, she had been impatient to grow up.

The memory was easily recalled, but Imoshen felt distanced from her younger self, as if that Imoshen was another person. Her family and their retinue had taken two days to make the journey, travelling at a comfortable pace. In mid-winter, in heavy snow, the journey could kill.

For the second time that day, the townspeople escorted them out of the township. Despite Imoshen's foreboding, the attitude of the elite guard, her stronghold guard and the townsfolk was positive.

In better times, the route to the capital had been a well-travelled road with a serviceable inn at the halfway point. Imoshen doubted if they would find it standing now.

As they pushed on through the snow, the sky darkened and Imoshen slept with her eyes open, hardly aware of where she was. The General ignored her. She felt despised, less than human. It would have hurt, if she could have felt anything beyond brain-numbing weariness.

Snow fell lightly at first, then with gathering intensity. It was clear that despite their fresh horses, they would not reach the inn, or what was left of it, before darkness closed in on them. Imoshen roused herself from her lethargy, rising in the saddle to look around. They must find shelter for the night.

If only they were near one of the hot springs. Even during the coldest winter they did not freeze over. The simple folk worshipped these places as sources of ancient power. But only someone in direst need would camp there overnight.

With a surge of inner certainty, Imoshen knew that Reothe was sheltering his rebels at one of the hot springs. Knowing him, he would dare to flout convention. It was an ideal winter hide-out, shunned by the locals and protected from the worst of the weather.

Should she tell the General what she suspected? Instinct told her she was right, but it was still only a guess, and there were many hot springs scattered over Fair Isle, especially in the highlands to the south.

Imoshen pulled the white fur close around her and peered resentfully from under the hood at the snow-dusted shoulders of the man in front of her. This was typical of the General's style of leadership. He made snap decisions and moved fast.

She understood Tulkhan wanted to seize power by filling the vacuum of leadership in T'Diemn. But what if Reothe was hiding in the forest, his scouts observing them even now? A concerted attack could see their escort slaughtered, Tulkhan's life at Reothe's mercy and herself faced with a bitter choice – join Tulkhan in death or take her place at the side of her betrothed.

A bitter smile pulled at Imoshen's cold lips. She shuddered. Could she live as Reothe's tool? A caustic laugh welled up in her. Hadn't she chosen to live as Tulkhan's tool, his tolerated oddity? But at least with the General she was not merely his tool. He needed her as much as she needed him.

She tried to make out the dim outlines of the tree trunks through the thick curtain of falling snow. Soon it would be too dark to choose a good camp for the night. They were exposed and vulnerable.

Fighting a wave of nausea caused by sheer exhaustion, Imoshen urged her mount toward the General. She had intended to convince him to stop, but when she caught up, he was already ordering his men to make camp.

Imoshen huddled in her furs and watched them build a basic shelter. Her stronghold guards all knew the tricks of surviving in the open in winter. They chose a protected overhang and built a crude snow wall. While they worked, the elite guard gathered wood.

They had food and warmth, but not peace of mind. Imoshen slept deeply, troubled by threatening dreams, where Reothe accused her of treachery and she begged his forgiveness.

Waking with tears on her cheeks, she found the General sitting across the fire from her, a silent sentinel in the cold predawn. Despite his suspicion of her, she found his presence reassuring. Was he regretting his hasty actions?

'Do your dreams trouble you?' he asked softly.

'No.'

'How can you deny you dream of Reothe? You weep for him.'

She flinched.

One of the men stirred and Tulkhan rose to walk the perimeter of the camp, leaving her to her cold, unhappy thoughts. Anger stirred in her.

If Reothe didn't attack them, capture her and kill Tulkhan, he was not the tactician she thought him to be, she thought sourly, rolling over to sleep.

But when dawn arrived they were still alive, unharmed. The camp broke up stiffly, leaving their crude shelter for other travellers, as was the custom.

While mounting up, Imoshen marvelled at their lucky escape. Possibly Reothe had elected to follow the young King and had already killed that party. Maybe their group would reach the capital unharmed.

Her only comfort was the knowledge that Reothe and his rebels would find it as hard to move about as they did, and that his people were underfed, under-armed and short of horses.

IN THE LATE afternoon of the third day out from Umasreach Stronghold, they spotted the towers of T'Diemn. Imoshen strained in the saddle, peering across the icy air to see if the town had changed much since her last visit.

She noted the blackened bones of buildings, the result of Gharavan's torching of parts of the town. She could not see any signs of revolt, but that meant nothing. The townsfolk could have murdered the Ghebite army while they slept and thrown their bodies into the river, for all she knew.

Or perhaps the army had seized control of the town. Had they panicked without their king? Even now they could be lying in wait behind shuttered windows, ready to spring on the General's small party, trap them in a blind alley and slaughter them all.

Imoshen shuddered. She was being morbid, letting her imagination run away with her.

The General was right. The capital had to be secured. It was the centre of trade, the source of wealth. If she was to help General Tulkhan hold Fair Isle, T'Diemn had to swear fealty to him, and she had to be at his side when that happened.

Imoshen felt a quiver of apprehension. She was not well known here. She had been the third child of a minor branch of the royal family, her only outstanding feature the luck, good or bad, of being born a throwback. As the first pure T'En to be born in her branch of the family since the Aayel, her parents had never ceased to be slightly surprised by her. She was an embarrassing blessing, a potential liability.

Her family had not wished to be social outcasts, unlike Reothe's parents who had bonded precisely because they had many of the T'En traits. His parents had been eccentric historians, who were shunned by the more modern members of the royal family. They had produced only one child, who arrived late in their lives when they had given up hope of children. Reothe was their joy, pure T'En. Yet their end had been so tragic.

Imoshen frowned, recalling the mocking rhyme she'd learned about them as a child. Only when she grew older had she understood its significance. It told how Reothe's parents had taken their own lives. No one really understood why. They had become recluses, abandoned by the royal family, served by one faithful servant. This servant found them both dead by ritual suicide, with ten-year-old Reothe at their side.

Reothe had inherited their combined wealth, but not their lifestyle. He hadn't been a recluse. The Empress had been appointed his guardian, so he spent his teenage years in the royal palace, where he'd charmed the servants and learned the intricacies of protocol.

Driven by his restless nature and relentless ambition, he found court life too restrictive. He had invested his capital in ships and men, and had sailed south-east to the archipelago, looking for wealth and fame, or so the story went. He forged new trade alliances with the prosperous island nations and recouped his investment so handsomely that he could finance an even more audacious voyage to find his ancestors' homeland, which was rumoured to lie northeast of the archipelago.

He had not discovered the legendary homeland of the T'En but had turned west and retraced his steps, finding a path through the ice-floes to the far west, where rich kingdoms were eager to trade. The prestige and wealth Reothe gained from his enterprise ensured him a place in minstrel songs and stories which carried his name to every corner of the island.

Reothe was relying on that popularity to help him escape the Ghebites. Imoshen shivered. How would the townsfolk of T'Diemn react if it was Reothe at the head of a rebel army about to enter the city?

Imoshen studied her companions thoughtfully. As with their entry to Landsend, General Tulkhan ordered them to stop and don their battle dress for their arrival at T'Diemn. The elite guard wore Tulkhan's vibrant colours and her own stronghold guard wore the more subdued and familiar royal colours of her family. What kind of welcome could they hope to receive?

The townsfolk of T'Diemn might see her as a reminder of the T'En Emperor and Empress who had failed to protect them. They might direct their anger at her. Of all Fair Isle, the T'Diemn townspeople had borne the brunt of King Gharavan's destructive vengeance. They might give lip service to the T'En church, but how would they react to a throwback like herself?

The General rode down the ranks, inspecting their party with a critical eye. Galloping back to the lead, he met Imoshen's gaze. She might have doubts about her welcome, but she would not reveal them. Sitting tall in the saddle, she dropped the hood so that her face was not hidden. She would not cower before the townsfolk.

'Ready?' General Tulkhan asked.

Imoshen nodded and adjusted the folds of the ornate ceremonial gown she'd changed into and settled the fur cloak around her shoulders. In white fur and red velvet, she was dressed for effect, and she noted with some satisfaction that it had not been lost on the General.

The Ghebite battle regalia was also designed for effect and to show off the might and muscle of its soldiers. However, as impressive as the combination of heavy armour and bare skin was, it was hardly practical in the depths of a Fair Isle winter. She knew the General must be cold, but there was no hint of it in his proud bearing. His men also bore the chill stoically, setting aside their borrowed furs to make a good impression on the townsfolk. Her own stronghold guard wore thick woollen padding beneath their battle gear.

Satisfied, the General gave the signal to move out. Imoshen urged her horse forward. She was sure their party must have been sighted from the town gates. The people of T'Diemn had opened those same gates and surrendered to the invader only to be betrayed. She was grateful the General was a man of his word. Otherwise the people of Umasreach Stronghold might have suffered the same fate.

The townsfolk lined the street, silent and sullen. Had they heard about King Gharavan's defeat? It was unlikely. The trail to the far north western port veered before T'Diemn, so unless someone had slipped away from the stronghold or the town and ridden ahead, the townsfolk could not know their persecutor had been vanquished by General Tulkhan and herself.

Imoshen searched the faces of the crowd. They had been a prosperous, almost smug town before this, basking in the patronage of the royal court. To find themselves at the mercy of invaders would have shattered their peace and complacency forever.

She saw people pointing in her direction. Someone called out the ritual phrase for T'En blessing. A little girl tried to break free from the crowd, presumably to touch her sixth finger for luck, but a woman pulled her back.

It felt wrong to ride through the gathered townsfolk without making contact. She noticed children watching her wide-eyed and realised fear was not far from their minds. A horse snorted and shied and those nearest stumbled back. A small boy yelped in fright and was comforted. Imoshen felt a sudden rush of gratitude and relief that her own people had not suffered at the hands of King Gharavan.

As General Tulkhan's party walked their horses slowly up the rise, Imoshen gradually dropped behind. She slowed her mount and let her own stronghold guard move on ahead.

Searching the faces of the townsfolk, she tried to understand their position. These were still her people, and she felt personally responsible, because her family had failed to protect them.

She stiffened – there, in the front row was an elderly woman, wrapped in nothing but a shawl. Her paper-thin skin stretched over her twisted knuckles as she pulled the material tightly around her stooped shoulders. It was poor protection from the bitter cold. The old woman reminded Imoshen fleetingly of the Aayel, who had stood so proudly to receive the terms of surrender. Her wise counsel had prevented Imoshen from taking rash action. The Aayel had saved them from disaster.

Before she knew what she was doing, Imoshen swung down stiffly from the horse and crossed the snow-covered cobbles to greet the old woman who stared uncomprehendingly at her.

'Grandmother, you are cold.' Imoshen unclasped her white fur cloak and shrugged it off, swinging it around the old woman's shoulders. 'Take this.'

As Imoshen kissed the withered cheek, tears stung her eyes.

The old woman lifted a cold, clawed hand to hers and grasped her sixth finger. 'Bless you, Lady T'En. Bless you.'

In a blur, Imoshen found herself surrounded by curious townsfolk. A small child tugged on her hand and she picked him up, feeling his fingers twine through her hair which hung loosely down her back. Others stroked her hands or her clothing. Voices were raised around her in exclamation.

She lost track of what they were saying, but tried to answer them, to reassure them. Theirs were the eternal questions of hope and fear, for their families, their homes.

Yes, she assured them repeatedly, wicked King Gharavan was gone, banished by his half-brother.

They could hardly believe it.

Tulkhan was aware of the crowd's resentment. When he heard voices, he wheeled his horse.

What was that disturbance? The crowd muttered, watching him uneasily. He glanced along the column of his small escort, automatically counting heads. Imoshen was missing.

Fear closed a cold hand around his heart. Had she been dragged from her mount, abducted and murdered?

Cursing fluently, he urged the horse back between the columns of his men.

'Crawen, where is your lady?' he demanded from the leader of the stronghold guard.

The woman flinched at his tone. 'Right behind me, General.' But when she turned, Imoshen was not there. 'I don't understand –'

'Come.' Tulkhan had no time for the guard's excuses. He rode on with the stronghold guard at his back until he saw a knot of people growing larger by the moment. At its centre was Imoshen's tall, fair head.

They'd tear her apart.

Even as he thought this, he realised the crowd's voice was reverent, excited and almost hungry, as they surged eagerly toward Imoshen.

There was no menace, yet. But all it took was one disgruntled individual with a knife and a grudge to settle with the T'En who had abandoned them, and Imoshen would be lying in the snow, bleeding to death. The image flashed through his mind, spurring him on.

Anger flooded him. What was she doing, risking her life pointlessly like this? What if there was someone who was loyal to King Gharavan in the crowd? They had too many enemies.

Furious, Tulkhan urged his horse through the people. They pulled back, stumbling in their haste to escape his battle-hardened mount. He saw nothing but Imoshen's fair head, rising above their heads. His heart pounded, his hands ached to grasp her. He would throttle her, he would...

Swinging down off the horse he thrust the last person aside. 'Imoshen?'

She turned, surprised. The smile died on her lips as she took in his expression. He noted her cheeks were flushed, and if he hadn't known better he would have sworn she'd been crying. She held a small, golden-skinned child in her arms.

Soothingly, she returned the boy to his mother, touching the tip of her sixth finger to his forehead in T'En blessing.

Tulkhan breathed a sigh of relief. Imoshen was perfectly all right. This time. But he could sense the crowd's resentment of him and all he represented.

'Come.' Tulkhan felt like an interloper. He grasped her arm, pulling her toward his horse. Where was her mount?

As his hand closed around her upper arm, he realised Imoshen was wearing nothing but the rich red gown she had donned to enter T'Diemn.

'Where's your cloak?'

She glanced over her shoulder and he noticed an elderly woman wrapped in the white-tipped fur. What was Imoshen thinking?

'Yours?'

She caught him as he went toward the old woman. 'The old woman needed it more than I.'

He caught a flicker of warning in her eyes. The crowd was muttering, drawing back as women pulled children behind the ranks of the able-bodied men.

Tulkhan cursed softly. With one action, Imoshen had won over the townsfolk of T'Diemn, then he had come along and undone her good work.

'You could have been killed.' He kept his voice low. 'One assassin with a knife –'

'I know.' Her voice was as soft and intense as his.

They had lost their entire escort now. The stronghold guard were cut off from them, surrounded by a sea of townsfolk. Even if they were to try to come to their aid, they would have trouble forging through the packed streets. Tactical training told Tulkhan they were hopelessly vulnerable.

'Take me up on your mount. Mine must have followed the others,' Imoshen whispered. 'Wrap your cloak around me.'

He focused on her face, on her compelling wine-dark eyes and, almost in a daze, found himself swinging into the saddle, hauling her up after him. As he settled her across his thighs and pulled his cloak about them both, he sensed the crowd's mood change.

There was a tentative cheer. Imoshen waved, then swung both arms around Tulkhan's neck and kissed him. The impact of her hot lips on his mouth broke the daze which had gripped him. He experienced an intense, overwhelming physical desire for her. It went beyond conscious thought. It was the call of her body to his. His hands slid inside the cloak to pull her closer. All the frustration and rage which had engulfed him spilled over into his instinctive response to her.

Roaring. There was a roaring in his ears.

The crowd was cheering them. It could just as easily have torn them to shreds.

Trust me. He heard her voice distinctly in his head, yet her lips were melded to his.

In that instant, he understood what had happened. She had manipulated him with her T'En gift, clouding his mind, prompting him to act the way she wished. Somehow she had slipped past his guard. When had he become so susceptible to her?

A shudder of alarm swept through him.

What had she said? She feared the power that lying with T'Reothe would give him over her? Tulkhan flinched. Surely then, in joining their bodies, he had made himself vulnerable in her power?

Furious, Tulkhan broke the kiss, and found his hands gripping her face. He could feel the fragile bones of her skull cupped in the merciless cradle of his hands. One twist and he could break her neck.

The thought horrified him. Yet with one action he could be free of her creeping power over him.

Fear flared in the depths of her eyes. Had she read his mind, again?

'Get out of my head.' The words were torn from him. Barely audible, they grated from between his clenched teeth.

She grimaced, whether in shock or annoyance he couldn't tell, and took his hand, prising the thumb from her throat. To the watchers it could have been a fond touch.

'You're choking me. Ride on, while we still can, General.'

Her advice was sensible and, as much as it galled him, he urged the mount forward. She did not have to tell him to wave as the crowd saluted them.

The goodwill Imoshen had won surged forward with them, changing the mood of the people as they rounded the bend, flanked by the stronghold guard. His entrance to the capital had become a triumphant welcome and he had Imoshen to thank for it.

He felt the sway of her body against his and the scent of her hair filled his nostrils. She had invaded his mind again, albeit to save them both when the crowd threatened to turn hostile. But he knew he had no protection from her, and the knowledge ate at him like an insidious poison.

Even now as they rode she waved, smiling at the townsfolk, who responded eagerly. He could not be sure how much of their response was natural, how much might be a trickery. After all, she had convinced everyone in the great hall that she was his half-brother. Mass hallucination... what next, mass mind control?

Tulkhan shuddered. He hated not knowing the extent of his enemy's power... That thought pulled him up sharply. When had Imoshen become his enemy?

Rather, he thought grimly, *when had she ever been anything but?*

She had allied herself with him to ensure her survival, nothing more. He must not forget that. She was Other, not True-woman at all.

When they entered the square in front of the Royal Palace, it was filled with milling men-at-arms. Those loyal to General Tulkhan were standing in ranks. He could identify his commanders in one solid block. Those loyal to the King were congregated in a resentful mass.

Imoshen sensed the danger as she took in the scene. There might yet be bloodshed. What if King Gharavan's men refused to swear allegiance to the General?

She felt Tulkhan tense and would have slipped from her perch across his thighs, but his grip on her tightened. She had an excellent view of the gathered army as he walked his mount between the orderly ranks of his own men. He paused here and there, speaking softly to individuals, inquiring after an old wound with one, a toothache with another. It confirmed what she had come to believe. General Tulkhan's men loved him, and he knew everyone by sight if not by name.

Then they crossed the sludgy snow to approach Gharavan's men. Several men of rank stepped forward and Tulkhan greeted them with quiet dignity. Would he order their allegiance or death? How would he resolve this stand-off?

Imoshen tensed as she saw the unfriendly faces of the young King's men. Tulkhan was mistaken to keep her with him. They feared and hated her.

The General cleared his throat. 'Well men, you know me. I served my father, the King, since I joined the ranks as a youth. Some of you have served under me on other campaigns, others of you worked with me when we settled the town recently. I am a fair man.'

They muttered and nodded.

'Gharavan is on his way to Northpoint. I've claimed Fair Isle for myself.'

There was a stunned intake of breath and a torrent of exclamations. The muttering and grumbling from the ranks grew louder. Tulkhan let them vent their surprise and outrage before calling for silence.

'If you feel you can't stomach serving me, you can take the clothes you stand up in and your kit and walk to Northpoint, under an escort of my men. You have until dawn tomorrow to make up your mind. Those who remain must swear allegiance to me.'

A grizzled commander stepped forward. 'I don't need till dawn to make up my mind, General. You served your father, but Gharavan's half the king he was. I'll take an oath of allegiance to you and my men will follow suit.'

Tulkhan thanked him. 'By tomorrow I will have the allegiance of the townsfolk and an army loyal to me.'

He wheeled the horse. It rose on its hind legs. Imoshen clutched the horse's neck to steady herself. He secured her, one arm pressing her to him. With a start, she realised the horse was trained to rear and walk on its hind legs. Though she felt precarious, she sensed she was quite safe. She was also aware of the striking sight they made as his own men broke into a spontaneous roar of approval.

Now she understood.

By keeping her with him, the General had sought his men's acceptance of her by unspoken demand. And they had given it.

At Tulkhan's gentle command, the magnificent black destrier gave voice, then settled and pranced toward the stables at the rear of the palace, almost as if it had enjoyed the display and approval.

Exhausted as she was, Imoshen knew no peace when they finally arrived at the palace. The town was far from secure and there was much to be done. She left the General speaking to his men in the stables and headed inside the palace, flanked by her stronghold guard.

She had known this building as an infrequent visitor, a minor member of the extended royal family. The first time she had come here was during the midsummer festival before Reothe and she were betrothed.

Although they were second cousins and the only throwbacks of the last two generations, their paths had not crossed before, because her parents had not thought her mature enough to visit the court. Even if they had, Reothe would probably not have been there. He had spent the better part of the last ten years at sea with only short intervals in T'Diemn between his voyages.

That midsummer, the huge formal rooms had been decorated and the public hall was open to the townsfolk. There had been impromptu dances, poetry recitations, musical performances and plays. The flower of T'En culture had been present.

Barely sixteen, Imoshen had been overwhelmed by the sophistication of the palace and its occupants. She had longed to remain in the background but already she stood as tall as any man and her colouring marked her as T'En.

Everywhere she went, people stared.

For Imoshen that festival had been a prolonged period of excruciating tension and formality, as she was escorted by various family members to different venues and introduced to the members of their extended family. She had been formally presented to the Emperor and Empress and listened in on several sessions of government, where the nobles met to formalise alliances within their own island and trade agreements with the mainland and the archipelago.

How different it was now. The long corridors were filled with fearful milling servants and the debris of the young King's occupation. Imoshen stepped over smashed crockery to enter one of the formal greeting chambers.

'Crawen, you may take your people and settle in. Send the cook and the master of the bedchambers to me.'

Left alone in the room, Imoshen stared unseeing at the opulent surroundings. Memories crowded her, making her face flame with shame as she recalled the first meeting with Reothe. She had been sent to collect her brother from a performance in the forecourt of the palace. Only she had taken a wrong turn and found herself in a group of young royals and nobles who were watching a poetic duel.

The first duellist had to create a rhyming quartet about something topical, then the other would take an idea from that rhyme and create another quartet, often turning it back on the originator.

She and her brother and sister had played a similar game as children. Being proficient in courtly speech was considered an important tool of etiquette.

Unfortunately for Imoshen, her arrival threw one of the duellists off his speech and, to recover himself, he chose her as his subject. Or perhaps it was simply a comment about the T'En.

At any rate, she stiffened as every eye in the room turned to her. It was a cruel jest at the expense of the T'En, but it was clever and the audience applauded him for that with their customary subtle little finger clicks.

Eager to outdo her opponent, the other duelling poet chose the T'En again and this time made a more intimate reference to Imoshen.

She stood stranded, under unbearably intense scrutiny and unable to flee because her pride would not let her, but not sufficiently versed at this level to produce a quartet of her own. She did not know the duellists by name or reputation.

As the female duellist wound down and everyone clicked their appreciation, Imoshen saw the first poet take a breath and knew he was about to use her as a topic again. His eyes glistened with anticipation, making her heart sink and her cheeks flame.

But from the seated ranks Reothe came to his feet. He was as ornately dressed as anyone there and as graceful when he gave the formal sign to show he was entering the duel, but he radiated a lethal quality which she now recognised. It stemmed from years of command. Then she had known instinctively that he was different from the others.

Reothe wasn't playing – he never played.

The first part of his quartet shifted the emphasis from her to the first T'Imoshen. It was not offensive but clever. It mocked those people who resisted change. Then he turned the rhyme back on the two poets themselves, likening them to their ancestors.

He rounded it off so neatly that even the two poets clicked their appreciation.

Imoshen met Reothe's gaze across the crowded room. His wine-dark eyes silently mocked her, angering her more than the poets' comments had. She could see he expected her to be grateful to him for coming to her rescue.

The two poets challenged by Reothe's skill were eager to reply. In the ensuing three-way duel, Imoshen slipped away.

Her brother wasn't even where he was supposed to be and she went looking for him.

Reothe found her. He might have been waiting on the landing between the wing of guest chambers and semi-formal chambers for her to pass, but she refused to believe he would lie in wait for her.

Seeing him there, she stiffened her shoulders and prepared to walk past but he caught her arm. 'What, no word of thanks?'

His assumption irritated her, yet good manners told her to thank him. She flicked her arm free using a simple escape break she had polished through childhood bouts with her siblings. Few of her peers bothered to maintain the skills of unarmed combat but she took pride in hers.

'Thank you, but I would have extricated myself –'

'That's what it looked like.'

She stiffened, knowing he was right. While she had been out of her depth socially, she felt her Reothe shouldn't have reminded her of this. She studied him, surprised that he should overstep the boundaries.

What she read in his narrow intelligent face did not reassure her. She knew instinctively etiquette was a tool he used and discarded when it suited him. There was an intensity about him which could not be contained by propriety. The expression in his dark eyes was too intimate. She felt as if he had looked into her heart and knew all her failings, and she hated the sensation.

'Thank you for bringing my deficiencies to my attention. I will make a point of not attending poetic duels until I am more skilled.' She spun on her heel. Dizzied by her sudden about-face and the implication she had read in his expression, she left him.

'You're running away,' he called softly, as she forced herself to walk up the broad staircase with what she hoped was stately dignity.

She tensed and turned, looking down into a face so like her own that they could have been brother and sister.

'She who runs away, lives to fight another day.' She used the High T'En speech, not the bastardised version of the old maxim.

Reothe's eyes widened and she knew she had scored a point. No one used High T'En now days, few people even read it. Only those church priests who made a study of law were proficient in it.

Imoshen gave a start, as the clatter of approaching palace servants brought her back to the present. Drawing a deep breath, she prepared to deal with them. She was no longer a gauche sixteen-year-old. She'd had a birthday since that midsummer, been betrothed, seen her world destroyed, lost her family and escaped death more than once.

Entering the palace as part of the conquering force, she could have retreated to her room and expected to be waited on, but that did not suit Imoshen. She was used to taking control. She knew how much organisation was needed to run a large establishment, though Umasreach Stronghold was not as complex as the palace.

If, as she suspected, the palace staff were in disarray after serving the King and his men, they would need firm guidance. Imoshen insisted on speaking with the servant responsible for each aspect of the palace administration. She inspected every state room and many of the informal rooms. She spoke with the cook and inspected the kitchen and storerooms to ensure they had plentiful supplies of food, spices and wine.

Finally, the master of the bedchambers reported to her for an inspection of the double wings of bedchambers. As she surveyed the chambers, disgust filled her. King Gharavan and his men had been living like pigs, wallowing in their own filth, surrounded by debauchery. She threw out the whores, male and female, then ordered the serving men and women to scrub the rooms.

To her relief, the servants acknowledged her natural authority and responded well. The master of the bedchambers promised to restore order. She knew he feared for his position. A little fear was good, but she preferred her people to serve and strive to please her because they loved her.

It was dark and the candles were lit before she was satisfied that the task of running the palace was under control. Imoshen was so tired her hands trembled, but she could not afford to let herself rest. There was still the evening meal to get through. She selected one of the semi-formal rooms, where she had the tables arranged in a u-shape. It pleased her sense of order and beauty to watch the well-trained servants spread out pristine white cloths and arrange the fine silver, delicate china and crystal.

When Tulkhan entered, she could tell by the tense set of his mouth that he had been busy shoring up lines of support within the ranks. A rush of purely physical relief swept her body and she fought an urge to go to him. It was as if an invisible thread united them, drawing her ever closer to him.

At that moment he looked across the ornate room to her, across the table with its sparkling setting and scented candles. His expression was carefully controlled. She searched his face for a hint of softening but his obsidian eyes were unreadable.

She felt excluded.

The room was quite plain compared to some of the other formal rooms, but it was more ornate than anything in the stronghold. Was that the problem? Did the General find the opulence of this setting repellent? Did it disgust him as a symbol of the rot which had led the Old Empire to collapse? Did she disgust him as a remnant of that richly decadent regime?

Imoshen could not tell. She only knew that she longed to go to him and must not reveal her weakness for a moment.

'General.' She acknowledged him and the men who had accompanied him, recognising several as members of his elite guard. Others she did not know and she marked their faces. They must have held positions of responsibility in Gharavan's army. Could their loyalty be trusted? 'Gentlemen. The meal is almost ready, if you will be seated. There is warmed wine and fresh bread.'

It smelt delicious. Imoshen had discovered in the cook an artist forced to serve the barbarians, and the woman had responded to Imoshen's overtures with a feast. Confronted with a T'En who understood the preparation of food and presentation of dishes, the cook had outdone herself. Imoshen was pleased.

But it had taken time and energy. Imoshen was not as good at reading people as the Aayel had been. By surreptitious touch and careful questioning, the Aayel had discovered people's needs and found the key to winning them over. Support freely given was much better than support gained by coercion.

It was exhausting, mentally and emotionally. And now she had to sit down to a meal. She felt too nauseous to eat while mixing with these men, many of whom clearly resented her. But she would do it. She would do whatever she had to do to survive.

Imoshen took a deep breath and lifted her chin. The u-shaped table created an intimate dinner setting which was still loosely formal.

'Wine, General?' She tilted the steaming jug. Her gaze ran over the lines of the vessel, instinctively enjoying its elegant shape. Candlelight glistened on its polished surface.

That midsummer long ago she had discovered the simple act of eating in the royal palace could be a sensuous experience, and now she was here, serving these barbarians who probably would not even know how to use the cutlery. A shiver ran over Imoshen's skin.

Life was strange... strange and cruel.

General Tulkhan's hand gripped her wrist. When his dark, scarred fingers closed around her white flesh she felt the strength in him.

'You would serve me?' His piercing eyes held hers.

She felt colour steal into her cheeks, very aware of the men who were taking their seats. It occurred to her, with the instincts schooled in diplomacy, that the table needed women, but she could not call in the whores she had banished.

They needed the wives and daughters of the minor nobles to normalise the situation. She suspected the Ghebites would act less rashly when there were women present, women they respected.

Tulkhan's fingers tightened on the tender bones of her wrist. 'I said, would you serve me like a common kitchen maid?'

She stiffened in silent fury as the truth of it hit her like a physical blow. Her position was tenuous at best, relying on his goodwill. Here, away from her own stronghold, she had simply assumed command of the palace servants, but if he chose, the General could undermine her position. She could be relegated to the role of a menial servant.

'What place do I have, General?'

He grimaced. 'Sit at my side.'

She baulked, the memory of King Gharavan's whores filling her with dismay. 'Am I to sit at your side as your equal or your whore?'

He flushed. She saw the rising tide of anger stain his cheeks. The knobs of muscle at his jaw-line gleamed in the candlelight as he ground his teeth.

'Now is not the time –'

'On the contrary.' Blood rushed in her ears as she felt all eyes turn to them. Conversations stopped. 'I have spent all afternoon soothing the cook's feelings so that she could produce this meal, working with the master of the bedchambers to throw out your brother's whores. Even now the servants are stripping the beds to make them fit for your honest men. I would like to know where I stand!'

He glared at her.

Though her heart was pounding, Imoshen did not flinch when he lifted his hand. Before she could protest, she found herself swept off her feet. In a rush, he lifted her with him as he climbed onto his chair. Towering above the table, Imoshen clutched the General as they balanced precariously on the chair. Its slender legs creaked ominously.

'Fill your mugs, men; I give you a toast. A toast to Fair Isle, my new land, and to Imoshen, my wife.'

Cold shock doused Imoshen. But, of course, it was the next step.

Tulkhan had laid claim to her and the land in one sentence. Reothe had wanted her because of what she represented. Tulkhan could not afford to let her remain unbonded. He would legitimise his claim to the land by binding her to him.

The knowledge that she had played into his hands filled Imoshen with shame. Once enslaved as his *wife*, what bargaining power would she have? The implications swamped her.

Tulkhan's men echoed his toast as the servants hurried forward with more warmed wine. Someone thrust a goblet in her numbed hand.

'Drink and smile!' Tulkhan hissed. His arm circled her waist, pressing her to his side.

Imoshen lifted the wine and sipped as the room swayed around her. Here she was standing on a chair in a lesser dining room of the royal palace, claimed as a prize of war by the barbarian who had murdered every member of her family.

It was too much.

She felt utterly numb. An almost hysterical urge to laugh threatened to overcome her as she recalled the last time she had eaten here, during the midsummer feast.

Only the Emperor and Empress's immediate family, about forty people, had been present. It was her first private formal evening since she had arrived, and Reothe had been present. With their argument still ringing in her ears, she had been careful not to notice him during the excruciatingly long dinner and the entertainment which followed. But when she was sure he was not looking, she had watched him avidly.

How dare he pity her.

He was as exotic as she was, with his silver hair. His slender rangy form exuded male strength. He made the more civilised men of the Emperor's table seem like fat, lazy tabby cats. He reminded her of a snow leopard she had seen once in the deep woods. Beautiful, deadly, unattainable but fascinating.

He must have sensed her scrutiny, because he looked across the room and met her eyes. Of course she stared back, secure in the knowledge that he would not cause a scene here before all their relatives.

Despite their rivalry she felt a kinship with him. Of all the inhabitants in that room only she and he were pure T'En. Had he experienced the veiled taunts she had known? Did he curse the differences which made him remarkable?

Then he had lifted his wine and offered her a silent toast, which she had chosen to acknowledge. For a moment, when she lowered the goblet and met his intense wine-dark eyes, all else faded. It had seemed to her that they were alone amid a swarm of bees and heat moved within her.

Had he been trying to influence her, even then?

If he had, it had not been successful, because she had smiled and deliberately turned her back to him so she could converse with the person beside her.

It had been her sister. They hadn't been close. Yet at this moment Imoshen willingly recalled her sister's face, the sound of her voice. Without warning, everything shifted. She felt as if she was seated at the formal tables. She could see her mother and her father. As always, her brother was showing off.

Pain lanced her.

'Dead, they're all dead –'

'Who's dead? ' A deep voice demanded, shaking her.

Superimposed over her laughing relations she saw the Ghebite barbarians, watching her and General Tulkhan's keen dark eyes.

'Are my people in danger?'

'Your people?' A bitter laugh shook her. 'No, *my* people, my family!'

She could even see her mother's small scar which she tried to hide by wearing her hair forward on her forehead. The curl had fallen aside. Imoshen fought the urge to let mother know. It would be so easy to slip away from the cold, dangerous present, into a fragile moment from the past...

'Imoshen!' Abruptly, Tulkhan swung her into his embrace. Her wine cup flew from her slack fingers to clatter on the delicate mosaic floor tiles. She resented his warm strength and was disoriented by the abrupt change as the world of the T'En was lost to her, lost to rapacious, unforgiving Time.

The General was flesh and blood, immediate and impatient. He made her intensely aware of sensation as she felt the rasp of his bristly chin on her cheek, the coarse pads of his fingers on her face and the strength in his arms.

Then his lips found hers and she was utterly confused, lost in the heat of his passion. This was General Tulkhan, self-styled ruler of Fair Isle. He had claimed her for political reasons, but she knew with a woman's instinct that when he took her to his bed it would be because he wanted her.

Dimly, she heard the catcalls and whistles, the thumping on the tables. It was so different from the refined finger-clicking of the royal courtiers.

Revulsion filled her. These Ghebites were barbarians. The absurdity of her current situation, contrasted with the restrained elegance of the setting and her intense memory of that last formal yet intimate evening with the doomed royal family of the T'En.

Her mind went blank.

It was too much. For the first time since Umasreach Stronghold surrendered, she had allowed herself to feel the loss of those people she loved, and she couldn't bear it. While they lived she had taken them for granted, dead they became precious. She couldn't live with the pain.

Desperate to escape it, she concentrated on sensation, trying to blot out all thought, all memory. The immediate pressure of Tulkhan's lips on hers elicited a physical response which she didn't bother to disguise. She was hungry for him, hungry for the oblivion his passion promised.

The General released her, his obsidian eyes glittering with a savage male hunger which she knew would not be easily sated. He lifted his crystal wine glass, threw back his head and gave the Ghebite battle cry. The blood-curdling challenge shattered the restrained elegance of the formal room, reverberating down the corridors and through the heart of the Royal Palace.

With sudden clarity, Imoshen knew the past was dead. General Tulkhan was the future.

Despite everything, she was drawn to him. Her heart swelled with the intensity of his passion. He had it all now: Fair Isle, the royal palace and herself, the last T'En Princess.

The Ghebite barbarians had triumphed.

A fey mood was on Tulkhan, and it didn't leave him as they took their seats and the food was served. She observed him as he steered the conversations with the leaders of his army. Each man vied to prove his loyalty. The Ghebite commanders saw General Tulkhan as the source of all power. Imoshen understood that to them, she was about as significant as the palace – beautiful, useful, but without will or choice.

The knowledge galled her.

As for General Tulkhan, she watched him eat his food with the same vigour he applied to everything. He would take her as fiercely and freely later tonight. Then – what – throw her aside as he threw aside the bone he had just finished with?

What was a Ghebite wife but a possession and a convenience fit only for bearing sons?

Imoshen tensed. At that moment, she hated the General because he held her life in his hands and hated herself because when their eyes met, she felt the insistent tug of her body to his. She ached for his lovemaking.

But she would not be a convenience. If he was taking her to bond for life, to consolidate his hold on Fair Isle, then he must abide by the laws and customs of Fair Isle. He must abstain from touching her until they took their vows. She smiled, because she knew he would not like that.

The servants cleared away the main course and there was a lull as they carried the sweets from the distant kitchen.

Imoshen leant closer to Tulkhan, lowering her voice. 'You have Fair Isle, General. But can you hold it?'

His dark eyes met hers, weighing, wondering. Good. She had his attention.

'The townsfolk are nervous. They fear your army, which has inundated the town. To consolidate your victory, you need to win over the people of T'Diemn.'

'I was going to call on the guildmasters and the town leaders to swear fealty tomorrow –'

She nodded, pleased. 'You think they will come willingly, considering what happened when King Gharavan did that? I suggest we stage a feast, declare a holiday, invite the guildmasters and their families. When you have them present, praise T'Diemn's prosperity. Promise that you won't interfere with the administration of the town. The townsfolk will only revolt if threatened. Make them feel secure under your leadership.'

'Why are you doing this?'

She felt his suspicious eyes on her.

'Why are you smoothing the transition of power?' Tulkhan caught her hand as she reached for her wine. 'Answer me, Dhamfeer.'

The use of that word told her all she needed to know. He felt alienated from her. Why? Because they were in the palace which was so obviously constructed by the T'En race and it represented a richer culture than his own.

With a deft twist she slipped her hand from his grasp and raised her wine goblet, watching him over the rim as she sipped. Should she try to minimise the differences between True-man and T'En? Anger seethed in her. She would never pretend to be less than she was.

'You have claimed me as your bond-partner, *wife* in your language. As bond-partner my role is to aid you, and yours is to aid me. According to T'En custom you are my equal, my other half. If I help you, I help myself.'

General Tulkhan looked down at his own hand where it lay resting on the tablecloth.

Imoshen noted the coppery skin criss-crossed by tiny scars. His broad, strong hand looked so out of place on the fine white cloth. She knew how those calloused hands felt on her delicate skin. A shudder of longing swept her body and she despised herself for it.

Here tonight, and over the ensuing moons, she would need all her wits about her, yet she was finding it difficult to separate her physical needs from the logical paths her mind told her she should take. Abstinence would give her a chance to overcome this weakness.

'The ways of the T'En are new to me,' Tulkhan confessed, his voice like deep honey, so rich she could almost taste it. 'If we are to be partners, then the sooner we are wedded the better. Tomorrow –'

'Tomorrow would be too soon.' Despite her best intentions, she laid her hand over his because she wanted to feel the strength in him. A slow burn of desire ignited in her core. 'True, the ceremony should be soon. But this must be done properly. The T'En church is very powerful and its leaders can influence how well your rule is accepted. They hold great wealth and the minds of the people. If we woo them to our side we will have their support. For the people to recognise our joining, the T'En church needs to be involved in the ceremony. And what of your own religious leaders?'

Tulkhan shrugged. 'I'm a soldier. I've little time for gods.'

'Your men?'

He rubbed his chin thoughtfully.

She nodded to herself. 'Your men might feel more at ease if you observe the rituals of the Ghebite religion.' She paused as his eyes flew to hers.

A smile lurked in their obsidian depths and he acknowledged she was right with a slight nod. That smile did more to threaten her resolution than anything else. With a shock, Imoshen realised she liked the General. She liked his ready understanding and his rueful humour.

'Why do you smile, General Tulkhan?'

He shook his head slowly. 'Is it all a game of tactics to you?'

She wanted to deny it, but she couldn't disclose her weakness. The General did not trust her, so he wouldn't believe her. It would be an agony to admit her feelings only to have them spurned. She smiled. 'I play to win, General. There's no point otherwise.' Imoshen let him believe that if he chose. It was safer for her. 'Now, it will take time to negotiate the cooperation of the religious leaders. The people of Fair Isle have a feast on the shortest day of the year. Declare the Midwinter Feast the day that we make our vows and you are officially crowned ruler of Fair Isle. It will allow time for the minor southern nobles to come in from their estates.

'They need to see that you are a fair man, they need reassurance. They need to know that you will not confiscate their estates –'

'I want to reward my loyal men.'

'There are empty strongholds and estates to the north. Reward them with those, and with bond-partners. Marry them to the eligible daughters of minor southern nobles. Blood ties are much stronger than the bonds of fear.'

The General's eyes flickered over her face and then away, and Imoshen knew she had lost him. What had she said?

Troubled, Tulkhan shifted in his seat, leaning away from Imoshen. The Dhamfeer's vivid, intense face was like a magnet drawing him in. He wanted to look on her forever, to drink in her features. Her intelligence glinted behind her eyes, brilliant as sunlight on water. Then, just when he thought he understood her, she revealed another facet. And he feared he would cut himself on her sharp edges.

Now this. Blood ties are stronger than the bonds of fear.

How true. He had loved his half-brother almost to his own death. And look at Imoshen. She had tricked him, seduced him. No... that was not fair. He had chosen her and now she carried his child – the child he thought he could never have. Imoshen was the key to Fair Isle and to the future.

But could he trust her? Dare he trust her?

Dare he not? Her words of advice were true, even if they were motivated by self-interest. He almost laughed. Of course they were motivated by self-interest, what better motivation?

Selfless interest? He pushed that thought aside as irrelevant.

Imoshen was his captive, willing to work for his good because it benefited her. By what right did he, the slave master, wish for love as well as devotion?

She came to her feet. 'You will excuse me, General. There is much I must organise for tomorrow –'

'Leave it.' He caught her around the waist, drawing her between his thighs. He could feel the gentle swell of her hips, the rise and fall of her ribs as she drew in a sharp breath. He had to tilt his chin to look up into her face. She was so much taller than the women of his race. And proud. He liked the way she met his eyes, liked the way she would not defer to him.

She was Dhamfeer, Other and dangerous. She was possibly the instrument of his death, but he wanted her and he would have her. He'd laid claim to her.

'I want my bed.' His voice was a low growl. He tightened his hands on her waist, felt the tension in her. He knew she understood his meaning. He wanted her in his bed, under him, preferably with her thighs wrapped around his hips. A shaft of desire flamed deep within him.

A wicked smile lifted the corners of her mouth and played in the depths of her garnet eyes. It should have warned him.

'I will show you to your bedchamber, General,' she told him. 'Then I will go to mine. It is customary for betrothed partners to practise abstinence until they take their vows.'

'Abstinence!' The thought was abhorrent.

She laughed. The throaty peal was like velvet rubbing across his skin. He sensed more than saw every head in the room turn to them, and knew instinctively that every man there desired her, whether he would admit to it or not.

She ran her fingers over his head, down the line of his jaw, lingering on the hollows of his throat. He could see the candlelight reflecting in her eyes, twin flames of desire. He wanted to immolate himself in those flames.

'As leader of your men, you set the tone of your army,' she said. 'Your half-brother set no example.'

The truth of it hit him. If he wanted to take Imoshen to wife, by his own laws he must observe the rituals. Abstinence.

He cursed softly.

As he caught a gleam of triumph in her eyes, he told himself to be wary. After all, this was a political wedding even if by good fortune it promised to soothe the physical ache which was driving him to distraction.

He studied Imoshen and she tilted her head, returning his gaze. How much of what he was feeling was his own body's response to hers? Was she planting thoughts in his head, manipulating him? She had sworn she wouldn't do it, said that it would be wrong, yet he could count the instances when she had invaded his mind.

'General?' She leant forward, peering into his eyes, unconsciously giving him a view of her high, firm breasts barely contained by the neckline of her gown. Desire flared through him again. Useless, potent flames of lust seared him from within.

He pulled her onto his lap, burying his face in her soft flesh, inhaling her womanly scent.

How long until midwinter? He tried to think, but could not recall the dates. He'd returned to the stronghold well after winter cusp. This meant they had...

'Thirty-seven days,' Imoshen whispered.

Anger lanced his mind, cutting through the cloud of desire. She had been in his head again, curse her!

Even as anger flared in him, he saw her eyes widen as she realised what she'd done.

'Please!' she hissed, pressing his face to her breast. He felt her strength, her soft curves on his cheek. The rapid pounding of her heart thundered in his ear.

He turned his head away, almost overcome by her physical presence.

Abruptly, Imoshen slipped from his lap and dropped to her knees, kneeling between his thighs.

'I didn't mean to,' she confessed in a low whisper.

He saw the truth in her eyes and the knowledge both repelled and fascinated him, because at that moment he realised Imoshen's ability to touch his mind was an instinctive reflex.

Could he live with that knowledge?

Tulkhan didn't know, but for now he would maintain a distance between them. So far she had invaded his thoughts only when their bodies were touching. It seemed safe to assume Imoshen's ability weakened with distance, or only worked on contact.

A grim smile warmed him. His body might crave hers, but he didn't want to the pay the ultimate price for his lust and become her instrument.

It was just as well their customs required abstinence.

Tulkhan pushed his chair back, coming to his feet. Imoshen also rose, withdrawing from him, and gathering her dignity about her like a cloak.

With a formal bow, he bid her good night. Tulkhan knew by her rigidly controlled features that he had hurt Imoshen, and it galled him to admit that it hurt him to see her pain.

FROM DAWN THE following day Imoshen was frantically busy. Messengers ran from one end of the palace to the other, delivering her orders, tallying information and co-ordinating the efforts of an army of servants.

Imoshen vowed that this time when the guildmasters, town dignitaries and their families met the Ghebites, they would not be greeted by treachery but with familiar entertainment. They would see General Tulkhan was not like his uncouth, treacherous half-brother.

The people of T'Diemn were not surrendering their city but greeting their deliverer from oppression. It was a fine distinction which Imoshen hoped to impress on them.

The day was bitterly cold, too cold to hold the ceremony in the square. She elected to open the public rooms of the palace, which necessitated cleaning them, heating and lighting them. Food had to be prepared and seating arrangements organised for several hundred guests. At her insistence, the leaders of Tulkhan's army were to be scattered through the civilian guests. All weapons were to be left at the door. It would not be a welcome request, but if both parties cooperated it would go a long way to reassuring the townsfolk.

At short notice, she had sent messengers to scour the town for the skilled performers who had fled the palace. Original T'En forms of entertainment would be staged, as well as the more robust Ghebite entertainments provided by the army's camp followers. Her aim was to blend the two cultures – a symbol, she hoped, for the blending of their people.

Shortly before midday she tracked General Tulkhan down and reported her plans to him for approval. He had to agree to disarm his men or the townsfolk's gesture meant nothing.

She watched the General anxiously as he gazed through the tall window of one of the palace's entertainment rooms which faced onto a formal garden, lightly dusted with snow.

'All weapons at the door?' he muttered, casting a swift glance back to the men who had remained at the table when he left it.

'To reassure the townsfolk,' Imoshen insisted.

Tulkhan read the list. 'Six jugglers, a set of balladeers, seventeen acrobats, two storytellers, and a pair of duelling poets?'

She smiled at the tone of his voice. 'A T'En custom. You'll see. The entertainment is to give the formal ceremony a festive air, to make it less threatening.'

He nodded, then glanced down at the list again. 'It starts at midday?'

She nodded.

'This ceremony will go on until after dark.'

'Yes. It will be a great occasion.'

'Pomp and ceremony,' he sighed. 'Very well. I will put my work aside for the rest of that day.'

Imoshen stiffened. It wasn't as if she had been waited on hand and foot, her every wish catered to. She hadn't eaten a scrap since dawn and her head spun with details. 'Pomp and ceremony has its place, General!'

He gave her a long-suffering look and she realised with a shock that he was teasing her. It was a new sensation; not unwelcome, just... different.

WHEN THE CHURCH bells of the great domed basilica across the square rang out at midday, Imoshen was ready to play her part. She greeted each of the leaders of T'Diemn personally, before passing them along to servants who escorted them to their seats.

The church was represented by the Beatific, its temporal leader. She was a handsome woman in her early forties with eyes that saw too much. She made Imoshen feel gauche. Determined to be as regal as the Empress, who had impressed her so deeply when she was sixteen, Imoshen greeted the large retinue of priests and priestesses in their formal finery. She made a point of leading them to their seats personally. Soon she would have to deal with the Beatific to negotiate the church's approval of Tulkhan's coronation and their bonding.

Something told her it would not be easy. The Beatific was young to have risen to this position, so she must be a skilled negotiator.

Imoshen returned to her post and continued with the greetings. The townsfolk were all seated before any of the Ghebites appeared and then it was General Tulkhan himself who entered, alone and unattended. He surprised her by arriving from the square.

Imoshen stepped back as she took in his appearance. He was dressed in full battle regalia, looking magnificent in his red and black. She was startled by his choice of apparel, since he had agreed they would not bring weapons.

But understanding dawned on her when, after the formal greeting, he unclasped his weapons and handed them to her. Piece by piece, he discarded his battle regalia till he was dressed in nothing but his tight-fitting breeches, boots and a simple white undershirt.

She had to admire his sense of timing. Divested of his cloak, breast plate and helmet, he stood before her simply a man, though no one could accuse Tulkhan of being a mere man. Even divested of all his finery he carried himself like the leader he was.

He gave her a formal bow and whispered, 'Satisfied?'

Imoshen had to smile.

'Very effective,' she replied as she returned his formal bow. 'But won't you be cold?'

'I can live with it and so can my men.'

As he straightened, she saw his commanders all waiting to greet her as their leader had done. She went forward to welcome them.

While she did, she was aware of the General making his way slowly toward the rear of the public hall. As he did, he paused to speak to certain people. They appeared to know him and look on him favourably. Imoshen deduced they were the guildmasters he had dealt with when King Gharavan had been in charge of the city and he had to repair the damage his half-brother had done.

Imoshen greeted each of General Tulkhan's commanders and their trusted men. They handed her their weapons and were escorted to their seats. So far it had gone well. Her mind ran through the plans for the next step.

When everyone was present, Imoshen turned and saw that Tulkhan had not taken his seat on the dais. He was waiting for her. She realised he needed to consolidate his position with the people by having her at his side when he took his seat.

A now familiar stab of sadness pierced her. Once again she was reminded of Reothe. Both he and General Tulkhan wanted her for what she represented. Still, she had her part to play and she would not falter.

Imoshen moved lightly down the length of the hall, lifting her hand to meet Tulkhan's as he waited.

A rueful smile lurked in his eyes and she felt an answering smile on her lips despite her sombre mood.

He kissed her fingers. It was unexpected. She felt his warm breath dust her skin and a stab of desire surged deep within her.

'I thought you had a soldier's hatred of pomp and ceremony?' she whispered.

'I do, but someone once told me, there is a time and place for it.' His words were meant only for her. They charmed her, as they were meant to. She ground her teeth and steeled herself against him.

Imoshen placed her hand along his raised arm, recalling that his was how he had led her from the great hall of the stronghold the night of the Harvest Feast. That reminded her of their joining and her cheeks grew hot. She silently cursed her betraying fair skin.

Together they mounted the two steps onto the dais. As she looked out at the sea of faces below, Imoshen reflected that at least she had no painful memories of the great public hall. The midsummer festival's formal ceremonies had been held outside in the square, and in the gardens of the palace grounds. But these town dignitaries would have memories. Were they comparing the Emperor and Empress with the Ghebite General?

Imoshen listened to Tulkhan give his speech of welcome, but her concentration was focused on the inhabitants of the hall. She was trying to weigh the reaction of the town's leaders and of Tulkhan's men.

The townsfolk had already met General Tulkhan, when he repaired the damage his half-brother's cruelty had caused. She could tell they were relieved with the General's reasonable tone. His own men must have been privy to the contents of his speech because they were not surprised by any of the concessions the General was making. It was for the best. T'Diemn was an orderly, prosperous town and it would remain so if the town's leaders were allowed to go about their business without interference.

Then Tulkhan called for the leader of each guild to step forward and swear loyalty to his rule. Imoshen did not doubt that they would. They were a practical people, intent on trade and wealth. There was a murmuring and shuffling as chairs were pushed back and people rose, moving forward to congregate before the dais. They were men and women of age and distinction, leaders in their own fields.

A finger of pure winter light found its way through the clouds. Its silver rays plunged through the high, ornate stained-glass windows so that the area surrounding the dais was bathed in multi-coloured patches of light.

The town's leaders congregated and after whispered consultation the first couple stepped forward to kneel and swear fealty. Imoshen knew they would be the representatives of the largest of the greater guilds. She smiled. Even within the guild system, there was a pecking order.

The man was ancient. To Imoshen's healer-trained eyes, he looked as if he normally walked with the aid of a cane, but had done away with it out of pride. The woman was a stout matron with intelligent eyes. Imoshen deduced she must be in training to take his place as guildmaster. She suspected the old man had been called out of retirement to groom her after the previous guildmaster had been murdered by King Gharavan.

As the old man stepped from the dimness into the multi-coloured light he faltered. The woman, possibly blinded by the transition into the light, did not notice. Imoshen saw the old man lift his hand, feeling for the woman's shoulder, and miss.

Her healer's instincts took over. If he fell on the hard tiles, he could break a brittle bone. Before he could miss his footing, she ran down the two steps and caught his outstretched hand.

He seemed startled to find her there supporting him and moved to pull away.

'Let me be your cane, grandfather,' she whispered.

'Lady T'En?' He stared, bemused.

She smiled and placed his hand on her arm. When he knelt, she knelt with him. There was a hushed, collective sigh from the crowded tables.

She saw that the General had come to his feet and started down the first step. Now he stood above them.

She found his expression unreadable. Would he think she was currying favour with the townsfolk? Anger flickered through her. Would he rather she let the old man fall?

It did not matter what she did, he could interpret her actions negatively.

The old man and his assistant gave the oath of fealty and General Tulkhan formally accepted it, giving in return an oath which bound him to fair treatment of all their guilds and their members.

The oaths finished, Imoshen rose to her feet with her hand cupped under the old man's elbow so that her assistance appeared minimal but she was there ready to offer him help if he faltered.

He lifted his eyes to hers. His bald pate came only to mid-chest on her. He raised her hand to his withered cheek and, as they stepped apart, he kissed her sixth finger for luck. The woman thanked her softly, taking her hand to stroke her finger.

As the next couple moved forward, Imoshen sensed movement behind her and found General Tulkhan had descended from the dais. He joined her.

Why? Was he annoyed with her?

She had not felt comfortable seated up there while her people bowed and swore their oaths.

Standing before the dais, the General linked his arm with her. She liked the feel of his strong body next to hers, but she told herself he was only aligning himself with her to bolster his position with the townsfolk. It was a political move.

Imoshen knew she could not let down her guard, there was so much to bear in mind. As yet, she had not approached the church representatives to ask for their oath of fealty. That would require delicate negotiation.

It was a long process. Each of the greater guilds and then the lesser guilds swore their oaths. The last to make his oath was the elected administrator of the city and his cabinet of six people.

The mayor rose from swearing fealty and took Imoshen's hand. 'Welcome, Lady T'En. The city has been too long without an Aayel.'

Imoshen was so surprised she was speechless. Did he think to flatter her? The title Aayel was not given lightly. He moved off before she could speak.

The formalities over, the food was served and the entertainment begun. Much later, as the guests broke into patterns for the dances, Imoshen found a middle-aged woman waiting at her elbow, obviously anxious to speak with her.

Imoshen's whole evening had been a series of intense conversations as people sought reassurance. She turned, ready once again to shore up the General's position.

But when the woman caught Imoshen's hand, her face was tight with tension, her wine-dark eyes glistening. With a jolt Imoshen recognised the T'En trait, though the woman bore none of the other signs.

'My son? Do you know what became of him?' she whispered.

Imoshen searched her mind for the identity of this woman. She was guildmaster of the silversmiths.

'You must be –'

'Drakin's mother,' the woman supplied.

Imoshen felt her mouth go dry. She did not want to be the deliverer of bad news. 'You should be proud of your son. He brought word to Umasreach Stronghold. His news convinced General Tulkhan to ride to T'Diemn. It was Drake's intervention which brought aid to the city.'

'But what of my lad?' the woman asked.

Imoshen's fingers closed over the woman's and gripped her hand. Without a word, she led her through the clusters of guests, until they could be private. Then she spoke softly. 'Drake left my stronghold to join the rebels.'

The woman groaned. 'Then his life is forfeit!'

'No. I have told no one. He could yet return and, if he does, I will never tell.'

'Tell what?' General Tulkhan asked.

Imoshen felt the woman flinch. She slid her arm around the guildmaster's shoulders. 'Tell how relieved I am it is you who have claimed Fair Isle and not your half-brother.'

Tulkhan met her eyes and she realised he knew she was prevaricating.

'General,' she said quickly. 'Let me introduce the Silversmith Guildmaster.'

The woman's gaze flew from Imoshen to the General and back. If General Tulkhan had been a man like his half-brother, one word from Imoshen could see the guildmaster's position lost, her property confiscated and her family imprisoned or executed.

Gharavan would not have hesitated to use Drake's family as hostages to prise Reothe's whereabouts from them. Would the General stoop to the same tricks?

Imoshen did not believe it, but she had no intention of testing him.

It surprised her to realise she did not want Tulkhan to fail her.

Chapter Ten

'THERE THEY GO again!' Kalleen rolled her eyes as the bells rang out. 'On and off, all day long!'

Imoshen looked up from her papers. Was Kalleen jesting? No, being a farm girl she had marked the passage of her day by the rising and setting of the sun. 'Those are the bells of the basilica. They call the priests to prayer and ring out the times of the day for the convenience of the townsfolk.'

Kalleen laughed. 'No wonder the townspeople of T'Diemn rush about with such worried faces. Life's too short to parcel up the day as it slips away!'

Imoshen felt a smile tug at her lips. Kalleen was good for her.

With an impudent grin, the girl darted out of the room, intent on some mission of her own. For a lady's maid she spent very little time in Imoshen's room, and was quick to give her opinion on any and every subject, but Imoshen would not have it any other way. Things were said in Kalleen's hearing which would not have been said in front of Imoshen. The girl was a fount of information, not all of it welcome.

Sighing, Imoshen went back to the book. Her morning had been devoted to studying the documents from the palace library, searching for a clue as to the extent of the church's autonomy. She suspected that the Beatific was trying to assume more power than the church had previously laid claim to. It was what she would have done in the same position. As yet, Imoshen did not have the woman's key and it frustrated her.

She read until the convoluted grammar of the High T'En tongue turned her thoughts to nonsense.

Arching her back, Imoshen stretched and wandered to the window. Looking out over the spires and towers of T'Diemn to the blue-white hills which ringed the capital, she tried to clear her head. A little more than half a small moon had elapsed since they had arrived in the capital, but already she felt hemmed in. If she felt trapped, how did the General feel?

He spent much of his time in the town, inspecting its fortifications and seeing to his men. Although she had vowed to keep him at a distance, when he made no effort to be with her and seemed to prefer the company of his men, Imoshen was perversely irritated.

She told herself it was better this way. Her negotiations with the head of the T'En church required a clear mind and just being in the same room as the General distracted her. Somehow his voice rang clear above every other man's. When he laughed, something deep within her stirred with unspoken longing – not that she would ever reveal this to Tulkhan.

Kalleen's spirits had improved markedly with the return of Wharrd and his small band of elite guards, who reported that Gharavan had sailed eight days previously without trouble.

Meetings with the T'En church did not go so smoothly. Not that voices were ever raised. The Beatific was all smiles and polite interest, but her position was solid. She knew General Tulkhan needed the church's approval.

Of course, the General could raze the basilica and confiscate the wealth gathered over six hundred years of devotion, but that would destroy the people's trust. He had to win the populace over to hold the island.

Imoshen and the Beatific knew he would not use force. Unfortunately Tulkhan's religious advisor was a relatively young man whose zealous devotion to his own faith made him intolerant of the T'En religion. Cadre Castenatus had the arrogance of youth, armoured with pious righteousness. Imoshen wished he was a battle-hardened realist like Wharrd or Commander Piers, who had offered the General his allegiance so willingly when they entered T'Diemn. It was not going to be easy to find common ground.

The basilica bells rang out again. Imoshen cursed. Despite the reminder of the bells, she was late for yet another meeting with the leader of the church. Luckily she was already dressed for the formal meeting. Head down, she slipped out of her chamber and ran lightly along the long corridor, grateful there were no servants to see her running down the halls of the Emperor's palace. Her poor mother would not have approved.

Imoshen was almost at the formal wing when she remembered she'd meant to bring a critical document with her. If she could cite decrees by her forebear and provide written evidence of the extent of the church's power, the Beatific's advisors would have to retract their stipulations.

It paid to have a working knowledge of the language of law, and Imoshen was glad she had kept up her study of High T'En. With a muttered imprecation she spun on her heel and this time ran in earnest.

Her supple dress-boots hit the floor with a soft thud. She flung open her bedchamber door and darted across to the worktable. Intent on rifling through the scattered documents, it was only when the vital scroll was in her hand that she heard an angry voice coming from Kalleen's antechamber.

Imoshen's mouth went dry. She listened, but could not detect a second voice. Still, she could not walk off knowing Kalleen was in distress. She hated to witness another's hurt, even a stranger's. It had always caused her physical discomfort, but even more so since her gifts had been awakened.

Stepping lightly across the rugs, she pushed the connecting door ajar. It looked as if Kalleen had flung herself across her bed. Even as Imoshen took in her silent despair the girl noticed the open door and rolled off the bed, silently wiping her face on her sleeve. Meeting Imoshen's eyes with a steady gaze, she almost dared the T'En to accuse her of crying.

Instinctively Imoshen crossed the chamber and went to touch her, but Kalleen jerked away.

'I won't have you seeing my thoughts, Lady T'En,' she said stiffly.

A shaft of pain stabbed Imoshen. Kalleen too?

No, she was certain the girl trusted her, which was more than could be said for most of the palace servants. She'd overheard the whispers, talk of how she'd assumed Gharavan's form to save General Tulkhan. She'd seen the hastily averted eyes, experienced the sudden absence of conversation when she entered a room. Since the night they had deposed Gharavan, Imoshen had noted the shift in her people's perception of her.

'I would never do anything against your wishes, Kalleen.' Imoshen was surprised to hear how reasonable her voice sounded despite the pain. 'I merely sought to comfort you.'

'So you say.' Kalleen sniffed, wiping her nose inelegantly with the cuff of her sleeve. 'You'd do it without thinking. Ten times a day I've seen you anticipate what people are going to say.'

Imoshen's heart sank. Was Kalleen right? Was she unconsciously alienating the palace servants? She licked her lips and forced herself to face this unwelcome revelation.

The girl took a step closer, very obviously placing her hand on Imoshen's arm. 'I do trust you, my lady, no matter what they say.'

Imoshen smiled wryly. Kalleen was a friend in the truest sense of the word. Who else would speak the unpleasant truth? 'I'm glad to hear it. So, if you trust me, tell me what's wrong.'

A tremor rippled through the young woman's features and she broke contact. 'Wharrd has asked me to bond with him, to be his *wife*, as he calls it.'

So she was to lose Kalleen. Imoshen said nothing.

The girl drew a shuddering breath. 'I told him no.'

'Why? If you care for him, surely –'

'I love him. But I won't be his slave.'

Imoshen's eyes widened.

Kalleen walked to the small window. The exterior of the thick glass was crusted with ice crystals glistening in the direct sunlight. 'Wharrd says the General will give him an estate and a title. I have nothing. ' She spun to face Imoshen. 'I might only be a farm girl, but I am not stupid. I've been asking questions. Ghebite women don't own their share of the family property. They *are* part of the property.' Kalleen shuddered, visibly revolted. 'They belong to their men!'

Imoshen stepped closer, pierced by ready compassion. 'Of course, I see your dilemma.'

Kalleen's golden eyes blazed. 'No matter how much I love him, I won't be his slave. I told him I'd rather stay here and serve you!'

Again a smile tugged at Imoshen's lips. So she was an acceptable alternative to slavery.

She could understand Kalleen's decision. As long as the girl's mistress retained her position, Kalleen ranked above almost all other palace servants.

Imoshen had no trouble empathising with Kalleen. If the girl bonded with one of her own people she would be an equal partner – half-owner of a farm was better than the wife-slave of a rich Ghebite.

Imoshen took Kalleen's small, golden hand in her own. 'Simple. I will gift you with an estate. I wanted to find some way to reward you for taking my place in the dungeon. I'll make over the Windhaven Estate to you and your heirs...' Imoshen broke off with a curse, dropped Kalleen's hand and strode into her own room, her cheeks hot with frustration.

Windhaven was no longer hers to give. It lay to the north and had probably been gutted by the Ghebite army. But the lands would still be good. She would have to ask General Tulkhan to release it to her so she could gift it to her maid. She hated to ask him for anything. The thought galled her.

Imoshen was aware of Kalleen watching silently and turned to her.

'General Tulkhan took Windhaven Estate when he took Fair Isle. I will have to speak with him.' The words left a bitter taste in Imoshen's mouth. Kalleen's golden eyes held ready sympathy.

Pacing the room, Imoshen tried to come to terms with her position. It infuriated her to know she had so little control over her own life. In truth, even Umasreach Stronghold was no longer hers. She had surrendered it to Tulkhan. As long as she strode the corridors of the palace and advised the General it was easy to forget that she was his captive, a prize of war.

She needed a lever on the Ghebite General.

The Aayel had indeed been wise.

Imoshen had to maintain her hold on the General, and what better way than through his own flesh and blood? She would see to it that her children held the reins of power and made the decisions of government. Fair Isle would not slide into barbarism in one generation.

'My lady?' Kalleen whispered. 'Even if you gift Windhaven to me, the moment I give Wharrd my vows he will own everything I own, including me. Ghebite women have no rights. I know what will happen.' Her top lip curled contemptuously. 'The Cadre has been most helpful. According to him I don't even have a proper soul!'

'Absurd!' Imoshen looked down into Kalleen's indignant face and had to smile. The girl was right. She could not let that happen, not to Kalleen, not to herself. 'True, you would lose everything if you married by the Ghebite religion, but what if the Ghebites were to recognise our church and its laws? Bonding is another thing entirely.'

In that moment, Imoshen understood what she had to do and she was sure if she handled it correctly the Beatific would comprehend the benefits for the T'En church. Imoshen's greatest opponent would become her ally.

Delighted, she hugged the smaller girl. 'Don't worry, Kalleen. I will see to it. You will own your own home and yourself. Every female of Fair Isle will retain her dignity.'

Kalleen searched Imoshen's face, hope warring with despair. 'We surrendered, my lady. We have nothing but what they choose to give us.'

Imoshen chewed her bottom lip. It was true. They were fine words, fine sentiments. But how realistic was she being? Possession was nine-tenths of the law. As of this moment, by custom she and Kalleen possessed the rights of ownership and self-determination. Imoshen vowed she would not give up these rights without a fight.

The basilica bells sounded again.

'Wait and see. I must go. I'm terribly late for my meeting.'

Imoshen tucked the document within her brocade vest and strode off, her mind racing with ideas.

As the last of the royal family she was the titular head of the T'En church, a position she found bizarre. Since the Aayel had opened her eyes she had been observing the church officials. It was clear to her now that the current religious leaders gave lip service to her status but jealously guarded their positions of power within the church structure.

Maybe long ago the T'En race been regarded as being touched by the gods, but as the T'En began to die out, the church had gained more and more control over the temporal world. Imoshen could understand why the religious leaders resented anything or anyone who rivalled their position. She was an anachronism, an embarrassing reminder of the spiritual side of the church which had lost significance as the church's hold on temporal matters of law expanded.

Imoshen frowned. She had to have the church's blessing.

It was a powerful, multi-layered beast whose fingers of influence spread into the smallest isolated village, but here in the city the greatest power lay in the basilica. This served as the religious and administration centre for the church's many branches. In her elected position the Beatific held the post for a term of five years. Imoshen suspected much manoeuvring behind the scenes had gone into securing that position.

As Imoshen entered the formal greeting chamber, the Beatific rose, her attendants rising with her. If the woman was annoyed by Imoshen's late arrival, she did not show it.

Etiquette demanded Imoshen make a formal apology.

Commander Piers hardly let her finish before opening the inner doors to a circular table laid with food and drink.

'Everything is ready, Lady T'En,' the grizzled commander announced. At his side Cadre Castenatus resumed a heated discussion with one of the high ranking T'En priests. Imoshen understood the commander's impatience. The Cadre could be trusted to irritate a saint.

She ushered the group into the inner chamber. The correct ceremony had to be observed. It was only after warmed wine and sweets had been consumed that Imoshen was able to broach the real subject of their meeting and she did it tangentially.

'Beatific, before we begin our discussions I thought the Cadre might like to tell us a little about his homeland, Gheeaba.'

The woman's sharp, golden eyes fixed on Imoshen. This was off the subject. The Beatific had been holding out for an increase in church powers before agreeing to officiate at the wedding ceremony or give the church's blessing to the crowning ceremony which followed.

'Tell me, Cadre...' Imoshen turned to the northern priest. His righteousness was so ingrained that she hoped he would speak without considering his audience. 'How many sisters do you have, and which positions do they hold in the governing council of your country?'

He blinked at her. 'I have three sisters, but they hold no official places. Their husbands sit on the council.'

'How then do they use their education to mould the laws?'

He laughed. 'They have no education in such matters.'

Imoshen turned to Commander Piers. 'You, sir. Will you take a wife and settle here?'

He was startled by her sudden change of subject. Imoshen caught his worried eyes. He knew she was up to something.

'I don't know...' he began slowly.

'Commander Piers could take several wives. His position allows him up to four,' Cadre Castenatus explained.

Imoshen sensed the stiffening of all the women present, but did not allow herself the luxury of looking at the Beatific.

Instead, she turned to the old commander. 'Surely that is a Ghebite custom. You would abide by our customs here?'

He hesitated, clearly aware that his answer could be detrimental to the negotiations. 'I am a simple soldier –'

'If women do not sit on council, then they must serve their country in some other way,' Imoshen remarked ingenuously, turning back to the Cadre. 'What do they do, administrate the townships, or disseminate information through schooling, or do they officiate at the religious ceremonies?'

He laughed. 'Everyone knows a woman has but a poor weak soul which cannot sustain itself without guidance.' With the conviction of absolute certainty he launched into a long speech quoting learned doctrines on the weakness of a woman's soul and the female's need for protective guidance. Imoshen had no trouble translating it as a justification for the males of Gheeaba to dominate their women. And it was clear every other woman present had come to the same conclusion.

It was only at this point that Imoshen allowed herself to meet Beatific's eyes. For a fraction of a heartbeat the handsome woman's political mask slipped and she exchanged a knowing look with Imoshen. It was underlaid with pure fury.

Neither the Beatific nor Imoshen could afford to let secular differences divide them when their enemy was so obviously determined to grind them down.

Sitting back, Imoshen let the Cadre win her argument for her.

When he paused to draw breath, she remarked. 'I am a little lost. Your system is new to me. If a man were to die, which of his wives would inherit the property?'

'The man's eldest son by his first wife, of course.'

'Not the first wife?'

'None of the wives. The property belonged to the man.'

'But surely the women –'

'Women cannot own property.'

The Beatific sprang to her feet, the movement at odds with her usual stately grace.

The Cadre fell silent as the Beatific's assistants also rose. His expression of surprise revealed how little he understood the people of Fair Isle.

Imoshen came to her feet. Stepping around the formal table, she placed a hand on the Beatific's arm. 'I feel we have a great deal in common, Beatific. I think we could work for the good of Fair Isle, particularly the women of Fair Isle.'

It was a simple, honest statement, but the Beatific only gave Imoshen a sharp look before formally taking leave of those present.

Imoshen was sure she had convinced the Beatific to give her support, but she could not understand the woman's suspicion. Of all the people Imoshen had met since coming to the palace, the Beatific remained elusive. Because she could not find the woman's key, Imoshen could only wait and hope her ploy had worked.

In the late afternoon she received a communication from the leader of the T'En church. Heart pounding, hardly able to let herself hope, she opened the brass cylinder and unrolled the vellum. Feverishly, she read the covering missive.

A surge of triumph flooded her. The communication contained two copies of a formal agreement in which the Beatific offered to host the ceremonies on Midwinter's Day on the understanding that the church's current systems of law, particularly those pertaining to ownership and inheritance regardless of sex, would remain in place. It meant General Tulkhan's position had the support of the church, but in acknowledging the church he had to give credence to their laws.

It was exactly what Imoshen was hoping for.

She replaced the documents and left the cylinder on the table. Feeling pleased with herself, Imoshen went looking for the General to give him the good news. The servants sent her to the stables, where the Ghebites had organised an entertainment. Trudging across the courtyard, Imoshen heard the throaty growl of the crowd and tensed.

She stopped, undecided.

Rumours of the Ghebites' penchant for bird-baiting had swept the palace. But her workload had been so heavy she had not had time to investigate and, Imoshen had to admit, she did not want to know the full extent of the Ghebites' barbarity, so she had avoided the stables. She'd heard that the birds were reared especially for the fate, bred winner's-get to winner. Their only purpose in life was to die at their owner's whim.

It was a typical example of Ghebite mentality. Everything must serve their purpose and damn the feelings of lesser creatures, be they female or dumb animal. To the Ghebite way of thinking, they were probably one and the same.

It was no good. Imoshen couldn't ignore the cock-fighting. What happened in the palace set the tone of the city. The townsfolk would take their cue from her, and if she condoned this barbarism what else might she condone?

Gritting her teeth, Imoshen strode toward the closed double doors. Her excuse to consult the General was legitimate. He could not accuse her of prying. She would just take a casual look while delivering her good news. Perhaps the whispers were an exaggeration.

Imoshen slipped unobtrusively inside the stable. The sound and stench hit her like a physical blow.

The long barn was crowded, filled with strident voices. Men bellowed as they placed their bets, competing with the music to be understood. The Ghebite musicians who had travelled with the army were set up in a stall, playing their rowdy, raucous excuse for music.

Wine flowed freely, as did the opinions of those who considered themselves experts. They argued over the skill exhibited in the previous match and the likelihood of the surviving bird beating the new contender.

As Imoshen forged through the thickly packed crowd of sweating bodies, disgust and frustration filled her. The Ghebites thought nothing of inciting birds to kill each other, feeding their own bloodlust with the male bird's frenzy.

Deep within her, Imoshen felt an innate sense of injustice. The cockerel was only doing what nature intended it to do. How could these men take perverse pleasure from so pointless a death?

She wanted to banish them and the invaders' sordid entertainment from the Royal Palace. At the very least, she wanted to confront General Tulkhan. How could he condone this?

But she was frustrated, unable to join him, because although she could see him standing on the far side of the fighting pit, she knew she couldn't simply march over and upbraid him.

Like herself, the General was treading a fine line. He had to retain the support of his commanders. She could not afford to undermine his position. His men would resent it if she didn't show the General proper deference. Tulkhan would have to retaliate by treating her as he would treat a Ghebite woman. If he didn't, he would lose the respect of his soldiers.

Imoshen drew a short, tight breath. Frustration welled in her. She looked around and tried to be fair. Was she overreacting? Was this only harmless entertainment?

It worried her to see so many of her own people present. There were male palace servants, stable hands and entertainers. No women, she realised. But the men of Fair Isle were obviously enjoying the spectacle. It concerned her to see how quickly they forgot themselves. They were only too happy to immerse their senses in mind-dulling violence. Was the beast so close to the surface in even the most civilised male?

Were they really closer to the animal than females? Was it only the strength of the women of Fair Isle that maintained their society's level of civilisation? It was a sobering thought.

She noticed the Cadre in the thick of it. Blood flecked his tunic from the last bird's death, staining the religious symbol of purity. How dare he claim Ghebite women had lesser souls than men? A sharp surge of anger flared inside Imoshen. She clenched her fists, trying to control her rage.

Densely packed bodies heated the air which was heavy with the scent of horses, men, wine, blood and...

A prickle of sensation danced across Imoshen's skin as she identified the last ingredient – crude, eager excitement. It was so thick she could almost taste it. How dare they sully the palace's rich culture with their Ghebite barbarism!

As the new bout started, an expectant, hungry hush fell over the crowd. Imoshen's heart pounded. Fury boiled inside her. A strange taste filled her mouth, making her teeth ache and her skin itch. She felt a rush of feverish hunger, as though the blood lust, which lay so thick on the air, was a dainty morsel she could inhale. It made her body sing and her head spin.

Across the crowd, beyond the fighting pit, she met Tulkhan's obsidian eyes. Why was he watching her so intensely?

The crowd roared. Dimly, she was aware that the fighting birds had drawn fresh blood.

Imoshen's nostrils stung. Her very flesh vibrated with the deep-throated growl of the crowd. A magnificent rage empowered her gift. The rush was so intense she felt weightless, as if she might rise off the dirt floor.

The birds in the pit drew her attention. One was weakening. She could feel its life force slipping away even as a joyous rage grew in her, but one part of her mind remained crystal clear. With a start, she realised that the spilling of life, even a life so insignificant as the cockerel's, could be channelled to empower her T'En gifts. It was enticingly, achingly sweet.

One by one, the men stopped shouting. Those who'd had their backs to her turned, eyes widening, lips pulling back from their teeth. She could smell their terror, taste it on her tongue. It was all so sweet, tempting.

Acting on instinct, the triumphant fighting bird attacked its weakened opponent, tearing out its throat. The shrill death screech sounded obscenely human in the sudden silence.

Imoshen knew the moment the bird's life left its body.

The combined life forces of the crowd and the bird joined within her, flooding her. Fingers curling, teeth aching, she caught her breath as her vision blurred and swam, filled with pin-wheeling sparks.

But she would not give in. The urge to manipulate this power was overwhelming. Instinct told her it would be too sweet and far too easy to grow dependent on it. How long before she began to crave this heady rush?

Fear was her anchor. It was the rock to which she clung in the tidal flood of new found power.

But the build-up demanded release. Imoshen sensed if she didn't channel it, it would consume her. She had to release this.

Brilliant white light engulfed her. Blinding her. Dread raced through her. She had lost control and immolated herself!

No.

The light consumed the birds. With an ear-numbing absence of noise they exploded in a ball of flame and feathers. Men ducked for cover. Shards of burning flesh and feathers sprayed the crowd, burning skin, hair and igniting straw. Men shouted. Horses screamed, sounding just as human and terrified.

Imoshen staggered back, nearly overwhelmed by the rush of those escaping the stables. The stench of burning feathers made her gag.

Disbelief warred with an instinctive knowledge that went bone deep. She had done this.

May the Aayel help her!

But the no one could. Imoshen was alone.

She clutched a stall wall and retched, tears stinging her eyes. The crackle of greedy flames added to the confusion. When the retching had stopped, she dragged a trembling hand across her lips and ran, fleeing with the last of the crowd.

In the press of bodies she was swept out of the stable and into the courtyard. Those around her were so shaken they didn't notice her. Could it be they didn't realise she was to blame, or had fear of the greedy fire overcome their fear of her?

Her mind reeled and nausea clawed at her.

Like swarming bees, the terror of those around her stung her senses. It was too immediate and raw, too easily tapped. She had to escape them.

Abruptly she changed direction, shoving her way through the bodies. Her footsteps took her away from the others into the bowels of the palace. Though Imoshen ran, she knew there was no safe harbour, for the enemy was within her. Tears blurred her vision. It wasn't fair. She'd been so careful. She hadn't once tried to use her gifts. Until now she'd had no idea they could be triggered by violence and death. Blood roared in her head, thudding in her ears in time to her pounding heart.

She had nearly lost control. Only a reflex action had saved her at the expense of the birds.

What must the General think of her? Would he assume she'd done it intentionally? When their eyes had met across that pit, he'd registered her disgust.

Others had turned to her, sensing something as it built. The Cadre's suspicious face remained imprinted on her mind. She snorted, seared by self-disgust. The tale would be all over the palace by evening.

Now Tulkhan's men, the palace servants and even the stable boys – all of them would be terrified of her. If only there was someone she could trust to help her with this.

Imoshen rounded a corner and met up with a group of women plucking chickens. Downy feathers hung on air made humid by the kitchen ovens. Death, blood and heat. It was too reminiscent of the stables.

In her quest for privacy Imoshen had fled to the kitchens, the place she always chose as a child. But this was not her childhood home. Even the stronghold was no longer hers.

Tears flooded her eyes.

There were too many witnesses here, too many people ready to judge and condemn. She ran down another long corridor. When she came to the door she knew it led into the gardens and the lake with its mock forest. She craved the peace and solitude of the silent snow.

Wearing nothing but her thin boots and a formal dress with a brocade vest, she ran out into the open. Cold cut into her bare skin, through the thin gown and boots. Her throat and chest burned with each breath of chilled air. But it was good to escape the confines of the palace and all it represented.

To clear her head Imoshen scooped up a handful of snow, crunching some in her mouth, rubbing more on her cheeks. It stung, but it was invigorating and cleansing.

Wiping her stinging palms on her thighs, she ran on not thinking, knowing only that she needed to escape. Her feet carried her into the hollow to the edge of the frozen lake.

The setting reminded her how one year when, she had been too young to attend the Midwinter Festival, her sister had returned with tales of an ice ballet on the lake.

Midwinter was fifteen days away, but now she would never see an ice ballet. All the beauty of the Old Empire was dead, consumed by the crude hunger of the Ghebites.

Without stopping, she ran out onto the ice. Her boots had no grip, their soft soles skidded and her momentum carried her forward awkwardly. She careered with her legs locked, arms wavering to keep her balance.

Letting her body go limp, she hit the ice and went with the skid until she felt her momentum slow and she came to a stop.

All was utter silence. Cold, uncaring quiet.

The folly of her mad run struck Imoshen. It was freezing, too cold for what she was wearing, and who knew if the ice was safe.

She tried to get to her feet, but her legs went out from under her and she dropped in an undignified heap, sliding across the ice on her backside.

'*Imoshen!*'

General Tulkhan's furious voice startled her. Heart sinking, she looked over her shoulder to see his dark form on the edge of the lake. The indignity of it seared her.

Did he have to witness her every indiscretion? Couldn't he leave her be?

'Go away!' Anger flooded her. With sudden insight Imoshen knew it could happen again. The power of her T'En gifts seethed just below the surface. She could lose control and hurt someone.

Cold fear cooled her rage. It was demeaning to admit she couldn't trust herself. Today she had discovered she was a child with an adult's weapon.

Pressing icy fingers to her heated cheeks, Imoshen closed her eyes and took a deep shaky breath. There was nowhere to run. She had to admit her failure and face the General. He deserved an apology.

Besides, sitting in a puddle of melting ice while Tulkhan looked on was not doing anything for her dignity. With a sigh, she rolled over onto her knees and rose carefully to her feet.

Tulkhan watched as Imoshen stood up and straightened her shoulders. He was going to tear strips off her. How dare she try to intimidate his men with careless displays of her T'En power? That he had been as startled as his men hadn't helped. He hated being at a disadvantage. Not to mention the damage she'd caused. Luckily the fire hadn't spread, but the rumour would and with it the damage to Imoshen and himself.

Imoshen lifted a hand and acknowledged him with a wave. She took one step forward and went through the ice.

Her disappearance was so abrupt Tulkhan stared, too stunned to move.

Then he was running across the slippery surface, his heart roaring in his head. He didn't even remember moving. His boots thudded on the ice, striking chips. One part of his mind told him, if he wasn't careful, he would go through the ice into the freezing lake with her.

Tulkhan slowed his mad dash and looked up, trying to judge the distance and the thickness of the ice. Frustration filled him. This wasn't his land. He came from the hot north. He'd be no help to Imoshen if he ended up in the lake with her.

He tried to stop, but his boots wouldn't grip and he went down on all fours, skidding across the ice.

Ahead of him he saw Imoshen's head break the surface of the icy lake, her mouth open in a silent scream. She lunged for the ice lip, trying to lever herself out. But the ice gave way, dragging her under the choppy lake water again.

His mouth went dry as his momentum continued to carry him toward the weak ice.

Imoshen's head broke the surface again. Her hair clung to her skull like spilt milk. Seeing him, she shook her head furiously.

'Stay back!' Her voice was a frantic, breathless cry.

He came to a stop. Fear sank its icy hand into his gut. To advance might mean his death, but to hesitate would condemn her. He couldn't let her drown. It was a cruel choice.

Frozen with indecision Tulkhan watched as Imoshen pulled her weight onto the ice lip. He was close enough to see skittering cracks race across the surface of the ice.

Though he hadn't grown up skating on frozen lakes, he understood it would precipitate both their deaths to approach her now.

Wordlessly she looked across to him, lips compressed, deliberately not calling for help. Her silent struggle to ease her weight onto the precarious ice tore at him. His heart swelled to choke him. No, he couldn't leave her to struggle alone.

He crept forward on his hands and knees.

She looked up and saw him coming.

'Stay back!' Fury ignited her face.

It made him smile.

Creeping laboriously forward, he watched the ice for cracks. His bare hands stung with the cold, then burned until they felt nothing.

'No further!' she warned.

This time her tone stopped him. Her eyes were dark pools in her white face. Shivers wracked her body and she could hardly speak for the chattering of her teeth.

He crouched there, impotent and hating it.

She was just a body length from him, trapped from her waist down in the lake, her upper body pressed to a cracked ice slab. Tulkhan knew if he returned to the palace for help, Imoshen would be dead before he could come back.

'Where are your men when we n-need them?' she whispered.

A painful grin escaped him. 'I told them not to follow.'

'Wh-why?'

It seemed ridiculous now. 'I wanted to confront you. What possessed you? Why incinerate the birds?'

She rolled her eyes and shook her head, then grew very still. He was afraid she had lost her strength and, with it, all hope. But abruptly she kicked with both legs, lunging up onto the ice.

His breath caught in his throat. Would the ice crack?

It held.

She was closer, almost within arm's length. If he could only pull her off that weak ice... Tulkhan edged towards her. She watched him, hope warring with desperation. Her arm stretched out him, fingers splayed.

Only a little further.

He lay on his belly and thrust one arm towards her. Their fingers touched. Convulsively hers closed around his. Chilled as his hands were, hers felt colder.

She smiled, her blue lips parting, teeth chattering. 'You f-fool!'

He grinned and flexed his arm, but he had no leverage and she was weighed down by her soaked clothes. The cold lake still claimed her from the thighs down.

With quiet desperation she raised her knee, shifting her weight onto the ice lip.

Tulkhan's grip tightened. 'Now the other...'

She nodded, clenched her chattering jaw, and eased her second knee out onto the ice. He dragged her toward him. The strain made his muscles protest.

Trembling with a combination of cold and effort, he drew her towards him until they were face to face, belly down on the ice.

Imoshen clutched his shoulders, panting with relief. He felt her bury her cold face in his shoulder. Even her breath seemed icy.

'S-so cold!'

Tulkhan realised she could still die.

He had to get her back to the palace, get her warm. 'This way.'

With painstaking care they slithered across the ice on their bellies. As soon as the ice appeared more solid, they clambered onto their hands and knees to crawl. Imoshen fell behind. When Tulkhan looked over his shoulder, she was struggling to keep up with him, her head down, trying to lift her shoulders. Her faltering efforts frightened him.

Furious, Tulkhan returned to her, knelt and pulled her into his arms. He shook her. 'Keep moving!'

She nodded but clung to him, great spasms of shivers wracking her body. When he looked into her face her eyes were dull, her concentration turned inwards. He was losing her. *No!*

Instinctively, he caught her head in his hands and kissed those cold lips, willing the desperate passion that warmed him to animate her.

At first her mouth remained unresponsive under his. He could feel only her reflexive shivers shaking him with their intensity. He pulled her hard against him, ignoring the icy cold of her clothes which seeped through his already damp clothing.

A shuddering sigh escaped her and he felt her respond to him, an unmistakeable sign that he had reawakened her fierce will to live. Desperately, she returned his kiss, her lips like cold liquid satin on his. The sensation was so potent he caught his breath. Now he felt her body's instinctive move to meet his.

She held nothing back.

His long years of battle experience told him Imoshen's response was a reaction to her narrow escape from death. He didn't care. He wanted her...

'General?' worried voices called.

Tulkhan detected frantic figures in his peripheral vision. Stunned, he lifted his head, peering past Imoshen's shoulder. Dark figures shouted and capered on the lake's shore. They insisted he acknowledge them.

He groaned and felt Imoshen tense as she registered the change in him. It took a determined effort to release her from his embrace.

He indicated the frozen lake's shore.

Imoshen turned, grimaced then sighed. '*Now* they come? What are they yelling?'

There were so many voices all shouting at once that the individual words were lost.

Imoshen went to stand and staggered. Tulkhan came to his feet, catching her before she fell.

'I'm so weak,' she complained disgustedly.

'Stop!' Someone called from the shore. 'Don't move. The ice is not safe!'

Tulkhan looked down at Imoshen. Laughter rose inside him. The same impossible laughter ignited her. He threw back his head and roared.

A peal of fey delight broke from her lips. The sound brushed across his skin like silk. He wanted to wrap himself in it.

Imoshen clutched his arm, grasping for breath. 'Don't laugh. They'll think you're touched like me.'

That sobered Tulkhan.

He judged the distance they had yet to travel. 'Can we walk to the shore from here?'

She nodded.

Together, hands clasped, for balance, they walked gingerly across the ice to the lake's shore. Men were just returning with planks of wood when they reached the bank.

'My lady,' Kalleen panted, as a party of palace servants scurried up behind her. 'You're soaked. You'll catch your death.'

Imoshen went to climb the bank but slipped. Tulkhan caught her before she could land in the snow. He swept her up in his arms.

She stiffened. 'Put me down.'

He ignored her, ploughing up the bank as the servants, men-at-arms and stronghold guard milled around them.

Imoshen lay in his arms, furious but unwilling to cause a scene in front of the others.

'*Put me down!*' She twisted in his arms. 'I'm too heavy for you. I'm as big as an ordinary man.'

'And I'm bigger than most men, but if you struggle I might drop you in the snow.' Tulkhan smiled when she stopped wriggling. Would he have dropped her in an ungainly heap in the snow?

Yes. She knew him well. He realised he was enjoying this.

The servants and men-at-arms shot questions at him. He answered them all with an edited version of the accident. Finally they fell silent, dropping away to accompany them in small groups.

Imoshen's arms slid around his neck. 'You risked a ducking in the lake to save me.'

He heard the serious tone behind her facetious words. He had risked his life to save her.

'I must be mad,' he muttered. 'I can't even swim.'

Her arms tightened compulsively around his neck.

'Mad, indeed,' she whispered. Then her tone changed. 'You can put me down. You must be getting tired.'

His arms were beginning to ache, but she wasn't the only one who could be stubborn. He was glad he'd inherited his grandfather's build. It had been a nuisance as a boy. At twelve he'd stood as tall as a man and been expected to act like one. At sixteen he'd been a head taller than most men. He'd discovered his size influenced the way people treated him.

'You know,' he said softly, pitching his voice so only Imoshen could hear. 'When I was younger, people used to think I was stupid because I grew so big. Tulkhan, the dim-witted giant!'

He glanced down and saw her sharp, wine-dark eyes on him. With a jolt, he sensed her Otherness. What was she learning of his past from this physical contact? Once again he was reminded that she was not like him, she was T'En.

Imoshen studied the General, surprised by his admission. 'I never thought you stupid. An arrogant barbarian, yes, but never stupid.' She saw him grin and lightness filled her. How sweet it was to know that she had driven those bitter memories from him.

They walked on, nearing the bulk of the palace. Tulkhan's admission about his youth made him seem more real to her. She felt compelled to share something of herself with him. 'Ever since I can remember, people have feared me, because I'm a throwback.'

He looked down into her face, his dark eyes alert but unreadable. He had closed himself away from her again. She was glad she hadn't added that she was beginning to fear herself now.

Their return caused a great commotion. Imoshen suspected that many of those who wished her well were secretly wishing the treacherous ice had done its job more thoroughly.

Kalleen would have had her bathed and tucked into a warmed bed, but no sooner was she dressed than Imoshen sent for the General.

'As for you, you can go, Kalleen. I won't sit by the fire with a blanket around me like some old grandmother,' Imoshen said, pacing up and down.

'What's so important that you must see me now and not go to bed like a sensible person?' the General demanded.

Imoshen wanted to run to him. Instead, she channelled her energy into achieving her goal and darted to the table where the Beatific's terms were waiting to be read. Unable to stop herself, Imoshen lifted the brass cylinder and waved it triumphantly.

'The T'En church will recognise our bonding and coronation, which means the rest of Fair Isle will follow suit. And you have me to thank for it!'

'Let me see.' General Tulkhan strode toward Imoshen. She opened the cylinder and slid out the scroll, passing it to him. He turned it to the light of the scented candles. Dusk fell early this close to midwinter.

He frowned. 'What manner of chicken scrawl is this?'

Imoshen bit her lips to hide a smile. 'The language of all official documents is High T'En.'

He held it out to her. 'Read it to me, word for word.'

'If I am to translate it, shouldn't the Cadre be here too?' Imoshen suspected the Ghebite priest intended to dismantle the T'En church once General Tulkhan was officially recognised as ruler of Fair Isle.

'Why?' Tulkhan snapped. 'I make the decisions.'

She took the scroll from him and turned away so he wouldn't see her smile. The General's dislike of the Cadre's company had not been lost on her.

She went closer to the fire, eager for its warmth and prepared to read, then translate. General Tulkhan settled into her chair with his long legs stretched out before him. Propping one elbow on the table, he cupped his chin to watch her thoughtfully.

She tried not to let her gaze wander to him as she read each sentence, then translated it. This manner of delivery made the meaning rather disjointed, as the grammar of the High T'En tongue was very different from its daughter language.

The General's keen dark eyes never left Imoshen's face, and she wondered if he was having trouble comprehending the ornate prose. When it came to the paragraphs pertaining to recognition of T'En church laws, Imoshen's heart pounded. She willed him to accept what she was interpreting. The General's expression did not change. Either he was keeping his reaction close to his chest, or he did not understand how civil laws and church laws intertwined.

Imoshen felt no guilt withholding this information. If he had asked, she would have explained, but he didn't. Finally she came to the end and indicated where the Beatific had signed and placed her seal of office.

'Two copies, one for the Beatific to keep, one for us. This is where you sign, and I sign here.'

'You?' His gaze flew to hers.

She tilted her head, surprised by his reaction. 'By recognising your position, the Beatific strips the rebel leader Reothe of his rights. As the last legitimate member of the T'En royal family, I become titular head of the church. Do you want a translated version of this before you sign?'

'Why? You read it word for word, didn't you?'

Imoshen nodded. She had read it word for word as he requested, though the meaning would have been clearer had she paraphrased it.

His stomach grumbled audibly and the General shifted in the seat. Reading the scroll had taken a good while. He held out his hand. Imoshen passed the document to him, aware of her heart hammering in her chest. She had gambled that if she did provide him with a translated version, he would have been too busy to read it thoroughly before signing. But it appeared he was ready to sign now.

After all, the Ghebite General was a man of action. Yet he had taken the trouble to learn her land's language before bringing his army to Fair Isle. He was a strange mixture of the primitive and sophisticated.

His obsidian eyes scanned the ornate pages of the document. 'So if I sign this now, the Beatific retains control over her church and will back me in controlling Fair Isle?'

Imoshen nodded.

'Have you ink and wax?'

Imoshen noted that her hands did not tremble as she indicated her own ink and wax, then sharpened the scriber.

'You first,' he said, when she offered it to him.

Imoshen swallowed and dipped the tip in the ink.

'You think this is a fair agreement?' Tulkhan asked.

'I do. The terms are fair to all inhabitants of this island, whether they are Ghebite or locals.' She paused as she tapped the excess ink from the tip of the scriber. 'General, you have enemies on the mainland, an unruly army of ex-soldiers, reluctant southern nobles and a competent rebel leader in Reothe. Any support from an entrenched body like the church must be useful.'

He laughed. 'You think like a Ghebite soldier.'

She stiffened. Was he attempting to insult her? No, she read only genuine amusement in his eyes.

'Statesmanship was one of my best subjects,' she temporised.

He nodded and gestured for her to sign. Imoshen wrote her full name and title. Then she melted the wax and, instead of using an official seal, she followed the ancient T'En custom. Dipping the tip of her sixth finger in the puddle of hot wax, she ignored the flash of pain.

It hurt more when she did the same for the second document. Her teeth grew chilled as she sucked in her breath.

Tulkhan's eyes met hers. She stepped back. 'Now you.'

Businesslike, he signed and placed his official ring seal on the document, first one then the other.

Imoshen went to Kalleen's door. The maidservant looked up, the remains of her evening meal on a tray on her lap.

'Give the Beatific's assistant this copy of the document, which has been signed. Place the second copy in the palace library and please have our meal delivered.'

'And then you'll go to bed?'

Imoshen sighed. 'There are a dozen palace servants who would be eager to take your place.'

Kalleen grinned. 'I wouldn't trust them to feed the pigs!' With that she scurried off.

Imoshen smiled as she shut the door. Kalleen was right. She dare not trust anyone else.

Weary though she was, she had to speak with the General. This was a perfect opportunity. The Ghebite Commanders had been monopolising their General's time. Today she and Tulkhan had shared a common threat. He'd risked his life to save her...

An unwelcome thought struck Imoshen. Would it have been more accurate to say that he risked his life to save the child she carried, his only chance for a son?

Imoshen shivered. She didn't want to know the answer. It was enough that Tulkhan not only needed her due to political necessity but he also desired her. She could hardly ask for more.

'Will you stay and eat with me, General?'

He looked at her, his expression inscrutable. 'After that, will you go to bed?'

She laughed. 'Yes. Kalleen would be honoured to know you agree with her.'

He smiled fleetingly. 'Then I will share a meal with you.'

So they ate, sitting before the fire in strangely companionable silence. When the last of the servants had departed and they were savouring the remains of their meal, Imoshen looked across the hearth to him. 'There is something I would discuss with you.'

He put his wine aside. 'What now? I've agreed to a formal dinner tomorrow night to celebrate the signing.'

She knew he was teasing her and it filled her with a warm glow which she found hard to ignore. 'Roasted nuts?'

He selected a handful and tossed the lot into his mouth, chewing vigorously. He ate with the same voracious hunger he tackled everything in life.

After draining his wine he reached for more. 'They don't have nuts like these on the mainland.'

'No. They come from the archipelago.' Imoshen found she was strangely loath to disturb the peace of the moment. And she had to admit she did not want to ask the Ghebite General for a favour, even if it was for her maid.

Observing Tulkhan surreptitiously, she thought he appeared relaxed. Strangely enough, he had said nothing regarding the incinerated birds. Imoshen decided if he did broach the subject, she would have to apologise, but she wasn't going to offer an apology right now. It would entail an explanation, and she didn't want to go into detail, which would reveal her weakness.

She picked up the bottle. 'More wine?'

Tulkhan nodded. It always amused him when Imoshen played hostess. She had such regal bearing and used what appeared to be Old Empire manners, so that she made the simple act of pouring wine almost a ritualised dance.

It secretly delighted him to know that beneath her formal exterior she was all woman and his touch could ignite her. He swallowed and felt his body quicken with need.

He had avoided being alone with her, but this had only exacerbated his need for her. Midwinter could not come too soon.

Imoshen sipped her wine.

'Yes?' he prodded, watching her over his wine goblet. He could tell she wanted to broach a subject she found distasteful.

Was it something to do with Reothe? His gut tightened.

She placed her wine on the table and turned to him, ready to face him no matter how unpleasant she found it.

It could not be Reothe, he decided. She would have simply told him and faced his anger. Tulkhan was intrigued.

'I ask a boon,' Imoshen said.

So that explained it. He knew she hated asking for anything. 'Ask. We are to be wed. I would be making you a wedding present.'

'This is not for me.' She licked her lips and grimaced. 'The estates to the south are still held by their nobles, but the estates to the north lie in ruins. Their rich lands are your prizes of war.'

Tulkhan chose not to remind her that the whole of Fair Isle was his. Two thirds had been taken by force, and the other third had surrendered by omission.

'I own an estate,' Imoshen continued. 'Or rather I used to own an estate to the north. It is not large, but –'

'It is yours once more.' He anticipated her.

She flushed as he knew she would. 'Thank you.'

He smiled. He could tell how much it galled her to say those words. 'Why just one estate? Are you planning to flee the capital?'

He couldn't let her do that of course.

'No. I'm going to gift it to Kalleen.'

'What?' Tulkhan's wine slopped on the floor as he thrust his goblet aside.

Imoshen lifted her chin and met his eyes. 'Have you forgotten that it was her bravery that allowed me to escape the dungeon and Gharavan's axe? You sit here, soon to be crowned King of Fair Isle, because she took my place at risk to her own life.'

He rubbed his chin thoughtfully. 'You would give her an estate?'

'And the title that goes with it. She would be the Lady Kalleen of Windhaven.'

Tulkhan was reminded that he had meant to assign estates and titles to his commanders. If they owned land, it would ensure their loyalty to him and Fair Isle. A mercenary fights for money, but a man who fights for the land under his feet, fights with fire in his belly – it was basic warcraft.

'Very well.' Tulkhan nodded, relieved her request had been so simple. 'I will have the papers drawn up.'

'You might wish to gift the neighbouring estate to Wharrd,' Imoshen told him. 'I know you were planning to reward him, and since you have recognised the T'En church, Kalleen can bond with him.'

'Wait...' Tulkhan sensed he was missing something. 'Why couldn't she marry him before?'

Imoshen simply looked at him, her face a beautiful mask. 'Kalleen refused his offer of marriage because it would have been unequal. When people are joined by the T'En church, they become bond-partners, equals. I explained this to you the night you claimed me for your bond-partner.'

The room swayed around Tulkhan and blood rushed in his ears, filling his head with a roaring noise.

Now he understood the significance of everything that had passed between them this evening. He had just signed a document recognising the laws of the T'En church. To gain the support of the people of Fair Isle, he had to marry Imoshen and have their *bonding* recognised by the T'En church.

For once political necessity happily coincided with his private desires. The prospect of taking Imoshen to wife made the cool political marriage his father had arranged pale into significance.

But because he had recognised Fair Isle church laws, as soon as the Beatific formalised their joining, Imoshen would legally be his equal. Half of everything he owned would be hers.

He had signed away half of Fair Isle to his captive!

Her face was turned away from him, presenting the curve of her cheek and the hollow under her jaw. Her perfect porcelain skin and a profile were so pure he could not imagine a cruel conniving thought ever crossing her mind.

Unaware of his scrutiny, Imoshen twisted to face him, her hand cupping a bowl. 'More nuts?'

'No.' He saw her start, surprised by the harsh tone of his voice. He watched closely for duplicity. 'You know what you have done?'

She turned away from him to place the roasted nuts on a low table.

Yes, she knew exactly what she had done. Manipulative, traitorous Dhamfeer. Anger hardened his heart against her beauty and her false innocence.

'When the people are secure, they are happy,' she lectured with calm precision. 'By signing that document, you have ensured their prosperity. They will not be open to Reothe's cunning tongue. News travels fast. Soon all of Fair Isle will know you have recognised the rights and laws of the T'En church. You cannot hope to hold what you have taken if the people do not support you.' She met his eyes, daring him to object. He could have drowned in those wine-dark depths. 'I have helped you hold Fair Isle, General Tulkhan.'

Burning with anger, he longed to denounce her for what she was, but on another level he knew she was right. A charged silence fell between them.

With deliberate care he caught her hand and drew her from her chair, to her knees. She waited compliantly between his thighs as though she hadn't just manoeuvred him into signing away half his kingdom.

'That is not all,' he told her.

'No.' She lifted her chin in that now familiar gesture. 'I have taken the first step to ensure the women of Fair Isle will not be reduced to slaves like your Ghebite females.'

'You've ensured half of Fair Isle for yourself.'

She stiffened, her eyes flashing. 'I belong to all of Fair Isle, General. If I didn't, I would have escaped with him when I had the chance at Landsend!'

What?

Imoshen stood abruptly. 'Have you sent the Midwinter Feast invitations to the southern nobles?'

'And the ambassadors of the mainland kingdoms and the princelings of the archipelago,' he answered automatically. Escaped at Landsend? Did she mean she'd planned to escape from there to the islands of the archipelago? If so, when? Before she surrendered her stronghold to him? He doubted it. Then when?

The answer came to him. She could have escaped when they were at Landsend together in the first moon after he took Umasreach Stronghold. But escaped with whom?

Reothe. Who else?

A flare of pure rage ignited Tulkhan. To think the rebel leader had dared to infiltrate the abbey while the Ghebite General was there. The Seculate, all of them... how they must have been laughing at him!

But Imoshen hadn't escaped when she had the chance.

'Why?'

She jumped at the tone of his voice, then calmly went on placing the remains of their meal onto the trays the servants had left behind.

'Why what?'

'Why didn't you run away with Reothe when we were at Landsend?'

A flush inflamed her pale skin and he had to smile grimly. She hadn't meant to reveal that she'd had the opportunity to escape. Knowing Imoshen, she was probably cursing herself.

Very slowly, Imoshen turned to meet his eyes. 'To abandon you there would have meant a bloodbath. The people would have revolted. The southern nobles would have turned and forced you to defeat them. Besides' – she sighed tiredly – 'I had given my word.'

Since the stronghold had fallen and Imoshen had become Tulkhan's prisoner, she had constantly opposed him, forcing him to confront his beliefs. He had seen evidence of her tactical training and her consummate statesmanship, but until this moment he had not personally experienced its effect.

After the assassination attempt, he had confronted Imoshen, demanding to know who Reothe was. She had admitted that the last T'En male had once been her betrothed but she had given him up for dead. Reothe was said to have been killed in battle. Yet she had known all along that her betrothed lived, because he had offered her a chance to escape with him at Landsend Abbey. She had refused, and because of this, had faced death at Tulkhan's own hand, averted only by the Aayel's sacrifice.

How she must have hated him, her Ghebite captor.

He had underestimated T'Imoshen, last T'En Princess. She had risked her life rather than betray the people of Fair Isle, who trusted her to look after their interests. She had stayed because she had given him her word. He would never again compare her with a Ghebite woman.

Tulkhan watched as Imoshen collected the trays, then carried them to the passage for the servants to take away. She was keeping him at a distance.

Why?

It was obvious she didn't want to discuss this with him. She had chosen to stay because she had given him her word, and for her that meant everything.

An unwelcome thought occurred to Tulkhan. She had also given her word to the rebel leader. A cold ball of certainty settled in his belly. 'You gave your word to Reothe. The pair of you were betrothed.' It was out before he could stop himself. 'You are forsworn.'

Her lips twisted in a painful smile. 'I was barely sixteen. The betrothal promise was a vow sworn on a dying empire.'

'Reothe is not dead.' He had to pursue it, had to hear her say the deposed T'En Prince was nothing to her. It ate at him.

She said something in an ancient language which made the little hairs on his body rise. A T'En curse? Once he hadn't believed in her race's gifts. But he had seen what Imoshen could do.

He sprang to his feet, heart thudding. 'What was that, a gift-laden curse?'

She shrugged. 'It is a line from an old T'En poem. It translates something like, *Dead man walks and talks, but doesn't know he's dead.*'

A shiver moved over Tulkhan's skin. Reothe had quoted the same line when they met in the mists. Tulkhan swore softly but with force.

Imoshen looked up, startled. 'What is it, General? My vow to Reothe is dead. I have made a commitment to you –'

'For the good of Fair Isle.'

'Exactly. You can trust me.'

Tulkhan itched to take her shoulders in his hands and shake her. How dare she speak of such things while looking so reasonable? 'Actions speak louder than words. Why did you incinerate the fighting birds?'

She flinched and he felt better, then perversely despised himself.

Imoshen turned and padded to the window. She picked up a plate of half eaten fruit she'd overlooked.

'Leave that. The servants can do it. There's enough of them.'

She replaced the plate, but hesitated with her back to him, fiddling with something on the table below the window. 'I must apologise –'

'I said leave it!' He'd strode across the room before he knew he meant to. When he spun her around to face him he could feel the firm flesh of her upper arms in his hands. 'I asked why you felt it necessary to stage that display for my people. You could have burnt down the stables, killing people and trained battle horses.'

With a liquid-quick movement she broke his hold, swinging her arms up against his thumb and down again so fast he couldn't hold her.

Her lips drew back from her sharp teeth and her wine-dark eyes blazed with an inner feral light which both frightened and fascinated him. He had pierced Imoshen's armour. Tulkhan was pleased.

'Why must your men act like barbarians, bringing their foul ways into the lives of my people? Fighting cocks, blood sports. What next, bear baiting?'

Since this wasn't far from the truth, Tulkhan remained silent.

Imoshen ground her teeth then shrugged past him disdainfully. She prowled the room before finally settling in front of the fireplace. 'You have inherited an ancient culture, with a legacy of knowledge rich beyond measure, General Tulkhan. Don't destroy it simply because you don't understand it.'

The fire's glow behind her bathed her body in light, illuminating her long legs through her gown, and creating a halo in the strands of her hip-length hair. He wanted to run his fingers through that pale, silken mane.

The ever-present need to touch her was overwhelming. He could feel it drawing him across the room. He wanted to step close enough to inhale her scent and grow drunk on it. He needed to feel that quicksilver response in her, to know that his touch ignited her body as she ignited his. He needed her.

On the lake he had been ready to make the ultimate sacrifice to save her. With a jolt he realised he would throw away everything to have Imoshen in his arms and in his bed. She was a drug he craved. Would his need for her destroy him?

Cool, rational thought made Tulkhan hesitate.

Already tonight she had outmanoeuvred him by tricking him into recognising the T'En church. But, to be truthful, he'd had little choice. He needed the church behind him. And in some ways he could see Imoshen's point of view.

Why should she give up her right to make her own decisions and own property? Had the Ghebite women he'd known during his youth despised the men they loved because they were slaves of their fathers and sons?

Tulkhan's head spun with the implications. He could sense Imoshen watching him, studying him. He must not let her guess how deeply she disturbed him. Would she use it against him? In her position he would have.

Cold certainty gripped him. The more he saw of Imoshen, the more she drew him. The more she knew of him, the easier she would find it to manipulate him.

No matter what it cost him, he must keep her at a distance. Bed her, yes, but welcome her into his heart – never!

He caught her watching him. Her faintly calculating expression confirmed all his suspicions. Furious with himself for ever thinking there could be trust between them, he advanced on her.

Imoshen stood her ground before the fire, proud but wary.

Despite his vow to keep her at a distance, he caught her in his arms, felt the curves of her strong body against the length of him. He wanted her to need him as much as he needed her.

Her lips parted in a sharp gasp and he felt a tremor run through her. An answering tremor ran through his as his body responded.

'Marriage or bond-partner, it's all the same to me,' he ground out. 'It means you're mine to have. Kiss me.'

'No. Not like this. Not in anger –'

He caught her face between his hands and captured her lips. The force of her fury ignited him. Her foot came down sharply on his instep, but she was only wearing soft indoor slippers and it wasn't painful. He laughed.

She cursed him, her knee surging up between his thighs, but he twisted, deflecting the blow.

'Tulkhan, I –'

The moment her lips parted he had her. He could already feel it, the surge of need building between them. He knew the instant her kiss became voluntary. Triumphant desire raged through him. She called to him. He wanted to drown in her.

A groan escaped him. Her breath fanned his cheek. 'Curse you, General!' Her lips moved on his. 'Why must you take, when a gift is more precious?'

Her words confused him. He could think only of his need.

Why should he wait? They'd publicly announced they were to wed. He'd already known her body twice.

'No!' Her voice cut through his thoughts.

Sharply, she twisted from his grasp. Darting back two steps, she snatched a brand from the fire.

Holding it by the blackened end she thrust the flame between them. 'One step closer and I'll put out your eyes!'

For a moment he believed her. Then he saw the sheen of unshed tears.

'You wouldn't. You want me. If I persisted I could have you now and you'd end up welcoming me.'

She gave a bitter short laugh. 'Is force all you Ghebites understand? You take my land by force. You claim me as a prize of war. Do you think you can take me by force?'

'Your fingers are burning.'

'Good. I'd rather burn than be defiled by you.'

'Defiled? You're no celibate Dhamfeer priestess. First, you broke your vows to your church by accepting Reothe as your bond-partner. Then you broke your vows to your betrothed because it suited your purpose. You bedded me to save yourself. You're no better than the Ghebite women you despise.'

'Get out!'

'I'm going.'

'Good!'

They stood there panting, the air charged with the force of their emotion.

Imoshen jerked the burning brand, indicating the door. The pain in her hand was nothing compared to the pain in her heart. She'd thought Tulkhan was different from the other Ghebites.

'I'm going,' he repeated and she could see him distancing himself from her. 'But mark this, Dhamfeer. I know what you are and I won't forget it.'

He turned his back on her and strode out of the room.

As soon as the door closed after General Tulkhan, Imoshen flung the brand back into the fire and ran to the window, opening it to thrust her fingers into the snow on the ledge.

A deep sob of despair shook her.

'Fool, fool...' she moaned, not sure whether she meant herself or Tulkhan.

When her fingers finally grew numb, she returned to her seat by the fireplace to put salve on her burns. Hugging her throbbing hand to her chest, she sat there as silent tears of despair slid down her cheeks.

She should heal her hand as Reothe had taught her, but perversely she felt she deserved this pain and besides, every muscle in her body ached. She was exhausted. The drenching in the lake had shaken her more than she cared to admit.

Kalleen was right, she should have rested. But she could not have taken to her bed when she did not know whether the General and his advisors were perusing the church document without her.

Now the document was signed, sealed and delivered. The Aayel would have been pleased. Imoshen had achieved her goal, but she didn't feel elated. She had paid a bitter price. It had cost her Tulkhan's trust.

While she had won for her people, she had lost for herself. But she could not think of herself, too much was at stake.

Leaning her head against the tall chair back, she groaned with pain. She wasn't strong enough for this. If only the Aayel had lived to advise her. Exhaustion, emotional and physical, had made her slip tonight. She hadn't meant to let the General know about her opportunity to escape with Reothe at Landsend.

Tulkhan might be angry with her, but in recognising the church's laws he had secured the church's support, and without it he could not hold Fair Isle. She had taken the first step to ensuring that her country did not sink into barbarism.

Weary beyond words, Imoshen dropped her good hand to her lap and peered into the flames. Her fingers splayed across her belly protectively. Had the General only been thinking of his child when he risked his life to save her? The child hardly seemed real to her. It was too early to feel anything, too early to show. There was no visible evidence to confirm that brief flare she'd felt when the new life began.

Since that night she had lain with Tulkhan – a shudder passed through her as her body quickened with the memory – so much had happened. Her T'En powers had grown with frightening rapidity. In her mind's eye she saw the fighting birds engulfed in a fiery ball of flames and feathers. Her hands tightened into painful fists and she groaned, lifting her burnt hand to her lips.

How could she admit to General Tulkhan that she had no control over her gifts when he already despised her T'En side?

What did she expect? He was Ghebite.

What did she want from the General? Trust? Love?

What did he expect her to do? Deny what she was?

Imoshen ground her teeth in frustration. She had done everything she set out to achieve. Fair Isle was hers, and one day her son would rule the island.

Yes, she had won the battle, but the war was far from over. Too many factors could upset the balance of power. The southern nobles, and Reothe and his rebels, weren't the only threat. She sighed. It would be only too easy for Tulkhan and his Ghebite army to make a wrong move and destroy their fragile alliance with the people of Fair Isle, then the conquered people would welcome Reothe and his rebel army.

And what of King Gharavan? What if he swore revenge and returned with a fresh army?

Imoshen shuddered. She may have reclaimed Fair Isle, but now she had to hold it. And to do that she needed General Tulkhan's support. But it had to be willing support. He would not take kindly to manipulation and, besides, she did not want to dishonour him with trickery. He had signed the agreement with the T'En church because it benefited them both, and united the population of Fair Isle behind him. Now that he understood the full ramifications of property ownership, he was angry with her, but the General was a fair man. He would come round. She was sure of it.

Her hand throbbed and she turned it over to the light. The blisters were already beginning to form. She had to heal the burn. Concentrating, Imoshen reached inside herself for that one T'En gift she felt secure enough to call on. But strive as she might, she could not find it. The familiar taste did not settle on her tongue and her teeth did not ache with the build-up of tension.

She was drained. Exhausted by the bone chilling dip in the frozen lake and the shattering outpouring of power she had directed at the fighting birds. At this moment, she felt like she used to feel when the gift first came to her and she had tried to heal at the Aayel's bidding. Her gift had limits. It would do well to remember that.

She unfolded her legs and padded to the window, plunging her hand into the snow again to ease the pain. With a sigh of relief, she let her mind drift.

A movement in the shadows of the courtyard attracted her attention. It was Tulkhan. She would know those broad shoulders and that proud bearing anywhere. He stood alone, staring up at the twin moons. The small moon would be full again soon, while the larger waxed more slowly. It would not be full again until spring cusp. The night was so clear that she could see the large moon's dark crescent silhouetted against the stars.

What did the Ghebite General see when he looked up at the twin moons? Did he see two brothers forever in conflict, the son of the first wife trying to outshine the son of the second wife and win his father's love?

Or was he remembering what she had told him about the role of the twin moons in the mythology of Fair Isle – man and woman, different but complete in themselves. For a while one would be in the ascendancy, then the other would dominate, but they were at their brightest and strongest when both shone together. Had he understood her unspoken message?

She looked down at him thinking, *we are different, you and I, from different backgrounds, different as a man and woman can be, yet for the good of Fair Isle we must not burn ourselves out in pointless conflict.*

But was it possible for a Ghebite male to overcome barbaric ways and his prejudices? Could Tulkhan accept her T'En self?

Reothe would. The thought came unbidden. Reothe was her other half. She might fear his superior T'En powers, but at least he would never despise her for her innate gift.

He believed that together they could unite Fair Isle and drive the Ghebites out. Would the sum of their gifts be greater joined? For a moment she let herself contemplate standing at Reothe's side, leading an army across the fertile plains of Fair Isle, driving the arrogant Ghebites into the sea and restoring T'En rule.

But she couldn't. Her people had seen too much death. They wanted peace. They needed to know that if they planted a crop they would live to harvest it for their children. They had the right to the simple dignity of their lives, lived without fear of being called upon to serve their rulers in a war not of their choosing.

She could not condone more fighting, and joining Reothe would inevitably cause more death. Besides, she hardly knew the man who had once been her betrothed. The General, for all that he was a Ghebite, was more familiar to her. She knew Tulkhan was an honourable man.

Imoshen had to believe that she had made the right choice when she rejected Reothe's offer of escape.

As though he sensed her gaze, the General looked up. Moonlight sculpted his broad cheekbones and shadows hid his eyes. What was he thinking?

He lifted his chin and raised his hand in a silent salute, acknowledging an equal. She returned the gesture. Then Tulkhan strode from the courtyard.

Imoshen flexed her fingers. The snow had numbed the pain at last. She closed the window. So much depended on her. She must not falter.

She was no man's puppet. Neither Reothe nor Tulkhan would use her to bend Fair Isle to their wishes. She was T'Imoshen, and the future was hers to shape.

The last T'En Princess would bow to no one.

BOOK TWO
DARK
DREAMS

To my editors,
thank you for your patience
and dedication

Chapter One

IN THE PAST the palace of a thousand chambers had overwhelmed Imoshen; now she strode its corridors the uncrowned Empress. But her position was as precarious as the man she would rule alongside.

General Tulkhan and his Ghebite army were the overlords of a conquered people who remained loyal to the Old Empire, but the invaders were in the minority. Every day the palace servants deferred to Imoshen, when in reality she was the General's captive. Every day the Ghebites flaunted their barbarian splendour, carelessly insulting her people.

Imoshen smiled grimly. Though she had seen her island conquered and been forced to surrender her family's stronghold to the Ghebites, General Tulkhan had claimed her for his own, which put her in a position of great tactical strength.

Much had been achieved since the Harvest Feast. Only last night Tulkhan had signed the document recognising church law, returning to Imoshen all she had lost and more. For, on their bonding day, she would stand before her people as co-ruler of Fair Isle, the first pure T'En woman to take a bond-partner in six hundred years.

The clash of weapons made Imoshen freeze, wary as a hunted woodland creature. She had become intimately acquainted with fear, and the knowledge that her life hung by a thread shadowed her every move. Heart hammering, she followed the razor-sharp sounds to a balcony where half a dozen servants were avidly watching a confrontation in the courtyard below. One glance told her the General and his men were at sword practice.

Relief flooded her, yet she was dismayed to see the Ghebite fascination for violence infecting her servants. 'Get back to work, the lot of you!'

They made guilty apologies and hurried away.

In the confines of the courtyard the swords' song resonated harshly. As Imoshen watched unseen from the balcony's shadows, she could not help but admire the Ghebites' skill, even as she abhorred their love of violence.

Once past boyhood, a Ghebite warrior practised with battle-ready weapons, scorning the use of blunt swords. It was not unknown for Ghebites to take a fatal wound in practice. The warriors were feared for their ferocity, and Tulkhan was the very embodiment of the Ghebite ideal. For at only nineteen he had assumed command of the army, leading it south, creeping inexorably across the mainland. In eleven years no kingdom had been able to withstand the General's onslaught, and it had appeared he would conquer the known world.

But instead of attacking the last of the southern kingdoms, he had turned his eye on Fair Isle, making a surprise assault. Betrayed by her allies, unprepared for war on her own shores, Fair Isle had crumbled in one spring-to-summer campaign.

The memory of those desperate times made Imoshen shudder, and she returned her attention to the scene below. General Tulkhan was renowned for his tactical skill and physical bravery. Given that, why was he taking on three of his trusted swordsmen while his elite guard watched? What was he trying to prove?

In a flash of insight Imoshen understood – once her position as co-ruler of Fair Isle became known, his men would think she had emasculated him. They might even suspect he had been ensorcelled by her. Some of them still refused to meet her eyes, believing the rumours of treacherous T'En powers. No wonder Tulkhan wielded his sword with such intensity that his men could barely defend themselves.

Metal grated, setting Imoshen's teeth on edge. She gasped as one man gave a guttural cry, dropping to his knee. At the last moment Tulkhan turned his sword, striking with the flat of the blade. The Ghebite sprawled on the slippery stone.

No one moved.

Imoshen took a step closer, drawn by the charged atmosphere. She could taste their intoxicating bloodlust in the air.

The sound of the men's ragged breathing was magnified, trapped in the snow-bound inner courtyard. In the brilliant early morning light, two remaining swordsmen faced Tulkhan over the body of their barely conscious comrade, steam rising from their skin.

General Tulkhan's naked back glistened with sweat as he stood poised to strike. He was magnificent and undeniably dangerous. Something tightened deep within Imoshen. With bittersweet self-knowledge, she recognised the sensation. She had known Tulkhan's body only twice, but her need for him was already so strong it made her vulnerable.

Moistening her dry mouth, she watched mesmerised as the confrontation unfolded. Swordsman Jacolm stood over his fallen sword-brother, bristling, ready to die for the man who was bound to him by the Ghebite warrior code. No wonder their army was invincible when the warriors shared this unbreakable bond and welcomed death in battle. Fallen Ghebite soldiers were ensured a place riding at the side of their warrior god. Imoshen's lips curled with contempt.

Then the grizzled veteran, Piers, deliberately lowered his weapon. Turning his shoulder to Tulkhan, he helped the injured man to his feet. Following his lead, Jacolm also sheathed his weapon.

The General gave a disgusted shrug, though whether he was annoyed with them or himself, Imoshen could not tell. With a word he dismissed the others.

From her vantage point she saw the elite guard and Tulkhan's trusted commanders leave the courtyard. The General walked towards her. He scooped up a handful of the snow, which had been swept into deep drifts, rubbing it vigorously over his face.

Imoshen's heart raced as she stepped into the patch of sunlight illuminating the balcony rail. 'General?'

Startled, Tulkhan looked up, his expression guarded.

'Only me.'

'Only?'

Imoshen smiled. She liked Tulkhan best when they were alone, when he did not have to play the public role of Ghebite General, nor she the role of T'En Princess.

With a tug Imoshen pulled the brocade tabard over her head, casting it aside so that she stood dressed only in her loose-fitting trousers, thin undershirt and soft-soled boots. 'Teach me to use the Ghebite sword.'

The General's eyes narrowed.

The women of Tulkhan's homeland never touched weapons. They hardly dared raise their eyes to a man, let alone a sword. Imoshen knew she was breaking Ghebite law; this was why she had waited until the others had left.

Before the Ghebites invaded last spring, she had taken for granted the ways of Fair Isle. Now she understood that her island was a beacon of enlightenment in a sea of barbarism. Everything she believed in was under threat, but she was determined the Ghebites would not erode the position of women in Fair Isle. If this meant confronting Tulkhan and constantly forcing him to question his assumptions, then so be it. There was an ancient T'En saying which translated as, *Truth is a precious but often bitter seasoning.*

Imoshen swung her legs over the balustrade and dropped two body-lengths into the heaped snow near Tulkhan. Aware of the General's keen dark eyes, she straightened, wiping crusted snow from her buttocks and thighs.

'What now, Imoshen?'

Holding Tulkhan's gaze, she tried to gauge his mood. For a Ghebite the General was a reasonable man, but he was proud, too. 'I began instruction with the T'En sword the year before you attacked. But the Ghebite style is different and I may need to defend myself, so teach me.'

He prowled around her. 'How casually you insult my honour.'

'All I ask is to be able to defend myself.' She kept her tone reasonable. 'Where is the dishonour in that?'

'Truly, you do not see. In Gheeaba a man is expected to defend his wife. His honour rests on –'

A surprised laugh escaped Imoshen. She caught herself, aware of the slow burn of his anger. 'I mean no insult, General. But I fail to see how you could protect me unless I never left your side, and even then, wouldn't you rather have me at your back with a weapon in my hand than clinging to you and encumbering your sword arm?'

Her question drew a reluctant grin from him and she smiled in return. She was not his wife yet, and she never would be. Bond-partners of Fair Isle stood shoulder to shoulder.

Tulkhan lifted his hands. 'In Gheeaba my wife would be safe within the walls of my estate. You would be escorted to events of importance, protected by the elite guard of my house-line. You would never set foot outside alone, you –'

'How boring. How could anyone live like that?'

Tulkhan grimaced. 'You wilfully misunderstand me, Imoshen.'

'Yes.'

'You are a trial!' His hands flexed as if he would like to use them on her.

Imoshen's heart rate rose another notch. 'All I ask is to learn to use the Ghebite sword.'

He glanced up at the balcony where she had been watching. 'So that is your excuse for spying?'

'Spying? If you call watching your men wield those ploughshares spying, then yes, I was spying.' She saw a flash of amusement in his obsidian eyes. Sweat glistened on his coppery skin.

'For a woman to touch a man's weapon is death in Gheeaba, Imoshen.'

She stiffened. 'This is not Gheeaba. And I will not be limited, by your... by Ghebite attitudes. Teach me.'

Tulkhan's eyes narrowed. 'Very well, I will enjoy teaching you your place.'

He turned and walked to the courtyard door, calling to someone in the passage beyond. Satisfied, he returned his attention to her. 'My servant is bringing you a ploughshare.'

Imoshen inclined her head, aware that she might have overreached herself this time. Her skills with the T'En sword were basic. The Ghebite weapon was much heavier and used in a different manner. Being a throwback to the T'En race which had settled Fair Isle, she was taller than an average True-man, but Tulkhan stood half a head taller again, and even a T'En female did not have the muscle bulk of a male.

Imoshen knew she had no chance of beating the General, but then she had no intention of besting him at swordsmanship. Her goal was to create a bridge between them. If he taught her to use the Ghebite sword, he would be one step closer to accepting her as his equal.

The courtyard door opened and a nervous servant handed Tulkhan a second sword. The General dismissed the youth and weighed both weapons in his hands, observing their blades.

'I suppose you would rather fight with a toothpick and a knitting needle?' he challenged. 'Catch.'

Instinctively she caught the sword by the hilt, gauging its weight and unfamiliar balance. At that moment she wished for a sharp short dagger and a tapered sword such as she had been training with. The T'En blade would have given her the advantage of speed and length of reach against the Ghebite sword's greater weight. Already she felt clumsy, and guessed that before long her wrist would be aching.

If she were using T'En weapons and this were a fight to the death, her only chance would be to strike fast before Tulkhan could use the advantage of his heavier blade and greater strength.

Like all pure T'En, Imoshen was left-handed. She turned her body side-on to the General to present as small a target as possible. Tulkhan took up the same stance. As he was right-handed, the two of them faced the same side of the courtyard, instead of opposite sides. It might unsettle the General, but only for a moment.

'At least the T'En way offers precision and style instead of brute strength,' she said.

'You're holding it all wrong.'

'Show me.'

When he stepped around behind her, she felt the heat radiating from his skin. His hand closed over hers and she forced her arm to relax, letting him lower the sword.

'Not high like that. Hold the sword more naturally.'

Imoshen swallowed, wondering how he could not be aware of her body's reaction. She ached for him. As he resumed his place opposite, she met his eyes and knew he felt it too.

She cleared her throat. 'In my lessons I was taught to use my wrist to deflect the attacker's sword. But after watching your men at practice I see the Ghebite style is more –'

'Crude?' he suggested with a hint of anger.

'I was going to say you appear to bring the whole weight of your body behind the blade, slashing as opposed to lunging.'

'Hmm.' Tulkhan's black eyes studied her. 'If you were a youth with those scrawny arms, I'd advise you to use a two-handed grip. These are hand-and-a-half grips, designed for two-handed fighting if necessary.'

Imoshen bristled. 'I am stronger than I look.'

'Really? Defend yourself.'

He struck, telegraphing his intention but not restraining his speed or force. Imoshen barely had time to bring her weapon up. She took the impact of his strike on her blade, ready to deflect it with a twist of her wrist. But the force jarred her arm right up to the shoulder, numbing her fingers. Only by an effort of will did she maintain her grip on the weapon and divert the blow.

'Wrong technique, Imoshen.' Tulkhan's white teeth flashed against his coppery skin. 'These are not T'En weapons.'

She darted forward, aiming for his throat, knowing that he would deflect her strike. With a laugh, he caught her blade, using the force of his swing to throw her off balance. She danced out of range, recovering in an instant.

'You are as light as a cat on your feet. It's a shame you're a female. You'd make a fine swordsman. If only you had the strength in your arms and shoulders. Try the two-handed grip.'

'Wouldn't that limit my range of movement?'

'Always an answer. Pity your tongue isn't a sword.' He advanced. 'Defend yourself. This time divert my weapon past your body. '

He struck, she diverted. The shock of it ran up her arms to her left shoulder.

He struck again on the other side and she understood why she should hold the sword two-handed. But there was no time to change grips.

Backing away with each strike, Imoshen barely maintained her guard. She suspected he was playing with her, and her suspicions were confirmed when he struck, skidding up over her weapon in such a way that she knew his energy hadn't been directed into the first strike. His sword passed inside her guard, striking her ribs under her left breast with the flat of the blade. The blow knocked the air from her lungs.

'That was a death blow,' he told her. 'Had enough?'

Each breath seared. She gritted her teeth. 'Teach me that trick.'

'It isn't trickery. It takes years of practice.' He punctuated his phrases with strikes, the blows coming faster and faster. 'Maybe one day I will show you the battle sword I inherited from my grandfather. Now there's a beautiful weapon!'

The force of his blows jarred her sword arm, numbing her fingers. It was all she could do to block his attacks.

Imoshen knew she did not have the strength in her upper body to counter his. She barely had the skill to defend herself. Backing across the slippery stones she realised it was only a matter of time before her boots sank into the heaped snow and she lost the ability to manoeuvre.

Each screech of the blades echoed around the courtyard, pounding in her head until she could hear nothing but the reverberating ring of steel on steel.

'I don't expect to become an expert overnight, General.' She grunted with the effort it took to hold him off. 'You said yourself I am light on my feet and willing to learn.'

'Why bother? By spring you'll be heavy with child!' He was barely sweating. 'That is why men fight and women don't. Only in Fair Isle is the natural balance disrupted.'

Anger flooded Imoshen. 'I won't be heavy with child forever!'

A familiar taste settled on her tongue, warning her that her T'En gift threatened to surface, but she refused to call on her powers to cloud his mind or distract his aim. To use her abilities against the General now would negate everything she had achieved.

Absorbed in her inner battle, Imoshen gave ground, and her heel sank into the snow. Her guard wavered. The General struck. She blocked.

The force of his blow tore the hilt from her useless fingers, sending her weapon spinning across the courtyard to clatter against the stone wall and drop blade-first into a snowdrift.

Silence filled the palace's inner courtyard.

Tulkhan smiled.

It pleased him to have Imoshen at his mercy. Two spots of colour flamed on her pale cheeks. Damp with sweat, her thin undershirt clung to her breasts as she struggled to regain her breath. He was reminded of the first time he'd seen her, restrained by five of his elite guard but far from beaten. She had been injured defending the treasures of a library of knowledge, crimson blood trickling down her white throat over her high breasts.

He had wanted her then and he wanted her now.

She glared at him. Her distinctive T'En scent, at once so familiar yet alien, drew him. It tempted him to forget all reason.

He needed to make her admit that she wanted him too. At the same time he despised himself and despised his hunger for her. How could he desire her, when she was the antithesis of Ghebite womanhood? There she stood, defiantly tall and strong-limbed, refusing to admit his mastery.

Unlike Ghebite women, Imoshen used no feminine wiles to arouse and entice him. Instead of diminutive womanly curves, delicate coppery skin and deferential dark eyes, he faced those accursed T'En eyes. Rich as ruby wine held to a candle flame, they blazed with keen intelligence. According to legend, the T'En could look into a man's soul.

He had grown up hearing tales of this legendary race and their ability to enslave True-people. But in Imoshen he had found a much more dangerous enemy – a living, breathing woman whose fierce pride and passion called to him against his better judgment.

His body urged him to ignore the stricture that forbade physical contact before their formal union. His blood was up. He saw the comprehension in her eyes. A flush of anticipation raced across the pearly skin of her throat, and he felt his own body respond. By the gods, he was but a breath away from taking her here in the snow. And who would know? Who would dare raise voice against him if he did?

Imoshen straightened. Dropping the defensive stance, she inclined her head, acknowledging him the victor. A ragged cheer echoed across the courtyard, startling Tulkhan. He spun to see a dozen of his men standing under the arch on the far balcony.

He grinned reluctantly and marvelled that they did not demand Imoshen be punished for daring to raise a weapon against him. Then he returned his attention to her. She had fought as well as any untrained man, and she had fought in the knowledge that she was outclassed.

He raised the sword point to her throat and she lifted her chin to avoid the blade.

'The Ghebite sword is not meant for a woman's hand. Kneel and concede me the victor,' he ordered in a voice meant to carry, then added more softly, 'Kneel, Imoshen. Do not insult me before my men.'

'And you do not insult me?' Her voice was breathy with anguish and exertion.

He frowned, surprised that she would see it this way.

As he watched, the feral light of battle faded from her eyes. She swallowed. He saw her wince and recalled the blow he had delivered to her ribs. He knew her every breath must hurt, yet she did not complain. Unlike Ghebite noblewomen she made light of being pregnant and did not hesitate to ride or work as hard as any man.

'You fight well,' he said, recalling another time when she had stood at his side and faced death. Curse his weak-willed half-brother, Gharavan.

Curse the Vaygharian's poisoned tongue for planting the seeds of betrayal in Gharavan's mind. The youth had been King only one summer when he let his adviser's words of treachery override Tulkhan's years of service.

Tulkhan would have served his half-brother as loyally as he had served their father, but he had not been given the chance. Gharavan had had Tulkhan and Imoshen arrested on false charges of treason and thrown into her own stronghold's dungeon. Only her handmaid's bravery and Imoshen's T'En trickery had saved them. 'You were not outclassed when you faced the Vaygharian's sword.'

'That night I fought for my life against an enemy I despised. Besides, the Vaygharian did not seek to kill me; his aim was to escape.' Imoshen's gaze flickered past Tulkhan to their audience on the balcony. When she spoke, her voice was low and intense. 'General, why won't you trust me?'

A bitter laugh escaped him. Trust a T'En, one of the dreaded Dhamfeer, as they were known in his own language? It went against everything he had ever been taught. 'Kneel and acknowledge me the victor.'

She hesitated.

Shouting down from the balcony, one of the Ghebites advised the General what to do with this recalcitrant female. Even though he spoke Gheeaban, his meaning was clear enough to make Imoshen's nostrils flare with fury.

Tulkhan smiled ruefully. He had been a heartbeat away from acting on just that advice.

Imoshen's eyes darkened to mulberry black, glittering dangerously as she dropped to one knee and slowly bent her head. The men cheered loudly. But when she raised her head, her eyes held defiance and a jolt of understanding hit Tulkhan. She might be on her knee to him, but in her heart she would never yield.

His mouth went dry. Her attitude goaded him. He wanted to lose himself in a battle for mastery. Only when she was in his arms, under him, could he appease his passion for her. But, if he guessed correctly, every touch, every look weakened his resolve against her, laying his mind open to her T'En powers.

Bed her? Yes. Trust her? Never!

'I yield to you, General,' she said, but her expression made a mockery of her words.

Tulkhan grimaced. Just as Imoshen had been forced to surrender her stronghold to him, he vowed she would ultimately admit him the master. Then Fair Isle and all it contained would be his.

It was imperative he hold Fair Isle, for he could not return to his homeland. Imoshen had advised him to kill his half-brother, but he had not been able to execute the boy who had been more like a son to him. Gharavan's betrayal still stung, for Tulkhan had loved him even though his half-brother's birth had meant his disinheritance.

Years of devoted service had earned Tulkhan the respect of his men and the command of the Ghebite army, but they could not make him the son of the King's first wife.

He had planned to kneel before his father as conqueror of the legendary Fair Isle. For hundreds of years this island had been growing rich on the trade routes between the mainland to the west and the eastern archipelago. Protected by its vigorous merchant navy, Fair Isle was the envy of the bickering mainland kingdoms. And Tulkhan had meant to present this island kingdom to the King.

But the invasion had gone sour. His father had fallen on the battlefield leading a secondary attack on the island. Tulkhan had sent Gharavan his fealty and continued the campaign, ultimately winning Fair Isle for the new Ghebite King.

And how had he been rewarded for his loyalty? Tulkhan skirted Gharavan's treachery like an open wound, returning to practical, tactical matters. After his half-brother's betrayal, Tulkhan had banished the young King and claimed this island, effectively exiling himself and his warriors from Gheeaba forever. He and his men were outcasts, Fair Isle their only home. And he could not hope to hold the island without Imoshen's support.

Tulkhan stepped back, sheathed his sword and offered Imoshen his hand. With a tug he pulled her lightly to her feet. In that instant, before she could mask it, he saw the hunger she felt for him. An answering need moved him. It was there between them, this primal pull, body to body.

He'd been a fool to think casual bedding would be enough. He licked his lips. Their bonding day could not come soon enough.

Unaware of these undercurrents, his men signalled their approval with the Ghebite battle cry.

Imoshen glanced at them, then back to Tulkhan. 'Thank you for the lesson in swordplay, General.' Once more the T'En royal, she gave him the obeisance between equals, inclining her head and raising one hand to her forehead.

When she met his eyes, he thought she seemed pleased. Why?

'Now I must issue invitations for the celebration tomorrow night. The townspeople have heard that you signed the document acknowledging church law, but when they see you sitting down with the head of the T'En church, they will really believe it.' She turned away from him.

Bemused, Tulkhan watched her leave the courtyard. Imoshen had deliberately humbled herself before his men, yet she had done it on her own terms. The old wives' tales were right, truly the Dhamfeer were a devious race.

Imoshen returned to her chambers, where she discarded her soiled shirt, wincing as she peeled down her trousers. Confronting Tulkhan was worth the pain.

Her mother had been right, she was a wilful creature.

Imoshen faltered, but there was no time to mourn her family, all lost on the battlefield. If they had agreed to take her with them, she would have died fighting by their side. But no, they had said she was too young at seventeen. Yet they had left her to run the family stronghold, responsible for the lives of a thousand people, her great-aunt her only support.

Hot tears of anger stung Imoshen's eyes. Even in death, her parents had not wanted to acknowledge their daughter was a throwback, a descendent of the legendary T'En. She brushed the tears away and glared at the marble bathing chamber. A bitter laugh escaped her. Soon she would be bonded with the General, a co-ruler of Fair Isle. Her parents could never have foreseen that.

But her great-aunt had. The only other member of their family to be born pure T'En, her great-aunt had devoted her life to the service of the church and on her hundredth birthday had been rewarded with the title of 'Aayel.'

It had been her great aunt who advised Imoshen to surrender Umasreach Stronghold and accept terms. Even so, their lives had hung by a thread. As the last remnants of the old royal line, their very existence would have fostered insurgence. To ensure their survival, they'd needed a lever on their captor. The Aayel had used her mind-reading gift to discover the General's secret fear and most fervent desire. In Gheeaba, a man's virility was judged by how many sons he produced. Tulkhan's only marriage had been annulled when his wife did not produce a child within three years. The Aayel had directed Imoshen to seduce Tulkhan and ensure she conceived a boy.

It had seemed an impossible task, yet, when it came to consummating the Harvest Feast, the General had played into Imoshen's hands. Every year the fertility of the land was ensured with a ritual consummation. Usually a young man and woman from one of the local villages were chosen, but the General had claimed Imoshen and she had told him the moment she felt his son's life flare into being.

However, she would not have lived to conceive this child if the Aayel had not saved her life by sacrificing her own.

When the rebels' assassination attempt on Tulkhan had failed, he had ordered the execution of the last of the old royal line. The Aayel had chosen to assume blame, absolving Imoshen, and had then taken her own life in an abbreviated form of the T'En ritual suicide.

Grimly Imoshen stared at herself in the silver-backed mirror. She hoped that if she was ever faced with such a choice, she would be as brave.

Tentatively she touched her flat belly, shaking her head in wonder. Her child broke with six hundred years of tradition. Pure T'En women were supposed to be chaste, devoting themselves to the church. Yet she should not feel as if she was committing a crime, for before the invasion the Empress of Fair Isle had granted dispensation for her to break with custom and bond with the only other full blood T'En, Reothe.

Imoshen swayed, sinking to her knees. She must not think of her betrothed and what might have been. When she had surrendered her stronghold to the General, she had believed Reothe dead and that, as last surviving member of the royal family, her duty was to help her people survive the Ghebite invasion. However, she had soon discovered that Reothe was very much alive. He had slipped into her chamber one night at Landsend Abbey, intending to complete their bonding vows, escape with her and retake the island.

Imoshen's left wrist tingled and she lifted it to her mouth. Licking the bonding scar, she urged it to fade. To remember was to feel, and she did not want to recall Reothe's arms around her, or his determination as he cut his wrist, then hers, to mingle their blood. She had not wanted to refuse him, but she had been unable to sanction more bloodshed. Reothe represented her lost dreams. Her loyalty must be to the people of Fair Isle and the General.

She looked down at her left wrist where the scar was all but invisible. So much rested on her. She had to believe she had made the right choice.

'How can I be your maid if you won't let me serve you?' Kalleen demanded, running into the room.

With a relieved laugh, Imoshen came to her feet. 'Soon you will be the Lady of Windhaven and have servants of your own.'

The girl used a choice farmyard word. 'I'm not the Lady of Windhaven yet.'

'It is only right that your loyalty and bravery be rewarded,' Imoshen said. She suspected there would be many who resented seeing a farm girl elevated to the nobility. But it was thanks to Kalleen that she and Tulkhan had ended Gharavan's brief reign.

Kalleen gasped as Imoshen turned. 'That bruise on your ribs... Did the General do that because you dared lift a sword to him?'

Imoshen sighed. 'Does everyone know already?'

'The Ghebites are saying that if you had been properly disciplined you would know your place. They say the General should beat you every day until he breaks your spirit.'

Imoshen cursed softly under her breath.

'Should I unpack the Empress's formal gowns for tomorrow night?' Kalleen asked, practical as always. Imoshen thought of the fearful town dignitaries, of the General's wary eyes; of the Beatific, the enigmatic leader of the T'En church.

Imoshen sighed. Her only experience of the Empress's court had been a short visit the summer before Tulkhan attacked. At the time she had not been aware of the subtle power interplay between the church and the Empress. She had simply accepted that the church venerated the T'En as sacred vessels and in return the T'En served the church. But since entering the capital as Tulkhan's captive, she had sensed a wariness in the woman who should have been her closest ally.

Imoshen turned to Kalleen. 'For the celebration I must remind them of the Old Empire. I must be T'Imoshen, the last T'En Princess. So yes, unpack the formal gowns and jewellery.'

'It is lucky the Empress was nearly as tall as you,' Kalleen said as she left.

Imoshen sank into the warm bath with a sigh of relief. The General might scorn Fair Isle's aristocracy and their complacency after six hundred years of uninterrupted rule, but he could not fail to be impressed by hot running water.

*   *   *

'My lady's in the bath, General Tulkhan,' Kalleen protested, darting forward as if she intended to restrain him. 'You can't go in.'

'Then you'd better tell Imoshen to come out, because I want to speak with her.'

Radiating disdain, the maid bundled up Imoshen's clothing and retreated to the bathing chamber.

When Tulkhan heard their voices, he imagined Imoshen, her pale flesh glowing from the hot bath as she dressed indignantly. He smiled to himself. Confronting Imoshen was always invigorating, any excuse would do.

Already once today she had stood before him, disarmed but not beaten. He should have refused to let her touch the Ghebite sword, yet he could not resist her challenge, and because of this he'd just broken up a fight between the palace stable workers and his own horse handlers.

'General Tulkhan?' Imoshen greeted him, weaving the ends of her long silver hair into one thick plait.

He turned, aware of her frank gaze. Clearly it did not trouble Imoshen that the damp robe clung to her body. The knowledge that it would soon be his right to join her in the bathing chamber made Tulkhan short with the maid. 'You are dismissed, Kalleen.'

Instead of obeying him, she looked to Imoshen, who nodded. This irritated Tulkhan intensely. The palace's army of servants were always deferring to Imoshen.

'You wanted to speak with me?' she asked.

'I will assign several of my elite guard as your private escort when you leave the palace.'

'I have my own stronghold guard,' Imoshen said. 'Besides, I can look –'

'Hear me out. By raising a sword to me you have broken Ghebite law and –'

'You hear me out, General. This is not Gheeaba. In this land anyone can bear arms in defence of themselves and their loved ones.'

'Don't lecture me, Imoshen. My army is quartered in T'Diemn. They hear garbled stories of how you insult me by taking up arms against me. The customs of Fair Isle confuse them. Every day they see women walking about the streets, running businesses, sitting in tea-houses and taverns, laughing and talking.'

'So?'

Tulkhan repressed a wave of frustration. 'In Gheeaba a woman covers her face to walk out in public. Don't look outraged. It is just the way things are. My men don't know what to make of women who look them in the eye and laugh.'

'Do them good!'

'Imoshen, be serious.'

She bit back a smile. 'I am listening, General. Surely in the years you've been on campaign your men have seen how other countries live.'

'Less than you'd think. We travelled as an army and camped as an army. They are good men, but simple. Even Wharrd is wary of you, and he has worked at your side helping with healings.' Tulkhan could tell his argument had not convinced her. 'By the gods, Imoshen, I am trying to honour you. If my elite guard escorted you, it would be the same as if I was at your side. It would look right to my men.'

She sighed. 'That may be, but it would not look right to the people of Fair Isle. Your elite guard would offend them. They expect the Empress to be approachable. And even though I do not claim this title, it is how they see me. From the poorest homeless worker to the master of the greatest guild, I must be accessible to them all. And now, if you'll excuse me, I have work to do.'

'Wait.' He caught her arm as she brushed past. 'I just broke up a fight in the stables. Some hot-heads were brawling in defence of your honour. This time there was nothing worse than a few bloody noses, but I cannot be at your heels every time you step out of the palace.'

She laughed and flicked free of his grasp with one easy movement. 'I am not so useless that I need protecting from my own people, or yours. Now, I must attend to the invitations.'

'Imoshen!'

She waited, regal and amused.

'All it takes is one zealot with a knife. You could be killed.'

All amusement left her face. She held his eyes, hers sharp as garnets. 'It is the same for every ruler. I have faced death many times since I surrendered my stronghold to you, General Tulkhan. You, of all people, must be aware of that. But this has not stopped me performing my duty.'

He wanted to deny that he had been ready to order her death on more than one occasion, but he could not.

She leant closer and raised her hand in what he thought was a caress, but instead she plucked a straw from his temple plait and tossed it into the fire. 'Don't worry, General. I will be on my guard.'

Imoshen walked off but she was not oblivious to the General's displeasure. Since they had arrived in the capital, she had watched Tulkhan study the palace and its people. He was quick to learn and adapt. He would not insist on assigning an elite guard to escort her if she could convince him otherwise.

She paused at the entrance to her chambers, where one of her people stood, and smiled at the youth, remembering how twenty men and women from her stronghold guard had accompanied her to the capital at a moment's notice. When Tulkhan had banished Gharavan, he'd had to move quickly to seize power.

In fact, he had moved so swiftly he had announced their betrothal the first night in the capital. She might be the last T'En Princess, but her twenty guards and a single chest of belongings were all that was truly hers in this great palace.

Despite this, she had to act as if she considered herself the Empress. It would impress the town dignitaries and church officials if their invitations were delivered by the leader of her personal guard.

'Where is Crawen?'

The young man flushed, lifting T'En eyes to Imoshen's. They shared a common ancestry, though only Imoshen carried all the traits of the pure T'En – six fingers, glittering silver hair and piercing garnet eyes. In the six hundred years since her people had settled Fair Isle, they had interbred with the locals until the pure T'En had all but died out. Her birth had been an unwelcome surprise for her family, both a curse and a blessing.

'Crawen is practising T'Enchu in the ball-court.'

'Thank you.' Imoshen turned to Tulkhan. 'I trained under Crawen from the age of ten. As leader of my stronghold guard, she is master of the sword as well as T'Enchu. Come see my people's skill at unarmed combat, then tell me I cannot defend myself.'

She led the way, but they did not reach the ball-court. Raised voices greeted them before they entered the connecting passage.

'...she should be made to know her place!' The Ghebite Harholfe's words became clear to Imoshen.

'Her place?' Crawen repeated softly. 'You insult –'

'She insults our general. In Gheeaba a woman would not dare touch a weapon,' Jacolm said. 'In Gheeaba she dare not raise her eyes to a man who is not her husband or blood relative.'

Imoshen would have rounded the corner to confront them but, Tulkhan caught her arm, his expression urging her to listen.

'You Ghebite barb –'

'Quiet,' Crawen ordered her companion, her tone sharp but level. 'This is not Gheeaba, Commander Jacolm. T'Imoshen is second cousin to the Empress and skilled enough to teach the art of T'Enchu. Once True-men and women did not raise their eyes to the T'En, but we have come a long way since then. One day, Gheeaba may do the same.'

'You call yourself a leader? Yet you fetch and carry these fairground disguises!' Harholfe kicked an arm guard which bounced off the wall and skittered around the corner to land at Imoshen's feet. She picked it up automatically.

Again Crawen's companion would have protested, but she cut him short, saying, 'In Fair Isle, the higher we rise the more we serve. I belong to an ancient, honourable fellowship of elite warriors.'

'What kind of guard accepts women into its ranks?' Jacolm sneered.

A charged silence followed.

'Your men are deliberately baiting my people, General,' Imoshen mouthed.

'What do you expect?' He held her eyes. 'You bait me, they are only –'

Furious, Imoshen turned the corner to find Jacolm and Harholfe and three of Tulkhan's elite guard facing three of her stronghold guard. Crawen and her two companions stood with their backs to a decorative arched niche. Behind them was a scene from the Age of Tribulation rendered with lifelike accuracy. The first two hundred years of T'En rule in Fair Isle had been spent containing bloody uprisings. As Crawen had said, Fair Isle had come a long way.

Imoshen faltered. Was the shedding of blood the only way to resolve ideological conflict? It seemed threat and might were the only things the Ghebites respected.

'Crawen,' Imoshen greeted them. 'Jacolm, Harholfe. The General and I wish to stage a tourney.' She caught Tulkhan's eye as he joined her.

He cloaked his surprise and, with a gleam of annoyed amusement, folded his arms and leant against the wall.

She realised he had abandoned her to sink or swim. She plunged on. 'When the Age of Tribulation ended, our people kept their martial skills alive with competition and display. I propose the stronghold guard stage a martial display of T'Enchu and T'En swordsmanship on the spring fairground east of town.' Imoshen turned to Tulkhan. 'Would your men like to stage a display of their own?'

He straightened. 'When?'

Imoshen glanced from the belligerent Ghebites to her beleaguered guard. 'Would this afternoon be too soon?'

Chapter Two

As THE TWO columns of Ghebite horsemen circled the field, Imoshen marvelled at their precision, born of discipline and relentless training.

Spellbound, the silent crowd watched the Ghebites' horses pound over the ground, kicking clods of snow and dirt high in the air. Taking up position opposite the painted-hide target, the two columns paused, one to Imoshen's right, the other to her left.

On the far side of the field, parents hurriedly herded children to safety, and there was a moment of hushed expectation. Uttering the eerie Ghebite battle cry, the first archer urged his horse to a gallop, charging diagonally at the target.

Before he had even let his arrow fly, the opposite rider surged forward. Standing in their stirrups, both archers approached the target. One mistake and the riders would collide, going down beneath sharp hooves.

First one, then the other, let his arrows fly, alternating like a rug-maker's threads, weaving a craft of whistling death. The bolts flew true, striking the centre of the target. No wonder the Ghebites had swept all opposition before them.

Their display finished, the Ghebite cavalry made a triumphant circuit of the field. As the people of Fair Isle cheered their conquerors, Imoshen repressed a bitter smile. Even though she had been the one to suggest the tourney, the crowd's response rankled.

The mounted men wheeled and saluted the far side of the field as their general appeared on his black destrier. Imoshen caught her breath.

Tulkhan wore no armour, nothing but boots and breeches. His long black hair hung free around his broad shoulders and he rode as one with his horse. To Imoshen he was the physical embodiment of his ancient Ghebite heritage, of those fiercely loyal tribesmen of the harsh plains who counted their wealth in horses.

A buzz of speculation spread through the crowd. Tulkhan circled the field at full gallop, then stood in the stirrups. Without warning he leapt to the ground, running beside the flashing hooves of his horse, hands on the saddle pommel. The crowd gasped. Imoshen glanced to the cavalry, who watched their general proudly, and she understood he was repeating the deeds of his ancestors, men who rode bareback as boys, men who worshipped bravery and skill. With a leap, Tulkhan regained his seat, rising to stand on the horse's back. Arms extended, knees flexed, he balanced above his galloping mount.

When Tulkhan finally dropped into the saddle, Imoshen let out her breath. He pulled his mount short, walking it backwards. With a flourish he urged the horse to rear. It danced on its hind legs to everyone's applause. Tulkhan's teeth flashed white against his coppery skin, triggering a need deep inside her.

Imoshen smiled. The General claimed to hate pomp and ceremony, but the barbarian in him clearly loved this kind of display.

A servant ran onto the field to present Tulkhan with his round shield and sword. The cavalry had discarded their bows, taking up swords and shields.

Tulkhan signalled the bout was to begin and Imoshen tensed as the men charged, striking right and left. Horses wheeled and went down screaming. At first she thought the Ghebites had gone mad. Their swords were wicked-looking weapons half as tall as a man. Then she realised the men were turning the flat of the blades on each other. Even so, some would pay with broken bones.

One by one the Ghebites conceded defeat, leaving the field, dazed and bleeding. At last only one horse and rider remained. General Tulkhan.

The crowd roared.

Tulkhan stood in the stirrups, black eyes flashing. Damp hair clinging to his broad shoulders, he took a victory lap – the model Ghebite warrior, fearless and terrifying.

On the battlefield Tulkhan was renowned as a brilliant tactician, able to make intuitive decisions which led his men to victory even against great odds. But it was his personal bravery that had earned him his men's devotion. They would die for him.

Imoshen studied Tulkhan. Could he hold Fair Isle? The skills of a general were not the skills of a great statesman.

By claiming her, he had consolidated his position, and by agreeing to honour the laws of the church, he had earned the support of this powerful body. The Beatific sat in the row behind Imoshen, flanked by her priests, lending the church's sanction to today's display. But Tulkhan no longer had the backing of the Ghebite Empire, and he held Fair Isle with only his loyal commanders and army. They were a formidable force, yet spread over the population of Fair Isle they were like pebbles on a sandy beach.

Then there was Reothe, the late Empress's adopted son turned rebel leader. The whole island knew he bided his time in the impenetrable Keldon Highlands with his ragtag army, awaiting the moment to strike.

To retain Fair Isle, Tulkhan had to win the support of its conquered people. Imoshen knew her people. If only Tulkhan would trust her enough to heed her advice. Irony warmed her. Since when did a Ghebite listen to a woman? She was not even a True-woman, but T'En, cursed Dhamfeer in their language. And when they called her by that name, they made it an insult.

Her hands shook with anger as she poured wine into the victory goblet and raised it high, to the applause of the crowd.

This martial display had not only given her stronghold guard an opportunity to display their skills to the Ghebites without bloodshed, but it had reassured T'Diemn's townsfolk.

As word about the tourney spread across the capital, shopkeepers had locked up and harnessed their horses, piling children, blankets and food in carts. Quick-thinking bakers had thrown hot buns into calico sacks, and by noon everyone had marched out to the field where the annual spring fair was held.

Determined to remind Tulkhan that she was not one of his slavish Ghebite women, Imoshen had taken her place in the T'Enchu display. She was wearing the traditional loose-fitting trousers, and her pure white tunic proclaimed her skill equal to that of a teacher. T'Enchu was more than a form of unarmed combat, it was a moving meditation; and it had come from the T'En homeland beyond the seas. The artform had been maintained and polished since then, and it was said a T'Enchu master could defeat an armed opponent. T'Enchu also placed males and females on an equal footing, because it relied on speed and used the opponents' strength against them.

Imoshen had delighted in the precision needed to pull her attacks so that she left no mark. Blows that could have broken bones merely brushed her sparring partner's tunic. Because this was a display match and she fought a partner of equal ranking, they wore no protectors.

But when it had come to the T'En swordsmanship bout, she had bowed out after the first round, having only just begun her training last year.

Heart racing from the exertion, she had returned to the hastily erected dais to take her seat beside the General. As the display bout continued, Imoshen had not been able to resist leaning closer to Tulkhan to say, 'See what a skilled sword player can do with a knitting needle and a toothpick!'

He'd had the grace to grin.

Having disarmed the last opponent, Crawen had approached the dais to accept the victory cup. She'd dropped a little wine on the ground before draining her goblet, an old custom that acknowledged the Ancients and revealed her peasant roots. The Beatific frowned. Worship of the Ancients was regarded as primitive.

When the stronghold guard's piper had saluted the victor, Imoshen had felt tears of pride prick her eyes. Her people had given a good account of themselves. Perhaps now Tulkhan's men would not be so quick to cast aspersions. But having seen the Ghebite cavalry, she had to admit they were impressive.

Now, as Tulkhan rode towards her, his men chanted a paean to the great Akha Khan. It was said that in times of danger the greatest of their gods took on a physical form. In some tales he appeared as a great black bear, or a stallion. In others he was a hybrid creature, half man, half beast and, on rare occasions, he took the form of a man, a giant in stature with brilliant black eyes. It was not surprising that Tulkhan's men regarded him as the embodiment of their god.

Triumphant, Tulkhan remained astride his destrier to accept the victory goblet from Imoshen. When he tipped a little of the wine onto the ground his gaze held Imoshen's, as if to say, *See, I honour your customs even if I don't believe in them.*

As formidable as the General's physical presence was, it was not his most dangerous attribute. She must never underestimate his intelligence.

'A most impressive display of skill, General, but how many of your men nurse broken bones?' Imoshen made her voice rich and mocking. Her stronghold guard had suffered nothing worse than bruises.

Tulkhan's eyes narrowed. A frisson of danger made Imoshen's breath catch.

The General drained the goblet then tossed it to his bone-setter, Wharrd. He offered Imoshen his hand. 'Trust me?'

'In matters of warcraft? Yes.'

His eyes narrowed. 'Then take my hand and I'll show you real skill.'

Imoshen stepped onto his boot and astride his thighs. The horse surged forward and she felt the solid wall of Tulkhan's chest at her back. When he turned the destrier she faced the ranks of his men dressed in their purple and red cloaks.

'Bring me three short spears and a target,' Tulkhan ordered.

Two men raced forward with them.

Tulkhan took the spears and handed Imoshen the target. 'You don't ask what I do?'

'You seek an opportunity to strut like the barbarian warrior you are!'

He laughed, then urged his horse towards the edge of the field where canny shopkeepers had set up spits. The scent of roasting cinnamon apples hung on the air, making Imoshen's stomach rumble.

He halted the horse beside a waist-high tree stump. 'Stand here.'

Imoshen slid off his thighs to stand on the stump.

He showed her how to thread her arm through the target's support and warned, 'Now brace yourself, and when this is over mock me no more.'

As she spread her feet Tulkhan wheeled his horse, galloping across the field. The crowd fell silent. The steady thud of the black horse's hooves echoed Imoshen's heartbeat.

The General selected his first spear, then with a shout spurred the horse on. The black destrier leaped forward, guided by the pressure of his rider's knees.

Tulkhan raised the spear.

Imoshen braced her shoulders, centring the target which barely covered her chest. One mistake and she would be dead, a spear through her head or belly. One calculated mistake and Tulkhan would be free of her.

Imoshen gritted her teeth.

Tulkhan rose in the saddle, slewing the horse sideways. Even as the first spear left his hands he plucked the second and threw, then the third, moving so fast that all three were in the air at once.

Thud, the first spear struck home. Two more followed in rapid succession. The impact rocked Imoshen and she had to fight to retain her balance. The cheering of the General's men drowned out the rushing in her head.

Suddenly Tulkhan was beside her, hand extended. His eyes blazed with triumph, reminding Imoshen that the savage in him was very close to the surface.

Accepting his hand she leapt up behind him. Aware that the Ghebites loved display, she took her cue from Tulkhan's earlier horsemanship exhibition. Planting her feet on the horse's broad rump, she steadied herself with one hand on Tulkhan's shoulder and held the spear-impaled target above her head. The crowd's loud acclamations made her heart race and she experienced the heady rush of battle fever.

When they reached the dais Imoshen tossed the target aside and jumped to the platform, where she signalled that the display was over. The court heralds sounded the closing notes while the General's black destrier pawed the ground restlessly.

Imoshen collected her cloak and caught Tulkhan's eye. 'Night comes early this close to midwinter, General. I will ride back to T'Diemn with you.'

As Tulkhan extended his hand, he wondered why Imoshen had chosen not to ride her own horse. She leapt up before him, settling across his thighs. When he wound one arm around her waist, strands of her silver hair tickled his face and he inhaled her scent like rare perfume. She might be pure Dhamfeer, but she was all woman in his arms. The blood sang in his veins and he threw back his head and laughed.

Imoshen twisted round to look up at him, searching his face. In Gheeaba an unmarried woman would not dare look a man in the eye. But then no Ghebite woman would have done what Imoshen had done today, turning what could have degenerated into a vicious fight into a celebration of martial skill.

'You did not doubt my spear's aim?' he prodded, full of admiration for her bravery.

Her lips quirked as she gave him a knowing look. 'You are a great tactician, General. If you had wanted me dead, you would have chosen a less public way of doing it.'

Anger replaced admiration and made his body tighten. The horse responded to the pressure of his knees, increasing its pace, and the General turned his mount towards T'Diemn.

Weary shopkeepers packed up their stalls and children cried sleepily for their dinner. In the clear winter twilight a long line of carts snaked down the road to the capital, making way for the General Tulkhan's black destrier and their escort, the elite guard.

Silhouetted against the setting sun's glow, the palace towers and Basilica's dome dominated the old city. But T'Diemn had long ago outgrown its defences, and the city sprawled outside the old walls, prosperous and exposed.

'I must design new defences and repair the old,' Tulkhan said.

'And I must oversee the restoration of the palace.'

The General grimaced. The capital had suffered when it had surrendered to his half-brother. King Gharavan had slaughtered the town officials and executed the guildmasters. The King's soldiers had camped in the palace, looting and destroying what they did not understand.

Imoshen had been quick to point out that Gharavan's cruelty threatened to destroy any trust Tulkhan might establish with her people. Conquering was one thing, holding was another. A conqueror had to win the people over or constantly fight rebellion.

'General...' Imoshen interrupted his train of thought. 'What do you think of combining your elite guard with my stronghold guard and giving them an official name like... oh, the T'Diemn Palace Guard?'

'You ask the impossible. My men would never accept women in their ranks.'

'But you saw Crawen's skill with the sword. Though the people of T'Diemn cheered you today, they are still uneasy. To restore their confidence we must be united.'

'You push too hard, too fast, Imoshen. I have signed an agreement to honour the laws of the church; that is enough for now.' It was more than enough. He needed the support of the church, but he dreaded his men's reaction when they realised he meant to acknowledge Imoshen as his equal. It was a delicate balance. Somehow he had to appease the people of Fair Isle, yet retain the respect of his men.

Imoshen radiated impatience but she held her tongue for once. A small mercy. Their escort was pressed close about them and it would not help matters for his men to hear her debating with him.

She brooded in silence as they entered the outskirts of T'Diemn. Mullioned windows glowed with welcome and the rich smell of roast meat hung on the winter air, making Tulkhan's mouth water.

Imoshen stiffened in his arms. 'Stop.'

A plump woman thrust through Tulkhan's elite guard to clutch Imoshen's hand.

'You must come, Empress. This way.' She ran off as though Imoshen's agreement was a foregone conclusion.

Tulkhan halted the horse. 'What is it?'

'Down the lane, General,' Imoshen said, face tight with foreboding.

Tulkhan turned his mount.

Wringing her hands, the woman waited outside a modest two-storey house which bore the Cooper Guild's symbol of two half-barrels.

Imoshen pointed. 'The new-life garland hangs on the door. The woman of the house must have given birth within the last small moon.'

A man threw the door open and staggered out, his face a mask of grief, a hat clutched in his hands.

'His hat bears the new-father's badge,' Imoshen whispered. 'I dread...' She dropped to the cobbles. 'You, cooper, what's wrong?'

He cast aside his hat as he made a deep obeisance, lifting both hands to his forehead. By this Tulkhan knew he accorded Imoshen the honour of Empress, just as the woman had. Old habits died hard.

'T'Imoshen?' The cooper used the royal prefix. 'You must help me.'

'Of course.' Imoshen threw Tulkhan one swift glance as she disappeared inside.

Responding to her unspoken plea, he swung down from his horse.

'Wait here,' he told his men, tossing the reins to Wharrd. He paused long enough to retrieve the man's hat. Only in Fair Isle would a man don a badge of fatherhood and decorate his house with a garland so that his neighbours could celebrate the birth of his child.

The plump woman watched Tulkhan anxiously as he ducked his head to cross the threshold. The man's voice carried down the stairwell to him.

'Larassa gave birth to our daughter this time yesterday. I offered to stay with her, but she urged me to go to the tourney.' A groan escaped him. 'Why did I listen?'

Tulkhan hung the hat on the hall peg and took the steps two at a time, but slowed as he came level with the landing. A young woman lay in a pool of blood.

'No one stayed with her?' Imoshen asked, incredulous. 'Right after birthing, a woman is –'

'I know. But all our relatives died in the war and we know few people in T'Diemn. I should not have left her!'

Imoshen knelt to touch the woman's neck. When her eyes met Tulkhan's he knew there was no hope.

'A woman walks death's shadow to bring forth new life,' Imoshen whispered. 'Sometimes...'

The cooper dropped to his knees, rocking back and forth. 'I failed her. I must not fail her soul. You must say the words over my Larassa. Send for your T'Enchiridion and say the words for the dead.'

'I know the passage off by heart,' Imoshen said. 'But you should send for the priests to do this.'

As she rose Tulkhan noted her strained face. Imoshen carried his son. Was she thinking that soon she would be facing the trials of childbirth? The thought of Imoshen lying dead in a pool of blood was too much to bear.

'My daughter.' The cooper sprang to his feet, darting through a door. He returned with a babe so tightly wrapped in swaddling clothes that only her face was visible. 'Does she live? I cannot tell.'

Imoshen took the baby from him, pressing her fingers to the infant's temples. 'Alive, yes... but her life force flickers like a candle drowning in its own wax.' She frowned at the father. 'Didn't the midwife deal with the afterbirth?'

'She did, but... You must call on the Parakletos to escort Larassa's soul through death's shadow. I have heard how mothers who die in childbirth refuse to be parted –'

Imoshen hissed, pressing the baby closer.

'T'Imoshen. I beg you.' The cooper fell on one knee. Taking her left hand, he kissed her sixth finger. 'You are pure T'En. The Parakletos will listen to your voice above all others. You must do this. Please.'

Imoshen closed her eyes. For an instant Tulkhan thought she would refuse. Then she took a deep breath and looked down at the man. 'Prepare Larassa. Place her on your bonding bed while I watch over your daughter.'

Tulkhan would have helped the man, but Imoshen drew him aside.

'None but a blood relative or bond-partner must touch the dead one's body. Come.' She studied the baby. 'We are lucky the babe still lives. The mother has been dead long enough for her skin to go cold.' She sniffed the air, her eyes narrowing. 'But her soul still lingers.'

Tulkhan shuddered. 'I don't understand. How could the dead mother take the baby? Who are the Parakletos?'

'Guides between this world and death's realm. When the priest says the words for the dead, the Parakletos answer her summons, escorting the soul through death's shadow. I have never sensed the Parakletos myself, but the danger to this baby is very real. New life is always fragile.' She frowned on the silent infant. 'Considering how the mother died, this little one would be vulnerable even with the proper words over the afterbirth.'

'I still don't understand.'

'How could you? As a trained midwife I learned how the soul of the baby is formed in the afterbirth, just as the babe's life force is housed in the growing body. At birth the soul transfers to the baby's body, animating the life force. The proper words must be said and the afterbirth disposed of safely to ensure the baby's soul is securely bound.'

'But my people don't...' Tulkhan hesitated. A Ghebite man avoided his wives when they were due to give birth.

'How often are Ghebite babies born dead or die unexpectedly? The new soul can drift, leaving the baby alive but its mind unformed. Sometimes this does not happen until the person is grown. Have you seen people whose minds wander, people who kill and have no memory of it? This is what happens if the soul is not properly fixed in the body. This little girl is barely one day old. The bond is fragile and the mother –'

'I am ready. Come quickly.' The cooper beckoned.

They ducked their heads to avoid the lintel. Wrapped in a rich cloth, the woman was laid out on the bed. Candles glimmered in the four corners of the room. The single mirror had been covered and the window was opened so as not to impede her soul's passage.

'My daughter?' The cooper peered anxiously at the pale little face.

'We must move quickly.' Imoshen put the baby in his arms. 'Hold tight to your daughter, fasten her soul and life force with your will. I'm sure Larassa would not wish to kill her baby, but the time immediately after death is very confusing. A soul that has been parted from its body by violent death often lingers for a day or more before beginning its journey through death's shadow, and this is a tragic death. Larassa will not want to leave you and the child.' Imoshen gave him a compassionate smile. 'Remember there is an honoured place in death's realm for women and babies who die in childbirth, a place alongside warriors who die defending their loved ones.'

Tulkhan frowned. In Gheeaba fallen warriors had the honour of riding with the great Akha Khan. Priests taught that women did not possess true souls. Once dead, their life force dissipated. They were mourned just as one might mourn the death of a favourite dog.

When told of his mother's death Tulkhan had told himself he felt nothing, but the knowledge that she had died alone and untended troubled him.

Imoshen's voice came to him speaking High T'En, then alternating with the language of the people. She called on the Parakletos by name, begging them to hear her plea, binding them to their task.

As she spoke, Tulkhan heard the people in the street outside singing a dirge.

Imoshen's voice faltered. Tulkhan's gaze flew to her face. The whites showed all around her garnet eyes as she fixed on something he could not see. A metallic taste settled on his tongue. He grimaced, recognising the sensation. How he despised the taste of T'En power.

Tendrils of Imoshen's long silver hair rose as if they had a life of their own. The room grew oppressively cold, filled with palpable tension.

The cooper held his daughter to his chest with fierce determination. He repeated Imoshen's last words and she recovered, continuing the passage.

Had it been possible, Tulkhan would have left the room to escape witnessing this mysterious T'En ritual, but his body was not his to command.

Although he could see Imoshen's lips as the words flowed from her tongue, he couldn't hear a sound for the pressure in his ears.

Without warning, the cooper's legs gave way. He sank onto the chest under the window. Burying his face in the baby's blanket, he wept softly with relief.

Imoshen gasped, dropping to her knees.

Tulkhan caught her as she pitched forward. He expected his skin to crawl with the physical contact, but she felt as warm and yielding as a True-woman. 'Imoshen?'

She moaned, her open eyes unseeing. 'This time I felt the words. The Parakletos came at my call. I never...' She shuddered and pushed him away, then pulled herself upright using the bedpost. She looked from the dead woman on the bed to the grieving father with his baby daughter. 'I have done what I can.'

Shouts came from the street below, a combination of Ghebite soldier cant and the common trading tongue delivered imperiously. Tulkhan strode to the window.

Imoshen rolled her eyes. 'What now?'

He had to smile. 'We are honoured. The Beatific herself is here.'

Imoshen's heart sank. Since entering this home she had been labouring under the dead mother's despairing heartbreak, which hung thick as a blanket, on the air. The effort of calling the Parakletos, then controlling them, had drained all her reserves. She did not have the strength for a confrontation with the Beatific.

Several pairs of boots sounded on the stairs. The door swung open and a priest announced the leader of the T'En church. The Beatific swept into the room, still dressed in the rich fur mantle she had worn to the tourney. Her elaborate headdress brushed the doorjambs.

Taking in the body on the bed and the four candles, she turned on Imoshen. 'What have you done?'

'I have done nothing but serve my people.' Imoshen chose her words with care.

The Beatific's eyes narrowed. 'You overreach yourself.'

'It was necessary. I could not refuse –'

'No? You have not given your Vow of Expiation. By what right do you perform this holy office?'

'By right of birth.' Imoshen lifted both hands, fingers splayed like fans before her face. Looking over the twelve fingertips, she held the Beatific's eyes until the woman's gaze wavered, then lowered her hands. 'I trained at the Aayel's side. Many times I have said the words to bind a baby's soul.'

'That may be so,' the Beatific conceded. 'But the words for the dead are powerful tools. You should have sent to the Basilica for –'

'T'Imoshen saved my daughter's life.' The cooper lurched to his feet. 'I begged her to say the words.'

The Beatific ignored him. 'You said the words without your T'Enchiridion, Imoshen? Or do you have it with you?' She looked pointedly at Imoshen's empty hands. 'What were you thinking? The Parakletos are not to be called lightly. One wrong word and they could take the soul of the caller!'

Tulkhan cursed. 'You risked yourself?'

Imoshen stiffened, meeting his eyes. 'I am a healer. I could not let the infant die. And I did not need the book because the Aayel made me memorise the verses.' She faced the Beatific. 'If we had sent for help, it would have been too late. The baby's life force was ebbing, its soul lured by the mother's restless –'

'You are not qualified to speak of such matters!'

There was a fraught silence.

Then the Beatific massaged her temples, sighing heavily. 'You thought you were acting for the best, this I understand, but the sooner you take your Vow of Expiation the better.'

Imoshen dropped to one knee, both hands extended palm up, offering the obeisance of a supplicant. 'Wise Beatific, hear me. I was ready to take the vow on the seventeenth anniversary of my birthing day, but Fair Isle was at war and I could not travel to the Basilica. I am prepared to take the vow –'

'Of chastity? Are you ready to follow the true path for a pure T'En woman, the one dictated by your namesake, T'Imoshen the First?'

Imoshen looked up startled. The Beatific knew she was supposed to bond with the General. Did this True-woman favour tradition over political expediency? No... Imoshen understood in a flash of insight. The Beatific feared Imoshen's throwback blood.

Tulkhan strode forward. 'I have claimed Imoshen. She cannot –'

'I cannot take the vow of chastity,' Imoshen spoke quickly before Tulkhan could reveal that she carried his child. According to the records, no T'En woman had given birth in six hundred years. Cloaking her pregnancy was instinctive. She came to her feet. 'Once I would have taken that path willingly. But the Empress granted me dispensation even before the Ghebites invaded

Fair Isle. Now I must serve my people in another way.' She felt for Tulkhan, who took her arm, linking it through his. He was reassuringly solid.

She drew on his certainty. 'In other circumstances I would have called on the church to say the words for the dead, and I concede it is wisest to speak those words from the T'Enchiridion.' Her mouth went dry as she recalled her discovery that the Parakletos were not merely an abstract concept. Even worse, they were not the benevolent beings of the church's teachings. She shuddered, forcing herself to go on. 'This is no longer the Old Empire, Beatific. We must bend before the winds of change or be uprooted.'

The True-woman's mouth tightened in an angry line.

Imoshen had not meant it as a threat. They were all vulnerable, none more so than she.

'What is this Vow of Expiation, Imoshen?' Tulkhan asked.

The Beatific replied for her. 'Before they can be accepted into society, all pure T'En must give the Vow of Expiation to the church, offering themselves in its service.'

Imoshen noted the Beatific omitted to mention that the only other pure T'En throwback, Reothe, had also given his Vow of Expiation, and now served only himself. Perhaps he regarded regaining Fair Isle as serving the people?

'Imoshen can give this vow when we make our marriage vows on Midwinter's Day, that is less than one small moon away,' Tulkhan announced, sweeping the problem aside.

Imoshen caught the Beatific's eye. Bonding was nothing like a Ghebite marriage.

'No harm has been done here today,' Tulkhan announced. 'And a life has been saved. My men wait outside in the cold, grumbling for their dinner. Come, Imoshen.' He gave the Beatific a nod, insulting in its brevity.

'Beatific.' Imoshen offered the leader of the T'En church the proper obeisance and waited for her to leave. Imoshen knew if General Tulkhan had had his way, he would have simply marched out, leaving them to trail after him. Every day was filled with a thousand small insults, salt in the wound of Fair Isle's surrender.

Chapter Three

THE RIDE BACK to the palace was swift but not swift enough. Their meal had spoiled. Imoshen had to soothe the cook's feelings. She had just left the royal kitchen behind, with its lingering smell of burned sauce, when a young boy ran into her.

'What's so important that you cannot walk the palace corridors in a civilised fashion?' Imoshen asked, hauling him to his feet.

He rolled his eyes. 'The Ghebites –'

What now? Distantly she heard their raised voices. 'Take me to them.'

The boy led her through a connecting passage to an old wing dating from the Age of Tribulation. Curious servants clustered in doorways, pointing and giggling.

A dozen of Tulkhan's commanders and elite guard marched past Imoshen. Some held braces of candles and wine flagons, others carried massive oak chairs between them, all sang at the tops of their voices. There was much laughter and they stopped every few paces to share the wine.

Imoshen experienced a strong sense of dislocation. In the Old Empire, ritual and protocol guided every moment of the day. This bizarre Ghebite parade was so out of place it left her disoriented and bemused.

As the song ended Tulkhan's voice echoed down the passage, ordering them to take care. Imoshen edged past the men, brushing against wainscoting and ancient weaponry. She entered a disused hall, where she found fourteen men staggering under the weight of a feasting table. Leaping candle flames cast frantic shadows on distant walls but could not illuminate the high ceiling.

'What are you doing?' Imoshen demanded of the nearest man.

He blinked owlishly, realised who she was and made the Ghebite sign to ward off evil, fist before his eyes.

'Imoshen?' Tulkhan located her. 'Is our meal ready?'

'Not yet. The cook is trying to muster up enough cold meat and cheese to feed forty people. Our spoiled food will be fed to the pigs.'

'Then we have time to get these tables and chairs upstairs. Come on, men!'

They launched into a rousing drinking song while manhandling the solid oak table out of the room. Imoshen winced as one corner chipped the doorway.

'Take care!' Tulkhan bellowed, then tilted a flagon across his forearm and drank deep. 'Take it up the marble staircase. Should be wide enough.'

Imoshen caught Tulkhan's arm. 'But why? What's wrong with the tables and chairs that we've been using?'

'Too small. I'm tired of sitting on chairs that protest every time I move. This furniture's more to my liking. A man can get his knees under that table!'

'That table was built at T'Ashmyr's command nearly five hundred years ago. He was the first throwback Emperor of Fair Isle.'

Tulkhan stared at her.

Imoshen realised the General was not drunk at all. 'You can get your knees under that table because it was designed and built for a pure T'En leader who could have looked you in the eye. In the parts of the palace built during the Age of Tribulation, all the furniture is T'En size. You might be a giant amongst your own kind, but you would have fitted right in with my people.'

Wax from Tulkhan's brace of candles fell on his wrist. He grimaced, then shrugged. 'Well, at least I'll be comfortable.'

And he strode after his men.

Imoshen lengthened her stride to keep up with him. They entered the royal wing, where upper-echelon servants clustered in statue niches, pointing and whispering. Tomorrow the tale would be all over T'Diemn, how the barbarians marched roughshod over palace treasures.

In the long gallery they found the elegant gilt-legged, red-velvet chairs piled carelessly on their matching table. Anger and dismay flooded Imoshen, but she did not reveal it. Turning to the servants, she directed them to clear the furniture away and store it. 'We will have our meal now.'

Tulkhan offered Imoshen his arm. When they walked into the formal dining room, the Ghebites gave a cheer. Raising their drinks, they indicated the new table and chairs. Well pleased, Tulkhan took his place at the head of the table and Imoshen joined him. None of them seemed aware how incongruous the heavy dark furniture looked set against the pale splendour of the room's mirrors and gilt-edged plaster work.

'Wine?' Tulkhan offered to pour Imoshen a glass. She declined. He took another mouthful from the flagon, then appeared to recollect that he was not on the battlefield and poured a generous glass. The fine T'En crystal looked fragile in his hands. 'A toast to the greatest army in the known world!'

The men echoed his sentiment, downing their drinks lustily. Crystal goblets slammed emphatically on the tabletop as soon as they were emptied.

A memory of the Empress graciously finger-clicking her approval for a pair of duelling poets struck Imoshen with renewed pain – the Old Empire was truly dead, supplanted by these barbarians. How would the remnants of the T'En nobles react when they saw this kind of behaviour?

Imoshen caught Tulkhan's arm, dropping her voice so that only he could hear. 'General, the nobles from the Keldon Highlands will be here soon. They have not formally surrendered and you have every right to expect an oath of loyalty. But...'

Servants entered with trays of cold meat and cheeses, presented in patterns which were works of art. The Ghebites fell upon them with gusto, grabbing chicken legs and tearing into the white flesh.

'Don't wrinkle your nose like that, Imoshen. The men are hungry. They've been out in the cold all day doing a man's work.'

'I suppose I am lucky they will even eat with me. Men don't share the table with women in Gheeaba, do they?'

He put his glass down. 'Business and battle plans are discussed at the table. These are not for women's ears. In the privacy of his own home a man might invite his favourite wife to eat with him. But this is not Gheeaba and my men have not been home for eleven years.' He gave her a shrewd look. 'We've seen all sorts of customs in mainland palaces. Eating with women is the least of it. Why, I remember one banquet which was served on the naked bodies of nubile virgins.' His dark eyes challenged her. 'They were dessert!'

Imoshen refused to rise to his bait. 'The southern nobles are a proud lot. They traced their blood lines back to the dawn people, children of the Ancients. They were the last to adopt T'En rule and there were sporadic uprisings for two hundred years. It was only at the beginning of the Age of Consolidation that the locals truly accepted their T'En nobles, and by then the highland T'En had grown away from their cousins in the north.

'The Keldon ravines might be rich in precious metals, but they don't provide an easy living. *Scrawny sheep and stiff-necked Keld*, as the saying goes.' She smiled at his expression. 'I'm asking you to go slowly with the Keldon nobles. Soon they will come to the capital to give you their oath of fealty, because they must. But they –'

'They shielded the rebel leader while they smiled and gave me false welcome,' Tulkhan growled. 'I hunted Reothe in those ranges. I know how wild and unforgiving they are.'

Imoshen nodded. 'The land shapes the people. The Keld are few and fiercely loyal. They cannot hope to stand against your army, but they are quick to take offence and slow to forgive. Unless you want to split Fair Isle with civil war, you need to win them over.' She felt General Tulkhan watching her curiously. 'Yes?'

'You advise me against your own people?'

'I advise you for the sake of my people. The fields lie blackened from T'Diemn to the north of Fair Isle. This is a fertile island. Once her towns had great stores of grain, but your men raided them.'

'An army on the move needs to eat.'

Imoshen sighed. 'We've had this conversation before and I argued for cooperation then. I don't want to see this spring's planting ruined because of more fighting. I will not watch my people starve.'

'What do you care? They are True-men and women, not even of the same race as you.'

Even though she knew Tulkhan was baiting her, Imoshen could not hide the heat in her cheeks. 'I belong to Fair Isle. In the centuries since the T'En took this island, my race has interbred with the locals. The blood of T'En, True-man and woman alike has enriched the soil. Only the land endures.'

Tulkhan grimaced. He could not argue with Imoshen's logic but he knew what she was saying. How long before his Ghebite army was absorbed into the larger population of Fair Isle? Would they one day cease to be Ghebites? Would his grandson don the badge of fatherhood and invite everyone to celebrate the birth of a daughter? In Gheeaba the father did not even bother to name a daughter.

'What is wrong with Jacolm?' Imoshen asked, changing the subject.

Before Tulkhan could stop her she hurried down the long table and ordered Jacolm to his feet. The man stood resentfully, favouring his right side. His thick eyebrows pulled together as Imoshen told him to open his shirt.

The room fell silent. Tulkhan tensed. Jacolm's hasty temper was renowned in the ranks. Yet he stood at this woman's command and bared his flesh to her eyes.

Imoshen ran her hands over the man's torso as he gaped, too stunned by her temerity to react. 'Just as I thought, a cracked rib. Let me –'

Jacolm stepped back. 'I will not be tainted by the touch of a Dhamfeer.'

Tulkhan saw Imoshen's face grow pale with the pain of rejection, but he also understood his man's reaction.

Imoshen was too much the diplomat to respond with anger.

'Let me heal your rib,' she offered. 'It must be painful. At least let me strap it.'

But Jacolm's answer was to lace up his shirt. His sword-brother came to his feet in a gesture of solidarity.

Imoshen glanced at Tulkhan, who could only shrug.

She lifted her hands and turned them over for all to see. 'I see no taint on these fingers.' She met Jacolm's eyes. 'True, these are T'En hands with six fingers, but they have healed many a True-man and woman, and it mattered not whether they came from Fair Isle or Gheeaba.' Gracefully she took three steps back and gave them the T'En obeisance among equals. 'I bid you sleep well.'

As Imoshen glided out of the room Tulkhan considered following her, but his men would not be impressed if he ran after *the Dhamfeer bitch*, as they called her none too quietly behind her back.

When the door closed on Imoshen, there was a long moment of silence, then Harholfe made a jest about what would help him get to sleep and the men laughed. But they spoke too loudly and laughed too long, anxious to ignore the issues Imoshen had raised.

Tulkhan could not. He poured himself another wine and drained it grimly.

As Imoshen walked the long gallery she seethed. Jacolm's rejection stung, particularly when she had offered nothing but help. It was two steps forward and one step back with Tulkhan and his Ghebites.

She made her way to her bedchamber, where one of her stronghold guard stood at the door. The young woman straightened at Imoshen's approach. All twenty of Imoshen's stronghold guard could not hope to save her if Tulkhan's elite guard turned on her, but it was the symbol which carried weight. These people were as loyal to her as the General's guard were to him and they had done her proud today.

Imoshen congratulated the young woman, then entered her room, where she found the fire set and candles laid out. She lit the candles and carried them to the bathing chamber beyond. Wearily, she checked that the burner was working, then let the water flow.

Alone at last, Imoshen dropped her guard. As she sank onto a low stool she shuddered, recalling the death ceremony. The Parakletos were things half-glimpsed in nightmares... From now on, she would leave such things to the T'En church priests trained for the task.

Many times she had stood at the Aayel's side while her great-aunt said the words for the dead, and not once had she sensed the Parakletos. Was it because her T'En senses had been less mature? Her gift had always been healing and it came more easily now.

Instinctively she knew she must hide her growing powers from the True-people, particularly the Ghebites. One wrong move and she would be dead, assassinated by enemies or even executed at the General's command.

Though she suspected Tulkhan would regret ordering her death, she knew he would do so if he thought it necessary. She'd heard how he had conquered the defiant mainland kingdoms in the early days of his career. He had been utterly ruthless. Yet, when Tulkhan met her eyes, she sometimes thought she read...

Anger fired Imoshen. She rose and prowled the chamber. A metallic taste settled on her tongue. With a start she recognised the first signs of the T'En gifts moving unbidden, and unwanted. Dismay flooded her. If only she knew how to harness her gifts. If only her great-aunt had lived long enough to instruct her.

Before the Aayel died, she had revealed that Imoshen's parents had forbidden her to instruct Imoshen in the art of using her powers. All those years she had walked at the Aayel's side, learning herb lore, memorising the T'Enchiridion, watching her great-aunt serve the people, she might have been learning about her heritage.

Instead she was ignorant.

Imoshen grew utterly still. The Aayel hadn't lived, but the palace library was even more extensive than her stronghold's. The palace library was sure to contain learned discourses on the T'En gifts. It might take all winter, but she would sift every ancient document.

If only she didn't have to organise the feast to celebrate Tulkhan's signing of the church agreement.

Resentment flooded her. She hated palace protocol and had never wanted to play a role in court life. Yet now she had the responsibility of running the palace. How her sister would have envied her!

Imoshen's eyes filled with tears. Her sister would never mix in the Empress's inner circle. Her brother would never compete at the Midsummer Feast for the duelling poet's crown of fresh flowers. All her kinsfolk had died in a futile attempt to halt the General's advance. How could she discard them so easily to plot for her own future?

Imoshen hardened her heart. To survive she had to look forward. She would not let the General relegate her to the position of a Ghebite woman – a piece of comfortable furniture to be used when needed then put away in a gilded room. She would be the architect of her future and the future of Fair Isle.

Imoshen tested the water and turned off the spigot. She sank into the bath, feeling her muscles relax.

Today she had saved the life of the cooper's child, but she had offended the Beatific, who was so ready to distrust her.

Yet the Beatific should have been her ally. After all, the church retained its position as arbiter of law only because Imoshen had convinced Tulkhan to sign the document.

Between the church, the proud Keldon nobles, the conniving mainland ambassadors and the arrogant Ghebites, she must somehow keep the peace while consolidating her position with General Tulkhan and his position with the people of Fair Isle.

So much was at stake, her head spun.

SATISFIED WITH THE menu for this evening's feast, Imoshen left the kitchen wing. She had only just entered the main gallery when she heard raised voices echoing through the great marble foyer.

Built during the Age of Consolidation, the palace entrance had been designed to impress, with huge marble columns, a grand divided staircase and an intricately painted ceiling which appeared to open up to the heavens.

Imoshen peered around a marble column and cursed softly. A party of Keldon nobles had arrived sooner than expected. Lord Fairban and his three daughters were welcomed by the flustered palace footman. Behind the old lord an entourage of servants waited, wary but curious.

This meant more places to set at the feast tonight, more volatile tempers to soothe. The Keld had not yet formally surrendered or offered fealty to General Tulkhan, and the situation was extremely delicate.

What must her southern cousins think of her, aiding and abetting the invader? Surely they realised she had to choose the path of least resistance to ensure her survival, just as they must give lip-service to General Tulkhan to avoid having their lands and titles forfeited?

What good was honour if you were dead?

Below her the master of the bedchambers arrived and hastened to greet Lord Fairban. Imoshen smiled. Let the palace dignitary earn his keep. He could escort the new arrivals to their chambers while she spoke with the master of ceremonies and adjusted the seating.

But after this was done, Imoshen decided to deliver the dinner invitation to Lord Fairban's daughters in person. She would need the support of the Keldon noblewomen if they were to civilise the Ghebites.

Imoshen plucked her metal comb from her key chain and scratched briefly on the door tang. To her trained ear every comb had a different sound. She could identify a servant or a noble by the note their comb made when run across a door's metal tang. The Ghebites' habit of thundering on doors grated on her nerves but it certainly identified them as a race.

Discarding protocol, she entered the suite's outer chamber. A maid gave a muffled shriek and ran off to get her mistresses. The Fairban sisters entered, followed by curious maids laden with clothing and jewellery.

Trying to hide their surprise, they gave the obeisance appropriate for the Empress. But the Empress would not have slipped unannounced into their rooms. The younger two Fairban women exchanged stiff smiles and Imoshen recognised that tolerant, half-embarrassed look. They could not ignore her height and her colouring. She was so obviously pure T'En that even her own family had found her an embarrassment.

But she was not going to apologise for her existence. Instead, Imoshen studied the three women. Would they suit her purpose? The two younger girls were very like their father – small, fine-boned and truly of the people – but the eldest who stepped forward graciously was nearly her own height.

'I greet you, T'Imoshen,' Lady Cariah said. In her bearing Imoshen recognised the polish of the Old Empire. The woman was several years older than her, in her early twenties.

A pang of insecurity stabbed Imoshen. How she longed to have that air of effortless elegance. Again she was reminded of the painfully self-conscious sixteen-year-old she had been on her first visit to the palace less than two years ago. Just finding her way about the endless rooms had been a challenge, without trying to unravel the politics of the court. But she was no longer that child. She had a role to play and she needed the Fairban sisters' cooperation to do it.

Imoshen took the older woman's hand, returning her formal greeting.

She couldn't help admiring Lady Cariah's hair. It fell around her shoulders like a shawl of burnished copper. Good. All three of the Fairban women were beautiful enough to arouse the interest of the Ghebite commanders.

'I am honoured to greet you and your sisters. We need the civilising influence of your presence at...' Imoshen's fingers curled around Cariah's, the invitation on the tip of her tongue, but all thought fled as she registered the oddity of the woman's hand. Lord Fairban's eldest daughter had six fingers. She did not have the wine-dark eyes, but she carried the T'En blood.

Startled, Imoshen's gaze darted to Cariah's face. She read tolerant amusement in the older woman's gaze.

Heat flooded Imoshen's cheeks. She was no better than the younger Fairban women. Yet, why did they find her T'En characteristics disturbing when their own sister carried T'En blood? Perhaps it was because Imoshen confronted them with something they wished to deny.

'Our mother bad the wine-dark eyes, as well as the six fingers,' Cariah explained, seeing Imoshen's confusion.

'Your... your mother?' Imoshen faltered.

'Long dead. Father would never bond again.'

The conversation was much too personal for Old Empire protocol, but then Imoshen had always had trouble containing her unruly tongue. Her own mother had despaired of her.

The enormity of her loss hit her.

'My mother is dead too. They are all dead!' Even as tears threatened, shame flooded Imoshen. But she could not contain the soul-deep sobs which shook her. She had not let herself grieve. There'd been no time, and now it was as if a dam had broken. Unable to contain the fury of her tears, Imoshen turned away, covering her face in despair.

Surely this worldly woman would despise her.

But Cariah slid her arms around Imoshen's shoulders, offering unconditional comfort, and for a few moments Imoshen knew the peace of compassion as she weathered the storm of her loss.

Then she pulled away.

Ashamed to have revealed her weakness, she walked to a mirror. As she composed herself she was acutely aware of the shocked noblewomen and their maids reflected behind her. They had been silenced by her social solecism.

'Forgive me.' Imoshen turned to face them, giving the lesser bow of supplication. 'I am here to invite you to the celebration tonight.'

'You honour us,' the Lady Cariah said, and though Imoshen searched that beautiful face, she could read no mockery.

Imoshen took formal leave of them and even as the door closed she could hear the buzz of comment behind her. Her cheeks flamed with humiliation.

Though they were stubborn Keldon nobles, poor cousins of the prosperous T'En court, they were still steeped in its traditions. The expression of grief, love, all strong emotions had been highly ritualised in the court.

Imoshen castigated herself. To weep in the arms of a stranger was unheard of. The Fairban sisters would think her as uncouth as the Ghebite barbarians. How could she look the Lady Cariah in the eye tonight?

But she had to. Somehow she would hide her discomfort, for she could not leave the General to host the evening alone. Bracing herself, she set off to ask the cook to prepare Keldon delicacies.

'T'IMOSHEN?' AN ANXIOUS voice called. 'Where is the Empress?'

The cook looked to Imoshen, who summoned a smile, even though the sound of running feet made her stomach cramp with fear. Hopefully, it was simply a crisis of protocol precipitated by an unthinking Ghebite.

A youth thrust the door open and stood there panting. By his dress he was one of the outdoor servants, and by his state he had searched the endless corridors of the palace for her.

'I am here.' Her voice sounded calm. Only she could feel the pounding of her heart. Absurdly, her first thought was for Tulkhan's safety.

'The Ghebite priest has gone mad,' the youth announced. 'He's destroying the hothouse!'

This was the last thing Imoshen had expected. A laugh almost escaped her. The hothouse supplied the palace with year-round fresh vegetables. Why would that pompous self-important priest object to fresh carrots?

'Come and see!' Even in his agitation, the youth did not dare touch her.

Imoshen marched out of the kitchen, followed by the kitchen staff. Human nature being what it was, they welcomed any excuse to stop work, and besides, this promised to be entertaining; for no one liked the Cadre.

She smiled grimly, but the smile slipped from her face when she heard the sound of smashing glass. Even in T'Diemn glass was valuable, especially glass crafted for large windows.

She caught the arm of the nearest scullery maid. 'Fetch General Tulkhan.'

The girl gave the Old Empire obeisance and hurried off.

With the youth dancing in front of her like an agitated puppy, and a growing crowd of spectators in tow, Imoshen approached the large hothouse. Several anxious gardeners ran up to her, their voices strident with outrage as they told her how the priest had marched into the hothouse raving about blasphemy.

It made no sense. No sense at all.

Imoshen thrust the door open and the heat hit her, followed by the rich smell of fecund earth. Tray after tray of sprouting seeds stretched before her. Inoffensive tomato seedlings lay bruised and trampled.

Unaware of his audience, the Cadre swung the rake at another window. The sound of shattering glass threatened Imoshen's composure. She tasted the forewarning of the T'En on her tongue, aroused by her anger.

'Cease this destruction immediately!' Her voice rang out as she strode through debris.

But the priest was too intent to hear her. He positioned himself before another window and raised the rake. Imoshen came up behind him, tore the rake from his hand and tossed it aside. She caught him by the scruff of his neck, swinging him off his feet.

Empowered by fury, it took little effort for her to hold the Cadre off the ground. The startled priest shrieked and clutched frantically at his collar, which had risen up under his chin.

'What is the matter with you?' Imoshen shook him like a dog shakes a rat and said the first thing that came into her head. 'Do you hate fresh carrots?'

The absurdity of it made the servants laugh. She suspected they were as relieved as she was to find the threat was not armed Ghebites slaughtering innocents. The priest clawed at his throat, his face going red. Imoshen opened her mouth to speak, but General Tulkhan forestalled her.

'What's going on here?' His deep voice cut through the nervous giggles, silencing everyone.

Imoshen dropped the priest in disgust, indicating the destruction. 'Isn't it obvious? Your priest objects to fresh vegetables!'

Tulkhan fought the urge to laugh. When frantic palace servants had summoned him, he'd expected the worst. He turned to the Cadre. 'Explain yourself.'

Glaring at Imoshen, the priest rearranged his elaborate collar ruff and dirt-stained robe of office. 'It is an abomination!'

'Since when is fresh food an abomination?' Imoshen countered.

Tulkhan gestured to the odd, glass-roofed building. 'What is this place?'

'The hothouse where the palace's fresh vegetables are grown,' Imoshen said. 'You wouldn't need this in Gheeaba. During our long cold winters the windows capture the heat of the sun.'

'It is an abomination in the eyes of the great Akha Khan!' the Cadre insisted and darted past Imoshen to pull a plant out by its roots, shaking it fiercely so that damp earth flew everywhere. 'This is the abomination, this and all its brothers!'

Imoshen wrinkled her nose. 'You object to a cup of herbal tea?'

Tulkhan felt his lips twitch but kept his voice neutral. 'This is a tea plant?'

'We dry the leaves, boil water and make an infusion which we drink,' Imoshen explained. 'It is one of many teas sold in the tea-houses throughout –'

'Tell him what it's used for,' the priest insisted, his eyes gleaming triumphantly.

'Women drink it to control their fertility,' Imoshen replied.

'Exactly!' The priest stepped forward, waving the plant under General Tulkhan's nose. 'This is the root of the evil in Fair Isle. This plant is an abomination. No wonder the women of this island know no shame. No wonder their men are emasculated!'

Spittle flew from the Cadre's lips and Tulkhan sensed the locals draw back.

'It is a woman's lot to bear children. She is the property of her husband, and the sons she produces are his heirs. The more sons the better, to make a strong house-line!' The Cadre glared at Imoshen. 'To interfere with a woman's natural bearing of children is an abomination, an affront to Akha Khan. Think of all the Ghebite sons who would never be born to take up arms if this plant were used in Gheeaba!'

Imoshen made a rude sound. 'I should prepare a shipload and send it –'

'You dare to mock me, Dhamfeer bitch?' the priest rounded on her. 'You are twice over an abomination!'

The palace servants gasped, turning fearfully to Imoshen. She towered over the priest, her brilliant eyes flashing dangerously. Even from half a body-length away, Tulkhan could feel the overflow of her T'En gifts rolling off her skin.

'Leaving aside my race,' Imoshen's control was more frightening than rage, 'leaving aside the fact that Ghebite men don't think their women possess true souls but are only one step above the beasts of the field, I would like you to explain to me what is wrong with preventing unwanted children? Surely it is better for a family to be able to feed the children they have than to breed irresponsibly?'

'See how she twists everything?' the priest demanded of Tulkhan. 'Cunning Dhamfeer. Listen to her long enough and you'll believe black is white. General, you must protect yourself from her. You must protect your men from the women of Fair Isle. These women would emasculate our men, play them false with their vile herb. What man does not want sons? What man would not believe himself a lesser man if his wife did not produce a babe every year, or at least every second year?'

'Like a prize pig?' Imoshen asked, her eyes glittering.

Tulkhan was aware of her fury, but he was also aware that a Ghebite warrior who had risen high enough to afford to keep three or even four wives expected to see them all heavy with child. Thirty, maybe even forty children was not unheard of. At least half would be male. With all those sons to further the interests of his house-line, while his daughters married to consolidate alliances, he would be considered a rich man.

But that was back in Gheeaba and this was Fair Isle.

The priest flung the herb to the cobbles and ground it underfoot. 'General, you must order all these plants destroyed. Send your men throughout the island to collect them. Pile these vile herbs in every village square and burn the lot. It is the only way to teach the women of Fair Isle their place!'

Imoshen felt her world tilt on its axis. General Tulkhan's Ghebite features gave nothing away. Surely he could not be considering this? The priest would undo six hundred years of civilisation and reduce the women of Fair Isle to slaves like their Ghebite counterparts.

She covered the distance between them, instinctively taking the General's arm, seeking contact with his mind. In the moment before he raised his guard she sensed his reluctance to shame the priest.

Her fingers tightened. 'Every woman of Fair Isle grows this herb in her garden. Every woman decides when to have a child. Would you deny her this? Would you make her fearful of physical love? As a healer I know there are women who cannot carry a baby. It would kill them.' Imoshen searched Tulkhan's face. His features remained impassive. How could she convince him? She recalled his one secret fear. 'There are other women who have trouble conceiving children. They use a variety of this herb to bring on fertility. Would you deny those women and their bond-partners the joy of their own child?'

She saw a muscle jump under the General's coppery skin.

'Cadre.' Tulkhan's voice was harsh in the strained silence. 'An agreement with the T'En church has been signed.'

Imoshen took a step back, releasing the General's arm.

'By the terms of this agreement,' Tulkhan continued, 'we will not interfere with their worship and they will not interfere with ours. I charge you not to force your beliefs on these people. This law you propose would be impossible to enforce. Any plot of dirt or windowsill pot can be used to grow this herb. Would you have my army reduced to gardeners, rooting out unwanted weeds?'

Put that way, it did seem absurd. The palace staff tittered and the Cadre glared at Imoshen. She held his eyes. He had brought this ridicule upon himself.

'Take care of your soldiers' souls, Cadre,' Imoshen advised, linking her arm through Tulkhan's. Whatever dissonance there might be between them personally, before his men and her people they had to present a united front. 'Leave the ruling of Fair Isle to us. Come, General.'

They left the Cadre fuming and walked towards the hothouse door.

Once they were outside, Tulkhan turned to Imoshen, deliberately removing her arm from his. 'Don't think I don't know what you are about.'

Imoshen stiffened. 'General, what is at stake here is much larger than you or me. It is the fate of the women of Fair Isle. Would you see half your subjects reduced to wife-slaves? Would you be the cause of a generation of unwanted children left to roam the streets, begging or stealing their bread, as I have heard they do on the mainland?'

'T'Imoshen, a word?' a gardener spoke, hovering at a polite distance.

Imoshen searched the General's face. He was a clever man but he was also steeped in the culture of his people. How far could she push him before he pushed back?

'I have work to do,' Tulkhan ground out, according her the barest, nod of civility.

Imoshen gave him the obeisance between equals, the significance of which would not be lost on her servants and, knowing how sharp he was, it would not be lost on the General either.

Imoshen turned to the aggrieved palace gardeners, assuring them repairs would be carried out in time for the seedlings to re-establish. But her mind was on the General. Tonight the two of them must sit side by side at the feasting table without revealing their differences.

Chapter Four

TULKHAN'S GAZE FOLLOWED Imoshen as she stepped lightly through the patterns of a complicated dance. Three pretty noblewomen made up the corners of the intricate pattern; together they partnered four town dignitaries. His commanders watched, waiting for a Ghebite dance so they could break in and claim the women.

Tulkhan noted how Imoshen moved with casual grace. She wore a deep plum velvet gown. It was the same vivid colour as her eyes and it made her pale skin look even paler. Her hair was loose, confined only by a small circlet of electrum inset with purple amethysts. When she turned, her hair fanned out over her shoulders like a rippling sheet of white satin. She came to the end of the dance, her hair and skirt settling around her long limbs. Tulkhan swallowed. He wanted to run his fingers through those long pale tresses, wanted to lean close and inhale her heady scent. Just watching her made him ache with need, and there wasn't another woman anywhere who could do that to him.

'T'Imoshen dances well,' observed his table companion.

He turned to the Beatific. In Gheeaba she would not dare to address him. An unmarried woman, or a married woman past child-bearing age, was thought fit only to mind the small children or feed the animals.

'You seem distracted, Prince Tulkhan.'

'I am not a prince.' He baulked at explaining the complicated family structure of his people. 'As first son of the King's concubine I was not given a title. I earned my position through merit and years of service in my father's army. I prefer to be called by the title I've earned.'

'And soon to be King of Fair Isle,' she agreed smoothly.

He caught her clever hazel eyes on him. Pinpoints of golden candlelight danced in her pupils. He reminded himself that he must not underestimate her simply because she was a woman. Imoshen had taught him that.

'I must congratulate you on your forthcoming bonding, General.'

The words were innocuous enough, but there was something in her tone which warned him to be on his guard. Did he detect a trace of mockery? Did these people think him presumptuous to crown himself king?

Of course they did. He was barely three generations from his nomadic herdsman grandfather who, through his wiles and great stature, had united the Ghebite tribes.

'Thank you,' Tulkhan said, turning to watch Imoshen, who was making the robust Ghebite dance a thing of precision and grace. How could he wait for their bonding?

'T'Imoshen is very... *beautiful* isn't the right word. The T'En are too dangerous to be beautiful. They have a kind of terrible beauty. You never met the rebel leader, T'Reothe?' The Beatific paused, making it a question.

Tulkhan shifted in his seat, trying to appear only mildly interested. He neither denied nor admitted meeting Reothe.

Deep in the Keldon Highlands, Tulkhan had inadvertently called on the Ancients by spilling blood on one of their sacred sites. Attracted by the surge in power, Reothe had appeared before him. The rebel leader had laughed when he had realised who Tulkhan was and cursed him, saying, *I am your death. You do not know it, but you are a dead man who walks and talks.*'

His words had often returned to haunt Tulkhan's darkest hours.

'I was surprised when the Emperor and Empress approved Reothe's betrothal to Imoshen,' the Beatific said. 'By custom she would have taken the vows of chastity at seventeen when she made her Vow of Expiation. Instead the Empress informed me I was to witness the historic bonding of the last two pure T'En. They were to be joined this spring, did you know?' She did not pause for him to reply. 'Reothe could have looked to almost any woman for his partner, any woman but a throwback. He went to the Emperor and Empress for special dispensation. By the time I learnt of it, they had already agreed. It was so unexpected. The custom has always been to marry out, T'En male to True-woman. Imoshen the First made it mandatory. Do you know much of the T'En history?'

Tulkhan no longer pretended only polite interest. He spoke slowly. 'There are rumours of great powers.'

She nodded. 'T'En gifts can also be a curse. The first Imoshen and her shipload of refugees fled their homeland to escape persecution. She ordered the ship burned.'

'I was told Imoshen the First was an explorer.'

'With small children and old people?' The Beatific smiled. 'No, she rewrote our history for her own purposes.'

Tulkhan met the woman's eyes frankly. 'How do you know this?'

'I have access to the journals of our early church leaders. When the first Imoshen set out to take this land, she was utterly ruthless. She had about her a band of devoted T'En warriors – the legendary Paragian Guard. They'd sworn a gift-enforced oath to serve her. Those who died in her service were destined to serve beyond death. They became the Parakletos.' She made a furtive sign before resuming. 'It was only through the dedication of this Paragian Guard that Imoshen the First was able to subdue the people. But once the island was taken, she disbanded the guard and ordered her own kind to mingle with the locals.

'She took a vow of celibacy and all pure T'En females since have followed her example. Her only surviving daughter became Beatific. Imoshen the First bonded her pure T'En son to the old royalty, just as you are doing. But she did it for an even stronger reason.'

Tulkhan contained his impatience, very aware that this woman enjoyed playing him like a fish on a line.

'Pure T'En are unstable. Even amongst Imoshen the First's people there were not many pure T'En. Throwbacks like Imoshen and Reothe can inherit great gifts, but they are also cursed.'

'Explain.'

The Beatific smiled. 'Well, even the royal family were wary of Reothe. They were happy when he absented himself on long sea voyages of exploration and trade.'

'Piracy, you mean. I have heard about his exploits.'

The Beatific held his eyes. 'Reothe was acting under a charter from the Empress herself. His task was to harry the trade of Fair Isle's enemies on the high seas. A small wealthy island such as Fair Isle must protect her trading interests or the greedy will think her weak. Reothe was a great sea captain. He explored the archipelago and opened new trade routes.' She shrugged. 'However, the pure T'En males are a danger to themselves and to those around them. Who knows what mischief Reothe might have caused if he had remained at court? As it was, the Empress had to remove one of her other adopted sons to preserve the peace. It is true that the Empress loved Reothe. She reared him from the age of ten, but as he matured, so did his powers. They first begin to manifest at puberty. The pure T'En have a range of gifts, from the ability to scry or manipulate the minds of others, to more practical abilities like healing. In the females the gifts are generally weak, but in the males they can be quite powerful. It was expected Reothe's gifts would be strong, but he was adept at hiding them. The T'En have ever been a secretive race and Reothe was true to his blood.'

She lowered her voice. 'Why, the Emperor himself confided in me that he feared Reothe might supplant his own children. And then there is the question of why the Emperor and Empress granted Reothe dispensation to bond with Imoshen. I advised them against it, but they were fixed on the idea, even though it flouted six hundred years of custom.' Her brilliant eyes held his. 'I often wonder whether Reothe used their trust and affection to sway their judgment.'

Tulkhan's hand tightened on the goblet's stem.

The Beatific sat back. With languid grace, she selected a cube of diced fruit, slipping the choice morsel between her lips. She dipped her fingers in the little bowl provided and wiped them fastidiously.

'I can only speculate as to why the first Imoshen led her shipload of refugees from our homeland. But it has long been the role of the church to limit any damage the T'En might do. When the remaining Paragian Guard were disbanded, they chose to serve the church. They formed the T'Enplars, warrior priests sworn to uphold the sanctity of the T'En gifts, but it was from their very ranks that the first T'En went rogue.

'Sardonyx led the revolt of sixty-four. His own cousin Empress Abularassa joined with the first Beatific to contain him. They created the Tractarians to balance the power of the T'Enplars. Balance, that is what *En* means in High T'En. After Sardonyx's death, T'Abularassa built a tower in his memory. Sard's Tower. Since then the families of the rogue T'En have commemorated their loss with a tower of tears, and the Beatific has been empowered to declare one of the T'En rogue if there is enough evidence of treason against the church and the Empress. For over five centuries the Tractarians have hunted down rogue T'En. You will have heard of the stonings?'

'It's been over a hundred years!'

'I know. There has not been the need. After the last stoning no pure T'En males were born for over seventy years, and the Tractarians withered. But since Reothe came to maturity they have been revitalised under the leadership of Murgon.' She gestured without actually pointing. 'That's him at the next table, third from the left. Tall thin man with the T'En eyes.' She saw Tulkhan's surprise. 'Those of part blood are particularly sensitive to the use of the gifts.'

'Would it not be simpler to kill all pure T'En babies at birth?' Tulkhan asked.

'We are not barbarians!' Disgust made the Beatific's voice sharp.

'I meant why wait? Why not contain the threat?'

Her eyes narrowed. 'Not all T'En go rogue. They, like all nobles, are taught that their duty is to serve Fair Isle. Their T'En gifts can serve True-men and women. Look at Imoshen's ability to heal. The people revere the T'En.'

'In abstract?'

He surprised a smile from her, but she did not acknowledge his question. 'General?'

Tulkhan looked up to see Imoshen's flushed, smiling face. Guilt stirred in him. On Imoshen's advice he'd signed the document that enabled the Beatific to retain her position of power, and now the woman was undermining Imoshen. Politics!

Disgust filled Tulkhan. He much preferred the knife-edge life and death decisions of the battlefield. At least when death held a blade to his throat it did not smile and whisper words of comfort.

Imoshen gestured to the small man at her side. 'Let me introduce the first of the Keldon nobles to accept our hospitality. Lord Fairban.'

Tulkhan came to his feet. 'So we meet again, my lord. This time in my keep.'

'No one can say the Keld dishonour the laws of hospitality,' Fairban bristled.

Tulkhan smiled grimly. 'I'm sure you will find my hospitality everything yours was and more.'

Silence hung heavy between them as Imoshen glanced from one to the other.

'General Tulkhan spent a night at my holdings while he was hunting rebels,' the old lord answered Imoshen's unasked question.

Imoshen's eyes widened.

'How are your beautiful daughters, Lord Fairban?' the Beatific asked.

Under the cover of their conversation Imoshen turned to Tulkhan. 'Come dance with me, General?'

'No.' Dancing was not something a general needed to be proficient in. Yet he longed to take Imoshen in his arms in front of everyone, to know that when he put his hands on her she was his.

What was he thinking? The Beatific had told him the T'En were unstable, a danger to others and themselves. Was Imoshen exerting some kind of mental pull on him?

'General?'

Looking into her teasing face Tulkhan could not believe she was consciously manipulating him. The only power she had over him at this moment was the pull of his body to hers. But that was powerful enough and that was too much.

'You mock me, Imoshen.' He made his voice hard and contemptuous as he sat down. 'What time does a general have for dancing? Ask someone else.'

She hesitated, her features briefly registering the humiliation of his rejection. Then she stepped closer, her voice dropping. 'Since you don't know the T'En dances, General, I could have the minstrels strike up a Ghebite jig.'

Just for a moment he thought he read something in her face beneath the teasing, a need. Perhaps she wanted him to step away from everyone else to be with her and her alone. He hesitated, surprised by how much he wanted to believe this. Shaking his head, he chastised himself.

A formal mask settled over Imoshen's face. Twice he had rejected her before the Beatific, who was certainly listening in to their conversation. He wanted to recall his hasty words, but Imoshen was already moving gracefully aside. Only he had seen her quickly veiled disappointment, only he knew the hurt she hid as she stepped lightly off the dais to join the others.

Or did he? Perhaps he was just a lust-crazed fool projecting these finer feelings onto a manipulative Dhamfeer. He craved her, yet he knew she was his by necessity and not by choice.

Imoshen took several steps from the table, not really aware of where she was heading. Only pride made her approach a group on the dance floor. Unshed tears stung her eyes.

The General had not seen the malicious gleam in the Beatific's gaze, but Imoshen had. That was good, she told herself, for now she knew that the leader of the T'En church had enjoyed her humiliation and was very likely working to undermine her. So be it, at least now Imoshen knew where she stood.

'T'Imoshen?'

It was Cariah. Imoshen's heart sank. Had Lord Fairban's daughter seen General Tulkhan reject her? Imoshen turned expecting contempt, but found instead understanding.

'The Ghebites want to start a fresh dance circle,' Cariah said, slipping an arm through Imoshen's. 'And I need another female to make up the numbers.'

'Then how can I refuse?' Imoshen replied with a grateful smile. 'When the rest of the Keldon nobles arrive we will have the numbers for the formal dances.' And more tempers to soothe. But she did not add this.

Cariah met her eyes, a rueful smile lighting her face. 'The Keld can be quick to take insult.'

Imoshen blinked. Had Cariah simply anticipated her, or did she have a little of the T'En gift for skimming thoughts? There was nothing in her expression to suggest it was anything more than a lucky guess.

'True, they can be touchy,' Imoshen said, 'but then the Ghebites are so good at giving unintended slights.'

A chuckle escaped Cariah.

Imoshen slowed her step before they joined the circle. Instinct told her to trust this woman. 'Cariah, I am all alone with no one to guide me in court protocol. Will you help me ease the transition of power? I need to find common ground for the Keld and the Ghebites.'

She saw her request had surprised Cariah, who hesitated mid-step then continued smoothly. 'Commander Jacolm, your partner.'

It appeared to be an unfortunate choice. The man's heavy black brows drew down, making it clear he would have preferred Cariah's company. Imoshen's stomach clenched – yet another rejection. Then she turned to see Cariah take her place in the dance circle with her father, Lord Fairban.

Cariah's answer had been to act on her request.

When the music started Cariah caught Imoshen's eye and for the first time since the Aayel's death Imoshen did not feel cast adrift. Then the dance swept them apart as they circled their partners before moving to the next. If Cariah was prepared to do her part, Imoshen must do hers. As they changed partners she set about winning him over.

Tulkhan watched Imoshen take Lord Fairban's hand. The top of the man's grey head came up to Imoshen's chin, but Tulkhan could tell she was charming him with a word, a teasing smile. When she moved away to join the women who circled the men, Lord Fairban's eyes followed her.

'That is another of their tricks.' The Beatific gestured briefly to the dance floor. 'When they choose, the T'En can be delightful companions. The males make notoriously good lovers. But it is said they can only know true release in each other's arms. Of course, with the women's vow of celibacy that is impossible.'

Though his gaze never left Imoshen, Tulkhan was aware of the Beatific sipping her wine.

'Discarding her vows of celibacy does not seem to trouble Imoshen,' the Beatific observed.

Tulkhan snorted. He could not believe he was having this conversation with the leader of the T'En church. In Gheeaba there were no females in the church hierarchy and the priests were celibate. Recalling the earthy Harvest Festival at Imoshen's stronghold, something told him celibacy was not a prerequisite for the priesthood in Fair Isle.

Did the Beatific have her choice of lovers? Turning to study her mature, sensual beauty he could well believe she did.

Imoshen laughed and his gaze was drawn irresistibly back to her. She looked over the heads of those around her and their eyes met. He realised she was willing him to share her amusement. An unexpected longing took him. He wanted to share her quick understanding, to know they had a special affinity.

The path he'd chosen would be a difficult one, but he would not relinquish Fair Isle and Imoshen at any price. If she was at his side and they were truly united in purpose, then it was not an impossible dream. He could have it all. He could hold Fair Isle and savour Imoshen's willing companionship.

Second wife's son, second best, supplanted heir. He desperately wanted the supremacy of Fair Isle, and Imoshen was the key. Politically he had to take her to his bed, but gut-deep he knew he would have had to have her even if it was political suicide.

What was he thinking?

If the Beatific was to be believed, a True-man could not even satisfy a female Dhamfeer. And he had arranged to marry the last pure T'En female in a 'bonding' ceremony which would make her his equal in the eyes of the law, a law she had manoeuvred him into recognising.

He was not fool enough to let his lust rule his head. He did not doubt Imoshen's devotion to Fair Isle, it was her commitment to him he was unsure of. Once his rule was cemented and accepted by the nobles of the Keldon Highlands, how long before she no longer needed him?

Perhaps she was merely buying time for Reothe to rebuild his forces. Cold suspicion shook Tulkhan. Were the last two T'En in league against him?

The dance finished and Imoshen returned to the seat on Tulkhan's right.

Her smile faltered when she met his eyes. 'What is it, General?'

Her hand rose to touch his arm, but he recoiled. She had used a touch like this to pluck the image of his mother's lonely death from his mind and had used it against him. 'Don't touch me.'

Her expression hardened into a beautiful mask. Once again she was that alien, unknowable creature, the Dhamfeer.

Imoshen's heart sank and she clasped her fingers tightly beneath the table. She didn't need to touch the General to read his emotions. At this moment he feared and hated her.

She detected a slight movement to his left. The Beatific was devouring the succulent white meat of a roasted bird with dainty but decisive bites. Imoshen knew this woman had been planting seeds of doubt, poisoning Tulkhan's mind.

Drawing a quick breath, Imoshen searched for a neutral topic of conversation. 'With Lord Fairban's arrival we can expect to see the rest of the Keld soon. It would be best to hold off awarding your men their estates until the nobles are here to witness the ceremony.'

Tulkhan's wary eyes met hers.

She lifted a hand to deny any ulterior motive. It was simply good politics to assuage the older nobility's feelings when investing new nobility.

'Very well,' Tulkhan conceded. 'We'll give them eight days.'

Imoshen had to be satisfied with that. He had said *we*, not I. Once they were bonded and Tulkhan lay naked in her arms she knew there would be no cause for mistrust. How could there be when they shared their bodies and their minds?

Wharrd beckoned, Tulkhan rose abruptly and left her to her thoughts. She watched as he spoke with his bone-setter. Both men wore the dark breeches and boots of the Ghebite soldier. Tulkhan favoured a red velvet thigh-length shirt. A heavy belt worked with gold filigree inlaid with niello was slung low on his narrow hips. He wore his thick straight hair loose on his shoulders. Two long plaits threaded with small gold beads fell from his temples. By Old Empire standards he wore too much vibrant colour and too much gold ornamentation. Despite this, he looked utterly at ease in his barbarian splendour, dwarfing the more soberly dressed males of T'Diemn.

'The General struts like a peacock, yet he puts our men to shame,' the Beatific remarked.

Startled, Imoshen met her eyes. 'I must be growing used to the Ghebite love of display,' she said to fill the silence. Alone with the church leader, now was her chance to find the woman's key, the secret weakness that would open her up to Imoshen's powers. Other than healing, Imoshen's gifts were weak. The Aayel had been good at reading people. Though Imoshen had attempted this skill many times, it was only on first meeting General Tulkhan that she had successfully plucked the key image of his dying mother from his mind.

Since coming to the palace she had been forced to develop her ability to read people. Every day she soothed tempers and assuaged hurt feelings. Everyone had a weakness, everyone could be reached.

Imoshen offered to refill the Beatific's wine glass. 'Let us toast to preserving the dignity of Fair Isle's women.'

She poured the wine, then they exchanged looks across the rims of the glasses. At least in this they understood each other.

Imoshen savoured her drink. 'Signing the document was an important step, but every day in subtle ways they grind us down. It will be a long battle, I fear.'

'A battle we must win.' The Beatific put down her glass.

Imoshen placed her hand over the other woman's. 'I need your help in this.' But when she gently probed the Beatific's mind, she discovered that it was sealed against her. Not only that, but she was very much aware of Imoshen's attempt to trawl her thoughts.

'Remove your hand!' The Beatific enunciated each word with icy clarity. 'In the Old Empire that would have been unpardonable.'

Heat flooded Imoshen's cheeks. None of the palace servants or guildmasters had been aware of her subtle mental touch. 'Forgive me, I –'

'Indeed?' True-woman eyes studied her and narrowed. Then the Beatific smiled, but it was hard and patronising. 'It seems I must forgive you, for how could you know better? Your parents deliberately kept you ignorant of your T'En heritage. If you had been born in the Age of Consolidation, one of the pure T'En would have been nominated as your mentor when you were ten. This T'En would have trained you in your obligations to Fair Isle, preparing you to take the Vow of Expiation at seventeen. But there was no one who could –'

'The Aayel could have.'

'No. She too was untrained. When T'Obazim went to her parents offering to mentor her, they broke with tradition and refused. He appealed to the church. For two years it went through different appeals, with a final submission to the Empress. But before she could give her decision, Obazim went rogue, demanding the girl be given into his care against her family's wishes. The Tractarians hunted him down and he was stoned.'

'I know. The Aayel told me how she witnessed his death. She was only twelve.' Imoshen shuddered, recalling how her great-aunt had described the rogue T'En's execution. The Aayel had lived the rest of her life in the shadow of that memory. Imoshen had not forgotten her great-aunt's ambiguous comments about the church's motivations either. 'The Aayel told me that T'Obazim captured her mind so that she experienced his death with him.'

The Beatific looked grim. 'That was cruel. Did the Aayel also tell you that Reothe's parents approached her to mentor him? No? She turned them down. Shortly after that, they committed ritual suicide.'

'I never understood how they could abandon him like that.'

The Beatific looked upon her with cruel pity. 'I believe they could not face the terrible grief of building a Tower of Tears for Reothe.'

'No.' The denial was instinctive. 'Reothe has served Fair Isle on the high seas and here at home. He had the love of the Empress, some say T'Ysanna's love too. With the protection of the Empress and her heir he would never have been declared rogue. Not that he would ever go...' Under the Beatific's frank gaze Imoshen ran down.

'Your great-aunt was investigated but exonerated of any responsibility for the deaths of Reothe's parents.'

'I did not know.' Imoshen was shocked.

'How could you? Your parents refused to admit your T'En nature. Before you turned ten my predecessor asked that you be gifted to the T'En church, but your parents refused.'

Imoshen was glad. It would have been terrifying to have been cast adrift at so young an age in a great building like the Basilica, surrounded by unfriendly True-men and women. Poor Reothe. On the death of his parents the Empress had become his guardian and the royal court his home.

'I see you are troubled.' The Beatific deliberately covered Imoshen's hand with hers.

Fighting a sense of entrapment, Imoshen understood the Beatific was making it clear that she felt secure enough in her defences against the T'En gifts to touch her.

'Let me advise you, Imoshen. You find yourself in an invidious position, forced to accept this Ghebite General as your bond-partner, forced to host this parody of a royal court. I know palace protocol and I have the experience of nearly seven years as Beatific behind me. I was the youngest person ever to be awarded this office. I can advise you.'

'I must admit I am out of my depth.' Imoshen felt relieved when the woman released her hand. She resisted the impulse to rub the imprint from her fingers. It would not hurt to appear to accept the Beatific's support. There was much she could learn from this woman. 'I thank you for your offer.'

The Beatific smiled like a contented cat, and Imoshen knew she must stay alert or she would become the mouse.

IMOSHEN STROKED THE cover reverently. 'So this is the oldest book in the palace library?'

'The T'En Codex of the Seasons.' The Keeper of the Knowledge undid the clasp.

'Beautiful,' Imoshen whispered. Although she marvelled at the great tome's workmanship, it was not the book she wanted. She had not dared to tell the Keeper she needed information on how her T'En ancestors controlled their gifts. Instead she had asked to see the rarest and oldest books in the library, hoping they would contain what she needed.

'But it is not the original. That was destroyed in the revolt of sixty-four when the palace library burned. We lost much during the Age of Tribulation.' The Keeper shook his head sadly. 'This reproduction is a labour of love. Each page is made of a wafer-thin sheet of wood. The words are incised with the most delicate of quills, and each drawing is a work of art. See how the phases of the moon are illustrated, two small moon cycles to each large one, and the twin full moons on the season cusps. Perfect En.

'There is a page for each season and its ritual celebration is described here. See the two full moons of autumn's cusp, and the instructions for the Harvest Feast?' He turned several pages. 'And here is midwinter, symbolised by the small full moon and large new moon –'

'T'Imoshen?' a palace artisan appeared at the library door, her clothes dusted with white powder. 'The master-builder would speak with you in the Age of Tribulation portrait gallery.'

Imoshen sighed. Brief though their reign of terror had been, Gharavan's Ghebites had done much damage. They had taken particular pleasure in defacing the portraits of her ancestors, and the gallery was in the process of being restored. She thanked the Keeper and followed the artisan.

The palace was a warren of wings, stairs that led nowhere, even rooms within rooms. It was built on the site of the original palace, which had been burned to the ground during the revolution. Sardonyx's failed revolt destroyed the treasures of the original palace and its library. This was when Imoshen the First's very own T'Elegos had been lost to posterity. How

Imoshen longed to read her ancestor's history of the T'En journey from their homeland and the trials of subduing Fair Isle. The T'Elegos had been written by her namesake in the autumn of thirty-one, just before she died and, unlike the Codex of the Seasons, it could not be replaced.

'T'Imoshen.' The master-builder greeted her with a branch of lighted candles, which Imoshen thought odd since it was only late afternoon. Tools lay discarded in the empty passage and the smell of fresh sawdust was the only evidence of the workers.

'Come this way. I thought the proportions of the gallery strange,' the craftsman explained. 'Your ancestors were great ones for building. Sometimes they pulled down the work of the previous generation, sometimes they just built over things. When we removed the damaged wainscoting we discovered this.'

He paused before a dark passage. Musty, stale air greeted Imoshen. The candles flickered.

'A secret passage.' She smiled with delight. The palace was supposed to be riddled with secret passages, but she had never seen one. 'Where does it lead?'

'I'll not go in there.' He handed her the candle brace. 'Anything that old has the taint of the pure T'En, if you'll pardon my plain speaking.'

Without another word he left. Imoshen peered into the darkness, her heart racing with excitement. Lifting the candles high, she ducked her head to enter.

TULKHAN OPENED THE door. Stepping aside, he let Lord Fairban and his daughters enter. Several of his commanders vied none too subtly for the attention of the young women.

'And this room has just been restored. Unfortunately my half-brother's men could not resist looting it.' Looking around he could just imagine his countrymen's reaction. Late afternoon sunlight poured through a single circular window in the centre of a dome. The room needed no more illumination, because every surface other than the black marble floor was golden. The dome was lined with beaten gold, impressed with intricate designs. The walls alternated gold-embossed panels with amber-lined niches housing statuettes of pure gold.

No wonder the Ghebites had been consumed with gold lust. Fair Isle was renowned for its wealth, but this was almost beyond belief.

'Imoshen insisted the room be restored precisely as it had been,' Tulkhan said.

Lord Fairban nodded. 'Very proper. After all, it is part of Fair Isle's heritage, even if it is in bad taste.'

Wharrd caught Tulkhan's eye.

'Bad taste?' Tulkhan asked.

Cariah nodded seriously. 'This whole wing dates from the Age of Consolidation.' She picked up a golden statuette of a couple amorously entwined and held it up for them to see. 'Too much decoration and ostentatious display, particularly during the middle period. In this, the Age of Discernment, we can look back on these rooms and their contents and appreciate them for their heritage value, if not their artistic value.'

Tulkhan's men looked stunned. He hid a smile.

When Cariah returned the statuette to its niche, Harholfe stroked its sensuous curves. The T'En claimed to be highly civilised, yet they thought nothing of portraying the naked body in varying stages of arousal. Tulkhan's people found the sculptures and frescoes disconcerting to say the least. If he was not careful Harholfe would make some crude joke and offend Lord Fairban.

'Let me show you the old portrait gallery,' Tulkhan said quickly. 'The portraits are away being repaired while the gallery itself is being restored.'

A LITTLE CROW of delight escaped Imoshen. The steps had led into a passage, down more stairs and finally through an archway into a long corridor. Someone had wedged the panel open with a broken tile. Imoshen left it wedged in place, not trusting that the old mechanism would still work.

Raising the brace of candles high, she turned full circle, marvelling. With its exquisitely rendered stonework and buttresses, this corridor clearly dated from the Age of Tribulation. She was standing in history. This had to be part of the palace rebuilt after Sardonyx's revolt.

She closed her eyes, inhaling the air of another age, and opened her T'En senses to the past. If only she could have lived in a time when the T'En were revered and accepted.

She opened her eyes and gasped with surprise as a boy wandered past her, his hands extended as if he were blind. He was pure T'En, and stood nearly as tall as her, although his chin was smooth.

'Who are you?'

He didn't hear her. Perhaps he was deaf and mute as well as blind.

Imoshen hesitated. There were no pure T'En left save herself and Reothe. Perhaps he had been hidden down here. Her heart went out to him.

Hands extended, eyes blindly staring, the boy felt his way along the corridor. Gently, because she did not wish to frighten him, she lifted one hand to touch his arm, but her fingers passed right through him.

Imoshen gasped, sagging against the wall. The apparition continued on. Was she watching some long-lost ancestor or someone from the future? His clothing consisted of simple breeches and shirt which could have been worn at any time in the last six hundred years.

Imoshen took a deep breath to slow her heart rate, then followed. Though he was blind the boy seemed to know his way around. He appeared to be counting the archways until he found the one he wanted. There he ran his fingers over the stonework, triggering a hidden panel which opened onto a narrow stairwell. He wedged the panel open with one shoe and went down the steps.

When Imoshen looked down to see a real shoe wedged in the doorway, dusty with age, she realised she was seeing an event from the past. She hurried down the steps, anxious not to lose the boy. They were below ground now, in the catacombs deep under the original palace. She shivered with awe as the brace of candles illuminated the wall niches where the dead lay, their forms carved on the stone lids of their coffins.

As a child she had listened to her older brother and sister whispering stories late at night. They'd told how T'Sardonyx had gone slowly mad. According to legend he would creep into the palace catacombs to lie on the marble slab destined for his body and commune with the Parakletos.

Imoshen shuddered. After the revolt it had become mandatory to burn the bodies of pure T'En and sprinkle their ashes on the sacred garden of their estates.

The boy felt his way until he missed a step and fell forward onto the ground where he lay weeping softly in despair. Imoshen hastened to his side, but her words of comfort could not reach him.

Setting the brace of candles down, she sat back on her heels. Maybe she could reach him with her gift. Lifting her face she closed her eyes and concentrated. This was not a healing, so she did not know how to begin, only that she must seek the familiar tension of the T'En powers. The metallic taste settled on her tongue, making her mouth water.

Ready to attempt contact, she opened her eyes and saw the ceiling of the catacomb's barrel vault above her. Dismay made her groan. Staring down from above were paintings of the T'En martyrs, the Paragian Guard who had died in the service of Imoshen the First.

Men and woman stood dressed in early T'En armour, their hands on their sword hilts. Their garnet eyes were alive in their pale faces as they watched her. These were the T'En warriors who had given their lives to secure Fair Isle, the ones Imoshen the First had commemorated in the T'Elegos.

When Imoshen read the high T'En name of the one directly above her she recognised him as one of the Parakletos. She bit her tongue, wishing the words unthought. Unbidden the verses of the death-summoning came into her mind. Somehow, she resisted saying them aloud. But it appeared that thinking them was enough, for a great oppression settled on her, filling her ears with roaring silence so that the sound of her ragged breathing faded.

The Parakletos were coming for her. Panic engulfed her, froze her to the spot. Her heart faltered. Time stretched. She could sense them approaching, eager and vindictive, questing for her. Soon they would fix on her, and when they did she would not escape.

Propelled by terror, she broke the trance and, with one last frantic effort, broke free of her paralysis. Snatching the candle brace, she ran. The flames winked out one by one so that by the time she reached the top of the stairs only one candle remained alight. She tripped and fell full length on the stone, skinning her hands. The last candle rolled away, winking out.

Fear stung her. The candle flared back to life and she scrambled to her feet, careful to shield its precious light.

Panting with fear, Imoshen found she could hardly think. Which way?

*   *   *

'Why aren't your people at work?' Tulkhan asked the master-builder who stood in the entrance to the old portrait gallery.

'We uncovered an old passage. T'Imoshen is exploring it.'

There was a buzz of excitement from Tulkhan's companions.

'Show me,' the General ordered.

The craftsman led them down the gallery and stopped before a dark opening to light a brace of candles, handing it to Tulkhan. 'You will need this.'

'Let's go!' Lord Fairban's youngest daughter exclaimed.

'There might be ancient treasures,' Cariah whispered.

'More gold?' Jacolm asked, nudging Harholfe.

Cariah laughed. 'Much more valuable. Lost knowledge.'

Jacolm frowned.

'Wait, General,' Lord Fairban began, but Tulkhan had already ducked his head and stepped into the steep stairwell. The others followed him down the staircase, complaining that there were not enough candles.

The steps led into a passage, down more stairs and through an archway.

'General, I –' Lord Fairban began, then pointed, muttering something in High T'En.

Light appeared at the end of a long corridor. The single candle's flame illuminated only the figure's face so that it appeared a disembodied T'En wraith was gliding towards them.

'Imoshen?' Tulkhan called uncertainly. She looked up. For a fleeting instant he read terror in her features.

Then she smiled and raised her voice. 'I did not expect all of you to come looking for me.'

'I was showing Lord Fairban and his daughters the restoration,' Tulkhan explained, holding Imoshen's eyes for a moment longer than was necessary. The candle flame trembled and he took the holder from her. The metal was so cold it burned his skin. Something had terrified Imoshen. 'What is it?'

'Yes, where have we come out?' Cariah asked.

'Only a long passage and old storerooms. Nothing more exciting than rat holes, I'm afraid.' Imoshen shrugged. She plucked the unlit candles from the holder and lit them, handing them out. 'Take these. We don't want to break our necks going up the stairs.'

'Yes, but what about exploring?' Jacolm asked.

'Nothing but rat holes and musty storerooms,' Imoshen repeated.

Tulkhan felt a thickness in his head.

'Let's go,' Imoshen urged.

A sense of urgency filled him. He wanted to get out of these confined passages.

Muttering under their breath, the others turned and shuffled up the stairs, their candles casting myriad shadows on the walls. Imoshen was right behind Tulkhan as he stepped out of the secret stair into the portrait gallery once more.

The master-builder greeted them.

Imoshen turned to him. 'You were right. Nothing of interest lies down there. Replace the panel and continue the restoration. It must be time for the evening meal.'

Linking an arm with Cariah she began to stroll out of the gallery. The others followed her.

The master-builder met Tulkhan's eyes, his expression grim. Tulkhan handed the candle brace to him, then hurried after his men. Imoshen's words carried to the General as he caught up. To his ear her tone was a trifle forced.

'Lady Cariah, General Tulkhan has been appointed patron of the Halls of Learning and I am patron of the hospices, so we must visit them tomorrow. Will you be hostess in my place?'

'I would be honoured.'

Imoshen stopped at the foot of the stairs. 'Oh, I forgot. There is one more thing I must tell the builder. You go on ahead.'

Tulkhan strode up the stairs with the others, ignoring their idle chatter. Something felt wrong. He paused on the landing. Wharrd met his eyes.

Tulkhan shook his head. 'Go on, I'll catch up.'

Careful to move quietly, he retraced his steps to the entrance of the portrait gallery, where he could observe Imoshen unseen. She stood halfway along the gallery in a pool of light, holding a candle high so the master-builder could position the new wainscoting. Tulkhan lifted his fingers to his mouth and blew on them. They still stung from the cold metal. Truly, Fair Isle was a place of mystery and Imoshen was the greatest mystery of all.

'Make certain it is sealed. And tell your people there was nothing but old storerooms below,' Imoshen ordered.

The builder replaced the skirting board then left by the servants' exit.

Tulkhan waited in the shadows until Imoshen walked past him, her head down in thought.

'Imo –'

She spun, a knife appearing in her hand, her eyes glittering dangerously.

Tulkhan lifted both hands in a no-threat gesture and she slowly dropped her guard.

'What was down there?' he asked, taking the candle.

'Nothing.'

'Since when were you frightened of nothing?'

A half smile lifted Imoshen's lips. The candle flame reflected in her garnet eyes. The flickering point of light lured Tulkhan, urging him to forget everything.

'Well?' he prodded, refusing to be distracted.

'Nothing,' Imoshen whispered. As she returned the knife to its hiding place under her tabard he caught a glimpse of pale thigh above the knife's sheath. 'Nothing you want to know about.'

'Let me be the judge of that.'

She shook her head silently.

'Imoshen?'

'This is better left undisturbed. Trust me.'

'How can I trust you when you hide things from me?'

'In this you must trust me.' She took his arm and he felt the insidious lure of her T'En gifts urging him to lose himself in her alien beauty, to trust, to devote himself to her.

He flicked free of her touch. 'Don't play your T'En riddles on me!'

'I did not mean to.' Her lids flickered down hiding her eyes. 'I only –'

'You seek to hide something. I will have it from you or I will tear the wainscoting off and go down there myself!'

'Fool! Nothing could induce me to go down to the catacombs again. If I can't face them, how can you?'

'Face who?'

She laughed bitterly. 'I see you will not let it rest. Very well, General. Far below us lie the catacombs of the original palace, built six hundred years ago. There the bodies of the pure T'En were laid to rest to protect them from grave robbers. You would be surprised how much gold the sixth finger of a pure T'En would bring on the mainland. But I digress.

'Among them lie the legendary Paragian Guard, who after death became the Parakletos.' Her voice dropped on that word, growing breathy and urgent. 'I used to think them nothing but legend, stories peddled by the church to keep the farmer folk in need of their services, but you were there in the cooper's house when they came at my call. And tonight... tonight I barely escaped them. They sought me, hungry for –'

'I don't want to hear.'

She stepped away, giving him an ironic obeisance. 'I will see you at dinner, General.'

Imoshen disappeared up the stairs, leaving Tulkhan alone in the dark with a single candle and his doubts.

Chapter Five

IMOSHEN WINCED AS Kalleen brushed her hair. Apart from the one day they had spent together touring the Halls of Learning and the hospices, the General had avoided her, occupying himself with riding the outlying reaches of T'Diemn with his engineers.

'...and who's to say what those Ghebite commanders will do once they get their hands on their new estates?' Kalleen asked, pulling vigorously on Imoshen's hair. 'Only yesterday, when I was in the market, I overheard an old farming couple. Talk about moan! You'd think they faced the loss of their livelihood and their rights when the new Ghebite lord takes over the estate where they live. I told them it is a noble's obligation to protect their people. At least, a noble should take care of them.' Kalleen frowned. 'Who knows what these newly ennobled Ghebite lordlings will do?'

Imoshen twisted from the waist to face Kalleen. Naturally the country folk would fear their new overlords.

Kalleen was experimenting with an ornate Old-Empire hairstyle. She gave a sharp tug. 'Hold still. I can't get your plaits straight.'

'I'd be just as happy with a simple twin-plait.'

'Well, I wouldn't. You should hear them in the servants' wing, talking about how I turn you out.'

'What do you care? Tomorrow you'll be Lady Kalleen of Windhaven with a maid of your own.' Imoshen grinned. Kalleen was still acting as her maid because she had refused to relinquish the position. 'I hope she snaps at you and pulls your hair –'

'I never...' Kalleen looked horrified, then contrite.

Imoshen smiled, holding her gaze in the mirror. 'Only a little. But you've given me an idea. I must go to the library to see what I can find on early T'En investitures of nobility.'

GENERAL TULKHAN CAME to his feet at last. The interminable monologue that passed as a performance in Fair Isle had been obscure at best.

Imoshen appeared at his elbow. 'General? Walk with me?' Sliding her arm through his, she guided him towards the windows overlooking the courtyard.

Tulkhan frowned at the many small panes of glass. One good swing with an axe and the enemy would be into the vulnerable underbelly of the palace. It was typical of the T'En to build for effect, not defence. Still, it could be argued that if the enemy had made it as far as this private courtyard, the palace was already taken.

Then he realised this was the courtyard where he had seen his half-brother's men burning books, destroying everything that offended the Ghebite church's dictates.

'Was the performance so bad?' Imoshen teased.

Tulkhan schooled his features and tried for a light tone. 'I've never heard such a long death-bed eulogy. I thought the poor fellow would never die.'

'I'll have you know that was one of the great tragic moments of T'En literature, portrayed by one of the greatest actors of the Thespers Guild.'

But he could tell she sympathised with him. For a rare moment, they were alone, removed from the Keldon nobles and Ghebite commanders. He took her hands in his – pale flesh encased in scarred, coppery fingers. Her palms were soft, unlike his calloused skin. She had never done a day's hard work in her life. She was representative of her people, of the Old Empire grown complacent. Contempt flashed through him, for he had walked the original fortified walls of old T'Diemn and seen where new buildings had weakened the walls' defences. Too much peace and prosperity made a people weak.

When Imoshen looked up, he could not fail to recognise the intelligence in her wine-dark eyes.

'Yes?' he prompted.

'Tomorrow you reward your faithful men with lands and titles.'

'There's no need for more delay. The nobles from the Keldon Highlands have arrived.'

'There is some resentment –'

He snorted. His men had been restrained in claiming their rights as the conquering army. He opened his mouth to say as much but Imoshen anticipated him. Or did she skim the surface of his thoughts? He could not tell.

'True, to the victor go the spoils, but we are trying to smooth the transition, General.' A rueful smile tugged at Imoshen's mouth. 'I have been researching T'En investiture. I think it would help reconcile the people if we were to use the old formalities.'

'Good idea,' he agreed swiftly, her talk of research reminding him of something. 'I heard some tale of the river being diverted from its original bed, past the walls of old T'Diemn. Surely it is only a tale?'

'Not at all. T'Diemn used to flood, so T'Imoshen the Third's brother diverted the River Diemn to run on three sides of the walls of old T'Diemn. Scholars have pinpointed the day he became Emperor as the beginning of the Age of Consolidation. Much was achieved. They built the river locks, and the port facilities were improved by dredging.' Imoshen's bright eyes fixed on him. 'But that's enough of a history lesson. If I have your agreement I'll organise the investiture and ensure the ribbons of office and deeds are ready.'

'A T'En investiture rather than a Ghebite?' Tulkhan muttered. 'Very well. I would have the men swear on something other than my faithless half-brother's kingship.'

Imoshen's fingers tightened on his arm. 'Honour knows no nationality, General. Your men serve you because they respect you.'

Her words warmed him. 'You are right, a man's honour knows no –'

'You mistake me,' Imoshen corrected swiftly. 'The full quote translates as, *Honour knows no nationality or gender.*'

Tulkhan frowned. 'You never miss a chance to remind me that you are heir to so much T'En culture. Scholars who studied the Age of Consolidation? Diverting the River Diemn? What next, flying machines?'

Imoshen's eyes flashed as she opened her mouth to reply.

'General Tulkhan?' a voice interrupted. 'Would you take a partner for a game of chance?'

He wanted to ignore them and confront Imoshen, but he forced himself to turn.

'Sahorrd,' he greeted him. 'What game?'

The tall commander grinned. 'Something T'En. Lady Cariah is organising the teams. Jacolm and I agreed to play as long as the loser does not have to compose a rhyming couplet!'

Tulkhan had to smile. He remembered his own dismay when he had discovered the variety of forfeits T'En games entailed. To his Ghebite eyes the intricacies of T'En culture were often absurd.

Imoshen slid her hand from Tulkhan's and lowered her voice. 'Join the game. I have much to do before the investiture. When I find the plans for old T'Diemn I will show you. River locks, dredging and more besides. Then mock the T'En if you can!'

She gave him the formal bow of leave-taking and left.

With her challenge still ringing in his ears, Tulkhan reflected that Imoshen was always careful to accord him the honour of his uncrowned position when others were there to observe, but she was quick enough to forget it when it suited her.

TULKHAN WRIGGLED HIS toes in his new formal boots and grimaced – velvets and silks when he was just a simple soldier – but the people expected him to dress like a king for the investiture of his commanders. A small boy fidgeted as he waited at Tulkhan's side with the first of the ribbons and deeds on a silver platter.

Imoshen signalled for silence in the great hall. She was dressed in white samite, the heavy silk threaded with silver. A small skullcap of woven silver formed a net over her hair, ending in delicate chains tipped with rubies which caught the light as she turned her head. A single ruby hung in the middle of her forehead, echoing the colour of her eyes.

As she lifted her arms the pale winter sun broke free from the clouds and a finger of multicoloured light pierced the nearest stained-glass windows, illuminating her. The air was heavy with expectancy. Anyone who could wrangle a place, from guildmaster to noble, soldier to entertainer and T'En church official, was present. A hush fell over the great hall.

The small boy by Tulkhan's side made a strangled sound in his throat, then sneezed loudly. An agonised blush flooded his smooth cheeks. As Tulkhan gave the boy's shoulder a reassuring squeeze, he met Imoshen's smiling eyes.

First to be ennobled and receive his estates was Wharrd. That Imoshen had given this honour to the veteran bone-setter pleased Tulkhan.

Wharrd strode up the two steps onto the dais. Even on the same level he had to look up to Imoshen.

Tulkhan waited ready to receive the oaths of service. There had been time for only a quick explanation of his part in the ceremony. Pomp and ceremony had always bored him, and his thoughts returned to the challenge of making T'Diemn impregnable, until Imoshen's words pierced his abstraction.

'You are being raised to this position so that you may serve the people of Fair Isle.' Imoshen went on to list the requirements of Wharrd's position. Tulkhan listened with growing surprise as his bone-setter promised to rebuild his estates' hospices and schools where none would be turned away.

Now he understood Imoshen's manoeuvrings. Anger stirred in him. The last T'En Princess was trying to educate the barbarian conquerors in her ways.

Wharrd signed his name to the land deed. Unlike many of Tulkhan's men, the bone-setter could read and write. In the Ghebite army verbal oaths were sworn before witnesses, for few of his commanders could do more than make their mark. At this rate a farmer who worked a noble's fields would have more education than his liege lord.

Once the document was signed, Imoshen draped the first of three ribbons across Wharrd's chest.

'In accepting the ribbons of office you accept what they signify. White for purity of purpose, to serve selflessly.' Her voice carried throughout the silent great hall as she draped the red across his chest. 'Red to signify the blood you have shed and are willing to shed to protect your people and all the people of Fair Isle.' When she took the third ribbon, a black one, Wharrd looked at Tulkhan questioningly. But the General had no answers.

Imoshen continued inexorably. 'Black to signify death which comes to us all, no matter how high we are raised in this world.'

Wharrd's mouth opened in silent surprise. Ghebite ceremonies did not mingle a man's inevitable death with his promotion. This was a strangely humbling ceremony.

'Now give your oath to the General,' Imoshen whispered to Wharrd, who was fingering the three ribbons.

Recollecting himself, the veteran stepped sideways to drop to one knee before Tulkhan. He gave his oath of allegiance, then hesitated. On impulse Tulkhan drew his sword, folding both hands over the hilt.

Wharrd touched the embossed seal-ring Tulkhan wore on his right hand. It carried his father's symbol of a rearing stallion. There were only two such seal-rings in existence, and the other was on King Gharavan's hand.

Following Ghebite custom, Wharrd kissed the sword's blade. When the man rose, Tulkhan could tell it had been the right gesture.

Kalleen stepped forward as Wharrd retreated. It was clear to Tulkhan that Imoshen meant to reward Kalleen before his men. They would see it as a calculated insult. Tulkhan caught Imoshen's eye, sending a silent warning. Two bright spots of colour blazed in her pale cheeks.

'Step forward, Kalleen,' Imoshen said. 'Your personal bravery saved my life when King Gharavan would have had me executed. Before everyone here I acknowledge that debt and honour my obligation. If you or yours are ever in need I can be called upon.'

Then to Tulkhan's surprise Imoshen repeated exactly the same formalities with the farm girl who had once been her maid, making it clear that in the eyes of T'En church law and state, Kalleen was Wharrd's equal.

A finger of sunlight moved across the dais as the ceremony wore on. At last Tulkhan sheathed his sword and offered Imoshen his arm. She took it, casting him a swift glance to gauge his mood. He smiled grimly.

She had orchestrated the contents of the oaths for her own purposes. Her people's war swords may have been sheathed when she surrendered her stronghold to him, but the battle continued. Only now she fenced with protocol.

MUCH LATER, AS the tables were removed and the musicians in the high gallery began to play, Imoshen looked for Kalleen.

'My lady?' Imoshen gave her former maid the correct T'En obeisance for an equal, then straightened to meet Kalleen's gaze.

Excitement and disbelief danced in the girl's hazel eyes. Imoshen smiled. It was like one of the epic poems. The farm girl had risen to become Imoshen's maid and then Lady Kalleen of Windhaven. Kalleen's delight, however, was tinged with sadness. On arriving in T'Diemn Imoshen, had sent a rider to contact Kalleen's family to share her good fortune, but they had been unable to find anyone from her village who had survived the invasion.

The little maid flushed, stroking her ribbons and the seal. 'If only my family had lived.'

'We are each other's family now.' Imoshen hugged her.

Kalleen bit her bottom lip and brushed angrily at her tears, giving a shaky laugh. 'No one in the servants' wing will talk to me after this. They'll think I've grown too grand!'

'What do you care? From this day forward you'll live in the nobles' wing.' Imoshen took her hand. 'You must promise never to tell me what I want to hear, only what I need to hear.'

'Spoken like a true empress,' Cariah said as she approached.

'Now you are telling me what I want to hear!' Imoshen chided.

Cariah laughed.

Imoshen grew serious. 'I'm concerned about the General's lord commanders. They will need guidance when they take control of their new estates.'

'Why not appoint a church official to advise them?' Cariah suggested.

Imoshen frowned. She did not want to give the Beatific any more power than she already had.

On the other side of the gallery Tulkhan watched Imoshen's expressive face, trying to guess her thoughts.

Lord Commander Jacolm nudged the General's elbow. The man's heavy eyebrows lifted suggestively and he gestured towards the trio. 'A woman like that redhead makes a man glad he's not a eunuch!'

Tulkhan grinned.

'It's the Lady Kalleen for me,' Wharrd admitted. 'It has been since we first took Umasreach Stronghold. I'd have married her without the Windhaven Estate. As far as I'm concerned, our bonding day can't come too soon.'

He said this with such relish that Tulkhan smiled. If only he could look on his and Imoshen's approaching bonding with the same unreserved enthusiasm.

'I usually like them with a bit of meat on their bones,' Jacolm remarked as if he were talking about a brood mare. 'But that head of red hair promises a fire a man could warm himself in!'

Wharrd chuckled. 'Beware you don't get burnt!'

Jacolm insisted he knew how to handle himself and their banter turned crude even by soldiers' standards.

Tulkhan studied the three women. Little Kalleen was a lively thing and the Keldon noblewoman was a beauty, but neither of them stirred him like Imoshen did. He wondered what three such disparate women could possibly be talking about. What did the women of Fair Isle chatter about while their men discussed matters of state?

At that moment, Imoshen and her two companions turned and glanced in Tulkhan's direction, their expressions disconcertingly intense.

Imoshen's perceptive eyes met his and he felt a tug. Tulkhan found himself walking towards her, wending his way through the revellers.

Imoshen stepped away from her companions, her gaze fixed on his face. 'General, I want to speak with you about your lord commanders. They will need help when they take over their estates.'

'Don't worry yourself about my men,' Tulkhan said. He turned to the redheaded beauty. 'Lady Cariah, you know my finest swordsman, now Lord Commander Jacolm.' As he suspected, Jacolm lost no time asking her to dance.

Wharrd spirited Kalleen away, leaving Tulkhan alone with Imoshen. It was the outcome he had both wanted and dreaded.

Imoshen's hand closed on his forearm and he responded immediately. Surely she must feel it too. Was he an open book to her, so transparent that she laughed at his hopeless craving for her?

He slipped her hand from his arm, intending to put her away from him, but instead he pulled her closer. 'Let's dance.'

'I thought you said you couldn't dance.'

'I lied.'

Imoshen laughed and shook her head.

He stared down into her upturned face, feeling a smile on his own lips. Why couldn't life be simple? If only he was a soldier and she a camp-follower. He would lead her away to a secluded corner and seduce her. Already he felt his body reacting to the thought of her uninhibited response.

Tulkhan knew Imoshen wanted him. He could feel it now in the way she melded against him. How could he wait until their official bonding day when his body raged at him to claim her?

'Not long till midwinter,' Imoshen whispered.

Furious, Tulkhan stepped back. She had invaded his mind again.

'What is it?' Imoshen asked, disconcerted.

She looked so innocent. Was she unaware of what she was doing even as she invaded his privacy?

'I have no time for this. I have matters of state to deal with.'

Imoshen watched the General stalk off, his back stiff with tension. What possessed him? Here she was trying to help his men assume control of their estates and he would not even listen to her.

Annoyance flashed through her but it was tinged with regret. She had to admit that she'd felt a heady rush of desire when he held her. And now her body thrummed with a need that made his rejection doubly cruel.

IMPATIENCE DROVE IMOSHEN as she glided across the empty anteroom to the door of Lady Cariah's private bedchamber. She scratched on the door tang, her comb sending its delicate clear notes ahead of her as she pushed the door open. 'Are you feeling better, Cariah?'

It was nearly time for the noon meal and Cariah had retreated to her bedroom, complaining of a headache. Imoshen hated to disturb her but already a day had passed since they had spoken of the General's lord commanders and their new estates. Imoshen was concerned for her people. They needed someone to explain their customs and beliefs to their new overlords.

'I have a tisane for your headache, Cariah,' Imoshen called.

The woman's tousled head thrust through the bed curtain and she laughed. 'A moment.'

Cariah reappeared a few heartbeats later, slipping through the closed bed curtains dressed in a simple undershift.

'I made you this.' Imoshen offered the prepared draught. 'The Aayel always gave it to me if my head ached. And I wanted a chance to talk to you about –'

'Wait. We must be alone.' Cariah put the tisane aside and raised her voice. 'Jacolm, get dressed. I will see you tonight.'

Imoshen's face stung with heat as she realised she had interrupted their lovemaking. There was a muttering and rustling from inside the closed bed before the man climbed out, still lacing his breeches.

'Cariah...' Imoshen began, but the woman gestured for silence.

Jacolm glared at the pair of them from under his heavy black brows, then recollected himself and made a perfunctory Ghebite bow before hastening away, shirt tails flapping.

When the bedchamber's door closed, Imoshen sank onto a seat, covering her hot face. 'Oh, Cariah!'

But she was laughing. 'Hush. The wait will make our joining all the sweeter tonight. Jacolm is oversure of himself anyway.' She sat down next to Imoshen, taking her hand.

Imoshen felt the warmth of Cariah's skin, noting the sensual flush in her face. Without meaning to, she registered the subtle change in Cariah's scent. Her friend glowed with life and passion, making Imoshen feel inexperienced and gauche.

'I am sorry.' Imoshen could not meet Cariah's knowing eyes. 'I forget the ways of the high court. I only visited once. For the most part my family kept me secluded, even from my own relatives.'

Cariah squeezed her hand. 'You wanted to speak with me?'

Imoshen bit her lip. Naturally Cariah did not want to hear how she lived as an outcast. The T'En traits Cariah bore were subtle enough to let her pass amongst True-people. A flash of resentment stung Imoshen, but she put it aside as unworthy.

'Of course,' Imoshen said. 'I have been thinking, and I don't want to send priests as advisers with the new lord commanders. I'd prefer to send lesser masters from the Halls of Learning' – Imoshen smiled – 'as interpreters.'

Cariah laughed. 'How could they refuse?'

Relief flooded Imoshen. 'Then I must select the most tactful of lesser masters for these posts.' Again she hesitated. 'The General might not believe this necessary, but if it is already arranged –'

'He won't argue. Use my chamber to interview them.'

'AND THEN?' TULKHAN asked, his voice as cold as the ache in his chest.

The little man flinched at his tone but continued. 'As she has done for several days, your betrothed entered Lady Cariah's bedchamber. The princess was in there from one bell to next. After she left, three men slipped away.'

Tulkhan winced. The thought of Imoshen's quicksilver passion being ignited by another man's touch enraged him. Nausea roiled in his belly. He could not believe it of Imoshen.

'Leave me!' He dismissed the man, a trusted Ghebite who had spied for him on many past missions.

Tulkhan rose, knowing he should be preparing for the hunt. It was one of the few pastimes both his own people and the Keld enjoyed.

He knew he should expose Imoshen, yet... With bitter insight he realised that he did not want to confront her because he did not want to face the truth.

*   *   *

'HE COMES,' KALLEEN hissed, hurrying past Imoshen and swiftly disappearing around the corner.

Imoshen straightened, her heart thumping. This was ridiculous, but every time she had tried to speak with the General he had been too busy to see her, forcing her to resort to this little ruse. She had asked Kalleen to watch for him and warn her of his approach.

She heard the thud of his booted feet. Good, he was alone. It was so much harder to speak when his commanders were with him.

Imoshen stepped out of the doorway and collided with him as he rounded the bend.

'General?' she gasped.

'Imoshen.' He accorded her a cold welcome.

She ignored it and plunged on. 'I'm glad to see you. I promised to show you the plans of old T'Diemn. Come this way.'

For a moment he looked blank, then he nodded grimly. It did not bode well. She was hoping that if she lured him away from his men and showed him something of interest, his manner might change.

They made their way to the palace library in silence. As the Keeper of the Knowledge scurried off to get the documents, Imoshen cleared her throat.

'I'm glad you asked me about the River Diemn. I was able to hunt up... Ah, here it is.' She thanked the old man and spread the large tome on the table. 'T'Diemn was originally built on several hills, with the river skirting their bases. Every second year it would flood, with much loss of life and livelihood. T'Imoshen the Third's younger brother diverted the river, taming it so that a small portion flowed through T'Diemn, bringing fresh water, while the rest flowed around the city walls. That was when he designed the palace's ornamental lake –'

'The lake is not natural?'

'No. Neither is the forest. Then he improved on the original design of old T'Diemn, which was laid out in concentric circles with streets running directly from the south to the north gates and from east to west. He built the ring-road within the city walls so that reinforcements could be rushed to the defences if the walls were breached. He designed the fortified bridge we crossed to enter the old part of the city.'

'That bridge? But you can't see daylight for the shops and homes.'

Imoshen nodded. 'They are more recent additions. Originally it was built for defence. You know where the bridge ends in an L-shaped bay before the outer and inner gates of the old city? If attackers managed to cross the river, they would be pinned there, by the defenders on the gate towers.'

Tulkhan shook his head. It never ceased to amaze him. The T'En had created great feats of engineering and built fortifications more sophisticated than any he had come across elsewhere, then they had let it all go by allowing shopkeepers to build on the bridges and obscure the defenders' line of fire.

'I thought you might like to see this.' Imoshen's smile warmed him.

Still, he was surprised when she opened the last pages of the book to reveal intricate faded drawings of complex machines.

'Imoshen the Third's brother attempted to build a flying machine. But he couldn't get a person off the ground for more than a gliding flight. And there's this.'

'Some kind of siege machine?' Tulkhan studied the drawing. 'The wheels would only work over smooth ground. The metal plates would stop defenders from setting fire to the machine, and protect the men crouching behind it, but it would be very heavy, hard to transport.'

'I don't think it was ever built. Reothe lived at the beginning of the Age of Consolidation, when Fair Isle no longer faced internal threat. The T'En –'

'What did you call him?'

Imoshen stopped, took a slow breath and raised her eyes to his. 'He was T'Reothe the Builder. My kinsman, Reothe, was named after him, just as I was named after T'Imoshen the First. They are common names.'

Tulkhan stared at Imoshen. It was always there between them, her heritage, her T'En traits and her broken vows to the rebel leader.

'Here.' She pushed the old volume aside and selected another, opening it. 'If you follow the family lines you will see the same names turn up again and again.'

Tulkhan stared at the indecipherable High T'En script. He couldn't even read the dates. 'More chicken scrawl.'

'It is our family tree. Here is Reothe the Builder, my ancestor.' Imoshen smiled as she turned the page. 'He heralded the Age of Consolidation which lasted around three hundred years. The Age of Discernment began with the stoning of the last Rogue T'En a hundred years ago.' She turned two more pages, tracing the line, and pointed. 'Here I am. Imoshen the Last.'

Then she blinked in dismay, as if hearing her words.

But Tulkhan had no sympathy for her. He found it hard to credit what he saw before him – six hundred and sixteen years of births, deaths and marriages. The written records of his Ghebite royal family went back only as far as his grandfather's time. Before that the histories and traditions of his nomadic people had been remembered by the tale-teller of each tribe.

Nomads did not carry such heavy items as books. It was only when Tulkhan's father was a boy and his people moved into the palace of their first conquered kingdom that they had begun to write down their histories, transposing a tent culture to a more permanent home. Strictly translated, they were not house-lines as he had told Imoshen, but tent-lines.

He felt her watching him now and tapped the page. 'In this book you have six hundred years of blood lines, father to son?'

Imoshen laughed. 'You're thinking like a Ghebite, General. This book itself was begun four hundred years ago at the dawn of the Age of Consolidation, transcribed from fragmentary older records. But yes, it traces the royal line from empress to daughter for just over six hundred years. The Empress's brother only inherited, as in Reothe the Builder's case, if she had no children. Emperor Reothe bonded with his second cousin to consolidate the royal line.'

Tulkhan's gaze returned to the book of war machines. 'I want to study this, particularly the parts referring to the defence of old T'Diemn. Have it sent to my bedchamber.'

'You can take it now if you like.'

'No. I'm late already. I'm supposed to view the Passing Out Parade at the Halls of Learning.' He could not hide his reluctance and saw her answering smile. 'Besides, I want a translation. Could you have those passages ready for me by tomorrow afternoon?'

'I can't. I have an engagement.'

Anger hardened in him. An engagement with her lover? 'Break it.'

'I can't. Like you, I have responsibilities.'

Was Imoshen betraying him? True, their vows had not been given, only a commitment to marry. Tulkhan frowned. She had betrayed Reothe after their betrothal.

'I must go.' He stepped back.

'I will have the book sent to your bedchamber.'

He wanted to tell her to bring it herself or not to bother. But he did not know what he would say if he opened his mouth, so he strode out in silence, leaving Imoshen looking confused and hurt.

How could she look so innocent if she was taking lovers? If his men believed he was being cuckolded, they would expect him to kill Imoshen to restore his honour.

Chapter Six

IMOSHEN STOOD BY the balcony door, tracing the lines of the bevelled glass. Tulkhan had not returned from the Halls of Learning. It was one of those clear, crystal cold nights of winter, and she longed to escape the confines of the palace. Opening the door, she stepped out onto the balcony overlooking the city. She wished she was an apprentice being granted her year's service, or a student of the Halls of Learning accepting her passing out for the year.

Soon it would be Midwinter's Day and the scholars had agreed the historic bonding of the last T'En Princess with the Ghebite General would determine the end of the Age of Discernment and the dawn of a new, as yet, unnamed age.

She had spoken only yesterday with the engravers at the royal mint to approve the design of a new coin to celebrate her bonding with the General, but Tulkhan had been too busy to accompany her. Resentment stirred in Imoshen.

She turned, resting her elbows on the balustrade to survey the palace, its windows blazing in the night, its towers dark against the stars. A movement on Sard's Tower caught Imoshen's attention. She frowned. It looked for all the world like the Keeper of the Knowledge struggling with a bulky object. Curious, she darted inside and retraced her steps to the long gallery before making her way to the tower.

By the time she found him, the old man had set up his equipment and was seated on a stool, a blanket wrapped around him, studying the stars.

'I thought so!' Imoshen crowed. 'Can I have a look?'

He stood up with good grace.

She took his place, peering through the enlarged farseer.

'Amazing. I can see patterns on the large moon!'

'Mountains.'

'You think so?' She studied it.

'Take a look at the smaller moon. I think the concentric circles are artificial constructions, primitive fortifications perhaps.'

Imoshen was not so sure. She pivoted the instrument to study the spires and rooftops of T'Diemn, looking for something she could recognise. A gasp escaped her. 'What's that glow? Something's burning.'

Leaving the farseer on its tripod, Imoshen went to the edge of the tower, and the Keeper of the Knowledge joined her there.

'Look.' She pointed. 'A building's burning within the old city walls.'

'That's the Caper Night bonfire in the main square of the Halls of Learning.

They'll celebrate, paint their faces and don their masks. Before long they'll be roaming the streets looking for mischief.'

'I've heard they fight pitched battles in the streets.'

He laughed. 'Last Caper Night they caught one of the guildmasters, stripped his shoes off him and painted his feet bright red. There's no harm in it. There's always been rivalry between the Greater and Lesser Guilds and the students from the Halls of Learning – battles with brooms and paintbrushes, guild symbols painted out, white-washed hall ensigns. Why, I remember the Caper Night I graduated...'

According to the Keeper it was all in good fun, youthful exuberance which sometimes got out of hand. As if to prove his point, Imoshen heard shouts of laughter and snatches of song from the streets of old T'Diemn.

Someone came up through the open trapdoor.

'Imoshen!' Kalleen chided. 'I've searched half the palace for you. There's a messenger waiting and it's urgent.'

'Urgent?' Imoshen's stomach clenched with fear for the General. 'Where?' Kalleen told her.

Imoshen's soft slippers flew over the polished wood of the palace corridors. When she opened the door to her greeting chamber and saw it was not one of Tulkhan's men but one of the hospice healers, with the T'En eyes, relief flooded her. She tried to recall his name. 'Healer... Rifkin. What is it?'

'T'Imoshen,' he greeted her formally, 'Dockside Hospice calls on your healing expertise this night.'

As patron of the Healing Guild she had an obligation to help, but it went deeper than that. She could not turn away someone in need. 'Kalleen, my cloak.'

It was lucky Kalleen did not know T'Diemn well enough to realise how dangerous it was to venture out on Caper Night. Despite the Keeper's view that it was all harmless fun, decent folk stayed indoors and barred their windows.

The girl returned with both their cloaks.

'Don't bother with yours. No need for you to have a late night too,' Imoshen told her. 'The healer will guide me.'

Kalleen looked dubious.

'I'm sure I saw Wharrd at the entertainments. Why don't you rescue him from the duelling poets?'

Kalleen smiled. 'You should take an escort.'

Tulkhan had said the same, offering her the use of his elite guard. But she did not want Ghebites hounding her every step. 'I know. I'll take Crawen, she's on guard at my door tonight.'

GENERAL TULKHAN WAS glad he had missed the duelling poets. Their ability to wrest a rhyme from thin air and wield it like a knife blade unnerved him.

Kalleen and Wharrd were occupied in the far end of the room, but he saw no sign of Imoshen.

Cariah swept forward to greet him. Instinctively he bristled. Was this woman providing a cloak for Imoshen's infidelity?

'General Tulkhan. Would you like to hear a reading?'

Anything but that. He never knew when the thing was over. According to the T'En nobles the pauses were as significant as the words. Clapping was considered gauche and finger-clicking your approval in the wrong place brought embarrassed silence.

'Where is Imoshen?'

'I don't know. She was here a little while ago.'

Nicely evasive. Perhaps she was with a lover right now. A rush of fury coursed through his veins like liquid fire. He stalked past Cariah to join Wharrd and Kalleen.

'Where is Imoshen, Kalleen?' Would the girl lie too?

Kalleen stiffened, responding to his unspoken threat. 'Doing what she must to serve her people.'

'Just what does that mean?'

'She's been called away to help in a healing. She may be on her way back already.'

'Back?' Tulkhan barked.

'From the hospice.'

Tulkhan's body tightened. 'Imoshen has left the palace on Caper Night?'

Kalleen nodded. 'A healer from the Dockside Hospice came for her. Where are you going?'

'To escort her back to the palace.'

Tulkhan didn't want a large group to accompany him that would attract attention. Luckily Sahorrd and Jacolm were within hearing distance and they caught his signal, following him out of the chamber. As he left he was aware of many curious eyes watching them.

Kalleen bustled after him like an officious little bird. 'T'Imoshen is –'

'Out alone on Caper Night!' He seized Kalleen's small wrist. 'What if someone with a grudge against the Old Empire catches her?'

'She took one of her stronghold guard,' Kalleen said.

'Who?'

'Crawen.'

Tulkhan cursed. 'Stay here. If Imoshen returns alone, tell her I would speak with her.' He did not wait for an answer.

A SINGLE CANDLE burned in the hospice's empty foyer, symbolising a welcome for anyone in need.

Imoshen left her cloak on the peg. 'I don't know how long I'll be, Crawen. The kitchen is down the back.'

Rifkin lit a second candle and led Imoshen up a set of narrow stairs to a small door. He scratched softly before stepping aside.

Imoshen entered a small room, closing the door after her. A candle burned beside numerous glass jars of dried or pulverised herbs. These jars stood stacked on a narrow table. The room's only occupant was a beggar, huddled on the low bed.

She smiled to herself. It seemed right to her that the highest should be called upon to serve the lowest. It symbolised all that was good in the Old Empire.

Imoshen lifted the candle and approached. 'How may I help you, grandfather?'

The beggar looked up and stood slowly, seemed to keep rising so that he grew taller than her. The hood fell back from his beggar's cloak to reveal silver hair, sharp cheekbones and wine-dark eyes.

'It is I who have come to help you, Imoshen.'

'Reothe.' The word was torn from her. Her breath caught in her throat. The healer had betrayed her. No. Rifkin had probably seen what she first saw – a lowly beggar.

The rebel leader stepped forward, his eyes glittering in the shuddering candle flame. Every time she saw Reothe she was reminded of her own T'En traits, and of how the True-people must see her. Tonight he looked ethereal and austere, inspired by an inner fire like a legendary warrior from the T'Elegos.

'I heard that the General has claimed Fair Isle and forced you to accept him,' Reothe whispered. 'These Ghebites have no respect for T'En women, for any women. Come away with me, Imoshen.'

'I can't.'

He caught her free hand, bringing it to his lips. She felt the warm rush of his breath on her knuckles.

'Why not? You refused me last time for fear of pointless bloodshed. But since the General has been betrayed by his own people he cannot call on the resources of Gheeaba to resist us. Join with me tonight and we will sweep him from the island by midsummer and fulfil our betrothal oaths.'

'No.'

'Think, Imoshen. Joined, we could be so much more than we are apart,' Reothe pressed.

His intensity made her body resonate. Imoshen's sight blurred with the visions conjured by his words. Fair Isle restored, Reothe as her bond-partner. Suddenly it seemed not just possible but the only viable alternative.

'Don't do that!' Imoshen twisted free from him. 'I won't let you use your gift to influence me. My decisions must be my own.'

His garnet eyes narrowed. 'Logic tells me General Tulkhan cannot hold Fair Isle without Gheeaba's support. Logic tells me that the people will unite behind us if we are united. Would you side with a Ghebite invader against your own blood kin?'

Imoshen's head reeled.

'We can do it, Imoshen. Come to me, this very night.'

Reothe's fierce will illuminated his features. She could drown in his eyes. Worse, she suspected he was right.

'The Ghebites were in the wrong to invade our peaceful Island,' Reothe whispered, his thumb caressing the back of her hand. 'They stole our future. This spring we should have made our bonding vows before your family.'

Imoshen moaned.

TULKHAN STRODE THE streets of T'Diemn with Wharrd and Jacolm on either side of him and Sahorrd at his back carrying a single lantern. The larger thoroughfares were lit at night, but down by the docks it would be pitch-black.

As they crossed the fortified bridge the shops and homes that perched precariously on its sides were closed and boarded shut. Their upper storeys almost met in places, excluding the light of the waning larger moon.

'Dockside Hospice is in the roughest area, catering to the merchant sailors,' Wharrd said as they passed under the bridge tower. 'There have been strangers in the dockside taverns asking questions about you, General. Gharavan won't rest –'

'You think this could be my half-brother's idea of revenge? But why? He has the rest of the Ghebite Empire. All I took was Fair Isle –'

'And his pride. You humbled him before his followers, sent him packing!'

Tulkhan shook his head. He still had trouble reconciling his half-brother's actions with the boy he had taught to ride.

As they emerged from the tower's archway a dozen apprentices ran around the corner, jostling them. The revellers laughed, waving torches and paint-sodden brooms. Six young people danced around Tulkhan, singing a doggerel which praised the Silversmith Guild and made jest of others. Paint slopped on his boots.

Another band of apprentices in different masks charged out of the laneway opposite, waving brooms and brushes. Tulkhan lost sight of his men in the crush.

Laughing faces with masks awry tried to stop him but he forged through, anxiety for Imoshen gnawing at him.

Once free of the crowd Tulkhan broke into a run, one hand on his sword hilt to steady it. Having studied T'Diemn's layout with a view to making it more defensible, he knew he could find the hospice alone. He ran down narrow lanes towards the smell of the docks. Several more turns and he saw the open hospice door, dimly lit by its welcoming candle.

Perhaps he was wrong and this was a perfectly innocent call on Imoshen's healing gift. He heard laughter coming from behind a closed door and marched down the hall. Throwing the door open, he found Crawen and a healer sharing warmed wine and hot cakes. So much for guarding Imoshen.

'T'Imoshen, where is she? I am here to escort her back to the palace.'

'This way.' The healer hurriedly put his wine aside. Crawen came to her feet with a hand on her sword hilt.

'Don't bother.' Tulkhan strode off.

*   *   *

'DON'T SPEAK OF my family!' Imoshen closed her eyes to shut Reothe out. With a great effort of will, she pulled her hand free of his. 'Don't speak of what might have been. The Ghebites are here. Fair Isle has surrendered. What you ask would bring more war to our people, more bloodshed.'

'Death in a righteous cause. It would not be the first time the T'En gave their lives for their people. The Paragian Guard laid down their lives to secure Fair Isle. Surely we –'

'Reothe?' Imoshen clutched his arm. She longed to tell him of her meeting with the Parakletos in the catacombs but was too ashamed to reveal her cowardice. 'I performed the ceremony for the dead. I called the Parakletos. When they came, they...' She shuddered. 'They are not the benevolent creatures the church claims.'

He laughed grimly. 'They have no power in this world. But once the veil is down you must be wary, for they will try to drag you into death's shadow with them.' A haunted expression shadowed his eyes. 'I've met with the Parakletos in their world and –'

'But I thought no one could escape?'

He focused on her and fear prickled across her skin because his eyes were windows to death's shadow, then the moment passed and he smiled grimly. 'Most of what the church teaches is distorted or simply not true.'

'I suspected this, but I cannot believe –'

'Believe me. There is much I could show you.' His voice grew intimate. 'No one can give you what I can, Imoshen.'

She could not break his gaze.

'This is our chance. We can influence events this very night. My rebels are hidden in the city awaiting orders. I could get us into the palace, into the Ghebite General's bedchamber. By dawn he could be dead, his elite guard captured, and the palace ours. Think of it, Imoshen. With General Tulkhan gone –'

'But that is murder!'

A short bark of laughter escaped him. 'And this is war!'

Imoshen turned away, her mind filled with a vision of Tulkhan dead in his bed. His blood staining the sheets, all his dreams and passion extinguished.

Tulkhan... Even now she thought she heard his voice. Startled, she darted to the door and swung it open. She was amazed to see him approaching with the healer. The General's broad shoulders filled the hall almost as if he had been conjured by her thoughts of him.

Rifkin greeted her. 'Your escort is here, T'Imoshen. How fares the beggar?'

Her heart sank.

Already, Rifkin and Tulkhan were waiting for her to step aside and let them enter. The General thrust the door open, peering past her into the room. Shadows clung to the far corners but no one hid in them.

'Gone.' Imoshen's throat was so dry she could hardly speak. She gestured to the table with its equipment. 'I was just cleaning up.'

Tulkhan thrust past her and strode to the window, looking down.

'He wouldn't leave that way,' Rifkin said. 'There's only the river below. He must have slipped out while I was with Crawen.'

Imoshen realised Reothe had leapt into the river. In his beggar's guise he could only have carried a knife, and for all he knew Tulkhan might have been accompanied by a dozen of his elite guard.

'Then you are free to go?' The General rounded on Imoshen. 'Come.'

Tulkhan thrust the candle into her hand, drawing her out of the room.

Imoshen shielded the flame as they sped down the steps to the entry, where Crawen awaited them. Tulkhan barely allowed Imoshen time to bid the healer goodbye before they were out on the street, their single candle casting a small pool of light.

'I don't know what possessed you to come out alone on this night of all nights, Imoshen.'

'I had to answer a call for help.'

'What if it had been a hoax?'

'I took my own guard. Besides, I trusted Healer Rifkin.' A mistake she was unlikely to make again.

A group of rowdy armed men rounded the bend. Imoshen tensed, poised for attack.

'General!' Wharrd exclaimed. 'You should have waited for us.'

Raucous laughter echoed down the street, drowning out the General's reply.

'Here.' Tulkhan snatched the candle from Imoshen, pinching it out. He took Sahorrd's lantern and thrust it into her hands. 'You carry the lantern to free up his sword arm. Come.'

Shame stung Imoshen. The meaning was clear. Tulkhan thought she was useless, capable only of carrying a lantern, and he ignored Crawen altogether.

As several laughing apprentices charged around a corner towards them, Tulkhan grabbed Imoshen's free arm and dragged her with him.

She wanted to explain that the whole point of Caper Night was to have a good time while poking fun at authority. But the pace Tulkhan set was so relentless she saved her breath. Besides, she heard glass shattering and a shrill shriek that made her heart lurch.

Tulkhan moved so swiftly she was hard pressed to keep up with him. Only the taverns and less reputable Tea-houses were open, their lights and patrons spilling into the streets. Snatches of song and laughter rang out on the otherwise quiet night air. Imoshen lost track of where she was.

Then she recognised a shop front and knew they were approaching the fortified bridge. Soon they would be in the brightly lit streets of old T'Diemn.

But before they could go any further a dozen or more revellers, students by their cloaks and masks, charged out of the laneway and collided with them.

'Come, Imoshen!' Tulkhan dragged her with him.

She followed at his heels, half stumbling to keep up, the lantern swinging awkwardly. From the shouts and laughter behind them she could tell the others had been waylaid. They were probably having their faces or some other part of their anatomy painted.

Imoshen's booted heels struck the bridge's stonework with a hollow sound which echoed off the closed shopfronts. She took the chance to catch her breath as Tulkhan slowed to a fast walk. A group of masked revellers left the dark entrance of a shop and wove drunkenly towards them.

Tulkhan cursed and the revellers' appearance assumed a sinister aspect. The General caught her arm again. She'd have bruises tomorrow. She strained to see the lower half of their faces.

Three steps, two...

The rasp of weapons being drawn made her mouth go dry with fear. Tulkhan's sword was already in his hand. She didn't remember him drawing it.

'Get behind me.' He shoved her into a doorway.

Imoshen unsheathed her knife. But it didn't have the reach of a sword and, if she risked a throw, she would leave herself disarmed.

A figure lunged, dancing around them ready to deal death. Tulkhan parried and struck. There was no time for finesse. Laughing, mocking masks hid their attackers' faces revealing only grim mouths.

Imoshen feinted with the knife at an overeager attacker, then lashed out with the lantern to defend Tulkhan's unprotected left side. The attacker's blow tore the lantern from her fingers. The oil spilled, carrying blue flames which clung greedily to the man's clothes.

'Fire!' Imoshen screamed. The word was guaranteed to bring the bridge's inhabitants out. The shops and houses were built of wood. 'Fire!'

Tulkhan kicked the nearest attacker in the thigh and darted out into the centre of the bridge.

'Now, Imoshen. Run!'

Her line of sight free, Imoshen threw her knife at the third attacker. Tulkhan's assailant rolled to his feet. Imoshen tore off her cloak and flung it in his face before fleeing. The heavy thump of Tulkhan's boots told her he was at her heels.

Down the dark length of the bridge she ran, heading for the pool of light beyond. Moonlight illuminated the courtyard. Ahead of her, she saw the narrow passage that led through the gates into old T'Diemn.

Skidding on the cobbles, she looked back the way they'd come. Their attackers were closing in, and behind them were more figures. She could not tell if they were the other Ghebites or students.

'Quickly!' Tulkhan dragged her down the dark passage. Running blind, they raced towards the crescent of light at the end.

Under the street light they hesitated. Before them were two paths, one into the ring-road which ran around inside the walls of the old city, the other into a square where she could see glimpses of jostling bodies and torches.

'This way.' She made for the square.

'No, Imoshen.'

She ignored him.

Frustration and fear surged through Tulkhan. He didn't want to enter a square full of potential killers, masked enemies who hid behind laughing young men and women. In that crowd someone could get close enough to sink a knife between his ribs or Imoshen's. But their attackers had almost caught up and his own men were nowhere in sight. Cursing Imoshen's impulsiveness, he charged after her.

She entered the square three long strides ahead of him, her silver hair glistening in the torchlight. Without missing a beat she broke into a line of dancers and tore a burning torch from someone's hand.

A torch was as good a weapon as any in the circumstances. Tulkhan shouldered a youth aside and darted forward to join her, also grabbing a torch. But the dancers had stopped. They stared and pointed as Imoshen leapt onto the rim of the fountain.

Tulkhan felt the instinctive awe of a people taught to deify their T'En royalty.

'T'Imoshen!' The cry went up.

Joyously the revellers surged forward, dragging Tulkhan with them. Arms reached for Imoshen. As he watched they hoisted her off the fountain and carried her high on their shoulders. Cheering, leaping people surrounded him. He saw Imoshen search the crowd for him and waved. She returned his signal.

'To the palace!' Imoshen gestured, pointing the torch.

Relief washed over Tulkhan as the crowd took up her cry. They broke into stirring song and surged through the streets towards the palace.

Studying the merry faces around him, the General strained to identify the masks of their attackers. Pressed amidst the bodies he could not manoeuvre, could not even use his drawn sword, but at least they were being escorted back to safety.

The singing, laughing crowd carried Imoshen right across the square and deposited her on the steps of the palace, where they began another song, linking arms and swaying as though this were some kind of ritual.

Tulkhan forced his way to the steps to join her. He saw surprise register on the unmasked faces of those nearest. Imoshen drew him to her side and kissed his cheek. Several revellers tore off their masks and tossed them in the air.

Imoshen lifted the burning torch high, her voice meant only for him. 'Smile, General. Caper Night has saved your life.'

'My life wouldn't have been at risk if you hadn't gone off alone.'

She tossed her head, eyes glittering with anger.

He wanted to shake her, to make her realise how close they had come to death. 'You should trust me, General.'

As the doors to the grand entrance opened, light spilled down the steps of the palace and Imoshen slipped away from Tulkhan to speak with the bewildered servants, then returned to his side, taking his hand in hers. 'Sing, General. They are singing of their love for Fair Isle.'

He realised what he thought was a rowdy drinking song was really a tribute to their homeland. By the time they were ready to repeat the chorus he was able to join in.

The last notes drifted away and the crowd looked up at them expectantly. Tulkhan tensed. Crowds were unpredictable animals. Then he heard noises behind him.

'Right on time,' Imoshen muttered with relief. She dropped his hand to direct the servants. 'Go out into the crowd and serve them.'

Tulkhan watched as a long line of servants moved past him, carrying trays laden with food. The revellers cheered and waited with surprising courtesy to be served. The people of Fair Isle would never cease to amaze him.

'We can slip away now,' Imoshen whispered, retreating up the steps.

He followed. Their footsteps echoed in the marbled foyer. Drawing her into an antechamber he snatched the torch from her hand and flung it into the unlit fireplace along with his. 'If those attackers on the bridge weren't waiting for us, who were they after?'

'Thieves looking for a party of drunken revellers?' She shrugged. 'How should I know? What does it matter? We escaped them.'

The wood in the grate burst into flame. Imoshen stepped closer and extended her hands towards the warmth. A shudder gripped her.

Of course she was cold. She had thrown her cloak at their attackers to buy him time. She had faced death at his side. Admiration stirred in Tulkhan. He knew of no Ghebite woman who would have stood by him like that, or would have been capable of thinking on her feet as she had. 'Imoshen?'

When she looked up at him, her eyes were haunted by the danger she had escaped. Before he could stop himself Tulkhan opened his arms and she went to him. True, she was Dhamfeer, the people's revered T'En Princess, but she was also Imoshen and not half as sure of herself as she pretended.

'Are you hurt?'

With a half sob she turned her face into his neck, her hot breath and damp tears warming his throat.

'How many times must I walk through death's shadow?' she whispered.

Tulkhan had no answer.

TULKHAN HAD JOINED the Keldon nobles and his Ghebites troops to watch a T'En display match. It was staged in a hall built specifically for this purpose with tiered seats on two sides.

The match was yet another example of T'En absurdity. Played with flat paddles and rag balls, it followed obscure rules. There was much explanation of points taken and loud guffaws from his own men who found the niceties of the game beyond them.

Tulkhan stiffened as Imoshen received a message from a servant. Was she leaving to go to her lover?

As she slipped away, Tulkhan decided he must discover the truth once and for all. His hand settled on his sword hilt and he stalked down the long gallery to the bedchamber wing. Imoshen was a distant figure ahead of him, sailing noiselessly through the fingers of afternoon sunlight which pierced the narrow windows. Even in this small connecting gallery the T'En had indulged their love of beauty. Lifelike paintings of vistas containing fantastic mythological figures filled each niche.

Imoshen entered the wing of bedchambers and he waited before following. If she was being unfaithful he wanted to catch her in an incriminating situation, something she could not talk her way out of.

Heart pounding, he marched up the stairwell after her, dreading what he would discover. As a Ghebite, Tulkhan could not live with the dishonour of her betrayal. He would have to kill her, and then himself.

IMOSHEN ENTERED CARIAH's bedchamber. Three young men turned to face her.

'I have their recommendations,' Cariah said.

Imoshen took the letters, saying, 'The post of interpreter will not be an easy one. The Ghebites –'

The door burst open, crashing against the wall. In the reverberating silence General Tulkhan stood in the entrance glowering, naked sword blade raised.

Imoshen looked up, horrified. Surely he had not imagined her in danger, not in the palace itself? Perhaps there was some heinous plot she knew nothing about. Imoshen's skin grew cold as she realised the door had been ripped off its hinges. Tulkhan must have feared for her life.

The General eyed the occupants of the room suspiciously and then sheathed his sword. 'What are you doing, Imoshen?'

'Interviewing prospective interpreters.'

'In Lady Cariah's bedchamber?'

Imoshen turned to the young men. 'Leave now. I will contact you.'

One of them plucked his recommendation from her hands. 'I was mistaken. I could not work with...' He glanced at Tulkhan then scurried out, followed by the others.

The General strode across to Imoshen, taking the rest of the letters from her. While he frowned over them she cast Cariah a pleading look.

But Cariah tilted her head as the Basilica's bells rang. 'Is that the time already? I must go. I am late to meet Sahorrd.'

'Sahorrd? I thought it was Jacolm,' General Tulkhan muttered, but Cariah had already departed.

'I can't keep track of her lovers,' Imoshen said.

He sank onto the chair. 'What are these letters of recommendation for?'

'I was trying to find tactful interpreters to assist your lord commanders when they take over their estates.'

'Is that what you have been doing these afternoons?' he pressed.

She hesitated, surprised by the urgency of his tone. 'I did try to speak with you the night of their investiture, but –'

'Why didn't you tell me?'

She recognised the pain in his voice. As a healer her instinctive reaction was to offer comfort. She searched his face. 'Surely you did not think I was in danger here in the palace itself? Have you had word of a plot against my life?'

'A plot?'

'You burst in with your weapon drawn.'

He stifled a bitter laugh.

She stepped back unnerved. 'I... I don't understand, General.'

Cursing, he sprang to his feet and marched towards the door.

Anger overrode Imoshen's confusion. 'In the Old Empire we did not reward kindness with boorish behaviour.'

He turned. 'Is that how you see us? Barbarians who need nursemaids?'

'No!' The cry was out before she could stop it. 'This was for my people as much as yours. Your men are loyal and skilled commanders, but they are not like you.'

'And what am I, Imoshen?'

Heart hammering, she dragged in a ragged breath. This was her chance. She had wanted to speak with him free of hangers-on and court protocol, but suddenly she found his intense dark gaze frightening.

'What am I to you, Imoshen?' he asked, striding back to search her face.

Resolutely she met his eyes. If there was going to be anything between them it had to be built on honesty and, when she spoke, her words sprang from a deep need to believe this was the truth. For if it wasn't, all her hopes and plans were laid on a foundation of shifting sand. Swallowing her trepidation, she closed the distance between them. 'You are a fair and good True-man who seeks to do what is right for all of Fair Isle, not just for your own Ghebite soldiers.'

Something like a groan escaped him as he caught her to him.

As he enveloped her in his embrace, a rush of warmth filled her. She could feel his great heart hammering under her palm which was pinned against his chest. Once she had thought conceiving his child would bind him to her, yet it was more complex than that. For a moment she wanted nothing more than to be held like this.

But Imoshen had to have answers. She pulled away. 'Why have you been so cold to me, General? What aren't you telling me?'

His lips found hers, drowning her questions, drowning all coherent thought. Desire ignited her. She wanted to forget everything in this moment. Only this was real, this passion and this man.

She felt tears escape her closed lids and did not care.

Everything weighed upon her – the resistance of the Keldon nobles and their unspoken condemnation of her, the knowledge that her every action was being watched by foreign ambassadors while they debated whether to support the rebel T'Reothe or the Ghebite general. Rights and wrongs did not bother these pragmatic brokers of power, only results. Yet she could bear all this if only she knew that she had the General's trust.

As his lips covered hers Imoshen gave herself up to the hunger of his kiss.

She knew they should not be touching like this, not when they were to be bonded soon, but she needed to feel his desire for her. He cradled her head and tenderly brushed her cheeks with his thumbs

'You're crying?'

'No.' She shook her head and would have pulled away but he caught her arm, making her wince. Her split sleeve parted to reveal livid bruises.

'I hurt you last night?'

She shrugged, not meeting his eyes.

'Forgive me?' he asked, voice thick with emotion.

A laugh escaped Imoshen. 'For what? How could I be so mean-spirited when you were only thinking of my safety?'

He shook his head, drawing back a little. 'I judged you by Ghebite standards. I listened to evil advice.'

'From the Beatific?' It was out before Imoshen could stop herself. When he pulled away sharply she ground her teeth in frustration.

'I told you to keep out of my head.'

'I wasn't in your head. I have eyes. I can see and I'm not stupid, although your Ghebite men treat me as if I were!' She lifted trembling hands to her face, brushing the hated weak tears from her cheeks. 'Oh General, is there any hope for us?'

'Us?'

'F... Fair Isle.' Imoshen hurried on. 'The peace is so fragile. The Keld watch your men like hawks, looking for any slight, imagined or real. Your lord commanders seem to seek ways to flaunt their rise in status. A hundred times a day Cariah and I have to soothe ruffled feathers.'

He snorted. 'I have seen the way Cariah soothes ruffled feathers. Which of my commanders hasn't she bedded?'

'Piers, I think. And Wharrd,' Imoshen replied automatically, then wondered why Tulkhan glared at her.

'In Gheeaba a woman of good standing would never take a lover!'

'In Gheeaba a woman is the property of her father, husband or son. No wonder she has no love for men!'

Tulkhan shook his head despairingly, but Imoshen thought she detected a faint gleam of amusement in his dark eyes.

'Ah, Imoshen, you have no idea,' he told her.

Relief warmed her but she stifled it, hardening her resolve. To need his approval weakened her. 'Then explain what I don't understand. Perhaps I don't know a great deal about your culture but I can learn. To keep me in ignorance demeans us both.'

He sighed. 'The Cadre would argue to keep a woman in ignorance is the only true kindness, for she does not have the ability to cope with the same mental complexities as a man.'

Imoshen laughed outright. 'That Cadre is a prime example of his own argument. Because his mind is closed he cannot see the Beatific for what she is. From the Basilica she weaves a magnificent web of power.'

Tulkhan gave a snort of laughter then rubbed his chin ruefully, as he studied her.

'What?' Imoshen asked, feeling strangely lighthearted.

He shook his head, offering his arm in a formal gesture. 'T'Imoshen?'

She laid her arm along his and closed her fingers over his hand. Regally, she inclined her head. 'General Tulkhan?'

'I believe there is an entertainment being performed in the forecourt to welcome the newly arrived nobles and ambassadors from the Amirate,' he said. 'Our presence is expected.'

'If we are lucky it will all be over before we get there,' Imoshen whispered, falling into step with him. She darted a quick look up at him and caught his grin.

'You are terrible, Imoshen.'

She sighed elaborately. 'Yes. My mother despaired of me. She said I was too wild for the high court.'

He squeezed her hand. 'You will have to prove your mother wrong.'

A little ball of sorrow formed inside Imoshen. It was true. She would have to succeed in the elaborate game of court life, because the fate of Fair Isle lay amid its seething factions. Yet she longed for her simple life at the stronghold, now irrevocably lost. If the Ghebites had not conquered Fair Isle she would have bonded with Reothe in the spring. The thought made her cheeks grow hot.

She frowned. Would Reothe dare to move against Tulkhan without her support? Because of the formality of the Old Empire, she had not come to know Reothe as intimately as she now knew the General, yet she had to acknowledge the powerful pull she felt towards him. They shared the same T'En heritage but the affinity went much deeper than that. How much deeper she did not know, and she did not want to find out.

Chapter Seven

IRRITATED BY THE scratching on the door, Tulkhan put aside his plans for T'Diemn's defence. Curse these palace servants with their little metal doorcombs, creeping about in their silent slippers, obsequiously bowing to him while smirking behind his back. 'Enter.'

Imoshen strode in and placed a sheaf of papers on his desk. 'I have selected fifteen interpreters for you to make the final selection from.'

Tulkhan was not convinced his men would accept the advice of Fair Isle interpreters. He missed Wharrd's counsel. After their bonding ceremony and the ensuing celebrations, Kalleen and Wharrd had followed custom and left to visit their estates.

Every day Tulkhan watched Imoshen win over ambassadors from both the mainland and the archipelago, securing her position. If only he could be certain of her motivation.

Tulkhan read the top letter. The man could read and write in three languages. The General fought a surge of annoyance. Few of his commanders could do more than sign their own names. If he foisted a Fair Isle scholar on them, they would be sure to take insult.

'You'll note I chose only men so as not to offend your commanders,' Imoshen said, eager to convince Tulkhan. He looked up at her suspiciously. 'Believe me, General, in all of Fair Isle you have no more loyal supporter than me.'

'For the good of Fair Isle,' he said, his Ghebite features impassive.

'What? Yes, for the good of my people, and yours.'

'And if you thought that T'Reothe stood a better chance of holding the island, would you throw your support behind him with as much ingenuity and vigour?'

She gasped, denial leaping to her lips.

'Think long and hard before you answer that, Imoshen,' he warned, 'because I can smell a lie!'

She swallowed, resentment flooding her.

'He was your betrothed,' Tulkhan continued. 'You broke your vows of celibacy to –'

'I had given no vows of celibacy. I wasn't old enough!'

'It was expected.' The General's expression was implacable. 'You thought little enough of your honour to break your vow to your betrothed.'

Fury consumed Imoshen. 'You stood at the gates of my stronghold with an army. You threatened to put my people to the sword. What would you like me to have done, sacrifice their lives for my personal honour?' She drew in a shaky breath. 'I took the path of peace.'

'So, from your lips I hear it. You support me out of necessity.' He smiled grimly. 'Do you wonder that I question your loyalty?'

'You twist my words.' She held his eyes. 'Whatever my reasons, I stand at your side now. The worm of doubt is in you, General, not me.'

When he did not respond she gave him the formal T'En obeisance and turned to go, sadness welling in her.

'I heard from Wharrd. He and Kalleen plan to be here for our bonding,' Tulkhan said to her retreating back.

Imoshen hesitated, then turned to face him. He sat sideways at the table, his long legs thrust out towards the fire. Even seated, he dominated the room.

Their bonding...

He was deliberately flaunting their imminent intimacy. She felt her cheeks grow hot. Her skin was so fair it was impossible to hide her reaction. She saw his features tighten.

Daring him to comment, she held his gaze. The silence stretched. She sensed that he wanted something from her, but was unable to determine what.

'Take these.' He shoved the letters in her direction. 'When my men assume control of their estates I will not be sending your watchdogs with them.'

Rejection made her stomach clench. She picked up the sheaf of papers, straightening them. 'The farmer folk speak their own language.'

'They'll find someone who can speak the trading tongue.'

'But –'

'Enough!' He gestured to the door. 'My men would have nothing in common with your over-cultured scholars.'

Deeply troubled, Imoshen returned to her room and left the letters on her desk. If her judgment was wrong in this, how could she trust her instincts? A wave of despair swamped her. She needed Cariah's coolheaded counsel and went to find her.

Heart thumping, Imoshen paused by the open doors of the crowded gaming salon. Slowing to a casual stroll, she wove through the tables.

Catching Cariah's eye, Imoshen used Old Empire signals to let her know that she wished to speak privately. With innate elegance Cariah made towards a door that led to the withdrawing room.

'Lady Cariah,' Jacolm called, 'stay and give me good luck. Sahorrd and I are losing hand after hand.'

'Later,' Cariah answered as she joined Imoshen.

'Why doesn't he ask you to advise him on what cards to play? At least then he might win a game,' Imoshen muttered.

Cariah bit back a laugh. 'Imoshen, you know he thinks the complexities of a card game too much for my feeble mind.'

'How can you bear it? Prove him wrong.'

Cariah's lips parted in a sensual, feline smile. 'When I am ready. Not everything can be achieved by direct confrontation. Now, what troubles you?'

Through the withdrawing room window Imoshen could just make out the shapes of a formal garden with knee-high hedges and topiaried trees – a classic example of T'En order and formality.

Jacolm and Sahorrd laughed raucously, crowing their victory over a turn of the cards. The sound rubbed on Imoshen's raw nerves, fraying the edges of her control. She felt the T'En power move in her, shifting like a restless, eager beast. It was more than she could bear.

'Do you fear your T'En heritage, Cariah?' she asked abruptly. 'Failing –'

'Hush!' The woman closed the connecting door, then returned.

A dim light filtered through the stained-glass window, illuminating Cariah's features as she spun to face Imoshen, her eyes luminous. 'How can you speak of failure? Soon you will be co-ruler of Fair Isle. You are on the brink of achieving everything. Why, you even carry his child.'

'How did you know that?'

Cariah blinked. 'Kalleen told me. Forgive me if –'

'Kalleen did not know.'

'She suspected. So I...'

'You what?' Imoshen pressed.

Cariah silently lifted her hand and placed it palm down over Imoshen's flat belly.

'I felt the growing life,' Cariah told her. 'This child is historic.'

Imoshen covered Cariah's hand with her own and opened her T'En senses, willing herself to feel that same fragile life. Her heart rate lifted and that recognisable taste settled on her tongue, sharp enough to sting.

Cariah gasped, pulling her hand away.

'What?' Imoshen asked, seeing Cariah's startled expression. 'You felt my T'En gifts?'

Cariah nodded. 'I've never come across it so strongly before. But then you are the first pure T'En I've known. T'Reothe's voyages coincided with my times at court, so I never met him, although I did hear rumours.' She shuddered. 'You made my skin crawl.'

Imoshen laughed. 'If I don't cloak it, even General Tulkhan knows when I use my gift on him, and he is pure Ghebite. I wanted to feel my child's life force stirring. Was I going about it the right way? Show me.'

Cariah shook her head slowly. 'I am not tutored in the gifts; anything I know I deduced myself.' She caught Imoshen's hand and placed her palm upon on her belly. 'By accident I felt the life force moving in you when we touched.'

A strange tension gripped Imoshen, a skin-prickling awareness. Until this moment Imoshen had assumed only the pure T'En were gifted. It was said their part-T'En cousins had an affinity for the gifts, but... 'You have innate power!'

'No! Only a little. I got it from both sides of the family. One of Father's ancestors trafficked with the Ancients. Don't tell anyone, I –'

'Cariah!' Imoshen dropped to her knees, clasping Cariah's hands to her face, kissing her palms. Tears of relief tightened her throat. 'Teach me what you know. I have been so alone, so frightened. The Aayel died before she could instruct me. I feel the gifts stir in me. I fear what I cannot control.'

'Hsst! You must not speak so.' Cariah sank to kneel with Imoshen, casting a swift look towards the closed door. 'They must never suspect.'

'Suspect? They know I am a cursed with the gifts. How can they not suspect?' Imoshen demanded. Then she saw Cariah's expression and understood the other woman's duplicity. It was her own power Cariah did not want revealed. 'You live a lie, Cariah. You deny what you are!'

'Don't be so quick to condemn me, Imoshen.' Her beautiful face twisted with emotion. 'I saw my mother sicken and die, locked away in the tower of my family's stronghold because as much as my father loved her, he feared her more. I will not be an object of fear and hatred!' Her face hardened. 'At best I could coach you to hide your gifts, but you already know how to cloak them.'

Guilt lanced Imoshen. How many times as a child had she longed to be accepted? What would she have done if she could have hidden her heritage? She could not judge her friend.

'I'm sorry. Forgive me, Cariah,' she whispered. 'I did not think of your position.'

Tears spilled over Cariah's lower lids, chasing each other across her cheeks. She fought to hold back a sob. Her pain touched Imoshen. Lifting a hand, she smoothed the tear track from Cariah's soft cheek. 'Forgive my cruel words.'

'Life is cruel!' Cariah turned her face away, wiping the dampness from her cheeks. The bitterness in her voice surprised Imoshen. 'We must take what we can, while we can.'

'I don't believe that.' Imoshen took hold of Cariah's shoulders, turning her, willing the woman to meet her gaze.

Cariah shook her head pityingly. 'You are so young. One day you will see.'

'No. I have to believe there is hope,' Imoshen whispered, fervently. 'If I did not, I could not bear to live. My family are all dead. The Aayel died so that I would live. I must believe we are capable of greatness —'

Cariah kissed her.

The gesture was so unexpected Imoshen froze, experiencing those soft lips on hers, salty with tears. The gentleness of the caress was unmistakable. Cariah offered love.

Imoshen gasped and pulled away.

Cariah sank back onto her heels. Her mouth trembled, unshed tears glistening in her pleading eyes. 'Don't reject me, Imoshen.'

Stunned, Imoshen stared.

Cariah's hand lifted imploringly.

'I...' Imoshen floundered.

Abruptly Cariah rose and stood before the mirror over the mantelpiece. In the dim light she made a great production of straightening her hair and smoothing her face to remove all traces of emotion.

'I surprise you. You are unsophisticated. This was the way of the Old Empire,' she explained with brittle casualness. 'T'Ysanna was my first lover.

She shared her men with me, taught me to enjoy them for what they could give but to look elsewhere for true love.'

Imoshen could hear Cariah distancing herself while denying what had passed between them.

With a smile Cariah returned to face Imoshen, offering a hand to help her rise. 'Come, tidy your face. They will be watching us.'

Imoshen stood stiffly, clasping Cariah's hand. She refused to release it, instead she lifted it to her lips, kissing the soft skin. 'Don't draw away from me, Cariah. I am out of my depth. I need your counsel.'

'You deny me in one breath then ask for my loyalty in the next.' Cariah stiffened. 'You are too cruel.'

'HERE WE ARE. Just for you.' The Keeper of the Knowledge beamed at Imoshen as he unwrapped the first of two packages. 'You would not believe what I went through to hide these from King Gharavan's men!'

Imoshen gasped. She had never seen anything like it. The edges of the pages were thick with gilt, but it was the cover and spine which astounded her. She stroked the plush velvet, her fingers tracing the inlaid jewels. 'This must date from the Age of Consolidation.'

'Middle period,' the Keeper nodded and gently unwound the calico wrapping of the second volume. 'This one is even more magnificent.'

'Pure gold?' Imoshen laughed.

'It is exquisite work,' he said. 'See the filigree, the granulation. This is real craftsmanship.'

Imoshen had to agree. 'May I?'

He hesitated, unwilling to let the book pass from his hands to hers.

'I will take care,' Imoshen promised. 'You know how much I value knowledge.'

At last he left her alone to search the books' indexes, but she was disappointed. Though the books themselves were invaluable works of art, they contained nothing more unusual than a collection of poems and a study of Keldon Highland customs. Still she would search them for any reference that might offer a clue to understanding her T'En gifts.

Imoshen sighed, rewrapping the volumes. She felt so alone. Cariah had drawn away from her and she could not blame her. The noblewoman helped with the entertainments, but instead of sharing her private time with Imoshen she spent it with her lovers. Imoshen tried not to begrudge this, just as she tried not to resent Cariah's popularity. It was curious. Lady Cariah of Fairban was enough like her sisters to be accepted. When she sang beautifully and danced with others from the Thespers' Guild, no one acknowledged that it was her T'En heritage which enabled her to move them to tears of joy.

In the days leading up to her bonding with General Tulkhan, Imoshen had walked the corridors of the palace with no one to call friend, cut off from Cariah and cold-shouldered by the General.

Food had no flavour and her life was as grey as the ever-shortening winter days. By the cusp of spring the babe would begin to show and she would be even more isolated as everyone would see how she had flaunted tradition.

'Finished already?' the Keeper asked. 'If you told me what you are after...'

Imoshen shook her head. She did not dare reveal her real purpose. 'Just curious. I am content to wander the library. You may go.'

She knew the old man liked to spend his days in the kitchen, sipping mulled wine near the ovens where the heat warmed the ache from his bones. There he enjoyed the company of the cook and bored the scullery maids with his stories.

He nodded and smiled, bright old eyes fixed on her.

'He was very like you, earnestly studying the old tomes.'

Imoshen's mouth went dry. Only one other person was like her. 'Reothe?'

'He was a pleasure to teach.'

Imoshen did not want to hear tales of Reothe's boyhood. She did not want to dwell on how lonely he must have been. Knowing the high court, he would have been an object of pity and ridicule. Her heart went out to that boy, but Reothe was no longer a defenceless child and she would do well to remember that. 'You were his tutor?'

'Yes, before he went to the Halls of Learning.' The Keeper's face glowed with pride. 'I have a copy of the treatise on philosophy he wrote when he was fifteen.'

But Imoshen had no time for philosophy. She tried to sound casual. 'Was there anything on the T'En that he particularly liked to read?'

'Everything. He devoured everything on the T'En, then he moved on to the great library in the Halls of Learning. He was disappointed because they don't study the T'En there, but his debates were legendary. When he took his place on T'Ashmyr's stone there was standing room only around the library stoves!'

Imoshen tried not to show her disappointment. 'Can you show me the books about the T'En?'

The old man laughed. 'Every book mentions the T'En.'

Imoshen looked down. She longed to trust the Keeper. But what would he say if she revealed she wanted to harness her gifts?

'No matter how high he rose, Reothe never forgot his old teacher,' the man continued fondly. He pulled something from inside his vest and unwrapped it. 'When he returned triumphant from his first voyage to the archipelago he brought me this.'

'What is it?' Imoshen asked. 'A religious artefact?'

'A shrunken human head.'

Imoshen shuddered. How primitive the dwellers of the archipelago were. Fair Isle was literally an island of culture in a sea of barbarism. She could not, would not let the heritage of her T'En culture sink into darkness.

TULKHAN RUBBED HIS eyes wearily. The old city of T'Diemn could be made secure again because it had been designed for defence, but the new city sprawled in an ungainly manner over the surrounding fertile basin, making defence all but impossible.

If he could have devoted himself to the problem, he would have come up with a solution by now. But for the time being he had to devote his attention to the visiting ambassadors so he could observe the interchange between them, particularly the triad of prosperous mainland kingdoms which he had not conquered.

He focused on the map of T'Diemn and its surrounds. Every street, every gate and spring was marked. It was all to scale, with the highest points in gradients of colour so that it appeared three-dimensional. There was no point in building fortifications around new T'Diemn if he did not include the hilltop to the south. Any general worth his salt would mount an offensive from that hilltop, yet it would mean taking the fortifications out to the hill since the outlying market gardens only reached its base, or pulling back and being prepared to sacrifice those people and their livelihood. Every decision was a compromise.

The door to his map-room flew open. Imoshen stood there in nothing but a thin nightgown, her feet bare, her hair loose on her shoulders. Her cheeks were pale and her chest rose and fell as if she had been running.

'You could not leave well enough alone, could you?' she demanded. 'You thought you knew better!'

Tulkhan put the scriber down with exaggerated patience. 'I have no idea what you are talking about.'

Her eyes widened with fear.

Tulkhan felt a prickling sensation travel across his skin. 'What is it?'

She took a deep breath. 'You had better come.'

As Tulkhan collected his sword from the back of his chair, she made a noise in her throat.

'What?'

'Cold steel will not help,' she whispered, then hurried off.

He followed, lengthening his stride to keep up with her, while buckling his sword belt. 'Should I call out my elite guard?'

'Not for this.'

The evening's entertainments had finished long ago and the servants had cleared away. Only the occasional sconce of candles lit the way.

Imoshen moved soundlessly. Tulkhan's boots struck the tiles and then the wooden floor of the older wing. When Imoshen glided down the steps to the Tribulation Portrait Gallery, Tulkhan fought a sense of foreboding.

At the entrance to the gallery Imoshen stopped. It was deserted and unlit except for a branch of candles which sat on the floor about halfway along, before a gaping hole in the wainscoting.

'The secret passage has been forced.'

'He fled,' Imoshen whispered. 'I don't blame him.'

'Who?'

'The servant who found this.' Imoshen spoke over her shoulder as she hurried down the hall. 'He was taking a shortcut through this gallery to meet his lover.'

When they reached the gaping hole, Tulkhan picked up the candles and peered through the splintered wainscoting into the secret passage. The stale smell of old air made him grimace.

He straightened and looked at Imoshen. 'What would you have me do? How do you even know it is my people? It could be some of your builders.'

'My builders would not be so stupid. They know better than to disturb the past. And they would not be so crude. If they wanted to explore the passage they would remove the skirting board and wainscoting, then replace it afterwards, not bludgeon a hole with a battle-axe. No. It is one or more of your men. My guess is Harholfe and his friends.'

Tulkhan frowned. 'They've gone looking for gold.'

'Isn't the gold room gold enough?'

'It's the challenge.' He grinned then sobered. 'What do you expect me to do? Go after them like misbehaving boys? Like as not they'll find nothing down there but storerooms and rat holes, just as you said –'

'That was not all I said.'

'No.' Tulkhan had not forgotten, merely tried to deny what he did not wish to face. He shook his head. 'We must bring them out.'

He ducked down, stepping through the jagged gap with difficulty. His shoulders were almost too wide. He'd taken four steps when he realised Imoshen was not following him. Turning on the stair he looked back up to her, her face framed by the splintered wood. Six candle flames danced in her fixed eyes.

Tulkhan's body tightened, responding to her fear. His free hand went to his sword hilt. But Imoshen had said cold steel would not help him against what lay below.

He cursed under his breath. 'They are my men and your ancestors. You can't turn your back, Imoshen.'

He saw a flare of anger displace her fear. Still she hesitated.

'If you want my respect you must earn it,' he told her. 'A good general has a responsibility to his people.'

'A good leader does not attempt the impossible.'

'What? What is so impossible?'

'Tulkhan, I am out of my depth!' Her hands lifted in a silent plea.

He did not let himself feel compassion. 'Suit yourself.'

Turning his back, he walked down the narrow stair. Though she moved soundlessly, he knew when she caught up with him because he could feel the skin-lifting tension of her T'En gift. It made his temples throb and left a metallic taste on his tongue.

As he came to the long passage Imoshen caught his arm. 'They brought this on themselves by forcing entry to the secret passages. If they have gone down into the catacombs, we must seal the door and leave them there.'

Cold horror closed like a vice around his chest. He hardened his voice. 'You know I cannot do that.'

She stared at him, her face pale and set.

With a string of High T'En curses, or perhaps it was a prayer, she darted around him. Still muttering, she plucked the candles from his hand and went ahead.

Tulkhan smiled grimly to himself. But the hand which gripped his sword hilt was slick with sweat as he followed.

Imoshen went unflinchingly down another staircase. At the base he noticed the exit panel was wedged open with a broken tile. They stepped into a long narrow gallery. The candles could only illuminate the nearest walls and part of the vaulted ceiling. Their lowered voices echoed.

'See the style of vaulting? This dates from the Age of Tribulation. This way.' Imoshen spoke as if she was conducting a leisurely tour of the palace, but her eyes never ceased searching the shadows.

Tulkhan followed, his senses on alert. The tension which rolled off Imoshen's skin was not so bad now. She had to be controlling it because she had not relaxed.

'How far along was it?' she muttered. 'All these archways look the same.'

A man's raw scream cut the air. Imoshen stopped still. Tulkhan strained to hear as the echoes of the cry faded. He was about to speak when the clatter of boots reverberated on the stonework.

'This way.' Imoshen ran, trying to shield the candle flames.

Tulkhan pushed past her. He could see light and leaping shadows coming from a narrow opening. He stopped as Sahorrd and Jacolm stumbled out.

'General?' Jacolm raised his candle.

'One of them. Behind you!' Sahorrd warned, lunging forward, his sword drawn.

Tulkhan spun, unsheathing his blade. Sahorrd aimed for Imoshen's throat. She parried with the candle holder, disarming him even as Tulkhan struck using the flat of his sword. The man went down with a grunt of disbelief.

Jacolm swore. 'The Princess.'

'Who did you think it was?' Tulkhan hauled Sahorrd to his feet. The man rubbed his head, avoiding Imoshen's eyes as she handed him his weapon.

'Much good it would have done you, if I'd been who you thought I was,' she told him. 'Let's get out of here. But first I must seal the catacombs.'

Jacolm stepped between her and the open passage. 'Harholfe's still down there, General.'

Anger flashed through Tulkhan. 'You left him down there?'

'He was right behind me!' Jacolm bristled.

'Harholfe had the battleaxe,' Sahorrd said. 'He used it to prise the lid off the coffin.'

Imoshen gasped. She made the sign to ward off evil, raising her left hand to her eyes then over her head. 'May their eyes pass over me, over all of us.'

'Your long-dead T'En warriors?' Tulkhan asked. 'The Para –'

She hissed, cutting him short.

Tulkhan looked to her for an explanation.

'Names have power.' Imoshen's voice thrummed with emotion. 'We invoke them by name to serve us.'

'But what of Harholfe?' Jacolm insisted.

'We go after him,' Tulkhan said. 'You two stay here, cover our retreat.'

He caught Imoshen's eye. She wiped the back of her hand on her mouth, then moved into the narrow stairwell. He stepped down after her, aware that Jacolm and Sahorrd were following despite his orders. He was not surprised. No matter how deep their terror they would not abandon their brother-at-arms. To display cowardice meant disgrace.

At the base of the stair Imoshen waited, holding the candles high to illuminate a long barrel-vaulted catacomb. Heavy stone coffins lay in wall niches.

Silently Imoshen pointed upward. Above them were life-size paintings of the legendary Paragian Guard in full armour. The inlaid gold and silver flickered in the candlelight.

There was no sign of Harholfe.

'This way, General.' Only the gleam of Sahorrd's fearful eyes betrayed his dread as he led them to the right. Their combined light illuminated a waist-high stone coffin resting under a High T'En inscription.

'Imoshen?' Tulkhan indicated the words.

She raised the candles and translated. 'Here lies the Aayel. First of the Last.'

'What does it mean?' Tulkhan asked.

'It is the sarcophagus of Imoshen the First's own son, Aayel, First Emperor of Fair Isle. After he abdicated in favour of his half T'En daughter, Abularassa, he served the church and the people of Fair Isle. The title *the Aayel* was created to honour him. He was the first to serve in this capacity and the last surviving pure T'En male to be born in the old country. Only children, those born on the long journey and those too young to remember, were left.' She touched her forehead, signalling the T'En obeisance to the first Aayel. 'This is almost worth the –'

'But where is Harholfe?' Jacolm took two impatient paces past them, then stopped. Holding his candle high, he looked back. 'Come on.'

Imoshen ignored him, studying the lid of the sarcophagus instead. Tulkhan joined her. The lid was decorated with a raised stone carving of an aged T'En male. He was richly dressed in clothes of state and carried no weapons. The individual hairs of his plaited beard had been intricately delineated first in stone, then silver thread.

'For Akha Khan's sake, can we move?' Sahorrd urged. 'The coffin is just around the corner.'

'The one you were foolish enough to open?' Imoshen snapped.

He did not meet her eyes.

'You desecrate my heritage,' she told him. 'These are the T'En of legend and you –'

'Imoshen!' Tulkhan barked. 'We must find Harholfe and get out of here.'

As he strode past Jacolm, he sensed the man's terror and knew he was not far from violence. Tulkhan's small pool of candlelight moved forward with him and soon he identified another stone sarcophagus. The heavy lid was off, tilted against the side.

'So small,' Imoshen whispered.

'It contains a child,' Sahorrd explained as they came abreast of it. 'The carving on the lid was inlaid with precious metal and jewels. That's why we –'

Imoshen's whimper cut him short. She swayed as if she might faint. Tulkhan steadied her only to find her skin was ice cold and her body felt stiff.

He peered into the opened coffin expecting a skeleton. Instead he saw a perfectly preserved ten-year-old child. She was richly dressed in red velvet embroidered with gold thread. Jewels were sewn into the broad yoke collar that lay across her shoulders. Her eyes were closed and he could see the individual lashes, the soft curve of her top lip. A single ruby lay on her forehead.

'Why didn't you plunder this one?' Tulkhan asked.

Sahorrd and Jacolm stared down at the child, their weapons forgotten. Then Sahorrd looked up like a startled deer transfixed by a spear.

'I don't understand.' Panic edged his voice. 'The ruby...'

Tulkhan felt a sense of time slowing down so that he could hear his own heart beating in his ears, echoing hollowly in his head, drowning all sense of urgency.

'Imoshen?' He had to force himself to speak.

She did not blink.

Tulkhan felt his skin crawl. 'Imoshen?'

She looked over her shoulder at him, wine-dark eyes awash with tears. 'My daughter...'

'You have no daughter. Who is this, Imoshen?'

She left his side, walking around the stone coffin to read the inscription on the lid which rested against the sarcophagus.

'Here lies Ysanna. Killed by rebels.' Imoshen touched the date. 'She was six years old. I've never heard of her.'

Tulkhan looked into the coffin again and felt himself falling away. He forced his tongue to work. 'What T'En sorcery is this and where is Harholfe?'

'He claimed the big ruby,' Sahorrd said.

'But he's put it back for some reason,' Jacolm muttered. His hand darted forward to take the precious stone.

'No!' Suddenly Imoshen's fingers were between his and the jewel, holding it in place on the child's forehead. She glared at him, her features austere, her eyes flickering red in the candlelight.

'Curse your witchy eyes, woman!' Jacolm spat, his sword tip lifting.

'Enough,' Tulkhan snapped. 'Where is Harholfe?'

They looked around but there was no sign of him, only empty stone walls.

'Tell me what happened,' Tulkhan ordered.

'They came for us when he took the ruby.' Sahorrd shuddered. 'Three Dhamfeer dressed in armour appeared from the shadows. The priests say a True-man should turn his eyes from the black arts and now I know why. These beings made the blood run cold in my veins. I've never known such terror...' He looked down in shame, then met their eyes resolutely. 'I fled.'

'We ran for the stairs.' Jacolm indicated back the way they had come. 'I swear Harholfe was right behind me.'

'Then where is he?' Tulkhan turned to Imoshen only to discover she was standing absolutely still, the big ruby pressed to the centre of her forehead between her closed lids. She opened her eyes and replaced the ruby. When she met his gaze, her garnet eyes were cold and contemptuous.

'I thought you didn't want the grave desecrated?'

She stared at him in silence.

Tulkhan fought a surge of fear. 'Where is my man, Harholfe?'

Closing her eyes, Imoshen lifted her left hand. Her splayed fingers seemed to feel the air.

'What is left of him is just beyond the next coffin, propped up against the wall.' Her voice was rich and strangely intimate.

Jacolm cursed. He darted away, candle held high, weapon drawn. They followed him.

'Nothing. I see nothing but his battleaxe.' Jacolm spun around, gesturing to the dressed stone walls and floor, which were bare except for the discarded weapon. 'Here is the stone coffin, but where – ?'

'Where is the body, Imoshen?' Tulkhan went to catch her arm, but before he could touch her, he felt a sharp, stinging blow. The flesh under his nails throbbed. He cursed with pain.

Imoshen pointed to a blank wall, lifting her candles high. 'There.'

The reflection of the flickering flames glistened on the stone's slick surface, glistened and coalesced into the outline of a man's body.

Sahorrd's indrawn breath sounded loud in the silence. 'It is his shadow. I mean...' But he had no words for what he saw.

Like oil dropped into water, the outline of a man appeared on the wall's stone. Tulkhan could see Harholfe's expression of frozen terror. He felt cold to the marrow. As a general he had seen men die in many ways – in battle, in agony, raving with fever, even too weary to care. But he had never seen a man die of fear, leaving his last moment of terror imprinted on stone.

'Where is Harholfe's body?' Jacolm turned on Imoshen, sword raised. 'His weapon lies at his feet unbloodied.'

'Of course. Steel cannot kill those who are already dead.' Imoshen held his eyes until he lowered his blade. 'Your companion broke the ward protecting the grave. His soul was forfeit.'

'Don't play your riddles on me, Dhamfeer bitch!' Jacolm's voice vibrated with terrified fury. 'Where is Harholfe?'

Imoshen's eyes closed. Tulkhan felt the overflow of her gift and took a step back, his fingertips still throbbing. Sahorrd and Jacolm made the Ghebite sign to ward off evil.

When Imoshen opened her eyes they glowed with an inner radiance. 'The

Parakletos are escorting him through death's shadow into death's own realm.'

'I thought you said...' Tulkhan stopped. It struck him as odd that Imoshen no longer evinced any fear and seemed at ease with her T'En gifts. Her expression was calm and she looked at him as though he were a stranger. His skin crawled with understanding. Some long-dead T'En being was animating Imoshen.

'I think it is time to go. Sahorrd, Jacolm?' Tulkhan used the battlefield gesture to signal retreat. They moved to stand behind him, never turning their backs on Imoshen as they edged away.

'We can't leave,' Jacolm protested. 'Harholfe has not been properly buried.'

Imoshen stabbed a finger at him. 'You and your two friends trespassed on a sacred place and desecrated an innocent's grave. Harholfe has paid, so it is finished, but first the stone must be replaced.'

She walked past them, unconcerned by their weapons. To Tulkhan she did not seem vulnerable, despite her bare feet and the thin nightgown which brushed her slender ankles.

He bent to retrieve the undamaged battleaxe. As he stood, stone grated on stone. He heard his men's surprised intake of breath and turned to see Imoshen straighten, pivoting the stone slab into place.

The abandoned candlestick behind the coffin illuminated her as she leaned over the stone statue to kiss the child's cold lips, whispering something in High T'En. She replaced the sarcophagus's lid and dusted off her hands. He glanced at the stone lid. It had taken three men to move it. She did not have the strength to move that slab.

Imoshen bent to retrieve the light.

The moment stretched. She did not rise.

Dread made Tulkhan's movements stiff as he walked around the sarcophagus to find Imoshen sitting on the ground looking dazed. 'General?'

Relief flooded him. He helped her to stand. Her skin was warm and soft.

'Come,' he said.

'What of your man?'

'Dead.'

She accepted this. In silence, except for the scuff of the Ghebite boots on stone, they hurried towards the first Aayel's sarcophagus. Jacolm and Sahorrd turned the corner, taking their light with them.

Imoshen stopped and flicked free of his grasp to stroke the Aayel's tomb.

'What?' Tulkhan asked.

Imoshen looked around the catacomb with awe and wonder. 'My feet walk on history's path. Sardonyx used to come down here and lie on the stone slab meant for his body.'

'We must go.'

'They said it drove him mad.'

Tulkhan took her hand even though it made all the hairs on his arm rise in protest. 'Come.'

'His own kinswomen condemned him to death.'

Tulkhan tugged on her arm. 'The others are waiting.'

'My heritage is one of tragedy.'

'Not now, Imoshen!' Tulkhan hurried her towards the steps under the cold long-dead eyes of T'En warriors.

As they stepped out into the gallery, Imoshen shuddered. 'Close the passage, seal the catacombs. No one must go down there.'

'How do we close the passage?' Tulkhan asked.

'The shoe.' Imoshen pointed to an old shoe wedged in the door frame. 'Long ago a boy used it to hold the door open.'

'What boy?' Tulkhan asked.

'Some lost boy. I don't know any more.'

Tulkhan sheathed his sword and worked the shoe loose. It came free with a tug and the panel slid into place, grating stone on dust. It did not close completely, however, remaining about a finger's breadth open.

He grunted. 'That will have to do. Let's get out of here.'

Jacolm and Sahorrd were already moving but Imoshen pressed both hands on the stone trying to force the door.

'Leave it be, Imoshen,' Tulkhan urged. 'We'll seal the secret passage from above.'

Regret and fear mingled on her face.

'What happened down there? Do you remember finding the child?'

Her eyes widened and she looked away, saying, 'I'm not sure it is safe to leave the door like that.'

'I'm not sure of anything. Not since I...' He had been about to say, *not since I met you.* 'Since I came to Fair Isle I doubt everything.'

Her sharp eyes sought his.

'General?' Jacolm called from the base of the stair.

'We'll seal the entrance at the portrait gallery. That will have to do,' Tulkhan decided.

'What about Harholfe's body?'

Tulkhan realised she did not remember. 'Harholfe has paid for his folly. There was no body.' He wondered how he would explain Harholfe's disappearance to his men. 'Come.'

They hurried after the others and stepped through the shattered wainscoting into the portrait gallery. Grimly, Jacolm and Sahorrd sheathed their weapons. Tulkhan knew by tomorrow night they would be boasting of this in their cups, denying their terror.

So much had happened since he had entered that secret passage Tulkhan felt as though it must be nearly dawn.

Imoshen inspected the damage done by the battle-axe. 'I will have the master-builder provide a stonemason. This will be sealed securely and the wainscoting replaced.' She turned to Jacolm and Sahorrd. 'You see, there was nothing down there but storerooms and rat holes.'

'But –' Jacolm began.

'Nothing but storerooms and rat holes,' Imoshen repeated.

Tulkhan's temples throbbed and his head ached. He saw Sahorrd rub the bridge of his nose.

Jacolm frowned.

'Nothing,' Imoshen urged. 'Nothing worth a man's life.'

'Harholfe...' Sahorrd moaned.

'Harholfe has taken a ship to the mainland in my service,' Tulkhan said. There was no corpse to dispose of, no way to make his death public and honour him. 'We will not speak of this to anyone.'

Jacolm and Sahorrd exchanged glances.

Tulkhan dismissed them both. When they had gone he turned to Imoshen. 'Well?'

'Well what?' she asked.

'What happened down there?'

She shrugged. 'They disturbed a sacred site. One of them paid with his life. The T'En look after their own.'

'What of the Para –'

'Don't!' She covered his lips, her fingertips gritty with dust. 'At least not here, not now.'

'You didn't look frightened.' Tulkhan sheathed his sword.

'Nonsense. I was terrified the whole time.'

'After we found the child's grave –'

'Do not speak of that.'

Tulkhan frowned. 'Do you remember the sarcophagus of the first Aayel?'

'Of course. And I would dearly love to explore the whole of the catacombs, but every time I think of them I am filled with such dread that I feel ill. So speak no more of this and I will have the entrance sealed up.' She frowned. 'I don't remember anything after Jacolm went to take the ruby. How do you know Harholfe is dead if you did not find his body?'

'We found enough.' Tulkhan shuddered and shook his head. 'Don't go down there again, Imoshen.'

A bitter laugh escaped her. 'You were the one who insisted I go. Believe me, nothing could get me into those catacombs again.'

Tulkhan stared at her, not sure if she was being deliberately obscure. 'Who was the child, Ysanna? You called her daughter.'

She flinched. 'Sometimes the gifts can be a curse.' Her gaze slid past his and he knew she was going to lie, or at least avoid answering the question. 'There have been many Ysannas. The most recent was the Empress's only daughter and heir. Like all my other relatives, she died defending Fair Isle. One by one they fell before your army, choosing to fight to the death rather than be taken captive.' Her face grew hard and proud, reminding him of how she had looked down in the catacombs. 'Why do you look at me like that?'

'I am tired. Go to bed.'

'I was in bed, in case you hadn't noticed,' Imoshen told him.

'Oh, I'd noticed. You are wearing nothing under that nightgown. If I were to undo the drawstring and slide it off your shoulders you would be naked in my arms.'

She lifted her chin. 'I might be naked, General, but I would not be in your arms.' She plucked a candle from the holder. 'Goodnight.'

He watched her go. The more he knew of Imoshen the less he understood. And after tonight he was not eager to pry too deeply.

With a sigh he walked across the gallery and sat down with his back to the wall and Harholfe's battleaxe across his knees. He snuffed out all but one candle and watched the dark entrance to the secret passage.

He did not really believe anything was going to come up that stairwell. And if it did, he knew cold steel would not stop it, but he could not rest easy until the entrance was closed and the shades of the legendary T'En warriors sealed away from True-men.

Chapter Eight

RECOGNISING THE OTHER occupants of the carriage as the elite of the Keldon Highland aristocracy, Imoshen hid her misgivings. They were leaders of the most powerful families, related by blood and bonding, and united, she suspected, in their plans for Fair Isle. What was supposed to be a tour of the sites of T'Diemn promised to be a grilling.

'T'Imoshen,' they greeted her.

'Grandfathers, Grandmothers,' she deliberately gave them the more intimate honorific instead of their titles. 'What do you wish to discuss?'

'So impatient,' Lady Woodvine, the iron-haired matriarch, muttered.

Frail, half-blood Lord Athlyn shook his head. 'In the high court the Empress –'

'The Empress is dead,' Imoshen interrupted, 'and the Old Empire died with her. The scholars are agreed that on the first day of the new year a new age will begin. We must make our peace with that.'

The Keldon nobles exchanged glances.

'To the Causare,' Lord Fairban told the driver, who urged the horses forward.

Imoshen stiffened. It was in this building that the Causare Council of the Old Empire met to debate policy. She had watched one of these sessions during her first visit to the capital. But the long-winded speeches had bored her and it had been much more fun to watch the spectators in the gallery. It had amused her when the nobles were unceremoniously bundled out on the bell of noon to make room for the other functionaries of the Causare, the traders.

From sun up till noon the building served the council, then from noon till dusk it served the traders. They were merchants, sea captains, guildmasters, anyone who thought they could turn an opportunity to profit. After the noon bell, the Causare Council became a place of furious buying and selling of profits as yet unearned. Traders bought and sold part ownership of planned voyages to the archipelago or the mainland ports. It was said a canny Causare trader could turn a profit on a crop of grapes three times before it was sown, let alone harvested, crushed and fermented.

Imoshen maintained her silence as the carriage passed through the streets of old T'Diemn and finally stopped at the Causare. Leading the party, she sailed up the wide steps and through the double doors embossed with symbols of Fair Isle's prosperity.

Once in the central chamber under the great dome, she hesitated. The

Beatific, accompanied by four high-ranking priests including Murgon, acknowledged her. Imoshen returned their brief nods. She had expected to see only the remaining Keldon leaders, but the gathering also included what looked like the elite of T'Diemn's traders. By their rich clothing and personal styles she identified merchants, bankers, guildmasters and a few ships' captains – an odd gathering, considering it was not yet noon.

Lord Fairban caught up with her, leading her to the Empress's bench, which looked no different from any other. In the Causare all voices were supposed to be heard with equal weight. But by custom this had become the seat of power.

The Beatific parted from her companions and took the seat on Imoshen's left, claiming the highest precedent after the Empress. Fairban retreated to join his faction, and for several moments there was a shuffling of feet as people found their places in the circle of tiered benches.

The Beatific said nothing. Imoshen vowed she would not give her the satisfaction of asking what was going on.

When a shaft of sunlight entered the dome far above, Imoshen looked up. The first-floor gallery was empty of spectators. Light shimmered on the central floor where a mural depicting Fair Isle and the known world was worked in tiny multicoloured tiles. Most of the council's seats would have been empty had it not been for the traders.

One by one people settled and Imoshen waited, her features schooled into an impassive mask.

In the ensuing hush the formidable Keldon matriarch came to her feet. 'T'Imoshen. Unlike others' – Woodvine paused to glare at certain people – 'I will not call you Empress, because you have not earned that title. We have two questions for you to present to the Ghebite general. First, when will the Causare reopen to serve the people of Fair Isle? And when it does, who will lead us?'

'Yes!' An eager merchant leapt to her feet. 'War is bad for business. I lost a whole shipment of mainland fruit left to rot because –'

'And I have not seen the profits from my last voyage because the banks have frozen their funds!' another cried.

At this a terrible clamour arose as the bankers argued that if they had not frozen funds the panicked populace would have bankrupted the country, and traders angrily debated the efficacy of this policy. A smile tugged at Imoshen's lips. Trust the people of Fair Isle to be concerned about profits before politics. Or was it simply the other side of the coin?

The double doors flew open and General Tulkhan strode into the centre of the Causare, his boots thundering in the sudden silence. His elite guard marched in single file to take up position behind the highest seats, where they stood, hands on their sword hilts. Half a dozen of the General's most trusted commanders formed a solid wall at the open doors.

No sound echoed in the great dome, no one moved. Imoshen feared the tiles would soon run with blood.

'What treason is this?' Tulkhan roared. He pointed to the Keldon nobles. 'You swore an oath of fealty to me. And you!' He turned on the traders. 'You also swore an oath. Yet you meet in secret!'

'General Tulkhan.' Imoshen left the Empress's seat to join him. 'No treason is being worked here. This building houses the Causare Council. During the Old Empire the leaders of Fair Isle debated policy here and traders met to arrange backing for their ventures.' She took his hand, feeling the tension in him. 'Come, hear them speak.'

As Tulkhan followed her relief washed through Imoshen, making her light-headed. He had entered the Causare as a general but it would take a statesman to resolve this.

'We must avoid bloodshed, General. Trust me,' she whispered, seating him next to her. Imoshen signalled for silence, coming to her feet. 'This is not how I remember the council.' Actually it was more like the energetic afternoon's trading. 'You wish to know when the Causare will reopen? Well, today is that day.'

The traders finger-clicked their approval, some going so far as to give the official traders' call of success.

'Pretty words.' Woodvine stood. 'But what of the council? We have no say!'

'What of the banks?' a merchant interrupted. 'We are losing money!'

'We are saving your gold!' insisted a banker.

The Causare erupted.

Imoshen turned to the Beatific, who appeared pleased. Tulkhan's disgusted expression made her smile.

Imoshen leaned so close to him that her lips brushed his ear. 'The day-to-day business of Fair Isle has resumed but the larger ventures which risk great capital are all halted until the political situation regains stability. The merchants cannot undertake their ventures if the banks have frozen their funds.'

'What do you suggest, Imoshen?'

'Give the Emp – Give your royal seal to the banks. If they know they have the resources of the royal house behind them they will release funds.'

'But I am not officially ruler of Fair Isle until the coronation ceremony.'

'The Causare will not meet again until the new year. Until then, the traders can negotiate business in the taverns and tea-houses, then get their agreements formally recognised when the Causare reopens its doors.' Imoshen hesitated, watching Tulkhan's features as he ran through the ramifications.

The Beatific raised her voice over the din. 'General, Fair Isle must not lose her position as centre of trade.'

'You both speak sense.'

'And that surprises you?' Imoshen dared to tease. She sat back, pleased.

The Causare grew silent as people realised the General was ready to speak.

'Hear this.' Tulkhan raised his hands. 'After the coronation ceremony I will underwrite the banks with the funds of the royal house...'

Furious trading drowned out his voice as every merchant, banker, sea captain and guildmaster touted their latest venture.

Woodvine left her seat to march across the floor towards the General. She was joined by Fairban and Athlyn. Imoshen took the General's arm, aware that only part of the original question had been answered. She noticed the Beatific move to stand on the General's other side.

Tulkhan was astounded by the sheer volume of noise. He eyed the belligerent Keld before him, ready to repulse their attack, but they rounded on Imoshen.

'Very clever, T'Imoshen,' Woodvine snapped. 'You have cut our support out from under us by giving the traders what they want. But the Causare is not just a trading forum. We represent the old aristocracy, we have a right to sit on council and direct the policy of Fair Isle. We will not rest until that right is acknowledged.'

'All rights are earned, including the right to serve,' Imoshen replied.

'Right?' Tulkhan repeated. The arrogance of these people astounded him. Though he had no proof, he knew they gave aid to Reothe and his rebels. He would have been within his rights to confiscate their titles and lands. These Keld were lucky to be alive.

'General Tulkhan will hear your petition in the new year after the celebrations,' Imoshen spoke quickly. 'Until then the palace is packed with mainland nobility and ambassadors. We must present a united front.'

'For Fair Isle's sake,' the Beatific urged.

Tulkhan noted how Imoshen and the Beatific exchanged looks as the others agreed. He took Imoshen's arm, escorting her from the Causare. His men filed out after him.

Imoshen would have spoken, but he signalled for silence, climbing astride his mount and offering her his hand. She placed her foot on his boot and leapt up across his thighs where their conversation would not be overheard.

As the doors closed on the noisy scene within, Tulkhan turned his horse towards the palace. 'The people of Fair Isle never cease to amaze me,' he muttered.

'Why?'

He did not reply.

After a moment Imoshen cleared her throat. 'I know you find the Keldon nobles' request to reopen the Causare Council presumptuous.'

He gave a bark of laughter.

She hesitated. 'When you are at war, you consult with your commanders, you listen to the locals, consider what you have learnt, and then you make the best decision based on all this. Yes?'

He nodded.

'Ruling Fair Isle is no different. You would heed the advice of your commanders. Among the Keldon nobles there are people who have seen eighty years of history unfold. Surely their advice is worth something?'

'True, but are their goals mine?' the General countered grimly.

They continued on, Tulkhan guiding his mount through the gates to the palace grounds.

'There is a T'En saying that loosely translates as, *A person who has nothing will risk everything*,' Imoshen told Tulkhan. 'Give your commanders and the Keldon nobles a say in the ruling of Fair Isle. As Fair Isle prospers under your rule they will also prosper, and their goals will become yours.'

'Truly the T'En are a devious race.'

They had reached the palace. Imoshen slipped from his thighs, landing lightly on the stone paving. 'There is another T'En saying, *Do not use a battle-axe to kill a fly.*' She grinned. 'It is more poetic in High T'En.'

He felt himself smile. 'These are dangerous flies.'

Imoshen gave him the lesser obeisance and walked off. Tulkhan swung his leg over the horse's back and dropped to the ground. Regretfully, he watched Imoshen enter the palace. He would welcome their intimacy if only she were not pure T'En.

IN THE DAYS leading up to their bonding Tulkhan gave Imoshen's words much thought. While his father had been King, he had gathered about him capable men, rewarding them to ensure their loyalty. There was merit in this but Tulkhan did not see how he could implement it.

While his men would not listen to the advice of a woman, he did not suffer from this prejudice. He only felt truly alive when he was in Imoshen's company. It appalled him to discover he craved her presence like a drug.

Now he hesitated on the brink of approaching her card table. The older Keldon nobles had retired when the Beatific left, leaving only the younger members of the court. A buzz of conversation rose from the other tables: the players consisted of visiting aristocrats from mainland kingdoms, politically minded church officials and several bizarrely dressed individuals from the islands of the archipelago. The evening's entertainment had continued later than usual, leaving Tulkhan bored and irritable.

Imoshen never bored him.

She was involved in a six-sided T'En game of cards which appeared to involve more laughter than skill this night. In Gheeaba gambling was a serious business. A man's honour was at stake. If his luck ran out he could lose his estates and his wives. Suicide might be his only option.

Imoshen and her partner were teamed against Cariah and Jacolm on one side, and Wharrd and Kalleen, who had returned from a tour of their estates looking like cream-fed cats, on the other. So far the luck had run Jacolm's way and he was not averse to letting everyone know.

'My Beatific and Empress-High outplay your hand of lesser nobles!' he crowed.

Tulkhan walked around the table to stand behind Imoshen so that he could see her cards. In the long winter evenings he had learnt the basics of this game and understood the system of playing alliances against alliances, while supporting your partner and undercutting the other teams.

He took the opportunity to observe Imoshen, drinking in the curve of her cheek, the line of her pale throat, the unconscious grace of her every movement. His mouth went dry with longing.

When the round finished, the cards were pushed Imoshen's way. Her partner Sahorrd reached for the pack, but she was quicker. Tulkhan knew she was unaware she had insulted him as she collected the cards. Her fingers moved deftly, shuffling and dealing. Watching the play, he looked for a chance to advise her, for any excuse to touch her, even if it was in a room full of people. But she won that hand and the next three, playing with an uncanny ability to guess which alliances her opponents favoured.

The shuffling and dealing made its way around the table again. Jacolm became progressively irritated, then belligerent as he received his new cards. At last he threw the painted paste-boards down in disgust.

Tulkhan stiffened. Was his commander going to accuse Imoshen of misdealing? In Gheeaba such an accusation would have occasioned a duel of honour. Silence fell.

Imoshen laid her cards face down. 'Is there a problem, Lord Jacolm?'

'No problem. I should know better than to play a game of chance with a Dhamfeer!'

Tulkhan tensed. The Ghebites within hearing went utterly still.

'If you have something to say, say it,' Imoshen told him calmly.

Tulkhan noted how Jacolm's sword-brother, Sahorrd, shifted in his seat, turning his shoulder away from his card partner. With this movement he withdrew his support from Imoshen.

'Well, Jacolm?' Imoshen pressed, one arm hooked elegantly over the back of her chair. Was she deliberately insulting him by omitting his new title?

The man's dark brows drew down as he flipped his cards over. 'Look. It's been the same rubbish for the past four hands. Why, I even have the T'En rogue again!'

Imoshen shrugged. 'The fall of the cards –'

'The cards fall in such a way that you win.' Jacolm sat forward. 'How else do you know what everyone holds in their hand?'

The spectators gave a collective gasp. Tulkhan sensed their speculative appraisal of Imoshen. Perhaps it was possible to use her gifts to manipulate the fall of the cards. He wondered whether he should intervene.

Several of his men looked past Imoshen to him, obviously expecting their general to respond. The day after tomorrow Imoshen would be his wife; any slight on her honour was a criticism of his. His body tensed but he ignored the instinctive urge to declare her innocent.

If a man were accused of cheating in Gheeaba, it would be up to him to prove his honour, but Imoshen was a woman and so unable to accept Jacolm's challenge or offer challenge of her own. Tulkhan hesitated. There were no precedents to guide his actions.

'You are mistaken, Jacolm,' Imoshen said, voice icy. 'I would never use my T'En gift for such a paltry purpose.'

Tulkhan saw the man flinch.

'So you say,' Jacolm sneered.

Imoshen made an impatient noise in her throat. 'Cariah, have I been using anything other than my wit and skills?'

Tulkhan saw the red-headed beauty swallow and lift her chin. He could tell she was preparing to lie.

'How would I know?' Cariah gestured as if bored by the whole thing. 'I have not seen Imoshen do anything other than count the cards and anticipate what people have in their hands by what they have played.'

'Thank you for your support,' Imoshen said dryly.

Tulkhan knew by her tone that Imoshen was rebuking Cariah, but he did not know why. If Imoshen was not cheating, why was Cariah lying? Before Tulkhan could ponder this, Jacolm rose, telegraphing his intention to challenge Imoshen's word. To offer challenge to a mere female would demean Jacolm, but Tulkhan realised Jacolm's honour would not allow him to back down.

Everything slowed as Tulkhan stiffened. Cheating or not, he had to defend Imoshen's honour. He had to redirect the challenge.

Before Jacolm could speak Tulkhan stepped forward. 'Are you offering insult?'

'There has been no insult offered,' Wharrd interjected soothingly. This was strictly true – no formal challenge had been laid down because Tulkhan had intervened before it could get that far.

Imoshen ignored Wharrd. Coming to her feet she glanced from Tulkhan to Jacolm. 'What goes on here?'

'I am merely asking this man if he offers challenge,' Tulkhan ground out.

Jacolm's resentful eyes studied the General.

'If insult is intended, it is to me, not to you,' Imoshen said.

'Any insult offered my wife is an insult upon my honour. A challenge,' Tulkhan told her. Then he returned his attention to Jacolm, trying to read the man's next move.

Silently Sahorrd rose and moved around the table to stand behind his sword-brother.

With all his being Tulkhan willed Imoshen to remain silent. Anything she said now was bound to inflame Jacolm. Imoshen was but a heartbeat from death for Jacolm was one of Tulkhan's finest swordsmen.

A muscle jumped in the man's cheek. Tulkhan sensed he was close to losing control. There was no chance of a formal duel here. Knowing Jacolm, he would favour the soldier's solution – challenge offered, accepted and honour decided on the spot.

'There is no cause for insult to be offered. No need to challenge.' Wharrd came to his feet. 'I have been watching the cards. No one can cheat this old campaigner.'

This attempt at humour elicited no laughter but it did lighten the atmosphere.

Imoshen drew a slow breath. 'And I choose to take no insult. Jacolm does not know me. I would never use my T'En gift on something so paltry – to save a life, yes, to win a game of chance, never!'

With a few brief sentences she had placed the man in the wrong and forgiven him. Tulkhan could sympathise with Jacolm as he bristled.

Cariah rose. 'Supper is being served.'

The sudden influx of servants carrying trays of food broke the stalemate. Imoshen turned her back on Jacolm with deliberate casualness, but her expression when she met Tulkhan's eyes was anything but casual.

She was furious. Not with Jacolm, with him.

Why? He had been about to defend her at the risk of losing one of his best men.

His body thrummed with unresolved tension as he escorted Imoshen to the sideboard where the servants had laid out the food. Every dish was a masterpiece of presentation, food sculpted to form animals, birds in flight, or intricate pieces of T'En architecture. Every morsel was a surprise to delight the palate.

Imoshen's fingers trembled ever so slightly as she poured wine for them both, though no one but he saw this.

All around them people talked animatedly, but their chatter was too bright and their smiles forced. They skirted Tulkhan and Imoshen, while appearing to defer to them. At the same time the General knew that every ear was strained to catch their conversation and every malicious eye was trained on them to observe the undercurrents revealed by their gestures.

'Wine, General?' Imoshen offered him a crystal goblet.

His fingers tingled when they brushed hers and his temples ached as though a storm were about to break. Experience told him the power was moving within her.

'Since when did my honour cease to be my own?' She spoke softly so that only he could hear.

'The day after tomorrow you will be my wife –'

'Bond-partner. Equal!' she insisted softly, turning her back to their audience. In a gesture that appeared affectionate she raised her hand and brushed a strand of hair from his throat.

His body responded to her touch but he found it disturbing because her eyes, which only he could see, held ice-cold fury. She was deliberately masking the content of their conversation from those who watched them. Again he had to admire her, desire her... and fear her.

'I will stand at your side, not behind you, General. If I am offered insult I will handle it, not you.' Her eyes glittered with suppressed fury. 'I am not your lapdog to be petted and protected from the real world.'

Her words hit their target. For an instant Tulkhan stood in her shoes. He saw her invidious position and empathised with her against his will.

With a nod of satisfaction Imoshen turned away and moved gracefully along the length of the sideboard. She nibbled this and tasted that, pausing to speak with minor church officials, then with Lady Cariah's two sisters and the young Ghebite commanders who rarely left their sides. Those she exchanged pleasantries with smiled and deferred to her, but when she passed on Tulkhan saw their relieved expressions. Something twisted inside him. It shocked him to discover he pitied Imoshen, destined always to be an outsider.

Amid the general conversation he caught the tone of Jacolm's voice. His man was still angry. Sahorrd and a few others stood with him talking intensely, their gazes on Imoshen.

Wharrd approached Tulkhan with Kalleen at his side. Tulkhan greeted them and they both glanced over at the angry group.

'Jacolm's a hothead,' Wharrd muttered. 'He'll grow out of it one day.'

'Or it will kill him,' Tulkhan amended.

Wharrd met Tulkhan's eyes in silent acknowledgment.

'He's lucky T'Imoshen didn't take insult,' Kalleen said.

Again Tulkhan felt that uncomfortable shift in his perception. To Kalleen that was the encounter in a nutshell. As far as she was concerned Jacolm was still alive to plot satisfaction only because he had not raised the ire of a full-blood T'En.

Tulkhan was reminded how little he knew of this place and these people. A prickling awareness of menace moved across his skin. If sufficiently angered what was a Dhamfeer capable of?

He had seen Imoshen furious and he had seen her frightened, but he had never seen her out of control. Or had he? He recalled a visual image so intense it seared his inner eye – two fighting birds exploding in a ball of fire.

Though Imoshen had refused to discuss the cockerel fight, he knew that she had been outraged by its barbarity. When she discovered his men betting on a fight to the death she had grown frighteningly still. He could see her now, standing across the pit from him, fierce eyes blazing. Then suddenly the birds had burst into flames. Was that evidence of Imoshen out of control?

Tulkhan wanted to find her, to warn her of Jacolm's hasty temper and explain why honour was so important to his commander.

Searching above the heads of those present Tulkhan could not see Imoshen's distinctive silver hair. Impatience drove him. He took his leave of Wharrd and Kalleen and crossed the room, having to pause to engage in conversation several times. He realised he was projecting the same casual air as Imoshen.

Deliberately stopping beside Jacolm, Tulkhan clapped a hand on the man's shoulder and passed a few innocuous words. They meant nothing. His real meaning was in the way he stood at their sides. He offered solidarity and he saw his men understood as their expressions eased, conveying their relief.

Leaving the crowded room, Tulkhan entered the relative quiet of the hall and felt the cool air on his face. One of Imoshen's stronghold guard stood at the door. 'Which way did Imoshen go?'

The young man stiffened and inclined his head to the left. Tulkhan set off, wondering what he had said to offend the youth.

He rounded a corner but did not see Imoshen. A servant approached. 'Have you seen Imoshen?'

With a nod of his head the old man indicated the direction from which he had come. 'T'Imoshen is with the Lady Cariah.'

Tulkhan managed a smile. He told himself it was a good sign that the old servant felt secure enough in his presence to reprimand him for not addressing Imoshen with sufficient reverence.

KEEPING A TIGHT rein on her anger, Imoshen had slipped from the crowded room at the first opportunity, intent on confronting Cariah, who had already left. Rounding a corner she saw the other woman. 'Cariah, wait.'

From the way Cariah turned and met her eyes, Imoshen knew she had anticipated a confrontation.

A servant approached with a fresh tray of food. Imoshen nodded to an open door and the two women stepped into the darkened room.

The only light came from the building across the courtyard. It spilled through the room's floor-length windows onto the polished floor and illuminated a graceful stringed instrument. As if drawn to this, Cariah glided over to stroke the sensual curve of the wood. Imoshen followed.

'You alone could have defended me against Jacolm's charge, Cariah. You chose not to.' She tried not to sound as hurt and betrayed as she felt.

Cariah did not turn to face her, but looked out through the window, her voice the merest whisper. 'What would you have me do?'

'Confirm that I was not using my gifts to cheat at a foolish game of cards.'

'You would have me reveal myself and risk ostracism, for what?' Cariah demanded raggedly. Her tear-filled eyes reflected the light, beseeching Imoshen's understanding. 'Why should they believe me, if they will not believe you?'

Imoshen's heart sank. She wanted to rail at Cariah, to complain at the unfairness of it all, but... 'You are right.'

Cariah's shoulders slumped.

Imoshen stepped closer, placing a hand on her shoulder. 'I'm sorry. I will not betray your secret.'

Cariah shook her head. She pushed Imoshen away and sank onto the seat next to the instrument. 'You make it hard for me not to love you.'

Imoshen gasped. 'All I ask is that you be my friend.'

A short, bitter laugh escaped Cariah. She brushed the tears from her face, then her hands travelled over the instrument's vertical strings, absently plucking them, drawing sweet notes into the air.

Imoshen watched Cariah's graceful fingers, the elegant line of her throat. 'How can you hide your power so well?'

'Years of practice.'

A tense silence hung between them.

Then Cariah sighed. 'My powers are negligible, so it was easy. I vowed when my mother died never to reveal the depths of my T'En inheritance. Can you imagine what it was like living in my own stronghold, constantly watched by Father and the servants, aware that one unconscious slip would see me a prisoner, locked away as my mother had been?'

'I am sorry.'

'So am I.' Cariah caressed the strings. 'I have only one acceptable power and I use it sparingly.'

Imoshen touched her fingers. 'Play for me, Cariah. First as you would play for them, then for me alone.' Cariah met her eyes, then nodded.

TULKHAN STRODE DOWN the dimly lit hall. The palace was so complex that if he did not find Imoshen soon he would not find her until she was ready to be found.

He froze as subtle T'En music drifted from the darkened room. Silently he slipped through the half-closed door. The room's occupants were too absorbed to notice him. Curious, he stepped into deep shadow.

Imoshen was a tall silhouette outlined against the window. Cariah played an elegant stringed instrument. Fingers poised she paused, then ended the piece with a flourish. Tulkhan had learnt enough by now to know that the pauses were as important as the notes.

'This time I play for you alone,' Cariah whispered. She stroked the strings with her fingers to create rippling waves of sound so sweet they flowed like water over Tulkhan's skin, bringing tears to his eyes. He felt as if she were plucking the strings of his soul.

Cariah's fingers grew still and silence followed. At last Imoshen let out her breath in a long sigh. 'How can you hold it back?'

Silently Cariah looked up at Imoshen. Tulkhan could not see her face, only the back of her head.

'Something so beautiful cannot be bad,' Imoshen whispered.

Cariah stood. When she spoke her voice was cool, dispassionate. 'I have chosen my path.'

'But is it right to make yourself out to be less than you are so that you can be accepted?'

Cariah's laughter sounded as sharp as breaking glass. 'You can talk!'

Tulkhan saw Imoshen's shoulders stiffen. The two women confronted each other. He did not understand the point of their argument.

'I am out of my depth.' Imoshen lifted her hands imploringly. 'All I ask is your friendship and counsel.'

'Is that all?' Cariah shook her head slowly. The same hand which had drawn that hauntingly beautiful music from the strings lifted to tenderly caress Imoshen's cheek.

The intimacy of the touch made Tulkhan flinch. When he had suspected Imoshen of taking lovers, he had never thought to be cuckolded by a woman.

'Do you wonder that I must refuse?' the redhead whispered.

'Cariah,' Imoshen pleaded.

'No. You ask for more than I can give.' Abruptly, she turned and strode towards the door, her eyes blinded by tears. Once Tulkhan had resented her, now he felt sorry for her.

The sound of her soft footfalls faded and Tulkhan returned his attention to Imoshen. She straightened, visibly gathering her composure, before walking towards him. As she stepped into the dim shaft of light Tulkhan moved, slamming the door closed. His eyes had adjusted to the dark, Imoshen's had been turned to the light, but the sudden closing of the door caused her to dart sideways.

As suddenly as he had moved, she was gone.

While he strained to see her, he registered that familiar metallic sensation. Fear closed a cold hand around his heart. 'Imoshen?'

'Tulkhan?'

He identified her tall dark shape amid the shadows where a moment before he could not see her. His skin prickled unpleasantly.

Silence hung between them. He felt vulnerable, exposed by the beauty of the music and the intimacy of the scene he had witnessed. When he made no move to speak she took a step closer.

'Why are you here, General?'

He closed the distance between them and lifted his hand to cup her cheek as he had seen Cariah do. He wanted to claim her with a kiss of slow, lingering intensity, to taste her lips and savour her response.

Her hand closed over his, and she used gentle pressure to break the contact. 'Don't. I cannot think when you touch me.'

The admission made his blood race. 'Nor I.'

The rawness of his tone surprised him. He heard Imoshen's quick intake of breath. He wanted to pursue that breath, to feel her gasp at his touch. Driven, he sought her lips. Just one kiss, he told himself.

But he knew it would never be enough when she opened at his touch, sweetly giving. She was the elixir of life, intoxicating and vital.

With a little moan, Imoshen broke contact. 'Why did you follow me, General?'

He knew he should warn her about Jacolm, but he didn't want to destroy the intimacy of this moment. Yet questions begged to be answered. 'What is there between you and the Lady Cariah?'

She turned her face from him.

'Imoshen?'

She sighed. 'Nothing that I can share with you.'

'But you share something with her? What unnatural creatures you are!'

She gave a snort of disbelief. 'And the love your men share as sword-brothers is somehow more natural?'

When he gave no answer she went to walk past him. He caught her arm, fighting the urge to pull her to him and bend her will with the force of his need for her. 'What do you plot with Cariah? Answer me.'

Her eyes were dark pools in her pale face. She gave no answer, no denial.

He tightened his hold on her. 'Imoshen, you tell me to trust you. How can I?'

Sadly she mimicked his earlier action, cupping his jaw in her hand. Her lids lowered as she leant close enough to brush her lips across his. 'Trust must be given.' Her breath dusted his face.

He returned the kiss. 'Earned, not given. I will not have secrets between us.'

She pulled back. 'So you say. But it is not my secret to share with you. Let me go, General.'

It was on his lips to deny her. As if sensing this she twisted her arm, breaking his hold.

'We of the T'En value our word,' she told him.

'You speak in riddles. You cannot expect me to trust blindly. I was ready to support you against my own man tonight.'

'That Jacolm is trouble. My honour is my own to –'

'Anything you do or say reflects on me,' he told her.

'I could say the same. How would you feel if I fought your battles for you?'

He tensed. 'You do. You did not even consult me before interviewing those interpreters.'

Her startled look amused him.

For a moment she said nothing. Then she lifted her chin as if facing something unpleasant. 'I see. If I have offended you, I am sorry, General Tulkhan. But I am used to making decisions and acting on them. What I did, I did for your own good.'

'I could say the same. You do not know what honour means to a Ghebite man.'

'And it means nothing to a Ghebite woman, to any woman?'

He lifted his hands helplessly.

Imoshen moved to the door. As she opened it the candlelight cloaked her with its golden glow. When she looked back he wanted to kiss the furrow from her brow.

'The day after tomorrow we will take our vows, General. Bonding is no dry legal transaction. It is not an exchange of property where a man acquires a wife to act as brood mare.' Emotion choked her voice. He could see tears glittering in her dark eyes. 'Bonding is a joining of the souls. I only pray we will not live to regret this.'

With that, she was gone.

He wanted to confront her, insist that what he felt for her had nothing to do with political necessity. But how could he reassure her when he had already promised himself to take his pleasure from her body yet keep his inner self private, shielded from her powers?

A Ghebite soldier reserved his closest friendship for his equal, his sword-brother. They faced death together on the battlefield. He trusted his sword-brother with his life. A Ghebite soldier shared something less with the wife he hardly saw. After all, she was only a woman.

Tulkhan's head reeled. Imoshen expected him to regard her as his equal. But could he share his soul with her? Would she settle for less?

Chapter Nine

IMOSHEN HID HER surprise as Tulkhan linked his arm through hers and drew her away from the others.

'In Gheeaba it is customary for the husband to give his wife a gift the day before their wedding,' he said.

It was on the tip of Imoshen's tongue to correct him – she would never be his wife – but she did not want to destroy such a rare moment of accord.

She was aware of the disapproving stares of Woodvine and Athlyn as Tulkhan led her out of the salon. According to the old customs, bond-partners fasted and purified themselves, abstaining from all contact from dawn the day before their bonding. But even before the Ghebite invasion, only old-fashioned people like Imoshen's family and the Keld had adhered to such customs. In the high court this observance had been reduced to fasting from midnight the night before the bonding, and this was what Imoshen planned to do.

Tulkhan opened the door to the map-room and strode to the table which, for once, was not littered with maps. Four mysterious objects were laid out there.

'First' – he picked up Reothe the Builder's tome – 'I wanted to thank you for supplying a translation of the passages on T'Diemn's defences. What a mind, and to think he lived four hundred years ago!'

Imoshen couldn't help smiling.

Tulkhan put the book aside and unrolled a rich velvet cloak to reveal the longest sword she had ever seen. 'I wanted you to see this. I know you think my people barbarians because we don't have written records dating back hundreds of years. But we are not ignorant. This is my grandfather's sword, which was gifted to me. As you see, the scabbard is not decorated for display, but the hilt is another matter.' He unwrapped the hand grip. It was decorated in niello with a surprisingly graceful design of a stylised rearing horse. 'This is my size, a hand-and-a-half grip. I take after my grandfather, Seerkhan the Giant, or Great. In our language, *giant* and *great* are the same word. In my grandfather's time a man's life depended on his sword and his horse. I was taught never to unsheathe this sword without drawing blood. The great Akha Khan demands his tribute. Come closer. I want you to see this.'

Drawn despite herself, Imoshen stepped towards him. He took her into the circle of his arms, her back to his chest. His deep voice enveloped her. She felt warm to the core.

'This sword should not be unsheathed in direct sunlight.' Silently he withdrew it from the fur-lined scabbard and held it before them so that Imoshen looked along the blade. 'Breathe on the blade and see Akha Khan's Serpent come to life.'

Imoshen took a deep breath and exhaled. As her breath moved up the blade, a pattern like the variations of a serpent's skin travelled up the blade and back. She gasped in wonder and reached out to touch it.

'No,' Tulkhan warned. 'It is dedicated to Akha Khan.'

Imoshen's fingers itched to stroke the gleaming blade to see if she could identify the power which animated it. 'How?'

'This weapon is a work of art. Its blade was made in three parts, entwined cold, forged, then twisted and reforged. Then it was filed and burnished with infinite care. This is not the work of an unsophisticated people.'

He released her to step away. His eyes met hers. She watched as he ran his finger down the blade's edge, leaving a smear of blood.

Holding Tulkhan's eyes Imoshen placed the tip of her sixth finger above the blade's edge. She knew she could seal a wound with her healing gift. Exerting herself, she concentrated on creating a wound. A drop of blood pooled on the pad of her finger, fell then trickled down the gleaming metal.

The General's black eyes widened. No word passed between them, but they understood each other. It thrilled Imoshen.

Tulkhan cleaned the blade before replacing it in its scabbard.

'I thank you for sharing this with me,' she said. 'It is a gift I will treasure always.'

He laughed. 'Your gift is more tangible than that.' With a flourish he opened the last object, a shallow chest. 'This is your gift. A torque of pure gold to match my ceremonial belt.'

Imoshen stared at the neck circle. Its line was elegant enough, a crescent moon. That was not what offended her. It was the subject of the filigree and niello design.

'See.' Tulkhan unwrapped his ceremonial belt, which was made of rectangular hinged squares of gold embossed with the same design. 'Let me see the torque on you.'

Imoshen opened her mouth to protest, but held her tongue. Tulkhan placed the heavy gold torque around her throat, then stood back to admire the effect.

Imoshen lifted her hand to the neck circle. It felt like a yoke of servitude, binding her to Tulkhan's perceptions of a wife. She undid the clasp and removed the torque slowly, replacing it in its bed of velvet.

'What is it, Imoshen?'

'Your men deck themselves in golden jewellery.'

'It is our way. We wear our wealth on our backs. It is not so long since we were a nomadic people, and old customs die hard.'

Imoshen sighed. He was defensive now. 'What is on the torque, General?'

Tulkhan grimaced but contained his annoyance. The design was obvious. 'The great Akha Khan in the form of a black stallion.'

'And what is he doing?'

'Crushing the enemies of his people.' Even as he said it, he understood. 'It is taken from a myth where he transforms into the stallion and tramples his opponents.'

'Death and bloodshed.' She lifted the heavy torque from its resting place and held it before him, anger making her voice tight. 'My island has been trampled by Akha Khan's stallion and my family are all dead. How can you expect me to wear this?' Tears stung her eyes. 'True, this is exquisite workmanship, but it deals with blood and death. Is the Ghebite mind so steeped in violence that it cannot create peace and beauty for its own sake?'

'You refuse my gift?'

'I will wear your gift with honour. But I will never be your *wife* and wear a yoke of servitude.' Imoshen replaced the torque, searching his face despairingly. She scooped up the great sword on its bed of velvet. 'I value the sharing of this more than anything else.'

Her declaration warmed Tulkhan. He took the sword from her and slowly rewrapped it. 'Every morning when I wake I wonder, what will Imoshen confound me with today?'

Silence hung between them, heavy with so many words left unsaid.

Imoshen touched his arm. 'Neither of us treads an easy path, General. We will be bonded and crowned on the last day of the old year. When the sun rises the day after tomorrow it will be dawning on a new age for Fair Isle.'

His hand covered hers. 'I did not mean to insult you with my gift.'

'It is the gifts you cannot see that I treasure most.'

He shook his head. 'You are a rare woman, Imoshen.'

She smiled. 'I will see you at the festivities this evening.'

Only when the door closed behind her did Tulkhan realise that she had forgotten to take the torque. He would send it to her room.

Crossing to the hearth he stirred up the coals then sat before the fire, resting Seerkhan's sword across his knees. His heart beat faster as he recalled Imoshen's words. The day after tomorrow the sun would rise on a new age for Fair Isle, one fraught with danger and challenge.

An age he would stamp as his own.

IMOSHEN SHIFTED IMPATIENTLY, causing her new maid to drop the comb. 'I'm sorry, Merkah.'

The girl flushed. Imoshen suspected she wasn't used to members of the royal family apologising.

'It will be a grand feast tonight,' Merkah ventured.

Imoshen nodded. This was her last evening unbonded. Tomorrow promised to be a full day with the bonding ceremony in the morning and the joint coronation after the midday meal. She longed to know whether her bonding with Tulkhan would bring peace to Fair Isle, and feared what would become of Reothe. The temptation to do a scrying was intense but she lacked control.

And she was still no closer in her quest for knowledge of her gifts. Though the Keeper of Knowledge had provided her with a raft of ancient documents, she could find no histories of her people and no treatises on the T'En gifts. If only Imoshen the First's journal had not been destroyed!

'There, T'Imoshen.' Merkah stepped back with a pleased expression and waited expectantly.

Imoshen studied her reflection. She looked quite unlike herself. The maid had created a hairstyle worthy of the high court. Imoshen's hair had been smoothed over padding on the crown of her head to create a fan of silver satin. A single deep blue sapphire hung in the centre of her forehead. She had argued against a diadem of zircons, preferring the simplicity of a single sapphire echoing the deep blue of her underdress.

'I look so... grand,' Imoshen said. 'Thank you.' But she could see it wasn't the response Merkah had hoped for.

Recommended by Kalleen, the girl was a capable maid, but Imoshen couldn't let her guard down with her. She longed for her old friend's company.

'You may have the rest of the evening to yourself.' Imoshen rose.

'Very well, T'Imoshen.' Clearly disappointed, Merkah knelt to adjust Imoshen's brocade tabard, which had been embroidered with the finest thread of spun silver. It hung to Imoshen's knees over the velvet undergown.

As Merkah rose she tripped. Imoshen caught the girl's arm but she pulled away sharply.

Just as quickly she offered an abrupt obeisance of apology. 'Forgive me, my lady.'

'It does not matter,' Imoshen whispered. But it did. It hurt when people pulled away from her touch.

She pretended to adjust her neckline in the full-length mirror. The truth of her position was not pleasant. In desperation the people might reach to her for reassurance, but in everyday life she was a pariah. In the Age of Discernment, enlightenment in Fair Isle did not extend to the T'En. 'You may go, Merkah. Join in the festivities.'

The maid gave Imoshen the traditional deep obeisance without meeting her eyes and silently withdrew.

Imoshen paced the room. She was ready before time because she had chosen not to attend the afternoon's formal entertainment. She had thought she needed time to compose herself for this evening and tomorrow, but now she was restless.

Surely it would not hurt to walk the corridors of the palace? She could pretend she was making a last-minute review of the arrangements for the festivities. Sweeping out into the long gallery, she strode off.

The palace of a thousand rooms was full. The Keldon nobles had all brought their own retinues, and entertainers of every kind were housed in the servants' quarters. Mainland ambassadors and nobles had been arriving steadily for the past ten days. This in itself was a good sign. It meant their rulers were willing to acknowledge General Tulkhan's sovereignty of Fair

Isle. From conversations with various parties Imoshen had learned that the General was well known and respected. Even the ambassadors whose countries had been annexed to Gheeaba spoke well of him.

She'd had to exercise diplomacy while greeting the ambassadors from the mainland triad. When the Empress had called on the southern kingdoms to honour the old alliance, they had claimed they could not mobilise their armies against the Ghebite invasion in time. Yet now they boldly presented themselves as though their excuse was not paper thin.

Imoshen suspected Tulkhan had received news of his half-brother from the copper-skinned men of the mainland's north. As far as she knew Gharavan had retreated to lick his wounds, though unsurprisingly no one had been sent from Gheeaba to bring them news. If the lack of an ambassador from his homeland troubled Tulkhan, he did not reveal it, least of all to her.

A familiar arrogant voice echoed up the grand staircase from the marbled foyer below. Imoshen's skin went cold. Hardly daring to breathe, she peered around a column.

Kinraid the Vaygharian! The sly manipulative traitor himself.

This was the snake who had convinced Gharavan to turn on Tulkhan. Unbidden, the memories swamped her. When she had not been in her stronghold to greet the Ghebite king and his Vaygharian adviser, they had declared her a rebel. In reality she had been abducted by one of Reothe's men, Drake. She had escaped and returned to her stronghold only to find the King and his Ghebites feasting in her great hall.

Within a day Tulkhan had returned from the Keldon Highlands after failing to capture Reothe. Seeing his chance, Kinraid had claimed that if the General were truly loyal to King Gharavan he would return at once to hunt the rebels.

When Tulkhan refused to leave until spring melted the snow in the high passes, Kinraid had marched into Tulkhan's bedchamber where Imoshen and the General lay entwined. Kinraid had laughed as his men beat Tulkhan senseless in front of her.

But, when Kinraid's bare flesh had touched hers, she had seen his death. The Vaygharian would meet his end in flames of agony.

Kinraid's voice jolted her and she looked down to see him dressed in the formal robes of the Vayghar, complete with sculpted beard and beaded hair. He was accompanied by several men in the same ornate costumes of Vayghar merchant princes. They carried themselves with assurance, full of their own self-importance. Imoshen had seen the same stance in other ambassadorial groups.

She flushed. How dare Kinraid presume on the immunity of ambassadorial status to invade her palace? The General must be warned. Swiftly, Imoshen left the upper gallery and sped to the salon.

When Imoshen saw the General's familiar profile she had to smile. He was watching a performance which the audience needed an appreciation of ritualised song and dance and a knowledge of T'En history to understand. The General would find it a terrible bore.

Imoshen could not catch Tulkhan's eye. Frustration churned in her. She must warn him, but it was against her people's strictest traditions to disrupt a performance. She must attract his attention by other means.

As Tulkhan watched the play, he marvelled that anyone could keep a straight face while decked out in such a ridiculous costumes. How they balanced on one leg while completing the delicate arm movements was beyond him. When a cymbal tinkled, the Keldon nobles clicked their fingers appreciatively.

Several of his men glanced his way. He bit his lip to hide a smile and thought about tomorrow's arrangements. Soon Imoshen would be his by every law known to man. Despite his impatience, dread made his heart beat like a drum, for no True-man had bonded with a pure T'En woman in over six hundred years. What had Imoshen the First tried to hide with her vow of celibacy?

Something stirred his senses. He felt as if silken fingers had stroked his skin. The touch was so sensual he had to swallow. Pinpricks of sensation dusted his lips. He wanted to find Imoshen and kiss her. The back of his neck tingled.

Very slowly, he turned.

There she was, standing in the entrance with her intense eyes focused on him. Curse her!

She beckoned, her expressive eyes troubled.

He sprang to his feet, weaving through the clustered tables and chairs, heading towards her like a dog called by its master. Fury built in him.

Wharrd met his eyes, looking for an unspoken signal to accompany him. Tulkhan shook his head. He did not want the world to know the Dhamfeer had tweaked his leash.

'General,' Imoshen whispered. She caught his hand and drew him with her, hastening across the wide gallery into a window embrasure where they could talk in private.

Though she radiated anger, it was not directed at him.

'I've seen Kinraid,' Imoshen whispered. 'He dares to come here as an ambassador of Vayghar. What will we do?'

Before he could answer, the regular thump of booted feet on the gallery's parquetry floor interrupted them. Tulkhan moved out of the embrasure to see a self-important servant escorting five richly dressed Vaygharians, Kinraid amongst them.

He sensed Imoshen at his side and he was surprised to realise he found her support reassuring.

Kinraid stepped from the ranks and gave a formal bow of greeting. He offered a sealed scroll. 'We meet again, General Tulkhan. I am ambassador to the Vayghar and these are sons of the merchant council, princes in their own right, come to celebrate your coronation.'

Tulkhan accepted the scroll and broke the seal, reading it swiftly. Imoshen peered over his shoulder.

As Vayghar's official representative, Kinraid could not be refused a welcome without insulting the trading nation. The princes were there to add weight to his reputation. Tulkhan did not want to insult one of the most powerful countries on the mainland. He felt Imoshen's tense hand on the small of his back.

'Welcome, Vaygharians.' He gave a small inclination of his head, the barest minimum for civility, then held Imoshen's gaze. 'T'Imoshen, would you find a suitable apartment for the Vaygharian entourage, and arrange for their seating during tomorrow's ceremony?'

He knew Imoshen would understand the political necessity of acknowledging the Vaygharians, but it was clear she didn't like it. He grasped her arm, willing her to rely on his judgment. If he sent the Vaygharians packing on the eve of his coronation, how would the other ambassadors react?

Only this morning he'd had news confirming that his half-brother was bitterly plotting revenge. It was not enough that Gharavan had inherited the extended Ghebite Empire, benefiting from years of Tulkhan's faithful service. He wanted Fair Isle too.

Tulkhan feared his half-brother, with good reason. He knew the strength of the army Gharavan could raise. If he had been in the King's position he would have mobilised a massive force by calling on alliances and auxiliary troops from the annexed countries. He would have struck swiftly and without mercy. Rebellion had to be put down before it could spread. Only one generation separated Gheeaba's annexed kingdoms from freedom, and they did not wear the yoke of servitude willingly.

If he did not want to see this island's fertile fields and prosperous townships reduced to rubble, Tulkhan had no choice but to make the Vaygharian ambassador welcome. Politics disgusted him.

Imoshen gave the General a sharp look, then turned to face the Vaygharians, giving them the formal T'En greeting. 'Welcome. Come take refreshment and watch the performance while I prepare your rooms.'

She escorted them into the salon then swiftly returned to Tulkhan's side. He was standing at the window, watching the swirling snow. It was almost dusk and he looked tired and depressed, as if he missed his warm homeland. Imoshen felt a tug of fellowship. She had lost her family, but in conquering Fair Isle, the General had lost his family and his homeland. She wanted to ease that frown.

'I know you welcome Kinraid because of political necessity, but I cannot forget –'

'Do you think I can? Because of Kinraid's lies my half-brother hates me.' Tulkhan expelled his breath in an angry sigh. He seemed older and more than a little cynical. 'I know what Kinraid is, Imoshen. I'd rather he was here where I can watch him than have him stirring up trouble elsewhere.'

'He will report back to the Ghebite King.'

Tulkhan's wolfish smile made her heart lurch.

'Yes, he will report back to Gharavan. And he will tell him what I want him to know.'

Imoshen's felt the twin of Tulkhan's smile tug at her lips but she was still uneasy. Her hand closed around the General's arm, seeking reassurance, contact. 'I don't like it.'

He straightened, looking down into her face, his obsidian eyes unreadable. 'And you think I do?' He smiled grimly. 'My father taught me many things, but one above all else. Keep your enemies close, where you can see what they plot.'

Cold fear lanced Imoshen. Was Tulkhan telling her that she was his dearest enemy, the one he would keep so close he would bed her?

Sickened by the thought, she pulled away. 'There are arrangements I must see to. Please excuse me, General.'

MUCH LATER, IMOSHEN unpinned her elaborate hairstyle and massaged her throbbing temples. There had been no opportunity to eat or relax, least of all to speak privately with General Tulkhan. The Vaygharians had to be housed in chambers befitting their importance and she'd had to give the same consideration to the seating arrangements for tomorrow's ceremonies. She was exhausted.

With a frown, she finished preparing a tisane to ease her headache. The bitter aftertaste clung to her tongue, so she washed it down with a goblet of wine. Tonight she needed to sleep well, because tomorrow she must not falter. Imoshen stared into the fire, watching its leaping patterns.

To think, once she had imagined her bonding day as a day of great joy and spiritual significance – the joining of her soul with Reothe's.

Dreamily she unclasped the lace tabard and laid it over the chair, followed by the rich velvet underdress.

Kicking off her formal slippers, Imoshen knelt naked before the flames on the fur rug. Her hair slid across her shoulders and down her back like a silken shawl. She felt the fire's warmth caress her bare skin.

The fur was deep and so fine it enticed her to enjoy its caress. Sinking into its embrace she vaguely understood that the herb was having a strong effect, mixed with the wine on an empty stomach. She let herself drift, safe at least for now. Come tomorrow, she would face the enemy.

At first her overworked mind ran on and on, replaying images like brilliant jewels – flashes of conversation, a peal of laughter, the flickering candles, the heat of sweating perfumed bodies pressed together... then it all faded away and she felt pleasantly empty.

Her limbs grew weightless and her body became an insubstantial thing which had no hold on her. It seemed as if she was slipping painlessly from her physical shell and floating upwards. She turned to look down on her pale slender form, lying with such innocent abandon on the fur before the fireplace. Did she really look like that, an alabaster sculpture, her blue-veined skin like fine marble?

This incorporeal state was so peaceful she doubted she would ever feel the need to return. What did that body have to offer her but responsibilities and cruel choices? She was content.

For once she wanted nothing but to relinquish all thought and she gave herself over to the warm haze which enveloped her.

'SO YOU NEVER felt that you truly belonged?' her companion asked.

She was dreaming, yet her leg muscles worked as she strode up the slope. Around them the amber leaves of autumn fluttered down to crunch underfoot.

'Did you?' Imoshen asked Reothe. She recognised the place and time now. They were walking their horses through the woods. He had just asked her to bond with him and she had said yes.

A strange excitement animated her. Every time she looked at him her breath caught in her throat. There was something unknown in his eyes, a presentiment of their joining which promised to be both thrilling and dangerous.

Yet she felt safe in his company. He was the one who had held back when she would have taken their kisses further. He had laughed, delighted with her response. She felt a heated blush stain her cheeks with the memory, and saw his knowing smile.

Annoyed because he could read her so clearly, she turned away from him and strode on. 'Don't tell me the Emperor and Empress welcomed you with open arms.'

'You forget, I was only a boy of ten. When my parents killed themselves I found their bodies. As my guardian the Empress tried to make up for that, rearing me with her own children. Because she was open to me it was easy to win her over.'

When Imoshen had first heard this she had taken it at face value, but this time she understood. Reothe was talking about finding the Empress's key. She was the centre of the palace, adored by the Emperor, revered by everyone else. Back then Reothe had been a vulnerable boy. He'd had to win her over to protect himself. Imoshen could almost believe it had been an instinctive thing. He was gifted indeed if he could use his T'En ability at ten years of age. Her healing gifts had not surfaced until puberty.

As if thinking of it brought on her powers, a prickle of T'En awareness made her skin itch with danger. What was that smell? Tallow dip candles?

Suddenly Reothe was beside her and she felt the hard planes of his body.

'You made a vow,' he whispered hoarsely.

His hands circled her waist, bare palms on bare flesh. A familiar flash of longing ignited her body as she recognised him.

She wanted him. Why hold back? They had just agreed to bond. Her parents would oversee the betrothal ceremony...

Her parents were dead and this was all a lie, an impossible dream.

'No!'

The illusion fell away, revealing cold reality. Reothe still held her, but she was naked in his arms. Desperate, she tried to orient herself. She was in a dimly lit cave. Plush rugs covered the ground and hung on the walls, yet the only furniture was a crudely made table. On its roughly hewn planks sat crystal goblets and a matching decanter filled with ruby wine.

'Where am I?'

Reothe laughed.

Instinctively she bought her knee up but he was already stepping back, leaving her off balance. Why wasn't she cold? They were in a warm cave. The hot springs.

'Answer me. What have you done, Reothe?'

His smile was triumphant. 'I proved my theory.'

'Theory? I am no theory!' She felt vulnerable because she could not hide her body's response to him.

He laughed delightedly and dragged the simple lawn shirt from his body, tossing it across to her. 'Here, cover yourself if you must.'

She caught the shirt, wanting to throw it back in his face. His expression told her he knew her dilemma and was amused by it. Defiantly she pulled the garment over her shoulders. His scent enveloped her. The fine material was warm from his body and it brushed her bare flesh like a caress.

Then she noticed the designs etched on his wiry chest in dried blood. Though she was not familiar with their meaning, Imoshen recognised the symbols of the Ancients.

'Your chest.' She tasted the air with her tongue. 'Blood and death?'

'Don't worry, it's not my own blood. I had to seal the pact.'

'With a death?'

'It was necessary. The Ancients crave a little blood and death. They are a greedy lot.' He smiled and she realised that this beautiful creature had no more true humanity than... than her.

No. She wasn't like that.

'What games have you been playing, Reothe?' Her heart thundered with fear but she would not reveal it. Planting her feet to confront him, she felt the uneven stone under the rugs. 'How did I get here?'

'I brought you to me. We made our vows and we are all but bonded. Your body calls to mine.'

'You killed tonight to do this?' She feared she was bound to him in ways she did not understand.

'Only a snow leopard.'

'Still. A creature's life force has been extinguished, and to what end?'

'To unite us.'

A trickle of dread made its way down her spine to settle in her belly. Was he brilliant or mad, or both?

Reothe poured two goblets of red wine, holding them to the crude candles, turning them back and forth.

'Your eyes flicker like this, red flame as dark as wine. Come, drink, Imoshen. Celebrate our bonding.' The timbre of his voice stroked her senses.

She found she was standing beside him, her hand on the crystal stem of the goblet, yet she didn't remember moving. Her head felt slow and her tongue thick.

'Tomorrow I make my vows with General Tulkhan, all is arranged.' But it took a great effort to speak.

'No. Today you make your vows with me. You did not think I would let you bond with another, did you? We are the last of the T'En. We owe our forebears this much. And we owe it to each other.'

She felt a delicious anticipation and a sense of completion, as if this was always meant to be.

As he raised the crystal and sipped the wine, she found her body mimicking his. The wine was tart on her tongue. Drugged?

A spurt of fear cleared her head. What would General Tulkhan think if she deserted him on their bonding day? He would never believe she had been abducted against her will. Panic spiralled through her.

'Drink,' Reothe whispered.

She put the goblet down with so much haste wine spilled on the crude table.

He laughed softly and took a deliberate sip of his wine. She saw it glisten on his lips but didn't see him swallow. Somehow she knew what he intended before he moved to take her face in his hands, yet she couldn't refuse him. The touch of his lips on hers was like velvet, warm, wine-flavoured kisses. And then she tasted wine on her tongue and swallowed instinctively, drinking from his mouth.

Imoshen moaned. It was the bonding in its most primitive form. In the modern version of the ceremony she and General Tulkhan would sip from the same cup, their lips touching the same place.

Reothe pulled away, a deep growl rising from his throat. She took an instinctive step back.

'How can you think of him when you're kissing me?'

She shook her head, unable to explain. 'I won't do this, Reothe. I gave my word –'

'To me!' His fist hit his chest. He stared at her then shook his head and lifted a hand in entreaty. 'Our vow predates your word to the General. Let's finish this now.'

He leant closer, eyes closing as he inhaled her scent. When he spoke his voice was raw with need, calling up an instinctive response in her. She wanted him, had always wanted him.

'I promise it will be like nothing else, nothing you've known with him. I heard how he chose you the night of the Harvest Festival.' His hands settled on her shoulders, tightening painfully. 'Yet you came to me that night with his scent on your skin. Why do you torment me like this?'

Imoshen wanted to deny it. That night she had walked the battlements alone and frightened. Her need for something familiar had taken her to Reothe, but she did not know how. She had never meant to torment him. What would Reothe say if he knew...

'Knew what?' His eyes flew open, alarmingly alert. The dark centres were large and flecked with the moving flames of the candles.

'I love the General.' She had said the first thing that had come into her head, but even as she said it she knew it was true.

He laughed. 'You can control him, you mean. You can't love less than your equal. Look!'

He raised his arm between them. Disbelievingly she saw the scar of his old bonding wound split open. A ragged gasp escaped him as blood welled to the surface, trickling freely down his inner arm.

Every instinct told Imoshen to run, yet she couldn't bring her body under control. As if in a dream she saw her arm lift between them to reveal her bonding wound to mirror his. The scar was so well healed it was almost invisible.

'You did this,' he whispered. 'Did you think you could erase our bonding by seamlessly knitting the skin?'

She shook her head.

He clasped his fingers through hers, palm to palm, wrist to wrist. She could feel his hot blood on the sensitive skin of her inner arm.

His eyes held hers. 'Bond with me. Bond our blood, our bodies, then our minds. There is no turning back what we began that autumn.'

'No.'

'Part the skin, open for me.'

Something shifted, warm and willing inside her.

A sharp sound escaped her. The old scar stung.

He smiled. 'Your body wants me.'

'No. You're doing this.'

'I don't have to.'

And Imoshen knew he was right. Her body had always wanted him, had recognised him before she did.

She was falling into an abyss.

'As our blood mingles, so will –'

'No!' She would not say the formal bonding words.

A scream rent the air. For an instant Imoshen thought it was her own. But Reothe's startled expression told her it was as unexpected as it was unwelcome.

He gave their interwoven fingers a squeeze. 'Say the words!'

'Not while there's breath in my body!'

Another scream filled the air. This time she recognised it for what it was. A great cat's death scream.

On a rush, sound permeated the cavern. Men and women yelled instructions. Their boots pounded on stone and metal scraped on metal.

Reothe cursed. Dropping her hand, he flicked aside a wall-hanging to reveal a passage, and left her without a word.

Imoshen ran after him, his shirt flapping around her bare thighs. As she ran she brought her wrist to her mouth and licked the old wound. It was all she need do to make the skin knit.

Her feet carried her through a short passage and out of a torchlit opening into the night. Flaming torches did little to dispel the mist. People rushed past her.

She heard another terrible feral scream, but this time it was an attacking scream closely followed by the ragged shrieks of someone dying in terror. She did not need to see them to know the cat was shredding its victim's belly with the claws of its powerful hind legs.

A white leopard loped out of the mist towards her. Imoshen's heart faltered. She glanced about but there were no weapons within grasp.

The beautiful beast slowed and prowled nearer, a growl trickling from its chest. It must have smelt her fear, yet its head lifted as if it was listening to something. Then she noticed the fur under its throat. Shocked, she saw the gaping neck wound but no blood dripped from the injury. A prickling sensation, part awe and part terror, travelled over her skin. If the beast was dead, what was animating it?

Instinctively she searched for the force which gave the cat life. Now that she probed she felt it, an unknown power source, both angry and ancient.

Shrieks and Reothe's shouted commands told her that his people were making a stand somewhere in the mist.

The beast looked into her eyes, primeval intelligence illuminating its feline features. She knew she was in more danger from this fell creature than from a hungry snow leopard. This had to be the beast Reothe had killed to bring her here.

Despite her fear, Imoshen knelt as if in supplication and extended her hand, fingers limp. The cat stepped forward. Dainty for such a large animal, it lifted its great muzzle. Jaws capable of crunching bone lightly brushed her flesh. She watched its nostrils flare as it inhaled her scent, identifying her. Then its tongue rasped across her skin.

'If you have been wronged. I will right the wrong,' Imoshen offered.

The screams of the dying drove her to her feet. The cat caught her hand in the feather-light grasp of its massive jaws and led her away, its great shoulders brushing her bare upper-thigh. With its guidance she found the defenders.

The snow cat at her side, she stepped out of the heated mists into a clearing. More than a dozen people were backed up against the far cliff face. Some swung blazing torches, others had weapons of steel. In their front ranks stood Reothe, bare chested, dressed in nothing but boots and breeches, his hair loose. He danced with death in the form of several white cats, swift and silent. Imoshen knew it was only a matter of time before they brought him down.

Already he was bleeding, or was it the blood of the beasts he had slain? He held a burning brand in one hand and an axe in the other.

The great cat let her hand drop, then lifted its head and gave an eerie yowl. At this signal the other cats ceased their attack. As if summoned they prowled over to join Imoshen and the great beast by her side.

Reothe's companions gasped. Some made the sign to ward off evil, others dropped to their knees, heads bowed, both hands raised to their foreheads in deep obeisance.

Reothe let the weapon drop. The axe hit the stone with a dull thud. His face held hope. 'Imoshen?'

'No, Reothe. I promised to right the wrong.'

The great cat nudged her and she stepped forward with it at her side. She saw Reothe's eyes widen as he recognised the beast.

'I think you know what to do,' she told him, though she had no idea.

Fear crawled across his face. He controlled it and handed the flaming torch to someone nearby.

Unarmed, Reothe sank to his knees to face the beast. Its head was level with his face, its jaws a mere breath from his throat. It could tear out that slender column quick as thought.

Imoshen could see the frantic flutter of Reothe's pulse. Her fingers twined through the beast's thick fur as if to restrain it. A jolt of pure energy travelled up her arm, almost knocking her back a step. The beast swung its head towards her, a low growl issuing from its throat, but she tightened her hold.

Why was she doing this? If the ancient ones used this beast to kill Reothe, she would be free of him. Reluctantly Imoshen released the great cat.

It sat facing Reothe, whose eyes never left its face.

He was communing with the Ancients. Had he stolen the power he needed to bring her here by spilling the great cat's blood and releasing its life force? Perhaps the Ancients had sent the cats to seek retribution.

Without warning the dead snow leopard lifted its paw and slashed Reothe's chest.

Burning streaks of pain raced down Imoshen's chest between her breasts. She staggered backwards.

Three parallel furrows appeared on Reothe's skin. For a moment they appeared bloodless, then they grew dark as the blood gathered. Reothe swayed but remained upright.

The beast lapped at the blood. Imoshen shuddered as she felt its rasping tongue on the flesh between her breasts, drinking from her life force.

She opened her eyes, unaware that she'd closed them, and saw Reothe watching her. His hands lifted to caress the fur of the great cat's head. In that instant the tension eased.

Hardly able to believe they had been released so lightly, Imoshen watched the Ancients' power leave the cat's body. Slowly, it crumpled to lie dead at Reothe's knees. He swayed, then collapsed over it.

She darted forward, catching him before his head could strike the stone. His body was limp and cold in her arms. The others stood immobile, stunned.

'Help me!'

They came, muttering fearfully. Between them they carried Reothe back to his cave and made up a bed. She sent someone to bring furs and whatever medicinal herbs they had.

Imoshen was not surprised to see Drake. She had not seen him since he had tried to abduct her. As she made her once-betrothed comfortable, Drake told her those present were Reothe's most trusted people. The rest of the rebels were camped two days' trek away through the ravines.

Drake and the others treated her with a deference they might have shown a vision, hardly daring to stroke her sixth finger.

'It is well you are here to care for him,' Drake told her.

Imoshen felt like a fraud as she arranged the furs to keep Reothe warm and prepared a healing drink for when – if – he woke.

'Leave me now, Drake.'

He obeyed her without question. She felt ashamed.

Numbly Imoshen knelt by the low pallet where Reothe lay, and pulled back the furs. Blood still welled from the parallel claw marks. With an instinctive knowledge she knew they were not normal wounds.

Bathing them only made it clear the skin would not knit without her help.

She brushed the damp silver hair from Reothe's forehead. His skin was hot and she watched as fever shook his body. Calling on her healing skills, she smoothed the frown from his forehead with her fingertips.

His closed eyelids quivered. What was he seeing in his mind's eye? Was the power of the Ancients stalking him in those visions?

Her heart went out to Reothe. She did not condone what he had done, spilling the snow cat's blood to call on ancient powers, but she did admire the strength of purpose which drove him to that desperate act. He was far braver than she.

Despite her better judgment, she could not distance herself from him. He was her kinsman and the last of her kind. No one else could save him. She could not stand back and let him wander, trapped in some other plane.

Imoshen clenched her hands in frustration. Here she was, untrained, floundering against something ancient and infinitely powerful. Fear left a bitter taste on her tongue, straining her nerves to fever pitch.

A shuddering breath escaped Reothe, but his chest barely moved. He was fading.

She would have to do it, she had no choice.

Closing her eyes she placed her fingers over the first of the long claw marks, willing the skin to knit. The hairs on her body rose in protest. A strange taste filled her mouth, making her teeth ache. Reothe's body tensed under her hands, his skin slippery with a sheen of sweat. An answering sweat broke out on her body, making her shiver despite the steamy air of the cave. She could feel the phantom claw mark on her own flesh burn as it closed in time with Reothe's visible wound.

With the sealing of each long welt she felt a path of itching pain etch itself down her chest. The very air grew heavy with tension. This simple healing act strained her concentration until her body felt taut as a drawn bow. Ignoring her own parallel pain, she forced the last wound to close.

When it was completed something snapped inside her, and she felt light-headed, almost dizzy with relief.

Now the air held nothing out of the ordinary. Experimentally, she parted the shirt's fine material to reveal the pale flesh between her breasts. It appeared unmarked. To the naked eye her skin was flawless yet she could still feel the wounds stinging.

A sigh escaped Reothe. He seemed to be deeply asleep. Sitting back on her heels, she studied his chest. Purple ridges rose where before the cuts had welled with blood. She suspected he would carry those scars till the day he died, just as she would carry the invisible ones.

He was lying so still. Before his skin had felt too hot, now it was cold. Instinct told her to warm him with her own body heat. But she suspected if she willingly touched his flesh, he would own her body and soul.

Leaning forward she touched her lips to his closed eyelids in a silent benediction. Then she pulled the furs over him and rose to go.

Leaving him helpless hurt her more than she cared to admit. The urge to sink down beside him and wrap her body around his was almost overwhelming.

In desperation, Imoshen turned and walked from the cave. She did not look back. When she stepped outside the sky was already growing light, though the torches still burned.

'Will he live, T'Imoshen?' Drake asked anxiously.

Reothe's people watched her expectantly. What could she say? She had healed his body, but what toll would Reothe pay for trafficking with the Ancients?

Suddenly their faces ignited with joy and Imoshen felt a presence behind her.

'T'Reothe...' his followers whispered reverently, greeting him in the old tongue with phrases she had never heard spoken aloud. It sounded like a litany.

Imoshen stiffened, unable to move, unable even to turn and face him. She had underestimated Reothe. Frozen with fear, she sensed his approach.

'See,' he whispered. His breath caressed the back of her neck, his words rubbed her senses like warm velvet.

'We are already bound.' His arms slid around her shoulders and she felt his hard thighs on her buttocks, his chest against her shoulders. 'You tamed the ancient ones, you saved my followers and then me.'

His people dropped to their knees one by one, giving the obeisance reserved for the Emperor and Empress, both hands going to their foreheads. Only Drake dared to lift his head and drink in their presence.

Reothe's words wove an insidious spell. 'They love us. They will die for us.'

Disgust overwhelmed Imoshen. It was wrong to manipulate the innocent love of a desperate people.

Reothe tightened his hold on her, his voice deeply persuasive. 'They want to worship something, Imoshen. It is in their nature. Why not us? We are the last pure T'En, our gifts are the true source of the church's power. For too long the church has sought to destroy us –'

'No.' But the word was a plea and she despised herself for her weakness.

'Together we could –'

She dropped into a crouch to escape his tender embrace. Throwing her weight forward she took several steps, then spun to face him. Her rapid movement made the light material of his shirt caress her body. His scent filled her nostrils, a mockingly intimate reminder.

She tore off the shirt and threw it at his feet. 'I won't be a part of it, Reothe.'

He smiled and looked up as the birds sang to greet the sunrise. 'Your bonding day dawns. Do you think the Ghebite General will forgive you for abandoning him?'

Frustration filled Imoshen. Tulkhan was never this devious. He always tried to meet her half way. He listened and learned. Her longing for him was a physical ache. She lifted her hand to the parallel streaks of pain between her breasts, discovering she could feel with her blind fingertips what she could not see with her eyes. Scar tissue.

'I did not ask to come here,' she whispered. Calling on the power of the Ancients she raked her flesh, drawing blood along those scar lines. 'Release me!'

Dimly she heard a shout and saw Reothe dart towards her, but he was much weaker than he pretended and he fell to his knees. Desperately he lurched forward with his arms outstretched to her.

Her heart contracted and she gasped with sharp dismay at the depth of her feelings for him. Fearful lest his touch undo her resolve, she turned to run and tripped.

Chapter Ten

IMOSHEN'S HANDS AND knees stung as she hit the polished wood. A cry of pain escaped her. She felt dizzy, a little sick and very frightened. Where was she?

That male smell? General Tulkhan... A disbelieving joy flooded her. The Ancients had answered her plea.

'Come to murder me in my sleep?' Tulkhan asked softly as he watched Imoshen turn with feral grace to face him.

Tulkhan had been sitting in the chair by his bedchamber window staring out at the cold winter's dawn, comparing it to other humid dawns in his homeland, when the room had suddenly grown warm and oppressive.

Even the air had taken on a strange tang, making him aware of unseen danger. He had been about to draw his weapon when, with a palpable, release of tension, the Dhamfeer had appeared naked and disoriented. She was bleeding from three parallel lines on her chest.

Now she stared at him as if she didn't believe she'd heard him correctly. What other excuse did she have for appearing unannounced in his bedroom?

Unless it was to bed him? Tension fed by weeks of frustration thrummed through his body. 'Either you are here to kill me or to bed me. Which is it?'

With understanding came anger and Imoshen stalked towards him, magnificent and furious. Her long hair hung around her body like a cloak. Every instinct told him to flee. It was only by exerting his will that he remained outwardly impervious.

'You seek to provoke me, Tulkhan. Haven't I proved my loyalty to you time and time again?'

He stared up into her face. With a jolt he noted the tears shimmering unshed in her eyes.

'Then why are you here?'

Her hands trembled as she pushed the hair from her face, muttering under her breath. He didn't need to understand High T'En to know she was cursing him.

Spinning on her heel she stalked off, all wounded dignity despite her nakedness. He was on his feet before he knew it, lunging forward to catch her around the waist. Her skin was icy cold. She arched against him, her body an exclamation of silent fury. The wiry strength in her surprised him.

Anticipating her reaction, he lifted her off her feet, still writhing, and threw her onto the bed. She twisted in the air like a cat, landing on her hands and knees, her hair splaying around her in an arc.

A shiver of instinctive awe rippled through him in response to her Otherness. She had never looked more Dhamfeer.

He tore at his vest. It was an elaborate brocade garment and the thin laces snapped easily.

Her eyes widened. 'What are you doing?'

He didn't bother to answer. The vest hit the floor. She scurried across the bed but he tackled her before her feet could hit the ground on the far side. They twisted, wrestling.

It struck Tulkhan that she did not mean to harm him. She used her strength only to repulse him, forbearing to deliver the killing or maiming blows to his eyes or throat he knew she could deliver with ease.

By the time she lay beneath him, both of them were panting with exertion, their faces only a hand's breadth apart.

'This is a lie,' he said and lowered his head to inhale her scent. It hit him like a physical thing. When he went on his voice was hoarse. 'You could have blinded me and escaped. You are here beneath me because it is where you want to be.'

She gave a wordless moan and lifted her face to his. He felt her smooth cheek on his throat, her soft parted lips as she traced the length of his jaw with her tongue. An involuntary shudder of pure desire went through him, triggering an answering shudder in her. His heart rate lifted another notch.

'Imoshen.' Her name was an invocation, drawn from him against his will.

His lips sought hers and instead he found a cheek wet with tears. Stunned, he shifted his weight onto his elbows and studied her tense face. What he saw made him smile. Her eyes were fierce, denying the tears on her cheeks and the trembling of her chin.

Silently he sat up so that she was free to climb off the bed, but she threw herself forward into his arms.

There was no mistaking the sincerity of her embrace as she wound her arms around him. He could smell fire and blood in her hair. 'Where have you been this night, Imoshen?'

She shook her head, either unable or unwilling to answer.

He cradled her against his chest, dragging the covers over her cold limbs. 'What –'

'Don't ask.'

There was such sorrow in her voice he could not pry. So instead he held her close until the trembling ceased.

Tulkhan realised he was whispering Ghebite endearments, things his mother used to croon to him, things he'd long forgotten. But now he recalled his mother's hands on him and her loving touch when he was too young to leave her side to live in the men's lodge. How strange – finding Imoshen had forced him to face his mother's loss, and in facing it he had found her again.

Imoshen pulled away from him, brushing the tears from her cheeks. The light from the open window had grown stronger and Tulkhan knew the servants would be coming soon. They must not find her in his chambers.

He went to warn her, but she placed her fingers to his lips. 'Hush.'

There were smudges of tiredness in the shadows beneath her eyes. Why did she look so haunted?

'We have little time,' she whispered. 'Know this, Tulkhan of the Ghebites. I will bond with you this day.'

He had to smile. All of Fair Isle knew that.

'No.' Her face was serious. She took his hand, placing his palm on her chest where he felt her heart beating strongly. 'I bond with you, here and now. I swear it. We don't need the church or a thousand nobles to witness this. It is between you and me.'

Tulkhan understood. The utter simplicity of Imoshen's vow went straight to his core.

He lifted her free hand, kissing her sixth finger. What was that scent?

He held her eyes. 'Know this, Imoshen of the T'En. I will bond with you from this day forward.'

Silently she eased her fingers from his to slip her hand inside his shirt. He felt her cold palm over his heart. His own hand rested on her chest, mirroring the gesture. It felt as if he held her rapidly beating heart in his hand. And, as she looked into his eyes, he felt his heart's rhythm change until their two hearts beat as one, resonant and strong.

Imoshen nodded once as if satisfied, then slid off the bed. 'I must go.' But she hesitated, looking down at him.

At that moment she seemed fragile. Tulkhan didn't want to part now, to spend the rest of the day looking at her, unable to touch, unable to share this intimacy until the last ceremony was over late tonight.

A noise in the hallway alerted him. 'Be careful, the servants come.'

A sweet sad smile illuminated her face. 'They will not see me.'

He knew it was true. He was mad to love a Dhamfeer.

THE DAY OF the Midwinter Feast dawned bright and cold as Kalleen and Cariah helped Imoshen prepare for the bonding ceremony.

'There...' Cariah stepped back to admire Imoshen's hair. A circlet of gold studded with yellow amethysts sat on her brow, and a thin gold net set with amethysts at every joint held her heavy hair in place. A second outfit was laid out on her bed for the coronation this afternoon.

Imoshen adjusted Tulkhan's bonding gift. 'The weight of this torque will give me a headache by midday.'

Kalleen smoothed her slim hands over Imoshen's gown of exquisite gold lace worn over an underdress of black satin. 'You are lucky you are tall. The babe does not show yet.'

'Does everyone know?' Imoshen asked ruefully.

Kalleen wrinkled her nose. 'It is the right and proper way to go to your bonding, rich with child, my lady.'

Imoshen shrugged to ease the tension in her shoulders. Kalleen still addressed her as *my lady*, only now it sounded like a term of endearment.

After this day she would be the Empress, she supposed, though by Ghebite custom General Tulkhan would accept the kingship, which in turn made her his queen. Imoshen grimaced. She did not feel royal. She felt dizzy with trepidation.

'Your hands are so cold.' Kalleen rubbed them between hers and blew on the icy fingers. 'What is it?'

Imoshen shrugged. She felt Cariah's sharp eyes on her. She had bathed Reothe's scent from her skin, but he remained in her thoughts. It felt as if she had left a piece of herself behind in that camp amid the hot pools. No matter how she rationalised it, she hated having to leave him. It had been a cruel choice. Yet she believed it was for the best. For all his talk of equality, Reothe threatened to dominate her in ways Tulkhan did not. She felt as if she had abandoned her younger, naive self when she had abandoned Reothe last night.

This very morning Tulkhan had sworn to bond with her, and she knew would stand true to his oath. Yet, as the day progressed, he was sure to draw away from her. If only she could get close to him, intimately close. She knew that if she could slip into his mind when he slipped into her body, she could imprint herself on him and... But no, that would not be right. What good was love if it was not freely given?

'What troubles you, Imoshen?' Cariah whispered.

'Tulkhan does not love me!' It was out before she could stop herself.

'He wants you,' Kalleen said. 'I've seen the way he looks at you. You are to be bonded –'

'You speak of bonding in the old way of the country folk,' Cariah corrected. 'In bondings of state the best you can hope for is companionship, and if you are very lucky a little fondness. Don't despair, Imoshen, love may follow, especially since his body pulls him to you. Make use of it.'

Cariah's Old Empire tone made Imoshen flinch. 'My parents raised me with the old values. Their bonding went beyond the flesh to their souls. From what I now know of life in the Empress's court, I'm glad my family avoided it.'

'You can't avoid your responsibilities,' Cariah said.

'Enough, Cariah.' Kalleen squeezed Imoshen's hands. 'It will be for the best. I have seen how Wharrd has changed since we were bonded. The General will grow to love you.'

Imoshen sighed. 'I am being foolish. Forgive me. As Cariah says, this is a bonding of state. Sometimes when I look into the General's eyes I think as much as he desires me, he hates me.'

Kalleen and Cariah exchanged swift glances, their silence damning. Imoshen stifled her dismay. The murmur of the approaching noblewomen who would be escorting her to the great hall filled the pause.

'They come,' Cariah said. 'Stand tall. Don't let them suspect.'

Kalleen hugged Imoshen. 'I wish you happiness. You have been so good to me.'

The women entered and for the rest of the day Imoshen knew she would have no peace.

*   *   *

FOR IMOSHEN THE bonding ceremony felt unreal, as if it were happening to someone else. For one thing it went on longer than was traditional because both churches played a role. The Cadre performed his with bad grace, having been relegated to giving his blessing before the Beatific oversaw the vow-giving in the manner of a Fair Isle bonding.

Standing next to her, Tulkhan seemed alien and distant in his barbarian splendour. He wore the ceremonial belt over a red velvet tunic with black sable trim. His long hair fell free down his back and two plaits hung from his temples, threaded with fine gold beads.

As the two of them clasped hands and the Beatific tied a slender red ribbon around their wrists, Imoshen recalled how Reothe had used the old form of bonding, cutting their skin and pressing their wrists together. When their blood mingled she had refused to make the vow. With the words unsaid they were not bonded by the laws of their church. Yet her unruly body had responded to Reothe by breaking the old bonding scar. She shuddered.

Hands still joined, they accepted the bonding chalice. Imoshen offered it to Tulkhan. When he had taken a sip he offered it to her, turning it so that her lips touched where his had. The memory of drinking from Reothe's lips made her dizzy.

The Beatific retrieved the chalice, then the moment came for Imoshen to make her vow to Tulkhan before the gathered nobles and town officials. It was a relief to say the words. This final step was irrevocable. It freed her from Reothe's claim. It must!

There was still the long noon feast and then the coronation ceremony to be endured, but tonight when she lay with General Tulkhan their joining would erase all thought of her once-betrothed.

AS THE PALE winter sun set on the great dome of the Basilica, Tulkhan and Imoshen faced the Beatific on their knees, ready to accept the coronation symbols of the Emperor and Empress.

They had crossed the square and entered the Basilica as supplicants, barefoot and bare-headed, but after the ceremony they would leave in the coronation chariot as befitted their new roles.

It was this aspect of their bonding which troubled General Tulkhan. The ornate coronation made him deeply uncomfortable. He was sure the Keldon nobles considered him a barbarian upstart, and with all this pomp and ceremony he felt he was being distanced from his own men. He wished this T'En rite over. But first Imoshen must be accepted by the Orb before she could be Arbiter of Truth.

With deep reverence the Beatific donned gloves so that her flesh did not defile the relic. She unlocked a delicate cage and withdrew the Orb. According to legend, it came from the land beyond the dawn sun. Tulkhan stared at the fragile glass and wondered cynically how many times it had been replaced in six hundred years of journeys and battles.

Imoshen seemed nervous. Her face was paler than usual and she wore Old-Empire make-up which heightened her T'En characteristics. The torque he had given her was nowhere in evidence, indeed her whole outfit was different from the gold and black of this morning's bonding ceremony. Now she wore a white underdress overlaid with fine silver lace. Her hair was loose on her shoulders like a satin cloak, and her head, like his, was bare, ready to accept the crown.

Her eyes closed briefly as she prepared herself. The tang of her T'En gift registered on Tulkhan's tongue, making him wonder about the source of the Orb's power.

Imoshen raised her arms, hands cupped to receive the Orb. It left the Beatific's grasp, falling into Imoshen's. The instant her bare fingers touched the Orb's surface it flared brightly, surprising Tulkhan.

A gasp of reverence escaped the masses gathered behind them. The Orb had responded to Imoshen's T'En blood.

The Beatific removed the Orb and replaced it. Then she returned her attention to them, ready to finalise the coronation. An awed silence fell as the Beatific raised the twin crowns for public blessing.

Stiff with inactivity, Tulkhan waited impatiently with Imoshen at his side. Self-derision twisted within him. Whether he called himself King or Prince, he would never be as respected as the rulers of the Old Empire. He ground his teeth.

'What is it?' Imoshen mouthed softly, though she continued looking straight ahead.

'I can't do it.' His own words surprised him. 'I won't claim to be something I'm not.'

'What do you mean?' Startled, Imoshen turned to him.

He had always despised hereditary rule which accepted a man's birth before his ability. The Beatific stepped towards them, her assistant carrying the twin crowns on their bed of velvet.

Revulsion stirred in Tulkhan. 'I'm no king. I'm a soldier!'

'If you can lead an army, you can lead an island.'

Tulkhan knew she was right.

He sprang to his feet, pulling Imoshen with him. The Beatific took a step back, her expression a mixture of annoyance and confusion.

'Trust me?' Tulkhan asked Imoshen.

She searched his eyes, then smiled. 'Yes.'

He felt an answering smile ignite him and faced the crowd.

'I am not your Emperor and I never will be.' His words carried, echoing in the great dome. Not surprisingly a murmur of confusion greeted his announcement. He lifted his free hand, signalling for silence. 'I am not the King of the Ghebites. I am simply a soldier, first son of the King's second wife. I claim no royal privilege for myself. I am a general. I will place no one, whether they be noble, guildmaster, Fair Isle farmer or Ghebite soldier, above any other.' The investiture of his men returned to him. 'Like my lord commanders I am here to serve Fair Isle.'

He paused to study the sea of faces, their expressions ranging from outrage to astonishment. Certain factions would not approve. The Keldon nobles for one, but he had already acknowledged their rights and the laws of their church.

'I declare myself Protector General of Fair Isle, and this is Imoshen, Lady Protector of the People.' He took Imoshen's hand, placing it along his forearm so that her fingers draped over his.

A tentative cheer broke from the ranks of his men, telling him his instinct had been right. The people of Fair Isle were harder to read. A furious whispering broke out in the crowd as they debated his repudiation of the emperorship.

Imoshen's fingers tightened on his. He expected to see anger, but pure joy suffused her features.

'Signal the musicians and choir,' Imoshen ordered over her shoulder to the Beatific. 'We will dispense the coins and make our triumphal ride around the square now.'

'The Vow of Expiation,' the Beatific hissed. 'You must give that vow or negate the bonding and coronation.'

'I had not forgotten,' Imoshen whispered, still facing the crowd.

Tulkhan squeezed her hand as the choir began their rehearsed piece, their voices soaring high into the great dome like streams of living sound.

'Are you disappointed?' Tulkhan asked under cover of their song.

Imoshen smiled. 'No, Protector General. You have confirmed my faith in you in a most unexpected way.'

'Good.' He smiled, enjoying her approval.

They stepped off the dais, making their stately way down the aisle under the centre of the dome. There, inset in the floor, was an ancient circle of stone, so old its engravings were almost worn away.

Before everyone, Imoshen sank to her knees and placed her left hand in the impression on the stone. Her six fingers fitted the indentations perfectly.

As she gave her Vow of Expiation, promising to serve the people of Fair Isle without fear or favour, Tulkhan noted the intense expression on the face of the man opposite. Dressed in a mulberry tabard, his wine-dark eyes glittered as they fixed on Imoshen's bent head.

For a moment Tulkhan could not remember who he was. Then it came to him. This was Murgon, leader of the Tractarians, the branch of the Church dedicated to hunting down rogue T'En.

Imoshen came to her feet and the choir resumed their paean of praise. At the doors of the Basilica two acolytes knelt to help Imoshen and Tulkhan slide their feet into their shoes. They had entered the Basilica barefoot and bare-headed, mid-afternoon.

Now it was dusk and they left it wearing the mantle of their office, although the crowns remained on their bed of velvet.

'If only the pomp of position could be escaped as easily as the crowns and titles,' Imoshen whispered, as if aware of his thoughts.

Tulkhan wanted to laugh. But she was right. There were still hours of formality ahead of them as they presided over the coronation feast where they would sign the charter giving the three largest banks royal endorsement.

When they stepped outside, the crowd greeted them with song. Along the steps of the Basilica two lines of people formed an honour guard. They were high-ranking nobles, Tulkhan's men amongst them, town officials and ordinary citizens chosen by lot.

The acolytes handed Tulkhan and Imoshen their chests of newly minted coins. The General paused to study the two-headed coin. Imoshen's profile graced one side, his profile the other. It was dated six hundred and seventeen, though the new year did not officially start until tomorrow.

'Time to share our good fortune,' Imoshen said. 'These coins will be collectors' items in years to come.'

They distributed the coins and accepted endless congratulations. At last the empty chests were returned to the acolytes and Tulkhan and Imoshen stepped into the open coronation chariot.

The square was packed with residents of T'Diemn and outlying farms, all come to witness this historical occasion. The chariot made its slow stately way round the square, its two horses led by a groom. Then it came to a stop directly in front of the palace's grand entrance where two tall towers stood like arrogant sentinels.

Imoshen's hand covered his. 'Now you will see the display I promised.'

A wizened little man scurried towards them, passing several objects to Imoshen.

'I always wanted to launch one of these things,' she confided as she pulled on a leather glove and took the cylinder.

It didn't look particularly inspiring. Tulkhan had expected jewels and gold.

The little man opened his coal pouch and blew on it to quicken the flame. 'Take care to hold it away from your body, Empress.'

Imoshen dipped the cylinder's wick in the flame. It sparked into life immediately, brighter than striking a flint. A tail of fire shot from the cylinder as it leapt into the air. Rapid as an escaped bird it arced across the sky, trailing sparks of light, only to burst star-bright above the palace.

Tulkhan blinked, stunned by the afterimage as much as by the improbability of what he had seen. But the crowd was not surprised. They cheered delightedly, then grew expectantly quiet.

'Watch the towers,' Imoshen whispered. She stripped the glove from her hand and returned it to the little man.

Tulkhan frowned. A spark flared on the nearest tower, followed by another. The crowd gasped as waterfalls of living sparks poured from the tower tops.

'The place will burn to the ground,' Tulkhan muttered.

'Not at all. Members of the Pyrolate Guild spend years learning their craft. Surely you've heard of the T'En fountains of light?'

Tulkhan had but he had discounted them, just as he had the rumours of the Dhamfeer powers. He stared in awe as from every tower fountains of golden light poured down, illuminating the palace. The crowded square was utterly silent. 'What are they made of?'

'I've no idea. The guild keeps their knowledge secret. But they are quite harmless.'

Tulkhan marvelled. How could Imoshen be so casual? 'I will inspect the apparatus that makes these fountains and that star-bird you shot into the sky.'

Imoshen laughed softly. 'You would have to convince the master-pyrolate himself and that would be no easy task. When they are apprenticed they take a vow of secrecy.'

She pulled him around to face her, pressing her strong body against him. Fey laughter danced in her eyes. 'Kiss me under the fountains of golden light, General.'

So General Tulkhan of the Ghebites claimed Imoshen, last T'En Princess, savouring the impossibility of the moment.

As THE CORONATION feast wound down, Tulkhan stretched, easing the tension in his shoulders. Imoshen was his now by every law of man, and by the gods he wanted her.

'A word, Protector General?'

Tulkhan turned to see the self-important Ghebite priest. He contained his annoyance and stepped back so that their conversation would be more private. 'Yes, Cadre?'

The smaller man glanced over his shoulder at Imoshen who was playing an elaborate game with a young Keldon noble.

The complexity and variety of games played by the people of Fair Isle never ceased to amaze Tulkhan. He supposed they had to find some way to amuse themselves. *Too much peace*, he thought sourly.

'Did you know she holds the records of all property ownership?'

Tulkhan grimaced. Obviously the Cadre was not talking about Imoshen. 'The T'En church has always held the records.'

'It is run by a woman!'

'It is their way.'

'It is not our way!'

Tulkhan looked down at his indignant priest. 'And this is not our land. But we will make it so.'

'Then relegate the Beatific to a lesser function. Give me the task and I will reorganise their church.'

Tulkhan almost laughed. 'Why should they give up what they have?'

The Cadre stiffened. 'Half of them are women, only women!'

This time Tulkhan did laugh. He gazed at Imoshen who was now performing an elaborate sequence of movements which could have been a dance. 'There is no *only*.'

Anger hardened the Cadre's features. 'You let your lust rule your head.'

'You let your anger rule your tongue.' Tulkhan warned. The Cadre went to apologise but the General waved him aside. 'No. Go now. We will speak again later.'

Tulkhan folded his arms and leaned against the wall. Obscured by shadows, he observed the game and the purpose finally struck him. Imoshen and her opponent were performing a series of dance moments. At the end of each sequence they added another movement.

The two competitors had to remember the whole sequence, perform it and add another each time. The first one to make a mistake lost.

He wished the game would end so he could lead Imoshen away. They had done their duty. Didn't she want him as badly as he wanted her?

'Protector General?'

'Beatific.' He straightened, cloaking his uneasiness.

She returned his acknowledgment with the elaborate obeisance reserved for the Empress and Emperor. Was she mocking him or did she seek reassurance because he had been speaking with the Cadre?

But the Beatific said nothing, instead her gaze followed his, and he realised he had looked past her to Imoshen.

'T'Imoshen is at her most charming. Unfortunately, it is an illusion. Forgive me, I am going to speak plainly. You are Ghebite and a True-man. Do not be lulled into a false sense of security. Imoshen is not one of us. The T'En are both more and less than True-people.'

Tulkhan did not want to hear this tonight. He wanted that part of Imoshen which was only too real and womanly, her quicksilver passion. But he had to placate the head of the T'En church. He met the Beatific's eyes expecting her to give another vague warning about Imoshen's gifts. What could she possibly say that he hadn't already thought of in the dark lonely nights?

'The flame burns bright attracting the moth but venture too close and it will be consumed. You may think you can warm yourself at Imoshen's fires and escape unscathed. But T'En work their way beneath your guard. Believe me, I know.' The Beatific's hand closed on his arm. Her smile was luminous with painful self-knowledge. 'Reothe and I were lovers. He coached me, helped me attain this position.'

Tulkhan was stunned. A married Ghebite woman would face death if she admitted this. An unmarried Ghebite woman would kill herself if defiled by a man.

'I went to hear Reothe debate in the great library of the Halls of Learning. His passion for knowledge and truth was inspiring. I was fascinated by the brilliance of his mind. It drew me with such intensity I had to walk away.' She shook her head wryly. 'I think that was why he first pursued me. It annoyed him to have someone walk out while he was speaking. When he came after me I should have been on my guard but I lied to myself. He was only seventeen, I was nearly ten years older. I let myself believe I could enjoy him and remain aloof.' She sighed. Tulkhan did not want to hear this, yet he knew he must. 'At that time I was working my way up through the church hierarchy. Knowing what I know now, I believe he saw ability in me and wanted a lever on the T'En church for the future. Reothe plans for the long term, you see, and he is utterly ruthless.' She held Tulkhan's eyes. 'He was under the Empress's protection, related by blood to her and her heirs, but that was not enough for him.'

Tulkhan said nothing. He suspected the Beatific would continue until she got the reaction she wanted from him.

'You know he and the Empress's heir, Ysanna, were lovers. Reothe wanted control of the royal family.' The Beatific shrugged. 'The Empress loved him when he came to her as a tragic youth. She reared him with her own children. Ysanna played her suitors off against Reothe. Could they sail, ride, hunt or write poetry as well as he? He never committed himself to Ysanna, for there were those who did not wish to see him the future empress's bond-partner. When he asked Imoshen to bond with him it was the lesser of two evils, or so they thought.' She fixed troubled eyes on him. 'You don't know what the T'En can do. With every touch they cement their hold on you, slipping insidiously into your mind, sifting for what they can use to further their own ends.'

Tulkhan nodded once, reluctantly. This time when he looked into the Beatific's face he understood that despite everything she still loved Reothe.

'What better way to control someone than through love?' she whispered.

Something twisted inside him. Hadn't Imoshen said the very same thing?

'She is not like that.' It was an instinctive denial.

The Beatific smiled tolerantly. 'Imoshen is T'En. They protect themselves. Reothe was a youth in a palace of intrigue, searching for a way to ensure his safety. You can forgive them anything. I know I did.'

Tulkhan sensed movement. The game had broken up and Imoshen was coming towards them, laughter dancing in her eyes. He watched that joy turn to wariness as she read his expression.

Before he could move, the Beatific glided forward, spoke softly to Imoshen, then made a formal obeisance and left.

Imoshen joined him and paused a little beyond touching distance. 'Well, General?'

'Protector General.'

She eyed him thoughtfully. He could tell she was trying to understand him. A True-woman would have tried to read his face and stance, Imoshen resorted to her gift. The overflow of her power made his skin crawl, yet he still wanted her.

'Bed.' The word left his lips unbidden.

'Yes.'

In a blur they slipped away unnoticed. Tulkhan knew Imoshen was cloaking them, but he did not care. A madness was upon him. The passage was long and echoed with the night's revelry. The servants were absent from their posts, even the stronghold guard.

Chapter Eleven

IMOSHEN FELT LIGHT-HEADED. Her feet seemed to fly over the glossy parquetry floor. She could see the same strange excitement in Tulkhan's eyes. It was heaven to escape the confines of their official roles. She had waited too long for this.

She could wait no longer. With a wordless cry of challenge she took to her heels. She heard the General give chase and laughed, increasing her speed.

Habit led her to her own bedchamber, even though they should have entered the grand suite reserved for the Emperor and Empress.

There was no fire or light in her room. She sprang to one side of the door and pressed her back against the wood panel. Her heart thundered, echoing the rapid thud of Tulkhan's boots.

He thrust the door open and charged in, stepping out of the shaft of light immediately. She saw his body grow still as he listened for her. He was the perfect warrior, poised for the hunt. She could not resist baiting him.

Silently she slipped her shoes from her feet, then slammed the door shut and tossed the shoes to different ends of the room, presenting Tulkhan with three sources of movement.

She heard him spin, heard his muffled curse.

With a laugh she sprang on his back. He staggered under the impact before regaining his balance.

She held an imaginary knife to his throat. 'Yield, you are my captive, General!'

'Never!' He hauled her over his shoulder.

She slammed onto the floor, the air driven from her lungs. Sparks floated in her vision and she gave a painful laugh. Then she felt a real blade at her throat and froze.

Her world swung crazily. Did he mean to kill her and blame it on assassins?

'I thought we were past this?' Imoshen played, for time. She heard him chuckle but it was edged with anger. Instinctively she clasped his bare arm, seeking his motivation.

The General sprang away, muttering Ghebite curses. She heard him walk towards the fireplace where the makings of a fire had been prepared but not lit. In a moment he had struck the spark and ignited the tinder.

She rolled into a crouch and watched as he lit the candles on the mantelpiece. 'What did the Beatific say to you?'

The broad planes of his Ghebite features were illuminated by the flickering flames, but his expression revealed nothing. Looking down at her his dark eyes were hooded, cloaking his expression even further. Again Imoshen felt the urge to touch him and discover his thoughts.

'It is time I made one thing clear,' he said.

She felt uneasy but kept her tone light. 'And what would that be, General?'

'We are no longer captor and captive. Come here.'

Though she was prepared for a battle of wits, her treacherous body was preparing for him. Every caress of her satin underdress was a foretaste of his touch.

She could sense the impregnable layers of his formidable will shutting her out. 'Speak, General.'

He grimaced. 'Why don't you touch me and learn what you want to know?'

'You don't like it when I do that.'

'No. Yet I can't live without touching you.'

It was a raw admission. Something inside her clenched with an answering need.

'I know. It is the same with me.' Heat stung her cheeks. It was hard admitting this to a distant Tulkhan. She would much rather embrace him and let him feel how much she wanted him.

'You say you already carry my child. I need never touch you again. I could walk from this room and our bonding would be nothing but a marriage of state,' he told her, yet his voice vibrated with repressed passion.

Pride made Imoshen school her features and call up an amused smile. 'You could try, but I doubt it would be workable.'

'No. This last small moon has proved that. I could not see you every day and want you as I do. Not without...'

Triumph flashed through her and he ground to a halt, visibly angered.

'Then you'll just have to accept me for what I am, General.'

'No. Either you vow never to invade my mind and use your T'En gifts on me, or I will turn my back on you.' His expression was implacable. 'I will have you escorted to the Beatific. Surrounded by a thousand priests and watched over by the Tractarians, the rebels won't be able to touch you or use you. The people will think you safe and I won't be tortured with the constant reminder of your presence.'

'Murgon's Tractarians.' How she hated those priests, betrayers of their own kind. A deep anger coalesced in her. Was she such a loathsome creature that she must be shut away from the light of day? She wanted to strike the General, to make him suffer the same pain she endured. He had admitted he craved her body, yet in the very next breath he had revealed his revulsion for her T'En traits.

Instinctively she weighed the odds. Physically he might be stronger than her, but was his will equal to hers? If it came down to this, only one of them would survive, and she would never give up.

Yet... she could not bring herself to hurt him. The thought of causing General Tulkhan pain caused her pain. Her feelings for him made her weak and she despised herself for opening her heart to this Ghebite.

Imoshen sucked in her breath, feeling the inrush of air chill her teeth and tongue. How had it come to this?

'Do you understand?' he demanded. 'I will not have the privacy of my mind invaded.'

She nodded, numbly. Yes, she understood that fear only too well. It was why she feared Reothe. But she did not seek to manipulate Tulkhan, and he should know this. It was the threat of incarceration which cut deepest. The General would use Fair Isle's own weapons against her – the Beatific and the Tractarians.

'You misjudge me, Tulkhan,' she said, hardly able to speak for the knot of sorrow which filled her throat. 'I might have offered such a vow freely. But –'

'But?'

She wanted to defy him, to declare that she would not be bullied. She wanted him to back down. With a flash of insight she understood what she really wanted was for him to accept her without reservation. But he was a Ghebite, and a True-man, with all the limitations of his birth and culture.

'Imoshen?' The word was barely audible. 'I will not be your puppet.'

Then she understood his deepest fear, and in understanding it was able to reach inside herself for a deeper compassion. 'You underestimate yourself and me. If it will satisfy you, I promise not to invade your mind except in an emergency. I won't let you come to harm if I can save you.'

When she held his eyes Imoshen thought she saw a flash of remorse.

'You would swear to this?' he asked finally.

She nodded.

He took her hand to place it palm down over her belly. 'Swear on this life.'

Imoshen felt an odd little flare inside her. 'I swear on the life of my... our unborn child not to use the mind-touch on you, except in an emergency.'

'Or any other T'En gift – no compulsions, no tricks of any sort,' he prodded.

Imoshen gave a moan of protest.

Tulkhan felt it like a knife slicing his soul. He had not thought it would cost him so dearly. He could see he had hurt her by devaluing her trust. With this vow he had reduced what they might have shared. But he had to have peace of mind. 'Well?'

'You are denying what I am!'

'If I cannot trust you, I will not touch you.' He steeled himself against her pain. 'The choice is yours.'

It was a bluff, but Imoshen could not know that. He had no choice where she was concerned. She was a compulsion which drove him to madness.

'You would have me deny myself to be with you? Is that truly what you want?' Her tortured eyes searched his face.

He wanted to tell her no, that she was everything to him and the rest of Fair Isle could rot. But even now he could not be sure that this feeling wasn't prompted by some T'En trick. 'Make this vow or there can be nothing between us.'

'I will make this vow, General.' Imoshen shuddered. 'But until the day you free me from it, it will stand between us.'

Despite the warmth of the fire a shiver passed over his skin. He could not imagine a day when he would willingly lay himself open to her gifts. 'The vow?'

'I vow on the life of our unborn child not to use my T'En gifts on you, except in dire emergency.' Her lips twisted in a parody of a smile. 'Will that satisfy you, General Tulkhan?'

He could feel the anger vibrating in her. His body was totally attuned to hers and he sensed the power building.

'You are angry with me. I'll leave you alone tonight.' He raised her hand and brushed his lips across her inner wrist. It was a gesture he had seen the Keld use, one which could be formal or very intimate.

Every instinct screamed at him to stay, but he made himself walk away. When the time came he wanted theirs to be a joyous union.

'Tulkhan...'

He turned to see her standing before the fire in her finery, her face taut, tear tracks in her ceremonial make-up. He waited.

'Would you have me beg?' The words were torn from her.

Her desperation called to something primal inside him. Yes, he wanted her to beg for him, to welcome him. He was greedy for her.

She lifted one hand in supplication.

As he approached she turned away, unwilling to reveal her naked need. He took her shoulders in his hands, feeling the tension in her body. An answering tension ignited him.

He noticed the delicate lace of her overdress had torn and that made him recall throwing her over his shoulder to the floor. He winced, sure he would find bruises on her tender flesh when he removed her formal robes. How could he treat her so roughly when she carried his child? Yet she demanded he give no quarter and she appeared to take no hurt.

Silently he lifted her thick hair to undo the lacing at the back of her neck. The silver tabard slipped from her shoulders and fell to her feet, glittering in the ruddy firelight. When he released her hair it ran through his fingers like silk. Unable to stop himself he stroked it, feeling the tension drain from her. Gradually she relaxed into him, her back pressed to his chest.

His arms slid around her body, pressing her closer so that she could feel his growing need. Her hips melded against his, her welcome unmistakable.

A spasm of naked desire made him arch in response.

'The body's needs are powerful,' she whispered, but he had no time for words.

Imoshen had intended to hold herself in reserve. Deep inside her a little knot of cold resentment burned to be expressed, but when he tilted her face with infinite tenderness and his lips claimed hers, she experienced a rush of completion.

The love she wanted to deny welled up, swamping her defences so that she gave herself utterly to the moment, luxuriating in his ardour.

Eagerly she turned within the circle of his arms to slide her hands inside his shirt, exulting in his hot flesh, the hard planes of his chest. His great heart hammered, pacing her own.

Impatient, she tore at the lacing of his shirt, shrugging it over his shoulders to reveal his coppery skin, criss-crossed by the fine silver scars of old wounds. To think one of those wounds might have been fatal and she would never have known him.

In that moment, he was unutterably precious to her and as necessary to her as the very breath she took. The realisation was luminous in its intensity.

His calloused hands closed on her, rasping across her shoulders as he fought to undo the ties of her underdress. In a fever of desire she came to his aid and they discarded their formal garments.

When her gown pooled at her feet he stepped back, a ragged gasp on his lips. Suddenly shy, she felt his gaze on her like a physical thing, illuminating her. Hardly able to breathe, she dared raise her eyes to his. Naked need suffused his features.

Wordlessly she opened her arms to him and he came to her. She pulled him down before the fireplace, accepting him even as she sank into the fur. There was nothing but this moment, nothing but this man.

MUCH LATER, as they lay on the furs before the fire, it struck Tulkhan that for the new rulers of Fair Isle, they had chosen to consummate their marriage in primitive surroundings, ignoring the royal chambers, rich with every decoration and comfort.

'Why do you smile?' Imoshen's skin was flushed, only a smudge of colour remained of her formal make-up and her hair lay damp and knotted, a riot of pale silk.

Tulkhan shook his head slowly and she blushed. Their lovemaking couldn't have been more perfect. Recalling it made him feel almost reverential. How could two people know such ecstasy in the union of their bodies and yet be strangers?

All this long day and for the long days leading up to it, he had waited for this night. Replete at last, the tension drained from him.

Imoshen heard Tulkhan's breathing grow deep and regular. Propping her weight on one elbow, she watched him as he succumbed to sleep.

Relaxed like this he looked much younger. His dark hair mingled with the dark fur. Drawn, she leaned closer to feel his warm breath on her face. With each exhalation she inhaled his breath, willing him to become a part of her. A delicious languor stole over her body as she absorbed his being, focusing on his essence. A tingling awareness of their two separate entities surfaced in her mind's eye and she...

Cold reality shocked her from this pleasant intimacy. She had vowed not to use her gifts. Reluctantly she relinquished the sweet contact. She hadn't known she meant to bind him to her. It had been an instinctive act.

Pulling away, she studied the perfection of his sleeping profile. When had his broad cheekbones and coppery skin become her ideal of male beauty? It had been a gradual thing, a shift in her perception.

A little worm of anger writhed within her. How dare he threaten her? She searched her mind for the trigger and recalled the General's closed face as she approached him as he stood with the Beatific.

What had the Beatific told Tulkhan?

He stirred in his sleep. She could trawl his sleeping mind without him knowing. Why stop there? Why not plant ideas, compulsions, even suspicions which she could later use?

Bitter self-knowledge shook her. It would be easy to make the attempt and far too easy to justify her actions. After all, she was only protecting them both from the Beatific's machinations.

She fought the urge to use her gifts, trembling with the effort. Finally the compulsion eased.

No wonder General Tulkhan did not trust her, she hardly trusted herself!

Imoshen sat up and hugged her knees, looking into the dying flames. It appeared she and the General were destined to share the kind of bonding True-people shared, one that went deep on a physical level but excluded the mind-touch. Was it enough?

He wanted her. He made her body sing. She even suspected General Tulkhan could grow to love her. But he expected her to live a half life. Could she be satisfied with that?

No.

Imoshen knew with utter certainty that she had to have it all. Tulkhan had to not only accept her T'En gifts, he had to embrace them, or she would grow to despise him and herself.

Unlike Cariah, she could not be less than she was.

Tulkhan wished he could have slipped away with Imoshen as Wharrd had done with Kalleen, to forge their bonding in private, but royal bondings required celebration and their duties never ceased.

He watched Imoshen perform the elaborate warmed wine ceremony. In front of each person stood a small porcelain cup, decorated with delicate High T'En symbols. The aromatic wine steamed on the still air. It was time to speak.

When Imoshen caught his eye, hers held a warning. Since their bonding there had been little time to discuss the Causare Council and now he faced its delegates, Woodvine, Athlyn, Fairban and others, leaders of the greater and lesser noble families of the Keldon Highlands.

He had not denied them their request for a formal meeting, choosing to greet them in his map-room. They sat around the large circular table, their features reflected in its glossy surface, their wine untouched.

Imoshen lifted her porcelain cup with Old Empire formality and took a sip. Everyone followed suit. Tulkhan rolled the wine around on his tongue. It was sweet and spicy, not really to his taste. He put the cup aside.

'We have been patient, Protector General,' Fairban began.

'Not a word of dissension has passed our lips before the mainland spies,' Woodvine said. 'When will you hold the first of your Causare Councils?'

Old Athlyn lifted a hand. 'There are those amongst us with hot heads who would see everything achieved before spring. Fair Isle was not established overnight. Give us a sign that you –'

'I have spoken with my lord commanders,' Tulkhan said. 'They understand the idea of this council, though it goes by a different name in Gheeaba. The Causare Council will reconvene, but with some changes.'

There was uneasy muttering.

'Have you no say in this?' Woodvine demanded of Imoshen. 'Will women be forbidden to take their seat on the council?'

Imoshen placed her palms flat on the table to each side of her wine. 'In keeping with custom, so that all voices will be heard equally, there will be a new Causare Council consisting of equal representatives from the Old Empire and the new. Six of the General's lord commanders will take their seats in the Causare. And you must select from your ranks six representatives.'

'You jest!' Woodvine exploded.

Tulkhan met Imoshen's eyes as the Keld argued against this restriction. He had deliberately selected his most trusted men, those who could be relied on to keep a cool head. Not only would they have to debate matters of state with their recent enemy, but some of those enemies were sure to be female. To Imoshen it was simply an accepted custom, to his men it was an insult. He could trust no more than six. Besides, he wanted the Causare Council to be a controllable size.

Argument raged around the table.

When Imoshen came to her feet voices faded. Tulkhan watched her lift one hand, fingers spreading elegant as an unfurling fan.

'Six people from the Old Empire.' She lifted the other hand. 'Six from the new.' She lowered her hands palms open. Her brilliant mulberry eyes met theirs in turn. 'Think on it.'

IT WAS FIFTEEN days after midwinter and the frozen lake had been pronounced safe for skating. This was the last evening of formal entertainments, for which Imoshen was deeply grateful. It would be a relief to farewell the majority of the mainland visitors tomorrow. Only the ambassadors and their aides would remain. Imoshen wanted those who left Fair Isle to report that the new Ghebite overlords had not destroyed T'En culture, so she and Cariah had organised tonight's farewell ice ballet to reinforce that impression.

Kalleen caught Imoshen's arm as she flew past laughing. Her wooden skates skidded out from under her, dragging them both off their feet. Being a farm girl, Kalleen had learnt to skate on the village pond, but this had not involved the fancy performance step she'd just tried to execute.

Perched on the bank overlooking the lake, the musicians played as the sedate nobles circled in pairs, studiously avoiding Imoshen and Kalleen, which made it seem all the more ridiculous.

Most of the Ghebite commanders had refused the chance to learn to skate. They sat in the large tent at one end of the lake, drinking and watching the festivities.

Kalleen gave Wharrd a wave, unworried by the disapproval radiating from the other skaters. Imoshen wished she could forget her role as Lady Protector of Fair Isle and play silly village games.

Her stomach rumbled. Hot food was being prepared in pot-bellied stoves on the bank. The tangy aroma drifted on the slight breeze stirring the multicoloured lanterns.

Cariah laughed as she swooped in, turning her skates to slow her advance. 'You are shocking my sisters, Kalleen!'

Imoshen wondered if Cariah was obliquely censuring the Lady Protector of Fair Isle.

Kalleen rolled her eyes. 'I won't pretend to be something I'm not and spoil my fun!'

'We don't all have that luxury,' Cariah snapped, her meaning all too clear.

Imoshen winced and came to her feet. 'Have I overstepped the mark?'

Cariah glanced around impatiently. 'There are some who would resent your behaviour if you sat in the tent and did nothing. Life's too short to worry about people like that.'

'Help me up,' Kalleen commanded imperiously. Imoshen laughed. What would she do without Kalleen to lend a breath of sanity? If only she could mend the rift between herself and Cariah. Together they pulled the smaller woman upright, steadying her.

Imoshen noticed General Tulkhan's large form weaving through the circling skaters towards her, and her body quickened at the sight of him.

'The entertainers are ready,' Tulkhan said, coming to a stop with surprising grace.

'Then we mustn't keep them waiting.' Imoshen lifted her arm to link with his.

'I'd better take my place.' Cariah slipped away.

The musicians ceased their playing and the skaters made their way over to the tent. The flap had been rolled up to give them a view of the lake and the floor was covered with rugs and low tables. Tonight they followed the old custom of reclining on rugs and pillows.

Imoshen sank down and slipped off her skates. It disappointed her to note that although the ambassadorial parties and mainland nobles mixed freely with both the Keldon nobles and the Ghebites, the two groups she most wanted to mingle were stolidly refusing to do so.

A hush drew her attention. Dancing skaters each carrying flowering fountains of light formed a sinuous weaving snake which whirled in time to the growing tempo of the music. Imoshen stole a look at the General. He was entranced.

Lord Fairban leant forward proudly. 'Here comes my Cariah.'

She swept across the lake, moving with fluid grace.

Imoshen's heart swelled with pride. Cariah skated smoothly past the tent, turning in a wide arc that allowed her time to jump, spin and land again. Against a backdrop of sparkling light fountains, she performed the ice ballet. It was a display that few could equal.

Once again Cariah was benefiting from her unacknowledged T'En gifts while Imoshen experienced the two-edged sword of hers. But she intended to live up to the tenets of the T'Enchiridion. In serving the True-people of Fair Isle she hoped to win their trust and acceptance. One day people like Cariah would not need to hide their gifts.

When the dance finished the audience applauded rapturously, and this time Imoshen did not find the rowdy appreciation of the Ghebites embarrassing.

As the entertainers moved off, servants sailed across the ice with the food. Imoshen couldn't help wondering what would happen if one of them lost their balance.

A smile tugged at her lips and she caught Tulkhan's eye. When he grinned she knew he had been thinking the same thing. A rush of warmth swept through her. It was a relief to know he shared her unruly sense of humour.

There was a mild stir as Cariah joined them. She bestowed a fond kiss on her father's bald head and sank gracefully onto the cushions, midway between the Keld and the Ghebites.

As those around her congratulated her, Imoshen watched Cariah throw back her head and laugh. Several of Tulkhan's commanders vied for her attention. Sahorrd played a game with her hand, making a point of discovering her sixth finger.

'You have T'En blood in your family, Lord Fairban,' Imoshen said.

'On my bond-partner's side. Three beautiful girls she gave me, but only my eldest takes after her. Did you hear?' he beamed at Imoshen. 'Cariah has been accepted into the Thespers' Guild as a full member?'

'Your daughter belongs to a guild?' Tulkhan remarked. 'But she is the daughter of a nobleman.'

Imoshen knew that the General was not trying to offend Lord Fairban, his reaction stemmed from genuine confusion.

'Acceptance into the Thespers' Guild is conditional on talent and ability,' Imoshen told Tulkhan. 'Anyone can learn to make shoes, and chance dictates whether you are born into the nobility. But very few people are truly creative. To be accepted by one of the creative guilds is a great honour.'

'I see.' He looked at Lord Fairban. 'My apologies. Things are different in Gheeaba. An artist is a craftsman hired to do a job, nothing more.'

The old man's lips thinned and Imoshen realised the General's apology had only served to further offend him. Tulkhan's dark eyes met hers with a silent question, but she shrugged almost imperceptibly. Intolerance stemmed from both sides. At least the General was trying.

The lavish meal continued. In between courses, ice-skating clowns performed. This was more to the Ghebites' taste. At Cariah's insistence, several of the Ghebite commanders sang in their native language.

Imoshen guessed from Tulkhan's expression that the words were rather crude, but since most of it was not understood by the gathered nobles, it did not matter.

When the meal finished, people left their places to mingle and Kalleen joined Imoshen, while Cariah spoke with a friend.

'Anyone would think a female incapable of conversation!' Kalleen muttered.

Imoshen smiled. 'I'm sure Wharrd does not think so.'

'Then why is he with the Ghebite men and not here with me?'

There was a grain of truth in Kalleen's complaint.

Imoshen felt uneasy. Kalleen had been raised to hold the old values dear. She would take it hard if her bonding was reduced to the shallow parody Imoshen had witnessed in the high court.

Cariah sipped her wine and nudged her friend, indicating the young Ghebites who were betting on the outcome of an arm-wrestling match.

'Such physical creatures,' she purred. 'Which one will I take to my bed tonight?'

Her friend studied the men, amused. 'Aren't they a little...'

'Crude?' Cariah suggested. 'Yes, but most enthusiastic. The tall one, Sahorrd, is very intense. The hairy one has amazing stamina, and Jacolm is extremely well endowed.'

The friend tilted her head. 'Why not all three?'

Kalleen gasped and covered her mouth.

Cariah's laughter rippled above the noise in the tent like beautiful birdsong. As the Ghebites looked over, Kalleen glanced to Imoshen.

'Old Empire customs,' Imoshen whispered.

Meanwhile, Cariah patted her friend's arm. 'You are a girl after my own heart. But now I must decide whether to have them one after the other, or all three –'

'Imoshen?' Tulkhan snapped.

She sat up, startled by his tone. His glowering expression did nothing to reassure her as he held out his hand. She placed hers in his and he hauled her upright with such vigour that she fell against his chest.

'Come watch the dancers.'

It was an order. Resentment rose in her. He bundled her out onto the ice and around the side of the tent where he rounded on her. 'Don't let me catch you talking of bedding three men!'

She bristled. 'What is it to you, General? Cariah is not bonded. She can pick and choose. It is the custom for a woman to –'

'It is not a Ghebite custom!'

'Are they not Ghebite men she is bedding?' Imoshen asked innocently.

'It is different for a woman.'

'Different? How so?'

He pulled her to him. She could feel his need for her and it triggered a sweet flash of desire, spiced by irritation.

'Imoshen!'

'Don't Ghebite women enjoy bedding their men?' she prodded.

'You are in need of a lesson,' he growled.

'Are you my tutor?'

His hands tightened.

With a laugh she let her weight drop and broke his hold. Darting past him she ran across the ice behind the tent. He was right on her heels as she ploughed up the snow-laden bank. He tackled her, knocking her to the ground, and they rolled down the far side of the bank into a hollow, pillowed by deep snow.

Wordlessly he pinned her beneath him, seeking her lips. Imoshen returned his kiss with equal fervour, her heart soaring. Their bonding could not fail. It was too good, too rich. If only he would accept her T'En self.

Desperation drove her passion.

When his lips left hers she could not resist, teasing, 'Aren't you glad I'm not a sighing, long-suffering Ghebite maid?'

'By the gods, yes!'

She laughed, reaching for him. He tensed as she freed him.

'Your hands are cold.'

A laugh bubbled out of her.

The brocade tabard parted. As was the custom, her gathered trousers had no centre seam. Bundled in their thick garments only the barest minimum of their flesh met, but it was enough. They writhed in the snow, eager, flushed with their mutual need. It was a delicious, stolen moment.

When Tulkhan could think clearly again he straightened his clothes, watching Imoshen rise and expertly arrange hers.

'There is much to be said for the way women dress in Fair Isle,' he told her.

She laughed and offered him her hand. He wanted to pull her back down into the snow, but they would soon be missed. They ploughed down the bank, pausing in the lee of the tent to make final adjustments.

'Do I look presentable?' Imoshen asked.

Her cheeks were flushed and her lips were swollen by his kisses.

'You look beddable,' he told her.

She thumped his chest with a good deal of force then returned to the tent.

He still wanted her. Tulkhan was grateful for the thick overjacket. He waited a few minutes, then joined the others.

'I THOUGHT I would find you here,' Tulkhan announced loudly.

Imoshen gave a guilty start. She had escaped to the library after fulfilling her official duties. It had been a day for leave-taking. The mainland nobles had sailed to reach the estuary with the morning tide, leaving only the ambassadors and their servants. The Keldon nobles would stay on to avoid the difficult travel over snowbound passes. By midmorning Wharrd and Kalleen had made their farewells.

Kalleen had promised to return in time for the baby's birth, but Imoshen did not know when that would be. The longer the pregnancy, the more T'En the babe would be. She sighed.

'Yes, General?' She put the tome aside.

'Three more of the stable boys are down with winter fever,' he told her, though she could tell by his tone that this was not why he had come.

'I'll see to them. By the way, Lord Athlyn has been talking to me. He has advised the Keldon nobles to accept the new Causare Council. Telling them to select only six representatives was a master stroke. They will be fighting amongst themselves for the privilege.' She smiled. 'Have you heard from Fairban or Woodvine yet?'

'Not yet. There is something...'

She waited but he did not continue. 'What is it, General?'

He didn't answer immediately, picking instead at the binding of the book until she retrieved it to save it from his aimless fingering.

'It's the Lady Cariah. You will have to speak with her,' Tulkhan said at last.

'I thought she was doing a very good job of bringing the Keldon nobles and town dignitaries together with your men. The younger, more flexible members have struck up friendships.'

Tulkhan grimaced uncomfortably. 'It's her lovers.'

Imoshen bit her bottom lip to keep from smiling. For such a passionate man, the General was strangely prudish. 'Surely that is her own business?'

'Not when it comes to my men.'

'Surely that is *their* business?'

The General frowned. 'Then you won't do anything?'

'There is nothing I can do.'

He sighed and slid a formal invitation across the table. 'The Beatific wants me to take a seat at the next Intercession Day, but I know nothing of T'En laws.'

Imoshen chose her words with care. 'We have a fair system of laws; different, I gather, from the system you have in Gheeaba. If disputes between guilds or individuals cannot be settled by priestly mediation on Intercession Day, both parties appeal to the Emperor and Empress. We would be called upon to arbitrate.' It was actually the Empress who was final arbiter, but Imoshen decided not to mention this. 'You should familiarise yourself with the laws of possession and inheritance to begin with.'

'More chicken scrawl?' He gave a mock sigh.

Imoshen swallowed. The familiar teasing note in his voice warmed her. 'I could teach you.'

Tulkhan rolled his eyes. 'Taught by a woman. In Gheeaba women don't read or write.'

She stiffened.

'Don't be angry with me, Imoshen. I did not make the rules.'

'You Ghebite men have a lot to answer for!'

He gave her a disarming smile. 'Here I am, at your mercy. Use me.'

His meaning was clear. Imoshen felt a smile tug at her lips.

'Very well.' She slid out the sheet of notepaper and dipped the scriber in the ink. 'The first letter of the T'En alphabet is shaped like this.'

Tulkhan groaned, but sat at her side to study. Imoshen felt the warmth of his body seep through her clothing. It was only by exercising great self-discipline that she continued the lesson.

These were the moments she savoured – when there was no one to observe or judge them, and their differences faded. Even teaching Tulkhan the T'En alphabet was a sinful pleasure she hugged to herself before she had to relinquish him once again to palace politics.

Chapter Twelve

'I DON'T KNOW what they expect me to do.' Lord Fairban was genuinely distressed. 'My daughter has already refused them both. Surely they can see it is her decision?'

Imoshen smiled for this was obvious. 'Then forget it. Cariah has her status as an independent noblewoman, not to mention the support of the Thespers' Guild. No one can force her to do anything against her will. Even if she were a poor farm girl, the choice of bond-partner would be hers alone.'

Lord Fairban nodded but he didn't look convinced. Imoshen felt impatient. What did he expect her to do?

She pushed that thought aside as unworthy. The old lord had turned to her, the least she could do was consider the situation carefully, but it was hard to think clearly. Late into the night and again since dawn she had been tending the sick. A debilitating winter fever had swept through the servants and begun to work its way through the nobles. She supposed it was inevitable, considering the number of people inhabiting the palace. To save her own strength she had used her healing gifts only on the worst afflicted, relying on basic herbal lore for the majority of cases. Even so she felt drained and fragile.

Finally, to escape the confines of the sickroom, she had slipped away to the balcony overlooking the courtyard where she knew the Ghebites would be practising their swordsmanship.

She had intended to lose herself in the secret vice of admiring the General, but she had not been allowed this indulgence, for Lord Fairban had approached her. She wished the old lord would take himself and his troubles away and let her enjoy Tulkhan in peace.

The Ghebites were stripped to the waist and their gleaming bodies steamed in the cold. Imoshen felt her gaze irresistibly drawn to the General. He was downing a drink in between bouts and she longed to go down and challenge him. Maybe later when the men left she would slip down, tie up her formal skirts and ask him again to train her in the use of Ghebite weapons.

Sword practice was one of the endless Ghebite customs designed to exclude and confine women. She suspected these traditions had evolved for the express purpose of bonding the males closer. In a society where your only equal was another male, it was no surprise to see that the relationships men shared went beyond mere friendship. King Gharavan had been following custom when he took the Vaygharian as his lover.

The mood of the fighting changed, piercing Imoshen's abstraction. There was trouble. General Tulkhan intervened. The two men bristled at each other like rabid dogs.

'That's them,' Lord Fairban whispered, making Imoshen jump. She had forgotten him. 'Sahorrd came to see me last night. He said he wanted to marry Cariah. I told him bonding was not a matter to bring up with me, that he had to ask her. If she accepted him, we three could discuss the joining of their estates. Later that night Jacolm came to me with the same request.'

'And she refused them.' Imoshen was not surprised. Bonding with a jealous Ghebite male would severely restrict Cariah's freedom.

Raised voices filled the courtyard, echoing off the walls. Imoshen caught Cariah's name, butchered by the soldier's harsh accents. Tulkhan strode between the two men. She half expected him to knock some sense into them, but instead a heated discussion followed.

'If Cariah has refused them both, why are they still arguing?' Imoshen asked Lord Fairban. He had no answer. As she watched, a decision seemed to be reached. 'The General is sending for something, or someone.'

While they waited Jacolm and Sahorrd were led to opposite ends of the courtyard by their companions.

Tulkhan strode over to stand below Imoshen. 'There will be a duel. Send for the Lady Cariah of Fairban. She should be present to greet the winner.'

'I will find her,' Lord Fairban said.

He stepped back from Tulkhan's view, turning anxiously to Imoshen.

'Do it,' she whispered. 'I swear no harm will come to her.'

When he had gone she leant over the balcony, speaking only for Tulkhan's ears. 'What is the problem, General?'

He grimaced. 'Cariah has come between Sahorrd and Jacolm. If they hadn't been sword-brothers it might not be so bad, but they are each determined to have her.'

'Surely that is her decision. Stop this before –'

'Be sensible, Imoshen. I cannot ask a man to dishonour himself before his brothers-at-arms!'

Imoshen opened her mouth to speak, but a Ghebite approached Tulkhan.

'Ah, the duelling swords. No lectures now, Imoshen. I have no choice.' Tulkhan went over to his men.

Annoyed by this dismissal, Imoshen watched Sahorrd and Jacolm select their weapons. As much as she wanted to, she knew she should not intervene. She only hoped the men could work off their ill feelings without too much bloodshed.

With formal signals the Ghebites touched the tips of their weapons, bowed, then stepped back, waiting grimly.

Imoshen stiffened. Those were wicked weapons. Surely this was no more than a fight to first blood?

'Imoshen?' Cariah approached, graceful even when hurrying. Her father hung back, perhaps reluctant to bear witness.

'Lady Cariah,' Tulkhan called.

Imoshen looked down into the courtyard to see both men give Cariah a formal salute then fall into fighting stance.

'What...' Cariah began but her words were drowned as the men leapt at one another, their swords ringing. She gasped, stepping closer to Imoshen. 'More sword practice? Why was I called?'

'Not practice. A duel.'

'The fools!'

'They fight over you, like dogs over a bone.' Imoshen could not keep the scorn from her voice.

Metal scraped on metal, obscenely loud in the charged silence. There was no mistaking the sword-brothers' concentration.

'Surely it is not to the death?' Cariah whispered uneasily.

'I trust not,' Imoshen answered. 'The General will stop them before it gets to that point.'

Cariah's hand closed over Imoshen's, telegraphing her distress. 'What do they hope to gain by this display? It will not make me change my mind.'

'Perhaps if they shed a little blood it would ease their hot heads,' Imoshen suggested. She heard Lord Fairban shift uneasily and glanced at him. His mouth was grim and he winced as the sound of screeching swords echoed off the courtyard walls.

The old lord pointed. 'One of them is down!'

Imoshen's gaze flew to the courtyard and a sickening certainty swept over her. For Sahorrd and his sword-brother this was a fight to the death.

Time slowed agonisingly. Down on one knee, Sahorrd lunged under his opponent's guard, aiming a killing blow to Jacolm's exposed upper thigh. But Jacolm leapt back to avoid the fatal strike, missing his chance to finish the bout.

'One of them is going to die.' Imoshen had not meant to speak aloud.

'Can you tell which one?' Cariah demanded.

Imoshen did not know. She studied the duellists, wondering whether foretelling death was part of her gift.

A subtle shift passed over her sight as she searched for signs. The strangely graceful movements of the fighting men slowed and the ring of metal on metal sang, lingering on the air in visible arcs of sound.

'Imoshen?' Cariah pleaded, her voice rustling across Imoshen's perception.

'I...' She shrugged helplessly. Both men were surrounded by an aura of vibrating air, but what this meant she could not tell.

'T'Imoshen?' Cariah pressed, resorting to formality in her desperation.

Imoshen met her eyes. In that fleeting glimpse she saw the same aura around Cariah's beautiful face. Fear clutched her.

'What is it? What did you see?' Cariah demanded.

A man's hoarse scream rent the air.

Stunned, Imoshen looked down to see Sahorrd on the ground clutching his belly. She knew without examining him that it was a fatal wound. Even with her skills she could not stem that much blood and repair those damaged organs.

Cariah gasped Sahorrd's name, her face pale.

Tulkhan stepped forward and took the weapon from Jacolm who stood frozen. He did not resist when his general led him towards their balcony and lifted his arm in a sign of victory.

'Jacolm will see you, Lord Fairban, to claim your daughter,' the General announced.

The old man shook his head, looking to Imoshen to explain the misunderstanding, but it was Cariah who answered.

'My father has no say in this. It is my decision and I won't have him.' Her voice rose with fury. 'You killed without cause, Jacolm. Murderer!'

Imoshen dragged Cariah into the shadows of the balcony out of the sight of the men below. 'Quiet. Think what you do.'

But Cariah was beyond thought. Her furious voice carried into the courtyard below. 'I despise them all. Ghebite barbarians!'

'That may be so but we are at their mercy,' Imoshen hissed, finally reaching Cariah through her grief. She slid her arm around the woman's shoulders to support her, then walked to the balustrade to face the Ghebites.

'The Lady Cariah of Fairban has already refused both men, as is her right,' Imoshen told them. 'In Fair Isle we respect the free will of the individual. This duel changes nothing.'

Even as she said this Imoshen felt a flare of heat and the force of Cariah's fury made her body tremble. It was a strangely seductive sensation. It called to her, wooing her with its dark passion. She wanted to bathe in Cariah's rage. Startled, Imoshen dropped her friend's arm, stepping away from.

The General glared up at them. 'Jacolm fought for her.' His voice sounded forced, as if he was trying to maintain a reasonable tone. 'She belongs –'

'I am not a prize,' Cariah stated.

Tulkhan indicated the body. 'A man lies dead!'

'By whose hand?' Imoshen asked, heart in her mouth. She would not see Cariah blamed for Sahorrd's death.

With an inarticulate cry, Cariah ran along the balcony and through the far door.

There was stunned silence then one of the Ghebites yelled, 'A man lies dead because of that bitch!'

'No! He lies dead because he would not admit she had a choice.' But Imoshen's voice could not be heard above the furious shouts of the Ghebites, and even if they had listened, she doubted they would understand.

Wordlessly General Tulkhan shook his head and turned away to rejoin his men. Only Jacolm remained, staring unseeing up at Imoshen. Her heart filled with a cold foreboding.

In his agitation Lord Fairban clutched Imoshen's arm, drawing her into the shadows. 'You should have stopped them.'

Imoshen gestured to the courtyard where the Ghebites seethed like a simmering pot about to boil over. 'How could I stop that?'

'But you are the T'En Empress.'

'To them I am nothing but a hated Dhamfeer, a female at that.' Imoshen heard the bitter edge to her voice and saw him register the truth of her words.

'Barbarians...'

'We must salvage the situation. Come, my lord. A man lies dead and the proper words must be said over his body.' She took the old man's arm. 'Sahorrd's death arose from a misunderstanding and the Ghebites will realise this when their heads are cooler.'

But her words sounded hollow even to her.

IMOSHEN RESTED HER forehead on the windowpane, relishing the feel of the cold glass on her skin. The Empress's rooms were larger than her own and designed to promote peace and serenity. Today they did nothing for her.

Her eyes ached with each heartbeat. Her skin felt fragile. She knew she was coming down with the same ague that had struck so many already. She had prepared a willowbark tisane but she was too weary to move.

Since the duel this morning, the palace had been in ferment. Several altercations had broken out in the entertainment wing as Keldon nobles and Ghebites argued over who was at fault. It had taken great diplomacy on Imoshen's part to soothe their self-righteous anger. At last she had retreated to her rooms, too disheartened and weary to move. It was growing dark and, according to Ghebite custom, the words for the dead had to be said before dusk. No matter how tired she was, she had to show proper respect for Sahorrd and attend the ceremony.

Someone scratched at the door, then entered before Imoshen could summon the strength to deny them.

'I must speak with you,' Cariah began. 'I keep asking myself if I am to blame...' She stopped, her shoulders sagging with despair. 'I am heartsore and want nothing more than to be alone. I have come to ask whether I should retreat to my estates.'

'If you left now it would be seen as an admission of guilt, when all you have done is insist on your rights.'

Cariah sighed. 'My guildmaster agrees with you. He advised me to stay. And so I must.' She managed a stiff smile. 'Even though all my instincts tell me to run. I feel threatened by every whisper, every look. Those Ghebites would kill me with a glance if they could.'

Imoshen slid her arm around Cariah's shoulder, offering wordless comfort. Without meaning to, she inhaled the scent of Cariah's hair. She could smell her pain and felt an instinctive urge to ease it. 'We must not reveal any sign of weakness. I will stand by you.'

Cariah shuddered. 'It is the whispering and watching. I cannot stand it.'

'You feel the force of their emotions. It is your gift. When this is over you and I can –'

Cariah pulled away. 'Half-bloods do not have the gifts.'

'Maybe once, but the Aayel once let slip that when our people blended their blood with the descendants of the Ancients we –'

'I feel nothing.' Cariah would not meet Imoshen's eyes. 'You frighten me with such talk. A part of me wants to run from you too.'

Imoshen felt as if she had been dealt a physical blow. She turned away in pain. If Cariah, who was more T'En than most, could still fear her, what hope was there that others would accept her?

'Why did Jacolm kill Sahorrd?' Cariah cried. 'He loved him.'

'Who knows what love means to them?' Imoshen muttered.

Cariah resumed pacing. 'I should have handled it differently.'

Imoshen restrained her impatience. 'If you cannot say no to a Ghebite male, then what chance have other women, women who are not independently wealthy with the connections of a noble family, women who do not have the power of a guild behind them? Do not berate yourself, Cariah. There is more to this than simply you, Jacolm and Sahorrd. The right of all the women of Fair Isle to control their lives is at stake.'

'I did not think...'

'Go now.' Imoshen was too weary to talk.

'Forgive me, T'Imoshen, you see further than I.' Cariah gave a formal obeisance and Imoshen was aware of a subtle shift in the balance of their relationship.

When Cariah retreated, closing the door softly behind her, Imoshen stared unseeing into the flames. It was too cruel – Cariah, of all people, feared her. She felt overwhelmed by the escalation of events. Everything was unravelling.

Her muscles ached with the onset of the fever. She added more wood to the fire to warm her cold bones. A heartbeat later, the door swung open and Tulkhan strode in without so much as a word of greeting. Imoshen straightened. He vibrated with repressed anger.

A dart of despair pierced her and she turned away from him.

'At least look at me, Imoshen.' Tulkhan's voice was raw.

She turned to face him.

'Get this woman to accept Jacolm.'

A bitter laugh escaped her.

He cursed. 'Is it so impossible?'

'What do you think?' She stared across the room at him, a cultural chasm between them. 'Cariah has rejected both men.'

Tulkhan gave an exasperated grimace. 'She would have his name.'

Imoshen snorted. 'She has her own name.'

'His protection.'

'She needs no protection. She is a respected member of the Thespers' Guild and a property holder in her own right. Why should she ally herself with Jacolm, or any man, unless she wants to?'

'Then why did she lie with him, with them both?'

Imoshen had to laugh. 'Why do you think? Don't your Ghebite women enjoy bedding their men?'

Tulkhan flushed.

Imoshen shook her head in wonder. 'Why did you not stop the duel?'

'You don't understand what honour means to us.' He made an impatient gesture but she could see the grief in his care-worn face.

Imoshen's head throbbed and her throat felt tight. She could hardly think and there was still Sahorrd's burial ceremony to endure. 'Please leave. I will dress now. In Fair Isle we wear our finest clothes to honour the dead, but I don't want to offend your people. What should I wear to honour Sahorrd?'

He shook his head in wonder. 'Imoshen...'

'What?'

'The Cadre would be horrified to see a woman at a man's burial ceremony.'

'I see.' Anger made her voice hard but this was not the moment to make a stand. 'My people will expect me to do the right thing. Someone from Fair Isle must be present to honour Sahorrd in death.' There was only one male of equal rank to her and she could hardly ask Reothe. 'With emotions running the way they are, I cannot ask any of the Keldon nobles. The Beatific would be ideal if she were not a woman.'

'Murgon the Tractarian?' Tulkhan suggested.

Her first impulse was to deny Murgon this honour. Of all church officials he was the last person she wished to represent her. It would elevate his importance in the eyes of the Ghebites.

'You have a better suggestion?' Tulkhan pressed.

She sighed. 'I will send a message to the Beatific, appointing him as my delegate. Wording it without offending her will be a challenge.'

Tulkhan gave her a wry smile and hope stirred within Imoshen.

'You see, all it takes is a little compromise,' Tulkhan said. 'If you would but speak with Cariah...'

'Enough! What you call compromise would see the women of Fair Isle reduced to property. I will not do it, General.' Imoshen's rage drained away, leaving her dizzy. She reached for the mantelpiece and missed, felt herself fall.

Startled, Tulkhan caught her, swinging her up into his arms. Her skin branded his. Remorse stirred him. 'You are feverish.'

'The Beatific,' Imoshen mumbled. 'I must –'

'I will speak with her. You should be in bed.'

'Trust you to think that,' she whispered.

He grinned and carried her into the bedchamber. 'Can I get you something?'

Imoshen frowned at him, her eyes glassy with fever as she lay back on the pillow. 'Bring the tisane.'

Imoshen was almost asleep when he returned, but she roused herself enough to drain the medicine.

He sat on the bed next to her, pulling the covers up.

She brushed his hands away. 'I can do that.'

'I know. But I want to.'

A tear slipped down Imoshen's cheek. 'Oh, General, everything has gone wrong and I try so hard.'

'We both do.' He pushed her fever-damp hair from her forehead.

Imoshen fought to open her eyes.

'Sleep.'

'But –'

'There is always tomorrow, Imoshen. For once, trust me.'

Her fingers reached out to feel for his. Tulkhan held her hand until she slept.

'GENERAL?'

Tulkhan looked up to see Lord Fairban's anxious face. The General had spent a restless night going over and over the events surrounding Sahorrd's death. He did not see how he could he have acted otherwise. Curse this Keldon noble and his beautiful, arrogant daughter. 'What is it, Fairban?'

'The Master of the Thespers' Guild tells me my daughter is missing. She did not meet with him this morning as arranged and her sisters have not seen her.' Lord Fairban began reasonably, but his voice gained intensity as he spoke. 'Unless she has taken refuge with T'Imoshen, I fear for her safety. Where is your man, Jacolm?'

Tulkhan ground his teeth as he saw the Vaygharians enter the room. Everyone was looking his way, making no pretence of polite conversation. The fatal duel and Cariah's subsequent rejection of the winner had provided the court with a feast of speculation.

'Commander Piers?' Tulkhan called his trusted veteran. 'Send for Jacolm.'

To maintain the appearance of normalcy Tulkhan joined in a game of chance, but his gaze kept returning to the doorway. When he caught sight of Piers, he rose, and the others made no pretence of continuing the game.

Piers gave a formal salute.

'Well, man?' Tulkhan heard the tension in his voice.

'Jacolm cannot be found anywhere. His bed has not been slept in.'

Lord Fairban moaned and people exclaimed.

Tulkhan signalled for silence. 'Piers, organise a search of the palace, then the grounds. Locate Jacolm's horse and kit.'

'I checked. Untouched. The kit is still in his room.'

Lord Fairban paled. 'If that Ghebite has –'

'Get moving!' Tulkhan rounded on his men. The Keld watched him silently. Though no one spoke, he could almost sense them withdrawing from him.

Tulkhan ran his hand through his hair. He needed to find Cariah and Jacolm before anything happened. In desperation he thought of Imoshen and the scrying platter. Without a word he strode from the room, heading for their chambers. Every servant he passed avoided his eyes.

Imoshen would understand the need to use her gifts just this once. He only hoped she was well enough.

The new maid gave a gasp of surprise as he threw the door open.

'Where is she?'

The girl glanced to the door of Empress's bedchamber.

He strode past the maid and thrust the door open. The bed was empty.

'You look for me, General?'

He spun to see Imoshen's blanket-shrouded form rise from the rug before the fire. Two bright spots of colour burned in her white cheeks. Her pale beauty glowed with the inner furnace of a fever.

'You are no better.'

'What's wrong?'

He didn't want to tell her.

'Is it Cariah?' Imoshen's voice was a croak.

'She's missing.'

'And the Ghebite?'

'Jacolm's missing too.'

'He has abducted her?'

'His horse and kit are still here.'

Imoshen clutched the back of the chair for support.

He tried to reassure her. 'I have men searching the palace.'

She sank to her knees before the fire. 'It's my fault. She wanted to run, but I told her to stay.'

'No, it's my fault. I should have foreseen Jacolm's reaction. What man could face such disgrace?'

'What disgrace?'

Tulkhan had no time to explain. He crossed the room, lifting Imoshen to her feet. 'We must find them before it's too late. Are you well enough to do a scrying?'

She stiffened. 'You insisted that I never use my gifts.'

'Lives are at stake.'

'So you would use my T'En gifts when it suits you?'

'Yes.' Why was she hesitating?

'If I do, what stops you from having me locked away like some unclean thing?'

'Have done with this.' He heard the maid's gasp. 'You, girl. I know you're listening at the door. Bring the scrying plate.'

Imoshen closed her eyes and stood absolutely still. Tulkhan's hands tingled. A prickling sensation ran up his arms.

Shocked, he released her, stepping back. 'So you don't need the plate?'

'Focus. The Aayel said it was all a matter of discipline and focus. I dread...' Imoshen grimaced in concentration. 'They are not in the palace buildings. It is very hard, people are running everywhere. There is so much tension.

'Search the grounds.'

'I am.'

Merkah returned with the plate, but Tulkhan waved her away. 'Go, and keep out.'

'I find no bright points of life, only...' Imoshen's knees buckled and she staggered. Tulkhan caught her. In that instant a wave of nausea swept over him. Roiling dark emotions blotted his vision.

Imoshen moaned. 'Heated fever dreams. The taste of death on my tongue.'

Tulkhan cursed. She was delirious. He should call for the maid and have Imoshen put to bed.

'Now I understand the visions,' Imoshen whispered. 'I thought them feverish nightmares, but it was Cariah trying to reach me.'

'What do you mean?' Tulkhan demanded.

Imoshen shook her head and pushed past him.

He watched her unsteady passage across the room. 'Where do you think you're going?'

'I must face this.'

He strode after her, sweeping her off her feet, blanket and all. 'You can barely walk.'

For once she did not resist him. 'The place I sense lies beyond the lake. You can't carry me that far.'

'We'll ride.'

By the time they had entered the stables they were accompanied by half the court, including Fairban and his two younger daughters.

'Saddle my horse,' Tulkhan called to a stableboy, ignoring all demands for an explanation. He stepped up into the saddle and held out his arm to Imoshen. She clasped his forearm, put a bare foot on his boot and he hauled her up into his arms.

Her face was starkly pale. Her eyes glittered strangely. Even with the blanket between them, he could feel the overflow of her T'En gifts, rolling off her skin like heat radiating from a blacksmith's forge. It made his heart race. And though he knew it probably damned his soul for all eternity, he liked the sensation.

Imoshen guided them out beyond the ornamental gardens to the lake and the woods. Tulkhan skirted the water. It was only a matter of days since the performance, but he didn't trust the ice to take a galloping horse laden with two people. He could hear horses and shouts behind him as the others followed.

'That way.' Eyes closed, Imoshen guided them unerringly through the winter-bare trees.

They slowed to pick their way over the treacherous ground, hollows hidden by deep drifts.

'Which way now?' Tulkhan asked. The others had caught up with them and were floundering through the thick snow.

She flinched. 'You have to ask?'

Then he saw a dark patch already half buried by the lightly falling snow.

Imoshen twisted from his arms and slid to the ground. Barefoot, she staggered through the drifts. He threw his leg over the saddle. When he caught up with her she was on her knees before the figures.

They could have been entwined in a lovers' embrace. Snow dusted their heads and clothes. Cariah lay in Jacolm's arms, her face swollen and distorted.

Tulkhan could see Jacolm had strangled her, then cradled her body while he cut his wrists right up to the elbow. His blood soaked them both, a great black stain.

'Poor Jacolm,' Tulkhan whispered. 'He could not live with the dishonour. He loved her –'

'Love?' Imoshen sprang to her feet, flinging the blanket aside. She wore nothing but a thin shift and her hair was loose. Already a crown of powder-fine snow clung to her head, her lashes.

'Love?' Imoshen repeated. 'Love does not kill what it cannot have!'

Lord Fairban leapt down from his mount with a keening cry of pain. His sobbing daughters waded through the snow to his side, trying to restrain him.

'Cariah...' he moaned, beside himself with grief.

Tulkhan looked over their heads to a contingent of his men awaiting his orders. They would have to bring the bodies in and prepare them for burial. Which church would claim precedence, or would it be each to their own?

It was a nightmare.

'You...' Lord Fairban turned on Tulkhan. 'You could have stopped this. Cariah had already refused them. It did not have to come to this!'

'The moment she refused them it led to this. Don't you understand? Jacolm could not face the disgrace. No Ghebite could!' Tulkhan felt his voice vibrate with anger. Why couldn't these people see? As much as he loathed the pointless loss of life, he understood it.

Lord Fairban launched himself at Tulkhan's throat. The General caught the old man's clawed hands, turning them aside. Deranged by grief, Lord Fairban fought with manic fury, while Tulkhan fought only to keep him at arm's length. Even in his prime, the smaller man would never had been a match for Tulkhan.

Lord Fairban's daughters and servants surged forward to restrain the old man. The Ghebites barrelled into the melee, pushing people down into the snow and drawing their weapons. Tulkhan bellowed instructions, ordering them to sheathe their swords, but his voice was drowned by the screams. Soon blood would be shed and the precarious peace shattered.

Frantically Tulkhan searched the crowd for Imoshen's fair head, fearing she would be struck down and accidentally killed, or left lying unconscious in the snow. In her feverish state the chill would be enough to kill her.

He thrust people aside, vaguely aware that Lord Fairban was being dragged away by three Ghebites. In the midst of the wrestling bodies Tulkhan saw Imoshen. She was a solitary figure kneeling before the corpses.

As he darted forward to comfort her, a woman collided with him. The force of the impact sent him to his knees and he barely saved them both from falling under the hooves of a frantic horse.

Imoshen stared at the dead lovers, seeing minute details. Unbidden, she relived the moments before their deaths. At first Cariah had argued, but Jacolm would not acknowledge her right to choose, then Imoshen experienced Cariah's terror when she realised he meant to kill her and relived her friend's battle for life and her defeat. She sensed Cariah's shade raging impotently, unable to leave the site of her murder.

At the same time, Imoshen felt the Ghebite commander's utter despair. He had killed his best friend and sword-brother, only to be publicly humiliated by the woman he adored. Even as he strangled her, he told her he loved her. But, dishonoured, he had no choice. Jacolm's shade had departed with his acceptance of death.

Imoshen's heart swelled with ferocious pity. Despair settled upon her like a great stone. Her grief was not only for those present, it was for all her people and for Tulkhan's men too. This terrible lesson must never be forgotten.

In her heightened state, Imoshen could feel everyone fighting behind her, a seething mass of True-people. Their anger, fuelled by loss, rose like a great tide of torment, threatening to engulf her. The force of their swirling passions almost overpowered her. Channelling it, she used the well of strong emotions to empower her T'En gifts.

As Imoshen stroked Cariah's sixth finger, she watched the young woman's features settle into a peaceful pose, all trace of violent death eradicated. Now Cariah lay in Jacolm's arms as if embraced. Dusted with snow, they were an island of stillness in a sea of emotion.

Cariah's impatient soul ate into Imoshen's awareness, demanding justice, demanding acknowledgment. The words for the dead spilled from Imoshen's desperate lips. This time she would not be bluffed by the Parakletos. She would bind them to her will. Anger filled her throat so that the words choked before they were born. It did not matter – the words had only to form in her mind and the Parakletos came. Eagerly.

This time she had no fear, she was an instrument channelling the rage of those present. Emotion impossible to contain consumed her. Her heart was stone. Stone was immortal, a timeless memorial, and the Parakletos were her stonemasons. Their purpose appeased Cariah's tortured shade, and with appeasement came acceptance.

Their task completed, the Parakletos returned to death's shadow with Cariah's shade.

Tulkhan felt a great pressure inside his head, a roaring which drowned all noise, then something snapped and he staggered, dizzy with relief. Around him grappling bodies parted, some dropping to their knees. One woman stood staring blankly.

Thrusting through disoriented people, he strode to Imoshen's side. At his touch she fell sideways into a snowdrift, still as a corpse. Horrified, he dropped to his knees and pulled her into his arms. Her skin was cold, her lips blue. Had he lost her and his unborn son? 'Imoshen...'

Remorse seared him. Desperate, he lifted her in his arms and carried her towards the horses.

Strange. A few moments ago everyone had been intent on wreaking vengeance, now they stood stunned as if their desperate emotions had turned to smoke.

He handed Imoshen's unconscious form to Piers and climbed into the saddle. 'Pass her up.'

Tulkhan focused on taking her weight, arranging her comfortably across his thighs and wrapping her in the blanket someone had retrieved. He shouldn't have asked this of her. He nodded to Piers. 'Bring the bodies in and have them prepared for burial.'

'No!' Cariah's youngest sister cried. 'It cannot be!'

'What now?' Piers muttered.

'See for yourself.' The girl stepped back, pointing to the bodies.

The other sister moved forward, accompanied by curious servants. There was silence as they inspected the bodies. One of the servants called on the T'En for protection.

'Frozen like stone,' Cariah's sister marvelled.

'What curse is this?' Piers asked uneasily.

'We can't move my lady Cariah. She has turned to stone,' the servant reported, close to panic.

'Impossible!'

'Frozen, that's all,' Piers said, going to inspect the bodies. He cursed in shock.

Their startled comments washed over Tulkhan. As the others sought to satisfy their curiosity, a strange certainty settled around his heart. Imoshen's flesh had been as cold as stone when he touched her and as smooth as marble.

He urged his horse forward. The others fell back.

Silently Tulkhan looked down at the bodies, trapped forever in stone's cold embrace. Even the dusting of snow had been transformed. A knife turned in Tulkhan's stomach. Imoshen had ensured Cariah and Jacolm would be a permanent reminder of his failure to understand.

'White marble,' he whispered, recognising the stone.

Someone cursed. Cariah's youngest sister declared it a miracle. Lord Fairban muttered something in High T'En.

Everyone fell silent, turning to Tulkhan. The General's arms tightened around Imoshen's unconscious form and his mount shifted uneasily, sensing the crowd's animosity and fear. Tulkhan watched them draw away, uniting against the unknown. Even the Keld averted their faces, lifting their left hands to their eyes then upwards, deflecting the evil so that it passed over them.

His own men stared at him, their faces filled with such awe and dread that Tulkhan sensed if he hadn't been holding Imoshen they might have leapt on her and torn her apart. Years of command told him he had to seize the moment.

He gestured to the stone lovers. 'They will be a permanent reminder to us all. They paid the price for our failure to understand each other. Let there be no more lives lost so pointlessly.'

Then he rode away as if he did not expect a knife in his back. Yet he knew that only years of Ghebite discipline on the battlefield and the nobles' natural awe of the T'En restrained the crowd from turning on him and Imoshen like a pack of wolves.

Chapter Thirteen

Tulkan's hands shook as he gripped the reins. What had Imoshen been thinking? A familiar suspicion crossed his mind. More than once he had wondered whether the T'En gifts were more of a reflex than a learned skill.

He glanced down at her still face. Her pallor was worse than usual, but it was the blueness of her lips that made his heart falter. This time she had over-reached herself. He could only hope warmth and gentle massage would help her emerge from this frozen state.

The outbuildings of the royal palace lay just ahead. Stableboys and servants ran forward to hold the General's horse as he dropped to the ground with Imoshen in his arms. His knees protested.

Around him people clamoured for news. He gave the servants only a brief explanation as he entered the palace.

Striding down the long gallery with Imoshen in his arms, Tulkhan called for the fire to be built up in their chambers and the bed heated. He ordered a warm bath drawn immediately. Somehow, he had to bring the colour back to Imoshen's cheeks.

He kicked the bedchamber door open and placed her gently on the bed. The maid appeared at his side, her wide eyes fixed on Imoshen's unconscious form with a mixture of awe and horror.

'Is she dying?' Merkah whispered.

'No, merely exhausted,' he said, hoping it was true. 'Leave us.'

When she was gone, he placed his cheek against Imoshen's mouth, trying to detect her breath. He felt nothing. Desperate, he tore open her thin shift and laid his face on her pale breast. For an agonising moment he heard nothing, then he felt a slow single beat and nothing more. What had happened to her out there in the snow?

A servant entered to tell Tulkhan the bath was ready. He would let no one else care for Imoshen. He stripped her single garment and lowered her limp form into the warm water. Though it did bring a little colour to her flesh, it did not wake her.

Before the water could cool, he carried her to the bed and tucked her between blankets which held warmed stones. Then he took her hands in his and waited.

By dusk that evening he had not left Imoshen's side and she had not stirred. If anything, she seemed even less responsive. The heat of the room made him sweat, but Imoshen's skin was like porcelain, cool and lifeless.

The Ghebite bone-setter who had trained at Wharrd's side had already been and gone. His skill was in the art of sewing up wounds. This was no True-man injury.

Tulkhan pressed the heels of his hands to his aching eyes as he waited for the Beatific to send a priest trained in the arts of healing. Someone scratched at the door and he rose hopefully. But it was the Beatific herself who entered.

'General Tulkhan,' she greeted him softly. Her alert gaze went past him to Imoshen's still form and she approached the bed slowly, as if drawn against her will. Gingerly she laid a hand on Imoshen's pale cheek.

'Have you ever seen anything like this?' he whispered, desperate for a word of comfort.

'No. How could I? The pure T'En have almost died out. And even when they lived they kept the use and extent of their gifts a closely guarded secret.' The Beatific met his eyes. He sensed she was studying him, weighing up possibilities. 'If she does not wake soon, she will die. Maybe the babe is already dead. It is for the best. No pure T'En woman –'

'The babe!' He sank onto the side of the bed. His son was probably dead, but he felt nothing. All his being was focused on Imoshen.

In that moment he knew she had come to mean more to him than life itself. The child she carried was his hold on the future and on Fair Isle, yet he would give it all up if Imoshen would only wake.

The Beatific opened her arms and pressed his forehead to her breast, offering wordless comfort.

He pulled away. 'Sahorrd, Jacolm and Cariah, all dead. I did not think, did not foresee... now this.'

The Beatific made a soothing noise and he looked up into her handsome face. Her hazel eyes glowed with compassion. She understood. Hadn't she confessed to loving Reothe against her better judgment?

'This is a T'En illness, General. It needs one of the T'En to bring her back.'

'Reothe!' The name escaped Tulkhan with all the hatred he felt for the rebel leader.

The Beatific stepped back as Tulkhan rose impatiently. He paced to the fire. If he were to invite Reothe into the palace to help Imoshen, what chance had he, a mere True-man, against a Dhamfeer male? Reothe had mastered his T'En gifts to such an extent that with a single touch he could deliver death. Tulkhan shuddered, recalling how one of his men had died after delivering Reothe's message, just as the rebel leader had foretold.

Frustration raged through Tulkhan. He might as well hand Fair Isle and Imoshen over to Reothe right now!

But if he hesitated Imoshen might die, and with her his unborn child. He could not contemplate such loss.

'General Tulkhan?'

'I take it you can get word to Reothe?' He knew he was asking her to implicate herself. He'd suspected all along that the Beatific was playing a double game by currying favour with both him and the rebel leader, while looking to the future to secure her power base.

Her golden eyes widened and she spoke slowly, as though surprised he would contemplate calling on his sworn enemy. 'It might be possible. I have people who watch and report. But it would not be safe to invite Reothe here. Better to let nature take its course. No, listen!' She caught Tulkhan's shirt in her hands, as if her woman's strength might sway him. 'You cannot sacrifice everything you have achieved for her. Already Imoshen has betrayed you. I heard she was at Reothe's camp the night before you were bonded.'

'What?'

The Beatific flinched as he grasped her shoulders. Tulkhan released his vicelike grip, already regretting his slip. He would not be manipulated. 'Rumour, mere speculation.'

'Not necessarily.' The Beatific worked her shoulders gingerly and looked up at him, gauging his reaction. 'The country people say she was with Reothe till dawn. They claim she saved his life after he was mauled by a snow leopard.'

Tulkhan recalled Imoshen's sudden appearance in his bedchamber, naked and disoriented.

'There is more,' the Beatific continued. 'It is said Imoshen and Reothe planned to lead a surprise attack on the palace, to strike while you were in disarray. If Reothe were to march into T'Diemn with Imoshen at his side, the people would lay down arms and join him. Only your Ghebite soldiers would remain loyal.'

It was nothing but the bitter truth. The strategist in Tulkhan knew he should let Imoshen die.

What chance would he have if Imoshen and Reothe united against him? He would never hold Fair Isle. Already this accursed island had robbed him of his father and his half-brother.

He looked across at Imoshen's pale, still form on the bed. Yet he longed to trust her.

Unable to stand still, he paced the room, aware that the Beatific was watching him carefully. Perhaps this woman hoped to gain from Imoshen's death. Did she imagine he would turn to her for comfort? Never! Yet, without Imoshen, he would need the Beatific's support to hold Fair Isle...

Full dark had fallen and he hadn't lit more candles. He found himself standing over the bed, staring down at Imoshen. She appeared pale even against the white covers. He sensed that the longer she stayed in this state, the harder it would be to rouse her. He had to make a decision.

'Leave us.'

'General Tulkhan?'

'Just go!' He wanted time alone with his thoughts. 'I will call you when I am ready.'

The Beatific retreated without a word.

Methodically, he lit the candles. Then he returned to the bed and stripped the sweat-dampened shirt from his back, removing his boots. Clad only in his breeches he slipped beneath the covers, rolling the warming stones onto the floor.

Despite the stones' residual heat, Imoshen's flesh was cold and her body limp. With infinite gentleness Tulkhan slid his arm under her shoulders so that she lay draped across his body, her face cradled in the crook of his neck. He guided her still hand to his lips and kissed her fingers, even her sixth finger. Pain twisted inside him.

He rubbed her wrist across his lips, inhaling her sweet scent.

Odd. He lifted her hand to study her left wrist. Why had he never noticed that pale scar before? It was barely visible, yet... He pressed her inner wrist to his lips, feeling the thin ridge of flesh where the skin had knitted. The scar felt more visible than it looked. Perhaps this was because her skin was so fine.

Imoshen was dying, and he should let her die, even though his heart railed against it. Tears stung his eyes. A great knot of sadness swelled inside his chest.

Despite the many blankets, her cold body leached the warmth from him. His eyes closed as a terrible weariness overcame him. His thoughts grew blurred and slow. It was a cruel choice. He wanted her to live... but if he called on Reothe, he lost her, lost everything.

Sleep, then decide.

Drifting away he felt nothing but a deep abiding sorrow. Then he sensed oblivion calling and welcomed it.

TULKHAN WOKE WITH a start. The fire had burned down to glowing embers and the candles had guttered into wax.

His body screamed a warning. Through half-closed lids he watched the air at the end of the bed shimmer. A figure took shape in the flickering candlelight.

Fear froze Tulkhan's limbs. His breath caught in his throat.

The last T'En warrior stood studying the two figures in the bed, his features unreadable.

Tulkhan kept his eyes mere slits, hoping Reothe would not realise he was awake. Had the Beatific betrayed him? If she had sent a messenger to Reothe, he could not have arrived so soon unless he was just outside the city gates.

'I can tell you are aware of me,' Reothe said softly. 'How does it feel to lie helpless before your enemy?'

As he said this Tulkhan discovered he was paralysed.

Reothe laughed softly. 'Your fear is sweet. I could drink it down in one gulp. Don't look so horrified. You hold Imoshen in your arms and yet you don't know her true nature? Her gifts grow, living off all of you, the fears and hopes of so many little lives. We T'En serve True-men and women because you serve us.'

He fell silent for a heartbeat then a sweet smile illuminated his face. 'I can feel the Beatific in the next room. She plots to console you once Imoshen dies. She desires you, admires your virility. But if I were to go to her now she would take me into her arms, her body and her heart. It is the fate of you, who call yourselves True-people, to serve the T'En for love.'

Tulkhan raged against the truth he heard in Reothe's words.

'How?' His voice was a mere croak, but at least he had spoken. 'How are you here? Now?'

Reothe tensed, studying him. 'You are a determined creature. I could enjoy your resistance for a long time before overcoming you.'

Terror clogged Tulkhan's throat. He could not protect himself, let alone Imoshen, from this alien creature.

Reothe walked around the bed to crouch at Tulkhan's side, bringing their faces level. 'You want to know how I come to be here?' He smiled. 'You called me. Ironic, isn't it?'

'Called you?' Tulkhan couldn't move his head. He could only see his tormentor from the corner of his eyes. The strain made his head ache and distorted his vision so that the fire's embers seemed to flicker through Reothe's features. 'Never!'

'But you did. You see, Imoshen and I are bound, betrothed in the old way. Earlier today I sensed a dimming in Imoshen's life force. When you touched our bonding scar you called me.' Reothe paused to observe Tulkhan's face. 'Didn't she tell you? The night before she was to bond with you, she joined with me. We mingled our blood and our breath to complete what we had begun last autumn. See.' He held his left arm out to reveal a scar that matched Imoshen's. 'Everything she has ever shared with you was meant for me.'

Tulkhan could not believe it. Would not!

'Deny this.' Reothe turned Imoshen's left wrist to Tulkhan's face. 'She may knit the scar seamlessly – she may cloak its very existence from you – but she cannot change what is!'

Before this day Tulkhan had never noticed the scar. Imoshen had been hiding it. Was she playing some deep, double game? She couldn't be, she had come to him so openly. He could not believe she would betray him, yet...

'This is too sweet!' Reothe crowed. 'You tear yourself apart. Let me ease your pain.'

If Tulkhan could have moved he would have screamed, but his body was not his to command. He could only lie writhing in mental torment as Reothe spread the fingers of his left hand over Tulkhan's face.

Instinctively the General closed his eyes, but instead of flesh on his skin, he felt six cool points caress his senses. Soothingly they sank deeper into his awareness, siphoning off the terror that threatened to engulf his sanity. He was aware of a sense of Otherness which was Reothe. It was not unpleasant, just... different.

He knew he should be horrified, but fear was a distant memory. When the presence that was Reothe retreated, he was almost sorry to lose contact. He had never experienced the intimate presence of another being like that. As he opened his eyes he was aware of a cruel separation.

Until this moment, he had never known how truly alone he was.

Reothe rose to stand beside the bed. A delighted laugh escaped him as he pulled back the covers.

'See what you have done for me. I grow more substantial on your emotions.'

Now Tulkhan understood that this Reothe was only a projection. There was something chillingly innocent in the T'En warrior's delight. It was as if he was so far removed from a True-man that the rules Tulkhan lived by could not affect him.

One part of the General knew he should be mortified to lie defenceless before his most dangerous enemy, but the mind-touch had left him strangely distanced, so that he could only watch as Reothe studied the way Tulkhan's body entwined with Imoshen's.

Reothe's six-fingered hand glided over Imoshen's thigh. His touch contained reverence and ownership. Resentment flooded Tulkhan. Yet an equal and opposite surge of hope filled him. Could Reothe help?

'Ask for any reward, anything.' Tulkhan's words were a breathy whisper.

'Anything?' Reothe leant closer, as though fascinated despite himself. 'There is nothing you can give me, True-man. Mere-man. By this time next winter I will have the palace, Imoshen and Fair Isle. You are merely holding them in safekeeping for me.' His hand passed over Tulkhan's face to rest on Imoshen's temple. A frown settled between Reothe's narrow brows. 'Why did you delay so long? I may be too late to escort her from death's shadow.'

'But you will try?'

Reothe gave a short, sharp laugh, his eyes as brilliant as the jewels they resembled. He searched Tulkhan's face. 'Did you know she saved my life the last time we were together?'

The General wanted to deny it. Reothe's satisfied smile told him the Dhamfeer was enjoying his reaction. Tulkhan tried to control his emotions. But how could he bluff Reothe when the T'En could sense his feelings, possibly even catch a whisper of his thoughts?

With what he had learnt of Reothe during the mind-touch, Tulkhan understood that every word was a weapon designed to wound him. He recalled the old nursery rhyme about Dhamfeers and tried to armour himself against Reothe's cunning.

'The bond Imoshen and I share is older and deeper than yours, Ghebite.' Reothe made the word an insult. 'One day she will look into your True-man eyes and realise what you are. Mere-man. Her place is with me, and so I will save her, not for you, but for that day. And when it happens you will remember this moment.'

Tulkhan closed his eyes. It felt as though Reothe had revealed a greater truth, something Tulkhan had always known but refused to acknowledge. Yet Tulkhan did not believe in fate, and he did not believe Imoshen was destined to be with Reothe. A man made his own future.

'You may feel a little pain. I haven't done this before,' Reothe warned.

Tulkhan met Reothe's eyes and read something he didn't want to acknowledge. Instead of mocking cynicism he saw a man who knowingly faced death, and for this he felt a grudging respect.

The Dhamfeer was naked now and insubstantial. Narrow parallel scars ran down his chest, weeping fresh blood. Had Reothe been wounded when he arrived? Tulkhan couldn't remember. The glowing coals of the dying fire flickered through Reothe's body as if he was consumed from within.

One part of Tulkhan wanted to shrink from the contact as Reothe stretched on the bed beside him. He felt the T'En male's intense questioning gaze.

'What?' Tulkhan mumbled.

Those insubstantial fingers pressed his lips closed.

'Pray to your gods that I succeed, Ghebite, because if I fail, you lose us both and possibly your own life, too, since I am going to anchor myself in you. Concentrate on that burning candle, do not let it go, and ignore me even if you find what I do disturbing.'

Tulkhan wanted to watch, to understand what was happening, but the words triggered a compulsion and his gaze focused on the flame at the end of the bed. He was fleetingly aware of Reothe's presence at his side and then his insubstantial body moving over his own, settling atop Imoshen's unconscious form.

Then the candle flame blurred and Tulkhan's heart pounded in his chest. Lightness filled his body so that he felt dizzy and vague. Fear closed around his raging heart. He must not lose sight of that flame. If he did, they were all lost.

He was aware of a heaviness filling Imoshen's body, then heat flashed through her limbs. She gasped as if in pain. Hope soared in him, sinking once again as she returned to the dreamless state.

The flame flickered and separated to become two points of light. Like the reflective eyes of a great white cat they stalked him. Terror filled Tulkhan's chest. He could not scream, could not defend himself. Sweat broke out on his skin.

Malignant intelligence pursued him. He wanted to close his eyes to deny approaching death, but perversely he knew to break contact was to die. He dared not even blink. His eyes burned and his breath passed through his parched throat in short sharp gasps.

Abruptly the twin flames broke into a thousand sparkles like sunlight on water, blinding him.

Tulkhan opened his eyes to find the room dark except for the dim glow of the fire's coals. The candles had all burned out. He felt so weak he could hardly move. But Imoshen lay warm in his arms, her body sculpted around his. She was pliable and dear to him. With a rush of joy he recalled how they would lie entwined like this after making love.

Experimentally he lifted a hand to stroke her upper back. Her skin no longer had that cool, marble-smooth feel. Hope flared within him, giving him renewed strength.

'Imoshen?' Rising on one elbow, he cradled her face in his free hand. 'Answer me, Imoshen.'

She frowned and Tulkhan's heart soared. Whatever Reothe had done, it had succeeded.

Trembling with relief he sat up, gathering her warm, body to his. Pure joy illuminated him. His fingers entwined in her hair as he cradled her face, kissing her temple, the hollow under her jaw.

The soft sound of protest she made in her throat was a blessing. He laughed, feeling tears on his cheeks.

'Imoshen,' he breathed, seeking her lips. She had come back to him.

Her mouth moved under his, her breath mingled with his. He could drink from her lips forever. He felt her smile.

Relief made him light-headed. He looked down into her face, seeking her dear familiar features, but her wine-dark eyes mocked him. The sad smile was not hers.

Cold certainty filled Tulkhan. 'No!' He pushed her from him, repulsed. The intelligence watching him from Imoshen's eyes was not hers.

The room spun. He had to clutch the bed frame to steady himself. Still reeling he watched Reothe's insubstantial form detach from Imoshen's body. As his wraith rose above her, she sank onto the bed.

Then Tulkhan saw two people – the sleeping form of Imoshen, with Reothe's wraith, kneeling over her.

Tulkhan could barely summon the strength to swallow. What he had witnessed this night was something no True-man should know. Yet he could not look away as Reothe stroked Imoshen's face. His incorporeal fingers failed to brush a strand of hair from her lips. Tulkhan watched him dip his head, pressing his pale lips to hers.

It was too intimate a gesture for another to witness. He had to look away. When he looked back Reothe had turned to him, his face a deadly mask. Tulkhan scrambled off the bed and backed away staggering, his legs hardly able to support him. He wished for a weapon, though he knew it would do no good.

As the Dhamfeer stalked towards him, one part of his terrified mind noted that the bed and Imoshen's sleeping form could be seen quite clearly through Reothe.

Perhaps the T'En's gifts were wearing thin with use. Tulkhan hoped so. It would be a relief to know the creature had limitations.

Reothe stopped before him. 'I have braved the Parakletos, searching death's shadow to find her and bring her back.'

Tulkhan barely breathed. 'I thank you.'

'I didn't do it for you.'

'I know.'

Reothe turned to gaze at Imoshen. He said something in High T'En. It sounded like poetry or a line from a song.

The Dhamfeer returned his attention to Tulkhan, a lingering smile in his alien eyes. It was a smile that held painful self-knowledge. 'You do not ask. It means, *Those we love have the greatest power to wound us.*'

'Reothe.' Tulkhan went to touch him but his hand slipped through the T'En's body. 'Can't we find a middle ground?'

'You would compromise?' Reothe shook his head ruefully. 'You don't want to do a deal with me, True-man. I have already bargained away my soul.'

He lifted his face as though looking for something beyond Tulkhan. The Dhamfeer winced as the slashes across his chest deepened and the blood ran freely.

Even so, Tulkhan felt there was something in Reothe, something he recognised because something similar lived in him. It didn't have to be this way. He went to tell the last T'En warrior, but Reothe was gone.

Stunned, Tulkhan searched the room. His senses told him that he was alone with Imoshen again.

Wearily he went to the bed. It was the darkest part of the night, the time when sick folk died and babies were born, the predawn of a winter's night.

As though waking naturally, Imoshen rolled over and stretched. Her eyes opened and she smiled as if recalling a pleasant dream. He made an involuntary sound in his throat. She looked at him.

There was no recognition.

Had Reothe stolen Imoshen's memory? But no, now she recognised him. As memory returned, her face grew haunted.

She sat up abruptly. 'Jacolm and Cariah!'

Tulkhan flinched. He had hoped to see pleasure light her face, not sorrow. Were they destined to bring each other nothing but pain?

Questions burned to be asked, but tonight he was not sure he could face the answers.

Imoshen's chest hurt. Every muscle in her body ached, as if she had been tested to the limits of her physical endurance. The last thing she recalled was kneeling in the snow before the bodies of Cariah and Jacolm and saying the words for the dead.

'How did I get here?'

'I carried you. You've been unconscious all day and most of the night.'

Tulkhan was watching her closely. He looked very weary and she could sense a difference in him – he had been touched by something beyond a True-man's understanding. 'What haven't you told me?'

He shrugged as if he did not know where to start.

'You're tired, come to bed,' she urged, but he made no move to join her. 'What is it, Tulkhan?'

'You hide things from me.' His eyes narrowed.

'Why do you look at me like that?'

He sank onto the bed and she ached for him to take her in his arms.

'You turned the bodies of Cariah and Jacolm to stone.'

'Impossible.' But even as she said it, she knew it was true.

'It nearly killed you. When I brought you back here you were as cold as stone.'

She shuddered and reached for him but he did not respond. 'Why won't you hold me?'

'Why don't you ask how it is that you still live?'

She shook her head, drawing back to study his face. His eyes held a deep glittering anger. It frightened her.

He snatched her left hand and turned her arm over, inspecting her wrist, then held it up for her to see. 'You say you do not use your tricks on me, then why is the bonding scar you share with Reothe hidden once again?'

Imoshen frowned. Had she been unconsciously cloaking the bonding scar from Tulkhan? 'The scar is not what it seems...'

The General grew pale and he dropped her wrist. 'Now that you admit it, it reappears.'

'Not intentionally. I don't mean to hide things from you.'

'Were you in Reothe's camp the night before our bonding? Did you save his life?'

Imoshen's skin went cold and she opened her mouth to deny it but she could not lie.

'Answer me!' Tulkhan caught her shoulders, shaking her.

Tears stung her eyes.

He released her. 'I must be mad!'

She drew back, seared by his derision. Deep sobs shook her. He would never trust her.

'Imoshen...' Tulkhan pulled her into his arms. 'I thought you were dead.'

She felt his lips on her forehead and sensed his relief. 'I don't understand. Why does it hurt when I breathe? What happened here this night?'

Tulkhan was unwilling to reveal that he had been useless while Reothe had risked his life to save her. Before he could confess, Imoshen leant forward and licked his throat.

Her eyes widened. 'I can taste Reothe on your skin.'

'He was here.'

'He couldn't have been. It would take days for him to ride here.'

'He didn't ride. He wasn't here in body.' Tulkhan shrugged. He didn't have the words. 'Reothe said he felt your life force dim, that you were bound to him in some T'En way. It was he who saved you. I... I could do nothing for you.'

Imoshen shivered with fear.

'Reothe said that I am only holding you in safekeeping, until he is ready to claim you.'

'You mustn't listen to him.' Imoshen's breath caressed the hollow under his jaw.

Then he felt her hands on him, needful and urgent. As her lips moved on his throat the knot of failure which had wound so tight inside him gradually eased.

'Reothe can tell the absolute truth and make it sound like a lie so that you doubt your own judgment.'

Tulkhan wanted to ask her if she could do the same. But the warmth of her breath on his skin was overwhelming. It drowned all caution. The need in her was great, calling up an answering urgency in him. He wanted only to bury himself inside her, to forget everything but her touch. She was a balm to his bruised soul. Yet...

'How could you give your bonding vows to me when you already had this?' He grasped her left wrist.

Imoshen gave a little gasp. 'Reothe cut our wrists before I could stop him. When he tried to say the words to complete the vow I refused.' She searched Tulkhan's face. 'I have been true to you. I swear.'

He wanted to believe her. 'I must be mad.'

He felt as if Reothe had stolen something intangible this night. Only Imoshen's touch eased his hollowness and he gave himself up to her.

Chapter Fourteen

WHEN IMOSHEN WOKE late the next morning the bed was empty, although the scent of their passion still clung to her skin. Every movement was an effort as she forced her trembling body to perform the simple act of dressing.

She had searched her mind but there was no memory of Reothe's presence, no memory of her time in death's shadow other than what felt like fevered nightmares. Tulkhan had told her how Reothe had risked the wrath of the Parakletos to save her. She was beholden to him and she hated it.

'T'Imoshen,' Merkah cried. 'You are up and dressed. Why didn't you send for me?'

'Where is the General?'

'He left word that you were to go to him once you were ready.'

Imoshen nodded. Her arms hurt so much she could not lift them above her head. She asked Merkah to do her hair and sat before the mirror.

As the maid set about her task she gossiped. 'It was such a surprise when the General told us you had recovered. The Beatific could not believe it. She was sure the baby would be dead –'

Imoshen gasped.

Merkah's startled eyes met Imoshen's in the mirror.

'I suppose it is common knowledge, or it will be soon.' Imoshen's hand closed over her belly. She feared that the fragile life had been extinguished while she lay unconscious.

Stiffly she came to her feet. 'Where is General Tulkhan?'

Before Merkah could reply a grey mist enveloped Imoshen's vision. She felt her legs buckle and, when she could think clearly again, found herself sitting on the floor.

'Stay here, I will bring a healer,' the girl urged.

'Nonsense. I'm fine.' But Imoshen came to her feet slowly and waited a moment to be sure. She didn't have time for physical weakness. 'Now, where is the General?'

Merkah hesitated. 'I will go with you.'

'Very well.'

As they walked through the palace galleries, Imoshen noted there were very few servants, and the few she did see slipped away quickly. 'Where is everyone?'

'In the woods, viewing the beautiful stone lovers. Half the city has been through the palace grounds today. The queue runs right out the gate.' Merkah paused by a window. 'You can see it from here.'

Imoshen peered over her maid's shoulder. A dark line of people snaked across the white snow.

They walked on in silence. Until this moment Imoshen had not really believed Tulkhan. But it appeared she had indeed turned the dead lovers to stone. Not only had she failed Cariah, she had unwittingly revealed gifts that would make True-people fear her.

'Here we are.' The maid scratched on a door tang. At the sound of Tulkhan's deep voice Imoshen's face grew hot with the memory of their urgent lovemaking.

She lifted her chin and walked in. The General stood behind a large table covered with maps. Wine bottles, goblets and several ink wells held the curling edges flat.

Merkah shut the door as she withdrew.

The planes of Tulkhan's face were tight with tension and he raised cold eyes to her.

Imoshen did not understand why he had distanced himself from her yet again. She let the tip of her tongue rest on her upper lip, tasting the air. Someone who didn't like her had been in this room recently.

'I have lain awake thinking,' Tulkhan said. 'You do not deny that you have been to Reothe's camp. Tell me where it is.'

Imoshen's heart sank as looked down at the maps.

'You say I have your loyalty,' Tulkhan persisted. 'Prove it. Point out his camp.'

'That was back at midwinter. If Reothe is half the tactician I believe him to be, he will have moved by now.'

Tulkhan did not seem disappointed. He slid something out from under a map and tossed it onto the table before her. The silver platter spun and settled heavily. 'Then do a scrying to locate his camp.'

Imoshen looked at the plate's dull surface. This was the scrying platter she had inherited from the Aayel. It annoyed her to think Tulkhan had asked Merkah to take it while her mistress slept. 'You made me vow not to use my gifts.'

'I'm making an exception. Do it!'

Pain unfurled inside Imoshen. He wanted to use her as a tool to locate and kill. How could this be the man who had held her so tenderly last night?

'If you refuse, I will –'

'Lock me up?' Imoshen whispered. 'Steal my child and wall me inside the palace somewhere, leaving me to starve to death?'

Tulkhan appeared shocked. 'Do you really believe that of me?'

Imoshen shook her head and picked up the scrying plate. The skin of her fingers crawled with distaste. Gingerly she lifted them to her face and inhaled. 'The Vaygharian has been here. Is that why you doubt me, General? Have you forgotten so soon that he poisoned your half-brother's mind?'

'I can see through Kinraid's manoeuvring. Besides, he is not the only source of my information.' His eyes narrowed. 'Just do the scrying, Imoshen. Think of it as a test. I would be a fool to have such a tool at my disposal and not use it.'

'I can't.'

'You mean won't.'

'No. I can't. The Aayel tried to explain it to me when I was younger. Back then I did not know enough to understand her. You probably won't understand me but I am going to try.' She sighed. 'Reothe is more versed in his gifts. I am just discovering mine. Scrying is not an exact science. If I were to pick up the plate and do my preparation, then try to locate Reothe, I might succeed too well. I don't want to give him access to my mind.' She shivered, hugging her body. 'I won't do it. Please... I'm afraid.'

Tulkhan rubbed his jaw thoughtfully. 'Let me see if I have this right. You and he are both sorcerous creatures.'

'No, we're –'

'That is the Ghebite word for someone who manipulates powers no honest True-person has. I will call you anything I like.' When Imoshen did not argue he continued, 'But even though you both have the T'En gifts, you are weaker than he. Are you telling me I have allied myself with the weaker of the two sorcerers?'

Imoshen nodded. She was a child where her skills were concerned.

The General studied her. Once again she was aware of his keen intelligence.

'What's to stop you from turning your back on me and joining Reothe?' Tulkhan asked. 'He shares your heritage. Last night he risked his life to save you. He was your betrothed by choice and... he loves you.'

Imoshen felt her cheeks grow hot. She did not attempt to deny Tulkhan's assessment.

'So why stay here, Imoshen? Are you playing a double game, passing information to Reothe? Did you go to him the night before our bonding then come back to me with false promises on your lips? Why do you persist in this farce?'

She heard the raw pain in his voice and she ached to reassure him. But he would not let her approach. Had Reothe planted gift-enhanced doubts in Tulkhan's mind?

She felt too weary for subterfuge. 'The night before our joining, Reothe made a pact with the Ancients. He sacrificed a snow leopard to appease their greed and drew me to him. They reanimated the snow leopard and demanded a price of him.'

Her hand went to her throat as she recalled the pain of the snow leopard's claws on Reothe's chest. She had raked her skin and pleaded with the old powers to return her to the palace. The small wounds made by her fingernails had healed because there were of a physical origin, but wounds made by the Ancients no True-man could see and she did not know if they ever truly healed.

With a grimace, she shrugged the memory aside. 'Reothe abducted me. I had no choice in going to him. Returning to you was my decision.'

General Tulkhan folded his arms, clearly unconvinced.

'You can place a guard on me if you choose. Though what the palace servants will think of that, I can't imagine.' Determined and defiant, she tucked her scrying plate under her arm. 'I am true to you, General Tulkhan. If there is a seed of doubt, it lives in you, not me!'

WHY WOULDN'T THE man die? Tulkhan's sword arm ached. His breath rasped in his throat. And still the man kept coming. Every killing blow Tulkhan struck was ineffective, while his own body grew steadily weaker. Sweat stung his eyes.

The swordsman hadn't been this hard to beat the first time Tulkhan had killed him. With a jolt the General realised this was a dream and he was reliving his first battlefield kill.

At seventeen Tulkhan had sent this man to his grave without a thought.

Now, he slipped on the bloodied ground, going down on one knee. He took a sword strike under his arm above the armour. The blade ran deep into his chest, burning, searing all the way. Each breath became agony and grew shallower as he drowned in his own blood.

He stared up at his opponent silhouetted against the sun. The swordsman pulled off his helmet.

Reothe!

Tulkhan woke gasping, drenched with sweat, his heart racing. As he rolled to his feet, his knees threatened to give way. Staggering, he crossed the room to the window and threw it open. The smell of death and despair clogged his nostrils. He felt utterly hollow.

He heard Imoshen moan in the room beyond and stifled the impulse to go to her. To lie in her arms now would be bliss, but each time he did he felt the bonds of passion bind him ever closer to her. Tulkhan could not forget the moment Reothe had revealed the bonding scar he shared with Imoshen.

Last night he had let himself believe her denials, but excuses sprang too easily to Imoshen's lips. After she had refused to search out Reothe's camp, Tulkhan had vowed to stay out of her bed. Instead he'd placed a blanket on the floor in the Emperor's private chamber and slept there.

Now Tulkhan strode to the fireplace to stir up the coals and keep back the night. Somehow he knew this feeling of despair was Reothe's doing and that he must fight it with every breath he took, yet he could not shake off the premonition that his time with Imoshen was destined to end with his death.

IMOSHEN ROUSED HERSELF from a doze. It was the day before the Spring Festival, though the snow still lay thick on the ground. She blinked and remembered that she had been working through the plans for the feast before she drifted off.

The scratching came again. Imoshen did not recognise the comb's metal tone.

She rubbed her face and straightened her hair. 'Come in.'

Lord Fairban's youngest daughter entered. 'T'Imoshen.'

'Lady Miriane.' Imoshen came to her feet. They were the same age, she and Miriane, but they were worlds apart. This woman was the youngest child of an indulgent father, while Imoshen carried the weight of Fair Isle on her shoulders.

Like the rest of the Keldon nobles, the Fairbans were preparing to return to their estates now that the worst of the snows had melted.

'My father wishes to speak with you before he leaves,' Miriane said.

'I would be honoured.'

'You'll need a cloak. Father wants to speak somewhere private.'

Imoshen did not like the sound of this. She'd thought Lord Fairban had become reconciled, as much as was possible, to Cariah's death.

She followed the young woman through the palace, out into the formal gardens.

'This is as far as I go. Father waits for you in the centre of the maze,' Miriane said.

Imoshen thanked her and moved on. The air was still, crisp and cold. Ideal for carrying sound. She heard the horn and the baying of the dogs. The Ghebites were hunting in the woods again. Disgusted, she wondered what animal they had flushed out this time. They had just about hunted all the game from the formal woods. There was even talk of freeing some of the animals from the menagerie. That would be cruel indeed, since these were rare animals, presented to the palace as gifts and bred over generations.

Imoshen's fine indoor slippers were sodden by the time she rounded the last bend of the snow-shrouded maze. Lord Fairban spun to face her. She could tell by the furrowed snow that he had been pacing the central garden.

Catching sight of her, he grew still. He had aged since Cariah died. A steely determination defined his face as he studied her.

She waited, then prompted him. Her feet were starting to go numb. 'I have come in answer to your summons, Lord Fairban.'

He indicated the stone seat, brushing last night's snowfall from its surface.

'Come, T'Imoshen. I have been made spokesman and it is time we revealed our plans to you.'

Imoshen's heart sank. 'Continue.'

'This may be painful for you but I must speak plainly. You are nothing but a tool to the Ghebite General, a prize of war to be used to cement his hold on this island. Even the child you carry is more important for his hold on Fair Isle than yours. He needs you. You do not need him.'

Imoshen raised an eyebrow. It seemed everyone knew of her pregnancy.

Lord Fairban nodded to himself. 'I came to see the General and I must admit I was favourably impressed. Tulkhan is a good man, for a Ghebite. But events have proved that we can never live with them. They are primitives.'

He took her hand, patting it kindly. A wave of sincerity washed over Imoshen. Lord Fairban believed what he was about to say.

'There are others who feel the same way. We want to see you and Reothe in the palace. If the royal family had been pure T'En as they were meant to be, Fair Isle would never have fallen to the Ghebite invaders.'

Imoshen was swamped by his vision of a future with a powerful T'En ruling class who protected the True-people of Fair Isle. She withdrew her hands, too dismayed to speak.

He appeared unaware of this. 'I will go back to the highlands and make contact with T'Reothe to aid him. When he is ready we will march into T'Diemn where you will be waiting for him.'

Imoshen dared not reveal how she really felt. If she objected to his plans, Lord Fairban would become her enemy, for he must surely know that what he had just revealed would result in his death and the destruction of everyone associated with him.

'I knew you were biding your time, playing out the charade until the moment of confrontation,' he continued, pleased with his sagacity. 'My daughters and I leave immediately after the festival tomorrow. It is time the Keld made a stand.'

'Lord Fairban, I urge caution.'

'No need. I know your hands are tied for now. But when the moment is right you will strike a telling blow for Fair Isle, turning the invaders to stone!'

Imoshen slumped on the low seat, feeling the cold seep through her cloak and gown.

'My Cariah admired you, Imoshen. I have lost a daughter. You have lost your family. Let my daughters be your sisters, let me stand in place of your father.'

Stunned, she could only stare at him. He radiated absolute faith in her, and she knew his heart was good. Imoshen was horrified. What could she do? She did not want to be the death of Cariah's father and the annihilation of what remained of Fair Isle's old nobility.

'I will leave first,' he advised. 'You wait a while, then follow me out. There are spies everywhere.'

Imoshen watched him go then buried her face in her hands. To think it had come to this. Her head spun with the implications. The Keldon nobles believed she was capable of turning the Ghebite army to stone. They believed she and Reothe could not fail to rout the Ghebites. Naturally they would be happy to rise against the invaders. To know her own unthinking actions had triggered this development was bitter indeed.

Imoshen rose, stiff with cold and shock. She had no idea how much time had passed. In a daze of worry she followed the footprints out of the maze. It was only when she came to the last turn that she noticed there was an extra set. A third person had stepped in her footprints, but their stride was not as long as hers.

Imoshen's heart faltered.

Who had overheard them?

One of Tulkhan's spies? Since he no longer came to her bed she knew he had set people to watch her. Or maybe it was one of the ambassadorial groups; their keen-eyed servants were everywhere.

Imoshen dropped to her knees, placing her bare hand in the snow hollow before lifting it to her nose. She knew that stench. Vaygharians!

By tonight Kinraid would have Tulkhan's ear, planting his poison to grow and fester. If only the General would let her touch him. She knew if she could lie naked next to him, she could ease his doubts and soothe his fears.

But she wouldn't get the chance. Frustration welled in her. She didn't want to betray Tulkhan. Somehow she had to convince him of that, while protecting Lord Fairban.

The horn sounded again.

Inhaling, Imoshen tasted the Ghebites' hunting blood lust carried to her on the breeze. Tulkhan was with them. Without another thought she took to her heels, running towards the woods.

A heaviness in her lower belly reminded her of the baby's presence but did not slow her. It was harder going when she entered the woods where the snowdrifts had piled up. She concentrated on finding Tulkhan. Something was being hunted through the woods. The tang of its fear and the hunter's male excitement hung on the air. An unpleasant aftertaste sat on the back of Imoshen's tongue.

She ran on, letting instinct guide her. Soon she found herself on a rise, hunting the hunters. They were on horseback moving parallel to her. The thick woods slowed their pace.

She identified the General's broad shoulders amongst the hunters. He didn't want her to use her powers, but she had to make him come to her. Everywhere she turned people were trying to drive a wedge of mistrust between them and she had to forestall their wicked whispers.

Tulkhan shifted in the saddle. He had the strangest feeling, a prickling sensation on the back of his neck. It told him he was being watched. He glanced up the rise. A cloaked figure stepped from the trees and looked down at him. He knew that pale form, those dark eyes.

An emotion which was equal parts dread and fascination gripped him. Right at this moment Imoshen looked Other, wreathed in T'En mystique. Yet none of his men seemed to notice her.

Tulkhan shuddered. Was he aware of her because he had been touched by both Imoshen and Reothe? It seemed he was growing sensitive to their gifts. Vulnerable, perhaps?

Anger warred with an urgency which was not his own. He realised she was calling him and he fought the compulsion to go to her. But it was overwhelming. Confronting her was the only way to escape her pull. He let the others ride on and turned his mount to the rise where she waited. Her red cloak was bright against the white snow, obscenely bright, a splash of fresh crimson blood.

At last he faced Imoshen who looked up at him, her chest rising and falling as if she had been running.

'Well?' he demanded, not bothering to dismount.

She would have stepped forward, but stopped when he jerked the horse's reins and the creature sidled away.

'I have news of a plot to aid Reothe,' she said.

It was so unexpected he snorted. 'Why tell me?'

She flinched. 'They will tell you that I am part of it and I'm not. Don't let them do this to us, General!'

The pain in her words lanced through his anger but he maintained his distance. If he let his guard down she would claim his soul, and then, he suspected, it was only a matter of time before Reothe's prophecy was fulfilled. Since the night the rebel leader had saved Imoshen, Tulkhan's dreams had been filled with visions of his own death.

He was growing to believe he would never rule Fair Isle, never live to see his son grow to manhood. It was all a shallow dream. The blood of his Ghebite army would enrich the soil of Fair Isle and his memory would be a tavern jest, no more.

'So tell me about this plot,' he said coldly.

'Why should I betray my own people when it's obvious you despise me?' Imoshen turned, her red cloak swinging in a defiant arc as she darted away through the silver trunks.

Tulkhan urged his horse forward in pursuit of her. Imoshen was hampered by knee-deep snow. He took his time catching up to her, letting her know who was in control. Yet, as she looked over her shoulder he caught a flash of something in her eyes and wondered if he wasn't playing into her hands.

Annoyed, he closed the distance between them. Coming abreast of her he leant out, caught her cloak and pulled her off her feet. She twisted and writhed, resisting him with surprising strength. Either he had to let her go or leap from the horse. Swinging his leg over the saddle he threw himself forward. They went down in a tangle of limbs as the horse galloped on.

Cursing, Tulkhan caught a flash of Imoshen's furious eyes before he hit the snow, pinning her face-down under him. The force of the fall knocked the wind from his chest. Stars flecked his vision.

She recovered before him. Only by tensing his muscles was he able to stop her from flipping him off.

She muttered something hard and angry under her breath.

He hugged her to his chest, pinning her arms. 'So who is in on this plot?'

She arched in silent protest, then the fight seemed to go out of her and she melted into the curves of his body. Without warning he felt the liquid heat of desire flow through his limbs and her scent made his head swim.

'Don't try to distract me!'

'I do nothing. If you lust after me, it is your weakness, not mine.'

'Don't tell me you don't know what you do.'

She laughed bitterly. 'If you would think with your head for a change, you'd ask yourself why I came out here to warn you.'

'Trick me, you mean. Do you think to win my trust with half lies?'

'You are a... a Ghebite dog!' she spat, panting with anger. 'All rutting and –'

He laughed. 'Is that the best you can do?'

'Tulkhan, listen. Because of what happened to Cariah and Jacolm, the Keld are mobilising support for Reothe. When he leads them to invade the city they will call on me to join them. They expect me to turn you and your army to stone.'

'As if you could. You'd die trying.'

'It is enough that they think I can do it.'

'Who thinks this?' He tightened his hold on her. 'Who, Imoshen? Name them and I will have them arrested, their lands confiscated.'

'That's right,' she gasped. 'That will really make the others trust you.'

'What do you expect me to do?'

No answer.

'Well?'

She remained obstinately silent.

At last he loosened his hold, allowing her to sit up and face him.

'The nobles plot to overthrow me. What would you have me do, Imoshen?'

'I don't know!'

The despair in her voice touched him. 'Imoshen?'

She shook her head, brushing impatiently at her tears. 'So much is against us, General. Sometimes I...' A sob escaped her.

He gathered her to him. Her tears were salty on his lips, her breath hot on his skin. How could her touch be a traitorous lie?

Earnestly she pulled away. 'We must be strong in ourselves, strong in each other for the sake of our people, and for...' She took his hand, guiding it to her belly where he felt a small, firm swelling.

It was his child, nestled safely within her. She smiled, shyly. A deep joy flooded him. He kissed the tears from her cheeks. It seemed to him that all his life had led to this moment in the pristine cold air with Imoshen in his arms.

She returned his embrace with fierce passion. Tulkhan didn't want to go back to the palace and his advisers, who sought to convince him Imoshen would be his downfall. He wanted her now, but that would mean laying himself open to her. He could not think for the urgency of his need.

Suddenly she froze.

'What?'

'It can't be!' She sniffed the air and her eyes widened. 'What were you hunting?'

'A big white cat. My men let it out of the keep to hunt.'

'A snow leopard?' Her nose wrinkled as if she was smelling the predator's rank scent.

He sniffed, then tensed for he could smell it now.

'Move slowly,' Imoshen advised.

Tulkhan uncoiled to his feet, searching the ridge. His mount had paused a body length away. The horse rolled its eyes fearfully but obeyed its training despite the instinct to run. Then Tulkhan saw the cat, a patch of deeper white moving through the drifts. 'It's below us, heading this way.'

Imoshen came to her knees. Dragging off her cloak she rolled it round her right forearm. 'Do you have a weapon?'

'Only a ceremonial spear. It is supposed to be a clean kill, man against beast.'

Imoshen muttered something derogatory in High T'En, then she was on her feet, backing up the ridge. Tulkhan spoke soothingly to his horse as he collected its dangling reins.

'Could we outride the cat?' he asked.

'Not two of us on a single mount through heavy drifts.'

'Then mount up,' he urged. 'I'll stay and distract it.'

'No.'

'Imoshen, don't argue. I'll have the spear.'

She laughed. 'I'd like to see you tackle a snow cat with a spear. I've seen what they can do!'

'You'll get on the horse, Imoshen. You have to, you can't risk the child.'

'Of course.' Her wine-dark eyes burned with resentment. 'I keep forgetting. That is all I am to you, a brood mare.'

He caught her around the waist, intending to lift her onto the horse. The sudden action startled the beast and it reared, knocking them both aside. Its hoof struck Tulkhan's thigh with great force and his leg crumpled under him. A groan of pain escaped his clenched teeth.

Imoshen scrambled out of his grasp. Her eyes searched his face as her hands felt his leg. 'The bone is not broken, but –'

Angry with himself, he pushed her away, struggling to one knee. His leg muscle protested as he tried to stand. In a few days he would have nothing but a limp and a fading bruise, but he didn't have a few days. 'Get on the horse, Imoshen. Leave me.'

'No.' She met his gaze steadily. 'I will not leave you.'

The horse wheeled, its body trembling with fright. Tulkhan called it softly, but the beast danced away, taking the spear with it. Cursing, he removed his cloak and wound it around his forearm.

Imoshen slid her shoulder under his, grasping him around the waist. He knew a moment of sheer frustration. Here he was without a weapon, injured, unable to defend himself or Imoshen.

'This way,' she urged.

Each time his injured leg took even a little weight, sweat broke out on his forehead.

The trees thinned out as they approached the crest where his mount waited. It snorted nervously, standing near the edge of the cliff. Behind it was only sky.

'Wait here.' Imoshen guided him to a small building where he sank down gratefully onto the step.

As protection the structure was useless. It had a roof, a circle of elegant columns and no walls. Tulkhan could just imagine the courtiers of the Old Empire strolling through the woods to this lookout to enjoy the view while servants brought them food and entertainment. What a strange idle world the T'En had created, where form outweighed substance.

'Is there a way down the cliffs?' Even he could hear the strain in his voice.

Imoshen darted to the edge to peer over the drop. 'There's no path down. The river lies below but there's a wide patch of broken rocks, we'd never make it if we jumped.'

'Good. I don't want to jump. I can't swim.'

She grinned and padded back to him. Crouching, she covered his hand with hers. 'We're trapped, General.'

'You should have taken the horse when you could!'

She smiled fondly. 'As if I would.'

'Heal me.'

Her eyebrows drew together in a frown.

'It is an emergency,' he told her. 'I'm not asking you to break your vow.'

Her nostrils quivered as she inhaled angrily. 'Does this mean you accept the T'En side of me?'

'Not now, Imoshen. Heal me,' he urged. 'Then at least I can defend us from the great cat.'

'You set it free to kill it for sport. It is only doing what wild cats do, following its nature.' Her eyes narrowed. 'You would have me deny my nature yet use me when it suits you.'

In that moment Imoshen looked so Other that Tulkhan fought an instinctive surge of fear. Then he noticed the horse had drawn closer. 'Get my spear.'

She looked down the slope to the snow leopard. 'There it is. The perfect killing weapon.'

The beast had crept into the open, where it crouched in the snow, so still it was almost invisible.

'When it charges you won't see it coming,' Imoshen whispered as though fascinated.

'If you will not heal me, at least escape. Get on the horse and flee. It will come after me. I'm the easier prey.'

She studied him sadly. 'It's kill or be killed with you, isn't it?'

'Imoshen...'

She ignored him, stepping forward to meet the cat.

'No, Imoshen!' With a groan he struggled to his feet. But the short rest in the cold had made his injured muscle seize up, and he could not stand. He fell to one knee, helpless and furious. 'Imoshen, I forbid it!'

Her soft mocking laugh hung in the air between them, reminding him forcibly of Reothe.

He wanted to howl with frustration. He looked for the shape of the white cat in the snow but couldn't find it. The beast had moved.

Imoshen's hands rose to her neck. The sharp rent of tearing material cut the air and the cat answered with a scream of its own. The primal sound elicited an equally primal response in Tulkhan. The sweat of fear rose on his skin, chilling him to the core.

A helpless groan escaped him as Imoshen dropped to her knees, baring her breasts to the beast, her head thrown back, arms outspread.

Desperate, Tulkhan slewed his weight around and called softly to his mount. As soon as the horse ventured close enough, he dug his hands into the saddle girth, using it to pull himself upright. The spear was strapped firmly in place. His fingers fumbled with it. He expected at any instant to hear Imoshen's scream as the cat attacked. His blood roared in his ears.

Clumsily, because he was holding onto the horse's saddle to stand, he turned and hefted the spear in his hand, praying for one clean throw.

Too late – the beast was on her.

What was it doing?

Stunned, Tulkhan tried to make sense of what he saw. The great white head of the leopard nuzzled Imoshen's neck, then it stepped back and sat looking at her for all the world like a tamed pet.

She rose unsteadily to her feet, her hand sinking into the winter-thick fur at the cat's neck.

When she turned, a gasp escaped Tulkhan

Between her small breasts were three parallel streaks, claw marks welling with blood. One part of his mind told him he had seen this before. But he could only think that she had somehow tamed the cat.

She lifted a trembling hand to her throat. 'I promised safe passage for it and its mate out of the city.'

'You talk to beasts now?'

She watched him from Otherworldly eyes, impervious to his humour. 'You must not let your men kill it. I cannot go back on a promise.'

A promise to a snow cat? The horn sounded and he heard the baying of the dogs.

'Get on your horse, Tulkhan.'

'I don't think I can.'

'Try.' Imoshen came up the slope to join him. 'I'll help.'

There was a strong smell of predator on her hands. The scent triggered a memory, he had smelled it on her once before. He frowned as he recalled it was the morning she'd come to him on their bonding day. Those marks were the same as the ones Reothe carried on his chest.

'What does this mean?' He took her by the shoulder.

She shook her head. 'Up.'

With a grunt of pain he swung his bad leg over the horse's back. 'I can't stop the dogs, Imoshen. They act on instinct.'

Even now he could see the pack heading up the rise towards them. The sun broke through the low clouds, bathing them with its ethereal silver glow.

Imoshen stood at his side. She picked up her cloak and swung it over her shoulders, covering her bare breasts. The great cat came to her and sat at her feet. Tulkhan felt his horse shudder with fear.

The hunters followed the dogs, crashing up the slope. Tulkhan expected the dogs to attack but they slunk back and forth at the edge of the tree line, howling eerily, not daring to come closer.

The Ghebites pulled their horses to a halt and looked across the open ridge top. At that moment Tulkhan knew he was no longer one of them. Because of what he had experienced with Reothe and what he felt for Imoshen, he had taken a step across an invisible line. He might jest and hunt with his men, but in his heart he would walk alone because he had been touched by the T'En.

'General?' one of his men called uncertainly. 'Are you all right?'

'I am unhurt. The hunt is over.'

'Witch!' someone hissed.

Tulkhan raised his voice. 'My horse threw me, kicked me in the leg. Imoshen tamed the cat.'

A round of uneasy comments greeted this.

'She's in league with the evil one!' someone cried. Tulkhan thought he detected a Vaygharian accent.

'There is no evil one.' Imoshen spoke softly, yet her clear voice carried. 'Only the evil in men's hearts.'

Tulkhan grimaced. Trust Imoshen to speak a truth his men did not want to hear. Their muttering grew louder.

'The hunt is over. Go back to the stables.' Tulkhan urged his horse forward, eager to break up the group before they resorted to violence.

Imoshen walked beside his horse, her head level with his knee. The cat matched her step, never leaving her side.

It was a long trek back to the stables. Imoshen and Tulkhan parted company from the hunters at the ornamental lake and made their way to the menagerie.

The keepers wept with joy to see the snow leopard returned unharmed and Tulkhan felt great shame to think that he and his men had been ready to kill the animal for sport.

Following Imoshen's instructions the keepers prepared the menagerie's barred cart and she climbed into the cage with the snow leopard pair.

'We will take the cats out of town to the outskirts of the farms beyond before setting them free. They will make their way into the highlands,' Imoshen told Tulkhan.

He wanted her to promise that she would not go south with the snow leopards, but his pride wouldn't let him. He hesitated, unsure what to say. After all, she had come to warn him of a plot against his rule. She was right, much was against them.

'Imoshen, be on your guard.'

A soft laugh escaped her. 'You have seen what I can do and yet you tell me to be careful?'

'I know how much you risk.' Risking his own arm, he slipped his fingers through the bars of the cage to grasp Imoshen's hand. 'Though you refused to heal me, you did not leave me.'

Imoshen's eyes narrowed. 'Remember that when they come to tell you of my treachery, General.'

On returning to the palace, Tulkhan found it abuzz with Imoshen's latest escapade. The servants whispered that even T'Reothe had not seemed so T'En. Truly, Imoshen was a throwback to her namesake, T'Imoshen the First.

Shape-changer, his men hissed. *White hair, white cat, white witch.*

It was the stuff of legend and the Ghebite warriors were as quick as the palace servants to spread the story.

Chapter Fifteen

THAT EVENING IMOSHEN lay alone in her bed, listening for Tulkhan's step. She was determined to mend the breach between them. They had grown close while escaping the snow cat and she was sure he would open to her, but she heard him walk right past.

Throwing back the covers, she padded to the connecting door and peered through as Tulkhan made up his simple bed before the fire. She ached to go to him yet dreaded his rejection.

As he lay brooding, Tulkhan heard the softest of sounds and looked up to see Imoshen illuminated by the fire's flickering flames. For a moment he wondered if his need for her had conjured her.

She crossed the chamber and knelt beside him. 'How is your leg? Let me...' Her hands went to his thigh but he pulled away, certain that if she touched him he would be lost.

Imoshen flinched. 'Why do you shun me?'

He looked up at her. Tears glistened in her eyes and her hair hung loose on her shoulders. She appeared vulnerable, yet he knew what she could do.

He swallowed. 'You bear the same marks on your chest as Reothe.'

'Not by choice. I told you he called on the Ancients to draw me to him.'

Tulkhan tore his gaze from her. If Imoshen with all her gifts could not stand against Reothe, what chance had he, a Mere-man? Truly, he was a dead man who walked and talked.

He turned away from her.

After an eternity he heard Imoshen rise and return to her room. Alone again, Tulkhan covered his eyes to hide his hollow soul.

IMOSHEN TRIED TO pretend that it didn't hurt when people refused to meet her eyes. Twenty days had passed since she had freed the snow cats. No one had broached the subject with her, but the rumours were more damaging than direct confrontation.

Tulkhan filled his days with feverish activity and by night she heard him pacing, consumed by something she did not understand and could not ease because he kept her at a distance.

'T'Imoshen?'

She glanced up to see a palace servant looking distinctly uncomfortable. The woman gave the old obeisance.

'Yes?' Imoshen straightened, putting aside her reading.

There was a muffled shout from the room beyond and several people shoved past the servant. Imoshen's hand went to her dagger but, even as her fingers closed around the hilt, she realised these people were not a threat.

'We won't be kept out. The Empress would have seen us!' declared a stout matron.

'And so will I,' Imoshen said easily, rising and approaching them.

For an instant the woman and her three companions simply stared at Imoshen.

The matron recovered first, making the deep obeisance. 'It is our right to be heard.'

Imoshen smiled at her belligerent tone. 'Then speak. I am listening.'

'For nearly three hundred years my family have lived in our home. We don't want to live anywhere else. You tell him that we don't want another house.'

The others joined in noisily.

'Wait.' Imoshen held up her hand. 'Who is asking you to leave your homes?'

'The Ghebite General. He's tearing down our houses!'

'What?' Imoshen bristled. 'When?'

'Right now. We were given notice the day after the Spring Festival. The Beatific said she would speak with him, but this very morning his men arrived and began destroying our homes.'

'I will see this for myself!'

Imoshen marched out of the palace with an escort of angry townsfolk following close behind. There were others waiting in the square.

As they led Imoshen through the streets of old T'Diemn, she heard wails of distress and the sound of builders at work. She rounded the end of the lane to discover the source of the disturbance. Ghebite soldiers had moved all the families' personal belongings out of a row of houses and were demolishing the buildings.

'What is going on here?' Imoshen demanded of the first man she saw.

He flinched at her tone. 'Following the General's orders.'

'And where is General Tulkhan?'

He pointed and Imoshen strode forward followed by a crowd of townsfolk. Little children skipped ahead of her, shouting and calling to their friends.

She found the General standing beside a kitchen table which was perched incongruously on the cobbles amid piles of pots and pans. The table was covered with large drawings and two men were discussing these with Tulkhan.

'General?' Imoshen greeted him, aware as always that his Ghebite companions resented her presence. 'I would speak with you, alone.'

'Of course.'

A boy chased his pet pig past them, calling it by name. Several children raced after him, eager to help. The General's eyes met hers and she smiled.

But she waited until Tulkhan's men moved away before speaking. 'Why have you thrown these people out of their homes?'

'They received notices. They'll be relocated.'

'That's not what I asked. Why are you doing this?'

'I'm securing T'Diemn,' Tulkhan said. 'Take a look at this.'

Imoshen glanced down at the plans for T'Diemn. 'What has this to do with my question? You can't turn people out of their homes.'

Tulkhan tapped the drawings. 'This other Reothe was an excellent engineer. See how he designed the streets of old T'Diemn so defenders could be marched to each of the four gates to hold off attackers. He also left the inside wall free of buildings so that troops could be rushed along the ring-road to reinforce a breach in the wall. But over the years people built right up against it, destroying access.' Tulkhan rolled up the plans. 'I'm removing the houses which interfere with the defensive integrity of the wall.'

'But these are people's homes, General. Families have lived in them for hundreds of years.'

'I'll build them new homes.'

'It's not the same.' She could tell he did not understand. How could he, when he'd spent the last eleven years travelling with his army? 'These people are part of a whole neighbourhood. They've known everyone from birth, their parents knew their neighbours' parents. You're taking more than their homes, you're taking their heritage.'

'They will be generously compensated for their hardship.'

'Tulkhan, gold does not solve everything. Think of the people.'

'I *am* thinking of the people!' He rounded on her, then seemed to collect himself. 'T'Diemn can't be defended as it stands, Imoshen. It is absurd to let perfectly good defensive works fall into decay because a few people built their houses in the wrong places. I am trying to make T'Diemn secure from attack. To save the city.'

'But what of all those people who have their homes outside the old wall? What will become of them?'

'I'll get around to them. My engineers and I are working on that.'

He looked so pleased and determined Imoshen sighed. 'General Tulkhan, we are not at war. The rebels are contained in the Keldon Highlands. All of T'Diemn accepts you as their Protector General. Is this really necessary?'

He studied her, his face unreadable. 'You stand before me, princess of a conquered people, yet you still ask this? I took Fair Isle because your people had grown complacent. No one will take Fair Isle from me!'

Imoshen flinched.

'Soon the rebels will be raiding the fertile plains, causing trouble for my commanders who hold estates in the south.' He urged her towards a lane which led directly to the old wall. A ladder stood against the stonework. 'Come up and see what I plan.'

She followed him up onto the walls of old T'Diemn. They were wide enough for four people to walk abreast. Her ancestors had designed well. To the west she could see the river gleaming in the sunshine as it wound its way through the countryside, dropping lower and lower, lock by lock, to the tidal flats and the sea. Closer still the new part of the city fell away below them, masses of pointing roofs and spires. It was a prosperous, proud city.

A complacent city?

'Look at T'Diemn sprawling before us, Imoshen. It is hopelessly under-defended. Where are the earth works, ditches and palisades? With the population and wealth of this city, the townsfolk could have built defences right around the new part. They had all last spring and summer to prepare their defences. But no. They sat here, turning a blind eye to my approaching army.'

'What approaching army are you preparing to defeat?' Imoshen asked.

Tulkhan frowned at her. 'Have you forgotten the threat of Reothe and the Keldon nobles? This is basic warcraft. Bluff and counterbluff. You suffer from four hundred years of peace. Your people fought their wars offshore: territorial wars, trade wars, diplomatic wars. But, ultimately, what is taken by force must be held by force.'

Imoshen drew a calming breath. 'Will you not reconsider, General? Why not build new defences around the whole of T'Diemn? You will raise the ire of the people if you pull down their homes. Does the security of old T'Diemn outweigh the goodwill of the townsfolk?'

He shook his head. 'I knew you would not understand. This must be done, Imoshen.'

'Will you pull down the shops and homes on the fortified bridges as well? When will you stop?'

'When I think T'Diemn is defensible.'

'Then make it defensible, but don't interfere with the old city.'

'What if the outer defences are breached? If an invading army took all of new T'Diemn, the people could retreat to the old city and hold out against their attackers.'

'Only if they needed to. Why do you think Fair Isle *suffered* from four hundred years of peace? We used diplomacy instead of force.'

'And when diplomacy no longer worked, what happened?' he countered. 'A wise commander plans ahead. I swore to be Protector General of Fair Isle and I keep my word!'

Imoshen searched his face for any sign of softening. He looked strained and tired but determined. 'I think you are making a mistake, General. It is not the size of the defences but the heart of the defenders which keeps the enemy at bay. If you lose the hearts of the townsfolk, you might as well open all the gates and invite Reothe in. Please reconsider.'

He folded his arms, looking out over T'Diemn. 'I do what I know to be right, Imoshen.'

It was clear he would not be swayed and she suspected he was right. She would have to persuade her people to accept his actions.

While Imoshen climbed down the ladder, Tulkhan remained staring out over the city. Thousands of people trusted him to defend them. He could not fail them just because a few families did not want to be moved.

He returned to the ground. As he strode out of the alley he could hear the impatient mutterings of the townsfolk and Imoshen's clear voice. If she was stirring up the people against him he would throttle her.

'You would come to me and cry, we have lost everything because you did not defend us.' Imoshen's words reached him. He stopped, surprised. She stood there on the kitchen table, waving the rolled-up plans in one hand. 'Four hundred years ago T'Reothe the Builder made our city safe from attack, but we have grown complacent. With these plans we will make T'Diemn safe from an invading army. Never again will you face the likes of King Gharavan. Never again will children and old folk be chased down the streets of T'Diemn and slaughtered.

'I congratulate those people who are giving up their homes for the good of T'Diemn. We must praise them and make them welcome in their new homes. And I thank the General Tulkhan for thinking ahead and planning for the safety of everyone in T'Diemn!'

Imoshen flung her open hand in his direction and the people turned towards him. Those who were being asked to move eyed him resentfully, but others cheered. They crowded around Tulkhan and soon he could not move for the crush.

When the crowd dispersed, he approached the table where Imoshen stood, leaning on both elbows to study the plans.

She straightened, greeting him with a quick smile.

'Thank you,' he said, his voice meant only for her. 'Even if you used your gift to sway them.'

Her eyes narrowed. 'You do not understand my people, General. The higher we rise the more we serve. To serve is to be elevated. I have called on these people to serve the greater good and they will do it because not to do so would make them social outcasts.'

'To what do I owe this change of heart?'

'I concede you may be right,' she told him with a grin. 'T'Diemn is prosperous. We can afford to build strong defences. It will reassure the people. The rulers of the Old Empire were too proud. I will not make the same mistake.'

Tulkhan met her glittering eyes and knew it was true. If he had delayed entering Fair Isle long enough for Imoshen and Reothe to be bonded and united in defence of Fair Isle, he would never have taken the island.

Imoshen offered her arm. 'Walk with me, General? It is good to let the people see us united.'

Tulkhan linked arms with her but did not drop his defences. As they strolled along, pausing to speak with the people of T'Diemn, he watched Imoshen charm butcher-boy and guildmaster alike.

'The people seem ready to forgive you the stone lovers and even tamed snow cats,' he remarked when they were alone again.

She looked up at him, her features solemn. 'When will you forgive me? My bed is cold and lonely. At night I hear you pace the Emperor's chamber. What troubles you, Tulkhan?'

But he shook his head. As much as he longed to share his fears with her, he could not.

IMOSHEN STUDIED TULKHAN'S design for T'Diemn's outer defence. She had to admire his clever use of the natural terrain, the hills and river locks.

But the defence of the capital was not what concerned her now. It was mid-spring and Reothe's rebels threatened the fragile peace. In the small moon since the Spring Festival, the snow had melted in the Keldon passes and the rebels had grown bold.

Reothe did not raid the farmers or the hard-working villagers; instead, he attacked the traders, whose tales of woe would be carried to the capital, and the merchants who could afford the loss squealed the loudest.

The Ghebites talked of capturing Reothe and executing him. They were eager to avenge the deaths of their brothers-at-arms, for on three separate occasions Reothe had surrounded Ghebites on their new estates and massacred them, leaving only one man alive to tell of the attack. Reothe flaunted his ability to come and go protected by the locals.

Many of the Ghebite commanders had dispersed to lay claim to their estates, others were prepared to accompany the General into the Keldon Highlands to answer Reothe's challenge. Imoshen knew Tulkhan must retaliate or risk losing half the ground he taken last summer, but she feared Reothe would lead Tulkhan's army on a wild chase through the Keldon Highlands, picking off his men one by one.

As Tulkhan strode into the room resplendent in his battle finery, her heart contracted with longing.

'We are ready to ride,' the General said. 'I will leave you Piers and a company of men to hold T'Diemn. You are my voice. While I am gone you must oversee the construction of the city's new defences.'

'I know what I must do.' Imoshen came to her feet. 'Won't you reconsider? Use me to draw Reothe out. I'll tell him I've had second thoughts and ask him to meet me somewhere between here and the highlands. But I must be there to meet him or he will sense it is a trap. I'm willing –'

'Well, I'm not.' Tulkhan feared once Reothe had Imoshen in his power she would succumb to his strange allure. 'I won't risk losing you and the child.'

'Not even to hold Fair Isle?'

He held her eyes.

'Then you could lose it all.'

Tulkhan turned his hand over in supplication. 'I will come back when the baby is due.'

'I fear...' Imoshen's voice faltered. 'I fear you might never return!'

Silence stretched between them.

Tulkhan opened his arms and she ran to him. He felt her shoulders shake with silent sobs and he found her lips, embracing her with all the strength in his body. If only he could put everything else aside, but that was impossible. He could not truly claim Imoshen until Reothe was dead, yet he travelled into the highlands knowing a Mere-man could not hope to defeat a T'En warrior.

Closing himself away from Imoshen, Tulkhan stepped out of her arms.

'Have you no kind word for me before you go?' she asked, searching his face.

'I am a warrior, not a courtier.' Steeling himself against her disappointment, he turned and strode out.

Imoshen stared at the place where Tulkhan had stood only a moment before. It still seemed to vibrate with the force of his personality and the words they had left unsaid.

Prowling to the window, she watched the men in the stable yards awaiting orders to mount up. What if Tulkhan was killed on the battlefield?

She would not be able to hold the Ghebites. If the General died, his commanders would turn on the island's inhabitants like ravenous wolves, breaking into factions, warring amongst themselves for the spoils. She couldn't allow this. If Tulkhan fell she would have to ally herself with Reothe to save Fair Isle from the remaining Ghebites.

This realisation frightened her. She feared Reothe, feared that he would try to dominate her with his superior T'En powers. But what frightened her most was the knowledge that she would not be averse to standing at his side – perhaps it was where she truly belonged. If Tulkhan was dead and she had done all she could to forestall another summer of war, then she would have no choice but to join the last T'En warrior.

She knew that an alliance with Reothe would not be a cold political joining. Never that. She felt her gift surge and forced it down.

The thought of losing Tulkhan was torture, but it was something she must face. Was it only last autumn that she has thought there was a right and wrong? Tears for the innocent she had once been stung her eyes. Bitter experience had taught her there was no right or wrong, only decisions to be made on constantly shifting grounds to ensure the one all-important outcome. Survival.

The shout went up. The men were moving out.

Clasping one hand under her belly to compensate for the weight of the child, she hastened out of the room and along the gallery.

Before stepping out onto the balcony overlooking the square Imoshen paused to straighten her hair and assume a regal stance. She watched as the mass of humanity below formed disciplined ranks, mounted men to one side, foot soldiers to the other, all wearing the traditional purple and red Ghebite cloaks. Imoshen wrinkled her nose. She must speak to Tulkhan about designing their own standard and colours. It offended her to see his men wearing King Gharavan's colours.

The ranks of Tulkhan's men filling the square were a grand sight, but their discipline would do them no good in the Keldon Highlands. The rebels knew the treacherous ravines intimately, and cunning traps awaited their enemies. Cavalry was useless. Battle-trained destriers were no match for wiry mountain ponies. Imoshen's heart twisted with pity. Few of these men would return to T'Diemn.

When General Tulkhan rode into view she caught her breath, already grieving for him. As he spoke to his men, the breeze carried his words over the ranks away from her. She watched him walk his horse backwards. The proud black beast reared, dancing on its back legs. A shout went up.

Imoshen had to smile. Tulkhan loved this kind of display. He had spent his formative years with the army, leading men. It was what he was.

The horse dropped back down onto four legs, pivoting in a circle, and Tulkhan caught sight of her on the balcony. She raised her arm above her head in salute and he returned the salute, standing in the stirrups.

Imoshen's heart swelled in her chest. She loved him but he would never believe it. Lowering her arm, her hand settled over her belly.

He brought his closed fist to his chest over his heart, then he flung his hand open toward her.

Her skin grew warm with the significance of his gesture. How could he love her, knowing her as he did, knowing how truly Other she was? Tears blurred her vision and she lifted her hand to cover her racing heart. Tulkhan had grown as dear to her as the very breath she took.

The men began a Ghebite chant.

Tulkhan wheeled his horse and rode through the ranks, leading the army through the city's streets to the fortified bridge.

'ANY WORD, MERKAH?' Imoshen asked, as she had every day for almost thirty days.

The maid looked up from her handiwork. She knew her mistress well enough now not to bother standing and making a formal obeisance every time Imoshen approached. 'No, T'Imoshen.'

'Very well. I will be in the library.' Imoshen handed Merkah her riding cloak. She had just returned from overseeing the progress of the T'Diemn's eastern defences.

As she walked down the gallery long slanting arrows of afternoon light filled the broad hall, making the woodwork glow. The sight should have cheered her, but she felt distant and cold. There had been no word from Tulkhan since he sent her a short communication soon after he left. Surely she would have sensed it if he had been killed?

He was due to return for the summer's cusp festival and stay on, because the baby could come any time after that.

What if the baby did not come? What if her son was more T'En than True-man and she continued heavily pregnant until the cusp of autumn? The child had to have a little of the General in him, but she had no way of knowing how much. She had only the official records to go by, and because of the vow of chastity no other pure T'En woman had given birth in six hundred years.

By the time she reached the library she was panting with exertion, for the baby lay like a great summer fruit nestled in her body. The Keeper of Knowledge did not greet her as she entered. She suspected the old man was in the kitchen courtyard, arguing with the cook and drinking apple cider. Not that she could blame him, the weather was too perfect to stay indoors.

Imoshen went to her favourite spot on the broad day bed. Spread on the low table before her were her inks and papers. She was making a list of works that were referred to in the library but were no longer available. It was the key to a mystery which had gradually presented itself to her. Poems and treatises on the T'En gifts which everyone took for granted in the old texts no longer existed. Why?

Imoshen immersed herself in her reading, cross-referencing the quotes and their sources. The movement of the fingers of light from the library windows marked the passing of time.

After a while she let the scroll fall, arched her back and closed her eyes. She was weary. Only so much of this could stem her anxiety, and then it returned. Where was the General?

Without warning, a hand clamped over her mouth. Terror froze her limbs as a cold blade stroked her neck. Assassins? Her attacker increased the pressure, forcing her into the cushions.

'Quiet, Imoshen. It's only me.'

Reothe's familiar voice did not comfort her. When she nodded her understanding he let her go. Disbelief flooded her as she propped herself up. Reothe pushed the papers aside and perched on the low table.

'Only you? Is that meant to reassure me?' It pleased Imoshen to detect no tremor in her voice. She was rewarded with a genuine smile from Reothe. Then she cursed herself for caring.

As she slid her hand casually across her body Reothe closed his fingers over the hilt of the knife she now wore sheathed between her breasts for quick access.

Slowly and deliberately, he withdrew the blade. 'Dainty, but deadly in the right hands.' He did not return the weapon.

'I have to know...' She played for time, trying to guess what he wanted. His fine silver hair was halfway down his back now and he wore clean but ancient peasant garments. He smelled of fresh herbs and dust. Dust? She must not let anything distract her. 'How did you get in here?'

He laughed softly. 'You forget I grew up roaming the palace. I doubt there is a secret passage I don't know. Our ancestors were great ones for intrigue. Anything built before the Age of Discernment is riddled with secret passages.'

He looked thinner. His narrow features, so like her own, were more defined, as though he had been living on the edge both mentally and physically. She felt an odd sense of recognition and an unwelcome anticipation warm her body.

Reothe had saved her life. He knew so much more about his T'En gifts than she. His knowledge both awed her and frightened her. Without warning she felt her T'En senses flex. A strong sense of Reothe enveloped her. He was a drawn bow string, all coiled power. Her heart rate increased in response.

'Why are you here, Reothe?'

A gasp of pleasure escaped him. 'Don't stop.'

'Stop what?'

His sharp eyes met hers. 'Your touch is exquisite.'

'I didn't touch...' The words died on her lips. 'I didn't mean to –'

'Don't.' He shook his head, slipping off the table to kneel on the floor beside her. 'Don't deny me, Imoshen.'

She drew back, making him smile.

'Is it me you don't trust, or yourself?'

His wine-dark eyes glittered intense and disturbing. For all that he was smiling and his voice sounded reasonable, even indulgent, she sensed a deep anger in him.

His gaze went to the laces on her underdress, where the swelling of her belly strained the material. She had not bothered to have special clothes made to accommodate her growing child, relying for the most part on the all-covering tabard on official occasions. Imoshen felt vulnerable, and wished she had worn one today.

'This explains much.' Reothe whispered. He gestured towards her belly with the knife.

'Reothe,' she warned.

'This should have been our child, Imoshen. You hid its existence from me. I did not think you so cunning.'

She shook her head, knowing only that the need to protect her child overrode everything else. Yet, when he cut the lacing she didn't protest. The material of her underdress parted, falling away to reveal the rise of her pale skin and the curve of her breasts, ripe with pregnancy. Her skin was patterned with fine blue veins like marble.

Reothe drew in his breath sharply. He swallowed and slipped her knife into his bootstrap. As his hand hovered over her flesh, Imoshen's skin tingled in anticipation of his touch. A luxurious longing crept through her limbs.

Imoshen looked down, silently cursing herself. It was always this way with Reothe.

'What will you do if the Ghebite rejects the baby?' he asked. 'It could be almost pure Dhamfeer.'

'Or more True-man.'

'So it is a male child.'

She nodded, regretting the slip.

'I heard a rumour. They say the General can't father children,' he smiled. 'They are saying the baby is mine.'

She flushed, trying to pull herself up, but the weight of the baby made her slow. Reothe casually grasped the back of the day bed. She didn't want to come in contact with his skin so she stayed where she was, half reclining. 'But you know that isn't true.'

Reothe met her eyes, amused, and she realised he was happy to let people believe the babe was his. Fury curled inside her. It would be the ultimate irony for Tulkhan to finally father a child and have everyone believe it wasn't his.

Reothe leaned closer and inhaled. 'You smell different. I like it.'

Imoshen swallowed. 'Don't do this.'

He nuzzled the heavy swell of her breast. 'Tell me to stop.'

'Stop.'

She felt him smile, his cheek on her flesh. 'You didn't mean it.'

Despair warred with desire. The first time he had touched her he had wakened something in her, something that was his to call, and no amount of logic could sway her body's response.

His breath tickled her throat and cheek, as he raised his head, exploring her. She felt his lips on her jaw, travelling across to her mouth. She could turn away or she could turn towards him.

She chose to do nothing.

With infinite delicacy he nibbled her mouth, his tongue brushed the crease of her lips. 'Part for me.'

She felt more than heard his words. The impulse was there, but she contained it, refused to welcome him. It would be all he needed to destroy her resolve.

A sigh escaped him and she opened her eyes to see him looking down at her, exasperated yet affectionate.

'You are an annoying creature, Imoshen. How do you know that I won't take by force what you refuse me? I know you long for me.'

She swallowed, making no answer because to say anything would be to admit more than she cared to.

He leant back, ruffling papers on the table. Absently he picked one up, reading it swiftly. Imoshen wanted to stop him. Her lack of skill was a weapon he could use against her.

Reothe looked up and fixed his gaze on her. 'You search for information on the T'En.'

She nodded. 'Our gifts are mentioned in passing, but –'

'I know. I've already travelled the same path. I can tell you why our ancestors came here. I can reveal what has been deliberately hidden from us.'

She sat up eagerly. 'Yes?'

He smiled. 'Come away with me now. Your general wanders the ranges, harried by my people. We could rout him, you and I.'

'And then you would share your knowledge with me?' Imoshen heard the bitterness in her voice.

'I would share everything with you.'

His meaning was unmistakable. A rush of heady longing swept through her. The urge to go to him was almost overpowering. She fought it, desperate to keep some kind of equilibrium. When she opened her eyes Reothe was watching her with intense fascination.

'It is only a matter of time,' he told her. 'The General knows it. He drives himself trying to deny it. Come away with me now. Put him out of his misery. He's only a Mere-man and a barbarous Ghebite, but I have to admit a certain admiration for him. Like a fish caught on the hook he is putting up a mighty battle, but the end is inevitable. He doesn't deserve it really.'

A knot twisted in Imoshen's chest. Tulkhan did not deserve a lingering agony.

'He saved us,' Reothe said softly. 'The night I came to find you wandering lost in death's shadow, he anchored us. I drew on his strength, without it we would have both been doomed.'

Fear made Imoshen's heart plunge. She had no memory of that time but the church taught that without the guidance of the Parakletos a soul might wander death's shadow for eternity, prey to the vengeful beings who were trapped there.

Heat stained her cheeks. 'You saved me at risk to your soul, I –'

'Don't demean what we share by thanking me.' Anger hardened his features.

Imoshen understood him only too well. 'We share nothing!'

'You deny what you know to be true. Besides, I have the Sight. I have seen our future. I recognised you the day we met.'

Dismay flooded Imoshen. 'It would be so much easier if I could hate you.'

'And it would be so much easier if I could kill you.' His smile was bitter.

Imoshen understood. If Reothe were to kill her now and plant something to implicate the Ghebites, Tulkhan's tenuous hold on the island would be shattered. Her death would smooth a path for Reothe to retake Fair Isle.

'Why don't you kill me?'

He laced his fingers through her left hand, lifting it up so that their forearms pressed together. The bonding scars touched.

Reothe pressed her knuckles to his lips. 'Because I would be alone forever.'

'There are other women, countless willing women, from what I've heard!'

His smile made her wish she could have cut out her jealous tongue.

'True, and I have had so many of them.' He cast her a teasing glance. 'But only you share our T'En heritage. For now you believe what you have with this Ghebite is enough. You might even love him a little. But he is only a Mere-man. You don't know what we could have.'

'Enough, Reothe.' She pushed him aside and surged to her feet, stalking away from the day bed.

'Go on, run away, Imoshen. You can't run from what you know is true.'

She could feel him watching her as she paced. The late afternoon sunlight could not dissolve the knot of cold terror around her heart. She hugged her body, pulling the material of her underdress together. 'Why are you here, Reothe? Why risk your life to taunt me?'

He stood across the room from her yet she felt his presence as intimately as if his breath stroked her flesh. She knew he was using his T'En gift on her.

'Don't do that!'

'Why? Because you like it? Surely you can't have forgotten what day this is?'
She stared at him appalled. No one else had remembered.

'It's the anniversary of your birthing day,' Reothe said. 'Today you are eighteen and we would have been bonded.'

Her eyes closed as she registered the blow, a cruel reminder of the decision she had been forced to make.

She sensed Reothe moving towards her. When she opened her eyes he stood before her. The sun's rays hit the polished floor, bathing them both in light. She read a calculating wariness in his features and suspected he was manipulating her feelings for him, for Tulkhan.

'I'm not going with you, Reothe, and you can't drag me kicking and screaming from the palace, no matter how many secret passages you know. Someone would notice.'

Defiant words, but Imoshen knew they sprang from desperation and so did he.

'I brought you a gift, Imoshen.'

'I don't want anything from you.'

'You'll want this. It is the last thing my parents gave me before they killed themselves.' He pulled a slim volume from his jerkin. It was about half the size of the T'Enchiridion. 'It belongs to the T'En.'

Despite herself Imoshen held out her hand.

Silently he joined her. The book looked unremarkable in his hand, its scuffed kidskin cover attesting to its great age.

Imoshen took it, turning the worn embossing to the light.

'T'Endomaz. The T'En laws,' she translated, her heart hammering with excitement. Her fingers trembled as she turned to the title page, where a name was scrawled in childlike script. 'T'Ashmyr? Could it have belonged to Ashmyr the First when he was a boy?'

'He was a pure throwback like ourselves,' Reothe said.

Imoshen's mouth was so dry she could hardly speak. Could this book really date from the Age of Tribulation? Five hundred years!

Reverently she turned to the first page. Disappointment made her gasp. 'It's encrypted.'

'Then you don't recognise the code? I thought perhaps the Aayel had taught you.'

'No. My parents forbade her to teach me anything about the T'En. All I now is what she let slip.' Bitterness tore at her. 'T'Endomaz. An encrypted set of laws. How do you know they are ours? This looks similar to the T'Enchiridion, which is for everyone. And Ashmyr is a popular name.'

'Close your eyes, Imoshen. Hold the book in your left hand. Tell me what you feel? No. Not with your T'En senses. I've tried that. It is as if someone has erased the book's past. You must rely only on your sense of touch.'

She frowned but did as he said. What was she supposed to feel?

To her T'En senses the book seemed blank when it should have held a sense of antiquity considering its age. That in itself was suspicious.

'Feel with your fingertips,' he whispered.

Then she understood. Her eyes flew open. 'There are six smooth patches on the cover. This book's cover has been worn by the touch of a left-handed person with six fingers!'

He nodded. 'It is ours, Imoshen.'

'But we can't read it.' She could have wept with frustration and loss.

His hands closed over hers, shutting the book. His face was suffused with evangelical passion. 'I give you the T'Endomaz. I charge you to unlock the encryption and reveal our heritage.'

And, in that moment, Imoshen feared what she might learn. 'No. Keep it. I don't want to be beholden to you.'

She thrust the book into his hands and would have pulled away but he caught her arm. His contained fury made her skin crawl.

'How can you deny what you are, Imoshen?'

Flicking free of his grasp she turned away. The swelling of her belly hit him and they both looked down.

Imoshen felt the baby kick in protest.

Reothe's free hand closed over the slope of her stomach, pressing through the gap in the material so that his flesh touched hers. There was an anticipation in him which made her teeth ache. She sucked in her breath with an audible gasp.

'Don't resist!' he hissed.

In that instant her guard was down. She felt a wave of tension roll through her body, her knees nearly gave way. The baby twisted inside her.

Imoshen swung her arms in an arc and broke all contact with him. 'I won't let you hurt –'

He laughed bitterly. 'You have a strange idea of me.'

'I have no idea,' she admitted.

'Like you, I am only ensuring my survival,' he said. 'Go on. Call the guards. You could have called them any time and had me arrested, had me killed attempting to escape. Ask yourself why you haven't called them.'

She drew breath to scream for the guards, but he caught her to him, his free hand covered her mouth.

His laughter unnerved her. 'I deserved that.'

She hated him yet recognised herself in him.

'I am going, Imoshen,' he whispered. 'And because I can't have you discovering my secrets, I'm going to have to do this.'

'What?' The word was muffled but clear enough.

'Kiss me and find out.'

His hand slipped from her mouth to her throat, cradling her jaw. His fingers slid up into her hair at the back of her neck.

'Why should I?'

'Because if you resist it will be painful for both of us. I am only going to steal a few minutes from you.'

He could do that? What a useful trick, one she would like to know.

Imoshen pretended to consider. 'Very well.'

He looked a little startled, as if he hadn't expected her to agree.

Imoshen kept her face impassive as she smiled inside. She was sure he could not do this without her discovering how. She would have all his secrets out of him. But no – she mustn't think, he might...

Lifting her face she felt his breath on her skin. And she knew at that moment she was fooling herself. She wanted to kiss Reothe, had always wanted him.

'Imoshen,' he whispered raggedly.

Her heart lurched.

Then his mouth was on hers and the sweetness of his touch negated all thought. It was the elixir of life. It flowed through her body, unbearably rich and fragile.

She heard his voice in her head, but his lips didn't form the words. 'This is just a taste of what we could have, Imoshen. But I can't let you learn all my tricks, you're much too clever already.'

Then everything faded.

Chapter Sixteen

SCREAMING...

Imoshen wished they would stop. Someone grabbed her.

'Get your hands off me!' Imoshen felt disoriented and nauseous with the sudden swing from deep sleep to awareness.

'T'Imoshen...' Merkah cried. 'You've come back to us.'

She was lying on the day bed with a shawl thrown over her. Its silky material covered her bare breasts and that made her recall Reothe slitting the laces of her underdress. As Imoshen struggled to sit up a book fell from her lap onto the floor. Reothe's gift.

She picked it up, tucking it under the shawl. She searched the room. A dozen Ghebites and palace servants stood clustered around something near the window. Fear gripped her. Was Reothe hurt?

'What happened?'

'He killed him,' Merkah supplied unhelpfully.

Imoshen's world went grey. 'Who?'

'T'Reothe killed the Keeper of the Knowledge.'

'No!' Imoshen's denial was instinctive. Reothe would not do that. The Keeper was a defenceless old man. But she could not afford to defend the rebel leader. 'What happened? I... I remember nothing.'

Merkah seemed to accept this at face value. 'The Keeper was returning to his post. When he opened the door he saw Reothe with you. He was...' Merkah coloured.

Imoshen pressed the material to her body. 'Tell me, I must know.'

'The Keeper says Reothe pressed his face against the bare flesh of your belly.'

Imoshen's hand pressed over her baby. Fear was a cold band around her heart. 'Then?'

'The Keeper was at the door. He called for help. Before anyone could come, Reothe dragged him inside and killed him.'

'How do you know this?' Imoshen asked.

'He told us.'

'But you said he was dead.'

'Almost dead.'

'Is he still alive?'

'Yes, but –'

'Enough.' Exasperated, Imoshen swung her legs off the couch. Despite Merkah's protests she hurried over to the knot of men. They were lifting the old Keeper to his feet. To save the Ghebites from embarrassment she tied the shawl across her breasts.

'The shadows are too deep. Bring candles. Place him here on the table,' Imoshen ordered. She noted Kinraid the Vaygharian watching her, but there was no time to curse the luck that would bring him of all men to her rescue.

Imoshen grasped the old man's hand. Yes, he was dying, but his gaze cleared as she looked into his eyes. 'What happened?'

He smiled. 'He was such a bright boy. No one else cared about the old manuscripts, but he read them all.'

'Reothe?'

The Keeper nodded.

Someone set candles on the table, illuminating the old man's features.

'What happened?' Imoshen pressed. 'They say he hurt you?'

She searched the Keeper's face, noting how one side drooped. He'd had a seizure. Reothe had not done that, unless the surprise of seeing him had triggered it.

'I had to call for help. I didn't want...' He seemed to recollect himself. 'Reothe grabbed me, dragged me into the room. He touched the back of my head then suddenly I had this blinding pain in my chest. I could not breathe. I knew nothing until I came around on the floor.'

Imoshen nodded. 'I'll brew you something to drink. It will help you sleep.'

But nothing would help him. In her work as a healer she had seen death too many times not to recognise it. Within a day or two he would have another seizure and his heart would simply stop beating.

'Before you go, Lady Protector...' Kinraid appeared before her. 'The men and I want to know how Reothe got in here and how he escaped.'

'I can't tell you.' Imoshen knew her dislike for the Vaygharian must have been evident. 'Reothe grabbed me, held something over my face, and the next thing I knew I was here with all of you.'

'Then you did not see him come, or go?'

'No.' It was the truth.

'Then you don't mind if we search the library?'

A protest leapt to the Keeper's blue lips and Imoshen had to smile.

'You may search, but you will not destroy or damage any of the valuable manuscripts stored here. Now I must go and brew this tonic. Have the Keeper carried to his room.'

She returned to her own room with Merkah at her heels. 'I must concentrate on my healing. Leave me.'

As soon as the door closed, Imoshen withdrew the slim volume, still warm from her body. T'Endomaz. The law of the T'En. She desperately wanted to believe it had belonged to the boy emperor, T'Ashmyr, greatest of all the T'En rulers.

What if someone stole the book before she could translate it? She strode to her chest and threw it open but it was too obvious a hiding place. Her gaze fell on the Aayel's T'Enchiridion. The book should have been burnt with her great aunt, in keeping with tradition, but Imoshen had saved it, knowing she would have to refresh her memory to say the words at the Harvest Feast the following day.

Swiftly she retrieved the T'Enchiridion. It was twice the size of the T'Endomaz. As she unsheathed her knife from its original hiding place, she realised Reothe must have replaced it. She slit the inner lining of the larger book's back cover and slid the T'Endomaz inside. Unless someone inspected her copy of the T'Enchiridion closely, they would not find it.

Reothe had given her more than a book. He had given her the key to controlling her gifts. She could not help comparing his bonding gift to Tulkhan's. How well Reothe knew her. But she was not going to bond with the last T'En warrior. He might claim to know the future but the Sight was often misleading.

She had bonded with Tulkhan and nothing could change that, not even Reothe's lure of a union so powerful it would unlock the secret of all her gifts.

It WAS THE talk of T'Diemn. Reothe had entered the palace unseen, seduced T'Imoshen and killed a dozen men before disappearing in a flash of light.

It brought Tulkhan back in less than ten days.

He returned without warning late one evening after Imoshen had already retired to her room. She was reading by the hearth when he stalked in. The sight of him made her heart leap with joy, then plunge in despair when she saw his expression.

Tulkhan threw his cloak and gloves on the table then strode towards Imoshen, thinking she looked more beautiful than ever, her fine features softened by the bloom of new life. This late in her pregnancy a Ghebite woman would have been hidden away from all but the women of his house-line. Instead of being repelled by her changed body he wanted to run his hands all over her, to savour every ripe curve. But he must know the truth first.

'Is it true what they're saying? Did he rape you?'

'Of course not.' She laughed and he wanted to strangle her. 'That is a Ghebite custom.'

Cursing, he ignored the insult. 'Then you submitted willingly?'

'I was not conscious when the Keeper found me with Reothe.'

'In every village or nobleman's keep I hear the same thing,' Tulkhan growled. 'They are saying this was not the first time, that the babe you carry is his and you two plot to kill me when it suits you.'

Imoshen came to her feet, pushing herself out of the chair. The added weight of the baby made her movements slower but no less graceful. It hurt him to look on her, knowing what was being said. According to the rumours she was sweet treachery itself.

She approached him with her hands out, palm up, her face gentle and mocking, but underneath he thought he read an urgency not quite masked.

'General, how can you worry about what they are saying when you know you were the first and only one for me?'

He knew it was true. He caught her to him, feeling the hard swelling of the baby between them. A number of swift kicks told him his son resented the pressure. Shocked, he met Imoshen's eyes. She smiled.

Any day now he would be a father. The evidence had just kicked him. A delighted laugh escaped Tulkhan.

'Our son is an active little being,' she said. 'Tell me, how many men did you lose fighting the rebels?'

The abrupt change of subject startled him. One minute she was all woman, the next she thought and spoke like a man. It unnerved him more than he cared to admit.

He shook his head wearily. 'Too many died for what we achieved. Enough for me to know that you were right. The rebels hide and strike without warning, melting into the ravines so that we can't pursue them. If we do chase them, my men get separated and picked off one by one.' He felt the weight of their deaths. 'But I won't try your way either.'

'So what will you do?'

'I am considering.'

She pressed her face into his neck. Her breath was warm on his skin and his body responded to her touch. She had to twist her hips so that the baby lay to one side of them. This was his child yet Reothe had stolen it from him without ever touching Imoshen.

'Why didn't you call for help?' he demanded. 'We could have had him!'

He felt her sigh.

'Take off your things, you smell of horse and sweat. Let me bathe you.'

She moved through to the bathing room where she checked that the burner was heating and released the valve. Water steamed as it poured into the waist-high tub.

Tulkhan watched in awe. He had not been so long in the palace that he took such extraordinary T'En inventions for granted, especially after a small moon of living rough in the inhospitable ranges.

Imoshen approached him, ready to help him disrobe. The thought of her hands running over his soapy body made him ache to have her despite the Ghebite stricture against such things. By rights they should not share any intimacy in the last small moon of her pregnancy.

But she was deliberately distracting him. Reothe had been here in this very palace. He caught her hands before she could touch him. 'Is there something you aren't telling me?'

She looked obliquely up at him. Her expression seemed calculating but it could have been the way the light fell on her features.

'I did not willingly invite Reothe into the palace. He grew up here. He knows of secret passages.'

'He didn't just appear?'

'In a flash of light? No.' She shook her head, smiling fondly at Tulkhan.

'He grows arrogant.'

'I don't know how he slipped in and out unseen,' she admitted, sounding disgruntled, then she grinned. 'But I'm glad he did, because it brought you back to me.' She tugged at his laces. 'You will stay here now?'

'I don't know. My men are withdrawing –'

'Consolidating.'

'It looks like a defeat. It stinks of defeat.'

'Defeat is when you are dead,' Imoshen told him. 'And not before!'

'True.' He smiled, admiring her spirit.

Imoshen turned her back to him. 'Undo my lacings.'

His heart pounded and his fingers trembled as he fumbled with the knot. Tulkhan swallowed, dry-mouthed.

'Wait,' Imoshen whispered.

She walked over to the door and slid the bolt, then turned to him and let the gown fall from her shoulders. As he drank in her naked splendour, he knew he would put aside all the strictures of his upbringing to have her. What wouldn't he do to possess her?

THE FOLLOWING DAY Tulkhan stood in the map-room studying the Keldon Highlands. If he were to build fortresses to hold the two passes into that region, it would contain the rebel army's freedom of movement. He was considering the reaction of the proud Keldon nobles when a servant scratched at the door.

Merkah entered with the ink and scriber he had requested.

'Close the door,' Tulkhan told her.

She placed the instruments on the table.

'So?' Tulkhan prodded.

'T'Imoshen asked for word of you every day.'

'Did she have any meetings with unexpected people?'

The girl looked perplexed.

'Any of the Keldon nobles or their servants?'

Merkah shook her head.

'So nothing out of the ordinary happened?'

'There was that time when T'Reothe –'

'Apart from that.' Idly Tulkhan wondered what the maid hoped to achieve by spying on her mistress. Surely she realised he would never trust her, and if Imoshen ever discovered her deceit Merkah would lose her position.

'No, General.'

He dismissed the girl and returned to the maps. His men expected him to lead them to victory even against overwhelming odds. But Reothe did not follow the standard rules of warfare. He attacked then melted away, shielded by the sullen farm folk who claimed they hadn't seen him come or go.

A knock on the door interrupted his thoughts.

'Yes?' he answered, expecting one of his men.

An unfamiliar servant backed in with a tray of food.

'I...' The General caught sight of the man who accompanied the servant. 'Come in, Kinraid, join me.' Tulkhan heard the false welcome in his voice and wondered at the man he was becoming.

Twice before, the Vaygharian had brought him news. Tulkhan preferred to let Kinraid believe he had won his trust with information. Besides, he would rather hear it from the snake's mouth than hear Kinraid's lies from people he trusted.

'You may leave,' Tulkhan signalled the servant.

'No, he should stay. What my man has to say will concern you,' Kinraid said.

Tulkhan nodded, masking his irritation. Shoving the maps aside to clear a space on the table, he sat down and stretched out his long legs. He knew he appeared casual and relaxed. It was a lie.

The little man poured a goblet of wine for Tulkhan then his master.

'Speak, Kinraid.' Tulkhan accepted his wine.

'The palace is riddled with secret passages,' he announced. 'That is how Reothe made his way in unobserved.'

'So Imoshen told me.'

'She also claimed to be unconscious. But my man here heard her speaking with the rebel leader.'

'They spoke?' Warily he watched the two men for any sign of complicity. 'Was your man able to make out what they said?'

Kinraid shook his head. 'Their words were muffled by the door, Protector General. But they spoke for a good while before the Keeper returned and caught him ravishing her.'

Tulkhan looked away. The room swam before him.

'My man was one of the first into the room,' Kinraid continued inexorably. 'He found the Keeper on the floor and your wife appeared to be unconscious. She was almost naked. The Keeper said he caught them embracing –'

'If she was unconscious, Reothe was the one doing the embracing,' Tulkhan corrected.

Kinraid's mocking silence presented a thousand possibilities to Tulkhan. Imoshen was a swift thinker. What better way to avert suspicion than to feign a faint?

'Whether she was unconscious or not, it is clear she had the opportunity to call for help,' Kinraid said. 'We could have had the rebel leader arrested and awaiting you even now in the cells below!'

The vision of Reothe brought low was a pleasant one. But Tulkhan doubted if a mere prison cell could contain the T'En warrior for long.

Exasperation filled the General. How was he to defeat Reothe? No one alive today knew the extent of the Dhamfeer's gifts. No one but Imoshen.

The thought drove him to action.

'Where are you going?' Kinraid asked.

Fury filled Tulkhan. He did not have to explain his actions to a man whose trade was treachery.

Seeing the General's expression, Kinraid stepped aside and made an obeisance of apology.

The corridors were remarkably busy with servants. No, Imoshen was not in the library. No, she was not in any of the entertainment rooms, nor the kitchen or storerooms. Someone had seen her go out for a walk.

Tulkhan's boots crunched on the fine white gravel path of the palace's formal garden. What had Reothe said?

The one you love has the most power to hurt you.

Tulkhan felt a bitter smile twist his lips. Love. He had no time for that weakening emotion. He would be utterly calm and trick the truth from her. There she was, through the trees.

Imoshen tilted her head to study the fruit tree. According to the gardeners this blossom-laden bush would produce masses of stone fruit. Now, if she could only take a cutting and graft it onto their fruit trees back at the stronghold.

'Imoshen!'

When she turned to face Tulkhan, his expression made her heart sink. But she waved and maintained her calm, snapping off a twig heavy with blossom before greeting him. 'I think I'll take some cuttings back home. They tell me not only is this tree exquisite in the spring, but it's an excellent fruiter.'

'Imoshen!' He caught her by the shoulders. 'You lied to me. You said Reothe knocked you out. But now I'm told you spoke with him.'

'Your spies took this long to report that?'

He glowered and she cursed her unruly tongue.

'You lied, Imoshen.'

'I omitted to mention it. Reothe did knock me out and I don't know how he did it.' That still rankled. 'But not before we talked.'

'What about?'

It was time for the truth. With a twist she freed her shoulders and rubbed the imprint of his anger from her skin. 'It was the eighteenth anniversary of my birthing day, the day I would have been bonded to Reothe. He came to see me, to ask me to go with him.'

Tulkhan blinked. She could tell he found the truth unpleasant but was not surprised.

'What was your answer?'

'I am here, aren't I?' Imoshen thumped his chest with enough force to let him know she was angry.

Tulkhan absorbed the blow but it appeared nothing would pierce his foul mood.

'Why didn't you call for help?' he demanded. 'We could have had Reothe arrested, awaiting execution even now.'

'I doubt that.'

'So you think a Mere-man couldn't hold one of your kind?'

Imoshen hesitated. She had never seen Tulkhan so furious. Why was he referring to his people as Mere-men? Then she recalled that Reothe had used that term. Had Reothe planted a seed of doubt in the General's mind to fester and finally destroy him?

Instinctively she lifted her hands to cup Tulkhan's face, but he caught her arms, pulling them down. His strength, fuelled by rage, threatened to crush the small bones of her wrists. She gritted her teeth.

'Don't play your Dhamfeer tricks on me!'

'On the contrary, I think Reothe may have played a trick on you.' She kept her voice even. 'I was going to search for a sign of him planting doubts in your mind.'

She felt Tulkhan shudder with revulsion before dropping her wrists.

'I am not your enemy, General.'

'If you wanted to convince me of that, you would have had Reothe lying in a cell when I came back.'

'That is easy for you to say.' A flush of warm, velvety anger rushed through her, leaving a metallic aftertaste on her tongue. 'I am not Reothe's equal. How many of your men would have died trying to restrain him?'

'They would have died gladly for me.'

'I am not so quick to order the deaths of others.'

Tulkhan flinched.

She lifted her hands, palm up. 'General?'

'What was he doing with you naked in his arms?' The agony in his voice cut her.

'I was not naked. The laces on my underdress were cut.'

Tulkhan snorted.

'I don't know what Reothe was doing. I wasn't conscious. He used his gifts. Maybe he was planning to carry me out through the secret passage. In which case you can be glad the Keeper found us when he did.'

The General took a step back from her.

'Tulkhan, please.'

'Answers trip too easily off your tongue, Imoshen. From this day forward I will not be coming to your bed. I no longer trust you.'

It was the final blow. 'Then you are lost, because I am the only one you can trust. I love you.' It was torn from her.

She saw him flinch. Was her love such a terrible thing? His rejection felt like a physical blow. She almost staggered. 'General?'

He turned on his heel and walked off.

Through a blur of unshed tears Imoshen watched the stiff angle of General Tulkhan's broad shoulders as he walked away. He rounded the corner. As the blossoming trees obscured him from sight, her legs gave way and she sank onto the gravel path. The pain in her knees was nothing compared to the pain in her chest.

This was beyond repair. The General would never trust her again. By withdrawing from her he was sealing his fate and fulfilling Reothe's prophecy of his death.

She stared at the gravel. The twig had fallen unnoticed from her hands.

Crushed blossoms lay all around her, trampled into the stones, the fine petals destroyed. Everything she had worked and planned for might be destroyed before the tree could bloom again. If Tulkhan died, she no longer cared if she saw next spring's blossoms.

When Imoshen returned to the palace, weary and desperate to rest, she found the General in their bedchamber. Servants scurried about packing his belongings.

She did not like having their private division witnessed by others. Imoshen met his gaze across the room.

'I will move into my old bedchamber. I stay here only long enough to see my son born,' the General informed her coldly.

Imoshen licked her lips. 'Take a walk with me in the courtyard.'

He would have refused but she let him see that this was not an idle request. Aware of the curious glances of the servants, Imoshen led him outside.

'Well?' he prodded when she did not speak immediately.

'I have not mentioned this before because I am not sure of things.'

'No T'En riddles, Imoshen. Get to the point.'

She rounded on him. 'I am not your Ghebite wife to be browbeaten and bullied.' She paused to draw a calming breath. 'To be frank, I don't know when your son will be born. My mother carried me a full year from conception to birth. Your son is part T'En so it could take –'

'You're saying he might not be born until the Harvest Feast?'

Imoshen nodded and held Tulkhan's eyes. His Ghebite features hid his thoughts too well. 'Throwbacks like myself take a full year, eight small moons to develop.'

'True-men babies take around six,' Tulkhan remarked. 'So you are saying the longer it takes, the more T'En my son will be?'

Imoshen registered his distaste but she would not give him the pleasure of knowing how much it hurt her.

Tulkhan turned away, surprising the servants who were openly watching them through the glass doors. He gestured angrily at them and they hurried back to their tasks.

It was already past the cusp of summer. His son would have been born any day now if he was a True-man. Tulkhan grimaced. Why had he denied the obvious? If the child was half Imoshen's he would be half T'En – an alien creature like Reothe.

His boy might as well be his enemy's son.

Tulkhan strode toward the doors.

'Where are you going?' Imoshen called.

He did not answer her, but flung the door open. 'Don't bother moving my things,' he told the servants. 'I leave to rejoin my men.'

They stared at him and then at Imoshen. Hastily recollecting themselves, they made quick obeisances and left the pair alone.

Tulkhan did not want to be alone with Imoshen. Just to look on her was agony.

'You will leave me like this?' Her voice was raw.

He gave her a cold look, closing himself away from her pain. 'I leave as soon as I am ready.'

IMOSHEN ALLOWED HERSELF to hope when she received Tulkhan's summons to the map-room, but as soon as she saw his grim expression she knew his heart was still set hard against her.

'I've marked the passes. Are there any others?' he demanded, indicating the Keldon Highlands.

Hiding her disappointment, Imoshen studied the map. 'Only those two. The Greater Pass leads directly to T'Diemn and most trade travels that way. The Lesser Pass is a longer, more difficult route and is only used by small parties. The highland ravines are steep and treacherous. A traveller might wander for days trying to find their way. What are you planning?'

'Fortifications. Once I control the passes I can monitor the comings and goings of the Keldon nobles, stop their trade if need be. The highlands are not rich and fertile. If I choose, I can make life very harsh for the Keld. Let them decide between fresh supplies and supporting the rebels!'

Imoshen hesitated. 'They are a proud people, used to austerity.'

'What would you have me do, Imoshen? Repeat the mistake of your ancestor, march into one of their villages, demand they give up Reothe and his rebels? Execute the villagers until the survivors cooperate?'

She shook her head, horrified.

'That is the alternative. Unless you have changed your mind about doing a scrying. No?' His expression was calculating. 'Then we'll do what you suggested. Send Reothe a message. Tell him you'll meet him, only I will go in your stead. I'll ambush him before he can reach the rendezvous. He need never know you betrayed him.'

At that moment Imoshen realised she would never betray Reothe. She might fear him and mistrust him but he was her kinsman, the last of her kind. She could not lure him to his death.

'It would not work. Reothe would know if I was not waiting for him.'

'I see.' Grimly Tulkhan rolled up the map. 'By closing the passes I contain the rebels' raids. That will reassure the people south of T'Diemn. I ride now.' But he stood silently looking at her.

Imoshen lifted her hands. 'If you would only trust me –'

She winced as a bark of laughter escaped him.

'I might be a barbarian, Imoshen, but that does not mean I am a fool. Bring me Reothe's head in a basket; only then will I trust you!'

Nausea roiled in her belly.

With a curse Tulkhan was gone.

She sank into the seat, too stunned to think. Absently she stroked the scriber Tulkhan had been toying with, sensing his determination. If Reothe were foolish enough to bring a large force to attack the fortresses, neither side would gain. But why would Reothe wait until the fortifications were completed? Why not attack while the men were vulnerable?

Imoshen knew Tulkhan did not intend to return until the fortresses were finished and manned. This would take until autumn, maybe even early winter. She could hardly believe Tulkhan would desert her before the birth of his son, yet she had been told it was the Ghebite custom to segregate women at this *unclean* time.

How she hated everything Ghebite!

Chapter Seventeen

THE DAYS OF summer passed. In a kind of stupor, Imoshen slept and ate mechanically, while the baby writhed inside her as if impatient to be free. It had reached its highest point under her ribcage but had yet to drop, so she had no relief from the pressure. She was always weary.

Imoshen dozed, dreaming she was back home at Umasreach Stronghold where her family were celebrating the imminent birth. It would be a great event. The Aayel had been giving her wise advice on handling the contractions.

A great foreboding gripped her and she awoke, her heart hammering. Was something going to go wrong with the birth? Why did she feel such a sense of dread?

She needed the scrying plate to help her focus. Imoshen was torn between her need to know and her fear of scrying, but the sense of foreboding won out. She strode to her chest, the only thing that was truly hers in all the palace, and rifled through it.

Merkah should not have touched her scrying plate. Imoshen hugged it to her chest, affronted. She took the plate to the bathing room to run a little water in it. Pricking her thumb with her dagger, she squeezed two droplets onto the water: one drop of blood for her soul, one for her son's. The drops hit the water's surface, spreading into whirls.

The spiral of fine blood drew her gaze to the plate. It had never done that before. She'd better focus on the birth, but the reflections held her captive.

General Tulkhan... She saw him astride his horse, supervising the earthworks of the fortification. The ground was treacherous, the pass steep. He swung down from his mount to consult with the engineers.

Imoshen watched the breeze lift his dark hair. She wanted to touch him. It was a physical need. But she mustn't give in to it. He might sense her.

The water's surface shimmered. She was still looking at Tulkhan, but this time he faced death. His men fell around him, poorly protected by the half-finished fortress. Why didn't they try to defend themselves? Rebels leapt over the walls crying Reothe's name.

Reothe!

Too late, she could not stop the thought. The plate already shimmered. Imoshen knew she should not look, but it held an awful fascination. Reothe stood by a hot spring. He appeared to be alone except for a child of about eight. From this angle it was hard to tell if the little one was male or female.

Both of them paused and turned towards Imoshen. Reothe's eyes narrowed suspiciously. But it was the child's gaze Imoshen could not hold. They were the oldest eyes she'd ever seen. With cold shock she knew she was looking into the eyes of one of the Ancients.

Her fingers locked on the plate. She had to break contact. With a burst of will that left her dizzy and breathless, she cast the plate aside. It flew out of her hands, spinning in the air, and crashed straight through the stained-glass window.

The sound of the shattering glass roused her. How could she be so stupid? She was too inexperienced to scry. The foreboding must have been a forewarning of Tulkhan's death, not her baby's.

'T'Imoshen, are you hurt?' Merkah threw the door open then gasped when she saw the smashed window. Lead curled like broken fingers, clasping at the empty air. 'What happened?'

Imoshen had no idea what to say. She straightened. 'Pack my things. Have my horse saddled. I ride out today.'

'But –'

'Now!'

Merkah ducked her head. Imoshen caught a flash of resentment in the maid's face. She had been too sharp with the girl. Though she tried, she had never established the easy friendship she'd had with Kalleen.

Imoshen strode into her chamber where Merkah was already laying out her clothes. 'No, nothing fancy. I am joining my bond-partner. I want riding clothes.'

The problem was nothing would do up over her belly. She tossed her dress aside and pulled on a pair of breeches, letting them ride under the swell of the baby. A borrowed shirt of Tulkhan's was large enough to cover her stomach. It fell to her thighs, and while it was not suitable for court, it was presentable. She took her cloak to sleep under.

'Who will be accompanying you, my lady?'

'No one. I travel faster alone.' And in disguise. She did not want any of Reothe's people reporting her whereabouts to him.

She felt buoyant. If she could reach Tulkhan in time to warn him of the attack, then he would have to believe her loyalty. If she didn't warn him he would die.

The need to get moving consumed her.

'But my lady, you cannot go alone!'

'No? I do not need a maid, or servants. I am not incompetent.' Imoshen winced as she heard her tone.

Merkah stiffened, retreating behind a wall of offended dignity.

'I am in a hurry,' Imoshen said more gently. 'Have the cook pack travelling food for me. I won't have time to hunt.'

Before long she was in the stables strapping saddlebags to her horse. After a moment she sensed someone observing her. She glanced over her shoulder.

The Vaygharian. Anger consumed her.

He lifted his hands in a placating gesture. 'This is not wise, Lady Protector. The General ordered me to watch over you.'

She made a rude noise. 'I can smell a lie.'

'At least take an escort,' he demurred. 'A woman in your condition cannot travel alone.'

Briefly she considered taking several of her stronghold guard but that would reveal who she was. She did not bother to reply to the Vaygharian, but took her horse's reins and prepared to walk the beast out of the stall.

The Vaygharian caught her arm.

Quick as thought she flicked free of him and drew her knife, holding it to his throat. The horse sidled away. She nearly laughed as Kinraid glanced around uneasily.

'I am only trying to serve you, Lady Protector.'

'I know who you serve.' She stepped closer. 'I know what you are. Remember I looked into your soul and saw your death!'

He went pale. She caught the smell of fear on his skin. Her lips pulled back from her teeth in a grimace of disgust. 'If you are here when I get back, I will slit your throat myself.'

'That is not the way the ruler of Fair Isle treats an ambassador of Vayghar.'

'No.' She smiled. 'It is the way I treat a traitor. General Tulkhan wants people to think he is civilised. I don't care what people think.'

She stepped away and picked up the horse's dangling reins. Silently she led her mount out. A dozen stable workers and palace servants gathered in the courtyard watching anxiously, but no one dared argue with her. She wondered who they would be serving this time next summer.

The rigours of the journey did not concern her. She had seen farm women work until the contractions started and had helped them deliver their babes on dirt floors. Then, once the proper words were said, those women would be on their feet preparing their family's evening meal.

Imoshen had no illusions about the birth either. The powder of a pain-killing root was tucked into her travelling kit. She intended to brew a tea to sip during the worst of the pain.

Pulling the cloak over her silver hair, Imoshen led her horse through the silent streets of T'Diemn. All her energies must be focused on reaching the General before it was too late.

AFTER FOUR DAYS in the saddle, Imoshen was heartily sick of riding. It was not something she would recommend to anyone in the advanced stages of pregnancy. The action of the horse's gait rocked her hips, triggering hot pokers of pain which shot down her legs without warning. Worse still, when she dismounted she found she could hardly walk.

On leaving T'Diemn she had heard a horse galloping behind her and had ridden into a grove of trees to escape pursuit. It was Crawen, leader of the stronghold guard, come to escort her. Imoshen was sorely tempted but in the end she had let her guard ride by.

She had concentrated on using her T'En gifts to cloak her appearance.

When she emerged on the far side she knew the Vaygharian's spies who followed her would not recognise her. They probably would not even notice her. She had chosen the form of a wandering T'En priest, a male at that.

But maintaining the illusion required deep concentration and once Crawen had ridden dispiritedly past her back to T'Diemn, Imoshen had let her concentration slip. It would be enough to will herself unnoticed when she saw people and to keep to the lesser known paths.

Now Imoshen's heart lifted, for she would reach Tulkhan soon. She was in the foothills of the Keldon Highlands. Here the people were distrustful of strangers, but surely they would not turn aside a weary traveller? She urged her horse towards a plume of smoke rising into the oyster-shell gleam of the dusk sky.

Before long, she approached the smoke's source, a crofter's cottage built of local stone, its roof made of sods. The rich smell of simmering stew made her mouth water.

Crouched behind the bracken Imoshen watched an old man chop wood while an old woman herded the chickens and goat inside for the night. For them life was an ever-turning cycle of seasons. As the old couple went inside, Imoshen almost envied them their place in the scheme of things. It looked like a safe haven for the night.

Picking her way across the dim ground she approached the door and scratched.

The wizened little man opened the door a crack. 'What do you want?'

'Is this the way the Keld greet a weary traveller?' Imoshen concentrated on projecting a bland image.

'Plenty of strange comings and goings near here,' the woman muttered from behind him. Her sharp old eyes took in Imoshen's pregnancy.

Imoshen had found her advanced pregnancy made women eager to help her. Tonight she cloaked only her T'En colouring, to attempt anything more would have been too hard to sustain in her exhausted state.

'That infant's nearly due. Come in,' the woman said.

Imoshen ducked her head to enter. 'The babe has not dropped yet.'

The old woman clucked under her breath, sounding for all the world like the disapproving chickens sheltering in the far end of the cottage. The goat added its opinion.

Imoshen felt light-headed. 'I can pay for food and lodging.'

The woman sniffed, offended.

'As if we would take your coins!' the old man muttered.

'Thank you Grandmother, Grandfather.' Imoshen used the honorific form of address for village elders. She watched as the old woman bustled around, stirring the food on the fire. When she saw the old woman check the bed of straw Imoshen told her, 'No, Grandmother. I will sleep on the floor before the fire. I would not turn you out of your own bed.'

But she did long for some warm water to wash the grime off her body. She wanted to be clean when she met General Tulkhan. It was her one vanity.

Despite the pain in her hips, Imoshen went outside to see to her horse. Everything was a chore, removing the saddle, rubbing the horse down. The beast appeared happy enough on a short hobble, and would have sensed predators if there were any about. For once Imoshen felt safe.

When she returned, the old woman had served up a tasty stew with thick crusty bread. Imoshen ate it gratefully. Then exhaustion overtook her. She just managed to thank the old couple for their hospitality before slipping to the floor in front of the fire pit, her arms cradling her belly, her head on her saddlebag.

It had been her intention to wait until the old couple went to bed but sleep was irresistible. As she lost consciousness, she felt her cloaking illusion fade and knew her true identity would be revealed. She would have to put her trust in the old people.

HER MOUTH TASTED foul.

Imoshen tried to swallow and gagged. Someone held a cup of water to her lips. It was elixir. She drank greedily. Cruelly, they took it away too soon.

It was still dark. Did she have a fever? She must remember to thank the old couple for bringing her water. At least she'd slept deeply. Since starting this journey she'd hardly been able to sleep through the night for the ache in her hips.

'Thank you.' The words were a croak. 'Have I been feverish?'

'No. You were drugged.'

Imoshen knew that voice. She struggled to sit up. Her companion would have helped her, but she pushed his hands aside. 'Why is it still dark?'

'It is the night of the following day. The old woman was free with the sleeping herb. She did not want you waking and taking your anger out on her.'

Imoshen moistened her lips. 'You might as well light a candle, Drake. I know who you are.'

'That doesn't worry me. We were sleeping. But yes, I will make a light.'

He stirred the coals in the fireplace, then coaxed a flame from a crude candle. Imoshen smelt the burning tallow dip. She looked around. They were in the crofters' cottage, or an identical one.

'Where am I?'

'Safe in the foothills of the highlands.'

So they had moved her while she was drugged. 'The crofters betrayed me.'

Drake laughed. 'T'Reothe could see you coming across the plains to him, bright as a beacon. He sent us to warn the old couple to bring you to him.'

'How?'

'We ride. Tomorrow you will join your betrothed.'

'No. I meant how could he see me coming?'

Drake tilted his head. 'You used your gifts to disguise yourself so that those who followed you would not discover Reothe's whereabouts. Every time you used your gifts, he sensed it.'

Imoshen hung her head. She knew Reothe could sense the use of her gifts when he was nearby, but if he was as sensitive as Drake claimed, he was powerful indeed. Her heart sank.

Reothe believed she had run away from the capital to come to him, not to warn the General. Or did he? If he truly believed that, he would not have ordered her drugged. Tulkhan would think she had deserted him for Reothe. She must warn the General of the attack, and that meant escaping Drake for a second time.

'Reothe trusts you,' she told Drake. He was her age, but seemed so much younger for all his bravado.

He nodded. 'I have proven my loyalty.'

Imoshen shifted uncomfortably. 'The baby presses down. Can I have some privacy?'

'You'll have to go outside like the rest of us.'

As Imoshen straightened, her gaze fell on her boots.

Drake noticed. 'You won't need them.'

Imoshen shrugged. Drake was wise not to trust her. Arching her back, she scratched her tummy. The skin itched. 'I'm so hungry. Is there anything to eat?'

'I'll cut some meat,' he offered.

Smiling her thanks she stepped over the bodies of Drake's snoring companions and went out into the night.

The large moon was on the wane and the small moon was not in the night sky, so she knew it was close to dawn. There was light enough for her to find a suitable bush. Her excuse to escape the cottage was genuine. The baby was sitting deeply.

By studying the stars Imoshen guessed the Greater Pass lay to the north-east, so that was the direction Drake would expect her to take. She would go south then double back. He would probably anticipate that too, but she was a country girl and knew how to hide her trail. She would not be able travel quickly without a horse and boots.

Hopefully Reothe had been too preoccupied to launch his attack. Drake would have been crowing if they had killed the Ghebite General. And if she kept them fully occupied searching for her, it might buy the time she needed to reach Tulkhan.

The enforced rest had done her aching hips good but it was not easy picking a path barefoot through country she did not know. At first she did not mind the effort. Then her stomach rumbled and she was reminded that Drake had been cutting meat for her. Poor Drake. She hoped Reothe would not be too hard on him.

When the birds began their predawn chorus Imoshen paused to drink. The water was not as cold as she expected, which meant she was near a hot spring.

At least she moved further from Reothe with every step. Pleased with herself she bathed her sore feet in the stream, rubbing the dirt and blood from her cuts. It was so refreshing that she would have liked to strip off and bathe her aching body, but she didn't dare. They would start looking for her soon.

Slipping into the water she waded upstream to hide her scent from her trackers. A wide pool lay before her.

As she stood debating whether to go through or around, a strange sensation gripped her. The baby's head ground down to her pelvis. She could almost feel it grating on the bones, wedging itself deep. Her knees sagged and a trickle of fear floated up through her body. The baby must not come now, not when she needed to escape her pursuers.

Determined to reach her destination, she waded across the rock pool. The water was warm and so clear she could see the large round boulders on the bottom. It was soothing and cleansed her gritty skin. When the water reached her chest she began to swim.

The first pain took her midway in deep water. It was so intense she could barely keep her head above the surface. Terror gripped her.

At last the pain slipped away, uncurling its tendrils from her body with a lover's reluctance. A burst of energy took her swiftly to the far side of the rock pool.

She stood dripping on a rock, considering her options. How far could she travel? How long did she have? The next pain rolled in like a summer thunderstorm, inexorable and intense.

Imoshen rode it. When it retreated, leaving the afterimage of its fury imprinted on her mind and body, she faced the truth. The baby was coming now. It could not wait for a better time or place and she thought longingly of the painkiller tucked safely in her saddlebags. So much for thinking ahead.

She had to find somewhere safe and warm. From the speed and force of the contractions she knew it would be a short, violent birth.

She also knew that the more she moved the faster the baby would come, but she couldn't stay out here in the open. Driven by necessity, she set off upstream looking for shelter.

There was no way for her to measure the passage of time other than counting, so she took to counting between each pain and the duration of the pain and placing all these numbers in a convenient place in her head to keep track of the birthing process. It helped to think she was in control of at least one thing.

Rounding a curve in the rock wall she stopped and stared in dismay. She had stumbled into a hot spring, a place redolent of the Ancients. The pools held steaming water and mist hung over the narrow ravine.

Imoshen was desperate. She did not want to use a place that belonged to the Ancients, but she knew Drake and his men would avoid it.

Without warning another contraction racked her. They were getting harder to ride. A silent, growing terror told her that soon she would be swamped, drowned by the sensation. From experience she knew there was a point where the body took over and the mind simply had to go with it. She wanted to be safe before that point came.

Walking on rocks warmed by hot pools, she made her way into the mist-shrouded ravine. Her damp clothes had been almost dry, but now they clung to her. A shiver shook her.

Was that a cleft in the rocks? Imoshen picked her way over slippery stones to investigate. It was the entrance to a cave.

Suddenly she felt an increase in pressure and her waters broke, flooding her legs with hot fluid. Her knees almost gave way. She wanted to cry out, but bit back the sound.

Trembling, barely able to walk, she felt her way into the cave. It grew lighter and opened into a natural cavern with a central pool. A shaft of sunlight poured in through a gap in the rocks above. Steam shimmered on the water's surface. It was a beautiful place. A good place.

Imoshen felt the tightening of her muscles, a sharp clenching as if she was about to cough. Already? She panted, fighting the urge to push. Picking a spot where she could rest her back against the rock, she stripped off her sodden breeches and sank to a crouch ready for the work of birthing.

That was when she saw the creature standing in the mist, aglow with light. It was a child, neither male nor female, a child with ancient eyes.

Imoshen would have screamed, but the urge to push gripped her. She caught her breath and went with it. The baby's head moved. There was barely time to catch her breath before the urge came again. She felt the baby move again and guessed that its head was emerging. Her skin stretched impossibly.

Panting, she looked up. The ancient creature was still there. Not threatening, just watching.

Once more her muscles contracted. She felt her skin tear as the bloodied head emerged into her hands. By feel she searched for the cord. It wasn't around the neck.

She gulped a breath and went with the last contraction. She had intended to manoeuvre the infant, easing first one shoulder then the other, but her body wanted to be rid of it. The force of the push tore her further as the shoulders emerged.

Panting, she looked up. The creature was watching intently.

Then the baby's body came, slithering out into her hands. Stunned, she stared at the baby boy, hardly able to believe he was her son, her flesh and blood. The cord pulsed with life. For now they were still one.

He writhed in her hands, his little head turning, black hair plastered to his head.

Alarm pierced her. The Ancient was still observing her.

She had to get out of here.

Imoshen lifted the baby to her chest and chewed through the cord, pinching it closed. She could not risk using her healing gift in case it drew Reothe, so she tied the cord off with a strip of material.

The baby sucked in a breath and exclaimed to the world. His mouth opened and his arms splayed out, fingers spread. Imoshen laughed.

Six fingers.

Pride stirred her. He was more T'En than True-man.

Would he ever stop yelling and look at her? She wanted to see his eyes. The hair was all Tulkhan.

Stupid man. He should have been here to greet his son. Imoshen frowned as another contraction took her. The afterbirth. It was not as painful as the baby.

True to her training, she checked that it was intact. She had no intention of dying of child-bed fever. The Aayel's T'Enchiridion remained safely hidden at the palace but she did not need it to recall the words. Imoshen shivered. She would have to find a safe place to bury her son's afterbirth then say the words to bind his soul.

But for the moment she let herself rest, leaning her head against the rock wall. It was so good not to be in pain.

Yet even as she crouched there cradling the hot, slippery body of her baby, her gaze never left the Ancient. What did it want? Was it merely observing because she had entered its sacred place? She felt a grim smile part her lips. Surely enough blood had been spilt to satisfy it.

Birthing was a messy business. She would have liked to wash herself and the baby in the warm pools but the presence of the Ancient oppressed her.

Collecting the afterbirth and her clothing she rose to her knees and then to her feet. She felt reassured by the warm bundle of life in her arms. Keeping a watch on the creature, she headed for the cave's entrance, walking carefully across the smooth rocks because her centre of balance had changed.

The Ancient began moving. Making no overt threat, it rose from the water's surface to the rock, its feet never touching the stone. It positioned itself between her and the patch of daylight.

Imoshen hugged her son to her chest, heart pounding so violently she thought she might be sick. 'Keep away!'

The voice was hers, but she'd never heard it sound so feral, so full of contained violence. It frightened her.

The Ancient said nothing.

Imoshen glanced around the cave. The only other way out was through the hole in the roof directly over the hot pool. It would have been an impossible climb even without the baby in her arms. She had no choice.

Though she could feel the power of the Ancient radiating like heat from an oven, she forced herself to step nearer, edging sideways in an attempt to slip past.

It shifted to block her path and extended its arms, palms up.

A moan escaped Imoshen. 'You can't have him!'

The ancient creature pointed to the afterbirth.

Imoshen gasped. She could not condemn her son to life without a soul. At best he would be a heartless killer, at worst dead within a day. 'No. The soul must be bound to –'

In her head she heard the Aayel reciting the T'Enchiridion. Only they were not the words of birth, but the opening of the death calling. She forced them from her mind. The last thing she needed now was to call the Parakletos.

But she understood the Ancients' message – they would either take her son's life force or his soul.

It was her decision.

If the Ancient had asked for her own life she would have given it willingly, but she could not bring herself to part with this new life.

Tears blinded her as she handed over the afterbirth.

The Ancients had claimed her son for their own. In life he would be theirs to call on.

TULKHAN GLANCED UP at the lookout's signal. It was just on dusk and the cooking fires were going strong. The smell of rich stew hung over the half-built fortress.

'What is it?' he yelled.

'You'd better come and see.'

He didn't like that tone. Something had startled the watch.

Tulkhan strode past the nearest campfire. He was careful to hide any trace of fear. His men had to believe in him. Once that had seemed so simple, because he had believed in himself; but all the rules had changed since he had taken Imoshen's stronghold, and now he doubted everything, his own decisions most of all.

Springing lightly up the ladder he climbed onto the lookout tower. The knuckles of his right hand hurt where he had injured them working wood.

Looking down he saw Imoshen. She stood there in one of his shirts, hugging something. His heart soared. She had come to him ready to renounce Reothe. Tulkhan's first impulse was to let her in. But he checked himself. There was no horse, no sign of companions.

It could not be Imoshen. It was a trick. It had to be Reothe baiting him with the illusion of Imoshen. The attack he had been expecting had begun.

'Should I open the gate, General?' the watch asked.

'No. Prepare for attack. That is not my wife.'

'You fool!' Imoshen cried. 'I am tired and hungry. I have walked a day and a night in bare feet through the ravines to bring you your son. Let me in!'

He had to grin. That certainly sounded like Imoshen.

'Who knows when my son is due, shape-changer.'

'Babies come when they are ready. If I don't get some food soon, I will drop!'

Tulkhan stared at Imoshen's upturned face, torn by his need to believe she was really there and the sheer impossibility of her appearance. How could it be Imoshen? She was back in the palace. She would not have come to him without attendants. In fact, he had expressly forbidden it. That made him smile – forbidding Imoshen to do something was not going to stop her.

Still, he had to be sure. 'How did my mother die?'

'She died alone from fever without anything to ease her passing. Now let me in, General.'

It was Imoshen. Only she called him General in just that tone, and only she knew his secret guilt about his mother's death. 'Open the gate.'

Tulkhan raced down the ladder, darted through before the makeshift gate was fully open and swept Imoshen off her feet.

'Careful, you'll hurt the baby!' she warned.

He glanced down, seeing a small face, its mouth opening to launch a cry. He was shocked, even though Imoshen had said she carried the babe.

'Shut the gate.'

He marched across the campsite, with Imoshen in his arms and a squalling infant in hers. His men stopped their tasks, mouths agape. Those nearest strained to see.

'Put me down. He needs to be fed,' Imoshen urged.

He let her slide to the ground by his fire. There were a hundred questions he had to ask, but the baby demanded precedence, tiny arms windmilling, hands splayed with frustration. That shock of dark hair stood straight up.

'He's mine!'

'Of course he's yours,' Imoshen muttered, struggling to unlace the shirt one-handed.

'You can't feed him here. My men will see.'

'I'll feed him where I please. He's hungry, and if your men don't like it they can look away. Besides, they were all babies once.'

Tulkhan saw the anger in her face but he also saw the exhaustion. 'Very well.'

'I don't need your permission.' Her fingers caught on the laces and she cursed, fumbling to undo a knot.

When Tulkhan took his son from her, the boy yelled so indignantly that he had to grin. He was unmistakably a Ghebite. Let Reothe try to claim him now!

Tulkhan turned and held the child out for his men to see. The naked bundle struggled in his hands, screaming lustily. A ragged cheer broke from his men.

'If you're quite finished?' Imoshen had knelt by the fire at his side.

He handed the baby to her and she leaned against the wall of the building behind them. Instinctively Tulkhan stepped between Imoshen and his men to shield her from their gaze. He could not help but watch as the baby turned his face to her breast, mouth open. Without any guidance from her he latched onto her nipple, sucking vigorously.

How could he be so little, yet know what to do?

'My feet,' Imoshen whispered. 'And food.'

He knelt to look at her feet. They were covered in blood and mud. 'How did you get here in this state?'

'I walked. I'll have some of that stew. I don't care if it's not ready.' She kept talking as he ladled out a serve. 'To escape from Reothe's people I had to leave my boots and horse behind.'

'What? Reothe had you abducted from the palace? How?'

'I was on my way here. Some bread too.' She accepted a bowl of stew, scooping up the sauce with the hard bread. The baby remained tucked in the crook of her arm and both of them fed with absolute concentration.

'How long since you last ate?' Tulkhan asked.

'Evening, three days ago. This one was born yesterday just after dawn.' She tore at a piece of bread with sharp white teeth, chewing vigorously. 'I was coming to warn you. You won't like this, but I did a scrying. I saw you fall defending this fort. I came to warn you that Reothe's going to attack.'

This was what he wanted to hear, proof of her loyalty, but perversely he found himself wondering if she had planned this with Reothe so she could open the fortress from within when his back was turned.

'You don't believe me.' Imoshen's voice sounded weary and indignant. 'Why do I bother?'

He stared across the fire at her. There were bruised circles under her eyes which shimmered with unshed tears. As he watched, the tears rolled down her cheeks, glistening in the firelight.

Before he could stop himself he crossed the fire circle to kneel before her. He used his thumbs to brush the tears from her face.

She blinked, twisting her head to be free of his hands.

Tulkhan rubbed his jaw, feeling the bristles of the beard he hadn't bothered to remove since leaving T'Diemn. 'If the scrying says I'm going to die here, what difference can warning me make?'

She shrugged. 'Scrying is not an exact science. I already told you that. I am here and the baby has been born, so things are not exactly as I foresaw them in the scrying. It was one possible path and now we are on another, hopefully one that will not lead to your death. Here, hold this.'

She gave him the half-eaten bowl of stew and changed the baby to the other breast. The babe protested vehemently but settled down when he found a fresh nipple.

Tulkhan had to admire his son's single-mindedness.

'My food.' Imoshen held out her hand. 'This is a good spot for a fortress, but we are vulnerable to attack right now. If I were Reothe I would make a clean sweep and be rid of us altogether.'

Tulkhan tried to concentrate on what she was saying. He had trouble discussing tactics with Imoshen in this situation. A Ghebite woman would never discuss such things with her husband, let alone do it while breastfeeding his son. Females were considered unclean while they were making milk, bleeding or pregnant. Even their normal places in the temples were forbidden to them at these times. The priests claimed they became channels for evil spirits because of their inferior souls.

'General, are you listening to me? I didn't come all this way to die in a surprise attack.' Imoshen fixed angry eyes on him.

Tulkhan concentrated on her features. Imoshen was not a channel for evil. He had seen too many different religions fail people to have any faith in the teachings of Ghebite priests.

'Do you have people posted outside the fortifications ready to give the alarm?' she asked.

He nodded.

She looked down tenderly. The baby had fallen asleep with her nipple in his mouth. 'Can I have a blanket to wrap him in?'

He took out his own blanket and laid it on the ground. She wrapped the baby and picked him up, then held him towards Tulkhan.

'What?' What was he supposed to do with a baby?

'Hold him. I want to get clean and treat my feet, then find some more clothes.'

Gingerly Tulkhan took the sleeping bundle. Imoshen called for warm water and spare clothes, then she climbed to the first floor of the central tower.

Tulkhan sank beside the fire, feasting his eyes on his two-day-old son. Who would have thought? So much black hair and perfect little features. Dark eyes. In the firelight it was hard to tell if they were black like his, or wine-dark like Imoshen's.

The baby gave a whimper, his hands splaying wide. Tulkhan blinked and caught one little palm, the baby's fingers closing around his finger, holding on tightly.

Six fingers.

His son was half Dhamfeer. How could he not be?

Tulkhan tried to withdraw his finger. The baby's hold tightened. The boy was a determined little thing. The General felt a surge of pride. His son had not taken the full year from conception to birth, but he was still half Dhamfeer. So be it.

Tulkhan leaned his head against the wall and looked up to the star-dusted sky. Their patterns were different this far south, but he had grown to know them as he travelled through Fair Isle. This was his island now and he would endure. His son was born of this land, half Ghebite, half T'En. He was the future.

With his finger encased in his son's firm grasp, Tulkhan felt the bitter kernel of distrust that had tainted his life for so many moons dissolve. As it slipped from him he realised its nature and its source. Reothe had planted that self-doubt.

Now it was gone and the world was his for the taking.

IMOSHEN PICKED HER way gingerly to the fire circle. Her feet were tender and she was still bruised and torn from the birth. When the General returned the baby she accepted him carefully. Her breasts were tender. She had nothing in reserve for healing herself.

She just wanted to sit and hold her son. It was amazing how good it felt to hug his little body to her. Warmth from the fire seeped through her. She was tired beyond thought.

Travelling the foothills with the baby had been a test of endurance. She had hardly dared let herself stop for fear of falling asleep and being recaptured.

It was so good to be safe at last. Through almost closed lids she watched Tulkhan leave the campfire to confer with his fortress commander. She had sensed something different about the General when he returned the baby to her. Tulkhan was lighter of spirit, more confident. She didn't know why, but she was relieved.

The familiar rumble of the Ghebite language hung on the air. There was something about the tone of the General's voice that she found very comforting.

'Imoshen?'

She looked up startled. Had she dozed off?

Tulkhan offered his hand, indicating she was to stand.

'Can't we just sit?'

He sank onto his haunches with the ease of a man used to living rough. 'The men are nervous, Imoshen. According to Ghebite custom a woman is unclean while she makes milk for the babe. Ordinarily no man but a woman's husband would see her for two small moons after the birth and even he would not touch her.' He gave an apologetic cough. 'You unsettle them.'

She snorted. 'Anyone would think they birthed and raised themselves!'

Tulkhan grinned. 'So it may seem to you. But these men are simple soldiers. They find it hard to think differently from the way they were raised.'

'You are a soldier, yet you can see things differently.'

He shrugged. 'As first son of the second wife, I have been on the outer looking in for many years.' He met her eyes, a rueful smile lighting his face.

Imoshen felt a tug of recognition. She knew what it was like to be an outcast.

Tulkhan seemed to recollect himself. 'To make matters worse, they fear attack. They know you turned Jacolm and Cariah to stone and they fear the same or worse from the rebel leader. Can you tell me how Reothe will strike?'

'I can't help you. I would if I could, but I am untutored in the T'En gifts. If the Aayel had lived I might know more. I am only finding my way. I don't know what Reothe is capable of. It frightens me too.'

His disappointment was palpable.

'I am sorry, General.' Regret made Imoshen abrupt. She touched his clasped hands. 'This is my gift.' She brushed his bruised knuckles, meaning to draw on the force of his own will to heal his graze because she was so exhausted. Strangely, she didn't have to. The food and rest must have restored her.

He lifted his hand, turning it over, flexing the fingers as he made a fist. The skin had healed perfectly.

'In time of peace it is a good gift,' she told him. 'But it's not much help at present.'

'Not true.' He squeezed her hand. 'We may have great need of you afterwards.'

Imoshen nodded, unable to bring herself to tell him that even if Reothe allowed them an *afterwards*, she doubted if she would have the strength to heal more than the mildest of wounds.

His knuckles brushed her cheek. 'Don't let yourself worry.'

It was a gentle gesture and it almost undid her. Weariness overtook her and she fell asleep sitting up, too tired to move.

Chapter Eighteen

A SCREAM RENT the air, a terrible keening note of pure terror. Imoshen pushed her hair from her eyes and struggled to sit up, her bruised body protesting. All around her men sprang to their feet, reaching for their weapons.

Tulkhan hurried around the fire to Imoshen, pulling her upright. She gasped as the myriad cuts on her swollen feet split open.

He pushed her towards the tower. 'Go up there, take cover.'

She hugged the baby to her chest. 'Give me a knife. Reothe's people took mine.'

He appeared startled and Imoshen cursed. Did he think she was some useless Ghebite female?

Several more screams cut the air, rising above the frantic shouts of the men.

Wordlessly Tulkhan dragged his own knife from its sheath and handed it to her. Imoshen grasped it in one hand, then turned to dart away.

'Imoshen?'

Tulkhan's tone stopped her.

His face worked with emotion. 'You came to warn me. Thank you.'

'Don't thank me. I probably led them here and provided the impetus for the attack.'

'I don't care.'

He took one step to cover the space between them and caught the back of her head in his free hand. His lips found hers in a bruising kiss. It made her heart leap. Her body recognised this for what it was.

A declaration.

She returned the kiss with all the fervour of her long-contained passion. Tears stung her eyes. Tulkhan might take his death wound this night. She might never have a chance to hold him again. So much was against them. Yet, at this moment, she knew he was hers, body and soul. Fierce joy filled her. If they lived through the night she would take him in her arms and love him with every fibre of her body.

He pulled away. The desire in his eyes warmed her to the core.

'Later,' he promised. 'If there is a later.'

'There will be. There has to be!'

Then he was gone.

Imoshen climbed the ladder, pulling it up after her. The tower was the fortress's last point of defence and there were no doors or windows on the ground floor. On the first floor there were no shutters to draw across its narrow windows. She scurried up the curved stairs to the floor above. Here there was no roof.

Her heart pounded as the screams rose to a crescendo. She made a nest in the darkest corner and, using strips of old material, quickly changed the baby, then rigged a sling to tie him to her chest.

Her hands flew, but her mind moved faster. How many rebels were attacking? At which point in the half-completed fortifications had they chosen to strike?

More importantly, what were they doing to cause those terrible screams?

She knew the sounds of physical pain, and this was more. This was agony of the soul.

The sweat of fear clung to her skin. No longer registering the pain of the cuts on her feet, Imoshen prepared to fight for her life and the life of her son.

She crept to a window. A pall of smoke hung over the campfires. Her nostrils stung and the back of her throat burned. This was no ordinary smoke. A glowing mist partially obscured the half-built fort. By this fell light she saw Tulkhan's men, their faces twisted in leering grimaces of mindless terror. Some had fallen to the ground, foaming at the mouth, while others ran about, slashing wildly at nothing. In their crazed attacks they knocked their own men to the ground. A few simply stood and screamed.

Fear for Tulkhan made her tremble. She could see rebels climbing over the ramparts, slitting throats methodically as they moved forward. Their helpless victims fell, blood spilling on the ground. As it hit the soil the blood steamed, adding to the mist...

The Ancients!

What evil pact had Reothe offered them to over-power the fortress?

Opening her T'En senses, Imoshen searched for Reothe; but instead she found the Parakletos. Beautiful in their full T'En battle armour, they strode insubstantial but irresistible amidst the slaughter. Some knelt beside the dying, waiting for them to gasp their last, others wrenched the dying Ghebites' souls from their bodies even as they fought for life.

Sickened, Imoshen shuddered. Terror stole her breath and pinned her feet to the floor. Reothe had said the Parakletos had no power in this world. Yet he had opened a path somehow and laid a feast before them.

Imoshen dry-retched. Tears blurred her vision. Gasping, she blinked to clear her sight. Tulkhan's True-men had no defences against the Parakletos. They appeared aware of the danger, but blinded, so that they did not see the rebels amidst them. Where was Tulkhan?

She identified him staggering towards the base of the tower. He fell to his knees, vulnerable.

Desperate, she ran down the spiral stairs, shoved the ladder out of the first floor doorway and scurried down.

Tulkhan was on his knees, his head in his hands, his body hunched and shaking. She knelt next to him. Cupping the General's head in her hands she searched his unseeing eyes. What was wrong? Then she sensed it on the mist – an overpowering terror. It stole her breath, her very sanity.

But it was an illusion.

'It's not real,' she told the General. 'It's a trick!' But the Parakletos were real and they waited greedily to claim men's souls. The rebels were killing for the Parakletos.

Imoshen grabbed two handfuls of Tulkhan's hair and jerked his head. The pain made him focus on her. Dragging in a deep breath, she blew into his mouth to drive out the poisonous mists which made him susceptible.

He pulled away from her, coughing. 'Imoshen?'

Coming to her feet, she hauled him upright. 'The rebels are amongst us. Your men are dying where they stand without lifting a blade.'

Stunned, he looked around, then cursed and bellowed an order at the nearest man, who writhed on the ground unaware.

'He can't hear you. The mist clouds their minds.'

'Then we are lost unless you can reverse it.' He spun to face her.

Imoshen shook her head. She could not do it. There were too many Ghebites. Even if she could, they'd be killed before she had brought enough of them back to make a stand.

The nearest Parakletos paused as he crouched over a dying man. T'En eyes that had seen too much horror met hers. Imoshen looked away, unable to hold his gaze.

Nearby, another Parakletos wept as she watched a man die. Her eyes widened as if she recognised Imoshen, and she lifted a hand in supplication. It came to Imoshen that not all the Parakletos were cold and cruel, but they were bound by their ancient oath and tonight they served Reothe.

'Imoshen!' Tulkhan pulled her around to face him.

She dragged in a shaky breath. 'You must find Reothe. If you strike him down, all his work will be destroyed.'

Tulkhan baulked. 'But if Reothe can do this, how can I hope to defeat him?'

'This costs. He'll be defenceless. Go after him and I'll do what I can here.'

Imoshen moved off, not bothering to see if Tulkhan would follow her advice. She searched for the fortress's commander. She would bring him back first. Between them they might be able to stem the tide.

Tulkhan turned in time to see one of his men fall from the gate tower with his throat slit. Furious, he scrambled up the ladder and struck down the rebel responsible. The man fell, landing across the body of the Ghebite. Their blood mingled on the ground, steaming and bubbling.

Someone leapt on Tulkhan's back. Instinct took over. He threw the attacker over his shoulder, breaking the man's neck before his feet hit the boards. Something unseen took the man's weight from Tulkhan's arms.

Unwilling to witness what a True-man should not, Tulkhan took one last look at the fortress compound where rebels were already opening the gate. So much for their defences. Tulkhan's lookouts had succumbed without giving a warning, and the rebels had been able to bring their ladders right up to the walls. The gate swung open. Rebels charged inside to slaughter the defenders who were preoccupied with their terrible dark visions.

Three men stood at Imoshen's side. Tulkhan fought the urge to go to her aid. He had to kill Reothe.

He climbed down the ladder, jumping to the ground outside the fortress wall. Where was the Dhamfeer? A glowing cleft in the rock wall to the south of the pass caught his eye. The rebel leader was sheltering in a narrow, dead-end ravine to work his evil sorcery.

Tulkhan ran, his feet flying over the uneven ground past a cluster of wiry mountain ponies. Three rebels drew their weapons as he approached the glowing cleft. Behind them, bathed in unnatural light, Reothe knelt in a trance. Imoshen had been right. Reothe was vulnerable now.

The first bodyguard charged Tulkhan, sword raised. The General deflected the attack and went for his knife, but remembered too late Imoshen had it. He grappled with the rebel, using his attacker's body to shield him from the other two. Furious with himself, Tulkhan caught the man's hand and turned his own knife on him, throwing the rebel at the second attacker. The third darted in. There was no time for finesse. Tulkhan parried the blow, stepped inside his guard and elbowed him in the throat, leaving him gasping his last.

The second rebel struggled free of his companion, ready to attack. It was a woman.

Tulkhan hesitated. She didn't.

She leapt forward. He staggered back, blocking awkwardly. The uneven ground betrayed him and he went down with her on top of him. Before she could turn her blade to strike, he knocked her senseless.

Casting her aside, he came to his feet.

The element of surprise was gone, along with the eldritch glow. Reothe had woken from his trance, though he still seemed disoriented as he fumbled to draw his weapon. With growing surety, he lifted the sword's point.

'She sent you, didn't she?' Reothe asked, beckoning with his free hand.

'Are you really here this time?' Tulkhan swung his blade and was delighted to feel the impact of metal on metal as Reothe blocked.

The T'En warrior's free hand surged forward, bringing a slender knife into play. Tulkhan sprang back warily, circling his opponent. Reothe matched him step for step, a long slender sword in one hand and a short knife in the other.

It was the T'En style of swordplay. Tulkhan regretted not testing Imoshen's skill to learn more about this technique. Though the slender sword was less able to deflect the slashing blows of his own sword, it had extra length and amazing manoeuvrability.

'She's playing a double game, Ghebite. Don't you realise it doesn't matter which of us lives? She will have it all in the end.'

Tulkhan ignored Reothe's taunts.

He wished he had a cloak to wrap round his free hand or cast over Reothe's dagger to put it out of commission. He knew he could break through Reothe's defence, but not without risking the dagger.

'I took your son, you know, stole him before he was born!'

In that instant, as Tulkhan tried to make sense of this, Reothe charged.

Instinct helped the General deflect the sword – his blade skidded up the shaft to strike the pommel – but he could do nothing about the knife. Twisting his body, he avoided the blow under his ribs to his heart and took a wound in the abdomen instead.

Tulkhan's free hand closed over the knife's grip. Reothe smiled and stepped back.

The General staggered, trying to keep his guard up. He knew that if this wound wasn't treated very soon he would bleed to death. It was better to die of blood loss than a festering stomach wound.

His hands and legs tingled. One knee gave way but he did not drop his guard.

'You are too much trouble to kill outright. I would like to stay here till you die, and watch the Parakletos take your soul, but I have to go. My people need me.' Reothe studied Tulkhan's face from a safe distance, his expression strangely intent. 'You can die knowing you did well, Mere-man. But you had no hope of winning.'

He straightened and strode off.

Tulkhan shifted. A sharp jab of pain made him gasp. If he pulled out the blade or tried to move, it would speed up the bleeding. He could not die here, but moving would hasten his death.

He blinked tears of pain from his eyes. His blood soaked into the soil, but there was no mist. Whatever fell sorcery Reothe had been working, it had faded when Tulkhan distracted him.

Imoshen!

Even if she had turned the tide with the rebels, Reothe himself was coming for her. Tulkhan felt the stain of failure.

Reothe had said she would win no matter which of them lived. Yet Imoshen had assured him that Reothe could tell the truth and make it sound like a lie.

Tulkhan's vision blurred. He had to move. He couldn't.

He should have been there at her side to face Reothe. Despair, more painful than the knife's blade, seared him.

IMOSHEN HAD KNOWN the moment Tulkhan confronted Reothe, because the mist had vanished and with it the Parakletos. Once free of the mist's effects the Ghebites had formed a solid core of resistance, their training coming to the fore. When the commander had asked for Tulkhan she'd explained he had gone to defeat Reothe.

But they fought on and still Tulkhan did not return. Imoshen hid her growing dread. Despite the disparity of numbers, the Ghebites held the rebels at bay. The battle could go either way.

Just as Imoshen thought this, she looked up to see Reothe ride through the gate. The dawn breeze lifted his silver hair as he looked down on the struggle.

She knew as soon as the Ghebites saw him they would lose heart. If only it had been Tulkhan.

Darting forward, she pulled the commander away from the fray, pointing. 'General Tulkhan has returned.'

The commander's gaze followed her gesture and he saw what she willed him to see. He gave the Ghebite war cry. His men echoed it, calling Tulkhan's name and attacking with renewed vigour. The rebels faltered.

Imoshen looked up at Reothe. Even from this distance she could tell he was furious. The air between them seemed to crackle. Her breath caught in her throat.

She cradled the baby to her chest and shouted, encouraging the Ghebites. The rebels lost heart, turned and ran. The defenders surged after them. But none of the Ghebites tried to stop Reothe as he dismounted and walked towards her.

Imoshen's stomach lurched. Her legs threatened to give way. Heart pounding, she stood her ground. Oblivious to the approaching threat, her son slept on.

When Reothe came to a stop within an arm's length of her, Imoshen could hardly breathe. She expected him to strike her down with one blow. She had no defences against a T'En warrior who could barter with the Ancients and bind the Parakletos to his will. She faced Reothe in the knowledge that, now he knew her loyalties, he would kill her.

And what did it matter? Tulkhan must be dead. Otherwise Reothe would not be standing before her, eyes blazing. She had wagered everything on one throw of the dice and lost. The baby woke and struggled against her. She cradled his warm head, feeling his fragile skull under his powder-fine hair and skin.

Why did Reothe hesitate?

Perhaps he did not want to hurt the baby. How could she be so naive? He was the ultimate pragmatist. He would not hesitate to kill Tulkhan's son before the boy grew old enough to cause trouble.

A flood of fury engulfed Imoshen. While there was still breath in her body no one would touch her child.

Reothe studied her. Amid the mass of fleeing, fighting figures only they were still.

'Very clever, Imoshen. This time you've won, but it is only a skirmish.'

Tension sang through her limbs. She did not understand why he hadn't dealt her death blow.

'Tulkhan is dead,' he said. 'Do you really want to stand alone against me?'

When she looked into his hard eyes she saw an image of Tulkhan, bleeding but still alive. Imoshen's heart leapt with relief but she was careful to hide this from Reothe.

'Think on it, Imoshen, then come to me. I will not be so patient again.'

He turned and walked unharmed through the milling Ghebites who were tending to their wounded.

Imoshen sank to her knees, dizzy with relief. Tulkhan lay out there, injured and alone. And if she knew Reothe, he was going back to deliver the killing blow.

'Tulkhan!' she cried silently, opening her T'En senses to search for him.

The merest flicker of his essence prickled on the periphery of her mind. She felt his fading strength. He lay dying without her.

As she ran out of the gate, the Ghebites called after her, but she ignored them.

TULKHAN SPRAWLED PROPPED against a rocky outcropping where he could see the entrance to the narrow gully. Dawn lightened the sky and he could make out hazy shapes.

Once Reothe had secured the fortress, Tulkhan expected him to send several rebels to make sure the Ghebite General was dead.

His hand still grasped the sword but he did not raise it, preferring to save his strength. He would take at least one or two of them with him before Reothe's prediction came to pass.

He heard running boots and shouts. This was it.

But they ran on past him. He heard hoof beats and suddenly a figure blocked the entrance. It was Reothe.

'Come to finish me yourself? I'm honoured,' Tulkhan grunted. He lifted the sword in greeting.

'You are a hard man to kill, Ghebite.'

Stepping forward, Reothe drew his sword. Tulkhan knew the end was inevitable but he would not go quietly.

At that moment three of the General's men charged through the cleft's opening. They looked from him to the rebel leader.

Reothe spun around, saw the odds and hesitated. For an instant no one moved, then Reothe dropped his weapon and leapt. With amazing agility be scaled the almost sheer rock wall.

The Ghebites charged after him, but not one of them could climb the wall. They cursed fluently. Tulkhan looked up to see Reothe's boots disappear over the crest.

The General's men returned to him and took in the extent of his wound. He saw from their faces that there was no hope. How had Imoshen and his men turned the tide of the attack?

Almost as if the thought had called her up, Imoshen slipped through the gap into the narrow ravine. She stepped gingerly towards him, muttering something about the stench of Ancient greed.

'We are too late. He's dying,' one man told her.

'You forget who you're talking to,' another said. 'This Dhamfeer can heal.'

When she crouched beside him Tulkhan noticed the baby asleep between her breasts.

'My son slept through it all?' he asked, his voice thick with equal measures of laughter and pain.

Imoshen smiled, but her heart sank as she inspected the General's wound. There was blood on his lips and it bubbled with each breath.

What could she do, exhausted as she was? She met the General's eyes. The sweat of pain stood on his greying skin but he looked at her with perfect faith. He trusted her to save him.

It was too cruel.

She took a deep breath. The stench of Reothe's sorcery was so thick she almost gagged, yet the Ghebites appeared unaware of it.

Tulkhan coughed. It was a horrible sound. She could not, *would* not, lose him now.

She pressed her cheek to his chest, where she could sense his heart labouring. The baby's weight made her back ache and she straightened.

'I failed you,' Tulkhan whispered. 'How did you defeat him?'

'No. You were victorious!' one of his men insisted. 'When you appeared in the gateway the rebels broke and ran.'

'I don't understand,' Tulkhan rasped, voice fading.

Panic seized Imoshen.

Looking into his eyes, she searched for a flicker of something she couldn't name. It was instinctive. Healing his grazed knuckles had drawn on his will, using only a small portion of her gifts, but this was a far greater healing. It would exhaust all her reserves and this time Reothe would not search death's shadow for her.

'When this is over, General, you must take me home.'

'Of course.'

'It could hurt,' she warned.

'You think it doesn't hurt now?'

That made her smile.

Closing her eyes, Imoshen called on the General's own fierce will. Whatever it cost her, she would help him to heal himself.

It was the second-hardest thing she had ever done.

TULKHAN WOKE FROM a disturbed sleep, his mind a jumble of half-remembered images – confronting Reothe, facing death, Imoshen coming to save him.

'Thirsty.'

The bone-setter helped lift Tulkhan's head and held a drink to his lips. It was the sweetest water he had ever tasted.

He lay back and looked up, seeing the framework of the roof over his head, raw wood against an endless blue sky. Above him the men sang as they fitted wooden slates to the staves.

'Don't drop one on my head,' Tulkhan tried to shout but it came out a croak. He pulled himself upright. 'How long have I been asleep?'

'One day.'

'Where is Imoshen?'

The man moved to one side and Tulkhan saw her asleep on a pallet in the far corner of the room.

'What, sleeping in the middle of the day?' Tulkhan laughed, rolling to his knees. The movement tugged at the pain in his chest, his muscles ached and his joints popped, but he was determined to wake her.

The man caught the General's arm, a warning in his eyes.

Tulkhan felt fear, by now a familiar companion. Forewarned, he crawled across the floor to kneel beside Imoshen. His son was asleep at her breast, her nipple still in his mouth. She lay completely still, her face pale.

He knew the signs, but this time he could not call on Reothe for help.

'How did this happen?'

'As the colour came to your skin, she grew paler.'

'But she is a healer. It's her T'En gift.'

The man shrugged. 'Maybe even she has limits. Remember in Gheeaba a woman would not rise from her bed for one small moon after giving birth, or take on her normal duties for another moon. She would be waited on by the other wives and her baby brought to her for feeding.

'This Dhamfeer crossed the ranges barefoot. She walked a day and a night to get here. She reversed the night terrors when the fortress would have fallen –'

'Then she saved me.' Tulkhan bowed his head. He had begun to expect the impossible of Imoshen.

The baby woke and opened wine-dark eyes. His gaze travelled up Tulkhan's chest to his face. There was no greeting, no recognition in those eyes, just impassive interest.

'Here, General.' The bone-setter lifted the baby. 'You'll have to give him a name.'

'A name?' Tulkhan had not thought of that, could not think of it when Imoshen lay so still. He would have to find a wet nurse. 'How are you feeding the baby?'

'Her milk flows. She rouses herself to take a little food and water –'

'What?' Then it was not the same as the last time. There was hope.

As the bone-setter moved off to clean and change the baby, Tulkhan grasped Imoshen's hand in his. He stroked her cheek. 'Imoshen, wake up and tell me what to call our boy.' Tulkhan grinned. His father would be turning in his grave. A Ghebite father always chose his son's name. 'I can't call him *babe* forever.'

He saw her lips move ever so slightly as if she would like to smile. Elation filled him. Stroking her pale hair from her forehead he leant closer. 'You can hear me. Is there anything I can do for you, get you?'

With great effort her lips formed the word, 'Home.'

Tears of relief stung Tulkhan's eyes and he kissed her closed lids. 'Rest easy, I will take you home.'

THEY RIGGED A cover over the supply wagon and Imoshen travelled in that. Their progress was slow by Tulkhan's normal standards, but he was pleased. Every day Imoshen regained her strength and the baby grew.

The day before the Festival of Midsummer they stood on the rise looking over T'Diemn. Tulkhan called a halt to the caravan and climbed into the wagon.

'We are home,' he told Imoshen and lifted her in his arms so she could see. 'There.'

He watched her face as she stared across at T'Diemn. It was one of the loveliest cities he had ever seen. Its spires and turrets shimmered in the rising waves of heat.

Yet Imoshen's face fell.

'What?'

She glanced quickly away. 'The stronghold is my home.'

He understood. What could he say?

'Where is your home, General?'

He could never return to Gheeaba. He knew that now. 'My home is with you.'

He saw her register his meaning. Her fierce hug warmed him.

She pulled away. 'Since we are here we must make the best of it. The people will want to see us and our son, Ashmyr.'

Imoshen had insisted they call the boy Ashmyr. She'd said T'Ashmyr had bound the island to him during the Age of Tribulation, uniting the T'En and locals alike. Only the Keldon Highlands had resisted him. So his son was named after a T'En emperor and Tulkhan did not mind

'Do you think you should ride?' Tulkhan was uneasy.

She had hardly so much as peeped outside the wagon except during their night camps.

'No. But you could carry me and I could hold the babe. The people of T'Diemn would like that.'

As they rode into town they received a rousing welcome. The people were celebrating the birth of the baby and the rout of the rebels, a tale he was sure had grown in the telling. The townsfolk came out of their houses and shops to cheer.

And they cheered loudest of all for Tulkhan's son.

'You won't reconsider?' Imoshen asked.

Tulkhan looked across at her. They were sharing a rare moment of privacy in the ornamental garden. Delicate blossoms hung from the trellis above them. It was a place of ethereal dappled light and sweet scent.

Nothing in Ghebite society was valued for its beauty. They valued wealth and military power, not aesthetics. In his brash youth he would have despised the creation of beauty as a waste of effort, but now he could admire a culture that had time for the pursuit of beauty for its own sake.

'Now that we've hosted the Midsummer Festival, I must return south. The fortress controlling the Greater Pass is almost finished, but I must complete the one sealing off the Lesser Pass before the harvest. Let the Keldon nobles winter in the ranges without fresh supplies.'

'I don't like it,' Imoshen said. 'It's a static defence. It gives the rebels a chance to study the fortresses, learn the patterns of your guards. In time they will spot a weakness and strike.'

Tulkhan knew Reothe could not afford to let the Protector General finish the fortresses. All trade and large caravans had to use the passes. If Tulkhan succeeded in barricading the Keldon Highlands, it would be a blow to Reothe's reputation. His supporters would be prisoners in their own estates.

'I must go.' Tulkhan joined her on the seat. 'I delayed only for the Midsummer Festival.'

She looked down, playing with the baby's hands. Imoshen never let the babe far from her side. Tulkhan had noticed her waking at night to check on him.

'Your workers will be attacked,' she whispered.

'I don't expect Reothe to disappoint me.'

'What will you do without me?'

Tulkhan sighed. Imoshen's gift had saved him and his men last time. Though she would say no more about that night, she often woke in terror, muttering in High T'En. And he had recognised the High T'En word, Parakletos.

Oh, he needed Imoshen all right, but she would not leave the baby with a wet nurse.

'I won't risk you and the baby. You can defend yourself, but my son can't.'

'I won't leave him behind.' She rose, her cheeks flushed with annoyance. The faint breeze played with wisps of her pale hair so that it seemed to have a life of its own. Anger and the stirring of her T'En powers exuded from her skin, making his heart race.

He ached for her but his bone-setter had warned him that there was good reason the Ghebite men did not touch their women for two small moons after the birth. The bone-setter's description of the injuries of an ordinary birth had horrified Tulkhan. No, he would not inflict himself on Imoshen until she was ready. But it had taken great self-restraint.

'You are my bond-partner,' Imoshen told him. 'And though I respect your wishes, I will do what I believe to be right. I could not live with myself otherwise.'

'Then we are at a deadlock,' Tulkhan said, and he left her.

Imoshen watched him walk away. Only yesterday Ashmyr had looked into her eyes and recognised her.

He had been born a little more than one small moon short of a full year. She suspected the exertion and the danger she faced had brought him on early. Even so, he was doing well and so was she. While she had recovered physically, she felt more vulnerable than ever. Reothe was ready to traffic with the Ancients and call on the Parakletos at risk to his own soul. To defeat Reothe she had to discover his limitations.

The palace library was no help. She had to get into the Basilica to search the archives. Somehow she would translate the T'Endomaz and use the knowledge against Reothe.

It was a cruel irony that he had given her the most valuable thing he possessed – his parents' last gift – and she hoped to use it to destroy him. Tears stung her eyes.

It was her lot to face terrible choices, just as it had been Imoshen the First's. Her namesake had bound the T'En warriors to her with oaths that went beyond death.

Pushing such dark thoughts aside Imoshen stretched, arching her back. Tonight was her last night with the General. The soft tug on her nipple as the baby fed made her other breast run with milk. She pressed it to stop the flow. Her body tingled and she thought longingly of Tulkhan's rough hands. If only he would hold her. She was sure she could overcome whatever scruples were restraining his ardour.

TULKHAN SPRAWLED ON the bed, watching Imoshen feed their son. He and his men were ready to move out. All that remained was this one night with Imoshen. He longed to hold her in his arms, but did not know if he could trust himself to do that without wanting more.

The baby fed eagerly. Tulkhan could hear him gulping milk. He grinned. 'My greedy son will get wind and keep you up all night.'

'Oh?' Imoshen fixed him with teasing eyes. 'So you're an expert now. I wager Ghebite men never care for their children.'

'Not true.' Tulkhan leaned against the headboard and linked his hands behind his head. 'When I was six I left the women's quarters and joined the men's lodge. There I was reared by the men who served my father. They trained me in the arts of war, preparing me for my role as first son of the King's second wife.'

She looked horrified. 'You mean you never lived with your female relatives after that? How sad.'

'Why?'

Imoshen shook her head. 'No wonder Ghebite men think women are a race apart.'

She detached the drowsy baby and tucked him into the basket by their bed before moving to sit in front of Tulkhan. A drop of milk still clung to her nipple. He found himself staring at it, unable to think of anything else.

Imoshen rose to her knees, her breasts tantalisingly close to his face. 'Are you thirsty?'

A shaft of urgent desire shot through him. Surely she wasn't suggesting? It went against everything he had been taught, yet it was so tempting.

He tore his gaze from the full expanse of her creamy white breast. 'Imoshen!'

She tilted her head, a smile playing about her lips.

'Is this how the women of Fair Isle act?' His voice was hoarse with the effort of denial.

Imoshen sighed and closed the bodice of her shift. 'I don't know. It was never mentioned in my lessons on how to share pleasure with a man.'

'You had lessons on... on –'

'Physical love?' Imoshen laughed. 'Of course. Everyone does. At least all well-educated people. I don't know about the farmers.' Her lips quirked. 'I suspect their education is more practical than theoretical.'

'How can you jest?' Tulkhan shifted across the bed, pulling the covers with him to hide his state. 'Imoshen, that is unnatural.'

'How can you say that? Didn't those men who reared you see to it that you learned how to lie with a woman?'

He could clearly remember them bringing a certain type of woman to his chamber when he was sixteen. It had been an enjoyable education, one he had partaken of regularly until he joined the army just after his seventeenth birthday.

Tulkhan folded his arms. 'That was different.'

'Different?'

For a moment he thought she was angry. Her eyes glowed like jewels. 'Imoshen?'

'How can you deny me when it is plain for all to see that you want me?'

The baby whimpered, responding to her tone. Imoshen glanced into the basket, then looked back to Tulkhan.

'I don't understand you,' she whispered.

He shook his head slowly. 'Nor I, you.' But it did not stop him wanting her.

'You could be killed,' she cried 'Reothe wants to lure you into the highlands so he can murder you.'

'What would you have me do?' Tulkhan reasoned. 'If I threaten the Keld to betray Reothe's hideout, they will grow to hate me. Yet I cannot let him undermine my hold on Fair Isle. I have no choice.'

'You go to your death!' Tears spilled down Imoshen's cheeks. Her balled fists hit his chest, pounding, thudding in time to his raging heart.

He caught her to him, pinning her arms against his chest, and kissed her forehead. He had no more words.

Her body trembled and he felt an answering shudder run through him. He wanted her so badly. He could feel her hot breath mingling with the moisture of her tears on his throat. His need to comfort her went core deep.

'Make love to me.' Her lips moved on his skin.

His arms tightened. 'I can't. It would hurt you so soon after the birth.'

She laughed and pulled away from him. 'I'm healed. Besides, do you think I care about a little pain?'

'I will be careful.'

She smiled and opened her arms in welcome.

Chapter Nineteen

THIS TIME WHEN the General marched out, Imoshen watched from the balcony with Ashmyr in her arms. The tenderness of their lovemaking had left her aching for him, vulnerable to the slightest nuance of his voice.

Sorrow formed a hard kernel in her chest as he gave her a farewell salute. She must not think of what awaited him. The last soldier disappeared from sight and she turned away. There was much to keep her mind from her fears, not least of all discovering the limits of Reothe's powers.

Imoshen made her way out of the palace and across to the Basilica. With deliberate casualness she strolled through the great double doors with Ashmyr in her arms. The priests clustered around her, delighted and honoured by the visit, fussing over the baby, who watched them all with curious unblinking eyes.

'So serious!' they laughed.

Imoshen's innocent request for a tour of the building was greeted eagerly and they were already halfway through the kitchens and storerooms when the Beatific caught up with them.

Imoshen knew the head of the T'En church probably wished her anywhere but inside her bastion of power, yet protocol demanded she welcome T'Imoshen graciously.

'There could not possibly be anything to interest you in this section of the Basilica,' the Beatific said. 'Let me escort you.'

Imoshen smiled. She knew the Beatific would not let her out of her sight, but that would not stop Imoshen meeting the Archivist and probing her mind.

'Our Basilica contains many great treasures preserved for posterity,' the Beatific said smoothly, leading Imoshen away from the acolytes. 'But first you must meet the leaders of each branch.'

The Beatific made a point of showing Imoshen the Tractarians' training chambers, where she felt as if she had walked into a nest of snakes. One by one the mulberry-robed priests fell silent, turning to watch her. Murgon came to his feet and said the words of welcome, but she read contempt in his eyes. A shudder moved over Imoshen's skin. This man was half T'En, yet he despised her.

'I will accompany you on the tour,' Murgon said, offering his arm.

Imoshen took a step back, unable to hide her revulsion. She could not bring herself to touch him.

Seeing her reaction, the Beatific's smile finally reached her eyes.

Imoshen felt the colour rise in her cheeks. Let them think her cowed by their display of force. It would make it all the easier for her to trick them.

The Beatific led her away and, after viewing countless trophies of war and tributes from long-dead mainland kings, they finally came to the Archives.

Imoshen was careful to appear only mildly interested. The Archivist and several of her staff came forward.

'Welcome to the Archives of the Basilica, T'Imoshen,' the Archivist greeted her. 'I think you will find this library is even greater than the palace's.'

While Imoshen pretended to admire the collection, she searched for something neutral to focus their attention. A multifaceted glass sculpture was on display beneath a window. It converted pure sunlight into shafts of rainbow light.

'Fascinating. How does it do that?' The delight in her voice was genuine.

She crossed to the captive rainbow. Spreading out her fingers within it, she watched the colours trickle over her pale skin.

'It is a prism, a child's toy.' The Archivist placed a hand on the glass sculpture.

'We had no such toys in the stronghold,' Imoshen said, trying to use the tenuous connection between them to sift the woman's mind. She turned her hand over and over, feeling the light, feeling the outer edges of the Archivist's mind. She had never attempted this with so weak a link.

'That's because your stronghold was one of the earliest built by your namesake, Imoshen the First. There was no time during the Age of Tribulation to indulge the senses. So many uprisings had to be put down.'

Imoshen sensed the Beatific grow tense, but what could the woman do? Imoshen was not touching the Archivist.

She had to keep the woman talking while she concentrated on finding out where the oldest cartularies were kept. They were the key to the T'Endomaz. 'Because I was named after her I have always felt a kinship with Imoshen the First. It was such a shame the T'Elegos was lost when the palace burned down.'

The Archivist smiled to herself. Imoshen felt the woman's reaction as though it was her own. The Archivist felt superior because Imoshen was mistaken. The T'Elegos had not been lost. It was safely hidden in the Basilica, in this very chamber!

Imoshen's mind reeled. She froze, desperate not to reveal herself.

'...Sardonyx's revolt of sixty-four,' the Archivist was saying. 'Some works predating the conquest did survive the sea journey, but they were lost to posterity along with the first Imoshen's T'Elegos. During the Age of Tribulation, not only was the palace burned, but your stronghold's library was destroyed twice.'

'What a shame,' Imoshen said softly. When she felt she could hide the triumph in her heart she looked up and smiled. 'I would like one of these prisms for Ashmyr when he is older. I think it would delight a child to make rainbows.'

'Of course,' the Beatific agreed readily. 'Now, would you like to see the music wing where the choir will be rehearsing?'

Imoshen nodded, hugging her impossible discovery to herself. Joy and outrage mingled freely. She did not understand why the church had hidden the T'Elegos from the people of Fair Isle, but she knew she was close to breaking the T'Endomaz encryption.

Even the arrival of Murgon and several of his Tractarians during the choir's rehearsal did not dispel her elation. They watched her closely but there was nothing for them to see.

DESPITE HER IMPATIENCE, Imoshen bided her time until Intercession Day. It provided her best chance to slip unnoticed into the Basilica. Every fortnight they opened the disputation hall where anyone from a landless worker to the richest guildmaster was welcome to consult the priests trained in matters of T'En law and its interpretation.

If a disputation could not be settled, applicants requested the assistance of a church representative to present their case to the Empress. Consequently there was always a long line of petitioners awaiting hearings in the public rooms of the Basilica.

Late that afternoon Imoshen fed Ashmyr and strapped him between her breasts. She would have preferred to leave him safely in his little basket, but she trusted no one. Always at the back of her mind was the fear of the Ancients.

Imoshen pulled up her cloak's hood and shuffled forward, blending with the crowd. She did not intend to use her gifts, which might attract Murgon and his Tractarians. Unchallenged, she moved past public rooms packed with busy priests, each full of their own importance. Excitement powered her legs as she glided up the grand staircase. The first time she had seen its marbled balustrades, she had been overwhelmed by its beauty, but now she barely took in the glistening stone. Thanks to her guided tour she knew her way to the Archives, which were deserted on Intercession Day. Her soft-soled boots carried her soundlessly across the mosaic floor.

She went straight to the false wall panel, recognising it from the Archivist's memory. The woman had even supplied her with the knowledge to open the panel. Imoshen felt no remorse about her methods. As far as she was concerned the T'Elegos was her heritage. The church had no right to hide it.

The baby stirred against her chest and she crooned under her breath as her fingers traced the design of the carved wood panel which was inlaid with ivory and gold. In her mind's eye she saw the Archivist trip the mechanism and her hands mimicked the action. It felt exactly as the woman remembered. How strange to have the tactile memory of another person.

The panel clicked and the catch sprang open. Imoshen's heart leapt. At last she would discover the secrets her namesake had inscribed. She would know what Reothe knew, how to uncover and exploit his weaknesses, and she would have the key to break the encryption of the T'Endomaz.

Sliding the panel across, she peered into the dusty vault.

Nothing?

She blinked in astonishment and her heart missed a beat. It could not be. The vault was empty.

Had she given herself away? Had the Beatific removed the T'Elegos?

Imoshen sank to her knees. There on the stone floor she could see the dust-rimmed outline where a single jar had stood. This corresponded with what she knew. According to legend and what she could glean from historical accounts, Imoshen the First had spent the last winter of her life working on a long scroll of vellum. She had been determined to preserve for posterity the story of the T'En odyssey and to honour her warriors. Imoshen knew that the best way to preserve a single ancient scroll, to protect it from insects and damp was to seal it in an earthenware jar filled with oil.

The T'Elegos had almost been within her grasp. Her hands clenched in frustration.

Who would have taken it and why? Had the Beatific decided to change the hiding place? And if it wasn't the Beatific, who else would have had access and the motive? The Archivist certainly believed the T'Elegos was still in its hiding place.

Imoshen straightened, her thigh muscles flexing with the added weight of the baby. Leaning against the wall she stared into the empty vault. Her mind went blank and her vision blurred.

Candlelight danced on the walls. Someone stood with his back to her, rolling a heavy jar into position. He knelt to pick it up, turning towards her.

Reothe!

The vision faded.

Imoshen blinked, startled and dismayed. She had not meant to use her gift. Never before had she called up the image of a past event. But then she had never tried.

Reothe had stolen the T'Elegos!

Anger stirred in Imoshen. Had he removed the jar with the Beatific's approval or by subterfuge? She knew he was capable of slipping in here even more easily than she had done.

Why had no one at the Basilica discovered the loss? Imoshen had received the distinct impression from the Archivist that this document was too dangerous to read, yet too precious to destroy. For generations it had been hidden, keeping Imoshen the First's insights into the T'En mysteries safe from prying eyes.

Reothe must have given her the T'Endomaz knowing she could not unlock the secrets without the T'Elegos. As furious as she was with him, she found it hard to believe evil of Reothe. Perhaps the T'Elegos contained information which could be used against the pure T'En.

There was no doubt that there were True-people who hated the pure T'En. Murgon of the Tractarians was their most virulent opponent. Imoshen shuddered, feeling vulnerable.

Backing out of the secret vault, she closed the panel. Before she knew what she was doing, Imoshen brushed the carved woodwork, erasing all memory of her touch.

Now no one with the T'En gift would be able to tell she had been here.

That made her stop. How had she known how to cover her tracks?

Simple logic had told her. If these steps did one thing, then by reversing them she removed the traces. Strange, before this her mind had not worked along such paths and she had struggled to focus her meagre powers.

Had she betrayed her presence? The Tractarians were only half T'En. Though they were trained to sense the use of the gifts, as far as she knew there was only one person who had the skill to trace her actions.

Imoshen made her way to the grand staircase. A forewarning of danger travelled over her skin. Sick dread filled her as she took in the cluster of mulberry-robed priests at the entrance. And there, wandering casually through the throng, was Murgon.

Somehow these part T'En traitors had sensed her presence. Murgon turned and looked directly at the staircase. Imoshen froze, willing herself to appear ordinary. Then she realised the very act itself would attract Murgon. Terror killed all thought. Three intercession priests chose that moment to pass her, arguing loudly over a case.

Imoshen moved up the steps with them. From the balcony she looked down to see Murgon call two priests over and confer with them before heading towards the stairs.

She fled.

The Basilica was a sprawling rabbit warren and she had only a rough idea of its layout. She had to find the nearest safe exit. Opening her T'En senses, she risked a quick search. The maze of passages and informal rooms assumed a three-dimensional shape in her mind as she sought an escape route not guarded by the Tractarians.

She felt them questing for her. They were weak but they outnumbered her. Scattered like ants on a rubbish heap they picked their way through the dross, looking for the source of power which drew them like honey. She might crush one or two but she could not stand against all of them.

Nausea rolled over her. She had endangered herself and Ashmyr for nothing. These Tractarians would find her and she had no excuse for entering the Basilica today. How the Beatific would crow!

Her T'En power rose to the surface. She was aware of tension thrumming through her body, as well as the vast well of emotions emanating from the True-men and women in the rooms around her. Instinct told her to use her gifts to escape.

But that instinct would get her captured.

Slipping into a deserted storeroom, she reeled in her T'En senses, even though it left her feeling exposed. Without her gifts she could not tell where the Tractarians were, could not tell if they were closing in. Like a trapped animal she could smell her own fear.

Ashmyr stirred, whimpering in his sleep.

Leaning against the cold stone wall of the cluttered room, Imoshen slowed her breathing.

With a trembling hand, she wiped the sweat from her top lip and listened intently. Far away she could hear the clatter of the great kitchen and smell the food being prepared.

The kitchen!

It was the perfect avenue of escape. The kitchen of any great establishment was always full of bustle, people coming and going, deliveries, flirting scullery maids and cheeky stable hands trying to steal freshly baked pies.

Hardly daring to think what she planned, Imoshen left the sanctuary of the storeroom. She followed the heady scent of spices, baking meat, pickles and preserves to the kitchen. At any moment she could be discovered by a servant loyal to the Beatific, and turned over to the Tractarians...

What was she thinking? She had not been declared rogue.

No one but the Tractarians knew she was in the Basilica illegally. As long as one of them was not standing by each kitchen door she had a chance of escape.

Stepping into the shadow of a deep doorway she watched the flow of human traffic across the cavernous kitchen. With over a thousand people to be fed, the kitchen staff formed an efficient army. Some were busy peeling vegetables, their heads down and hands flying over long preparation tables. Others dragged loaves out of deep ovens, swinging around to slide them onto cooling trays. The scent of the fresh bread almost made Imoshen gag.

A mulberry-robed priest stood by the far door. The workers averted their eyes when they passed her. So they disliked this priest. Did they dislike all Tractarians or just this one?

Heart pounding, Imoshen slipped away before the priest could sense her. Her hair, her eyes, her sixth finger all marked her for what she was. A surge of hatred for her pursuers overtook her.

Imoshen headed towards the familiar smell of soap and sunshine. The laundry was deserted, the coppers emptied of their loads of washing. No one guarded this door, for it led to an enclosed courtyard which contained nothing but flapping priestly garments drying in the sun.

A mulberry tabard caught Imoshen's eye and she had an idea. Crossing the scrubbed tiles she entered the courtyard. No one was about. Who would watch washing dry? With a sharp tug she pulled a Tractarian robe off the line. Throwing it over her shoulders, she raised the hood to hide her hair.

Mouth dry with fear, Imoshen went inside. Now she noticed how the other priests avoided her eyes. That the priests would fear one of their own branches had not occurred to Imoshen, but under the circumstances she was grateful.

Taking care to appear at ease with her surroundings, she crossed the floor of the kitchen. The Tractarian by the door met her eyes briefly. Imoshen willed herself to appear familiar, willed her son to be silent.

'No sign?' the woman asked in High T'En.

Imoshen realised they kept the old language alive to exclude others. She slipped into the language as easily as she had slipped into the mulberry robe. 'No. I've been sent to check the carts.'

'Good idea.'

With one hand on Ashmyr she moved off, careful not to appear hurried. Once she entered the outer courtyard it was simple enough to follow one of the many delivery carts through the lane and out into the sunshine of old T'Diemn.

Imoshen felt light-headed with relief. This day had taught her a valuable lesson. She had more than one enemy within the church. If the Beatific was a cunning cat, Murgon was a ravenous wolf, leading his pack in pursuit of her.

Walking steadily away from the Basilica, Imoshen joined a crowd outside a tea-house then darted into a side lane to remove the mulberry robe. Without remorse she tossed it onto the rubbish a nearby shopkeeper had left burning. She stirred the coals until the material caught light. As she watched the robe burn she vowed never again to leave herself vulnerable to the Tractarians.

She had risked so much today – and for what?

Reothe had the T'Elegos. But she could wait no longer. Tulkhan was in danger and she must face the most difficult decision of her life.

EXHAUSTED BY HER close escape, Imoshen slept all afternoon and into the evening. Late that night she packed her travelling things. Then she debated over the wording of a message for Kalleen and Wharrd. She called on their friendship, asking only that they meet her at Umasreach Stronghold as soon as possible.

As she watched Ashmyr asleep in his basket, tears blurred her vision. It was because she loved him so fiercely that she had to remove him from danger, for she believed the inevitable confrontation between herself and Reothe was fated to be her last.

She would not leave Tulkhan to die alone. She must stand at his side, and if by some miracle they survived, Kalleen would restore Ashmyr to her. However, if she fell at Tulkhan's side, then Kalleen and Wharrd would know to flee Fair Isle. It demanded a lot of their friendship to ask them to raise her son, but if Reothe recaptured the island they would lose everything anyway, their estates, their titles and their lives.

Secreted in her family's stronghold was a king's ransom in portable wealth. With her great-aunt, Imoshen had collected and hidden it during the spring and summer of the Ghebite invasion so that they could ransom their relatives. Now it would be put to good use. With this wealth Kalleen and Wharrd could take Ashmyr and flee to one of the mainland kingdoms, far from Reothe's influence and the taint of the Ancients.

Safe and unknown, her boy could be raised in peace. When she saw Kalleen and Wharrd in person, she would tell them not to encourage Ashmyr to recapture Fair Isle. There was nothing to be gained by frittering away his life in fruitless revenge. She wished only that he be happy.

Imoshen smiled. Maybe when he grew to adulthood he would travel into the dawn sun and discover his T'En origins. But in truth she did not care what Ashmyr did as long as he grew up free of fear and Reothe. Imoshen folded the note and sealed it with a daub of wax and the pad of her sixth finger.

Unable to resist she knelt beside her sleeping son. Her heart swelled with love as she stroked his shock of fine dark hair.

'Merkah?' Imoshen looked up as the girl passed by with an armful of clothes. 'I won't need anything so fancy, just my travelling things. And you'll need yours too.'

'I am to come with you this time?' Merkah was still resentful.

'As far as the stronghold. But before you finish packing, please send for Crawen.'

'Yes, my lady.' Merkah hurried away, eyes bright with curiosity.

Imoshen picked up her son, cradling his soft head against her cheek. If she and Tulkhan lost, she would not see Ashmyr grow up and he would never know how much she loved him. She felt his head bob against her cheek, his little mouth open, looking for another feed.

She held him away from her to memorise his perfect little features. Tears ran unheeded down her cheeks.

He would never know what it cost her to give him away. Perhaps she should touch his unformed mind and leave a message there for him to find one day. No, she must let him be his own person. One day Kalleen and Wharrd could tell him that his mother had given him up so that he would grow up free. She had to content herself with that.

'Crawen, my lady,' Merkah announced.

Imoshen indicated the message. 'I want this to reach Windhaven as soon as possible. Deliver it into Kalleen's own hands.'

The woman took the sealed missive. 'Am I to wait for an answer?'

'No. I'm going to my stronghold. You can escort Kalleen and Wharrd there.'

Crawen smiled. 'It will be good to go home.'

Imoshen nodded but there was no smile in her heart.

IMOSHEN MEANT TO leave early the next morning, but both she and Ashmyr woke during the night hot and fretful. Merkah talked of the spotted-fever which had swept through the children of T'Diemn. Though Imoshen had had it as a child, it appeared she was still susceptible to a milder version.

Rather than take her son on a journey when he was ill, Imoshen sat by his cot and bathed him, speaking softly to soothe him and using her gift to cool his body. All day he lay on the bed next to her, safely tucked in the crook of her body. As she tended to his needs she savoured every moment, knowing she must soon give him up.

By evening he was cool and sleeping naturally. There was no sign of spots and her own fever had broken.

'Merkah?' Imoshen sat up, careful not to disturb the sleeping baby.

The maid paused as she tiptoed across the chamber.

'We'll leave tomorrow. There's no point in setting off this late in the day.'

The girl nodded and left.

Imoshen tucked a pillow on each side of the baby then slipped into the bathing chamber to wash the weariness from her body.

Rubbing her damp hair dry she entered the room to find Merkah beside the bed, the baby in her arms. 'He was stirring so I picked him up.'

'Thank you.' As Imoshen stepped forward she noted the glow of colour in Merkah's cheeks. 'Are you feverish?' Imoshen touched her forehead. The girl's skin was hot. Strange, her mind was closed. Imoshen would not have thought Merkah had the strength of will to resist the T'En gifts. 'I will mix you something –'

'No, I'll use my mother's remedy.'

'I am a healer, Merkah, I know my herbs.'

But the girl would not be swayed. Imoshen was not surprised. Some healers guarded their knowledge jealously. 'Then get some rest and we will see how you are tomorrow.'

But the next day Merkah was feverish. She kept to her room, refusing Imoshen's offer of help.

Imoshen spent the day pacing impatiently. Now that her mind was made up, every day was an agony of waiting, and yet the longer she delayed the longer she had with her son.

Over the next few days Merkah's fever worsened. Imoshen could have left without her but she allowed herself the painful indulgence of prolonging this time with Ashmyr. Besides, it would take several days for her message to reach Kalleen and Wharrd, and they would need time to pack and travel to the stronghold. Imoshen longed to see the home she had been forced to abandon at a moment's notice last autumn.

It was six days before Merkah was finally well enough to attend to her duties, and Imoshen faced the fact that their leaving could no longer be delayed. She stared down at her sleeping son and her heart ached with love for him. She could not bear to think of giving him up but it was the only way to keep him safe.

MIDMORNING THEY SET out with two servants and six of her stronghold guard, all of whom were happy to be returning home. Imoshen had not told them that she intended to leave them there and continue south to meet up with Tulkhan at the Lesser Pass.

They made good time and were soon into the woods, where the trees almost met over the road above their heads. Imoshen smiled as Merkah frantically brushed an insect off her shoulder. Her maid was not a good traveller.

As they travelled through the balmy summer afternoon, Imoshen's heart lifted at the thought of going home. She would see how Umasreach

Stronghold and the new town had fared through the winter. She would show off her son. For the moment she allowed herself to think only that far ahead.

Trying to make the halfway point, the party rode late into the long summer twilight. Finally they came to the burned-out ruins of what had once been a bustling inn. Imoshen was surprised no one had taken up residence. True, there was no roof and weeds had sprouted in the walls, but it was an ideal spot. Perhaps the people south of T'Diemn did not have the confidence to rebuild until this trouble with the rebels was settled.

Others had camped here before them and cleared out a hearth space, so they lit a fire on the stones and prepared the evening meal. Merkah seemed distracted. Imoshen had to call the maid twice to get her attention and even then the girl was slow to bring Imoshen the baby's change things.

While her companions sat back and ate their meal, talking happily of the stronghold, their friends and families, Merkah sat alone, watching the darkness fearfully.

'You must not be afraid,' Imoshen told her, growing exasperated with her timidity. 'We are a long way from the rebel camps.'

'True,' one of the stronghold guard said. 'But I have heard tales of Reothe and his people travelling far into the north while the Ghebites are busy building their fortress.'

'There are many tales,' Imoshen said dismissively. And there were. If you believed half of the sightings, Reothe would have to fly from one end of Fair Isle to the other. 'Get some sleep. We'll make an early start tomorrow.'

Imoshen tucked Ashmyr into the crook of her arm and closed her eyes. The thought of losing her son haunted her. She gave up trying to sleep and reviewed her plans. Were they safe from attack?

Imoshen tried to weigh up the chances. To escape notice she had chosen to travel with a small group and only her palace staff had known she was going.

IMOSHEN WOKE WITH an odd taste in her mouth. The larger moon was waxing and their campsite was bathed in its silvery glow. She sniffed. The air had that strange tang which foretold a thunderstorm, yet the stars were clearly visible.

Stiff from the saddle, she struggled to her feet with the baby cradled in her arms. Her head was thick with sleep, only the sensation of something impending drove her to move. 'Merkah, wake up. We must take cover.'

Her maid did not stir.

Exasperated, Imoshen searched the sky. There was not a cloud to be seen. No storm. Then what...

Reothe leapt up onto the ruined stone wall directly opposite her, his silver hair glowing in the moonlight.

Chapter Twenty

'YOU...' IMOSHEN GASPED. She tried to warn her companions. 'To arms. We are attacked!'

But her people did not stir and Reothe's people did not attack.

He jumped down into the shadows and prowled towards her. Instinctively she covered the baby, pressing him closer to her chest. Fear closed her throat, robbing her of speech.

Frantically, she kicked the nearest guard in the back. He grunted but did not wake.

'They are asleep,' Reothe told her, his soft voice hanging on the still night. 'And will remain that way until dawn, when they discover you have run away during the night to join me.'

'No.' It was a breathless denial.

He came to a stop before her and held out his hands. 'Give me the baby, Imoshen.'

Her heart sank. Selfish fool. If she had already given Ashmyr into Kalleen's safekeeping, she could have resisted Reothe with every fibre of her being, but as long as her son was vulnerable she dare not resist. Every contact with Reothe had confirmed that he was the master of his gifts and she the novice. She could not stand against him – better to play along with him for now.

Reothe smiled as she passed the sleeping baby to him. Turning Ashmyr's face to the light, he studied the boy.

Imoshen could hardly think for the rushing of blood in her ears.

'So much black hair... but at least he is half ours,' Reothe muttered. 'Come, Imoshen.'

He cradled the small baby against his body and held out his other hand.

She was too devastated to move.

'Bring his things and your own,' Reothe ordered. 'Do it, or I will walk off with him. I imagine even on his own, Ashmyr is enough to bring the General running –'

'I'm coming.'

'I rather thought you would.'

Numbly she collected their belongings. Reothe carried the baby and she followed him out of the ruins. None of her people stirred. They would assume she had gone of her own free will. Would Tulkhan believe them?

A dozen rebels mounted on wiry mountain ponies waited in the shadows of the trees, with two horses. She could just make out their sturdy peasant clothes and weaponry.

Imoshen felt a lightening of the atmosphere when she stepped onto the road. As her head cleared she realised she had been betrayed. Someone had told the rebels her plans. With a sickening lurch Imoshen understood Merkah must have slipped them a herb to mimic the fever, then taken it herself to cover her tracks. Yet Kalleen had recommended the girl. Merkah had to be passing information to someone of influence.

'Wake up, Imoshen, your horse is waiting,' Reothe chided.

She looked up to see him swing into his saddle.

Taking the reins in one hand, he cradled the baby in his free arm.

Imoshen put her foot into the stirrup and mounted her horse. All the while, her empty arms ached. She wanted to rail at Reothe, to plead with him to give Ashmyr back, but she was in no position to bargain.

Reothe wheeled his mount. 'Ride out. We will follow.'

The rebels rode off and left her with their leader. Imoshen twisted in the saddle, confused. Reothe laughed and pulled a brass cylinder from inside his jerkin. He tossed it onto the grass outside the entrance to the ruin.

'What's that?'

'An invitation to your Ghebite lover.'

His tone made Imoshen's skin turn to ice. Reothe was preparing a trap and she and Ashmyr were the bait.

'What did you promise the Beatific in return for betraying me?' she prodded.

But he gave nothing away. 'Ride on, Imoshen.'

She raged against her impotence. As long as Reothe held her son she would obey him.

DURING THAT LONG night Imoshen never left Reothe's side. Her son slept peacefully in the arms of the man who had sworn to kill his father. A burning anger grew inside her. Not only had she been betrayed but Reothe was using her child as bait.

At first she paid no heed to the direction they rode, thinking only of escape. But then she noticed as the dawn chorus began and the sky lightened that they were headed north, not south. Trust Reothe to lay a false trail for their pursuers, who would be expecting him to return to his hideout amongst the loyal Keld.

Shortly after dawn the baby began to squall. Reothe halted and the others waited, watching.

'He must be fed,' Imoshen said. She had been waiting for this. When Ashmyr was safely in her arms she would create a diversion, anything she could lay her gift on. While they were distracted she would gallop off. She had enough skills now to cloak her passage from all but Reothe, and if he followed her, well... she would find a way to kill him. She had to.

Reothe urged his horse closer to hers. 'You are ready to feed him?'

She nodded, leaning forward. They were thigh to thigh. She was eager to take the babe and her breasts ached in anticipation. Reothe swung his free arm around her waist, dragging her off her mount. Frightened by the thought of him dropping Ashmyr, Imoshen twisted and clung to Reothe.

She found herself sitting across his thighs as he passed the baby to her.

'Forgive me if I do not trust you, Imoshen,' he said above Ashmyr's screams. 'I want you where I can hold you.'

Then he laughed at her expression and urged his horse forward.

Reluctantly she undid the laces of her bodice. With the baby feeding hungrily at her breast, she had no choice but to remain where she was. Reothe's arms encircled her. Holding the reins with one hand, he clasped her firmly to him with the other.

If she tried to struggle free and get to the ground, she risked dropping Ashmyr and being trampled by the rebels who rode with them.

The rocking motion of the horse and the relief of holding Ashmyr again finally soothed her. They made their way through the deep woods, fording clear streams where she could see every stone on the riverbed.

As morning passed, Reothe made no attempt to return her to her own mount and she did not suggest it. Just holding her son was enough for now.

Her eyes felt gritty from lack of sleep. The dappled sunlight passed over them, alternately blinding her and warming her, then plunging them into a green-tinged twilight.

Ashmyr slept safely in her arms. Despite her exhaustion, she refused to let herself succumb to sleep. She would not sleep.

IMOSHEN AWOKE WITH a start, feeling something brush her face. It was dusk. Her cheeks burned when she realised she had slept in Reothe's arms. That would have amused him.

The others had already dismounted by the time Reothe swung his leg over the horse, stepping down. He wound his fingers through the reins, effectively ruling out any attempt to kick the tired horse to a gallop, and lifted one arm to help her dismount. She longed to shun the offer, but she was stiff from sitting in one position and didn't want to stumble with Ashmyr in her arms.

'Give me the baby.'

'No. I must change him.'

'I'll change him. You go with Selita and tend to your needs. You must be hungry.'

As soon as he said this she realised she was ravenous. Already someone had started a fire. With great reluctance Imoshen handed her son to Reothe.

'This way.' Selita was a farm girl much like Kalleen in size and colouring, but with a more pronounced Keldon accent. Imoshen could have overpowered her and escaped, but Reothe knew she wouldn't while he had Ashmyr.

The rebel girl waited as Imoshen splashed cold water on her face and hands, willing her mind to clear. Looking up at the sky through the gap in the leaves, Imoshen tried to get her bearings. They would have to turn south soon. The longer they stayed in the territory occupied by the Ghebites, the greater the chance of Reothe's band being captured.

As they returned, a foreign, spicy smell hung over the camp, making Imoshen's stomach rumble.

Reothe sat with his back against the rock, his knees raised. The baby was wedged in an upright position, facing him. Wide awake, Ashmyr waved his arms around, tasting the air with his tongue.

Imoshen's heart turned over because her son was so terribly vulnerable, a pawn in this endless game of power.

'Your share is there.' Reothe indicated a bowl on the ground next to him.

Holding the bowl in her hands she found she could not eat, despite her hunger. 'Give Ashmyr to me.'

'He likes it where he is.' Reothe rubbed the babe's cheek with one knuckle. Ashmyr turned his face and sucked on the knuckle.

'I can't eat unless I hold him,' Imoshen confessed.

Reothe's sharp eyes turned on her. She tried to smile but she could not hide the urgency of her feelings.

He frowned. 'I did not know how strong it was.'

He put his bowl aside and passed the baby to her. As soon as she held her son, her body relaxed. Propping the bowl on her knee, she ate quickly as she fed Ashmyr, only too aware that Reothe was watching her. He seemed amused.

'Food's good,' she said to distract him.

'It's a speciality of Amarillo's. He's from one of the spice islands of the archipelago.'

The cook tilted his head in her direction. Imoshen didn't want to know their names. She didn't want to get to know these people because she might have to kill them.

But she nodded and smiled. 'Thank you. Very good.'

Reothe nodded. 'Amarillo has served me since my first voyage. I bought him when his master was going to have him whipped –'

'Bought him?' Imoshen asked around a mouthful.

'Yes. Slavery is common in the archipelago. Each island preys on the others.'

'I thought they made beautiful crafts, pottery, exquisite mechanical things.'

'They do.' Reothe glanced at her, then rolled with catlike grace to his feet. 'They also cut off their enemies' heads, shrink them and hang them in their household temples.'

As soon as Imoshen had eaten, Reothe ordered them to break camp. He held out his arms for the baby.

She handed Ashmyr over, then climbed into the saddle, keeping close to Reothe's horse. Their thighs brushed.

'Such devotion,' he purred. 'What a pity it isn't for me.'

A shiver of fear ran up Imoshen's spine.

They rode through the night, pausing at dawn for fresh horses. Imoshen watched Reothe closely but he never let Ashmyr go or passed him to anyone else. She had no choice but to follow his lead, still north.

Why hadn't he returned to the safety of the Keldon Highlands?

TULKHAN STOOD ON the lookout tower of his fortress, staring down into the valley. A single rider worked his way up the treacherous switchback path.

As the figure drew nearer Tulkhan could see he was pushing his horse at a reckless pace. His message must be urgent. Abandoning the tower, the General swung through the trapdoor and down the ladder.

'Open the gates. He's one of ours,' Tulkhan ordered. The gates eased open to let the horse and rider enter. The mount's sides were flecked with foam.

Tulkhan caught the exhausted messenger as he fell from his saddle. 'What is it?'

The man thrust a cylinder into Tulkhan's hands. He tore it open, unrolling the thick paper. It was written in the common language of Fair Isle but his mind refused to take in the meaning.

'Forgive me, General,' pleaded the messenger. 'Your wife... she ran away to join the rebel leader.'

'She was abducted,' Tulkhan snapped. He didn't recognise his own voice. The man flinched. 'Reothe has laid down a challenge. It says here that I must meet him at Northpoint Harbour.' It actually said that Imoshen and the child were with Reothe. Typically ambiguous.

'It makes no sense,' the fortress commander muttered. 'That's the northernmost harbour in Fair Isle, far from the rebels' territory. Why would he risk a confrontation there?'

Tulkhan shrugged. He had planned to man the fortresses in the passes and so contain the rebels and the insolent Keld. Pulling back his forces to face a threat in Fair Isle's north was an unwelcome complication. If the Keldon nobles sensed a weakness they might join forces with the rest of Reothe's people and attempt to regain the capital.

To save time he set off with a small band of men, planning to collect more in T'Diemn before he advanced further north. But he would not need an army. The battle ahead was not of the physical kind.

Tulkhan ground his teeth. Imoshen might be the key to Fair Isle, but he knew now that he could not live without her. Frustration and fear tore at him. Imoshen and his only child were in the hands of an unstable Dhamfeer warrior who would stop at nothing.

SELITA PEERED THROUGH the steam. 'Are you out of the tub already, T'Imoshen?'

Imoshen wrapped herself in the drying cloth. She was grateful for the chance to bathe in warm water, but finding herself a 'guest' at Chalkcliff Abbey was disturbing. It was the largest abbey outside T'Diemn, and though the Seculate had been careful not to be seen, he was clearly aiding Reothe.

Since the Seculate answered directly to the Beatific, Imoshen was left in no doubt where the leader of the T'En church's loyalty lay.

She turned to Selita. 'Your turn.'

'I'll only be a moment.' The girl discarded her clothes eagerly.

'Take your time.' Imoshen finished drying herself, then finger-combed her damp hair as she walked through to her chamber.

Reothe lay stretched across her bed, playing with Ashmyr.

Making no attempt to hide her nakedness, Imoshen selected a fresh nightgown and pulled it over her head. Her hands trembled as she tightened the drawstring under her breasts then the second one at her throat. So as not to betray her nervousness, she took her time braiding her damp hair into one long plait.

Reothe watched her silently, his expression unreadable.

When Selita entered the room, wrapped in a cloth, Reothe dismissed her. Imoshen wanted to protest but she held her tongue as Selita tugged on her clothes and departed.

It had been in a chamber almost identical to this one that Reothe had confronted her at Landsend Abbey. Reminding her of their vows, he had urged her to join him and retake Fair Isle, but she had refused. Even as she thought this, the scar on her wrist tingled.

She hugged her left arm to her breast. 'I am ready to feed the baby now.'

'Come and get him.'

Feeling his eyes on her, Imoshen walked stiffly across the chamber to the bed. Every nerve protested at his presence. From her pounding heart to her rapid breathing, her body recognised him.

Ashmyr lay on his back, contentedly sucking his fist. At least he had not suffered during their forced march.

Imoshen scooped her baby up and backed away. She heard Reothe chuckling as she turned, heading for the chair by the fire.

She sank into the deep chair and loosened the upper drawstring, freeing her aching left breast. Ashmyr had only to feel the warm curve of her flesh on his cheek to realise what was coming. He latched onto her nipple.

'Is it that I am so terrible?' Reothe asked. 'Or is it that you don't trust yourself?'

'You need to ask, when you do not hesitate to threaten my child to control me?'

She heard the rustle of Reothe's clothes as he moved. Her skin prickled.

Reothe crouched beside the chair. She looked away from him, into the baby's face.

'Don't hate me, Imoshen. I am only trying to protect what is mine.'

She could not speak for her fury.

Reothe drew a sharp breath.

The urgent tug of the baby's sucking triggered the flow of milk in her right breast. Before she could press her hand over the left nipple to stop the flow, she felt a familiar tug.

Imoshen found Reothe's fair head at her breast. Her heart turned over. He had not pulled the material down, but between the heat of the milk and his mouth it felt as if the thin nightgown had melted away. His teeth grazed her nipple as she felt him draw on her aching flesh, triggering an arrow of sweet desire straight to her core.

A groan escaped her.

Her free hand sank into his silver hair, feeling its fine texture. She leant forward to experience that silken touch with her lips and inhale his scent. The melt began deep within her, dissolving her limbs and her will.

'No...'

'No?' He lifted his head, his lips glistening, his eyes hungry.

She felt her body respond, impossibly urgent. How could she expect him to understand when she didn't? 'Reothe, please.'

'No.' He smiled. 'Not till the moment is right.'

A flash of anger ignited her. 'I wasn't asking –'

'Yes, you were. I can feel how much you want me. It sears my senses. It always has.'

She shook her head. She did not like to think what his admission revealed.

With the nail of one finger he circled the damp patch of material around her nipple. 'You taste so sweet.'

A clench of desire seized her. Unlike Tulkhan, Reothe would accept her for what she was. He would revel in her Otherness.

'Even if I desire you, you must know I have made a vow. I am Tulkhan's bond-partner.'

'Only by necessity, and only after breaking your vows to me.'

'Nevertheless, Tulkhan and I are bonded.'

'Only until his death.'

Her mouth went dry. 'You mean to kill him?'

'I won't have to. At most he would only live another twenty years. Fifty is a good age for a True-man. But you and I have another eighty years or more.' He leant closer to her, brushing her cheek with his lips. 'Imoshen, don't deny what you know to be true.'

She drew in a shaky breath, senses scorched by his nearness. All those years alone...

'You want me,' Reothe whispered. His breath dusted her skin. 'We would already have been together if the Ghebites hadn't chosen to launch their campaign last spring. Don't deny me, Imoshen.'

Drawing a deep breath she met his eyes as honestly as she could. 'True, I want you. I may even love you a little, Reothe. But I gave my vow to Tulkhan, the truest of True-men. I am bonded till death parts us and I hope he lives another fifty years!'

She wanted to anger him. It was easier to keep her distance from an angry Reothe.

He lifted her free hand, stroking her bonding scar. 'With me you can bond beyond death.'

'No.'

'I speak the truth. Test me.'

He was offering to mind-touch with her.

She wanted it. It was awful to acknowledge how much. She had been so lonely, shut out by Tulkhan's resistance to her gifts.

Reothe smiled and leaned closer. Imoshen gasped as she felt the first tingle of awareness brush the surface of her mind. But that forbidden fruit was too sweet to taste without risking her strength of purpose, so she shut herself away from Reothe. It surprised her to discover that she could.

'You may believe the T'En can bond beyond death, Reothe, but I do not want to end up like the Parakletos, a restless shade, bound between this world and the next. Besides, I gave my word to the General.'

'You gave your word to a Ghebite, a man blinded by his upbringing, a man who does not understand your true value.'

'Nevertheless, I gave my word.'

'Under duress! Why does it always come back to this?' Reothe sprang to his feet. 'Why do you find it so easy to break your word to me?'

The baby jerked in her arms, responding to his tone. She changed Ashmyr to the other breast, reminded again of Reothe's touch. Then she looked up to see him watching her, one elbow propped on the mantelpiece, a frown drawing his narrow brows together.

'You gave your word under duress, Imoshen. I know you believed you were saving our people from further warfare, but it is coming...' He stopped himself as if he was about to say more. 'As for us, you gave your word freely to me, but you cannot say the same for that Ghebite. To which of us do you owe your true loyalty?'

She pressed the fingers of her free hand to her closed eyes, weary beyond belief. Every word he said made things more tangled. With a sigh she looked up. 'There is no right, Reothe, only survival.'

A smile lit his face, igniting him from within.

'What?' She regarded him warily.

He crouched beside her, earnest and intense. 'I'm glad you said it all comes down to survival. For I am also a pragmatist and I will do whatever I must to ensure the right outcome.'

Imoshen went cold. That wasn't what she meant at all. Or was it?

Reothe stroked the baby's foot. Ashmyr's toes curled in response, eliciting a smile from the rebel leader.

A servant scratched on the door, then backed in carrying Imoshen's meal.

Reothe rose, cupping her cheek with casual affection. 'Eat up. You will need your strength. We ride tomorrow –'

'South?' It was out before Imoshen could stop herself.

An impish smile lit Reothe's face. The more time she spent with him, the more she realised he was not like other men. Did Tulkhan find her as fey and disturbing as she found Reothe?

'You will see.' He left with a mocking grin.

The servant placed the dish on the table beside Imoshen. She dismissed him and tried the food. This time it was chicken and just as thickly spiced.

Reothe's words returned to her. He would stop at nothing to regain Fair Isle. Hadn't she vowed almost the same thing? She'd vowed her children would rule Fair Isle. Now that seemed a hollow goal. If Tulkhan fell she would not hand Ashmyr over to Reothe to rear as his tool. She refused to live out her days as Reothe's puppet empress, with her son's life hanging in the balance. If Tulkhan fell she would have to flee. If Tulkhan died...

Pain curled through her. It was impossible to imagine his brilliant mind and forceful personality gone forever. But he was as vulnerable as any True-man against Reothe.

Did contemplating the General's death make her as bad as Reothe? No. Unlike him, there were things she would not sink to, such as invading people's minds against their will.

What of the Basilica's Archivist? True, that wasn't against the woman's will, but it had been without her knowledge.

Imoshen sighed then licked the spoon clean. Was evil only a matter of degrees and perspective?

According to different legends T'Imoshen the First had been either a glorious saviour of her people or an ignoble invader who stole Fair Isle from its inhabitants.

In time to come, would Imoshen herself be regarded as a turncoat who betrayed the last of her kind, or a devoted servant of Fair Isle whose statesmanship saved the island from destruction? It all depended on which victor wrote the history books.

She shivered.

Reothe or Tulkhan? A True-man who had invaded a peaceful people for gain and now strove to unite them, or a T'En warrior who would do anything to return the rightful rulers to power? Was there a difference?

And what of Fair Isle?

If only Reothe was totally despicable then she could hate him. But he was too much like herself...

Imoshen stood with her baby snuggled in the crook of her arm. Completely trusting, Ashmyr had dozed off while she pondered their fate. A glow of pure love filled her. What ever happened, he was hers to protect.

TULKHAN GLARED AT Kalleen as he tossed Imoshen's letter onto the table between them. 'How can you claim you don't know what she wanted?'

The opinion of T'Diemn was divided and rumour ran rife. Half the townsfolk believed Imoshen had run off to join the rebels, the other half sided with the General, believing she had been abducted.

'I know as much as you, General Tulkhan.' Kalleen bristled. 'If you can read more into Imoshen's letter, let me know.'

'When we arrived at Umasreach Stronghold, she had already been abducted,' Wharrd explained, a restraining hand on Kalleen's arm. 'So we hastened to T'Diemn.'

'Then I am no closer to solving the puzzle.' Tulkhan retrieved the letter and smoothed the fine paper.

'What will you do, General?' Wharrd asked.

Tulkhan tucked the letter inside his jerkin. 'Go after her and my son.'

'But it's a trap!'

'Of course.'

'I will go with you.'

'And I,' Kalleen spoke up.

Tulkhan saw Wharrd's face go grey. The bone-setter caught Kalleen's hands in his. 'You carry our child. I can't risk losing you.'

The familiarity of it made Tulkhan wince.

Kalleen smiled sadly. 'If you fail I will lose everything.'

Wharrd shook his head but she remained obstinate.

Tulkhan knew Imoshen would do what she thought was right and he was almost certain that would not entail running away to join the rebels. He had to believe in her. 'I must organise my escort and plan my route.'

Tulkhan left Wharrd and Kalleen to sort out their differences. He strode down the corridors of the palace, throwing open the doors to his map-room.

'General Tulkhan?' A servant paused in the other entrance. 'The Beatific is here to offer her support.'

He groaned inwardly. He did not doubt the Beatific was here to plant more insinuations about Imoshen's loyalty. 'Send her in.'

Tulkhan studied the woman as she approached the table.

'Why does Reothe lure me north?' he asked abruptly.

She looked surprised. 'I have no idea. I am not a tactician.'

'No?'

She had the grace to flush and look down.

Tulkhan spread the map on the tabletop and indicated the town of Northpoint. 'This harbour offers excellent anchorage for deep-draught ships and it is barely a day's sail from the mainland with the right wind. Why would Reothe ask me to meet him there when his noble supporters and rebel army are in the Keldon Highlands?'

'Perhaps he feels the highlands are secure?' the Beatific hazarded.

'Could he be getting support from one of the mainland kingdoms?'

'The mainlanders support a Dhamfeer?' Scorn laced the Beatific's voice. 'Why do you think none of them honoured our alliances? They wanted to see Fair Isle humbled. And they fear the T'En.'

It was all too familiar. He had once thought that way.

'That's what I suspected.' He rubbed his chin, glad to be rid of his beard. 'Then it comes back to why. What does Reothe hope to gain?'

'You are going to meet him?' The Beatific regarded him closely.

'Yes, I –'

'It's a trap.'

'What Reothe doesn't know is that I have a trap of my own to spring on him.' He noted the way her eyes widened, but she remained otherwise impassive.

'Really?' she remarked. 'How fortunate.'

Tulkhan nodded and hoped the message would disturb Reothe when it reached him. His only regret was that he didn't have a trap – not yet anyway.

EARLY THE NEXT morning Tulkhan set out with a band of hand-picked men and Kalleen, who could not be persuaded to stay behind. She had threatened to follow them, and in the end Wharrd had been forced to give in.

They could travel fast with only a small band. Commander Piers was to follow as soon as he could organise a company large enough to quell any ragtag rebels Reothe might have gathered around him.

Tulkhan hoped Reothe expected him to move slowly north with his main army. In truth he was prepared to move swiftly, strike fast and get out. At this point surprise was his only strategy.

He had lost his chance to seize the initiative by using Imoshen and the babe to lure Reothe out. In fact the T'En warrior had turned the tables on him.

Tulkhan raged at his impotence. He would not sacrifice Imoshen and his son.

It was eight days since she had been abducted. Reothe's band might have reached Northpoint by now. The rebel leader had to be expecting support from one of the mainland kingdoms, otherwise he would have gone to ground in the Keldon Highlands. Yet who would deal with a Dhamfeer?

IMOSHEN STOOD AT the window looking down into Northpoint Harbour where a single merchant ship sat on the glistening sea.

Ashmyr stirred and grumbled, so she padded back to him. Like her own stronghold, the oldest part of Northpoint's defences dated from the Age of Tribulation. Protected from attack by the sheer cliffs below, her room at the top of the tower was an ideal prison. Short of throwing herself to her death, there was no escape.

The Ghebite commander who had briefly ruled Northpoint had renamed T'Ronnyn's Citadel after himself and filled it with luxurious booty, looted on his travels across Fair Isle. The bed was draped with brocade hangings and jewel-bright carpets lay three deep on the floor. Gilt-edged mirrors and paintings covered the walls. Crystal and fine porcelain littered every tabletop and sideboard. It was so opulent it was obscene.

But he had not enjoyed the luxury for long.

She chose not to ask what had happened to him. He had vanished along with his men. The servants were all loyal to Reothe, and the townsfolk they had passed on their way had seemed overjoyed to see the T'En warrior.

The baby whimpered. Imoshen picked him up.

'Can I get you anything, my lady?' Selita asked.

'The key.'

Selita grinned impudently. She had overcome her initial shyness. If the girl hadn't been her guard, Imoshen could have grown very fond of her.

Selita lay sprawled on the rug before the unlit fireplace, peeling a mandarin. Imoshen watched her, while soothing Ashmyr absently.

'I don't know why you are complaining,' Selita remarked. 'T'Reothe has forgiven you. He holds no grudge, despite the way you've treated him. Before the Harvest Feast you will be back in the capital, Empress of Fair Isle, and my people's honour will be restored.'

Imoshen's hand froze. The Harvest Feast was twelve days away. How could Reothe hope to reverse the Ghebites' advantage in such a short time?

Her thoughts in turmoil, Imoshen resumed rubbing Ashmyr's back.

Selita believed her people's honour would be restored. She had to be talking about the Keld. Imoshen could just imagine the Keld's stern matriarch Woodvine strapping on armour and riding into battle. According to Fairban, the Keld were ripe for revolt.

Imoshen joined Selita and sat down, resting her back against a heavy chest. Casually she settled Ashmyr across her lap.

Selita tossed her plait over her shoulder and nudged the tray of fruit towards Imoshen.

'What pretty hair you have.' Imoshen stroked the girl's braid. 'I knew someone once who had just this shade of coppery hair.'

It hurt her to recall Cariah. She had failed her friend. She must not fail her son or his father.

Selita changed position so she could face Imoshen. 'Reothe said I wasn't to let you touch me. He said you would seduce me. Were you about to trick me?'

Imoshen shrugged. 'I've no idea what he meant. I don't have a fraction the gifts he has. I'm only really good at healing. I was just going to offer to brush your hair.'

She selected a mandarin and began peeling it. The skin came away easily and juice dripped down her arm.

Selita's golden eyes studied her thoughtfully. 'You know, I'd trust you less if you pretended to go along with all this. But you make no pretence of wanting to be here. What do you see in this Ghebite General? Surely he can't compare with T'Reothe!'

The girl was impudence herself, but Imoshen laughed and licked the juice off her wrist.

'What a question. What does any woman see in a man?' She offered a mandarin wedge to Selita.

The girl bit into the fruit and spoke around it. 'But the General is only a Mere-man and you are pure T'En like T'Reothe. He will not bed a Mere-woman. He says it is but a pale imitation.' Resentment tinged her voice. 'What does he mean?'

'I've no idea. I think he boasts!'

Selita giggled, then frowned. 'You can't charm me into letting you go. I love T'Reothe. I think you're mad to refuse him.'

'You can think what you like,' Imoshen said. She offered the girl another wedge, concentrating on the tenuous contact they shared. Already she could taste the mandarin's tang on Selita's tongue. 'Tell me, how did you join the rebels?'

Selita hugged her knees and stared out the window. As she began her story, Imoshen sifted through the upper layers of her mind, careful not to disturb the girl with her presence.

When Selita paused, Imoshen made encouraging sounds while she continued searching for Reothe's plans. While much of Selita's mind was occupied with thoughts of Reothe, they were not the kind Imoshen found useful.

She discovered the rebel fighter resented her and was sceptical about her ability to satisfy Reothe. But it was hard to find an errant memory when the mind was thinking of other things. Perhaps she should ask Selita a question to trigger the right thought? Imoshen settled in, waiting for the right moment.

The door swung open and Reothe stalked in. Striding across the chamber, he grabbed Selita by the arm, dragging her upright. 'Get out, Lita!'

'Why? I've done nothing wrong.'

Heart thudding, Imoshen snatched up Ashmyr and scrambled to her feet. 'You little fool. She nearly had you!' He dragged Selita across the room, pushed her into the passage and slammed the door after her.

Chapter Twenty-One

REOTHE TURNED TO face Imoshen. She backed off. He advanced. 'Put the baby down.'

'No!' She held him closer.

'Put him down, Imoshen. You don't want him to get hurt.'

She blanched. Silently, she tucked her son into his basket.

'Come here.'

'You can't bully me.' But her heart hammered painfully as she stepped around the basket towards him.

'Closer.'

'This is close enough.'

A gasp escaped her as he covered the distance between them in one long stride. His hands grasped her shoulders. 'That was very foolish, Imoshen. I could feel you using your gifts from the other end of the citadel.'

'Then why don't I feel you when you use yours?' It was out before she could stop herself.

His eyes narrowed and he smiled slowly. 'Why do you think? I am no novice. I cloak my gifts. Don't you try to turn Selita or anyone else into your tool. I'll feel it. I will stop you and it won't be pleasant.'

Fear made her heart skip a beat. Did she want to force him to hurt her? No, better to...

'Good. I don't want to hurt you, Imoshen.'

Reothe didn't want to hurt her, but she knew he would if he had to. She tried to divert him. 'Whose ship is in the harbour and why do they fly no flag? What will you do when Tulkhan gets here?'

'So many questions. Do you really expect me to answer any of them?' He tilted his head, watching her.

Imoshen noticed the tip of one of the snow leopard's scars peeping through the gap in his shirt.

'Why do your scars show when mine don't? The leopard's claws marked us both yet they only touched you. What price did the Ancients ask of you?'

His hands tightened on her shoulders. She thought she detected a flicker of fear in his eyes. Then he pulled her close, until their bodies touched.

'If you would only trust me, Imoshen, I would share my knowledge with you.' His arms encircled her. She wanted to back away but she felt drawn to him. His breath tickled her face as his fingers stroked her hair.

His voice was rich velvet rubbing across her skin. 'Trust me, Imoshen.'

A soothing, sweet warmth flooded her. It would be so easy to accept his lure. He promised everything, his love and the gift of knowledge. Together they could unfold the mysteries of the T'En.

But the price was too high.

'Trust?' Bitterness tightened her throat, thinning her voice. 'That is a strange thing to ask when you threaten my son and hide so much from me. You give and take in the same breath. How can I break the encryption of the T'Endomaz when you have the key? I know you stole the T'Elegos from the Basilica.'

His eyes widened and he laughed with delight then shook his head sadly. 'The T'Elegos does not contain the key to the T'Endomaz.'

She ignored this. 'The T'Elegos is my heritage, too. Where have you hidden it?'

Immediately she felt him think of the hiding place – a cavern appeared in her mind's eye. Then the thought was shut down like a door slamming closed. Her mind reeled with the impact and everything went dark.

When the blinding pain eased she found herself lying across the bed with Reothe kneeling at her side.

'Are you all right?' he whispered.

She nodded and winced.

'I told you it would hurt if I used my gift to limit yours.'

Tears stung her eyes. She would not cry in front of him. 'I had to try.'

'Imoshen!' The despair in his voice made her flinch. He pulled her into his arms, stroking her hair, pressing her cheek to his throat. 'When will you stop fighting me?'

There was no answer to that.

She felt him lower his head and inhale her scent.

'Only three more days,' he whispered brokenly.

She stiffened. Three days until Tulkhan got here? Three days until Reothe murdered him?

'Reothe, I was thinking...' Shakily she pulled away from him to kneel on the bed, taking one of his hands in hers. 'What good is Fair Isle? It is just one small island. You have ships and loyal followers. Why stay here to battle for an ungrateful land? Why not go east into the dawn sun? I've always wanted to see our homeland. There must be more like us. You could... Why do you look at me like that?'

His hand slipped from hers as he swung his legs off the bed and strode to the semi-circle of windows. The setting sun's rays gilded his fine features and pale hair. She could see the tension in his shoulders as he gripped the sill.

'You must know the truth, Imoshen. We are outcasts. We have no homeland.' He did not turn to face her and his voice vibrated with contained pain. 'You know that Imoshen the First brought her people here, but you don't know there were three ships. Two did not survive the crossing.

'Our ancestors weren't brave explorers, Imoshen. There were old people, women and children on those ships. They were outcasts, selected for their

T'En traits and banished. I have read the first Imoshen's own account of their flight and the reasons for it. Terrible things happened in the name of the T'En. The people could no longer suffer us to live. They banded against us, they offered us death or banishment.'

'No. It is a lie.'

'I have read the T'Elegos, written in her own hand.' He turned to her, glowing with the intensity of his emotion. 'The T'En are fallen angels.'

'You must have misinterpreted the T'Elegos. High T'En is designed to carry many shades of meaning. And even... even if Imoshen the First's people were banished for some reason, it has been more than six hundred years. If you were to make the journey to our homeland beyond the dawn sun, they would not deny us.'

'You don't know what I know.'

'How can I, when you hide things from me? Why did you give me the T'Endomaz and where does it fit in?'

He hesitated. 'I believe the T'Endomaz is the hidden lore of the T'En. During the Ages of Tribulation and Consolidation the pure T'En left their parents at ten years of age. They were taken by a pure T'En mentor who trained them in their gifts. I believe the T'Endomaz is the very book they would have been trained from.'

Imoshen moaned. 'Why didn't you tell me? Why not share the T'Elegos with me? Why hide it?'

'I didn't hide it from you. The leader of the Tractarians hates me, Imoshen. I saved Imoshen the First's history from Murgon's prying eyes.' He grimaced as though even the man's name tasted foul.

She could easily believe Murgon hated him. 'But why?'

Reothe shuddered. 'When I was a boy of ten, raw with the suicide of my parents, I was sent to the palace to be reared by the Empress. Because Murgon was three years older and related through my father, she gave me into his care. We took our lessons with the royal heirs, explored the palace and attended functions at their side. We were being groomed to become royal advisers.

'Murgon was mad for T'Ysanna and she used my adoration of her to keep him at a distance. He took out his spite on me. At first it was little cruelties which might have been accidents. But he grew bolder until I was nearly killed by a jest gone wrong. He startled my horse, causing it to throw me. The Empress must have suspected because she arranged with the Beatific to have the church request his services.

'I thought that was the end of it. We gave him gifts and he was inducted into the priesthood. But he bided his time. The day before the Harvest Feast, he forged a note from Ysanna asking me to meet her in the underground passage we had discovered below the portrait gallery. When she did not appear I tried to leave but found the door locked. What with the festivities, no one missed me for two days. And then when they did begin searching they could not find me.

'I wandered alone in the dark without food or water. I tried all the false panels I could trigger until I discovered the catacombs. To be sure I could get out, I wedged the entrance open with my shoe.'

Imoshen's gasp made him pause, but she indicated he should go on.

Reothe smiled wolfishly. 'If only he knew, Murgon did me a favour. I believed I was dying. I lay on the slab like legend says T'Sardonyx used to, and said the words for the dead, for my soul. The horror of it triggered my gift and I left my body behind. The Parakletos came, some curious, others resentful.

'The Parakletos found me wandering lost in death's shadow and led me back to this world. In my dealings with them I have learned all is not what it seems.'

'You said they have no power in this world.'

'They don't. Some are filled with a thirst for revenge and will try to steal your soul, but others pity the True-men and women they escort into death's realm.' He shook his head sadly. 'Woe betide the caller who summons them without the will to withstand them!'

'Yet you say they were kind to you?'

His sharp eyes met hers. 'Did I say kind? One day I may tell you what passed between us before they returned me to this world.'

'So they returned you to the catacombs. How did you escape?'

'By then Ysanna had revealed our dangerous games and the underground passages were being searched. When they found me I had been lost for five days. The Empress was furious. But I did not reveal Murgon's role. For one thing I had no proof – Ysanna's note had disappeared – and for another Murgon had been transferred into the Tractarians. Anything I said against one of their number would have been suspect.

'Besides, I thought that was the end of it.' Reothe grimaced. 'I was wrong. When the old leader of the Tractarians died, Murgon was named his successor. He promised to make them a power once more and they loved him for it.

'For most of the Age of Discernment the Tractarians' strength had been fading. The only living pure T'En was your great-aunt, and she was no threat. But with my birth they began to lobby for more resources, more priests. There is nothing like a threat to make True-men and women band together. The T'En blood runs strong in Murgon. He has the eyes and six-fingers. In any other branch of the church, he would be treated with caution. He joined the Tractarians because he saw it as a route to power. As their leader he meant to discredit me.

'But when the old Beatific retired I made sure I had the new Beatific's ear. I had picked her for her potential, had been cultivating her for years.' Reothe smiled across at Imoshen. 'Yes, politics. I can see you despise the power play, but you must learn to use it for your own survival as I have done. Murgon and his Tractarians fear us. What True-people fear, they destroy.'

'You speak as if we were at war with True-people.'

'Except for the occasional throwback like us, the church has almost succeeded in wiping out the T'En. For centuries they've kept us in ignorance. What right did T'Abularassa have to rewrite our history? She and Imoshen the First's own daughter, the Beatific, deliberately hid the T'Elegos. They used the T'Enchiridion to bind us to serve them. I heard how you gave your Vow of Expiation. What crime have you committed that you must ask for expiation?'

He stepped closer to search her face. Though he did not touch her, the force of his presence made her body thrum.

Reothe held her eyes. 'Do you know how lonely it is to live in a palace full of True-people and know that while they laugh with you and love you with one breath, they could turn on you with the next and stone you to death? A decree from the Beatific is all it takes to declare one of us rogue.'

So that was why he had 'cultivated' the Beatific. Imoshen could understand self-preservation.

'The last rogue T'En was stoned over a hundred years ago,' she objected. 'Murgon may be a fanatic, but this is – or was – the Age of Discernment.'

'Discernment? Age of Denial more like!' Reothe muttered. 'They thought we T'En had died out. They had your great-aunt cowed. They claimed to be enlightened because they believed us a spent force.'

Imoshen shook her head. 'Who is this *they*? Besides, it is different now that the Ghebites –'

'Hate us. The Ghebites are more dangerous than you realise. They despise us because we are not True-people. And look at what they do to their own women!' He gestured in frustration. 'What if the current Beatific was a man instead of a woman? What if the Beatific and the Ghebites joined forces? Who signs the decree to declare a T'En rogue? Imoshen the First chose celibacy, but who enforces the practice? The church. The church represents the True-people. They are our enemies, yours and mine.'

Imoshen shook her head. Fair Isle was her home, its True-people were her people.

Reothe prowled away. He paused by the mantelpiece, staring into the cold fireplace. 'Light a fire, Imoshen.'

She blinked. 'Light it yourself, the flint is there.'

'No. I mean light it.'

She understood. A frisson of excitement made her skin prickle. 'I don't know how.'

'Oh, come now. You nearly had Selita enthralled and you weren't even touching her.'

The prickling of her skin increased. She looked at the pyramid of wood arranged in the hearth. All it needed was a spark. A stinging sensation snapped behind her eyes and when she opened them little flames consumed the kindling.

Delight flooded Imoshen. She darted over, kneeling before the fire to admire her handiwork.

'Very nice,' Reothe said dryly. 'Now you see why they want to wipe us out.'

'But it was only one little spark!'

'It only takes one spark to start a fire.'

Fear chilled Imoshen. She wanted to deny the truth of his words but could not. Reothe held her eyes. 'Mere-men and women kill what they fear.'

She thought of her people cast out of their original homeland, then persecuted in their new island home. 'I must read the T'Elegos. Are you sure you interpreted the old language correctly? Its meaning can be ambiguous.'

He laughed. 'Yes, my little scholar. Remember that first time you quoted High T'En to me? I wanted to hug you. But you would have run away.'

'Nonsense!' she said, only he was right. She had been wary of him, fascinated yet frightened by the force of his personality.

He sighed. 'All along, our timing has been out. If you had been older, we would not have had to wait so long for our bonding. We would have been bond-partners when the Ghebites attacked. The Empress would have –'

'Would have, could have! It's too late to talk of what might have been!'

'You are right.'

The last of the sun's setting rays faded, casting the room into darkness except for the flames of the fire.

Imoshen felt as if she had travelled a lifetime since Reothe sent Selita away.

He took one of her hands in both of his. 'I promise when all this is settled we will read the T'Elegos together. Somehow we will break the T'Endomaz's encryption. You can't stand against me, Imoshen. Stand at my side, my equal in every way.'

Her heart turned over. She trembled as she pulled her hand free of his. He called her equal yet he hid things from her. And when Reothe spoke of sharing the reins of power it would mean Tulkhan's death.

She shuddered. Nothing, not even Reothe's promise of a shared T'En heritage, could make her sacrifice the father of her child.

Imoshen touched Reothe's face, felt the lean line of his jaw. 'Second cousin, last of my blood kin, last of my kind, don't let this war consume you. Sail east. Provision your ships and make your way via the archipelago. You know the sea –'

'And you'll come with me?'

She let her hand drop, startled by the prospect.

'I jest, Imoshen. I would not ask it of you even if you said yes. It is not something to be attempted lightly. The sailors of the archipelago don't venture east. They say to go into the dawn sun is death.' He gestured. 'Imoshen, ask yourself, it has been six hundred years, why haven't we had visitors from the land beyond the dawn sun?'

It was a good question. She tried to read his face. 'You tell me.'

'I don't know,' he answered with simple honesty.

'Then why don't you sail into the dawn sun? It would be a glorious adventure.'

'Don't patronise me, Imoshen. And don't try to influence me with your gift.'

'I wasn't.' But she was. Even as she said the words, she had instinctively added a push, willing him to feel her enthusiasm.

'No?' He gave her a half-smile.

Again she felt that dangerous attraction and would have pulled away but he caught her hand, lifting her arm to press his bonding scar to hers.

'It is you and I against the rest, Imoshen. For the moment the Ghebites accept you. But I heard about the stone lovers. How long before they cease thinking of you as their pet Dhamfeer and begin to fear you? How long before your General smothers you in your sleep and drowns his half-Dhamfeer pup.'

'No!' She sprang away from Reothe, heart thudding. Tulkhan would never do that.

Her tone made the baby stir and cry. At the same instant there was a scratching at the door.

'Enter,' Reothe called, then lowered his voice. 'Don't fool yourself, Imoshen. I am your only true friend because we share the same enemies. Our goals should be the same.'

She turned away from him to retrieve Ashmyr from his basket.

'T'Imoshen's food.' A servant waited with a tray. Reothe gestured for him to enter as he lit the candles.

Imoshen wanted to send the meal away but she would need her strength for what was to come. In three days Tulkhan would arrive.

'Bring it here, please.' She sat down by the fire.

'I'm going to send Selita to you,' Reothe said. He did not need to warn Imoshen against trying to influence the girl.

She ate slowly and methodically. Today she didn't even taste the delicious spices.

Reothe lingered. His hand brushed her shoulder. A tingle of awareness moved across her skin. It was the overflow of his T'En gift, questing for an opening, a welcome. But Imoshen closed herself away from him, knowing that he was probing for the mind-touch. It hurt her to shut him out, as much as it hurt her to know Tulkhan had shut her out. But she remained obdurate.

Grimly Reothe left.

The events of the afternoon made Imoshen's head spin. She could still see Reothe gilded by the sun, declaring they were fallen angels.

Wearily she returned Ashmyr to his basket. Her mind reeled with the implications of what she had learnt. Reothe had asked who deserved her loyalty, Tulkhan and the True-people of Fair Isle, or Reothe and the T'En?

She had three days to decide.

ANOTHER DAY'S HARD ride, Tulkhan estimated, before they approached Northpoint. His people were tired. It was midafternoon and they had been riding since dawn. He was weary himself but driven by the knowledge that every step brought him closer to Imoshen and his son.

'General?' Wharrd called.

'Yes?' He knew they should stop to eat and let the horses rest, but he was loath to delay.

Wharrd said nothing, his expression eloquent.

'Very well, first likely spot we'll take a break.'

Tulkhan could almost feel their relief. Little Kalleen never complained and consequently none of his men dared grumble.

'Down there?' Wharrd asked. He pointed to a single fishing hut halfway up the hillside, far above the pebbly beach.

Tulkhan recalled this place from his campaign last spring. There had been a whole village here bustling with life before his people attacked. In the first small moons of the campaign they had been brutal, wiping all resistance before them. The little fishing huts built to withstand storm had offered no protection from armed men.

Tulkhan experienced a twinge of regret. He'd had no argument with these innocent fisherfolk. He had simply decided to take Fair Isle and had unleashed his army. The island was too ripe a plum not to pluck. For the first time Tulkhan faced the unpleasant truth. Reothe stood on the moral high ground. The T'En warrior was only defending his homeland, his heritage.

'General?' Wharrd pressed.

Tulkhan reined in his thoughts. 'Very well.'

He turned his mount towards the beach. The others followed. He needed to approach Northpoint undetected, to find out where Imoshen was being kept. A tight, well-coordinated raid might succeed in freeing her. But it was exactly what Reothe would expect of him, that or to lay siege to the town itself.

Tulkhan noticed the fisherman's boat pulled up beyond the high-tide mark. Reothe would expect an attack from the land, not from the sea. But they would need more than one boat...

IMOSHEN PACED THE length of her chamber, unable to relax. Her decision was made. Fair Isle was her home and its people were her people, no matter what their race. She would continue Imoshen the First's work and see the pure T'En race accepted by the True-people.

Sometime today the General would reach Northpoint and she would stand at his side, against Reothe.

Selita had fled after lunch, complaining of a headache. Reothe had been in twice to check on Imoshen, but had refused to answer her questions. He had simply satisfied himself that she was not up to anything and left. Like her, he could feel the tension in the air, the heavy foreboding of a thunderstorm about to break. It made her teeth ache.

Sensing her anxiety, Ashmyr had been fretful all day.

Imoshen stood at the windows of her prison, staring down at the harbour. The evening stars dotted the emerald sky. She frowned, counting the ships. Another two had arrived with the evening tide.

She hadn't seen Reothe since mid-afternoon. For all she knew Tulkhan might be attempting a raid on the eastern wall of the harbour town at this very moment.

Imoshen returned to the chair by the fire. Tonight was the best time to attempt her escape. Hopefully Tulkhan's arrival would distract Reothe and keep him too preoccupied to monitor Imoshen's use of her gifts.

She went through her normal routine, even putting on her nightgown and sitting by the fire with Ashmyr's basket at her feet. But her body burned with restlessness.

She had to find a way of giving Tulkhan an advantage, but first she and Ashmyr had to escape Reothe. Time to test him. He was not all-powerful. He had to have a weakness.

Settling her body into the chair, she forced herself to relax. Gradually she became aware of her heartbeat slowing. Her T'En senses spread out until she could feel the servants in the lower rooms bustling about, clearing up after the evening meal.

Her perception was only minimal, just a general sense of purpose with no individual personalities rising to the surface. Could she manipulate one of these people, make them come up here on some errand? She'd never attempted anything like this before but she was desperate.

First she had to select someone who seemed susceptible. Maybe a probe to test...

Even as she thought this, she felt the sharp flare of Reothe's perception. He was coming for her.

Gasping, she retreated, reeling in her awareness until she had nothing but a True-woman's senses. She strained to hear his footfalls along the corridor. Heart pounding, she waited, dreading the inevitable confrontation.

From her brief contact she had felt the formidable strength of Reothe's will, but he also seemed preoccupied.

He was already in the corridor.

Imoshen must distract him, soothe his suspicions. She began unravelling her plaits, her heart beating as rapidly as a snared bird's.

Reothe scratched on the door.

She had to clear her throat before she could speak. 'Enter.'

She glanced up, feigning calm. Reothe strode in and came to an abrupt stop before her, ignoring the baby at her feet. Waves of tension rolled off him. His narrow nostrils flared as he inhaled, his eyes narrowing. 'What have you been up to?'

Though it cost her, she remained in her chair and continued to unravel her hair, ignoring him.

'Imoshen?' he pleaded.

Startled, her gaze flew to his and connected. Why did he look so strained? All her healing instincts told her he suffered mental anguish.

'What is it?'

His lips parted, then he shook his head and strode to the fireplace. He stared into the flames, his back to her.

Imoshen came slowly to her feet. 'Has General Tulkhan come?'

'Why?' He turned sharply. 'Do you sense him?'

'No, I...' She shrugged, not about to reveal that the General had forbidden the mind-touch. In closing himself away from her he had prevented her contacting him even in an emergency like this. 'No, you said three days and it has been three.'

His bitter laughter cut her short.

Imoshen could not read Reothe's mood, but she could sense the danger of his barely restrained gifts. She dare not provoke him.

The silence stretched between them as he stared at her. Tonight Reothe was vulnerable and troubled. But he was also Other. And it called to her.

A heat dawned in her centre, creeping through her limbs. Imoshen felt her face flood with betraying colour. Reothe's lips pulled back from his teeth. She knew he could sense her arousal.

She turned, but there was nowhere to run. Still, her feet carried her to the windows. The sea breeze cooled her cheeks, lifting the loose strands of her hair.

Her hands closed on the cool wood grain of the windowsill. Across the bay each ship was a small self-contained world illuminated by lanterns. If only...

'No, you don't!' Reothe's hands closed on her shoulders.

She could feel him down the length of her body. He radiated heat, tension and purpose.

She focused on the bobbing lights in the bay, the sea breeze, anything but his need for her.

His breath brushed her ear.

She tilted, her head to avoid it, but the melt continued deep inside her, the call of her body to his, answering his unspoken need.

His hands tightened. 'Tell me to go away.'

'Go away.'

'Cruel, your head tells me one thing but your body tells me another.' His voice rubbed across her senses like raw silk. 'If the Ghebite General had not come, we would have been bonded. Life would have been sweet for us. Can't you see it, Imoshen?'

At his insistence she could. Visions appeared before her – the pair of them riding together, poring over the T'Elegos together, deciphering the T'Endomaz. A well of longing, long suppressed, opened within her. Reothe would accept her T'En self. He would put no limitations on her gifts. For him, she simply was. She saw herself meeting him on the deck of a ship. She carried a small fair-haired baby, and when Reothe's arm rose in welcome she went to him as she was meant to.

'Don't plant visions in my head!'

'Don't insult me. I see the same visions myself. Sometimes they fade and I fear one of us will die. At other times they grow so strong I forget where I am and think you are with me.'

'Don't. I don't want to know.' She did not want to acknowledge his vulnerability and need for her. It would weaken her resolve.

'We were meant for each other, Imoshen.' His voice dropped. 'We are the last of the T'En. It is time to save our people. I want to gather all those with T'En blood. I want to create our own T'En Hall of Learning where we develop our abilities and share what we have learnt.

'Our race would no longer be a source of anxious curiosity, worshipped in one breath and feared the next. In every village there would be a T'En healer. Every bonded couple who produced a child with T'En traits would consider themselves blessed. This is my dream and I need you to help me make it possible.'

Imoshen bowed her head. The pain caused by her Otherness, the unspoken jibes, the fear and awe which had come to mark her interaction with other people, all this mingled inside her. Reothe's vision would imbue her differences with a holy purpose.

'We will renew Fair Isle. It will be the renaissance of the T'En, the Age of the T'En. Do you dare to dream with me, Imoshen?'

She tried to think clearly. Instinct told her Reothe was sincere. He wanted to redeem the fallen angels and create a golden age. But she feared the power he promised.

'True-people –'

'Need us. It is in their nature to look for a higher authority. Why should we be hunted down and eradicated like vermin? I have lived on the outside too long. Join me, Imoshen. Restore the T'En.'

She drew a ragged breath.

It seemed to draw his hands upward from her shoulders. His fingertips traced the line of her throat where he must have felt her pulse racing. No doubt it pleased him to know how he moved her.

She felt the heat of his body down the length of hers, knew that he desired her. The gentle pressure of his questing gift increased, insistent, eager, demanding.

Anger stirred in Imoshen. 'I will fight with the last breath I take.'

'Why? When we both know you want me. Your T'En gifts perfume the air. I could feel your desire from across the room. Your scent intoxicates me. Even as I speak, you tremble.'

'With rage!' It was too much. 'You bring me here against my will, hold my son to ensure my cooperation, then think I will welcome you into my bed?'

Furious, she whirled around to face him. His jaw clenched so tightly she could see the hard knobs of muscle. Good. Let him storm out of here in a fury. Or better yet, let him strike her so she could hate him.

He stepped away, cold and enraged. 'You back yourself into a dangerous corner, Imoshen. You leave me no choice.'

Her heart plummeted. She glanced uneasily at the slumbering baby. But Reothe turned on his heel and stalked to the door.

She wanted to ask what he meant to do. Biting her tongue, she contained her fears.

Before he opened the door Reothe turned to face her. 'I'm placing a special lock on this door. If you try to force it, I will know.'

She nodded her understanding.

He stepped through the open door then looked back, his expression hard to interpret. 'You had your chance. Next time we speak things will stand differently between us.'

The door closed and Imoshen sank to the floor, pressing the heels of her hands into her closed eyes. Reothe meant to move against her. He would capture Tulkhan and kill him while she was trapped here.

Without moving, she probed the door. Nothing disturbed her senses. If she could only identify the T'En lock Reothe had fashioned, she could disarm it.

She.... a sharp white pain stabbed into her unshielded senses.

Tears bled from her eyes. Blood roared in her ears. Shivers shook her body. It was a force she could not escape. It chilled her to the bone. She had to get warm. Hardly able to see, Imoshen crawled to the bed and pulled up the covers.

Pain obliterated her will, leaving her anxious only to escape the pressure inside her head. She gave up the unequal fight and lay gasping on the bed, waiting for it to pass.

As abruptly as it had started, it stopped, leaving her wrung dry, too weak to lift her head. For a long time she lay there, tears seeping from her eyes onto the pillow.

She was useless. She had tried and failed.

So fragile did she feel that she dared not even probe beyond this room. Any attempt might bring back the excruciating pain.

Chapter Twenty-Two

TULKHAN CLAMBERED UP the rope ladder to the deck. The merchant captain of this ship owed no allegiance to Fair Isle, so for him this would be a simple business transaction. Once Tulkhan had hired this vessel they were assured of an escape route. This ploy had to work.

He felt that familiar mixture of fear and excitement which preceded a battle, the knowledge that he faced death with only his wits and skill. But this time he did not face a True-man.

Reothe was expecting an attack from the land. If Tulkhan had been willing to wait a few more days, Commander Piers might have provided one and created a diversion, but the General wanted to move before their presence was discovered.

Once their escape route was secured, Tulkhan planned to enter Northpoint with a select band of men. The port was full of sailors, a few extra would not be noticed.

Informants had told him Imoshen and his son were locked in the citadel's tower. He had even seen the light of her window, impossibly near yet so distant. Below it was a sheer drop to the rocks. If it had been possible he would have scaled those sea cliffs, but he was not an accursed Dhamfeer warrior.

Instead he planned to infiltrate the citadel, free Imoshen and slip away. He was gambling on the fact that Reothe would be concentrating his defence on the town's perimeter, leaving the citadel's people relatively unprepared. But if his band was detected, Tulkhan was prepared to fight a pitched battle back to the wharfs to escape by sea.

As his feet hit the deck, a sailor greeted him in a thickly accented version of the trading tongue. 'Captain's waiting below.'

Tulkhan had dealt with Lowland merchants to ensure safe passage for his army to Fair Isle, and knew he would have to haggle. Those Lowlanders had no god but gold.

He followed the sailor down the steep steps and headed along the narrow corridor, ducking the beams as he went. The small cabin door swung open and he stooped to step through.

The captain's chair was empty.

Before he could draw a weapon they jumped him. With no room to manoeuvre he staggered. Hands closed on his throat, others tried to wrest his half-drawn sword from his fingers. Driving himself backwards he smashed into a wall, crushing the man on his back. The pressure on his throat eased.

With an effort, he shook off the one who hindered his sword arm and was about to draw the blade for a telling blow when a flash of blinding pain clouded his vision.

He fell to his knees. His arms buckled and a boot hit his ribs as he pitched forward. His breath escaped in a helpless groan.

'Don't hurt him,' a familiar voice warned. 'I want him unharmed.'

'You tell him that,' someone muttered.

Tulkhan blinked as he was rolled over. A blinding light seared his eyes.

'This will hurt more if you resist,' Reothe said.

Of course he resisted.

Reothe's free hand splayed over Tulkhan's face. He tried to keep the T'En warrior out, then he was falling through the back of his skull. Falling, falling...

FIGHTING NAUSEA, TULKHAN sagged against the stone wall. It was cold and metal bands hurt his wrists.

Voices. Hated laughter.

'Trust him to put up a fight,' the Vaygharian said and laughed again.

Tulkhan blinked. The Vaygharian was aiding Reothe?

He tried to focus on the face opposite him. It was definitely Kinraid.

'What are you doing here?' Tulkhan's voice was raw but clear enough.

'He's awake,' Kinraid announced.

Reothe stepped into view. He studied Tulkhan critically. 'He'll heal in a day or two. You can tell your master I've delivered him as I promised. Now he must honour his part of the bargain. I want those mercenaries.'

'You'll get them. They're waiting to sail. With the weather and tides the way they are, it will take two days for them all to disembark.'

'Then send your message.'

Kinraid gave a slight bow and left.

'So you've sold me?' Tulkhan asked. 'Who would want me that badly?'

'Why, King Gharavan of course. He'll try you for treason before he executes you,' Reothe explained. He lifted a bowl of water sprinkled with crushed herbs. 'I'm not a healer like Imoshen, but –'

'Why bother?' Fury and betrayal swamped Tulkhan. His own half-brother had colluded with this vile Dhamfeer.

Reothe shrugged and stepped closer to bathe the blood from Tulkhan's head. His hands were cool and competent. A droplet of water trickled down Tulkhan's neck and inside his jerkin.

'You nearly succeeded, True-man. I wasn't expecting an attack from the sea. Luckily my people are vigilant.' Reothe pressed a dry cloth to Tulkhan's head and held it there. 'You should have killed Gharavan when you had the chance.'

'Do you have a brother?'

'No.'

Tulkhan grimaced. 'Then don't presume to judge me.'

Reothe tilted his head to study him. 'You are right.'

Tulkhan was taken aback. He glared at Reothe. He wanted to hate the Dhamfeer. 'Are you afraid to kill me yourself?'

'That would be a waste. You're worth more to me alive, in exchange for trained soldiers I can use to crush your leaderless men.'

'Beware any mercenaries my half-brother sends. They will serve his purpose, not yours,' Tulkhan snarled.

Reothe smiled. 'Unlike you, I did not make the mistake of underestimating Gharavan's treachery. Mere-people are an open book to me. They come to serve me for wealth, in the end they will serve me for love. Love is more powerful than fear.' He stepped back to put the bowl and cloth aside, then turned to watch Tulkhan. 'No. I don't need to kill you. Besides, why should I make a martyr of you for Imoshen to mourn when your own miscalculation will be your downfall?'

Tulkhan winced. Imoshen would despise him. He was as good as dead.

Reothe stepped closer again. Tulkhan saw his nostrils flare as he inhaled. 'I smell no fear on you. Why don't you fear me?'

'I don't care how much you mock me.' Tulkhan swallowed. Failure left a bitter taste on his tongue. It wasn't his own fate he cared about. 'Just don't hurt Imoshen and the boy.'

Reothe almost smiled. 'That is too sweet. You see, the boy already belongs to me. I touched his mind before he was born.'

Tulkhan tried to hide his anguish.

He was aware of Reothe intent gaze on him. Why was the rebel leader studying him so closely?

'As for Imoshen' – this time Reothe did smile – 'I can't hurt Imoshen.' He saw Tulkhan did not understand. 'Have you ever wondered why the men and women of Fair Isle share everything equally, from ownership of wealth to political rights?'

Tulkhan shrugged. He didn't want a history lesson.

'Have you come across this arrangement in any other land?' Reothe persisted.

Tulkhan shook his head.

'Why are the women of your homeland slaves to their men?' Reothe asked, sounding like one of Tulkhan's childhood tutors, patient and persistent.

'Slaves?' Tulkhan stiffened. 'I... I suppose it's because the women are not as strong as the men.'

'Exactly.' The T'En male watched him closely, waiting. 'The strong always rule.'

Surely Reothe could not mean what Tulkhan thought he meant?

'Did you think the balance of power in T'En society sprang from some obscure altruistic motive? No. Power is wielded by the powerful.' Reothe stepped closer, his eyes sparkling with inhuman amusement. 'Imoshen does not know it. How could she? It was all written in the T'Elegos, but T'Abularassa hid our heritage.

'Her pure T'En cousin, Sardonyx, went rogue, demanding the information in the book be made public. There was an uprising in T'Diemn itself. The palace burned. T'Abularassa claimed the T'Elegos had been destroyed. She and the first Beatific hid it. Eventually I discovered the location and an ambitious priest helped me gain access.'

'The current Beatific.'

Reothe glanced at him consideringly. 'Yes. She has been very useful.'

Tulkhan wasn't going to let him gloat. 'If Imoshen is more powerful than you, why doesn't she know it?'

'How could she?' Reothe smiled. 'No one knows. For the past six hundred years, pure T'En females have been celibate by law.'

'Imoshen told me her T'En gift was healing. She fears your gifts.'

Reothe nodded. 'People fear what they don't know. But my gift is this.'

He brushed his fingers on Tulkhan's forehead. The sensation was a cool breeze ruffling his thoughts, strangely refreshing, if unnerving.

'Mind skills. I can make people think they are hurt, so that they become hurt. I can make it seem I have healed myself. I can bring people what they most desire. But it is all illusion. Already Imoshen outstrips me. It has been a gamble all along to keep ahead of her. When I heard...' He stopped and looked at Tulkhan.

'Imoshen the First forbade pure T'En females to breed because it brings on their gifts. With the growing babe, the power grows. So it was they and not the men who ruled our homeland. It is that residual power which still runs our society. The Beatific, our last Empress and the women who rule the guilds, they wield power and don't realise who they have to thank for it. Even now, Woodvine of the Keld awaits my signal to lead the nobles against your men in T'Diemn. She is but one in a long line of female leaders.'

Reothe fell silent, his thoughts turned inward. Tulkhan watched him, fascinated despite himself.

'Why do you tell me all this?' Tulkhan asked.

Reothe smiled sweetly. 'Because you are as good as dead, Mere-man, and I thought you would appreciate the irony of knowing you always had it within your power to destroy me, if only Imoshen had understood her own potential. It is her mistaken belief that I am more powerful that allows me to control her.'

Victory had been within his grasp all along? Tulkhan wanted to rage at the unfairness of it all, but he shut his eyes, vowing he would not give the rebel leader the pleasure of knowing how he felt.

When he opened his eyes, he saw Reothe's sympathetic expression and he knew his enemy understood only too well.

'Do you like to watch me suffer?' Tulkhan snarled.

'Yes. Part of my gift is the vicarious enjoyment of emotions, the more intense the better.'

'You're insane!'

'No. Just different.' Reothe leaned closer.

Tulkhan wished his hands were free. Chained like this, he could do nothing but glare at the Dhamfeer male.

'I think I have enough now. I just need one more thing: taste.' With that, Reothe licked Tulkhan's throat, lingering the hollow beneath his ear.

Anger vibrated through the General's body.

Reothe stepped back and gave an odd little formal salute. 'I thank you.'

Tulkhan wanted to ask Reothe him what he meant, but he dreaded the answer.

'Wait,' he whispered. 'I have a question.'

'Ask.'

'The night you came to the palace and saved Imoshen... if you aren't as gifted as her, how did –'

'You ask; don't blame me if you don't understand. I have some knowledge of death's shadow.' Reothe repressed a shudder as he undid the laces of his shirt. Parallel ridges scarred his chest. 'I used my gift to anchor myself in you. If only you knew it, we are closer than blood kin. And I borrowed power from an outside source.'

'A snow leopard.' Tulkhan had seen those same marks on Imoshen. 'But how?'

'Imoshen and I are bound in a way that you and she can never be. I have trafficked with the Ancients and compromised principles because of you. You threw my plans into confusion.' Reothe pulled his shirt laces tight. 'Power exacts a price and there will be a price to pay for regaining Fair Isle, but I am willing to pay. My people have been persecuted too long. Imoshen and I will introduce the Golden Age of the T'En and you will be but a memory. You damned yourself the day you stepped onto this island. It was already mine but I wasn't ready to move. You forced my hand.'

Tulkhan said nothing.

Reothe shrugged. 'Think on it, Mere-man. You were in the wrong to invade a peaceful island. I am redressing that wrong.'

'I'll escape if I can,' Tulkhan warned. 'I'll tell Imoshen about her gifts and I'll see you dead!'

Reothe gave a mock bow. 'I would expect no less.'

The General watched him climb the ladder out of the windowless cell, taking the only light with him.

Alone in the cold darkness, Tulkhan faced his own mortality. And he cursed the day he made Imoshen swear not to use her gifts on him.

IMOSHEN AWOKE TO find a hand on her mouth and a body pressed to hers in the darkness.

She recalled huddling in the bed crippled by the mental blow Reothe's lock had dealt her. Sleep must have overcome her. She glanced over to the fireplace but the baby had not stirred.

'Imoshen?'

'Tulkhan?' Her heart rejoiced in his familiar scent and the rasp of his whispered voice. 'How did you get in here?'

'I slipped in by sea. They're all busy watching the entrances to the town.'

She nodded. That made sense, and Reothe's lock was to keep her in, not someone out. Hugging him, she ran her fingers through his silky dark hair. 'I missed you so much. I never thought to see you again.'

His lips were achingly familiar, his kisses so sweet. She wanted to drink him in. Tears of joy stung her eyes and slipped across her cheeks. He kissed them away, as loving and gentle as she knew he could be.

His ragged breath spoke of such longing she had to respond to his touch. An impossibly savage surge of desire ignited her. They had been parted, faced death and now were united. It was only natural to want him like this, but...

'We must escape –'

'Everyone's gone, watching the roads.' He caught her hand, guiding it inside his shirt. She could feel his pounding heart under her fingers. Her own heart thudded erratically.

His free hand undid the drawstring on her gown and pulled the neckline down. His palm pressed over her heart. She covered his hand with hers, just as she had done that morning when they swore their bond. She felt her heartbeat steady to thud in time with his. Words weren't necessary.

Silently she tugged at the laces of his breeches. When he moved to take over she pulled her nightgown above her head and tossed it aside, looking up to see him magnificently naked before her in the light of the larger moon.

Extending one hand, she drew him down onto the bed and pulled him to her. Tomorrow they might die but tonight they had each other. She wanted him fiercely and wanted him to know it.

He hesitated. She welcomed him with a subtle tilt of her hips. When she felt him fill her, a shudder of repletion shook her. His body trembled in sympathy.

It was beyond her control. Her body's needs overcame all thought. Her lips sought his, their breath mingled. The urgency in him spurred her on. If only he would let her touch his soul. She longed to make that final contact.

Threading her fingers through his hair she drew his face to hers.

'General,' she whispered, 'if we die tomorrow, know that I love you.'

He froze. She felt his fingers dig into her shoulders. His hands moved up through her hair as his mouth took hers. It was a brutal kiss, but she welcomed it because she wanted to shut out everything else, to imprint this moment forever.

Again, tears burned her eyes and her throat grew tight.

Then she felt it, the faintest whisper of cool contact, brushing the fevered plains of her mind.

Impossible. But it was there and she recognised that sentient sensation. Dawning panic took her.

Like a great blue-white sun, she felt Reothe's essence rise above the horizon of her perception. The mountains she built could not keep him out and he blazed forth across her mind, searing her with his presence.

Turning her back on that intense coolness, she tried to escape.

Wordlessly he sought her. *Imoshen, let me love you.*

It was a plea from the heart. It demanded nothing. She was already caught.

A spasm of desire rolled through her. She lost the perception of where her body ended and his began. Rippling waves of passion built around them, sweeping her ever closer to the edge, driving her to clutch him as they were swept over.

When she found herself again, she clasped him close. He was her only solid point in the chaos of her heightened perception.

Stunned, she turned her face away and the tendrils of intermeshed awareness parted, prickling all over her body. At last he was just a cool, soothing presence in the dark stretches of her mind. There was no room for thought, no words for what she had experienced.

Time seemed to stretch. He demanded nothing of her, seemingly content to linger in contact. And she, who had never known the intimacy of such contact, marvelled.

Was this what it was meant to be like with one of her own kind, a sharing of complete trust?

But he had tricked her.

She tried to ease away from the mental contact. He held on, passive but determined. Fear made her heart lurch and he reacted with a soft breeze allaying her fear.

'Reothe?'

He covered her lips with his fingers, cool, calming, calculating.

Calculating?

Then she felt it, the familiar pinprick as new life flared within her. It was a tiny star-burst of sensation so intense she gasped.

She felt his flash of triumph. Fury engulfed her. She chased him down a long tunnel. His blazing essence escaped her and his own walls sprang up. This time she pulled back before she hurt herself.

The transition was so abrupt her head reeled with impressions and nausea threatened.

'Imoshen?'

She scrambled across the bed away from him.

'Imoshen, don't do this.'

'You tricked me!'

'Yes. The drug was in the food, disguised by the spices. It was three days until the night you were fertile, not three days before your General arrived. His arrogant Ghebite pride won't let him accept you once he knows you carry my child.'

'It was him I took in my arms, not you!'

'Not in the end.'

That was true. A flood of sensations rolled over her, memories so intense she gasped. She felt raw. 'So this is what you promised?'

He was a pale form glowing on the bed. In her heightened T'En state, all surfaces gleamed with an inner radiance.

His hands lifted in a pleading gesture.

'You did wrong to trick me, Reothe.'

'Sometimes you must do a little wrong to achieve a greater right.'

Imoshen snorted, rejecting this utterly. Chaotic impressions rushed through her. She pressed her hands to her closed lips, fighting nausea as her head filled with sensations. 'What's happening to me? I feel strange.'

His touch was reassuring. She sank into his arms and he cradled her against his chest. The unnerving sensations passed. His cool essence was so calming she had to fight to remind herself he had betrayed her.

'Oh, Reothe,' she whispered, 'why did it have to be this way between us?'

TULKHAN LIFTED HIS head and blinked. The single candle flame seemed brilliant after the dark.

It was Reothe again, descending the ladder.

'Come to gloat?' Tulkhan tried to goad him. Anything was better than hanging here like piece of butchered meat waiting to be served up to his half-brother.

Reothe crossed the stone floor and stepped close, wordlessly offering the inside of his wrist to Tulkhan, holding it just below his nostrils.

'Do you smell her on my skin, Mere-man?'

As he said it Tulkhan experienced a flash of jumbled sensations. He felt Imoshen's body under his, felt her quicksilver passion ignite.

He wanted to deny them, but the impressions were too vivid to be a lie. Devastated, he turned his face away.

'The next time you see her, know this: she carries my child. As her true mate I have awakened her T'En potential. Whatever she may have felt for you will be coloured by this. Once she might have loved you, but can you bear to be pitied?'

It was the final blow. A groan escaped Tulkhan.

'Accept your fate, General,' Reothe whispered, satisfaction strong in his voice. 'You were outclassed.' Stepping back, Reothe called up the ladder. 'He's ready.'

Tulkhan turned to see several armed rebels descend.

'It is nearly dawn,' Reothe told him. 'At the Vaygharian's signal from the cliff-tower, Gharavan's ships made a night crossing with the wind behind them. There is only the exchange to get through, General, then you go home to your people and die.'

In that moment Tulkhan was overwhelmed with a longing to see the brilliant sun of his homeland, the brightly dressed people in the markets, the proud Ghebite men riding at one with their horses.

When they released him, Tulkhan rubbed his wrists and stretched to loosen his stiff muscles. One of the rebels moved forward with a chain, but Reothe waved him off.

'There is no need. Come, General.'

They walked side by side towards the ladder. Three of the rebels climbed up first. Tulkhan thought briefly of forcing Reothe to kill him, but the rebels might simply maim him, and besides, he discovered a nub of resistance deep within him. He would not go down without a fight.

Yet why did he feel so useless?

It was Reothe's doing. It had to be.

'Climb.' Reothe gestured to the ladder.

Tulkhan obeyed. When they were on the next floor the ladder was pulled up and a stone slid over the opening of the cell to create a living tomb.

He shuddered.

'Come take your place in history, General,' Reothe said.

They were escorted out of the gates of Northpoint citadel and into the township. It was the darkest part of the night, just before the dawn. The small moon had already set and its larger mate was waxing. Tulkhan looked down to the bay where a low fog clung to the water.

Reothe and their escort marched silently down through the curving streets to the wharfs. Incongruously, the smell of freshly baked bread made Tulkhan's stomach rumble with hunger.

A large bonfire burned on the stones of the wharf. Reothe lifted a brand and waved. Tulkhan saw a man return the signal from the ship. He could not see the Ghebite flag, but then the Ghebites would hardly advertise that they were supplying rebels to a Dhamfeer prince in exchange for the black sheep of their royal family.

The cruel irony of it tortured Tulkhan.

IMOSHEN WOKE FROM a troubled doze with a start. Ashmyr slept in her arms. The baby had woken after Reothe had slipped silently away. She had refused to speak to him, turning her face to the wall. All her perceptions of herself had been overturned, and she'd been too confused to confront him, her dearest and most dangerous enemy.

Now a sense of foreboding made her anxious. She slipped out of bed. The room looked normal. Instinct took her to the window. The bay was still dark, but a bonfire burned on the wharf.

Its leaping flames drew her gaze, reminding her of something. Before she could pinpoint the memory several figures stepped in front of the bonfire. Amid them was a broad-shouldered man, taller than all but one other. Even from this distance she recognised Tulkhan.

And Reothe was with him. The General must be Reothe's captive, yet he seemed unharmed; unarmed, yes, but not restrained. She couldn't imagine Tulkhan giving up without a fight.

It was so strange.

No time to wonder, this was her chance.

Eagerly Imoshen darted back to the bed to collect Ashmyr. Barefoot, her hair loose, dressed in nothing but her nightgown, she hurried to the door. With Reothe down on the wharf intent on the General, she could risk breaking his lock.

Experimentally she ran the fingers of her free hand over the door. There was nothing, no tingle, no pain waiting to cripple her mind.

Amazed, she concentrated on the mechanism within the lock chamber, felt it shift and the door swung open.

There was no T'En lock keeping her in, only her belief that it existed. Hot shame flooded Imoshen. Reothe had fooled her. He must have remained outside the room ready to rebuff her first attempt on the lock, blocking it so firmly that she would not dare try again. She had played right into his hands.

Furious with herself, Imoshen ran down the dark corridor with Ashmyr in her arms. Nothing was going to stop her.

But the tower rooms were almost deserted. She had no trouble finding her way out and into the township.

TULKHAN SHIFTED AS mist flowed around his boots. It drifted up to creep across the wharf around him and into the streets. He had heard there were times when the buildings of Northpoint were shrouded in fog and only the citadel tower rose above a sea of fog.

He could hear the gentle slap of water hitting the approaching boat's prow, mingled with the creak of the oars. Tulkhan watched the evidence of the boat's passage as it approached. The mist swirled around it so that at times the heads of the men looked like disembodied shapes. A rope sailed up towards them and was made fast.

His captors stepped up onto the wharf.

Kinraid! Bitterness closed Tulkhan's throat.

The Vaygharian made a mock bow. He turned to Reothe. 'Three boatloads of mercenaries are ready to disembark, and you'll get the rest when the Ghebite traitor stands on the mainland. I'll take him off your hands now.'

A surge of despair gripped Tulkhan.

No! This was not his emotion. Reothe was manipulating him.

Like the sun breaking through clouds, the pall that had been crushing him lifted. He heard Reothe gasp and the Vaygharian curse.

The rebels stepped back, muttering uneasily amongst themselves. Tulkhan turned to see what had startled them.

Imoshen! Fog curled its insubstantial tendrils around her. She was illuminated by an eerie inner radiance. With her silver hair loose and her white gown floating around her, she seemed to be carried on a sea of glowing mist.

The Vaygharian and his companions made the sign to ward off evil, calling on their gods to protect them. Even the rebels backed away, mouthing something in High T'En.

Tulkhan's teeth ached and his tongue registered the metallic taste of power. For an instant he thought he read fear, quickly masked, in Reothe's features.

'Imoshen.' The T'En male stepped forward, his hand extended in welcome, but when she made no move to accept it he let it drop. 'The General was just leaving. The events of this last summer have been set to rights. Soon Fair Isle will belong to the T'En.'

Tulkhan could not bear to look on Imoshen. Her choice was clear – she had renounced him for her own kind.

Though he felt the intensity of her gaze, he shut himself away from her, too proud to let her discover the blow she had dealt him.

This accursed isle had stolen everyone he had ever loved, but it would not take his self-respect. He would return to Gheeaba and restore his honour by killing his half-brother.

Imoshen shivered. Tulkhan would not meet her eyes. Reothe must have told the General she had given herself to him willingly. No wonder Tulkhan despised her.

Desperately she reached out to him but he jerked away, as though he found her touch was repellent.

His revulsion ate into her flesh like acid. The pain of it made her gasp and stagger. Reothe supported her, taking the baby as a wave of dizziness swamped her vision.

All along she had known the General found her Otherness unnerving, but she had believed they could overcome that. Now she knew he did not merely hate her, he was disgusted by her.

'Take him away,' Reothe gestured to the boat.

She watched in stunned despair as Tulkhan stepped willingly into the boat. When he sat down the mist closed around him, shrouding all but the crown of his head from sight.

Imoshen could not believe he had rejected her. But he had.

The Vaygharian went to leave.

Reothe stopped Kinraid. 'You will stay until the last mercenary stands on this shore. I know how the Vayghar fulfil their bargains.'

Kinraid hesitated, resentment colouring his features. 'So be it. Push off.'

The rebels uncoiled the rope and tossed it to the boat.

'Here. Take the traitor's brat with you!' Kinraid tore the baby from Reothe's arms and threw him into the mist.

Imoshen gasped. The white cloth of Ashmyr's gown fluttered like useless wings as he sailed out and down into the fog-shrouded sea.

She screamed, calling on Tulkhan with every shred of her being to catch their son.

A small splash filled the void left by her cry.

Shouts came from the boat. Several large splashes followed. It sounded as if the boat had over-turned.

Imoshen spun to face Kinraid. Rage engulfed her.

Drawing his sword, the Vaygharian stood ready to fight. Behind him the bonfire roared and leapt like a rampaging beast eager to consume. Imoshen recalled her vision of his death.

'You will die by your own hand in flames of agony,' she told him, hardly able to speak for the fury which closed her throat.

Terror engulfed his features. Against his will, he turned to the bonfire. As though fighting every step, Kinraid dropped his sword and ran clumsily, leaping into the flames. His screams rose on the night, piercing and utterly abandoned.

The confrontation had taken no time at all.

Imoshen ran for the edge of the wharf. White noise rushed in her head.

Reothe caught her, absorbing the impact.

'Ashmyr's dead, Imoshen. I felt his life flicker out!'

No. She could not believe it. Frantically she twisted in Reothe's arms, but he knew the T'En breaks and holds as well as she. At last he caught her body to his, using his superior strength to pin her arms.

'He's dead, Imoshen. Believe me!'

She stiffened in refusal.

'Imoshen?' He cupped her face in his hands. She felt him probe. It was too much. Instinctively she snapped back, retaliating against his intrusion. The strength of her gift was unleashed by desperation and he gasped, staggering. Even as he crumpled to the wooden planks she leapt over him.

In her mind's eye she still saw Ashmyr falling with his gown flapping uselessly, still heard that terrible small splash echo over and over.

He could not be dead.

Where was he? Where should she dive?

She couldn't see the boat for the thick mist, but she could hear the splashing, the shouts from the men in the water.

'Tulkhan!' she cried, probing for him.

'Here!'

Two hands surged from the mist, holding a small, still form. In the same heartbeat they sank down, hidden by the thick fog.

'Help! I can't swim!' Tulkhan called, panic edging his voice.

She recognised his fear. Her body reacted, heart pounding furiously.

Dropping to her knees, she searched the swirling mists, identifying the occasional dark shape which might have been any of the Vaygharian's men struggling to stay afloat.

'Accept me, Tulkhan. I can swim.'

She closed her eyes and probed for his mind. There it was, familiar for all that it was filled with cold terror. She slipped into him, felt the baby clutched to his shoulder, their shoulder. The pair of them went under.

As cold dark water closed over his head, panic roiled through him. She fought him for control. At last he understood and relaxed enough for her to kick, driving his strong limbs in a thrust that would bring him and Ashmyr to the surface.

She forced his free hand to form a scoop and drove his arm in an arc which carried him forward, kicking at the same time.

Now that he could feel the results, he let himself go with her, trusting her to save them. She could feel his great heart raging, powered by his determination to live.

With another stroke, his hand hit the barnacle-encrusted pole of the wharf. Desperately he clutched it, trying to keep his head above water. The still baby was wedged safely in the crook of his neck.

Imoshen detached herself from Tulkhan's perception and stretched full length so that she hung over the edge of the wharf. Her hands plunged into the mist and encountered Tulkhan's head. 'Give Ashmyr to me.'

Silently, Tulkhan passed the baby's limp form to her. She hugged the little body to her chest and rolled away from the edge, huddling in a crouch.

In the growing dawn light she saw that the life had left Ashmyr. She probed, but not a flicker remained.

It could not be.

She would not let it be.

In desperation she tore the neckline of her gown and raked the scars of the Ancients. Fiery tendrils of pain raced down her chest, but it was nothing compared to the pain of her loss.

With all her will she called on the Ancients. Ashmyr was theirs already. She could not begin to understand their purpose, but surely they would not let him die!

Tulkhan heaved his cold, wet body onto the wharf.

Imoshen's tragic figure riveted his gaze. She knelt, her breasts bared. Parallel rivulets of blood stained her white skin. With her arms extended she held the limp form of their son before her.

He did not need to be in touch with her mind to share her agony. It was written clearly on her face and it mirrored his own.

Tulkhan would have gone to her then but Reothe hissed a warning.

Startled, he glanced at the rebel leader and his skin went cold. Blood trickled from the Dhamfeer's nostrils and ears. Even his eyes wept tears of blood. He lay sprawled on the wharf, barely able to lift his head. The rebels had deserted them. Reothe lifted a trembling hand. 'Help me.'

Tulkhan found nothing incongruous in this plea. His only son was dead. Nothing mattered.

He scrambled across the wharf. Sliding an arm under Reothe's back, Tulkhan lifted the T'En warrior against his chest. Reothe's hands clutched him in a spasm of pain. A raw groan escaped him.

Then Reothe went very still.

Tulkhan followed his fixed gaze and stiffened as he recognised the same childlike being he'd seen when he had inadvertently spilled blood at an ancient site.

'The Ancients answer her summons,' Reothe whispered.

Tulkhan studied the apparition which hovered in the mist above the sea. He could not bear to meet its fathomless eyes as it glided through the fog towards Imoshen.

'I don't –'

'Imoshen called on the Ancients to save Ashmyr,' Reothe explained. 'That much is clear even to me.'

Tulkhan shuddered at Reothe's tone, equal parts fear and scorn.

An inner light suffused the Ancient, making Tulkhan squint and his eyes water.

As the strange being's hands closed on his son's body he felt a surge of panic. He fought it. The boy was dead, nothing could hurt him now.

Imoshen's arms dropped to her sides. Except for the rapid rise and fall of her breasts she was utterly still. Her eyes were fixed on the Ancient, her face naked with desperation.

Hope rose in Tulkhan's chest. He forced it down. Death could not be denied. Could it?

'Can they save him?' Tulkhan asked, unable to tear his eyes from the eerie tableau.

'For a price.'

The Ancient extended its free hand and touched Imoshen's closed eyelids. She shuddered visibly, took a deep breath, then gave a slight but firm nod.

Taking the baby in both hands the Ancient lifted Ashmyr's head and breathed into him. The little body jerked in a painful spasm. A grunt of sympathetic pain escaped Tulkhan, but his heart raced as hope surged, closely followed by revulsion. This was not right. No one returned to life from beyond death's shadow.

It was too much for Tulkhan to grasp. He strained to see through the radiant glare that consumed Imoshen, the Ancient and his son.

Was it possible? Would the baby's life be returned? If it did, surely he must be tainted?

Tulkhan wanted to ask Reothe for reassurance. Only by an effort of will did he hold his tongue, straining for the slightest sound.

A piercing cry broke from the baby. Imoshen gasped, her hands lifting, pleading.

The Ancient held the baby in one arm and floated closer to Imoshen. It leant towards her until its forehead touched hers. They might have kissed. For an instant they stayed thus then the Ancient transferred Ashmyr to Imoshen's hands and retreated.

She swayed, steadying herself with difficulty, the baby pressed to her body.

'What did it do?' Tulkhan whispered.

'I can't tell, I am as blind as you.'

'Reothe?' He studied what he could see of the T'En's face. His eyes were not blank like a blindman's. Did he did mean his T'En gifts had been destroyed? 'What happened to you?'

Reothe grimaced, raw pain and despair passing across his features. 'Look!'

Imoshen now held the baby, a living breathing child. As Tulkhan watched, the glow which had illuminated both her and the Ancient faded and with it the apparition, until only Imoshen and Ashmyr remained.

She sank to her knees. Oblivious to them, she stripped the wet gown from the baby and lifted him to her breast.

A sliver of silver dawn light illuminated the horizon behind the township, bringing the first hint of natural colour to their surroundings. Tulkhan shifted Reothe a little to ease his tense muscles. He felt the other give an involuntary shudder of pain.

Behind him he could hear voices, and guessed the rebels had drifted beck and would soon find them. Quick as the thought, he slipped the knife from Reothe's waist and held it to the rebel leader's throat.

A painful laugh escaped Reothe. It scraped across Tulkhan's raw senses like salt on an open wound. But he would not falter. The T'En warrior was his bargaining tool. Tulkhan had the rebel leader where he had always wanted him – helpless. Why then did he feel no rush of victory?

'Imoshen?'

Imoshen looked up, startled to hear her name. She felt like a sword's blade forged beyond recognition by the fires of pain.

Dawn's subtle light revealed the two men dearest to her.

'Ashmyr lives.' She stroked the soft dark head at her breast, joy and wonder suffusing her.

'But at what price?' Reothe whispered.

His question was an unwelcome intrusion. She glanced his way, noticing for the first time how he lay limply in Tulkhan's arms. The General's blade was pressed into Reothe's throat, making her flinch.

Cradling the baby, she crept over to them.

Already Tulkhan's long dark hair was drying in the breeze that carried the mist away. He held the knife so tightly his knuckles were white.

But it was Reothe who made her gasp. Blood had dried in painful paths where it had trickled from his nose and ears. It looked as if he had wept tears of blood.

Her heart turned over with outrage. 'Who did this to you?'

His eyes closed and he gave a wordless, almost imperceptible shake of his head. A rueful smile touched his lips. When he opened his eyes the knowledge was there for her to read.

'No, impossible!' she cried. 'I would not, *could* not, hurt you!'

Tulkhan muttered something in the Ghebite language. She glanced at him and registered his pain, but there was nothing she could do.

Silently she offered Tulkhan her apology. He looked away, unable to accept it. Her heart faltered.

Dragging in a tight breath, Imoshen returned her attention to Reothe. Blood-tinged tears slid from under his closed lids.

'Are you in pain?' Imoshen touched his temple, anxious to ease his discomfort, and felt a blankness.

Tulkhan shifted, stretching his cramped muscles. 'He says his T'En gifts are gone.'

Instinctively Imoshen splayed her fingers over Reothe's face. She probed. His body stiffened, a guttural groan escaped him. It tore at her. Sweat broke out on her skin, making it grow chill in the dawn breeze as she searched.

'I can't find you.' She could not believe the essence she had felt so acutely was dulled to a point where she could not perceive it. Gone forever?

'He said your gifts are greater than his,' Tulkhan told her softly, almost sympathetically. 'That they always have been.'

'But –'

'You did this to him,' Tulkhan said bitterly. 'Had you but tried, you could have withstood Reothe at any time.'

Imoshen's gaze shifted from Tulkhan's remote eyes to Reothe's pain-ravaged face.

'All bluff, Imoshen,' Reothe whispered. He held her eyes silently, asking forgiveness. 'A great gamble. And I almost won.'

His smile wrenched at her.

'Stay back!' Tulkhan barked suddenly.

Imoshen turned to see the rebels approaching, followed by a stream of townsfolk.

The baby at her breast gave a soft whimper. She soothed him automatically and came to her feet to face Reothe's rebels. As they edged forward, weapons drawn, the townsfolk hung back behind them, torn between fear and curiosity.

Imoshen studied the wharf and the bay, now visible through a thin film of retreating mist. The Vaygharians in the water had slunk off like rats.

'There will be no more fighting.' Imoshen met the eyes of the rebels. 'Sling a sail between two poles to make a stretcher. T'Reothe is hurt. I want him carried to T'Ronnyn's Citadel.'

As the rising sun chased the last of the mists away, Imoshen watched the rebels work. Tulkhan sheathed the knife and released Reothe, placing him gently on the deck. The Ghebite general did not approach her when he stood.

The rebels seemed subdued, concerned for their injured leader, and unsure of their own status as prisoners.

The creaking of a boat's oars made Imoshen turn.

'Wharrd comes,' Tulkhan announced. 'I must have the Vaygharian ship's captain captured before he can carry a message back to my half-brother.'

He strode past her to the end of the wharf.

Tulkhan did not trust himself near Imoshen. This night he had looked into the dark depths of his soul and he did not like what he had seen. It was as the Beatific had said. A True-man forfeited much if he loved one of the T'En.

Logic told him to climb into Wharrd's small boat and leave Fair Isle while he still owned his soul, but that would mean deserting his son, his only heir. Common sense told him his son was dead, that this creature Imoshen cradled was a changeling, but he could not bring himself to leave.

A spear of insight stabbed Tulkhan. Would his son grow into a being like Imoshen? Would the adult Ashmyr look upon Tulkhan with T'En eyes and scorn him as a Mere-man?

No wonder the T'En had been cast out of their home beyond the dawn sun. How could True-people live with the knowledge that Tulkhan was now privy to?

Wharrd lifted an arm and waved.

Tulkhan returned the signal automatically.

'Don't leave me, General,' Imoshen whispered suddenly at his side.

He snorted. 'I have no intention of relinquishing what I have taken. And do me the courtesy of keeping out of my head, T'En.'

She gasped softly. 'I was not... I did not mean to. I need you, General Tulkhan.'

'Oh?' He felt like laughing. What could Imoshen possibly need from a Mereman like himself? 'You have my son, you have Fair Isle, and now you have your betrothed, suitably chastised. What could you possibly want with me?'

He looked down into her face, illuminated by the soft morning light. She looked tired, fragile and vulnerable. He knew his words had hurt her. The irony of it was that in hurting her, he had hurt himself, because despite everything he still loved her.

Against his better judgment he cupped her cheek, feeling the softness of her skin on his calloused palm. Wisps of her pale hair lifted in the breeze.

She turned her face into his palm and kissed him. It was the gentle gesture of a supplicant, but her eyes were as sharp as ever.

'I need you to rule Fair Isle, General Tulkhan. The people are afraid of the T'En. I need someone they trust to represent their interests.'

He almost choked. 'So I am to be your puppet king? Truly, I am honoured.'

'Don't!' It was a plea from her heart.

'Think what you ask, Imoshen. I won't be your tool. I could not live with myself.'

'I know.' She edged closer to him, pressing against his side.

He had to acknowledge how much he craved her touch.

'I don't want a public life. You are a good True-man. You have earned Fair Isle, General Tulkhan. Keep it. I know you will rule wisely. And –'

'Kill him!' The words were out before he knew he meant to say them. 'Have Reothe executed.'

He felt her stiffen as the boat with his supporters bobbed nearer.

'I can't do that.'

'Why not?'

'He is the last of my kind. I can no more kill him than you could kill your half-brother. Remember what you said to me when I advised you to kill him?' Sorrow made her eyes luminous. 'You said if you could kill that easily, I would be dead. Now I give you the same answer. There have been moments when I could have taken another path, one that would have led to your death, but I did not. Don't ask me to kill Reothe.'

'Then banish him.'

'I need Reothe. He has T'En knowledge which I must have for my people and my own peace of mind. And, for the time being, he is harmless.'

Tulkhan laughed bitterly. 'We should stone him now while we can!'

He looked into her eyes and saw the knowledge there. They both knew that if Reothe should regain his gifts he would be too powerful and cunning to contain.

She did not attempt to deny this but offered Tulkhan a rueful smile. 'Reothe is the last of my kin.'

'And the father of your child?' It cost Tulkhan to ask this.

She nodded, searching his face. He waited for an explanation, a plea for forgiveness, but she said nothing.

'Imoshen, tell me he took you against your will. Offer me cold comfort.'

A rope snaked up through the air towards them. Tulkhan caught it on reflex and made it fast.

As he straightened he met Imoshen's gaze. A charged silence hung between them. Then Wharrd and the Ghebites clambered up onto the wharf, demanding an explanation, and the moment was lost.

Imoshen stepped back as Tulkhan moved forward to lift Kalleen onto the wharf. In a few moments he was surrounded by his own people. They greeted him exuberantly, knowing only that the rebel leader lay strapped to a litter, unable to move, while their general stood with Imoshen at his side, apparently victorious.

The irony of it was bitter. Yet he could not help but smile and accept their heartfelt congratulations. They had feared for his life. They had stood by him when all was lost and he had worked a miracle. He was their legendary General Tulkhan, a man capable of pulling victory from the jaws of defeat. Fair Isle was his and they shared a golden future.

Not one of them knew he was bound by chains of love to a creature more dangerous than his worst nightmares. He met Imoshen's garnet eyes above their heads and saw only her Otherness. Her expression reminded him of Reothe.

Imoshen slipped away from the celebrating Ghebites. Their hearty joy grated on her raw emotions.

Kalleen darted after her and hugged her with a thousand questions on her lips. Kalleen attempted to take the sleeping baby, but Imoshen would not part with him.

Ashmyr was more precious to her than life itself.

Returning her friend's hug Imoshen felt the rush of new life illuminating Kalleen and smiled, though the sudden expansion of her T'En gifts startled her.

Kalleen wrinkled her nose as she studied Imoshen. 'What is it, Imoshen? You look... different.'

Tears stung Imoshen's eyes. Kalleen grasped her arm impulsively, offering comfort.

Imoshen blinked the tears away and shook her head, dredging up a smile of reassurance. 'I need you to go to the citadel. Have chambers prepared and food laid out. Tell them the General has triumphed and is reconciled with the T'En. The rebels must not panic. There will be no executions.'

Kalleen nodded and called Wharrd to her side to explain what was to be done.

Imoshen left them. She crossed to where Reothe lay strapped to the makeshift stretcher, and knelt down beside him. The rebels stepped back to a respectful distance.

She touched his cheek, feeling the crust of dried blood. 'Are you in pain?'

He grimaced. 'What does it matter? I have lost and I'm as blind as a Mere-man. Kill me now before I recover, because I will not rest until I have restored the T'En.'

She splayed the fingers of her free hand across his forehead, concentrating on easing his pain. When his fine features relaxed, she let her hand drop.

'I don't want to kill you, Reothe.'

He turned his face away from her. Sadness settled in her core. Tulkhan had withdrawn from her and now Reothe.

'I am alone and frightened by what I've learned this night, Reothe. I thought I could shut the T'En gifts away and use them only when I chose. But...'

'What did you promise the Ancients?' he asked.

'What did *you* promise them?'

His eyes clouded, but he would not answer.

Imoshen sighed. 'All I ever wanted was to ensure my survival and a future for my child.'

'What will you do with me, Imoshen?' Reothe asked.

Tulkhan joined them and Imoshen came to her feet. Rebels and townsfolk watched uneasily, fearing purges and executions.

Imoshen raised her voice. 'People of Fair Isle, tell the rebels who hide under your beds that there will be no more killing. Fair Isle has seen enough death. We take T'Reothe to the citadel, as our honoured guest.'

As four men came forward to lift the litter, Imoshen turned to Tulkhan, extending her hand. For a moment she thought he would refuse to touch her, then he raised his arm and she closed her fingers over his.

She wanted to reassure him but he was too remote. He had made his acceptance of her conditional on Reothe's death, and she could not order the execution of the last T'En warrior. Reothe had a vision for the future of the T'En race that inspired her. Reothe was her other half, closer than a lover or a brother. Without Reothe to anchor her gifts, she doubted she would survive, and she was afraid of what she might become.

No wonder the T'En were so unstable.

Pain curled around Imoshen's heart. To think it had come to this.

Last autumn when General Tulkhan's forces had prepared to storm the Stronghold, it had all seemed so simple – death or honour. Every decision she had made had been with the best of intentions. She wished she had never uncovered her T'En powers. But here was Ashmyr in her arms and another life growing inside her, and she could not turn back the passage of events which had led her here.

Imoshen lifted her chin and prepared to face the township.

In the growing light of a new day they made a slow, stately procession through the winding streets to the Citadel. The shopkeepers stood in the doorways and solemn children watched history unfold.

The smell of freshly baked bread made Imoshen's stomach rumble. She veered towards a baker's apprentice who had run to the front of the shop.

He brushed flour from his apron as he balanced a tray of fresh loaves, hot from the oven.

Imoshen's mouth watered. She met his awed eyes. 'May I?'

The baker nodded proudly. 'Best in all Northpoint,' he announced. 'Take as many as you want.'

'Thank you.' Imoshen took one and tore into it. Warm crusty bread melted in her mouth. She smiled. 'Excellent!'

The baker beamed and his apprentice cheered. The crowd surged forward. First one then another stroked her hair or touched her sixth finger.

'T'Imoshen...' they whispered reverently, their relief and pleasure evident. She tried not to think how easily their feelings for her could turn to hatred.

With the baker's consent, Imoshen offered a loaf to the General.

Tulkhan's fingers closed on the crusty bread and his mouth watered in anticipation. He looked into Imoshen's eyes with rueful understanding. She had done it again. With a simple gesture she had won the people over.

Was it by design or pure luck?

It didn't matter.

He tore a chunk from the loaf and ate it, giving the baker his compliments before they resumed their journey.

Imoshen's gaze met his. 'It appears you have won, General.'

He looked into the eyes of the creature he should despise, but if truth be told he adored her. 'Appearances can be deceptive, T'Imoshen.'

BOOK THREE
DESPERATE ALLIANCES

*To my friends and colleagues who have helped
bring the T'En trilogy to life*

Chapter One

TORN BY CONFLICTING loyalties, Imoshen sat beside Reothe's bed. With the arrival of evening, scented candles now burned in the chamber that had so recently been her prison. In the space of one day, their positions had been reversed.

She should let Reothe die. He had sworn to reclaim the throne whatever the cost, and if he regained his gifts he would be too powerful to contain. But to stand by and let someone die when she could heal them went against her instincts. All day she had fought to save him, easing his pain with herbs and, when this failed, drawing on her healing powers.

'Here, sip this.' She lifted Reothe's head, holding the tisane to his lips. His suffering had pared back his features, emphasising his high forehead, narrow nose, prominent cheek bones. He grimaced at the bitter taste. 'It will lower your fever.'

Obediently he drained the goblet. She smoothed the damp silver hair from his pale forehead and his hand squeezed hers in gratitude. Her heart contracted.

After what he had done she should hate him, but she could not. Before Fair Isle fell, they had been betrothed. Reothe was the last of her kind. They were throwbacks to the T'En race which had settled Fair Isle, marked by their wine-dark eyes, striking colouring and six-fingered hands. Last survivors of the old royal line, they possessed the T'En gifts, powers which were both a blessing and a curse.

And since General Tulkhan had captured their island kingdom, they had both clung to life with determination and, when necessary, guile.

Even she had been a victim of Reothe's trickery. The memory stung, making her cheeks flame with anger. Last night Reothe had come to her in Tulkhan's form, slipping into her arms and planting a seed of dissension which she feared would drive Tulkhan to reject her. The proud Ghebite general would never accept another man's child. The prospect of losing Tulkhan's trust was particularly cruel, for even though he had taken her as co-ruler to cement his hold on Fair Isle, she had let herself hope he had begun to love her.

The General's bone-setter entered the chamber, bringing her warmed wine. With an effort she came to her feet. 'Thank you. I think the worst is over.'

'I will watch him. Get some rest,' Wharrd urged.

'Yes.' However, she clasped the goblet to her chest and stared down at Reothe. She had to admire his daring. In a decisive gamble he had kidnapped her and the son she had borne Tulkhan, luring the General into a trap.

In exchange for a mercenary army Reothe had offered to deliver Tulkhan to King Gharavan. The Ghebite king was the legitimate heir and Tulkhan's younger half-brother, but any love he bore Tulkhan had been eroded by the General's popularity and military success.

With the mercenaries and his own rebel army, Reothe had intended to retake Fair Isle. He had come so close to making the exchange that Imoshen felt ill.

Strange. This time last year she would have given anything to see Tulkhan in chains, but now the thought brought her no joy. It was ironic that after surrendering her stronghold she had set out to woo the conqueror, only to fall in love with the man.

THROUGH THE PARTIALLY open door General Tulkhan watched Imoshen. She claimed to love him, but doubt consumed Tulkhan. He could not understand the strange hold Reothe had over her. In his darkest moments he feared it was like calling to like.

Only last night, when he had been held captive in the tower's dungeon, Reothe had come to him with Imoshen's scent on his skin, boasting that she carried his child.

Tulkhan refused to accept it.

Fury surged through him. As a tactician he knew that if he wanted to hold Fair Isle, Reothe must die. The rebel leader commanded the love of the people and the loyalty of the old nobility in the Keldon Highlands, and Tulkhan had good reason to suspect certain high church officials quietly favoured Reothe's plans. But it was the thought of another man's hands on Imoshen that made Tulkhan resonate with rage.

Reothe would die this very night.

As Imoshen bade Wharrd good night, Tulkhan stepped into the shadows behind his guards.

Blinded by exhaustion, the last T'En Princess passed by, her straight nose and determined chin a beautiful mask. The General wanted to break her terrible composure. He wanted her to beg his forgiveness and declare her love for him. But he let her walk down the hall, a stiff-shouldered, tall figure with a deceptively fragile air.

Pain twisted inside Tulkhan. How could she betray him after everything they had shared?

IMOSHEN CLIMBED THE stairs to her room, numbed by the speed of events. Even the knowledge that her life would be forfeit if the church learnt she had used her gifts to kill a True-man left her unmoved. She did not regret killing the Vaygharian. He had signed his own death warrant when he threw her infant son into the sea. The shock had unleashed her nascent powers and she had turned on him, driving him to immolate himself in the bonfire's flames, fulfilling her vision of his death.

Recalling the Vaygharian's cruel nature, a sense of foreboding overcame

Imoshen and she longed to hold her infant son and rejoice in Ashmyr's innocence. But even this simple joy was a double-edged sword, for she now carried a child she had not chosen to conceive.

Resentment urged her to take control. As a midwife, she knew the herbs. One draught of womansorrow would dislodge the babe and circumvent Reothe's trickery.

She staggered, reaching for the wall. In a flash of understanding so intimate that she felt nauseous, Imoshen realised she could not do it. She sank onto the steps, with her head in her hands. As a healer she was devoted to preserving life. But, more than that, she was a mother.

Tears burned her eyes. Just as Ashmyr was an innocent pawn in the game of power, this child was innocent of their father's treachery and she would defend the babe with her life.

Yet she knew the General would never accept Reothe's child. Taking a deep breath, she stood and straightened her shoulders. Despite everything, she must make Tulkhan understand.

PRIMED FOR MURDER, Tulkhan pushed the thick oak door open, revealing the injured rebel leader. Wharrd looked up, a single candle flame illuminating his sun-lined features. Silently the bone-setter nodded to Tulkhan and led him to the canopied bed, raising the candle. By its flickering light Reothe lay utterly vulnerable.

'I have never seen an injury like this. The whites of his eyes are blood red,' Wharrd whispered. 'And it is almost as if Imoshen's presence sustains him. Since she left he has faded rapidly.'

Without warning, Reothe's body convulsed. A moan was torn from him and he lay panting, his skin glistening.

'He sinks deeper still and radiates heat like a forge,' Wharrd said. 'I doubt he'll last the night.'

'Then he will save us the trouble of killing him.'

Wharrd met Tulkhan's eyes. 'The Princess –'

'Not only is he the last male of the old royal line, but he is pure T'En.' As Ghebite war general, Tulkhan had made many hard decisions but, despite the danger Reothe represented, betraying Imoshen's trust tore the heart out of him. 'If the rebel recovers his sorcerous gifts, he will unite Fair Isle against me. Better to suffocate him now and face Imoshen's wrath.'

'Why face her anger when you could console her?' Wharrd countered. 'As I watched Imoshen battle to save her kinsman, I felt for her, knowing that we could not let him live. Like you, I sought a soldier's clean solution, but after consideration I offer you a courtier's solution. My herbal knowledge comes from the mainland. Pains-ease is odourless and swift and, in his state, a double dose would snuff his flame.'

Tulkhan's mouth twisted with repugnance. 'A courtier's solution.'

'Imoshen trusts you. This way –'

'She will not realise that I have betrayed her trust.' Tulkhan knew Wharrd was right, yet he felt this subterfuge diminished them both. He longed for an honourable solution which would not conflict with his warrior code, the Gheeakhan. Finally, he expelled his breath. 'So be it. I have fought beside you these eleven years, and never thought to see you murder a sick man. Never did I think I would give you such an order.'

Wharrd looked down.

'Just do it and do it quickly,' Tulkhan said. 'I'm going to see Imoshen.'

On the mainland much was whispered about the mysterious T'En of Fair Isle. Tulkhan was only just beginning to understand their strengths and weaknesses. His people called them the Dhamfeer and the Ghebite priests believed them closer to beasts than True-men.

Accordingly, the General should have been repulsed by a woman who stood as tall as a tall True-man, whose milk-white skin and garnet eyes proclaimed her tainted T'En blood, but her Otherness fascinated him and he found Imoshen's refusal to admit him her master exhilarating.

He had discovered that this proud, passionate woman was far more dangerous than any mainland myth. Tulkhan could not pinpoint when it had happened, but in the space of one year she had ensnared him, heart and soul. Imoshen was his addiction and he ached to confront her.

As conqueror of Fair Isle he had dictated the terms of surrender. Imoshen had negotiated many concessions for her people, but tonight she would be the one making concessions.

The soft sound of running feet coming down the spiral stair made him hesitate, hand on his sword hilt.

'General Tulkhan?' Kalleen gasped. The little True-woman wore nothing but a nightgown and her hair hung loose to her waist. In the candles' glow, it was the colour of honey held to sunlight. Though she was the Lady of Windhaven now and no longer Imoshen's maid, she would let no one else serve the Princess. 'It's Imoshen, she –'

Mouth dry, Tulkhan rushed past her and threw open the chamber door. Imoshen lay crumpled on the brilliant carpet like an abandoned toy. 'What happened, Kalleen?'

'She had just given the baby to me when she convulsed and fell to the ground.'

Crossing the room, Tulkhan spared a glance for his son sleeping in the basket and then knelt beside Imoshen. 'Can you hear me?'

She did not respond.

He slid his arms under her and stood, fear making the movement effortless. Even as he carried her to the bed, he felt the heat rise from her skin. 'Did she give any sign that she was sickening?'

'She was very quiet. I thought her tired after nursing T'Reothe all day.' In her distraction, Kalleen gave the prisoner his royal title. 'General...' As she reached out to Tulkhan, the fear in her hazel eyes made his stomach clench. 'This is no ordinary fever. Before it came on there was that tension on the air. You know the way it feels when Imoshen uses her gifts?'

Tulkhan nodded briefly. For him, warning that Imoshen's T'En powers were roused came as a prickling of his skin. His concern deepened. The first time Imoshen had overextended her powers and fallen into a stupor, no-one had been able to wake her. That night Reothe had come to her rescue after sensing a dimming in her life force.

But Reothe had only been able to save her because they had once been betrothed and, according to Reothe, the last two T'En were bound in ways a True-man could not understand.

Cold certainty gripped Tulkhan. 'Wait here.'

He ran down the steps. Command meant never revealing doubt, so he forced himself to slow down and stride past the guards as though Imoshen's life didn't hang in the balance.

When he entered the prisoner's chamber, he found Wharrd leaning over the unconscious man, trying to get him to swallow something. 'Stop. Kill him and you kill Imoshen!'

Wharrd straightened, letting Reothe sink back onto the pillow.

'She lies upstairs in the same state as him.' Tulkhan gestured to Reothe. 'I fear...'

Wharrd gave a grunt of understanding and glanced at the mixture in the mug. Tulkhan realised with one act of treachery he could be free of both the dreaded Dhamfeer. The thought revolted him.

Grabbing the mug, he strode to the oriel window and flung the potion into the night. Far below Northpoint Citadel's tower, where the rocks met the sea, the waves would obliterate all trace of 'the courtier's solution.'

Closing the window, Tulkhan turned to Wharrd. 'Through Imoshen I command the loyalty of her people. If she did not support me the Keldon nobles would rise up in revolt. They know that since my half-brother turned on me I don't have the backing of the Ghebite Empire, and without it I cannot hope to put down a rebellion in the highlands.' Battle strategy was second nature to Tulkhan, but in his heart, he had to admit that, although he taken the last T'En Princess as his wife out of political necessity, it was not cold necessity that took him to her bed, nor simple lust that bound him to her. 'I need Imoshen.'

'To hold Fair Isle you need her, but that means' – Wharrd gestured towards the unconscious man – 'letting this snake live.'

They both stared at Reothe. Once Tulkhan would have given almost anything to have Reothe in his power. Now, he felt no surge of victory. 'Come and see if there's anything you can do for Imoshen.'

In the room above, Kalleen was sponging Imoshen's face. She turned at the sound of footsteps. 'Wharrd.'

'Kalleen.'

In that one exchange Tulkhan heard their love confirmed. A stab of guilt assailed him, for he knew the bone-setter wanted nothing more than to retire to his estates with Kalleen.

Wharrd examined Imoshen. 'She appears to suffer just as he does. I fear there is nothing we can do but watch and wait.'

'I will watch over her,' Tulkhan said, pulling a chair up beside the bed. 'Take my son for the night.'

He wrung out the damp cloth while Kalleen collected the baby. Consumed with fear for Imoshen, Tulkhan hardly heard them slip away. His hands trembled as he sponged the beads of perspiration from her forehead.

Unaware of him, she lay there, her pale skin flushed, silver hair spread across the pillow. She gave a soft moan and her lids moved as if she were watching events played out on another plane. The tension of her gifts made his head ache and frustration ate at him. He was only a True-man, unlike Reothe. But try as he might Tulkhan could not revive his anger.

'Ahh, Imoshen, how could you betray me?' he whispered. He had to believe that she had not gone willingly into Reothe's arms. But how could he be certain?

Threading his fingers through hers, the General pressed her hot skin to his lips, savouring the satiny texture. Loving Imoshen might yet be his downfall, but that did not stop him willing her to live with every fibre of his being.

UPON WAKING, IMOSHEN gave silent heartfelt thanks to see another dawn. Nothing had prepared her for what she had experienced when she returned to her room last night. While nursing her son she'd sensed the approach of the Vaygharian's vengeful soul, and had only just managed to pass Ashmyr to Kalleen before the man's shade had latched onto her.

Cruel in death as he had been in life, the Vaygharian had tried to drag her through death's shadow with him and into the realm beyond. Only her fierce will had saved her. A shiver passed over her skin, leaving her feeling raw and fragile.

In all her studies of the T'En she had not read of this phenomenon, but then she had only read the works available to True-people. Her ancestor's account of how the T'En conquered Fair Isle was sure to contain the truth about death's shadow, but Reothe had hidden the T'Elegos. He knew so much more about their heritage, she must convince...

'Imoshen?'

'Tulkhan?' Her voice was a mere thread. She turned her head to find the General by her bed. The shadow of a beard was dark against the coppery skin of his jaw. His temple plaits had unravelled and his long black hair hung dishevelled around his broad shoulders. She longed to smooth the lines of worry from between his brows, but he had avoided her since they had taken Reothe captive yesterday morning.

She fully expected him to insist on executing the rebel leader, and prepared to argue for Reothe's life.

The General clasped her hand. 'I prayed the fever would break, but when it did you went so cold and still, I feared you would never wake.'

'Water,' she croaked. He helped lift her head so that she could take a sip. Sinking back onto the pillow she was touched to see him so careworn. 'You stayed by me, thank you.'

'Ah, Imoshen.' He brushed this aside gruffly. 'Your servants will come soon. We have very little time, I must be frank. After Reothe's capture the town seethes with rumour. You cannot deny your powers when your features proclaim your T'En blood. But for my men to accept you, they must believe these gifts are nothing more than the useful ability to hasten healing.'

'As you see, even my healing gift deserts me if I overextend myself,' she whispered, then wished she had not reminded him that she had spent the previous day by Reothe's bed. Tulkhan must wonder why she hadn't fought off Reothe's advances. If he discovered how Reothe had tricked her he might march down the tower steps and kill the rebel leader with his bare hands.

'I am no fool, Imoshen. That was more than a passing fever. You suffered something only the T'En can endure.'

'True,' she admitted, but would not elaborate.

'Very well.' He stood, expression unreadable. 'When you are ready we will tour Northpoint. I must speak with the captains of the mercenary ships. Reothe's rebels watch us, ready to strike at the first sign of weakness. The people must see that we are united and our heir unhurt.'

Imoshen sat up, alarmed. 'Where is Ashmyr?'

'With Kalleen. I will send for her.'

But the little True-woman was already at the door with the hungry baby, issuing orders to draw Imoshen's bath. Imoshen hardly noticed Tulkhan slip away. Joy blossomed within her as she cradled her son and bared her breast, marvelling at the boy's perfection. Intent on suckling, his lids were closed, hiding his wine-dark eyes. Thick black lashes formed crescents on his pale cheeks. She touched his hand and his six fingers closed around her little finger. Imoshen gave thanks for his precious life from the depths of her heart.

As soon as the servants left, Kalleen climbed onto the bed next to Imoshen. She stroked the baby's fine hair. 'The tower servants kept stopping me to touch him. I can't believe he nearly drowned. How could you let... I mean –'

'I am not all-powerful, Kalleen.' The near loss was still too immediate for Imoshen. Her voice shook as she tried to speak dispassionately. 'The General was in the boat about to be rowed out to the ship and exchanged for the mercenaries when it happened. The Vaygharian was acting as go-between for Reothe and King Gharavan, but he'd always hated me. In a moment of spite he snatched Ashmyr and threw him into the sea.' She closed her eyes, seeing her son fall into the mist-shrouded bay, hearing that terrible small splash.

In white-hot fury she had turned on the Vaygharian, driving him to suicide. Reothe had sought to console her but she refused to believe that Ashmyr was dead, and had lashed out and crippled his gift. 'I ran to the wharf's edge and called on Tulkhan to save our son.'

'But Ghebites cannot swim.'

'I helped him.' How simple it sounded. But only in desperation had Tulkhan dropped his guard and accepted the mind-touch, letting her guide his body.

'My sweet boy,' Kalleen whispered, cupping one tiny foot which had escaped the blanket. His toes curled in response, making her smile. 'It was lucky Tulkhan reached him in time.'

But he hadn't. Ashmyr had been dead when Tulkhan passed him up to Imoshen. In despair she had called on the Ancients to restore Ashmyr's life. That she held her living son in her arms was due entirely to those old powers, and her willingness to make a bargain. And a poor bargain it was for, in her extremity, she had promised them anything. And the Ancients were known to have long memories.

She shuddered, then told herself there was no point dwelling on something she could not change.

Servants arrived with a copper bath and others followed with buckets. In the old tower they did not have the luxury of hot water piped to each floor.

Kalleen took the drowsy baby, tucking him in his basket. Still weak, Imoshen was grateful for her help. It was wonderful to sink into the warm, scented water.

The General returned while Kalleen was rinsing Imoshen's hair. Without explanation he went to stand before the windows, his hips resting on the sill, his arms folded across his broad chest. He faced Imoshen and the light from behind hid his expression, revealing only the glint of his eyes as he followed Imoshen's every move.

Very aware of him, she bent her head as Kalleen twisted her long damp hair into a knot. Kalleen sent Imoshen a questioning look but Imoshen had no answer. Coming to her feet, she placed one hand on Kalleen's shoulder for support as the little woman gently rubbed scented soap into her skin.

Imoshen's body grew hot under Tulkhan's gaze. As water sluiced over her, rinsing off the soap, her pulse throbbed through her limbs. Still Tulkhan said nothing, neither leaving nor sending Kalleen away.

Dizzy and breathless, Imoshen stepped from the tub. Kalleen wrapped the bathing cloth around her. She undid Imoshen's hair, letting it fall heavy and damp to her hips. Then Imoshen knelt before the fire as Kalleen finger-combed her hair, spreading it to dry.

Hardly able to swallow, Imoshen dared a quick look at the General. He stood rigid, his eyes devouring her.

When Kalleen began to divide Imoshen's nearly dry hair to plait it, Tulkhan straightened. 'Leave us.'

Kalleen looked to Imoshen, who nodded.

Alone with the General, Imoshen's breath caught in her throat. She looked up. His eyes, black as obsidian, bored into her. She could sense the force of his emotion, barely contained. Would he reject her because she had not fought off Reothe?

He offered his hand palm up. Her skin looked so pale against his and his flesh felt hot as his fingers closed around hers. Pulling her to her feet, he drew her into his arms. She welcomed his touch. Without a word he sought her lips, hungry and demanding.

Tears of relief stung her eyes.

She had been so afraid he would reject her. Pressed to the length of his body she felt the strength in him, but she wanted more. She ached to share the absolute intimacy of the mind-touch that came with true bonding. Only when he lowered his defences and opened to her would she know how he truly felt. She needed to be absolved by his love.

She gasped as he lifted his head. His great body trembled and his ragged breathing made her heart race. He pressed his lips to her forehead, his large hands cradling her head.

Opening her senses she sought his essence. She knew him now, having shared his mind. It had been impulse which made him leap into the bay to save their son, but it had taken cool-headed bravery for him to accept the mind-touch which he had fought so long. He had trusted her enough to guide his limbs and swim for the wharf. It was that willingness to accept new ideas and the ability to think under pressure which she admired in Tulkhan. But when she sought to make contact with him she discovered his barriers were clamped firmly in place.

'No, Imoshen. You promised not to try this.'

'I thought, with what we had shared...' She ran down as he pulled away from her. 'Tulkhan?'

He stood before her, arms out. 'I am but a True-man, Imoshen. Accept me for what I am.'

'We could share so much more.'

'Where would it end? When I am your puppet king?'

She shook her head, cut to the quick. 'Never, Tulkhan. I respect you too much –'

'Then respect my wishes in this one thing.' He caught her hands in his. 'Imoshen?'

She looked down at his strong hands, scarred by years of battle. Respect his wishes in this one thing... but it was such an essential thing. By denying her T'En nature he was denying an intrinsic part of her. Could she live with that? Did she have a choice?

She searched his face, aching for him to hold her.

'Imoshen!' He pulled her close. She felt his mouth almost bruising hers, his hands almost too hard on her shoulders. It was as if he was trying to erase her doubt with the force of his passion. If this was all they could share then it would have to be enough.

THAT AFTERNOON TULKHAN stepped off the mercenary ship's gangplank, pleased with the results of his meeting. The captain had been only too eager to describe the Ghebite king's forces. Satisfied that he had found a chink in his half-brother's defences, Tulkhan looked around for Imoshen.

She had accompanied him on this tour of Northpoint to reassure the townsfolk, who were understandably wary with the Ghebite army across the straits and Reothe's rebels in the countryside. Their town had suffered the brunt of Tulkhan's invasion, and they were anxious not to provide the stage for another confrontation.

But Imoshen was nowhere in sight. Wharrd answered Tulkhan's unasked question. 'The Princess went to inspect the hospice. I insisted she take three elite guard.'

Tulkhan was not really surprised. Considering Imoshen's gift was one of healing, she was a natural choice for patron of the hospices. As a minor member of Fair Isle's royal family she had been raised to believe a noble's duty was to serve her people. Still, he did not trust these people. They had been too quick to support Reothe. 'Which way?'

He needn't have asked. Shouts and splintering wood urged him to hurry. Striding up the steep lane, he followed the sounds to their source, a grand building of the same white stone as the Citadel. A plump man was scurrying about the steps, collecting damaged candles and cursing the Ghebites. Seeing Tulkhan he fled.

The General stepped over the debris, thrusting the double doors of the hospice wide open. The public hall was festooned with market paraphernalia. 'What's going on here?'

Tulkhan's elite guards greeted his arrival with relief. They were no match for Imoshen in full stride. With Ashmyr strapped to her chest, she was berating a little man.

At the sound of Tulkhan's voice she spun to face him. 'This is, or was, the hospice. They have turned it into a market!' Imoshen rounded on the man. 'This building was dedicated by Imoshen the Third to serve the sick. The church should never have allowed –'

'The priests were killed in the invasion, like the hospice healers. Our markets burnt down. What could we do?'

'I heard how your township suffered in the early days of the invasion,' Imoshen said soberly. 'But now I want the hospice restored. I will send for more healers and priests.' She gestured to the elite guards. 'See that this building is emptied and cleaned.'

Tulkhan's men bristled. They were warriors, not common labourers. Before the silence could grow uncomfortable, the General swung a bale of wool onto his back. 'Where do you want this, Imoshen?'

She smiled her thanks. 'Outside. They can rebuild their markets.'

'Why rebuild when another invasion threatens?' someone muttered.

Imoshen silenced the traders with a look. 'In a few days Tulkhan's army will arrive, and he will sail across the T'Ronnyn Straits to forestall Gharavan's invasion. Thanks to the Protector General your town won't be a battleground again. You can not only rebuild the markets, but your lives!'

Much heartened, the townsfolk assisted the General and his men in dismantling the stalls.

When this was progressing well Tulkhan joined Imoshen. 'Now I understand why this building bears the T'En royal sign over the door and not the anchor and sword of the Citadel.'

'Do not mention that symbol to these respectable townspeople. They will not thank you for reminding them of their pirate ancestors.' She met his eyes with a rueful smile. 'There are many minstrel tales about T'Ronnyn and his T'En brothers. They were given a Charter to keep the Pellucid Sea free of pirates. It was not long before they were more feared than those they hunted. Most of Northpoint are descended from them, though they're too proud to admit their T'En blood...' She frowned, her gaze going past him. 'You, child, come here.'

A scruffy urchin approached, her eyes fixed on the ground. Unlike the mainland towns where gangs of homeless children roamed the streets, there were few poor in Fair Isle.

Hugging her son to her chest, Imoshen knelt in her fine velvets to feel the child's thin legs. 'This girl's broken leg has not been set properly. That's why she limps.' Imoshen's eyes glistened with real anger. 'Who is responsible for her?'

A tall man, his red hair silvered at the temple, put aside a crate of late-ripening melons. He raised both hands to his heart and then his forehead, giving the deep obeisance reserved for the Empress. The child sidled over to him like a puppy. His head remained bowed. 'I am responsible for Almona.'

Imoshen straightened. 'Why haven't you sought treatment for her leg?'

'It had already knitted poorly when I took her in. It was beyond the skills of all but a T'En healer.' He raised wine-dark eyes to Imoshen. Tulkhan stiffened. It always startled him to find half-bloods. 'Her parents are dead.'

'But families and friends have always taken in orphans,' Imoshen said. 'Children are valued in Fair Isle. Why is she with you?'

'Whole villages have been wiped out.' The man's large hand cupped the child's face, lifting her chin so that she raised the same garnet eyes to Imoshen. 'And no one wanted a half-blood. I have taken in seven others like her.'

'What happened to your...' Imoshen took his hand, turning it over.

Drawn by her pained gasp, Tulkhan moved closer. With a jolt he realised the farmer had once had six fingers on each hand, but all that remained of both sixth fingers were stumps.

'I have read of these mutilations during the Age of Consolidation,' Imoshen whispered. 'But I did not think to see such barbarity in my time. Who did this to you?'

'My parents. Out of love. They witnessed the stoning of the last rogue T'En. Rather than abandon me at birth, they –'

'That was over a hundred years ago!' Tulkhan objected.

'I carried both the T'En traits, too close to a throwback for comfort. Everyone knows the males are dangerous. So...' He shrugged eloquently.

Tulkhan caught Imoshen's eye. Everyone believed the T'En males more powerful and so they were, but only if the females' greater powers weren't triggered by the birth of children. Since Imoshen the First had ordered all pure T'En women to take a vow of chastity, this knowledge had been lost to memory.

The night before last, when the General had been in Reothe's power, the rebel leader had revealed it was only Imoshen's belief that his gifts were greater than hers that made her his captive. The irony of it had delighted Reothe.

Now Imoshen stood beside Tulkhan, his bond-partner and mother of his child, powerful enough to cripple a T'En male. Tulkhan looked on her with fresh eyes.

'To cut off a child's sixth fingers. So cruel!' Imoshen's arms closed around her son protectively. Her shoulder met Tulkhan's chest as she stepped back and he felt the tension in her. With her ability to skim minds he guessed she had absorbed the mutilated man's memories, and this was confirmed when her trembling hand sought Tulkhan's. With the T'En gifts came strength but also vulnerability. He squeezed her fingers and she cast him a grateful smile. She turned to the farmer. 'Your name?'

'Eksyl Five-fingers.'

'Let it be known that all unwanted children are welcome here. Food and bedding will be sent from the Citadel. I will be back tomorrow to begin the healings. Then I will see what I can do for Almona. I can do nothing to right the wrong that has been done to you, Eksyl.'

'All I ask is your blessing, Empress.'

Imoshen cast Tulkhan a quick look, the colour rising in her cheeks. 'I am not the Empress and make no claim to that title. The day I took General Tulkhan for my bond-partner we became co-rulers of Fair Isle. I am your Lady Protector, Eksyl.'

He sank to one knee. 'Forgiveness, T'Imoshen.'

Tulkhan smiled ruefully for, after denying the Old Empire title, Imoshen regally raised her left hand, the one closest to her heart, and placed the tip of her sixth finger in the centre of the half-blood's forehead. 'You have my blessing. I name you Malaunje Protector.'

Later, as they walked up the rise to the Citadel, Tulkhan remarked, 'Malaunje? I don't know that word.'

'It is an old High T'En word. It means half-blood, but the connotations were different then. Once the T'En were respected and the Malaunje were their closest kin.'

Nowadays it was a curse to be born a throwback and half-blood children with T'En traits were unwanted. Tulkhan noticed how Imoshen brushed her lips across Ashmyr's soft head. He did not want his son to be ostracised.

'How long before you leave to confront your half-brother?' Imoshen asked.

'I sail as soon as Commander Piers gets here with the army and the ships are prepared,' he said.

She licked her lips as if she might say something.

'What?'

Imoshen smiled sadly. 'Nothing. I know you must go. It is just that I –'

'Had a premonition of disaster?'

She laughed. 'Nothing so dramatic. Mine is a purely selfish motive. I will miss you, General.'

With him gone, would she attempt to seize Fair Isle? Tulkhan looked into Imoshen's smiling eyes and could not believe the worst of her.

Chapter Two

WITH THE ARRIVAL of his army four days later, General Tulkhan was ready to go to war. Though Imoshen matched him stride for stride on the Citadel's parapets, once he set sail her position would be precarious. She was co-ruler of Fair Isle, but Tulkhan's men feared her and his absence would test their respect for her authority.

Behind her the General's commanders vied for position with his elite guard. Not so eager, the dignitaries of the township kept a cautious distance. Like Imoshen, they were trapped. Reluctant hosts to Tulkhan's army, they feared his half-brother, who brooded across the straits threatening a spring invasion.

The last of the sun's setting rays illuminated the top of town's gate tower, while the township below was shrouded in twilight. The General came to a stop and looked down on his army, a sea of upturned faces. Seeing him, his men shouted his name, striking their sheathed swords on their shields: *Tulkhan*, clap, clap... *Tulkhan*, clap, clap.

Imoshen gasped, assaulted by the army's wave of devotion for their General. She could taste the men's hunger to shed blood in Tulkhan's name. Reining in her T'En senses before the Ghebites' emotion overwhelmed her, she turned her focus on the township which spilled down to the harbour. This had been a wealthy, complacent port. The four-storey mansions of the merchant aristocracy were built of the same white stone as the Citadel, and the great families had striven to outdo each other, making each building more ornate than the last.

Come spring, it would be two years since the invading Ghebites had ransacked and looted in a frenzy of greed. The inhabitants had fled, only to return and rebuild when the General took Imoshen as his bond-partner. Now they crowded every available balcony and window. Some even perched on the rooftops to witness this historic occasion.

Not for the first time Imoshen wondered if the people really cared who ruled Fair Isle, as long as they could live their lives in peace. She had thought a sense of tradition prompted them to call her Empress, but now she wondered if they thought her most likely to provide stability.

Tulkhan signalled for silence and raised his voice. 'Tomorrow we sail across the T'Ronnyn Straits to crush my half-brother once and for all!' The General took his infant son from Imoshen's arms, holding the boy so that all could see him. A wail broke from the startled babe. 'In crushing Gharavan I ensure Fair Isle for my heir, for all our sons!'

A cheer and scattered chanting followed. Tulkhan's men picked up the rhythm, making Imoshen shiver.

Retrieving Ashmyr, she soothed the fretful baby. 'You seem as eager as your men to shed your half-brother's blood!'

'I must destroy Gharavan. He will not rest until he has avenged the insult.'

'What insult? After you had given years of service to Gheeaba he turned on you. He was the one who arrested you on trumped-up charges of treason, forcing you to claim Fair Isle for yourself!'

'You still don't understand Ghebite honour and our warrior code. When I banished my half-brother from Fair Isle and sent him packing with his tail between his legs, I insulted him. To erase the dishonour he must retake this kingdom and kill me.'

She swallowed, her mouth suddenly dry. 'You should have killed him when I urged you to.'

'If I killed so readily you would not be alive today. I would have had your kinsman smothered before he could recover his sorcerous powers!'

Imoshen's heart faltered. 'Reothe is no danger.'

'For now... No, our greatest threat is my half-brother.' Tulkhan smiled wolfishly, as he gestured to the west where the mainland lay. 'Gharavan has made a fatal mistake. I've learnt he is accompanied only by his courtiers and one company of Ghebite soldiers. The mercenaries he hired outnumber his men ten to one, and paid killers can be bought by the highest bidder.'

'Is that what you intend to do, buy their loyalty?'

'I may not need to. In all the years that I led the Ghebite army I lost a few battles but never a war.' Tulkhan spoke simply, stating a fact. 'There is no profit for the mercenary who fights on the losing side. They will switch allegiance and leave Gharavan defenceless.' He grinned then sobered. 'I don't look forward to shedding my half-brother's blood. But tonight we celebrate because, as my old tutor used to say, a battle is fought in the field but a war is won in the hearts and minds of men!'

Something stirred deep within Imoshen. She had to admire Tulkhan's military ability, even if it had been the downfall of Fair Isle.

The General held her gaze, his black eyes impenetrable. 'I have no illusions, Imoshen. I leave this island seething with revolt. My spies tell me the remains of Reothe's rebels are hiding in the hills outside Northpoint. I must ensure my hold on Fair Isle while I am away.' He faced his commanders and elite guard, drawing his sword and planting it between his feet. 'Wharrd?'

The grizzled veteran approached, going down on one knee.

'Until I return victorious, I name you leader of the capital's garrison, answerable only to me.'

Wharrd accepted this position, renewing his fealty by kissing the naked blade, as was the Ghebite custom.

'Jarholfe?'

Imoshen recognised the man as one of Tulkhan's elite guard, fond of fine clothes but deadly with a sword.

'Jarholfe, I name you leader of my elite guard, which will remain on Fair Isle, sworn to protect me and mine.'

Jarholfe accepted the honour and stepped back.

Tulkhan's arm slid around Imoshen's shoulders, drawing her close in what appeared to be a fond embrace. His lips brushed her ear as he whispered. 'Kneel and swear fealty before my men.'

Anger constricted her throat. 'Do you doubt me?'

'Should I?' His eyes narrowed. 'Imoshen, I ask my men to risk death. What guarantee do they have that you will not reclaim the throne while my back is turned? Swear fealty before them and you will be my Voice while I am gone.'

Though she understood the necessity of this oath, it did not make it any easier. She beckoned Kalleen, passing her son into the little woman's arms. 'He's tired. Take him to my chamber.'

Silence fell as Imoshen knelt before Tulkhan and looked up at him. The General was dressed in full Ghebite armour. His helmet hooded his eyes and his cloak billowed in the stiff sea breeze. Now that the last of the sun's rays had left the tower only flickering torch flames illuminated the narrow blade of his nose, the line of his jaw. His wide cheek bones were hidden by the helmet's cheek guards. Imoshen marvelled that she had once thought Tulkhan's Ghebite features harsh.

'T'Imoshen, Lady Protector.' He combined her old title with her new. 'I name you my Voice. Until I return, your words will be obeyed as mine.'

The joy of vindication filled her for this publicly acknowledged not only Tulkhan's trust in her loyalty, but his belief in her statesmanship.

'Protector General.' Imoshen pitched her voice to carry. 'On behalf of the people of Fair Isle I thank you for defending our shores.' She did not kiss the blade but came to her feet offering her left hand to Tulkhan, palm out, forearm towards him. He copied the gesture, threading his fingers through hers. Their wrists met, arms joined to the elbow, mimicking the T'En bonding ceremony. 'I vow to keep your trust and pray that, one day soon, our people will sit by their hearths in peace and plenty.'

Her words were greeted with a cheer from the Ghebites and polite finger clicking from the townspeople.

Tulkhan smiled ruefully. Imoshen had worded the oath so that his men would hear her vow of fealty but the people of Fair Isle heard their Empress thank her war general. Though she denied the title, Imoshen was made for the role. No wonder he was drawn to her. 'Then let us break open the Vorsch and drink to victory!'

'Yes, but first the people of Fair Isle wish to give your army due honour.' She cast him a cat-with-the-cream smile and beckoned a little townswoman. As the birdlike woman scurried forward with a bundle over her arm, Imoshen said, 'To you goes the honour of releasing the first star-bird, General. The Pyrolate Guild have been busy.'

The woman's gloved hands produced a cylinder which she offered to Tulkhan. Then she blew on the embers in her coal pouch to bring them to flame. Tulkhan recognised this procedure from their coronation celebration on Midwinter's Day, when fountains of light had poured from the palace towers. He lit the star-bird's tail and it leapt, rising high, to burst, a bright flower of light against the night sky. Sparks of gold rained down upon the Citadel.

On this signal a series of star-birds left the highest tower, lighting up the night sky over and over. His men gave their piercing war cry, and the townspeople murmured in awe.

With a smile of delight Imoshen linked her arm through his and gestured to the mainland. 'I've heard that on a clear day the people of Port Sumair can see the white stone of the Citadel's towers. Tonight your half-brother will see the lights in the sky above Fair Isle and it will be remembered as an omen of his fall. Let him quake in his bed, for his days are numbered!'

Imoshen inspired him. With her at his side Tulkhan felt anything was possible. Pulling her close he claimed her lips, savouring her sudden intake of breath. He sensed the moment her quicksilver passion ignited and gloried in the knowledge that the last T'En Princess was his, while above them the sky lit up, over and over again.

Tulkhan pulled back to gaze down on Imoshen's upturned face. Patterns of sparkling light played across her features. He was not blind to her T'En beauty but it was her mind and spirit he valued. 'Truly, I am a lucky man. If you had been Empress I would never have conquered Fair Isle.'

Imoshen stiffened. 'Please excuse me, General. I sent Kalleen to put our son to bed. I must see if he has settled.'

She would have left him but Tulkhan caught her hand. 'Imoshen, I did not mean –'

'In winning Fair Isle you lost your half-brother and your homeland, while I...' She could not finish, managing only a sad smile. 'Neither of us has won, Tulkhan. But we may yet.'

IMOSHEN PAUSED AT the tower door to let her eyes adjust to the dimness. Then she sped down the steps and entered a passage to the great hall, taking a short cut. This part of the Citadel dated from the early Age of Consolidation but later owners had added gleaming mosaics, mirrors and gilt. Four hundred years of prosperity had done much to hide the gracious lines of the original building.

No servants or guards were present in the public hall. She suspected they had climbed to the parapets and balconies to watch the display. Tables were laid with food and crystal glittered in the candlelight, awaiting the revellers.

Without warning, Imoshen's vision shifted. She saw was laughing people, True-men and half-bloods and amongst them, she saw herself as a child sitting at the high table looking lonely and lost.

Only she had never been here as a child.

The T'En girl, probably some distant ancestor, stiffened and looked straight across the room of phantom feasters into Imoshen's eyes. With a shudder Imoshen slammed a mental door on the vision.

Nausea threatened as she fought for control of her gifts.

She needed Reothe's advice but all along he had held his T'En knowledge to ransom. Anger curled through her, turning her hands into fists. When she had heard that Reothe had woken weak but clear-headed four days ago, she had refused to see him, using the valid excuse that she was needed in the hospice.

Moving on soft indoor slippers, she entered the passage to the central courtyard where T'Ronnyn's Tower stood. On the second top floor, Reothe lay imprisoned, still too weak to rise. She would have to confront him soon, but not tonight. She was tired and wanted to check on Ashmyr.

As she crossed the courtyard, light flashed above, illuminating every stone. Little gold sparks fell like rain. Delighted by the beauty, Imoshen held out her hand to catch a spark.

It faded before her eyes and in the sudden darkness a man grabbed her, his blade pressing between her ribs.

'Keep walking,' her captor growled.

'Drake!' It was a relief to identify him even though she knew Drake served Reothe. She obeyed his order, her legs stiff with fear. 'What do you want?'

'I have come to free T'Reothe.'

'He cannot be moved.'

'I'll be the judge of that. Take me to him.'

Recalling Drake's reverence for everything T'En, Imoshen did not believe he would kill her. 'There is no need to threaten me. I will take you to T'Reothe. He is my honoured guest.'

'Don't play word games with me. And do not dream of giving me away. I'll slide this knife between your ribs quicker than you can say my name.' Hatred laced his words. 'I know you for what you are, a traitor to your T'En blood.'

Her mouth went dry and a familiar taste settled on her tongue. She fought the urge to use her gifts. Drake was but one man, she had to win the support of all rebels if she was to hold Fair Isle.

'I've been searching for a way to get into the Citadel since you captured Reothe. Unlike you, I would willingly die for him, so do not think to call the guards,' he said. 'Now move.'

Imoshen walked towards the tower. It rose before them solid and windowless on the ground floor. She climbed the external steps to the first floor. There were no balustrades, so that defenders could pick off exposed attackers before they could get to the internal stairs. This caution did not help her now, not with a knife at her back.

'If you serve Reothe then you serve me, because he is in my service now,' she bluffed.

Drake gave no answer.

As they climbed the steps Imoshen considered calling for help from the guards stationed outside Reothe's chamber, but she didn't want Drake to have to prove his loyalty to Reothe by killing her.

At last they stood outside Reothe's chamber. Every nerve in Imoshen's body screamed in protest. The guards sat opposite the doorway, speaking with two of their brothers-at-arms, who were urging them to take a look at the Pyrolate display. The men hardly spared Imoshen and Drake a glance.

'Open the door,' Drake whispered.

Before Imoshen could take her doorcomb and run its teeth across the door's metal groove to announce herself, the door swung inwards, revealing a corner of the canopied bed. But confronting them was Kalleen, possibly the only person in the Citadel who could identify Drake and knew him for the rebel he was.

Imoshen froze, cursing the trick of fate that had brought Kalleen to Reothe's room. Though Drake was now a much hardened man, there was little doubt Kalleen would recognise him as the youth who had briefly been her lover.

'My Lady?' Kalleen's smile faltered as she looked past Imoshen to the man behind her. 'D... Drake?'

He cursed.

Kalleen frowned. 'What are you doing here? I heard –'

Drake lunged. Imoshen saw the knife flash. Kalleen's cry was cut short by the impact of his strike. A useless scream of protest tore from Imoshen's throat.

Drake darted into the room. The guards exclaimed and their chairs scraped on the floor. Kalleen sagged against the doorjamb then slid to the floor, her skirt belling around her, the rich brocade firmer than her limbs.

Imoshen dropped to her knees, horrified by the blood dripping from Kalleen's chin. A knee thumped into Imoshen's back as men charged through the doorway, but she felt no pain as she focused on her friend's injury. From the knife's angle Imoshen could see that it had plunged between Kalleen's ribs, carrying with it all Drake's anger and frustration. Guilt lanced Imoshen.

'I'm dying.' Kalleen's words frothed on her lips.

'No.' Imoshen's denial was instinctive. She used the hem of her gown to wipe the blood from Kalleen's face. She had once saved Tulkhan when Reothe dealt him a mortal wound, drawing on the General's own willpower. 'Think of the child you carry. That life depends on you!'

Beyond Kalleen, Imoshen was aware of struggling men, smashing crockery, grunts of pain and hoarse shouts. She ignored the turmoil.

Bending over Kalleen she willed her to believe. 'You are stronger than you think. Trust me.'

Kalleen's eyes fixed on Imoshen's face. She nodded, but when she coughed her fingers tightened, the nails biting into Imoshen's flesh.

A man's death scream made Imoshen flinch.

Shutting everything out, she sought the familiar source of her healing gift. Somehow she must stem Kalleen's blood loss, repair the torn tissue and ward off festering. Anger swamped her senses as she absorbed the violent energy of the struggling combatants across the chamber. Imoshen felt that primal force pool within her. It rose, flooding through the pores of her skin, almost beyond her control. The origin of this power was a death struggle, but she would turn its purpose, using it to save Kalleen's life.

Desperation lent Imoshen the strength to focus the power and channel it into healing. Kalleen's hazel eyes widened.

'We have him, my lady,' one of the guards bellowed.

Imoshen ignored him.

'He killed –'

'Silence!' Imoshen concentrated on willing the knife to slide from its resting place between Kalleen's ribs. The effort required to knit the tissues behind the withdrawing blade caused beads of perspiration to gather on her forehead, stinging her eyes.

Dimly, she heard the guard call on his warrior god to protect them from sorcery. Imoshen clenched her teeth.

Kalleen's eyes never left her face. Her fingers never eased their claw-like grip. Imoshen took the knife as it emerged and then slit the bodice of Kalleen's gown, dragging it apart to reveal her small golden breasts and the bloodied flesh where the blade had penetrated.

Imoshen leant forward, only just resisting the instinct to lick the wound clean. Instead, she tossed the knife aside and slid her fingers over the flesh.

'Bring water.' She hardly recognised her own voice.

The guard stumbled away and returned with a pitcher.

'Pour a little over the wound.' Imoshen used the hem of her gown to wipe the blood away, revealing a fresh scar.

'Great Akha Khan...' The man's curse was cut short as the pitcher smashed at his feet. Water sprayed them. A pottery fragment stung Imoshen's cheek.

Kalleen's gasp had barely left her lips when Imoshen swept one arm under the little woman's knees and the other under her shoulders. Anger empowered her as she stood.

'Fool!' With Kalleen in her arms she turned to face the man. 'Take the Lady Kalleen to her bedchamber and send for Wharrd.'

The man's features flushed with something that could have been anger or shame. As he extended his arms to accept the burden, Kalleen's mouth opened in a protest.

'Sleep and heal,' Imoshen whispered, touching the sixth finger of her left hand to Kalleen's forehead. Her friend's eyes closed and the tight contours of pain upon her face eased. 'Go now.'

The same fury which had enabled Imoshen to rise with Kalleen in her arms now drove her into the room. Two guards held Drake on his knees, his wrists twisted up behind his shoulders. He glared at her.

Another guard lay in a puddle of dark blood, unmoving. There was nothing Imoshen could do for him.

Disgust filled her 'Death dealt in the name of honour. Is this what you want for Fair Isle, Drake?'

Winding her fingers through his hair, she hauled him across to the bed, freeing him from the guards. 'Here is your rebel leader.' She snatched a sword from the nearest man and flung the weapon so that it lay across Reothe's chest. 'Rise and strike down your captors, T'Reothe!'

On reflex one of Reothe's hands closed on the hilt, but he did not have the strength to lift the blade, let alone rise.

'You are cruel, Imoshen.' Reothe thrust the weapon off the bed in disgust. It clattered on the floor at their feet.

'Are you satisfied, Drake?' Imoshen demanded.

The rebel youth spat. 'Order your dogs to kill me, T'En traitor.'

Dismayed that he still courted death, Imoshen faltered. Drake wrenched free. Snatching the sword, he twisted up under her guard. With dreamlike slowness she watched the sword point arc towards her throat. One clean slice and she was dead.

Pressure snapped inside her head. She saw nothing, heard nothing but the rush of blood in her ears. Something struck between her shoulder blades, driving the air from her chest. The back of her head hit the upright at the end of the bed, jarring her teeth and filling her sight with pinpricks of light.

Chest burning, she fought to drag in a breath. Like a cat, she had sprung backward the length of the bed to escape Drake's strike. He knelt before her, sword hanging from his limp fingers. She watched as a great gout of blood erupted from his mouth, spraying across her skirt.

One of the men must have stabbed him in the back. But they were too far away and still staggering backwards.

Imoshen drew a painful breath and stepped around Drake. His back was free of injury. If not a stab wound then how...

It did not matter. She had to heal him. Placing a hand on his back she sensed the damage and sought to repair it. Drake fell into a deep healing sleep and she lowered him to the floor.

Reothe hung half off the bed, supporting himself with one trembling arm. 'Help...'

'What goes on here?' Tulkhan demanded, thrusting his men aside as he strode into the room.

Imoshen could not speak.

Reothe's expression was an odd mixture of wariness and admiration as he explained, 'Imoshen turned her gift on Drake, just as she turned it on me.'

She shook her head, unwilling to admit it

'No?' Reothe mocked. 'He has no visible wound.'

Tulkhan cursed, turning shocked eyes to her.

Overwhelmed by the discovery that her healing gift was as capable of tearing flesh as closing it, Imoshen fled to the sanctuary of her room.

She threw open the door, startling the old woman who was changing the bedding. Imoshen tore at the fastening of her stained gown and flung it into the fire. Ashmyr woke with a cry. She longed for the balm of his touch. 'Bring me the baby, Dyta.'

The old woman scurried to obey.

Feeling unsteady, Imoshen backed away until her thighs met the bed. She sat abruptly, recalling the guard's expression as she put Kalleen in his arms, the way his companions had fled from her. She hadn't meant to cripple

Drake. It had been self-defence, but that would not stop the rumours. In a few heartbeats she had undone all the good she had achieved at Tulkhan's side these last few days.

She opened her eyes to find Dyta watching her warily.

'Bring me a damp cloth. Help me sponge the blood from my hands.'

But blood remained under her fingernails. A rush of despair flooded Imoshen. In her mind she saw Reothe's covetous expression, and the fearful intensity in Tulkhan's face.

She was not a killer. Tears of determination stung Imoshen's eyes as she silently vowed to use her powers only to heal. Her gift was a tool, one she must learn to control.

TULKHAN STEPPED ASIDE as, with due solemnity, the guards removed the body of their dead brother-at-arms. Then he faced the man he had been avoiding.

'Why don't you kill me?' Reothe asked.

'You insult me, Dhamfeer.' He made the Ghebite word an insult. 'Do you think me some crude barbarian who would kill his sworn enemy as he lay helpless?'

Reothe lifted his head to glare, then winced. His hands spasmed with pain, one clenching in a fist, the other twitching feebly. So it was true, one half of his body was crippled as well as his T'En gifts. And Imoshen had done this to the man whose power she had feared.

'First she cripples me, now she despises me, yet she keeps me alive,' Reothe whispered. 'Cruel love.'

'You assume much,' Tulkhan said, but Reothe's suffering struck a reluctant chord with him, a disconcerting echo of his own mixed emotions.

'May the Parakletos feast on that Vaygharian's soul,' Reothe cursed, his thoughts following another path. 'I should never have trusted him to be Gharavan's go-between!'

Tulkhan shuddered. Reothe's curse was intrinsically T'En. The Parakletos were legendary T'En warriors, bound by a terrible oath to serve beyond death. They answered the priests' summons to escort the souls of the departed through death's shadow to the realm of the dead.

Yet, like everything else on Fair Isle, the truth was not so simple. Back in the capital, Tulkhan had stood at Imoshen's side when she had said the words for the dead for the cooper's wife. He had been unaware that she risked her own soul if her hold on the Parakletos faltered. That day she had revealed that the Parakletos were not the benign creatures of legend. So, he was certain Reothe was not wishing the Vaygharian's soul a safe journey.

'For all I know the Parakletos have feasted on his soul,' Tulkhan said. 'No one has claimed responsibility for his death. His charred remains were found in the fire's ashes as Imoshen foretold.'

Reothe gave Tulkhan a sharp look, reminding him that the rebel leader might be physically crippled and his powers destroyed, but that he still had his wits. It was clear Reothe suspected something but Tulkhan would not give him the satisfaction of asking.

Jaw clenched, he strode from the room.

TULKHAN THRUST THE door open to find Imoshen standing over their sleeping son. Blue shadows haunted her pale skin and her eyes held a lambent glow, as though she were consumed by an inner furnace. He hated seeing her so fragile. 'I will order Drake executed at dawn and his head spiked on the gate tower.'

'That is sure to convince the rebels to support you.'

'You can't be suggesting I let him live?'

But she gave no answer, rubbing her temples.

Remorse pierced him. He knew how healing exhausted her. 'You saved Kalleen's life.'

'And terrified your men, I fear.'

'You could have helped Drake escape with Reothe. You could have betrayed me.'

Startled, she met his eyes and he knew this had not occurred to her.

'Ahh, Imoshen.' He opened his arms and she went to him. Fine trembles ran through her body, reminding him of a highly strung horse.

Her lips moved against his neck as she spoke, her breath hot on his skin. 'Drake went for my throat. My reaction was instinctive.'

'What else is instinctive for the T'En?'

She pulled away from him, distressed. 'Truly, Tulkhan, I don't know. My family forbade my instruction in the gifts. They tried to deny their throwback daughter, when all the world could see . . .' She lifted her six-fingered hands to her face.

Tulkhan had once found her luminescent colouring, high cheekbones and narrow features strange. Now he thought Imoshen as exquisite as the Fair Isle porcelain which was prized on the mainland while its manufacture was a closely guarded secret. This island contained too many secrets. He expelled his breath in frustration.

'I have not come to berate you, Imoshen. I'm running out of time. Even now my carpenters work by lantern-light to build catapults. Soon it will be the Harvest Feast and –'

'It will be just over a year since you captured my stronghold,' she whispered. 'Since we...' She flushed and he was reminded of their first joining in the Harvest Bower when he had claimed her for his own.

His mouth went dry with longing. 'This is our last night together before I go into battle.' But when he tried to pull her close she resisted. 'What is it?'

'You could die confronting Gharavan.' She searched his face. 'There is something not right between us. Each time you've come to me you've been almost...' she quivered. 'You've been fierce. I feel no gentleness in your touch. I don't understand. Not once have you mentioned Reothe.'

He released her, driven to pace the chamber as if it was a cage.

Imoshen was torn between the need to know Tulkhan's thoughts and fear of what she might learn. 'I don't understand, General. You have not asked me how it happened.'

He spun to face her. 'You have already admitted it is true. By taking him to your bed you dishonoured us both. At least now if you carry a child there is a good chance it will be mine!'

She gasped, her hand going protectively to her belly.

His eyes narrowed. 'I let myself believe... But it is different for the women of Fair Isle. You are trained in the arts of lovemaking. You told me the moment you knew my son was conceived.' His shoulders sagged and he looked drained. 'When Reothe boasted that you carried his child it was already true. Wasn't it?'

She could not deny it.

'By Ghebite law I should strangle you and my half-blood son!'

Tulkhan's explosive anger frightened Imoshen into revealing the truth. 'Reothe tricked me. I did not knowingly betray you. He came to me in your form. I thought it was you I welcomed to my bed.' Her voice dropped. 'I did not tell you before because I feared your anger would drive you to kill him.'

'I knew it. I knew it had to be trickery.' Tulkhan sank into the chair by the fireplace. 'But it makes no difference. By Ghebite law you are in the wrong –'

'But I thought he was you.'

'That is of no consequence.'

'What kind of justice makes the injured person guilty?'

He smiled wryly. 'Trust you to see it that way.'

Fury kindled in Imoshen but she forced it down, placing her left hand over her heart. 'I swear I have never knowingly betrayed you, Tulkhan. Do not be hampered by the boundaries of your upbringing.'

'Boundaries don't blind my thinking, Imoshen. But my men are simple soldiers. To lead I must have their respect. They'll believe that you dishonour me. Do you think if I truly doubted you, I would have made Wharrd and Jarholfe answerable to you while I am gone?'

She went to him, her bare feet registering the warmth of the carpet before the hearth. Sinking to her knees in front of his chair, she took his hand in hers. He was leaving to go into battle tomorrow and she longed to join with him. 'If you trust me, why do you come to my bed with anger in your heart?'

He made a helpless gesture. In that instant his barriers were down and she sensed his most private and primitive emotions. She had been stolen from him. Every time they made love he was reclaiming what was his.

'Ah, Tulkhan.' She smiled. 'You say you are free of your Ghebite upbringing but I fear it runs deeper than you think.'

He opened his mouth to argue, then withdrew his hand, eyeing her thoughtfully.

'What?' Imoshen prompted.

'How can you speak to me of being shaped by my upbringing when you are shaped by your blood? You gave your solemn promise not to use your gifts on me. Yet, what did you just do?'

'That was not, I mean...' She felt herself colour and saw his knowing look. 'It was not intentional. We were touching and it just happened.'

'How convenient.'

She saw anger in his face, but also a glint of humour, and realised he was teasing her. Her heart turned over. Slowly she stood up, offering her hand. 'No man can take what I do not give, Tulkhan.'

His fingers entwined with hers. But he resisted when she would have led him to the bed. He cleared his throat. 'I will welcome you into my arms but not into my mind. That is how it must be, Imoshen.'

'Then I must be satisfied with that.' But deep within her heart his rejection stung.

Chapter Three

IMOSHEN WOKE TO the golden light of late afternoon. She stretched, surprised to discover she had slept through most of the day. But then she had only fallen asleep at dawn when Tulkhan left her bed with a lingering kiss and a loving word.

Ashmyr stirred and she gazed at him dreamily. He might as well have been pure T'En, only his sable hair marked him as Tulkhan's son. She smiled fondly as his mouth worked, sucking in his sleep.

A figure detached itself from the shadows near the door. Imoshen tensed, then she recognised Wharrd. The bone-setter stepped into the light, his expression curiously guarded.

'Where's Tulkhan?' Her voice was rusty from lack of use.

'On the wharves. He sent me to bring you.'

Her heart sank. Tulkhan must go, but she dreaded their parting. She felt empty, cast adrift. Resolutely, she swung her feet to the floor. 'I will get dressed.'

'First hear me out. You saved Kalleen's life. Kalleen is my wife but I love her as I would love my sword-brother. If he was killed, I would avenge his death. If someone saved his life, I would be under a Ghiad until I had repaid them with an equal service.' Wharrd gave a variation of the Ghebite salute. 'By the Gheeakhan, warrior code of the Ghebites, I am under a Ghiad to you.'

Imoshen hid her annoyance. Wharrd claimed he valued Kalleen as highly as he would value his sword-brother, yet he meant no insult. 'Then I release you from your Ghiad.'

'You can't release me. My honour must be satisfied.'

She shrugged, not about to argue further.

'The rebel Drake still lives,' Wharrd announced. 'When do you want to execute him?'

'I don't want him executed. Not everything can be resolved by killing. Fair Isle needs unity. I must win the rebels to our cause.'

'But Drake invaded the citadel, threatened your life, spilt Kalleen's blood and killed a Ghebite. You must –'

'I will not kill him. Would you have this go on forever? A life for a life until no one lives?' She paused, struck by that thought. 'Is this the way in Gheeaba? A life for a life?'

He nodded. 'A man must seek revenge or be thought weak.'

'Sometimes it takes more strength to forgive.'

Wharrd did not look convinced. 'What will you do with him?'

She didn't know. 'If he is hurt, see that he is tended. I must go to the General.'

TULKHAN PACED THE docks, impatient to confront his half-brother. Much had been achieved since he turned the tables on Reothe. The mercenaries who would have been exchanged for Tulkhan had been escorted to the army's encampment outside the township. Their leader had been quick to see reason. Dying for profit was one thing, but dying without profit was unthinkable.

Every fishing boat and seaworthy skiff within a day's ride had been commandeered. The carpenters had completed the merchant ships' modifications. Catapults would be mounted on the ships' decks when they reached port.

Tulkhan felt the little hairs on his neck rise and knew that Imoshen approached. She had sworn not to use her gifts on him, and he believed she did not consciously do so, but surely this intensity was not normal? If he was under some kind of T'En compulsion he hoped it would fade with time and distance. Then he would know how things really stood between them.

As IMOSHEN APPROACHED Tulkhan, she wrapped her cloak around their sleeping son. She knew the General was aware of her.

The Ghebites embarked, torches blazed and firelight danced on the sea's black surface. The men filed past, singing rousing war songs.

Imoshen studied the sky. The season was about to turn and autumn would be all too brief. Soon winter snows would blanket the ground and make fighting impossible. The General did not have long if he wanted to destroy King Gharavan and incite the repressed countries of the mainland to revolt against Ghebite domination.

Since he had become war general at nineteen, Tulkhan had consolidated and increased the conquests of his father and grandfather, subjugating most of the known world. Imoshen smiled grimly. It would be ironic if Tulkhan was the one to drive the Ghebites back to the far north.

The call of the battle horns startled her. The tide was turning, the wind was right. She looked to Tulkhan.

As he strode towards her she was reminded of their first meeting, when he had appeared in full battle regalia, alien and unknown. His unusual height was emphasised by his helmet's plume. His black temple plaits swung as he walked, his long hair lifting around his shoulders.

Once she had thought his appearance barbaric and ostentatious. Now she was bound to him in ways that went deeper than words. 'Strike swiftly, return safely.'

His hands closed on her shoulders. As he searched her face she wondered what he looked for.

'If I am killed you will have it all: Fair Isle, your crippled consort and what's left of my army.'

'How can you say that?' It was a cry from her heart. 'Besides, the remaining Ghebites are loyal to you, not me.'

'Ultimately self-interest must motivate my men. None of us can return to Gheeaba. What will you do? Go to the palace at T'Diemn?'

'Yes. When Reothe is better we will go slowly, stopping along the way so the people can see that Reothe is under my protection. Only strength will unite Fair Isle. We –'

'Imoshen, since Gharavan declared me a traitor, my life is forfeit on the mainland. Any man may take my head for the bounty.'

She was horrified. 'I did not know.'

He smiled. 'I did not want you to know.'

'Oh, Tulkhan!' It was on the tip of her tongue to beg him to stay.

'I have returned from many battles and I have every intention of surviving this one. You hold my life in your hands, Imoshen. Fair Isle is the only home I have. Do not betray my trust.' He gave her no time to reply. 'Reothe's gifts might be crippled but he still has his wits. Beware his honeyed tongue.'

She nodded, unable to speak.

Tulkhan raised an arm to acknowledge the townsfolk. 'Smile for your people, Imoshen.'

Lifting her chin she waved, but she could see little through the veil of her tears. Tulkhan saluted his men, his teeth white against his coppery skin. Flinging one arm around his neck, she lifted onto her toes to kiss him, felt his surprise and then the heat of his response. A soul-deep stab of need pierced her. 'Think of me.'

He pressed her hand to his heart and, with great reluctance, stepped away.

Alone on the wharf, she watched the General stride towards his ship. The gangplank bounced under his weight. The sailors shouted and withdrew the board. Ropes writhed across the growing chasm of roiling black water. Torches diminished but all she saw was Tulkhan's mask-like face, eyes fixed on her as if he were memorising her features.

As his form grew ever smaller Imoshen felt as if a long cord connected them, straining to stretch the distance, sucking her soul from her with painful intensity. A part of her was leaving and she did not know if she would ever be whole again.

As TULKHAN PACED the command ship's deck in the predawn chill, mist lay thick on the water.

'There it is, General, the beacon fire. I knew they'd have the tower lit in weather like this.' Kornel pointed, then adjusted the belt of his trousers to sit comfortably below his belly. As a merchant ship's captain, he ate well and took few risks.

Tulkhan nodded. His makeshift flotilla of fishing boats and commandeered merchant ships had to negotiate the harbour entrance safely under cover of the mist, yet their signal bells might betray their presence. He cursed softly. He had campaigned on land for eleven years and knew little about coordinating an attack from the sea, but if all went well he would not have to. 'Send for the mercenary leader, Tourez.'

Tulkhan had dealt with Vaygharian mercenaries before and he was willing to forego a surprise attack on the port to send Tourez ahead with an offer. Since the lives of Tourez's mercenary band back in Fair Isle were being held as surety of his cooperation, Tulkhan felt sure Tourez would argue his case well. The General fully expected the mercenaries to switch allegiance and support him. After all, he was the more experienced leader, with eleven years of victories behind him.

They waited in tense silence as the ships negotiated the sand bars and floating islands. Their bells dulled to cloak their arrival, they entered Port Sumair's harbour unable to see the famous sculpture of the merchant scales through the mist.

As the mercenary approached, Tulkhan slipped the message cylinder from his pouch. 'Now that we are inside the harbour you'll be rowed to the wharves. We will sit off the docks under cover of this fog until the rising sun starts to burn it away. Then we will strike. If the mercenaries deliver Gharavan, I will reward them. If not, I'll treat them as loyal Ghebite soldiers and slaughter them to a man.'

Tourez nodded. A boat was lowered for him and the soft sound of its oars could be heard as it moved away from the ship. Then that sound faded and Tulkhan could only wait.

THE GENERAL HAD been sure the Vaygharian mercenaries would change allegiance. But it was dawn and Tourez had not returned.

Tulkhan stepped forward to order the attack. Before he could open his mouth, an arrow, buzzed like an angry bee, sailing past his ear to thud into the mast. He stared in disbelief at the mercenary who was already notching another arrow, one leg over the ship's rail. The man's brothers-at-arms clambered aboard with knives between their teeth.

Tulkhan cursed, throwing his dagger. The archer let his second arrow loose prematurely and fell back clutching his side. His cry and the following splash heralded the attack. Stealth discarded, the mercenaries boarded. Cries of battle came from the other boats. With a jolt Tulkhan realised Tourez had not only betrayed him, but also his own men back in Northpoint.

A man charged. Tulkhan blocked the strike, countering automatically. All about him he heard the clash of metal on metal, grunts of pain, agonised screams. His boots slipped on the blood-slick planks. Furious, he fought his way to the catapult, but the mercenaries had already disabled it.

Dislodging his weapon from a man's spine, Tulkhan looked up and saw the silhouettes of bowmen on Port Sumair's rooftops, ready to strike as soon as the mist cleared. That was all he needed – flaming tar-dipped arrows.

Tulkhan hauled the ship's captain aside. For a merchant who lived the good life, Kornel wielded a sword efficiently. 'Up anchor, Captain.'

Tulkhan sounded the horn, signalling retreat. The sails bellied down and the growing dawn breeze filled the canvas. Imperceptibly at first, the ship gathered momentum. To Tulkhan's relief the other great merchant ships also spread their sails.

Shouts, then screams, rent the air as two merchant ships rode dangerously close. Tulkhan could do nothing but watch helplessly as his ships crushed a small skiff between them.

Anger drove him back across the deck into the mercenaries but they realised they were about to be carried from the harbour. On an unseen signal they sheathed their weapons and leapt overboard. It was what Tulkhan expected. Only a zealot fought to the death.

The ships turned ponderously and there were still the sandbars to negotiate. Burning arrows now hit the decks and sails. Men downed weapons to drown the flames and throw bodies overboard. Tulkhan saw a fishing boat burning unhindered to the water line.

When cheering broke from the observers on the docks, fury consumed Tulkhan. Dousing his head in a pitcher of water, he shook the droplets from his skin, shoved the damp hair from his face and turned to assess their situation.

A sailor threw a bucket of sea water across the deck, sending the entrails of the fallen sliding like foam on a wave's crest. Tulkhan strode across to Kornel at the helm. 'We'll go over the sea-wall and come at them across land.'

'Can't be done. These ships can't get in close enough.'

'We'll lower the boats and row in.'

'Can't be done in these numbers. We'd churn up the mud, be stuck like beached whales.'

'Then where is the nearest harbour?'

'The Lowland harbours are defended. But there is another way to get at Port Sumair. A way they wouldn't expect.' The captain glanced at Tulkhan, his features defined by cunning.

The General felt a surge of interest. 'Go on.'

'It is difficult, but not impossible. I did it before I commanded ships this size. You'd have to use the small vessels.'

'That's good. The merchant ships could blockade the port, misleading them about our intentions,' Tulkhan muttered, thinking aloud. His spirits lifted. He had learnt to surround himself with men who had local knowledge, and he knew how to heed advice. 'Tell me more.'

As the ship left the harbour Tulkhan saw the sun break over the distant cliffs of Fair Isle. He was not going back to Imoshen until victory was his.

Chapter Four

IMOSHEN EXPECTED NEWS of Tulkhan with the following dawn's tide, but the new day brought no news, and when the late tide arrived with no message, Imoshen felt the mood of Northpoint change. From the candle trimmer to the harbourmaster, cautious optimism had been replaced with growing concern. She hugged Ashmyr closer.

As Imoshen approached T'Ronnyn's Tower a servant's gesture reminded her of Selita, the rebel who had been her maid while Reothe had her imprisoned. On impulse, Imoshen called, 'Selita?'

The girl responded instinctively to her name.

Imoshen beckoned. Selita cast one desperate glance around the bustling courtyard, then followed her up the tower's steps.

'What are you doing here?' Imoshen whispered. After Drake's attempt to free Reothe, Tulkhan's men were eager to avenge their comrade's death.

Selita stiffened. 'I am ready to die for Reothe!'

'Dying is easy. It is living that's hard.' Imoshen chewed her bottom lip. She had discussed nothing of importance with Reothe, at first because he was so ill, and later because she was careful never to be alone with him. The last she had heard, the nobles of the Keldon Highlands were ready to rise up in rebellion. She came to a snap decision. 'As it happens, Reothe does have a task for you. He wants you to carry a message to his supporters.'

The girl looked sceptical.

'I haven't called my guards to arrest you, have I?'

'I would hear this from Reothe's own lips.'

'Very well. We shall go to him.' Imoshen strode up the circular stairs with Selita at her side.

Acknowledging the guards, Imoshen drew the girl into Reothe's room and closed the heavy door. 'I bring you a visitor, kinsman.'

As Reothe struggled to lift his head Selita ran to the bedside and fell to her knees with a sob. 'My T'En Lord, your beautiful eyes!'

'Selita, you'll get yourself killed,' Reothe rebuked.

'I have explained that we decided to call off the Keldon uprising because Fair Isle cannot afford civil war while Tulkhan is on the mainland,' Imoshen bluffed. 'Selita wants to hear the orders from your own lips before she carries your message to Woodvine of the Keld.'

Holding Reothe's gaze, Imoshen dared him to rise above personal ambition and consider Fair Isle's fate. All along he had claimed to be working for the good of the people. His response would reveal the truth.

'Since you don't have the strength, I will write your message,' Imoshen told him.

A rueful smile tugged at Reothe's lips. 'I heard how Woodvine refused to call you Empress because you had not earned that title. She does not know you as I do.' He sighed. 'You are right, Imoshen, we cannot have civil war.'

Relieved, she went to the desk and selected paper, tapping the excess ink from the scriber's sharpened nib.

After a moment Reothe began to dictate a letter to Lady Woodvine, the iron-haired matriarch of the Keldon nobles. Imoshen wrote swiftly. Finally she sanded the paper, blowing off the excess.

'What if Lady Woodvine does not believe they are truly your words?' Selita asked, still kneeling by Reothe's bed.

'Tell her to go to Lord Athlyn of the Keld. He will remember how two of his grandsons had an argument in the stronghold library. Tell Woodvine to tell my grandfather that Reothe begs his pardon. It was him and not his cousin Murgon who spilt ink, ruining the mainland map.' He flashed Imoshen a charming smile. 'I let my temper get the better of me. Even then Murgon and I were rivals.'

Imoshen turned away to hide the pull he exerted on her. When Reothe's parents died he had been adopted by the Empress and raised with her children. His cousin Murgon had also been in training to become a royal advisor, and their rivalry over the Empress's heir, Ysanna, had intensified until Murgon was sent to the Basilica. It was strange, the paths their lives had taken, for Murgon was now a high ranking church official, leader of the Tractarians who were trained to hunt down rogue T'En.

'Satisfied, Selita?' Imoshen asked. She held the candle over the folded message until a pool of wax formed. Then she went to Reothe, who pressed the tip of his left hand's sixth finger into the wax.

Imoshen held it to the light. 'So it is true, only the T'En have the double spiral.'

He laughed. 'Ever the scholar. And if you were to compare ours they would differ. When there were more of us we were taught to recognise the patterns at a glance.'

A sense of loss overwhelmed Imoshen. The mysteries of the T'En were her heritage but Reothe had hidden the T'Elegos. She needed to control her gift and to do that she needed to read the history her namesake Imoshen the First had written the autumn before she died.

'From my hand, to yours, to Lady Woodvine's.' As Imoshen gave Selita the sealed missive there was a knock at the door.

'Ghebites!' Selita hid the message.

Imoshen placed a calming hand on her arm. 'Yes?'

A guard opened the door. 'Lord Commander Wharrd awaits you, Lady Protector.'

'Very well,' Imoshen said. Tired of waiting for news from Tulkhan, she had summoned Wharrd. 'Come, Selita.'

Imoshen walked the girl from the room, turning to the guard. 'Provide a safe escort for my servant. She is returning to her family for the birth of her sister's child.' Imoshen saw the man's eyes glaze over and smiled to herself. The Ghebites' lack of interest in anything that belonged to the female world made them easy to manipulate.

Imoshen held Selita's eyes. 'The fate of one individual, no matter how dear to us, does not compare to the fate of our people.'

When Selita had gone, Imoshen went upstairs to her chamber, where she found Wharrd waiting by the fireplace. She crossed the room to place Ashmyr in his basket. 'Send a ship to Port Sumair. I must know how it goes with Tulkhan. Defeat I can deal with, but this silence...'

Wharrd nodded, gave the salute he would have given his General and departed.

Thinking of the T'Elegos had reminded Imoshen of Reothe's bonding gift to her. She wedged a chair against the door, then opened her chest, taking out the T'Enchiridion, the T'En church's book of prayers. This was her great-aunt's volume, worn by her many years of service to the church. On her hundredth birthday her great-aunt had been named the Aayel in recognition of that service.

When Imoshen was a child, the Aayel had made her memorise the prayers for the dead and the newborn. But the T'Enchiridion Imoshen now held in her hands contained something more.

Imoshen's heart thudded as she eased her fingers inside the T'Enchiridion's back cover, sliding out a slender, scuffed volume.

At risk to his own life, Reothe had come to her on the day they had planned to bond, the eighteenth anniversary of her birthing day. And even though she had broken her vows to him, he had given her this. She should not have accepted it but...

Imoshen stroked the embossing on the kidskin cover. T'Endomaz, the T'En book of gift lore. Opening the book to the title page she read the childlike script: 'T'Ashmyr.' Her son, Ashmyr, was named after the greatest throwback T'En emperor of the Age of Tribulation. During those turbulent years, Fair Isle had needed a warrior emperor. She hoped she had not foretold her son's future.

If this book had once belonged to T'Ashmyr himself, it was five hundred years old and should have been redolent of great age. But when Imoshen flexed her gift she sensed no trace of time in the book. One of the T'En had wiped it clean to hide its importance. This convinced Imoshen that she held an artefact dating from the first hundred years of settlement. She closed her eyes and concentrated on what her fingers told her. The book's fine kidskin cover was worn in six places by the fingertips of many T'En hands.

Frustration coursed through her. She was heir to the knowledge the T'Endomaz contained, yet she could not read it because the contents were encrypted. The T'Elegos had to contain the key, but Reothe would not reveal where he had hidden it. Tulkhan was right, she could not trust him.

* * *

As the General's small skiff pulled away, he looked up at the merchant ship riding tall above the waves. Its sails glowed in the sunset while Tulkhan and his craft were already in twilight. It seemed symbolic of their separate tasks. Commander Piers was to return to the harbour and blockade the port with the three merchant ships.

The remaining fishing vessels and small skiffs, heavily laden with men and supplies, were to follow Kornel upriver through the marshes to a village, where they would force one of the marsh-dwellers to show them the safe path to the marsh wall. Beyond that wall lay the reclaimed Lowlands, ripe and unready for battle.

Tulkhan intended to force-march his men across the plain and attack Port Sumair's landward gate while its defenders were watching the sea. But if he couldn't get his men across the marshlands and into position to attack Sumair at the agreed time, Piers's sea attack would fail and his men would be slaughtered.

The skiff nudged a larger fishing vessel and eager arms helped Tulkhan and his crew aboard. Now his flagship was a fishing trawler with no cabin and a shallow keel which, according to Kornel, would carry them deep into the marshlands before they had to abandon it. Without Kornel's local knowledge, Tulkhan could not hope to spearhead an attack through the supposedly impenetrable marshlands. But he had not told Imoshen this. His message to Imoshen merely informed her of his intention to blockade Port Sumair, and ordered the mercenary troop's execution.

Ducking the low beam of the sail, Tulkhan strode to the bow to join Kornel. His odd fleet was already moving into the mouth of the river.

Tulkhan had been warned there would be times when they would have to carry the boats across sand banks, and he searched the water, wondering what might lurk beneath it. He lifted his eyes to the landscape beyond. Strange, the trees had not looked so tall and menacing when he'd stood on the merchant ship's deck. Then the marshlands had spread out before him like a tapestry laced with gold thread as the setting sun gilded the many small pools and waterways. Edging those sinuous river paths were the saltwater trees of the Lowlands. They hung over the river's banks, marching boldly into the water itself.

'We're making good time,' Kornel observed, as the sky darkened.

A sailor gave them their evening meal, two chunks of salted meat and wine. Gnawing on the tough flesh, Tulkhan noticed something moving on the far bank. 'What's that?'

The captain took a lantern to the side of the boat. Tulkhan joined him. It was hard to distinguish anything among the blur of the tree trunks in the water.

'Look for their eyes. They will reflect the lantern light. The narcts are the reason we couldn't risk getting stuck in the mud at the foot of the sea-wall.'

'Sea-going predators?'

'They hunt them out of the port. But here... watch this.' Kornel tossed the remains of his meat over the side. It fell halfway between the ship and the tree line. Before it hit the water, creatures slithered out from the cover of the trees, ploughing through the river, moonlight glowing in the rippling wake they created.

The narcts converged on the meat. Jaws flashed, teeth gleamed. The snap and crunch as they fought was sickening.

Tulkhan grunted. 'Greedy beasts.' He tossed his bone overboard. A protest died on Kornel's lips. A series of barks sounded up and down the river bank.

'They sound like dogs and they're just clever enough to hunt in packs. One narct couldn't bring a man down on dry land, but in the water it's another matter, and when you get a hunting pack...' Kornel spat.

Tulkhan watched as the frenzy of feeding slipped behind them, but the barking of the narcts echoed up and down the river. Any carrying of boats across sand banks would be fraught with danger.

IMOSHEN NURSED ASHMYR as she read Tulkhan's message. Four long days had elapsed since the General had set off to attack Port Sumair. Before Wharrd could find a seaworthy craft to make the crossing, a small fishing skiff had arrived with a hasty note scribbled in the General's own hand. After failing to take the port, Tulkhan had set up a blockade. This did not surprise Imoshen. She had known that he would not return until he could claim victory.

It was his order to execute the mercenaries that worried her. She met Wharrd's eyes. 'By now all of Northpoint will know I have heard from the General and guessed the worst. The mercenaries will be sharpening their weapons.'

'They were held as surety. Their lives are forfeit.'

Imoshen laughed. 'You speak as if they will simply put down their arms and march to their deaths at the hands of my people.' She did not want to sacrifice her people in a blood bath. Perhaps something could be salvaged from this. 'Send for the town officials, the merchant leaders, the guildmasters and the new leader of the mercenaries. I will see them in the public hall.'

When Imoshen walked into the Citadel's great hall it was so closely packed she could not see the mosaic floor tiles. With Kalleen at her heels carrying her son, she made her way to the dais, stepping into a growing well of silent expectation.

Imoshen raised her voice. 'Sumair did not fall to a frontal attack. The Protector General has blockaded the port. But do not despair, tell your families and friends that in the eleven years General Tulkhan has led his army, no fortified town ever withstood him. It is only a matter of time before Sumair falls and King Gharavan is captured.'

A wave of comment greeted her words. The harbourmaster approached Imoshen. 'We thought victory was certain. What went wrong?'

'The mercenary leader, Tourez, revealed General Tulkhan's attack to the defenders at Port Sumair.' Imoshen beckoned the new leader of the mercenaries. 'Step forward, Lightfoot.'

He wore the serviceable boots, breeches and jerkin of his mercenary trade, his weapons better cared for than his garments. His sun-lined features reminded Imoshen of the veterans Wharrd and Piers. Good. If he had survived this long in his profession, he would not be hot-headed. Like many of the mainlanders, he would not meet her eyes but this time the Dhamfeer tales served her purpose. Let him fear her.

'Tourez betrayed your mercenary troop.' As Imoshen spoke the crowd renewed its angry muttering. 'In doing this he forfeited your lives.'

Lightfoot's mouth thinned but he did not argue.

'General Tulkhan lays siege to Sumair while Tourez shelters within its walls. By rights I should honour the General's agreement and have you all executed.'

A muscle jumped in Lightfoot's jaw.

'But I seek a more practical solution. I assume Tourez's actions negate the validity of any contract he negotiated on your behalf?' Imoshen asked.

'What?' He was startled by her change of subject.

'This leaves you free to negotiate a new contract of hire. Am I right?' Imoshen asked, watching him closely. Within a heartbeat, she saw his leap of understanding.

He wanted an honourable, bloodless solution as much as she did, and he wanted revenge on the leader who had betrayed him.

Imoshen nodded. 'While I could order the execution of your troop, I am sure your men would sell their lives dearly, and I see no point in shedding their blood or that of my own people.' She smiled at Lightfoot's expression. He had not expected such plain speaking. 'In return for your lives, I ask that your men take up arms against King Gharavan. Will you fight at General Tulkhan's side?'

'We will.'

'Bring me ink and paper.' Imoshen signalled Wharrd, who was ready with the agreement she had already drawn up. Even so she felt lightheaded with relief. 'We will sign a new contract which you will deliver into the General's hands.'

Fortuitously, the mercenary was a lettered man. He read the document and signed his name with a flourish that spoke of penmanship learnt in childhood under an exacting tutor.

'Lightfoot is not a Vaygharian name,' she remarked.

'It is the name I have gone by for nearly twenty years.'

The man was hiding his true identity. Imoshen wondered if he would be as treacherous as Tourez. She did not want to send Tulkhan a faulty tool, or worse, a tool which would turn on him. If only there was some way to ensure that Lightfoot would honour the contract.

After dripping the wax onto the document Imoshen held up her left hand and curled all but the smallest sixth finger into her palm. 'This is my T'En seal.'

She pressed the pad of her finger into the hot wax, closing her mind against the small burn. When she removed her finger the whorls of her skin remained there, imprinted on the document. If only she could seal the mercenary's cooperation as easily.

'The contract carries my sign. Lightfoot, I look into your eyes, and claim you in my service until you fulfil this contract.' Like a rabbit terrified by a snake, Lightfoot remained transfixed. Without questioning her action, Imoshen placed her fingertip, still hot from the wax, on the centre of his forehead. Pressure built inside her head and sparks swam before her vision. With an internal rush the pressure snapped, returning her hearing and sight. 'You are mine, and I will know if you dishonour our contract.'

She smelt his fear.

When she removed her finger a red blister appeared on his skin in the shape of an inverted tear. Strange. She had not thought the touch of her finger hot enough to brand him.

The memory of something Tulkhan had once told her flashed through her mind. A Ghebite soldier had been captured by Reothe and told to deliver his message to Tulkhan but once he had, Reothe had said the man would die. The Ghebite had been whole and healthy. There had been no reason for him to utter the message then drop dead, no reason except Reothe's touch.

Now she had used a similar trick on Lightfoot. Imoshen did not even know if it would work, but it was clear the mercenary believed her. She smiled slowly, seeing confirmation in Lightfoot's eyes. It was enough that he believed he was her creature. 'Go now and remember, T'Imoshen granted your life and the lives of your companions when she could have taken them.'

As he backed away, giving her a deep obeisance reminiscent of the Vaygharian merchant aristocracy, she caught Wharrd's eye and lowered her voice. 'I will go to Tulkhan.'

'You can't. The townspeople fear the mercenaries will murder them in their beds. They won't be happy until they see the back of Lightfoot and his men. The rebels watch the Citadel. They await Drake's execution as a signal to strike. If you left Northpoint now the people would panic. I'll go to Tulkhan.'

'You are right. Tell Tulkhan the mercenaries have agreed to support him. I'll send them over as soon as he sends word.'

Wharrd slipped away and Imoshen's head swam. This time last year she had been plotting against General Tulkhan to save her life and secure Fair Isle. Now Tulkhan's second in command was answering to her, and she was consumed with worry for the General's safety.

TULKHAN EXPECTED TO hear a bark at any moment but Kornel had been right. The marsh-dwellers had hunted the narcts out around their village.

During the night, the General and his men had crept forward. Now they crouched behind boggy hillocks, watching the pole-houses of the village as the sky lightened.

Narct skins were strung from one high verandah to the next, flapping in the dawn breeze, their shimmering fur glistening. Smoke issued from the central hole in the nearest roof, bringing the smell of cooking fish.

Tulkhan gave the signal. They crept towards the headman's pole-house. Kornel's advice was to take this man and the village would surrender. Avoiding the slippery green patch where a freshwater spring fed into the river, they crept ever closer. Several chickens squawked, cooped in a cage built under the base of the house's platform, but no one bothered to investigate.

Tulkhan swung up onto the platform and dropped the house's ladder into place for his men. He slipped past the woven mat hanging in the doorway to find a woman cooking breakfast on a small metal brazier, with a baby at her breast and a child of about four at her side.

She stared, too surprised by their sudden arrival to react. The headman stood before a polished plate, plucking the whiskers from his chin with a pair of shells.

He dropped the shells and leapt for a weapon but Tulkhan grabbed the small boy, holding his knife to the child's throat. The woman moaned. A whimper escaped the lad and he wet himself.

The General cursed. 'Kornel, tell them the boy will not be harmed if they cooperate. We have captured their village.'

When Kornel spoke, Tulkhan caught a lilt to the language which reminded him of the common trading tongue, but he didn't understand individual words.

The headman spoke to his woman, who lifted the mat at the window. When she reported what she saw outside, the man held his hands out palm up.

'He is yours to command,' Kornel told Tulkhan.

But Tulkhan saw the anger burning in the man's eyes and he knew his service had been earned through fear, not gratitude. 'Kornel, tell him to pack enough food to travel to the marsh wall. We'll take the child to ensure his cooperation.'

As Kornel translated, Tulkhan watched the mother's face, and found he did not like the man he saw reflected in her eyes.

IMOSHEN LAUGHED TO see Almona dance across the grass. It had taken several intensive sessions but the child's leg was straight. 'I'm sorry, one leg will always be shorter than the other.'

'She is lucky,' Eksyl said. 'We all are.'

Just then a Citadel servant hurried into the hospice garden. 'A delegation approaches Northpoint flying the pennant of Chalkcliff Abbey.'

Imoshen had long suspected the abbey's Seculate of supporting Reothe. Tomorrow was the Harvest Feast, a holy day, and a good excuse to visit and see how the rebel leader fared. Smiling to herself she caught the servant's bewildered expression and recalled her own confusion when she had questioned her great-aunt about the church's role. This time last year she had not understood their subtle power plays.

Imoshen bid Eksyl and the half-blood children goodbye. They insisted on escorting her up the rise to the Citadel, where she went straight to her bedchamber.

She was determined to put on a good show for the Seculate. 'Dyta, it seems we must dip into the Citadel's treasures to find a garment to impress the Seculate. It is just as well the late Ghebite Lord of Northpoint had an eye for riches and sticky fingers to match.'

Imoshen suspected the Lord and his men had been murdered in their sleep by the locals when Reothe arrived at the Citadel. This had happened while she was Reothe's prisoner and she had not inquired too closely. As far as she could remember the man had been one of King Gharavan's men who changed allegiances when Tulkhan banished his half-brother. Judging by the way the locals reacted whenever he was mentioned, his death was not a great loss.

The old woman muttered something under her breath, then asked, 'Will I find something for T'Reothe to wear as well?'

Imoshen stopped unfastening her bodice. Dyta was right. The people would expect Reothe to play a part in the ceremony. If she hoped to defuse the situation with the rebels, Reothe must be seen to be raised high, while serving her. 'Yes, thank you.'

She pulled her ordinary gown over her head and draped it on a chair, staring at the mirror. It was silver-backed glass, as fine as any found in the palace. Under her feet the carpets lay three deep. Dyta was sure to find a garment fit for an empress, which was how she had to appear before the Seculate. She hated power politics, but if she had to play the game, she would play it to win.

When the maid returned, Imoshen selected a red velvet tabard, edged with gold brocade. Settling the skull cap of beaten gold on her hair, Imoshen adjusted the single large ruby to hang in the centre of her forehead and ordered a formal ceremony of welcome.

As High T'En music played, Imoshen completed the warmed wine ceremony, grateful to her mother for the boring hours of practice. Seven priests sipped their wine, eyes downcast. On her signal to speak, the Seculate explained his plans for the Harvest Feast and the restoration of Northpoint's church.

Imoshen was sure everything the Seculate saw would be reported to the Beatific, the head of the T'En church. The Beatific had supported Tulkhan, but Imoshen had long suspected the canny power broker was playing a double game.

Imoshen put her porcelain cup aside and came to her feet. 'I'm sure you wish to see T'Reothe, Seculate Donyx.'

She did not miss the quickly masked eagerness in the Seculate's beak-like face. Lifting her arm, Imoshen waited for him to join her. As her hand closed over his, she discovered the man was shielded from her gift. This was either innate, or he had experienced the T'En ability to sift the surface of a True-man's mind via touch and had learned how to guard against it.

Imoshen did not reveal her discovery by so much as a moment's hesitation. Instead, she escorted the Seculate to T'Ronnyn's Tower. In silence they climbed the internal staircase, which spiralled right so that True-man defenders could back up away from attackers, while protecting their shielded sides. Once her ancestors had known who their enemies were, she thought. Now she was surrounded by smiling threats, Reothe not the least of them.

When they entered the floor where he lay, Imoshen saw her people had prepared for this visit. The guards were absent and their *honoured guest*'s door was ajar. Gliding into the room, she smelled freshly crushed herbs and caught the tang of the sea breeze. The windows were open to the bay.

As Imoshen gave Reothe the formal obeisance, lifting both hands to her forehead, she noticed the floor. Scrubbing had removed the blood, leaving a pale patch. Unbidden, the memory of her encounter with Drake returned and a dizzying revelation seized Imoshen. If Seculate Donyx discovered that she had used her gift to strike Drake, he could petition the Beatific to declare her rogue. Tulkhan's men had sailed, leaving Reothe the only witness.

He would not betray her, would he?

Her gaze flew to Reothe. He was watching the Seculate closely and he did not look like a man about to greet an ally.

Straightening, Imoshen masked her turmoil with Old Empire formality. 'T'Reothe, Seculate Donyx of Chalkcliff Abbey has come to help us stage the Harvest Feast. You will have the honour of leading the festivities.'

Though the whites of his eyes had returned to their normal colour, he looked thin and pale. He sat upright, propped on pillows, but he lifted only one hand in greeting.

'T'Imoshen.' Her name rolled off his tongue with all the cadences of High T'En. He continued in this language, offering the True-people of the church formal greeting. He appeared to be honouring the Seculate and the priests, but Imoshen suspected Reothe was subtly reminding them that the church was supposed to worship the T'En gifts.

As Reothe's hand hung in the air between them, Imoshen saw his fingers tremble. Before the Seculate could notice his weakness, she caught Reothe's hand in hers. It surprised her to discover that she could not reveal Reothe's vulnerability to these priests. His skin was cool and her heart skipped a beat. It was the first time she had touched him since he had recovered from the fever's delirium and she realised she had missed Reothe, missed him fiercely. She should not have made physical contact. It weakened her resolve.

As she fought the urge to initiate the mind-touch the moment spiralled down until she was aware of no one but Reothe and nothing but her need to rediscover his T'En essence.

Despite the crippling of his gifts, Reothe sensed something, and he searched her face for the subtleties he would have once been privy to. His garnet eyes narrowed in pain.

'T'Reothe, is something wrong?' Seculate Donyx was perceptive.

'Not at all.' Reothe sank back, pale against the pillow. 'I will host the Harvest Feast with honour, but I am still recovering.'

'A carry-chair will be provided. I see we have tired you. We will withdraw,' Imoshen said. As she slipped her fingers from Reothe's, she saw raw need in his face and understood that he was powerless, marooned in a hostile world of True-people. It touched her to her core.

Secretly horrified by the discovery that Reothe could still affect her so deeply, Imoshen escorted the Beatific's spies from the room.

IT WAS JUST as well the General had the marsh-dweller's son to ensure the man's cooperation. He would never have picked the path to the marsh wall. For two days they had tramped through tussocky hills and bogs which all looked the same. Still water punctuated by needle-sharp grass filled every hollow.

When the dark line first appeared on the horizon, Tulkhan had thought it was mountains, then hills, then finally he understood it was the marsh wall of legend. Somehow he had led his army across the festering marshes without losing a single man to the bogs or the beasts.

They camped a little way from the wall because the ground before it was low, made that way to stop the predators, who could not climb. They burned dried clumps of the bog. Just on dusk the narcts began their nightly chorus. Tulkhan knew they would prowl outside the fire circles, fighting amongst themselves, ready to take down an unwary man.

'Climb the wall, Kornel, see if you can get your bearings. I want to attack Sumair at dawn the day after tomorrow. We'll travel by night.'

'With the twin full moons against us?'

'The moons are going to favour us. We attack the dawn after Harvest Feast, when everyone will be sleeping off their revelry. Don't tell me you object on religious grounds?'

Kornel grinned and shook his head.

Tulkhan dug into his travelling bag for sweet nuts and offered some to the child. To show they were harmless, he cracked the shell and ate one himself, then cracked another for the boy who, after catching a nod from his father, tried the crisp white flesh.

Tulkhan grinned at the child's delighted expression, then casually offered the father a nut. He took it, cracking it as the General had done, indicating he found the flesh good. But it would take more than a nut to win him.

As Kornel began to make his way towards the wall, the marsh-dweller stopped him, asking something in a low, intense voice.

'What does he want?' Tulkhan asked.

Kornel snorted. 'This fool thinks you'll let him go home now we've reached the wall.'

If Tulkhan let the man go, he could make it home in two days. Two days from now the General would either have Sumair or be staging a siege. On the other hand...

'There's nothing stopping him going over the wall after us, raising the alarm and warning Sumair. Then your plans would come to nothing,' Kornel said, voicing Tulkhan's concerns.

The General nodded. He could exact a vow from the marsh-dweller to return to his home, but what good was a vow given under duress?

Reothe had claimed that Imoshen's vow to Tulkhan had been given under duress. Reothe had said that he, and not Tulkhan, had been Imoshen's first choice. But Tulkhan believed that when she gave her bonding vows to him on Midwinter's Day they had been freely given. He had to believe it.

He rose, throwing the nut shells onto the fire as he returned to the issue at hand. 'Tell... what is his name?'

'Banuld,' Kornel said.

'Banuld-Chi,' the man corrected.

Tulkhan looked to Kornel.

'The Chi is an honorific, because he is the headman,' Kornel explained impatiently.

'Banuld-Chi,' Tulkhan acknowledged the man. 'Translate this, Kornel. In two nights from now you will be free to go.'

The marsh-dweller understood him even before Kornel translated the words and Tulkhan saw his despair. He did not believe they would live.

Tulkhan caught the captain's arm. 'Kornel, tell him I give my word. He and his son will be free to return home when their release no longer endangers us. And I'll reward him for his service.' Tulkhan did not miss the eager light in Kornel's eyes at the mention of a tangible reward.

IMOSHEN PACED HER room with Ashmyr in her arms. When he fell asleep, she paced with empty arms. Finally, she slipped on her cloak and climbed to the top of T'Ronnyn's Tower. From the top she could glimpse Port Sumair.

Imoshen did not take a torch, preferring the glow of the large and small moons as they neared their full glory. As she left the stairwell, she recognised a small silhouette. 'Kalleen, what's wrong?'

The little woman turned, her cloak wrapped high under her chin, her small face cold and imperious. 'You sent my bond-partner on a mission of state and he has not returned.'

'Wharrd serves Fair Isle.'

'He serves you, under a Ghebite oath that comes between bond-partners!' Kalleen's intensity made her seem larger. Her eyes were luminous in the moonlight. 'His Ghebite honour is greater than his love for me.'

Imoshen lifted her hands, asking for understanding. 'I must know if there is some way I can help the General forestall Gharavan's invasion. I have heard nothing since that first hurried message, which I suspect Tulkhan was loath to write. He does not enjoy failure. I'm hoping he will tell me what supplies he needs. The General trusts Wharrd.'

'Then why hasn't he returned? How do you know Piers hasn't betrayed Tulkhan for his true king? How do you know Wharrd isn't swinging from the ship's mast or feeding the fish?'

All these thoughts and more had crossed Imoshen's mind.

'T'Imoshen, I request permission to return to my estates.' Kalleen gave the Old Empire obeisance, reminding Imoshen of Lady Cariah, so gracious and elegant.

The memory stung her. Alone of all the Keldon nobles, Cariah had befriended Imoshen and helped soothe the transition of power during that first winter under Ghebite domination. But Cariah had made the mistake of rejecting her Ghebite lover's offer of marriage. Unable to live with the dishonour, he had murdered her before committing suicide. This angered and saddened Imoshen every time she thought of it.

Tulkhan had said she did not understand a Ghebite warrior's sense of honour. Wharrd's insistence on serving out his Ghiad to her made no sense, and Jacolm and Cariah's deaths had been equally pointless. Heartbroken over Cariah's loss, she had called on the Parakletos to escort her friend's soul into death's realm. Imbued by the power of this tragedy, Imoshen had turned the lovers into marble and death's own guardians had served as her stonemasons. Even now the stone lovers stood in the palace grounds, a permanent reminder of the cost of misunderstanding and intolerance.

Imoshen bowed her head. She had failed to anticipate that tragedy because she had not understood the Ghebite mind. Self-doubt wracked her. Had she sent Wharrd to his death?

'T'Imoshen?' Kalleen prodded.

'So formal...' Imoshen whispered sadly. 'What of Wharrd? Surely you wish to wait for his return?'

'My bond-partner has placed something before me.' Kalleen's chin lifted. 'I will go where I can be useful. If Wharrd returns, tell him where I am. If he does not come, I will know what to think.'

'At least stay for the Harvest Feast,' Imoshen said and Kalleen nodded. As she went to leave, Imoshen caught her arm. 'War is coming. Though you return to your estates, events may soon come to you.'

'I pray not.'

'As do I.'

Imoshen was surprised by a swift hug, bringing with it the scent of lavender. Kalleen's soft lips brushed her cheek, her breath hot on Imoshen's skin.

'I am not suited to this life of leadership,' Kalleen whispered. 'I long for my own hearth, the turn of the seasons and my family around me. Forgive me, Imoshen.'

After Kalleen left the tower top, Imoshen felt bereft. Kalleen had been with her at Umasreach Stronghold when her great-aunt was still alive. Kalleen had helped sustain her through the first winter under Ghebite rule. They shared so many memories.

A knot of pain swelled to fill Imoshen's chest. Walking blindly to the parapets, she gripped the stone, registering its cold solidity. Tears stung her eyes, blurring her vision as she stared across the T'Ronnyn Straits. The night was so clear she could almost see the lights of the blockading ships. She hoped that the reason Wharrd had not returned was because there was no news.

A sound made her turn.

'T'Reothe asks for you,' Dyta said.

'How does he fare?' Imoshen asked, recalling the unspoken plea he had made to her earlier that day.

'The left side of his body is weak, but he forces his fingers to work a little more each day.'

This news only gave Imoshen more concern. If Reothe's body was healing, how long before his gifts returned? Frustration flooded her. She needed to read the T'Elegos. Reothe might lie in the bed weak as a kitten now, but he still held the cards she needed to play a winning hand.

'Do you have a message for him?' the old woman asked.

Imoshen studied her closely. Was Reothe already exercising his gift to win people over?

All she read in Dyta's face was concern for an injured fellow; that this person was Reothe, the last T'En warrior, and that he was both beautiful and crippled, was only chance.

Or was it? Did True-people find the T'En beautiful? Imoshen did not know. General Tulkhan had looked on her with reluctant lust so many times that she could not trust her own judgment. 'Tell T'Reothe I will see him soon.'

The old woman left.

Imoshen imagined Reothe lying in bed two floors below listening to the sounds of the sea, vulnerable and alone. Her heart went out to him.

Having been under the watchful eyes of the Seculate and his priests all day, she could understand why Reothe felt persecuted by True-men. Imoshen was sure that Seculate Donyx was her enemy. Right now she felt as wary of True-people as Reothe was.

By the T'En heritage they both shared, she owed her kinsman her loyalty. It was loyalty of a different kind from that which she had vowed to share with Tulkhan, but she doubted if the General would understand the distinction.

She had to go to Reothe.

Chapter Five

IMOSHEN PADDED DOWN the stairs. As she approached the two Ghebite soldiers playing cards outside Reothe's room, she was filled with misgivings.

Between the rebels and the priests, she did not know who might be carrying treasonous messages. She felt as out of her depth as she had been during her one and only visit to the Empress's court. 'Has anyone been to see Reothe?'

'Only the old woman.'

Opening the door, Imoshen slipped into the chamber. Moonlight silvered the floor and the edge of the bed. She smelled the sea and Reothe's familiar scent. Her heart rate lifted.

Not bothering to light a candle, she went to the foot of the bed. When Reothe did not move, she stood with one hand on the bed's upright, unsure if she should go.

'Come to mock me, Imoshen?'

'How did you bear growing up amongst all those True-people in the Empress's court?'

'At least then I could protect myself. Now I am a husk. Why are you here?'

'The General failed to take Port Sumair. His ships blockade it. Wharrd is missing. The mercenaries sit outside the gates of Northpoint and grow fat while they sharpen their weapons. Their leader betrayed the General to Gharavan. Tulkhan ordered their execution but they've agreed to fight on Tulkhan's side.'

'What did you offer them?'

'Their lives and revenge.'

He gave a short bark of laughter. It plucked at something deep within her. Imoshen swallowed, senses strained to interpret his sudden silence, but the crippling of his gift acted as a barrier between them.

'Your rebels eat at the tables of the townsfolk and plot to rescue you,' she continued. 'My every move is watched.'

He pulled himself upright with his good arm, using a rope slung from the bed frame. The speed of his movement surprised her. 'What do you want of me, Imoshen?'

The moonlight sculpted his fine features. With a jolt she recognised him on an intrinsic level and, like a sleepwalker, she was drawn to him. Wordlessly, he curled his arms around her waist. She sensed the strength in his good arm and the weakness in the other. Cradling his head, she felt the warmth of his breath.

Tears stung her eyes and she longed to unburden herself. She ran her fingers through his fine, long hair. When she lifted her hand to the twin moons' light she saw several strands, glistening like spider webs on her fingers. The healer in her understood.

She had dealt his body such a severe blow that his hair came away in her hands. Would he ever truly recover? The urge to ask his forgiveness was almost overwhelming. Again, she ached to reach out with her T'En senses and greet his familiar essence.

The force of her longing to initiate the mind-touch triggered a flash of insight. When Reothe had come to her in Tulkhan's form he had revealed himself only at the last moment. With her barriers down, his mind had melded with hers and because of this she missed him as she would miss a severed limb. She suspected he had established some sort of link at that moment and she would never feel complete again without him. The revelation rocked her.

Dry mouthed, Imoshen slipped from his arms and backed away.

'You must beware of Seculate Donyx, too,' Reothe warned. 'He claims to be true to the old ways but he is a churchman first and foremost. Crippled like this, I cannot help you. I need to be whole again.'

'I don't know how to heal you.' She had not begun to think how it might be done.

'Try.' Reothe's eyes blazed a challenge.

'No.'

'Why not? Because it suits you to have me at your mercy? Does it amuse you to keep me as your gelding?'

'No.' Imoshen dragged in a quick breath. She suspected she would have no defences against Reothe once he was healed. 'Even my healing gift can kill. You saw what happened to Drake.'

'It was self-defence.'

'That would not protect me from the Tractarians.'

'I will not accuse you, Imoshen.' He studied her closely. 'You were raised to be a True-woman and you think like one. You don't realise your full potential. Fair Isle could be yours and yours alone. This is my honest advice. Act swiftly. Execute Drake and me, hire the mercenaries to consolidate your power, rout the remaining Ghebites, and slay everyone who resists.'

'No! I couldn't.'

'I know,' he said, and she could hear the smile in his voice. 'What will you do?'

'I don't know.'

He sighed and sank onto the pillows. 'Then I don't know how I can help you, Imoshen. Or even why I should.'

'You mock me.'

'Then stop pretending to be what you aren't – a True-woman, a Mere-woman – when I know you could be so much more!'

'I see we cannot agree.'

'What did you expect?' He caught the rope, pulling himself up to confront her again. Moonlight illuminated his face, austere and beautiful. 'Heal me and I will guide you to the T'Elegos. Heal me and, with the Keldon nobles at our back, we can unite the island and take the capital before the General can capture Port Sumair. Seize the day, Imoshen!'

She shook her head and backed away as his soft, derisive laughter followed her from the room.

THE DAY OF the Harvest Feast dawned fine and cool. Imoshen wrinkled her nose as she held up a pair of leather breeches and tried to judge the size. Reothe was taller and more slender than the late Lord of Northpoint, but the silk shirt was broad enough for his shoulders and the brocade tabard suitably ornate.

As for herself, she would spend most of the day barefoot with her hair down, dressed in nothing but a thin white shift. She was supposed to feel the earth beneath her feet when she gave the blessing for next year's harvest and catch.

Shivering, she dropped the shift over her shoulders. It made her feel exposed. At least Reothe would have the dignity of his ornate clothing. Imoshen turned to Dyta. 'Take these clothes to Reothe.'

The carry-chair would support him during the day's ceremonies and Seculate Donyx would be at his side, giving them the perfect opportunity to plot against her.

She was gambling that Reothe had not ordered his rebels to attack today. Her people had reported an influx of strangers in the port's taverns, but this was to be expected at festival time. As for the mercenaries, they had no reason to complain. They were well treated.

'The Ghebites are talking of an execution for today's entertainment,' Dyta said when she returned. 'It won't do to kill the rebel lad on Harvest Feast Day. No crops will grow, no cows will calve if blood is shed.'

Imoshen was shocked. 'I've ordered no execution.'

The old woman shrugged. 'You hear things.'

'Hear this. I have not ordered Drake's death.' Imoshen's bare toes gripped the thick carpet as she stepped closer.

'I just repeat what is being said, T'Imoshen.'

'Then repeat what I say to those who would spread false rumour. And send for the Custodian of the Citadel.' Dyta nodded and hurried away.

Imoshen brushed her hair until it crackled, lifting with a life of its own. She must quash these rumours. With a start, she felt the gifts stirring within her, empowered by her anger. She thrust the brush aside and took a long, deep breath, concentrating until the sensation passed.

BAREFOOT, IMOSHEN PROWLED into the crowded square before the Citadel. Looking resplendent in a purple tabard embroidered with fine gold thread, Reothe sat on the carry-chair with his four porters behind him. But she noticed he raised only his right hand when he was called upon to give his blessing. Every household had brought a portion of their Harvest Feast for Reothe to bless. This far north the festival's details varied from those of her own stronghold.

Because Reothe represented the church's kingdom and she the worldly kingdom, she had to present the Citadel's portion for his blessing. Did it amuse Reothe to see her kneel before him, she wondered?

Against custom she met his eyes, brilliant as garnets. He looked composed, his face thin but unmarked by his recent illness. Without his gifts, he could not know how vulnerable she had become to him. His advice had been brutal – kill him, or kill Tulkhan. But Imoshen refused to believe it was weakness to show compassion.

She accepted Reothe's blessing and rose, passing the tray to a servant. Then, instead of stepping away, she placed her hand over Reothe's weak left hand where it lay on the arm of the chair.

'Bring the prisoner.' She pitched her voice to carry.

The crowd muttered uneasily and she felt Reothe tense. Several Citadel guards appeared, escorting Drake between them. A hush fell. The air grew thick with expectation.

Drake squinted in the sunlight. She saw him flinch and knew the picture she and Reothe must present. Safe, pampered, secure in their power. How wrong.

Drake stood shivering on the flagstones.

Imoshen had to raise her voice to be heard over the crowd's murmur. 'Everyone here knows how this man almost killed Lady Kalleen of Windhaven, and how he attempted to free T'Reothe. But my kinsman is here by my side and it is his honour to host the Harvest Feast.' She felt Reothe's hand clench under hers. Imoshen focused on one dark golden head whose features revealed fear, quickly masked. 'Lady Kalleen, step forward.'

Kalleen picked up her skirts and moved through the smaller children who jostled for position at the front of the crowd. Crisp sunlight bathed Kalleen's face, gilding her hair and her skin.

Her beauty made Imoshen catch her breath. 'The wrong was done to you, Kalleen. You must decide Drake's fate: death or freedom?'

'Freedom,' Kalleen replied without hesitation, just as Imoshen expected. Her friend might have been born in a dirt-floored cottage, but her heart was pure and generous.

'So be it.' Imoshen turned from Kalleen to the rebel youth. 'You are free to go, Drake. You are pardoned of all association with the rebels. Return to your family.'

He stared at her in disbelief.

'You wonder why? For the second time in less than two years, Fair Isle faces the threat of invasion from the mainland.' Imoshen paused to give the crowd a chance to quieten. 'The people of Fair Isle need to be united against the common enemy. We can learn from the Lady of Windhaven. Let it be known that all rebels are pardoned, free to go to their homes, their farms and families.'

Her last few words were lost in the happy cries. Imoshen smiled at Kalleen's surprise and beckoned the bewildered Drake who approached, the force of his emotion making his body tremble.

He dropped to his knees, hands raised in deep supplication. 'I thank you, T'En Empress.'

'T'Reothe wants you to have this, in acknowledgment of your faithful service.' Imoshen dropped a draw-string purse into Drake's upturned palms. She hadn't bothered to correct Drake when he used the old empire title. It didn't surprise her. He was a traditionalist. 'Go to your family with peace in your heart. Go with the blessing of the last T'En.'

Drake snatched Reothe's free hand, kissing it. 'My service cannot be bought. It comes from the heart.'

'I know.' Reothe's reply was thick with emotion.

Heat filled Imoshen. It was the first time she had seen Reothe appear vulnerable before others.

Now Reothe slipped his weak hand from hers, briefly touching the tip of his sixth finger to Drake's forehead in the T'En blessing. 'Ride swiftly, ride safely.'

Drake stepped back a pace. He turned to Kalleen, who had been watching their interaction. She glanced over her shoulder as if she might run, but before she could, he knelt at her feet. Clasping her hands in his, he begged her forgiveness.

Kalleen's bemused expression made Imoshen smile. But when she glanced down at Reothe, his face was flushed with scarcely suppressed fury. She had dismissed his rebel army.

Let this be a lesson for him. Soon she may have to call on the people to defend Fair Isle, and the rebels would stand behind her, believing she and Reothe were united in purpose. She could be as ruthless in her compassion as he was in his willingness to fight.

As Seculate Donyx approached, Imoshen went to slip away, but Reothe caught her arm and tugged so that she lost her balance. With a twist she avoided falling into his lap, and found herself on one knee before him. His good hand clasped her chin and he leant forward, their eyes almost level. She could feel his tension as he inhaled her scent.

'This garment is indecent.' His eyes grew deep and dark.

Imoshen felt a rush of desire and this time she could not blame it on his T'En tricks. Hanging her head, she let the fall of her long hair hide her face. She felt more than heard Reothe's sharp intake of breath.

'I don't need my gifts to feel your response. Why do you deny me?'

She could give no answer, none that he would want to hear.

'Curse that Ghebite General!' Reothe hissed beneath his breath, then studied her. 'It was a master stroke to pardon my rebels, Imoshen. Truly, if you had stood at my side we would have ruled Fair Isle. We still can.'

A buzz of speculation rose from the crowd. To them it must appear that she bowed before Reothe. 'You play a dangerous game.'

'I play to win.'

'As do I.' She came to her feet. 'I am expected down at the wharves.'

Under Reothe's taunting eyes she strode away with her escort of priests scurrying to keep up. The townspeople lined the road waiting to shower her with late-blooming flowers and golden leaves, while on the wharves the fisherfolk awaited her blessing in the hope of a plentiful catch.

She could not falter, not for a moment.

As THE MOONS rose above the T'Ronnyn Straits, the Harvest Feast culminated in the selection of the young woman and man who would receive the corn sheaf and bull's horn. The town's populace followed the couple outside the gates to celebrate their joining in the Harvest Bower and the Citadel's public hall became even noisier. Imoshen tried not to recall this moment during last year's festival. She missed Tulkhan fiercely.

Reothe glared at her and she noticed the whiteness of his knuckles. She did not want him passing out, though the way the revellers were behaving it would not have been remarkable.

Rising, she gave the Seculate a formal bow. 'T'Reothe has overextended himself. I will see him to his room.'

It took a while to locate four servants sober enough to be entrusted with the carry-chair. Silently she followed them to T'Ronnyn's Tower. When the servants placed the chair in the hall outside Reothe's door, Imoshen dismissed them.

'Where is Ashmyr?' Reothe asked.

'Asleep.' Imoshen found Reothe's interest in the child unnerving considering who the baby's father was. 'Can you walk as far as your bed?'

'What would you do if I said no?' he asked sweetly.

'I would help you.'

'Ah, Imoshen. Then I fear I am too weak to walk that far.'

She felt a smile tug at her lips as she guided his hand to her shoulder. His fingers bit into her flesh but she did not complain, matching him step for step.

When Reothe nudged the door shut after them, Imoshen's heart thudded uncomfortably. Within two breaths her eyes had adjusted and she could see the room. The moons' light was so bright the furniture cast shadows. 'Not far to the bed.'

'I'll go to the windows. I want to bathe naked in the moonlight.'

Imoshen refused to imagine Reothe's pale form. 'Do you expect me to undress you?'

'Would you deny me the solace of the twin moons' light? It is beneficial to the T'En. I will feast in my own way tonight.'

'Really?' She felt more than heard Reothe chuckle and resentment stung her as, once again, she was reminded of the knowledge he kept from her.

In the silver light that streamed through the open windows, Reothe stood unaided. He raised his good arm to the ornate tabard. 'Remove this.'

Anticipating his needs, Imoshen helped him. He wore soft indoor slippers, which he eased off while steadying himself on her shoulder, then he let his breeches drop, stepping unconcernedly out of them.

She would not let herself look on his nakedness. Her gaze stayed firmly on his chest. His good hand lifted between them to cup the moonlight as if it were a physical thing.

Imoshen's breath caught in her throat.

'You feel it?' His voice was a forceful caress. 'You must. This is our night. Every double full moon belongs to the T'En. It is an ancient custom from the land beyond the dawn sun.'

'I've never heard –'

'What, of the moondance?'

'But that's performed by villagers on the seasonal cusps,' Imoshen objected. 'I thought it was one of their customs dating from before our time.'

'Many of their customs overlap ours. Imoshen the First deliberately melded our practices with theirs, just as she melded our blood with theirs. She knew the blood of the Ancients ran through the tribes of Fair Isle and that the mix would change our gifts forever. In the T'Elegos I read of T'En dances performed –'

'I must read the T'Elegos!'

He caught her eager hands, placing her palms on his chest where she felt the steady beating of his heart. 'Heal me tonight under the twin moons.' His voice resonated through her and her heart beat in time with his. 'Heal me and I will share the knowledge of the T'Elegos with you.'

She could hardly breathe. To deny him was to deny a part of herself. Only he knew the burden of their shared birthright. He promised beauty and knowledge when her T'En blood had brought her nothing but ostracism. She longed to open to him, but... 'I am sorry, Reothe.'

His hands tightened on hers. She sensed the force of his will and realised he was trying to use his gift.

But he gasped, his legs giving way.

She sank with him, cushioning his fall. As he lay naked and vulnerable in the moonlight, she leaned closer to inhale his scent, letting her hair trail the length of his body. Something inside her clenched and she could not deny her desire for him.

It seemed only right to let their bodies join and to open herself to the mind-touch. Only this would assuage the hollow ache inside her. Yet she was sure she would not crave him like this if she had not succumbed to his trickery. He must have implanted this need, knowing it would be triggered by his nearness and the timbre of his voice. Swimming in a sea of sensation she fought to centre herself, for she could not afford to restore his gifts, not when she had no defences.

Reothe moaned and his eyes flickered open. They were windows to his soul, containing his fierce intelligence and the pain of his loss. 'I cannot live a T'En cripple, Imoshen. You must heal me.'

Unable to speak, she pressed her face into his throat. As if in benediction he stroked her hair. Tears burned her eyes.

'You cry for me, yet you let me suffer. How cruel is that? You leave me defenceless, surrounded by adversaries. Even I would not be so cruel to my enemy.'

A sob escaped her. She sat upright in the moonlight, her hair around her shoulders like a satin cloak.

'I don't understand you, Imoshen. Your tears insult me.' A shiver wracked him. 'Bring the bed fur.'

Silently she dragged the heavy white fur off the bed. It felt luxurious against her skin. She wanted to lie naked in the moonlight with him. Instead, she knelt at his side. It was painful to watch him roll onto the fur with a stifled curse. Unable to stop herself, she stroked his long flanks.

'Lie with me in the moonlight, Imoshen.' He gestured to his body. 'Surely you do not fear me?'

Imoshen kissed his closed eyelids, then she stretched out on the fur beside him. Gradually she felt the tension ease from him. Closing her eyes she savoured this moment. They were like two children naked in their innocence, but it was an illusion. She desperately wanted to heal him, and she knew she could not take that risk.

Imoshen stayed only until she felt Reothe's breathing lengthen into the rhythm of sleep, then she covered him and left him lying there wrapped in the pale fur, caressed by the silver moonlight. She had not willingly betrayed Tulkhan, but it cost her dearly to deny Reothe and the bond they shared.

TULKHAN EASED HIS shoulders and flexed his hands, looking up at Port Sumair's landward wall. This was the ultimate test of his mad gamble. Leaving the marsh-dweller and his child under guard, he signalled Kornel to come with him. They approached the port, its walls and peaked roofs silhouetted against the stars. The large moon hung low in the western sky and the smaller moon had already set. The revelry of Harvest Feast had long since faded.

He had force-marched his men through the night. March all night then fight at dawn. He asked the impossible of his men before, but he asked nothing of them that he did not ask of himself.

His commanders each had their assigned task. He had chosen to lead the assault himself with a band of seven men. Tulkhan hefted the grappling-hook and coiled rope over his shoulder, thinking all it would take was one guard not too soused by drink to discover him.

Kornel spat and eyed the gate towers. 'The winch is in the base of the left tower.'

Tulkhan nodded. He covered the distance to the wall at a run. Here there were signs of hastily destroyed dwellings. The poor had been taken inside the walls.

Planting his feet, he swung the grappling-hook. It scythed the air with a sound that was loud in the predawn quiet. Then he let it go, watching it sail dark against the star-speckled sky. A soft chink told him the grapple had hit stone. He pulled steadily until it caught and held.

Tulkhan hauled himself up, his boots finding purchase on the wall. Any moment he could be discovered and the rope cut. In his mind's eye he saw himself falling backwards and fought a wave of vertigo. At last he hauled his weight over the parapet, sinking low.

He signalled the others and drew his weapon to stand guard as they made the climb. Tulkhan led his party towards the gate tower and the sound of a guard snoring. Entering the tower, he could just make out his army through the narrow window. They lay like the shadows of clouds on the flat land.

Hefting the drunken guard upright, the General pressed his knife to the man's throat. At Tulkhan's whispered command and the man led them down the narrow circular steps to the winch room, where Tulkhan set his men to raising the outer and inner gates. As soon as the outer gate was waist high, his men darted under it, entering the tunnel designed to bottleneck intruders. Silent except for the scuff of boot on stone, the attackers poured into the passage, passing through the inner gate.

Tulkhan tightened his hold on the guard, grimacing with distaste as fear made the man sweat, bringing the stench of alcohol through his skin. 'Where does King Gharavan sleep?'

His captive grunted, speaking in the common trading tongue. 'I'll not get my throat slit for a Ghebite King. You can tell your General Tulkhan he's welcome to use his half-brother's skull for a soup bowl. Gharavan commandeered the Elector's Palace.'

'Kornel, do you know where that is?' Tulkhan asked. He nodded. The General handed the guard into the custody of his gate holders.

At the General's signal a group went to attack the merchant quarter as a decoy while Tulkhan headed for the Elector's palace with a party of thirty men. Once Gharavan was his captive the mercenaries would lay down their arms, and Tulkhan believed he could reason with the remaining Ghebites, many of whom had served with him on other campaigns.

With Kornel in the lead they headed down the main thoroughfare, then plunged into a winding lane where the upper stories of the houses almost met overhead.

They had gone several blocks when a mercenary patrol rounded the corner. The light of their torches flickered on the closed faces of the narrow houses. The mercenaries gaped, stunned to discover the enemy within the walls. With a roar the nearest attacked.

Cursing his luck, the General drew his sword. Behind the mercenaries Tulkhan saw a man run off, no doubt carrying a warning to rouse the port. But there was no chance of catching the messenger when death danced just beyond his sword tip. The clash of metal on metal sounded loud and harsh in the cobbled street. Tulkhan's men fought silently, while the mercenaries bellowed their battle cries, and soon answering calls filtered through the twisting lanes.

Tulkhan cursed again. Forced to fight four abreast in the narrow lane, his men could not pass the mercenaries.

'Separate. Cut around behind them,' Tulkhan ordered, then grabbed Kornel. 'Take me to Gharavan.'

Charging down a dark alley on Kornel's heels, Tulkhan and his small party of men soon left their pursuers far behind. When they entered a more prosperous merchants' quarter, Kornel bent double to catch his breath.

Pealing bells and shouts of 'fire!' came from the merchants' quarter. More cries echoed from the wharves, heralding Commander Piers' attack. Above the rooftops the sky glowed. He had to find his half-brother before the defenders could mount a cohesive defence. 'Kornel?'

'I know the wharves and merchants' quarter best, but I think the Elector's Palace is this way.'

They cut through several lanes, then entered a square with an ornate central fountain. Kornel spun around to get his bearings. 'There, that building with the spires.'

Mercenaries poured down the palace steps. With a shout they bore down on Tulkhan's much smaller party.

'Fall back.' Tulkhan ran with his men at his heels. It was typical of Gharavan to stay safely indoors while hired swords fought his battles. 'We'll go around.'

But when they entered the lane beside the palace, they ran into another band of mercenaries, holding a party of Tulkhan's men at bay. The General charged, leaping onto the back of the nearest man and cutting him down.

Driving through the melee, he forged on to unite his men. Before they could enter the Elector's palace, more port defenders arrived. With one frustrated glance to the palace, Tulkhan signalled his followers to fall back. 'Take us around another way, Kornel.'

The ship's captain led them down narrow alleyways that all looked the same. Smoke billowed from the merchants' quarter. Tulkhan's breath rasped in his throat. They fought as they ran, leaving the dead where they fell.

Half blinded by the smoke and barely able to breathe, Tulkhan caught Kornel by the arm. 'Can you get us back to the gate? We must retreat.'

Grey with fatigue, Kornel nodded. 'We're nearly there.'

Rounding a bend, they found a hastily constructed barricade of household furniture manned by mercenaries. Beyond it the gates had been recaptured and closed.

Tulkhan had no breath to curse. Soon it would be light enough for archers to send down a rain of arrows. His people were armoured for speed and stealth, not for defensive battle. Bitterly, he raised the horn and sounded the retreat.

'To me!' Tulkhan cried. They had to retake the gate before his men were massacred. Charging the barricade, he grasped a massive oak table. His thighs screamed in protest as he lifted it. Men joined him. They ploughed through, smashing all before them. At his side men tripped over broken furniture, and some fell defending their backs, but the way to the gate was cleared.

Leaving others to deal with the barricade defenders, Tulkhan made for the winch room. A single local fled as he entered. Tulkhan threw his weight behind the winch mechanism, but the massive cogs were slow to move. Finally, the heavy gates screeched and began to lift. Three of his men joined him in the winch room to lend their strength to the effort.

Their escape route secured, Tulkhan returned to the barricade. In the growing light he saw more of his men approaching, fighting as they attempted to retreat through the narrow street.

The Ghebite battle cry leapt from his lips and he ran out to meet them. For a few moments it was life and death on the cobbles under the swinging business signs of tailors and hatters. He held the gap in the barricade to let the others through, then he dug his hands under the oak table.

Seeing what he was about, several men helped him. Together they turned and rammed the table into position, blocking the gap. As they held back the defenders, Tulkhan took stock. If he could keep the gate open long enough, he could get a force inside and make it a fight every step of the way to the Elector's palace.

At that moment the deadly hum of a flying arrow made his decision for him.

He fought a rearguard action, holding the narrow gate passage to let the last of his men through. Oil poured from the slits above, landing on the stones between him and freedom. A flaming brand followed. Covering his face with his forearm, Tulkhan leaped through the flames.

As the outer gate made its ponderous descent he ducked under. Then it was a mad scramble to run beyond bow shot. From narrow slits the defenders sent whistling death.

Even though he knew his unprotected thighs were more vulnerable, the space between Tulkhan's shoulder blades ached with the expectation of an arrowhead. Finally Tulkhan reached Kornel in the ranks. Then he turned to face the port's walls, putting his hands on his knees to catch his breath.

The defenders did not make a sortie, contenting themselves with shouting abuse. Tulkhan smiled. Though the surprise attack had failed, by now the defenders would have reported the impossible to Gharavan – Tulkhan's army was camped outside the gates of Port Sumair, ready to lay siege.

His stomach rumbled as he turned to his commanders. 'Break out the stores. I want my breakfast!'

They grinned, catching his enthusiasm.

Chapter Six

THE DAY AFTER the Harvest Feast Imoshen escorted the Seculate and his party to the city gates and bid them farewell. The wind carried a foretaste of the winter to come and Imoshen shivered. Fair Isle had seen too much war. The peaceful years of her childhood now seemed halcyon and unreal. She did not want her son's childhood shadowed by violence.

Her people had reported a great exodus on the roads south and east as the rebels headed home. There was much to be done to prepare for the winter with the prospect of war in the spring.

Finally Imoshen turned and, accompanied by the officials of Northpoint, retraced her steps to the Citadel's public hall. In her heart she dreaded returning to her chamber and Kalleen's anxious, accusing eyes. For despite having permission to return to her estate, Kalleen lingered, hoping for her bond-partner's return.

IT WAS MIDAFTERNOON before the port defenders signalled they were ready to talk. Tulkhan commandeered a draught horse, the only mount sturdy enough to carry him, and rode out to meet them. He wished he had his battle-hardened destrier, but the horse was still on Fair Isle, doubtless growing fat and sleek on too much grain and not enough exercise.

He had dressed in full armour, wearing the purple and red colours of his Ghebite father, the old King. He waited as the gates opened, allowing seven ornately dressed horseman to ride out.

Tulkhan's hands tightened on the reins as he recognised his half-brother. It was all very well to swear Gharavan's death, but it was another thing to meet the youth face to face. He had taught Gharavan to ride, had made his first wooden practice sword, and now he was sworn to kill him. It left a bitter taste in Tulkhan's mouth.

The General did not recognise a single Vaygharian mercenary among the company. He cursed. Since it was clear that the Lowlanders did not support Gharavan, he'd been hoping to strike a bargain with Gharavan's mercenaries. If the mercenaries could be persuaded to change allegiance, Tulkhan could cut the body from the head of Gharavan's army and the war would be all but won.

The party halted and a single horseman rode out. His ornate clothing proclaimed him one of Gheeaba's new military elite, a breed of young man who played at war while never having to bloody his hands.

'General Tulkhan,' the man greeted him.

'I will speak with my half-brother or no one!' Tulkhan roared. 'And I am Tulkhan, Protector General of Fair Isle.'

The others conferred, then Gharavan ventured forward with the six men at his side. His horse shifted nervously.

Tulkhan could smell the perfume on him from here. Their father would have turned in his grave. 'Gharavan.'

'King Gharavan to you, Protector General!' The youth made Tulkhan's title an insult, his thin voice carrying on the still air. 'I see you have torn yourself away from your Dhamfeer bitch long enough to come to meet me. Or did you bring her along to warm your bed and hold your hand?'

Tulkhan forced his hands to unclench from the reins. 'T'Imoshen holds Fair Isle. I have Port Sumair surrounded. Surrender now and I will discuss terms.'

'How many men and ships did you lose? It is a wonder they follow you at all,' Gharavan sneered. 'It would be better to take your horse and put it to the use it was bred for, ploughing a furrow. Or would you rather be back in Fair Isle ploughing the Dhamfeer's –'

'You have until dusk to surrender.' Tulkhan spoke over him, but contained his rage. 'I will take no retaliation against the people of Port Sumair because I know they want no part in this. As for the mercenaries –'

'They are loyal to me,' Gharavan crowed. 'What does your traitorous army call themselves now, Fair Weather Men of Fair Isle?'

The laughter of Gharavan's supporters sounded forced, but it was all Tulkhan could do to stop himself leaping off his horse and dragging his half-brother from the saddle.

'Why should we surrender?' Gharavan asked. 'There's food for two years in the granaries. Long before that, your Dhamfeer bitch will have bedded her rebel prince. And long before *that*, my auxiliary forces will have marched across the Lowlands to crush you. And when you're mine, there will be no axe for your neck. No.' Spittle flew from Gharavan's lips as he rose in the saddle. 'You will die the death of a Ghebite traitor, tied between four galloping horses, your limbs pulled from their sockets while you scream in agony!'

Tulkhan grew cold and still inside. He lifted his eyes from Gharavan's white knuckles to his maniacal features. His half-brother hated him with an irrational intensity Tulkhan recognised but could not comprehend.

Silence stretched between them. A gull called, reminding him that the sea was not far away.

'I thank you for telling me your contingency plans.' Tulkhan kept his voice dispassionate. 'And I thank you for killing the last love I bore the boy I knew. When I banished you from Fair Isle, I said I no longer had a half-brother. But it took until today for you to make this true. Ride away, little king, scurry back inside your gate and hide under your bed, for you have had the last easy night's sleep you will ever know.'

Gharavan jerked on the reins, making his horse dance in a half circle. 'I call down a curse on your house and your blood. The bastard child you claim to have sired will never sit on the throne of Fair Isle, because I will take the island and execute all of your traitorous commanders, saving the Dhamfeer bitch and her half-breed cub for last. When I have finished with her she will beg me for death.'

Tulkhan felt a muscle contract in his cheek, but he remained impassive.

Still cursing, Gharavan and his supporters galloped back to the gate. Tulkhan watched him go, his heart hard as stone.

When the General returned to the campsite, he discovered his hands were shaking, but there was much to be done. Teams of men had been sent to scour the farmlands for food and useful tools. They returned laden with cartloads of stores from the farms and reported the land deserted. Hardly a mongrel dog remained. Tulkhan had left orders not to pursue the Lowlanders. He wanted an ally, not an enemy on Fair Isle's doorstep.

His men were exhausted, yet despite the failure to take the port, they were in good spirits as Tulkhan planned his defensive earthworks. To win this siege they needed to be secure from attack from the port and from Gharavan's auxiliary army.

FULL DARK SAW the General's campfires dotting the plain like stars. Not having slept in more than two days, Tulkhan rotated his shoulders wearily, then turned, surprised by a familiar voice.

'Wharrd?' He turned to greet his old friend. 'I thought I left you in Northpoint. What's that stench?'

'Mud. You try crossing the mud flats below the seawall!'

Tulkhan grinned. 'What brings you here?'

'I had to come myself to stop Imoshen coming.' He offered the formal salute of a Ghebite to his leader, but Tulkhan grabbed him by the shoulders, hugging him.

Wharrd cleared his throat. 'You had us fooled. We thought you blockaded the port by sea.'

'That was the idea.' He glanced around. Kornel was nearby, as always, but out of hearing. Even so, Tulkhan lowered his voice. 'My surprise attack failed, so now I lay siege. How did it fare with Piers?'

'He bombarded the wharves and dockside as planned. Spot fires broke out all over the city. A third of the merchants' quarter burnt down, which will make Gharavan very unpopular.' Wharrd chuckled, then sobered. 'When Piers heard you sound the retreat, he recalled his men. The port remains sealed by sea.'

'And we have her sealed by land. But they have two years' supply of grain and Gharavan was foolish enough to let me know he has sent for support from the annexed kingdoms. He looks forward to watching me die a traitor's death. He threatened to execute every Ghebite loyal to me.'

Wharrd cursed softly. 'How much time do we have before Gharavan's auxiliaries arrive?'

Tulkhan squinted into the flames. 'If the Lowlanders are anything to go by, there's a good chance the annexed countries will delay to see which way the wind blows.'

'I'd be happier knowing your army was up to strength.'

'So would I. This plain is perfect for cavalry and I haven't a decent horse to call my own. Have Imoshen send over siege machines, and two companies of my best cavalry in case Gharavan does get his auxiliaries. You'll have to negotiate for their passage with one of the southern kingdoms. Diplomacy...' Tulkhan muttered disgustedly. 'And I don't have the weight of the Ghebite Empire at my back to exercise diplomatic muscle.'

'You would claim Fair Isle for your own.'

'What choice had I?' Tulkhan countered. They grinned, then fell silent. A man brought them local beer served warm and flat. Tulkhan sipped his, deep in thought.

'I have some good news,' Wharrd announced. 'Imoshen bargained with the mercenaries, offering their lives for revenge. They've agreed to serve you. She'll send them over as soon as you are ready for them.'

Tulkhan smiled ruefully. Trust Imoshen. She could not simply follow his orders, she had to go one better. 'I hope they prove more loyal than their leader.'

Wharrd shrugged and stretched. 'I'm getting too old for this.'

'Never say!'

'I want no part in the fate of kingdoms. A warm fireside, Kalleen and my children; that is all I ask.' He hesitated. 'You know I am sworn to T'Imoshen's service.'

Tulkhan looked up at his old friend. 'You undertook a Ghiad.'

'Imoshen saved Kalleen's life. Until I repay that debt, I am under an obligation to her.'

'Does she understand what a Ghiad means?'

'I don't think she will ask me to fall on my sword. In fact she tried to release me. So no, she doesn't understand.'

Tulkhan came to his feet, clasping the older man's shoulder. 'Then I don't envy you, my friend, for Imoshen is Dhamfeer and almost beyond a True-man's protection. I fear you will be under this Ghiad until death releases you.'

'Then so be it. My honour allows nothing less.' Wharrd returned the pressure on Tulkhan's shoulder. 'There is honour in serving the last T'En Empress.'

Tulkhan frowned. Even his man, Wharrd, thought of Imoshen as Fair Isle's Empress. Yet if Wharrd knew Imoshen carried Reothe's child, he would not use the word *honour* in the same breath as her name. Worse, he would despise his General for not avenging himself. Frustration ate at Tulkhan, but one problem at a time, for now he had to deal with Gharavan.

'Is there some private word you would have me carry to Imoshen?' Wharrd asked.

Tulkhan shook his head.

'I must go.' Wharrd swung his cloak around his shoulders.

'Tell her...' Tulkhan stopped. It was not the Ghebite way to speak of such things.

Wharrd nodded. Then he was gone, slipping into the shadows while Tulkhan stared into the fire.

IMOSHEN WAS UP with the sun, seeing to Ashmyr's needs. She could have asked a servant to care for him, but she wanted to see his eyes light up when he recognised her. Her maid's doorcomb sounded discreetly, identifying her by its tone.

'Enter, Dyta.'

Imoshen smiled with relief as the woman escorted Wharrd into the room. She placed Ashmyr in his basket before greeting the veteran. 'Do you want something to eat?'

Wharrd shook his head and, as the door closed, Imoshen realised it would be rumoured that she had taken the General's closest friend for her lover. Kalleen would know better. She had been put aside not for lust but for honour.

'Kalleen and I feared for your safety when you did not return or send word.'

'Secrecy was essential for the General's plans.'

'Tulkhan is alive and well?'

'Yes. He took his army across the marshlands.'

'Impossible.'

Wharrd grinned. 'They attacked Port Sumair the dawn after Harvest Feast, but the port's defences held, so now he lays siege.'

'War games.'

'This is no game. If Tulkhan fails, Gharavan will have him dismembered, before attacking us. The General is all that stands between Fair Isle and his half-brother's greed for revenge!'

Hiding her dismay, Imoshen walked to the oriel window.

'Tulkhan needs you to negotiate safe passage for cavalry and siege machines. And he needs men and supplies immediately.'

'As soon as I have the ships I will send the mercenaries and more supplies. You look tired, Wharrd. You should see Kalleen.'

He agreed, but she could see he was oblivious to the anxiety his mission had caused his bond-partner.

Imoshen looked out over the T'Ronnyn Straits, almost blinded by the sea's intense blue. Tulkhan's army needed supplies. The merchants of Fair Isle would not be pleased to find their profits taxed yet again. She would have to select an ambassador to negotiate with the Amirate, the kingdom to Sumair's south. With a sigh she returned to her desk and opened her writing case.

Imoshen smiled to herself. The old tales did not dwell on the business of war. It was won or lost on supplies and manoeuvring, and she was going to make certain the General won this encounter.

*   *   *

IMOSHEN ARCHED HER tired back. She had been working since she sent Wharrd to the capital laden with messages.

'Here's your fresh bread and hot spiced milk, my lady.' Dyta placed the tray on the chest before the fire. 'It's a cold day for travelling. I tried to get the Lady Kalleen to have some warmed wine, but –'

'Kalleen has gone?'

'Her entourage gathers in the forecourt.'

Imoshen ran out the door and down the spiral staircase to the first floor balcony. From there she could see travellers milling in the courtyard below. Recollecting her dignity, Imoshen slowed as she went down the steps and approached Kalleen, taking the horse's bridle. 'You are leaving?'

Kalleen nodded, arranging her cape over her legs to keep out the wind.

Imoshen led the horse a little away from the others. 'I'd hoped with Wharrd's return you would reconsider.'

'He has already left for T'Diemn in your service.'

'At least let me provide you with an escort.' Imoshen called Jarholfe and told him to organise this. Then she returned her attention to Kalleen. 'They will be ready soon enough.'

For a few minutes they stood in stiff silence, Imoshen at the horse's head, Kalleen straight and cold in the saddle. Around them the men shouted, horses were saddled and there was the sound of running boots on the stones as guards went to collect their travelling kit.

'I am sorry it has come to this, Kalleen.'

'Ask Wharrd what it means for a Ghebite to be under a Ghiad.'

But Imoshen was concerned with other things. 'If Fair Isle is attacked from the mainland, Windhaven will be one of the first places to fall. Promise me you will head for T'Diemn at the first sign of attack?'

Kalleen eyed her solemnly. 'Is war so certain?'

'Nothing is certain. Which is why we must be ready.'

TULKHAN'S FARM HORSE picked its way through his men, who wielded shovels instead of swords. He rose in the saddle to study the layout of his camp. On horseback he was the tallest point. He could see the smudge which was the seawall, and closer still another smudge which was the old seawall. Nearly two hundred years ago the Lowlanders had reclaimed this land from the sea, building Port Sumair on a rocky outcropping.

The Lowlands were a maze of landlets encircled by walls until you came at last to the most recent seawall, where even the industrious Lowlanders had decided it was too much effort to reclaim the land from the sea.

With no high ground on which to mount a defence, he needed ditches, deep and broad, to protect his army's back and flanks in the event of attack from Gharavan's auxiliaries. Earth was being rammed into place to form a thick-based wall within the trench works. This defence faced inland, stretching in a great half-circle from the seawall south of his position to the northern seawall.

Yet it was not enough if the defenders tried to break the siege. So a second defence works was also under construction, its ditches and earth wall facing the port.

Tulkhan grinned to himself. All this work kept his men busy. And the digging provided good cover for their attempts to mine under the port's walls. Tulkhan didn't intend to let this siege grow dull.

But it frustrated him that there was so little timber. The houses were made of dried sods which formed hard bricks. He could not build siege machines or watchtowers without decent wood.

On the breeze he heard the laughter of a child and saw the marsh-dweller's son dashing through his men. The father caught him, cast an anxious glance about and retreated.

Tulkhan hadn't seen anything of the man and his son since he failed to take the port. Banuld was probably afraid Tulkhan's temper would find an outlet in him. But it was a matter of honour with the General to treat his men firmly yet fairly. Soon he would reward the marsh-dweller and send him home.

Leaving his mount with the horse-handlers, Tulkhan greeted Kornel. 'It would be quicker to bring my supplies over the seawall than through the marshes. I want to see this seawall.'

They rode through the abandoned fields under the light of the waning moons, which were still bright enough to cast shadows. Tulkhan gave the port a wide berth, and before long he was facing the seawall. On the landward side it was a steep hill, twice as tall as Tulkhan on horseback. He dismounted and clambered up the slope.

Heart thudding with the effort, he reached the crest, where it was wide enough for three men to walk abreast. Tulkhan peered over the seaward side. No water lapped at the sea-wall's base. Mud stretched for a great distance before he made out the glimmer of moonlight on water.

'Why do they build so high?' he called down to Kornel, who had hobbled the horses and was scuttling up to join him.

The captain paused a moment to mop his face with his shirt tail before answering. 'Storm surge at high tide. This is low tide just after the twin full moons. See how far the mudflats stretch? Even at the highest of high tides a deep draught ship would have to send the men in by the boatload. Any other time they'd churn up the mud so badly they'd be stuck like beached whales and then the narcts would get them.'

'We could stand guard. Kill a few and scare them off.'

'The beasts are attracted by blood, and out in the channel...' Kornel pointed to a dark smudge in the moonlit sea. 'See the islands drifting with the currents and tides? The narcts nest on them.'

Tulkhan realised what he had thought were the shadows of clouds were actually the drifting islands. He would have to bring supplies and men through the marsh. The lights of his blockading ships bobbed on the sea. 'I need to signal the ships. Have you something to burn?'

Kornel dragged off his grimy coat. Tulkhan took out his flints. Setting fire to Kornel's coat, he swung it an arc above his head.

It seemed to take an age before a boat rowed across the moonlit sea towards them. Impatient, Tulkhan slid down the seawall's steep incline.

'Wait!' Kornel began, but too late. The General sank knee-deep in thick, sticky mud. It gave off foul bubbles as he struggled to pull his legs out.

'Stay there, Kornel. No need for you to get filthy too.'

No need for Kornel to hear Tulkhan's plans. The merchant captain had been helpful so far, but Tulkhan suspected Kornel worshipped only one god and it gleamed gold.

CLOSETED IN HER chamber, Imoshen studied the mainland map, trying to imagine how Tulkhan had marched his army through the marshlands.

'Deep in thought?' Reothe's rich voice startled her.

She pushed the books aside so that the map rolled closed, before walking around the desk to stand before him.

After discovering how much she craved Reothe's presence, Imoshen had deliberately avoided him. Now he confronted her, one side of his face lifting in a painful smile while he leant heavily on his walking stick. It hurt her to see him like this, yet she was relieved to know his menace was contained in the crippled shell of his body.

'You pace the floor at night, this night even more so, Imoshen. I hear Wharrd has returned and gone again.'

'What excellent spies you have. What else do they tell you?'

'That Fair Isle is a ripe plum waiting to be plucked by the Ghebites, or any mainland power.' He made his way to the desk, nudged the chair and let his weight down carefully. And there he sat for a moment, battling dizziness, she suspected.

Imoshen fought the need to stroke the line of pain from his forehead. 'The General lays siege to the port. I must send more men, siege machines and cavalry.'

'That will take time to organise.'

She shrugged. 'That's what a siege is, a waiting game. Unfortunately Gharavan has called on the allied kingdoms to send auxiliary armies.'

'The T'En once had treaties with the triad of southern kingdoms. It would not hurt to remind them of this.'

'They did not come to our aid when we asked for help against General Tulkhan,' Imoshen said bitterly.

'No. They were eager to see us brought low,' Reothe agreed. 'But now that the Ghebites are on the move again, they will side with the stronger force. You must convince them that the Empress of Fair Isle and her war general are that force. If you do not, you will have trouble securing a safe port to unload your cavalry and siege machines.' He cursed softly. 'If only I were whole!'

Imoshen studied him. Reothe, her ambassador? What would stop him playing a double game, ensuring support to usurp Tulkhan? Perhaps it was just as well he was not *helping* her.

'What?' Reothe asked. 'I dislike that expression.'

'Your counsel is good.'

'Then why do you avoid me?'

Imoshen looked away. Whenever she closed her eyes she saw him lying on the fur in the moonlight and she ached to go to him and claim her T'En heritage in every way. 'I have been busy with matters of state.'

'How convenient.'

She hid a smile. Ashmyr made a soft mewling sound in his sleep and she went over to settle him.

'The Ancients returned his soul but... You could delve into his mind to see if he is recovered,' Reothe suggested.

'It is against my principles to invade an unwilling mind.'

'Unwilling?'

'Uninvited, then.'

'Seriously, Imoshen how can you afford such principles?'

She flushed, meeting Reothe's eyes. He was stroking the vellum map. He pushed it aside. 'Do I disgust you?'

'No. How can you say that?'

'You've been avoiding me.'

She stood and poured some wine, offering him a glass, but he shrugged impatiently.

The goblet was exquisite blown glass, more evidence that the Ghebite Lord of Northpoint had not stinted himself. Everyone looked after their own interests, it seemed, except her. She wanted what was best for Fair Isle. There was no time for doubts.

She wound both her hands around the goblet's stem. 'I will speak plainly, Reothe. Tulkhan is the only one who stands between our island and the greedy mainlanders who have long resented our wealth and power. If the General defeats Gharavan, every petty prince will rise up to snatch what they can of the crippled Ghebite Empire and that means they will be too preoccupied to bother Fair Isle.' She swirled the wine around, watching its deep burgundy surface glisten in the candlelight, rich and dark as Reothe's eyes which gave nothing away. 'But if Tulkhan falls, we face invasion. I need your support.'

'Fair Isle almost bled to death during the General's invasion,' Reothe said. 'He must crush his half-brother. Port Sumair's granaries are deep. Can the General wait out the winter?'

'I'm hoping he won't have to. I'll send the mercenaries and more supplies. Meanwhile my ambassadors will negotiate safe passage for cavalry and siege machines. Who knows, with the right rumours the conquered countries may yet rise up and revolt. King Gharavan could find himself king of nothing.'

Reothe smiled. 'I will not insult you by saying you think like a man.'

Imoshen felt the blood rush to her face and a sweet pain filled her. Shortly after their first meeting Tulkhan had accused her, with typical Ghebite blindness, of thinking like a man because she talked tactics. Reothe would never make the mistake of thinking her gender limited her intelligence.

Again she felt compelled to reach out to him, and placed her hand on his shoulder. When Reothe pressed his lean cheek to the back of her hand she felt the heat of his skin. Her lips brushed his head. She longed to open her T'En senses, reach out and touch his essence. She felt so empty she ached. The moment stretched impossibly.

With great effort she pulled away and walked around the desk to top up her wine. 'Drink to our bargain?'

'What bargain? I have agreed to nothing, Imoshen.' His features hardened. 'Or did you think to seal my agreement with the offer of your body? Tantalising as it is, I must decline.'

She froze. Seeing his knowing expression, she realised he could read her actions, even if he could no longer sense her thoughts. Shame and fury lashed Imoshen, but she schooled her features, putting her glass aside. 'All I ask is your support to hold Fair Isle.'

'I called off the Keldon nobles, didn't I? I am loyal to Fair Isle. Can you say the same?'

'All I have done has been for Fair Isle!'

'Perhaps,' he conceded, suddenly tired.

Imoshen took a step towards him, her hand extended. He flicked it aside. 'Your maid is a terrible gossip, Imoshen. She will know exactly how long I have been alone with you. By tomorrow morning everyone will believe we are lovers.'

'We've been discussing matters of state. If I were a man they would not think otherwise.'

He smiled slowly. 'But you are not a man. You are a beautiful woman made more desirable by the power you wield. And besides' – Reothe's eyes gleamed with painful self-knowledge – 'we both know the only reason we are not lovers in deed as well as intent, is because this body of mine is –'

'But I have never sought to seduce you.'

'True. Now tell me you've never desired me.'

She swallowed, determined to ignore his challenge. 'You must tell the truth, Reothe, or does such gossip amuse you?'

'As you wish. I will explain that we were discussing how to hold Fair Isle in the event of the General's death.' He cut short her protest with a shrug. 'Let them believe what they choose, Imoshen. It is only a matter of time. The General will disown you because you carry my child.'

'Is that why you...?' She laughed bitterly. 'He told me by Ghebite law he should strangle me and our son.'

Reothe's eyes widened in surprise.

'What did you expect? Ghebites think differently.'

'Yet you still live.'

'Yes. As do you. And I don't know why.'

'It is a simple thing to find out.' Reothe frowned when she would not hold his eyes. 'Let me guess. He made you promise not to use your gifts on him and your honour won't let you break a promise. Why do you find it so hard to break a vow to him, when you broke your vows to me?'

'How can you speak of vows and honour?' Tears stung her eyes as she realised how deeply his betrayal had hurt. 'You tricked me!'

He uttered a short bark of laughter. Her hand lashed out but he caught her wrist in his strong right hand and pulled her against his chest. Her heart raced, her breath caught in her throat. Everything else receded but his nearness. She could have freed herself in an instant yet, dangerously, she longed for his touch.

'Yes, I tricked you. But your body recognised me just as it does now. We were meant for each other. Only in your company do I feel truly alive, and when our minds touch...' He shuddered. For an instant Reothe's features glowed with a fierce passion. His beauty stole her breath. He was so Other, she feared her instinctive attraction to him.

She sprang away shaking her head.

He gestured to himself. 'You did this to me. You are more powerful than you realise.'

But she did not dare unleash the powers he seemed so sure of. At least for the moment they were equal. His abilities were crippled and hers untutored. 'How can I discover my true potential when you hide the T'Elegos from me? It is as much my birthright as yours.'

'You have only to ask and I will share everything with you.'

She fought a heady rush of desire. He promised so much more than the knowledge of their T'En legacy, but her choice was made. 'I'm sorry, Reothe. I must stand by my vow to Tulkhan.'

'You surrendered to save your life, Imoshen. Your vow to me is of an older making and sprang from your own free will.'

'Our betrothal belongs to a lost future.'

'I have the Sight. I've glimpsed many futures. I believe we can claim the future we want. Look at your left wrist.'

A sharp sting made her gasp and she covered her wrist. But she could not deny that the bonding scar they both shared had split open.

Shortly after General Tulkhan had accepted her surrender, Reothe had come to her at Landsend Abbey. He had offered to help her escape, but she had already given the General her word, and the people of Fair Isle relied on her to smooth the transition of power. Before she could explain this, Reothe had cut their wrists to begin the bonding ceremony. She had refused to complete the oath.

In Landsend Abbey she had made a decision to follow her head and not her heart. Now just over a year later, she hoped it had been the right decision. Imoshen gritted her teeth as blood welled between her fingers.

'Imoshen?' The tone of Reothe's voice made her look directly at him. She watched transfixed as he raised his left arm and a thin trickle of blood seeped from the wound across his wrist. 'I once told you it would stop bleeding on the day we were properly joined. We have shared our bodies and our minds, yet you still refuse me. This might not be a perfect future, but it is all we have and I will not give up.'

His vehemence frightened her. She sealed her bonding wound with her tongue, tasting the bitterness of her blood. 'You forget I hold your life in my hands.'

'Then kill me and stop this farce. I find it too painful to bear. You see, compassion is but another name for cruelty, sweet T'Imoshen.' His voice rang with truth. He turned his wrist again to reveal the bleeding wound. 'Heal me.'

'Never.'

'Then I will never reveal the T'Elegos, and you will destroy yourself and everything you love because you cannot control your gifts.'

Imoshen staggered, reaching blindly for the table.

'Think on it, Imoshen. I am your anchor. You need me.' Tortuously slow, but with great dignity, he left her.

Chapter Seven

TULKHAN STRODE TO the entrance of his makeshift command shelter. The smoke of many cooking fires rose on the still dawn air. Men called to one another, their voices carrying. After eleven years of campaigning this was a familiar and reassuring sight.

Tulkhan cleared his throat. 'Kornel, where's Banuld?'

'Probably by the kitchen fires, gambling away his beer rations,' Kornel muttered.

'Fetch him.'

By the time Kornel returned Tulkhan was seated under the awning at a table scavenged from some farm kitchen, drinking warm beer and eating honey cakes. Banuld looked wary, if hopeful.

'Tell the marsh-dweller I have good news and bad. I will be sending him to his village, but without his son.' Tulkhan saw the marsh-dweller quickly swallow his anger as Kornel spoke.

'Ban?' Tulkhan lifted his arms to the marsh-dweller's son. The boy glanced to his father, who signalled that he should obey. Eagerly, the child ran into Tulkhan's arms. He had won the boy with sweet nuts and rides along the earthworks. Absently he stroked Ban's head, feeling the many tiny plaits the Marsh-dwellers used to confine their long hair. He met the father's eyes. 'Banuld-Chi, you will lead Kornel and his men through the marshes.'

The General watched as Kornel translated. The boy nudged Tulkhan's arm and pointed to the nuts. Tulkhan cracked one between his fingers. Ban tried to do the same trick with his small hands. The General grinned, and taking the nut from Ban he cracked it in his teeth as he would have done as a boy.

Kornel ceased his translation and turned back to the General. 'He asks why.'

'I have three boatloads of mercenaries coming across the T'Ronnyn Straits. I need you, Kornel, to take the shallow draft boats to the river mouth. By the time you get there, all the mercenaries will be waiting. You'll bring them over the marsh wall to me. That is why I need Banuld to guide you through the marshes. I will pay him for his services.'

Kornel nodded. 'Warn the mercenaries to build big fires and post watch when they make their camp at the river mouth. That should keep the narcts at bay.'

While he was aboard Piers' ship, Tulkhan had sent a message to Imoshen requesting the dispatch of the mercenary force. He poured three mugs of warm beer, offering them to Kornel and Banuld, who accepted his with surprise. 'To a swift passage through the marshes and a short siege!'

When the captain translated, Banuld added his own toast with an elaborate hand signal. Tulkhan looked to Kornel who explained, 'It's their blessing. *May your feet always find dry ground.*'

Tulkhan laughed and drained his beer, wiping his mouth. 'After crossing the marshes I can appreciate that!'

Kornel grinned, eyeing the remaining beer, and Tulkhan obliged. He needed their loyalty, even though he would send his own men with them; if either one betrayed him, he would be left here with the barest minimum of men and supplies.

Tulkhan lifted his mug. 'Sumair is a rich port. I hear her merchants live like princes. To the spoils of war!'

'The spoils of war!' Kornel's deep-set eyes gleamed.

'A BLOCKADE SHIP has arrived with a message.' Dyta stepped back to let a young soldier with a gingery moustache and freckled skin enter Imoshen's chamber.

He gave her a Ghebite bow and dug inside his jerkin to remove a sealed missive. 'Rawset, on behalf of General Tulkhan. I made the night crossing.'

'Bring food and warmed wine for two, Dyta,' Imoshen said. The woman departed and Imoshen accepted the message, noting that Rawset was careful not to meet her eyes or let their fingers make contact.

The residue of Tulkhan's presence remained on the paper, making her skin prickle with the memory of his touch. Lifting the missive to her face, she inhaled. What she learnt reassured her. Tulkhan had not written this under duress.

She rocked Ashmyr's basket while she broke the seal and read. As Tulkhan's words formed in her mind, his voice, his scent and his manner returned to her. She felt dizzy with his presence and the rediscovery of her love for him. Tears of longing swam in her vision but she blinked them away with fierce determination. So the General wanted his supplies and men to travel through the marshes. 'You know the contents, Rawset?'

He nodded.

The old woman returned with a tray.

'Dyta, tell Lightfoot the first shipload of his mercenaries will sail this morning,' Imoshen said. 'Eat while I write a reply, Rawset.' She took her scriber, dipped it in the ink then thought long and hard over a reply; so long, in fact, that the ink dried and she had to re-ink the scriber.

Telling the General her plans did not require a great deal of thought. It was how to word her reassurances that troubled Imoshen. She was sure some rumour of how things appeared between herself and Reothe would eventually reach the General. Finally she opted for formal courtesy. When the mercenaries reached Tulkhan, he would not doubt her loyalty.

'I want you to put this in General Tulkhan's hands, Rawset.' She placed the message on the table. 'And I want all communication that passes between the General and myself to come via you.'

Rawset swallowed, his Adam's apple bobbing. He pushed the plate aside. 'I will not see the General until after all three boatloads of mercenaries have been delivered to the marsh river mouth.'

Imoshen nodded and lifted the candle, pointing to her message. 'Hold it flat.'

She let hot wax drip to form a puddle then pressed her sixth finger into it to seal it. The heat stung. A rush of urgency filled her as she looked down into Rawset's face. She wanted to ensure his loyalty as she had ensured Lightfoot's. 'Can I trust you, Rawset of the Ghebites?'

He nodded. 'But I am no longer a Ghebite. I am General Tulkhan's man.'

'Then you are my man,' Imoshen whispered. She fought the urge to touch him with her sixth finger. 'You are mine.'

His eyes never left her face. 'I am yours.'

Imoshen smiled, stepping back. 'Good. Go now.'

FOUR NIGHTS LATER, torchlight flickered as the last shipload of mercenaries left for the marshlands and Imoshen stood on the docks to see them off. Tomorrow she would leave for the capital, escorting Reothe as her *honoured guest*. Once there she would prepare for a possible invasion, but she needed the support of the Keldon nobles, the church and the Ghebites to do this.

'T'Imoshen?' The harbourmaster approached.

Since this was her final evening in Northpoint, Imoshen had invited the town officials for warmed wine. In a blur of weariness, she led them back to the great hall where she performed the leave-taking ceremony, serving them with her own hands, a symbol of her service to Fair Isle. She said all the right things, but nothing could change the facts. From the lowliest candle trimmer to Imoshen herself, they faced an uncertain future.

At last they departed and Imoshen retreated to T'Ronnyn's Tower. She felt Ashmyr's weight as she climbed the stairs. All was quiet. The servants, their preparations completed, were already in bed.

The door to her room had been left ajar and she saw that the windows were also open. The candles had not been lit and the fire had been allowed to burn down to embers. Imoshen sniffed in annoyance.

Ashmyr slept soundly as she placed him in his basket, tucking the down-filled comforter around him. She straightened, arching her back, and slipped off her boots, wriggling her bare toes on the rug. It was cold, but there was no point in stirring up the flames until she closed the windows.

Padding lightly across the floor, she went to the semi-circular wall of windows and leant out to pull each one closed. The night was so clear she could almost see the lights of Tulkhan's ships across the straits. He had entrusted her to keep Fair Isle safe. She missed her great-aunt's advice; now, more than ever, she needed it.

If the rebels hadn't tried to assassinate Tulkhan, the Aayel might still be alive. Unarmed, he had fought off three attackers, which hadn't done his reputation any harm. But it was the Aayel's bravery Imoshen recalled. Her great-aunt had taken the blame on herself, saving Imoshen by committing suicide. That failed assassination attempt had cost Imoshen dearly.

As she crossed to the fireplace, a shape detached itself from the shadows. An assassin?

Fear ignited Imoshen. Light arced across the room, a thousand small comets of fire. Flames roared up in the grate, throwing crazy, leaping shadows, illuminating Reothe's arrested expression as he balanced precariously without his walking stick.

'Imoshen, don't!' Reothe's warning cut through the roaring in her head.

She staggered back several steps, almost tripping over the baby. With a gasp she discovered live coals glowing on his blanket, eating their way through to him. With a soundless cry of horror she plucked the coals from the cradle and threw them into the roaring fire.

No pain registered.

'Imoshen, the bed curtains.'

Hungry yellow flames licked at the thick material tied back against the bedposts. Pushing Reothe aside, she snatched the water pitcher and doused the fire.

The fire in the hearth dropped as suddenly as it had risen, but the room was still thick with the smell of smoke. All around her on the floor, the chair and her desk were the winking, glowing eyes of live coals.

Cursing under her breath, she snatched the hot coals from the furniture, dropping them into the jug, and stamped out those on the floor. Reothe lit the candles and rebuilt the fire, coaxing it to burn brightly. The sweet scent of fresh popping resin filled the room, overlaying the smell of charred material.

Imoshen went to the windows to empty the water jug of its charcoal sludge. When she turned, Reothe was just rising, one hand on the mantelpiece to steady himself.

He met her gaze, a rueful smile lighting his sharp features. 'Remind me never to surprise you.'

'I was thinking of the assassination attempt on Tulkhan.' She put the jug aside.

'Did you get all the live coals?'

'Yes.' Only then she did become aware of the pain in her fingers and feet. Gritting her teeth, she confronted Reothe. 'Why are you here?'

'I bribed your maid to go to bed early.'

'That is how, not why.'

'That was quite spectacular. If I had been an assassin, I would have been surprised enough for you to incapacitate me before I could strike. But it was also dangerous. Ashmyr –'

'Don't you think I know?' She inspected the sleeping infant, but he was blissfully unaware.

'You're burnt,' Reothe said. 'Where are your herbs?'

Imoshen was so weary that she found the idea of Reothe taking care of her insidiously sweet. 'The herbs are in the small cabinet behind my desk.'

Sinking into the chair, she watched him limp to the cabinet and study its contents. 'You don't need your walking stick?'

'I pace the parapets three times a day.'

Imoshen watched as he sniffed the glass jar's contents. 'You will find the –'

'I know what I am looking for. Healing might be your gift, but I have a working knowledge of herbal lore.'

She smiled at his tone. In pain but perversely happy, she waited as he returned with the soothing ointment. It was odd to find Reothe kneeling at her feet. A little quiver swept through her. His strong hand closed around her ankle and she turned her face away to hide the pain he caused her.

'Curse me, if it will help,' he urged.

Imoshen had to smile. She stole a look at him. He was watching her fondly. If only... A stab of loss made her gasp.

'I'm clumsy,' he apologised.

Imoshen shook her head, unable to speak. She resented the fact that she'd never had the chance to know Reothe without the fate of Fair Isle coming between them. He took her other foot and she looked into the flames to hide her thoughts.

'Now your hands.'

'I can do them.'

'Show me.'

When she did, she realised that bending her fingers around a bottle to take out the stopper would have been a challenge.

'Do not weep, Imoshen.'

'I am not weeping. My eyes leak.'

He laughed, and that hurt her far more than the burns, she wanted to hug that laugh and never relinquish its intimacy.

'My beautiful liar,' Reothe whispered. 'Don't look at me like that. I swear I will forget my vow.'

'What vow?'

He smiled mysteriously. 'You will not be able to hold the reins tomorrow. We will have to share my invalid wagon.'

Imoshen wanted to argue but he was right.

'Now your other hand,' he said.

Obediently, she offered her hand. The sweep of his long fingers was almost hypnotic. She could have sat like this for hours, bearing the pain just to have him near her, caring for her.

A quick smile illuminated his features. 'Now that I know I will have your company in the wagon, I will not insist on riding until you are well enough to do so. That was why I wanted to see you. It did not suit me to ride in a wagon like someone's grandfather.'

Imoshen snorted. 'I nearly set fire to the room because it did not suit your dignity to ride in a wagon? It would have been easier to send a message.'

'Easier, but not nearly as instructive.'

She drew a quick breath. 'You are an unprincipled creature, Reothe. Is everything and everyone grist for your mill?'

His smile faded, revealing his dagger-sharp intelligence. 'Ask yourself this, Imoshen. What is really important to you and what would you give up to ensure that outcome? I know my answer.'

'There we differ, Reothe, because my question is not what, but who. I will not sacrifice people for ideals –'

He laughed and stood. 'That is what you say. Maybe it is even what you believe. But I see you using True-people every day to serve your purpose. In denying your T'En nature you deny what you could be. Look what happened tonight.'

'This was an accident. You surprised me.'

'But why didn't you sense my presence?'

Imoshen looked away.

'What game are you playing, Imoshen? Pretending to be a Mere-woman when we both know –'

'I will not be lectured by you of all people!'

The baby woke with a shrill cry of panic. Coming to her feet, Imoshen gasped in pain and almost fell. Reothe caught her. The pair of them swayed as he struggled to keep his balance.

'Sit down, Imoshen, I'll bring him to you.'

When Reothe lowered the baby into her arms, she tried to undo the bodice of her gown but her hands were too sore. Wordlessly, Reothe knelt at her side, and his long fingers undid the lacings. Her breasts ached with the rush of milk. An equal rush of heat pooled within her.

Reothe tucked the bodice under her swollen breast and helped guide the baby's urgent mouth to her nipple. A gasp of relief escaped Imoshen. She pressed her forearm to her other breast to stem the flow of milk.

Reothe drew in a ragged breath. When he lifted his eyes to her face, she knew that he wanted her with every fibre of his being and her body responded with an instant tug of recognition that went beyond conscious thought.

She looked down and took a long, deep breath. It was a mistake. His body's scent had changed, triggering a rise in her heart rate. A dangerous, sweet languor stole the strength from her limbs.

'I...' She had to clear her throat. 'I will not compromise my vows.'

'I know.'

But he drew nearer to inhale her scent and shame filled her, flooding her cheeks, because she wanted him.

'You intoxicate me, Imoshen.'

'Please, don't do this.'

'Don't fear me.' The gentleness of his tone surprised her and he held her eyes. 'I won't trick you again. When you come to me, it will be of your own free will. That is my vow. Nothing less will satisfy me.'

Her mouth went dry and she seemed to feel her heart beating like a great drum, throbbing through her limbs, each beat a tide of desire, ebbing and rising through her flesh.

When the secondary meaning of his words hit her, tears stung her eyes. 'I trusted you –'

'I did not ask you to trust me. I asked you to join me. I told you I would win whatever the odds.' His voice was sweet and reasonable. Yet...

'Am I nothing but a tool to you, Reothe?' Imoshen asked, sadly.

'Come to me freely. You will be the breath in my body.' His eyes flared, the leaping firelight dancing in their dark depths. 'As one, we would be invincible.'

It came to her that T'Reothe was totally ruthless but honourable by his own code, and she realised that to bond with him meant much more than she had anticipated when she had agreed to their betrothal. A single tear, shed for her lost innocence, slipped down her cheek. Now she would never know the true bonding of the T'En.

She looked away, staring into the fire.

'You deny me,' Reothe whispered. 'I offer everything I am, and could be, yet you turn your face from me. How cruel is that?'

Swaying a little, he came to his feet. Stunned, he slowly made his way across the chamber. It pained her to see his limp was more pronounced.

He paused by the door, as she knew he would.

'I am weary of our battles, Imoshen. Tonight I am weary beyond thought. But my body heals, growing stronger every day.'

'What of your gifts?' It was out before she could stop herself.

'My gifts?' His eyes glittered. 'The T'En in me is an open wound. Every day I prod it without meaning to. Every touch sends me to my knees. The pain robs me of the power of thought and speech. You did this. You emasculated the last T'En warrior. Now who will save our people?'

'I didn't mean to,' Imoshen whispered. 'If it hurts you to use your T'En gifts, don't –'

He laughed softly. 'It is instinctive, Imoshen. Every day I am reminded of your cruel love. A love that would let me live in pain.'

'I am more sorry than you can know.'

His angry gaze met hers, frankly sceptical. 'Do not mock your gelding, T'Imoshen. The beast may throw you yet.'

Imoshen's heart redoubled its pace but she would not look down. For a long moment she dare not blink, then Reothe winced and felt for the doorjamb to steady himself.

She flinched in sympathy, understanding he had reached for his gift. 'Reothe?'

But he shook his head, closing the door on her sympathy.

Ashmyr stopping suckling, squirmed and gave a little cry. She lifted him to her shoulder, gritting her teeth at the pain in her hands. Though Reothe was gone, Imoshen's body trembled in the wake of his presence. Seeing to Ashmyr relaxed her.

'That's what you get for gulping your food,' she told the baby. A satisfied burp escaped him. She looked into his face. He was falling asleep again. 'No, you don't. You haven't finished.'

Her other breast ached. She tilted Ashmyr across her body and he woke up enough to latch onto her nipple and resume his feed. She leant her head against the back of the chair. Reothe had deliberately startled her. A rueful smile warmed her. She hoped he had enjoyed the show, but it worried her to have so little control.

Reothe believed she could heal him and she suspected he was right, but if she did, he would become the wild card in her deck. Reothe returned to his full capabilities was someone to be feared. Yet how could she live with herself if she let him suffer? Bitter self-knowledge filled her. She would let him suffer because it was safest. But she did not want to ride in the wagon with him.

Imoshen cursed softly and sought to heal herself.

Closing her eyes, she reached for her gift, only to find she'd exhausted it. Panic flared. This absence was worse than what she had felt when she had been training at the Aayel's side. Then she had not always found the little surge of warmth that hastened healing, but now she felt utterly drained of power.

Wearily, Imoshen opened her eyes and her gaze fell on a smear of ash, triggering a memory of flying coals, roaring unnatural flames. Comprehension shook her. The defensive burst had exhausted her reserves. Already she could feel a mind-numbing fatigue creeping upon her. It seemed there was a price to pay for the use of her gifts. What else was Reothe keeping from her? If only she knew how the T'En trained their young.

Imoshen closed her eyes as waves of pain and weariness swept over her. She could not stop an assassin now.

This jolted her. Was there no way to defend herself? Sifting through her reserves she found nothing and she opened her T'En awareness.

A bright flare of external anger drew her questing senses. Somewhere in the tower below her, a group of True-men were gambling, and their avaricious intensity called to her. She could taste it on her tongue, sharpening her awareness.

The sensation reminded her of the time she'd caught the Ghebites betting on their fighting birds. The build-up of their lust for blood and violence had almost overwhelmed her. That day she had only just managed to channel it into destroying the birds. Now understanding flooded through her as she grasped the principle involved.

Four men crouched two floors below her. She could sense their eager reaction to the turn of a card. One was a Ghebite, the other three were locals. It was the Ghebite who interested her. He was a mass of impulses, anger because he was losing, brittle fear because he suspected the Citadel guards of cheating him, though he couldn't prove it, and underlying all this was the threat to his honour. He was looking for an excuse to challenge one of them. To lose was one thing, to lose all night to men who had so recently been his enemy was too much.

The flames of his fury licked at his composure. Imoshen realised it would take only one little push to make him draw his weapon, and she could siphon off the energy of this confrontation to rebuild her reserves.

She needed it. Her hands and feet cried out to be healed and her vulnerability urged her to arm herself, but... She would not trigger violence and death to supplement her gift. What manner of creature would do such a thing?

Imoshen looked up, aware of the room, the dying fire and the sleeping baby. She was not that T'En creature.

Not now, not ever!

TULKHAN SAVOURED THE productive buzz of his men at work. They'd widened the ditch until it was twice as broad as he was tall and as deep. Normally it would have been filled with sharpened stakes but there was little timber. What little there was had been used to support the tunnels. He had two teams digging under the port's walls but it was hard work in the boggy soil.

The General stamped his feet to get the circulation going and started out, only to be stopped by a cry from little Ban. Since Kornel and the marsh-dweller left to escort the mercenaries, the boy had followed Tulkhan everywhere. Ban slipped his hand into Tulkhan's large one, a question on his lips. Without Kornel to translate, the General could only guess what the boy was asking. Ban pointed eagerly to where the horses were picketed.

'We're not riding that sorry excuse for a horse today,' Tulkhan told him, aware that the child was listening to the tone of his voice. 'Today we will choose the place for our cavalry to practise.'

The boy watched as Tulkhan paced out the area within the defences, while his men waited for orders. 'I want this earth dug up to a depth of one hand, turned over then levelled.' It was almost level now, but the soil needed to be soft and evenly turned so that the galloping horses could wheel without injury. It took years of training for man and beast to act as one and Tulkhan did not intend to waste that with avoidable injuries. 'I need hides prepared for target practice and shelters built for the horses. Get moving.'

He did not know how long it would be before the cavalry arrived, but the knowledge that he considered it a certainty would cheer his men.

Come dusk the boy fell asleep and, as Tulkhan tucked the furs around him, the General looked up to see Rawset had returned. 'What news?'

Rawset stepped into the shelter offering two sealed messages. 'I dropped the last shipload of mercenaries at the river mouth this morning. Kornel was already waiting there. I bring you word from T'Imoshen and the Commander of your elite guard.'

'Good.' Tulkhan hardly heard him. His hands closed on Imoshen's message. 'You must be hungry. Go.'

As Rawset, left rubbing his forehead, Tulkhan slid his thumb nail under the wax seal and tilted the paper to the candlelight. The words were those of one official to another, Imoshen the statesman to Tulkhan, her war general. There was no word from Imoshen the woman to Tulkhan, her lover. Imoshen's hasty flowing script made her come vividly to life. He could almost see her elegantly chiselled features and feel her presence so strongly that for a moment he wondered if she had laid some T'En trick upon the message. When he lifted the finely made paper to his face he could smell her scent and ached for her touch.

Removing the wax seal, he held it in his hand, noting the tear-shaped impression of Imoshen's fingertip. Turning it to the light, he studied the whorls of her fingerprint, fascinated by their double loop. The recurring pattern seemed to draw him in.

'General?' Rawset's voice recalled him. Something in the man's tone told him it was not the first time he had spoken.

Tulkhan looked up, surprised and a little unsettled to see the candles now guttered in their own wax.

'T'Imoshen will be in T'Diemn soon. She said any message was to go from your hands to mine to hers.' Rawset rubbed his forehead as if he had a headache.

Tulkhan understood Imoshen's fears. 'You will be my personal emissary. The merchants of T'Diemn can supply a fast ship.'

Rawset looked relieved and when his hand fell to his side, Tulkhan noticed what appeared to be a red birthmark where he had been rubbing his forehead.

'Stay until the mercenaries arrive and you can take back news of that. Have a seat.'

Rawset seemed to have difficulty switching from correct junior officer to companion, so Tulkhan poured him a warm beer. 'Why don't I remember you?'

'I was part of King Gharavan's auxiliary army,' he answered uneasily. 'When you offered us the chance to join you, I decided to stay.'

'Why?'

Rawset looked down.

'Answer freely,' Tulkhan urged. 'I am a fair man.'

A relieved smile lit his young face. 'That is what I heard, and partly why I took my oath of allegiance to you.'

'Only partly?' Tulkhan was amused by his ingenuous reply.

Rawset's eyes widened and he held Tulkhan's gaze earnestly. 'I never wanted to fight, General. I wanted to be a priest, but my village had to supply men for the Ghebite king. Remember the far western desert campaign? I had no choice.'

'Tell me, lapsed priest. Why didn't you agree to go with King Gharavan, then desert him and return to your family?'

Rawset wiped the beer's froth from his moustache. 'There would be no honour in desertion. Besides, with the things I have seen these last three years...' He shrugged sadly. 'I have lost my faith. It is a terrible thing to believe in nothing.'

'Is it?' Tulkhan asked, surprised.

'Of course. I felt adrift until...' He ran down.

'Until?'

But Rawset would not be drawn.

The General changed the subject. Questioning Rawset, he learned how the Ghebite Empire's never-ending wars were resented by the conquered countries which had to supply men and arms for the insatiable army.

Tulkhan could not remember a time when Gheeaba hadn't been at war. In his grandfather Seerkhan's day, the wars had been tribal and had been to unite the Ghebites. Then, to conquer and expand became the point of Ghebite existence; but now Tulkhan wondered how long this could go on. How long before Gheeaba splintered into a dozen warring kingdoms?

Would it matter if it did? His own ambivalence surprised Tulkhan.

He caught Rawset watching him and realised he had taken out Imoshen's message and was smoothing it between his fingers, over and over. 'She gave you no word for me?'

Rawset shook his head and Tulkhan folded the message, slipping it inside his jerkin, where he could feel it lodged against his skin, above his heart. He dismissed Rawset, then remembered there was another message to be read.

Jarholfe had hired a merchant scribe, who had written in the common trading tongue, but Tulkhan could detect Jarholfe's forceful personality in the words. According to this man, Imoshen had taken Reothe for her lover. They had been meeting in her chamber late at night.

Tulkhan refused to believe it. There had to be a simple explanation. Resolutely, he held Jarholfe's note to the candle flame and watched it burn. But he could not erase the seed of doubt the words had planted.

Chapter Eight

LYING ON THE farmhouse's best bed, Imoshen waited for Mother Reeve to change her bandages. Their journey had proved more tiring than she had expected, and when the Reeves offered the hospitality of their prosperous home, Imoshen had gratefully accepted.

All day Reothe had driven the wagon, playing her servant as though he hadn't threatened to unseat her from the throne only the night before. He was also exhausted and had retired early.

At last Mother Reeve arrived with warm water, clean cloth and herbs. While the bandages were being changed, Imoshen heard how the woman's family had rebuilt the shell of their farmhouse when it was burnt out during Tulkhan's campaign. Now several bonded sons and daughters and the rest of the younger children all lived under the one roof. But they had plans for two more wings to house their large brood. Doubtless, Imoshen would have been treated to the life histories of every family member if the woman hadn't been called away to serve dinner.

Propped up against the duck-down pillows, Imoshen watched as Ashmyr was bathed by the three youngest daughters. They fussed over him until he fell into an exhausted sleep from a surfeit of attention.

Alone at last, Imoshen wriggled, sinking deeper into the pillows and, now that her gift had been restored, she set about healing her burns.

Clearing her mind of all extraneous thought, she concentrated on the source of her healing gift. It was like walking a familiar path. She no longer had to strain to discern the markers, and when she reached the pool of her power, it had refilled. This time it was pure and clear; it was her own reservoir, not the absorption of external violent passion.

She visualised her hands dipping into the healing pool, slipped her feet in, and relaxed. A warmth flowed through her body. She sank deeper into her self-induced trance, willing the blistered skin of her hands and feet to heal. When the process was finished, she felt sleep steal upon her and welcomed it, not stirring until the cock crowed at dawn.

With Ashmyr's first cry, the young Reeve girls entered. The middle one picked the baby up, laughing when he smiled at her.

The older girl placed a bowl on the bedside chest. 'Are you ready to have your dressings changed, T'Imoshen?'

Last night the changing of the dressings had elicited hot tears of pain. Today she hoped there would be no more dressings.

'Baby's hungry,' the littlest girl announced, and her big sister brought him to the bed.

Imoshen bared her breast, still clumsy with the bandages. She fed Ashmyr while the eldest girl pulled back the covers and carefully peeled the linen away from the soles of her feet. Her gasp made Imoshen look up.

'What?' asked Mother Reeve, entering with a breakfast tray.

The girl pointed wordlessly at Imoshen's feet.

The mother put the tray on the blanket chest and came over. 'Bless us, there's not a sign of blisters.'

The others demanded a look. Their mother let them see, then chased the girls out and poured Imoshen a hot spiced milk.

'Thank you,' Imoshen said softly. The woman would not meet her eyes. 'I did appreciate your care last night.'

'It was not my herbs that healed those burns. Why come here and call on my help when you could heal yourself?'

'I needed time to prepare and... this was the first chance I had to heal myself.'

'That baby needs a change.' Mother Reeve took him before Imoshen could put him to the other breast.

When the woman returned Ashmyr to Imoshen, her hands brushed Imoshen's bare skin and Imoshen caught a clear impression of a small boy of about three. He had the same red golden hair as the youngest girl, but he also had the T'En eyes. Imoshen sensed sorrow. 'What is wrong with your little boy?'

Mother Reeve gasped and made the sign to ward off evil.

Imoshen caught her arm. 'You have been kind. Let me help.'

'Even you cannot help. His is no simple affliction that can be set to rights by a few herbs and a little healing.' The woman went to the end of the bed.

'At least let me see him,' Imoshen urged. 'If I cannot help, he will be no worse off than he was before.'

The woman's work-worn hands slowed as she unwrapped Imoshen's other foot. 'This one is as good as the first.' She met Imoshen's eyes. 'No, T'En healer, there's nothing can be done for my boy. I've seen it happen before. I took sick while I was carrying him. He looks perfectly normal, but he cannot hear a word we say. It...' Her face worked as she fought her sorrow. 'It makes it hard for him. The other children – not ours, you understand – the others tease him because not only can't he hear but he –'

'Has the T'En eyes,' Imoshen finished for her.

The woman nodded. 'My mother had the T'En eyes. Sometimes it will skip a generation.'

'I'm sorry. You are right. There is nothing I can do if his hearing was damaged before he was born. The T'En can aid healing but they cannot replace –'

There was a shout of laughter from the hall and the door swung open. A small boy darted inside, followed by his sister. He slipped under the bed and there he stayed crowing delightedly as both his mother and sister tried vainly to drag him out.

Imoshen laughed and cut short the woman's apology. 'He won't bother me.'

Mother Reeve looked doubtful. 'Have it your way. I've got enough to do, what with the leader of your guards and T'Reothe himself sitting down to eat at my table, not to mention three dozen Ghebite soldiers camped in my fields. I've no time to play games.'

She bustled off with her daughter, leaving Imoshen to eat her breakfast. The boy soon tired of hiding and climbed out to peer over the bed base at Imoshen.

She smiled. He smiled back. She tore off the honeyed crust of the hot roll and used it to lure the child closer.

In no time he was sitting on the bed spilling crumbs on the covers. He drank all her spiced milk and finished the last of the bread, then looked hopefully for more. He was so bright. It was cruel to think he would always be excluded from conversation because of his hearing loss and then excluded again because he had the T'En eyes.

She placed a tentative hand on his head and probed as the boy looked up at her trustingly. His awareness was bright and untouched by sound, but so sharp with colours, scents and sensations that it flooded her like a fresh awakening. She opened herself to it, searching for something she could trip or trigger.

Then she felt a snap inside his small being. With a leap of understanding, he recognised what she was doing and rushed to meet her mind. His laughter filled her with joy. A physical embrace followed a heartbeat after the mental touch.

'What's going on here?'

Imoshen pulled back, terribly tired. She had no strength to protest when Mother Reeve snatched the boy.

'Even the T'En healers of old could not restore a severed limb. You reach too high, T'Imoshen!'

Mother Reeve's words pierced Imoshen. She had been arrogant to invade the boy's privacy without his mother's approval. 'Forgive me. I should have asked.'

'What's wrong?' asked the teenage daughter.

Imoshen opened her mouth to speak but the girl laughed and turned to her little brother. 'No, you cannot have another honey bun. You've had two already.'

'Three,' Imoshen said. 'He ate mine as well.'

Then the three of them fell silent, staring at the boy who wriggled until his mother put him down. He ran over to the window where a bird had landed on the sill and was pecking at the glass, framed by one of the little wooden squares.

'How did you know he wanted another bun?' Imoshen asked.

The girl shrugged. 'I... I saw a bun and –'

'Now he wants me to open the window so he can touch the bird,' Mother Reeve whispered, awed.

Understanding came to Imoshen. 'I tried to help him communicate. I felt something open up inside him.'

'But half-bloods don't have gifts,' the mother protested.

Remembering Cariah, Imoshen asked, 'Do you have ancestors who served the Ancients?'

The girl glanced to her mother.

Imoshen nodded.

The mother went so pale her daughter helped her to the blanket chest, where she collapsed, leaning against the wall.

The girl fanned her mother with her apron until the woman pushed her aside to confront Imoshen. 'Think what you have done to my boy. I loved him when he could not hear, now you've taken him from us.'

Imoshen was appalled. 'At least now, he can let you know when he wants things. He won't be so lonely.'

'Lonely?' The mother fixed Imoshen with bright, angry eyes. 'How can you say that when everyone he meets will shy away from him? T'En eyes were bad enough, but power as well? Ehh, now they'll say he's T'En touched!' And she burst into tears.

Imoshen's heart contracted. Had she condemned the boy to even worse ostracism? 'I'm sorry. I was only trying to help.'

The child wandered over to his mother. Climbing up into her lap, he put his arms around her neck. Abruptly her tears stopped and she stared at him in wonder.

'By the Aayel,' she whispered. 'I can feel his love for me!'

Imoshen's eyes stung.

Mother Reeve looked at Imoshen, her sun-lined face serious. 'I'll admit you meant no harm, T'Imoshen. But this?'

Imoshen shrugged. 'I will not lie to you. The gifts are a two-edged sword. I awakened something that was already in him. It might have slept all his life, or it might have wakened when he reached puberty and was driven to communicate. I only hope you and he can live with this.'

'Why shouldn't we?' The girl smiled, but the mother's expression told Imoshen she could foresee difficulties.

'My door will always be open to you,' Imoshen said.

A deep voice yelled up the stairs.

'The others are ready to go,' the girl said. 'Come, T'Imoshen, we'd best get you packed.'

'I can manage.' Imoshen tugged at the bandages on her hands. The young woman came over to help her. 'At least today I can walk down the steps.'

But she discovered when she stood that her new skin was too tender to walk on. By the time Imoshen had been carried down the steps and out to the wagon by two healthy farm lads the daughters had brought down Ashmyr and the rest of their things.

Imoshen looked up to see Mother Reeve at the open window with the boy in her arms. They were not smiling, but he waved and she had a feeling of sudden happiness and a visual picture of a bird taking flight. It was a lovely sensation. But what if the child was angry? What images might a fierce temper tantrum produce?

Normally the T'En powers did not arise until puberty when the young person was mature enough to cope with them. Perhaps it would have been better if she had left well enough alone. Imoshen decided from now on she would confine herself to simple, physical healings.

'YOU HAVE OVEREXTENDED yourself with these healings,' Reothe said reprovingly.

Imoshen gripped the back of the chair, as her head spun. She reached blindly for the wine jug, but it was empty. 'Would you have me turn away those in need?'

'What about your needs? You will do them no good if you burn down like a candle.'

Imoshen sank into the chair. It was only natural that she minister to the townsfolk of Lakeside, but the sheer number of people who needed healing overwhelmed her. The effort made her ravenously hungry. 'I will be fine. Besides, it is mostly herbs and tinctures. I only add a little of the gift to aid the healing, if I must.' The baby gave a cry from the back room. 'See to Ashmyr and ask the tea-house keeper to send in more food.'

'Your servant.' Reothe gave her a mock obeisance.

Imoshen peered through the windows to the square outside where people waited patiently under delicate umbrellas of painted silk. Music and singing came to her through the many glass panels of the tea-house entrance. A troupe of entertainers were performing for their captive audience.

She had stopped in Lakeside to gauge the townspeople's mood. They had suffered twice during the Ghebite campaign. Once under Tulkhan's initial attack and the second time when King Gharavan overran the town. He had burned the outlying houses on the lake's banks, but the older stone buildings, linked by their intricate arched bridges above the lake's shallows, had escaped the brunt of Gharavan's anger. He had saved that for T'Diemn.

This was her first visit to Lakeside, and it was every bit as beautiful as the minstrels claimed. Originally the inhabitants had built fortified houses on the lake's scattered islands, only to link them as time passed. This square was the largest area of open land in old Lakeside, faced by three-storey houses dating from before the Age of Consolidation four hundred years ago.

Imoshen had feared the townsfolk of Lakeside would resent her, after the late Empress had failed to protect them. But when she had arrived with Ashmyr in her arms, Lakeside officials had turned out to greet her. People packed the square, singing a canticle in praise of the T'En. Imoshen realised that she and Reothe represented Fair Isle's glorious past and the people's hope for a prosperous future.

This was confirmed when the mayor had given them the deep obeisance reserved for the Empress and her consort, saying, 'We heard that the rebels had been pardoned and sent home, that T'Reothe himself stood at your side, T'Imoshen. Truly, Lakeside is honoured to host the T'En.'

'The honour is ours,' Imoshen had replied. It was rumoured Lakeside was loyal to the rebels. She needed to win over the townsfolk. 'Let your people know I am ready to heal the sick.'

But she had been healing since noon and now the shadows lengthened. Jarholfe's men stood outside the shop where normally people would be drinking and eating. The little outdoor tables had been pushed to one side and people waited, the weakest on carry beds under the shade of the awning.

The tea-house keeper delivered a tray of fresh food and Imoshen thanked the woman who had turned her premises over to them at a moment's notice. 'I am sorry to have lost you your afternoon's custom.'

'You did at that. But come tomorrow they'll all be here again, sitting in the very chair where you sit, telling of how their cousin's youngest was healed by you. So don't you worry.'

Imoshen had to smile. 'Did Reothe say the baby needed me?'

The woman shook her head. 'He's in the private room back there, singing to the babe.'

'Reothe's singing?'

The woman nodded.

Unable to stop herself, Imoshen crept to the far door to find Reothe sitting in a swing-chair slung from the ceiling with Ashmyr in his arms. He faced a courtyard, its ornamental garden designed to promote peace and harmony, and he was unaware of her as he swayed gently. Once she could never have crept up on him like this. She felt as if she was intruding.

His voice was a deep murmur, inherently musical. Though she did not recognise the song, she knew the words were High T'En. Imoshen was enchanted. She wanted to go to Reothe and cup his face in her hands, but she contented herself with approaching and stroking Ashmyr's soft cheek.

Reothe looked up. Imoshen leant closer. She wanted to kiss Reothe, not with desire but...

'T'Imoshen?' The woman spoke from the doorway with the empty tray in her hands. 'They are asking for you.'

'Thank you.' Imoshen met Reothe's eyes. 'I must go.'

'Do not overwork your gift for, unless you heal me, I cannot walk death's shadow to bring you back,' he warned.

He was speaking of the day she turned Cariah and her lover's dead bodies to stone. The effort had drained her to the point of death. Only Reothe's willingness to risk his soul in death's shadow had saved her. 'I never thanked you –'

'I never wanted thanks!'

She heard voices in the front room. 'Nevertheless –'

'Just go, Imoshen. Do not insult me.'

Hurt, she left him.

Six people waited. Imoshen's heart sank. One man lay on a stretcher which had been placed on a long table, his body covered by a blanket, his face turned away from her. Four of them looked to her. The fifth lifted his head. His eyes were milked over with the blindness that came on some people in old age, even though his body was still vigorous. The woman who led him placed a hand on his shoulder.

Imoshen had never attempted to heal blindness before. She suspected that this man's kind of blindness could be reversed. But if she healed him she feared it would exhaust her.

Crossing to the table where the tea-house keeper had laid out food and spiced wine, Imoshen poured herself a drink and drained it quickly. Then she tore into the pastry with its tasty filling, licking her fingers before dusting the crumbs from her lips. The food stopped her limbs trembling but she knew she could not go on much longer.

Imoshen was aware of them waiting expectantly.

'One moment.' She beckoned Jarholfe from his post at the door. 'Please tell the people this will be my last healing for today.'

Jarholfe nodded and objections greeted his announcement. Imoshen steeled herself. She doubted she had the strength to help the blind man today, so she would see what she could do for the sleeping man on the stretcher. Stepping closer, she took his hand in both of hers. 'Tell me what is wrong with him.'

Too late, a surge of awareness shot up her arm.

Hard garnet eyes sprang open and the man's sword leapt up from under the blanket. Its point pressed under her breast bone. From behind his bandages the man's fierce T'En eyes fixed on her. 'We want to see T'Reothe.'

Imoshen schooled her features. 'You had but to ask.'

Taking the blade, she turned the point gently away from her body, her eyes never leaving the rebel's. But if she had blocked this man's immediate threat, she had not deflected his purpose. Two of his companions stepped behind her, their desperation palpable. One arm snaked around her neck, and she felt the sharp edge of a blade nudge her exposed throat.

Urgently she tried to touch Reothe's awareness to warn him, but he was blind to her questing senses. Regret and frustration raged through her, for she had made them both vulnerable by refusing to heal him.

She swallowed. 'You do not need to threaten me. All rebels have been given amnesty. Why not go home?'

'My home no longer stands. And what is a home without the ones you love?' a woman asked, voice harsh with heartbreak.

Imoshen sensed stark desolation. She licked her lips. 'A home without love is a shell. Yet what is violence but a –'

'Don't listen to her T'En tricks,' the man with the hard garnet eyes warned, as he swung his feet to the floor.

The blind man's head lifted like a dog who had caught an interesting scent. He pointed revealing six-fingered hands. 'Someone is in there!'

Imoshen's heart faltered. Her son must not be used as a lever. Anxious to deflect them, she raised her voice. 'T'Reothe, put your plaything away. You have visitors.'

While the rebel leader unwound the bandages from his head, the two who held Imoshen shuffled around to face the back of the room.

If Reothe was surprised to see Imoshen held at knife point, he did not reveal it. He lifted his arms. 'My people, why have you come to me with violence in your hearts?'

'We had to see for ourselves,' the leader said.

'See what, Amyce? That I am unharmed? No one holds me at knife point.' Reothe glided towards them. Only Imoshen knew how much it cost him to move so smoothly. 'Release T'Imoshen.'

The woman relaxed her grip but the knife stayed at Imoshen's throat.

Reothe's eyes narrowed. 'Please forgive my people, Imoshen. They are foolish but sincere.'

She felt the wariness of her captors and smelled the change in their body scent.

'All rebels have been granted amnesty. I have no quarrel with these people.' Imoshen noticed the blind man whisper something to his guide, who darted into the back room. Praying the woman would not find Ashmyr, Imoshen almost missed Reothe's subtle signal. He beckoned her.

Imoshen took a deep breath and raised her hand to meet Reothe's. His fingers closed on hers. She stepped forward into the knife. The blade slipped harmlessly past her throat as the woman's arm dropped to her side. Relief flooded Imoshen, but only for a heartbeat, then she heard furniture being moved in the back room.

Every nerve in Imoshen's body screamed a warning but she remained outwardly composed. Reothe's hand squeezed hers and he pulled her towards him, turning her so that she stood on his weak left side. She could feel the trembling of his muscles.

Imoshen faced the hardened veterans, all armed with weapons which had been concealed from Jarholfe's men. The Ghebites would come in answer to her cry, but by then she and Reothe could be dead. Although she did not believe the rebels intended to kill them, the tension in Reothe's body was not reassuring. And what would she do if the woman found her child?

Imoshen tried to reach for her gifts, but she was drained by the afternoon's healing and unfocused by her concern for Ashmyr.

Reothe slung his arm over Imoshen's shoulder, letting her take some of his weight. 'We are the last two T'En. We –'

'Look what I found, the Ghebite General's brat!' crowed the woman. She ran into the room with Ashmyr held out in front of her, his little legs kicking in distress. A cry of protest escaped Imoshen.

'The child is mine!' Reothe said, his arm tightening on Imoshen's shoulders. The woman hesitated. 'But he has the Ghebite's hair.'

'I touched his mind before he was born. He will be my tool when he grows up. Return him –'

'To me.' Imoshen stepped forward, her arms trembling with fury. She wanted every last one of them dead.

The air seemed to vibrate between them as Imoshen took Ashmyr from the woman's unresisting hands. At the first touch of her son, a rush of heat flooded Imoshen's body, bringing with it that familiar metallic taste of power on her tongue.

Her senses became heightened. She sensed the rebels' pounding hearts and their strained minds opened to her. Fever-pitch tension sang on the air, swamping her senses.

'Go quietly now, and quickly,' Reothe urged. 'You do not know how close you have come to death. Just as T'Imoshen can heal with a touch, she can kill.'

Had Reothe regained enough of his gift to sense her state? She tried to search his perception, but he was a blind spot. No, not blind. She saw his eyes widen and knew if he was bluffing before, now he was aware of the gifts moving in her.

'Go,' Reothe ordered.

The woman backed away from her, hands raised in a defensive gesture.

'There are Ghebite guards outside,' the leader growled, his voice thick with hate. Imoshen could taste it, rich as gravy.

'Those Ghebites obey my orders,' Reothe said.

Imoshen saw Reothe beckon her. Choosing not to move, she remained between him and the rebels. Like her, Reothe carried a knife, but two short blades would be poor protection against swords in the hands of killers. Worse, Reothe was crippled and she was holding Ashmyr.

The rebels made no move to leave. Tension rose another notch, wooing her senses with its cruel promise of violence.

Imoshen felt empowered. A laugh escaped her. Why was she thinking like a True-woman when she could turn their own violence back upon them? It was so tempting. Power trickled from the pores of her body. Not one of them would meet her eyes.

'My people,' Reothe whispered. 'Have you forgotten? I said the day would come when Imoshen and I would unite and lead Fair Isle.'

'But the Ghebite General isn't dead,' the bitter woman objected.

The blind man had gravitated to his guide's side, and Imoshen could see his six-fingered hands opening and closing. His senses were sharpened by the lack of sight. She could tell he was reacting to the build-up of her T'En gifts. Beads of sweat clung on his sun-bronzed forehead. The smell of his fear assailed her nostrils, exotic as any perfume.

'Yes, the General still lives.' The leader was oblivious to the danger.

Imoshen focused on him. Bringing this man to his knees would be sweet.

'Tulkhan lives,' Reothe conceded, 'because it suits me.'

Imoshen sensed the path Reothe wove between lies and half-truths. It made her wonder how many lies he had told her to gain her trust.

The rebel leader frowned. 'General Tulkhan –'

'Serves me!' Reothe said. 'He serves me by capturing Port Sumair and killing King Gharavan. Do you think I want Fair Isle swarming with mainland soldiers again this summer?'

Imoshen's vision faded as everything fell into place and she understood why Reothe was cooperating with her. She could feel him at her back, her beautiful betrayer.

Her gift readiness rose another notch. The power had to be expelled. She wanted to strike out. Their suffering and deaths would further empower her. Exultation filled her.

The street door opened.

'T'Imoshen, the people will not leave. They...' Jarholfe stiffened as he saw the drawn weapons. He looked to Imoshen for orders. He was her tool. He would kill at her command. Death and bloodshed. It was hers to call down.

A savage joy flooded Imoshen. It both frightened and exhilarated her to discover the T'En part of her would thrive on their deaths. No. The power was only a source, the outcome was hers to choose. Death or life.

'Not death. Hold your sword, Jarholfe.' Imoshen moved before she could give in to the urge for violence. Her free hand covered the blind man's face, fingertips spanning his closed lids.

His scream cut the air. As he dropped to his knees, she sank with him. The blind man plucked weakly at her arm and a keening moan issued from his throat with each ragged breath. Imoshen was only vaguely aware of the others, of chairs turning over, of Reothe's raised voice and of fierce Ghebite accents. She focused on searing the blind man's eyes clear of their milky film. It took three long breaths and it was not gentle.

When she felt no more obstructions, she let her hand drop and he pitched forward, falling face first to the floor. His guide caught him. Cradling his head, she cast Imoshen a look of pure hatred.

Reothe pulled Imoshen to her feet. She found the room still and silent. The Ghebites stood in the doorway, weapons drawn, uncertain while the rebels looked confused, as if they had forgotten the reason for their anger.

'How could you do this?' A sob escaped the woman on the floor. Everyone turned. She hugged the injured man to her breast. 'You are a healer!'

'It was not gentle. I am sorry,' Imoshen whispered.

'Sorry?' the rebel leader repeated, but even he fought to recall his anger. 'She reveals her true nature. Now do you see what she is, T'Reothe?'

'T'Imoshen?' Jarholfe prompted uneasily. He and his men were ready to kill at her command but, to her relief, Imoshen no longer craved violence.

She had averted it, yet the knowledge that it had come so close sat heavily on her. 'These people are free to go. I will have no blood shed in anger this day. Go!'

The rebels sheathed their weapons and left.

Jarholfe crossed the room to join Imoshen. 'Do you want them followed and killed?'

She flinched. Was murder so easy for some people? 'No. Let them go.'

Trembling, Imoshen reached for Jarholfe's arm. The physical contact told her that he was confused and angry, but too afraid to speak out. A grey mist of weariness obscured her vision and she leaned on him. 'Help me to the table and then see to your men.'

When he had gone, Reothe tried to place a wine glass in her hand. 'Drink this.'

'Reothe.' The baby gave a cry, startled by her tone. 'How can you offer me wine when you will betray me the first chance you get? I have it from your own lips!'

'You mistake me, Imoshen.' Reothe took one step back. 'I told them only what they needed to hear. I had to buy time.'

'Time for what? Time for you to betray General Tulkhan?'

He backed into a table, steadying himself. 'They were ready to kill and so were you. I saw it in your eyes. You are the one who talks of compassion. Today I averted bloodshed. You could have taken one or two of them down with you, but what of Ashmyr and me? Do you think I could stand by and let them kill you? What possessed you to take vengeance on the blind one?'

A bitter laugh escaped her. 'You are the one who is blind. And don't talk to me of Ashmyr. I have often wondered why you treat him as if he were your own child. What did you do to my child before he was born?'

'T'En healer must see me!' a familiar voice cried.

Imoshen went to rise, but before she could, the door was thrown open. The blind man broke free of Jarholfe's men. He stumbled into the room, stopped and glared around, blinking fiercely. When he saw Imoshen, he ran to her, dropping to his knees. 'Why did you do it? I would have killed you.'

Smiling, Imoshen lifted his face so she could study his eyes. They were the clear golden-hazel of the Dawn people who had lived in Fair Isle before her kind; another hybrid, part Ancient, part T'En. 'I am sorry it hurt you.'

'T'Imoshen,' he whispered, tears running freely down his cheeks. Clasping her free hand, he kissed her sixth finger. 'I have done terrible things in the name of the T'En, but today I have seen what that name means.'

Imoshen shook her head, for today she had seen what she could become.

'Let me serve you, T'En healer.'

'Serve me?' Imoshen shook her head again. 'All I ask is that you and your friends hold yourselves ready should I call for help. You owe me nothing.'

He gave her the deep obeisance, lifting both hands to his forehead and backing out of the room.

'Do you win them over intentionally, Imoshen?' Reothe muttered softly. 'Or is it part of your gift?'

The thought surprised her. Her gift was a dangerous thing. When Reothe was whole, did the T'En side of him grow drunk on the suffering of others? She could tell he was trying to catch a glimpse of her thoughts. But he pushed too far, and collapsed in a chair.

She should heal him. It was wrong to leave him vulnerable. It weakened her as well. Her first instinct was to go to him, but she didn't. She sat there, listening to his ragged gasps, as she battled the urge to restore his gifts.

'Look what you have done to me,' he whispered, voice vibrating with anguish. 'Crippled, I cannot help you. All I have left is my tongue. But when I use it to save us, you accuse me of betraying you!'

'I don't know what to believe anymore,' Imoshen admitted. 'Everything you say is plausible.' Guilt assailed her. He spoke with such sincerity and his suffering was real. Imoshen poured wine, her hand shaking.

Ashmyr bobbed against her breast, hopeful for a feed. Absently, she changed his position. He drank greedily.

His sucking slowed and he looked up at her. Imoshen could not help smiling.

His little six-fingered hand grasped her bodice as if he would not let her escape. He was so precious. How could she protect him when her own life hung in the balance?

Like a physical sensation, she could feel Reothe watching them, and his claims about the baby returned to her. But she was too tired to think. Already she could feel the mind-numbing weariness caused by the over-extension of her gifts creeping up on her.

'Imoshen?' Reothe's breath dusted her cheek. Startled, she looked up to find him kneeling at her side. 'You must heal me. You need me at your back.'

He was right, his weakness made her vulnerable. But her eyes wouldn't focus. 'I must sleep.'

She heard him call the tea-house keeper. They urged her to stand. She walked through a mist of nothingness, then climbed steps, so many steps. At last she felt a bed and welcoming cool sheets. When hands tried to take Ashmyr from her, she tightened her grip.

'Let him go. I'll look after him,' Reothe urged.

No. Reothe would steal his soul. But the Ancients had already done that, and returned it for a price.

'Very well. Rest easy, Imoshen. I will watch over you both.' Strangely enough, she knew in this she could trust him.

Chapter Nine

WHEN THE LOOKOUTS signalled the mercenaries' arrival, Tulkhan climbed the earthworks and held little Ban so that he could see his father's return. Then Tulkhan sent orders to the cook to break out the beer and not stint on the evening meal.

But before they could celebrate, he had to meet the new mercenary leader and see this contract which Imoshen had signed on his behalf. In Gheeaba a woman would never sign a contract on her own behalf, let alone her husband's. He smiled fondly. Typical of Imoshen, she had no idea how deeply she had insulted him.

It was just on dusk when Tulkhan met Lightfoot. After reading the contract, he had to admit he could not pick fault with the terms. He pointed to the signature. 'This is your name?'

The man nodded. 'Lightfoot. Leader of the mercenaries. When I told the men the news...' He looked up at Tulkhan, his expression hard. 'Tourez betrayed us. The men want his blood.'

'Get in line. I'll add my signature and you can sign again.' Tulkhan said. 'You made good time through the marshes.'

'I wouldn't have said it was possible.'

'That's twice we've done the impossible marsh trek. Your leader betrayed his men when I sent him into Port Sumair, Lightfoot. Why?'

The man spat. 'My guess is, he was outvoted by the other mercenary leaders in Gharavan's employ.'

'But my offer was generous. My reputation as a commander outstrips my half-brother's. Why would the mercenaries choose to fight on the losing side?'

'You wish me to speak frankly?'

'Always.'

'Gharavan's mercenaries don't believe they fight on the losing side.'

Tulkhan accepted this without bluster. 'Why not?'

'Vestaid,' Lightfoot said. The name was vaguely familiar to Tulkhan. 'In the last year he has united three troops. His battle strategy is brilliant. The men are happy to follow him for profit and, who knows...'

'Glory?' Tulkhan suggested. It was not unknown for a mercenary leader to gain so much power he unseated the lord who had hired him. But surely this Vestaid did not think he could supplant the king of the Ghebites? If he did, he was playing for high stakes indeed, and he would not consider the loss of one mercenary troop too great a price to pay. Of course, he would not succeed. Tulkhan had yet to meet a man who could outwit him on the battlefield. 'What do you know of this Vestaid?'

'There are two types of leaders: those who lead by example and those who lead by fear. Vestaid lets no strong man rise under him.'

'My half-brother should look to his back,' Tulkhan said. The dinner horn sounded. 'Come, meet my men.'

As they stepped out of the shelter their way was blocked by Rawset. He gave the Ghebite version of a bow to a foreigner whom he considered of lesser rank and, as he straightened, the flickering torchlight fell on his face. The mercenary muttered a surprised oath.

'Do you know each other?' Tulkhan asked.

'No.' Rawset frowned.

'I was mistaken. Your men are waiting,' Lightfoot muttered.

At the table, Tulkhan opened a bottle of Vorsch and made the introductions as the drinks were poured. His men jokingly disparaged the locals' warm, flat beer. If Tulkhan hadn't seen Lightfoot's reaction to Rawset, he would have said the man was at ease, but he knew the mercenary leader was hiding something.

Tulkhan studied the men around his table. Kornel took a seat, though it was clear to Tulkhan that some of his men did not believe the captain deserved it. The marsh-dweller had retreated to the cooking fires with his son. The General missed little Ban.

The talk was of the journey, the trouble with the narcts and the problems of getting even the relatively light supplies through the marshes.

'A toast.' Tulkhan stood. The men followed suit. 'To our new allies, Lightfoot's mercenaries.'

They drank, slamming their empty mugs on the table.

Tulkhan would have sat down, but Lightfoot touched his goblet to his chest as was the Vaygharian custom. 'To T'Imoshen and all who serve her.'

Tulkhan could understand impressionable young Rawset being overwhelmed by Imoshen. The youth probably half fancied himself in love with her. But Lightfoot was a hardened veteran who killed for profit.

The General's men looked to him for explanation.

'To my woman.' Tulkhan raised his Vorsch. 'May we all soon be back between the thighs of our women!' He detected a note of relief as his men roared their agreement.

'To General Tulkhan, Destroyer of the Spar!' One of his men announced. 'Leveller of Port Sumair!'

Tulkhan acknowledged their support as he resumed his seat. He had been utterly ruthless in suppressing the Spar uprising. This victory had won him his father's respect and the generalship of the army at nineteen.

Tulkhan grinned as conversation grew steadily more ribald. Kornel was telling a long story in extremely bad taste about a camp follower and a soldier. The others joked and egged him on.

The men's laughter and jests flowed past Tulkhan into the night. There were many campfires within hearing distance and this jovial meal would reassure the common soldiers.

Once again the talk had turned to women as the men bemoaned the lack of camp followers. Just then Tulkhan looked up and caught Lightfoot watching him. Imoshen had seemed certain of the man's loyalty. The General's hand went to his chest where he felt Imoshen's message pressed against his skin, its creases as familiar as the words.

In salute Lightfoot lifted one hand to his forehead, touching the first two fingers of his hand to the place where some cultures believed the third eye lies dormant in all but the greatest of Seers. Tulkhan found the gesture oddly familiar, but he did not recognise it as Vaygharian.

FOR TWO DAYS now Imoshen had fought a silent mental battle with herself. If she left Reothe's gifts crippled, it made them both vulnerable to True-men. But if she healed him, Reothe would use his gifts to achieve his goals, and these were not hers.

Pausing before the polished mirror, Imoshen wondered what to wear. Tonight she needed her wits about her, for they stayed in Chalkcliff Abbey and she was to dine with Seculate Donyx and Reothe, under the guise of friendship.

She selected a skull cap of finely beaten electrum, setting it on her head. Tiny pearl beads hung on small chains in an arc across her forehead, linked to a central ruby which caught the light with the same inner fire as her eyes. To complement this, she chose a mulberry gown of richest velvet, laced tight under her bodice. Lastly she wore a choker of pearls with a central ruby.

Taking Ashmyr in his basket, she stepped out of her room to find Reothe waiting across the hall from her. He wore mulberry velvet, too, with deep brocade cuffs. These were embroidered in the finest silver thread, so that they flashed when he straightened and prowled towards her, making her heart thud. She had noticed his limp was more pronounced of an evening, but tonight there was no sign of it. He had ridden in the wagon today and now she knew why. He wanted to be alert and physically capable. Her skin prickled with a presentiment of danger.

'T'Imoshen.' Only he could roll her name off his tongue with full High T'En intonation. He offered his strong right arm.

'T'Reothe. You appear to be well,' she said, letting him know she understood his tricks.

'And you appear to be everything the T'En should be.'

'Should I take that as a compliment or an insult?' she asked softly as they walked down the hall towards the abbey's refectory where the Seculate and his priests awaited them.

Her arm lay along his, her fingers closed over his hand. Through this touch she could feel the slight roll to his step as he compensated for, and hid, the weakness in his left side.

'I merely made an observation on your appearance. You must know you are beautiful.' His voice caressed her senses, deep and intimate. 'Whether you have the strength of purpose to match that beauty, only time will tell.'

'And I suppose you have the strength of purpose?'

He laughed but said nothing as they entered a courtyard illuminated by small lanterns hanging from the surrounding arches. The air was cool, perfumed with the heady scent of night-blooming roses. Exquisite singing drifted from the chapel, touching Imoshen with its beauty.

He held her eyes. 'I do not doubt myself. Can you say the same?'

She gasped at his arrogance then chose to reply with a High T'En saying. *'The wise know in life, only death is certain.'*

He laughed. 'How can you say that when you cheated the death of your own son? What price did the Ancients ask of you, Imoshen?'

But she would not answer and they traversed the courtyard in silence. Stepping through an arch, they entered the refectory. A stillness settled on the hall's inhabitants. Even the Seculate stopped in mid-step.

Balancing the baby's basket on her hip, Imoshen gave them the Empress's blessing. She smiled but she felt heavier, weighed down by the knowledge that she was slipping deeper and deeper into a role she had never wanted.

Seculate Donyx hurried forward, as fast as his dignity would allow. The formal words of greeting tripped from his lips, but all the while he watched them. Imoshen returned his gaze, careful to reveal nothing.

When the Seculate introduced them to the elders of the abbey, Imoshen sensed Reothe's strength fading. She should heal him. She would speak with him later tonight and extract some kind of promise.

The Seculate led them into his private chamber, where a low table awaited them, bounded on three sides by cushioned couches. Apparently Seculate Donyx followed the old high court practice of eating while reclining, something the Emperor and Empress had retained for intimate dinners.

Imoshen placed Ashmyr's basket beside her and began the elaborate warmed-wine ceremony. A pot of sweetened, spiced wine sat on the brass burner to maintain the right temperature. Aware of the Seculate and Reothe watching her, Imoshen's hands moved in the formal patterns of preparation, pouring then presenting the fragile porcelain cups.

The ceremony over, she stretched out on the couch while the meal was served. Imoshen nibbled a little of this and that, one hand gently stroking Ashmyr's back as Reothe and the Seculate discussed a theological argument which had been going on for two generations. The finer points were debatable but the basic question was impossible to resolve. She had never found it interesting since the whole point of the argument seemed to be to outdo the opponent by quoting tracts from obscure T'En tomes.

It amused her to learn that Reothe had written a book on the subject, and a copy was delivered from the abbey library so that passages could be quoted.

The remains of their food were cleared from the table and palate-cleansing sweets arrived. Then these too were removed and still the Seculate and

Reothe showed no signs of quitting the table. The evening stretched out like a long tunnel before Imoshen. Sounds became thick and disjointed. Waves of weariness washed over her as her eyelids grew heavy. Though she tried to stay awake, she caught herself slipping lower and lower on the couch. She must not fall asleep at the Seculate's private banquet.

Struggling to lift herself onto one elbow, she swung her legs over the edge of the couch and felt the floor heave beneath her feet. This was not right. She'd been drugged. Panic made her fight it.

'Reothe?'

Next thing she knew, he knelt before her. Focusing on his face with great difficulty, she lifted heavy arms to his shoulders to hold herself upright.

'The food was drugged.' Her words were slurred.

'I know.'

'I cannot stay awake.'

'That you can still talk is an achievement.'

She blinked, trying to focus on his face. With a start she realised he was not drugged. 'You... you –'

'Go to sleep, Imoshen. No harm will come to you and what you do not know, you cannot reveal.'

This seemed to make sense. Reothe had asked Seculate Donyx to drug her so that they could talk treason.

She caught Reothe's arm as he went to rise. 'Why now? Why not talk later when I would have been sleeping?'

'Jarholfe watches me like a dog with a bone. He cannot carry back word that I have met privately with the Seculate if he believes you are present.'

Imoshen nodded, already she was slipping away. 'One thing. Ashmyr...'

'Is safe. Sleep, Imoshen.'

And then she was lost, drifting down through layers of consciousness. What had they given her? Her herbal training prompted her to analyse the sensations but all too soon she lost the thread, lost all sense of time and place.

IMOSHEN WAS WOKEN by Reothe's insistent voice and an abominable scent. 'Phew!'

'I'm afraid you will have a headache. I cannot let you sleep off the drug. You must walk to your chamber,' Reothe said.

She struggled to focus on his face. The room was empty, the candles had all burned out, except the one Reothe held. Her head thumped.

'I will carry Ashmyr,' Reothe said. 'Can you walk?'

'Of course I can walk!' she snapped, but then she had to bend double because she'd stood up too quickly. 'I hope your treasonous talk went well!'

He laughed softly. 'Put away your claws. The mouse has gone.'

He urged her through the door. She blinked several times to clear her vision. But the walk to her bedchamber was strangely disjointed. At one point they were in the deserted refectory, then the next in the courtyard with the cool night air sighing over the bare skin of her shoulders, and then she was in her room with no memory of walking down the hall. Fear replaced anger.

'...my lady?' It was Jarholfe speaking.

Imoshen wondered how she appeared to him. Stunned and drugged, or tired and aloof? He did not look suspicious.

'Will there be anything else, my lady?' he repeated, glancing at Reothe, who was placing the baby's basket beside the bed.

She could not betray Reothe to a True-man, a Ghebite at that. 'Leave me.'

Jarholfe gave a cold, furious bow and walked out.

'And you can go, too, Reothe.' Imoshen was mortified. She had come close to healing him, only to discover her judgment was wrong. 'I do not like being drugged. Why must you flaunt your treason before me?'

'Only those who write Fair Isle's history will know who worked treason. Was it T'Imoshen who joined with the invader of Fair Isle, or T'Reothe who sought to restore –'

'You twist everything,' Imoshen muttered. But he had made his point and the fight went out of her. 'Curse you.'

Reothe stroked her cheek. She looked up at him, feeling a kinship that went beyond the blood they shared. If only...

'You want me to absolve you of all other vows so that you can give yourself to me without guilt. But I can't do that, Imoshen. You must renounce your vow to General Tulkhan. Only then can we know the full potential of our T'En gifts. Renounce him and heal me. It is that simple.'

She froze. 'You sensed my thoughts.'

'I read your face.'

But she did not know what to believe. If he was regaining his gifts, he might realise how deeply he had penetrated her defences. 'You would have me believing black was white. Leave me. My head is thumping fit to burst!'

He mocked her with the Old Empire obeisance reserved for the Empress, then left.

TULKHAN RODE ALONG the newly constructed rampart. Below him the mercenaries' campfires were already alight, their thin plumes of smoke rising on the still, dawn air. The troop's standard lay limp against its pole. Every mercenary would follow it to their death. He needed his own standard to lead his men into battle. Gharavan's slur on his parentage and right to rule still cut him.

The night had been very cold and now the sun rose over distant Fair Isle. His heart swelled. For him Fair Isle represented beauty and promise, and Imoshen was Fair Isle.

Imoshen had once begged him not to destroy what was good in T'En culture in his haste to claim the island. He had already taken steps to fashion a new society, one after his own heart. He would invite the greatest minds of the mainland to T'Diemn. It would be the dawn of a new era.

Tulkhan's vision glazed over. At that moment the sun's rays pierced the low cloud, breaking through in golden shafts, and he knew that the symbol of his reign would be the dawn sun.

He smiled ruefully. The dawn sun was most appropriate, since the royal T'En symbol was the twin moons on a midnight blue sky. As the moons set on the house of T'En, he and Imoshen would create a royal house that was both old and new. Ashmyr was their dawn. At that moment Tulkhan realised the Ancients had returned Ashmyr's life because the boy had a destiny to fulfil. His son would unite Fair Isle. Tulkhan left his horse with the handlers, returning to his shelter, eager to set ink to paper.

A short while later Kornel backed through the flap with a tray. He placed the fresh bread cakes on the table. The scent of warm beer and hot bread made Tulkhan's mouth water.

'Take a seat. Have something to eat.' The General put his drawings away and lifted a leather thong strung with triangular gold beads. 'What do you think? This much for Banuld-Chi?'

The merchant captain eyed the yellow metal with carefully concealed avarice. 'What use is gold to a marsh-dweller? It won't keep his feet dry.'

Tulkhan laughed. 'True. But I promised him payment.'

Kornel's comment was crude.

Tulkhan acknowledged this. Banuld and his son were lucky to be alive. Most commanders would have killed them once their usefulness was past. But if Tulkhan wanted to see his vision for Fair Isle come to fruition, he had to be at peace with his neighbours, even if they were lowly marsh-dwellers.

The General watched the triangular gold beads catch the light. Funny. Gold meant nothing to him. It was only a means to an end. What better use for gold than paving the path of peace? With a smile, he added two more beads to the leather thong.

'I value those who are loyal to me,' Tulkhan told Kornel. The merchant captain would be more helpful if he thought he would be well rewarded. 'Tell me, Kornel, could you find the way back through the marshes to the village?'

The man's mouth opened and closed once. 'Yes.'

'You're sure? I will have need of that route to bring in more supplies.'

Kornel nodded.

'Then send in Banuld-Chi.'

While waiting for Banuld-Chi, Tulkhan wrote to Imoshen, telling her of the marsh-dweller and little Ban. He wrote of Lightfoot and his mercenaries, and of providing Rawset with a fast ship and appointing him their emissary. But he did not write of the way he ached to hold her and how he missed her quick mind and wry humour. If anything, distance had sharpened his need for her.

Rawset pushed the flap open. 'I heard you were about to dismiss the marsh-dweller?'

Tulkhan let the letter roll shut. 'Yes. Why?'

'You may need to use the marsh path again.'

'I intend to. Kornel will be the guide.'

'I returned by ship, so I was not with Lightfoot and Kornel, but...'

Tulkhan had noticed an unlikely friendship developing between the failed priest and the grizzled mercenary. 'What?'

'Lightfoot told me Kornel insisted on leading their way, and twice he would have taken the wrong path but the marsh-dweller stopped him, scouted ahead and came back to report the way had closed. Lightfoot likened the marsh paths to the maze of floating islands which are carried by tides and winds.'

Tulkhan sank his chin onto his cupped hand.

'I thought you should know,' Rawset offered, then glanced through the shelter's flap. 'Here they come.'

Rawset stepped aside as Kornel entered with the Banuld-Chi and his son. Tulkhan realised that he should have learnt more than the marsh-dweller's words for food and sleep, but he had thought their association was going to be brief. 'Have you told Banuld-Chi I am about to send him home, Kornel?' The man's eager expression was his answer. 'Translate this for me. Do the marsh paths move?'

Kornel's mouth opened and closed. He cast Rawset a swift glance, his eyes narrowing. 'They move, but I can find my way.'

'You might be willing to risk your life, but I will not risk the lives of my men,' Tulkhan stated. 'I want the truth, Kornel.'

The marsh-dweller asked something, his concern evident. Kornel's answer was swift and brutal. The man's expression darkened. The boy clutched his father's hand.

On impulse Tulkhan beckoned. 'Come, Ban.'

The father stiffened as his son went to Tulkhan without hesitation. The General stroked the boy's head, feeling his braided hair. 'Kornel, tell Banuld-Chi he can take his son home to his mother. I ask him to return to serve me.' Tulkhan held up the necklace of gold. 'Pretty Ban?' The boy nodded, understanding the meaning if not the words. Tulkhan slid the necklace over his head. 'This is a present for his mother.'

Kornel's translation faltered and a spasm of anger coloured his face.

'Tell Banuld-Chi' – Tulkhan emphasised the honorific – 'that there will be more if he returns to serve me of his own free will.'

The words had barely left Kornel's mouth when the marsh-dweller stepped forward and dropped to one knee. Grasping Tulkhan's free hand, he raised it to his lips and uttered the Ghebite word for thanks.

Tulkhan noted that when Banuld-Chi's hands went to the boy it was to hug him, not to paw the necklace, and he knew his assessment of the man's character was correct. Still speaking his words of thanks, the marsh-dweller backed out.

'Why did you give him the gold?' Kornel demanded. 'It would have been enough to tell him it was to be his after he served you. Now you'll never see him again!'

'We will see which of us has judged the man correctly. Meanwhile go with him. Take the boats back to the river's entrance and await the supplies.'

Realising he had overstepped his position, Kornel gave a stiff bow and backed out.

'Do you think I have thrown away my guide?' Tulkhan asked Rawset.

The young emissary shook his head. 'I can see why T'Imoshen believes in you.'

Tulkhan thought it was a strange thing for a Ghebite soldier to say but he was eager to get Rawset's reaction to the new standard. 'Take a look at this. It will be the dawn of a new royal house. The sun and its rays will be golden. The lower section will be sea-blue. I want you to take this design to Imoshen. Her seamstresses can make up the banners. They will fly from every ship and from every tower of T'Diemn. I want them gleaming on the battlefield.' He gestured towards his cloak which was flung over a chair. 'If Gharavan were to lead a sortie from the port tomorrow, my men would be wearing the same colours as his. I need cloaks of sea-blue for all my men and plumes of gold.'

Display was vital. Tulkhan knew from experience that if a man looked the part, he felt part of a greater whole. He wanted his new banner flying on the field so that when Gharavan looked down he did not see the banished concubine's son of a dead Ghebite king, but the ruler of Fair Isle. 'Leave me now.'

Rawset departed and Tulkhan felt the fire of his vision stir in his belly. This was not the fire of conquest for its own sake. The riches he saw in Fair Isle's future were not the kind you could measure on a jeweller's scale. He was imbued with a sense of purpose greater than himself, and he longed to share this with Imoshen, sure she would be as inspired as he was. With this in mind he sat down to finish the letter.

At last he stretched his cramped hand and read back what he had written, adding one last sentence: *I know you see this future too, because you spoke of it the day we stood overlooking Landsend.* He wanted to write of how he had taken her in his arms that day and how he longed to do so now, but it was not the Ghebite way to speak of these things.

Dropping melted wax on the folded message, he stared at the growing wax blob. He needed his own official seal. So far he had used his father's ring seal. But he had no right to that seal, to anything Ghebite.

With the tip of his knife he drew a rising sun in the wax puddle before it could dry. Would Imoshen notice? Would she make the connection and have a ring fashioned for him? He smiled to himself. It was a little test.

Rawset returned and Tulkhan gave him the sealed message. 'Deliver this into her hands and see that she breaks the seal herself. '

'So be it. I sail tonight for T'Diemn.'

'Kornel will take the skiffs back to the mouth of the marsh river to await the supplies. Unless there is a message for me, stay with T'Imoshen.' Tulkhan wondered how he could tell this idealistic young man that he wanted him to report on what was happening in T'Diemn. He needed to know if there was any truth behind Jarholfe's accusation. 'Be aware of what goes on around her. There are many enemies who would do harm to our cause, and not all of them live on the mainland.'

'I understand,' Rawset said, but Tulkhan doubted.

As the youth left, Lightfoot joined Tulkhan at the entrance to the shelter. 'You sent the marsh-dweller and his son home?'

He nodded. 'If Banuld returns, it will be because he chooses to serve me.'

'Choice!' Lightfoot muttered, rubbing his forehead and Tulkhan wondered if he was missing something. Lightfoot looked up at the sky, no stars were visible tonight. 'Looks like rain.'

Tulkhan nodded. His miners would not welcome more rain. Already one of the shafts had collapsed because of the boggy soil.

THAT EVENING IMOSHEN and Reothe ate in Windhaven Hall, where the farm girl Kalleen was now the mistress.

'My ambassadors should be on the mainland by now,' Imoshen said as the servants took away the last of the plates, leaving Kalleen, Imoshen and Reothe alone. Jarholfe had opted to eat in the courtyard with his men.

Imoshen pushed her plate aside. The meal had been uncomfortably formal. 'So, tell me, Kalleen, what do you think of Windhaven? The soil is good and the people are friendly.'

'My lady?' A tentative voice spoke from the shadows.

Kalleen signalled for the woman to approach.

'Some people want to see the T'En healer. One has the bone ache, another coughs blood, two more –'

'Send them in.' Imoshen came to her feet. 'Have someone bring my healing bag.' She put the sleeping baby in his basket on the floor in front of the fire and leant closer to Kalleen. 'I would speak with you later.' She turned to Reothe. 'You might as well go. This could take hours.'

Ashmyr stirred and Reothe soothed him. At that moment the woman returned with the first of the locals, a farmer whose body was twisted with the bone ache. As Imoshen dealt with the old man, he glanced to Reothe. And she saw, what her patient saw, the rebel leader rocking the conqueror's son. No wonder people whispered that Ashmyr was Reothe's child.

A constant stream of locals shuffled across the ancient flagstones. Some needed only a few herbs and words of encouragement. With others Imoshen had to call on her gift to encourage healing.

When Ashmyr fell asleep, Reothe placed the basket on the floor by his chair and observed her. She tried to ignore his presence. But even if she had been able to disregard the tension in her body, she couldn't ignore the way the villagers glanced shyly at him, offering their thanks to both the T'En as though she and Reothe were two sides of a coin.

At last there were no more True-people to be healed and Imoshen packed away her depleted herbs, weary yet satisfied. Reothe rose, stretching like a great cat, flexing and tensing the muscles on the weak side of his body.

'I'm sorry if you were bored,' Imoshen said, unsettled.

'Bored? Never. Besides, it is good for them to see me with you when you heal.' He saw she did not understand. 'When you use your gifts, I am included in your nimbus of power.'

Imoshen gasped, annoyed because she should have anticipated this.

He shrugged, amused.

She slung the herb satchel across one shoulder, then knelt to pick up Ashmyr's basket. 'I thank you for reminding me what you are, Reothe.'

'No one can forget what we are, Imoshen. We wear our heritage on our faces.'

'I must go.'

'Yes. Kalleen will be waiting, no doubt.'

Imoshen felt the heat rise in her face. 'She is my friend.'

'Kalleen is a True-woman who fears you.'

'You don't understand. You see betrayal everywhere, and because of it you cannot trust or be trusted.' She felt sick at heart. 'I won't become like you, Reothe.'

'You didn't grow up in the court of the Old Empire.'

But she refused to acknowledge this and climbed the stairs to her room, where she found Kalleen dozing in a chair by the fire. At the soft click of the latch, Kalleen gave a little start. For a heartbeat her unguarded face betrayed her wariness and Imoshen's heart sank.

She knelt to place Ashmyr before the fire then looked over his sleeping form to Kalleen. 'Thank you for waiting.'

'Have you had word from Wharrd?'

'Only on matters of state,' Imoshen said, and Kalleen looked away to hide her disappointment. 'I am here to place a special trust upon you.'

Kalleen's face was a mix of caution and curiosity.

Imoshen stroked Ashmyr's cheek, tears blurring her vision. 'He is so small and defenceless. If anything were to happen –'

'Please don't ask this of me!'

'These are desperate times. Unless Tulkhan defeats King Gharavan, we face war in the spring. Fair Isle is rife with dissension. The Ghebite commanders, Reothe's rebels and the Keldon nobles are ready to take up arms against each other. I must ask this of you. If something happens to me, look after Ashmyr.'

Kalleen's eyes widened. 'Have you seen your deaths?'

Imoshen shook her head and brushed tears from her cheeks. 'Swear you will take care of my son if I die.'

'I swear,' Kalleen whispered. 'But I don't see how I can save him if you can't. If the worst comes to pass, I will be fleeing Fair Isle with nothing but the clothes I wear and two children. Or did you forget I am with child?'

Imoshen had not forgotten. Kalleen could expect to carry her child around six small moons. Imoshen knew her pure T'En babe would be carried eight small moons, one year from conception to birth. It would be nearly the cusp of autumn before her child would be born. If Tulkhan denied her, the birth would drive her into allegiance with Reothe. No wonder she found it hard to take joy in the pregnancy, but the babe itself was innocent. Her hand settled protectively over her flat belly.

'What is it?' Kalleen covered Imoshen's hand. 'Are you ill?'

'No.' Imoshen smiled. 'I want to leave a message in your mind for the day you may need it.' She saw Kalleen's imminent refusal and hurried on. 'I promise that is all I will do, and the message will not surface unless you need it.'

'How...' Kalleen swallowed. 'How will you do it?'

Relief flooded Imoshen. 'It won't hurt. I promise.'

'Very well. Let's get it over with.'

Imoshen stood. 'Come to the bed. Is your wound healed?'

'Yes. Only the proud flesh of the scar remains.' Kalleen climbed up onto the bed and lay back. She undid the drawstring of her night gown, turning her face away as Imoshen pulled the material apart to reveal her breasts, now swollen with her pregnancy. Below her left breast was a puckered scar, evidence of Drake's attack.

'Do you trust me, Kalleen?'

Their eyes met. 'I want to.'

'Then listen to me.' Imoshen began to sing a T'En lullaby which her great-aunt used to croon to her, tracing a circle on Kalleen's abdomen in time to the rhythm. When she felt the familiar metallic taste on her tongue and the ache in her teeth, she knew her gifts were moving. Kalleen's breathing slowed as her body relaxed.

Imoshen focused on the scar. She ran her finger over its puckered surface. The skin stirred like soft white sand. Still humming, Imoshen drew a map of her family's stronghold on Kalleen's abdomen, stretching and elongating the thin, silver scar tissue to define the shape. When this was done she touched the tip of her sixth finger to the spot where she and the Aayel had hidden the family's wealth.

It was a king's ransom, because that was what they'd thought it would be for. They had feared the Ghebite General would capture their family and demand gold for their safe return. But he hadn't. He had simply slaughtered them. She must not forget what kind of man Tulkhan was. Strange, the man she knew did not mesh with his past actions.

The treasure cache contained more than enough gold and precious jewels for Kalleen to flee Fair Isle a wealthy woman. Imoshen placed this knowledge in the secret cavern of Kalleen's mind, safely hidden until the day she might need it.

When it was done, Imoshen discovered she was weary beyond thought. Kalleen slept deeply. It was all Imoshen could do to lie down beside her before she lost all sense of self.

Imoshen woke at dawn with Kalleen's warm body tucked around hers and the woman's soft cheek on her shoulder. If the baby hadn't been working up a cry, Imoshen would not have moved. She nudged Kalleen, who pushed the hair from her face, blinking owlishly.

As Imoshen went to the baby, Kalleen sat up, then noticed her night gown was still undone.

'I tried to smoothe your scar but –'

'It does not matter.' Kalleen pulled the drawstring closed as Imoshen undid her bodice. 'So, you left your message?'

Imoshen nodded. 'To thank you seems inadequate.'

'Then don't.' Kalleen laughed, but it was almost a shudder. 'I pray the day never comes.'

'So do I.'

Chapter Ten

IMOSHEN'S HEART LIFTED as she approached Fair Isle's capital. Truly, T'Diemn lived up to its fabled beauty. Bathed in gentle afternoon light, the sandstone buildings glowed. The old city was built on hills, bounded by defensive walls constructed during the Age of Consolidation. New T'Diemn lay around the outskirts, twice as large again.

Riding down the broad road to the new city's north gate, Imoshen was relieved to see Tulkhan's fortifications were progressing well. The ditches and towers were almost completed.

She had intended to slip quietly into the capital, but from the moment she identified herself to the gate guards, news of her arrival preceded her. People came out in droves to see T'Imoshen with T'Reothe riding proud beside her. They pointed and whispered and she knew every conceivable rumour was taking life.

Was T'Reothe reconciled, or was he playing a double game? The Protector General was on the mainland laying siege to Port Sumair. What if he failed to defeat his half-brother? The people of T'Diemn had experienced King Gharavan's cruelty first hand and Imoshen felt the weight of their expectation.

A crowd gathered in the square before the palace of a thousand rooms. Once Imoshen had dreaded entering the palace, overwhelmed by its myriad passages, army of servants and seething court factions. Now she saw it as a beautiful, flawed pearl, an aggregate of buildings added to and literally overlaid by her ancestors during six hundred years of T'En rule.

Directly opposite the palace, the Basilica's great golden dome gleamed in the afternoon sun. This building rivalled the palace in complexity and beauty. Careful to accord the church's leader due honour, Imoshen led their party to the Basilica's steps where the Beatific stood flanked by high ranking officials. While offering formal greetings to the Beatific, Imoshen wondered what report Seculate Donyx had sent by fast horse.

She deliberately turned away so that she did not have to watch the meeting between the Beatific and Reothe. Did the woman within the Beatific still love Reothe?

Imoshen sensed an intense scrutiny and searched the ranks of the church hierarchy to discover its source. She found Murgon, Leader of the Tractarian Order. His unguarded expression was a window to his mind. He not only feared Reothe – he envied him. It was a dangerous combination.

With a sigh, Imoshen urged her horse across the square to greet the palace staff who had assembled on the steps. It wasn't until she had met with all those persons who thought it necessary to receive direct instructions that Imoshen could retire to her small study. She enjoyed the simple lines of this room, with its desk of inlaid polished wood and tripod chairs. It had been decorated in the Age of Discernment, when elegance was valued above opulence.

Taking over the candle lighter's job, she instructed him to send for Wharrd, but he returned with a report that the commander was in the south, conferring with the Keldon nobles. Imoshen sighed. She had hoped to hear Wharrd's news. 'Then please send something to eat.'

Servants soon arrived. Soundlessly, they placed food trays on the desk before leaving. Spreading out paper and tapping the ink from her scriber, Imoshen prepared to read petitions, only to be interrupted by Jarholfe.

'Yes?' She looked up.

'When the General took half the elite guard with him, it left my ranks greatly depleted. Do you want me to assign men from the general army to be trained?'

Imoshen frowned. Unlike her own stronghold guard, she did not trust the elite guard. She wished she could dismiss Jarholfe, wished there was no need to fear treachery and assassination. 'Provide me with a list of the elite guard who remain in T'Diemn and their skills.' Even as she spoke she recalled that he could not write. Someone knocked. 'Enter.'

Imoshen's heart sank as the Ghebite priest strode in, his ornate surplice swinging with each step. Since arriving in T'Diemn the Cadre had been as contemptuous of other beliefs as he had been vocal in preaching his warrior god's path. Jarholfe met his eyes, then looked quickly away.

The Cadre gave an abbreviated Ghebite bow. 'I am here to offer my services, Lady Protector. In his haste to defeat his half-brother's army, General Tulkhan has been remiss. He cannot expect a woman to rule Fair Isle in his absence.'

Imoshen came to her feet. 'On the contrary, before his commanders and elite guard the General said I was to be his Voice.'

But the Cadre continued as though she hadn't spoken. 'Fortunately Lord Commander Wharrd remains in Fair Isle. Together with myself and Jarholfe, we will be able to guide you.'

'What would you advise, Cadre?' Imoshen asked silkily.

'Make an example of this rebel leader. Execute him and outlaw all those who would support him. I had reports that the Keldon nobles were massing on the plains. They have since returned to the highlands, but their threat must be contained. Confiscate the estates of the troublemakers. As for the rest, take their eldest sons hostage –'

A doorcomb sounded and silenced the Cadre. By the comb's tone Imoshen knew it was a noble from the Old Empire and guessed it to be Reothe. He entered before she could think of a way of dismissing him. Reothe's gaze swept the gathering and when his eyes met hers they held a question.

'The Cadre was offering me much the same advice you offered in T'Ronnyn's Tower,' Imoshen explained. The priest's confusion made her smile.

'Palace intrigue is not for the faint-hearted,' Reothe said.

A spasm of hatred, quickly concealed, travelled across Jarholfe's features, and the Cadre would have spoken, but Imoshen forestalled him. 'I thank you for your offer of assistance, Cadre. If I am need of your advice I will send for you.' She included them both in a gesture. 'You are dismissed.'

They backed out seething.

'A pair of snakes,' Reothe remarked. 'The Cadre hates you. It's not surprising when minstrels from one end of Fair Isle to the other sing of how you shamed him.'

'I caught him smashing our hothouses. I could not let him destroy the herbs that control fertility. If he had his way, he would reduce women to breeding cows.' Imoshen sat wearily. 'Every day I battle to educate these barbarians, but the Ghebites are blinded by their culture.'

'That, and fear. I don't need my gifts to smell Jarholfe's fear of us.' Reothe lopped off a wedge of cheese, eating it from the knife like a farmer. 'Watch him.'

'I have plans for Jarholfe. The security of the palace will not be his responsibility.'

'And what is my responsibility? Or am I to be your lap dog?' Reothe gestured with the knife. 'Give me something to do, Imoshen!'

His barely contained tension made her gift flare. She forced it down and poured a glass of wine. Since Chalkcliff Abbey she had decided caution was the safest path with Reothe. She dare not heal him. 'I need you to inspect the city's new defences. I want to know how close they are to completion. Tell me if you can spot any weaknesses.'

A servant's doorcomb sounded. 'Emissary Rawset wishes to speak with you.'

Imoshen rose, pushing her untouched wine aside. She could not bring herself to read Tulkhan's message under Reothe's mocking gaze. She picked up the baby's basket. 'Send Rawset to my chamber.'

Reothe stabbed a piece of cheese. 'Entertaining yet another man in your bedchamber, Imoshen?'

'I work for the good of Fair Isle. Be grateful I do not drug you while I discuss matters of state!' She headed for the door.

'Do not be so sure of your high moral ground. Remember, the historians decide who works treason!'

The sound of his laughter followed her out of the room, echoing in her head as she strode through the long gallery. She doubted if the palace would ever be big enough to share with Reothe.

Her chambers had been warmed and lit, and her clothes unpacked. She was used to the opulence now and barely noticed the inlaid amber panels, other than to appreciate the way they reflected the candles' glow.

Imoshen placed Ashmyr's basket before the fire and tucked the blanket under his chin. There was barely time to straighten before a servant scratched discreetly at the door, announcing Rawset.

He gave her the Ghebite obeisance, then the T'En court greeting, taking her hand and kissing her sixth finger. 'You have arrived safely.'

'Why would I not be safe?' Imoshen asked.

'There is talk of rebel bands roaming the countryside. I'd heard stories –'

'We took our time and we had no trouble on the road. What word from the General?'

Rawset removed a message from inside his cloak. 'From his hands to yours.'

Imoshen smiled. She felt much older than Rawset, yet she suspected he was at least five years her senior. Taking the message to her desk, she wished him gone so that she could pore over every word, alone with the General's memory.

The seal was odd. It looked as if someone had drawn in the hot wax. Why hadn't Tulkhan used his usual seal, the rearing stallion, symbol of the Ghebite god? Perhaps this new seal was visible evidence of a shift in the General's thinking.

With care, Imoshen prised the wax away from the paper and spread the sheets. It was all as she expected until she came to his plans for a new standard. Blue and gold – the dawn sun rising over a new era for Fair Isle. Her throat tightened and tears of loss stung her eyes. She had witnessed the Old Empire's death throes, but General Tulkhan's plans reopened the wound.

The T'En twin moons had set and Tulkhan's house was in ascendancy. So be it. Wiping her eyes, Imoshen focused on the design for Fair Isle's new standard. 'I will inspect the merchants for appropriate materials and speak with the clothworkers' guild on the morrow, Rawset.'

'General Tulkhan said I was to return with the finished banners and cloaks.'

'Cloaks for a whole army? I will have to see what the cloth merchants have in stock.' Imoshen felt a familiar fire ignite her. She loved a challenge. In her mind she could already see the new standard, its finely spun thread of gold on the purest azure blue.

She glanced down at the General's letter. There was no private word for her, nothing but a fleeting mention of the time they had stood on the lookout above Landsend and shared a vision for Fair Isle's future. Imoshen closed her eyes, recalling the sharp sea breeze and the way Tulkhan had taken her in his arms and kissed her. She wondered if this was what he had intended.

She wanted, needed, to believe that Tulkhan, with the limitations of a True-man, had deliberately written of that moment to reach out to her.

Imoshen cleared her throat. 'When everything is ready, I will write to the General and I'll have a fast, seagoing ship assigned to you in case we need to contact him quickly. I'm hoping to have good news from my ambassadors in the Amirate. Until then, take your pleasure about town.'

Alone at last, Imoshen considered how she would handle Jarholfe and his men. Though it was entirely logical to combine the elite guard and her stronghold guard, she knew the Ghebites would resist. They did not respect a fighting force that accepted women.

Tired of confined spaces, Imoshen opened her door to find one of her stronghold guard on duty. 'Ashmyr sleeps. I'm going for a walk. Let no one in.'

Deep in thought, Imoshen strode down passages and up steps, eventually finding herself in a portrait gallery dating from the Age of Tribulation. She paused before the panel to the secret passage, which she had ordered sealed. It led to the catacombs and no one must venture down there for fear of rousing the Parakletos.

The bodies of the Paragian Guard might be entombed, but those who had died while under oath to Imoshen the First knew no rest. They had given more than their lives to subdue Fair Isle, they had given their deaths as well, becoming the Parakletos, death's guardians.

Imoshen pressed her cheek to the dusty wood grain.

Though she longed to explore those ancient catacombs, her fear of the Parakletos was greater. Reothe had said they had no power in this world, but she had sensed their animosity.

Resuming her pacing, she found herself in a narrow gallery. Its alcoves were decorated with life-like paintings of mythical and historical scenes.

In the alcove facing her, Parakletos escorted the soul of Causare Imoshen from this world to the next. The artist had chosen to illustrate not the darkness of death's shadow, but Imoshen's the First's destination. The dawn sun blazed behind the Parakletos, who were depicted as fierce creatures with great white wings. In this representation they were stern beings of beauty and majesty, escorting the soul of one who had devoted her life to the service of others.

Imoshen frowned. How different the beliefs of Fair Isle were from Ghebite beliefs. For a bonding gift Tulkhan had presented her with a torque of pure gold, embellished with exquisite filigree work picked out in niello. It was a work of art, yet the scene it illustrated was the great Akha Khan trampling his enemies beneath his hooves. All the Ghebites knew was violence, and their god reflected this. He appeared in several forms: a black bear, a black stallion, half-stallion-half-man, or as a giant of a man like Tulkhan.

The General's elite guard would not take kindly to being amalgamated with her stronghold guard, but she needed a palace force loyal to her.

Imoshen's vision swam and she saw the half-stallion-half-man, as it appeared on Tulkhan's torque, overlaid on the image of the Parakletos in the painting before her. Pure light glowed through the man-stallion, making it appear a white-winged protector.

When Wharrd returned to T'Diemn, Imoshen ordered a meal laid in her favourite dining room. The Jade Room dated from the early Age of Consolidation. Jade deities, gifted by a mainland king long dead, stood in niches around the room. A central low table was bounded by three couches suitable for intimate dining.

At his knock she told Wharrd to enter but it was Reothe. 'Were you expecting someone else?'

'You know I was expecting Lord Commander Wharrd, else why did you knock, rather than use your doorcomb?'

He smiled disarmingly. 'Wharrd reports on matters of state. The fate of Fair Isle concerns me. I know the General has designed a new standard for Fair Isle. I know Rawset will get a ship of his own. Why bother to hide things from me, Imoshen? I gave you my report on the defences and you agreed the wharves are the city's weakest point.'

'Yes, but your plans to make the wharves safe would drive the merchants mad, obstructing the unloading and loading of stores. Besides, an invader would have to take every river lock between here and the Pellucid Sea, killing each of the lock keepers between, before they could attack the wharves. Impossible.'

'They said taking an army across the marshland was impossible, yet your General did it. And forget the merchants, they are only interested in profit. You will get nothing but complaints from them until they are under threat. Then see how quick they are to blame you for not taking adequate precautions. I know where I would attack if I wanted to take T'Diemn.'

His threat hung on the air. Imoshen felt her body and gifts quicken to his challenge. Reothe stood across the room from her, his eyes glittering with febrile brilliance. A T'En warrior in the full capacity of his gifts was a terrible thing to contemplate. Thank the Aayel, Imoshen had not healed him.

'What?' Reothe pressed.

He was too perceptive. Imoshen opened her mouth to put him off but there was a knock at the door. 'Enter.'

As Wharrd let the door swing shut behind him, Imoshen caught the veteran's uneasy glance in Reothe's direction.

'Have you eaten?' Imoshen asked, gesturing to the table.

'I'm not hungry.' He did not sit down.

'You can speak before T'Reothe. He does not want a spring invasion any more than we do. We have called a truce, haven't we, kinsman?' She held Reothe's eyes.

'Yes, kinswoman. As you say we are allies, Empress.'

Imoshen wondered what Wharrd would make of the use of that title. Reothe's antagonism was clear enough. But Wharrd ignored Reothe, explaining that ambassadors had been sent to all three southern kingdoms, though the Amirate capital was the preferred port. Following her advice, he had selected bond-partners, Ghebite lord commanders and Fair Isle noblewomen. No word had returned as yet.

'As for the siege machines I checked them personally,' Wharrd continued. 'They are safely stowed and the ships are ready to sail at a moment's notice. The cavalry drill every day. It is good exercise for the men and their horses. They have grown fat with too much easy living.'

'I would like to see this Ghebite cavalry,' Reothe announced.

Yes, Imoshen thought. Study your enemy, Reothe. One day you may be facing this cavalry, much better to know their strengths and weaknesses.

From Wharrd's expression the same thought had occurred to him.

But she gave Wharrd a nod. 'Arrange a display.' Ashmyr stirred and she rocked his cradle. 'That will give me a chance to invite the Beatific and the guildmasters. It would not hurt to make a display of strength. Let the news of our battle-readiness filter back through the mainland spies to the Amir and his allied kings. Let them think twice about dishonouring their old alliances.' She smiled with relish.

Reothe silently lifted his wine glass to her, the echo of her smile in his eyes. She felt that familiar tug of like to like.

'You rock the cradle with one hand while you rule Fair Isle with the other. You think like a man, I don't...' Wharrd seemed to realise he had spoken aloud. The bone-setter-turned-diplomat bowed stiffly, his coppery skin growing dark with shame. 'Forgive this old campaigner, T'Imoshen. I have been in the saddle since dawn. I bid you good night.'

With that he left the room.

Reothe's gaze met hers. 'These Ghebites do not know what to make of you, Imoshen. They are not used to a woman who can reason with the best of them. I raise my glass to Imoshen the Diplomat.'

She flushed. As a compliment it touched her far more than any flowery phrase. 'I wish only for peace and the chance to sit by my own fireside, Reothe.'

He laughed. 'So you say, but you would be bored within a small moon.'

Imoshen shook her head. 'Give me peace and quiet any day.'

He studied her sceptically. 'I think you honestly believe that. But I think that will not be our fate, Imoshen. We are the last of the T'En. Death will not come to claim us in our dotage by our firesides.'

She knew at a visceral level that Reothe was right, and she longed to ask him if he'd seen their deaths. He claimed to have the Sight. Perhaps he fought so feverishly because he tried to wrench the path of destiny into one of his own making. She looked over at him.

'Ask,' he prompted.

But she would not reveal her thoughts. Reothe was a law unto himself and for all his apparent compliance she remained suspicious of his motives.

IMOSHEN LOOKED UP as a servant announced the Keldon lord, Athlyn.

'Have warmed wine prepared in the greeting room,' Imoshen ordered, and the servant departed. She sorted the notes on her desk. The cloth merchants' guild had been quietly ecstatic at the thought of so much business. Their most gifted artists were inspired to refine Tulkhan's design.

Since Wharrd's return, Imoshen had left Reothe to oversee the completion of T'Diemn's defences. Every day he grew stronger in body. He had resumed the wing of rooms which had always been his and she suspected, though he rode the defensive earthworks every morning, Reothe was also contacting old friends and calling in old favours.

The Beatific had paid a courtesy call and offered support in the war against King Gharavan. Because General Tulkhan had formally recognised the T'En church's laws, Imoshen had the support of Reothe and the Beatific, albeit motivated by self-interest. Now she needed the support of the Keldon nobles.

She opened the connecting door. 'Lord Athlyn.'

'T'Imoshen.' He gave her the formal obeisance.

Imoshen took her seat and performed the warmed-wine ceremony. Only when the porcelain cups were steaming before both of them did she meet his T'En eyes, recalling how he had confronted her with the other Keldon nobles. They had demanded that the Causare Council reopen so they could have a say in the running of Fair Isle.

The General had thought them incredibly arrogant for a conquered people. Luckily she had been able to negotiate a compromise. Tulkhan had agreed to accept the advice of the Causare Council as long as six of his men and six of the Keld took seats. 'Have the Keldon nobles selected their six representatives for the Council?'

'You toy with me, T'Imoshen. In times of war the Council has no power.' He met her eyes frankly. 'No, I am here unofficially. We –'

Athlyn broke off as Reothe entered the room.

His spies were most efficient, Imoshen thought.

Reothe smiled as he met her eyes, then greeted the old lord. 'Grandfather.'

Casting back through their shared family tree, Imoshen realised she was speaking with the man who had bonded with her great-aunt's sister. Even though Athlyn's relationship with Reothe was through the lesser, paternal line, it explained the support Reothe had received from the Keld.

Reothe sank gracefully into the seat on Imoshen's left. His hand settled on her forearm.

Athlyn's wine-dark eyes rested briefly on Reothe's hand. 'They told me the last of the T'En were reconciled. I came to see for myself.'

'Fair Isle cannot afford division,' Imoshen said. 'I want confirmation that the Keldon nobles will stand at the General's side if Gharavan invades. Tell Woodvine and the others that the Causare Council will be reopened when Gharavan is dead, and the six Keldon places on that Council will be filled by those who have proven their loyalty.'

Reothe chuckled. 'Imoshen believes in speaking plainly.'

'Imoshen can speak for herself,' she told him.

Lord Athlyn smiled as he came to his feet, an old man grown whip-thin with age. 'I will return to the highlands this very day. All along I have argued for temperance.' He gave Reothe a hard look. 'My greatest ambition is to die of old age in my bed, surrounded by my family. How many of us have died in our sleep in six hundred years, Reothe?'

'Not enough, Grandfather.' Reothe embraced him.

Athlyn gave Imoshen the obeisance for the Empress and departed. With a start, she realised that she was Empress T'Imoshen to almost everyone now, and she was not yet nineteen. Few people saw past the power to the young woman who had risen to meet the challenge of her position.

IMPATIENCE SEIZED TULKHAN as he shaded his eyes against the midday sun, watching his ships on the brilliant sea. If only he had the siege machines. He could not attack by land without the machines, and the ships alone were not strong enough to break the siege.

He swore softly under his breath as he realised he had been thinking like a landsman. He could erect siege machines on the ship's decks and bring them right up to the wall. The more pressure he placed on the people of Port Sumair, the more likely they were to turn on Gharavan.

Skidding down the landward side of the seawall, he caught his mount's reins, already planning his message to Imoshen. Unfortunately, Rawset was in T'Diemn. How could the General convince Imoshen his message was genuine if it did not come from the hand of a trusted emissary?

'THE ELITE GUARD are waiting in the sword practice courtyard, along with your stronghold guard,' Wharrd reported.

'Thank you.' When Imoshen had first told him her intention to unite the two guards, Wharrd had advised against it. He had talked of the Gheeakhan code of honour, and of a Ghebite soldier's ambition. This had given Imoshen the insight she needed to devise a strategy to win the Ghebites over.

Followed by two servants carrying a hastily painted banner, Imoshen approached the courtyard with some trepidation. Stepping into the sunshine, she sensed the elite guards' resentment. Her own stronghold guard, the twenty men and women who had accompanied her to T'Diemn, waited uneasily.

'Crawen and Jarholfe.' Imoshen acknowledged the leaders of both guards. 'I have called your people here today because Fair Isle faces her hour of greatest need. King Gharavan threatens a spring invasion –'

'General Tulkhan will trim his wick!' a Ghebite called. Someone added a ribald comment and the men laughed too loudly.

Imoshen let the laughter die down. 'But Fair Isle also faces internal threats. In the southern highlands there are stiff-necked Keld who whisper treason, and bands of leaderless rebels wander the countryside terrorising decent folk. Meanwhile, in the palace of T'Diemn, the people who should be protecting the royal family are intent on each other, ready to take insult at the slightest provocation. I speak of my stronghold guard and the elite guard.'

Jarholfe muttered under his breath. Imoshen signalled Wharrd, who stepped forward. He outranked Jarholfe, and without his support she could not have hoped to carry this off.

'The General gave me the protection of T'Diemn,' Wharrd said. 'But I find myself under a Ghiad to T'Imoshen and unable to fulfil this role. Jarholfe, I call on you to take over the role entrusted to me by General Tulkhan. I name you leader of the city's garrison.'

No ambitious career soldier could resist the promotion, and Jarholfe was quick to give the Ghebite salute, arm across his chest, fist clenched. 'I am honoured. By the great Akha Khan I will not fail this charge.'

The elite guard were now leaderless. Wharrd stepped back and caught Imoshen's eye. She raised her voice. 'My faithful stronghold guard, you left your homes and families at a moment's notice and have not returned for over a year. I release you from your oath. You are free to return home. As for the elite guard, they are free to return to the regular army or follow Jarholfe into T'Diemn's garrison.'

This was greeted with uneasy muttering.

Imoshen signalled for silence. 'Behold the symbol of the new palace guard.'

She undid the banner's ribbons so that it unfurled to reveal the white man-stallion, wings outstretched as he leapt over the dawn sun. Her own people would understand the reference to Imoshen the First's Paragian Guard. The Ghebites would believe she honoured Tulkhan and the Akha Khan.

'Anyone who can meet the high standard of the Parakhan Guard is free to join.' She caught Crawen's eye and smiled. 'They will be trained in unarmed combat under Crawen, and in the use of the Ghebite sword by Edovan.' Imoshen beckoned him. Travelling with Jarholfe's men had given her a chance to study them, and she believed Edovan, though he appeared startled now, would adapt quickly. 'Jarholfe has recommended your skill with the sword, Edovan. Will you accept this honour and become Sword-master of the Parakhan Guard?'

To refuse would be disloyal to Jarholfe. He gave the Ghebite salute. 'I would be honoured to serve General Tulkhan as Sword-master of the Parakhan Guard.'

Imoshen indicated Crawen and Edovan were to turn and face their fellows. 'We of Fair Isle believe that, like the small and large moon, men and women are different. Each has their strengths and weaknesses, but like the moons they shine strongest when they shine together.' She wanted to say more but held her tongue. This was one small step towards her ultimate goal of uniting Fair Isle.

IMOSHEN'S HEART LEAPT in anticipation of the unveiling of Tulkhan's banner. She signalled the servants to release the ties and the heavy material unrolled, revealing its rich blue and gold, brilliant even in the dull light of the autumn day. The huge banner hung across the rear wall of the palace's great public hall. She had to step back to take in its magnificence.

The cloth-workers had used finely spun gold thread to highlight the rising sun and its shafts of light. The sea was a deep, royal blue, the sky an intense azure, and in the top left-hand corner she had instructed the embroiderers to illuminate the twin moons of the T'En in silver thread. All about her the workers and their guildmasters congratulated each other.

The house of Tulkhan rose with the dawn, watched over by the T'En. The people of Fair Isle would understand the significance.

A familiar voice made Imoshen turn.

'Wharrd?' She beckoned him and gestured to the banner. 'What do you think? We will have new flags on all the towers of T'Diemn. Tulkhan's cloaks and the battlefield banners are loading even as we speak. And, by the way, the Parakhan Guard are looking fine in their new uniforms.'

'Fine fittings do not make a lame horse whole.'

She lowered her voice. 'You think the Parakhan Guard a lame horse, Wharrd?'

'No.' He grimaced. 'Merely unused to the bridle.'

'That can be remedied. In time we –'

'Time is what we don't have. Can we speak?'

Imoshen's stomach clenched. 'A moment.' Raising her voice she thanked everyone but, even as they beamed at her, she was trying to anticipate Wharrd's bad news.

When they returned to her private chambers, she turned to him. 'Speak.'

'We've had a reply from the Amirate.' He handed her a message scroll.

Imoshen frowned, reading quickly. 'They regret they cannot honour alliances drawn up with the Old Empire... General Tulkhan, bastard son of the Ghebite invaders, has no authority.' Imoshen lifted her head. 'They are refusing to give us port access. But it is only one kingdom of the triad. One of the other kingdoms may yet agree. They constantly vie for an advantage –'

'Keep reading.'

Imoshen returned her attention to the message. 'Treason? Our ambassadors are imprisoned, accused of treason against the Amir himself?'

Wharrd nodded. 'It gets worse. They expect us to pay an enormous sum in compensation before they will consider releasing our people.'

'What happened?' Imoshen sat down heavily.

'Our ambassadors arrived in the middle of a feud between the maternal and paternal relatives of the infant Amir. By Amirate law the boy cannot be crowned until he is sixteen, so the paternal grandfather was declared Amiregent. The maternal uncle arranged for the old man's assassination and seized the chance to lay the blame on our people.'

Imoshen cursed softly.

'If we don't reply, it will be seen as an admission of guilt and our people will be executed. If we don't pay the compensation, it will be seen as an admission of guilt and our ambassadors will be executed. We have until the large new moon to deliver the compensation.'

'Ten days,' Imoshen whispered. She had not expected such treachery.

'Can we find the gold?' Wharrd asked.

She shook her head. 'We won't pay.'

The veteran opened his mouth to speak, then stopped.

'What haven't you told me?' Imoshen prompted.

'The ambassadors are Lord Commander Shacolm and Lord Fairban's youngest daughter, Lady Miriane.'

Imoshen fought a wave of nausea. Already that family had paid for her misjudgement with Cariah's death. Now this...

Wharrd cleared his throat. 'I thought sending bond-partners would –'

'It was what I recommended,' Imoshen agreed. 'We could not know the political situation was so volatile. We... I have been concentrating on Fair Isle, without giving thought to the intrigues on the mainland.' She frowned.

'The new Amiregent and his confederates probably hope King Gharavan and Tulkhan will worry over Fair Isle like two dogs over a bone and forget their miserable kingdoms. While the Ghebite army expends itself on internal warfare, the triad is safe from invasion. It appears Fair Isle will not get help from the mainland unless we prove we are stronger than Gharavan with all of Gheeaba behind him.' She could feel a tension headache building. 'What will I tell Tulkhan?'

'The truth. The ambassadors' servant is waiting, if you want to speak with him.'

Imoshen nodded. 'In time. You may go.'

As Wharrd left, she realised she should expect a visit from Lord Fairban. For a moment she wondered why Miriane had accepted a Ghebite for her bond-partner. After Cariah was murdered, both of her sisters had broken off all involvement with their Ghebite admirers.

Imoshen dipped her scriber into the ink, then hesitated. Not wanting to reveal her failure, she told the General only that negotiations with the Amirate were continuing. Then she wrote of the new Parakhan Guard and enclosed the banner, closing with the news that his army's new cloaks and standards were on their way.

She sent for Rawset and was ready when he arrived just on dusk, dressed for sailing.

'For the General's own hands.' She gave Rawset the message. 'And this is to be placed around Tulkhan's neck.' She held up a thin chain. The large brass seal swung heavily. 'It is the General's new seal.'

She dropped it over Rawset's head and tucked it inside his shirt. Her hand rested for a moment over his heart which she could feel thudding under her palm. 'This must not fall into enemy hands. If your ship is lost, throw the seal overboard.'

'I understand. What's this?' He pointed to a large travelling satchel.

'The General's own clothes, standard and a banner. Be sure to take this to him along with my message.'

'What will you do about the ambassadors?'

Imoshen groaned. 'Does all of T'Diemn know?'

'I heard it from my ship's captain.'

'Very well.' Imoshen sat down to tell Tulkhan that she would deal with the Amiregent. As she waited for the ink to dry she turned to Rawset. 'And what does T'Diemn think of the Amiregent's actions?'

'They are outraged. They want you to save our people but they don't think you should pay the gold. What will you do?'

Imoshen sealed the message. She did not know how she was going to save Miriane, but she owed Cariah this. 'You can tell General Tulkhan that I will not let our people down.'

Chapter Eleven

When a servant announced the General's emissary, Imoshen frowned. Rawset has set sail only the evening before. Her frown deepened when the mercenary leader entered.

'Lightfoot,' she greeted him, wondering if he had proven as untrustworthy as his former leader. 'When did you become the General's emissary?'

He reached under his cloak to unbuckle the sword he wore. 'The General said I was to show you this weapon.'

'I know it.' Imoshen formally accepted the massive sword, palms up, head bowed. This sword had belonged to Tulkhan's grandfather, Seerkhan, who had united the Ghebite tribes. The General's father had honoured him with the weapon. It was thought to be imbued by the character of the men who wielded it.

The day before their bonding, Tulkhan had drawn this sword to reveal how her breath made the metal's snake skin pattern dance up the blade. Then he had spilt a little of his blood, explaining that Akha Khan demanded a tribute every time the sword was drawn. Imoshen treasured the memory of that shared moment.

She wrapped her hands around the hilt. It was a hand-and-a-half grip for a giant of a man. Even so, Gharavan could have found a similar sword and trusted she would not recognise the difference. Ignoring Tulkhan's edict not to use her gifts, she opened her T'En senses to the weapon.

Many life forces had been dissipated by this blade, but she ignored the pain and quested for the identity of the person who had held this weapon before Lightfoot. A sense of Tulkhan enveloped her. It was as unmistakable as it was intimate, and she missed him fiercely.

Turning away from Lightfoot, she pressed the hilt to her lips.

Then Imoshen returned the sword with the formal salute the T'En reserved for weapons of great antiquity. 'You speak truly.'

Lightfoot gave her Tulkhan's message. She liked the General's plans for ships armed with siege-breaking weapons. 'Tell Tulkhan I will speak with the engineers.'

But when Lightfoot departed, Imoshen went straight to Reothe in the library. 'Those siege machines...' She began, then stopped as the absurdity of asking advice from Tulkhan's sworn enemy struck her. But they shared a common enemy in Gharavan and Reothe was Fair Isle's greatest sea captain.

'What about the siege machines?'

'Could they be mounted on ships?'

'The giant scaffolds with their protective shields could be mounted. Planks could be thrown across from the top of the scaffolds to the port's wall. But the whole thing is academic. Such heavy machines on deck would make the ships unseaworthy.'

'What if the machines were assembled while lying off the port and taken apart when the ship was at sea?'

'That's a possibility...' He frowned. 'Why do you ask?'

Imoshen hesitated.

Reothe's eyes widened. 'The General learns quickly. Send him his siege machines, but hold some in reserve. He still needs to build up his land forces.' He frowned. 'If you send Tulkhan the means to take Port Sumair, what becomes of Fair Isle's people held hostage in the Amirate?'

'What can I do?' Imoshen leant on the table. Old maps of the city were held in place by statuettes made for this purpose. Everything of the Old Empire was designed for beauty, even these paperweights. The one before her portrayed a couple locked in an amorous embrace of exquisite sensuality. She admired the lines, then put it aside. Distress made her abrupt. 'I cannot let Cariah's sister die!'

'You cannot pay the compensation.'

'No.' Imoshen paced. 'I need to break the siege of Port Sumair. The longer it goes on, the weaker it makes Fair Isle appear. The Amirate will side with the winner. We must crush Gharavan.'

'We must free our people. If the petty princelings of the mainland believe they can flout the old alliances with impunity, they will soon be vying to divide our island between them.'

'Exactly. But how can I save them?'

'I know how hard it is to negotiate from a position without power,' he said.

But Imoshen would not be diverted. 'The Amiregent sees only the fate of the regency. Who knows if the infant Amir will live to be crowned?' She paused. This could be her son's fate. If she were killed and the General fell in battle, Tulkhan's loyal commanders and the Keldon nobles would both try to seize Fair Isle in Ashmyr's name.

'What will you do?' Reothe asked.

'Send Tulkhan his siege machines for now.'

TULKHAN ENTERED HIS shelter to find both Lightfoot and Rawset had returned.

The mercenary presented him with Seerkhan's sword, saying, 'I think she used some Dhamfeer trick to be sure I was not lying. T'Imoshen said she would speak with the engineers about the siege machines.'

As Tulkhan strapped the weapon around his hips, his hand caressed the hilt, but he could draw no sense of Imoshen from the gleaming surface.

Rawset placed two bundles on the table. 'I left more food and men with Kornel at the marsh river mouth yesterday evening.'

'What news?' Tulkhan asked.

He dug into his jerkin to pull out three messages, then felt around his neck to remove a chain. Tulkhan accepted the chain, catching the seal to hold it to the light. It was his new standard repeated in miniature. He smiled. Little escaped Imoshen.

Dismissing them, he lit the candles. He was sure the small, hasty-looking message from Imoshen was something private. But as he read the note he cursed.

Their ambassadors taken prisoner? The Amiregent's insult called for immediate action. Digesting the bad news, Tulkhan slowly broke the seal of the larger letter. This was all good news about the delivery of his standards, banners, flags and cloaks. Imoshen wrote in glowing terms of the new Parakhan Guard, bidding him to view their banner.

When Tulkhan unrolled the banner he had to admire her daring. She had adapted the symbol of the great Akha Khan himself, combining it with figures he recognised from palace paintings. Even though he knew she had designed the image to manipulate, it still made his heart race with reluctant recognition, calling on his Ghebite heritage.

Putting the banner aside, he unpacked his new standard. The sun's surface flickered in the candlelight. Unable to resist, Tulkhan ran his hand over the embroidery, marvelling at the golden thread, spun so fine it could be sewn.

He stood the banner upright. The dawn sun blazed forth against an azure sky. In the candlelight something flashed silver. His fingertips brushed the material at the top left-hand corner. Raising the candle, he identified twin moons sewn in silver thread. A rueful smile tugged at his lips. Ever the diplomat, Imoshen had found a way to include the T'En symbols.

Tulkhan unwrapped the last bundle to reveal his cloak, helmet and crest. Never again would he wear the red and purple of Gheeaba, colours of violence and death. His new colours promised life and hope.

When the rest of the new cloaks and banners arrived, he would have a symbolic burning of the old ones before the gates of Port Sumair. The colours of Gheeaba would turn to ashes while his half-brother watched.

He heard Lightfoot's voice outside and lifted the flap beckoning him. 'Come see my new standard. Your men will wear my blue cloaks. In the heat of battle we don't want soldiers forgetting whose side they are on.'

Lightfoot rubbed the material between his fingers. 'Fair Isle cloth. Finest there is. Why the newly risen sun?'

'Because Fair Isle will see a new dawn. I'll build on all that was good in the T'En Empire to create an island of culture and learning, an island where a man is valued for his worth, not his birth.' He paused, hearing Imoshen's mocking voice in his head. What was this vision worth if it excluded half of Fair Isle? Tulkhan amended his words. 'A *person* will be valued for their worth, not birth. Everyone will have a voice. From the landless to the titled, all will be heard and all will be held accountable, even the rulers.'

Lightfoot stood, rubbing his forehead thoughtfully. He let his hand drop. 'She should have trusted me to keep my word. She shouldn't have done it!'

'Done what?'

'This.' He gestured to his forehead. 'The T'En stigmata. I would have served out my contract. And now, knowing you, I...' He knelt. 'I offer my services beyond this contract.'

'I accept your service.' Tulkhan pulled Lightfoot to his feet.

'Can you get her to remove the stigmata?'

He stared at Lightfoot. 'Remove what?'

'It is there for all to see. The T'En sign!' Lightfoot touched his forehead indicating an inverted teardrop scar. 'T'Imoshen touched me with the tip of her sixth finger. It burned my skin like a brand. She looked into my eyes and left me naked in her sight. She said if I betrayed you, she would know.'

Imoshen's interference angered Tulkhan. 'In my very next letter I'll tell her to remove it. Rawset will deliver the message.' Lightfoot's expression hardened. 'What now?'

'You do not see what is before you, General Tulkhan. Next time you speak with Rawset, look for the T'En stigmata on him, too.'

Was it possible that, in his absence, Imoshen had become the dreaded Dhamfeer of legend, manipulative and cunning?

There was still one message remaining. Tulkhan opened it. This one was from Jarholfe. He boasted of his new commission and made unprovable accusations against Reothe.

'Ask your emissary who he truly serves, and why,' Lightfoot said.

'Call Rawset. Say nothing of this to him.'

When Lightfoot left, Tulkhan reread both of Imoshen's letters, looking for anything which might reveal her hidden plans. Soon Lightfoot returned with Rawset, who was wiping his wispy moustache.

'Is there some message for me to take back to T'Imoshen?' he asked. 'I thought you would want to tell her how to handle the Amiregent. He can't be allowed to execute our ambassadors. The large new moon is only –'

Tulkhan cursed, for Imoshen had not revealed this detail. 'Tell me all you know.'

'The Amiregent arrested our people on trumped up charges of treason. He demands a massive payment in gold or he will execute them. If we do not reply, he will execute them anyway.'

'I see.' Tulkhan selected a sheet of fresh paper. The Amiregent had overstepped himself. The general laid down his terms decisively, then waved the paper in the air to dry. 'I've demanded the release of my ambassadors. I also insist that the Amiregent honours the old alliance and allows the passage of my cavalry and siege machines. I will regard anything less as an act of war.' Tulkhan caught Lightfoot's nod of approval. 'I have asked for an immediate reply.'

'But... but that would mean a war on two fronts,' Rawset whispered.

'If need be.'

Rawset swallowed. 'What if the Amiregent doesn't agree? He threw the other messengers in prison.'

Tulkhan understood. 'I won't be sending you, Rawset. You are too inexperienced for this.'

'I'll take your demands,' Lightfoot said. 'I insist the honour is mine.'

Tulkhan folded the message and used his new seal. 'Take my fastest horses, Lightfoot. How many men will you need?'

'A dozen soldiers will not protect me if the Amiregent takes offence. I ride alone,' Lightfoot announced.

'But...' Rawset croaked. 'You could be executed!'

Lightfoot smiled. 'Then the General will have his answer. I serve the General. Who do you serve?'

'Yes, who do you serve, Rawset?' Tulkhan raised the candles. Flickering light fell across the young man's freckled face, illuminating his sensitive features and the T'En sign, which Tulkhan had mistaken for a birthmark. 'You're right, Lightfoot. It is there.'

'What is? Why do you look at me like that?'

'No time for lies,' Tulkhan told him. 'There is no dishonour in admitting you bear the T'En stigmata. After all, what True-man can stand against a Dhamfeer? Why did you not tell me that Imoshen forced this service on you, Rawset?'

'You appointed me to this position. I am your emissary.'

'So you say. But who do you really serve?' Lightfoot countered.

Rawset dropped to one knee. 'I serve the T'En Empress who serves Fair Isle. You are her bond-partner and her war general, so I serve you, General Tulkhan.'

'No double talk,' Tulkhan insisted. 'She forced this service upon you with the touch of her sixth finger and held you with threats.'

But Rawset rose shaking his head. He glanced to Lightfoot, then back to Tulkhan. 'No, my General. I serve because I choose to.'

'But the T'En stigmata?' Tulkhan indicated the blemish on Rawset's forehead.

'This?' Rawset shrugged. 'It itches. As the conviction came upon me that I must serve T'Imoshen so did the itching and this blemish.'

Tulkhan frowned. 'There's no coercion involved in your service?'

Rawset straightened his shoulders. 'Since I failed in my priestly studies I have been cast adrift. In Lady Protector T'Imoshen I have found my purpose.'

Tulkhan shook his head. Itching stigmata, what next? Just when he thought he understood the T'En, some new facet arose to confound him.

'Was it not thus with you, Lightfoot?' Rawset asked.

'No, it was not! I had already signed my agreement to serve the General when she forced her sign on me and with it, my compliance. But I will be free of it soon. The General has promised.'

Both men turned look to him. Tulkhan had promised to free Lightfoot but as for Rawset, how could he free a man who wanted to serve?

'I must pack my travelling kit and select a horse,' Lightfoot announced. 'I ride at dawn.'

When Lightfoot had gone, Rawset turned to Tulkhan. 'The Amiregent will have him killed. Why did you let him go?'

'He claimed the honour.'

Rawset looked as if he might argue, but seeing the General's expression, he made a quick obeisance and left.

Tulkhan sat down stiffly. He had sent men to their deaths before in the full knowledge of what he did, but it did not get any easier. Perhaps he should be grateful for this.

IMOSHEN FOUND REOTHE reading his namesake Reothe the Builder's journal on the fortification of T'Diemn.

'You may go, Karmel.' Imoshen dismissed the new Keeper of the Knowledge, who retreated, her bird-like eyes bright with curiosity.

Reothe closed the book with a snap. 'I must thank you for my new assistant.'

'The Keeper?' Imoshen was lost.

'No, Jarholfe. As leader of T'Diemn's garrison, he has asked me to prepare a report on the city's readiness to repel attack.'

Imoshen smiled. 'I trust you will be very helpful. By the way, I've implemented your suggestion. In time of war no one will be able to get past the lock keepers without the passwords.' Her smile faded. 'I've spoken with the engineers and the ships' captains, General Tulkhan will have three ships with siege machines as soon as they are ready to sail. And I have decided to go to the Amirate to free my people.'

'Why would the Amiregent listen to you?'

Imoshen hesitated. He would have to listen because she would use her gifts. 'The Amiregent will listen to me.'

Reothe's eyes kindled like twin flames. 'I will come with you.'

'No.'

'Yes. I can sail across the Inner Sea by the stars. None of this coast-crawling. I can have you there in three days, less if the winds are good. But I have my price.'

She had foreseen this and had her response ready. 'I will not attempt to heal you. I might do more damage and you need to be able-bodied to captain my ship.'

'You mistake me. I want to see you work your gifts!'

'Why?' Imoshen felt drawn to him.

'It excites me.'

Her heart skipped a beat and she fought the irrational urge to unburden herself, to admit how she missed the intimacy of the mind-touch and how she longed to trust him. She walked to the window, watching the sunlight glint on the bevelled glass. 'I shall take you as my captain, nothing more.'

'I am yours to command,' he said, but his deference was feigned, and she knew it.

Next she sought out Wharrd and told him her plans. He was not pleased.

'You must not put yourself in danger. I will go. I am your Ghiad.'

'I have my reasons for going,' Imoshen temporised. She was not about to reveal that she meant to use her gifts on the Amiregent. 'Your task is to maintain order while I am gone. Have the cavalry and remaining siege machines readied. I intend to free our people, and negotiate safe passage for Tulkhan's supplies.'

'What will I say to the General if you are killed? At least leave his son here.'

'Ashmyr comes with me.'

'What will the people of Fair Isle think?' Wharrd asked.

'I am not deserting my island. The mainland kingdoms need to see that Fair Isle cannot be bullied.'

'I understand, but heed me at least in this. Don't go with the rebel leader.'

'Enough. Before Reothe was the rebel leader he was Fair Isle's greatest sea captain. He mapped half the mysterious southern land. I think he can sail across the Pellucid Sea.'

Wharrd closed his mouth, but he remained unconvinced. Imoshen dismissed him. She had her own reasons for keeping Reothe with her. While he was by her side, he could not be working treason with the Beatific. Fair Isle faced threats on too many fronts for her to contemplate a threat within the capital.

'I wish you luck, T'Imoshen,' Wharrd said formally.

'I believe in making my own luck!'

As TULKHAN RODE up to Port Sumair's gates, the golden crest of his helmet gleamed in the sunlight. His brilliant blue cloak lifted in the dawn breeze, and behind him his army stood rank upon rank, cloaked in his new colours. He grinned, aware that the defenders would be madly sending for Gharavan.

Escorted by Kornel and the marsh-dweller, the supplies had arrived late the previous evening. Tulkhan had ordered the new uniform to be passed out, and an extra ration of food and wine distributed. Banuld's voluntary return had proven the General's judgment of his character correct.

Tulkhan was about to strike a blow at the hearts and minds of the defenders. He wanted Gharavan to see how his army had grown and despair. The thickest walls in the world could not protect a city if the men did not fight with fire in their bellies.

All the Ghebite cloaks and banners had been collected and were stacked high before the gates of Port Sumair, ready to be torched. His trumpeter rode up and down, playing the Ghebite battle signal, reminding Tulkhan that he did not have a call of his own. But using the Ghebite signal would irritate Gharavan, just as burning the Ghebite colours would incense him. Hopefully it would drive the little king to lead a sortie. This could be the opening Tulkhan needed to crack the shell of Sumair's defences. And to his frustration these defences were proving hard to crack. He had even had to temporarily halt any attempt to mine under Sumair's walls since the second tunnel had collapsed, killing two men.

Soon heads clustered thick as flies on a corpse along the defending walls and gate towers. Tulkhan galloped towards the Ghebite standard. He caught it on the end of his spear and carried it to the heaped Ghebite cloaks and banners. Tossing the standard onto the pile, he took a flaming torch.

'When I am finished there will be nothing left of Gheeaba but ashes and memories!' he roared. His horse sidled, snorting nervously. 'They'll say that King Gharavan was the man who lost the Ghebite Empire. Every kingdom that bowed to our father will spit on your memory. Watch your standard burn, Gharavan, King of the Ghebites. King of Nothing!'

As Tulkhan tossed the burning torch he felt a savage surge of pain mixed with elation. Hungry flames licked over the oil-doused material. The fire roared into life and his men gave a spontaneous cheer.

Tulkhan hoped his half-brother was spitting with rage. He hoped the useless arrows, which even now fell short of their targets, were an indication of a sortie to come.

He rode back and forth in front of his men as they cheered. The flames leaped high on the air. The smell of burning cloth stung his nostrils. He was reminded of the Aayel's funeral pyre, how Imoshen had let no one but herself touch her great-aunt's corpse. It had come the full circle. Now he had lost his family and his home to gain Fair Isle.

His thoughts turned not to the lifeless land itself but to Imoshen, her quick mind and wry sense of humour. She would understand the value of this display. He longed to have her at his side, sharing the moment with him.

'How they yell. I'll lay odds the Ghebite King launches an attack!' Rawset crowed at the General's side.

'Gharavan was ever one to act and think later,' Tulkhan said. But this time wiser counsel prevailed and the defenders of Port Sumair did not retaliate.

ON REOTHE'S ADVICE, Imoshen had taken two ships and half the Parakhan Guard, led by Crawen. While making the crossing she had interviewed the ambassadors' servant, a one-armed Ghebite veteran. Imoshen had used every opportunity to skim the surface of his mind, absorbing his description of the Amiregent's court and the tower where his master and mistress were imprisoned. Her greatest danger was the overuse of her gift. If she overextended herself, she would drift into a vulnerable stupor of exhaustion.

Just on dusk their ship had crept into the deep river estuary which housed the Amiregent's capital and taken shelter in one of the many secluded inlets. Now the pulleys creaked as the sailors lowered a dinghy.

Reothe caught her arm, leading her away from the others, his voice low and intense. 'If you don't take me with you, how will I know if you are in danger? If only my gifts were healed!'

'Tonight I go to observe the Amiregent and find his weakness. Rest easy,

I will not take any unnecessary risks. Trust me, as I trust you to care for Ashmyr.'

Before he could protest, she left him, swinging her weight over the side of the ship and scrambling down the rope ladder to the waiting boat. She took the oars and pulled away into the darkness, as Reothe glowered over the side, holding the lamp high.

As she rounded the bluff, Imoshen looked over her shoulder up to the Amiregent's city. Many lights winked from windows, just as the ambassadors' servant remembered it.

Overlooking the port stood a sturdy old tower silhouetted against the large moon. The tower was thick at the base and at least four storeys high. It was built within the city walls and situated on the cliff edge. Tulkhan would have described it a good last line of defence. She winced, aware that he would not have agreed with her plans.

Soon she heard the cries of the night seabirds scavenging in the waste from the fish markets. The smell was enough to tell her she drew close. This was the greatest city of the Amirate. Many ships were berthed here, but the fishmarkets were quiet.

Imoshen pulled into a deserted wharf and tied the boat up. Dressed in the garments of an Amirate palace servant, with the cowl drawn up over her head and her face masked from the nose down, she climbed the steps of the wharf. As long as she kept her six-fingered hands hidden and her eyes lowered, she could pass unnoticed. The wharves were strangely deserted.

Even the dockside taverns were closed, their light and laughter hidden behind shutters. Several sailors and their women came out of a bawdyhouse. Though they passed within touching distance, they ignored Imoshen. Following the servant's memory, Imoshen climbed steadily, past the prosperous merchants' quarters which reminded her of the merchant townhouses in Northpoint, to the palace itself. With a start she recognised the tower where Cariah's sister and her bond-partner were imprisoned; because she had touched the servant's mind, however briefly, she experienced the man's fear. Her mouth went dry.

Imoshen entered the palace through the kitchens. It had been her experience that, with the many comings and goings of a great household, the kitchen's entrances were the least carefully observed. She made her way through the storerooms and preparation rooms, just another servant, ignored by everyone, including the over-servants who thought her someone else's responsibility.

Stepping into the quiet passages, Imoshen followed the Ghebite servant's memory to the wing where the Amiregent entertained. It was in these interconnecting rooms that Miriane and her bond-partner had been arrested. Their servant's memories were vivid and laced with dread.

Imoshen slipped through the servants' door, to join a group of workers behind an ornately carved screen at the end of a mirrored gallery. The room beyond the screen was all subtle shadows and wavering candlelight, reflected in the highly polished floor, which glistened like water. On their left, behind another screen, musicians accompanied the mummers who performed for the Amiregent and his courtiers.

At the sight of one particular ornately dressed man, Imoshen felt a jolt of terror, as she recognised the Amiregent from the servant's emotion-laden memory. With his painted face and elaborately dressed hair, he appeared a strange creature. He might look like a court jester to her, but the man had not hesitated to assassinate the last Amiregent, then blame this murder on Fair Isle's ambassadors.

Imoshen was familiar with the Amirate's language, so she was able to understand when the mummery ended and the Amiregent dismissed the performers, calling for servants to remove their meal.

She waited until all but the last of the performers had filed past, then caught the remaining mummer's arm. 'Where is the boy Amir?'

Her words triggered the man's recent memory. He stood on a busy street in late afternoon amid a crowd who were watching an old woman and a boy pass by in a gilded carriage. Only Imoshen could see the bars which held them prisoner. She had a strong impression of a tall, thick-based tower, broodingly dark. The tower on the bluff.

'Didn't you hear? He's with his grandmother. They were sent to the tower after the assassination for their safety.' The man looked as if he might add something but shook his head disgustedly.

She let him go. What had kept him quiet was another memory of a cage suspended from the palace's walls. Carrion birds whirled around, fighting over its grisly human remains.

Imoshen's head reeled with the implications. Opening her T'En senses, she discovered the court of the Amiregent was thick with fear. Its taste was so rich it hit the back of her throat, making her gag. She reined in her awareness.

So much for taking the heir hostage to ensure the Amiregent's cooperation. It was more likely the boy and his grandmother would not leave that tower alive.

'Send for the Dreamspinner,' the Amiregent called. 'I will have a foretelling. Dim the candles.'

After a few minutes, a woman entered carrying a delicate cage. Imoshen could just make out something flashing through the bars. The woman wore a simple gown compared to the courtiers but she carried herself with pride.

'Dreamwasps!' gasped a servant.

'They say it hurts,' another muttered, her eyes and the veil beneath them illuminated by the patterns of light which came through the screen. 'But only at first. Then it feels sublime.'

'My mistress built up a tolerance to their poison until she could bear the first sting,' the other whispered. 'She rewards us with lesser stings.'

'What visions do you have for us tonight, Dreamspinner?' the Amiregent asked. 'I want to know what the General of Fair Isle plans.'

'My Amiregent, the wasps' dreams cannot always be spun into cloth of our choosing,' she warned. 'But I will see.'

The courtiers sat forward eagerly, their eyes glittering as the Dreamspinner raised the delicate cage. With a smile she unclasped her gown, letting it fall from her shoulders to bare her breasts. From her pocket she withdrew a small jar. She offered it to the Amiregent, who uncapped it eagerly. Dipping an applicator in the contents, he rubbed a little on the pulse which beat at the base of her throat.

'I will have the second sting,' he said eagerly. Voices rose, claiming the privilege of the lesser stings. 'Quiet, you will have your turn. This must be done properly.'

When they were sufficiently composed, the Dreamspinner crooned a soft, seductive song. Opening the cage, she coaxed the Dreamwasp out onto her finger. It sat there, the size of a small bird. The nobles' envious gasps were tinged with admiration. It was an exquisite creature, all iridescent wings.

Imoshen could sense their anticipation. Her heart pounded. She had heard rumours of this practice. It was frowned upon in other mainland countries, but the Dreamspinners of the Amirate were trained from childhood to endure the stings and weave a vision from the dreams. It was said many were called but only a few survived the training.

Was it a true seeing, or wish fulfilment? Imoshen flexed her gifts, questing... The Dreamspinner stiffened. Her eyes widened and her gaze went to Imoshen's screen.

Startled, Imoshen reeled in her T'En senses.

'Why do you delay?' the Amiregent asked.

'It moves!' a noble cried.

Enticed by the sweet scent of the ointment, the Dreamwasp climbed up the woman's arm. All eyes focused on its progress.

The Dreamspinner's croon changed tone to a higher pitch, an almost insect-like hum. Imoshen realised the Dreamwasp was singing in reply to her, its tone just on the edge of hearing. She wanted to extend her senses to discover what was passing between the Dreamspinner and her wasp, but dared not.

Everyone, servant and noble alike, held their breath as the Dreamwasp's body pulsed. A build-up of inner light flashed through its dark abdomen in rhythmic patterns.

In a flash of radiance, the wasp struck. The Dreamspinner gasped and swayed.

The Amiregent snatched the wasp, carefully holding the stinger away from him. 'The ointment. Quickly. I am next.'

Someone applied it to his inner wrist and he held the wasp against his flesh. The wasp's body pulsed and flashed again, then it was passed on. Nobles swarmed around the Dreamwasp, each begging for a lesser sting.

Imoshen grimaced disgustedly. Perhaps she should leave the Amiregent to his visions. The snap of boots on the stone made her hesitate. Soldiers entered, escorting a captive.

The Dreamspinner swayed, lifting one hand to point to the captive. 'Death's messenger has come.'

'Step forward.' The Amiregent's voice was high and breathless.

The soldiers moved aside to reveal the mercenary leader, Lightfoot. Imoshen bit back a gasp.

Chapter Twelve

'HONOURABLE AMIREGENT.' LIGHTFOOT gave the mercenary bow and tossed his sea-blue cloak over his shoulder. 'I carry a message from General Tulkhan.'

A servant scurried forward to pass it to the Amiregent, bending low. Imoshen shifted impatiently as he read it.

The Amiregent flung the message to the Dreamspinner with a curse. 'And how does this figure in your spinning?'

The Dreamspinner caught the scroll, her cheeks flushed, eyes ablaze with inner visions. She did not read it. 'I see a kingdom in flux. I see a great leader rise.'

'I am that leader!' the Amiregent shouted. 'Arrest this man. I'll have his hands – no, his head. That will be my answer to the Ghebite upstart. Protector General of Fair Isle? Let him see how he protects his men now.' The Amiregent paced the floor. 'I see visions, too. I see the Amirate more powerful than Gheeaba!'

'If you harm me or the ambassadors, General Tulkhan will regard it as an act of war,' Lightfoot stated.

'War?' the Amiregent snarled. 'Your General can't even put down his half-brother, that snapping pup, Gharavan.' He gestured to Lightfoot. 'Throw him in with the ambassadors. He can tell them they will die at midday tomorrow and that their heads will be sent to General Tulkhan as a token of my esteem!' The Amiregent turned back to the Dreamspinner. 'This is how I make my dreams come true. Now, what do your dreams tell you?'

He and his nobles gathered close, but Imoshen had no time for dreams. Slipping out of the formal chamber, she headed for the tower room where the ambassadors were being held. On the way she passed a long table where trays of half-eaten food had been stacked. Hastily she selected the best of several meals so that it looked like she had a fresh tray. Even condemned prisoners would expect a meal.

Waiting in the shadows, she joined the end of Lightfoot's escort. The soldiers met up with the tower guards where there was much cruel jesting at Lightfoot's expense. He endured it in silence. When they could get no entertainment from him they unlocked the doors and marched into the chamber beyond. Imoshen followed, carrying the tray.

Miriane and Shacolm stood hand in hand, fear written large in their faces. Theirs was a gilded cage, complete with thick carpets and scented sandalwood screens.

'We have a friend of yours,' the soldier announced. 'He brings you news!'

They stared at Lightfoot in confusion. When Lightfoot did not speak, the soldier pushed him forward and he fell to his knees. He was slow to move after the bruising they'd given him. Miriane and Shacolm helped him to his feet.

'That's right,' the man jeered. 'Treat his hurts. Make him well for tomorrow's execution. Oh, didn't he tell you? The General has demanded your safe return. Tomorrow we'll send your heads as a token of the Amiregent's regard.'

Shacolm lunged, but the nearest guard struck him with the flat of his sword, sending him staggering into Miriane's arms.

'Enjoy your meal,' the soldier said, shoving past Imoshen as he and the others left. She recovered her balance and the door closed behind the guards.

'He can't execute us. Fair Isle will not allow it,' Miriane insisted.

'Fair Isle's anger does us no good after our execution,' Shacolm told her, then turned to Lightfoot. 'You are Vaygharian, by your accent, but I don't know your colours. How do you come to be carrying General Tulkhan's message?'

'Lightfoot.' He gave the Vaygharian bow. 'I am the General's man and I wear his new colours.'

'I fear General Tulkhan's message will be the death of us all, Lightfoot,' Miriane whispered.

Imoshen put the tray aside. She had meant to find the Amiregent's weakness then bargain for their release, but events had forced her hand. 'How many men guard your door?'

They turned in surprise.

'How many?' Imoshen pushed back her servant's head-dress, letting the veil fall.

'Dhamfeer!' Shacolm gasped and Lightfoot made the Vaygharian sign to ward off evil.

'Imoshen!' Miriane ran to hug her. 'You have come for us.'

'It is pure chance that I am here tonight. Lucky chance for you and for Fair Isle. I did not know the General had moved to confront the Amiregent.' Anger tightened Imoshen's voice. Suddenly ravenous, she devoured the sweet flesh of a roasted bird. 'And nothing more marvellous than a merchant ship brings me to you. It lies off the port with another small ship, awaiting our return. Now... the guards?'

'Two, no more,' Shacolm said. 'But there is the palace and the town to get through.'

Tossing the bone aside, she wiped her fingers. 'The townspeople dare not peep outside their doors. The servants go about with their eyes downcast. The nobles are drunk on Dreamwasp visions and we can deal with the guards. There is an old T'En saying, *Why use force when deceit will do?*' She smiled at their confusion. 'Miriane, I know you can play-act, last winter you took a part in the entertainments.'

'Yes, but –'

'I want you to pretend you are furious with Lightfoot. Try to scratch his eyes out. Shacolm, you call for help. Here, take this.' She handed the young

Ghebite her own knife. 'We will lure the guards in, attack them, then slip away.'

'How will we get out of the palace?' Lightfoot asked.

Imoshen resumed her cowl and veil. 'Leave that to me.'

She looked into their faces one by one. Their fear and faith mixed oddly, bittersweet on her tongue. She no longer felt hungry and shaky. The tension they exuded was enough to sustain her. 'Now, Miriane. Scream!'

The young woman opened her mouth, but no sound came out. Imoshen slapped her. Shacolm shouted and started toward them. Imoshen thrust Miriane into Lightfoot's arms so that he stumbled.

The girl sprang to life, uttering a bloodcurdling scream. 'You've killed us. You and your arrogant Ghebite General!'

Lightfoot stood stunned by the attack, then her nails raked his cheek, drawing blood. He caught her wrists and bellowed with rage as her teeth sank into his hand. 'Get her off me. I swear I'll strangle her!'

Shacolm glanced to Imoshen, who had moved to one side of the door.

'Help, guards,' Imoshen cried in the Amirate language. 'They're going to kill each other!'

The soldiers opened the door. They laughed as Miriane, whose head came no higher than Lightfoot's shoulder, kicked him in the shin. He cursed her. The guards ploughed in. One grabbed Miriane and threw her across the room. She careened into the table, sending crockery and food flying.

Imoshen swung the door shut and darted over to help Miriane to her feet. Miriane bit back a scream and pointed. Imoshen spun in time to see Shacolm dodge the guard's lunge. The man's own momentum carried him onto Shacolm's knife. The guard plucked futilely at the blade's hilt, staggered and fell. Imoshen felt a rush of heady warmth as the life force left him. She reeled in her T'En perception, unwilling to partake in death.

Businesslike, Lightfoot broke his attacker's neck and let him drop. Silently, his hands moved over the body, removing all weapons. He straightened. 'Let's go.'

Imoshen fixed on his sun-lined face. He did not kill for pleasure, yet he killed without compunction. She went to touch him and discover how he could extinguish life without remorse, then thought better of it.

Miriane ran to Shacolm. 'You are unhurt?'

He caught her to him, laughing shakily.

'What's the next step of your plan?' Lightfoot asked.

If she could get them safely down to the docks and out to the boat where Reothe waited, the Amiregent would have no leverage on her, but she still had none on him.

'One thing at a time,' Imoshen said. She opened the door to peer out. The anteroom was empty. The cards lay face down, the game never to be resumed. 'Bring the bodies.'

Imoshen arranged the dead guards in the chairs with their backs to the entrance so that they appeared to be dozing. A casually thrown cloak obscured the worst of the blood. At a quick glance it seemed they would spring to attention and apologise for sleeping at their posts.

Locking the prison door after them, Imoshen turned to the others. 'Into the hall and keep to the shadows.'

'This way,' Shacolm urged. He was headed towards the public rooms of the palace.

'No. We want to pass unnoticed. We go through the servants' passages.' Now she wished she had thought to take three of the household tabards. 'Hold hands. I will lead us down empty passages.'

Miriane grasped her hand, fingers trembling. Shacolm was next and Lightfoot last. Even now Imoshen could feel the need of these three people sustaining her. She called on that T'En part of herself which had wanted to feast on the death of those guards. Tension built in her. She could discern that the corridor as far as the steps was empty.

'My head hurts,' Miriane whispered. 'Why do I feel like this?'

'Come,' Imoshen urged. She guessed Miriane was more susceptible to the gifts than most, due to her mixed heritage.

Relying on her senses to tell her if passageways were clear, she led them back to the storerooms just off the kitchens and into the deserted courtyard. When Imoshen had entered the palace, the larger gates had been open for delivery wagons. Now these were closed and only a small gate stood open, manned by a single sentry.

Lightfoot reached for his knife. 'I'll –'

'No. You deal too freely in death. We'll do it my way. Hold hands.'

'I think I'm going to be sick,' Miriane warned.

'Just a little longer.'

The guard grimaced, then strode off around a corner. In a moment they could hear him relieving himself.

'Quickly.' Imoshen darted through the gate.

They hurried after her, keeping to the shadows of the narrow street until at last they reached the wharves and the boat. It looked inviting. Imoshen was weary, but she would achieve nothing if she could not gain a lever on the Amiregent.

'Go quickly now. Once you round the bluff, you will see the lights of the two ships. When you reach them, tell Reothe to send the boat back for me. I'll look for it here.'

'You're not coming with us?' asked Lightfoot.

'No.'

Imoshen moved into the shadows as the boat slipped quickly away on the dark water.

The sky was lit only by starlight and the large moon. Silhouetted against the stars was Imoshen's destination, the sturdy old tower. She picked her way through the quiet streets.

Away from the town, a path wound towards the bluff. There was not enough light to cast a shadow on the grass. Imoshen slipped off her shoes to walk over the bare earth of the wheel ruts and opened her T'En senses. The grandmother and the boy Amir had passed this way. The old woman did not expect to leave the tower alive.

Hearing horses, Imoshen stepped into a hollow and watched as two riders passed. They roused the guard and he opened the tower gate. Torchlight fell on the men's faces. Foreboding gripped her as she recognised the Amiregent without his court finery.

He swung down from the saddle saying, 'I have not been here this night, guard. Whatever you hear, do not climb the stairs.'

The man nodded and took the horses aside. Imoshen slipped inside the courtyard.

The light of a single flaming torch danced on the stonework as the Amiregent climbed the tower stairs, followed by his companion who carried something under a silken cover. Imoshen clung to the shadows just beyond the curve of the steps.

'If we are to have war with Fair Isle, I want no civil unrest. No one will use this brat to unite the people against me. He and his grandmother die tonight. And there must be no one to claim this was anything other than suicide. Kill that gate guard before you leave,' the Amiregent ordered softly.

'Then it will be war?'

'Oh, yes. Fair Isle is ripe for plunder. And whether Gharavan or Tulkhan win, the Ghebites are a spent force. Internal strife will consume their empire.'

'What of the T'En?'

'Only two of the throwbacks live, and they are at each other's throats, from what my spies tell me.'

Imoshen went cold.

'You have my jewels?' the Amiregent asked. 'Good, open the door.'

There was a soft jingle as his companion selected a key. The mechanism clicked as the tumblers fell inside the lock and the door creaked open. The men entered the room, leaving the door a little ajar. The keys swayed in the lock. Imoshen edged closer to listen.

'Wake, old woman. Your time has come!' the Amiregent said.

A soft scuffle followed and Imoshen imagined them dragging the Amir's grandmother from her bed.

'Take your hands off me. What manner of man are you?' a querulous voice demanded. 'Why do you come at this late hour?'

He laughed. 'You should be honoured I come in person. General Tulkhan has forced my hand. Wake the boy.'

The old woman uttered a sharp cry of denial. A child's frightened whimper urged Imoshen to act, but she held back.

'Remove the cover.' A high-pitched buzz filled the air.

'Hush, my jewels,' the Amiregent purred.

'Dreamwasps?' the old woman gasped. 'You can't –'

'By tomorrow evening all of the Amirate will know how you bribed the guard to bring Dreamwasps. You induced them to give you and the boy a fatal dose of their sweet venom, bringing you eternal sleep instead of brilliant dreams.' He laughed softly. 'How can I be blamed for your suicide?'

Imoshen felt the old woman's terror and the little boy's fearful confusion. She sensed the bright points of anger within the enraged Dreamwasps. They knew nothing of their role in the larger world, wanting only to vent their fury.

Imoshen swung the door open. By the light of the single torch, she saw the old woman with a small boy clinging to her and the two men. The Amiregent held a delicate cage. His concentration was on the contents, four glistening creatures, their iridescent wings flashing.

The other man noticed her and raised the torch. 'Evil eyes!'

'Run.' The old woman thrust the boy towards the door. 'Run for your life.'

'No, you don't!' the Amiregent lunged for him.

Imoshen kicked the back of his knee. His leg crumpled. He cursed, dropping the Dreamwasps. Their cage fell to the stone with a tinkle of breaking glass.

But Imoshen was still moving. The ball of her foot caught the Amiregent's conspirator in the midsection. He grunted as the torch fell from his hand, rolling under the bed. They were plunged into darkness except for four whirling points of angry light.

'My jewels!' A flash of light from a passing wasp revealed the Amiregent's horror-struck features as he reared back.

Imoshen dragged the old woman towards the door, colliding with the boy, who had stopped to watch. Shoving them out of the room, Imoshen gripped the door handle.

'No!' The conspirator lunged across the floor on his knees. A Dreamwasp landed on his face. Its body flashed with rage as it attacked. His roar changed to a high-pitched scream.

Imoshen slammed the door and spun the keys in the lock. Another scream rent the air, muffled only slightly by the thick walls and solid wood.

'I hope he dreams his death a thousand times before it comes!' the old woman whispered with relish.

'This way,' Imoshen urged. 'The guard was told not to investigate, but the screams might bring him.'

'I doubt it. The Amiregent ruled by fear.'

'Even still, we must hurry. I want to speak with you.' Imoshen felt for the stairs. 'Link hands.'

Silently they made their way down the dark steps, leaving the tortured male screams and splintering of furniture.

At the foot of the stairs they found the guard standing irresolute, a flaming torch in his hand.

'Amir.' He dropped to his knees before the boy and the old woman, then he recognised Imoshen for what she was. With a cry of terror, he drew his sword. 'Beware the accursed Blood-eyes!'

'Fool,' the old woman hissed. 'Bring me a branch of candles, then saddle some horses. The usurper is dead. I am Amiregent.'

He lit the candles, then hurried away.

'Will he betray you?' Imoshen asked.

The old woman smiled. 'Not if he wants to live. Now, what do you want of me? Are you really T'Imoshen of Fair Isle?'

'I came to seek the lives of my ambassadors.'

'They will be freed. That fool let greed make his decisions. I am not so certain the Ghebites are a spent force.'

The child pulled on her hand. 'Hungry.'

'Hush, boy. Listen and learn. One day you will have to lead your people. We will gather my loyal followers, then enter the palace. By dawn we will have the city. My first official act will be to release your people.'

'They are already free,' Imoshen said.

The old woman's sharp eyes fixed on her. 'Then why are you here?'

'I came to strike a bargain. I need safe passage for my army's cavalry and siege machines to the borders of the Lowlands.'

'Done.'

Imoshen laughed.

'I've no time for anything but straight talking tonight,' the old woman said. 'The balance of power shifts and it must shift in our direction. Tomorrow my grandson will be restored to his rightful place as Amir of the Amirate!'

'I must go. Tomorrow we will renew the old alliance,' Imoshen said. Tonight four men had died. She did not have to strike the killing blow to feel the weight of their deaths. She was weary, and she ached to hold Ashmyr and feast on his innocence.

Across the room the boy Amir was playing with wood chips, fighting imaginary battles on the cold flagstones. Were they all tools of destiny?

'Till tomorrow, then,' the new Amiregent said.

When Imoshen returned to the wharves all was quiet, misleadingly so. Soon the new Amiregent would begin her night of blood-letting to consolidate her power. Imoshen knew before dawn the streets would ring to the sounds of soldiers loyal to the dead Amiregent making their last stand. She wanted to be gone long before that. The sight of the empty rowboat at its mooring was welcome. Imoshen ran the last steps down to the pier then hesitated. Where was the sailor who had rowed the boat? Someone grabbed her from behind.

She knew that scent. 'Reothe.'

'This time. But it could have been a trap. Have care, Imoshen.' He shook her briefly then released her. 'Into the boat.'

Knowing that he was right, she took the stern seat.

Reothe bent his back to the oars, his silence oppressive. Imoshen watched his shadowed face.

After they rounded the bluff, before they neared his vessels, he shipped oars. 'You lied to me, Imoshen. You said you were only going to discover the Amiregent's weakness.'

'My ambassadors are safe, and tomorrow when we –'

'– meet the Amiregent we bargain from a better position. But this wasn't what we agreed!'

Beyond his shoulders the dark silhouettes of their vessels rose up and down with the swell. Imoshen licked her lips. 'General Tulkhan forced my hand. He demanded the release of Fair Isle's ambassadors and the Amiregent's response was to order their deaths.'

'So Lightfoot said.'

'There's more. The Amiregent is dead and by the time we dock tomorrow, the infant Amir's grandmother will be regent. She has promised to honour the old alliance.'

'Imoshen...'

She waited, but he said no more. There was nothing but the sound of the night birds calling over the sea. Weariness overcame her. 'They said Fair Isle was ripe for the taking, Reothe. They did not fear us because they believed that the last two T'En were at each other's throats!' She forced herself to think ahead. 'Tomorrow I will renew the old alliance with the Amiregent and then return to T'Diemn. I must get word to the General. The Amiregent can send her fastest rider as a sign of good faith. We'll be back in T'Diemn by then. But I want to send support sooner. If the people of Sumair know the siege machines are coming, they might try to break the siege. How long will it take to send the ships from T'Diemn, then drive the wagons across the Amirate to the Lowlands?'

'These things always take longer than expected,' Reothe answered. 'Why not send Lightfoot with my second ship straight up the coast to the blockade at Port Sumair?'

'Good. With luck Tulkhan will be planning Gharavan's execution –'

Reothe dropped to his knees and gripped her shoulders. The boat rocked. 'You're lucky it isn't your execution.'

Imoshen clutched the sides of the boat and said nothing.

'You could have been killed!' Reothe's cruel grasp softened as he pulled her closer. He pressed his lips to her forehead, then pulled back. 'If you face death again, I want to be by your side.'

Imoshen's breath caught in her throat. 'You have no right to make that demand and I make no promises.'

He released her. 'No, you promise me nothing.'

'I did what needed to be done.'

'You cripple my gifts. Then you leave me to mind your child while you risk your life. You have a hard head and a hard heart, Imoshen.'

She looked away. Let Reothe believe her heartless.

He resumed his seat, taking the oars but not dipping them into the sea. 'I wish I had been there to see you exercise your powers!'

She thought of the screaming men and the angry Dreamwasps and shuddered. 'Luck was with me. I hardly used my gifts at all.' Her voice caught. 'Take me to the ship. I am responsible for four deaths tonight.'

'You did not kill, death's shadow walked by your side, our ambassadors' lives for theirs. It is a fair bargain.'

But she shook her head and would not speak again.

*   *   *

IMOSHEN SEALED THE message with the print of her sixth finger and handed it to Lightfoot, who was about to sail up the coast to join the blockade of Port Sumair. 'For General Tulkhan.'

Lightfoot tucked the message inside his jerkin then hesitated. 'I owe you my life.'

'There is no obligation.' Imoshen read his face. 'Speak your mind.'

'We mercenaries have a saying that service given freely is more enduring than service bought by fear or wealth.'

'The T'En have a similar saying,' Imoshen replied. The rhythmic chant of Amirate wharf workers unloading cargo came through the open cabin window.

'Would you have me beg?' Lightfoot ground out.

Imoshen stared blankly at him.

'I cannot live enslaved by your stigmata!' He gestured to his forehead.

And she recalled touching him with her sixth finger. She had not known Lightfoot would prove loyal beyond his mercenary contract. She was not even sure if her touch had done more than mark his skin.

'Forgive me. I was not mocking you. Much has happened since that night.' She called on her healing gift and brushed the pad of her thumb across the mark on his forehead. The inverted teardrop scar was gone, as was the frown line which had marked his forehead. 'There, you are your own man.'

With evident relief, he gave the mercenary salute. 'I swear to serve you and your war general, T'En Empress.'

'I accept,' Imoshen said. It was strange, by removing her sign she had made him more her servant.

TULKHAN RECOGNISED NEITHER the horse nor the rider, who wore the colours of the Amirate. He expected bad news, but the man offered obeisance and presented him with a message sealed with the imprint of Imoshen's sixth finger.

Curious, Tulkhan broke the seal. He gave a bark of laughter. By luck Imoshen had been in the Amirate ready to negotiate a new alliance when his messenger arrived. 'The Amiregent grants our cavalry and siege machines safe passage. Port Sumair is ours!'

The men nearest him cheered and the cry went up through the encampment.

'Send in Banuld,' Tulkhan told Kornel.

By the time the marsh-dweller arrived, every man in the camp knew the Amirate had agreed to honour the old alliance with Fair Isle.

Tulkhan threaded several gold beads onto a leather thong. 'Kornel, tell Banuld-Chi that I have valued his service. And that he is free to go.'

'You've already paid him,' Kornel muttered.

'He has proven his loyalty. Tell him what I said.' Tulkhan came to his feet and grasped the marsh-dweller's arm.

Kornel translated, his tone ungracious.

When they had gone, Tulkhan looked up to see Rawset.

'Do you wish me to carry a message to T'Imoshen?'

Tulkhan shook his head. 'Not until Port Sumair is mine. Share a mug of Vorsch. We'll drink to Lightfoot's safe return!'

ON HER RETURN to T'Diemn, Imoshen had not expected to be greeted with pomp and display, but neither had she expected silence, shuttered doors and windows. It reminded her of the climate of fear that had hung over the Amirate and she grew more uneasy with every passing moment.

Anxious to give Wharrd the good news, Imoshen did not bother to send servants on ahead, but set off in the growing dusk with Reothe, Miriane and Shacolm.

Changing Ashmyr's basket to the other hip, she left the lower city behind and crossed the fortified bridge to enter old T'Diemn. Beyond the lanes, the formal square was empty. No servants clustered on the steps of the palace awaiting instructions, but then they were not expecting her.

Imoshen entered the palace and rang for a servant. 'I want to see the Lord Fairban and Lord Commander Wharrd. Have the kitchen send up a festive meal. I will await them in the Jade Room.' The man hurried off and Imoshen turned to the others. 'Dine with me. Your safe return and the honouring of the old alliance will be celebrated throughout Fair Isle, but for tonight let us have an intimate celebration.'

When they reached the chamber, Imoshen placed the sleeping baby's basket in a quiet corner and lit the candles while Miriane and Shacolm moved the low couches to the table for an intimate Old Empire meal.

'Something feels wrong, Imoshen,' Reothe said softly.

'Your gifts?'

'I don't need the gifts to sense the tension. Don't you feel it?'

Imoshen did. She lit the last candle and pinched out the taper. 'Wharrd will know what's going on.'

The door flew open. Kalleen stood there, grief distorting her features. 'Wharrd died this morning!'

Imoshen reached for Reothe. 'How can this be?'

'You would follow the Empress's example. You would flaunt your lover.' Kalleen pointed to Reothe. 'The Ghebites don't understand. They think you've dishonoured their general. Wharrd died bound by his warrior code. Curse the Gheeakhan!' A sob escaped her. 'This very morning I held him in my arms and begged him to live long enough for you to return but –'

'Miriane?' Lord Fairban thrust the door open. He had aged since Cariah's death, but his face lit up at the sight of his youngest daughter. 'When they told me of your plight, I lost all hope; but here you are.'

'Father!' She laughed and ran across the room to throw her arms around him. 'Imoshen saved us.'

'Blessed be the Empress,' Lord Fairban whispered in High T'En, then put his daughter aside, turning to Imoshen. 'But evil has been at work in T'Diemn. The –'

Shuddering on its hinges, the door was flung open a third time. Imoshen froze as a dozen fully armed Ghebites entered the room, Jarholfe at their lead.

He pointed to her. 'Arrest the whore and her Dhamfeer lover!'

Chapter Thirteen

JARHOLFE GESTURED TO Reothe contemptuously. 'Don't hesitate to take the male. His gifts are crippled and he has no strength in his left side.'

The T'Diemn garrison guards spread out, circling Reothe, who moved to keep the wall at his back.

'Stop this!' Lord Fairban ordered, but they ignored him.

Sick disbelief filled Imoshen. She realised this was what Kalleen had come to warn them about but had been too caught up in her grief to explain.

'Betrayer, get out of my sight!' Imoshen grabbed Kalleen and shook her, but in the instant before she pushed the young woman aside, she whispered. 'Take Ashmyr. He's by the door. If you bear me any love, get him to safety.'

Off balance from Imoshen's push Kalleen tripped, falling between two low couches. The Ghebites ignored her.

Imoshen spun to see Reothe strike out, a slender jade statuette his weapon. One man's sword went flying, another fell with a broken wrist. As Reothe ducked to grab the fallen sword, Jarholfe pounced, brutally pinning his arms behind his back.

From behind the strands of dishevelled silver hair, the last T'En warrior glared up at his captors. One of them struck the back of Reothe's head and he collapsed. The impact made Imoshen's head ache in sympathy. Nausea threatened to swamp her.

'Now the Dhamfeer bitch!' Jarholfe ordered. As they turned on Imoshen, she recognised the Ghebite priest at Jarholfe's side. The Cadre's eyes gleamed with malevolent satisfaction and she realised it was he who pulled Jarholfe's strings.

'Not T'Imoshen!' Miriane's cry pierced Imoshen's abstraction. 'She saved us. She has organised safe passage for siege machines. She –'

Jarholfe's slap sent her flying. 'Get your woman out of here, Shacolm, or I must question your loyalty, too?'

Miriane's bond-partner swept up her limp body and, casting Imoshen one swift glance, slipped away.

'You call this loyalty, Jarholfe?' Imoshen asked. 'Who appointed you leader of T'Diemn's garrison?'

'Don't listen to her, she twists everything with her Dhamfeer cunning,' the Cadre warned.

Imoshen faced the circle of men. They had served her on the road back from Northpoint, and now they hesitated to act against her. 'I forgive your actions so far because you have been misled. But from this moment forward, I will forgive nothing. Step aside. I must speak with your commander.'

They glanced at each other. They had seen her restore a blind man's sight. Respect, or perhaps self-preservation, overcame the conflict of orders.

Untouched, Imoshen stepped through the men to confront Jarholfe and the Cadre. 'By what right do you take this action?'

'The Gheeakhan!' The Cadre was exultant.

'The Ghebite warrior code? I don't see the connection.' Imoshen focused on Jarholfe, believing him more reasonable. 'You served me well on the journey south. I would hear this from your lips. Why do you betray my trust?'

'Acting under his Ghiad, Lord Commander Wharrd defended your honour against the charges of dishonouring General Tulkhan. Two days ago he took a mortal wound and he died this morning, confirming your guilt.'

'Only your death and the death of your half-blood brat can restore the General's honour,' the Cadre announced.

Imoshen forced herself not to search the room to see if Kalleen had escaped with her son. A rush of potent anger made her vision swim with a thousand fireflies of fury. Desperately she sought to influence the men but, without physical contact, both were impervious to her gift.

As she went to touch Jarholfe's hand, he pulled away and she changed the gesture into a plea. 'This brings me great sorrow. You have assumed the role of judge and executioner, murdering Wharrd, a good True-man. This is Fair Isle, not Gheeaba. By General Tulkhan's signed agreement, the laws of the T'En church govern our society. In this land might is not right.'

Her head spun with the implications. If the Ghebite priest could overturn the Beatific's ruling, how many other basic rights could he overturn? Would she live to see Fair Isle go the way of the mainland, where most women could not own property or speak for themselves?

'The General has been bewitched by your black sorcery. We must act to save his soul,' the Cadre said piously.

Imoshen snorted. If the priest had his way, she would not live long enough to see the women of Fair Isle brought low.

Behind the Cadre, she was aware of movement as Kalleen scuttled out the door with Ashmyr's basket in her arms. Praying the baby would not choose this moment to wake, Imoshen glared at the men. 'You have overstepped your authority, Jarholfe. General Tulkhan ordered you to serve me. It brings me no joy to place you under arrest for the murder of Lord Commander Wharrd.'

Jarholfe would have protested but Imoshen overrode him, gesturing to one of his men. 'Send for the Beatific. Tell her to prepare a hearing. She must bring representatives for both the Lady of Windhaven, on behalf of her dead bond-partner, and Jarholfe, who stands accused of Wharrd's murder.'

Reothe groaned as he regained consciousness.

Imoshen blocked out the sound. She must not to think of him restrained and vulnerable. She focused on Jarholfe, but her words were for the Cadre. 'The Beatific will be your judge, by the laws of Fair Isle.'

'The Ghebite priesthood does not recognise those laws,' the Cadre said.

Lord Fairban bristled. 'The Empress's word is law!'

'This is all the law I need!' Jarholfe grabbed Lord Fairban, bringing his knife to the old nobleman's throat. 'I won't take orders from a stinking Dhamfeer!'

Imoshen's heart faltered. She had failed Cariah, she must not fail her father. 'Let Lord Fairban go, I will not resist.'

'No. You won't resist. You'll be too busy with this!' Jarholfe shifted the blade lower and drove it into Fairban's abdomen in a cruel, gouging movement.

The old man screamed. Jarholfe shoved him into Imoshen's arms. His blood stained her travelling clothes.

Jarholfe strode past them to kick Reothe in the face. 'Take the rebel leader away. He's nothing but a powerless cripple. It's the woman we have to be wary of and she has her limits.'

While Imoshen fought to stem Fairban's blood, the men dragged Reothe away. She had not trusted him enough to restore his gifts, and the knowledge seared her.

Jarholfe crouched beside her, his malignant expression a revelation. 'I have seen you wear yourself out healing worthless peasants. Heal this old man if you can, Dhamfeer.' He sprang to his feet. 'Lock him in with her.'

'You can't move Lord Fairban. It might kill him.' Imoshen pressed the wound closed, her hands warm and slick with blood. The old man was barely conscious.

'Then you'll have to make sure he lives!'

Without apology, the Ghebites swung Fairban off the floor. Half tripping in her attempts to keep up with the men, Imoshen hurried at their side. They carried the old nobleman along the hall, down the steps and into the store room near the upper servants' quarters. The door opened on darkness and they threw the injured man inside, pushing her after him.

'Wait. Search her. She carries a knife!' Jarholfe ordered.

When none of his men moved, he strode into the storeroom to confront Imoshen. Before he could lay hands on her, she pulled the knife free and held it out hilt first.

He hesitated as if he expected a knife thrust.

'Fool!' she hissed. 'Unlike you, I value life.'

Cursing, he took the weapon and shoved her. She fell onto the cold stone and the door swung shut. The bolt shot home. Imoshen knew that she could urge the bolt to do her bidding, but not yet, not until she was certain she could escape with Lord Fairban.

His soft panting came to her, every few heartbeats it would stop as a moan escaped him, then start up again. Despairing, she strove to staunch the bleeding.

Lord Fairban caught her hands. 'You mustn't waste your gifts on me. Save yourself. The Cadre means to wipe out the last of the T'En.'

She shook her head and prayed that Kalleen had escaped with her son. But she must not let fear for Ashmyr shatter her concentration. For now, his fate, like Reothe's, was beyond her control. Imoshen concentrated on the wound and prepared to fight the one battle she knew she had a chance of winning. She called on her gift.

A SINGLE SHOUT alerted Tulkhan. By the time he had stepped out of the shelter, a dozen or so of his men arrived, dragging a prisoner. Torchlight fell on Kornel's bruised face.

'We caught him trying to sneak out of the camp.'

Unless he was contacting spies from the port, Kornel had no reason to leave the camp. Tulkhan frowned. 'Turn out his pockets. The penalty for treason is death.'

'I'm no spy,' Kornel insisted. 'Haven't I proved my worth? Without me, you would never have taken your army through the marshlands.'

Rawset joined them as one of the men handed Tulkhan something wrapped in a rag. A heavy gold necklace unrolled and fell into his hand. Tulkhan recognised it as belonging to Banuld-Chi. 'Where is the marsh-dweller, Kornel?'

'How should I know? He lost the necklace on the fall of a dice. I haven't seen him since he left yesterday.'

'Why were you leaving the camp?' Tulkhan asked.

'I wasn't. I couldn't sleep. Went for a walk. Needed to take a leak, so I went to the outer ditch rather than the latrines. They don't half stink.'

It was true. The logistics of providing fresh water and latrines for an army this size was staggering.

'If the smell offends you, we'll move the latrines. You can be on digging duty.' Tulkhan laughed at Kornel's expression. He nodded to his men. 'Let him go.'

Kornel straightened his clothes and left.

Rawset lowered his voice. 'Answers spring too easily to that man's tongue.'

Tulkhan felt the same way. He weighed the gold in his hands.

'You two.' He gestured to the men who had brought Kornel in. 'Take the three fastest horses and go after the marsh-dweller. Bring him back to me. I will have verification of Kornel's words from the marsh-dweller's own lips.'

At least he had good news. That very evening three ships had arrived from T'Diemn and were in the process of erecting siege towers. The pressure on Port Sumair was growing.

MUCH LATER IMOSHEN woke to blazing torchlight and shouting voices. Dried blood encrusted her hands and her tabard. Lord Fairban slept with his head on her lap.

Squinting into the glare, she identified Jarholfe and his men. A rush of fear washed away her weariness but did not restore her drained gifts. Her vulnerability was terrifying.

'Not so proud now,' Jarholfe sneered, fingering his sword hilt.

Surely they did not mean to kill her like this? They needed the sanctity of a trial to change her death from murder to execution.

Jarholfe gestured. 'Stand up.'

Careful not to reopen the tender new skin covering Fairban's wound, Imoshen slipped his head from her lap. His hand sought hers. She squeezed his fingers briefly.

Jarholfe's men waited at the door, as he moved towards her he waved a sheet of paper covered with fine Ghebite writing. 'The Cadre has drawn up your confession, Dhamfeer bitch. Sign it and save yourself the grief of torture.'

Mouth dry, Imoshen met his eyes. No spark of empathy stirred in their depths. 'I will sign nothing.'

'You will sign. Be sure of that. Everyone signs eventually. I see the old man still lives.'

Imoshen heard the implied threat and her heart sank.

'You think you're so clever,' Jarholfe snarled. 'But we have your lover and he will break soon. He will sign his confession and implicate you. As for the half-breed brat, he will not get out of T'Diemn alive!'

Imoshen felt triumphant. Kalleen had escaped with her son. But they were torturing Reothe. She must divert them. 'I am innocent of the charges and I can prove it. The Orb of Truth will vindicate me before all of Fair Isle. Call on the Beatific to bring the Orb of Truth!'

'The Beatific has no authority here,' the Cadre said, stepping out from behind Jarholfe's men. 'Besides, your own actions have condemned you. Only one who deals in the black arts of sorcery could heal this man.'

'The only blackness is in your hearts and minds. It clouds your vision. When General Tulkhan hears of this, he will have your heads on pikes over the gates. He made me his Voice.'

'We act to save him from himself!' the Cadre shouted. 'Lock her away before she poisons your minds.'

Jarholfe slammed the door.

Only a sliver of light came under the gap between the door and the floor. Imoshen could hear them walking away. In the darkness, she sank to her knees. If only she could contact Tulkhan. He had refused the intimacy of the mind-touch and now, in an emergency, she could not reach him. The irony of it hit her. She had not trusted Reothe enough to heal him and Tulkhan had not trusted her enough to let down his defences.

'I am sorry,' Lord Fairban whispered.

'We are not dead yet.'

'Hope is the province of the young,' he said, quoting an old T'En saying.

But Imoshen had no time for philosophy. If the Cadre and Jarholfe did not take the Orb as bait, she would have to move swiftly. She must free Reothe before they could force a confession from him. But first she needed rest to restore her gifts. Her greatest consolation was knowing that Kalleen and Ashmyr were safely hidden somewhere in the old city.

*   *   *

THE DAWN BEFORE the large new moon found Tulkhan preparing to ride the camp's defensive perimeter. He pulled his hood up against the fine drizzle. A shout drew his attention just as he put his foot in the stirrup.

Rawset ran up to him. 'Lightfoot's returned!'

Tulkhan walked his mount back to the horse-handlers and went to meet Lightfoot, who was waiting under the awning of the shelter.

Tulkhan clasped his shoulder and caught Rawset's eye. 'Send in some Vorsch.'

Lightfoot turned his face to the dim sun beyond the clouds. 'Do you see the T'En stigmata?'

Tulkhan searched the man's forehead. 'Not a sign.'

'She removed it. I...' He shook his head.

Rawset returned with the drink and food.

'Pour a drink and raise your glass,' Tulkhan said. 'To the fall of Port Sumair.'

He grinned as the men echoed his toast. It might be raining and the camp ankle-deep in mud, but the siege was about to turn in their favour.

IMOSHEN WOKE WITH the bitter taste of fear on her tongue. The storeroom was dank and dark, yet her inner senses told her it was late morning. When she touched Lord Fairban, his skin was hot with fever and she knew despite her best efforts the wound was festering. Another day in this place and he would be dead. She stood, arching her back, and wished for warm water, food and a change of clothes.

Searching her T'En senses she found her gifts restored at least for now. She was ravenously hungry and if she eased the old lord's fever, she would deplete her resources again.

Imoshen concentrated, sifting through the minds of those nearest for something that might help her. Not surprisingly, the palace servants walked the corridors in terror. Of the two Ghebites at her door, one had gone to relieve himself and the other was asleep, snoring loudly. Imoshen concentrated on the door's bolt. It slid without a sound and the door swung inward at her touch.

Heart thumping, she glanced up and down the hall. The stench of alcohol was strong on the sleeping man's breath. Returning to the storeroom, she lifted the old lord onto her shoulders, her leg muscles straining as she straightened. It was the work of a moment to close the door and send the bolt home.

Carrying the old man, she went up the passage. At the entrance to the servants' quarters she paused to ease Fairban's weight, then entered Keeper Karmel's room.

Leaving Lord Fairban on the bed, she stripped off her blood-stained clothes and refreshed herself, bathing in a basin of water still lukewarm from the servant's use. Then she cleaned the old man, sponging him down to cool his heated flesh.

She had not fed Ashmyr since the evening before. Her breasts ached with the build-up of milk and the onset of the milk fever. Huddling in the chair she sought to heal herself. The effort left her so weary, she slept again.

'T'Imoshen?' the Keeper whispered.

She woke with a start, momentarily disoriented, then everything came back to her. 'Shut the door, Karmel. Have you any news of my son?'

'They look everywhere for him. All gates out of the old city are closed and soldiers search the houses, but they rob and drink as much as they search.'

'Good. And Reothe?'

'They have him in the ball-court. None of the servants are allowed near.'

'What of the Beatific?'

'She is under arrest in the Basilica.'

'My Parakhan Guard?'

'Some died in the initial confrontation. The rest have gone into hiding.'

'Murgon and his Tractarians?'

'I have heard nothing of them.'

Relief swept Imoshen. Her greatest fear was that the Cadre would use Fair Isle's own weapons against her.

'Lady Miriane and her bond-partner have retreated to their chambers,' the Keeper said. 'I spoke with their servant during noon meal. No one knows what to do. With Jarholfe's men roaming the palace I thought it safest to hide in my room.'

Imoshen's stomach rumbled. 'I fear I must ask you to bring me food, my formal clothes and healing herbs. See if you can bring Miriane here.'

Keeper Karmel slipped away. She was an old woman, worthless in Ghebite eyes. Imoshen hoped her comings and goings would not be remarked.

As Imoshen bathed Lord Fairban's forehead she considered her position. It would take only a small trigger to tip the balance of power. Did she want the townsfolk to pick up kitchen knives and tools of trade and turn on the Ghebites? If only Woodvine and the other southern nobles had not returned to the highlands. She could have used Reothe's Keldon supporters now.

An image of Reothe as they dragged him away returned to her. Resolutely, she turned her mind from him and the fate of her son. She had to think like a statesman – not a mother and certainly not a lover. But a wave of weariness rolled over her. Anxiously, she felt her forehead, fearing the milk fever would burn up her gift's reserves.

For once she had to place her trust in another. She sat in the chair beside the bed and dozed, waking every now and then to bathe Fairban's head. The afternoon passed in a haze of grey exhaustion and feverish dreams.

Imoshen's stomach told her it was late afternoon when the Keeper returned with Miriane and Shacolm.

'I'm sorry I took so long,' the old woman whispered.

'You are safe, that is all that matters,' Imoshen said, aware of Miriane and Shacolm watching anxiously. If she failed, their lives were forfeit.

She accepted salted meat and wine, draining half a cup in one gulp. While chewing the meat, she mixed a herbal drink for the old man and something very similar for herself. She handed Fairban's drink to Miriane to administer and drank her own, ignoring the acrid taste.

With the Keeper's help she dressed in an elaborate formal tabard with a shimmering undergown. If she was to unite the people against their oppressors, she must look the part. Her pregnancy did not show and would not for a while. She was glad no one knew. If the Cadre suspected who the father of this child was, he would have killed her himself!

'I must free Reothe before I make a move against Jarholfe and the Cadre. And we must hide Lord Fairban.' Imoshen thought back to Reothe's unexpected arrival in the library. She turned to the old woman. 'Do you know the secret passages?'

The woman smiled.

Imoshen felt an answering smile on her own lips.

COLD ANGER CONSUMED Tulkhan as he crouched over Banuld's lifeless, mud-stained body. 'Where did you find him?'

'Less than halfway to the marsh wall. One of the dogs led us to him.'

Tulkhan nodded and came to his feet. They were under the awning of his shelter. A stinging sleet fell, its icy needles piercing all but the thickest clothes. 'Bring Kornel.'

The man was not a spy. He was something much simpler, a greedy murderer. Tulkhan heard Rawset and Lightfoot behind him, conferring. As he looked down at the corpse at his feet, it came to him that he had failed Banuld.

'What will you do with him?' Rawset asked.

'Send his body back to the marsh-village with his gold and my apologies. It is the least I can do,' Tulkhan muttered.

Rawset cleared his throat. 'I meant Kornel.'

'Execute him.'

'General?' A soldier approached. Water dripped down the man's face, plastering his hair to his head. 'Kornel is gone.'

Tulkhan cursed. 'Search the camp.' But he suspected Kornel had already escaped. The man was too cunning. The clouds to the west parted and the westering sun's pale golden light bathed their camp, slanting through the icy rain. It was late afternoon.

THE KEEPER LED the way while Shacolm carried Lord Fairban to the safety of the secret passages. Imoshen was grateful for his assistance. Weak from the milk fever, she could not have carried Lord Fairban far.

Leaving the wounded man in the care of his relatives, Imoshen took the old woman aside. 'Why haven't they noticed my escape?'

'The Cadre and his acolytes are ransacking the Basilica. Jarholfe's men dice for the largest treasures in the square even now.' Keeper Karmel pulled out a knife. 'This was all I could get away with.'

'You have done well.' Imoshen hid the knife. The Ghebites were playing into her hands. It would only take a leader among the townspeople to unite them, someone familiar with weapons and tactics. 'Reothe has followers in the city. Find them. Tell them to unite with the remaining Parakhan Guard, lead the people against Jarholfe and the Cadre's supporters. Can you do that while I free Reothe?'

The old woman repeated the message, her memory trained by years of study.

Imoshen slipped out of the secret passage and concentrated on cloaking her presence from the few servants who scurried nervously about the palace. Reothe was being held in the very ball-court where only a few moons ago the Ghebites and Keldon nobles had gathered to watch a display match.

It was nearly dusk. Imoshen realised she hadn't heard the Basilica's bells all day. Once the bells had rung the prayers, now nothing marked the passage of this black day. It was a powerful symbol of the destruction of T'Diemn society, of civilised society.

Avoiding the usual entrance to the ball-court, Imoshen climbed the steps and slipped through the door which opened onto the highest row of tiered seats. She looked down into the court, empty except for Reothe, who was tied to the far post. His arms were pulled above his head, the bonds slung through the ring which usually supported the net. He was naked and blood seeped from vivid welts on his back. His long hair had been roughly hacked off, revealing bloodied scalp in places.

She had failed him. She should have restored his gifts.

Reothe leant against the pole as though his will was broken. Her heart went out to him. What had they done to crush him? The thought brought her heightened T'En senses a visible answer – Jarholfe laughing as his men abused their prisoner. Sickened, she shut down her gift, unwilling to witness the Ghebite's calculated cruelty.

Heart hammering with rage, Imoshen ran lightly down the tiered seats. She leapt over the balustrade, dropping a body length to the polished floor below Even though she had hugged her swollen breasts, the jolt as she landed made her lurch with pain, and nausea threatened.

She paused to gather her strength. The court appeared empty but she could not be sure without using her T'En senses and that would open her to Reothe's pain. He would not welcome her sympathy. He was opposite her now, with his back to her. She saw his shoulder muscles tense, though he gave no other sign that he was aware of her presence.

Imoshen darted across the court to slip under Reothe's outstretched arms. One eye was swollen shut, the other widened at the sight of her.

'Imoshen?' The word cracked his bruised lips.

'Did you think I would abandon you?' Her voice was thick. She brushed the bruise over his temple willing it to heal, so he could open his eye. 'Where are your captors?'

'They went to dice for the riches of the Basilica.'

'We are in luck. Jarholfe's men run amok.'

'Luck!' He turned away from her.

Imoshen longed to beg his forgiveness but nothing would undo events. Rising on her toes, she sawed at the leather thongs that bound his hand so tightly his fingers were blue. One arm swung free and he gasped, flexing his shoulder before raising his free hand to his mouth to catch the leather thong in his sharp white teeth and tear at it.

A buzzing sliced the air. Reothe hissed with pain, swinging by his left arm which was still bound to the pole. An arrow shaft had impaled the muscle of his right shoulder.

Heart in her throat, Imoshen spun to confront their attacker. 'Jarholfe!'

Chapter Fourteen

'THROW DOWN THE knife. The next arrow goes through his heart,' Jarholfe ordered from the safety of the gallery opposite. He had another arrow notched.

Imoshen tossed the knife aside.

'I knew you would come for your lover. Now, where is the brat? I will wipe out this nest of Dhamfeer!'

Imoshen flinched, placing her body between Jarholfe and Reothe. 'Truly, I don't know. And even if I did, I'd die before I told you.'

'That's what I thought. I'm an excellent shot. At this distance I could put an arrow through his eye before you could get anywhere near me. My men claim you escaped from a bolted room while they were both on guard but I don't believe it. I know you have limits. I should have come back and gutted the old man a second time to keep you busy. I won't make that mistake again. I should have set Murgon on you. He was eager enough.'

'Jarholfe, I –'

A messenger ran into the gallery. 'Commander. The square is full of people, the town officials are demanding to see the Empress. They say we dishonour the Basilica and call on us to release the Beatific.'

'The townspeople outnumber you a thousand to one, Jarholfe,' Imoshen said. 'Kill me and they will rise up.'

'But if you convict yourself with your own words, they will have to sanction your execution!' he countered, then turned to the messenger. 'Tell the Cadre to bring the Beatific and that relic he finds so fascinating. Send in the town officials. We will give them their Empress, convicted by their own laws!'

The messenger scurried off and Jarholfe remained, cross bow primed. Imoshen stood before Reothe, unwilling to take her eyes from the Ghebite.

'The Cadre has been studying this Orb of Truth. They say it can tell if a man speaks the truth, and that it exacts punishment from those who lie. Are you prepared to place your palm upon the relic and swear you have never taken this Dhamfeer for your lover?' Jarholfe sneered.

Imoshen hesitated, for she had taken Reothe as her lover, even if it was only the once and only because he had deceived her by coming to her in Tulkhan's form. Her mind raced. When she had defied them to bring forth the Orb it was to buy time. She had never meant it to come to this.

Seeing her expression, Jarholfe laughed.

The passages beyond the ball-court echoed with the clamour of approaching town officials. As they took their seats, they radiated an air of trepidation and a desperate dignity.

'Imoshen?' Reothe whispered at her back. 'Heal me!'

'If I heal you, he will hurt you again. You heard him.'

'No. I mean really heal me,' Reothe pleaded. 'He cannot see my T'En gifts. It is only because they do not fear me that they dare to abuse me.'

He was right, but... 'It could render you unconscious.'

'I am willing to take that risk.' His expression told her he would risk anything for revenge.

Imoshen shook her head. 'If I am to make my move, I want you physically able.'

'Imoshen!' His despair tore at her.

But already events were moving, dragging her along like debris on a flood tide. The Cadre and his acolytes entered, escorting the Beatific and Murgon, who carried the Orb of Truth in its caged chalice. From Murgon's expression, he revelled in Reothe's downfall. Warm, velvety anger rushed through Imoshen making her gift stir despite the milk fever.

When the Beatific caught sight of Reothe, her eyes widened with pain and she glared at Imoshen, fury kindling the woman's mature beauty.

To arms! To arms!

Tulkhan sprang to his feet as a soldier charged into the shelter. 'Sumair's gates are open and mercenaries pour out.'

'Saddle my horse.' He sent a servant to bring his armour. Had the Ghebite auxiliary army arrived and somehow gotten word to the defenders of the port? His men had not reported any movement during their scouting forays. 'Watch for a secondary attack.'

When he stepped out of the shelter, he found several fleet-footed youths waiting, ready to carry his orders. Other runners would bring him reports. Striding across the soggy soil, Tulkhan approached the man who led his horse. Swinging into the saddle, he felt the familiar welcoming rush as his men prepared for pitched battle. Beyond the defensive earthworks, he heard the drums of Gharavan's mercenaries.

Forcing the horse to tackle the incline of the earthwork's inside slope, Tulkhan made the crest and surveyed the plain before Port Sumair's city walls. Mercenaries swarmed across the flat ground, but they were not a rabble. They were well prepared with defensive hides made of wood and straw, and they carried ladders to throw across the rampart's outer ditch.

He glared into the twilight. Dusk was a strange time to attack. Death whistled overhead and a man screamed. From behind by their hides, mercenary archers were firing in high arcs, trusting their arrows would find a mark in the crowded camp.

Tulkhan saw no Ghebite foot soldiers. It appeared Gharavan did not trust his own men.

Riding down the mound's incline, the General walked his horse through the bustling camp, pausing to speak with his men as they prepared for the first strike. All the while arrows fell about them. Some landed harmlessly on the ground, others carried soldiers to their knees. A man did not know when random death would claim him. But this was what they had been waiting for, the breach in the port's defences.

Why had they attacked now? Perhaps Kornel had taken word that the siege machines and cavalry were on the way. If so, Tulkhan thanked him, for now all he had to do was sit tight and let attack wear itself down on his defences and then, when the moment was right, send his men out.

How he wished for cavalry to pummel Gharavan's mercenaries and spearhead the counterattack.

He glanced at the sky again. By the look of those clouds, they might have the first snow of the season tonight. There was little daylight left, but the battle could be won or lost before the sun set.

'General Tulkhan?' Rawset rode up to join him. 'King Gharavan's mercenaries are trying to force the north entrance.'

The defensive ditch was knee-deep in water. Tulkhan threw back his head and laughed, and his men took heart as he meant them to. 'Pour oil in the ditch and set it alight. Then go to the seawall and signal Piers to mount a counterattack.'

IMOSHEN BLINKED AS torchbearers filed into the ball-court, now a court of trial. Heavy, snow-laden clouds dulled the light that filtered through the high windows, and with the arrival of the torches came an early night. None of the Ghebites thought to light the lamps which were designed to be raised and lowered by pulleys. The Ghebites were blind to the marvels of the Old Empire.

The murmuring of the crowd ceased as, on the Cadre's signal, Murgon stepped into the centre of the polished wooden floor carrying the chalice containing the Orb of Truth. Imoshen caught her breath. Insidious fear left an acid taste on her tongue. The townsfolk in the gallery stared down in awe. Everyone knew the significance of the ancient relic. Older even than Imoshen the First, this relic had come from the land beyond the dawn sun. It was revered, and the mystery of its making was lost.

The Cadre raised his voice, turning to confront the town officials. 'By Ghebite law the Lady Protector is already guilty of dishonouring her husband, Protector General Tulkhan.' He raised his hands to stem their angry muttering. 'But we are fair men. We understand you wish to see her guilt for yourselves. What is the sentence for a rogue T'En, Murgon?'

'Death by stoning.'

'Death!' the Cadre repeated.

But the Beatific would not see her authority undermined. She raised her voice. 'Only the Beatific can declare one of the T'En rogue, and then only if it can be proven that the accused has used their T'En gifts to take a True-person's life, or overthrow Fair Isle's rulers.'

'We can prove this Dhamfeer dishonoured Fair Isle's ruler by taking a lover. You will sign the decree,' the Cadre told her.

The Beatific glared at him. 'Declaring one of the T'En rogue is not something to be done lightly. Over the centuries, many have given their lives to bring in the rogues. Because of their weak affinity with the gifts many Tractarians are required to contain one T'En rogue so that the sentence can be carried out.'

The crowd whispered uneasily.

The Cadre spoke to Murgon. 'And this Orb senses the truth?'

'It glows with the pure light of truth,' the Beatific answered for him.

Murgon was quick to qualify this. 'But if the accused lies, the Orb will glow dull and dark.'

Imoshen saw the Cadre exchange a look with Jarholfe, who was flanked by six of his men. More waited up in the seats. They stood by the entrances, hands on weapon hilts. Imoshen suspected Jarholfe planned treachery, whatever the Orb's response.

The Cadre beckoned. 'Bring me the Orb.'

A collective gasp came from the crowd. Once in a century this Orb might be called upon. Those who failed to prove their innocence had been known to lose their minds, for the Orb not only exonerated the innocent, it punished the guilty.

Imoshen shivered. In her heart she knew the truth. She loved two men and there would be no peace for her. But she had not dishonoured Tulkhan, not by choice. She felt Reothe touch the small of her back where no one would see.

'Remember how I tricked you,' he whispered. 'Your words of love were for him, not me.'

'Give me the Orb.' The Cadre held his hand out, palm up.

'Only one of T'En blood may unleash the power of the Orb by asking the question and holding it against their skin,' the Beatific announced, stepping between him and Murgon. When the Cadre looked perplexed she explained, 'In the hand of a True-man or woman the Orb remains impervious.'

'I claim the honour of holding the Orb,' Murgon said.

'No!' Reothe protested. 'Only one without bias can hold the Orb.'

While the people in the gallery whispered in agreement, Jarholfe turned to the Cadre but the Beatific spoke up. 'By tradition it is the Empress herself who holds the Orb. Always the Empress has carried T'En blood.'

'You can't give it to that Dhamfeer bitch!' Jarholfe objected.

The town officials muttered.

'I will hold the Orb.' Murgon was eager to see her convicted.

'Is there no one amongst the townsfolk of T'En blood?' Imoshen cried. 'Someone who is without bias?'

The crowd shifted in their seats, one stood and pointed. 'The silversmiths' guildmaster.'

'Where? Step down,' the Cadre ordered.

Imoshen heard the whispers grow as a woman was escorted onto the court floor by Jarholfe's men.

'You have the Dhamfeer's accursed eyes. Who are you?' the Cadre asked.

'Guildmaster Maigeth, of the Silversmiths.' It was Drake's mother. She met Imoshen's gaze briefly, revealing the fear behind her composure. 'But I relinquish this honour. I am unworthy.'

'Will this woman do, Murgon?' the Cadre asked.

Before Murgon could open his mouth, the Beatific gave her approval.

The Cadre ignored her. 'Murgon?'

He nodded.

'Then proceed.'

'Bring the Orb,' the Beatific ordered. She unlocked the cage and turned towards the silversmith. But before Maigeth could move, the Cadre stepped between them, taking the Orb in his bare hand. The Beatific's mouth tightened in annoyance.

'Sacrilege!' Murgon hissed.

'Take this Orb and reveal the truth, woman,' the Cadre ordered.

Maigeth hesitated.

'Take it,' he urged.

'I can't. I have the T'En eyes and fingers, but I have no affinity with the gifts.' She cast Imoshen an imploring look.

'What is she talking about, Murgon?' Jarholfe demanded.

'Well?' the Cadre pressed.

'Not all half-bloods are cursed with the lesser version of the T'En gifts,' Murgon said at last. 'I have harnessed and trained mine. Give me the Orb.'

'No!' Imoshen fixed her gaze on the silversmith. 'Take the Orb, Maigeth.'

The woman shook her head. If she touched the Orb and it flared into life, it meant she had been hiding her affinity for the gifts from her family and her friends. They would never trust her again. If she did not, Imoshen suspected Murgon would ensnare her.

'Maigeth. I have stood by you. Stand by me.' Imoshen had not revealed that Maigeth's son had joined the rebels. She had never intended to use it against the woman. Only desperation drove her now. 'Do this for me. I am ready to swear that I have taken no man but General Tulkhan into my bed and into my arms.'

'Do it!' the Cadre ordered.

The silversmith's wine-dark eyes focused on the Orb as, almost against her will, she took it from the Cadre. At her touch it flared once in recognition.

The watchers gasped and murmured.

Imoshen knew that from this day forward, Maigeth would be regarded with suspicion by the True-people she had counted as friends.

'I've read that in rare cases the power can lie dormant for years until some crisis triggered them,' Murgon whispered.

The Beatific shook her head. 'I thought if the gifts did not come on at puberty, they –'

'Enough!' the Cadre snapped. 'You people could debate while T'Diemn burned.' He turned on Maigeth. 'Ask the Dhamfeer bitch if this male is her lover.'

Maigeth licked her lips.

Imoshen locked eyes with Maigeth. The fingers of her left hand hovered over the Orb. The brief glow had faded but she sensed its awareness, almost as if it were a living thing. Its surface was alive with palpable tension.

In her head Imoshen heard her own words and watched them fall from the silversmith's lips. '...taken no man but General Tulkhan to your bed and into your arms?'

'I have never taken any man but General Tulkhan into my bed and into my arms,' Imoshen repeated, her mouth so dry she could hardly speak. Her fingers splayed over the Orb, expecting to feel a cold slick surface or heat, but instead she felt resistance. It flared, illuminating her hand so brightly she could see the bones inside her six fingers.

The townspeople exclaimed her innocence as the residual image of the light danced on Imoshen's vision, blinding her.

'The Dhamfeer manipulated the Orb!' Jarholfe roared.

The townspeople of T'Diemn surged to the balustrades protesting.

'The Orb is false!' the Cadre screamed. 'Murgon. Tell me the Dhamfeer manipulated the Orb.'

The Tractarian opened his mouth. Imoshen tensed. Would he lie for the Ghebites?

'The Orb cannot lie,' the Beatific insisted. 'To manipulate the Orb brings on madness. Others have tried and failed.'

Her words were echoed by the townsfolk, who clamoured from the stalls.

'Jarholfe, get them out of here before they riot,' the Cadre ordered. Then he spun and snatched the Orb from the silversmith, knocking her aside.

Imoshen broke Maigeth's fall, asking under cover of the noise and confusion. 'Is Drake with you?'

'He was all for attack but I wanted to seek justice.'

'Tell him to move against the Cadre and Jarholfe. Their supporters must be found and –'

The Cadre dragged Maigeth away from Imoshen. 'Get out, woman. Or do you want to suffer the same fate as a full-blood Dhamfeer?'

Maigeth fled.

Imoshen held Murgon's eyes. 'Look deep into your heart. To hate us you must hate yourself.'

Murgon lifted his left hand to his mouth and mimed biting off his sixth finger then spitting it aside. Imoshen was stunned by his hatred.

Cries of outrage rent the air as Jarholfe's men drew swords on the unarmed townsfolk who had come expecting to see a fair trial conducted by the laws of the Old Empire. Instead, they faced naked steel and overzealous soldiers. Even as Imoshen watched, some were slain and the rest fled. She had failed her people.

'Imoshen, free me,' Reothe urged.

She retrieved her knife and ran to his side, sawing at the bonds which held his left arm.

Before she could free him, the Cadre snatched a handful of her hair, dragging her away.

Tears of pain burned in Imoshen's eyes. She clamped one hand over his, pressing his fingers to her skull. Then she dropped and twisted inside his hold, wrenching his wrist. Bringing her knife up, she aimed for his heart. The Orb, which was pressed to his chest, flared eagerly.

Jarholfe's boot took her in the ribs. The force of it sent her flying into the near wall. The knife spun from her fingers and the breath was driven from her body by the impact. She sank to the floor stunned.

'I warned you not to go near her, Cadre!' Jarholfe growled.

Imoshen fought for air. Specks of light flecked her vision. Each breath seared. She saw the last of the townspeople escape, pursued by Jarholfe's supporters. Only Murgon and the Beatific remained, along with Jarholfe, the Cadre and his acolytes.

Jarholfe cursed and advanced on Imoshen with his naked sword.

Fingers splayed, she reached for the knife hilt. Jarholfe's heel came down on her hand, crushing the fine bones. Her cry was drowned by the Beatific. 'Cadre, you must return the Orb. Murgon, tell him!'

Hugging her injured hand to her chest, Imoshen looked up to see the Cadre backing away with the Orb held above his head.

'It played us false, Murgon. You told me it would convict the Dhamfeer. Accursed relic!' The Cadre cast it down.

The Beatific's mouth opened in a silent scream as the Orb shattered at her feet.

Imoshen was reminded of the smashing glass of the Dreamwasps' cage and foreboding swamped her. 'Run!'

Before the Beatific could take a step, something intangible was released from the Orb. It had no shape or colour, yet Imoshen could see its essence distorting the terrified features of the Cadre's acolytes beyond. Murgon made the sign to ward off evil.

'Engarad!' Reothe used the Beatific's private name. Her form wavered. As Imoshen watched, the unknown presence invaded her and the Beatific crumpled.

The Cadre and his men backed away.

'Imoshen, help her!' Reothe urged, trying to lift his injured arm to undo the bonds which held him.

She had no idea how to help. Even so, her healing instincts drove her to the Beatific's side.

Imoshen rolled the woman over with her good hand. Already the Beatific's skin was waxen, her features lifeless.

Imoshen leaned down to listen for her heartbeat. She could sense the vengeful presence of a force long caged.

Calling on her gift, Imoshen placed her good hand over the Beatific's still heart and pressed, willing that heart to beat. The woman's mouth opened in a silent gasp. Imoshen leaned close, expelling her breath into the Beatific's open mouth, propelling her gift.

The rush of power jolted the dead woman. The Beatific exhaled and Imoshen inadvertently inhaled the vengeful presence.

Frightful cold filled her chest.

As though looking through imperfect glass, she saw Murgon drag the Beatific away, his features contorted with piteous fear. From a great distance she heard Reothe calling her name and Jarholfe's harsh voice demanding to know what was going on. She felt his hand on her arm as he pulled her upright. The Orb's presence was going to kill her, already she could feel it overcoming her resistance. She must pass it on or die.

In her mind's eye Imoshen saw Jarholfe gut Lord Fairban, saw him laughing as his men abused Reothe. With the last of her strength, she swung her free arm around Jarholfe's neck and planted her lips on his.

Exhaling, she drove the vengeful presence from her body into his. It went eagerly, sensing his defenceless life force.

As she pulled away from Jarholfe, his eyes met hers, revealing dreadful comprehension. Imoshen knew he felt a cold embrace, closing around his desperate heart, leaching the life from him. His mouth opened.

Before he could speak, Jarholfe dropped to the floor, dead at her feet.

Imoshen stared at his still body.

The Cadre's acolytes tried to flee but they were hindered by the return of Jarholfe's men.

Imoshen noticed the Beatific and Murgon exchange glances. They had witnessed her drive the Orb's power into Jarholfe. She'd used her gift to kill a True-man.

'Fiend!' the Cadre shrieked. 'The Dhamfeer must be killed.' He gestured to the frightened acolytes. 'Take Murgon and the woman back to the Basilica and hold them.'

Imoshen marvelled. Blinded by his contempt for females, the Cadre refused to use the Beatific's title.

Eagerly the acolytes drove the two church officials before them. Jarholfe's soldiers had returned, reeking of sweat, blood and death. They were dismayed to discover their commander dead. Several would have lifted Jarholfe's body.

'Don't touch him if you value your lives,' Imoshen warned. 'The Orb's presence is still dissipating.'

They glared at her. Imoshen knew her life hung in the balance. How many could she take with her: one, maybe two? She felt drained of her gift but was unsure what capabilities this crisis might unleash. She could have tried to escape, but she would not leave Reothe.

Four of Jarholfe's men advanced on Imoshen, their swords raised. A boot caught the remains of the Orb's crystal, sending it skittering across the polished wooden floor to the wall. The sound scraped Imoshen's raw senses.

'Hold your weapons,' the Cadre ordered, his voice rich with malignant triumph. 'The Dhamfeer has played into our hands. Tomorrow, if I am not mistaken, we will have a double stoning with the full approval of the Fair Isle's church.'

Imoshen straightened, aware that she had gained a reprieve for now 'What did you promise Murgon to betray Fair Isle, Cadre?'

He laughed, then shuddered. 'Fair Isle? Rather Fell Isle, filled with feral creatures.'

'You were the one who smashed the Orb. You are responsible for Jarholfe's death, not I.'

'Silence!' the Cadre roared. 'I will not listen to your poisoned words. You are convicted by your own actions, Dhamfeer bitch. Tomorrow you die. But first the pair of you must be safely secured for the night.'

He retrieved her knife and went over to Reothe. Imoshen expected him to slit the bonds which held Reothe's wrist. Instead he pressed Reothe's hand against the pole and hacked off several of his fingers.

A cry left her lips, its twin came from Reothe.

With satisfaction the Cadre tossed the severed fingers aside and slit the bonds which held Reothe. He fell to his knees clasping his hand as blood pumped from the finger stumps. Imoshen tore the hem of her underdress to stem the bleeding. She urged the wound to seal.

The Cadre watched in satisfaction. 'I've heard you two can climb like mountain goats. Let's see you try it now. Take them to the top of the tallest tower and shut them outside.'

Soldiers pulled Imoshen away from Reothe. She twisted free of their grasp. 'He'll die from blood loss if I don't pack the wounds.'

'Then you'd better heal him, bitch,' the Cadre urged. 'Jarholfe told me each time you heal it reduces your powers. So heal him if you can. And we'll see how much T'En trouble you give Murgon's Tractarians after you have spent a night exposed on the tower.'

TULKHAN FROWNED. IN the gathering gloom he could just make out the ebb and flow of battle. The ditch still burned, topped up with oil. All about him, men fought amid the roar of commands, the clash of metal and the stench of burned flesh. The camp's north entrance had held despite repeated attempts to breach it. Each time. Gharavan's mercenaries threatened to breach the defences, Tulkhan sent reinforcements. There had been no secondary attack and now he detected a slowing in the pace of the onslaught.

'Look, over by the port gates.' A man pointed.

Squinting past the glow of the ditch fires Tulkhan strained to make out what was happening. 'They've closed the gate on their own men!'

'Why?'

'The Lowlanders wanted nothing of this war. It would not surprise me if...' Tulkhan headed down the embankment, letting his momentum carry him far into the camp. It was the perfect opportunity to catch Gharavan's mercenaries in the open. 'Form a column!'

Tulkhan grinned as his men fell into formation. Now that the Lowlanders had cut off the mercenaries' retreat, it wouldn't surprise him if the port officials handed his half-brother over, trussed like a pig for the slaughter. His good mood infected the men and soon he had an attack force ready to form a pincer.

'The gates have been shut and the mercenaries fall back in dismay,' a runner reported.

'This is the night we take Port Sumair,' Tulkhan roared.

His men took up the cry. Tulkhan rode out with a small contingent of mounted men to spearhead the attack. Their horses' hooves sounded over the hastily lowered bridge.

With the burning ditch behind him, he faced the darker plain, littered with scattered fires caused by the burning hides. He heard the furious shouts of the betrayed mercenaries. He signalled the attack, while his men cheered from the ramparts.

Gharavan's mercenaries formed a hasty square to meet the General's onslaught, but the force of the heavy farm horses broke their ranks. Tulkhan found himself in the midst of struggling bodies, fighting in the dim twilight where it was hard to tell friend from foe. He stood in the stirrups as the battle raged around him and raised the victory horn to lips, believing the sounding of the horn would be enough to prompt the cornered mercenaries to lay down their weapons.

At the horn's call the tone of the fighting slowed as the enemy surrendered.

Tulkhan wheeled his horse, pulling back to assess their position. A strange sight greeted him. Several burning wagons dotted the plain between him and the seawall. One by one these winked out as if a black veil of darkness rolled towards him. A dull, hungry roar filled the air. Men turned towards the darkness.

They screamed as they were swept off their feet and carried towards him. Too late, Tulkhan realised the darkness was a wall of raging water engulfing friend and foe alike. Too late, men cast down their weapons to flee. Tulkhan's horse screamed and reared up against the boiling wave. As it came closer he could see the froth upon its crest and the limbs of men trapped in it. Then it was upon him. He was swept off his horse, carried away, turned over and over so that he didn't know which way was up or down.

His helmet was torn from his head, his sword from his fingers. Dragged under by the force of the water, held down by the weight of his armour, he struggled against ignominious, impartial death.

His head broke the surface and he barely had time to snatch a breath before he went under again. Spinning in cold blackness, he tried to undo his chestplate clasps. He felt the ground under his feet and he broke free of his armour, surfacing for a breath, only to lose his balance as something collided with him.

The breath rushed from his body. Frantic for air, he drove his legs down, but the ground slid out from under him. Then hands clasped his arms and hauled him up. He discovered he had been pinned halfway up the steep embankment of the defensive earthworks. His rescuer helped him to his feet.

Dragging in a deep breath, he looked about. By the light of scattered patches of burning oil and the few stars that pierced the cloud cover, he watched the water pour through the camp's northern entrance, tearing down parts of the ramparts. A great foaming flood engulfed the camp, abruptly silencing the screams of his terrified men. He seethed with impotence.

'The seawall must be down,' his companion muttered.

And Tulkhan understood. The townspeople of Port Sumair had locked the port's gates and breached the seawall, deliberately flooding their land to rid themselves of both the invaders and Gharavan's mercenaries. He could not fault their tactics.

Most of Tulkhan's men could not swim, but they would survive if they could make it to the embankments which bounded the camp.

'What's that?' The man pointed. 'A boat?'

Tulkhan turned to see a dark shape sail past. The outline was too irregular to be a boat. Then he heard the hunting bark of the narcts and fear curdled in his belly. The sea swirled around the embankment, rising steadily. He spotted another of the floating islands swept in from the channel. It surged past them with its deadly cargo.

'Are you armed?' Tulkhan demanded.

'Just my knife, I lost my bow.'

'Draw your blade and put your back to mine. The water is full of narcts.'

The man muttered an invocation to Akha Khan.

Tulkhan had nothing but his ceremonial dagger. He wished for a sword or a spear. To his left the water frothed and roiled. A man's screams were silenced as the narcts tore him apart.

Cries of despair rose from the men along the ramparts.

'We must band together!' Tulkhan roared.

'Something swims towards me!' his companion warned.

Tulkhan swung to face the threat.

'By the Akha Khan, help,' a man cried, thrashing through the water in his desperation to reach safety.

When Tulkhan stepped forward to take the man's arm, his leg went straight down the embankment. Only his companion's quick actions stopped him from going under. Regaining his balance, the General grabbed the struggling soldier's outstretched hand and pulled him up.

'Beware, Vaygharian. The top of the earthworks is only wide enough for two men,' he warned. He had not been fooled by the man's choice of invocation.

The mercenary tensed and would have thrust off their helping hands.

'Truce, man. We have a common enemy,' Tulkhan said, and as if to confirm this, they heard another chorus of barking.

'We were betrayed,' the Vaygharian mercenary spat.

'Doubly so,' Tulkhan agreed. 'The gates were locked, then the seawall opened to the ocean. I think you can consider your contract with Gharavan cancelled.'

The mercenary cursed.

'Take heart, men,' Tulkhan yelled. 'It could be worse. It could be snowing!'

Chapter Fifteen

'IT'S SNOWING,' IMOSHEN whispered, as the first flake caressed her cheek. Wearing only her underdress, she could not repress a shiver. 'Now don't argue, Reothe, put this on.'

He pushed away her offer of help but she could tell it was an effort for him to cover his nakedness with her brocade tabard.

They had been driven at sword point up the ladder to the top of Sard's Tower. Before the trapdoor was bolted, the Cadre had crowed, 'If you can force that bolt with your gifts, these men will be waiting. I give them leave to hack off any limb that comes through this trapdoor. You'll bleed to death as quick as a True-man!'

Recalling the fearful, glittering eyes of the guards, Imoshen knew they would be only too eager to follow the Cadre's command.

She came to her feet and went to the tower's edge to peer down. It was a sheer drop to the steeply sloping roof below. Even if she risked the jump, the icy roof slates would give her no traction. She imagined sliding off to plunge four floors to the ground below and shuddered.

'How far down is it?' Reothe asked.

'Too far to climb.'

But he had to study the drop for himself. 'It could be done if the roof were not covered in ice.'

'I doubt if I would attempt it even then. Now I must heal your wound and bind it properly.' Imoshen's reserves were pitifully low. She'd had little to eat, and worse, her body still burned with the milk fever.

Reothe hugged his wounded hand to his chest. 'Why should I be whole in body if my powers are crippled? You must heal my gifts!'

Despite everything, her instinct was to deny him. The memory of his trickery still stung.

'Imoshen?' His face was a pale oval and his features ill-defined in the dim light, yet she did not need to see him to know his expression. His bitter, desperate tone conveyed it all. Knowing how Jarholfe's men had abused him, she understood his rage, but she did not make the mistake of offering pity.

'I cannot return your lost fingers but I can promise to heal your wounds. To be frank I am too exhausted to attempt more.'

He pushed her entreating hand aside and she gasped in pain.

'You burn with fever and your hand is broken. Why haven't you healed yourself, Imoshen?'

'Your need is greater. Show me your hand.'

'So that you can tire yourself healing me? Would you leave me a useless T'En cripple but physically healed so that I can witness your stoning?'

'What would you have me do? There are so many Ghebites and I am almost exhausted.' Blinking tears from her eyes, she looked across at the Basilica's dome silhouetted against the cloudy sky. Everything was covered with a layer of snow. Tomorrow the Ghebites would come for them, strip them naked and lead them into the square. 'They will have to send wagons to the quarries outside of town to bring in cart-loads of stones. The snow will make that difficult. How many stones does it take to kill? I suppose it depends how well they are aimed.'

'Stop it!' He pulled her to him. 'Do you always let your head rule your heart?'

'And you don't?' She waited but he said nothing. At last, she kissed his cracked lips. 'Let me heal your body.'

'What good is that if we are to die?' Reothe's breath dusted her face with his despair.

'I have sent word to your rebels.'

Reothe cursed. 'I'm afraid you'll get no help from my people until the Cadre orders the old city gates opened.'

'I sent the guildmaster of the silversmiths to Drake. He can organise the townspeople –'

'To do what? You saw them today. The people of T'Diemn are sheep to the slaughter.'

Imoshen had to admit the truth of this. 'After today they will be better prepared.'

'Much good that will do us!' The moment stretched between them. 'Why did you come back for me, Imoshen? Why didn't you escape when you had the chance?'

Wordlessly she slid her good hand inside his tabard. As her fingers travelled over his back she willed the lacerated skin to seal, felt the warmth flow from her into him.

He gasped. 'Your touch is sweet, T'Imoshen.'

'You used your T'En tricks on me from the first, Reothe.' Anger thinned her voice. 'You tried to manipulate me into your arms.'

'A little,' he admitted, resting his forehead on hers. 'But my gifts have been crippled since Northpoint and you can't deny what we share.'

'You dishonoured me by your trickery. It was wrong.'

'I was desperate.'

'Still wrong.'

'A small wrong for a greater good.'

She shook her head, surprised to discover that despite her pain and weariness, her anger was raw and immediate.

He straightened, but before he could speak, she indicated the arrow. 'Now I must break this with my good hand.'

'Do it quickly.' He leaned against the tower's stonework, bracing himself. She caught the shaft in her teeth, took the feathered end in her good hand and snapped the shaft. Even so, she felt him shake with the shock of it. With the arrow broken, she felt behind him for the barbed head which protruded from his flesh and pulled it through, using her gift to knit the flesh behind it. The heat of her anger faded with the effort it took to seal the wound.

Dropping the arrowhead from numb fingers, she nearly lost consciousness. Reothe caught her before she could collapse. 'Heal yourself, Imoshen. We must be gone from here before dawn.'

'No. Your hand next.'

'Why did you save the hardest for last?'

'Because you never know what you can do until you must.'

A soft laugh escaped him and he kissed her forehead. 'Can you wonder that my love for you made me careless of honour?'

It was the closest he had ever come to an apology. She stared into his pale face pierced by the twin pools of his dark eyes. 'I thought love made a person strong, not devious.'

He flinched.

She took his injured hand to study the wound. His first two fingers had been sheared off at the base, the third was severed at the knuckle. 'So cruel.'

'They threatened worse.'

Behind the bitter humour in Reothe's voice, she heard fear. Guilt tore through her.

He tilted his head back, his face turned up to greet the falling flakes. As she held his hand, she sensed him growing receptive, opening to her touch. Concentrating on his injury, she called on her reserves to knit and seal the stumps of his fingers. It was surprisingly easy to work her healing on Reothe and she understood the dual nature of their bond. With the most intimate of the mind-touches she had grown to need him. But he had also become vulnerable to her. This was why she had been able to injure his gift when she had lashed out. The revelation left her trembling.

'Ahh, to be without pain. Bless you, T'En healer.' He used the High T'En invocation. Then, pulling the tabard around his body, he sank down with his back to the wall. 'Come close. Your skin is wondrously warm.'

She was burning up with fever and her maimed hand throbbed with every beat of her heart, but if she expended any of her gift to heal herself, she would have no reserves to maintain their body heat during the long night.

'You must not sleep.' Her teeth chattered, breaking up her words. There would come a point when they no longer felt cold and a curious warmth would spread over them. But she would not let it come to that. 'To sleep in the snow is fatal.'

'Sweet death, they say. It would cheat those Ghebites of their stoning.'

Imoshen flinched. The abuse Reothe had received at the hands of his Ghebite captors was designed to destroy his pride. Imoshen knew it was possible to die of this kind of injury. Her ears buzzed in the absolute silence of the snow-bound night. At least there was no wind, only the ever-falling snow seductively luring her to sleep in its deadly embrace. Though her fever raged, she shook with cold.

'Look down into the square,' Reothe urged. 'Are the townspeople gathering? They must come to us soon for I doubt we will last the night.'

She could distinguish nothing moving. The old city of T'Diemn slept peacefully under its blanket of fresh, crisp snow.

'What do you see?'

'Nothing. The snow falls too thickly,' she lied.

'Let us hope it aids our supporters. Come to me, Imoshen.' He took her injured hand and again she could not conceal the pain. 'You haven't healed yourself?'

'I'll use what's left of my gift to keep us warm.'

'So that we may be stoned in the morning?'

'By then Drake will have organised a revolt.'

'Now that I can think without pain, we must attempt to escape. If Drake does lead an uprising, the first thing the Cadre will do is have us killed. We must make our move before then.' Reothe's voice dropped. 'There is something you could try. Sometimes it is possible for one of the T'En to draw on the True-people around them.'

Imoshen went very still as the horror of the confrontation in Lakeside returned. Was Reothe asking her to renew her flagging gifts by driving someone to murder?

'Just as people have distinctive physical features, they give off distinctive emanations,' Reothe whispered. 'I can taste it on my tongue, sense it lingering on the air after they leave the room.'

Imoshen fought the memories of Lakeside.

'What is it?' Reothe prodded.

'I said nothing.'

'Don't shut me out, Imoshen, there is so much I could share with you.'

'What were you going to tell me about the T'En gifts?'

After a heartbeat Reothe continued. 'Open your senses. Trawl the minds of those in the building below. Find someone engaged in an intense moment and open yourself to them. Use them to sustain us.'

Imoshen yearned to know so much more. Perhaps this skill was mentioned in Imoshen the First's memoirs. 'The T'Elegos –'

'Will be ours to explore when all this is over, when you stand at my side and Fair Isle is ours.'

'How can you put a price on knowledge?'

'Everything has a price, especially knowledge. That much is very clear to me. There is so much I must achieve. This Ghebite General destroyed my plans and forced a terrible choice upon you, and you have been regretting it ever since.'

'I love Tulkhan.'

'I know. But this isn't about him, or you and me. It is about the fate of the T'En.'

'The Golden Age of the T'En?'

'Don't tease me, Shenna.'

Imoshen ducked her head. No one else used her pet name.

'Open your senses,' he urged. 'I will hold you safe until you find a source.'

She settled in Reothe's arms, cradled against his chest. The cold was fierce. Uncontrollable shivers wracked them both. But when she tried to open her mind, she could not. 'Don't watch me.'

'I can see very little!'

She could hear the smile on his voice. 'Turn your face away.'

'If that is what you want.'

With the pain in her hand and her breasts it was hard to find that peaceful place where she could leave her body. Would she be able to return to it, she wondered with a flash of panic?

'Trust me,' Reothe whispered.

She wanted to ask why she should, when he had lied and manipulated her from the moment they met, yet somehow she believed she could trust him in this.

At last she was able to relax and her awareness drifted.

Individual True-people called to her like beacons. As Reothe said, each one had a particular flavour. The palace servants radiated enticing fear. She paused at each one to draw off a little, leaving them more peaceful and herself stronger. The Ghebites were easy to identify by their rampant hostility, but strangely enough they, too, radiated fear. It was the motivating force behind their aggression.

In this state there was no up and down, yet Imoshen found she was able to orientate herself by relating back to her point of origin. Far below Sard's Tower, she found a Ghebite terrorising one of the serving girls. The man was drunk but not drunk enough to stop him raping her. Before he did, he wanted the girl to beg.

Revulsion filled Imoshen but she knew she had found her source. She disciplined herself to siphon off a little at a time as she milked the man's anger. Its rich and heady force urged her to drive him further, but she restrained the impulse, recognising it as her own terrible craving, one which she must keep secret even from Reothe.

Using this Ghebite as a source, she let one part of her awareness return to her body, consciously increasing her heart rate, lifting her temperature, until her flesh radiated heat. She used this to burn the last of the milk fever from her body.

Now that fever was gone, she could think clearly. Her gift was empowered by the Ghebite, and his fires were fed by the serving girl who suffered so that Imoshen and Reothe might live.

Revulsion roiled in Imoshen. She could not condone this. Better to release the girl from her torment. She drew on the Ghebite's energy until he collapsed.

The moment he did, Imoshen transferred her awareness to the girl, who burned with the bright flame of anger. It seemed a waste not to absorb her fury.

Imoshen concentrated on opening herself to the girl, only vaguely aware of the servant's grasp on a knife. Triumph flashed through them both as the knife plunged into the unconscious Ghebite's heart. His death was rich beyond measure, for with it came the rush of his fleeing life force.

Mentally reeling with the impact, Imoshen lost all sense of self.

In a leap of understanding she thought she saw the relationship between the Parakletos and the souls of the dead, and almost grasped how Imoshen the First had bound them under oath.

She was aware of the Parakletos waiting in death's shadow, each curious, eager or vengeful according to their nature. They had been drawn to her like predators to an injured beast.

They would consume her with their need. Terror engulfed Imoshen and she fled, retreating to her physical self.

'You're back,' Reothe whispered. 'I feared your soul lost and your body consumed by fever.'

Numbly she shook her head. Pressing her fingers into her closed eyes, she rediscovered her injured hand. At least she could heal it now. It was the work of a moment. 'Wake me near dawn and I will try to shield us while we escape.'

'Imoshen?'

But she would not answer.

THE SEA STOPPED rising when it reached Tulkhan's thighs, and then the tide turned, leaving them shivering on the embankment in ankle-deep water. The surviving men had formed a long snake-like column along the inner ramparts. Tulkhan knew that there were men on the outer ramparts because he'd heard their cries as they fought the narcts.

When the sea began rising again his men became concerned.

'It will rise no further than it did before,' Tulkhan assured them. 'Be ready for the return of the narcts.'

'I can't feel my fingers to hold my knife,' the man next to him muttered. 'The narcts will have us for breakfast.'

It was the coldest part of the night, when despair was closest to a man's heart. If only there was higher ground. Then it struck Tulkhan that the highest ground was the seawall. Surely it had not been completely demolished.

'This way. We'll outwit those narcts yet!' he called.

Tulkhan moved through the ranks to take the lead along the defensive embankment. Men lost their footing, but their companions pulled them up. Meanwhile the narcts waited, ready to snatch the stragglers.

As Tulkhan slogged through the rising water, he prayed that the seawall remained standing where it joined the ramparts. It was hard to judge distance in this watery world. The clouds had cleared and starlight revealed a flat expanse of sea, with the occasional floating island.

In the grey light of dawn Tulkhan spotted the dark band which was the seawall, rising like a causeway above the water. The incline was steep and muddy.

Tulkhan struggled up the slope onto the top of the sea-wall then turned to help the next man. Port Sumair rose out of the ocean surrounded by its stout walls, an island fortress. There was no sign of fire or cries of battle coming from the port. He feared for Rawset's life.

When he came to the place where the sea-wall had been eaten away by the in-rushing ocean he could see the silhouettes of his blockading ships. Tearing off his undershirt, he waved it above his head.

He had survived and the remnants of his army had regrouped. On this high tide, his ships, armed with their new siege machines, could come right up to the port's walls and demand its surrender.

When the defenders closed the gates on the mercenaries they must have turned on Gharavan. Sumair would surrender his half-brother and he would return to T'Diemn triumphant.

WITH GREAT RELUCTANCE, Imoshen let Reothe drag her back to awareness of her cold, miserable state.

So cold...

'They will come for us soon, Imoshen. We must move.'

'When this is done, I will have nothing left.' Her voice was a croak. 'I'm going to cloak us.'

He nodded.

Imoshen sought the most susceptible of the two minds below. She was familiar with them because of her earlier wanderings. In this guard's mind she planted the idea that the prisoners had escaped.

'They're coming. Join me, Reothe.' She drew him down beside her and gripped his good hand, willing them both as white as snow. She had to hold this illusion for only a few heartbeats.

Through a veil, she saw the trapdoor swing up, sending powdered snow flying. Snow dusted the man's head.

'I tell you they can't have escaped,' he was saying. 'What?' Cursing, he searched the tower top.

A second head appeared. 'I knew it. They flew away.'

'Impossible!'

'Where are they, then?'

'More to the point, what's the Cadre going to say?'

The younger man went pale.

'Come on. We must report their escape.'

They retreated, leaving the trapdoor open, and Imoshen let the illusion fall away. Already, waves of nausea washed over her.

Reothe darted across to the trapdoor. 'Come on.'

Holding her tender, newly healed hand to her chest, she crawled towards him. Her greatest desire was to find a warm place to lie down and sleep. She was beyond hungry.

'You can't give up now, Imoshen.'

'I'll never give up!'

He smiled and she realised he was deliberately baiting her.

Waiting at the base of the ladder, he looked up. 'I'll steady you.'

A neutral grey mist settled on her vision, so that it was by feel alone that she made her way down. Reothe caught her around the waist, turning her to face him. His features swam before her. He cursed softly, then swung her over his shoulder.

She gasped indignantly. 'Put me down.'

He did not bother to answer. As he strode off, she gave a moan of discomfort. The floor passed under her, dimly lit, then deeply shadowed. After several twists and turns, Reothe stopped and did something to open a concealed door, then stepped inside a musty passage. He lowered Imoshen to the ground, and she leant against a cold stone wall.

'Just leave me here in the secret passage to sleep.' Her words were as slurred as a drunkard's.

'I need you at my side to unite the people against the Cadre.'

A wave of despair swamped Imoshen. 'I used my gifts to kill Jarholfe in front of the Beatific. She will have me stoned!'

'Engarad is a pragmatist. We'll go to her now.'

He went to lift Imoshen again but she refused. She did not want to arrive at the Beatific's door carried like a sack of potatoes.

Reothe led her on a short trip through the secret passages to his own rooms. 'If we are to defeat the Cadre, we must look like conquerors.' He turned her towards the bathing room. 'Go wash. I'll get dressed.'

She would have loved a warm bath but there was no time. Her skin looked thin and there were dark circles under her eyes. So much had happened since she'd returned to T'Diemn. At least Kalleen and Ashmyr were safe. The Cadre would have wasted no time in telling her if they'd found her son.

'Ready?' Reothe scratched at the door.

Imoshen came out to find clothes laid on the bed.

'My boots will be too big,' he said. 'Try the indoor slippers.'

He went into the bathing room and she heard him curse. 'They've butchered my hair!'

Imoshen smiled. Reothe had been raised in the high court of the Old Empire, where a person dressed and spoke with elegance. Spots floated in her vision. It was an effort to remember to breathe.

'Ready?' Reothe asked. She had not even started to change her clothes. 'Dreamer!'

Despite her protests, he tore off the damp underdress and helped her into trousers, shirt and tabard, all slightly too big. Then he knelt at her feet to draw the laces of the indoor slippers tightly about her ankles. Reothe's lowered head revealed raw scalp. Imoshen touched his head, longing to heal him completely.

He looked up smiling. 'There. A bit loose but better than nothing.'

'Reothe,' Imoshen whispered. Since the General had captured her stronghold, she had repeatedly rejected Reothe, yet he remained loyal. 'I am not worthy of your love.'

He gave an odd laugh. 'Come.'

It was imperative that they seize the moment. The trip through the secret passages passed in and out of her awareness as she fought the encroaching fog of exhaustion. She found herself watching Reothe's back, willing her body to keep moving.

He paused at an intersection. 'This leads straight to the Basilica. How do you think I used to meet Engarad?'

Imoshen wished she had her wits about her to memorise the way. After what seemed an interminable walk, Reothe led her up several narrow flights of stairs, then stopped.

'I must leave you here to find the Beatific.'

Imoshen nodded, noting how he opened the hidden door. She waited. When she judged he had gone far enough, she tripped the door's mechanism and followed him. She did not want the Beatific and Reothe making bargains without her.

Though she felt flat and stale without her gift, she had no trouble following Reothe discreetly. She saw him hesitate at a door where a sentry waited. The man was too interested in what was going on inside the room to notice Reothe until it was too late.

Reothe caught the sentry around the neck, and pulled him backward into an anteroom. When Reothe reappeared, he was holding the man's sword in his maimed left hand. With a curse, he transferred it to his right hand. He felt its weight and balance thoughtfully before stepping into the Beatific's room.

Even from the end of the hall, Imoshen could hear raised voices. Eager to miss nothing, she hurried after Reothe. There was an untouched food tray on the chair by the door. Suddenly ravenous, Imoshen drained the wine, then grabbed the bowl of stew and a freshly baked bun.

Hugging the bowl to her chest with her tender left hand, she peered through the open door. The room was lit by a branch of candles which sat on a desk. A roaring fire burned in the hearth. It was the Beatific's private sanctum, richly decorated with thick carpets and intricately carved wood panels, picked out in gold leaf, yet it looked lived-in, with papers strewn on the desk and a discarded over-gown draped across a chair.

Imoshen longed to lie down before the fire and sleep, but Reothe held the sword at the Cadre's throat. The man backed up until he came to the far wall. They did not notice Imoshen, who hid in the shadows, devouring the stew.

'You can't kill him here!' the Beatific protested.

'Where do you want me to kill him?' Reothe asked.

The Cadre squeaked.

'He's the head of the Ghebite church and must be dealt with according to the laws of Fair Isle.'

'Law and order did not help us when the Orb declared Imoshen innocent.'

The Beatific stepped from behind her desk. 'I was working on freeing you.'

'And Imoshen?'

The leader of the T'En church hesitated.

Reothe spared her a hard glance. 'She saved your life, Engarad.'

'Imoshen killed a True-man with her gift, Reothe.'

'It was self-defence. And she saved you from the Orb's power!' His tone scalded. 'Hurry, Beatific. My arm grows weary.'

'I have not signed the decree. In the eyes of the church, you aren't rogue and neither is Imoshen, yet.'

'Don't threaten me, Engarad. When I entered this room you were the Cadre's prisoner and he was bullying you into signing away the rights of the church.' Reothe lifted the sword point until the Cadre strained on tiptoes to avoid it. 'We must rid ourselves of this malignant fool. At least the General is a statesman, not a fanatic.'

'I am ready to die for my beliefs!' the Cadre insisted.

'Then let me oblige you,' Reothe growled.

'No, Reothe!' Imoshen crossed the room. She felt the Cadre's angry glare as she put the empty bowl on the Beatific's desk. 'Tulkhan must be the one who orders the Cadre's death. Only that will legitimise our position.'

The Beatific and Reothe exchanged glances.

'What of the Cadre's supporters? Jarholfe's men fought pitched battles in the palace corridors,' the Beatific said. 'They displayed the bodies of your Parakhan Guard in the square.'

Anger boiled through Imoshen, but she refused to dwell on her people's pointless slaughter.

The Beatific tilted her head as the Basilica's bells rang out for the first time in two days. 'Dawn. Our people will strike now. Without a leader, the Ghebites will not stand long.'

But Imoshen was fast losing track of the conversation. The fire's heat combined with the food to swamp her senses and the room swayed about her.

'Where will we imprison the Cadre? On Sard's Tower?' Reothe asked.

'No, in the Basilica,' Imoshen mumbled. 'The Cadre's greatest crime is against the laws of Fair Isle. He threatened the right of every individual to a fair trial. The Beatific must lay charges against him on behalf of the church.'

'True,' the Beatific agreed. 'I –'

But Imoshen heard no more. The carpet met her face with a suddenness that should have hurt but didn't.

THE GENERAL STRODE the deck of Piers' ship, impatient to be moving. Rawset had not delivered Tulkhan's message. It seemed the flood had claimed the young emissary.

The General gripped the seasoned wood of the ship's sides. Before him, Sumair rose from the ocean. Its church spires and pointed roofs were reflected in the sea, which was as smooth as glass on this cold, still morning.

He had dressed in borrowed armour and eaten a hot breakfast. The horrors of the night so narrowly escaped still pressed on him, but there was no time now for reflection.

'Everything is ready, General,' Piers announced.

'Then sound the attack.'

With no wind to fill the sails, the men had to row the ships towards the island-port. Cumbersome with their new siege machinery, the ships bore down on Port Sumair like great beasts of prey, slow but inexorable.

As they approached the walls, Tulkhan studied the port's defences through the farseer, watching the hurried consultations of gathered heads on the parapets, and the frantic signalling from tower to tower.

Tulkhan closed the farseer with a snap and looked up at the siege machine's hide. It was made of beaten metal wrapped around braced wood, and with this protection they could come abreast of the walls, attack the defences directly and throw ladders across to the parapets.

'They're surrendering!' Piers pointed.

Fierce elation filled Tulkhan. He felt the same rush of conquest he had known when the Spar fell to him. Then he had shown no mercy, putting everyone to the sword, and his father's war advisors had respected him for it.

In his mind's eye he saw himself kneeling before his father to receive generalship over the entire Ghebite army. But it wasn't his father who turned to him from the royal dais, it was Imoshen. Disgustedly she pointed to his hands, covered in the blood of the defenceless women and children he had ordered slain. *Murderer!*

The people of the Spar had been fighting for their freedom. Tulkhan had quashed their rebellion in his father's name, but it had been his choice to slaughter the vanquished.

Revulsion filled him.

His vision returned to Port Sumair, glistening in the early morning sun. A slight breeze had sprung up, rippling the surface of the water and stirring the pennants on the spires, drawing his gaze to the flag of surrender.

'I'll take the ship alongside,' Piers announced. 'You can accept their surrender on the ramparts.'

Only a few heartbeats had elapsed from the first sighting of the surrender, and within that time Tulkhan's world had shifted. He felt cold and hollow. He had been young, full of hubris and eager to make his name. That was no excuse. He was a murderer tens of thousands of times over. While he could not bring back those innocent lives, he could deal differently with the people of Port Sumair.

The ship manoeuvred parallel to the wall as the sailors on the siege tower prepared to throw lines across. The gentlest of swells made the ship's deck lift and fall.

'How many men do you want at your back?' Piers asked.

Tulkhan cast his gaze over the assembled soldiers and indicated a dozen men. 'Come with me.'

The soldiers eagerly followed him up the ladder of the siege machine and across the plank onto the walls of Port.

Half a dozen port dignitaries, dressed in the heavy brocaded collars and half-skirts of Lowland merchants, waited anxiously on the rampart.

Behind him, Tulkhan heard the chink of his soldiers' armour and weapons as they took up position. He leapt down onto the walkway. 'Where is Gharavan?'

Only when he asked this did he realise how much he dreaded confronting his half-brother. He had no choice but to order his death.

One death, no more.

A man stepped forward, grey with fear. He bowed low, as was the Lowland custom. 'General Protector of Fair Isle, as Elector of Port Sumair, I want you to know that we did not choose to side with the Ghebite King. He arrived with his mercenaries and took up residence in our town.'

'Where is he?'

The man exchanged looks with his companions and lifted his arms in a Lowland gesture of helplessness. 'He escaped sometime last night after the seawall went down.'

Tulkhan cursed. He should have expected that his cowardly half-brother would scuttled away. 'What of the Ghebite soldiers who were with him?'

'Those who did not escape with their king are safely locked away, awaiting your pleasure.' The Elector looked relieved to report this. 'Execution by drowning is the Lowland way.'

'I'll make that decision.'

'We do have one prisoner you will want to see,' another merchant volunteered eagerly. 'Captain Kornel.'

'Take me to him.'

But when they escorted him to Kornel's cell, Tulkhan found the captain had escaped his revenge. Kornel had hung himself by his belt from the cell bars.

The port officials apologised profusely. They took Kornel's body down, tied his corpse to a chair in the Elector's square and had Tulkhan pronounce sentence. Then, as though the traitor still lived, they suspended Kornel's body, still tied to the chair, over the wall and lowered it into the sea until he was pronounced drowned.

Tulkhan went along with all of this, understanding that this custom served the purpose of expiating the man's sins. It was evident his own men took some comfort from the procedure, too.

The General's hand went to his chest where the messages from Imoshen had lain, but they had been lost in the flood, along with his grandfather's sword. He felt the loss keenly.

Once Kornel's bizarre trial and execution ended, Tulkhan turned to the Elector. 'Now, about the terms of surrender.'

Chapter Sixteen

WHEN IMOSHEN AWOKE, she knew by the pattern of sunlight on the polished wooden floor that it was mid-afternoon. Hearing Ashmyr's soft crow of laughter, she smiled sleepily.

Ashmyr!

It all came back to her. She sat up to find herself in her own chamber. Reothe leaned against the far bedpost watching Kalleen play with Ashmyr. A wave of relief rolled over Imoshen.

'You wake at last.' Reothe greeted her with a smile.

It was so normal, as if the Cadre's attempted coup had been nothing but a bad dream. Then she noticed Reothe's maimed left hand and she knew all of them had barely escaped death. 'Kalleen, bring Ashmyr. What's been happening in T'Diemn?'

Reothe stepped aside as Kalleen came to the bed. But when Imoshen took her son in her arms and bared her breast, she discovered her milk was gone, burned up by the fever. Ashmyr gave an indignant yell.

'Never fear,' Kalleen said. 'I will feed him. I have some milk warming. It should be ready now.'

Imoshen blinked back tears. Her arms ached to hold her son. Had she been alone, she would have wept with gratitude to have him safely returned. 'Where did you hide, Kalleen?'

'With the silversmith guildmaster.' Kalleen tested the warmth of the milk and settled the baby, who gulped hungrily. 'Don't rush, you'll get wind, my greedy boy.'

Reothe laughed softly.

Imoshen had to remind herself that he was still an enemy of the state, but he did not feel like an enemy. 'What has happened since I fell asleep this morning?'

'That was yesterday morning. I appointed Drake leader of the Parakhan Guard.' Reothe gave her a secretive smile. 'He swore on your name. I told him how Imoshen the First appointed T'Obazim, leader of her Paragian Guard.'

Reothe was quoting from T'Elegos, teasing Imoshen with glimpses of their hidden heritage. She didn't rise to the bait.

'They scoured the palace and the old city searching for the Ghebites who had turned against us,' he said. 'I fear many a Ghebite soldier is still in hiding.'

'It will not serve us if those loyal to Tulkhan are killed, Reothe.'

He shrugged. 'As for these Ghebite traitors, the Beatific has been trying them by the laws of Fair Isle, which is probably more of a hearing than they would have given us.'

Imoshen bowed her head in the knowledge that he was right.

'This morning the Beatific declared the trials over and the gates were reopened. The people of T'Diemn poured into the old city by the thousands. The square is packed. They want to see you for themselves.'

'Let me bathe and eat,' she said, and Reothe gave her the Old Empire obeisance reserved for the Empress, then left them. 'How is Lord Fairban?'

Kalleen's face fell.

'When?'

'This morning. He was old, Imoshen. You did all you could. May the Parakletos guide his soul.'

Imoshen kept her silence. The old saying no longer offered her comfort. She padded across the room to kneel at Kalleen's side and gaze on her son.

Tentatively, she stroked the baby's fine dark hair. It hurt to see Ashmyr feeding peacefully in Kalleen's arms, oblivious to her. He stopped sucking long enough to regard her seriously, deigned to smile, then returned to the teat.

'He is a charmer,' Kalleen whispered.

Pain twisted inside Imoshen. He was her son. She would die for him, had nearly died protecting him from Jarholfe. She forced herself to banish the resentment.

Imoshen met Kalleen's eyes. 'You saved my son. I am forever in your debt. I will watch over you and yours all the days of my life.' It was a deliberate reversal of the usual Fair Isle custom of assuming responsibility for the life saved. It sounded almost like a Ghiad.

Kalleen's face grew solemn as she took in the significance of this pledge. Tears of sorrow filled her eyes. 'I could not let them kill Ashmyr, too!'

And Imoshen remembered that Wharrd had died protecting her honour. Helplessly, she opened her mouth, but no words came.

'The man of my heart died in the service of the Empress. I wanted to hate her,' Kalleen whispered. 'But I cannot.'

A sob escaped Kalleen and Imoshen embraced her. They both wept freely. Finally, Imoshen smoothed the tear-damp hair from Kalleen's face, kissing her. 'Bless the day you fell at my feet. I'm proud to call you friend.'

'It is hard to be a friend of the T'En.'

Imoshen gave a rueful smile. 'It is hard to be the last of the T'En.'

Kalleen uttered a short laugh and held up the baby. 'Take him while I run your bath and lay out your clothes.'

Imoshen cradled Ashmyr, delighting in his soft skin and the smell of him. 'You don't have to be my maid, Kalleen.'

'I do what I do because I choose to,' she replied, and Imoshen understood it would always be this way with her.

Kalleen went into the room beyond where Imoshen heard the water running. Alone at last, she held her son and gave thanks that they had both survived the Ghebites' treachery.

*   *   *

TULKHAN WATCHED THE Lowland dancers perform for the assembled port officials and his commanders.

Lightfoot, back from the dead, sat opposite. Only this morning the townspeople of Port Sumair had gone out in their boats to scour the drowned land for survivors. Lightfoot had been found clinging to a church spire.

Silently, Tulkhan raised his wine glass to the grizzled mercenary, who returned the gesture. Tulkhan saw a word leave his lips. *Rawset.*

The youth had not been found and now it was unlikely he would be discovered alive. Tulkhan scowled. A high price had been paid for this victory. He was impatient to return to Fair Isle, but the signing of the terms of surrender had to be celebrated. He tried to show an interest in the performance as several dancers, wearing long blue-green gowns, swirled around others, engulfing them.

'Those dancers represent the sea?' Tulkhan asked.

The old man next to him nodded. 'We Lowlanders do not worship the sea, nor do we fear it, but we do respect it. The dancers in white symbolise the moons, which govern the tides.'

Tulkhan nodded. Earlier in the evening he had spoken with Sumair's engineers about the enormous job of draining the flooded land. It had been made clear to him that the breaking of the seawall had been deliberately delayed until it would do the most damage. That it happened to coincide with Kornel's betrayal was all the better from the Lowlanders' point of view.

'Before spring we will have the seawall rebuilt and the land ready for planting,' the old man said.

'So much work.'

Faded eyes studied him. 'I will speak plainly. You have been generous in your terms of surrender, General Tulkhan, offering the service of your men to rebuild. But we do not regret flooding our land. It is the price we pay for freedom. We wrest our land from the sea and, if we choose to return it to the sea, that is our business.'

HOLDING ASHMYR, IMOSHEN stepped onto the balcony overlooking the square. As she raised her left arm and gave the Empress's blessing a sibilant sigh of relief swept the crowd. A minstrel struck up an Old Empire song of praise and the crowd joined in. Tears stung Imoshen's eyes. This was her home, her people, and they had not deserted her.

When the song came to an end she raised her voice, willing it to carry across the square, aware that the words would be carried across Fair Isle. 'People of T'Diemn, I thank the Beatific for upholding the laws of the T'En church. And I thank Drake and the Parakhan Guard for standing true. Though the Cadre, and the Ghebite usurpers, are vanquished, we are not safe. Fair Isle faces a time of travail as dangerous as the Age of Tribulation. This is why

I am reviving an old branch of the church. Today I recreate the T'Enplar warriors. And I appoint T'Reothe, Sword of Justice, leader of the T'Enplars.'

She smiled at the crowd's joyous reaction. Reothe's tantalising mention of the T'Elegos had made Imoshen think. Recreating the T'Enplars appealed to her sense of history, and she had hoped it would inspire confidence in the people.

By conferring the leadership of the T'Enplars upon Reothe, she was protecting him within the mantle of the church's power. But she had another motive. She turned to him. 'When General Tulkhan returns, I don't want him to find you in the palace, Reothe.'

His face was a mask. Imoshen held her left hand out to the Beatific. Though Engarad inclined her head and kissed her sixth finger, the True-woman's mind remained closed to Imoshen. By the glint of triumph in her golden eyes, Imoshen knew that the Beatific believed she had made a wrong move in the game of power. The Beatific supported her only so long as it suited her own goals and now she had given the woman Reothe to lead a band of armed church warriors.

So be it.

In a way, Imoshen was grateful to the Cadre and Jarholfe for weeding out those Ghebites most loyal to the old way of thinking. She would tell Wharrd to... Imoshen almost staggered as his loss hit her. She had not realised how much she had come to depend on the veteran bone-setter.

In a daze of grief, she left the balcony to find the palace over-servants awaiting her. She spoke to each one, thanking them for their loyalty. When she came to the woman who ruled the kitchen, she paused to order food and drink to be distributed in the square.

At last Imoshen came to Keeper Karmel and she led the old woman into the library. 'You risked your life in my service. Is there anything you want or need?'

The woman pondered, then a cunning look came over her face. 'I want access to the Basilica's archives. For years the master-archivist has jealously guarded them.'

Imoshen laughed. 'T'Reothe will see that you have it.'

She returned to her room to write to Tulkhan. Her message would leave with the evening tide and she had to trust a new emissary. She missed Rawset.

Without anything being said, Kalleen moved into her old room next to Imoshen's and the days passed in a rush of activity. The families of the murdered Parakhan Guard had to be notified and provision made for their future. Imoshen rewarded Drake's initiative and loyalty by officially giving him the title of captain.

The Parakhan Guard's numbers had been greatly depleted. Townspeople wanted to be compensated for the destruction of property. Imoshen's head spun with the myriad repercussions of the failed Ghebite coup. Frightened Ghebites kept coming out of hiding and she had to consult with the Beatific as to how they should be treated. Simply returning these men to the community would imperil their safety, so arrangements had to be made for many of them to be relocated. A hundred times a day Wharrd's loss returned to her with renewed pain. Kalleen mourned privately, spending most of her time with Ashmyr.

Someone knocked at the door. Imoshen looked up from her desk with a sigh. 'Enter.'

'General Tulkhan!' Kalleen gasped.

Imoshen nearly knocked the ink well over.

The General strode into the room, making it seem small. Imoshen's heart raced with joy and she longed to feel his arms around her, but she had bad news for him. Imoshen came to her feet, speaking calmly to hide her trepidation. 'You are returned sooner than expected, General.'

'Port Sumair has fallen.'

'When?'

'These five days past.'

She blinked. The port must have fallen around the time she and Reothe regained the capital. It appeared her messenger had missed the General and he was not aware of Jarholfe and the Cadre's treachery.

'I bring you victory, yet you grow pale as milk,' Tulkhan said. 'What is it?'

Imoshen signalled Kalleen to take Ashmyr into the far room. But before she could do this, Tulkhan strode past both women. He picked up his son, who gnawed anxiously on his fist.

'He's teething,' Imoshen explained.

'You'd never know he had walked death's shadow and returned. He looks just like any other baby.'

'You mean apart from his T'En eyes and his six fingers?' she asked, then wished the words unsaid.

Tulkhan was not amused. 'Kalleen, take my son for now.'

Imoshen's mouth went dry. A charged silence filled the room as Kalleen took the boy from the General and retreated. The little woman held Imoshen's eyes before closing the door and Imoshen knew if help was needed Kalleen would come. It was typical of her, loyal and forthright. Loyal like...

'Wharrd is dead.' Imoshen confessed. Tulkhan looked stunned. She knew how he had treasured the veteran's friendship. Tears burned her eyes as she sought to comfort him. 'It happened while I was returning from the Amirate. There was nothing I could do.'

A great rushing filled Tulkhan's head, he stepped back, felt the chair behind him and sat unsteadily. He could hardly think. 'How... how did it happen?'

'Jarholfe and the Cadre attacked my honour and Wharrd defended it.'

'As your Ghiad, he could not do otherwise,' Tulkhan said, then shook his head. 'What possessed them?'

'They wanted a legal excuse to have me executed.'

Tulkhan cursed Jarholfe. Suddenly aware that Imoshen's hand rested on his arm, he pulled away from her, wondering what she might have gleaned from the contact.

'The Cadre and Jarholfe tried to force the Beatific to sign a declaration to have Reothe and I stoned,' Imoshen revealed.

Her words drummed in his head, the import too much to absorb. He sprang to his feet and paced to the fireplace, gripping the mantelpiece in both hands. One thing was clear. The Cadre and Jarholfe had caused Wharrd's death. He spun to face Imoshen. 'Where are they now?'

'Jarholfe is dead and the Cadre is being held by the Beatific for crimes against Fair Isle. Where do you go?'

He thrust past her, heading for the door. Imoshen fell into step at his side. Despite her height, she almost had to skip to keep up with him.

Tulkhan found the man he wanted waiting in the hall outside.

'Lightfoot, send a message to the Beatific. She is to escort the Cadre into the square. I want twenty of my elite guard in full uniform and I want them in the square as soon as possible. Tell them to bring the duelling swords.'

'Lightfoot,' Imoshen caught his sleeve. 'Drake is leader of the Parakhan Guard. Convey the General's message to him.'

In the heat of the moment Tulkhan had forgotten that Imoshen had disbanded his elite guard.

'Jarholfe's Ghebites hunted down our people, Tulkhan. They displayed their corpses in the square.'

He was eager to translate anger into action.

'General, wait.' She hurried after him. 'Do you intend to fight a duel with the Cadre?'

'If he has the stomach for it.' He headed down the steps with Imoshen at his heels.

'But General, the Cadre has broken the laws of Fair Isle. As leader of the T'En church, the Beatific must preside over his trial. Your role should be to advise on punishment. You are the wronged party. Not only you, but Kalleen has been wronged, and her unborn child. Slow down and listen, Tulkhan!'

She caught his arm before he could throw open the small door to the square. 'Think of your position. As Protector General of Fair Isle, you set the tone for the whole island. If you resort to violence, you are no better than the Cadre and Jarholfe, who ignored the letter of the law when the Orb of Truth proclaimed my innocence!'

'My men expect me to act swiftly and decisively against any threat to my leadership.' He thrust the door open, then stopped, surprised to see the square full of townspeople, gathered in the early morning sunshine. The season's first snow had melted but the air was cold and crisp. The smell of roasting nuts and cinnamon-apples came to him. 'What...'

'They expect a celebration, General. Your men will have spread the good news by now. They want to honour your victory over your half-brother.'

'Gharavan escaped. The merchant leaders of the port dropped the seawall and nearly drowned my entire army. Hardly the victory I planned.'

Imoshen's mouth opened, but before she could reply someone recognised them standing on the steps and the shout went up.

Reacting to the cheers, Imoshen threaded her arm through Tulkhan's, drawing him down into the square. 'Smile, General. In their eyes you are victorious. Let appearance become substance.'

He found himself walking through a crowd of well-wishers. They came from every strata of T'Diemn society, from street sweepers to rich merchants, from blue-fingered cloth dyers to grey-haired masters from the Halls of Learning. And all of them wanted to touch him. This time he was as sought after as Imoshen. He felt an unexpected sense of homecoming.

The rush and surge of the crowd carried them across the square. The clamour of voices drowned out individual comments, but the tone was one of welcome and still they pressed. Was every citizen of T'Diemn here today?

Imoshen sensed intense scrutiny and lifted her gaze above the throng to find Reothe watching her. Only the thin line of his mouth revealed his fury. His eyes were hooded by the shadow of a half-face helmet. The ceremonial T'Enplar weaponry looked as if it was made for him. Like a physical assault, Imoshen felt Reothe's silent accusation of betrayal. Her heart contracted as the dual tug of loyalties threatened to tear her apart.

Reothe marched through the crowd towards them, followed by his T'Enplar warriors. The townsfolk reacted with instinctive awe to the sight of the last T'En warrior and his supporters, resplendent in ornate chest plates, embroidered cloaks and half-face helmets complete with dyed horse-hair crests. The armour dated from the middle of the Age of Consolidation, when Fair Isle's ceremonial weaponry was designed for display.

Imoshen felt the shudder of recognition run through Tulkhan's body when he saw Reothe. People kept moving back so that by the time Reothe reached them, they stood alone in a sea of watchers.

Rage pulsed in the muscle of Reothe's clenched jaw. The moment stretched impossibly. Imoshen willed him not to antagonise the General, who was primed for violence.

'Protector General Tulkhan, Lady Protector.' The Beatific stepped into the silence, sweeping them a regal obeisance which claimed as much honour for herself as it accorded them. She was dressed in full regalia. Her long mantle of rich velvet brushed the cobbles as she bowed and the tassels of her ornate headdress dipped and swayed as she straightened.

'All of T'Diemn speaks of your munificence, General. When you could have ordered death, you showed mercy. The people of Port Sumair will remember your restraint.' A priest approached and the Beatific inclined her head to listen to his report. Behind her, priests waited with chairs and a large portable dais. 'My people are ready. I must prepare for the trial.'

Imoshen was relieved. With her usual acumen the Beatific had stepped in to prevent General Tulkhan's execution of the Cadre by trial of combat.

'Protector General Tulkhan.' Reothe delivered the Old Empire military salute, lifting his sword hilt to his forehead then re-sheathing the weapon. 'I stand before you, the church's Sword of Justice, leader of the T'Enplar warriors, to deliver the prisoner, the Ghebite Cadre.' Behind Reothe a dozen T'Enplars repeated his salute.

Imoshen thought she recognised a few of them and doubted very much if their loyalty was to the Beatific. It seemed some of Reothe's rebels had found redemption in service to the church. As for the Cadre, he stood unrestrained in their midst, his hate-filled eyes fixed on Imoshen.

A flash of mulberry robe in the crowd indicated the presence of Murgon and his Tractarians. As Sword of Justice, Reothe was now on the same level of the church hierarchy as Murgon.

While he had been leading the rebels, Reothe had received covert support from the church, but Imoshen wondered how those canny brokers of power would react to finding him in their midst. Imoshen did not envy Reothe his position. But then, she did not covet her own position either.

'Sword of Justice?' Tulkhan muttered.

'I recreated the T'Enplar warriors and appointed Reothe to this position. They serve the Beatific to uphold the laws of Fair Isle; your laws, General.'

But Tulkhan knew they weren't his laws. Most of the laws of Fair Isle were unknown to him – like this pomp and pageantry unfolding around him.

The crowd parted as Lightfoot arrived with the Parakhan Guard. The mercenary moved to stand behind Tulkhan. Drake approached Imoshen and Tulkhan, offering his salute to both of them, before opening a case in which rested two swords on a bed of black velvet.

'Violence was ever the Ghebite way.' Reothe's voice dripped scorn.

'We Ghebites may not be as civilised as the T'En, but we protect what is our own.' Tulkhan held Reothe's eyes across the duelling swords.

Reothe's features revealed his understanding but they held no deference. Tulkhan seethed. Didn't Reothe know he lived on sufferance?

But Tulkhan could not order Reothe's execution now. His army was scattered from Fair Isle to Port Sumair. He was surrounded by townsfolk who could just as easily turn on him if the hereditary heirs of Fair Isle tried to reclaim the throne.

'General?' Imoshen held his eyes. 'There is more than Wharrd's death at stake here. What the people witness today will travel all over Fair Isle on the lips of the minstrels. Do you want them to sing of barbaric bloodshed or of the justice shown by the Protector General of Fair Isle?'

Even though Imoshen was right, he was annoyed that she dared to counsel him before others. But then, she was not a Ghebite female. She was T'En, more royal than the Empress herself.

'Here comes the Empress's heir!' a voice cried and the crowd parted to let Kalleen through with Ashmyr in her arms.

'I see you brought T'Ashmyr, Lady Kalleen. Good,' the Beatific said as she rejoined them. 'His life was also threatened. Come everyone, take your places on the dais. We are ready to proceed.'

A church servant waited with a silk shade cunningly stretched over supple wood. He held it above the Beatific to keep off the sun as she took her seat.

Tulkhan glared at the man who would have held a similar piece of nonsense over him, but Imoshen did not remonstrate. She and Kalleen sat in the shade of the church's beneficence as the trial began with Reothe reading the charges. His words fell in absolute silence. The people of T'Diemn seemed to find this real-life drama better any Thespers' Guild performance.

When Reothe finished, the Beatific asked, 'How do you plead?'

'Yes, speak up, Cadre,' Tulkhan urged.

The T'Enplar warriors had stepped back to form a semicircle behind the Cadre. Behind them the Parakhan Guard formed a larger semicircle and beyond them was the crowd. People stood on wagons, clustered on balconies surrounding the square. The air was filled with a hushed expectancy.

Although the Cadre was dressed in his blood-stained surplice, his stance was not one of defeat. Raising his hand, he gestured to the Beatific, his eyes alight with the fervour of fanaticism. 'I do not acknowledge this female. It has been proven women's weak souls are channels for evil. I appeal to you, General Tulkhan.' He stepped closer to the edge of the dais, which came up to his thigh. 'Do not forget the ways of your father's people. It was your honour I was defending, and your dishonour that I sought to erase. This...' His voice grew scathing as he pointed to Imoshen. 'This Dhamfeer killed Jarholfe with her vile sorcery. She should be stoned. She, her half-breed brat and her lover should all be –'

'Enough!' Tulkhan roared. He ached to choke the poison from the priest's tongue.

Imoshen's voice cut through Tulkhan's fury like cold water on hot coals. 'I call on Silversmith Guildmaster Maigeth to speak for me. It was her honour to hold the Orb.'

In that instant Tulkhan understood that to kill the Cadre would not remove the accusations. Imoshen had to be seen to be cleared of these crimes.

'Come here, Maigeth,' the Beatific ordered.

'Yes. Step forward,' Tulkhan urged, determined to wrest control of the proceedings from the Beatific.

The spectators parted to let the woman approach the dais.

'Can you vouch for Imoshen's innocence?' Tulkhan asked.

'I can and so can everyone else who was there that day. We all saw the Orb glow bright with the light of truth.' The words fell from the woman's tongue as though she was reciting an ancient formula.

The crowd sighed and whispered in agreement.

'I say the Orb lied!' the Cadre cried.

People gasped. *Sacrilege!*

'Can the Orb lie?' Tulkhan asked the Beatific.

'All those who have tried to use it to further their own ends have died horrible deaths, in fear of their immortal souls.'

Again the crowd voiced their agreement.

'Then bring forth this Orb and let everyone see if the Cadre will venture his soul on the truth!' Tulkhan ordered.

The townspeople became strangely silent. Even the Cadre looked down. Tulkhan turned to the Beatific for an explanation.

She glared at the Ghebite priest. 'The Cadre smashed our holy relic.'

'It was the Cadre who released the Orb's presence.' Reothe said. 'He is responsible for freeing the ancient power which killed Jarholfe, not Imoshen.'

'The Dhamfeer killed a True-man with her vile T'En gifts,' the Cadre crowed. 'And by the laws of the T'En church she must die. Deny me that, Beatific!'

Silence hung heavy on the air.

Imoshen sprang to her feet. 'I call on Murgon, leader of the Tractarians.'

Reothe sent Imoshen a charged look which Tulkhan found hard to interpret but the Beatific was already calling for Murgon.

As he stepped from the throng, Tulkhan tried to place the man. He had the T'En eyes and wore deep mulberry robes. Then he recalled how Murgon's malevolent gaze had settled on Imoshen as she knelt to give her Oath of Expiation on their coronation day. And this man did not look any more ready to absolve her now.

'I ask only that you speak the truth, Murgon,' Imoshen told him.

The man's mouth worked as if he chewed on something bitter. 'I saw T'Imoshen breathe death into Jarholfe's body. She killed him as surely as –'

'She killed in self-defence after saving the Beatific,' Reothe insisted.

But the crowd stirred, unable to deny the ancient law. Tulkhan saw it all slipping away from him. He met Imoshen's eyes and knew it was true. She had killed Jarholfe. The why of it did not matter. It was the *how* which would be her death.

'No! Not Empress T'Imoshen!' a new voice cried.

Tulkhan spun to see a weatherworn member of the Parakhan Guard push through the T'Enplars.

Sibilant whispers echoed. *Empress T'Imoshen, Empress T'Imoshen.*

'I am the blind man who sees and I will be heard!' the Parakhan Guard shouted.

'Speak,' Tulkhan directed.

The man looked at each of them in turn, meeting Tulkhan's eyes last.

'I am the blind man who sees,' he repeated, gesturing to his eyes. 'And these eyes of mine see beyond the Ghebite priest's lies, beyond the Tractarian's half-truths. I see our Empress who has served Fair Isle in honour. I also acknowledge the old laws of Fair Isle. A True-man died by T'Imoshen's gift.'

As he unsheathed his sword the shrill sound rang on the silence. 'I assume the guilt for the death of the Ghebite, and through my own death absolve the Empress of all –'

'No!' Thrusting Ashmyr into Kalleen's arms, Imoshen ran to the edge of the dais. 'I won't let you die in my place!'

The crowd moaned like a wounded beast, Imoshen lifted her hands, pleading for their understanding. 'People of T'Diemn, I used my gift to kill Jarholfe, but it was self-defence. And the Beatific knows this. I call on the

Beatific to look into her heart and ask herself, if she is not here today because I saved her life. Am I to be condemned because I saved our lives in exchange for the Ghebite's?'

As the Beatific reluctantly joined Imoshen on the edge of the dais, her servant kept pace with her so that she remained under the silken shade's protection. Imoshen went down on both knees, lifting her hands, palm up, in deep supplication. 'You have the power to absolve me, Engarad. Look into your heart.'

The Beatific flinched. Her lips parted. Tulkhan could tell she was going to pardon Imoshen.

'No!' The Cadre snatched the blind man's sword.

Tulkhan drew his knife but could not risk a throw. Imoshen was between him and the Cadre.

Time slowed.

Helplessly Tulkhan watched Imoshen scramble backwards as the Cadre leapt onto the dais. He stood over her, his sword blade flashing in the autumn sun. Tulkhan threw his knife. But even as it left his hand, the tip of a ceremonial sword plunged into the Cadre's chest, its slender blade quivering. An instant later, Tulkhan's knife struck home too, and the Cadre collapsed on Imoshen's thighs.

Tulkhan hauled Imoshen upright, spinning her to face him. For a heartbeat her eyes betrayed her terror. Tulkhan had seen that look before on the faces of men who had survived death against all odds.

'Death stalks me,' she whispered, 'claiming others when I escape.'

Dimly Tulkhan heard the exclamations of the crowd. Reothe crossed the dais and knelt at the Cadre's side to retrieve the sword he had thrown like a spear.

'Good throw,' Tulkhan said.

'Surprising, considering.' Reothe flexed his left hand, revealing missing fingers.

'Dead?' The Beatific did not deign to examine the Cadre.

'Dead,' Reothe confirmed as he cleaned his sword. Tulkhan was struck by the maiming of his left hand.

'What happened?' Tulkhan gestured to Reothe's hand.

'The Cadre envied me my six fingers, so he removed a few,' Reothe said, then leapt down from the dais, gesturing to his T'Enplars. 'Take the traitor's body away.'

'Wait,' Tulkhan ordered. 'Say the words, Beatific.'

She looked confused.

'Say the words. Condemn the Cadre.' Tulkhan recalled the effect of Kornel's trial and ritual execution after his death. He wanted Imoshen absolved of all guilt so these events could not be used against her in future. 'Speak loudly, Beatific. I want all of Fair Isle to know that Imoshen is free of guilt.'

The Beatific made this declaration and the crowd looked on as justice was seen to be done. Then the T'Enplar warriors carried the Cadre's body away.

Imoshen beckoned Kalleen. Retrieving her son she turned to Tulkhan. 'Protector General, Kalleen's quick thinking saved our son. Wharrd's widow carries his unborn child. All of his estates are now hers, in accordance with the laws of the T'En church. Wharrd died in our service. Such loyalty deserves reward.'

'I want no reward,' Kalleen protested, her eyes glittering with unshed tears. She bit back an angry sob. 'I held Wharrd in my arms as he died. Nothing can restore him to me. Nothing!'

Imoshen shifted her son to one hip and hugged Kalleen. Seeing the two women embrace, Tulkhan was struck anew by the loss of his old friend. When he looked away, he noticed the Beatific was watching him closely.

Imoshen pressed her cheek to Kalleen's and whispered urgently, 'Every woman in Fair Isle depends on us. The Cadre is dead, but his thinking lives on. General Tulkhan must acknowledge your rights of ownership and your right to Wharrd's estates. We cannot let Ghebite thinking disinherit the women of Fair Isle. Do you understand why I do this?'

As Kalleen met Imoshen's eyes, hers glowed with fury. 'You use me for your own ends.'

'The higher we rise, the more we serve,' Imoshen said.

When she returned to the General and slid her arm through his she felt the tension in his body. 'As the Beatific is our witness, General, we must reward Kalleen. In Fair Isle the punishment for treason is death and forfeiture of lands and titles.'

'It is the same in Gheeaba,' Tulkhan conceded.

'Then it is only fitting you reward Kalleen with the estates and titles Jarholfe held. The Beatific can have the new deeds and titles drawn up.'

'It will be done.' The Beatific signalled to one of her people, who ran back to the Basilica. The news spread through the crowd, which broke into spontaneous singing.

Imoshen held the General's obsidian eyes. 'The traitors have been vanquished and your army is victorious. Let us call upon the Thespers' guildmaster to organise entertainments in the square while the palace kitchen prepares food for a celebration.'

Tulkhan returned Imoshen's gaze, thinking that with this morning's trial she had not only vanquished her Ghebite accusers, she had also consolidated her position as co-ruler of Fair Isle.

Yet, when he looked past Imoshen's shoulder to Kalleen's miserable face, he had to agree. Kalleen should be compensated and the future of Wharrd's unborn child secured.

How had the reins of power slipped from his fingers into Imoshen's?

Chapter Seventeen

LATE THAT EVENING, when Imoshen and Kalleen had retired to the Empress's chambers, Kalleen looked blankly at the estate deeds.

Imoshen joined her. 'How does it feel, farm girl, to be one of the richest women in Fair Isle?'

'My child's father is dead. Yet today I feel nothing. Am I heartless?'

'No.' Imoshen took her hand. 'You are weary, my friend. All too soon, you will feel again.'

'I will never love again. Not like I loved Wharrd.'

'No,' Imoshen agreed, and squeezed her hand. But when she looked down she saw not her own hand holding Kalleen's, but Tulkhan's battle-scarred coppery hands. Was it a warning vision? Suddenly she was consumed with fear for Tulkhan and for the love they shared.

'Imoshen?' Kalleen asked. 'What troubles you?'

'Nothing.' She gave Kalleen's hand a reassuring rub and let her go. 'Can you watch Ashmyr?'

Since the General had returned, she had not had a private moment with him. Going down the main stairs, Imoshen glanced up at the ceiling frescoes of the T'En royal line's great deeds and wondered if her ancestors had also longed for peace and quiet.

Tulkhan was not in the great hall. Drawing on her gift, Imoshen discovered he was in one of the small private chambers. She slipped down the dim passage and paused outside the door, wrinkling her nose as she opened her gift to discern what lay behind it.

The person with Tulkhan was her enemy.

'WITHOUT HIS T'EN gifts, Reothe is no more dangerous than a True-man,' the Beatific said. 'If you wish, I could give him the title of the Aayel. He would find himself busy from dawn till dusk in the church's service.'

Tulkhan understood what she was offering, but it was not true to say that Reothe was no more dangerous than a True-man simply because his gifts were crippled. 'Reothe needs no more honours.'

'Very well.'

'Go, and thank you for your support, Beatific.'

Before leaving, the woman offered him the obeisance between equals, raising only one hand to her forehead.

Tulkhan strode to the multi-paned window and looked out into the dark courtyard. If only there was a way to kill Reothe without endangering Imoshen or igniting rebellion.

The skin on the back of his neck prickled. As he gazed out of the window, he became aware of Imoshen's pale face and hair reflected in one of the squares of glass. His heart faltered and he felt as if his thoughts had been exposed.

Disguising his disquiet, he turned to greet her. 'So now you come and go like a ghost?'

She gave a soft laugh. 'The extent of T'En powers is greatly exaggerated, General.'

'I wonder... Today the Beatific absolved you of a True-man's death.'

She glanced down then up, candlelight glistening in her pleading eyes. 'It was self-defence, and at least I did not suffer like I did with the Vayg...' She gave a guilty start.

'So you did kill the Vaygharian.'

'He deserved to die!'

'If I went around killing everyone who deserved to die –'

'Don't judge me. I paid for his death.' She shuddered.

Tulkhan fought the need to take her in his arms.

She misinterpreted his silence. 'You don't believe me? You thought me ill with a fever, but it was far worse. For the T'En, the barriers between this world and the next are much frailer. The Vaygharian's vengeful soul tried to drag me through death's shadow with him while the Parakletos watched and mocked, or turned their faces from me. I barely escaped.'

Tulkhan had to turn his face away from her to hide his savage surge of triumph. With Imoshen's admission, he understood it was only coincidence that she and Reothe had both suffered the night he'd nearly ordered the rebel leader's death. He was free to kill Reothe and the shock of the revelation ran through his body.

'Tulkhan?' Imoshen whispered. Her hands slid around his waist.

He froze.

'Don't shut yourself away from me. I feared for your life and, when my own was in danger, I longed to reach out to you. But because you always resisted the mind-touch, I could not reach you.'

'Never...' He cleared his throat then turned in the circle of her arms. 'I will never open up to your gifts. I must have the privacy of my thoughts.'

She tilted her head, her eyes reflecting the many candles like the rubies they resembled. 'I know your warrior code belittles women, but I live by my own code of honour, General, and I have given my word not to take advantage of your trust. Do not hold yourself aloof from me.'

'As if I could!' His arm circled the small of her waist and he pulled her close. Imoshen melded to him, but even though his body responded to hers and he ached to open to her, he held back.

If he was to plan Reothe's accidental death, he could not risk discovery.

*　　*　　*

'THE ROYAL LINE descends through the Empress, so she selects the best males to father her children,' the Keeper of the Knowledge explained, her deep-set eyes keen with intelligence. 'It is not so different from what you were telling me of your Ghebite customs. Only instead of quantity, with many wives and children, the ruler of Fair Isle looks for quality.'

'Enough,' Tulkhan said. 'Leave me.'

He stared at the complicated family tree. Imoshen had shown him this chart once before, pointing to her own name. She had even said something about the royal line following the women, but he had not understood. Imoshen might claim he thought like a Ghebite, but she thought like a woman of Fair Isle.

'General?'

Tulkhan looked up. 'Lightfoot.'

'The town officials are ready to view the city's outer defences.' The mercenary had assumed command of T'Diemn's garrison.

Tulkhan thrust the book aside. To fund the massive defensive works, he had called for a levy from all businesses and households. The defences he was constructing would surpass those designed by Emperor T'Reothe four hundred years ago.

Though the townspeople of T'Diemn were incredibly wealthy by the standards of the mainland, they were not eager to part with their gold. Imoshen had suggested that a tour of the new defences might make the townspeople realise where their money was going.

Imoshen... her good counsel and leadership could not be denied. She deserved the respect of his men and they now believed her innocent of Jarholfe's accusations because the Orb proclaimed her so. But when her pregnancy began to show, he would have to acknowledge another man's child as his own, or admit Reothe had cuckolded him. Tulkhan felt like a bear in a trap. There had to be a way out of this dishonour.

IMOSHEN MET KALLEEN'S eyes as a servant announced that General Tulkhan wanted to speak with her. She glanced down at her notes. New standards, flags and cloaks had been ordered to replace the ones lost in the flood. But the cloth merchants' stocks were depleted.

Imoshen had decided to send a message to the Amiregent requesting supplies. Better to let it be known that Fair Isle was preparing for war than to pretend it would not happen.

'I will watch over Ashmyr,' Kalleen said.

Imoshen nodded and came to her feet. In the long gallery she passed servants busily trimming wicks and lighting candles. Just lighting the palace of a thousand rooms was a huge expense. If they faced another season of war, Fair Isle would have to tighten her belt to finance her defences.

Imoshen opened the door to Tulkhan's map-room where she found him lighting a branch of candles.

'If your half-brother mounts a spring campaign, the cost of refitting the army will have to be met somehow. Did your tour of the new defences loosen the pockets of the town officials, General?'

'Yes. Shut the door.' He pinched out the taper and the smell hung on the air. 'I have come to a decision.'

'Oh?' Imoshen did not like his strained expression.

'I know the women of Fair Isle control their fertility. I am sure you can rid yourself of an unwanted pregnancy. Get rid of Reothe's child and I –'

Imoshen turned to go.

Tulkhan strode after her, swinging her around to face him. 'Don't walk away from me!'

With a flick Imoshen freed her arm and would have pushed past him, but he thrust one hand against the door, holding it shut.

Imoshen's heart raged, one giant drumbeat of denial. Knowing her strength was no match for his, she made no attempt to leave. The familiar metallic tang settled on her tongue as her gift rose, but resorting to her powers would only alienate him further. 'I will not discuss this!'

'Before long all of T'Diemn will know you are with child.'

'What of it?'

'When the child is born they will know I am not the father! Think of my position.'

'How does that compare to the life of a child?' Outrage made her voice resonate.

'You would have me accept another man's cast-off?'

'I will not kill my own child.'

He ground his teeth. 'Look, they'll say. There goes Tulkhan. While he was away defending Fair Isle, his wife took the Dhamfeer rebel for her lover. Poor fool. He cannot see past his lust!'

'Tulkhan...' Imoshen reached out to him. In that moment he was exposed to her. She perceived that another layer had been added to the General's being while he had been away. In a flash she understood it was not generosity that had led him to spare the defenders of Port Sumair but guilt. Words spilled from her lips. 'Would you add the killing of the unborn to your list of murders?'

Tulkhan's coppery skin went grey. 'Is that what you think I am, a murderous barbarian?'

She wanted to deny it. She knew he was so much more, but she remained silent because it gave her power.

'How you must despise me. I marvel that you can bring yourself to stand at my side,' he whispered.

Imoshen caught his hands in hers. 'Mainland spies watch us. Their masters wait like carrion birds to peck clean the bones of Fair Isle's carcass. I know you find it hard to understand my people, but –'

He pulled his hands free.

'Don't close me out, Tulkhan.'

'I must. Is it any wonder, when I can feel power radiating from your skin?'

Imoshen looked up into Tulkhan's face. His features, once so alien, were now so dear. 'It is true I surrendered my stronghold to the superior force of your army, but since then I have come to know you. As T'Imoshen, on behalf of the people of Fair Isle, I have tried to make our alliance work. But I ask this of you as your bond-partner. Can you not find it in your heart to mend this breach between us?'

'You don't understand, Imoshen. By the warrior's code a man must have the respect of his peers!'

'Where is the honour in killing an unborn child?'

'You ask the impossible of me.'

Imoshen closed her eyes and recalled that dawn morning when she held her dead son in her arms and faced the blinding presence of the Ancients to restore his life. 'Don't talk to me of what is impossible. We can make anything happen if we want it badly enough. Think of Ashmyr.'

'But think of the cost,' Tulkhan countered. 'What price did you agree to pay?' When she wouldn't answer, he went on. 'You saved Ashmyr from death's shadow; I have seen you call the Parakletos and death's own guardian angels obeyed you. Perhaps that is why you will not admit defeat, but I am only a True-man. My life has boundaries.'

'I too, have boundaries. Tulkhan, I... I fear for us.'

He pulled her into his arms, crushing her with the force of his emotion. His words were a deep rumble in his chest, muffled by her hair as he pressed his lips to her head. 'Imoshen...'

She held him with all her strength, as if she could halt the forces which strove to drive them apart. If only they were simply a man and a woman, and not the embodiment of their separate peoples. Tears stung her eyes. She pulled away to search his face. 'Promise at least to listen to me.'

He removed the Ghebite seal ring. 'My father gave me this after my first victory. There are only two, and the other rests on Gharavan's finger. If you are ever in trouble or it seems there is no hope for us, send me this and I will listen, even if it goes against all reason.'

Imoshen slid the ring onto the longest finger of her left hand, where it became a symbol of hope. She made a fist to keep it safe.

'Why do you cry now?' he asked, his voice gentle.

Angrily, she brushed at the tears. 'Will you take your meal with me, General Tulkhan?'

He smiled. 'If that is what you wish.'

'I would pretend for this evening that we are simply a man and woman with no greater decisions than which fields to plant in the spring.'

He laughed and Imoshen felt lighter.

'We should have a feast.'

'Another feast?' he teased.

'When the defences are finished.'

'The first phase will be finished come spring, but I could go on fortifying T'Diemn forever.'

'Aayel forbid!' Imoshen grinned. 'I was taught a leader should use every opportunity for celebration to impress on her people the power and achievements of her rule.'

'If the royal line passes through the women, why did Imoshen the First marry her son to the old ruling line of Fair Isle and not her daughter?' Tulkhan asked abruptly.

'Imoshen the First's daughter was pure T'En. It was decreed that all pure T'En women were to remain chaste and that daughter became the first Beatific.' Imoshen regarded him fondly. 'You have been reading the old histories in the original High T'En. Your scholarship is to be admired.'

'I may be a Ghebite, Imoshen, but I am not stupid.'

She held his gaze. 'I may be a woman, but...'

'Will you never stop?'

'Never!'

He laughed again and it warmed her to the core.

TULKHAN WATCHED THE servants clear away the remains of the feast. Tonight's celebration was to acknowledge and reward his faithful lord commanders who had returned from the mainland.

The high table was positioned under his huge standard. The dawn sun, embroidered with thread of finely spun gold, glittered in the candlelight of the public hall, which was as crowded as the day he had awarded Wharrd and his men their titles. Again he felt the tug of that loss. The old bone-setter had served in honour, blood and death, just as the white, red and black ribbons of the T'En investiture signified.

Tulkhan stood aside while the servants removed the table. The musicians struck up a dance and the floor became crowded.

'That one bears watching,' Lightfoot remarked softly.

Reothe was dancing with Imoshen. Before the whole hall, he held her hand and looked into her eyes as though she was the sun to him. It stung Tulkhan to acknowledge that they formed a perfect pair, stepping to the measured paces of the Old Empire dance with innate T'En grace.

'The rebel's claws have been clipped,' Tulkhan replied. He was only awaiting the opportunity to have Reothe assassinated. Lightfoot would have been an ideal assassin but, even though Imoshen had removed the T'En stigmata, Tulkhan suspected that under the right circumstance she could call on the ex-mercenary. 'When Imoshen destroyed Reothe's gifts, he became an empty shell, nothing but a symbol of the Old Empire.'

'The people need symbols. That one gathers about him a brotherhood of fanatical warriors. The T'Enplars swear an oath to the Beatific, and Reothe claims to serve the church, but I know where their loyalties lie.'

This confirmed Tulkhan's suspicions.

'Here comes another cat that needs declawing,' Lightfoot muttered.

Tulkhan repressed a grin as the Beatific joined him. He greeted her and they both sat down. She had taken the seat on his left. Imoshen's seat was on his right – not, as he had once thought, because this acknowledged her importance to him, Protector General of Fair Isle, but because it placed him on her left hand. Since the T'En were left-handed, the left was the position of honour. Tulkhan had had to unlearn much to understand the people of Fair Isle.

The Beatific smiled on him, beautiful, worldly and... malicious?

'You do not dance?' he asked.

'Dancing is for children, not for leaders of state.'

Tulkhan winced. The woman was flattering him because he never danced. But she had reminded him that the T'En lived so much longer. Here he was over thirty, with maybe another twenty years to live, and there was Reothe. They were roughly the same age, yet Reothe could expect to live another seventy or eighty years.

'You were curious as to how Reothe's hand was maimed,' the Beatific said.

Tulkhan nodded. By tacit agreement, he and Imoshen had not discussed her kinsman.

'The Cadre sliced off his fingers to prevent him helping Imoshen escape from Sard's Tower. They were shut out there, exposed to the first snowfall, so they would be weak but alive when they were stoned. Imoshen sealed Reothe's wounds but even the greatest of T'En healers could not replace a severed limb. Somehow Reothe escaped from the tower and saved Imoshen.'

Twice now Reothe had saved Imoshen's life, once with his T'En gifts and this time with nothing more than bravery. The General frowned. He did not want to admire his enemy.

Feeling herself observed, Imoshen's cheeks grew warm. She did not have to turn her head to know that Tulkhan watched her with Reothe. She had only danced with him once before, on the celebration of their betrothal.

On that day so long ago she had laced her fingers with his and bathed in the glow of his admiration, knowing he wanted her. The memory made her writhe with resentment. She did not want to be reminded that her first, freely given vow had been to Reothe.

Standing on the ball of her foot, she turned under Reothe's outstretched arm. Her skirts settled around her with soft sigh. 'You should not have asked me to dance.'

'It would have been remarked if I hadn't.' His arms circled her without actually touching. His breath caressed her ear, intimate, mocking. He spoke as concisely as the steps they performed. '*What are the last T'En hiding?* people would have said. *Why don't they acknowledge each other?*'

Though their bodies did not touch anywhere but at the fingertips, she was aware of tension radiating from him. She stepped back and held his eyes. 'Everything you do is remarked, Reothe. They tell me more T'Enplar warriors join you every day. Beware or you'll be perceived as a threat.'

He laughed bitterly. 'How could the Ghebite General perceive me as a threat? You have denied me before everyone.' Fury ignited him. 'The Orb of Truth lied for you, Imoshen.'

'My words were true. You came to me in Tulkhan's form. You even told me how to speak the truth without incriminating myself.'

'Yet you carry my child and it is only a matter of time before he denies you!'

Reothe's triumph washed over her, making the little hairs on her skin rise up in protest. Was his gift healing? The heat, the scented candles, the press of the bodies... everything faded. Her vision blurred and narrowed down to an aura of light surrounding Reothe's shorn silver hair. The room spun. Couples moved around them in time to music Imoshen could not hear for the roaring in her ears. She stumbled.

Reothe caught her, then flinched as he attempted to sense her thoughts.

'I have had enough of dancing, Reothe.'

Aware of the Beatific's sharp eyes on her, Imoshen would have dismissed Reothe as soon as she reached her seat, but he made the formal obeisance of supplication, going down on both knees before the General, hands lifted palm up.

Light glinted on Reothe's closely cropped hair. The T'Enplars were all wearing their hair shorn in honour of their leader. 'I ask a boon of Protector General Tulkhan.'

'Ask.'

'As Patron of the Halls of Learning, you can grant me the right to establish a new Hall of Learning.'

'A Hall of Learning?'

'I ask only for a wing of the palace to house the children no one wants. There I will establish a Malaunje Hall of Learning.'

Tulkhan noticed Imoshen and the Beatific exchange glances. The word was familiar. 'Malaunje?'

It was the Beatific who answered. 'Malaunje is the High T'En word for half-blood.'

In a flash Tulkhan understood. Reothe meant to build a power base – an army of rebels wearing T'Enplarian warriors, and a school of half-blood children all loyal to the last T'En Prince. 'The half-blood T'En can study in the Halls of Learning now. What purpose would this new school serve?'

'Across Fair Isle there are many children of part T'En blood who are grudgingly accepted in their own homes and villages. I want to gather them together and restore their self-worth.' Reothe began dispassionately, but as he went on his voice grew fervent. 'Even the name, Malaunje, has faded from our language as if to deny their very existence. Once there were levels of Malaunje, just as once there were ranks within the pure T'En. Now there are only unwanted half-bloods and throwbacks. Ask Imoshen what it is like to live as an outcast in your own family.'

Tulkhan glanced to Imoshen and glimpsed the naked dismay in her face before she masked her feelings.

'What of your service to the church?' Tulkhan demanded. Did he want a palace full of Dhamfeer half-bloods? He heard his father's voice: *Keep your enemies close, the better to see what they plan.*

'I will continue to serve the Beatific, but there is not enough for me to do,' Reothe said. 'I need more.'

Imoshen was sure Tulkhan would refuse Reothe his Malaunje Hall of Learning.

'Very well,' Tulkhan said. 'You have your school.'

Imoshen's gaze flew to Tulkhan. He was watching Reothe, who offered formal thanks, then turned to the Beatific. 'I ask to be excused from my church service for as long as it takes to travel Fair Isle and find these children.'

'You would leave soon?' the Beatific asked.

Reothe nodded. 'It is nearly winter's cusp. I must leave before the snows set in.'

'Then go with the church's blessing.'

'Where will you go?' Tulkhan asked.

'The Keldon Highlands before the snows close the passes.'

Tulkhan smiled. 'Excellent. I was planning to inspect our defences. I will go with you.'

'I intend to travel lightly, with only a small band of T'Enplar warriors,' Reothe said quickly.

'Good. I also mean to travel swiftly with a handful of men,' Tulkhan announced.

Though the General smiled, Imoshen saw there was no humour in his eyes, only determination. Her teeth ached and the T'En taste grew strong on her tongue.

'As you wish.' Reothe rose with Old Empire grace.

Tulkhan stood. As Imoshen looked on, a great gash appeared in the General's thigh and he fell forward into Reothe's arms, crying *Betrayer!*

Imoshen leapt to her feet with Tulkhan's name on her lips.

Everyone turned to her.

She blinked. Tulkhan stood before her uninjured, his long legs planted firmly on the dais. A rushing noise filled her head as normal sounds and sensations returned. She could only stare at him. Was Reothe going to kill Tulkhan at the first opportunity?

'What is it?' Tulkhan asked.

To reveal what she had foreseen would condemn Reothe.

'What alarmed you, T'Imoshen?' Tulkhan asked formally.

'I have had too much wine. Please excuse me.'

Aware that this was hardly a worthy excuse, she collected Ashmyr's basket and Kalleen. Imoshen did not need her gift to tell her that everyone watched her departure with speculation.

After Kalleen closed the door to the Empress's bedchamber, she turned to Imoshen. 'You have the Sight.'

'It has come on me like this only once before, when I foresaw the Vaygharian's death.'

'Whose death did you foresee this time?'

Imoshen shook her head and placed the sleeping baby's basket safely on the floor. Again she saw Tulkhan stagger with the force of the blow as he fell into Reothe's arms, injured and vulnerable.

'Imoshen?' Kalleen crouched at her side.

She shook her head again.

'If one of them murders the other, it will be on your conscience,' Kalleen warned.

'It will be no more than everyone expects!'

'I can guess no good will come of this journey,' Kalleen said. 'But if I had the Sight, I'd feel duty bound to warn –'

'Warn him of what? If I say anything, I precipitate the death of someone I love and if I don't, I let my love go to his death!' Imoshen swallowed a sob. 'I can't bear this, Kalleen. I am torn in two.'

Firelight danced in Kalleen's golden eyes, belying her serious expression. 'All of Fair Isle is torn, Imoshen. Would it be kinder to send one of them away?'

If only it were that simple. Tulkhan would not relinquish Fair Isle. Since his half-brother had named him traitor he had no other home. And as for Reothe, Fair Isle was his home and she, his once-betrothed. 'Which hand will I cut off, Kalleen, my left or right?'

'Don't linger. Winter comes early to the Keldon Highlands,' Imoshen advised.

Tulkhan checked the saddle's girth for the second time. Fifteen of the Parakhan Guard, selected because they were loyal to Tulkhan, were already mounted. And behind them milled an equal number of Reothe's T'Enplars, dressed for cold weather.

'I want the outlying defences finished before spring,' Tulkhan told her.

'No one attacks in winter. Besides, your half-brother is probably licking his wounds.'

'If I know Gharavan, he will be planning revenge; don't rule out a winter attack. Fair Isle is weakened from repeated warring.'

It was more than he had said to her since the feast. As Tulkhan swung his weight up into the saddle she caught the reins. 'Beware a betrayer.' The words escaped Imoshen before she could stop herself

Tulkhan looked down on her, his Ghebite eyes sharp. 'Did your vision tell you who this betrayer is?'

Imoshen shook her head numbly.

'And your scryings are never accurate either.' His voice grew gentle, teasing even. 'What are these marvellous Dhamfeer gifts the old tales speak of? In real life they are nothing but market day tricks to amuse small children.'

Imoshen's heart turned over. His tone warmed her to the core. But why tease her so lovingly when he was about to leave? She caught his hand in hers, peeling back the leather glove to plant a kiss on the pulse inside his wrist.

'Take care, General Tulkhan.' With tears blinding her vision she stepped back, hugging her body to keep out the chill presentiment of death. The horses shuffled past.

Boots appeared on the ground before her and she looked up to find Reothe holding his horse by the reins.

'You cry for him, yet you won't even say goodbye to me. How cruel is that? Did you tell him which one of us died in your vision, Imoshen?'

She shook her head. 'You take no female Parakhan Guard?'

'General Tulkhan would see that as a sign of weakness.' He surprised her by sinking to one knee, offering the Old Empire formal salute of leave taking. 'I ask your blessing, T'En Empress. I go in the service of our people.'

Imoshen lifted her left hand, placing the tip of her sixth finger on his forehead. Would she see Reothe alive again? Her heart twisted within her. Reothe or Tulkhan. Why did it have to be this heart-breaking choice? She let her hand drop. 'If you return alone, I will kill you myself.'

'Those are not the formal words of blessing, Empress.'

'That is what my heart tells me.'

'And what does your head tell you?'

Imoshen stared into Reothe's wine-dark eyes, then stepped back. 'Nothing. My head tells me nothing.'

'Perhaps you are not listening.' He swung up into the saddle with a little smile on his lips.

But Imoshen would not meet his eyes.

Chapter Eighteen

ON THEIR FIRST night out, Tulkhan selected a campsite just off the main south road. The weapons of the T'Enplars remained in view, just as his own men had not disarmed to make camp.

While the men lit their cooking fires, he approached Reothe. 'Walk with me. I would like to know what can be seen from the top of that rise.'

Reothe glanced to the rocky outcropping silhouetted against the afterglow of the setting sun. 'Much the same as what can be seen from here, I hazard. But sight and perception are two different things.'

'Another T'En proverb?' Tulkhan asked.

Reothe shrugged and straightened stiffly, favouring his left side. They walked in silence through the gloaming to the rise and climbed it. Standing there with the afterglow of the sun's rays illuminating Reothe and himself, Tulkhan was aware that their men would be able to see them as two silhouettes.

'We must call a truce while we travel,' he said.

'And why is that, True-man?'

'Don't spar with me. Your T'Enplar warriors and my Parakhan Guard are at dagger's point with each other.'

As Reothe looked back towards the camp, Tulkhan realised it would be so easy to stab him in the back, or knock him off this rock and spring down to dispatch him as he lay injured. But the last T'En warrior had to die by accident.

'Give me one good reason why I should trust you,' Reothe said at last.

That gave Tulkhan pause and the Dhamfeer laughed softly, goading him to respond. 'I asked Imoshen to order your execution, but she wouldn't do it.'

Reothe eyed him. 'Did it occur to you that if she were to hand over General Tulkhan to his half-brother to prevent a spring war, it would give her time to rebuild Fair Isle's army? But she wouldn't do that either.'

Tulkhan scowled. He knew Reothe's assessment was right. And it irked him to learn Reothe had been discussing matters of state with Imoshen. 'I could kill you myself.'

'Why don't you?'

Tulkhan lifted a hand in frustration. 'Imoshen –'

'Exactly. Where she leads, the people will follow, and without the support of the people, neither of us can retain Fair Isle. Your army is reduced to a scattered mass of men and a few loyal commanders. My rebel army was never more than that. It all comes back to Imoshen. She embodies Fair Isle's history and the people love her.' Reothe rounded on him. 'Why can't you move on, General? I have. My goal is to preserve the T'En. If I can restore the people's faith in us, Fair Isle will grow strong again. No one would dare attack an island with an elite band of T'En warriors like Imoshen the First's Paragian Guard.'

The General's mind raced. It would only take a few generations of bonding half-bloods to create a band of throwbacks loyal to Reothe. If that happened, he would never have to regain his gifts. He could wield all the power of the T'En through his followers.

It only confirmed what he already believed. Reothe had to die. 'I am but a True-man. I cannot touch you to discover the truth of your words. Imoshen once said you could make the truth sound like a lie. For now, for the sake of Fair Isle, I suggest a truce. Do you agree?'

Reothe lifted his left hand, forearm open to Tulkhan. 'A truce.'

Tulkhan mimicked the action and their fingers interlaced.

'Agreed.' Tulkhan let his arm drop, secretly relieved that Reothe no longer had his gifts. If he had, he would have known that Tulkhan meant to break his word.

The General had put his plan in motion before leaving T'Diemn, which was why he had been avoiding Imoshen. His defences against her were good, but he could not be on his guard every waking moment.

When Imoshen had warned Tulkhan to beware a betrayer, his heart had faltered and he had only just managed to divert her with a jest. He smiled grimly. It was lucky for him her gift was erratic. Somewhere on this journey, their group was going to be attacked by bandits.

His own man, Commander Haase, would arrange it. In the heat of battle no one knew where each and every sword strike came from. He would carry Reothe's body back to T'Diemn in state, accompanied by at least one T'Enplar warrior who would swear the General was blameless of his leader's death.

As for Imoshen, she would mourn Reothe's loss but if Tulkhan was not to blame, she would accept him back into her arms. All that remained was the child Imoshen carried. If it was a girl, he might let her live. If it was a son, he would have to have the boy killed by subterfuge. It was cruel, but young children died all the time. They caught fevers or played dangerous games. What was one more murder to add to his long list of killings? A bleakness enveloped Tulkhan.

'It grows dark,' Reothe said. 'Deepdeyne Stronghold lies two days from here.'

'I want to inspect Deepdeyne. If my half-brother attacks south of T'Diemn, it could be our first line of defence.'

'We must be out of the Keldon Highlands before winter sets in. We can stop at Deepdeyne on the return journey.'

'Very well,' Tulkhan agreed. This suited his plans. It gave Commander Haase more time to prepare an ambush. Reothe's death had to appear a random act of violence and would be better happening on the return journey when everyone was less vigilant.

Tulkhan turned to climb down from the outcropping, giving Reothe a chance to strike treacherously. But he didn't.

'See,' Reothe greeted the camp sentry. 'We are returned safely. Neither of us stabbed the other in the back!'

The man laughed uneasily and Tulkhan did not blame him.

IMOSHEN'S HEART WENT out to the two brothers, the most recent Malaunje children to arrive escorted by one of the T'Enplars and one of the Parakhan Guard.

Willingly turned over by their parents, the boys found themselves in the palace where everything was strange. She watched them put their small bundles in the chests at the foot of their beds.

By housing the Malaunje children in T'Reothe's Hall, Imoshen hoped the peace and solidarity of his long reign would be associated with her Reothe's venture. T'Reothe the Builder had been the First Emperor of the Age of Consolidation, but the hall still had the characteristics of the Age of Tribulation, thick walls and narrow windows, as though the T'En did not feel truly secure even in their own palace.

'Now that you know which are your beds, you can go outside to join the others,' Imoshen told the boys. 'Drake is showing them how to use the T'En sword.'

They glanced at each other. Imoshen sighed. The brothers were probably used to being ostracised by their village playmates.

'This way.' She walked them down the stairs and into the courtyard where the boys approached the group warily.

Imoshen became aware of Maigeth in the doorway behind her. She took the silversmith's arm. 'I wanted to thank you for hiding my son.'

'You shielded my son when he joined the rebels.'

Imoshen nodded. Drake was showing the eldest girl how to hold the sword correctly while the others waited impatiently for their turn. Imoshen picked her words carefully. 'Have you noticed your power growing since the day you touched the Orb?'

A shutter came down, cloaking the woman's expression. Though Imoshen still linked arms with her, she could sense nothing.

'I have been replaced as guildmaster. I have lost the friendship of my dearest friend who was like a sister. I have seen everyone but my son turn away from me.'

'I am sorry.'

Maigeth looked at her. 'I believe you are, but that does not give me back my life.'

*   *   *

IT WAS A small village, like many Tulkhan had passed through in the Keldon Highlands. The rugged country-side was too poor to support large towns. According to the elders of the last village, a family lived here with four half-blood children. Some even had both traits, the six fingers and the wine-dark eyes, nearly full throwbacks.

Smoke drifted from the central holes of the snug dwellings, but they were deserted except for a cat which watched from a windowsill. When Tulkhan had met with his commander of the Greater Pass, the man spoke of roaming rebel bands robbing honest merchants, but this village was not wealthy enough to attract thieves.

Tulkhan turned in his saddle to Reothe. 'Where is everyone?'

The Dhamfeer dismounted. He stepped carefully over the churned mud and half-melted snow to the entrance of the largest cottage. The door opened at his touch and he disappeared inside.

Tulkhan's horse snorted. The beast did not like the cold. Tulkhan did not like living intimately with someone he planned to murder. It was not easy to break bread and joke with a man, knowing he would soon be dead.

Reothe came out of the house and looked up at the ridges behind the village, frowning. The trees were coated with snow, still and silent.

'Well?' Tulkhan prodded.

'There is bread baking in the oven above the fire-place.' Reothe took his horse's reins, put his boot in the stirrup and swung up into the saddle. 'They must have run away.'

'Why would the whole village run away? Everyone else has been glad to hand over their half-bloods, why not this family?'

Reothe met Tulkhan's eyes as they left the village. 'Because they think their children will be murdered once you have killed me.'

Tulkhan's body tightened. The horse responded to the pressure of his knees, sidling. He brought it under control before speaking. 'What nonsense is this?'

'Each time I have been given a Malaunje child, I have had to promise on my life that no harm would come to them.'

Tulkhan digested this in silence. So far he had not detected the Dhamfeer in a single lie. Reothe had been the perfect travelling companion, uncomplaining and ready with a jest when the going got tough. This empty village, however, did not make sense. 'But wouldn't the villagers be glad to be rid of a half-blood family in their midst?'

Reothe's expression reminded Tulkhan forcibly of Imoshen, alert, intelligent and just slightly amused.

When he spoke, Reothe pitched his voice to carry as though he suspected there were watchers in the undergrowth. 'This far south the people respect the old ways, the ways I wish to restore.' Then he lowered his voice. 'You know the saying, *Scrawny sheep and stiff-necked Keld*. It's likely everyone in the village is related to the Malaunje family. They may be loved and revered.'

A whole village steeped in the old ways? Tulkhan glanced back with a shudder. Already the snow-shrouded trees had closed around them. He doubted if he could find his way back here again.

'I fear there will be no more part-T'En children for us to find if this village is anything to go by,' Reothe muttered.

'Good.' The General urged his horse forward. 'I'm tired of ravines and snow. The sooner we return to the plains the better.'

Tulkhan urged his horse forward. The sooner they were attacked and Reothe killed, the sooner he would rid himself of the taint of betrayal which sat like under-ripe fruit in his belly.

'ELEVEN CHILDREN AND the snows have set in,' the Beatific remarked, as they watched the small figures riding sleds down the hillside overlooking the ornamental lake.

Imoshen tucked the fur around her knees. Ashmyr and Kalleen were sleeping in the warmth of the palace, but Imoshen had greeted the Beatific's invitation with relief. She was already tired of being cooped up and winter had barely begun. Besides, if the Beatific had something to tell her, she would rather speak where no one could overhear. 'So what did you wish to talk about?'

'Move on,' the Beatific told her sleigh driver. He cracked his whip and the horses responded, surging forward.

They followed the curve of the lake and Imoshen frowned as she identified the well-worn way to the stone lovers. On the fresh snow she could see the marks of horses, boots and several sleighs. 'Not that way, driver. Take us to the lookout.'

The delicate rotunda with its tall columns stood silhouetted against the winter-blue sky. When the sleigh slid to a halt, the Beatific threw back her furs to climb down. Imoshen watched this with misgivings. She was wearing only a knife, strapped to her upper thigh accessible under her brocade tabard, but the Beatific would not assassinate her here, not when everyone knew they had ridden off together.

Placing her boots in the indentations left by the Beatific's steps, Imoshen followed the woman to the rotunda. One of the stone seats was cracked. No one bothered to come up here anymore. The Old Empire fashion for eating outdoors was not popular with the Ghebites.

Directly below the lookout's cliff was the rock-edged river, beyond the river was old T'Diemn. The air was so clear that she could see individual tiles on the roofs of the buildings. The spires of new T'Diemn stood tall beyond the old city's walls and far beyond that the rolling foothills were dressed in a mantle of pure white snow. Would Gharavan attack in midwinter, she wondered? It was lucky they had restored the city's old defences.

But enemies surrounded her even here. 'I am listening, Engarad.'

The Beatific's golden eyes held resentment. 'I know you don't like me, Imoshen, but I am here today as your friend.'

'I don't trust you. That is different,' Imoshen replied. 'I am listening.'

The Beatific waved a hand towards T'Diemn. 'The people don't like change, and so much has changed in the last two years. They are alarmed by Reothe's plans. These children claim the name Malaunje and Reothe creates a Hall of Learning where half-bloods seek to tap into their nascent gifts!'

'Isn't that what Murgon's Tractarians do?'

'Yes, but they serve the church. Besides, it is impolite to speak of the lesser gifts of the Malaunje,' the Beatific corrected primly, then frowned. 'People fear what they do not know. They whisper that you and Reothe flew down from Sard's Tower and that you absorbed the power of the Orb into yourself.'

'I nearly died, as you well know!'

The Beatific had the grace to flush. 'When Reothe comes back, talk him out of this.'

Imoshen shook her head. If Reothe did not have his Malaunje Hall of Learning, she dreaded to think where his energies would drive him.

'At least try,' the Beatific urged.

'You try. He is your lover!'

The Beatific smiled. 'I have known Reothe since he was a youth of seventeen, passionate and ambitious – so ambitious he would stop at nothing to achieve his goal of ruling Fair Isle.'

'Maybe that is what he was like, but Reothe is no longer that youth,' Imoshen said, regretting her hasty tongue. 'He has other goals now.'

'If you believe that, you fool yourself. If Reothe could sacrifice his own parents to be near to the Empress and the seat of power, what makes you think he will be satisfied with these scraps you throw him?'

Reothe sacrificed his parents? Imoshen shook her head. 'He was discovered beside the cold bodies of his mother and father after they committed ritual suicide.'

'Reothe drove his parents to kill themselves,' the Beatific insisted.

Again Imoshen shook her head. 'He was only a child.'

'Children are totally self-absorbed. Reothe is absorbed in his own goals, he –'

'Reothe is not like that.' Imoshen read pity in the woman's face. It goaded her beyond belief. 'You hold a mirror to the world and so attribute your motivations to others!'

The Beatific's hand flew up in an arc. Imoshen could have stopped her, she had time to block and counterattack, but she did nothing. Instead, she took the full force of the slap in the knowledge that she had handled that badly.

Imoshen's face stung and her left eye watered as the Beatific stalked back to the sleigh. Waiting until the tingling in her cheek eased, Imoshen pretended to study the city. The thought of riding next to the Beatific made her uncomfortable, but any sign of a breach between herself and the Beatific would be gleefully noted by the mainland spies.

Imoshen glanced over her shoulder to see the Beatific seated in the sleigh and her servant staring stoically ahead.

Taking a deep breath, she picked her way carefully down the slope to the sleigh. Before she could arrange the fur over her knees, the Beatific signalled the driver. With a jolt, the horses strained against their harnesses.

As they began the ride back to the confinement of protocol and thousands of watchful eyes, Imoshen thought of her family's stronghold. It was more than a year since she had ridden away from her home on short notice. Homesickness welled within her, making her gifts stir. The Beatific glared, shifting away as far as possible.

Imoshen marked this. Most True-people were not so sensitive. Perhaps it was because the Beatific had known Reothe intimately. Imoshen cleared her throat. 'I spoke in haste, Engarad.'

The Beatific inclined her head in acknowledgment, but her expression did not soften.

Imoshen tried again. 'I value your advice. After all, we both want the best for Fair Isle. We both want to protect ourselves and our sisters from Ghebite arrogance.'

This time the Beatific met her eyes.

Imoshen forged on. 'Although Kalleen has the deeds to seven estates, her hold on them is tenuous. If she were to take a Ghebite for a bond-partner, he would expect the ownership to transfer to him.'

Contempt twisted the Beatific's face. 'The church will do all it can to curtail these Ghebites. It is lucky so many of them were killed in the Lowlands. It will be easier to absorb them without their ways influencing our people.'

Imoshen nodded, but the Beatific's comment had revealed one of Imoshen's hidden fears. General Tulkhan's army was greatly reduced, making his hold on Fair Isle even more tenuous.

Again she saw him fall wounded in Reothe's arms with the word *Betrayer* on his lips, and her stomach churned with anxiety. Perhaps the Beatific was right and Reothe was a subtle creature of great cunning and cruelty, capable of such deception that he would drive his own parents to suicide. But she could not believe it.

The dual loyalties of her heart threatened to tear Imoshen apart, yet not by so much as a sound did she betray her fears to the Beatific. They were allies, but only due to necessity.

TULKHAN SHIFTED IN the saddle, stiff with cold. The eight remaining men, four Parakhan Guard and four T'Enplars, did not complain. They had been riding since before dawn, looking for something Reothe expected to discover in the deserted foothills of the Keldon Highlands.

'There.' Reothe pointed with satisfaction.

Tulkhan could just distinguish the thin plume of blue woodsmoke against the ice-blue sky. Distance was hard to judge in the glare of these clear conditions but it appeared two hills separated them from the lonely cottage.

'Wait here.' Reothe dismounted.

Tulkhan watched him pick his way up the rise, wondering if Reothe was planning to circumvent Tulkhan's betrayal with a betrayal of his own. The General waited until Reothe had crossed the crest of the hill before dismounting. 'Watch the horses.'

Without explanation, he followed Reothe. The air was cold enough to make his chest ache and his nostrils sting. Tulkhan reached the crest and looked down into a little valley. Steam rose from vents in the rocks reminding him of the Ancients. Tulkhan's mouth went dry. The last time he had visited a hot pool, he had woken the power of the Ancients, drawing Reothe in his insubstantial form. Reothe had laughed, saying, *I am your death. You do not know it but you are a dead man who walks and talks.*

Only Reothe's death would prove his prophecy wrong.

Tulkhan frowned as he watched his enemy creep silent as a snow cat up the slope to a small crofter's cottage. It built into the hillside, and so laden with snow that it was almost invisible.

A huge, shaggy dog lifted its head. In the clear air Tulkhan could see the dog's ears twitch. Reothe straightened. There was no chance to creep up on the inhabitants now. The dog was big enough to fight off wolves, maybe even a bear. The beast charged Reothe, leaping on him. Its paws rested on his shoulders, its head level with his. To Tulkhan's amazement the dog's tail waved in greeting and it barked joyously.

The cottage door swung open and a small woman or child came out. She froze.

'I told you I would come back,' Reothe said.

'Six years!'

Reothe had no answer for that. 'I've come for Ysanna.'

'You can't have her.'

'I told you this day would come. I'm collecting Malaunje children.'

'There's nothing of the T'En in her.'

'Untrue.'

A tiny child stepped out of the cottage armed with a bow bigger than she was. She already had an arrow notched, aimed at Reothe. 'Shall I shoot him, Mam?'

She looked no more than three. Tulkhan was surprised she could speak so clearly.

When the mother did not answer, the girl shifted her feet. 'My arms are getting tired. Who is this man?'

Silence.

'Why don't you tell her?' Reothe prodded.

The little woman flung up her arms in despair. 'It is your father.'

'My father died last spring. Killed by bears.'

'That was your step-father. This is your father.'

The girl did not lower the bow.

'I have a company of soldiers waiting over the rise,' Reothe said. 'I could have ridden in here and taken her, but I didn't. I came to take her with your blessing.'

'You came to take her with or without my blessing!' the woman snapped.

'I don't want to go anywhere,' Ysanna said.

The little woman turned her back on Reothe and walked over to her daughter. Their two fair heads leant close together as they spoke. At last the child lowered the bow.

The woman sent her daughter into the cottage, then approached Reothe. Tulkhan could not hear her words, only the intense tone of her voice. She came no higher than midchest on Reothe but she was not intimidated. She seemed to have a lot to say, to which Reothe was agreeing.

When Ysanna reappeared with a bundle, the woman gave her a quick hug then called the dog and walked into the cottage without looking back. The child stood there undecided. Reothe beckoned her and she went to him.

Tulkhan waited for Reothe and Ysanna. As they made the crest, the child's golden eyes widened at the sight of him. 'So True-man giants are real!'

Reothe laughed. 'This one's real enough. It's Protector General Tulkhan come to check up on me, because he does not trust me.'

The girl studied Tulkhan frankly. Her five-fingered hand held a bundle to her small chest. She had the deep golden skin of the True-people, but her hair was almost white.

She wrinkled her nose. 'Does he always scowl?'

'He scowls because he does not understand.'

'If this girl is yours, why does she have none of the signs?' Tulkhan asked, goaded.

'Often T'En males don't breed true, but she is part T'En, nevertheless.' He smiled on Ysanna. 'You will like T'Diemn. The Empress is beautiful and clever, and she will be your teacher.'

When they rejoined the others, Reothe selected one of his T'Enplar warriors and one of Tulkhan's men to escort the child back to T'Diemn.

She cast the men uneasy glances.

'You will be safe with these men. Be good for the Empress, Ysanna.' Reothe stepped back and the girl's small frame was hidden from sight as the T'Enplar rode away.

Tulkhan wondered briefly why Reothe would go to so much trouble for a daughter, and then he concentrated on what lay ahead. 'Commander Haase's estate lies west of here, two days' ride.'

Reothe nodded. He glanced back towards the cottage where the woman now lived alone.

Tulkhan swung into the saddle. Was he regretting taking the child?

It did not matter. Within two days Reothe would be dead and Tulkhan would be freed of this burden. The children could all be returned to their homes. That little woman would not spend the winter pining for her daughter and Tulkhan would retain the respect of his men.

It all hinged on his willingness to kill Reothe.

*　　*　　*

TULKHAN LOOKED DOWN at Haase's stronghold. It was an odd shape, having been built on a bend in the river. The river had been partially diverted to flow around the high walls to create a constantly flowing moat filled with icy water. A bridge linked Deepdeyne Stronghold to the shore. The bridge was bent, and protected by a small tower at the bend.

'Looks sturdy,' Tulkhan muttered.

'Deepdeyne dates from the Age of Tribulation, so it was built for defence, not appearance,' Reothe said. 'Lying west of Imoshen's family holdings, Deepdeyne was the last great stronghold built to contain the highlands in the early years of T'En rule.'

Tulkhan studied the path down the slope. There was nowhere for bandits to hide. His party consisted of Reothe and himself and six men, easy targets. Haase's scouts would have reported their approach, and Tulkhan had expected an ambush by now, but Haase must have decided the bandits would attack after their visit.

Tulkhan urged his mount down the slope towards Deepdeyne.

When they entered the stronghold courtyard, Haase did not reveal by so much as a glance that he planned murder. By Ghebite standards his greeting to the fallen rebel leader was polite.

Tulkhan accepted his commander's formal salute, then clasped his arm. These years in Fair Isle had aged Haase. Tulkhan was reminded that the man was only three years older than himself. Before the year was out, Tulkhan would turn thirty-one. He was middle-aged by Ghebite standards. Haase was thinning on top and growing thicker around the waist.

Tulkhan gave Haase a mock punch in his belly. 'Too much easy living!'

Haase grinned and gestured to the scaffolding. 'The work never stops. At least when you lead the men, there are breaks between battles and the decisions are simple.'

Tulkhan understood that dilemma only too well.

'Your men can take their horses through to the stables.' Haase indicated the way. 'Come share a bottle of Vorsch with me. We're still living in the original keep while they finish work on the new hall.'

'Vorsch? Reothe, come try a real man's drink.' Tulkhan wanted the Dhamfeer where he could see him.

Reothe's lips twisted in a parody of a smile as he relinquished his mount's reins.

After climbing two flights of tower stairs, they entered the great hall. Even though it was midafternoon, little light filtered through the high narrow windows. The scrubbed table had been laid with fresh food and fine goblets. Sweet-smelling herbs had been sprinkled on the floor, releasing their scent when crushed underfoot, and a fire roared in the huge hearth. True to Haase's word, a bottle of Vorsch awaited them.

Tulkhan walked to the fireplace, noting how the three ribbons of office Imoshen had awarded Haase hung from the tip of a spear mounted above the mantelpiece.

Tulkhan pulled off his gloves and dropped his cloak on the high-backed chair, unclasping his sword. He caught Reothe's eye and the Dhamfeer followed suit. If Haase chose to go unarmed, then so must they. The man was playing his part of host with consummate skill. Even knowing that Haase was party to the plan to have Reothe killed, Tulkhan could not fault his manner.

Tulkhan turned and stretched, feeling the heat of the fire warm his travel-weary muscles. The smell of roasting meat made his mouth water. As Haase uncorked the Vorsch, Tulkhan repressed a pang of envy for the simple life. Strange: the higher he rose, the less freedom he had.

When Haase poured three goblets, Tulkhan raised his. 'To Fair Isle and her rich bounty.'

It would all be his again as soon as Reothe was dead. He drained the goblet in one long gulp.

Reothe was more tentative. He seemed unsure of the flavour. It was not the best Vorsch Tulkhan had tasted, but then this was not Gheeaba.

'Another drink?' Haase refilled their goblets.

'A toast to peace, a warm hearth, a willing woman and a full belly!' Tulkhan drained his goblet. He noticed Reothe give him a sharp look. 'Don't the T'En drink to peace?'

'They do,' Reothe acknowledged. 'But they don't insult women by equating them with basic necessities. If you want to see sparks fly, salute Imoshen with that toast.'

'What, drink a toast with a woman?' Haase muttered. 'You jest!'

Even as Tulkhan laughed, he saw the gulf between himself and his fellow Ghebites widen. He stood with a boot in both worlds. 'It's just as well you aren't keen on palace life, Haase.'

Reothe caught his eye and grinned.

Tulkhan swilled the Vorsch around in his goblet, watching the liquid glint in the candlelight, thinking it was a cruel thing to discover a kindred spirit in the man he was sworn to kill. He had first suspected this the night Reothe risked his life searching death's shadow to save Imoshen. The General might fear Reothe and he might not trust him, but he respected him.

Tulkhan drained the last of the Vorsch. The alcohol was bitter on his tongue, bitter with the knowledge that he intended to betray Reothe. At least in battle you know who your enemies were. The silence stretched, growing uncomfortable.

'Reothe of the T'En, would you offer us a salute?' Haase spoke with more diplomacy than Tulkhan would have given him credit for.

As Tulkhan turned to Reothe, he felt his head spin.

Reothe lifted his goblet. 'There is a T'En saying which translates something like this: *Better the enemy you can trust, than a weak friend.*'

It was an odd toast. Tulkhan drained the Vorsch, then went to put his goblet down on the table and missed. It fell to the floor, hitting the planks with a dull thud.

'I'll ease off on the Vorsch, Haase.' Tulkhan was surprised to hear his words slurring. 'What's to eat?'

Blearily, he focused on his commander, who was speaking earnestly about his relatives in Gheeaba, something about them being held prisoner. Tulkhan could see the man's mouth opening and closing, but his voice sounded like it was coming down a long tunnel. This was not the effect of the Vorsch on an empty stomach.

The Vorsch was drugged!

But he'd seen Haase pour out of the same bottle. The goblets must have been prepared. Perhaps Haase had changed the plan. If he had, he should have drugged only Reothe's Vorsch. Had the Dhamfeer poisoned him?

Tulkhan's heart pounded. He glanced to Reothe, expecting to see triumph in those wine-dark eyes. Instead Reothe was frowning into his own goblet.

Armed men charged into the hall.

Tulkhan lunged for his sword and spun about, intending to grab Haase and hold the blade to his throat, but Haase was already closing in on him, a weapon suddenly in his hand.

Tulkhan blocked. Too slow. Haase's sword travelled down his blade's length, the force of the strike taking it past the tip. Tulkhan saw the sword slice through the material of his breeches, saw the bright stream of blood. He felt nothing, nothing but the ignominy of discovering his own man had betrayed him.

'Betrayer!' Tulkhan lunged for Haase, who darted away.

The General would have fallen, but Reothe stepped in, catching him. The impact took them both to the floor. Where were his men? Probably ambushed in the stables.

'So this was her vision,' Reothe muttered.

Light flashed on a blade. The hilt struck Reothe from behind and he pitched sideways.

Helpless to save himself, Tulkhan collapsed.

'Three goblets each and they were still standing. I'd have a word with your healer if I were you,' a sneering Vaygharian remarked.

As the full impact of his predicament hit him, Tulkhan realised Imoshen had foreseen this and had tried to warn him. But he had been too consumed with his own plans of betrayal to heed her.

The General lifted his head. A boot collided with his face, laying him out on the floor. Though he felt no pain, he knew his nose had broken, and he drifted helplessly into unconsciousness.

Chapter Nineteen

IMOSHEN WOKE, HER cheeks wet with tears, the echo of her cry still ringing in her ears. She turned at a slight noise and found Kalleen peering around the door, holding a candle.

'You called for the General.' Kalleen crept over, her face alive with fear and curiosity. 'What does it mean?'

'Too much relish on my meat?'

'Imoshen, how can you jest? Has harm come to Tulkhan?'

The baby stirred in his basket beside the bed, reacting to the tension. Imoshen lowered her voice. 'I don't know what it means, because I was not trained in my gift.'

'What did the Sight show you?'

'Tulkhan crying *Betrayer* as he fell wounded into Reothe's arms.'

Kalleen paled. 'Then he is dead?'

'I don't know!'

'Will you do a scrying?'

'It shows only possible paths and I will not exhaust myself searching false trails.' She wrung her hands, consumed with frustration.

'Oh, Imoshen.' Kalleen knelt on the bed, her nightgown billowing over the slope of her pregnant belly. Sympathy made her golden eyes glisten.

'Now do you understand why I must save Reothe? Only he has... knows our heritage.' She almost let slip that the T'Elegos had survived Sardonyx's revolt and ended up in Reothe's hands. 'Without him, I am cast adrift. I... I am afraid of my T'En powers.'

Kalleen's eyes grew wide. Imoshen waited, heart in her mouth. The little True-woman opened her arms and Imoshen went to her. She could feel Kalleen's heart beating against her cheek, reassuring and solid.

'Everyone calls me Empress,' Imoshen whispered. 'But in the depths of my soul I am only Imoshen. And I am alone.'

'We are all alone,' Kalleen said.

They comforted each other, with only a single candle to hold back the night.

WHEN TULKHAN WOKE his head felt fragile, as if the slightest movement would split his skull. His nose seemed three sizes bigger than normal and stuffed with padding. It was so cold his limbs were numb. He knew he should be worried but, for the moment, he was in too much pain to remember why.

'Can you hear me?' Reothe whispered.

Tulkhan opened one eye but this achieved nothing. Either they were in a windowless prison, or it was night.

'They will send us to the coast at dawn,' Reothe said. 'We must escape now. It will be light soon.'

'How...' He had to work his tongue in his mouth to speak. 'How do you know?'

'The drug affected us differently. It paralysed me, but I was still aware.'

Tulkhan strained but all he could see were the dancing patterns produced by his night-blind eyes. 'Where are we?'

'In the chapel off the great hall. Ironic, really. It was dedicated by a distant ancestor of mine. Deepdeyne had been in my family for over five hundred years.' Reothe's tone was hard and bitter. He fell silent. When he resumed, his voice had regained its usual timbre. 'Haase and his Ghebites feasted late, celebrating our capture. You are to be returned to your half-brother for trial and execution.'

'And you?' Tulkhan did not know why Reothe still lived.

'The Ghebite king is having trouble with his alliance kingdoms. He wants a chained Dhamfeer to exhibit throughout his empire. He thinks it would restore respect for his rule if he recaptures Fair Isle and subjugates the legendary T'En. He intends to keep Imoshen alive too, if he can. But I don't –'

'Why? Why did Haase betray me?'

'Why does any man betray another? Love or wealth...' Reothe paused as if to shrug. 'Haase tried to tell you. His family are imprisoned back in Gheeaba. They treated your injured leg, by the way. They want you alive for your execution.'

Of course. 'Our men?'

'Dead.'

Tulkhan nodded to himself, then winced. He flexed his body and bit back a groan. As sensation returned, he realised he had been tied to a cot bed which was too short for him. His arms were tied behind his head, one to each leg of the bed, and his knees hung over the end of the cot, where his ankles were strapped to the uprights. 'Are you tied up?'

'Same as you.'

'Can you see?'

Reothe was silent, as though considering what answer to give. 'I may be crippled, but I still have the eyes I was born with. Do you feel as if you could walk?'

'I can't even feel my feet.' He heard Reothe chuckle. There was a soft crack of splitting wood. 'What was that?'

'These bunks are old and brittle.' More soft cracking and rustling followed.

Tulkhan flexed his arms, welcoming the pain in his hands as sensation returned. Could he crack the cot's legs, and if he did would his head hit the floor to add to his woes?

'Careful, don't start the leg wound bleeding.'

By the sound of his voice, Tulkhan could tell Reothe was kneeling beside him and guessed the Dhamfeer could see better than he would admit. The bonds fell away from Tulkhan's hands and he sat upright, repressing a grunt of pain. His head felt as if it might burst. Nausea threatened.

Reothe freed his legs. 'Can you stand?'

Tulkhan wondered if Reothe was helping him because they stood a better chance of escaping together. Perhaps Reothe planned to exchange his life for Tulkhan's if they were recaptured. Should it come down to a fight, he could not be blamed if Reothe was killed attempting to escape. Catching these thoughts, Tulkhan felt a pang of contempt for the man he had become.

'If I can find it after all these years, there's a secret passage leading from one of the lower storerooms,' Reothe said.

'Another secret passage?' Tulkhan felt his bandaged thigh and flexed the muscle carefully. 'I can barely walk. Can we lead horses through this passage?'

'No.'

Would Reothe leave him to his fate? One thing was certain, Tulkhan was not going back to his half-brother alive.

'We can get horses from the stables,' Reothe said at last. 'We'll need food and blankets. Winter is a cruel time to be living off the land.'

Reothe spoke from experience. Only last winter he and his rebels had been hiding out in the Keldon Highlands.

'Come, Tulkhan. The door is not locked.'

'Weapons?'

'The wall displays hold effective, if outdated, weaponry. But it would make more sense to slip away quietly.'

'To the stables, then.'

The door to the main hall opened on silent hinges. Tulkhan could hear the snores of a score of men. He was sure if his nose hadn't been completely blocked, he would have smelt their stale breath and sweaty bodies.

'Walk where I walk,' Reothe whispered.

It was all very well for the Dhamfeer. He could see. Tulkhan felt his way, senses strained. They made it across the hall to the stairwell without discovery. In silence and darkness, Tulkhan kept one hand against the wall as they descended. His injury pained him and the warm dampness down his leg told him the wound had broken open.

Two floors below, they unbarred the door and moved out onto the tower's external stairs. It was the darkest time before dawn. Nothing stirred as they stepped into the stone-flagged courtyard.

'This way to get the horses,' Reothe said softly.

The stables were snug, much warmer than outside. Tulkhan wished for light and worried they would disturb the stablelads. His horse greeted him with a soft whinny. He slipped the bridle over its head. Getting onto the horse's back was not easy. He levered his weight up onto a mounting block and swung his wounded leg over.

Reothe led his horse out into the courtyard. After a little urging Tulkhan's mount followed. The beast was not eager to leave the stable's warmth. Relieved to be upon the creature's back, Tulkhan thought about Deepdeyne's defences. It was a well-designed stronghold – a pity, because he would have to come back and take it before he could kill Haase.

'The gates are locked. I think our unknown ally cannot help us here,' Reothe muttered.

'What ally?'

Reothe looked up at him, his silver cap of shorn hair glinting in the starlight. 'The healer who gave Haase a weaker drug than he requested. The people of Deepdeyne are mine, General.'

Now Tulkhan understood the ease of their escape, but there was still the gate. He urged his horse into the deep shadows, holding the reins of Reothe's mount while the Dhamfeer unbarred the gate. The heavy wood creaked on its hinges.

It was enough to wake the dozing sentry, who staggered out of his warm nook, drawing his weapon. Reothe struck swiftly, but not before the man gave a strangled cry. A dog barked and more joined it, raising the alarm.

They made it through the first gate, onto the short arm of the bridge. But Haase had stationed men on the tower at the bridge's bend, and they had been alerted. These men brandished torches, swords drawn. Tulkhan knew Haase's men would be assembling in the courtyard behind them.

Reothe's horse shied. The reins tore from Tulkhan's fingers. He urged his horse forward, intent on getting past the guards at the tower.

The narrow bridge had no rails. The General's horse barrelled into the men trying to block his way. One man fell into the water. Tulkhan's boot smashed into another man's face. His mount screamed and went down. Before his wounded leg could be trapped, Tulkhan rolled aside and dodged a strike to his head. He tried to rise but his weak leg gave way.

Then Reothe was at his side hauling him upright. The defenders regrouped, blocking the bridge. Behind them Tulkhan saw the gleam of torches and a crush of figures pouring from Deepdeyne Stronghold.

'The river,' Reothe urged.

Tulkhan glanced at the icy black water. 'I can't swim. Save yourself.'

Instead of diving into the river, Reothe shoved Tulkhan in the chest. Off balance with his leg wound, he could only stare up in horror as he fell backwards. As his back hit the river he saw Reothe leap after him. Then the water closed over his face, so shocking, so cruelly cold that he gasped, taking in a mouthful.

He was a dead man.

The irony of it hit Tulkhan. Reothe would turn the tables by murdering him in such a way that he could not be blamed.

Then Tulkhan collided with someone. Arms grabbed him, legs kicked with a purpose. Their heads broke the surface. Tulkhan gasped and coughed. He tried to grab something but there was nothing. They were in midstream.

Torchlight danced crazily back on the bridge. Men shouted, pointing in their direction.

'They've seen us!' Reothe muttered. 'Take a deep breath, we're going to drown.'

Tulkhan drew breath to protest. Before he could, they were under the water. He had swum only once before and that was the night he dived into Northpoint harbour to save his son. Only by opening his mind to Imoshen had he been able to swim. She had driven his arms and legs, propelling him to the wharf. Now he tried to recall those actions. The force of the swiftly flowing river drove them along. Reothe was trying to swim across the current. Tulkhan kicked until his chest ached.

Just when he could last no longer, their heads broke the surface. This time the lights of Deepdeyne were far behind and they were much closer to the riverbank.

'Under again, before they spot us,' Reothe urged.

Tulkhan took a breath and let himself go.

The next time they surfaced, the banks consisted of black trees and pale snow. The cold had him in its clutches. Bone deep, the pain seared his whole body and his teeth chattered uncontrollably. 'H – have to get out of the river.'

'Not yet. They'll search the banks for our tracks.' Reothe kept kicking, now driving them along with the current. His body, too, shook with cold. 'Must let the river carry us further. We're lucky no one jumped in after us.'

'Ghebites don't swim.'

Reothe snorted. 'So how did you learn to swim?'

'I'm not swimming. I'm d – dying of cold!'

They stayed with the current, keeping near the bank. At last Reothe caught ahold of a tree trunk which had collapsed into the river. Shaking uncontrollably, Tulkhan hauled himself onto the steep, snow-laden bank. With despair, he realised his wounded leg was useless. Unable to walk across the snowy fields to find a warm cottage, he was doomed to freeze before Haase and his men could find him. Reothe would be the one to escape, the one to return to Imoshen, guiltless of Tulkhan's death.

Reothe held out his hand.

Tulkhan looked up, seeing him silhouetted against the starlit sky. 'Why?'

'Give me your hand. The falling snow will cover our tracks.'

Self-preservation won out. Grunting with the effort, Tulkhan took his weight on his good leg and Reothe wound his arm around Tulkhan's waist. They ploughed up the uneven slippery bank, in silence.

On the high ground, they paused to catch their breath. Tulkhan dragged in great gulps of air between bouts of shivering. They faced rolling, snow-covered fields. It was hopeless. If the cold did not kill them, then riders on horseback would find them easily by circling in ever-increasing spirals from the riverbank.

Tulkhan cursed. 'Without shelter we will die.'

'You forget. I know Deepdeyne. On this side of the river there is a secluded hot spring. If I can just find it...'

Tulkhan gave a grunt of understanding, then put all his energy into moving. Snow fell silently about them. For a while he could not tell if it was getting light, or if it was just the snow filling the air. Every now and then, Reothe stopped to get his bearings in the winter landscape.

Soon moving became an impossible effort for Tulkhan, and the snow began to look inviting. No longer cold, Tulkhan wondered if it would not be simpler to tell Reothe he was right. Fair Isle belonged to the T'En and he, Tulkhan, was an unworthy usurper. Even the reason Reothe was helping him ceased to plague him.

But something deep inside him urged him on. He would not give up. Survival became his imperative. For what seemed an eternity he concentrated on lifting one foot after the other.

Then he sensed a change in Reothe's pace and looked up to discover it was light enough to see. Hope surged.

They stumbled down a steep embankment, sliding into a snow drift. At the base Reothe dropped Tulkhan's arms and staggered forward to scrape at a dark patch in the wall of snow, which collapsed to reveal the entrance to a steamy cave.

Tulkhan crawled towards it.

HER SECRET FEAR hidden deep within her, Imoshen entered T'Reothe's Hall. No word had come from Tulkhan and Reothe's party except for this girl who had arrived last night. The child's escort knew only that Tulkhan and Reothe were going on to Deepdeyne Stronghold.

Imoshen climbed the stairs and stopped at the door. 'I greet you, Ysanna.'

The little girl was a striking creature with white hair, golden skin, five fingers and the golden eyes of Fair Isle original people who were descended from the Ancients.

The child stood beside the bed and met Imoshen's eyes with unblinking concentration. When she spoke it was with a maturity that belied her size. 'I want to go home.'

Imoshen joined her. Dropping to her knees she took the girl's small hand in her own. 'Everyone will be kind to you. You must not be afraid.'

'I am not afraid.'

'Of course not.' Imoshen used the contact with the child's hand to probe her thoughts, but she met a blank wall, an impressive wall. Few adults could resist her so thoroughly. Imoshen studied Ysanna's sweet face. The girl's chin might tremble but her mouth remained closed in an obstinate line. Imoshen's heart contracted in sympathy. 'Wouldn't you like to live in the palace, wear fine clothes and study with the other Malaunje children?'

'No. I only came with the T'En lord because my mother said I must.'

'If you don't like it here, you can go home. But will you stay just for a little while to see if you like it?'

'How long must I stay before I can go?'

Imoshen smiled. 'Just until T'Reothe comes back.'

'Very well.'

Imoshen left the girl with Maigeth, who had become a fixture of the palace. Five girls, nine boys, all with T'En traits except for the last child. Now there was a mystery. It was said the T'En males did not breed true, so unless Imoshen was mistaken, this girl was Reothe's daughter. Ysanna would be half-sister to the child Imoshen carried. By Fair Isle custom Imoshen was duty bound to care for her unborn child's blood relative, even though the girl was not hers. As Imoshen wondered what Reothe planned for this spirited little girl, a protective instinct surprised her.

The Malaunje children had not yet begun their training, because Reothe had left instructions only for their accommodation and welfare. Imoshen hoped he would return with the T'Elegos. How could she teach the children if she hardly knew her own potential?

Excitement surged within her, followed by a stab of anger. How dare Reothe return if he betrayed Tulkhan? She would not be able to look him in the eye knowing he was a murderer. She could not believe it of Reothe, would not believe it. Yet in her vision it had been Tulkhan who took the wound.

Imoshen massaged her temples. Why was she tormented with these gifts if they obscured more than they revealed?

'T'Imoshen?' Lightfoot approached her. 'There is a man with a message.'

'Where is he?'

'I will escort you.'

She fell into step beside him. 'Do you know this man?'

'No. He is one of Lord Commander Haase's men from Deepdeyne.'

Imoshen increased her pace, sure it was a message from Tulkhan. Eagerly she entered the room then stopped. 'I thought you said he was waiting?'

'He was.' Lightfoot strode to the table where food had been served. 'And here's the message.'

He glanced uneasily around the room, as though the man might be standing behind one of the hangings with a knife at the ready. But Imoshen knew he wasn't. The room was empty, yet it held the tang of something she did not recognise.

She removed a single sheet of paper from the brass cylinder and broke the plain seal. Imoshen frowned, then sniffed the paper. 'Strange, it is written in the speech of Fair Isle but by a mainland scriber.' She scanned the words, taking in the first three lines, then going back to the beginning. She could not believe what she was reading. The brass message cylinder fell from her hands, clattering on the tiles.

'What is it?'

Silently, Imoshen handed the paper to Lightfoot. Her trembling fingers smoothed the front of her gown where there was as yet no sign of the life she carried. The child's father, if this message could be believed, was as good as dead.

'General Tulkhan is to be tried for treason by King Gharavan?' Lightfoot whispered. 'I swear this is fell news.'

'And must not go beyond this room. Haase did not write this.' Imoshen indicated the paper. 'He can barely make the letters of his own name. Gharavan ordered this written on the mainland, to be delivered to me in the event of their capture.'

'How many days to Deepdeyne?'

'Three by fast rider. I fear Reothe and Tulkhan are already out of Fair Isle and sailing for the mainland.'

'Betrayed by his own commander!' Lightfoot muttered.

The words pierced Imoshen's abstraction. *Betrayed*. Now she understood the meaning of her vision, and a wave of relief swept her. But this was just as bad.

Worse. With Reothe and Tulkhan dead, how would she hold Fair Isle against the Ghebite King? How could she even think this, knowing Tulkhan faced execution and Reothe degradation before Gharavan had him killed?

She must harden her heart against their loss. Since the Ghebites invaded she had faced many cruel choices. Her loyalty was to Fair Isle. But she could not let them die... Imoshen's head swam with anguish and she bent double with a moan.

'Imoshen, my lady?'

Imoshen was startled to find herself on the floor with Kalleen at her side and Lightfoot hovering over them.

Kalleen turned on the servants. 'Stop gawking. Bring warmed wine and food.'

'What happened?' Imoshen asked.

'Lightfoot sent for me because you went white as a sheet and sank to your knees,' Kalleen said. 'He tells me you've had a shock.' She helped Imoshen to her feet. 'That is not good for women in our condition.'

Imoshen fixed on this. 'I said nothing.'

'No, but I have seen you push your breakfast away. You forget I kept you company through your last pregnancy, and I've experienced the same things with mine.'

'A pregnant Empress and an infant prince. What will become of the General's kingdom?' Lightfoot groaned.

'Fair Isle is mine,' Imoshen told him.

Lightfoot bowed in apology, but when he straightened his eyes met hers unchastened. 'You are the T'En Empress, but you are still only one person and soon to be heavy with child.'

He was right. Imoshen kicked the empty brass cylinder across the room in disgust. 'Where have you put that accursed message?'

'What message?' Kalleen asked.

Lightfoot removed the folded paper from inside his jerkin.

'Give it to Kalleen.'

'But, she's –'

'What? A woman?'

Lightfoot stiffened as he handed over the message. 'I meant only that Lady Kalleen is not trained in the craft of war.'

'And you are,' Imoshen acknowledged. 'I would hear your advice, too.'

As Kalleen read the message her face grew visibly paler. 'So this is what the vision and dreams meant. Can we buy their freedom? I know where...' She stopped abruptly, her cheeks colouring.

Imoshen signalled for silence.

'What is gold to King Gharavan, when he has the resources of the Ghebite Empire?' Lightfoot countered. 'He wants revenge!'

Imoshen folded the message. 'There is only one chance to save their lives, and I pray I am not too late. I must discover where the King is and sail in time to prevent Tulkhan's execution. Gharavan will want to make his revenge a public spectacle.' She licked dry lips. Her experience in the Amirate had made her bold.

'What if you fall into Gharavan's hands?' Kalleen whispered.

'Then I will die.'

They both stared at her.

Lightfoot stiffened. 'T'Imoshen, you have a responsibility to Fair Isle.'

'Don't speak to me of responsibility. I have always acted for the good of Fair Isle. Just this once I will follow my heart. Kalleen, I lay this charge on you, you must keep Ashmyr safe. If I do not return, I name you Regent.'

Kalleen took a step back, appalled.

Imoshen ignored Lightfoot's exclamation, turning to him. 'As leader of the garrison I name you Protector of T'Diemn. Commander Piers I name War General of the army of Fair Isle. As captain of the Parakhan Guard, Drake serves you, Kalleen.'

The young woman shook her head.

'Kalleen, Piers and Lightfoot will form a triumvirate of power. You three will serve the interests of Fair Isle until my son is of age to take an Empress. A council of three, with majority rules.'

The mercenary stared at her, as astounded as Kalleen was horrified. Imoshen supposed it was a long step from farm girl to regent and an equally long step from leader of a mercenary band to co-ruler of Fair Isle.

Imoshen strode to the table. 'We must move quickly. Kalleen, send for the Beatific. I need her to draw up the legal documents.' She frowned. 'No doubt Engarad will want a finger in this pie. But which piece will I give her?'

Kalleen would have argued but Imoshen sent her away. 'Lightfoot, I want you to go to Deepdeyne. If that snake, Haase, is still there, I want him dead and his head spiked on the city gates.'

This order was more to Lightfoot's liking. 'He will expect this.'

'He may, but these Ghebites always underestimate a woman. He probably thinks me cowering in my palace, terrified of the Ghebite King's wrath. Select your force and go.'

He saluted her as he would salute the General.

*   *   *

WHEN TULKHAN AWOKE, he found himself alone in the hot spring cave. Shifting to ease the ache in his body, he realised the fever had eased and the festering poisons had left his body. If his hunger was anything to go by, several days had passed. Where was Reothe?

Grunting with the effort, he pulled himself to his feet, bending almost double to avoid the low roof. The position triggered a memory. With the painful clarity of a fevered hallucination, he recalled finding Reothe huddled in pain.

Reothe's skin had been stretched over his bones so tightly Tulkhan saw the pulse beating in his temple. When he'd asked what was wrong, Reothe had glared at him. 'I took a life while we were escaping. The man's shade stalks me through death's shadow and I am crippled on that plane.' Dread had widened his eyes. 'He comes for me again.' And he passed out.

Tulkhan frowned as the memory faded. At that point he had believed they would both die.

Then a third person had appeared, a healer with soothing hands. Those hands had packed his wound with herbs and forced him to drink a vile-tasting mixture. He could feel the bandages around his thigh so it had not been a hallucination. Perhaps Reothe had died and the healer taken his body.

Painfully slow, Tulkhan limped to the mouth of the cave. He was stiff and hungry but he was alive, thanks to Reothe. And if Reothe still lived, where was he? Perhaps the Dhamfeer had left him to his fate. That made no sense. Reothe could have abandoned him many times.

Shame scalded Tulkhan, for he would have abandoned Reothe. He had meant to. Yet, when it had seemed there was no escape for him on the bridge, he had urged Reothe to save himself.

Tulkhan stepped out of the cave, blinking in the blinding light. Snow lay pristinely beautiful in the midday sun, individual crystals glinting like carelessly scattered diamonds.

Nothing moved, not even the air.

Tulkhan blinked and stared at a patch of darkness that eventually revealed itself to be Reothe's face, shadowed under the hood of a white cloak. He slid down into the hollow to join Tulkhan.

'When I woke and found you gone, I thought you dead.' Tulkhan's voice rasped from lack of use.

The Dhamfeer pushed back his hood, exposing his narrow face, his cheek bones painfully prominent. 'You confront death in your way, I in mine.' Reothe looked past him to the sky. 'Haase's men have not come searching this way for two days.'

'How many days has it been?'

'Six, I think.'

'And the healer. Did I imagine her?'

'Is that bandage on your thigh a dream?'

'Then I didn't dream your suffering. When the soul of the man you killed stalked you through death's shadow, did the Parakletos come to your aid?'

Reothe's eyes widened and Tulkhan was pleased to have startled him.

'Don't mention their name, True-man. They rule death's shadow, but they are capricious beings and I am no longer in their favour. My mentors have abandoned me since I failed to take your fort at the Greater Pass. More T'En riddles for you, Mere-man.'

Seeing Tulkhan's expression, Reothe laughed bitterly.

Then he sobered. 'I know exactly how many men I have killed, because I died a little with each of them. I am here now only because I have escaped death's shadow yet again.' Contempt narrowed Reothe's garnet eyes. 'You True-men think yourselves superior to the T'En. You call us beasts. Yet you kill without compunction. Do not speak to me of this again!'

Heart pounding, Tulkhan watched as Reothe stalked towards the cave mouth. 'You saved my life. Why?'

The Dhamfeer hesitated, then turned to face Tulkhan. 'If one of the T'En saves someone's life, that person becomes their responsibility. They must see to it that the person is looked after in a worldly sense and if possible in a spiritual sense. But Ghebites customs are different. Do you follow the Gheeakhan code, General Tulkhan?'

He stiffened. 'I hold my honour highly.'

Reothe nodded, as if Tulkhan's reply confirmed what he knew. 'Wharrd died in service to Imoshen, honour bound by his Ghiad.'

Reothe had saved his life, knowing Tulkhan would be under a Ghiad to him? The General's head spun. Sunlight glinted on Reothe's silver hair. Light flashed.

Tulkhan found himself on all fours in the snow. Pushing Reothe's helping hands away, he came to his feet. The full implications of his position hit him. He was honour bound to serve his deadly enemy.

'We must leave soon,' Reothe said. 'The healer won't be back. It is worth more than her life.'

Tulkhan limped into the cave. 'How did she find us?'

'Deduction. After we escaped from Deepdeyne she guessed we would head for this place. None of my people will reveal the location of the hot springs.'

Reothe unwrapped bread, roasted meat and a flask of wine. He cut off a chunk of meat, offering it to Tulkhan. 'Eat. You need your strength.'

Hunger made Tulkhan's mouth water. He was honour bound to serve Reothe, but did the Dhamfeer really understand what a Ghiad meant to a Ghebite?

'Don't worry.' Reothe smiled sweetly. 'I won't ask you to fall on your sword.'

The meat turned to ash in Tulkhan's mouth.

'I have only one stipulation. Do not share Imoshen's bed.'

A flare of anger engulfed Tulkhan, but he bowed his head to hide his fury, for under the Ghiad Reothe could ask for much more.

He could ask for Imoshen.

*   *   *

IMOSHEN PACED THE map-room. From the information she had gathered, she knew that Gharavan was not in the Amirate. She longed to confront the little Ghebite King, but she would not make a move until she knew where he was. To set off too soon might mean Tulkhan's death.

Chapter Twenty

TULKHAN IGNORED THE pain in his leg. He hoped walking was good for it, they had done enough, skirting upstream to avoid Haase's men. It had been on his insistence that they had come back to Deepdeyne, and he had not revealed how much trouble his leg was giving him, not wanting to give Reothe any excuse to veto his revenge on Haase.

Being under Ghiad to Reothe placed Tulkhan in a peculiar position. It was many years since he had followed another man's orders. Reothe could have refused Tulkhan his revenge, just as he could have asked him to fall on his sword, but he did not. Haase had to be killed and Reothe understood the need to set an example.

It was better to lead through love than fear, but sometimes a little fear was necessary.

'The secret passage will get us inside Deepdeyne. There will only be the two of us against Haase and all his men,' Reothe said. 'If my gifts were healed, I could slip in there and bring out your commander without anyone noticing.'

Tulkhan frowned. 'And why would you do that?'

'Because I need you to help me hold Fair Isle, General.' Reothe smiled disarmingly.

Tulkhan cursed silently as he headed up the slope to study the stronghold. 'You get us into Deepdeyne and I will do the rest.' He knew if he killed Haase, the commander's men would surrender.

'Very well. We'll take a look at the defences, but we'll wait until the small hours before dawn to strike.'

They kept low so as to present no outline, though it would have taken an alert sentry to notice them from this distance. Once on the crest it was clear their care was not needed. Deepdeyne was under siege.

Tulkhan was amazed to see that the encircling soldiers flew his own standard, the dawn sun. 'Who?'

Reothe chuckled. 'Imoshen, of course. She wouldn't let this insult pass. I expected as much.'

Was Imoshen herself down there? How did she know of their capture? 'Are you in contact with her, Dhamfeer?'

Reothe's eyes narrowed at the tone and term, then he smiled. Tulkhan was learning to dread that expression.

His back to a tree trunk, Reothe rolled down his sleeve to reveal the bonding scar on his wrist. 'My gifts are crippled. But Imoshen and I are still bound in ways a True-man would not understand.'

Tulkhan wondered if his original suspicion hadn't been correct. Perhaps killing Reothe would endanger Imoshen...

'Isn't that rider your mercenary leader, Tulkhan?'

The General shaded his eyes. 'Lightfoot! He'll know what's going on.' Tulkhan ploughed down the slope, limping in his urgency.

Crossing the snow-covered field, he signalled the sentries, who gave a shout of recognition. His men charged out with their weapons drawn, running past him. Tulkhan turned to see Reothe surrounded by Ghebites.

Reothe held the General's eyes.

A rider approached. The horse pawed the snow, breath misting on the cold air as Lightfoot dismounted.

'General? We had word... But I see reports of your capture and execution were greatly exaggerated.'

The mercenary glanced at Reothe, then shot a questioning look at Tulkhan. Only the General knew he was under obligation to Reothe. He could deny the Ghiad and blame Reothe for the betrayal, ridding himself of the Dhamfeer.

'Reothe saved my life. I am under a Ghiad,' Tulkhan said. Even Lightfoot knew the Ghebite term.

To a man, Tulkhan's soldiers were appalled.

'I am not awaiting execution or drowned in this river because of Reothe. Put away your weapons.'

Reothe's eyes were unreadable. Did he think Tulkhan a fool for not ordering his death?

'Well, you are alive at least. This calls for a celebration!' Lightfoot filled the silence. 'Come into my tent.'

Tulkhan fell into place at his side. He had the men and the means to enter Deepdeyne. Before dawn tomorrow the dishonour of Haase's betrayal would be removed.

Lightfoot stopped midstride with a curse.

'What?'

He lowered his voice. 'I must send a fast horse with word of your safe escape. I only hope it reaches the Empress before she sails for the mainland to confront King Gharavan.'

Tulkhan was astounded. 'She wouldn't.'

Reothe laughed outright.

THE SECRET PASSAGE into Deepdeyne led through a damp tunnel under the river itself. The weight of water and earth above made Tulkhan's gut twist. Ahead of him, Reothe led the way. Dressed in borrowed mail a size too small, he carried a branch of candles, his weapon drawn.

'My parents saw to it that I knew the history of each of my estates,' Reothe explained softly. 'Deepdeyne's defences are impregnable, but if the defenders wanted to make a sortie against their besiegers, they could use this tunnel. Commander Haase will know nothing of it.'

'Where does it come out?'

'In the old tower.'

At last they came to a stone wall. Reothe removed a small plug and peered through. 'Good. This wall should come down without too much trouble.'

The men moved in and demolished it, removing each stone quietly. Finally only an unlocked inner door stood between Tulkhan and revenge. At this time of night, except for the sentries on the outer wall, all the inhabitants of Deepdeyne would be asleep.

'Do not hurt the locals if you can help it,' Tulkhan told his men. 'Lead me to the bedchambers, Reothe. We'll capture Haase before the alarm is given.'

They searched the private chambers above the great hall, finding evidence of Haase's habitation but not the man himself.

Tulkhan returned to the great hall where the men-at-arms slept, sprawled like so many dogs in front of the fireplace. Stepping carefully through the sleeping bodies, Tulkhan looked for Haase's sword-brother. He would know where the commander was. Tulkhan found them together.

The General signalled for his men to spread out. Weapons drawn, they stood over the sleeping men. Tulkhan had selected an equal number of his loyal Ghebites and Lightfoot's mercenaries for this attack. His soldiers had served with Haase's men. He knew it would not be easy for them to kill their companions-at-arms, but he hoped it would not come to that.

Holding his sword point to Haase's chest, Tulkhan roared. 'Stand and face your fate, betrayer!'

The man awoke with a jerk, scrambling for a weapon before he knew who confronted him. Tulkhan gave him no chance, kicking him so hard he flew into the wall.

The startled cries of the men-at-arms faded as they woke to find themselves captured.

Haase glanced from Tulkhan to Reothe. He made the sign to ward off evil.

'What is the fate of a traitor, Haase?' Tulkhan demanded.

'No!' a voice roared.

Tulkhan spun to see Haase's sword-brother charge him, armed with a dagger. With precision, Reothe took his legs out from under him and sent the flat of his sword into the man's skull. Even as he was going down, Tulkhan sensed movement and ducked. Death whistled over his head.

Haase had wrenched a long sword off the wall-mounted display. It stood almost as tall as him. Tulkhan wondered which of Reothe's ancestors had wielded this grisly weapon.

Before Haase could regain control of the unfamiliar blade, Tulkhan stepped inside the range of the sword, blocking it with the guard of his own. He drove his ceremonial knife up under Haase's ribs straight to the heart. The commander was as good as dead.

Dispassionately, Tulkhan saw him accept his fate.

Haase met Tulkhan's eyes. 'Pray to Akha Khan, General, that you never have to choose between your honour and your family!'

He toppled forward into Tulkhan's arms. Hiding his regret, Tulkhan placed the man's body on the floor. The General looked up at Reothe, wondering what honour might yet force him to do.

Then he straightened, cleaning his dagger. 'That is twice you have saved my life.'

A fey smile lit Reothe's eyes. 'By T'En custom, twice over I am beholden to care for you and yours.'

'By Ghebite custom, twice over I am under a Ghiad to serve you.'

'General?' Lightfoot prodded. 'What will you have me do with Haase's men?'

'First, there is a wrong I must redress.' Tulkhan went to the fireplace, where Haase's ribbons of office hung. The men parted for him. He unhooked the three ribbons with the tip of his sword. They slid down the length of the blade to the hilt.

'Come here, Reothe of the T'En.'

Silently, Reothe approached Tulkhan and dropped to one knee. But the subservient stance did not match the gaze he lifted to Tulkhan. His mocking expression seemed to say, *Do you expect me to be grateful to you for returning what is rightfully mine?*

Tulkhan cleared his throat. 'For hundreds of years your family were the masters of Deepdeyne Stronghold. You have proven a truer friend that my own man, Haase. I confiscate his estate and return Deepdeyne to your care.' He dropped the white ribbon over Reothe's head. 'White to symbolise the purity of service to the people of Deepdeyne.' He slipped the red ribbon into place. 'Red symbolises the blood you have shed and are willing to shed in their defence.' As he let the black ribbon fall, his fingers brushed Reothe's short hair. It was soft and so fine that the sensation barely registered. 'Black symbolises death which comes to us all.'

As the words faded, Tulkhan felt himself to be more T'En than Ghebite. He recalled how Imoshen had surprised him with this ceremony. Now he understood its significance. No matter how powerful you became, everyone faced death, and the higher you rose, the more you served.

If he had been a Ghebite, Reothe would have kissed the naked blade Tulkhan still held. Instead he stood and met the General's eyes. Tulkhan read a reluctant emotion, quickly concealed. Then Reothe stepped aside, to stand just behind Tulkhan on his left. With a start he realised Reothe was honouring him.

Facing the others, the General sensed a shift in the balance of power. His men did not despise their general because he was under a Ghiad to the last Dhamfeer warrior. Somehow, Reothe's position at his back, their miraculous escape and the taking of Deepdeyne had all added to the aura surrounding him.

Tulkhan raised his voice. 'Men of Deepdeyne, you have a choice. Swear fealty to me, or join your commander in death.'

*   *   *

LATE THAT EVENING, Tulkhan sat at the table in the great hall, where the fire had burned low. He had sent Lightfoot back to the capital with word for Imoshen and all day the locals had come into Deepdeyne to swear fealty to their hereditary leader, honoured by the new regime. Tulkhan had legitimised Reothe, but he could not leave him at Deepdeyne.

What was he thinking? He was under a Ghiad to Reothe. The Dhamfeer could do whatever he liked. Tulkhan's head ached. He dreaded returning to T'Diemn and Imoshen.

Reothe dropped a bottle of Vorsch beside Tulkhan's elbow. 'Share a drink with me, General? I promise it's not drugged.'

He sat two small glasses next to the bottle. Their solid bases rattled on the scrubbed boards.

Tulkhan dredged up an acceptable reply. 'So, you have taken a liking to Vorsch?'

'No. I chose it because you like it.' Reothe uncorked the bottle and inhaled the scent. 'Though it does have a certain –'

Reothe's eyes widened at something behind Tulkhan. The General turned to see death charge out of the shadows. A naked blade flashed. Tulkhan reached for his own weapon, but before he drew it Reothe lunged, his sword flying past Tulkhan's left ear.

Haase's sword-brother screamed. Tulkhan's chair hit the floor. The corpse lay twitching in a steadily expanding pool of blood. Several men who had been drinking on the floor below charged up the stairwell, weapons drawn.

'Who was watching Haase's sword-brother?' Tulkhan demanded.

A man stepped forward. 'He was asleep a moment ago, General.'

Tulkhan did not pursue this, glancing instead to Reothe, who was staring grimly down at the corpse.

'Throw him into the moat,' Tulkhan ordered, denying the man the honour of a Ghebite warrior's burial. 'And get out.'

They dragged the man away, leaving blood smears on the floor. Tulkhan righted his chair and poured two more drinks. 'Again you have saved my life.'

'You would have saved yourself. I acted on reflex.'

Tulkhan considered this. 'Yes. But I would probably have been wounded for my lack of wariness.' The General wanted to ask Reothe how long before he suffered for the man's death, but his expression did not invite these confidences.

Reothe drained the Vorsch in one gulp.

The General watched the candle flame through his glass. He knew Reothe did not wish to discuss this, but Tulkhan had always thirsted for knowledge. 'You killed him on reflex. But I have known you to kill with forethought. Two days after you touched one of my commanders, he delivered your message, and dropped dead at my feet.' Tulkhan shuddered at the memory.

Reothe said nothing.

Tulkhan sipped his Vorsch. Before long Reothe would lie in a delirium, hurting and vulnerable. The Ghiad prevented Tulkhan from killing him but, if Reothe challenged him, he was entitled to defend himself.

'You call yourself greater than a True-man who kills and does not suffer for it. I put this to you. The T'En are less than True-men because they know what death is, and yet they still kill!'

Reothe's face registered shock, then cold fury.

Tulkhan shrugged and poured himself another glass.

The Dhamfeer stood abruptly, pacing across the floor to the open hearth. Placing his hands on the mantelpiece, he stared into the glowing coals.

Despite his casual stance, Tulkhan's heart pounded.

Reothe stalked back. Tulkhan's body tightened in anticipation. His hand closed on his sword hilt. He knew the speed of the T'En warrior's reactions. If he failed to block Reothe's killing stroke, could he drag the Dhamfeer through death's shadow with him?

Reothe came to a stop.

Tulkhan schooled his features, waiting for the first sign of attack. Reothe stared down at him, the single flame barely illuminating his face so that his eyes appeared as dark pools.

The silence stretched until Tulkhan felt the tension thrum through his body like a tightly drawn bow string.

Abruptly Reothe gave him the Old Empire obeisance. 'You are right, Tulkhan.'

The General's skin crawled. How could Reothe make him feel vulnerable simply by uttering his name?

With formal courtesy Reothe topped up Tulkhan's glass and refilled his own, resuming his seat. The General had to force his fingers to release his sword hilt.

Reothe sipped his Vorsch thoughtfully. 'If I still had my gift, I would trawl your mind, True-man. You think differently.'

Tulkhan repressed a shiver, grateful that this was impossible. Feeling he had the advantage, he pursued the point. 'If your gifts are crippled, why does killing still affect you?'

Reothe stared morosely at the candle, playing casually with the flickering flame. He circled it, just avoiding scorching the remaining fingertips of his left hand.

Eventually, Reothe reply. 'The T'En are different. This difference lies deep within our minds. Once, I could have caressed the flame and wooed it to do my bidding. Now I am only aware that it exists.' He saw that the General did not understand. 'You know this flame will burn if it touches your skin and you know how to put it out. Imagine that you have lost the ability to put out the flame, but it can still burn you. That is what Imoshen has done to me.'

For an instant Tulkhan glimpsed Reothe's agony and unwelcome sympathy moved him. But he would not be distracted. 'Does this mean your powers are healing?'

'If I'd had even a fraction of my gift, I would have known Haase meant to betray you. I would have smelt it on him.'

Reothe's revelation opened Tulkhan's eyes to the difference between a True-man and the T'En. Every time Tulkhan thought he was growing to understand Imoshen and Reothe, he discovered how much he still had to learn. 'If your gifts are crippled, how did you survive death's shadow?'

Reothe laughed. 'My gifts might be crippled, but I still have my wits!'

Tulkhan found this just as cryptic. He changed the subject. 'Tomorrow we return to the capital. I'm under a Ghiad to you. Why don't you send me away on a mission I can't hope to survive?'

'Your men are loyal to you, not me. Even if you died, Gharavan might choose to revenge himself on Fair Isle. I need you to hold Fair Isle until I am ready to retake it.'

Reothe used the truth like a knife to cut to the bone of the matter.

'Why tell me?' Anger closed Tulkhan's throat making his voice a low growl. 'Surely you must know I will kill you?'

Reothe held his eyes. 'Not until you are free of the Ghiad. How can you forget, Tulkhan? You are thrice bound by the Gheeakhan code.'

Fury and three glasses of Vorsch drove Tulkhan to speak before he considered his words. 'Maybe I will kill you while you wander death's shadow!'

Reothe rose, graceful and utterly Other. 'You will abide by your Ghiad because you are an honourable man and that is why Imoshen loves you.'

DETERMINED TO HIDE her misgivings, Imoshen greeted Reothe and Tulkhan in the map-room. She stood on the far side of the table so that she could observe them. Tulkhan's broken nose was a visible reminder of how close she had to come to losing them both.

She pushed the message across the desk towards the General. 'Gharavan boasts he will take Fair Isle from you.'

The force of Reothe's gaze was almost physical. She knew that he was waiting for her to meet his eyes, but she would not give him the satisfaction.

With Wharrd's death, she understood what a Ghiad meant to a Ghebite. Tulkhan would die for Reothe. She wanted to be certain he did not have to. As for Reothe...

What double game was he playing? Her gaze strayed to his face and what she read there did not reassure her. Reothe's narrow features were even more sharply defined. If she had not known better, she would have said he had been deathly ill. His eyes, brilliant as garnets, blazed with keen intelligence.

When Lightfoot had explained Haase's betrayal, Imoshen had cursed herself. If she had healed Reothe he would have known the man plotted treachery. Her lack of trust in Reothe had placed Tulkhan's life at risk.

The General made a disgusted noise as he finished reading the message which proclaimed his capture and ended with Gharavan's threats. He passed it to Reothe without being asked.

'Does the little King have the ability to raise an army of sufficient size to do what he threatens?' Reothe looked to Tulkhan, revealing a familiarity that was both unexpected and unnerving.

As Imoshen waited for the General to answer, she marvelled at how quickly Reothe appeared to have gained Tulkhan's trust.

'Gharavan might be able to raise an army of sufficient size. I could have done it.'

'Then we face invasion come spring,' Imoshen spoke, her mouth dry. Tulkhan had taken Fair Isle with less men. The strength of the army depended on the leader. Fair Isle's army was depleted, but Imoshen had General Tulkhan. His leadership would be their salvation. Reothe caught Imoshen's eye; their minds ran along similar paths.

Tulkhan's brows drew down. 'What's this about Kalleen being made Regent?'

Imoshen gave a little start, surprised by the change of subject and the speed with which Tulkhan had caught up with events. 'I see you have been speaking with Lightfoot. I had to make provision for the future of our son and Fair Isle in case I was killed confronting Gharavan.'

Tulkhan met Imoshen's challenging eyes across the table littered with the letters of state and maps. She had held the reins of the kingdom since the day he sailed for Port Sumair and she had not faltered. 'But Kalleen? You would make a farm girl Regent?'

Imoshen came to her feet. 'Do you object because she was born a farm girl, or because she is a woman? If it is because of her sex, you insult me. If it is because of her origin, you insult yourself, first son of the king's second wife. You are the one who claims a person should be judged by their worth and not their birth.'

Tulkhan felt the overflow of Imoshen's gifts exude from her skin and into the air around her, making the little hairs on his body rise and his heart race. He wanted to bathe in that sensation. At her most T'En, Imoshen fascinated him. He found himself on his feet, torn between anger and admiration.

A slow hand-clapping pierced the roaring in his head and he looked around to see Reothe ridiculing them with the Ghebite form of applause.

'Reothe!' Imoshen's eyes narrowed.

He offered the Old Empire obeisance and left.

Imoshen waited only until the door closed, then she rounded on him. 'How could you give him power over you, Tulkhan?'

'He saved my life. I am thrice bound under a Ghiad to him.'

She gasped, her fair skin draining of all colour. 'Thrice bound? This is fell news, indeed.'

'How so?' Anger drove him. 'What could be better, Reothe crippled and your war general forced to serve him?'

Imoshen's lips parted as if she would say something but instead she only stared at him. He hated to see her distraught and ached to take her in his arms. 'Don't play your tricks on me, Imoshen. I cannot be influenced by your gifts!'

Imoshen cursed in High T'En. 'I would not stoop to influence your thoughts, but if his gifts were restored, Reothe would. When will you learn, General? I am not the enemy!'

'You don't need to tell me Reothe is my enemy.'

'For now Reothe is your ally against Gharavan. To quote an old T'En saying, *My enemy's enemy is my friend.* And your half-brother's greatest ally is your lack of trust in me. If we are to leave anything to our son, we must unite to defeat Gharavan. It's nearly Midwinter Feast. We don't have long to prepare for war. What will the people of Fair Isle do?'

'They will fight or die.'

'If only all life were that simple!' Imoshen sighed. She had been ready to confront Gharavan and risk death for Tulkhan. Her throat felt tight as she moved around the table to him. 'I thought I had lost you to your half-brother's thirst for revenge.'

'Not yet. Not ever.'

Yearning filled her and she stroked his broken nose. 'Let me heal you.'

'It is healed.'

'I can smooth it.'

'I am what I am, Imoshen.'

She laughed and the warmth in his black eyes thrilled her. 'Why wear –'

'I will wear my broken nose until the day I die to remind me how close I came to playing into Gharavan's hands.'

'I feared you lost!' She embraced him with all her strength.

When Tulkhan kissed her tear-damp cheeks, she wanted to abandon herself to his touch. She could feel the need in him but Kalleen's doorcomb sounded.

'I request an audience with the Protector General,' she said formally.

Imoshen wondered what Kalleen wanted, but Old Empire protocol forbade the question, so she left them alone.

Kalleen looked up at Tulkhan earnestly. 'General, you must reason with Imoshen. I don't want to be Regent!'

He laughed. As if Kalleen would ever be Regent of Fair Isle.

'Please?' She caught his arm in her small hand. He was reminded of the women of his own race, but Kalleen was no subservient wife-slave. Her fierce will illuminated her. 'Please, do this one thing for me. The decree remains in the Beatific's safe keeping. If anything were to happen to you and Imoshen, I would be Regent.'

'Nothing will happen to us.' He held her shoulders, feeling the fragile bones. Already she was big with Wharrd's child.

'You cannot know that, but the T'En can. Have you asked yourself why Imoshen has done this?'

Her words struck a chill in him.

'She has the Sight,' Kalleen whispered. 'It comes on her without the use of the scrying plate.'

'Imperfectly. She sees things and misinterprets them. Like Haase's betrayal.' When Tulkhan slid an arm around the little woman's shoulders he was surprised by a protective urge. 'Do not fear, Kalleen. You will never be Regent.'

IMOSHEN LED REOTHE down the path to the courtyard near T'Reothe's Hall to see the Malaunje children. Screened from view, they watched them play for a moment. Imoshen noticed Drake's covetous expression as he supervised the children, making her wonder if he was sorry that the T'En gifts had skipped his generation. She had never thought someone might desire the T'En curse. 'As you see, they are all well cared for and happy.'

'I did not expect less.' Reothe stepped around the screen.

When they saw Reothe and Imoshen, the children dropped their coloured balls and came running, all but Ysanna.

A little boy tucked his hand inside Imoshen's. 'Will you show us how to do the fire trick, Empress T'Imoshen?'

'Just T'Imoshen,' Imoshen corrected and glanced to Reothe. 'You have already been to see them, carrying tales, I see.'

Reothe nodded. 'Come inside.'

And Imoshen was reminded that their every move was watched.

As they entered the hall, Imoshen paused to absorb the splendour of the room. Narrow fingers of afternoon sunlight pierced the deep-set windows, picking out the tiny imperfections in each small pane of glass. Imoshen liked the aura of age here: the wood panelled wainscoting, the rich wall hangings and the T'En sized furniture, chairs and tables. Why hadn't she been born four hundred years ago?

Reothe led her to the huge fireplace where wood had been laid but not lit. The children stamped their feet to warm them, shedding snow on the flagstones.

Imoshen knelt before the fireplace.

'Quiet now,' Reothe ordered. 'Watch and open your senses. Afterwards, see if you can tell me how the Empress does this. Go ahead, Imoshen.'

It felt strange to be encouraged to use her gift. A small child climbed into her lap and two more sat to each side of her. For the first time in her life, Imoshen felt truly accepted. She relaxed and reached for the power, welcoming the familiar taste on the back of her tongue. A rush of awareness travelled through her body, scents became sharper and she knew it would be easy to ignite a spark in the kindling. Like tripping a trap, she felt a snap in her mind. The children laughed, clicking their fingers in approval.

'Now,' Reothe said. 'Who knows how it was done?' One by one they shook their heads.

'Ysanna?' Reothe asked. She glared at him. An older girl licked her lips but did not speak. Reothe looked disappointed. Drake made a sound in his throat.

Imoshen came to her feet, smiling on him. He had been honoured to learn she meant to leave her son and Kalleen in his care, though he had argued against Lightfoot and Piers' involvement. He would have been happier to see the triumvirate consist of Kalleen, himself and the Beatific. 'How goes the Parakhan Guard, Drake?'

Before he could speak, Maigeth arrived. 'Time to eat, children. Thank your T'En mentors.'

Well trained, the children formally lined up and paraded past, giving the Old Empire obeisance. They formed pairs behind Maigeth and Drake to walk to the room where their meals were served. Imoshen caught the hand of the girl who would have spoken. When she probed, she felt the bud of her gift lying dormant, waiting to bloom. Imoshen squeezed the girl's fingers. 'One day soon, Larassa. Join the others.'

After the last two had gone, Imoshen turned to Reothe, who had been watching her closely.

'She sensed something?' Reothe asked. 'I hoped there would be some among them who could already use their gifts.'

'Perhaps it is for the best that the gifts do not bloom until we reach puberty.'

'My gifts were moving before then.'

Imoshen recalled the Beatific's poisonous words. Had Reothe triggered his parent's joint suicides? It had to be a lie. 'Mine did not start until I became a woman. And then the ability came on slowly, until...' She did not need to finish. Reothe had known her powers would grow with the birth of her children. 'But I'm sure Imoshen the First mentioned this in the T'Elegos?'

'The T'Elegos is waiting for you, as soon as you are ready to meet my terms.'

'Terms?' Anger warmed her. How dare he lay down terms? But then it dawned on her that she'd had a bargaining tool of her own. Once she knew the secrets of the T'Elegos there would be no need to fear Reothe's restored gifts. 'Maybe I have my own terms.'

She saw him accept this and understood he'd been waiting for this moment. He was far more devious than she.

'And what do you offer me, Imoshen?'

Chapter Twenty-One

'YOUR GIFTS RESTORED,' Imoshen said. A muscle flexed in his cheek. It thrilled her to be in control.

'What are your terms?'

'Bring the T'Elegos to the palace and...' Here she paused, suddenly unsure. 'Swear that you will not harm Tulkhan.'

His surprise gave way to anger. 'I saved his life. Do you think me so dishonourable that this counts for nothing?'

Her heart lurched. 'I can only judge you by your past actions. You did not hesitate to cloak your form in that of Tulkhan's to come to my bed.'

He flinched. 'I did what I had to do.'

'Exactly!'

'Would you respect me if I did not? How can you accuse me when we both know you are using the General to hold Fair Isle? When the time comes and Fair Isle is safe, which of us will you choose, my Empress?'

'It's not like that.'

'No?'

Imoshen turned to the fireplace, remembering that Reothe had been reared in the royal household of the Old Empire, where the Empress's word was law. But this did not mean he would not try to influence her choice. His every action proclaimed his belief that she would eventually honour her vows to him.

'You are no longer that girl-woman I first met, out of her depth in the Empress's court, Imoshen. I loved you then because I could sense the fierce flame of your being.'

His breath stirred the fine hairs on the back of her neck. She felt him standing just behind her, not actually touching, but then he did not have to touch her.

'Shenna?'

Blindly she grasped the mantelpiece and rested her head on her hands. The heavy indentations of Tulkhan's Ghebite seal ring bit into her brow, reminding her of her dual loyalties.

'Don't tell me you feel nothing. Events have come between us, but what we share goes deeper.' He slid his arms around her waist. His lips brushed the back of her neck, sending a rush of warmth through her. A sigh escaped her as her body moulded against his. She felt him smile.

'Heal me and I will bring you the T'Elegos,' he urged, lips moving like living silk on her cheek. 'It must be done in secret. Only Engarad and the master-archivist know the history still exists and they have no reason to consult it, so they do not know I have taken it. I promise not to kill Tulkhan until he has served his purpose.'

She spun to confront him then realised... 'You would not kill him. You are testing me.'

He laughed. 'I knew the day would come when I could no longer play you.'

'You mock me. I was barely sixteen when we met. You've always had the advantage of experience. But I have only sought to do what is right.'

'Whatever the cost?'

She shrugged. Without explanation she went to the inner door, locking it, then she locked the courtyard door.

At that moment Imoshen understood why she had chosen this fortress-like hall for the Malaunje children. They were in a state of siege, the T'En. She was protecting her own.

As she approached Reothe, her heart raced. The mind-touch was like an addiction, one that laid her open to his gifts. It had also made him vulnerable to her, allowing her to cripple him. So much of what she did was instinctive, but she had learnt a great deal about the use of her gifts in these last small moons.

He waited, intense and contained, as she joined him on the hearth.

'This could hurt. Close your eyes,' she said, and without question he obeyed. 'Open to me.'

He took a ragged breath.

Imoshen stood on tiptoe to kiss his closed lids, first one, then the other, the healer in her bestowing a ritual blessing. She inhaled his breath as he exhaled, seeking his essence – that cool bright spark she had known during their moment of intimacy.

The room, the fire, all sounds faded. She focused only on the pursuit of Reothe. Once before, when their minds had touched, she had not been able to escape the force of his will. This time she used her will to pursue him to his source, past the scarred landscape of his gift. At last she found him, trapped and bitter, but still recognisable. Knowing that she had been the cause of his destruction tore at her.

As he welcomed her, his overwhelming emotion was one of relief. She felt as if she had come home. But it would have been too easy to remain there with him. Disciplining herself, she sought to repair the damage. She smoothed the scars which had barricaded his power, blocking its use. When this was half completed she broke contact, gliding away from him, through the tortured terrain of his gift, leaving him stranded.

Imoshen returned to her senses to find herself kneeling on the floor in front of the fireplace with Reothe's head in her lap. She could see his eyes moving under the closed lids.

On a gasp, he returned to the waking state with bitter comprehension. Imoshen smoothed his fine hair, feeling its blunt ends. 'Do you know what I have done?'

He pulled away from her. 'You hold my gifts to ransom. Do you delight in your cruelty, Empress?'

'I had a good teacher, T'Reothe.' She saw him accept this and continued. 'When the T'Elegos is in my possession, I will fully restore your power. At least now you will not be so vulnerable to the Ghebites.'

IMOSHEN CREPT ACROSS the study to the fur rug before the hearth where Tulkhan slept. This was the third night he had not come to her bed and she ached to touch him. Breath tight in her chest, she knelt beside him, admiring the line of his jaw.

Licking dry lips she tentatively lifted her hand. As her fingertips hovered above his chest, his hand flashed up and caught her wrist. With a flick he pulled her off balance and rolled, pinning her to the ground.

She bit back a cry of protest and wriggled against him.

'Ah, Imoshen,' he whispered regretfully. 'Don't do that.'

'Why not?' When he did not answer she pursued it. 'Why haven't you come to my bed? I can feel how much you want me.'

With a curse he sat back on his heels.

She knelt by the fire. Had he somehow discovered that she had partially restored Reothe's gifts? 'What troubles you, Tulkhan?'

In frustration he flicked his heavy dark hair over his shoulder. 'You know I am under a Ghiad, Imoshen.'

Did this mean he could not sleep with her? Perhaps this was why Kalleen had felt rejected by Wharrd. 'I don't quite understand...'

'I think you do. Reothe has forbidden me to lie with you.'

Imoshen's cheeks flamed. 'He does not have the right –'

'He does, and more.'

She met Tulkhan's dark eyes, seeing the regret and longing there. How Reothe must be laughing.

'There is one consolation,' Tulkhan confessed. 'He does not realise that if he asked I would have to relinquish you to him.'

Imoshen snorted. 'You could not relinquish me because I am not your property and Reothe knows that!'

His mouth opened then closed. He shrugged. 'I find it hard to walk the line between the Ghebite world and your world. Every day I grow further away from my people.'

'And a little further from me, if Reothe has his way.'

'I will not dishonour my Ghiad.'

She stared at Tulkhan. The flickering flames sculpted his broad cheek bones, making his coppery skin glow. She wanted him to defy the Gheeakhan, but the warrior code defined him and she could not ask him to dishonour it. 'What must you do to serve out the Ghiad?'

'I must save Reothe's life three times. A life for a life, Imoshen. It is the Ghebite way. If someone killed a member of my family I would have to take their life to revenge them. If someone saves my life, I must repay that debt.'

'Three times?'

He nodded.

Imoshen's heart sank. Now that she had partially restored Reothe's gifts it would make Tulkhan's Ghiad harder to serve.

'What is it?' He was too perceptive.

Shaking her head she went to him, kneeling between his thighs. 'Reothe would know if you broke your word. He would smell your scent on my skin.' She traced the line of his mouth with her fingertip, feeling the bristle of his jaw and the heat of his breath. 'Kiss me before I go back to my cold, lonely bed.'

Tulkhan swallowed.

Imoshen lifted her face to him and closed her eyes, concentrating on the touch of his lips as they explored hers. Liquid heat pooled deep within her. Her breath caught in her throat. Everything reduced to this one moment and him.

Breathing rapidly, Tulkhan pulled back. 'Go now.'

She did not argue, slipping away, her body sensitised but unfulfilled.

As THE LONG day of Midwinter celebrations stretched into an even longer evening, Tulkhan's eyes narrowed. Across the great hall, the Beatific was in deep discussion with Reothe. What mischief were they planning?

Lightfoot approached him. 'I've been challenged to a practice duel, General. Will you stand at my back?'

Tulkhan grinned. He'd suspected his men would not put up with these civilised entertainments for long. If he had to sit through another session of duelling poets, never knowing when they would turn their razor-sharp tongues on him, he would not be answerable for the consequences.

'In the long gallery?' Tulkhan asked.

Lightfoot nodded.

'I'll be there.'

Tulkhan came to his feet, weaving through the clustered townspeople, Keldon nobles, entertainers and loyal Ghebites. This time last year he had shared the bonding ceremony with Imoshen, then they had slipped away together. He had felt a presentiment then that this would not last, and less than a year later he was fighting to retain Fair Isle.

His thirty-first birthday had come and gone with no one knowing. But even so his True-man body would betray him, growing old while Imoshen was still in her prime. As if his thoughts called her, Imoshen met his eyes above the heads of the crowd. She sent him a questioning glance which he ignored.

He was intent on clipping Reothe's wings.

'Beatific.' Tulkhan acknowledged her, then addressed Reothe. 'My men are giving a sword display. I thought you would like to see it.'

'Swordsmanship?' Reothe grinned. 'How can you honour it with this name when you wield ploughshares instead of swords?'

Tulkhan recalled Imoshen had once said much the same thing. 'I suppose you think the knitting needles the T'En call swords are superior?'

Reothe smiled slowly, his challenge evident. The last time they had faced each other with swords in hand, Reothe had wounded the General with one of those knitting needles.

A rush of anger warmed Tulkhan. 'I challenge you to a practice duel with Ghebite weapons.'

'I accept. But not before you accept my challenge. Let me show you why a T'En sword requires more precision than brute strength.'

'Very well. In the long gallery before the next bell!' Tulkhan spun on his heel and stalked off, hardly aware of the revellers who parted for him.

Imoshen's hand closed on his arm. 'General, would you dance with me?'

He held her eyes. 'Does your touch satisfy your curiosity? Can you tell what Reothe and I were arguing about?'

'I don't need to touch you to know you play games of male bravado. I thought we might dance to appease those who look for division.'

Tulkhan fought the need to take her in his arms, to lay claim to her before everyone here, before Reothe. 'You know I can't dance.'

'So you say, but I've seen your sword work. You could dance if you chose!' She held his eyes, always a challenge. 'Will I have the minstrels strike up a Ghebite pair dance?'

Wanting Imoshen consumed him. It was on the tip of his tongue to agree, but then he thought of his men waiting in the gallery and Reothe watching, planning to belittle him in swordplay. 'No dancing. But you can kiss your husband goodnight, my wife.' The words had barely left his lips when he realised his mistake. To Imoshen, husband meant master.

Her eyes flashed red with fury. But she surprised him by stepping closer. 'Is it a kiss you want, General Tulkhan?'

That and so much more...

Imoshen lifted her face, eyes angry, lips parted.

Knowing others could not see her anger, only the supposed surrender of her lips, he kissed her from the depths of his soul. He felt the instant her quicksilver passion ignited. He groaned. Her answering gasp told him she was as shaken as he.

Dimly, he heard the music stop and recalled where they were. With difficulty he broke contact, lifting his head to draw breath. Imoshen smiled up at him like a satisfied cat. He recollected himself and took his leave.

Imoshen met Reothe's eyes across the crowd. Forbidding Tulkhan to make love to her had only strengthened her hold on the General. Reothe's garnet eyes blazed. She felt the force of his gift as the people between them laughed too loudly and spoke too quickly, responding to the rush of energy. But Imoshen withstood it and Reothe faltered, his hand going to the Beatific's shoulder for support. The woman's glare told Imoshen she had committed a breach of high court etiquette.

Impervious to the Beatific's censure, Imoshen returned to Kalleen, who asked, 'What was that all about?'

'Tulkhan and I do not agree on the roles of bond-partners.' Imoshen opted for the simplest answer. 'He called me *wife*.'

Kalleen rolled her eyes. 'Oh, Imoshen. You mustn't let him tease you. The General might be a Ghebite, but he is a good man.'

Imoshen scooped up Ashmyr, who had fallen asleep in his basket, and drew Kalleen to her feet. She was a little awkward now with the weight of her pregnancy. 'Let us escape while we can.'

Heading for the staircase, Imoshen swayed with the weight of the baby and basket, but Kalleen lingered to look through the multi-paned doors that gave a view into the well-lit gallery.

When Imoshen focused on the scene beyond, her heart turned over. Tulkhan and Reothe were at each other's throats, swords flashing.

The slender T'En sword went spinning out of Tulkhan's hand and Reothe laughed, lowering his. 'You see, it is all in the wrist, General.'

Relief flooded Imoshen.

Tulkhan retrieved his blade. 'Once more and I'll get this right!'

Reothe saluted him.

Tulkhan returned the salute. 'You know I'm only letting you disarm me because when you get the Ghebite sword in your hands, the tables will be turned.'

'Of course. Defend yourself!' Reothe lunged, coming perilously close to skewering him.

Kalleen gasped. 'Tulkhan!'

Jealousy stirred in Imoshen's breast as she watched from the dark stairwell. She had asked Tulkhan to teach her the use of the Ghebite sword, but he always put her off because in his mind a woman did not touch a weapon. Yet there he was, sharing this skill with the fallen rebel leader. How could Reothe be accepted by Tulkhan and his men when she, who had done everything in her power to support the General, received only grudging respect?

Frustration seared Imoshen. How long before Tulkhan revealed Seerkhan's sword to Reothe? She guarded the intimacy of that memory, aware that Reothe with his insidious T'En charm could take even this from her.

Tulkhan's sword spun away across the floor again, and Reothe saluted him. 'Well done. It takes years to master this.'

'Let's see how you fare with a Ghebite weapon.'

The General's men hurried forward with the weapons and he selected two. After testing them for weight and balance, he handed one to Reothe. Imoshen watched as Reothe grasped the unfamiliar hilt, assessing its differences.

'I never thought to see it,' Kalleen whispered. 'Only a short while ago they were ready to kill each other, and now they are sword-brothers.'

Astonishment flooded Imoshen. She had been blind. Sword-brothers. That was why it was so easy for Tulkhan to accept Reothe – it was the Ghebite way.

Kalleen arched her back. 'I don't think I can stand much longer. I'm for bed.'

Still coming to terms with this revelation, Imoshen accompanied her. Anger powered her steps as she climbed the stairs. She must not let all she had worked for slip away, stolen by Reothe.

*   *   *

BUT REOTHE WAS cunning, and monopolised Tulkhan's time. They rode the new defences of T'Diemn together, they went hunting and, as the days passed, Imoshen seethed.

Knowing that Reothe visited T'Reothe's Hall daily, returning via the narrow stairwell, Imoshen lay in wait for him. The sound of his soft footfalls made her body tighten in anticipation. She stepped out of the shadows.

'Imoshen?' he greeted her warily.

'When will I see the T'Elegos?' she whispered. 'You have had the benefit of my part of the bargain for almost one small moon now.'

'I cannot leave T'Diemn without an escort of spies. Who would you trust with the knowledge that the T'Elegos survives?'

'Then when?'

'It's twenty days until the cusp of spring. When the snows melt –'

'So it is in the Keldon Highlands?'

'When the snows melt, the General will continue his inspection of Fair Isle's defences. I will collect more Malaunje children. Then I will retrieve the T'Elegos. Have patience, Imoshen. It is not what you think. Believe me, I've studied –'

'What have you studied?' Tulkhan asked as he rounded the bend in the narrow stairway.

Desperately Imoshen searched for a suitable answer.

'Shields,' Reothe said. 'Come, I'll show you.' He retraced his steps.

Heart thumping, Imoshen followed.

Reothe led them past the entrance to T'Reothe's Hall through a dark connecting gallery to T'Ashmyr's Hall, built in the first century of T'En rule.

Reothe strode across the worn flags. The first throwback Emperor T'Ashmyr himself had paced this room, planning his campaigns to consolidate his hold on Fair Isle.

Dragging a chair against the wall, Reothe climbed up to remove a shield from the display. Imoshen hoped there would be substance to Reothe's presentation, or else Tulkhan's suspicion would be raised.

'Here.' Reothe tossed the shield to Tulkhan, who slid his arm through the grip and tested its weight. Imoshen caught Reothe's eye as he jumped down, trying to warn him to tread carefully, but his expression held laughter.

'Light and strong.' Tulkhan turned the shield so that it glowed in the dim light. 'Beautifully made. But what –'

'It's the shape.' Reothe said. 'Ghebite cavalry shields are small and round, this one tapers to a point. Your shields leave a rider's legs unprotected. Five hundred years ago, T'Ashmyr designed these shields. Tomorrow I'll meet you on horseback. Arm yourself as you normally would and we'll see which shield offers better protection for a mounted warrior.'

'Done!' When Tulkhan grinned, his teeth flashing white against his coppery skin in the darkness, Imoshen felt a tug deep within her.

She missed his touch. The more Tulkhan withdrew from her, the harder she found it to resist Reothe's lure. Although Reothe had not invaded her dreams, her senses were so open to him. She felt him watching her. She knew if he had been in a room before her, and sensed his essence on objects he had recently touched. She did not know if this was deliberate or just the effect of his half-healed gifts.

The General stood opposite her, barely visible in the twilight of the old hall, the shield in his grasp, shielded from her by his warrior code. Imoshen was very aware of Reothe only two steps away. Like spider's prey they were caught in a web, a tangle of events and broken promises, bound by the fabric of their positions and their natures.

Struggle as they might, Imoshen could see no honourable solution which did not include the death of one of these men, and that she could not bear. She dreaded to make a move in case it precipitated her worst fears. The silence of things unsaid stretched between the three of them. The air grew heavy with expectation. Imoshen licked her lips and drew breath to speak.

Three servants entered armed with brooms, their candles held high.

'Empress,' the first gasped. 'We heard voices and feared –'

'Ghosts of T'Ashmyr's reign?' Imoshen laughed, surprised to hear how natural she sounded. 'I'm afraid we must disappoint you. There are no apparitions here, only scholars of ancient weaponry.' She glided over to the servants. 'But I thank you for bringing light. We let our enthusiasm carry us away.' Holding the candle high she turned to Tulkhan. 'Do you want to inspect the weapons?'

He hefted the shield. 'Trial by combat will suffice.'

As he and Reothe walked from the hall they fell into easy conversation comparing cavalry training exercises, shutting her out.

Imoshen repressed a surge of annoyance.

TULKHAN LOOKED UP from his maps to see Imoshen sweep into the room, radiant, imperious and untouchable. He ached for what he could not have.

'Nearly spring,' she said, 'and new T'Diemn's earthworks –'

'Will progress whether I am here or not. I must review the defences of northern Fair Isle. I leave Lightfoot to oversee the work here.'

'And I suppose you take Reothe with you?'

'Of course.' He could hardly leave him here to stir up trouble. 'Besides, Reothe is still looking for half-blood children. He has searched but a third of Fair Isle.'

'When you go to Northpoint, take Reothe to the hospice. Eksyl may wish to accompany the children back here.' She chewed her bottom lip. 'Tulkhan, Reothe seeks to win your trust with the cavalry drilling and the new shields.'

'Whatever his motives, my cavalry benefit.'

Imoshen looked down then up again swiftly. 'Have you shown him Seerkhan's sword?'

'No,' Tulkhan said, then wondered why she seemed relieved. 'It was torn from my hand in the Lowland flood. I meant to bestow it on my son but I fear it lost, buried in Lowland mud.'

'I am sorry,' Imoshen said. 'Will you teach me to use the Ghebite sword?'

He did not understand why Imoshen watched him so intensely. Perhaps she feared Gharavan would invade before he could return. 'Lightfoot commands T'Diemn's garrisons. With his years of experience, you will not need to use a sword.'

'I see,' Imoshen said, as though he had failed a test. 'I may not be here when you return. Kalleen's baby is due soon and I will accompany her to Windhaven for the birth.'

Tulkhan frowned. 'Can't Kalleen have her baby here? Windhaven is too near the west coast for my liking.'

Imoshen sighed. 'You're a man and a Ghebite, so you cannot understand. Windhaven is where the babe was begun. Windhaven is the ideal place for the child's birth.'

Tulkhan did not see the logic of this. 'If she must go, then surely there is a midwife on the estate?'

'I am her closest friend and trained for this task. Would you ask me to turn my back on Kalleen while she walks through the shadow of death to bring forth new life?'

'What's this talk of death's shadow?'

'Have you forgotten?' Imoshen pushed the maps aside to perch on the table. 'A woman must traverse death's shadow to bring forth life. There is a special place in the T'En afterlife reserved for women and babies who die in childbirth, alongside warriors who die defending their homes.'

As Tulkhan listened intently, Imoshen felt close to the General. She wanted to stroke his broken nose and heal it, but he wore his scars like badges of honour and she must respect that.

He frowned. 'I believe your place is here in the capital.'

Anger made her voice grow thin. 'According to the teachings of the Ghebite priests, females don't have proper souls. I suppose a woman lost in childbirth is mourned like a mare lost in foaling?'

He shifted uncomfortably.

'Well, General?'

'You won't like it,' he warned. 'Only after females have proved their worth by giving birth to a son are they accorded burial in the husband's family plot. As for the afterlife... If the correct burial is observed, a warrior who dies in battle joins the great Akha Khan's host, riding the plains.'

'And women?'

'There is no afterlife for women.' He shrugged an apology.

Imoshen held his gaze. 'And what do you believe?'

'Me? I have seen too many men die to believe there is an afterlife, at least... that is what I thought until I met the T'En. Now, I question everything!'

'Questions are good.'

'Answers are better!'

Imoshen smiled, then sobered. 'Sometimes knowing is more terrible than not knowing.' She thought of the Parakletos and leant closer to Tulkhan. 'What if I said I have walked death's shadow and know there is something beyond?'

'You are T'En. I am but a True-man. What is true for you may not be true for me.'

Imoshen flinched. Perhaps they were destined to live apart forever because of the differences of their race, differences which stretched beyond death. Longing filled her and she stroked Tulkhan's jaw.

He pulled her across the desk onto his lap, burying his face in her throat. 'I can't get enough of the smell of you. It haunts me. I left for the Lowlands wondering if distance would help me escape your strange allure.'

Imoshen wrinkled her nose. 'And did it?'

He shook his head. 'I missed your voice, but not because it held some T'En trickery. Your wise words of counsel are what I value, even when they make me question the very principles by which I live. Ah, Imoshen. I would not leave T'Diemn if I had a choice.' He cleared his throat. 'But I must review Fair Isle's northern defences. And I take Reothe with me because my father taught me to keep my enemies close by. This spring we face the final cast of the dice. We may all die and everything we worked for will turn to dust: your T'En legacy and my plans for Fair Isle.'

She was torn by the knowledge that this was true.

'I do not order you,' Tulkhan said. 'I ask. Stay in T'Diemn. I fear for your safety in Windhaven.'

'I cannot fail Kalleen,' she said, though she wished she could grant him his request. 'Tulkhan?'

'What?' There was a ragged edge to his voice.

'You were nearly killed the last time you left T'Diemn. I do not ask you to dishonour your Ghiad, but grant me this.'

'Ask.'

Unable to meet his eyes she pressed her lips to his throat. 'Stay with me this night and hold me in your arms. Nothing more.'

Heart hammering, she waited for his answer.

It came in a bone-crushing hug. 'You must think I have a will of iron.'

She smiled, warmed to the core.

'I CAN'T BELIEVE I'm still pregnant!' Kalleen muttered. Nearly one small moon had passed and she was long overdue. She had been urging Imoshen to return to T'Diemn for days. 'I swear I'm never going to have this baby!' Fanning herself energetically she glared at Imoshen. 'If you laugh, I will throw something at you.'

Imoshen smiled, enjoying the company and the beauty of Windhaven's orchard. Ashmyr lay on a blanket on his stomach, trying to lift himself onto his knees. His eyes were fixed on a butterfly, which had landed just out of his reach.

Chickens cackled contentedly and farmers sang as they worked in the fields. Soon it would grow dark and the workers would come in, hungry and tired. This last small moon had been the most relaxed Imoshen had known since the Ghebites invaded Fair Isle. She was reminded of her own stronghold and she longed to go home, but when she left Windhaven she would have to return to T'Diemn.

It was time to broach a delicate subject. Perhaps Kalleen's baby had not come on time because it was not ready. The longer she carried the baby, the more likelihood of it being part T'En. 'Did any of your family carry the T'En traits?'

'I know what you are hinting at.' Kalleen levered herself up on one elbow 'My grandmother had the T'En eyes. This baby –'

'Is late and getting later by the day.' And Imoshen had healed her friend while she was pregnant. Had the rush to T'En power triggered T'En traits in the baby that might have remained dormant? 'Face it, Kalleen. There is a good chance your child will be part T'En.'

Kalleen threw her hands up in despair. 'I just want to live a quiet life. I don't ever want to be Regent, and I don't want this for my child!'

'We don't always get what we want,' Imoshen said softly.

Kalleen had the grace to look down.

The farmers' singing changed to shouts of greeting and Imoshen shaded her eyes to study the distant figures on horseback.

Tulkhan and Reothe. Her body tightened in a knot of anticipation, part pleasure, part dread. She rolled to her feet, hardly impeded by the weight of her pregnancy. She was nearly five small moons along now, but she had been bigger with Ashmyr.

'You must return to T'Diemn with them and leave me in the hands of Grandmother Keen.' Kalleen named the local midwife. 'After all, the Ghebite King will not halt his invasion plans for the birth of one baby.'

Imoshen laughed and went to greet Reothe and Tulkhan.

WHEN THE EVENING meal was over Tulkhan watched Kalleen lever herself out of her chair. She was huge. 'Surely that baby is due soon. Will you present us with Wharrd's son tomorrow?'

'If only!'

'Kalleen is long overdue,' Imoshen said and Tulkhan caught her exchanging a quick look of understanding with Reothe.

He hid his uneasiness behind a jest. 'Should I expect to see the boy by morning, Kalleen?'

'What if it is a girl?' Kalleen challenged.

He shrugged, aware he was on thin ice. 'So long as the child is healthy.'

'Spoken like a true diplomat.' Imoshen laughed and lifted her glass to him. 'Have you left your soldiering days behind to take up diplomacy, General?'

'The gods forbid!'

They laughed and, as Kalleen went to bed, Imoshen dismissed the servants for the night. Tulkhan had the opportunity to observe her. Her loose summer gown only hinted at her pregnancy. But it would not be long before everyone knew he had been cuckolded and there wasn't a thing he could do about it.

Once the servants had gone, Imoshen turned to him. 'What news?'

'I've ordered all the strongholds' defences improved, and the towns' fortifications rebuilt. But if Gharavan's army make landfall under cover of darkness, they could get a toe-hold on the island and prove hard to dislodge. My spies report the Ghebites massing. Who is to say they won't sail around Fair Isle's southern tip and attack the east coast?'

'Gharavan is playing a cagey game,' Reothe observed. 'I wonder who advises him.'

Tulkhan shrugged. 'He has a dozen advisors, all eager to win his favour.'

'But this delaying and deploying is not the act of a headstrong youth.'

'Perhaps it is the act of an indecisive youth?' Imoshen suggested.

Tulkhan cracked a nut. 'Possibly.'

'You think it is only chance that his actions prevent us from anticipating where he will attack?' Reothe was not convinced. 'Am I reading too much into this?'

'Whatever his motives, we know he will attack.' Imoshen's eyes swept them. 'And we must be prepared.'

Tulkhan felt a familiar attraction. At first he had feared it was Imoshen's gift which drew him to her, now he understood it was an intrinsic attraction. He admired her intelligence and determination. She was a natural leader. No wonder the people of Fair Isle responded with love and loyalty.

'Will you return to the capital tomorrow?' she asked.

'Yes.' He wanted to insist she leave Windhaven, but... 'Do you travel with us?'

'I don't know.' She tilted her head listening. 'Ashmyr has woken. I mustn't let him disturb Kalleen.' She stood. 'If Kalleen has her baby tonight, I will come with you.'

'Let us hope she does,' Tulkhan said, then could not resist prodding. 'Gharavan is sure to have spies on Fair Isle. You could be needlessly risking yourself and my son.'

Imoshen's mouth opened as if she might argue.

'He is right,' Reothe said.

She glared at them both, then left.

Tulkhan met Reothe's eyes, seeing the mirror of his own rueful expression. 'You should insist she returns to T'Diemn,' Reothe said.

Tulkhan put his feet up on the chair, aware that Reothe was baiting him. It was so easy to forget that they were enemies, seductively easy to lower his defences. 'You think she should come with us? You tell her.'

Reothe laughed. 'Never give an order you know you can't enforce.'

Tulkhan acknowledged the truth of this. 'Then pray Wharrd's child comes soon.' He made a silent vow to watch over Wharrd's son or daughter.

Though Reothe's knowledge had proven invaluable in planning Fair Isle's defence strategy, he missed the bone-setter's frank advice.

Who would have thought...

Here he sat in companionable silence with his most dangerous enemy, bound by the warrior code. Frustration ate away at Tulkhan.

Chapter Twenty-Two

IMOSHEN STROKED ASHMYR'S back, waiting for the first sounds on the stairs. All evening she had been observing the interplay between Tulkhan and Reothe and it dismayed her to discover how the General had come to rely on her kinsman. She wanted a few minutes alone with Tulkhan, but when she heard the steps, there were two sets of boots and she seethed with resentment.

Imoshen paced the room. Ashmyr twitched in his sleep like a puppy and Kalleen showed no sign of going into labour.

When she could not stand being closed in any longer, Imoshen crept onto the top of the stairs. The large moon was still up but the little moon had already passed overhead on its quicker journey. Holding her hand in a beam of moonlight, she turned it over and over, recalling Reothe's words. Moonlight was beneficial for the T'En. He was right, she'd denied her T'En nature. Tonight she needed to feel the night air on her skin to clear her head.

Without stopping to put on shoes or a cloak, Imoshen ran lightly down the stairs and out into the courtyard. A dog whimpered in its sleep but did not wake as she let herself out the orchard gate. She headed for the knoll, feet flying over the grass. This was a sacred place, whispered to belong to the Ancients and avoided by the locals. It was bare of trees and high enough for her to glimpse the sea.

The air was warm with a foretaste of the summer heat and lightning flickered like fretful spirits behind the scattered clouds, illuminating them from within. The build-up of tension in the atmosphere made her heart sing. She could smell no rain on the air. No release for the restless lightning.

Lifting her arms, Imoshen turned slowly. Her bare feet opened her to the power of the earth. Moonlight caressed her skin like a soothing balm. She was tempted to shed her clothing. Charged night air filled her chest, sharp and fresh to taste. Lightning flashed and for a heartbeat the night was so bright she cast a shadow. A delighted laugh escaped her.

Swaying to music only she could hear, Imoshen glided across the knoll.

'Imoshen!' Reothe's voice was raw. 'I thought I would find you here feasting.'

She spun to face him, disconcerted. Lightning flickered. 'Why did you follow me?'

'How could I not? You call me like a beacon.'

She exhaled, acknowledging they were bound in ways she did not understand. Even now an awareness stretched between them. She could feel it drawing them closer. Trapped in a timeless moment, she felt as if there was nothing but this bare hill top, the moon's lambent glow and the lightning prowling the horizon. It enticed the T'En in her to forget her True-woman upbringing.

'No closer,' she ordered, when Reothe stood within arm's length. 'Why are you here?'

'You stand there, glowing with an inner radiance, and you ask why I am drawn as the moth to the flame?'

She touched his face silvered by the moonlight, seeing the glint of the lightning reflected in his eyes. Her fingertips registered the silken softness of his lips, his hot breath.

Reothe caught her hand. She felt his kiss, the touch of his tongue as he tasted her. She yearned for him.

Then he pulled away and let her hand fall, tormenting her. 'I will not accept crumbs, Imoshen. It is all or nothing!'

'Then it can be nothing.'

'How can you say that when we share this child?' He sank to his knees, his arms sliding around her waist to press his face against her body. 'Is our babe male or female?'

Reluctantly she cradled his head against the pounding of her heart. 'I believe it is not my right to touch the mind of an unborn child, so I choose not to know the answer.'

She felt him smile.

'Your principles make you weak, Imoshen.'

That familiar wariness returned. 'I must do what I believe to be right.'

He came to his feet catching her hands in his. 'When Gharavan is defeated and Fair Isle is ours again, I will come to you and you will have to make a decision.'

'My decision is already made.'

Reothe dropped her hands and stepped back.

Relinquishing his touch was painful, but she would not give him false words of comfort. He stood before her, radiating such intensity that she could still sense him when she closed her eyes. How could Tulkhan fail to realise Reothe's gifts were returning?

'Have you sent the T'Elegos to the palace?' she ventured.

'Perhaps.'

Anger sizzled through her. 'Don't you want your gift fully restored?'

'How do I know you will honour your part of the bargain once you have the T'Elegos?'

She laughed bitterly. 'Surely you can't expect me to restore your gifts first?'

'That would require trust, wouldn't it?' he whispered sadly.

'What would you know of trust, Reothe? You have stolen Tulkhan's trust of me.' Her mouth went dry. 'Is it true?'

'Is what true?'

'They say you and Tulkhan are sword-brothers.' The baldness of her question made her wince and her cheeks grew hot. She strained to distinguish every nuance of his answer.

He shrugged. 'You know the Ghebites.'

She gasped. 'I love him for himself, not for what use I can make of him. Would you take everything from me?'

'Name one thing I haven't lost!'

'Then it is true.' Her blood roared in her ears. 'You would use anyone and anything to gain your ends, even driving your own parents to suicide to be near the Empress!'

He grasped her shoulders. 'Who told you that?'

Fury shimmered off his skin, leaving the T'En aftertaste in her mouth as she inhaled. She shook her head, regretting her outburst.

'Who told you?' His hands tightened.

She could have broken his hold as easily as blinking, but instead she placed her palms on his chest. She could feel the rapid beating of his heart, sense his pain and betrayal. 'I have wronged you, Reothe. I should never have repeated what I know could not be true.'

'You say you know it is not true, yet you still doubt me enough to make the accusation.'

'I spoke in anger. Forgive me.'

He backed away. 'Why should I? Yet I forgive you everything else. You vow to bond with me then take another. You say you love me in one breath then turn me away. You make it clear you want me only for my knowledge of the T'En. Then you accuse me of murdering my own parents!'

'Please...'

'Please what? Forgive you again so that you can go on torturing me?' He cursed softly in High T'En and walked off.

Imoshen wanted to stop him but her choice had been made the day General Tulkhan surrounded her stronghold.

If truth be told, she'd had no choice.

THE DOOR CLOSED. Tulkhan sensed more than heard Reothe's cat-light steps across the boards. He schooled his breathing so that it would not betray him. He had heard Reothe leave and, imagining him in Imoshen's arms, time had passed with excruciating slowness.

He wanted to confront Reothe but if he did, he would endanger his Ghiad. Painfully aware, he lay on his shadowed bed and while Reothe stood over him, radiating violence.

When Reothe spoke, his voice was corrosive. 'You have come close to death so many times, True-man. How does it feel?'

Tulkhan felt the immediate danger pass and countered with a question of his own. 'I am bound by the Gheeakhan code to serve you. What restrains your hand?'

'The knowledge that I cannot have your blood on my hands.'

Tulkhan sat up and swung his legs to the floor. 'Then our hands are tied.'

'Unless something changes. She carries my child, General. Why don't you do the honourable thing and take a fatal wound in this coming battle?'

'Are you asking that of me under my Ghiad?'

'No!' Reothe stalked away and threw himself into the window seat beneath a patch of moonlight.

Tulkhan crossed the room, ducking his head to accommodate the slope of the roof. He dropped into a soldier's loose-limbed crouch in the shadows. 'How did Imoshen pass the Orb's test of truth if she carries your child?'

Reothe turned and his smile made Tulkhan's heart falter. 'I went to her cloaked in your guise.'

Tulkhan looked down, pleased to hear Imoshen's words confirmed.

Reothe's eyes narrowed. 'Ask yourself this. Why was Imoshen willing to believe the lie?'

All night Reothe's words ate away at Tulkhan's peace of mind. By morning, Kalleen had not had her baby. The General left Imoshen with the request she return to the capital as soon as possible. Had she been his Ghebite wife, he would have simply ordered her bags packed, but Reothe was right. There was no point in giving an order he could not enforce and, after his restless night, Tulkhan had begun to believe there was a lie within a truth.

WHEN IMOSHEN HEARD the pounding hooves, she feared the worst. It had been five days since Tulkhan and Reothe had returned to T'Diemn and Kalleen's baby still had not come.

A single rider hastened into the cold cellar where Imoshen and Kalleen were checking the state of last autumn's preserves, as if that was the worst of their worries.

He gave the Ghebite bow and delivered a message cylinder. Imoshen opened it. As she read, her heart missed a beat and her head swam with the implications.

'What is it?' Kalleen asked.

Imoshen folded the paper carefully, hiding her consternation. 'The General needs me to return to T'Diemn. Come upstairs while I pack.'

She picked up Ashmyr, told the messenger to take refreshments in the kitchen, then sent a servant to the stable. Once in her room Imoshen dismissed the maid and threw garments into her travelling bag.

'I can't believe it. The Beatific is dead by her own hand and Reothe is missing. T'Diemn is in an uproar and Tulkhan fears Reothe has gone rogue. If Gharavan gets wind of the city's disorder he will strike.' Imoshen closed the tapestry flap of her bag and buckled it, hands shaking. 'Will you be all right?'

'Go where you are needed.' Kalleen hugged her.

An overwhelming sense of loss engulfed Imoshen, making her eyes sting with an emotion that wasn't hers. It was not a vision but a presentiment of sorrow. She had to return to the capital before disaster struck.

*   *   *

Tulkhan looked up as Imoshen walked into his map-room, Ashmyr in one arm, her travelling bag in the other.

'How did it happen?' she asked.

'Poison.'

'No. What drove Engarad to this?'

'You tell me.'

She dropped the bag and set the boy on the floor. Ashmyr pushed himself up on his hands and knees and crawled straight for the open fireplace. She darted past him to adjust the grate, then turned him towards a chair.

Tulkhan watched in fascination as his son pulled himself upright and let go with one hand. 'Look at that. He'll be walking soon!'

'Not for ages yet,' she said. 'Tulkhan, this makes no sense. Did she leave no note? Is Reothe still missing?'

'Yes.' He frowned. He always had trouble reconciling Imoshen's role as mother of his son and head of state. In Gheeaba a woman might be considered a good mother, but she did not advise her husband. 'The only communication the Beatific left is this, her final decree.' Tulkhan pushed the document across the table. 'It fell into my hands after I sent for you.'

'The seal has been broken.'

'I read it.'

'But it is addressed to me.'

'It was addressed to the Empress,' he corrected.

She flushed.

'Where is Reothe, Imoshen? What are the signs if one of the T'En go rogue? I've put Murgon off three times. I swear that man is too eager for Reothe's blood.'

But Imoshen gave no answer, intent on reading the Beatific's final decree. Her fair skin went so pale he thought she might faint.

'Imoshen, are you all right?'

Dimly, Imoshen heard her name. Blood roared in her head. The Beatific was dead because of her. No, the woman was dead because she had tried to poison Imoshen's mind against Reothe. He must have guessed who had made the insinuations about his parents' suicide and confronted the Beatific.

Engarad had taken her own life in despair. Or had she?

Perhaps the Beatific had been right to suspect Reothe of driving his parents to their deaths. Could his partially healed gift be strong enough to drive a determined woman like the Beatific into a despair so profound she would take her own life?

Tulkhan cleared his throat. 'Unless you read something there that I cannot see, it is a simple decree. The Beatific named Reothe her successor. How much weight will this have with the Abbey Seculates? Could Reothe become the Beatific?'

Imoshen sank into a chair, forcing herself to think. 'Reothe has not come up through the church hierarchy, but his education equals the masters of the

Halls of Learning. He was writing discourses on philosophy and obscure religious debates when he was fifteen.' She tried to focus on the point. 'By appointing him Sword of Justice, I placed him in the upper echelon of the church hierarchy, among the ranks from which the next Beatific would be drawn. I did not foresee...'

The General came to his feet. 'How can you tell if Reothe has gone rogue? Concentrate, Imoshen!'

When she lifted her eyes to his, Tulkhan read stark despair. She must believe Reothe had gone rogue. He would have to order Reothe's death. All along he had wanted a legitimate reason to have the last T'En warrior executed, and one that could dissolve his Ghiad, yet now he regretted it.

Ashmyr gave a crow of delight. Tulkhan looked past Imoshen in time to see his son take five tottering steps then drop. 'Look at that. He walked!'

'Impossible. He isn't a year old yet.'

'I swear he took five steps on his own.'

Imoshen laughed. 'Oh, Tulkhan. Let the poor boy be a baby. All too soon he will have to grapple with matters of state.'

'But –'

'I'm going to consult with Keeper Karmel.' Imoshen came to her feet, picking up the child. 'The last rogue T'En was executed over a hundred years ago. I don't know the precedents. I need time to think.'

Tulkhan joined her. 'I tried to persuade the Basilica not to send for the Abbey Seculates, but they have already done it. They will hold the vote in three days.'

'The church needs a Beatific.'

'But it leaves the abbeys without leadership if Gharavan attacks.' Tulkhan noted how Imoshen stroked the boy's fine, dark hair as if seeking reassurance. 'What is it? Do you suspect the Beatific did not write that message? It was not delivered to me until the evening after her body was discovered. Do you think Reothe forged it?'

Imoshen glanced around the room as if looking for the answer. Two tears rolled unheeded down her cheeks. 'I don't believe it!'

'There's another thing I find strange. The Beatific did not strike me as the kind of woman who would kill herself.' Tulkhan waited for a response. 'Imoshen?' When she met his eyes he realised she knew the answer, or thought she did. 'Imoshen!'

She shook her head. 'All I know of the last rogue's execution was what my great-aunt told me. When the Aayel was twelve years-old T'Obazim tried to abduct her. That was considered a sign of going rogue, rising up against the lawful authority of the church or the royal line.'

'The church recognised my right to rule Fair Isle, but Reothe continued to lead his rebels against me.'

'I have reason to believe the Beatific had been secretly supporting Reothe.' Imoshen gave him an apologetic smile. 'Another sign used to be if one of the T'En killed a True-man or True-woman with their gifts.'

'We both know Reothe has done that, and in cold blood.'

'As have I, though not in cold blood,' Imoshen whispered. She nuzzled Ashmyr's soft head. 'I don't know enough about rogue T'En. I must consult with the Keeper.'

'But Reothe's gifts are crippled. Surely he is no more dangerous than a True-man?' Tulkhan said. Imoshen's expression made him wary. 'Is Reothe healed?'

'No. No, I...' She pressed her hand to her throat and took a deep breath. 'I have felt his gift flare on several occasions but I know he is not healed.'

'Partially healed?'

She nodded reluctantly.

Tulkhan took a step back, cursing. His elbow hit an onyx stallion. It toppled off the table and he caught it on reflex.

Ashmyr laughed. Imoshen smiled and handed the boy to Tulkhan. 'Watch over our son while I do my research.'

'I don't –'

But she was gone, leaving Tulkhan holding the baby. He turned Ashmyr to face him, admiring the boy's brilliant T'En eyes and pale skin, topped by hair black as sable. Twenty years from now, the women would be hot for him.

Ashmyr kicked his legs.

'You want to get down?' Tulkhan lowered him to the floor only to discover the boy wanted to stand, his legs planted wide. 'Well, walk then, and prove I am not a liar.'

Holding on to the tips of Tulkhan's fingers, Ashmyr walked across the room. With a laugh the General hugged his son, Fair Isle's fate forgotten for the moment.

IMOSHEN STROKED THE polished wood of the library's shelves, inhaling its scent, redolent with age and learning. Usually this place made her feel at peace. Today she paced, waiting for the Keeper's return. According to Karmel the books on containing rogue T'En were kept in the Basilica's archives, and she'd gone to retrieve them.

When Imoshen heard a soft footfall, she looked up expecting to see the old woman, but it was Drake and his expression was grim.

She gave him a wary smile and tried for a light note. 'Do all of the Malaunje children wish to join the Parakhan Guard?'

'There are nearly sixty of them now, but I am not here to speak of the children,' Drake said. 'I come on behalf of someone who wishes to be heard by the Empress.'

If someone felt they had been wronged they could present themselves to the Emperor and Empress, who would hear their case without prejudice. The last thing Imoshen needed was another complication, but she knew her duty. 'I am always ready to listen.'

'Good. You must come with me now and you must wear this.'

Imoshen eyed the long silk scarf uneasily. Even though she had appointed Drake captain of her Parakhan Guard, his ultimate loyalty was to Reothe. She guessed who this seeker of justice must be and her heart raced. 'Very well. But I tell you that this colour does not go with my gown.'

The last thing she saw was Drake's smile before he bound her eyes with the silk. 'This way, T'Imoshen.'

He took her hand, leading her to the back of the library towards the secret passages. She had to believe Reothe would not endanger her life and that of their unborn child. Dry mouthed, she stepped into the stale air of the dusty passages. Her body sang with tension and dread.

Yet she could not deny Reothe a hearing. Fair Isle's system of justice was one of the things which made her people more civilised than Tulkhan's.

Drake led her down stairs and underground, too far for Imoshen to guess where they were. When they came out in the open again she could feel the gentle breeze on her skin and the air tasted fresh. They walked uphill for a little way before Drake stopped.

'We are here, T'Imoshen.'

He undid the scarf and backed off.

Imoshen blinked. The afternoon light had a pearly quality, which made the delicate columns glow and the distant spires and roof tops of T'Diemn seem soft and mellow. How ironic to think that Reothe would meet her here, where the Beatific had fired her poisoned barbs.

Drake retreated and, as Reothe stepped away from the rotunda's columns, Imoshen's senses strained to detect every nuance.

Reothe greeted her with the Old Empire obeisance of deep supplication, kneeling and lifting both hands palm up, before bringing them to his forehead.

Imoshen understood he was treating this as a formal request to the Empress. Feeling a little reassured, she looked down on his bowed head.

'Empress T'Imoshen,' Reothe said. 'I ask to be heard without prejudice or preconceptions.'

'Then speak, for I am listening.'

'I have been grossly wronged by one I trusted.'

'Who is this person?'

'She was greatly admired and of high position.'

'The Beatific?'

Reothe looked up, his recent suffering etched on his features. She ached in sympathy. She must be wary, her love for him made her vulnerable.

'Imoshen, I am lost if you do not believe me. Engarad sought my destruction.'

'But she is dead by her own hand and has named you the next Beatific!'

'So I heard.'

'Is that the action of someone who would destroy you?'

'It is the action of a devious woman.' He sprang to his feet. 'I guessed she was the one who told you the lie about my parents' deaths, so I confronted her. That was when she revealed her hatred for me.'

'I gave you into the church's care because I thought she loved you.'

'Hate is the other side of the coin.'

'Is it?' Imoshen murmured but he did not hear her.

'She thought to resume our old friendship.'

'You were lovers.'

'Once. But when Engarad realised I could not lie with my body, her feelings festered. She tried to poison your mind against me and nearly succeeded, yet all the while she turned her smiling face to me.'

'Did you drive her to kill herself?' Imoshen asked.

'That is what she wanted you to believe. She wanted you to think I had gone rogue and driven her to her death so that I could take over the church and regain Fair Isle!'

'You could be telling me the truth. Or you could have driven the Beatific to suicide and this could be a plausible lie.'

His shoulders sagged and he sank onto the cracked stone seat, his head in his hands. 'Then the Beatific has succeeded in destroying your faith in me and she has given Tulkhan the excuse he needs to kill me.'

He looked up, despair written large on his features. Fighting the need to reassure him, Imoshen took two steps back.

His compelling eyes held hers. 'You can search my mind for the truth of what I say. I will not resist.'

'You could cloak the truth from me. You are so much more practised than I.'

'Possibly,' he admitted. 'Then there is no reason why you should believe me.'

She dared to touch him, tracing the line of his jaw with her fingertips. 'So thin and pale. Where have you been?'

'In the passages. Drake has been bringing me food. I thought the General might have me killed.'

'He sent for me straight away.'

'Tulkhan is an honourable man,' Reothe conceded then he caught her hand, bringing it to his lips. 'I have given you many reasons to doubt me, Imoshen. I have done things which cross the boundaries of my own honour because I believed it was necessary, but I swear I am innocent of Engarad's death, just as I was innocent of my parents' suicide.' He released her hand and knelt at her feet. 'What is your judgment, my Empress?'

Imoshen swallowed. In the absence of a Beatific, it was she who would have to sign the declaration condemning Reothe. The thought revolted her. 'My heart tells me you speak the truth.'

He wrapped his arms around her waist and she felt the heat of his flesh pierce her thin gown. Sinking to her knees, she held him close. This one embrace was all she would allow herself. His lithe frame trembled.

Relief and surprise filled Imoshen, for Tulkhan could have blamed the Beatific's death on Reothe, but clearly he hadn't. She drew a little away to search Reothe's face, his hands in hers. 'Tulkhan never suspected you of killing the Beatific. Why did you flee?'

'When they told me of Engarad's suicide, I wandered into the woods, stunned. Then Drake brought me news of her decree, and I –'

'So it is general knowledge?'

'The church's high officials would have opened her decree, then resealed it. I went into hiding believing even if the General did not suspect me of her death, he would never let me become Beatific.'

Though the General was co-ruler of Fair Isle, the church retained much of its power and prestige. If Reothe became Beatific, he would be more powerful than anyone but herself and Tulkhan. Imoshen sat on her heels, heart racing as the implications rushed her. 'It takes a majority vote to elect a new Beatific. How many of the five Seculates would vote for you?'

'I'm sure I have the votes of the Seculates from Chalkcliff and Landsend. If you added your vote I would only need the General's, but why would he –'

'What of Murgon?' Imoshen asked. She longed to be free of the fear of the Tractarians. 'He hates you. Why?'

'Because I was born a throwback and he was born Malaunje, forever to suffer the indignities of his birth with none of the advantages. Murgon chose the Tractarian path to power because he had no alternative.' Reothe smiled at her expression. 'I know Murgon. We were boys together. If I were Beatific of the church, the T'En would not live in a climate of fear. I would bring a public acceptance of the T'En, an honour for our race. It is for people like my cousin that I am trying to restore the T'En.' Reothe's hands tightened on hers. 'We must seize this opportunity!'

Her head swam with the force of his vision and she pulled back, unwilling to let him influence her decision. Dusting off her gown she walked a little way away.

When she turned he stood waiting. 'If I ensure that you are named Beatific, will you swear to protect all T'En, even Tulkhan's son?'

'You should not have to ask.'

She held his eyes.

He placed his left hand on his chest, covering his heart. 'I swear to restore the T'En. We will have a golden future.'

'That was not what I asked and it might be too much, too soon.'

'It is only with a strong power base that we will be safe from True-people.'

Imoshen gave a sigh of frustration. 'As long as it is them and us, we will never be safe. Surely you see that since the Ghebites invaded, there is no them and us, only Fair Isle?'

Silence stretched. He turned his hand over in entreaty. 'Imoshen, we must not argue. We need each other.'

'True. Tulkhan and I will endorse your Beatificship.'

'Why should he give his approval?'

'The church's power is more entrenched than his. As Beatific you can bring the church's massive resources behind the defence of Fair Isle.'

'All the more reason for him to fear me, if I become Beatific. Because of his Ghiad, he is honour bound to protect me, but he believes he has no such lever to hold over me.'

Reothe's words triggered Imoshen's realisation that they did have a lever over Reothe. She smiled. 'Leave it to me.'

*   *   *

TULKHAN RECOGNISED IMOSHEN'S graceful stride as she crossed the stable courtyard. 'Imoshen?'

She changed direction to join him. 'What are you doing with Ashmyr?'

'He wanted to see the horses.'

She rolled her eyes. 'I suppose you were picking out a pony for him? Will he be riding as well as walking before his first birthday?'

'In my grandfather's time, when we lived as wandering tribes on the plains, children rode as soon as they were big enough to sit astride a horse. They fell asleep at their mother's breasts, swaying in the saddle. The minstrels still sing of it.' His eyes narrowed. 'I thought you went to the library?'

Imoshen caught his arm, drawing him away from the stable. She took him into the formal gardens to a pond with a central statue.

He stood his ground. 'I am not a fool, Imoshen. You've been to see Reothe.'

'Yes, I have seen him and he has not gone rogue.'

'Then why did he go into hiding?' Ashmyr wriggled to be let down. Tulkhan handed him to Imoshen.

'The Beatific was Reothe's first lover. When she killed herself, he wandered off, lost in grief. It was only when he heard about the decree naming him the new Beatific that he went into hiding. He thought you would order his execution.'

'I can't let him become Beatific.'

'You need the church behind you to unite Fair Isle and defeat Gharavan. If Reothe is Beatific, you will have that.'

'Do you think me a fool? Once Gharavan is defeated, Reothe will use the T'En church's power base to usurp me.'

'He won't dare.' Imoshen's intense eyes held his.

'Why not?'

'Because you will have power over the one thing he cares for more than Fair Isle.'

Tulkhan's heart skipped a beat. Was Imoshen offering herself as a surety of Reothe's support? Could he accept Imoshen on those terms? 'You mean –'

'His child!' Imoshen whispered. 'Acknowledge Reothe's child as your own and he will support you.'

Tulkhan's head spun.

'Don't you see?' Imoshen gave an unsteady laugh. 'He thought it would be the one thing to drive us apart. You could not accept another man's child. But it is the one lever he has given you over him.'

'Imoshen.' Tulkhan backed away to sit on the fountain's rim. 'Reothe's child will be full T'En. Everyone will know it is not mine.'

'Who says?' Imoshen turned Ashmyr to face Tulkhan. 'Look at your son. Apart from his dark hair, he is pure T'En. Who knows what kind of children I will produce? Why do you think the first Imoshen decreed all pure T'En females must be celibate? Perhaps the blood of a pure T'En female is stronger?'

'You could argue night is day, Imoshen. You say I can use Reothe's child as a lever, but that is an empty threat, because you would protect your children with your life!'

She frowned. 'Surely you do not think I would kill my own child for power?'

'Then what are you suggesting?'

'The same as what happened to Reothe and his cousin Murgon. If a child was orphaned, or at the request of their parents, they would be given into the care of a high ranking relative. At ten years of age, Reothe was accepted into the Empress's family to be reared with her heirs. He and Murgon were trained to be royal advisors and their loyalty to the royal family was ensured, bound by bonds of love.'

Imoshen joined Tulkhan on the pond rim. Ashmyr stood on tiptoe, dipping his fingers in the water. She turned the mechanism to make the central fountain work. Ashmyr gave a crow of delight.

They both smiled.

'Fair Isle must be united to defeat Gharavan, General. The people know Reothe. They respect his leadership, and that is why they were ready to follow him. But it works both ways. If he were leader of the church, their loyalty would ultimately be to us, because the final veto for Beatific rests with the Emperor and Empress. Reward Reothe with the Beatificship and he will have a vested interest in seeing that Fair Isle's power structure remains intact. Tulkhan, if you can offer the people stability they will support you in this, Fair Isle's time of greatest need!'

Tulkhan looked down at Ashmyr's dark head as the infant stood between them and thought of the unborn child who might literally come between himself and Imoshen. 'You ask me to accept a child that is not my own to use as a lever on my most dangerous ally. Desperate measures, Imoshen.'

'It is time for the most desperate of alliances.'

'I must think.' He stood and turned away from her.

'You have three days until the Seculates vote. Would you rather Reothe became the next Beatific, or someone the Seculates select for their own purpose? Better the enemy you know than –'

'You have a hard heart and a strong head, Imoshen.' Tulkhan held her eyes. 'Do you never doubt yourself?'

'All the time,' she admitted, feeling the colour rise in her cheeks. 'But I am fighting for our survival. Remember this, General. Your son and Reothe's child are blameless. If we want them to have a future, we must hold Fair Isle against Gharavan.'

She saw him accept the truth of this.

'What if the Seculates vote against Reothe's appointment?'

Imoshen cloaked her surge of victory. 'The last Beatific decreed it. The Seculates from the five great abbeys are jealous of each other. They will want to protect their own interests.' She sensed him withdraw. 'What is it, General?'

'When I first laid eyes on you, I saw a dreaded Dhamfeer. But I thought, *She is only a woman, a girl at that. She is no threat.* I was blind. I will not insult you by saying if you had been born a man, you could have done anything.'

Imoshen laughed outright. 'I did not choose to be born the last woman of the T'En, but I will do what I must.'

'And damn the consequences? Reothe loves you, yet you have shown me the way to control him. Strangely, this coincides exactly with what you want. I can see through you, Imoshen.'

She looked down, glad he did not know how desperately she wanted Reothe to become Beatific and win over Murgon and his Tractarians. When she looked up, the General was watching her from hooded, obsidian eyes.

'To all of them I am T'Imoshen, last T'En Princess.' She felt suddenly vulnerable. 'But to you I would be Imoshen. Do not close your heart against me, Tulkhan.'

He pulled her to her feet and into his embrace.

Tears of relief filled her eyes as he hugged her. Pinpoints of light spun in her vision and she pleaded, laughing, 'Not so tight. I can barely breathe!'

He released her, letting her feet touch the ground. 'I swear I love you more than is good for me, Imoshen.'

Joy flooded her. She raised her face to his and found his lips, losing herself in him. She was not the cold conniving creature he imagined. She was this fragile, vibrant being enfolded in the General's arms.

THEY HAD OVER sixty Malaunje children living in T'Reothe's Hall now, with Maigeth and Eksyl Five-fingers. It seemed Drake was always visiting when Imoshen dropped by. This afternoon he was teaching the older children how to fall without hurting themselves.

Reothe stripped off his ornate tabard and let the smaller man throw him to show it could be done. When he rolled cat-light to his feet and laughed, he looked so young Imoshen ached for him. She had never known him as a careless youth.

'You have given us hope, T'Imoshen,' Eksyl said softly, his eyes on the children. 'In the past a half-blood was welcomed only by the Tractarian branch of the church.'

'Tomorrow Reothe will become Beatific and the church will honour all T'En. We live in an age of change,' Imoshen said. In private sessions over the previous days, she had spoken with each of the Seculates and let it be known that she and Tulkhan approved of Engarad's choice of successor. No other candidate had been nominated and the vote had been unanimous. Imoshen believed this was thanks to Gharavan's threat. It was time for a warrior Beatific. 'People will read about Beatific Reothe and General Tulkhan in their history books and think what an interesting time it must have been.'

'But not a good time to live,' Maigeth remarked. Then she raised her voice calling the children for their midday meal.

As they lined up and thanked their instructors, Imoshen asked Maigeth, 'Has Ysanna settled in?'

'I wish I could say yes.'

The children marched off single file and Imoshen wondered what to do. If she singled the child out, the others would resent it. For Ysanna's safety it was better if no one guessed Reothe was her father.

'Dreaming with the Ancients, Imoshen?' Reothe teased.

She laughed but that old saying reminded her that one of these days the Ancients would ask her to fulfil her part of the bargain and she would have to, or forfeit Ashmyr's life. She must not falter when that moment came.

Reothe touched her cheek. 'Why so serious, Shenna?'

She shook her head, moving away so he could not use touch to skim the surface of her mind. 'Seculate Donyx said something which made me think that Murgon –'

'I will win Murgon over.'

'And how will you do that?'

'I will take a leaf from your book.' He would say no more.

To witness Reothe's investiture, Imoshen wore an under-gown of purest white samite with an overdress of silver lace, paired with an electrum skull cap, inset with fiery rubies. She wanted to remind the Seculates of the Old Empire. The formal lines of the gown hid her pregnancy, but soon it would be impossible to hide the baby. She wished she could rejoice in this child as she had rejoiced in Ashmyr.

The church's choir filled the space under the great dome. On the dais Reothe was flanked by his T'Enplars in full ceremonial armour. He wore nothing but a simple white robe, ready to accept the mantle of Beatific and all it entailed.

For once the sight of Murgon and his Tractarians did not make Imoshen's palms grow damp with fear. General Tulkhan stood at her side, resplendent in full battle armour. His eyes met hers and she smiled, wishing her great-aunt were here to see their plans come to fruition.

Imoshen had travelled a hard path from captive royal to co-ruler of Fair Isle. Now, with Reothe's investiture, she would ensure the future of the T'En.

Reothe served warmed wine to the five Seculates, symbolising that, as Beatific, he served the church. Then he accepted the mantle and crown of the Beatificship.

Before the Basilican choir could break into song Reothe signalled for silence. 'I have sworn on my honour to serve the church and Fair Isle, but I need an assistant to advise me in the role of Beatific.'

He walked slowly past the five Seculates. His eyes met Imoshen's for a moment and she saw he was laughing inside. When he stopped before Murgon she understood. Like the General he would keep his enemy close and make his success their success. 'Murgon, cousin, will you accept this honour?'

Imoshen saw a muscle clench in Murgon's jaw. It was an honour he could not refuse.

*   *   *

IMOSHEN RETURNED FROM the investiture to discover Kalleen's belongings in the hall outside her room. Joy filled her, for she intended Kalleen's child to be raised with Ashmyr.

'Kalleen?' Imoshen threw the door open, but her friend's stiff face made her falter. Kalleen's gaze swept past her to a servant who was cleaning the grate.

Imoshen placed her sleeping son in the small bed he had been using since he had outgrown his basket. 'Bring food and wine for Lady Windhaven.'

The girl gave a quick obeisance and scurried away.

Imoshen approached her friend. 'Kalleen?'

Anger glittered in Kalleen's eyes. 'My daughter was born dead. Grandmother Keen said I will never have another child!'

And Imoshen understood her presentiment of loss when she had taken leave at Windhaven. She gasped, dropping to her knees as she wept. Kalleen fell into her arms, sobbing fiercely.

When the storm of Kalleen's grief eased, Imoshen drew her gently to the hearth chair. Then she poured water and sprinkled herbs in the bowl before bathing Kalleen's tear-stained face.

The little woman sat weak and listless.

'I should have been there,' Imoshen whispered.

Kalleen caught her hand. 'Six fingers, just like yours, but dead. Three days it took. I nearly died. They told me not to travel, but I had to see you.'

'I will try to heal you.'

'No!' Kalleen shrank back. 'I never want to go through that again. It would kill me.'

Ashmyr woke, saw Kalleen and gave a crow of delight. Her face opened like a flower in the sun. But when the little woman lifted the boy onto her lap, she winced.

'I will mix you something to dry up the milk and encourage mending,' Imoshen said. As she measured herbs she listened to Ashmyr's happy sounds. Already she could sense the healing that was taking place. Herbs to heal the body, Ashmyr to help heal Kalleen's heart.

As a midwife Imoshen knew the journey through death's shadow to bring forth new life was fraught with danger. Her vision swam with tears, for she believed, if only she'd been there, she could have saved Kalleen's child.

A sound from the doorway made her look up to see Tulkhan watching Kalleen. From his expression, he had heard the news.

Unaware of him, Kalleen spoke, her voice bitter. 'I said I did not want my child to have the T'En traits, but I was wrong. I would have loved her even if she was a throwback!'

Tulkhan hastily backed out.

Imoshen smiled grimly and stirred the herbal mixture. When it was ready, she handed Kalleen the cup. 'You will feel weak and weepy for a while yet. Drink this.'

Kalleen took a sip, wrinkling her nose at the taste. 'I don't feel weak. Wharrd, my child and my family. Everyone I ever loved has been stolen from me. I feel angry!'

Imoshen squeezed Kalleen's hand. 'You have suffered just as the people of Fair Isle have suffered, but we will overcome.'

Chapter Twenty-Three

As Imoshen waited alone at the entrance to the ball-court, she tried not to recall those desperate moments when she and Reothe had faced the Cadre. Footsteps warned her of someone's approach, and a prickling across her skin told her it was Reothe.

'So you have answered the General's mysterious summons too?' he said.

Imoshen nodded. She was relieved to see Reothe was equally at a loss.

Tulkhan opened the door. 'Good, you are alone. Inside, quickly.'

Curious, Imoshen studied the table-top model in the middle of the ball-court, recognising Deepdeyne Stronghold in miniature. It was complete with tiny trees, and river and moat painted blue.

'What is this?' Reothe asked uneasily.

'I wanted you two to be the first to see it,' Tulkhan said. He then gestured to a young man at his side and drew him forward. 'This is Ardon, a fifth-year man from the Pyrolate Guild. He has been working with me.'

Imoshen cast Reothe a swift glance. Ardon risked much. The guilds were notoriously miserly with their knowledge.

'For hundreds of years the Pyrolate Guild has been making star-birds and similar toys,' Tulkhan said. 'But I knew they could do more.'

Reothe nodded. 'So you set up the watchtowers armed with star-birds, ready to carry news of invasion. But –'

'But you mean more, don't you?' Imoshen walked to the table. 'Why else have you built this model?'

Tulkhan took Imoshen's arm. 'The demonstration will speak for me. Come.'

He led them up to the first tier of seats and nodded to Ardon, who opened his coal pouch, lighting a long string which fizzed and hissed just like a star-bird's tail. The string trailed right up across the model toward Deepdeyne keep.

'It is only a model but –' Tulkhan's voice was cut off as, with a flash and a dull crack, Deepdeyne disappeared in a cloud of smoke. The General laughed, swung a leg and dropped over the balustrade.

Reothe leapt after him and Imoshen went down the steps. Small flames licked at the paper trees. Imoshen's nostrils stung from the acrid smoke. The model's blocks were scattered over the table top. Deepdeyne's walls were breached.

Tulkhan smiled. 'If only I'd had this knowledge when I was trying to take Port Sumair!'

Seeing Reothe's expression, Imoshen knew Tulkhan had chosen this particular stronghold for his own reasons.

'With the right mixture and placing, not even the greatest wall could withstand this!' Tulkhan announced, one hand on Ardon's shoulder. The young man glowed. 'I call them my Dragon's Eggs.'

'The knowledge must not fall into the wrong hands,' Reothe said.

'Of course. Why do think we've been experimenting in secret?' Tulkhan turned to Imoshen. 'You are very quiet.'

'Secrets have a way of escaping. If news of your Dragon's Eggs gets out, you will change the world. The greatest cities will no longer be safe from any barbarian with the right tools.' She looked up into Tulkhan's pleased face and said the first thing that came into her head. 'How typically Ghebite, to take a beautiful thing and turn it into a tool of destruction!'

But Tulkhan shrugged this aside. 'Today you think like a woman, Imoshen. I'm sure Reothe has the vision to appreciate my Dragon's Eggs!'

Reothe met Imoshen's eyes.

'It is because we have vision that we hesitate to release this dragon of destruction,' Imoshen said. 'If Gharavan had this tool, all your work on T'Diemn's defences would count for nothing.'

Tulkhan looked grim. 'There are only four people who know the secret of this discovery. Ardon, who is sworn to silence, and we three.'

'I will say nothing,' Reothe vowed.

'Think how the mainland kingdoms would respect Fair Isle if they knew of this weapon, Imoshen. Power protects.'

'I am thinking of the T'En who are hated because True-people fear their power.'

Tulkhan threw up his hands in disgust. 'At least promise you will say nothing.'

'That I can promise without reservation!'

He glared at her and she wondered how she could love him so deeply, yet disagree on such a fundamental issue.

IMOSHEN SMILED FONDLY. Tulkhan had been right about Ashmyr. With his first birthday only a few days away, he was already trying to run. Misjudging the slope, Ashmyr tripped and Kalleen scooped him up, spinning him around. He shrieked with joy.

Kalleen's body had healed and she laughed often. But when she thought no one was looking, she would sit and stare, her heartbreak clear on her face.

Gharavan still had not attacked and, when Imoshen had confronted Reothe about the T'Elegos, he had claimed that while travelling with Tulkhan he had been too closely watched to retrieve it.

But she could not complain about his appointment as Beatific. Since his investiture he had mobilised the church's resources. In every abbey and every village, young people trained under T'Enplar warriors. It was the age-old problem: what kingdom could afford a standing army that might turn on those in power? Yet, when threatened, what kingdom could afford not to have a trained army?

Imoshen had appeased the Keldon nobles by convincing Tulkhan to admit a select few to his war council. Even now Woodvine, Athlyn and the others were in the city, ready to take up arms at a moment's notice.

Imoshen arched her back and shifted her weight. She had been standing too long. Had she been a True-woman she would have had her baby by now, but it was almost midsummer and her pregnancy would drag on for another small moon.

The laughter faded from Kalleen's face and Imoshen turned to see Reothe approaching through the ornamental gardens, his expression foreboding. Hiding her trepidation, she crossed the lawn, meeting him under the clipped arch.

'As Beatific I must advise against the General's plan to tour the western coastal defences,' he told her.

Imoshen hid a smile. Since Reothe had come to her it must mean he had been unable to sway Tulkhan. 'The General believes Gharavan's invasion is imminent.'

'All the more reason to stay in one place, the better to coordinate the army when the attack comes.'

'I suspect he hopes to draw Gharavan out. The longer the delay the more edgy our people become.'

'You could be right. I might send Murgon with him.' Reothe's voice became intimate. 'I have a gift for you. It is a bit late for your birthday, but...'

Imoshen flushed, remembering how Reothe had risked his life to enter the palace on the eighteenth anniversary of her birthing day. She rarely took out the T'Endomaz now, frustrated by her fruitless attempts to break the encryption. 'Not another unbreakable code designed to drive me to distraction?'

He grinned. 'No. The T'Elegos.'

'Reothe?' She caught his hands, touched to discover he trusted her with this treasure.

'The T'Elegos is safely in its old hiding place in the Basilica. And you would not believe what I went through to get it there without True-people discovering its existence. Imoshen the First writes of events in the T'Elegos which would disturb them. Still, I promised you the T'Elegos and when you have finished healing me, we will read it together.'

'Must you remind me of our bargain?'

'I have taken a step towards trusting you, Imoshen. The next step is yours.'

She opened her mouth to assure him of her good faith, but the Basilica's bells cut her short. It was not time for prayer. It was not a festival. It was...

'The signal. Gharavan has attacked!' Reothe darted onto the gravel path to get a view of the palace. As Imoshen caught up with him star-birds leapt from Sard's Tower, informing all of T'Diemn that they were at war.

She caught her breath, elated and terrified at once.

Reothe pulled her to him, 'We've run out of time, Shenna.' His fierce eyes fixed on her. 'Promise me this. If I do not survive, look after the Malaunje children.'

'Have you had a premonition of your death?'

He nodded. 'The General is an honourable man, but he will have a moment of choice and I don't know which path he will take, honour or pragmatism. At least now you know where the T'Elegos is hidden.'

'Reothe!' Only when faced with his loss did she realise how much she had grown to love him.

TULKHAN LOOKED UP to see Imoshen enter the map-room with Ashmyr, followed by Reothe and Kalleen. His commanders shifted uneasily, annoyed to see women and a child invade the war council. Only Woodvine and Athlyn looked relieved.

'Where have they landed?' Imoshen asked. Two bright spots of colour illuminated her pale cheeks.

Tulkhan indicated the markers on the map of Fair Isle.

'Windhaven?' Kalleen cried. 'My people!'

'Who will meet them?' Reothe asked. 'The nearest abbey is Chalkcliff. Their T'Enplar warrior can organise resistance and be there in two days.'

'And so can we.' Tulkhan was fired by a fierce determination. He had spent many long evenings studying the maps with Reothe, who had been able to suggest the best way to use natural features in defence and offence. Tulkhan knew he was lucky Reothe had not been Emperor when he invaded Fair Isle. The lack of preparation and incompetence of Fair Isle's defenders had been his allies in that campaign. How Reothe must have seethed to see his island thrown away by his own flesh and blood!

Tulkhan straightened. 'Gharavan has chosen to make landfall only two days' ride from T'Diemn, which places the capital under threat. Piers, prepare the cavalry for a forced ride. I want to surprise my half-brother with our speed.'

Ashmyr gave a little cry, tugging at Imoshen's skirt. She picked him up and passed him to Kalleen. 'He's ready for his sleep.'

'What of my people at Windhaven?' Kalleen whispered.

'Dead, I fear,' Imoshen said, glancing to Tulkhan, who nodded.

'Gharavan chose to strike closest to our hearts,' he said. 'Your people... our people are already dead.'

Kalleen paled and hugged Ashmyr as she slipped away.

Then they discussed weapons, men, horses, time to travel, stores to bring up, where to meet, the innumerable what-ifs. Tulkhan was glad he had completed T'Diemn's new defences and Lightfoot lead the town's garrison.

'The capital cannot be taken except by siege. But we will defeat Gharavan before he gets here.'

In a flurry the war council broke up, leaving him alone with Imoshen.

'Two years ago you were invading Fair Isle. Now you defend her,' Imoshen said.

'Two years ago I was the General of the Ghebite army, concubine-son of the king. Now I go to defeat my own half-brother, who is not half the king my father was.' It was such a waste.

Imoshen leant her head against his shoulder. 'Gharavan did not value you as he should and neither did your father.'

He cleared his throat. 'There are four outcomes that I can foresee. At worst, Gharavan defeats us and attacks the capital. If he does, you can hold out until winter. His army will have to prey upon the farmlands to survive. If we are defeated, torch the surrounding farms, bring everyone inside the city. He will be far from his lines of supply in a hostile land. Even if Reothe and I are both killed, enough resistance will survive to plague his every move.'

A half-sob escaped Imoshen, but he continued inexorably. 'At best, we defeat Gharavan and return triumphant. Fair Isle will be ours. No mainland power will threaten us because the mainlanders will be busy fighting over the carcass of the Ghebite Empire.'

'And the other two alternatives?' Imoshen asked.

He looked at her. 'I believe you know them. Either Reothe or I may be killed. Men die in battle. I am under a Ghiad to serve Reothe, but I cannot be everywhere on the battlefield. I ask this, if Reothe dies, will you accept that it was none of my doing?'

'I know you are an honourable man, General.' Imoshen offered her hand. 'Touch me and feel the truth.'

Dry mouthed, Tulkhan let his fingers meet hers. Dropping the shields he had constructed against her gift, he felt the force of her love for him. It made the knowledge that he must ride off and leave her all the more bitter.

'All this could be yours and so much more if you would only trust me, Tulkhan.' Her voice moved like a silken touch through his mind. He longed to bathe in her love and rise reborn.

Unable to bear the intimacy, he broke contact. 'If I am killed and Reothe lives, fulfil your vows to him.'

She shook her head, tears sliding unheeded down her cheeks.

'When a man faces death, Imoshen, there is no time for pretence. Fair Isle will unite behind Reothe. If I die, what is left of my people will have to follow the majority. I must prepare to ride now.'

She stepped into his path, pale but determined. 'When a man or woman faces death there is not time for pretence, General. True, I took you for my bond-partner because I had to. But I grew to love you. Won't you kiss me before you go?'

He held her face in his hands and touched his lips to hers, savouring the impossibility of his love for her. Letting his guard drop he accepted her questing mind-touch, sensed her surprise, then joy. But it was too much when he felt so raw and vulnerable.

He pulled back so that only their bodies touched. 'You have taught me a great deal, Imoshen of the T'En. I would be the poorer for not knowing you.'

*   *   *

A POTENT ENERGY powered his every step as Tulkhan strode the palace corridors. He needed to remind Imoshen to keep Ardon under watch. Gharavan must not learn of the Dragon's Eggs.

In Imoshen's room he found Kalleen rocking his son to sleep and, in a flash of understanding so powerful it was a physical revelation, he realised that he was not fighting for glory or power, but the safety of his hearth and home. All his years as General of the Ghebite army now appeared to him as nothing but a desert of destruction, conquering for its own sake.

Kalleen smiled and lifted a finger to her lips, pointing down the hall. 'The library...'

A group of servants passed Tulkhan as he strode into the library, their chatter masking his footsteps. The chamber seemed deserted, until he heard a sound from behind the great shelves at the far end. He was about to call Imoshen's name when he recognised Reothe's deep tone.

As far as he knew, Reothe had gone to the Basilica and not returned. A worm of disquiet prompted him to approach silently, his presence screened by tall bookcases. Through a narrow chink he saw a private nook, illuminated by a finger of golden sunlight. Beyond it was yawning darkness, the entrance to one of the secret passages he knew riddled the palace. T'En architecture reflected its builders' minds – full of beauty, artifice and deception.

Imoshen stood in the light, her hair and her skin aglow.

'...have paid the highest price, Imoshen,' Reothe was saying. 'I have lain with you only the once and that was by trickery and now I won't even know my own child!'

'You can't be certain.' The heartbreak in Imoshen's voice made Tulkhan flinch.

Reothe dropped to one knee, hands raised in supplication. 'The dishonour of my actions sit heavily with me. Will you forgive my trickery?'

Imoshen did not hesitate. 'You are forgiven.'

Reothe kissed her sixth finger. When she pulled him to her breast and pressed her lips to his head Tulkhan turned away, unable to watch. Now he understood Reothe's question at Windhaven. It was true that Reothe had come to Imoshen in Tulkhan's form, but in the depths of her heart she had loved her T'En kinsman when she had given her betrothal vows, and although she denied those vows to bond with Tulkhan, Reothe remained her first love.

Shattered, Tulkhan stepped back. The scuff of his boot betrayed his presence. In a flash they both confronted him, weapons drawn, eyes narrowed. For a heartbeat Tulkhan felt a True-man's awe of the T'En.

'Tulkhan?' Imoshen's cheeks flamed as she tucked her knife under her tabard. Reothe re-sheathed his sword.

The General cleared his throat. 'Gharavan must not discover the power of the Dragon's Eggs. Have Ardon arrested for his own safety.'

Imoshen's lips parted as if she might say something, but Tulkhan turned on his heel and marched out.

*   *   *

IMOSHEN WAITED ON the palace balcony to accept the salute of the army. For the moment the men faced the Basilica where Reothe stood, resplendent in the red and gold robes of the Beatific. He certainly understood how to use ceremony to inspire devotion. Even the Ghebites were moved to join in as the massed voices of the Basilican choir rose, weaving streams of exquisite sound. The beauty of it flooded Imoshen. T'Diemn was the jewel in the crown of Fair Isle, the pinnacle of T'En culture.

The blessing over, Reothe retreated to the Basilica to remove his garments of office and Tulkhan rode around the square, the people breaking into spontaneous cheers as he passed. He stopped before Imoshen to salute her.

She placed her clenched hand over her heart, then opened it towards him. Smiling through her tears, she recalled the first time he had used that gesture, before words of love had ever left his lips.

Tulkhan wheeled his black destrier. It reared, walking on its hind legs. The people cheered and when he let the beast settle, she saw him smile, teeth flashing white against his coppery skin. On his signal, Tulkhan's army marched out of the square towards the north gate.

A day had passed since Reothe told her the T'Elegos lay in its old hiding place, but she could not risk collecting his gift. With Reothe gone, Murgon ruled the Basilica and Imoshen dare not venture into the archives to retrieve the T'Elegos in case he caught her. It wouldn't do for one as conniving as Murgon to discover its damning secrets.

The last of Tulkhan's men were still leaving when Reothe and the T'Enplar warriors appeared below her balcony. He was dressed in modern, lightweight armour, his only concession to display the red and gold of the church's rich mantle. Behind Reothe the Keldon nobles waited, each with their own small army of loyal followers. Among them she recognised the stern matriarch, Woodvine, and Athlyn, Reothe's grandfather.

As Reothe saluted Imoshen with Old Empire formality her heart went out to him. He believed he faced death. She whispered his name and he rode out to collect the church's army from every village along the way.

Imoshen waited until the last red and gold cloak had filed from the square, then she went inside. Her head ached and her back was weary. Remembering her naivety the first time she had delivered a baby, she smiled. What was the hardest, she had asked the new mother, the waiting or the birth? The woman had simply looked at her.

'Lightfoot,' she greeted the mercenary. 'I want T'Diemn secure. Place lookouts on the hilltops. The people must be ready to vacate their farms at a moment's notice.'

HAVING PUSHED HIS cavalry to the limit, Tulkhan rode into Windhaven after dark the following day. The destruction, visible by the light of the small moon, was all the harder to take since he had been eating in the hall and watching the local children play in the orchard only recently.

With his sword tip Tulkhan stirred the building's ashes, revealing hot coals. Scouts returned to tell him the Ghebite army was headed inland towards Chalkcliff Abbey.

As Imoshen greeted Tulkhan's messenger, she was reminded of Rawset's loss. The youth before her trembled with fatigue, his face stained by dirt and grime. His news was grim, confirming the worst. Windhaven was destroyed. The General had gone to meet King Gharavan on the fields below Chalkcliff Abbey.

Imoshen nodded, aware of Kalleen's initial soft moan and now her silence. When the messenger left, Imoshen turned to find Kalleen staring blindly out the window.

'I thought the people of Windhaven would resent me, the farm girl who became their lady, but they didn't. And now I've failed them, just as I failed my child.'

Imoshen took Kalleen firmly by the shoulders. 'Is that what you really think?'

'No. That is what I feel!'

Imoshen kissed her damp cheek. 'I've said it before, but I bless the day you fell at my feet!'

Kalleen managed a smile. 'I still have the knife you gave me and I remember how to use it.'

Imoshen hugged her and prayed T'Diemn's people would not be reduced to fighting in the streets. She pinned her hopes on Tulkhan. Meanwhile she had her own plans. Tomorrow morning, Murgon would meet Lightfoot on the ramparts of the new city to discuss how the church could help defend T'Diemn. There was still the Master Archivist to slip past, but hopefully by tomorrow afternoon the T'Elegos would be in her hands.

Kalleen picked up Ashmyr. 'Time for your bath, my beautiful boy, who will be one year old tomorrow?'

With a start Imoshen realised she had forgotten the celebration planned for the royal heir's first birthday. The Thespers Guild were going to perform in the square and the palace would hand out sweet biscuits impressed with the first letter of Ashmyr's name in High T'En. She had decided to go ahead with the celebrations despite Gharavan's attack.

The door flew open and a boy of about ten ran into the room. 'You must come, Empress. Gharavan's army is in the city!'

'Impossible,' Kalleen said.

Spots of light danced before Imoshen's eyes. 'Who told you this?'

'Commander Lightfoot.'

Then it was true.

'He wants you, Empress. He's on the tower. Come quick!'

Imoshen squeezed Kalleen's hand. 'See to Ashmyr's bath.'

Kalleen searched her face. 'Imoshen?'

But she had no words of reassurance.

Imoshen followed the boy from the room. As he led her down the long passages, the servants watched aghast. Bad news travelled fast.

She followed him up the steps to the top of Sard's Tower, one hand under her belly to help support the baby's weight.

Climbing through the trapdoor was a tight squeeze. Lightfoot helped her to stand. As soon as she did, she saw smoke rising from the wharves, dark against the setting sun.

'The wharves!' Imoshen cursed. 'The lock keepers wouldn't let anyone past without the password. How could they overpower all seven lock keepers without raising the alarm? We must turn them back, retake –'

'Too late. We weren't prepared for attack from that quarter. Dockside has been gutted,' Lightfoot reported. 'Gharavan's men already have a toe hold in the new city. People are streaming into old T'Diemn. We have to close the inner gates.'

Silently she thanked Tulkhan for restoring and reinforcing the defences of old T'Diemn. 'We will keep the gates open as long as we can. Muster the city's defences, fight a rearguard action.'

'Street fighting from house to house, townsfolk trapped in their homes...' Lightfoot grimaced. He spoke from bitter experience. 'There will be fires and panic.'

He was right, but Imoshen believed if people saw her, they would take heart. 'Have my horse saddled and call on the Parakhan Guard to escort me. The inner west gate leads directly to the docks. Is that the one we must hold at all costs?'

'Yes. But you can't risk yourself.'

'I must be seen for my presence to be felt. Send for T'Imoshen the Third's ceremonial armour.' Imoshen's ancestor had been Empress at the end of the Age of Tribulation, when a ruler could expect to lead her army in battle. The chain mail would cover her belly.

AT DUSK, THE vision that lay before Imoshen was a nightmare. People streamed uphill carrying their most prized possessions. Members of the Parakhan Guard escorted her as she stood in the saddle carrying a torch. It was symptomatic of the fall of T'Diemn that no one had bothered to light the street lamps. But as she had anticipated, her presence helped restore calm and order.

Leaving most of her guard at the entrance to the fortified bridge, Imoshen rode through the crowd trying to estimate how many more people still had to get through the west gate and how close Gharavan's army was.

Here the press of bodies was worse. Smoke flowed up the street as if it were a chimney flue. Her horse snorted with fear and pawed the cobbles.

'Empress T'Imoshen!' the people cried, reaching for her. They were townsfolk, old and very young, no match for seasoned fighters. For the second time in less than two years, the people of T'Diemn saw their town invaded.

'Come away, T'Imoshen,' Drake urged, and Imoshen realised the press of folk were flowing past her, leaving her with three of the Parakhan Guard facing an empty thoroughfare.

Shouts and running feet echoed up the smoky street. From around the corner a burning building cast the shadows of people running.

'Imoshen!' Drake urged.

She quested with her gifts, then remained where she was. Several young apprentices ran around the corner. In a cruel parody of Caper Night, they were armed with weapons of their trades – dipped in blood, not paint. On seeing her they cheered, brandishing hammers, and scissors sharpened to a razor's edge.

Imoshen stood in the stirrups, holding the torch high. They trusted her and she was going to ask them to die. 'We must keep the west gate of the old city open for as long as possible to let our people into old T'Diemn.'

'We will hold it!' a girl cried, leaping onto a water trough to wave her butcher's cleaver. The others followed her lead.

Imoshen turned to the Parakhan Guard. 'Will one of you stay to lead them?'

She was asking which of them would die at the west gate.

'I will.' Drake urged his horse forward. 'But you must go back now, T'Imoshen.'

Imoshen met his eyes, recalling the earnest youth who had delivered news of the sack of T'Diemn just after her stronghold fell. Then Drake had longed for glory, now he volunteered for duty in the full knowledge that it would bring him death. She wanted to refuse but could not deny him this honour.

Sad at heart, Imoshen touched the tip of her sixth finger to Drake's forehead, then guided her mount back towards the bridge.

IT WAS NEARLY dawn when Kalleen entered the map-room at a run. 'They just closed the last gate to old T'Diemn.'

Silently, Imoshen bid Drake farewell and moved a barrier over the corresponding gate on her map of T'Diemn. Lightfoot met her eyes.

She hadn't slept. All night the baby had writhed within her, mirroring her agitation. The inhabitants of new T'Diemn were camped in the streets of the old city, sleeping in doorways.

'If we need to reinforce the walls, we must have clear access to the ring road. The people will have to move off the streets.' Imoshen remembered Tulkhan pulling down the houses which had obstructed this road. 'Open the palace gardens. They can camp in the ornamental woods.'

Lightfoot nodded.

'Empress?' A messenger stood in the doorway. 'Their General is calling for our surrender in the name of King Gharavan.'

'And who is this General?' Lightfoot snarled.

'Vestaid of the Vaygharians.'

Lightfoot's expression hardened.

'Is he the one who thwarted Tulkhan's first attempt to take Port Sumair?' Imoshen asked.

Lightfoot nodded. 'He was the one who led the attack on the plain outside Sumair. I thought him drowned.'

'Apparently not.' Imoshen straightened her aching back. 'I will speak with him. Where is he?'

'He stands on the west gate bridge.'

'Come, Lightfoot. Let us hear what he has to say.'

Kalleen scurried after them, looking determined.

Imoshen caught Kalleen's arm, lowering her voice. 'I want you to take Ashmyr and go to T'Reothe's Hall. Tell Maigeth...' She faltered. How could Imoshen tell Maigeth she had left her son to die? 'Stay there with them. If T'Diemn falls, you must take the Malaunje children and supplies, and hide in the secret passages. I'm sure Drake has shared his knowledge of them with Maigeth. Stay there until Tulkhan retakes the city.'

She only hoped the General was not already dead.

Lightfoot escorted Imoshen from the palace, through the streets and up the steps to the west gate tower. The city was laid out below her in the crisp light of dawn. Smoke from dockside had been blown inland, some fires were still burning.

'Empress, he has archers on the far defences,' one of her people warned.

'Will he order us killed if we show our faces, Lightfoot?'

The mercenary strode to the wall, signalling in an elaborate manner. Imoshen saw the same signal returned. She had to remind herself Lightfoot and Vestaid were countrymen, part of the brotherhood of mercenaries.

Lightfoot beckoned and Imoshen joined him looking down onto the bridge. No bodies littered the stonework, but there were blood stains. The river ran under the uprights, the water gleaming in the early light.

A man stepped out of the shadow of the tower opposite.

She pitched her voice to carry. 'I am T'Imoshen of the T'En, Empress of Fair Isle. What do you want?'

'I am Vestaid, General of the Ghebites,' he roared. 'Who is your Vaygharian lap dog?'

Lightfoot answered in his own language.

Vestaid laughed. 'You choose strange commanders, Dhamfeer; a traitorous Ghebite whoreson and a disinherited Vaygharian merchant prince!'

Imoshen filed away the revelation about Lightfoot's past and raised her voice. 'Make your point, Vestaid, my breakfast is getting cold.'

'Enjoy your hot breakfast, for I will have your surrender by nightfall, Dhamfeer.'

'Talk is cheap, Vestaid.'

'So is life!' He stepped into the shadow to haul someone out with him.

Imoshen knew that head of gingery hair.

'Rawset!' Lightfoot's gasp of dismay went knife deep.

One of the emissary's shoulders hung at an odd angle. Imoshen's heart contracted. She felt the baby within her recoil in sympathy.

Rawset had escaped the flood only to be captured by Vestaid. This explained how T'Diemn had fallen, for Rawset knew the passwords and the lock keepers. Imoshen took a deep breath to slow her racing heart.

'Greet your friends, Rawset!' Vestaid urged, kicking him in the back of the knee so that he fell to the stones. Unsheathing his knife Vestaid curled his fingers through Rawset's hair, pressing the blade to the emissary's throat.

Now that Rawset had served his purpose, Vestaid was going to kill him while they watched. Imoshen could not let this happen.

She opened her T'En senses and everything went deadly quiet as her perception changed. Scents became stronger. She tasted fear on the air and extended her awareness, centring on the savage essence of Vestaid, but the man was guarded against her intrusion.

Entwined with his, she felt the fragile essence of Rawset. She brushed his senses and he welcomed her. They had mistreated him, tortured him, but nothing compared to the pain he felt knowing he had betrayed her. He craved her forgiveness. Imoshen gave it without qualification. He bathed in the pure flood of her absolution.

'He whispers your name like a prayer, T'Imoshen. It is clear the Dhamfeer cannot protect their own. Your marvellous powers are nothing but rumour!' Vestaid gave a bark of laughter and in that heartbeat his guard dropped.

The instant he was susceptible, Imoshen struck. 'You don't see because you are blind, Vestaid. Blind!'

Shifting her concentration to Rawset, Imoshen felt as if she was on her knees with Vestaid's knife at her throat. Vestaid's hold loosened as he staggered, his hands going to his eyes. She gave Rawset the impetus to act, urging him to spin under his captor's arm, to tear the knife from the mercenary's grasp, to drive it straight up under his ribs and into his heart.

Rawset's satisfaction was hers.

Even as Vestaid's death cry rang out, a dozen soldiers surged forward, weapons raised. Imoshen felt Rawset fall under their blows. His pain was her pain. His death caught her ill-prepared, wrenching at her senses.

Something buzzed past her ear. Lightfoot pulled her out of the arrow's path, bringing her back to the reality of her physical body with awful suddenness.

From his touch Imoshen knew the mercenary blamed her for Rawset's death. She had appeared all-powerful when she saved Lightfoot from execution in the Amirate. But instead of saving Rawset, she had made him her killing tool.

All around them men screamed as arrows flew true.

Imoshen felt the aftershock of Rawset's surge of desperation as his life force left him. Her heart cried out at the injustice of it. Rawset's life was worth so much more than Vestaid's. 'He died well, Lightfoot.'

'Serving the T'En to the last!' the mercenary hissed, then straightened. 'Take the Empress back to the palace. She has bought us time with Vestaid's death.'

Without argument, Imoshen let the men lead her down the steep steps and into the cobbled lane where the mayor waited.

'King Gharavan's General is dead,' she said. People cheered and shouted this news up the street and along the ring road. 'Tell the townsfolk they are welcome to camp in the ornamental forest. We must have the streets free to send support to the walls where it is needed.'

The mayor nodded his understanding. Imoshen recalled how she had distrusted him the first time they met. At least he kept a clear head under pressure. Together they walked up the rise through the streets of old T'Diemn to the palace. Her back ached abominably. She felt nauseous with the shock of Rawset's death and the baby never ceased moving within her.

It took time to coordinate her plans with the mayor and palace staff, time to reassure people. When at last she closed the door to her private chambers, Imoshen found Kalleen placing fresh food on the low table before the fire.

'Where is Ashmyr?'

'Safe with Maigeth. I came back to see to you. Good news, I hear?'

'No, Rawset is dead.'

'But the mercenary General is dead too.'

Imoshen looked at the food. 'I don't think I can eat. I don't feel well.'

Something shifted inside her, making her bend double with pain. She looked down to find blood pooling at her feet. Kalleen gasped and Imoshen saw her own shock reflected in Kalleen's face. Now, when she could least afford to show weakness, she was going to lose the baby.

With a moan of dismay, Kalleen led Imoshen into the bathing room and helped her undress. 'I will send for a midwife.'

Trembling with dread, Imoshen caught Kalleen's hand. 'No one must know.'

'But you could die!'

Imoshen closed her eyes, focusing on the force of the first contraction. It was not a preliminary warning, it was earth-shattering. She uttered an involuntary moan. 'The baby is lying on my spine. Bring me my herbs. This is going to be fast and bad. Here it comes again.'

Unable to stand, she sank to the floor. Kalleen left and Imoshen counted two more contractions in the time it took her to bring mothers-relief. Panting with the effort to ride the pain, Imoshen waited for the aftershock to leave her spine before trying to speak. 'No point. I couldn't hold it down, even if we had time to mix up something.'

Kalleen knelt on the floor beside her. 'What do men know!'

Imoshen grinned, then went under again. It was going to be faster than the first birth, but then this baby was pure T'En and not due for another small moon. The babe was too early to live. Tears stung her eyes.

She hiccupped. Then the urge to push surprised her, overwhelming her. No time to mourn, no time to grow accustomed to the loss. Her body was expelling the child.

'It comes,' she warned Kalleen.

Her waters burst and the child slid from her. Imoshen caught her breath, opening her eyes in time to see Kalleen lift the little body.

'So blue and still.'

Imoshen moaned.

As Kalleen placed the infant on the blanket, Imoshen wondered if she could ignite his spark. Should she try? Physically he looked formed, but... Before she could decide, the contractions began again and the afterbirth was expelled.

'You've lost too much blood,' Kalleen whispered. 'I must fetch a healer.'

'Give the babe to me!'

As Kalleen lifted him, he gave a mewling cry and Imoshen's heart turned over.

'By the Aayel,' Kalleen gasped. 'He lives!'

'Cut the cord.'

Kalleen did this, then wrapped the blanket around the infant and placed him in Imoshen's arm. Their eyes met, full of wonder and trepidation. To have hope was crueller than to lose the child outright.

'He breathes,' Imoshen marvelled, wiping the grease from her son's eyes. His head turned instinctively to follow her hand. He would not give up, this one. Why should this baby live and Kalleen's die? She looked up to see Kalleen wrapping the afterbirth. 'That must be disposed of safely to secure his soul in the temple of his physical body.'

'But first we must clean you up,' Kalleen said. 'How are you going to cope with a baby that's come too early and T'Diemn under siege?'

Imoshen didn't know, but fierce determination flooded her. Just as this baby would not give up, she would never relinquish hope.

Chapter Twenty-Four

THAT EVENING IMOSHEN decided to dress for effect. Through the closed window of her chamber she could hear the joyous pealing of the Basilica's bells announcing the birth of her new son and celebrating the anniversary of the first birthing day of the royal heir. Those bells would carry to the mercenary army occupying new T'Diemn.

'The pearl circlet?' Kalleen asked.

Imoshen nodded and settled it into place so that the single large pearl hung in the middle of her forehead. Tonight people would be watching their T'En Empress for any sign of weakness and, although she was still tender from the birth, she had to appear strong.

Ashmyr played on the floor by his new brother's basket, unaware that their lives hung by a thread.

'Are you ready, Kalleen?' Imoshen asked, rising and looking at herself in the full-length mirror. The lacings of the heavy brocade gown supported her back and pulled her body into shape. Her skin looked paler than usual and her eyes very dark.

Kalleen picked up Ashmyr. 'Come, let the people wish you happy birthday, my beautiful boy.'

Imoshen cradled the new babe. Every time she looked she expected to find him cold and blue, yet he still breathed, no bigger than a small True-man's child, but pure T'En. Fine silver hair covered his body. If he lived, it would fall out. As a midwife she had seen other early babies covered in fine hair. This little life was as frail as a candle flame, yet her love for him burned so fiercely it was painful.

In the hall outside they joined Lightfoot. Palace staff lined the corridor, eager to see the new baby. Imoshen realised it would take a long time to reach the stables. Serving girls rushed forward, but the master of the bedchambers called them back. Imoshen walked slowly, letting each person stroke the little six-fingered hand.

'A miracle!' they marvelled.

In the faces of the palace servants, Imoshen saw wonder and hope, and understood what the birth of this baby meant to the people of T'Diemn at this dark time.

The Keeper of the Knowledge met Imoshen's eyes knowingly and stroked the baby's sixth finger. 'Sacrare.'

Imoshen's world shifted. She had never heard the High T'En word spoken.

A Sacrare was a pure T'En child born of pure T'En parents. The last recorded Sacrare was Causare Imoshen's daughter, who had become the first Beatific.

'That word must not be repeated,' Imoshen warned.

Kalleen held Ashmyr's hand, while Imoshen cradled the baby in one arm and greeted the mainland ambassadors, the remaining Keldon nobles, the few Ghebites who had not accompanied their General, the guildmasters and the town's elected council.

The mayor made his obeisance. 'The streets are cleared, Empress. The palace woods are now full of families camped under blankets.'

'Let us hope it does not rain. Come with me, we will tour old T'Diemn.'

The mayor's eyes glowed. He was eager to bask in the reflected glory of the Empress. But he would not be as eager to share her fate if old T'Diemn fell.

Lightfoot waited in the stable courtyard beside the ceremonial carriage.

'Come with us,' Imoshen said as she stepped up. Directly opposite her, Kalleen settled Ashmyr on her lap. They drove through the palace grounds and out into the square to the sound of the festive pealing of the bells, and the townspeople's cheers. Imoshen tilted the basket so that the baby could be seen.

Waves of fear washed through her, for if he died in the night everyone would despair.

When they passed the Basilica, she beckoned Murgon, who would not look at the baby. 'I want my son's arrival sung in the square by the full Basilican choir. And tell the Pyrolate Guildmaster that I want fountains of lights pouring from the gate towers of old T'Diemn.'

The town had celebrated Ashmyr's birth with these symbols. This child deserved nothing less and besides, the encircling army would be aware of their celebrations. Vestaid had delivered death, the T'En Empress delivered life. Their attackers would see how the spirit of T'Diemn rose above their besiegers unbowed.

THAT NIGHT IMOSHEN slept with her tiny infant on her chest. With every breath he took, she willed him to take another, and the long night passed.

When she sensed Rawset's soul questing for her, she met it squarely, expecting recriminations, but he did not seek to drag her through death's shadow with him. He wanted only to acknowledge her before making the final journey. Imoshen quested for the Parakletos, dreading their discovery, but they were too busy amusing themselves with the hordes of lost souls to notice her. Eventually she fell into an exhausted sleep.

All too soon she was awakened by Kalleen's indignant voice denying someone access.

'Who wants me?' Imoshen called.

After some furious whispering the Basilica's master-archivist and Keeper Karmel entered the bedchamber, accompanied by Lightfoot.

Imoshen sat up, cradling the sleeping baby.

'Your pardon, Empress,' Lightfoot said. 'This is the moment to strike. I know Vestaid. He would not have let strong men gather power beneath him. His soldiers will be leaderless. These people claim there is a secret passage from the old town of T'Diemn under the river to the new town. We –'

'Trust the T'En!' Imoshen laughed. 'We will send our people into new T'Diemn to strike when Vestaid's men least expect it. Give me time to get dressed.'

Lightfoot's mouth dropped open. 'You've just delivered a baby. You can't mean to –'

'I most certainly do. Just imagine their dismay when they see me!'

Lightfoot gave this some thought. 'I will ensure you have your own escort of Parakhan Guard.'

'To keep me out of trouble?' Imoshen smiled sweetly.

'In keeping with your importance.'

'You should have been a diplomat, Lightfoot.'

But he did not smile and Imoshen suspected she had lost him.

When the others left, Imoshen pushed back the covers. 'We must hurry, Kalleen. I don't want to give Lightfoot any reason to question my ability.'

'You'd rather he questioned your sanity?' Kalleen muttered.

'I will be fine. The farm women drop their babes in the morning and work the fields after the noon meal. I am no less capable than one of your sisters.'

'What of the babe? He's so small and fragile.'

'Don't you think I know?' Imoshen whispered. She undid the tie of Kalleen's bodice and opened the material to reveal her golden skin. 'Hold him next to your flesh like this. He needs to feel you.' She did not explain further.

'And if you are killed?'

'I will not be killed. I have too much to achieve to risk myself. My presence will be enough to dismay the attackers.'

'And then what?' Kalleen asked.

'We rid T'Diemn of these vermin and send word to Tulkhan.'

THE GENERAL STOOD in the stirrups, observing the evidence. Gharavan and his army had been through here. They travelled the countryside like a plague of locusts, destroying what could not be carried and murdering anyone unlucky enough to be caught. But they had not attacked Chalkcliff Abbey. 'Have they gone inland and south to T'Diemn, or north?'

Reothe tilted his face into the wind. His nostrils widened, then narrowed, and his eyes closed in concentration.

Tulkhan watched this uneasily. 'Surely you can't smell an army on the move, not with all these men around us?'

'Your kinsman has a peculiar stench,' Reothe said softly. 'He is half mad and it taints his...' He used a word which Tulkhan knew to be High T'En, though he could only guess at its meaning. 'I think they went west to the coast.'

'That makes no sense. There is nothing of strategic value between here and the coast. He left Chalkcliff untouched, so he must be saving his strength for somewhere else.'

'Send out the scouts,' Reothe advised. 'Don't assume he will reason logically.'

'Very well. But he has delayed attacking Fair Isle until now, and succeeded in dragging us up the coast and inland without confronting us. Why?'

'Perhaps it is to distract us from his true purpose. T'Diemn?'

'Can't be taken without a prolonged siege. We would come at him while he camped around the town and crush him against the city's defences. I planned for that contingency.'

'Then what?'

'I don't know!' Tulkhan seethed in frustration.

'THIS IS WHERE we crawl,' Lightfoot whispered. 'The passage runs directly through the west bridge, hidden within the roadway itself, and comes out on the riverbank below the west tower. We'll be at our most vulnerable coming out of the tunnel.'

Imoshen was content to let him take the lead. Even T'Imoshen the Third's light armour tired her and the tunnel seemed interminable. Crawling under the roadway of the west bridge, she marvelled at her ancestors' ingenuity, and cursed it. How her back ached.

At last she came to the exit. Light greeted her along with the mercenary's strong hand. She swung down onto the bridge's footings.

'Move along.' Lightfoot indicated the deep shadows under the bridge. Early morning sunlight sparkled on the fast flowing river. 'I'll secure the tower, then send for you.'

Imoshen nodded and picked her way over the damp stones, further into the shadows. Light came through the broad arches of the bridge. Across from her, the first massive pylon stood in shadow. Above the murmur of the river she could just hear the furtive shuffling of her companions as Lightfoot prepared the assault.

A body had been pinned against the footing of the pylon directly opposite. The man's arm waved, so he wasn't dead after all. Imoshen waved back and signalled for silence. The man's head lifted.

'Drake!' Elation filled her. Imoshen indicated she would get help.

Scurrying back to the tunnel entrance, she discovered that Lightfoot had already left with his raiding party. She found someone with a rope and several more with sturdy arms. They followed her unquestioningly. The rope sailed across the water and Drake grasped it on his first attempt. He wound it around his arm, then pushed away from the pylon into the river.

The current caught him immediately, swinging him out into the centre of the channel between the pylon and the tower footing. But the rope was short enough, and growing shorter as they hauled it in quickly, to prevent him being seen by anyone on the riverbank or the bridge. They dragged him out of the river, wet and shaking, barely able to stand.

'I did not think to see you alive, Drake!' Imoshen hugged him. 'You're injured?'

'My leg. I fell off the bridge during the fighting. Clung to the pylon since. What happened?'

'Vestaid's dead. We're about to break the siege.' She checked the wound. Putrefaction was the biggest danger after being exposed to cold and damp for so long. 'My people will help you back to old T'Diemn's hospice.'

Someone called for her and she left him, going inside the tower where Lightfoot's men had taken several prisoners.

'It was as I suspected,' Lightfoot said. 'Vestaid's officers have wasted time arguing whether to retreat, attack or send for King Gharavan. Their men, released from the threat of Vestaid's discipline, have been drinking and looting. They fear Gharavan won't honour the contract. If we capture the officers, the men will lay down arms.' He led her outside, where half a dozen horses waited. 'Mount up.'

Imoshen blinked in the bright sun as the Parakhan Guard mounted up around her. Beyond them marched Lightfoot's garrison. As they headed down the street towards Jewellers' Square, it saddened her to see store fronts broken open and possessions smashed in the streets. The few enemy mercenaries unlucky enough to cross their path were quickly silenced.

Entering the square, they surprised four men on the steps of the Jewellers' Guildhall, cutting them down before they could close the huge double doors. On Lightfoot's signal Imoshen and the Parakhan Guard rode up the steps, straight into the hall, their horses' hooves ringing out hollowly on the polished wooden floor.

Vestaid's officers overturned tables and chairs in their haste to escape, but Lightfoot's garrison swarmed over them. They were caught and killed, or dragged back to kneel before Imoshen. It was over in a matter of heartbeats.

Her horse sidled uneasily. She tightened her knees to control him as she removed her helmet. The captured men muttered uneasily. 'These are all Vestaid's officers, Lightfoot?'

'And a Ghebite lordling.' He kicked a man, driving him to his knees.

'Who speaks for you?' Imoshen asked.

They glanced to each other. So Lightfoot was right, Vestaid had let no strong man rise beneath him. She met their eyes one by one. 'Your choice is simple, surrender or die.'

As Lightfoot had predicted, they surrendered. When the signal horn echoed across the roof tops, her own people on the walls of old T'Diemn cheered.

Before long the gates were open and the defenders poured out, ready to restrain any of Vestaid's army foolish enough not to lay down arms. Imoshen watched all this from horseback, with Lightfoot at her side.

*   *   *

THAT EVENING THE people of T'Diemn celebrated in the streets. Imoshen was bone-weary but her responsibilities were not over. Lightfoot waited for her at the entrance to the public hall.

'Are you sure this Ghebite is privy to the Ghebite King's plans?' Imoshen asked.

'He's Gharavan's man, probably assigned to Vestaid's army to spy on the General. If any man knows what Gharavan means to do, it will be him.'

As Lightfoot strode into the great hall, the sound of their echoing footsteps told of its size. The lamps only illuminated the nearest of the slender twin columns, hinting at the majesty of the T'En architecture. A bound man stood alone in its vastness amongst enemies. Although he stood proudly, Imoshen could smell his fear. Terror crawled across his face as she approached.

'Kneel before the T'En Empress, Cavaase,' Lightfoot ordered.

The Ghebite glared up at her, refusing to bow his head. 'I would rather die than reveal King Gharavan's plans.'

'Dying is easy,' Imoshen told him.

He flinched.

Slowly she walked around him. Her own men stepped away. She opened her T'En senses and probed Cavaase, testing his resistance. Behind it was fatalism. 'Were you there when they tortured Rawset? Did you watch while he screamed?'

She saw the sweat start on his forehead and noted how his colour faded under his coppery skin. Again she probed, sensing panic and despair. 'That is a crude way to get information, fit only for barbarians. The T'En do not need to cripple the body when we want something from a man's mind.'

She came to a stop before him and leant forward. Despite his terror, his gaze went to the rise of her breasts. She saw him swallow painfully. He would not meet her eyes.

'If you resist me, this will hurt. Either way, I will discover what I want to know, Mere-man.' She was surprised to hear an echo of Reothe's tone in her voice.

A muscle jumped in the prisoner's cheek.

Imoshen lifted her left hand, little sixth finger extended. He jerked away as though she meant to strike him.

'Hold him,' Lightfoot snapped.

'No.' Imoshen waved the men back. 'It won't be necessary. Will it, Cavaase?'

In that instant she sensed despair overwhelm his will.

'You are mine!' She pressed the tip of her sixth finger to the centre of his forehead between his eyes. In a rush she understood as much as he did. Gharavan despised and feared the mercenary war general. Cavaase believed Vestaid meant to murder the young king and claim the Ghebite Empire for himself. He was not sure whether to tell his king this, or bide his time and see who was victorious. Gharavan's task was to distract the army of Fair Isle, evading battle until T'Diemn fell, and then he would march into the city and lay claim to it.

Imoshen broke contact, disgusted. She stared at the Ghebite lord who was willing to betray his own king if it was to his advantage. He blinked, his blank expression clearing to sullen lines of hatred as his will returned.

At least T'Diemn was safe for now, but Gharavan still wandered Fair Isle with a formidable army.

'I have what I need to know, Lightfoot.' She arched her back, still aching with the strain of the birth.

'I will decorate the tower of the west gate with the prisoner's head,' Lightfoot said.

Imoshen went to say no, then she looked into the man's eyes. 'I will ride past the gate tomorrow morning. Lightfoot, we must send word to General Tulkhan. T'Diemn has suffered because he did not anticipate this attack. I want him back here, ready to pay for this oversight!'

Lightfoot's sharp eyes met hers but he was shrewd enough not to reveal that this outburst was out of character.

'Take this craven creature away, his will is broken.' Imoshen did not have to tap Lightfoot's arm to tell him to stay.

After the others had filed out of the great hall, she turned to him. 'Arrange it so that Cavaase escapes. Don't make it too easy. I want him to think himself lucky to get away with his life. He will run straight back to his little king with the news of Tulkhan's discomfort. What do you think Gharavan will do? Run for the coast or attack Tulkhan from behind as he comes back to T'Diemn?'

The veteran narrowed his eyes. 'He will attack. He won't be able to help himself.'

Imoshen nodded. 'I must send a message to the General. For all I know Gharavan is already on his way here to claim T'Diemn.'

A silence fell between them. Imoshen looked up to find Lightfoot's eyes on her. She raised an eyebrow. He shook his head and would have turned away.

'I have no hold over you,' Imoshen said. 'When this is over you may wish to return to your family.'

'Forget what you heard from Vestaid. I cannot return. Twenty years ago my father declared me a dead man. My younger brother became heir to our merchant holdings and now has heirs of his own.'

'I am sorry.' Imoshen hesitated. 'I am not all-powerful, Lightfoot. If I could, I would have saved Rawset.'

'I have seen many men die. Rawset's death was one to be proud of.' He rubbed his forehead where the sign of his servitude had been smoothed away.

'If I had known the man you are, I would never have imprinted you with the T'En stigmata,' Imoshen said. 'And I removed it when you asked.'

'You cannot remove the knowledge that I could not resist the T'En. It remains a stigma on my mind.' Lightfoot gave her the bow of a Vaygharian merchant prince and backed away.

Imoshen frowned and rubbed the inner curve of the ring which Tulkhan had given her. Was there some way she could use this Ghebite seal to trick Gharavan?

*   *   *

TULKHAN STARED INTO the fire. He was determined to precipitate a battle before his men lost heart. Tonight they made camp in a vineyard that Gharavan's army had trampled.

Raised voices made him look up to see a messenger dismount, his horse's sides flecked with foam. The man pulled two folded messages from inside his jerkin and handed them to Tulkhan. The first was addressed to him, the second to Reothe, both written in Imoshen's hand. As if the thought had called him, Reothe walked into the fire circle.

Silently, Tulkhan handed him his message and broke the seal on his own. Before he could begin reading, Reothe muttered under his breath, 'Better for him to die!'

'Who?' Tulkhan whispered, aware of his men on the far side of the fire circle.

Anger and despair tightened Reothe's features. 'Not only is my child a boy, but he has been born before time. If he lives, his gift will be crippled.'

Tulkhan marvelled that the child he had dreaded had been born without the T'En gift. Then the rest of Reothe's speech sank in. Only a son. And one that might not live. Tulkhan had intended to let the child live if it had been a girl. But a T'En daughter would have inherited Imoshen's gifts. Reothe could have trained and manipulated her. Tulkhan had been blinded by his culture. Relief made him light-headed.

'What message does Imoshen send you, General?'

Tulkhan held the page to the firelight, reading with growing anger and astonishment. Wordlessly, he handed it to Reothe.

He seemed to read it in one glance, then looked up. 'We must return to T'Diemn.'

That had been Tulkhan's first thought, but... 'It will be what Gharavan expects.'

'The capital lies like a great beast with its underbelly exposed and outer defences breached in key places, from what Imoshen writes,' Reothe said. 'What if Gharavan has another attack prepared for T'Diemn?'

Tulkhan stared into the flames.

'Are you considering breaking up the army to go on ahead with the cavalry?' Reothe asked. 'The foot soldiers can only travel so far in a day and the majority are unblooded. What if Gharavan doubles back and attacks the stragglers? Do you plan to let him butcher me and my contingent, then ride in to mop up?'

Tulkhan spun to face Reothe, ready to deny this, but realised Reothe was deliberately provoking him. Once he would not have recognised this. Somehow Reothe had become his confidant, someone to argue strategy with, someone who knew him well enough to speak the truth and risk his displeasure.

'Even now Gharavan could get to T'Diemn before us if he pushes his army in a forced march,' Reothe said.

'Until now, Gharavan has been avoiding battle. But Imoshen has planted the misinformation that I am being recalled to T'Diemn.'

'Then let him think you have been recalled, draw him after us until we find a place where the lie of the land gives us the advantage, then turn to face him.'

This was what he had decided, but he wanted to see if Reothe would come to the same conclusion. 'I'll let it be known that T'Diemn nearly fell, and that the city is safe but vulnerable. We will give the appearance of returning to the capital.' Tulkhan raised his free arm to clasp the T'En warrior's shoulder. 'For what it is worth, I am sorry about your son.' And Tulkhan was surprised to discover his condolence was sincere.

But Reothe would not meet his eyes.

Calling for paper and ink, Tulkhan wrote to Imoshen. He would return to T'Diemn as soon as he had defeated Gharavan. Meanwhile, she was to stay safely behind T'Diemn's walls.

IMOSHEN FRETTED. SOMEWHERE between the capital and the west coast, Tulkhan and Reothe would face Gharavan's army, and the fate of Fair Isle – *her* fate – hung on that encounter. She suspected only one of them would return.

Seeking comfort, she knelt by the sleeping boys. She stroked her nameless newborn son's pale cheek and his lips moved as he suckled in his sleep. It made her smile but still she raged at her impotence.

Imoshen threw open her chest and found the scrying platter. She hesitated, recalling her previous attempts to steal a glimpse of the future. Her heart might be tearing in two with fear for Reothe and Tulkhan, but she would not let fate mock her by revealing a half-truth. Though it cost her dearly, she closed the chest.

Soberly she went to her desk to reread Tulkhan's message, but in her distraction she bumped the goblet, spilling the claret across the wood. The deep red liquid gleamed in the candlelight, reflecting the shimmering flame, drawing her in and awakening her Sight.

Sharply silhouetted against the molten gold of the setting sun stood the jagged rock sentinel that guarded the mouth of the River Diemn. Tulkhan knelt on the sand before his half-brother. Gharavan's naked sword blade flashed with reflected torchlight as he raised it to deliver the killing stroke.

The goblet continued to roll off the desk, clattering on the floor. Her vision had taken less than a heartbeat, but she could not ignore it. Reothe was going to die on the battlefield and Tulkhan would be executed on the beach at the mouth of the River Diemn.

Not while she lived.

Imoshen opened the door of the bathing room. Kalleen looked up from the tub, her face flushed, her long hair pinned on top of her head. With a pang Imoshen noted her beauty. It would not be long before some man tried to steal her away. 'I have to go to Tulkhan.'

'The little one needs your touch and constant feeds.'

Imoshen knew if she left the babe, he would die. 'I saw Tulkhan about to be executed. I need you, but if you come with me, you could die.'

Kalleen's mouth hardened. 'I will see this out.'

Imoshen nodded.

For the first time on this campaign Tulkhan was within striking distance of his half-brother's army. To lure him into attacking, the General had selected a campsite which appeared vulnerable. His hardened veterans and the Keldon nobles were camped on low ground by a lake. Their flanks were protected by lush green grass which hid boggy soil, impossible for cavalry to cross. His unseasoned troops were held in reserve behind a ridge to the south. As soon as Gharavan attacked, Reothe was ready to lead a pincer attack.

Tulkhan had pitched his tent conspicuously on the low ground and spent a restless night expecting battle at first light, but none eventuated. Frustrated, he had sent out scouts to discover Gharavan's movements. They reported his half-brother in retreat. With Reothe at his side, Tulkhan had ridden out to investigate.

'Gharavan leads us a merry chase, but to what purpose?' Reothe muttered, riding through the Ghebites' deserted camp. Only wheel ruts, blackened fire circles and trampled ground remained.

'I don't know, but I'm tired of playing cat and mouse. We'll confront him if we have to chase him all the way to the sea.'

Reothe stood in the stirrups, studying the land. 'The estuary of the River Diemn lies to the south and the sea lies one day's fast march to the west.'

'Then we'll force-march the men and pin Gharavan between the river and the sea. He'll have to fight or drown.'

All day they drove the army. That afternoon Tulkhan's scouts reported that Gharavan camped on the dunes at the headland.

Satisfied, the General settled his forces in position. The feeling as the men made camp was optimistic.

Tulkhan stood on the last dune, staring into the west, the sky lit by the setting sun. Gharavan's army was a dark shadow on the wide sandy flats.

'When the sun rises tomorrow we face Gharavan and this business will be decided one way or the other,' Tulkhan said.

Reothe gave no answer. The General was sure something troubled him, but what could he say to the man whose death meant his future happiness?

Imoshen helped haul the boat up the sandy bank. Although the sky still blazed with the setting sun's light, the hollow was shrouded in twilight.

They unloaded the boat in silence. Imoshen handed a weary Ashmyr to Drake, while Kalleen picked up the newborn. They'd left Lightfoot to hold T'Diemn. He was none too pleased with Imoshen's plan, but had agreed to hide her absence after she had explained her vision.

Imoshen climbed up the bank and pointed across the dunes. 'That's Tulkhan's army, Kalleen. Stay here until I return. If I do not come back by midnight, go to the General's camp.'

Imoshen hugged Ashmyr, who had fallen asleep in Drake's arms, then she stroked her nameless son's head and turned away. She walked along the river bank determined not to look back.

If her vision was to be trusted, Gharavan would be camped on the beach. Her plan was simple. She would make her way into his tent and kill him. According to Tulkhan, Gharavan was not a leader to inspire men. Once they learnt of his death and Vestaid's failure, the Ghebite army would surrender.

As she approached she caught the scent of Ghebite cooking fires. Ahead of her, the sentinel that marked the entrance to the River Diemn stood stark against the setting sun, just as it had in her vision. But she was going to circumvent events by killing Gharavan tonight.

She noticed a man with his back to her, derelict in his sentry duties. To enter the camp she would have to assume the Ghebite colouring. In her heightened state of desperation, it was not difficult to focus her gifts and she felt the sting of a thousand ants as she transformed. Now she looked like a Ghebite, down to the boots and cloak, and the long black plaits.

A row of torches stood before Gharavan's tent on the beach. Weaving through the campfires, she passed unnoticed right up to the back of the tent. Freeing her knife, she slit the canvas and slipped inside, but the tent was empty. Imoshen fingered the knife hilt, looking about for a place to hide.

A man thrust the flap open and marched in, colliding with her. She spun him around, pulling his arm up behind his back, bringing the knife to his throat. 'Call your king.'

'Why should I betray my king?' he countered and she recognised his voice.

'You were ready enough to betray him for Vestaid, Cavaase.' Then she replayed his words in her head and mimicked his voice, calling, 'My king?'

'What is it, Cavaase?' Gharavan thrust the flap aside. His eyes met hers. 'You!'

Leaving his countryman to die, Gharavan fled the tent.

Imoshen cursed. She should have guessed that Gharavan, for all his bluster, would be a coward. But how did he recognise her?

Taking advantage of her momentary distraction, Cavaase dropped and darted under her guard. Tearing her knife from her hands, be brought the blade to her throat. 'I'd kill you myself if I didn't know how much pleasure Gharavan will have slitting your throat, Tulkhan.'

Imoshen was astonished. In assuming a Ghebite form she had unconsciously adopted the one she knew best.

Cavaase forced Imoshen outside, where curious Ghebite soldiers gathered. 'I have your traitorous half-brother, my king.'

'Bring the torches nearer, the better to see Tulkhan beg!' Gharavan ordered.

Cavaase turned her to face Gharavan, who held his drawn sword ready. The rock sentinel stood silhouetted against the setting sun. With cold certainty, Imoshen understood that she had precipitated the vision herself. The absurdity of it made her laugh.

'You can laugh?' Gharavan demanded, his blade flickering in the torchlight as he advanced.

She recognised the weapon. 'Seerkhan's sword!'

'My sword. How do you think I felt seeing our father give away what should have been mine?' He frowned, then grabbed her hand, dragging the Ghebite seal-ring from her finger. Stepping back, he held the ring for his men to see. 'Our father never guessed he'd sired a traitor. But tonight I take back the seal, just as I have taken back Seerkhan's sword, and tomorrow I will take back Fair Isle!' His hate-filled eyes settled on Imoshen. 'I'll wash away the shame of your betrayal with your own blood, Tulkhan. Release him.'

Cavaase shoved Imoshen so that she fell to her knees in the sand. Her head whirled, superimposing the vision over reality. Was it the fate of the T'En to foresee their own deaths? Would Reothe die tomorrow and their line be extinguished except for one sickly, nameless babe?

'Come, Cavaase,' Gharavan ordered. 'I give you this ring in honour of your service. And I award you my traitorous half-brother's estates.'

The man accepted the ring triumphantly.

Cavaase's duplicity revolted Imoshen. 'He bears the T'En stigmata on his forehead. Ask him who he truly serves!'

'No.' Cavaase rubbed at his forehead. 'The Dhamfeer bitch touched me, but –'

'And sent you back to Gharavan to lead the army into this trap!'

Cavaase stared at her, squinting in the glare of the torches. Then his eyes widened in horrified recognition. He lunged for her throat, but two men held him back.

'Bring the torch closer,' Gharavan urged. 'I would see this T'En sign Tulkhan speaks of.'

'That is not the General!' Cavaase cried. 'I can smell the Dhamfeer from here. She wears his form.'

'Look for the T'En sign!' Imoshen focused her will on Gharavan since he was proving an easy target. 'Do you see it?'

'Hold his head still!' Gharavan yelled.

'She's doing it. She's branding me,' Cavaase cried. 'It burns my skin!'

Gharavan's men restrained Cavaase, as the stigmata on his forehead grew more pronounced.

'Every word you have said, all you have done, has been made known to your enemy.' Imoshen let her voice persuade. 'He has been the T'En's eyes.'

She willed them to see the stigmata elongate, become an eyelid and open to reveal a single wine-dark eye.

With a scream, Gharavan drove his sword straight through Cavaase's forehead, releasing the hilt as the dead man fell. His men stumbled away as Cavaase's blood seeped into the thirsty sand.

'Look around you, Gharavan,' Imoshen purred. 'How many of them do you trust?'

Those men who were susceptible to her radiating power clutched their foreheads, moaning, while others backed off. Gharavan snatched a sword from a man who staggered with his hands to his head, cutting him down. All around him his men drew weapons against their fellows.

Imoshen retrieved her knife and lunged for Gharavan, who turned and ran. She darted after him. Around her, torches toppled setting tents alight, adding to the mayhem. Someone collided with her. She fell to one knee.

Gharavan leapt on her, rolling her over, hands at her throat. His weight forced her into the soft sand. Stars peppered her vision. His knee on her chest drove the breath from her body. Her skin stung as her guise dissolved, exposing her true form.

'Dhamfeer!' Gharavan's grip slackened.

She gulped air and, with what little strength she had left, she reached for her knife, half-buried in the sand.

Gharavan recovered from his surprise. 'Know this, blood-eyed bitch. I'll choke the sense from you before I rape you. Then I'll hand you over to my men. You'll wish you were dead!'

Imoshen drove the knife up between his ribs. His grasp on her throat didn't falter. She twisted the blade. Patches of grey swam in her vision. Which of them would pass out first?

Chapter Twenty-Five

IMOSHEN FOUND HERSELF crawling through cool, silken sand. The damp air shimmered with a pale light. Perhaps this was the Empyrean Plane reserved for those who died protecting their fellows, but she did not remember traversing death's shadow.

Under her hands, the dune was threaded with silvery strands of runner vine, each perfect little star-shaped leaf bejewelled with dew. Looking about, she realised the world was cloaked by a pearly mist and she was alive.

The night's events returned in a rush of revulsion. Imoshen tried to stand, but her knees gave way. The merest whisper of a questing awareness called her and, opening her T'En senses, she recognised Reothe. Relieved, she sank into the sand, concentrating on drawing him to her. Soon she heard the soft susurration of his boots in the dunes.

'Imoshen, what have you done to yourself?' His face swam above hers, familiar and dear.

She tried to say his name, but her throat was too tender.

He frowned. 'That necklace of bruises...'

'I think I killed Gharavan,' she croaked.

He leant closer. 'I cannot sense his death on your skin.'

Tears of failure burnt her eyes as others joined them.

'Carry her between you,' Reothe directed and she held onto the broad shoulders of two men as they ploughed through the sand.

'Reothe, what of Kalleen and the boys?' she asked.

'Safe.' He was right behind her. 'She came to us during the night. Told us of your vision and what you were attempting.'

Imoshen concentrated on staying conscious. She wanted to ask him if he had seen his son, but could not speak of this before True-men.

People appeared out of the mist, their muffled voices alarmed but oddly disjointed as her consciousness wavered.

As the General took her in his arms she confessed, 'I failed you. Gharavan still lives and he has Seerkhan's sword.'

'In safe keeping only.' Tulkhan was horrified to find her so frail. He ducked into the tent and knelt to place her on the bedding. His knees cracked. Imoshen caught his arm and he squeezed her hand.

Tulkhan sat back to let Kalleen bathe Imoshen's face with warm herbal water to remove the dried blood, but she could not remove the bruises. Imoshen swallowed, wincing with pain.

Tulkhan cursed. Under cover of this mist Gharavan and his army might escape. 'Did you wound my half-brother, Imoshen?'

She nodded.

'We heard...' Tulkhan hesitated, loath to recall the screams. Despite Imoshen's injuries he had to know how things stood in the enemy camp. 'What happened last night?'

Imoshen slipped her left hand free from his. Trembling with the effort she touched Reothe's forehead with the tip of her little finger. Reothe stiffened, his lids lowered over his eyes, as he focused inward. His mouth narrowed in a thin line and he gave a soft exclamation of surprise.

Kalleen's small hand closed on Tulkhan's arm and she raised frightened eyes to him. He could feel the backwash of Imoshen's gift. It set his teeth on edge and made his heart race.

Kalleen picked up the bowl. 'I can't stand this.'

Tulkhan followed her from the tent, which was isolated in a world of glowing mist. She threw the water onto the sand, barely visible under their boots.

Kalleen gave a sob of relief. 'I thought her dead.'

Tulkhan hugged her. 'Even though Reothe insisted Imoshen still lived?'

He had wanted to invade Gharavan's camp as soon as the screaming started, but Reothe had argued against it, claiming it would place Imoshen at risk.

Tulkhan's fingers tightened on Kalleen's shoulder as the tent flap opened and Reothe stepped out.

'Well?' Tulkhan asked.

Reothe glanced to him, his face shadowed by knowledge Tulkhan did not want to share.

'Go see to Imoshen, Kalleen,' the General urged. After she slipped inside the tent, he turned to Reothe.

'Imoshen lost consciousness while Gharavan was trying to throttle her. I believe only her T'En instinct preserved her life, cloaking her from them, driving her to crawl away like a wounded animal.'

'But the screams... the fires?'

'Mere trickery.' But when Reothe met his eyes, what Tulkhan read there belied his words. 'The sooner we attack the better.' Reothe inhaled. 'The sea breeze will drive the mist away soon.'

'Your gifts are healed.'

He gave a soft laugh. 'I am only male, I never had Imoshen's gifts, never... Did you know in High T'En the word for *gift* also means *curse*?'

Tulkhan repressed a shiver. Then he felt the sea breeze on his face as Reothe had predicted. 'Time to move.' He led the way to the tallest dune to see the headland revealed by the clearing mist.

Gharavan had drawn up his army in a defensive position, with the river and sea curving around behind them so that they could only be attacked on two sides. 'We could drive them back, force them into the river.'

'You both think like landsmen,' Reothe said. 'By the time the sun is directly overhead the tide will have gone out and the sand will be hard enough to send the cavalry in on his flanks. His defences will crumble. We must divert him with the attacks he expects while we keep the cavalry in reserve.'

Tulkhan held Reothe's eyes. 'You have given me victory with this advice.'

'You would have realised it when the time came.'

'Still, I give you the honour of leading the cavalry.'

A strangely pained smile illuminated Reothe's face and for a moment Tulkhan thought he would refuse, then he gave the Old Empire obeisance of acceptance, and walked off.

IMOSHEN WOKE TO find herself lying on the mat with Ashmyr asleep on one side and her nameless son at her breast on the other. Kalleen was preparing food. Smoke drifted up to the hole directly overhead, hanging in the shaft of noonday sun. It was peaceful except for the distant roar and shouts of battle blown inland from the beach.

'I...' Imoshen began, then swallowed painfully. 'My voice will never be the same. How goes the battle?'

'They will tell us when there is news.'

Imoshen nodded. She did not want to discuss what was closest to her heart. Only time would tell if Reothe would die as he believed, or if Tulkhan would be defeated by Gharavan's army and fulfil the vision she had tried to circumvent.

The babe made a soft noise and she stroked his head. The fine silver down had fallen off, leaving his skin soft as silk and pale as milk. On Fair Isle it was customary for the mother to name her sons and the father to name his daughters. Imoshen had been waiting for Reothe to meet his son, to see if there was a name he preferred, but she had never admitted before Kalleen that the child was Reothe's. 'Perhaps I should name him. Then if we are all killed, at least he will die with a name.'

'Imoshen, what have you seen?'

'Nothing, my gift has ebbed away. I am useless.'

'Then you will just have to wait for the outcome like True-people do.'

Imoshen winced. 'I am sorry, Kalleen.'

'Sorry doesn't mend a broken pot.'

'But it may appease the potter.'

Kalleen smiled despite herself.

AS THE SUN approached its zenith, Tulkhan arched his weary back and flexed his sword arm. He had pulled back to the dune to see how the battle was going. Gharavan's army formed a solid core of seasoned men who were succeeding in holding off Tulkhan's troops. His half-brother rode up and down behind the lines. Imoshen had stabbed Gharavan, yet there he was in full battle armour.

The sea had retreated, leaving a wide band of hard-packed sand. Reothe had chosen to lead the cavalry which would attack from the sea flank. A second charge of Keldon nobles, led by Woodvine and Athlyn, would come from the river flank where the tidal flats had been revealed. Tulkhan raised the cavalry horn to his lips and the signal rang out loud and clear.

Pride filled him as his men poured down from the dunes to form two spearheads. They out-flanked the Ghebite army and were aiming for its soft underbelly.

Gharavan's own cavalry were hemmed in. Armed foot soldiers, no matter how well drilled, could not withstand a mounted charge.

He saw Gharavan attempt to send reserves but before he could, Reothe's mounted division broke Gharavan's flank, allowing Tulkhan's foot soldiers to attack the less seasoned reserves.

Tulkhan kneed his horse. Now that it was clear the attack would work, he wanted to be at Reothe's side in the melee. If ever there was a chance to redeem his Ghiad this was it.

Galloping down the soft sand of the dune, he felt his mount gain confidence on the hard-packed tidal flats. He followed the path his cavalry had taken, picking through the bodies, forging to the front ranks where he'd seen Reothe's red and gold helmet.

Rising in the stirrups, Tulkhan slashed at a mercenary. When he straightened, Reothe had disappeared. The General headed for the place where he had last been. Now Tulkhan was in the thick of the battle, screaming horses, roaring men and flying hooves. His own mount kicked and bit as he had been trained to do. For several heartbeats he fought with no time for thought.

At last the pace eased and Tulkhan wheeled his black destrier. A space had cleared around him. Reothe lay amid the fallen, one leg trapped under his slain horse, his sword broken. Three men bore down on him, weapons raised.

Tulkhan rode down the nearest man, taking his sword arm off. A pike man lifted his weapon. Another leapt for the destrier's bridle. Tulkhan concentrated on keeping his seat. He broke the man's pike and kicked him in the chest, sending him onto a protruding spear.

Tulkhan's horse lost its footing, dragged down by the man at the bridle. The General jumped off his mount, coming up in time to block a killing blow. He followed through with a counterstrike that opened the man's belly. His horse rolled upright. It stood shivering and snorting as it pawed the ground.

In one of those odd moments of battle, Tulkhan found himself in an island of stillness. The fighting had moved on, leaving him and Reothe amid a sea of bodies, dead and dying.

'Your Ghiad has been served,' Reothe said. The meaning of the words reached Tulkhan through the roar of battle and the pounding in his head. 'This is your chance to kill me.'

It would be the perfect murder. When Reothe's body turned up with the slain they would assume he had been killed in battle. Fair Isle, and Imoshen, would be Tulkhan's.

The General saw the foreknowledge in Reothe's eyes. With a shock, he realised Reothe had suggested the battle plan and agreed to lead the cavalry charge knowing this moment would come.

Time stretched impossibly.

And Tulkhan knew he could not kill Reothe. Silently he extended his left hand.

Behind him, his horse snorted. Tulkhan spun. The man who had fallen on the spear charged him. There was barely time to bring the sword point between them before his attacker was upon Tulkhan. The man's impetus and weight drove Tulkhan's blade into his body and carried them both down. His attacker was dead before Tulkhan could get out from under him. He rolled the corpse aside and came to his feet, disengaging his sword.

If he had paused to slay Reothe, this man would have killed him. In sparing Reothe's life he had saved his own.

'That part I didn't see,' Reothe said. 'Free my leg.'

Sweaty and soaked in the blood of the men he had killed, Tulkhan put his hands under the horse's rump and lifted. Reothe struggled out. Tulkhan searched the bodies for a sword, cleaned the scavenged weapon and presented it to Reothe.

'Why didn't you kill me?'

Tulkhan shrugged.

A fey laugh escaped Reothe. 'If you don't know, then I surely don't. Your walls are much too strong for my crippled gift.'

Tulkhan signalled his destrier, which picked its way carefully through the bodies to join him. Another abandoned horse followed his mount. Reothe caught its reins, swinging into the saddle with care to avoid putting weight on his injured leg.

Tulkhan surveyed the beach from high in the saddle. The battle had turned with the tide. Gharavan's army could drown or surrender. He would offer the survivors seven years' service. By Ghebite custom a surrendering soldier could accept death or indenture. While in service, if he refused an order, his life was forfeit. If he survived the seven years, he was free.

'Gharavan's tent is down,' Reothe said.

Tulkhan watched his father's standard fall. Seeing it trampled in the bloody sand brought him no joy.

Gharavan's army threw down their weapons. They wore the colours of Gheeaba and, despite everything, Tulkhan found he still thought of them as his men. He recognised many who had served him on other campaigns.

As he approached the ruined tent, soldiers dragged Gharavan before him. It should have been a moment of supreme triumph but, like the moment just past when he had looked into Reothe's eyes, Tulkhan felt no surge of killing lust.

They had torn the helmet from Gharavan's head and the armour from his chest. Tulkhan noticed blood seeping through his clothing and guessed the wound Imoshen had inflicted was bleeding.

'Tulkhan, brother!' Gharavan greeted him.

The General clenched his teeth.

Reothe urged his horse nearer and spoke for Tulkhan's ears only. 'If he dies of the wound Imoshen gave him, she will suffer for it. If you don't kill him, I will. I already face vengeful shades in death's shadow tonight and I am skilled on that plane.'

Tulkhan swung down from the horse, drawing his weapon. A soldier rushed forward, presenting him with Seerkhan's sword. Tulkhan took his grandfather's blade, feeling its familiar weight and balance.

'Think of the blood we share!' Gharavan cried. He would have fallen to his knees, but Tulkhan's men held him upright.

'Let him go.'

The men stepped back. Tulkhan became aware of his numerous small wounds, making his skin sticky with blood and his limbs weary. He tossed his borrowed sword across the gap between them, so that it speared into the soft sand at Gharavan's feet. 'I offer you honourable death. Defend yourself.'

Gharavan hesitated.

Someone in the ranks muttered. 'He does not deserve –'

'Quiet!' Tulkhan barked.

Gharavan attacked.

Tulkhan deflected and countered on reflex. The huge blade cleaved Gharavan diagonally from shoulder to hip. He was dead where he stood. He blinked once in disbelief, then toppled, his blood soaking into the sand.

'The Ancients will be pleased,' Reothe said softly. 'They belong to the land and they feed on the life force.'

Imoshen's words returned to Tulkhan: *Conquerors come and go, but Fair Isle endures.*

'Throw Gharavan's remains in the sea,' Tulkhan ordered. It was the ultimate insult to deny a proper burial.

Before they could move the body, Tulkhan reclaimed his Ghebite seal-ring and took Gharavan's ring in memory of the boy he had taught to ride.

Then he mounted his horse and rode through the battlefield with Reothe at his back. It came to Tulkhan that Fair Isle was truly his. And then another realisation hit him – the Ghebite Empire was also his for the taking.

RESTORED BY FOOD and sleep, Imoshen soothed the wounded, relying on herbs and stitching for the most part. It would have exhausted her to the point of death if she had tried to heal them all, yet it made her weep to turn her face from their desperation and let them die. She needed a hundred, no, a thousand, healers with her gifts.

Someone touched her arm and she recognised Woodvine, the woman who would have led the Keldon uprising.

'T'Imoshen, will you come this way?' Woodvine led her through Tulkhan's men to the Keldon encampment. Silently the iron-haired matriarch opened a tent flap.

Imoshen ducked to enter.

Lord Athlyn lay on the low bed with his kin clustered around. She met Reothe's eyes briefly across the tent.

'Empress T'Imoshen,' the others whispered, drawing back.

Lord Athlyn's pain-glazed garnet eyes focused on her.

She knelt by his low bed. 'I regret I cannot save you.'

'I am ready to go. I have lived to see my children die of old age before me. That is a terrible thing.' His gaze went past her to Woodvine and Reothe. 'There are those who counsel war and death before dishonour, but I believe you see with vision beyond your years. Take the path of peace, Imoshen. You were given that name for a reason. Carry on her work.' His breath rattled in his chest and he reached out, eyes closed. 'Reothe, are you there?'

'I am here, Grandfather.' Reothe knelt at Imoshen's side, tears on his cheeks. His long fingers threaded through the old man's six fingers.

'This time heed my advice, boy, take the path of peace. The Ghebite General is a worthy True-man. Build on what he has begun.'

Woodvine tapped Imoshen's shoulder. Although she wanted to comfort Reothe, she came to her feet and let the matriarch lead her out of the tent.

Woodvine shook her head. 'With his passing, the Keld lose a great statesman.'

'We are not Keld or Ghebite or T'Diemn merchant,' Imoshen replied. 'We are Fair Isle.'

Woodvine's eyes widened and she gave her the obeisance reserved for the Empress. 'Athlyn was right, you see with vision.'

Heart-sore and sad, Imoshen continued her work with the sick until she had emptied her herbal pouch. A little later she heard the pipes playing and knew Lord Athlyn was dead. Many Keldon pipes played that afternoon.

At dusk she returned to her tent to eat and to feed her smallest son. For all her talk, she had still not named him.

Tulkhan opened the tent flap. 'Have you seen Reothe?'

'No,' Imoshen said. 'Is something wrong?'

Tulkhan shook his head. He let the tent flap drop and kept looking. After asking around the camp, he learnt Reothe had walked into the dunes alone.

Tulkhan found the T'En warrior on a tall dune, wrapped in his cloak, watching the last of the sun's setting rays fade from the sky.

As the General joined him, Reothe met his eyes, then looked away. Tulkhan knew Reothe did not want to discuss what he faced when the souls of the men he had killed tried to drag him through death's shadow, but... 'Wouldn't it be safer in the tent?'

'I take no pleasure in killing. I tried to disable rather than kill, but even so I killed more than I could count in the rush of battle. Their souls linger after violent death. They cannot believe they are shades. But soon they will realise. And one by one they will come for me.' His eyes were dark pools. 'I don't want to frighten your people.'

'Do you need food?' Tulkhan asked.

'I have my cloak and a water skin. You should go back.'

Tulkhan stretched, working the kinks from his muscles. 'I think I will watch the path of the moons tonight. When my people still roamed the plains, a boy on the verge of manhood took his horse, a blanket and water, and left the tent circle. He meditated and waited for a sign. Eventually, he would see an omen and know what his private name would be, usually a bird of prey, wolf, wild cat or bear. After that, he would never kill that creature and, if he was in trouble, he would call on them. By the time I was of that age, my people no longer lived on the plains. More often than not, the priests assigned our private names.'

Reothe did not ask Tulkhan his private name, and for that he was grateful. He hadn't meant to reveal so much. The silence stretched. Tulkhan studied the endless sky as it darkened to reveal the stars.

'Do you expect a revelation tonight?' Reothe asked softly.

'May the gods forbid. I've had enough revelations!'

'I don't understand you, True-man.'

Tulkhan smiled. Sometimes he did not understand himself. 'I may not be T'En, but I have also been tainted by death's touch. I will stand guard while you walk death's shadow.'

Reothe met his eyes, surprised. 'It would be best if you returned to camp.'

'Tell me stay or go, but tell me truthfully.'

Reothe pulled the cloak tighter about his shoulders. 'Stay, if you will.'

Tulkhan was aware that some corner had been turned but he hadn't recognised the signpost until it was past.

In silence they watched the night deepen. Waves rolled onto the sand, their rhythmic roar hypnotic. Foam glistened in the light of the rising small moon.

The night was still, still enough for Tulkhan to hear Reothe's hiss of indrawn breath. The little hairs on Tulkhan's body lifted in response to the unseen threat.

'Don't come too close,' Reothe advised. He slid down the dune into the hollow where he sat cross legged with the cloak wrapped around him, impervious to this world.

Tulkhan shook his head. The Ghiad was over. Gharavan was dead. Nothing threatened his hold on Imoshen and Fair Isle but Reothe, and he was ready to protect him.

Truly, life was strange.

DEATH HAD COME close to them all and now Imoshen wanted Reothe to meet his son. She wandered the camp looking for him. One by one the Ghebites denied knowledge of his whereabouts. If it had been an emergency, she would have opened her T'En senses to search for him, but it wasn't and, besides, she was drained.

At last she came to a campfire at the far edge of the army. Only the rolling, moon-silvered dunes stretched beyond. She approached the men by the fire as she had done many times in her search. 'I look for Beatific Reothe.'

The Ghebites exchanged glances. One of them pointed out into the dunes. 'The General and his sword-brother went out there at dusk.'

Understanding rushed Imoshen. The slow burn of anger consumed her. How the men must be laughing. Presumptuous female. As if the General would prefer her to his sword-brother.

She was only fit for bearing sons!

Furious, she returned to her tent. Letting the flap drop behind her, she realised Reothe would be facing the shades of the men he had killed, and a deeper jealousy consumed her because he had trusted Tulkhan before her to stay with him.

THE BABY WOKE at dawn and Imoshen tended to his needs, marvelling at his tenacity as he clung to life. She fed him and sleep tried to reclaim her. She took a deep breath of contentment, then wrinkled her nose. Opening her T'En senses, she identified the dusty dry aftertaste of death's shadow.

Holding the babe against her body, she rolled to her feet and stepped through the tent flap to see Reothe lying pale and weak under the awning. His lids flickered and she knew he was aware of her. Suffering etched his features. All her anger evaporated and she knelt to smooth the lines of pain from his forehead.

'Your touch is a balm,' he whispered.

'I sense death coming from the pores of your skin. There was no mention of this T'En burden in the T'Enchiridion. Does Imoshen the First explain how to cope with it in the T'Elegos?'

Reothe gave her a wry smile. 'The T'Elegos is not what you think it is. It assumes the reader knows much, too much.'

She remained unconvinced.

'If I told you that on no terms must you attempt Traduciation, what would you say?'

'First I must know what it is.'

'Exactly.'

Imoshen expelled her breath. 'If only I had been able to break the encryption of the T'Endomaz.'

'With what I have discovered I think that some secrets are best left undisturbed.'

'How can you say that?'

'All my life I have carried the expectation and the burden of being a throwback. My parents killed themselves when they realised there was no T'En mentor to train me. They could not face the thought of their son turning rogue. Everything I know I've had to uncover for myself. I am infinitely weary, Imoshen.' He closed his eyes, his voice a soft, dry rustle. 'In the heat of battle yesterday I took the lives of True-men. Seven times I walked death's shadow as their shades tried to drag me into death's realm with them, and it was because of my T'En legacy that I was vulnerable. But I would rather that than kill without compunction.'

In sympathy, Imoshen undid the lacing on Reothe's shirt, pulling it to one side to reveal his pale skin. She placed his son's soft cheek over Reothe's heart. 'Here is a blameless life to bring your soul peace.'

With great reluctance, he cradled the baby's downy head. Tears rolled unheeded down Reothe's cheeks. He lifted his son so that the little body hung from his large hands, vulnerable as a day-old kitten.

'Because he came too early, our Sacrare son's gifts will be crippled, Imoshen. All his life he will suffer the mistrust of True-men with only crippled gifts for his defence.' Reothe kissed the baby's forehead. 'I fear one day you will curse us for giving you life, my son.'

Imoshen retrieved the babe. A fierce protective fire burned within her, as she recalled Mother Reeve's son. Like Reothe, she had made her own discoveries about their powers.

The sounds of the camp awakening came to her. Soon they would return to T'Diemn, the responsibilities of their positions and the expectations of their people.

'Imoshen?' Reothe whispered.

'Ask and if it is within my power, I will grant it.'

At that moment Tulkhan walked around the tent and Imoshen wondered if he had been listening.

He towered above them, his expression unreadable. 'Will you ride, Reothe?'

'Of course.' He rolled upright and by the time he was standing he had shrugged off the pallor of death.

Imoshen rose with the baby in her arms. Tulkhan held out his hands for the child. Heart hammering, she relinquished him.

When she had suggested Tulkhan use Reothe's son to control him, she had not actually envisaged handing the child over. Every nerve strained as Tulkhan turned the boy to the dawn sun. The baby's eyes closed in reaction to the light and his tiny arms came up. His six-fingered hands splayed out, then furled closed.

'There doesn't seem to be anything wrong with him,' Tulkhan said. The baby looked ludicrously small in his large hands. 'Truly, I am blessed. I never thought to have two sons. As princes of Fair Isle, my boys will have the best education, and I will see that they are not ashamed of their T'En heritage.' He held Reothe's eyes. 'In Gheeaba a man names his sons. What do you suggest, Reothe?'

If Reothe rejected Tulkhan's overture, there was no hope for them. Imoshen realised this was the last thing Reothe had expected Tulkhan to do. But much had happened since he had planted this seed of dissension.

Silence stretched. Reothe cleared his throat. 'Do you have a name that means, one who will overcome?'

'Seerkhan. It was my grandfather's name. He united the tribes. They say I take after him.' Tulkhan smiled. 'It is only right, since my first son bears the name of the greatest T'En Emperor of the Age of Tribulation, that this boy should carry the equivalent Ghebite name.'

'Seerkhan...' Imoshen whispered. Images rushed her.

'Catch her, Reothe,' Tulkhan warned as Imoshen crumpled. 'She's exhausted.'

But this was not the reason for Imoshen's collapse.

'Will she be able to ride?' Tulkhan asked.

She pushed Reothe's helping hands away. 'Of course. The T'En are a hardy race.' And vulnerable in ways a True-man wasn't.

'We leave for T'Diemn,' Tulkhan said. 'But first come with me.'

When he ducked inside the tent to give the baby to Kalleen, Reothe turned to Imoshen for an explanation, but she could only shrug.

Tulkhan reappeared and led them through the camp to the last dune. Before them the sand fell away to the sea. The towering sentinel rock which marked the entrance to the River Diemn stood bathed in crisp morning light. Everything looked renewed. Imoshen sensed they hovered on the brink of many paths, but the imminence of the moment prevented her from foreseeing the outcomes.

The sea breeze blew her hair in her eyes and she flicked it aside as she turned to Tulkhan. 'Well, General?'

He gestured to the central mountains of Fair Isle. 'When I landed at Northpoint with my army, I never thought to pay so high a price for this island – my father, my half-brother and my homeland. Reothe, you once told me that I was wrong to launch an unprovoked attack for gain. In those days I was my father's war general. The purpose of the Ghebite Empire was to expand and I did not think beyond that. I... I am not the man I was. Fair Isle and the T'En – you two – have taught me much.' His honesty was painful.

'None of us are the people we were.' Imoshen could barely speak.

'I am weary of war and killing,' Tulkhan confessed. 'I don't want to return to T'Diemn knowing I cannot sleep easy in my bed because the last two T'En plot my death.'

Reothe grew as still as a stalking cat.

'What do you want from us, General?' Imoshen asked.

Reothe gave a sharp laugh. 'Tulkhan wants a bloodless victory!'

He nodded. 'My army has been travelling nearly twelve years. My men are ready for peace. Your people have suffered, and they, too, are ready for peace. Today we stand at a crossroads. We can return to the capital and further plotting, or we can make a vow to put our differences behind us. To build on what we have.'

Imoshen's heart soared. Here was proof that she had not been mistaken in the General.

'I would make a truce with you, Reothe,' Tulkhan said. 'As Beatific of the T'En church, you are second only to the royal house in power and prestige. If you make restoring the T'En your life's work, will that be enough for you?'

Imoshen felt Reothe's eyes on her and her awareness spiralled down to this one moment. Her breath caught in her throat.

'Is this what you want, Imoshen?' Reothe asked.

She understood if she said no, he would take the path that led to Tulkhan's death. She could not unleash the last T'En warrior. To save the General's life, she would have to deny her love for Reothe.

'Is this what you want?' Reothe repeated.

'Yes. It is what I want.' The words left her lips in a rush.

Reothe faltered as if he might drop to his knees in the sand. Imoshen could not go to him.

'You have her answer,' Tulkhan said. 'Reothe?'

He walked a little away, his profile to them. Tension radiated from him, rousing her gift so that she could taste Reothe's essence on her tongue. At last he seemed to come to a decision and faced them. 'I never thought to be bested by the honour of a True-man, Tulkhan. You offered me a compromise once before and I refused. This time I accept. Like you, I grow weary of death. I will make war no more.'

Relief made Imoshen dizzy. At the same time, though, she could not believe Reothe had accepted her decision. Could he truly put her aside for an ideal?

She had put him aside. She had chosen to stay with the General to ease the transition of power, to preserve Fair Isle, never dreaming that she would grow to love Tulkhan. Now she hoped Reothe's compromise would bring its own compensation.

Numbly she watched the General remove his ceremonial knife and turn the blade on his left arm. With a start she realised he meant to make a T'En vow. She winced as he slit the skin over his wrist, then offered Reothe the knife. But Reothe refused it. Instead he lifted his arm and stared at the old bonding scar.

His mouth thinned as the scar opened. 'See, Imoshen, I once told you this scar would never be healed until we were joined.'

The extent of what she had lost made her gasp. Silently Tulkhan offered his arm and Reothe met it, hand to hand, forearm to forearm.

'You have my vow,' Reothe said.

'As Imoshen is our witness,' Tulkhan said.

When Reothe dropped his arm and turned to Imoshen, she felt the need in him. It robbed her of all pretence and she had to look away.

'I ask for a moment with Imoshen,' Reothe said.

Without a word, Tulkhan strode to the end of the dune and put his back to them, arms folded. The wind played with his long black hair.

'Imoshen?'

She could not meet Reothe's eyes. He would see her pain and she had no right to inflict it on him.

'You love him?'

She nodded.

'He is the best True-man I have ever known,' Reothe said. 'He will bring honour to Fair Isle.'

Her throat swelled with tears she could not shed. The bonding scar on her wrist throbbed and she hugged her arm to her chest.

Reothe touched her cheek, turning her face to his. Tears lapped over her lower lids, sliding down her cheeks. 'I misjudged you, Shenna. You do not have a hard head and cold heart.'

'I do what I must.'

'As do I.'

'I wish –'

'No wishing. We must walk the path fate has presented.'

'I don't believe in fate!'

He smiled with painful self-knowledge. 'In the T'Elegos, Imoshen the First writes that a T'En couple rarely risked the deepest bonding, because while it enhanced their power, it left them vulnerable to each other. Already you have proved that true. I took a mad gamble when I offered the deep bonding in the old way but I do not regret it.' He took her left hand, lifting it between them so that their fingers entwined, wrists met.

She felt the warmth of his blood and her own bonding scar ached. 'What are you doing?'

'Amending our vows.'

'I don't understand.'

'There can be no other for me, Imoshen. But I can wait. Enjoy your True-man. Watch him grow old and die. I don't envy you. And when your heart is healed, I will be ready. On that day we will complete our bonding vows.'

He pressed his lips to the back of her hand then released her, and raised his voice. 'I'll tell the army to break camp, General.' And he was gone.

Imoshen stared out to sea, hearing only the rush of the breakers, the cry of the sea birds.

Tulkhan joined her on the dune. 'Imoshen?'

She looked over her shoulder at the General. He had aged since he took her stronghold. Experience had marked his features with compassion and wisdom.

'When I first met you, Tulkhan, you were a great war general. Now you are a great statesman, one who will bring peace and prosperity to Fair Isle.'

'Don't speak of Fair Isle, Imoshen. I know you became mine by necessity not choice. Fate forced you to make cruel choices, but I had begun to hope that you might love me –'

A sob escaped her and she reached for him. They would have a few precious years together. She would not seek to know how many.

His arms tightened about her and when he spoke there was a catch in his voice. 'I did not know if you could love a Mere-man.'

'Mere... nothing!' She held his eyes fiercely. 'There must be no more Mere-man and T'En, only us and we.'

'But what of you and me?'

'You know that I love you.'

'But you love him, too. And I have been second best all my life, first son of the king's second wife, supplanted heir. I must be your one and only. I would have it from your lips.'

'I have renounced the last of my race. Doesn't that tell you how I feel?' She pulled back and searched his face. 'My T'En heritage has always been denied by the people who loved me. On our bonding day you made me vow not to use my gifts. But since then you seem to have grown less hostile. Can you accept me for the throwback I am?'

She saw him hesitate and her heart sank.

'If I have faith in you then I must accept your gifts, but I cannot pretend they do not trouble me,' Tulkhan admitted.

'Honest at least,' Imoshen whispered. 'If truth be told, my gifts sometimes frighten me.'

His eyes widened, then he smiled wryly.

She traced his mouth with her fingertips. 'Know this. For me you will always be the truest of True-men, Tulkhan.'

He removed one of the two seal-rings from his finger. 'I want you to have this.' His voice caught as he slid the Ghebite seal-ring onto her finger. 'There were times when it seemed too much to ask for Fair Isle and your love.' He kissed her palm and closed her fingers. 'You hold my heart, all that I am, right here.'

And she knew it was true. When he caught her face between his hands they were both vulnerable. Imoshen opened her T'En senses and closed her eyes as she gave herself over to him, exulting in his love for her.